C000220017

Lincoln's Dreams

For Jeff Johnston, a young historical researcher for a Civil War novelist, reality is redefined on a bitter cold night near the close of a lingering winter, when he meets Annie, an intense and lovely young woman suffering from vivid, intense nightmares.

Haunted by the dreamer and her unrelenting dreams, Jeff leads Annie on an emotional odyssey through the heartland of the Civil War in search of a cure. On long-silenced battlefields their relationship blossoms – two obsessed lovers, linked by unbreakable chains of history, but torn by a duty that could destroy them both ...

Passage

Dr Joanna Lander is a psychologist specialising in near-death experiences. Study is all very well, but she needs to experience near-death for herself. Her wishes are answered by Dr Richard Wright – a brilliant young neurologist who has come up with a way to manufacture the near-death experience using a psychoactive drug.

Joanna's first NDE is as fascinating as she imagined – so astounding that she knows she must go back, if only to find out why that place is so hauntingly familiar – but each time Joanna goes under, her sense of dread begins to grow. Because part of her already knows why the experience is so familiar, and why she has every reason to be afraid.

Yet just when Joanna thinks she understands, she's in for the biggest surprise of all ...

Also by Connie Willis

Novels

Lincoln's Dream (1987)
The Doomsday Book (1992)
Uncharted Territory (1994)
Remake (1994)
Bellwether (1996)
To Say Nothing of the Dog (1997)
Passage (2001)

With Cynthia Felice

Water Witch (1982)
Light Raid (1989)
Promised Land (1997)

Collections

Fire Watch (1985)
Impossible Things (1993)
Even the Queen: And Other Short Stories (1998)
The Miracle of Christmas (1999)
The Winds of Marble Arch: And Other Stories (2007)

Connie Willis

SF GATEWAY OMNIBUS

LINCOLN'S DREAMS
PASSAGE

GOLLANCZ

LONDON

This omnibus copyright © Connie Willis 2014
Lincoln's Dreams copyright © Connie Willis 1987
Passage copyright © Connie Willis 2001
Introduction copyright © SFE Ltd 2014

All rights reserved

The right of Connie Willis to be identified as the author
of this work has been asserted by her in accordance with the
Copyright, Designs and Patents Act 1988.

First published in Great Britain in 2014 by
Gollancz
An imprint of the Orion Publishing Group
Orion House, 5 Upper St Martin's Lane,
London WC2H 9EA

An Hachette UK Company

A CIP catalogue record for this book is
available from the British Library

ISBN 978 0 575 13107 1

1 3 5 7 9 10 8 6 4 2

Typeset by Jouve (UK), Milton Keynes

Printed and bound by CPI Group (UK) Ltd, Croydon, CR0 4YY

The Orion Publishing Group's policy is to use papers
that are natural, renewable and recyclable products and
made from wood grown in sustainable forests. The logging
and manufacturing processes are expected to conform to
the environmental regulations of the country of origin.

www.orionbooks.co.uk
www.gollancz.co.uk

CONTENTS

ENTER THE SF GATEWAY . . .

Towards the end of 2011, in conjunction with the celebration of fifty years of coherent, continuous science fiction and fantasy publishing, Gollancz launched the SF Gateway.

Over a decade after launching the landmark SF Masterworks series, we realised that the realities of commercial publishing are such that even the Masterworks could only ever scratch the surface of an author's career. Vast troves of classic SF and fantasy were almost certainly destined never again to see print. Until very recently, this meant that anyone interested in reading any of those books would have been confined to scouring second-hand bookshops. The advent of digital publishing changed that paradigm for ever.

Embracing the future even as we honour the past, Gollancz launched the SF Gateway with a view to utilising the technology that now exists to make available, for the first time, the entire backlists of an incredibly wide range of classic and modern SF and fantasy authors. Our plan, at its simplest, was – and still is! – to use this technology to build on the success of the SF and Fantasy Masterworks series and to go even further.

The SF Gateway was designed to be the new home of classic science fiction and fantasy – the most comprehensive electronic library of classic SFF titles ever assembled. The programme has been extremely well received and we've been very happy with the results. So happy, in fact, that we've decided to complete the circle and return a selection of our titles to print, in these omnibus editions.

We hope you enjoy this selection. And we hope that you'll want to explore more of the classic SF and fantasy we have available. These are wonderful books you're holding in your hand, but you'll find much, much more ... through the SF Gateway.

www.sfgateway.com

INTRODUCTION
from The Encyclopedia of Science Fiction

Connie Willis is the working name of US teacher and author Constance Elaine Trimmer Willis (Born 1945). She began publishing SF with 'Santa Titicaca' in 1971, but appeared only intermittently in the field until the early 1980s, when she became a full-time author, winning several awards almost immediately. Most of her best work of the 1980s was in short-story form; her first book, *Fire Watch* (1985), assembled a remarkable range of tales, mostly from the 1980s. 'All My Darling Daughters' – published as an original in *Fire Watch* because its language and theme were still unacceptable in the American magazine market of 1980 – is a significantly harsh tale of alienation and Sex set in a boarding school in an L5 orbit, where the male students rape small animals (apparently products of Genetic Engineering) which have vagina-like organs, making them scream in pain; and the female protagonist tries to make sense of her hyperbolic adolescence in terms strongly reminiscent of the work of J. D. Salinger (1919–2010). Among other tales of interest in this first collection are 'Daisy, in the Sun' (1979), 'A Letter from the Clearys' (1982), which won a Nebula, 'The Sidon in the Mirror' (1983) and the comic 'Blued Moon' (1984). A later novella, 'The Last of the Winnebagos' (1988), won Willis both the Hugo and the Nebula; 'At the Rialto' (1989) won a Nebula; 'Even the Queen' (1992) won a Hugo and a Nebula for Short Story and 'Death on the Nile' (1993) won a Hugo for Short Story.

As a novelist, Willis began slowly with the relatively lightweight *Water Witch* (1982) with Cynthia Felice, set on a sand planet where the ability to dowse for water is a precious gift. *Light Raid* (1989) with Felice also skids helter-skelter through an SF environment, in this case a balkanized Ruined-Earth America fighting off Canadian royalists, featuring the adventures *en route* to spunky maturity of a young female protagonist much like those found in Robert A. Heinlein's less attractive books. But it seemed clear that both Willis and Felice were treating their collaborations as *jeux d'esprit*, and Willis's first solo novel, *Lincoln's Dreams* (1987), aimed successfully at a very much higher degree of seriousness (see below).

Perhaps her most popular and certainly her most extended work is her Time Travel sequence, beginning with the title story of her first collection. 'Fire Watch' (1982), which won both Nebula and Hugo awards, applies a

Time-Travel premise – a distant Near-Future institute of historiography connected to Oxford University that sends individuals back in time to study artefacts *in situ* – in order to embed its protagonist in a richly conceived London at the time of the Blitz during World War Two, where he engages himself in attempts to save St Paul's Cathedral from bombing. The tale is told with reverence for time and place. Her second novel, *Doomsday Book* (1992), which won the 1993 Hugo and Nebula awards, continues the Time Travel sequence. The frame setting is the same mid-twenty-first-century institute, but the tale itself is set at a more remote and less minutely recorded time, the period of the Black Death (around 1350), and mounts gradually to a climax whose intensely mourning gravity is rarely found in SF, even in novels of travel to times past, where a sense of irretrievable loss is not commonly expressed. *Doomsday Book* attracted some claims of historical inaccuracy, which did not seriously diminish the burden of the tale. The same cannot be said of *To Say Nothing of the Dog; Or, How We Found the Bishop's Bird Stump at Last* (1998), which also won a Hugo award; it is a long (perhaps excessively long) *jeu d'esprit* set in 1880s England along the River Thames, where its model – *Three Men in a Boat (To Say Nothing of the Dog)* (1889) by Jerome K. Jerome (1859–1927) – is also set. The oddness of the tale may lie in the fact that Willis's nostalgia about Jerome's 1888 seems as intense as though – like St Paul's in 1941 – it had actually existed; but in fact Jerome created his own, concise idyll as a counterfactual homage to an imaginary England.

No such oddness afflicts what may be the copestone of the Time Travel sequence, the 2010 novel published in two separate volumes as *Blackout* (2010) and *All Clear* (2010), which, treated as a single consecutive narrative, once again won the Hugo award for best novel and also the Locus Award. The enormous tale is set, like *Fire Watch*, in London during the Blitz, and details in great (and sometimes overwhelming) detail the travails of three visitors from 2060 who are desperately afraid that their temporary inability to return home is fatally linked to their frequent involuntary transgressions against what they deem to be the proper flow of reality at a time of terrible fragility in the flow of the time of the world. Their plight is only resolved when they learn that their own future, which is ours, the future in which Hitler does not win World War Two, is in fact an Alternate World. The utter *wrongness* of the far more likely future in which Hitler Wins has inspired some force – Willis is not clear about the nature of this force, which may be no more than a convergence of right outcomes of history prescriptively conceived, but which also be something like the *spiritus mundi*, or perhaps even Gaia – to trick the three visitors into creating our own less plausible world. As with *Doomsday Book*, there is a sense of reverence about the world; in this case, though some very well-known details of life then are presented here as though newly discovered, the reverence is strengthened by Willis's clear, attentive love for the England of 1940.

During the years in which she primarily focused her energies on the Time Travel sequence, Willis continued to win Hugo awards for her shorter work: for best short story, 'The Soul Selects Her Own Society: Invasion and Repulsion: A Chronological Reinterpretation of Two of Emily Dickinson's Poems: A Wellsian Perspective' (1996); for best novella, 'The Winds of Marble Arch' (1999), *Inside Job* (2005) and *All Seated on the Ground* (2007). Most of her best short work can be found in *Impossible Things* (1994), in *The Winds of Marble Arch and Other Stories: A Connie Willis Compendium* (2005) and in *The Best of Connie Willis: Award-Winning Stories* (2013), which assembles all her stories which have won awards under a title that may seem tendentious, though in fact the collection does present an ample conspectus of her best-known work. Her concurrent fascination with the intersections of film realities and worlds of the past or future may constitute something of a byway in her career, though the hilarious spoofing of Hollywood Westerns in space in *Uncharted Territory* (1994), and the delving into the Marilyn Monroe mythos embedded into *Remake* (1995), are of sustained interest. But her major non-Time Travel tale is *Passage* (2001) (see below).

In the best of Willis's stories, as in her longer work, a steel felicity of mind and style appears effortlessly married to a copious empathy. Perhaps most memorably in the Time Travel books and the tales selected for this omnibus, she is a celebrator, and conveys in her written work much of the pleasure she gives in her frequent, masterful public appearances. She was inducted into the Science Fiction Hall of Fame in 2009 and received the 2011 SFWA Grand Master Award for life achievement.

The first novel presented here is *Lincoln's Dreams* (1987), her finest early novel, which won the John W. Campbell Award. As with much of her most deeply felt work, the enabling SF instrument is Time Travel, in this case via a psychic linkage between a contemporary woman and General Robert E. Lee (1807–70); at the same time the male protagonist, without a breath of frivolity on Willis's part, seems gradually to be taking on the psychic attributes of General Lee's famous horse Traveller, himself a few years later the protagonist of *Traveller* (1988) by Richard Adams (1920–). The relationship between the two protagonists, one of whom literally rides the other through the haunted landscapes of the American Civil War, aches with achieved intensity. Overall, Willis has created in *Lincoln's Dreams* a vision of the Civil War that deeply shapes our understanding of that long ordeal.

Passage (2001), the second substantial novel included in this omnibus, won the Locus Award, and makes an ideal companion for the first book. At some levels they are similar – both are constructed as dream-like trips into the past on the part of female protagonists whose experiences are involuntary but convulsive – but they treat, gravely and persuasively, of very different events. The protagonist of *Passage*, who is involved in a medical study of near-death experiences, falls deeply into corridors and passages aboard the doomed *Titanic*, which increasingly becomes a living/dying emblem of the one inevitable passage we all must make. But the joy of Willis's style, and the smooth depths of her feeling for the human condition, lifts this novel into regions more glowing than any death given here. *Passage* is a very big novel, and it leaves a very big wake.

For a more detailed version of the above, see Connie Willis's author entry in *The Encyclopedia of Science Fiction*: http://sf-encyclopedia.com/entry/willis_connie

Some terms above are capitalised when they would not normally be so rendered; this indicates that the terms represent discrete entries in *The Encyclopedia of Science Fiction*.

LINCOLN'S DREAMS

To
Courtney and Cordelia

Special thanks to my research assistants,
the Smiths – Brooke and Karolyn, Brien and Julie –
for wandering among the tombstones of Fredericksburg and Arlington,
asking questions and taking notes, searching for clues.

Foreword

While I was working on *Lincoln's Dreams*, any number of people asked me why I was writing a book about the Civil War, but no one at all asked me why I was writing a book about dreams. Instead, when I told them what the book was about, they began telling me about dreams they had had, as if I could tell them what they meant.

I had no idea. I have no idea what any dreams mean. All the latest research seems to indicate that they don't mean anything – that they are nothing more than the nervous system's charwoman, tidying up after the day's events, taking out the trash. And that makes very good sense. (Why else would we dream about empty creamer packets that steal a parakeet?) But something in us rebels at the idea that they're the day's detritus, because dreams so obviously *mean* something.

Freud thought so, too. He wrote his dreams down in painstaking detail (they are as ridiculous as ours – full of flower monographs and false teeth) and pored over them, trying to decipher their meaning. He decided they were dispatches from our unconscious: longing sighs and murmured memories and cries for help, all sent in a complicated code.

And that seems logical, too, until it comes to the deciphering. ('The creamer packets clearly represent your yearning for your mother's breast …') Because it's not a code, it's another language. And their images can't be reduced to symbols. Dreams are something more, something else.

Abraham Lincoln dreamed his own death. He heard the sound of crying and asked the guard, 'Who is dead in the White House?' and the guard said, 'The President.' And it's perfectly clear what that dream meant. You don't need a codebook to tell it's a warning. Yet I find myself puzzling over it, and over that other dream of his, the one he dreamed 'before every significant event of the war,' the one he dreamed the night before he died. In that dream, he was in a boat, drifting toward an unknown shore, and you don't need Freud for that one either.

Or if you insist on the charwoman theory, it is scarcely unusual that death was on his mind – there was at least one assassination attempt a week, and he had already heard the sound of crying in the White House when Willie died. And yet, in spite of all this logic, I find them staying with me like a dream, the code impossible to decipher, troubling me, haunting me.

As the Civil War haunts me. In the first part of *Lincoln's Dreams*, Jeff is offered a job researching the long-term effects of the Vietnam War. He turns it down. 'I'm busy studying the long-term effects of the Civil War.' And I guess that's what I was doing, too, writing this book. Because the Civil War isn't over. Its images, dreamlike, stay with us – young boys lying face-down in cornfields and orchards, and Robert E. Lee on Traveller. And Lincoln, dead in the White House, and the sound of crying.

The Civil War disturbs us, all these long years after, troubling our sleep. Like a cry for help, like a warning, like a dream. And we pore over it, trying to break the code, its meaning just out of reach.

Connie Willis

It may be that life is not man's most precious possession, after all. Certainly men can be induced to give it away very freely at times, and the terms hardly seem to make sense unless there is something about the whole business that we don't understand. Lives are spent for very insignificant things which benefit the dead not at all – a few rods of ground in a cornfield, for instance, or temporary ownership of a little hill or a piece of windy pasture; and now and then they are simply wasted outright, with nobody gaining anything at all.

– BRUCE CATTON
Mr Lincoln's Army

CHAPTER ONE

They bred such horses in Virginia then,
Horses that were remembered after death
And buried not so far from Christian ground
That if their sleeping riders should arise
They could not witch them from the earth again
And ride a printless course along the grass
With the old manage and light ease of hand.

— STEPHEN VINCENT BENET

Traveller died of lockjaw two years after Robert E. Lee died. I looked that up one day in February, the day I went out to see where Abraham Lincoln's son Willie had been buried. I had been looking for the grave for over a year, and when I finally found it in a biography of Mary Todd Lincoln, I ran out of the library still carrying the book. It set off an alarm, and one of the librarians came out on the steps and shouted after me, 'Jeff, are you all right? Jeff!'

It was snowing hard that day, a wet spring snow. It took me nearly an hour to drive out to the old cemetery in Georgetown. I don't know what I thought I'd find, some clue maybe to where Annie was and what had happened to her, some message that would tell me what had happened to all of them, Tom Tita and Ben and the rest of the soldiers who had died in the Civil War and were buried together under granite squares no larger than a scrap of paper.

But there wasn't anything there, not even Willie Lincoln's body, and I went back to Broun's house and got out Freeman's four-volume biography of Lee and tried to find out what had happened to Traveller.

As with everything else that had happened, there were both too many clues and not enough. But eventually I found out what I needed to know, the way I had found out where Willie had been, the way I had found out what was causing Annie's dreams. After all, that was what I was good at, wasn't it, looking up obscure facts? Traveller had lived two years. He had picked up a nail and gotten lockjaw. They had had to shoot him.

I met Annie two years ago, the night of Broun's press reception. The reception was supposed to be an advance publication party for Broun's twelfth novel, *The Duty Bound*, with bound galleys passed out to the press, but there weren't any galleys. There wasn't even a finished book.

The press reception had been scheduled for the last week in March, but at the end of February Broun was still fiddling with the copyedited manuscript, making changes and then changing the changes, and a week before the reception I was back in West Virginia, trying to find out exactly when Lee had bought Traveller.

It was a detail that didn't matter one way or the other to the book, since Lee had definitely been riding Traveller at Antietam in September of 1862, but it was the kind of thing Broun had been fussing over the entire book, and it worried me.

He was having all kinds of trouble with *The Duty Bound*. He usually turned out his Civil War novels like clockwork: proposal to outline to manuscript to corrected galleys, which was why his publisher, McLaws and Herndon, had gone ahead and scheduled this reception before they had the copyedited manuscript back.

I might have done the same thing. In the four years I'd been doing research for Broun, he'd never missed a deadline. But with *The Duty Bound*, he hadn't made a deadline yet, and when I called him from West Virginia he was still making major changes.

'I'm thinking of adding a chapter at the beginning of the book, Jeff,' he said. 'To explain why Ben Freeman enlists.'

'I thought you'd already sent the copyedited manuscript back,' I said.

'I did, son. Three weeks ago. But then I got to worrying about Ben. He signs up just like that, for no reason. Would you do that?'

'No, but a lot of recruits did. Listen, I'm calling because I've run into some trouble with Traveller. In a letter to one of his daughters, Lee says he bought Traveller in the fall of 1861, but the records here show he didn't buy him until 1862, during the Carolina campaign.'

'They must have had some reason for enlisting,' Broun said. 'What if Ben's courting a girl who's in love with somebody else?'

McLaws and Herndon would kill Broun if he started adding new characters at this late date. 'I think the beginning's fine,' I said. 'Ben doesn't have to have a good reason to sign up. Nobody else in the Civil War did. Most of the recruits couldn't have told you what the war was even being fought about, let alone why they were in it. I'd go ahead and leave it as is, and that goes for Traveller, too. I'm going up to Lewisburg tomorrow to check the courthouse records, but I'm almost sure Lee didn't buy the horse in 1861.'

'Will you be home in time for the reception?' Broun asked.

'I thought they'd postpone it since the book's late.'

'The invitations were already out. Try to get home for it, son. I need you here to explain why the book's taking so long.'

I wanted to ask him to explain it to me, but I didn't. Instead, I chased all over Greenbrier County for three days, trying to find a scribbled note or a preliminary agreement that would settle the matter one way or the other, and then drove home through an awful snowstorm, but I made it in time for the reception.

'You look like you've been through a campaign, son,' Broun said when I got there late in the afternoon.

'I have,' I said, pulling off my parka. The snow had followed me all the way from White Sulphur Springs and then turned into icy rain fifty miles from D.C. I was glad Broun had a fire going in his upstairs study. 'I found out what you wanted to know about Traveller.'

'Good, good,' he said, taking books off a straight-backed chair and setting it in front of the fire. He draped my wet parka over the back of it. 'I'm glad you're home, Jeff. I think I've finally got a handle on the book. Did you know Lincoln dreamed about his own assassination?'

'Yes,' I said, wondering what on earth this had to do with a novel about Antietam. 'He dreamed he saw his dead body in the White House, didn't he?'

'He dreamed he woke up and heard the sound of crying,' Broun said, dumping his Siamese cat out of his big leather armchair and pulling it around to face the fire. He didn't seem to be in any hurry, even though the reception was supposed to start at seven. He was wearing the ratty-looking gray cardigan he usually wrote in and a pair of baggy pants, and he apparently hadn't shaved since I'd left. Maybe they'd canceled the reception after all.

Broun motioned me to sit down. 'When he went downstairs he couldn't see anyone,' he went on, 'but there was a corpse lying in a coffin in the East Room. The corpse's face was covered by a black cloth, and Lincoln asked the guard standing at the door who was dead, and the guard answered, "The President. He was killed by an assassin."'

He was looking at me eagerly, waiting for me to say something, but I didn't have a clue of what that something was supposed to be. 'He had the dream, what, a month before he died?' I said lamely.

'Two weeks. April the second. I'd read it before, but while you were gone, McLaws and Herndon's publicist called and asked me what book I was going to do after *The Duty Bound*. She needed it for the press release they're going to pass out at the reception tonight, and I told her I didn't know, but then I got to thinking about the Lincoln book.'

The Lincoln book. That was what all this was about. I supposed I should be glad. If he got involved in a new book, maybe he'd quit messing with *The Duty Bound*. The only problem was that the Lincoln book wasn't a new book. Broun called it his midlife crisis book, even though he hadn't started it till he turned sixty. 'I was afraid I'd die before I wrote anything important, and I still might. I never could get a handle on the damned thing,' he'd told me laughingly when I first came to work for him, but I suspected he was more than half serious. He'd tried working on it again a year later, but it still wasn't much more than an outline.

'Tomorrow I want you to go out to Arlington, Jeff.' He scratched at the grayish stubble on his cheek. 'I need to know if Willie Lincoln was buried there.'

'He's buried in Springfield. In the Lincoln tomb.'

'Not where he's buried now. During the Civil War. His body wasn't sent back to Springfield until 1865, when Lincoln was assassinated. Willie died in 1862. I want to know where he was buried for those three years.'

I had no idea what Willie Lincoln had to do with Lincoln's assassination dream, but I was too tired to ask. 'You aren't still having the reception, are you?' I said, hoping against hope that he would say they weren't. 'The roads are terrible.'

'No, it's still on.' Broun looked at his watch. 'I've got to go get dressed. Those damned reporters always come early.' I must have looked like I felt, because he said, 'The battle won't be joined till eight o'clock, and I'll take care of the preliminary skirmishes. Why don't you go have a nap?'

'I think I'll take you up on that,' I said, and heaved myself up out of the chair.

'Oh, would you do one favor for me first?' Broun said. 'Would you call Richard Madison and make sure he's coming tonight? His girlfriend said they'd be here, but I'd like you to call and make sure.'

Lincoln's dreams and Willie Lincoln's body and now my old college roommate. I gave up even trying to look like I knew what he was talking about.

'He called while you were gone,' Broun said, scratching at the stubble. 'Said he had to get in touch with you right away. I told him I didn't have a number for you but you'd be calling in and could I give you some kind of message, but he just said to tell you to call him, and then when you called I didn't have a chance to pass the message on, so I called him to tell him you'd be back today.'

There had to be a connection here somewhere. 'You invited him to the reception?' I asked.

'I invited the girlfriend to the reception. Richard wasn't there. The girl said he was at the Sleep Institute, and I asked her what he did there, and she said, "He tells people what their dreams mean," and after I hung up I got to thinking about Lincoln's dreams and wondering what a psychiatrist would say they meant, so I called her back and invited them to the reception so I could ask him. But since I never talked to Richard and since he wanted you to call him, I think it would be a good idea for you to call and make sure they're coming. And then you'd better go lie down, son. You look like you're about to fall over.'

He went out. I stood in front of the fire for a minute, wondering why Richard had called me. We'd been good friends when we were roommates at

Duke, but we'd hardly seen each other in the six years since we graduated. He'd gone to New York to do his internship and then come back to D.C. for his residency at the Sleep Institute, which meant he was too busy to see anybody. He'd called me exactly once in the last year, and then it was to make me a job offer. One of his patients, a Pentagon big-wig, was doing a study on the long-term effects of the Vietnam war and needed a researcher.

'Not interested,' I'd said. 'I haven't figured out the long-term effects of the Civil War yet.'

'This would be a job where you could do something important instead of wasting your time looking up obscure facts nobody cares anything about for some hack writer,' he'd said.

I had just spent that whole day trying to find out why General Longstreet was wearing a carpet slipper at Antietam. He'd had a blistered heel, a fact that Richard would most certainly put in the category of 'facts nobody cares anything about.' Longstreet had probably cared, though, since he was trying to run a war, and so did Broun, which was why I worked for him, but I hadn't been about to try to explain that to Richard.

'If this Pentagon job is so great, how come the guy's a patient of yours?' I'd said instead.

'He has a sleep disorder.'

'Well, I sleep great nights,' I'd said. 'Tell him thanks but no thanks.' I wondered if he was calling now with another job offer. Broun had said Richard wouldn't tell him what he wanted to talk to me about, which meant it probably was, and I was in no shape to listen to it.

I took a hot shower instead and then tried for a nap, but I found myself still thinking about Richard and decided to call him and get it over with. I went back into Broun's study to use the phone. I thought maybe the girlfriend Broun had talked to would answer, but she didn't. Richard did, and he didn't have any job offers.

'Where in the hell have you been? I tried to call you,' he said.

'I was in West Virginia,' I said. 'Seeing a man about a horse. What did you want to talk to me about?'

'Nothing. It's too late, anyway. Broun said he'd have you call me,' he said almost accusingly. Why was I constantly finding myself in conversations I couldn't make heads or tails of?

'I'm sorry I didn't call. I just got home. But listen, whatever it was, we can talk about it tonight at the reception.'

There was dead silence on the other end.

'You are coming, aren't you?' I said. 'Broun's really anxious to talk to you about Lincoln's dreams.'

'I can't come,' he said. 'It's out of the question. I have a patient I—'

'We're closer to the Sleep Institute than your apartment is. You can give the

Institute Broun's number, and they can call you here if there's an emergency. I'd really like to see you, and I want to meet this new girlfriend of yours.'

Another dead silence. He said finally, 'I don't think Annie should—'

'Come with you? Of course she should. I'll take good care of her while you talk to Broun. I'll tell her all about your wild undergraduate days at Duke.'

'No. Tell your boss I'm sorry, but I don't have anything to tell him about Lincoln's dreams that he'd want to hear.'

Somewhere along in there I started to ache all over. 'Then tell him that. Look,' I said, 'you don't have to come for the whole thing. The reception starts at eight. You can talk to Broun and still have this Annie person home in bed by nine watching her rapid eye movements or whatever it is you psychiatrists do. Please. If you don't come, Broun'll send me to Indiana in this blizzard to look up nightmares Lincoln had as a kid. Come on, for me, your old roommate.'

'I can't stay after nine.'

'No problem,' I said. I gave him Broun's address and hung up before he could say no, and then just sat there in front of the fire. Broun's cat jumped on my lap and I sat there petting it, thinking I should get up and go lie down.

Broun woke me up. 'How long was I asleep?' I said, rubbing my hands over my face to try and wake up. However long it had been, the aches were worse than ever.

'It's six-thirty,' Broun said. He had changed into a dinner jacket with a pleated shirt and string tie. He still hadn't shaved. Maybe he was trying to grow a beard. If he was, it was a terrible idea. The grayish black stubble seemed to take all the color out of his face. He looked sharp and disreputable, like an unscrupulous horsetrader. 'I wouldn't have wakened you, but I wanted you to take a look at this.' He thrust a sheaf of typewritten pages into my hand.

'What's this?' I said. 'Willie Lincoln?'

He poked at the fire, which had died down to almost nothing while I was asleep. 'It's that first scene, the one I was worried about. I just couldn't see Ben signing up for no reason at all, so I rewrote it.'

'Do McLaws and Herndon know about this?' Broun's cat jumped off my lap and started batting at the poker.

'I'm calling it in to them tomorrow, but I wanted you to look at it first. Ben had to have some motivation for enlisting.'

'Why? What about later in the book when he falls in love with Nelly? He doesn't have any motivation for that. She gives him one spoonful of laudanum, and bang, he's ready to do anything for her.'

The cat wrapped a paw firmly around the poker, but Broun didn't notice. He stared into the fire. 'It was the war. People did things like that during the war, fell in love, sacrificed themselves—'

'Enlisted,' I said. 'Most of the recruits in the Civil War didn't have any motivation for enlisting. There was a war, and they signed up on one side of it or the other.' I tried to hand the scene back to him. 'I don't think you need a new scene.'

He put the poker back in the stand. The cat lay down in front of it, tail switching. 'Anyway, I'd like you to read it,' Broun said. 'Did you call your roommate?'

'Yes.'

'Is he coming?'

'I don't know. I think so.'

'Good. Good. Now we'll run this dream thing to ground. Be sure and tell me when he gets here.' He started out the door. 'I'm going to go check on the caterers.'

'Hadn't you better shave?'

'Shave?' he said, sounding horrified. 'Can't you see I'm growing mutton-chop whiskers?' He struck a pose with his hands in his lapels. 'Like Lincoln's.'

'You don't look like Lincoln,' I said, grinning. 'You look like Grant after a binge.'

'I could say the same thing about you, son,' he said, and went downstairs to talk to the caterers.

I tried to read the new scene, wishing I had the time to run a few dreams of my own to ground. I felt tireder than I had before the nap. I couldn't even get my eyes to focus on Broun's typing. The reporters would be here any minute, and then I would stand propped up against a wall for endless hours telling people why Broun's book wasn't ready, and then tomorrow I would go out to Arlington and poke around in the snow, looking for Willie Lincoln's grave.

If I could find out where he was buried, I might not have to spend tomorrow out wiping snow off old tombstones. I put down the rewritten scene and looked for Sandburg's *War Years*.

Broun has never believed in libraries – he keeps books all over the house, and whenever he finishes with one, he sticks it into the handiest bookcase. I offered once to organize the books, and he said, 'I know where they all are.' He might know, but I didn't, so I had organized them for myself – Grant and the western campaign in the big upstairs dining room, Lee in the solarium, Lincoln in the study. It didn't do much good. Broun still left books wherever he finished with them, but it was better than nothing. I had at least an even chance of finding what I needed. Usually. Not this time, though.

Sandburg's *War Years* wasn't where I'd put it, and neither was Oates. It took me almost an hour to find them, Oates in the upstairs bathroom, Sandburg down in the solarium underneath one of Broun's African violets. Before I even got upstairs with them, a young woman from *People* showed up and tried to pump me about Broun's new book.

'What's it about?' she asked.

'Antietam,' I said. 'It's in the press release.'

'Not that one. The new one he's starting.'

'Your guess is as good as mine,' I said, and turned her over to Broun and went back into the study with the books I'd found and looked up Willie Lincoln. He had died in 1862, when he was eleven years old. They had had a reception downstairs in the White House while he lay dying upstairs. And probably people had kept ringing the doorbell, I thought, when the doorbell rang.

It was more reporters, and then it was somebody from the caterer's and then more reporters, and I began to think Richard wasn't coming after all, but the next time the doorbell rang it was Richard. With Annie.

'We can't stay very long,' Richard said before he even got in the door. He looked tired and strung out, which wasn't much of an endorsement for the Sleep Institute. I wondered if the way he looked had anything to do with his having called me when I was in West Virginia.

'I'm glad you both could come,' I said, turning to look at Annie. 'I'm Jeff Johnston. I used to room with this guy back before he became a hotshot psychiatrist.'

'I'm glad to meet you, Jeff,' she said gravely.

She was not at all what I'd expected. Richard had dated mostly hot little nurses when he was in med school, and Washington's Women on the Way Up since he started working at the Institute. He had never so much as glanced at anyone like Annie. She was little, with short blonde hair and bluish gray eyes. She was wearing a heavy gray coat and low-heeled shoes and looked about eighteen.

'The party's upstairs,' I said. 'It's kind of a zoo, but ...'

'We don't have much time,' Richard said, but he didn't look at his watch. He looked at Annie, as if she were the one in a hurry. She didn't look worried at all.

'How about if I bring Broun down here?' I said, not at all sure I could get him away from the reporters. 'You can wait in the solarium.' I motioned them in.

It was, like every other room in the house, really a room for Broun to misplace books in, even though it had been intended for tropical plants. It had greenhouse glass windows and a heater that kept it twenty degrees hotter than the rest of the house. Broun had stuck a token row of African violets on a table in front of the windows and added an antique horsehair loveseat and a couple of chairs, but the rest of the room was filled with books. 'Let me take your coats,' I said.

'No,' Richard said with an anxious glance at Annie. 'No. We won't be here that long.'

I tore up the stairs and got Broun. The caterers had just set out the buffet supper, so he wouldn't even be missed. I told Broun that Richard was here but couldn't stay and herded him toward the stairs, but the reporter from *People* latched on to him, and it was a good five minutes before he could get away from her.

They were still there, but just barely. Richard was at the door of the solarium, saying, 'It's almost nine. I think ...'

'Glad to meet you, Dr Madison. So you're Jeff's old roommate,' Broun said, putting himself between Richard and the front door. 'And you must be Annie. I talked to you on the phone.'

'Yes,' she said. 'I've been wanting to meet you, Mr Brou—'

'I understand you wanted to talk to me about Abraham Lincoln,' Richard said, cutting across her words before she even got Broun's name out.

'I do,' Broun said. 'I appreciate your coming. I've been doing some research on Lincoln. He had some mighty strange dreams,' he smiled at Annie, 'and since you told me Dr Madison here tells people what their dreams mean, I thought maybe he could tell me about Lincoln's dreams.' He turned back to Richard. 'Have you had supper? There's a wonderful buffet upstairs if the reporters haven't eaten it all. Lobster and ham and some wonderful shrimp doodads that ...'

'I don't have very much time,' Richard said, looking at Annie. 'I told Jeff on the phone I didn't think I could help you. You can't analyze somebody's dreams just by hearing a secondhand account of them. You have to know all about the person.'

'Which Broun does,' I said.

'I mostly need some information on what the modern view of dreams is,' Broun said, taking hold of Richard's arm. 'I promise I'll only take a few minutes of your time. We can all go up to my study. We'll grab something to eat on the way and—'

'I don't think ...' Richard said, with another anxious glance at Annie.

'You're absolutely right,' Broun said, his hand clamped firmly on Richard's arm. 'Why should your young lady have to be bored by a lot of dry history when she can go to a party instead? Jeff, you'll keep her company, won't you? Get her some of those shrimp doodads and some champagne?'

Richard looked at Annie as if he expected her to object, but she didn't say anything, and I thought he looked relieved.

'Jeff'll take good care of her,' Broun said heartily, like a man trying to make a deal. 'Won't you, Jeff?'

'I'll take care of her,' I said, looking at her. 'I promise.'

'The dream I'm having trouble with is one Lincoln had two weeks before his assassination,' Broun said, leading Richard firmly up the stairs to his study. 'He dreamed he woke up in the White House and heard somebody crying. When he went downstairs ...' They disappeared into the roar of noise and people at the top of the stairs. I turned and looked at Annie. She was standing looking up after them.

'Would you like to go up to the party?' I said. 'Broun'll be upset if you don't have some of the shrimp doodads.'

She smiled and shook her head. 'I don't think Richard will be that long.'

'Yeah, he didn't seem all that enthusiastic about the prospect of analyzing Lincoln's dreams.' I led the way back into the solarium. 'He kept talking about having to leave. Is one of his patients giving him a rough time?'

She went over to the windows and looked out. 'Yes,' she said. 'Richard told me you're a historian.'

'Did he also tell you he thinks I'm crazy for spending my life looking up obscure facts that don't matter to anybody?'

'No,' she said, still watching the rain turn into sleet. 'That's a term he reserves for me these days.' She turned and looked at me. 'I'm a patient of his. I have a sleep disorder.'

'Oh,' I said. 'Can I take your coat?' I said, to be saying something. 'Broun keeps this room like an oven.'

She gave it to me, and I went and hung it in the hall closet, trying to make sense of what she'd just told me. Richard hadn't contradicted me when I'd called her his girlfriend, and Broun had told me she answered the phone at Richard's apartment, but if she was his patient, what was he doing living with her?

When I came back into the solarium, she was looking at Broun's African violets. I went over to the windows and looked out, trying to think of something to talk about. I could hardly ask her if she was sleeping with Richard or if her sleep disorder had anything to do with him.

'I've got to go out to Arlington National Cemetery in this mess tomorrow,' I said. 'I've got to try and find where Willie Lincoln was buried, for Broun. Willie was Abraham Lincoln's little boy. He died during the war.'

'Do you do all of Broun's Civil War research for him?' Annie said, picking up one of the African violets.

'Most of the legwork. You know, when Broun first hired me, he would hardly let me do any of his research. It took me almost a year to talk him into letting me run his errands for him, and now I wish I hadn't done such a good job. It looks like it's turning into snow out there.'

She put the flowerpot back down on the table and looked up at me. 'Tell me about the Civil War,' she said.

'What do you want to know?' I asked. I wished suddenly that I had had that nap so I could give my full wits to this conversation, tell her stories about the war that would get that somehow sad expression out of her blue-gray eyes. 'I'm an expert on Antietam. Bloodiest single day of the Civil War. Possibly the most important day, too, though Broun will argue with that. General Lee needed a victory so England would recognize the Confederacy, and so he invaded Maryland, only it didn't work. He had to retreat back to Virginia and …'

I stopped. I was putting myself to sleep, and God only knew what I was doing to Annie, who had probably never heard of Antietam. 'How about Robert E. Lee? And his horse. I know just about everything there is to know about his damned horse.'

She brushed her short hair back from her face and smiled. 'Tell me about the soldiers,' she said.

'The soldiers, huh? Well, they were farm boys mostly, uneducated. And they were young. The average age of the Civil War soldier was twenty-three.'

'I'm twenty-three,' she said.

'I don't think you'd have had too much to worry about. They didn't draft women in the Civil War,' I said, 'though they might have had to if the war had gone on much longer. The Confederacy was down to old men and thirteen-year-old boys. If you're interested in soldiers, there are a whole slew of them buried out at Arlington,' I said. 'How would you like to go out there with me tomorrow?'

She picked up another of the potted violets and traced her finger along the leaves. 'To Arlington?' she said.

Richard and I had roomed together at Duke for four years. I had never even looked at one of his girls, and tonight I had told him I would take care of her for him. 'Arlington's a great place to visit,' I said, as if I hadn't spent the last three days and nights living on No-Doz and coffee and wanting nothing more than to get back to Broun's and sleep straight through till spring, as if she weren't living with my old roommate. 'There are a lot of famous people buried there, and the house is open to the public.'

'The house?' she said, bending over another one of the violets.

'Robert E. Lee's house,' I said. 'It was his plantation until the war. Then the Union occupied it. They buried Union soldiers in the front lawn to make sure he never got it back, and he never did. They turned it into a national cemetery in 1864. I've done a lot of research on Robert E. Lee lately.'

She was looking at me. And she had put her hand in the flowerpot. 'Did he have a cat?' she said.

I turned and looked behind me at the door, thinking Broun's Siamese had come down here to get away from the party, but it wasn't there. 'What?' I said, looking at her hand.

'Did Robert E. Lee have a cat? When he lived at Arlington?'

I was too tired, that was all. If I could just have gotten a nap instead of looking up Willie Lincoln and talking to reporters, I would have been able to take all this in – me asking her out when she was living with Richard, her asking me if Lee had a cat while she scrabbled in the dirt of the flowerpot as if she were trying to dig a grave.

'What kind of cat?' I said.

She had pulled the violet up by its roots and was holding it tightly in her hand. 'I don't know. A yellow cat. With darker stripes. It was there, in the dream.'

I said, 'What dream?' and watched her drop the empty flowerpot. It crashed at her feet.

'I've been having this dream,' she said. 'In it I'm at the house I grew up in, standing on the front porch, looking for the cat. It's snowed, a wet, spring snow, and I have the idea that he has gotten buried in the snow, but then I see him out in the apple orchard, picking his way through the snow with little, high, funny steps.'

I did not know what was coming, but at the words *apple orchard* I sat down on the arm of the loveseat, looking anxiously over my shoulder to see if Richard and Broun were coming. There was nobody on the stairs.

'I called to him, but he didn't pay any attention, so I went after him.' She was holding the violet like a nosegay in front of her, tearing the leaves off in absent, desperate movements. 'I made it out to the tree all right, and I tried to pick the cat up, but he wouldn't let me, and I tried to catch him and I stepped on something …' She had torn all the leaves off now and was starting on the flowers. 'It was a Union soldier. I could see his arm in the blue sleeve sticking out of the dirt. He was still holding his rifle, and there was a piece of paper pinned to his sleeve. Somebody had buried him in the orchard, but not deep enough, and when the snow had started to melt it had uncovered his arm. I bent down and unpinned the paper, but when I looked at it, the paper was blank. I had the idea it might be some kind of message, and that frightened me. I stepped back, and something gave under my foot.'

There was nothing left of the violet but the roots, covered in dirt, and she crushed them in her fist. 'It was the cap of another soldier. I hadn't stepped on his head, but where the snow had melted I could see him lying face down with his gun under him. He had yellow hair. The cat went over and licked his face like he used to lick mine to wake me up.

'Whoever had buried them had just shoveled sod over them where they'd fallen, and the snow had hidden them, but now it was melting. I still couldn't see them except for a foot or a hand, and I didn't want to step on them but everywhere I stepped I went through to the bodies underneath. And the cat just walked all over them.' She had dropped what was left of the violet and was looking past me at the door. 'They were buried all over the orchard and the lawn, right up to the front steps.'

I could hear somebody clattering down the stairs, and I moved, for the first time that night, as if I were wide awake. I reached past Annie and scooped up a handful of dirt and torn leaves off the floor. When Richard came in with his coat over his arm, we were both bending down, heads together, picking up the shards, and my hands were as dirty as hers.

I straightened up with a handful of dirt and clay triangles. 'Did you two figure out what was causing Lincoln's dreams?' I asked.

'No. I told you I couldn't tell him what he wanted to know,' Richard said. He looked past me at Annie. 'We've got to go. Get your coat.'

'I'll get it,' I said, and went out to the hall closet.

Broun came plummeting down the stairs. 'Is he still here?'

I motioned toward the solarium. He hurried in, and I followed with Annie's coat. 'I'm so sorry, Dr Madison,' Broun said. 'That damned *People* reporter caught me on the way down. I wanted to say …'

'You asked me my opinion, and I gave it to you,' Richard said stiffly.

'That's right,' Broun said. 'I appreciate your giving it to me. And maybe you're right, and Lincoln was heading for a psychotic break, but you have to remember, there had been a number of attempts on his life already, and it seems to me that it would be normal for him to …'

Richard shrugged on his overcoat. 'You want me to tell you the dreams are normal? Well, I can't. A dream like that is obviously a symptom of a serious neurosis.'

I looked at Annie. She hadn't moved. She was standing beside me, her hands full of leaves and pieces of flowerpot, with an expression on her face that told me she had heard all this before.

'Lincoln was in need of immediate professional help,' Richard said, 'and I'm not going to stand by and say nothing. It's my duty as a doctor to …'

'I think Lincoln is pretty much beyond help even for a doctor,' Broun said.

'We have to go,' Richard said angrily, buttoning his overcoat.

'Well, even though we disagree, I'm glad you came,' Broun said, putting his arm around Richard's shoulder. 'I'm just sorry you can't stay and have some supper. Those shrimp doodads are wonderful.' He led Richard out into the hall.

I held the gray coat and wondered if I were really asleep and dreaming all this. Annie came and took the coat off my arm, and I helped her into it. 'What was the cat's name?' I said. 'In your dream?'

'I don't know,' she said. 'It's not my cat.' She looked down to button her coat, and then looked back up at me. 'It's not my dream,' she said. 'I know you won't believe me because Richard doesn't. He thinks I'm heading for a psychotic break, and you probably think I'm crazy, too, but it's not my dream. I'm dreaming it, but it's somebody else's.'

'Your … he's getting the car,' Broun said, taking in the whole scene.

'I'm sorry about your African violets,' Annie said. 'I was looking at one of them and …'

21

'No harm done, no harm done.' He led her to the front door and out, talking the whole time. 'I'm so glad you could come to our reception.'

When he came back, I was on my hands and knees in front of the bookcase, looking for volume two of Freeman. 'I had a very peculiar conversation with your roommate just now,' he said. He sat down on the arm of the loveseat and looked at the pile of dirt and flowerpot fragments that had been his violet. He scratched his scruffy beard, looking more than ever like a horsetrader. 'He told me that Lincoln's dream was a symbol for some deep-seated trauma, probably in his childhood.'

I found *The Gray Fox* and looked up 'Cats,' and then 'Lee, love of pets,' in the index. 'Well, what did you expect from a psychiatrist?' I said, wishing he would go back to the party so I could find out whether Lee had had a cat.

'I told him I thought the deep-seated trauma was probably the Civil War, and that it seemed perfectly normal for him to dream about assassinations and coffins in the White House. Did you know Willie's coffin was put in the East Room?'

'Did Robert E. Lee have a cat?' I said.

Broun looked at me. 'Lincoln had cats. Kittens. He loved kittens.'

'Lee, damn it, not Lincoln. When he lived at Arlington, did he have a cat?'

'I don't know,' he said, and it was the same placating tone he'd used with Richard. 'Maybe Freeman says something about a cat.'

'Maybe it does, but I don't have a goddamn clue as to where Freeman is. You keep volume one in the attic, volume three under your bed, and volume four you tear up for mulch and use in your African violets. If you had a library like other people instead of this goddamned disorganized mess ...'

'Your roommate said,' Broun went on, 'that all the half-buried bodies in the dream showed that Lincoln was obsessed with death.'

I looked up from the book. He was watching me with his bright little horsetrader's eyes. 'Do you have any idea what he was talking about?' he asked.

'No,' I said. I picked up the scattered books and started to put them back on the shelf. 'I'm going to bed. I've got to go out to Arlington in the morning.'

He stood up then and patted me on the shoulder. 'Don't bother with it,' he said. 'It can wait. You've just gotten home from a long trip, and I know you're tired. Go on to bed, son. I'll take care of that mob upstairs.' His hand was still on my shoulder. 'Did you get a chance to read that scene I gave you?'

'No,' I said.

'I had Ben have a fight with his brother over a girl. I wonder how many soldiers did that, enlisted because of some girl?'

I looked down at the book I was holding. It was the missing volume two. 'I don't know,' I said, and moved away from him.

CHAPTER TWO

Robert E. Lee first saw Traveller during the Big Sewell Mountain campaign in western Virginia. He was riding Richmond then, a big bay stallion that had been given to him by a group of admirers in Richmond. The horse Richmond didn't have the stamina or the disposition for war. He tired easily and squealed and bucked whenever there were other horses around. When Lee was ordered to the south, he didn't take Richmond. He took a horse called the 'Brown Roan', who later went blind and had to be retired. After Manassas, General Jeb Stuart gave Lee a gentle mare named Lucy Long to spell Traveller. In 1864 Lucy gave out, and Lee sent her behind the lines to recuperate. She was stolen by stragglers and sold to a Virginia surgeon.

I didn't wake up till ten the next day, and when I did it was with the idea that the phone had been ringing. It must have been. The message light was on. I turned on the answering machine and listened to the messages while I got dressed. There were two of them. The first was Broun. It had the grainy sound of his car phone. 'Jeff, I'm on my way to New York,' he said. 'I called my editor this morning. He says it's too late to add a scene, that they're already printing the galleys, so I'm taking the scene up to him myself and making sure it gets in. I'll be back tonight. Oh, and forget about going out to Arlington. I got to thinking this morning. Arlington wasn't made into an official cemetery until 1864, and Willie died in 1862. We'll figure out where he was buried later. Stay home and get some rest, son. It's supposed to snow. Oh, and I straightened up the books.'

I looked out the window. It had apparently just sleeted enough to put an icy glaze on the streets last night and then stopped, but now it was starting again. There were only a few large flakes, and they were melting before they even hit the sidewalk, but it had started that way in West Virginia, too, and then turned into a blizzard.

The message was over for a while before the machine and I realized it. Broun had refused to buy a regular thirty-seconds-and-beep kind of machine. 'Nobody worth talking to can state his business in thirty seconds,' was what he said, but what he really wanted was to be able to read long passages of the galleys over the phone or have me dictate the research I was doing in Springfield onto a tape that he could listen to and I could transcribe when I got home. He had had a whole elaborate setup built into the wall behind his desk, with a voice-activated tape that could hold up to three hours of messages and all kinds of fancy remote codes and buttons for fast-forwarding through messages and erasing them.

I pulled on a sweater and waited for the second message. It was Richard. 'I'm at the Institute,' he said. 'I want to talk to you.' He sounded as angry over the phone as he had when he left last night.

I erased both messages and called Annie at Richard's apartment instead. 'It's Jeff,' I said when she answered.

'I just tried to call you,' she said, 'but your line was busy. Do you still have to go out to Arlington to do your research? I want to go with you.'

'I was going out this morning,' I said. 'Are you sure you want to go? It's supposed to get pretty bad.' The snow was coming down faster now and starting to stick to the sidewalk. I could imagine her standing at the phone in Richard's living room, looking out at it.

'It isn't snowing very much over here,' she said. 'I'd like to go.'

'I'll pick you up,' I said. 'I'll be there in about an hour.'

'Don't come all the way across town. There's a Metro station right outside of Arlington. I'll meet you there, all right?'

'Okay,' I said. 'I'll be there in half an hour.'

I got a Styrofoam cup and put what was left of Broun's breakfast coffee in it to take with me. I had been up half the night, trying to find the answer to Annie's question about whether Lee had had a cat. It hadn't been in volume two of Freeman either, or in Connelly's *The Marble Man*. I'd found a letter from Lee to his daughter Mildred that mentioned Baxter and Tom the Nipper, but they were Mildred's cats, and anyway, there was little chance that they had made it through the many moves of the war. Robert E. Lee, Jr. had annotated the letter with the remark that his father was fond of cats 'in his way and in their place,' which seemed to indicate that Lee hadn't had any special cat after all. Nothing I could find in the mess of Broun's books said anything about the family owning a cat when they lived at Arlington. I had finally had to call one of the volunteers who guided tours at Arlington House. I woke her out of a sound sleep, but even half-awake she knew the answer. 'It's in the letters to Markie Williams,' she said, and told me where to find it.

The snow turned into something that was half-rain, half-snow, and slicker than either as soon as I pulled onto the Rock Creek Parkway. It took me almost twenty minutes to get past the Lincoln Memorial and across the bridge.

Annie was waiting on the sidewalk next to the stairs of the Metro station, hunched against the sleet in her gray coat. She was wearing gray gloves, but she didn't have anything on her head, and her light hair was wet with snow.

'I've already been in this storm once on my way back from West Virginia,' I said as she got in. I turned the car heater up to high. 'What say we forget the whole thing and go have lunch somewhere?'

'No,' she said. 'I want to go.'

'Okay,' I said. 'We may not be able to see much of anything, though.' Arlington was always open, even on days like this. It was, after all, a cemetery and not a tourist attraction, but I had my doubts about the house.

The sleet was coming down progressively harder. I couldn't even see as far as the Seabees Memorial, let alone back across the bridge. 'This is ridiculous,' I said. 'Why don't we ...'

'I asked Richard if he'd take me out to Arlington last night. On the way home. And again this morning. He wouldn't. He says I'm trying to project repressed feelings onto an exterior cause, that I'm refusing to face a trauma that's so terrible I won't even admit it's mine.'

'Is that what you think?' I asked.

'I don't know,' she said.

'How many times have you had the dream about the dead soldiers in the apple orchard?'

'I don't know exactly. I've had it every night for over a year.'

'Over a year? You've been at the Sleep Institute that long?'

'No,' she said. 'I came to Washington about two months ago. My doctor sent me to Dr Stone because I was what they call pleisomniac. I kept waking up all the time.'

'Dr Stone?'

'He's the head of the Institute, but he was in California, so I saw Richard. I stayed at the Institute for a week while they ran all kinds of tests, and then I was supposed to be an outpatient, but the dream started getting worse.'

'Worse? How?'

'When I first started having it, I couldn't remember very much of the dream. The dead soldier was in it and the snow and the apple tree, but it wasn't very clear. I don't mean fuzzy exactly, but distant, sort of. And then, after I'd been at the Institute for two weeks, it suddenly got clearer, and when I woke up from it I was so scared I didn't know what to do.' Her gloved hands were clenched tightly in her lap.

'Did you go back to the Institute?'

'No.' She looked down at her hands. 'I called Richard up and told him I was afraid to stay alone, and he said to get a cab and come right over, that I could stay with him.'

I'll bet he did, I thought. 'You said the dream was clearer? You mean, like focusing a camera?'

'No, not exactly. The dream itself didn't change. It was just more frightening. And clearer somehow. I started noticing things like the message on the soldier's arm. It had been there all along, but I just hadn't seen it before. And I noticed the apple tree was in bloom. I don't think it was in the first dream.'

The windshield wipers were starting to ice up. I opened my window and reached around to smack the wiper against the windshield. A narrow band of ice broke off and slid down the window. 'What about the cat? Was it in the dream from the beginning?'

'Yes. Do you think I'm crazy like Richard says?'

'No.' I pulled very carefully away from the curb and onto the wide road.

I couldn't see the curving stone gates until we were almost up to them, and I couldn't see Arlington House at all. You can usually see it all the way from the Mall across the Potomac, looking like a golden Greek temple instead of a plantation, with its broad porch and buff-colored pillars.

'Robert E. Lee had a cat, didn't he?' she said.

'Yes,' I said, and turned in at the iron gate that led to the visitors' center, flashed the pass Broun had that let him drive into the cemetery instead of parking in the visitors' lot, at a guard in a raincoat and a plastic-covered hat, and drove on up the hill to the back of Arlington House. We still couldn't see more than a bare outline of the house through the sleet, even after I'd parked the car at the back of the house next to the outbuilding that had been turned into the gift shop, but Annie wasn't looking at the house. As soon as I'd parked the car, she got out and walked around to the garden as if she knew exactly where she was going.

I followed her, squinting through the snow at the house to see if it was open to visitors. I couldn't tell. There weren't any other cars in the parking lot, and there weren't any footprints leading up to the house, but the snow was coming down fast enough that it could have hidden them. The only way to tell would be to go up to the front door, but Annie was already standing in front of the first of the tombstones at the edge of the garden, her head bent to look at the name on the wet tombstone as if she wasn't even aware of the snow.

I went over and stood next to her. The snow still wasn't sticking to the grass except in little isolated clumps that melted and refroze, making webs of ice between the blades of grass, but the wind had blown enough snow against the tombstones to make them almost unreadable. I could barely make out the name on the first one.

'"John Goulding, Lieutenant, Sixteenth New York Cavalry,"' Annie read.

'These aren't the soldiers who were originally buried here,' I said. 'Those were all enlisted men. Officers were buried on the hill in front of the mansion.'

The second gravestone was covered with snow. I bent and wiped it off with my hand, wishing I'd worn gloves. 'See? "Gustave Von Branson, Lieutenant, Company K, Third U.S. Vermont Volunteers." Lieutenant Von Branson wasn't buried here till 1865, after Arlington had become a national cemetery.' I straightened up, rubbing my wet hand on my jeans, and turned around. 'Then Commander Meigs had the enlisted men moved to—'

Annie was gone. 'Annie?' I said stupidly and looked down the row of tombstones, thinking maybe she had gone past me, but she wasn't there. She must have gone into the house, I thought. It must be open today after all.

I walked rapidly back along the gravel path and up the slick steps onto the porch. The wind was blowing snow up onto the brick-tiled porch and against the buff-colored pillars so they looked almost white.

I tried the door and then pounded on it. 'Are you open?' I shouted, trying to see in through the windows. There weren't any footprints on the porch except mine, but I kept on pounding for another full minute, as if I thought Annie might have gotten locked in, before my rational self told me she'd probably gotten cold and gone back to the car, and I went back around the house to see.

She wasn't in the car, and the gift shop was locked up tight, and I gave up all pretense that I wasn't worried and went tearing back to the front of the house to look down the hill at the lawn where the bodies had been buried.

The wind had picked up in the time it took me to get to the car and back, and I couldn't see more than a few yards down the hill. 'Annie!' I shouted.

I wasn't sure I'd be able to hear her if she answered, but I shouted again, ready to take off down the hill, and then I caught a glimpse of gray moving between trees on the far side of Arlington House and took off running after her. She must be on the Custis Walk, the wide cement sidewalk that came up from the road below. It made a wide curve around the hill so the view of the house wouldn't be spoiled, and I wondered as I ran if that was why they had moved the bodies, too, because they had spoiled the view.

The walk was hardly snowy at all, protected as it was by the big trees that were planted all along its length, and I took the cracked, uneven steps two at a time, trying to catch up with her, and found myself suddenly at the curved wall and marble terrace of the Kennedy Memorial. The eternal flame burned on the grave in the center of a circle of rough, smoke-charred stone, melting the snow around it as it fell.

I looked back up the hill. The snow was blowing almost horizontally across the hill and I couldn't see Arlington House, but I could see Annie. She stood halfway up the hill behind a low wall, looking down at the snow-covered lawn where nothing was buried anymore. I must have gone right past her, missing the turnout in my headlong pitch down the stairs. She didn't see me, standing there looking helplessly up at her, or the eternal flame that seemed to flinch away from the wet flakes of snow falling on it, but I could see her clearly in spite of the snow and the distance between us. I could see the expression on her face.

She had looked frightened last night, telling me her dream, but it was nothing compared to the terror in her face now. I could see them, the yellow-haired soldiers with their arms flung out across the snowy grass, their rifles still under them, and the ink on the scraps of paper pinned to their sleeves beginning to blur as the snow hit the paper and melted. I could see all of it, even the cat, reflected in Annie's face, and I knew I had had no business bringing her out here.

'Annie!' I yelled, and sprinted up the steep slope, my shoes slipping on the icy grass. 'Hold on!' I shouted as if I thought she might fall. 'I'm coming!'

I scrambled over the pebbled cement wall. 'I lost you,' I said, trying to get my breath. 'Are you all right?'

'Yes,' she said, still looking down the hill. 'Tell me about Robert E. Lee.'

The shoulders of her coat were covered with snow. Her hair was wet past curling. She must have been standing there the whole time I was looking for her.

'I had no business bringing you out here,' I said. 'You're going to catch your death of cold. Let's go back to the car.'

'Did he ever come back here?'

'I know a great place just across the bridge. Big fireplace. Great coffee. We can talk about Lee there.' I took hold of her arm. 'I'll tell you whatever you want to know.'

She gave no indication that she even felt my hand on her arm. 'Did he come back here after the war?'

'No,' I said. 'He saw it once. From a train window.'

She nodded as if I had confirmed something she already knew.

'Let's at least go up on the porch of Arlington House. We'll be out of the wind there.'

'He was a good person, wasn't he? They always say that, that he was a good person, don't they?'

I wanted to get her in out of the snow and out of her wet coat and sopping shoes and in front of a fire so she wouldn't catch pneumonia, but I was never going to get her to budge until I had answered her questions. I let go of her arm. 'He was a good person, I guess, if you can call anybody who directed the slaughter of two hundred and fifty thousand men good,' I said. 'He was brave, dignified, forgiving, kind to children and animals. Everybody loved him, even Lincoln.'

'His soldiers loved him,' Annie said. She had taken off her gloves and was twisting them in her hands.

'Yes,' I said. 'One time at Cold Harbor, a column of his soldiers saw him resting under a tree and passed the word that "Marse Robert" was asleep. The whole column went past him practically on tiptoe so they wouldn't wake him up. His soldiers loved him. His horse loved him.'

'Two hundred and fifty thousand men,' she said. 'If he was a good man, how could he bear that, all those young boys? He wouldn't ever be able to get over it, would he?'

'I don't know.'

'Maybe that's why he can't sleep. Because of all those boys.' She turned to look at me. 'This is the house in my dream. In the dream it looks like my house, but it's not my house. It's this house. And it's not my dream.' She turned and looked back down the hill at the Kennedy Memorial. The eternal flame, burning inside the circle of blackened stone, looked like a soldier's campfire. 'Tell me about the cat.'

'Did you ever have a cat? When you were a child?' I asked.

'No,' she said. 'You think I'm crazy, don't you?' she said. She had dropped both gloves. Her hands, flat on the low rough wall, were red and wet.

'No.'

'Richard says something happened to me when I was little, something I don't remember, that's causing me to have the dreams, and that the apple tree and the bodies and the cat are all symbols for what happened. He says the blank paper pinned to the soldier's sleeve is a symbol for the message my subconscious is trying to send me only I'm too afraid to read it.'

'Robert E. Lee's daughter had a cat named Tom Tita,' I said. 'A yellow tabby. He was left behind accidentally when the Lees left Arlington. When a cousin, Markie Williams, went to Arlington to get some of their things and send them to the Lees, she found the cat. It had been locked in the attic, living on mice.'

'What happened to it?'

I stooped to pick up her gloves. 'I don't know.' I handed them back to her. 'She didn't say anything about taking it with her. I suppose she left it there with the Union soldiers who were occupying Arlington. I don't know what happened to it.'

'I feel cold,' she said, and walked ahead of me back to the sidewalk and up to the house.

The porch wasn't much protection. The snow was starting to pile up on the wooden steps and had blown across the hexagonal brick tiles in curving drifts. 'Why don't we go sit in the car and talk?' I said. 'It's freezing out here.'

She sat down on a black painted bench. 'Did you find that in a book?' she said. 'About the cat?'

'In a letter,' I said.

'I could have read it, too, a long time ago, and forgotten I'd ever read it. I could have read somewhere that Arlington was Lee's house and forgotten that, too.'

'Like Bridey Murphy,' I said. 'She was hypnotized. She didn't have dreams.'

'Richard says dreams aren't really the way we remember them. That they're emotions projected as images or symbols, but the second people wake up they try to hide the meaning of the dream from themselves by adding things and forgetting things so it means something else. Maybe that's what I'm doing. I'm making them dead Union soldiers and they're really something else.'

'What?' I said.

'I don't know.'

'What kind of gun did the soldier have? The one you stepped on. You said he was still holding on to his rifle. What kind of rifle was it?'

'I think it was a toy gun,' she said. 'It looked like a rifle, but it had a roll of paper caps in it, like a toy pistol.' She looked up at me. 'Does that mean I shot somebody with a cap pistol in our apple orchard, and then made myself forget it?'

The snow was coming down like a curtain around us. I could barely see past the edge of the porch. 'One of the guns used in the Civil War was the Springfield rifle. It fired a Minié ball by using a paper roll of percussion caps, like the roll of caps in a toy pistol.'

'I had another dream last night,' she said.

'We can't sit out here. You can tell me about it in the car,' I said, and stood up, offering her my hand. She took hold of it with her icy one, and I helped her up, wanting to grab both her hands and hold them against my chest, rubbing some warmth back into them, but she let go as soon as she was on her feet, and put her sodden gloves back on. We walked back to the car.

I started it and turned up the heater and the fan as far as they would go. I didn't turn the windshield wipers on, and the collecting snow shut out the sight of the house and the garden and the graves.

'I was standing under the apple tree, only it was on a hill and down at the bottom of it was a stream, and where my house was supposed to be was the Presbyterian church that I went to when I was a little girl,' she said. She took off her gloves, started to twist them in her hands, and then stopped and stuck them in her pocket.

'It was afternoon, and Richard was there. He was wearing his slippers, and he was looking down the hill, but I couldn't see what he was looking at, and I was angry that he was doing that instead of helping me look.' She stopped and stared at the blinded windshield.

'Helping you look for what?' I said.

'The message. There were supposed to be a hundred and ninety-one of them, but one of them was missing, and I said to Richard, "We've got to find it," but he wouldn't put down the telescope, he just pointed down the hill and said, "Ask Hill. He knows where it is," and at first I thought he meant the hill we were standing on, but then I saw a man on a gray horse and I went down and said angrily, "Where is it?" but he didn't pay any attention to me either. He was trying to get down off his horse, but the horse had fallen forward, onto its knees sort of. Its knees were bent under ...'

She tried to show me, but her elbows wouldn't bend the right way, and I already knew how the horse had looked. I shut my eyes.

'He had one foot in the stirrup and he was trying to get his other leg over the saddlehorn, but he couldn't, and after a while I went back up the hill to Richard and said, "We've got to find it." He didn't answer me either because he was looking through his telescope past the church to the south. I was going to take the telescope away from him, but just then I saw what he was looking at. It was a whole line of Union soldiers, coming up from the south. I said, "Whose troops are those?" and Richard handed the telescope to me, but my hands were bandaged and I couldn't hold it, so I made him look again, and he said, "They're Federals," and I said, "No. It's Hill," and just then the man who'd been on the horse that was on its knees came riding up on another horse, only now he was wearing a red wool shirt, and I was so glad to see him because it meant that even though we couldn't find it, he had still gotten the message.'

I didn't say anything. I ran my hands around the rim of the steering wheel and thought about how I should take her home before the snow got any worse and we were both trapped up here.

'Maybe Richard's right,' she said, 'and whatever's in that lost message is whatever it is I can't remember.'

'What about the bandages on your hands? What about the Confederate soldiers in blue uniforms? And the number one hundred and ninety-one? What are they supposed to mean?'

'I don't know,' she said lightly, and put her gloves back on. 'Richard will have to tell me. He's the psychiatrist.'

'Broun's new book is about Antietam,' I said. 'I've spent the last six months researching everything in print about that battle.'

'And you know why my hands are bandaged?'

'Lee broke his right hand and sprained his left just before the march into Maryland. He was still wearing the splints and bandages at Antietam. Lee had sent an urgent message to A. P. Hill at Harper's Ferry, telling him to bring his men up as fast as he could, so when he saw some soldiers coming up from the south he hoped it was Hill's troops, but the soldiers were wearing blue uniforms.

'He asked one of his aides, "Whose troops are those?" The aide told him they were Union soldiers and offered to let Lee use the telescope, but Lee held up his bandaged hands and said, "Can't use it. What troops are those?" The aide looked again, and this time he could see the Confederate battle flags.

'It was A. P. Hill's men, just up from Harper's Ferry after a forced march of seventeen miles. Hill was riding ahead of them. He was wearing a red shirt.' I gripped the steering wheel. 'They were wearing Union uniforms they had taken from the Federal stores they captured at Harper's Ferry.'

Annie turned and looked out the side window at the graves she couldn't see. 'I want to go home,' she said.

CHAPTER THREE

Lee didn't buy Traveller 'in the mountains of Virginia in the autumn of 1861,' as he wrote his cousin Markie Williams after the war, but he thought of the horse as his from that meeting on, calling him 'my colt' when he saw him again in North Carolina and going out to the stables to visit him. The hostler complained that he was 'always pokin' 'round my horses as if he meant to steal one of 'em.'

Broun had called again, from New York, and left a message on the machine. The weather was even worse to the north. He hadn't been to McLaws and Herndon yet, but he'd seen his agent, and she'd hit the roof about the scene. She'd told Broun that the galleys had already gone to press and there was no way they'd be willing to stop the presses for a scene Broun's editor hadn't even okayed, but Broun was going to try anyway. He'd be home tonight if the weather let up. Otherwise, he'd come back tomorrow morning.

'I want you to call your friend Richard and see if he knows anything about prodromic dreams.' He spelled the word, and then, as if he knew what he was asking was impossible, he said, 'Or better yet, call Kate at the library and see if you can get a bibliography on them. And see if you can find out where Willie Lincoln's buried. Lincoln dreamed about Willie after he died. I'm determined to run this dream thing to ground.'

I looked at the books lying jumbled on the shelves under the African violets. Broun must have been at them again after he straightened them up. There was a biography of Lincoln lying open on top. I rescued a Freeman from the mess and then put it down again.

I wondered what Annie was doing. I hoped she had gotten out of her wet clothes and taken a hot bath, had something to eat, gone to bed, but I had an image of her standing, like myself, looking out at the snow, still in her gray coat, dripping all over the carpet like I was, and beginning to shiver.

I picked up the biography of Lincoln and went up to the study to put it away. The phone rang.

'I want you to stay away from Annie,' Richard said.

'Are you asking me as her doctor or her boyfriend?'

'I'm not asking you at all. I'm telling you. Stay away from her. You had no business taking her out to Arlington.'

'She asked me to drive her out,' I said. 'She told me she asked you to take her, and you refused. So I figure you had your chance.'

'Annie's emotionally unstable. By taking her out there, you could have sent her into a complete psychotic break.'

'Like that nutso Lincoln?' I said. 'You told Broun old Abe was heading for a psychotic break because he'd dreamed, of all things, about his own assassination. Are you trying to tell me that anybody who dreams about the Civil War is crazy?'

'She's not dreaming about the Civil War.'

'Then where in the hell did the Union soldiers come from?'

'You did this, didn't you? While I was upstairs talking to Broun, you were filling her head with a lot of nonsense about soldiers being buried in the front lawn out at Arlington, encouraging this neurotic fantasy of hers. You told her Robert E. Lee had a cat, didn't you?'

'He did have a cat.'

'And as soon as you told Annie that, she told you the cat in her dream was exactly like Robert E. Lee's cat, didn't she?'

I didn't answer him. I was thinking of Annie clutching the African violet and saying, 'Did Robert E. Lee have a cat? A yellow cat? With darker stripes?'

'During dream recall the dreamer's extremely suggestive,' Richard said. 'Anything that's told to the dreamer then can influence his memory of the dream. It's called secondary elaboration.'

'Like telling her she'd shot somebody with a cap pistol?' I said. 'The Springfield rifle had a percussion cap, did you know that? It looked just like a kid's cap pistol. The Springfield rifle was used in the Civil War.'

'Did you tell her that?' he said, sounding almost frightened. 'You had no business telling her that. You're interfering with her therapy. As her psychiatrist, I have a duty to ...'

'To what? Hit on your patients?'

'I wasn't trying to hit on her, damn it. It just happened. I was trying to help her. She was afraid to be alone at night. It just happened. Damn it, you've seen her.'

I'd seen her, standing in the solarium in her gray coat saying, 'You won't believe me either.' I would have driven her out to Arlington right then, in spite of the snow, if she had asked me to. I would have scaled the locked gates and broken into the attic with an ax to look for Lee's lost cat. I would have done anything to help her. Help her. Not take advantage of her fear and her helplessness.

'So you told her she was crazy and then climbed on top of her?' I said. 'Is that how you helped her?'

'Keep away from her. You're interfering with her therapy.'

'Is that what you call taking your patients home and fucking them when they're too scared and tired to say no? What other therapies are you using, Doctor? Have you thought about drugging her so she'll cooperate?'

He waited so long to say anything that even Broun's patient answering machine would have switched off. I waited.

'You know what's really ironic,' he said bitterly, 'I tried to call you last week, but you weren't there,' and hung up.

I looked out at the snow some more and then called the clinic to find out if Richard had phoned me from there. His secretary said, 'I'm sorry. He's not in right now. Can I take a message?'

'Will he be in at all today?'

'Well ...' she said as if she were looking at an appointment book. 'He has a general staff meeting at four, but that may be canceled because of the weather.'

I didn't wait for her to ask for my name. 'Thanks. I'm a friend of his from out of town, and I've got to catch a plane in about five minutes. I just thought I'd give him a call while I was in Washington.'

The phone rang as soon as I pressed down the button. I had the crazy idea that Richard had been listening in on the call and was going to threaten me again, but it was Broun.

'I didn't make it up here with the last two pages of that damned scene,' he said. 'It's probably on my desk. Can you look for it?'

I rummaged through the pile on his desk. He had stuck it in Randall's *Lincoln the President*. 'It's right here,' I said. 'Do you want me to Federal Express it?'

'There's no time for that. They've got the book all set up to print. If these changes don't go in right now, they don't go in at all. You'll have to read it over the phone. McLaws and Herndon are set up to record your call at this number.' He gave me the number.

'Are you going to try to come home tonight?'

'No. It's a real blizzard up here,' he said, and then seemed to catch something in my voice. 'Are you all right?'

No, I thought. I've just had a conversation I would never have believed I'd have with my old roommate over a girl I've just met, and I want you to come home and tell me she's not crazy. I want you to come home and tell me I'm not crazy. 'I'm fine,' I said. 'I was just wondering.'

He still sounded worried. 'You got my message this morning, didn't you? You didn't go out to Arlington in this mess?'

'No,' I said. 'The weather's terrible here, too.'

'Good,' he said. 'I want you to take care of yourself. I thought you looked kind of peaked last night.' He paused, and I could hear voices in the background. 'Listen, they're getting impatient on this end for that scene. Get some rest, son, and don't worry about anything till I get back.'

'I'll call it in right away,' I said.

I hung up and then wished I hadn't. What would Broun say if I called him back and told him I'd gone out to Arlington after all, and with somebody who'd dreamed about the battle of Antietam and Lee's lost cat?

He would say, 'There's a logical explanation for this,' and I had already told myself that – that and a lot of other things. I had gone through every argument there was last night, one after the other, the way I had gone through Broun's books looking for Tom Tita.

They were only dreams. She was ill. She was crazy. It was all an elaborate scam so she could get close to Broun. There was a logical explanation for the dreams. She had read about the cat somewhere. She'd been to Arlington as a child. It was all a joke. She'd been put up to it by Richard. It was some kind of dopey Bridey Murphy phenomenon. It was just a coincidence. Lots of people dreamed about yellow tabby cats. They were only dreams.

There was no point in calling Broun back. He wouldn't be able to add any new arguments to that list. Worse, he might not even try to convince me there was a logical explanation. Fascinated as he was by Lincoln's dreams right now, he might say, 'Has she ever dreamed she saw herself in a coffin in the East Room? Do you think you could try to get her to dream Lincoln's dreams?'

I called the number Broun had given me for calling in the scene, and they put me on hold. I read the scene over while I was waiting.

'You can begin recording now,' a woman said, and I heard a click and then a dial tone. I called again, but the line was busy, so I set the machine to redial the number every two minutes, plugged in the auxiliary mike, and read the revised scene onto the answering machine:

The picket fire slowed up toward dark, and Malachi went back into the woods a little way and built a cookfire.

'What you Rebs havin' for supper over there?' a voice called from across the river.

'Yankees,' Toby said, and then ducked as if he thought they'd shoot at the sound. There was laughter from across the river, and another voice called, 'Any of you Rebs come from Hillsboro?'

'Yeah, and we are on our way to Washington,' Toby shouted back. He put his gun down and leaned on it. 'Myself, I hail from Big Sewell Mountain. What you want to know 'bout Hillsboro?'

The voice across the river shouted, 'I am looking for my brother. His name's Ben Freeman. You know him?'

Toby stepped forward in plain sight to say something funny. Ben stood up and fired across the river. There was a rapid volley of rifle fire, and Toby dived for the ground, his arms around his gun. Ben walked into the woods and sat down by Malachi's fire. Malachi didn't say anything, and after a minute Ben said, 'I don't think we should go talking to the enemy thataway.'

35

Malachi stirred the fire and hung a can over it to boil the coffee in. 'How'd you and your brother come to be on opposite sides of this thing?'

'We just did,' Ben said, staring at the can.

Toby came up to the fire and squatted down in front of it. 'You and your brother fight over some girl?'

'We didn't fight.' Ben reached for his rifle and laid it across his lap. 'He just one day signed up, and I knew I had to, too, and there we was, enemies.'

'Me, I was drafted,' Toby said. 'I bet there was a girl in it somewheres, you signing up thataway.'

'You keep on like that, you might get yourself shot,' Malachi said mildly, 'setting yourself up for a target that way.'

I rewound the tape and waited. The call-completed button came on. I picked up the phone and gave the editor the remote code so she could receive the recorded message without redialing and waited again while she set up a recorder on her end.

'We're all set here,' she said.

'Call me again if it doesn't work,' I said, and hung up.

It was two-thirty. The snow looked like it had let up a little. Richard should be able to make it to his staff meeting. If he wasn't sitting by the phone making sure I didn't talk to Annie.

I picked up Randall's *Lincoln the President*. Maybe he knew where Willie was buried. If he knew, he wasn't telling, but he did say what Willie had died from. It was something called bilious fever, and God only knew what that was. Typhoid probably, though that was already a disease with a name in 1862, and a lot was made of his having caught a cold from riding his pony in bad weather, so it might have been a simple case of pneumonia.

Finding out what people died of a hundred years ago is almost impossible. Letters written by the grief-stricken relatives say that the daughter or son died of 'milk fever' or 'brain fever' or frequently just 'a fever,' and even that is something. Sometimes the patient simply died, 'having progressed weaker and more sickly through the winter till we held out little hope.'

Doctors' accounts are no better. They diagnose agues and heavy colds and 'diffusion of the heart.'

Robert E. Lee, who had almost certainly suffered from angina throughout the war and died of a heart attack, was variously diagnosed as suffering from rheumatic excitement, venous congestion, and sciatica. The modern diagnosis had been pieced together only because somebody thought to write down the symptoms. Otherwise, nobody would have the slightest idea what he died of.

At any rate, Willie Lincoln 'took cold' and died of pneumonia or typhoid or possibly malaria – whatever it was was probably contagious, because his brother Tad was sick, too – or something else altogether, lay in state in the Green Room, and then was moved to the East Room for the funeral.

The funeral was well documented, though I had to put down Randall and rummage through the mess in Broun's study to find the details. The government buildings were closed on the day of the funeral, which irritated Attorney General Bates, who commented that Willie had been 'too much idolized by his parents.' Lincoln, his son Robert, and members of the Cabinet attended, and Mrs Lincoln didn't. The Reverend Dr Gurley performed the service, Willie was bundled into a hearse, and then, like Tom Tita the cat, dropped out of sight.

Randall stopped cold after the funeral; everyone else I read quoted Sandburg, and Sandburg said blithely that Willie's body had been sent back west for burial. It had, but not until 1865. I was sure of that. Lloyd Lewis had chronicled every detail of Lincoln's funeral and the long train trip to Springfield, including Willie's coffin, which lay in front of his father's in the funeral car, so it wasn't 'sent back west' for over three years, and Sandburg, of all people, should have known that.

Sandburg had known Lewis back in the Chicago newspaper days. He had called him Friend Lewis when he wrote the introduction to Lewis's *Myths After Lincoln*. I wondered if Sandburg had forgotten what Lewis wrote about Willie, or if something else had happened between them, something that made Lewis no longer a Friend, something that meant they didn't read each other's books anymore. And was there a girl in it somewhere?

But even Lewis, who was a treasure trove of Lincolniana, didn't say where Willie's body had been for three long years. Was I supposed to assume that it lay in the East Room all that time, giving Lincoln bad dreams? Or had they buried it in the front lawn of the White House?

It was a quarter of four. I put the books back where maybe they would be next time I wanted them and called Annie.

She sounded sleepy, and that reassured me. She hadn't been standing by the window in her wet coat looking out at the snow, listening to Richard tell her she was crazy. She had been asleep.

'How are you?' I asked.

'Fine,' she said, but slowly, with a question in her voice.

'Good. I was worried about you. I was afraid you might have caught a chill out at Arlington.' Caught a chill. I sounded like a Civil War doctor.

'No,' she said, and this time she sounded a little more sure of herself. 'Richard fixed me some hot tea and made me lie down. I guess I fell asleep.'

'Annie, does Richard have you taking anything? Any medication?'

'Richard?' she said, and that faint note of questioning was there in her voice again.

'Is Richard there?' I asked.

'No,' she said, and it was the only thing she'd sounded sure about so far. 'He's at the Institute.'

'Annie,' I said, and felt like I was shouting to her from the bottom of a hill, 'are you taking any medicine, any pills?'

'No,' she said through a yawn.

'When you first came to the Sleep Institute, did Richard prescribe anything for you? Any medicine?'

'Elavil,' she said, and I grabbed my notes on Willie and scribbled it in the margin. 'But then he took me off of it.'

'Why?'

'I don't know. He just took me off of it.'

'When did he do that? – take you off the Elavil?'

It took her a long time to answer. 'It was after the dreams got clearer.'

'How long after?'

'I don't know.'

'And he didn't put you on anything else?'

'No,' she said.

'Listen, Annie, if you have any more dreams or if you need anything, if you want me to take you somewhere, anything, I want you to call me. All right?'

'All right.'

'Annie, last night you said you thought you were dreaming somebody else's dream. Are you sure it was a dream?'

There was another long wait before she answered, and I was afraid the question had upset her, but she simply said, 'What?' as if she hadn't heard the question.

'How do you know it's a dream, Annie? Could it be something that really happened?'

'No, they're dreams,' she said, and her words were blurred a little, as if she still weren't awake.

'How do you know?'

'Because they feel like dreams. I can't describe it. They ...' She all of a sudden sounded more awake. 'What message was I looking for? Was it the message I sent to Hill at Harper's Ferry?'

'No,' I said. 'On the twelfth of September Lee issued campaign orders for the drive into Maryland. One of them was lost. Nobody knows exactly what happened, but a Union soldier found the order and gave it to McClellan.'

'There couldn't have been a hundred and ninety-one copies of it, though,' she said, as if she were trying to convince herself. 'Lee didn't have that many generals. There probably weren't that many generals in the whole Civil War.'

I said, 'You've had a rough day. I don't want you to catch pneumonia. Go back to bed, and we'll talk about this tomorrow.'

'If there weren't a hundred and ninety-one copies, why did I dream that number?'

'It was Special Order 191. It was addressed to D. H. Hill, the man you saw on the gray horse in your dream. He claimed the message was never delivered.'

She hung up. I stood there holding the receiver until the phone began beeping. Then I went and stood by the window and looked out at the snow till it got dark.

It had started snowing again, thick heavy flakes that would cover the graves at Arlington like a blanket. I hoped Annie was asleep and dreaming of something pleasant, a dream without dead Union soldiers in it, a dream without messages.

She hadn't asked me about D. H. Hill, and I hadn't told her. Hill had ridden a gray horse at Antietam. He had been surveying the troops on an exposed knoll when Lee and Longstreet rode up. They dismounted to scan the field, but Hill stayed in the saddle in spite of the artillery fire. 'If you insist on riding up there, and drawing the fire, give us a little interval,' Longstreet had said angrily.

Hill hadn't even had a chance to answer. The cannonball took the horse's front legs off, and it plunged forward onto its stumps. Hill had had one foot in the stirrup, and when he tried to get off the horse he had been unable to get his other leg over the croup of the saddle, just the way Annie had described it. Just the way she had seen it. In her dream.

CHAPTER FOUR

Traveller was a Confederate gray gelding with a black mane and tail. He was probably not a thoroughbred, though historians have gone to incredible lengths to provide him with aristocratic breeding lines, one of them even claiming he was descended from Diomed, the famous English Derby winner. He did have a thoroughbred's intelligence and courage and incredible endurance. 'He never needs whip or spur,' his owner wrote to Lee, 'and will go anywhere.'

I got up early and went to the library to see what I could find out about Elavil. The drug compendium said it was a fairly mild tricyclic antidepressant with a sedative effect, and that it was frequently used in connection with insomnia. It had an assortment of minor side effects and a couple of major ones. It was contraindicated for patients with heart conditions and those who had shown a previous hypersensitivity. It didn't say anything about dreaming of dead Union soldiers. In fact, if Richard had had Annie on Elavil she shouldn't have been dreaming at all. The tricyclic antidepressants increased the amount of time spent in delta sleep and decreased REM sleep, which was the stage most dreams occurred in.

I asked the librarian what she had on dreams. 'Not much,' Kate said. 'Some pseudoscience things and Freud's *Interpretation*. No, wait, I think that's checked out.' She hit some buttons on her computer and waited for the book's status to come up. 'Yeah, that's checked out till April ninth. Do you want to reserve it?'

'I was really looking for current research.'

She tapped some more buttons. 'We've got a few things in the one hundreds, but nothing very up-to-date. If you know exactly what you want, I can get it through interlibrary loan. If not, I suppose the Library of Congress. Have you tried the Sleep Institute? They've got a really good reference library.'

'I'll take my chances in the one hundreds,' I said.

Kate was right. There wasn't much, and what there was was do-it-yourself dream interpretation: 'To dream about a house means you are sexually repressed,' that kind of thing. Cats were a symbol of animal instincts, guns of sex, dead bodies of – surprise! – death. Horses with their front legs shot off weren't mentioned.

I asked Kate to see if she could put together a bibliography on prodromic dreams for Broun, and went home.

The phone was ringing when I opened the door. I had set the answering machine to 'message' before I left. It shouldn't have rung more than twice before the taped message kicked in, but I counted three rings while I wrestled to get the key in the door and one more on my way up the stairs. I burst into the study.

Broun was hanging up the phone. 'Who was that?' I demanded breathlessly.

'It wasn't anyone,' he said mildly. 'Whoever it was hung up before I answered. Jeff, I want you—'

'It rang four times, and you were standing right there. Why didn't you just leave the damn thing on "message" if you weren't going to answer it?'

'Dr Stone and I were going over some material on dreams,' he said, still mildly, and gestured toward his club chair. 'Dr Stone, I don't think you've met my researcher, Jeff Johnston. Jeff, Dr Stone is head of the Sleep Institute.'

The man who had been sitting in the club chair all this time stood up and extended his hand. 'How do you do?' he said. My first thought was that Richard had sent him over to tell me to keep away from Annie, but he as smiling a polite, mildly ingratiating smile, the kind you use when you meet a total stranger, and Broun was smiling, too. My name obviously hadn't been brought up before I got there.

'I think I may know a friend of yours,' he went on. 'Richard Madison?'

I used to know him, I thought, but that was before he started telling his patients they were crazy. That was before he started seducing his patients.

'We were roommates in college,' I said.

'He's a good man,' Dr Stone said, dropping his hand easily, as if I had shaken it. 'He's been doing some research on insomnia, I believe.'

He's been taking advantage of one of his patients, I thought, and he could hardly tell his boss that, so maybe Richard wasn't the reason he was here after all.

'How well do you know Richard?' I asked.

'I've been in California for the past six months, working on a neurological dream-study project. I met him when I got back, but I haven't had a chance to discuss his work with him yet,' he said, still smiling, and sat back down. 'I'd only been back a few days when Mr Broun asked me to come over and explain Lincoln's dreams to him. I was flattered to be asked, of course, but I'm afraid I haven't been much help. I don't know what Lincoln's dreams mean. Or what any dreams mean, for that matter. If they mean anything.'

'He's had some very interesting things to say,' Broun said. 'Sit down, son. I want you to hear his ideas. I called on the way down from New York and left a message telling you Dr Stone was coming over, but I guess you didn't get it.' He motioned toward the only other chair in the study, a rickety wooden chair he used for reaching the top shelves. The seat was piled high with books, and his cat was on top of them, sound asleep.

'I was at the library doing research on dreams and getting nowhere,' I said, relaxing a little, 'so I don't know what Lincoln's dreams mean either.' Or why you're here, I thought. Broun had been curious about Richard's odd behavior the night of the reception. I wondered if he had invited Dr Stone over to try to find out why Richard had reacted so violently to his questions about Lincoln or whether he was simply trying to 'run this dream thing to ground.'

'Tell Jeff here what you were saying to me about Freud,' Broun said eagerly.

Dr Stone leaned back into the depths of the leather chair, his hands resting easily on the padded arms, and smiled. 'As I was telling Mr Broun, dream interpretation is not a science, although Freud attempted to make his colleagues believe it was one. He claimed that dreams were a stage on which people symbolically act out the traumas and emotions that were too frightening to deal with when they were awake. A Freudian would say Lincoln's dream was a symbolic enactment of Lincoln's secret wishes and fears, that not only the coffin but the stairs, the guard, everything in the dream was a symbol hiding the real meaning of the dream.'

I went over to the chair, shooed the cat off, and started stacking the books on the floor beside the chair. The cat went over to the leather chair, looked speculatively at Dr Stone's lap, and then went over by the fire to sulk.

'Which is?' I asked.

'I'm a scientist, not a psychiatrist. I don't believe dreams have a "real" meaning. They're a physical process, and any "reality" they have lies in the physical. Freud made no attempt to understand the physical. He felt the key to understanding dreams lay in content, and came up with an elaborate system of symbols to explain the images in dreams. In Lincoln's dream, for instance, the stairs represent the descent into the subconscious, of which Lincoln is both curious and afraid, symbolized by the crying that he hears. The guard and the cloth over the corpse's face are both symbols of Lincoln's unwillingness to find out the secret his unconscious holds.'

I thought of Annie standing in the snow saying, 'Richard says the blank paper pinned to the soldier's sleeve is a symbol for the message my subconscious is trying to send me only I'm too afraid to read it.'

'What about the corpse?' I asked. 'And the coffin.'

'Oh, the coffin is the womb, of course. The entire dream's about Lincoln's desire to return to the safety of the womb.' He smiled. 'According to the Freudians.'

'But that's not your interpretation,' Broun said.

'No,' Dr Stone said. 'In my opinion, dream interpretation as practiced by most Freudian psychiatrists, including some of mine at the Institute, is nothing more than a fancy system of guessing. I think trying to understand the "real" meaning of a dream without reference to the physical state of the dreamer is as pointless as trying to understand what a fever "means" without studying the body.'

In spite of the fact that I still thought Richard might have sent him, I found myself liking Dr Stone. He said things like 'I think' and 'in my opinion' and didn't seem to think he automatically knew all the answers where dreams were concerned. If Annie told him her dream, at least he wouldn't tell her she was crazy, and he might be able to help her. She was supposed to have seen him anyway. Maybe if I called her and told her he was back from California, she could change doctors and get out of Richard's clutches.

'Dreams are a symptom of physical processes,' Dr Stone was saying. 'They don't "mean" anything. Lincoln could have dreamed what he did for any number of reasons. He could have been to a funeral that day, or seen a hearse. Or he could have been reminded of someone who had died recently.'

'Willie,' Broun said. 'Lincoln's son. He died in the White House. His coffin was in the East Room, too.'

'Exactly,' Dr Stone said, looking pleased. 'He could have been dreaming about Willie. The person in the coffin could have represented both Willie and Lincoln's own fears of assassination. The combining of two people into one is very common in dreams. It's called condensation.'

I thought of Annie and the way she had combined the two generals, A. P. Hill and D. H. Hill, into one.

'Or,' he leaned back into the chair, 'it could have been something he ate.'

'So you couldn't tell if someone was emotionally disturbed just from the dreams they were having?' I asked.

'Hardly,' Dr Stone said. 'If that were true, we'd all be certifiable. I remember a dream I had where I was using a cattle prod on my patients.' He laughed. 'No, dreams by themselves can't offer adequate evidence of emotional illness. Why?'

I realized, too late, that we shouldn't have gotten into this. 'Somebody told Broun that Lincoln's dreams indicated that he was heading for a nervous breakdown.'

'Really? A layman, I assume. A psychiatrist would never try to diagnose on the basis of a dream.'

Well, a psychiatrist – one of his psychiatrists, as a matter of fact – had done just that, and I would have liked to tell him that Dr Richard Madison, that good man doing research on insomnia, had done more than that, but telling him about Richard meant telling him about Annie, and I wasn't ready to do that just yet, not until I knew a little more about Dr Stone.

'You said dreams can be caused by something you ate?' I said before Broun had a chance to tell him who had diagnosed Lincoln as crazy. 'Is that really true? Can you get nightmares by eating Mexican food before you go to bed?'

'Oh, yes. Eating causes certain enzymes to be released into the dreamer's system, and those trigger …'

The phone rang. I turned and looked at the answering machine. Broun put his pen down. Dr Stone leaned forward in his chair watching both of us.

'Do you want to get that?' Broun asked.

'No,' I said. I pushed the message button. 'It's probably only the librarian. She promised to get me some information on Lincoln's dreams. I'll call her back.'

The phone rang a second time, finally, and the message light came on. I could hear the click as the recorder started its spiel, telling whoever it was that there was no one here and would they leave a message at the sound of the tone. And who was it? Annie, saying, 'I had another dream'? Or Richard, calling to tell me to stop interfering with his treatment? The message light went out.

I turned back to Dr Stone. 'You were saying?'

'Digestion can have an effect on dreaming because the digestive enzymes in the bloodstream trigger chemical changes in the brain.'

'What about drugs?' I said. 'Drugs cause chemical changes in the blood, too, don't they? Could Lincoln's dreams have been the effect of some drug he was taking?'

'Yes, certainly. Laudanum was known to cause—'

43

'What about Elavil? Could it cause dreams?'

He frowned. 'No, actually Elavil represses the dream cycle. All the anti-depressants do, and of course the barbiturates: Seconal, phenobarbital, Nembutal. The patient usually doesn't dream at all when he's on those drugs. Of course, when he's taken off them, the number and vividness increase dramatically, so I suppose you could say in that respect they cause dreams. But of course those are modern drugs,' he said, looking at Broun. 'Lincoln wouldn't have taken any of them.'

'What do you mean, increase in vividness?' I asked.

'The drugs produce a dream deficit that is compensated for by a dream rebound as soon as the patient is taken off the drugs. The patient experiences what we call a "storm of dreams," for several days, powerful, frightening nightmares that rapidly succeed each other. It's the same thing that happens when a patient's been deprived of sleep for several days. We usually advise against abrupt discontinuation of antidepressants and sedatives to avoid triggering a storm of dreams.' He gave me a look almost as sharp as one of Broun's. 'Are you on Elavil?'

'No,' I said. 'Lincoln had insomnia after Willie died. I thought maybe his doctor might have prescribed something to make him sleep that gave him bad dreams, so I looked up "insomnia," and it said Elavil was a recommended treatment, but obviously I was in the wrong century.' I stood up. 'Speaking of sleep and drugs and digestion, would anybody like some coffee? Or does coffee give you bad dreams, too?'

'As a matter of fact, caffeine has been shown to have marked effects on dreaming.'

'I'll make it decaffeinated,' I said, and went downstairs to the kitchen.

Broun had another phone there, a separate line. I called the number of the phone in the upstairs study, and before it could ring, punched in the remote code that would play back the message. The only message on the machine was Broun's. 'I'm on my way down from New York, Jeff. I should be there around ten. I'm meeting with a Dr Stone from the Sleep Institute at eleven. He's been doing dream research in California, and I thought I'd see what he had to say about Lincoln's dreams.'

I put the coffee on and tried to call Annie. There was no answer. I found a tray and put Styrofoam cups and the cream pitcher and sugar bowl on it. I tried Annie's number again. Still no answer.

She's sleeping, I told myself. Her subconscious is trying to make up for the REM sleep she lost when she was on the Elavil. It was a logical enough explanation. When Richard took her off the Elavil, she had had a 'storm of dreams,' that was all. The dead Union soldiers and the horse with its legs shot off were nothing more than her subconscious trying to make up for lost time. When her dream deficit got caught up, she would stop dreaming about lost dispatches and Springfield rifles, and there was nothing to worry about.

But I had asked her, 'When did Richard take you off the Elavil?' and she had told me it was *after* the dreams got suddenly clearer and more frightening, not before. Besides, the 'storm of dreams' was only supposed to last a few days. Annie had had the dream about Antietam at least two weeks after Richard had taken her off the Elavil. And she had been dreaming about the dead Union soldiers for over a year.

Broun's cat had followed me downstairs. I looked in the refrigerator to see what the caterers had left behind and found half a plate of soggy crackers with shrimp salad on them. I set it on the floor and tried to call Annie again, and then went back upstairs with the tray.

They were talking about prodromic dreams. 'A Dr Gordon did a study on prodromic dreams a couple of years ago at Stanford on tuberculosis patients,' Dr Stone said, 'but I don't think he found anything conclusive. The study I was working on in California ...'

Dr Stone stopped talking when I came into the study. Broun stood up and began heaping papers and books on one side of his desk to clear a space for the tray. I set it down.

'Dr Stone was just going to tell me about his project,' Broun said.

'Yes,' Dr Stone said. 'The project I headed up in California involved using a probe on different parts of the brain. The probe produces an electrical charge that provides a stimulus to a localized region of the brain, and the patient, who's under local anesthetic only, tells us what he's thinking. Sometimes it's a memory, sometimes a smell or a taste, sometimes an emotion.

'The probe is used randomly, touching a large number of areas in a very short time, too short a time for the patient to respond individually to the stimuli. Then the patient is asked to describe everything that he's seen, and we compare the transcript of his account with transcripts of dream accounts obtained by traditional methods. We've come up with a statistically significant correspondence. And the most interesting aspect of it is that even though we know there's no connection between the images in the account, the patient connects them all into a coherent, narrative dream.'

Well, so much for suggesting Annie change doctors. Dr Stone might not tell her she was crazy, but what if he decided the best way to get at the 'real' meaning of the dreams was to put her on an operating table and open up her head? What Annie needed was a doctor who would listen to her dreams and try to find out what was causing them instead of trying to force his own theories on her, and I was beginning to think there wasn't any such thing.

'You mean there was some kind of electrical shock in Lincoln's brain and he saw a coffin and then made up the rest of the dream?' Broun said.

'*Made up* is the wrong word,' Dr Stone said. 'We have to remember that although the dream occurs in the subconscious, the memory of it occurs in the conscious mind. The dream is translated into the conscious mind, and it may be in that translation process that the dreams take on their narrative aspect. It may be the same kind of process that takes place when we watch film. We're seeing individual frames, but it looks like they've moving. Persistence of vision, it's called. Maybe there's a corresponding persistence that translates unrelated impulses into the dream we remember.'

Broun poured a cup of coffee and handed it to me. 'These impulses,' he said, 'where do they come from?'

'The initial results of our study indicate that the brain is processing the factual material of the day for storage.'

Broun handed him a Styrofoam cup full of coffee. 'Do you take anything in your coffee?' he asked.

Dr Stone leaned forward a little, making the leather in the chair creak, and took the cup. 'Just black,' he said. 'We're also getting indications that external stimuli have a marked effect on dream content. Everybody's had their alarm clock show up in a dream as a scream or a cat meowing or the sound of someone crying.'

Broun poured himself a cup of coffee and stirred cream into it. 'What about recurring dreams?' he asked. 'After Willie died, Lincoln dreamed about him for months.'

'The same dream?'

'I don't know,' Broun said. He set down his cup and scrabbled in his notes. '"Willie's death had staggered him, haunting his sleep until the little boy's face came in dreams to soothe him,"' he read aloud. 'That's from Lewis. And Randall says he dreamed Willie was alive again.'

'Our study has shown that most recurring dreams aren't the same dream at all. We used the probe randomly, repeatedly stimulating one selected region of the brain in each test. After each session, the patient would report that he had had the same dream as before, but when questioned about individual details he told an entirely different dream, though he persisted in his belief that the dreams were identical. Persistence of dreams again. Lincoln would naturally have many images of the living Willie stored in his memory that could be stimulated.'

'What about Lincoln's dream of his own assassination?' I asked. 'That couldn't just be Lincoln putting all the day's junk in some kind of mental file cabinet, could it? All the details fit – the coffin in the East Room, the guard, the black cloth over the corpse's face.'

'Because his conscious mind *made* them fit. Remember, we have no idea of what the dream was really like.' He turned and smiled crookedly at Broun, then turned back to me. 'What we have is Lincoln's account of the dream, which is something completely different.'

46

'Secondary elaboration,' I said.

'Yes,' he said, looking pleased. 'You *have* been doing a lot of research, haven't you? Lincoln's real dream would have been a sequence of unrelated images, a stairway, a memory of Willie Lincoln in his coffin, a cloth of some kind, a napkin or a handkerchief or something. It wouldn't have to be black or even cloth, for that matter. It could have been a scrap of paper.'

A scrap of paper, a cat, a Springfield rifle. It won't wash, Dr Stone.

'... and in the process of bringing the dream up to the subconscious and then telling it, the dream took on a coherence and an emotional importance it simply didn't have.' He put both hands on the arms of the chair. 'I'm afraid I'm going to have to get back to the Institute.'

'What if *I* dreamed I was upstairs in the White House and heard crying but couldn't see anyone?' I asked. 'What if when I went downstairs there was a coffin in the East Room?'

Broun reached for his cup. Coffee slopped onto his notes.

'I'd say you'd spent the whole day doing research on Lincoln's dreams,' Dr Stone said.

'Did you dream that?' Broun said, still holding the cup at an angle. More coffee spilled out.

'No,' I said. 'So you don't think Lincoln's assassination dream means anything, even though everything in it happened two weeks later? You think it's all just a matter of what he did that day and what he had for dinner?'

'I'm afraid so.' Dr Stone stood up and set his cup on the tray. 'I know this probably isn't the sort of thing you wanted to hear, especially when you're trying to write a novel. One of the greatest difficulties I encounter in my research is that people want to believe that their dreams mean something, but all the research I'm doing seems to indicate just the opposite.'

You didn't see her standing there in the snow, I thought. You didn't see the look on her face. I don't know what's causing her dreams, but it's not random impulses and it's not indigestion. Annie's dreams do mean something. There's a reason she's having them, and I'm going to find out what it is.

'You've been a great deal of help, Dr Stone,' Broun said. 'I appreciate your giving us so much of your time. I know you're very busy.'

He walked Dr Stone downstairs. I waited till they were almost at the bottom of the steps and then went over and hit the play button on Broun's answering machine. There still wasn't any message.

I tried to call Annie. She didn't answer. Broun's cat jumped up on the desk and dipped its head into Broun's Styrofoam cup and began lapping delicately at the coffee. I put down the phone and picked him up by the back of the neck to throw him off.

'I take it you didn't think too much of Dr Stone's theories,' Broun said from the door.

'No,' I said, depositing the cat on the floor. 'Did you?'

'I thought he had some interesting things to say.'

'About Lincoln's indigestion or about taking a cattle prod to his patients?'

'About the real meaning of Lincoln's dreams being physical.' He sat down heavily in the leather chair. 'And about the persistence of dreaming, how we take a lot of unconnected images and make them into one continuous dream.'

Unconnected images. A carpet slipper, a red wool shirt, a horse with its legs shot off. 'I thought it was all a lot of hogwash,' I said.

'Jeff, are you all right? You've seemed upset about something ever since you got back from West Virginia.'

'I'm just tired. I haven't caught up from the trip yet,' I said, and then wondered why I didn't say, No, I'm not all right. I'm worried sick. That young woman you met at the reception is dreaming things she couldn't possibly know about. I might not be able to tell Dr Stone, but I could surely tell Broun.

'Have you been sleeping all right?' He was sitting the way Dr Stone had sat, his feet flat on the floor and his hands resting on the leather arms of the chair, watching me.

'Sure. Why?'

'I thought maybe you ... when Richard called from the Institute and wanted to talk to you, I got the idea that maybe you were a patient of his, and then you asked Dr Stone all those questions about Elavil causing bad dreams. I thought maybe he'd put you on some kind of tranquilizer.'

'No,' I said. 'I'm not taking anything. And I'm not having bad dreams.' But Annie was. And now was the time to tell him, to explain my behavior and Richard's and tell him about Annie's dreams. The cat made a flying leap onto the desk and right into Broun's coffee. I dived for the cup and Broun's notes at the same time. Broun pushed himself up out of the chair and came over to get the cat. I moved the notes out of the way.

'Broun,' I said, but he had the cat by the scruff of the neck and was putting it out the door. He shut it on its indignant yowl and sat down in the chair again.

'I'm glad you're all right,' he said. 'I was worried about you. Did you know Lincoln had trouble sleeping? After Willie died? I think he must have almost gone crazy.' He was looking past me now, as if I wasn't even there. 'He had Willie's body disinterred twice so he could look at Willie's face, did you know that?'

'No,' I said.

'Poor man. I was thinking about what you said, about dreaming Lincoln's dreams. That would be wonderful, wouldn't it?'

'No, it wouldn't,' I said, thinking of Annie. 'It would be terrible,' but it was obvious he didn't hear me.

'When you were asking all those questions about having Lincoln's dreams, all I could think of was how wonderful for the book it would be if you were having them,' he said, still not looking at anything.

'For the *book*?'

'Imagine, if you were having Lincoln's dreams, we'd finally know what he really thought, what he really felt. It's what every writer dreams about.' He slapped the arms of the chair and stood up. 'Jeff, I want you to go to California for me.'

'No.'

He was finally looking at me, and his sharp eyes were taking in everything the way they had the night of the reception. 'Why not?'

The phone rang. I snatched it up, knocking the cup of coffee flying, wanting it to be Annie and hoping against hope it wasn't. I didn't want to talk to her in front of Broun. A minute ago I had wanted to tell him. I still wanted to tell him, but I couldn't. He thought Dr Stone had had 'some interesting things to say' about how dreams were only unconnected images. He thought it would be wonderful 'for the book' if I were having Lincoln's dreams.

He's not like Dr Stone, I told myself, or Richard. He's never been anything but kind to you. If you tell him about Annie, he'll be as worried as you are, he'll do anything he can to help her. Maybe, I thought, and maybe he'll look at her with his bright little eyes and say, 'This is what every writer dreams about.' I couldn't risk it. Not with Annie.

'Hello,' I said cautiously into the phone.

'Hi, this is Kate from the library. How do you spell "prodromic"? I've looked through our stuff, and we don't have a thing on it, so I'm going to call over to the Library of Congress, but I wanted to make sure I was spelling it right. Is it ...' She spelled it for me, and I held the phone, hardly listening.

I couldn't tell him about Annie, but I would have to tell him something. I had to talk him out of sending me three thousand miles away from Annie when she might call anytime, when she might need me.

'That's the way it's spelled,' I said to Kate, not knowing whether it was or not. 'Thanks.' I hung up and started wiping up the spilled coffee with one of the paper napkins on the tray.

'I'm determined to find out what caused Lincoln's dreams,' Broun said, still watching me. 'There's a man in San Diego who's been working on prophetic dreams.'

Broun's notes were soaked. I blotted them with the napkin.

'I want you to fly out tomorrow and talk to him about Lincoln's dreams,' he said.

'What about the weather? They said on the radio this morning that the airport was closed.'

'Then you can go the next day.'

'Look, I really don't see the point of all this running around. I mean, can't you just call the guy? There's nothing he can tell me in person that he can't tell you over the phone, is there?'

'You can watch him while he says it,' Broun said, watching me dab at the sodden notes. 'You can tell whether he's telling the truth or not.'

'And what difference will it make if he is?' I said angrily. 'Lincoln's dead, and this guy won't know what caused his dreams any more than Dr Stone or Richard did. No matter how many experts you ask, you're never going to find out what really caused the dreams. You've already got plenty of explanations. Pick the one you like the best. What difference does it make?'

'It made a difference to Lincoln,' he said slowly. 'It makes a difference to me.'

'The way it made a difference to you when Lee bought Traveller? You didn't need to know that. No matter when he bought him, it was before Antietam. But you sent me chasing all over West Virginia looking for bills of sale, and now you want to send me to California on another wild goose chase.'

'Never mind,' he said. 'I'll go myself.'

I looked down at Broun's notes, afraid my relief would show in my face. The sodden pages were matted together. I tried to peel the top sheet off, and half the page came off and half the page came off in my hand. I looked at it. The ink was blurred so badly I couldn't read what he had written.

'Look, I just think you should keep a little perspective on things. You got totally wrapped up in *The Duty Bound,* and look what happened. And now you're getting obsessed with this.'

'I said I'd go myself, damn it.' He stood up. 'Give me the damned notes before you ruin them. And call McLaws and Herndon. Tell them to wait on the galleys. I'm changing another scene.'

'You can't do that,' I said. 'They've already set the type. What am I supposed to tell them?'

'I don't care what you tell them. Tell them I'm obsessed with *The Duty Bound.*' He grabbed for the notes, and they tore across without any sound. He yanked the torn pieces out of my hand. 'Tell them you think I'm a little tetched in the head like Lincoln was after Willie died. Tell them I want to dig up the body to have one last look at it before it goes to press. Like that crazy Lincoln.'

When I went downstairs to the kitchen to call McLaws and Herndon, he shut the door of his study, and I could hear the uneven stutter of his typing like sniper fire from across the river.

CHAPTER FIVE

Around Christmas of 1861, during the Carolina campaign, Robert E. Lee bought Traveller for a hundred and seventy-five dollars, adding an extra twenty-five dollars to counteract the falling value of Confederate money. 'He has been my patient follower ever since,' he wrote Markie. 'He carried me through the Seven Days battle around Richmond, Sharpsburg, Fredericksburg, the last day at Chancellorsville, to Pennsylvania, at Gettysburg, and back to the Rappahannock ... to the final days at Appomattox Court House.'

Broun didn't ask me to call in the scene this time. He called it in himself the next morning and then left to talk to a Lincoln expert in Georgetown. 'I'm leaving for California tomorrow,' he said belligerently. 'Did you find out where Willie Lincoln was buried?'

'No,' I said. 'I'm going over to the library right now. Do you want me to go get the ticket first?'

'You can pick it up this afternoon,' he said.

'Fine,' I said, wishing I could say something that would make him less angry with me. I couldn't apologize because an apology meant an explanation, and I couldn't explain. Maybe it was just as well he wasn't talking to me because then there wouldn't be any questions either. 'What about the galleys?'

'What about them?'

'McLaws and Herndon called this morning before you were up. They said they were sending them down Federal Express, they want them back in two weeks at the latest, and no major changes.'

'You can give them the first reading, and I'll finish them when I get back.'

'Which will be when?'

'I don't know. A week maybe.'

I waited till he had left for Georgetown and then went upstairs and made sure the answering machine was set on 'message.' I drove over and picked up Broun's ticket from the travel agency and then went to the library.

Kate didn't have the bibliography ready, and I told her I wasn't in any hurry, I was going to be there awhile. I spent the rest of the day there, looking up information about Willie Lincoln and thinking about Annie.

She hadn't called last night. Broun had gone out for dinner, and I had spent the whole evening in his study waiting for her to call, but the phone hadn't rung even once. By ten o'clock I had come to the conclusion that Richard was somehow keeping her from using the phone, but this morning I didn't really believe that.

Richard had made it plain he didn't want me talking to her, but he was hardly going to have the phone disconnected or tie her up to keep her from answering it. She was his patient, not his prisoner, and she had disobeyed him before. He hadn't been able to keep her from going out to Arlington. He wouldn't be able to keep her from calling me either, if she really wanted to.

If she really wanted to. Maybe she didn't want to. She had seemed almost uninterested when I called her and offered her my services. What made me think she wanted to hear about Special Order 191 any more than she wanted to hear about traumas in the subconscious? She hung up on you, I told myself, and she's still at Richard's. You don't need Freud's *Interpretation of Dreams* to tell you what that means. She doesn't want to talk to you. So stop calling her and find out what the hell they did with Willie Lincoln.

I didn't believe that either, but I pulled out every book on Lincoln and tried to concentrate on the research. I couldn't find a word about Willie's burial. I found out what had happened to the pony he'd been riding 'in bad weather' when he came down with whatever it was that killed him, though. Several months after Willie's death, the White House stables caught fire. Lincoln ran across the lawn and leaped a boxwood hedge to save it, but he was too late. The guards hurried him back into the White House, afraid the fire had been started by an assassin to lure him out. Willie's pony was burned alive.

Every hour or so I went outside to the pay phone and called the answering machine, but there weren't any messages. By two o'clock I had run out of change and had to ask Kate for a dollar's worth of quarters. 'I'll have the bibliography ready for you in a few minutes,' she said.

I went out and called the answering machine. Broun's agent had called, wanting to know why in the hell Broun was still making changes. She'd just talked to McLaws and Herndon and they'd had to reset the type for the galleys. They were talking about charging Broun for the extra plates.

I called Annie.

'I'm glad you called,' Richard said. 'I wanted to apologize for my outburst the other day.'

'I want to talk to Annie.'

'She's asleep right now,' he said, 'and I don't want to wake her up. I know I was out of line the day before yesterday. I was just so upset about her condition. She was obsessed with the idea that she could obtain factual verification for her dream.'

He sounded completely different from the man who had warned me to keep away from Annie. His voice was calm and professional. 'It's a common phenomenon, but a dangerous one. The patient attempts to distance threatening dream images in his dreams by believing they have an objective reality of their own.'

I recognized the voice now. He had worked on it all through medical school. The voice was one of the psychiatrist's most important tools, he had told me when he was studying psychoanalysis. The proper voice could be used to obtain the patient's trust, inspire confidence, and convince the patient that the psychiatrist had his own best interests at heart. I had told him I didn't care what it could do, just not to use it on me.

He was using it now.

'By convincing herself that the house in her dream is Arlington House,' he said, 'she is trying to protect herself from the latent material in the dream. The half-buried dead man becomes a Union soldier instead of the image of her own personal trauma, the cat becomes a real cat instead of the symbol of her need to uncover the repressed memory that's causing the dreams.'

'The cat *is* a real cat. His name's Tom Tita. He got left behind when Lee moved out of Arlington.'

'You're confusing manifest content with latent content,' he said, inspiringly, compassionately. 'We all dream real things, objects and people we've seen, things we've read about or seen in the movies, memories. They make up the visible content of our dreams. But the subconscious puts those real people and objects and memories to its own uses. It's a process called dream precipitant conversion. Let's say Annie had a cat as a child.'

'She never had a cat. And she didn't see this cat, either, or read about it someplace. It's Tom Tita.'

'I'm sure she was convinced of that when she insisted on going to Arlington, and that was why I objected to the trip. But I was wrong. The trip produced a catharsis, a breakthrough. She realized the house in the dream was really her own house, and that the half-buried soldier was a symbol of her own repressed guilt.'

'What's the cat a symbol for?' And what about her bandaged hands? I was about to say when I realized that Richard, calm and inspiring and compassionate, hadn't said a word about the second dream. And what did that mean? That she hadn't told him? Or that she didn't want to believe what I had told her and had chosen to accept Richard's explanations: repressive guilt and manifest content and dream precipitant conversion. Terms that meant no more than bilious fever and rheumatic excitement and were as much help to the patient.

'I want to talk to Annie,' I said.

'I'll let her know you called as soon as she wakes up,' the Good Shrink said. 'I have to warn you that she may not want to talk to you. She identifies you with her rejection of her psychosis.'

I hung up on him and went back inside to Lincoln, who had had terrible dreams, too. But nobody had tried to convince him the East Room wasn't the East Room. Nobody had told him the corpse with the black cloth over its face was a symbol for repressive guilt or a neural impulse chosen at random by his hormones. Nobody had asked him what he'd had to eat before he went to bed.

Kate brought the bibliography over to me. 'I've starred the ones we have,' she said, pointing at ink notations in the margin, 'and marked the branches these are at. Do you want me to have the branches send them over here?'

'No, that's all right. I'll go get them tomorrow.'

'What's Broun's new book about?'

'Abraham Lincoln,' I said.

'Oh, I didn't know Lincoln was sick.'

'What?'

'Prodromic dreams are dreams people have when they're sick and they don't know it yet. What disease was Lincoln suffering from?'

'Bad dreams,' I said.

Broun was back when I got home, standing in the solarium looking at his African violets. I handed him the bibliography. 'Did anybody call?' I asked.

'I don't know,' he said stiffly. 'I left the machine on so you wouldn't miss any of your messages. Did you find out where Willie Lincoln was buried?'

'No.' I started up the stairs. 'Was Lincoln sick when he was shot?'

'He was obsessed with the Civil War,' he said bitterly.

I went on up the stairs and into the study and shut the door, but there were no messages on the answering machine, and Annie didn't call.

I spent most of the next day rounding up the books listed in the bibliography so Broun could take them with him. The galleys came Federal Express in the afternoon. It was overcast all day, and cold. Broun's plane didn't leave till five-thirty, and by the time we left for the airport it was getting foggy.

'I want you to go down to Virginia for me,' Broun said stiffly as soon as we turned onto the Rock Creek Parkway. 'I know you disapprove of these wild goose chases, but I need you to talk to a doctor in Fredericksburg.'

Fredericksburg was only fifty miles away. If Annie called I could drive back in an hour and a half's time. If she called. 'What's the doctor's name?'

He rummaged in his jacket pocket. 'Barton. Dr Barton. Here's the address.' He had fished out a folded piece of paper. He unfolded it. 'Dr Stone gave me his name. This Dr Barton has acromegaly. That's usually treated before there are any overt symptoms, but he's old enough that his wasn't. I want you to find out what kind of dreams he has.' He paused as if waiting for me to object.

'When do you want me to go? Tomorrow?'

'Whenever it's convenient for you to go,' he said.

I drove past the Lincoln Memorial and onto the bridge. 'I had no business saying that about the wild goose chases,' I said. 'I know how important this book is to you.'

'An obsession, I think you called it.'

I could see Arlington House up ahead on its snow-covered hill. I thought of Richard telling Annie she was obsessed with war and killing. 'I had no right to say that either.'

We turned onto the parkway heading south. 'Lincoln suffered from acromegaly,' Broun said as if he were apologizing for his rudeness before when I had asked him if Lincoln was sick. 'It's what made him so tall. It's a gland disorder. The bones grow too much. The hands and nose get wide and the feet get big. People with acromegaly get rheumatism and diabetes and suffer from melancholia. It can be fatal.'

'And you think that's what killed him?' I said, sarcastically, and then was sorry.

'I thought it might explain the dreams,' he said, and turned and looked out the side window at the foggy darkness.

I wondered if it had occurred to him, through all these theories of repressed guilt and neural impulses, that the dreams didn't need any explanation. Lincoln dreamed that he had been killed by an assassin, and two weeks later he lay dead in the East Room. He lost his son, and the little boy's face came to comfort him in dreams. And where in all this did a gland disorder figure?

I didn't ask him. I wanted some kind of truce before Broun went off to California. When we pulled into the airport, I said, 'I'll go see this Dr Barton tomorrow.'

He turned and looked at me, and I knew he didn't want a battle either. 'Just have Mrs Betts next door take the cat and tell her to water the plants. I left the answering machine on "message" and didn't say where you'd be in case you wanted to take some time off. I've been working you too hard. There's a nice inn in Fredericksburg. You could drive down and stay for a couple of days, take a little vacation. Stay till I get back from California if you feel like it.'

'Somebody's got to do the galleys,' I said, 'and you won't have time in California. Listen, don't worry about me. I'll take it easy. I'll run down to Fredericksburg and then I'll come back and work on the galleys.'

'Well, at least get somebody to help you with them. It takes so long the other way. Why don't you ask that girl to help you, the pretty little blonde at the reception the other night, what was her name?'

'Annie,' I said. 'But I doubt if she'd want to sit for hours reading a book out loud and checking for typos.'

He scratched at the stubble on his chin. 'I watched you two the other night. I got the idea she'd do about anything if you asked her. And vice versa.'

'She's Richard's girlfriend.'

'Did you hear that from the horse's mouth? Or did Richard tell you?'

'You're going to miss your plane,' I said. 'Don't worry about the galleys. I'll get them done if I have to read them onto a tape recorder and listen to myself.'

He got his suitcase out of the back and then reached forward to give me the piece of folded paper. 'Take care of yourself, son,' he said.

'You, too,' I said. 'If you find out what caused Lincoln's dreams, let me know.'

I went home and started in on the galleys, a long chapter about Ben's brother, who was in Mansfield's doomed Twelfth Corps, another, even longer one about Colonel Fitzhugh, whose men called him Old Fancypants and who went on for pages about a gentleman's duty and the glorious South.

'I thought the book was about Antietam,' I had told Broun the first time I'd read those chapters. 'And here it is chapter two and still the spring of 1862. The battle of Antietam didn't happen till the middle of September.'

'It's not about Antietam,' Broun had thundered, the only time I've ever seen him angry at one of my criticisms. 'It's about duty, damn it.' He had refused to take any of it out then, and now I saw that, although he had made so many changes I hardly recognized the book, all the passages about duty had been left in. It was chapter nine before we made it to the morning of September seventeenth and back to Malachi and Toby and Ben:

It was still dark when Ben woke up. 'I thought I heard something,' he said, sitting up.

'Not yet,' Malachi said. It was too dark to see him.

'What time is it?' Ben asked. 'I thought I heard guns.' It had stopped raining and there seemed to be a little light there to the east, but he couldn't be sure.

'No more'n three o'clock,' Malachi said, and then Ben must have gone back to sleep because when he opened his eyes again, it was light enough to see Malachi. He was sitting by his little cookfire, stirring the cold ashes, trying to get a spark, but the fire was completely out. A cold fog was drifting through the cornfield they had camped next to, so low he couldn't see the tassels on the corn.

'How'll we see to fight if there's fog?' Ben said, huddling his blanket around his shoulders. His teeth were chattering.

'Fog'll burn off as soon as the sun comes up, and then it'll be hot,' Malachi said, and he sounded as calm and wide awake as if he were back on the farm, up at three in the morning for a big day of planting.

'What would happen if we lit out beforehand?' Ben said. His teeth were chattering so hard he wouldn't be able to hear the guns. 'Couldn't nobody see us in this fog.'

'I thought you was the one just had to sign up. This here's what you signed up for.'

'I know,' he said. 'I just hadn't figured on getting killed.'

'How's a body supposed to get any sleep with you two clucking like hens?' Toby said. He yawned. 'Should you run? Will you git kilt? Me, I can't get kilt. Not Toby Banks. No, sir, I promised my mama I wouldn't.' He pushed his blanket down so it covered his feet and rolled over, and Ben lay down again and watched the fog drift across Malachi and the cold fire.

Toby poked him awake with his foot. 'You set up all night worrying and then you sleep through the battle,' he said. 'Don't you let Old Fancypants see you sleeping.'

Ben sat up. The sun was up and the fog was gone. Steam was rising like smoke over the cornfield. Malachi had another fire going. He was roasting ears of corn in the coals. 'Me, I been up practicing my Rebel yell for close on an hour,' Toby said.

Ben got up and folded his bedroll, trying to wake up. Toby was whistling something, a jig tune, but when Ben turned to look at him he stopped. He was writing something on a dirty white handkerchief. 'I want them Yankees to know who's shooting at 'em,' he said. He whittled a twig down to nothing and used it as a pin to stick the handkerchief to his shirt. 'Not that I'm letting any of 'em get close enough to read it.' He went over to the fire and plucked one of the roasting ears out of the coals. The husk was charred. It smelled wonderful.

She woke me out of a sound sleep. I had the idea that it was almost morning, and I couldn't think who would be calling at that hour. I answered the phone, and, as I did, it rang again, and I thought, 'It's the answering machine,' and punched what I thought was 'play' and had time to be surprised that there was no message before it rang again and I recognized the sound finally as the doorbell.

Annie was standing on the front steps. She had her gray coat on and was carrying a duffel bag. There was a suitcase on the step beside her. It was dark and foggy out, and I thought, 'That will burn off when the sun comes up, and it will be hot tomorrow.'

'Can I stay here?' she said.

I still had the idea that the phone had rung. 'Did you call?' I said.

'No,' she said. 'I know I should have given you some warning, but … if this is a problem, Jeff, I can go to a hotel.'

'I thought I heard the phone,' I said, rubbing at my face as if I expected a scraggly stubble of beard like Broun's. 'What time is it?'

She had to transfer the duffel bag from one hand to the other to look at her watch. 'Ten-thirty. I woke you up, didn't I?'

No, you didn't, I almost said. That was the problem. She had not, with all her ringing of the doorbell, managed to wake me up. I was still asleep and dreaming her, and they were not somebody else's dreams. She looked beautiful standing there in her gray coat, her light hair curling a little from the damp fog. She looked as if she had just awakened from a long and refreshing sleep, her eyes clear and bright, and healthy pinkness in her cheeks.

'Of course you can stay,' I said, still not awake enough to ask her why she was here, or even to wonder. I opened the door and leaned past her to pick up the suitcase. 'You can stay as long as you want. Broun's not here. He's in California. You can stay as long as you want.'

I led the way up the stairs to the study, still unable to shake the feeling that it was very late. The answering machine was blinking rapidly – I must have put it on 'call return' in my sleepy fumblings. I wondered what poor soul I had been calling for the last ten minutes. I hit the 'pause' button and yawned. I was still not awake. I'd better make some coffee.

'Do you want some coffee?' I said to Annie, who was standing in the door of the study looking rested and wide awake and beautiful.

'No,' she said.

I still had my hand on the answering machine buttons. 'I've been worried about you. I tried to call you. Did you have another dream?'

'No,' she said. 'The dreams have stopped.'

'They've stopped?' I said. 'Just like that?' I still wasn't awake.

The answering machine was still flashing. I stabbed at the buttons. The tape clicked. 'Annie's gone,' Richard said. 'I think she'll come to you. You have to make her come back. She's sick. I only did it to help her. I didn't have any other choice.'

'Did what?' I asked.

She pulled something out of the duffel bag. 'He's been putting these in my food,' she said, and handed me two capsules in a plastic bag. One of the capsules was cracked and there was a dusting of white powder along the bottom edge of the bag.

'What are they?' I said. 'Elavil?'

'Thorazine,' she said. 'I found the bottle in his medical bag.'

Thorazine. A drug strong enough to stop a horse in its tracks. 'Richard gave you these?' I said, looking stupidly at the plastic bag.

'Yes,' she said. She sat down in the club chair. 'He started putting them in my food when I got back from Arlington.'

When I called her I had asked her if she had been asleep, and she had said Richard had made her a cup of tea and sent her to bed. She had been so sleepy she could hardly answer my questions. Because Richard had put Thorazine in her tea. Thorazine. 'They use Thorazine in mental hospitals. With uncontrollable patients.'

'I know,' she said.

'How many of these did he give you?'

'I don't know. He … I didn't eat anything last night and all day today.'

I had taken her out to Arlington three days ago. She couldn't have been on the drug more than two and a half days, so there couldn't be that much in her system, but what kind of dose had Richard given her? Any dose was too much.

'Annie, listen, let me call the hospital. They'll know what to do. We've got to get this stuff out of your system.'

'Jeff, tell me what happened to the horse,' she said quietly. 'The gray horse I saw in my dream. It didn't fall forward on its knees, did it?' I looked at her hands, expecting them to be gripping the arms of the chair, but they were lying quietly in her lap. 'Please tell me.'

I knelt down in front of her and took hold of her hands. 'Annie, the dream's not important. What's important is that you've got a dangerous drug in your system. I don't know what symptoms it can cause, but we've got to find out. There might be withdrawal symptoms of some kind. We've got to get you to a hospital. They'll know what to do.'

'No,' she said, still quietly. 'They'll give me something to stop the dreams.'

'No, they won't. They'll try to get the Thorazine out of your system, and they'll run tests so we'll know exactly how much Richard's been giving you and for how long. What if he's been giving you drugs for weeks? What if Thorazine isn't the only thing he's been giving you?'

'You don't understand. They'll put me on medication.'

'They can't give you anything without your consent.'

'Richard did. I can't go to a hospital. The dreams are important. They're the most important thing.'

'Annie ...'

'No, you have to listen, Jeff. I figured out he was giving me something when you called me. When I got up to answer the phone I was so dizzy, and then when you asked me if Richard was giving me anything, I knew that must be it. But I didn't tell you.'

'Why not?' I asked gently.

'Because it stopped the dreams.' Her hands were ice cold. I chafed them gently between my hands. 'When you'd called I'd been asleep all afternoon, and I hadn't had any dreams at all. Then you called and told me about Special Order 191 and I didn't even want to listen. I just wanted to go back to sleep. I wanted to sleep forever.'

'That was the Thorazine,' I said.

'I wanted to sleep forever, but I couldn't. Even under the Thorazine, even when I was asleep, I knew the dreams mattered, and that I had to have them. That's why I came here. Because I knew you could help me. I knew you could tell me what the dreams meant.'

'Annie, listen.' I looked anxiously into her blue-gray eyes, trying to see if they were dilated. They weren't. They looked clear and alert. Maybe she *had* only been on the Thorazine for a couple of days. 'Will you at least let me call Broun's doctor? He's not a psychiatrist or anything. He's just a G.P.'

'He'll call Richard.'

'No, he won't,' I said, and wished I could be sure of that. If I told him that Richard had given Thorazine to one of his patients without her knowledge, he would immediately think she was a mental patient. He would call Richard, and Richard would tell him that she was highly unstable, that she suffered from delusions of persecution. He would use his Good Shrink voice and

Broun's doctor would believe him. And then what? Would he take Annie back to the Sleep Institute, or would he have Richard come and get her?

'At least let me make you some coffee,' I said, patting her hands. 'We need to get that junk out of your system.'

She wrapped her fingers around mine. 'Tell me about the horse. Please.'

'It was D. H. Hill's horse. It was shot out from under him.' I held on to her hands as if I expected her to pull away from me. 'Its front legs were shot off.'

'Did Lee see it happen?'

'Yes,' I said.

'I didn't want to believe it when you told me about Tom Tita and Hill's red shirt and the lost order,' she said, and her voice was still calm, but her grip tightened. 'But I knew it was true, even under the Thorazine. I knew what the dreams were that night at the reception as soon as you told me about the house at Arlington, but I didn't want to believe it.'

She bent her head so that it almost touched our hands. 'That poor man!' she said. 'The Thorazine made me sleep all the time, and even when I was awake it was as if I were asleep. It was wonderful. I hadn't been able to sleep before because I was so afraid I'd dream about the soldier in the orchard, and now I slept and slept and didn't dream anything. It was wonderful. I was so glad Richard had given it to me.'

She looked up at me. 'But even when I was asleep I kept thinking how terrible it was that they didn't have Thorazine in those days, that there wasn't anything to stop those awful dreams. He had to keep dreaming them over and over again till he was afraid to go to sleep, too.' She was holding my hands so tightly they hurt. 'That's why I have to have the dreams, that's why I came to you. You have to help me have the dreams. So he can get some sleep.'

'Who?' I said, but I already knew the answer.

'Robert E. Lee. They're his dreams, aren't they?' she said, and it wasn't even a question. 'I'm having Robert E. Lee's dreams.'

I could almost smell the corn, hear it rustling in the still, hot steam of the morning, and I knew the guns were about to open up and the slaughter begin.

'Yes,' I said.

I got Annie something to eat and made her drink some coffee. I wondered if I should walk her around to try to keep her from falling asleep the way you did for a drug overdose, but she had been asleep for days. I wished Broun had a medical book from later than 1865 so I could look up Thorazine's side effects.

The phone rang. 'It's Richard, you know,' she said, and took hold of my hands again. 'He'll come and get me.'

The answering machine clicked on. 'He won't know where we are,' I said. 'The message on the answering machine says Broun's in California. He'll think I went with him.'

'What if he comes over?'

'We won't be here,' I said. 'I have to go to Fredericksburg to do some research for Broun. You can come with me. He won't have any idea where we've gone.'

Annie was asleep before I'd finished talking, still holding on to my hands, her head turned slightly against the back of the club chair, her cheeks as pink as a child's. I eased my hands out of hers and went and got a blanket from my room to put over her, and then, wide awake finally, I packed a bag and put it and Annie's things into the car and then came back to the study and read galleys.

Richard called every ten minutes for the next three hours and then stopped, and I turned off all the lights in the study and went downstairs and made sure all the doors were locked. I went into the dark solarium and stood at the window, watching Richard pull up and park across the street and thinking about how the Civil War started.

Lincoln had offered Lee the command of the Union army, but he couldn't take it, even though he was opposed to secession and hated the idea of war. 'I have not been able to make up my mind to raise my hand against my relatives, my children, my home,' he wrote his sister. 'I know you will blame me; but you must think as kindly of me as you can, and believe that I have endeavored to do what I thought right.'

'I could have taken no other course without dishonor,' he wrote after the war, after he had killed two hundred and fifty thousand of his own men; and Lincoln, that other good man entrusted with mass murder, had said, 'Let us have faith that right makes might, and in that faith let us do our duty as we understand it.'

Our duty as we understand it. 'I had to do it,' Richard had said, and had slept with a patient, had given her a dangerous drug without her knowledge, and I had promised I'd take care of her, so I couldn't let him get away with it, even though he was my old roommate. 'He just one day signed up,' Broun's character Ben had said, 'and I knew I had to, too.' And there we were, enemies.

At seven o'clock I went back upstairs and woke Annie up. I called the woman next door and told her I'd changed my mind about going to California with Broun and would she watch the cat, I'd put its food by the door and she could come and get it and the cat anytime she wanted.

Then I said, 'And would you tell the police we're gone? Broun doesn't usually bother with that kind of thing, but there's been a car parked across the street with a man sitting in it ever since I got back from taking Broun to the airport last night. I can't tell if he's watching the house or not, and I'm probably crazy to think it means anything. But Broun's got a lot of first editions.'

When the police car pulled up next to Richard's, I took Annie out through the back door to the garage, and we fled south, into the land of dreams.

CHAPTER SIX

Traveller was a perfect horse for Lee. He could stand the bad weather and the parched corn, and he had incredible stamina. When Lee reviewed the troops, Traveller would start out at a long lope and never once change his stride. The men would be lined up for sometimes as much as ten miles, and Traveller would gallop the whole distance while the other officers' horses dropped out, one by one.

Fredericksburg was only fifty miles south of D.C., but it was an entirely different world. The redbud and forsythia were in bloom, and the martyred blossoms of the dogwood were everywhere.

I checked us in at the Fredericksburg Inn, a big old building with a wide porch. I asked for two adjoining rooms and then told the clerk I wanted to see them before we signed in. The clerk gave me a key and we went upstairs. The two rooms were really a suite on the second floor at one end of the building. I could see the parking lot from the window of one of the bedrooms and the Rappahannock from the other. There was a fire escape at the other end of the hall that went down to another, smaller parking lot that couldn't be seen from the front of the building.

I left Annie in the room and went down and signed us in as Mr and Mrs Jeff Davis. The clerk grinned when he read it. I debated telling him that an angry husband might show up and giving him twenty dollars to tell the husband we weren't there. Instead, I grinned back and said, 'No, no relation. Everybody asks that,' and went out to move the car around to the little parking lot by the stairs and get the bags.

When I got back up to the suite, I put my bag in the bedroom with the view of the big parking lot and Annie's in the other.

'You can relax,' I told her. 'Richard will have no way of knowing we're here. The only person who knew I was going to Fredericksburg is Broun, and he's in California. You can go ahead and unpack and then we'll go get some breakfast.'

I went into the other bedroom, shut the door, and called Broun's answering machine to make sure Broun hadn't left the name of his hotel or the number on the machine. 'I'm in sunny California doing research on my new book,' Broun's voice said. 'If you'll leave your name and number and any messages, I'll be picking my messages up remotely, and I'll try to return your call as soon as possible.'

Good. He hadn't left a number, and he hadn't said anything about his research assistant picking up his calls. He had meant it when he said he wanted me to take some time off. I tried to think of anybody else he might have given his California number to. His agent probably, but she wouldn't give out information to a stranger, even if he claimed to be an old roommate of Jeff's. McLaws and Herndon maybe, though I doubted if he'd told them he was running off to California when he was supposed to be working on the galleys.

I punched in the remote code that would play me any messages left on the machine. There was a click and then a short whirring sound while the machine rewound, another click, and Broun said, 'Jeff, I'm in California, and I must have brought the damned fog with me. I'm going to see the prophetic dreams man tomorrow. Call me if you run into any trouble with the galleys. And get some rest. I'm worried about you.'

I unpacked the bag I'd thrown together the night before and opened the box I had brought the galleys in. There were books lying on top. I didn't remember packing any books. I picked the top one up. It was volume two of Freeman. I sat down on the bed and pulled out the other three hefty volumes, one after the other.

A soldier running from battle would sometimes find miles later that he was still clutching his rifle, or his hat, or a half-eaten square of hardtack, and had no more memory of doing it than he did of running away. And here we were fifty miles from the battle with a suite at the Fredericksburg Inn and Freeman's *R. E. Lee* and who knows what in Annie's duffel bag, two Johnny Rebs on the run. But sooner or later that soldier would stop running and decide what to do next, and I had no idea. I hadn't thought any farther than getting Annie safely away from Richard.

I had done that, and we could stay here for at least a week and maybe longer if Broun stayed in California, but sooner or later we were going to have to go back to D.C., and sooner or later we were going to have to talk about the dreams.

But not yet. There was no telling how much Thorazine Annie still had in her system or how long it would take to work its way out. Dr Stone had said taking somebody off a sedative abruptly might cause a 'storm of dreams.' I wasn't going to insist on figuring out what was causing Robert E. Lee's dreams if she was having nightmares of her own. What she needed right now was breakfast and some rest and a vacation from the whole crazy mess.

There was a slick colored brochure lying on the oak chiffonier by the bed. I picked it up. Maybe we could take a walk around historic Fredericksburg, see some of the sights. 'America's Battlefield,' the brochure said. 'Visit the Historic Civil War Battlefields. Where 100,000 fell! Stand in the shoes of the generals. Self-guided tour.'

I thought of Annie standing halfway up the hill at Arlington, looking down at the snowy grass. Fredericksburg's battlefield had been made into a national cemetery, too, with twelve thousand unknown soldiers buried in it.

Maybe I shouldn't have brought her here, I thought. She hadn't dreamed about Fredericksburg yet, and I didn't want her to. The battle had been a complete slaughter, with the Union soldiers trying to cross a flat plain to the defended ridge called Marye's Heights. But Lee won, I thought. Maybe he doesn't dream about the battles he won.

The other attractions were minor, to say the least: James Monroe's law office, Mary Washington's cottage, and Kenmore, a southern plantation where George Washington's sister Betty Fielding Lewis lived, but when I checked the map, they weren't anywhere near the battlefield, which meant we could go sightseeing and read galleys and do what Broun had sent me to do, which was interview a doctor about his acromegaly.

I dug the number Broun had given me out of my wallet and called Dr Barton. The number had been disconnected. I opened the drawers in the oak chiffonier till I found the phone book and looked him up under 'Physicians' in the Yellow Pages. There wasn't any listing. There was a Barton listed in the white pages, but no 'doctor' after his name. Broun had said he was old enough that his acromegaly hadn't been treated. Maybe he'd retired. I called the number.

'Dr Barton's office,' a woman's voice said.

'Good,' I said. 'This is Jeff Johnston. I'm Thomas Broun's researcher. I'd like to make an appointment with Dr Barton.'

'Is this about a horse?' she said.

'No,' I said, squinting at the paper Broun had given me. 'Is this Dr Henry Barton's office?'

'Yes.'

'Dr Barton's name was given to my employer, Thomas Broun, by Dr Stone in Washington, D.C. I'm doing research on Mr Broun's new book, and I wanted to ask Dr Barton a few questions.'

'Oh, how interesting,' she said. 'I know my husband will want to see you. Let me look at the appointment book.' There was a pause. 'Could it be next week sometime? He's very busy. It's spring, you know.'

I didn't know why spring was so busy, but I didn't say that. 'What about in the evening?'

'Tomorrow's Sunday. Could you come out tomorrow?'

'Sure,' I said.

'Do you know how to get here?' she said. 'We're out of town.' While she gave me directions, I thumbed through the yellow pages again. Yep. There he was, Dr Henry Barton, DVM. Practice Limited to Large Animals. No wonder his wife had wanted to know if it was about a horse.

I put the phone book back in the drawer, picked up the brochure of 'Historic Fredericksburg,' and took it into Annie's room. 'Dr Barton can't see me till tomorrow, so we've got the whole day. What do you want to see? Mary Washington lived here. We could go tour the house. There's a mirror in her bedroom that …'

'I shouldn't have come with you,' she said. She was sitting on the four-poster bed. It had a green-and-white sprigged muslin coverlet with a ruffled flounce. Annie had her hands flat on either side of her, trying not to clutch at the muslin flowers the way she had Broun's African violet. 'When I started having the dreams I was so scared I didn't know what to do. I was afraid to be alone at night, and Richard was trying to help me …'

And it just happened.

'I'm not Richard,' I said. 'I don't know what kind of ideas you've got about me, but I didn't bring you down here for a fun weekend on Broun's expense account. I brought you down here because you were running away from Richard, and I thought this was a safe place for you to hide. That's it. I'm here to read the galleys for *The Duty Bound* and talk to some guy with long bones and big ears. I got a suite and registered us under a phony name because that way Richard couldn't call and find out you were here, but if you want a separate room, I can …'

'That's not it,' she said, crushing the coverlet in her clenched hands. 'I didn't think you … the suite is fine, Jeff. I'm glad you didn't get separate rooms because I need somebody in the room at night. And you shouldn't blame Richard for what happened. It was my fault. I shouldn't have gotten involved with him. It just made things worse.' She let go of the coverlet and looked up at me. 'The dreams scared Richard. He was afraid they were hurting me, and so he tried to stop them, but I couldn't let him. I have a duty to the dreams.'

'And you're afraid I'll get scared, too, and start putting Thorazine in your food. I told you, I'm not Richard.'

'I'm all right. The Thorazine's almost out of my system. I know. I'm feeling a lot better. There's no reason to go see a doctor. He'll try to stop the dreams. He'll put me on some other drug.'

'I didn't say anything about going to see a doctor,' I said helplessly, and then realized I had. 'You mean Dr Barton? That's the guy Broun asked me to interview. He's got acromegaly, the same growth disorder Lincoln had, and he's not even a doctor. He's a vet. When I called, his wife asked me if I wanted to see him about a horse.' I tried to smile at her. 'I know it's your duty to have the dreams. It's my duty to take care of you while you do. I promise I won't try to stop the dreams.'

'Okay,' she said. She smoothed out the coverlet where she had wrinkled it. 'Now how about some breakfast, and then we'll hit all the hot spots of

Fredericksburg? Mary Washington's got this mirror that people flock from miles around to see.'

'All right,' she said, smiling. 'Who was Mary Washington?'

'I don't know,' I said, looking down at the brochure. I had twisted it into an unreadable wad of colored paper. 'George Washington's mother? Or his daughter maybe? Did George Washington have any daughters?' She was staring at the brochure. 'I'll pick up another one in the lobby.' I dropped it in the wastebasket.

'Annie, it's going to be all right,' I said. 'I'll take care of you.'

'I know.'

Mary Washington was George's mother. We had breakfast in a coffee shop across from the inn and then walked downtown to see Mary's dressing glass and her sundial in a little house at the foot of the formal gardens of Kenmore.

I watched Annie anxiously all morning, but she looked fine. Better than fine. The warm spring air and exercise seemed to be doing her a world of good. She laughed at my comments on what sort of person Mary Washington had been, considering that her daughter had stuck her as far away from the house as possible, and said, 'She probably talked as much about that awful dressing glass as the tour guide did.'

She smiled, a beautiful, untroubled smile. Oddly, it made her look older, more like a woman and less like a ravaged child, and I thought, Good, I'm doing the right thing.

But after lunch, browsing through our third antique shop, she started to look tired. She picked up a china cat and started to say something, and then stopped in mid-sentence and went over to the window of the antique shop and looked anxiously out toward the south as though she were waiting for A. P. Hill's men to come up.

'Are you all right?' I said, worried that this was some side effect of the Thorazine.

She was still holding the china cat.

'Let's go get some coffee,' I said. I'd been pouring coffee into her all day, in spite of Dr Stone's theory that caffeine caused bad dreams. I couldn't think of any other way to get the Thorazine out of her system.

'I think I've had enough coffee,' she said, smiling. 'I'm fine. I just have a headache.'

'Well, how about some aspirin then?'

'No, I'm fine. I'm just tired. Maybe we should go back to the inn.'

'Sure thing. Do you want to walk? If you're tired, I can run back and get the car. Or we can call a taxi.'

'I don't think Fredericksburg's got taxis,' she said, putting the china cat down carefully on a drop-leaf table. 'There isn't any reason to panic, Jeff. It's a sinus headache. I get hay fever. It's probably the apple blossoms.'

She seemed fine on the walk home. A breeze had come up, and it blew the light hair back from her face and colored her cheeks. 'This is a pretty town,' she said, 'all these old houses. Was there a battle here? In the Civil War?'

'Yes.' I pointed at a dilapidated blue Ford sedan with a hand-lettered sign on its side as it drove past. 'I told you they had taxis in Fredericksburg.'

We went up the outside staircase of the inn to our rooms. A black cat with white paws was sunning itself on the second step from the top. It made no effort at all to get out of our way.

'Hello, there,' Annie said, reaching down to pet it. The cat closed its eyes and allowed itself to be petted as if it were doing Annie a favor. 'I've always wished I could have a cat. My father was allergic to them.'

'Your father?'

'Yes. They gave him hives.'

'You know, I don't know anything about you. Your family, where you come from, what you were doing before you started having Lee's dreams. Where do you live?'

She straightened up, her smile gone. She looked the way she had that night when Richard had been ranting about Lincoln's psychological problems. 'A little town. About the size of Fredericksburg.'

'Broun has a cat,' I said hastily. 'It's a selfish brute. Like this one here.' I chucked the cat under its black chin and walked on up the stairs to open the door for Annie, hating Richard at that moment more than I had ever hated anyone.

I didn't know anything at all about Annie. Correction: I knew she had a father who was allergic to cats, and that she came from a little town, and from the look on her face that was all she was going to tell me. I didn't blame her. Richard knew all about her. If it wasn't on the forms she had filled out at the Institute or the records her doctor had sent, Richard had found it out in his therapy sessions, and whatever he knew he had used: 'I see your father died last year. Did you feel responsible for his death? What did he look like? Did he have a white beard? Like Robert E. Lee's? Isn't that what your dream is really all about?'

And as if that wasn't bad enough, he had probably spent the morning calling those numbers on the forms, Next of Kin Not Living at Above Address, and demanding to know where she was. No wonder she didn't want to tell me anything. I might turn out to be another Richard, and when she ran from me, she would want to make sure I couldn't follow.

'Broun's really going to be mad when he gets back,' I said, opening the door to my room and smiling reassuringly. 'I gave his cat the leftover shrimp doodads.'

She followed me into the room. 'What did they taste like?'

'Well, I wouldn't want Broun to find out, but I think they're awful. I was afraid that night of the reception he was actually going to force us to eat some of them. Now you go ahead and take a nap if you're tired. Is there anything I can get you?'

She rubbed her hand across her forehead. 'Jeff, I think I could use some aspirin after all.'

'I'll see if I've got any,' I said, knowing full well I hadn't packed any in the mad dash down here, and went into my room. I had almost offered to go get some for her, but there was something I had to do first. I shut the door and called Broun's answering machine.

Broun's California-fog message repeated itself, and Richard had called.

'I'm calling to tell you that I'm not angry about your getting me hauled in for questioning by the police this morning,' the Good Shrink said. 'I know you felt threatened, and I know Annie feels threatened, but I want to reassure you that my only concern is my patient and her welfare.'

The psychiatrist must convince the patient he has her own best interests at heart.

'Running away isn't the answer, Jeff. You have to bring Annie back so she can get the proper treatment. I know you choose not to believe me, but this neurotic fantasy of hers is dangerous. She's completely dissociated herself from her dreams. She told me they're Robert E. Lee's dreams. She's on the edge of a complete psychotic break, and taking her to California is only going to precipitate it.'

Good. He thought we were in California. That meant he wasn't going to show up here while I was gone. I didn't want to leave Annie alone, but I had to find out about the Thorazine Richard had given her. I hung up and went back into Annie's room. She was standing by the window, looking out at the trees that lined the river.

'I didn't bring any aspirin. I'll run get you some. I saw a drugstore on the way back here.'

'You don't have to …'

'I've got to go anyway. I forgot to pack my razor, too, and, unlike Broun, I have no desire to grow a beard. Is there anything else I can get you?'

'No.' She managed a fair smile. She was looking flushed again.

'You're sure you'll be okay here? I'll just be a few minutes.'

'I'll be fine,' she said. She tried for a better smile. A truck rumbled past the front of the inn, and Annie raised her head and gazed out over the trees as if what she had heard was the low thunder of artillery fire.

I took the car, bought the razor and some aspirin at a convenience store, and then drove downtown to the library. I'd seen it on our way back to the inn, a three-story brick building that looked like it had been a school.

The reference books were in a drab basement room lit by fluorescent lights. The only drug compendium they had was badly out-of-date, and it didn't say anything about how to get Thorazine out of a person's system, but it said abrupt withdrawal from a high dosage could cause nausea and dizziness.

It didn't say what a high dosage was, and it didn't particularly matter anyway since I didn't have any idea how much Richard had given her, but how could he have given her any at all? The compendium described it as being just as dangerous as I thought it was.

Dozens of contraindications and warnings were listed, drowsiness and jaundice and fainting spells, and there was a note set off in double borders that read, 'Sudden death, apparently due to cardiac arrest, has been reported, but there is not sufficient evidence to establish a relationship between such deaths and the administration of the drug.' I wondered if in the ten years since the book had been published they had managed to establish a relationship, and if Richard cared.

He had to have known exactly what Thorazine could do to Annie, and yet he had given it to her anyway. Why? It wasn't used to cure mental patients. It was used to keep them under control.

I couldn't find anything about headaches or fever in the list of side effects, although it said infections could result after the fourth week. All of the side effects and warnings seemed to be related to long-term use of the drug, and the last page reassured me. In spite of all the warnings, it was recommended in the treatment of everything from hiccups to lockjaw.

I went back to the inn and found Annie sitting on the outside steps, playing with the black cat. 'My headache's gone,' she said when I handed her the aspirin. 'I feel much better.'

We ate dinner at the coffee shop where we'd had breakfast. 'How are you feeling now?' I asked her when the waitress brought our check. 'Have you been dizzy at all today?'

'No.'

'Nauseated?'

'No. Why?'

'You still may have some Thorazine in your system.'

'I don't see how,' she said. 'Between you and the waitress I've drunk enough coffee today to get anything out of my system. You don't have to worry about the Thorazine.'

'Okay,' I said, picking up the check. 'Then I won't.'

She stood up and looked across at the inn as if she were afraid of it. 'Now all we have to worry about is the dreams.'

I went back to the table to leave the tip. Her paper napkin was lying on the seat of the booth. She had shredded it into tiny pieces.

When we got back to the room, I said, 'I thought I'd read galleys in here for a while.' I pulled a green chair over near the foot of the bed, and went to my room to get the galleys, taking a while to gather up Broun's copyedited manuscript and a couple of blue pencils so Annie could get ready for bed, and whistling the whole time so she'd know I was there.

When I came back in, she was already in bed, in a long-sleeved white nightgown, sitting up against the pillows, her hands clenched together.

'Is that Broun's book about Antietam?' Annie asked.

'More or less,' I said. 'He keeps making changes. That's why I need to get these done before he comes back from California, so he'll quit fooling with it.'

'What do you have to do with them?'

'Read them over. Look for mistakes, typos, missing lines, punctuation, that kind of thing.' I moved the chair closer to the bed so I could prop my feet on the end of it.

'Can I help?' She said it calmly enough, but the knuckles of her clenched hands were white. 'Please. I don't want to just sit here and wait to go to sleep.'

I put the galleys down. 'Look, I don't have to work on these right now. We could watch some TV or something.'

'Really, I'd like to help with the galleys. I think reading would take my mind off the dreams. Do we take different parts or do we read it out loud to each other?'

'Annie, I just don't think it's a good idea.'

'Because it's about Antietam?'

Because it's about Lee's bandaged hands and a horse with its legs shot off and dead soldiers everywhere. 'Yes.'

'You read those out loud, don't you?' she said. 'That's exactly the reason I should help you. I can see if Broun made any mistakes. After all, I was there.'

There was nothing I could say to that. I handed her the galleys and a blue proofreader's pencil. 'I'll read from the copyedited manuscript and you follow along to make sure everything's there and they haven't left out a line. You can check for typos, too. Just mark an X in the margin, and I'll go back and put in the proofreader's marks.' I handed her a pencil and put my feet up on the footboard and began to read:

'What time is it, do you reckon?' Ben said. They were crouched in a cornfield a little behind the sunken road where all the fighting was. They had fired over the heads of the men in the road until they ran out of cartridges and then had begun working their way backwards between the rows of shredded corn, taking rifles away from dead and wounded men and firing them. It seemed like they had been doing it for hours, but there was so much smoke Ben couldn't even see the sun. He wondered if maybe they had been here all day and the sun had gone down.

'It ain't noon yet,' Malachi said. He had his hand under a soldier whose left shoulder had been shot off and who was lying face down in the broken corn stalks. He had yellow hair. His arm was lying on the ground beside him, still holding on to his Springfield. There was a scrap of cloth pinned to his sleeve with a stick. Ben put down his rifle and unpinned the cloth. It was a handkerchief.

Malachi turned him over and rummaged in his pockets. It was Toby.

'Come on,' Malachi said. 'Looks like he ran out of minnies, too, before they got him.' He thrust Ben's rifle at him and yanked him backwards. 'Listen. They're bringing the guns up,' Malachi said, and Ben could feel the rough dirt shake under his feet.

'I have to ...' Ben said and started forward again.

Malachi stood up and grabbed him by the back of his shirt. 'What in tarnation do you think you're doin'?'

He showed the handkerchief to Malachi. 'I gotta pin this back on Toby. How will they know who he is? How will his kin know what happened to him?'

'They'll have a right good idea, but they won't find out from that,' he said, and jerked his finger at the handkerchief Ben looked at it. It was covered with soot from the powder so badly he couldn't even make the letters out. 'Now come on! What the hell you doin' now?'

'I know him,' Ben said, scrabbling in his pockets. 'I know where he's from. Do you got some paper?'

A bullet hit Toby's arm and gouged out another red hole. 'Come on,' Malachi shouted, 'or that gal back home's gonta be findin' out about you.' He took hold of Ben's coat and yanked him back through the corn till they couldn't see Toby anymore.

After a while the shooting let up a little and Malachi said, 'Me, I stick my pertinents in my boots.'

'They can shoot you in the foot, too,' Ben said.

'They can,' Malachi said, 'but most likely you won't get kilt straight off and you kin tell 'em who you are before you die.'

'I'm sorry,' I said. 'We had no business reading that.'

She was asleep. I took the galleys back from her and put in the proofreader's marks till I began to feel sleepy myself, and then went and looked out the window a while at the Rappahannock. Union troops had camped on the far side of the river, no more than half a mile from here, their campfires hidden by the fog along the river, waiting for the battle to start. Everyone who had written about the Civil War, generals, platoon historians, journalists, said the waiting was the worst part. Once you were in the battle, they said, it wasn't so bad. You did what you had to do without even thinking about it, but beforehand, waiting for the fog to lift and the signal to be given, was almost unbearable.

'It's so cold,' Annie said. She sat up and tugged at the blankets with both hands, trying to pull them free of the foot of the bed.

'I'll get a blanket,' I said, and then realized she was still asleep. She yanked hard on the coverlet and it came free.

'Get Hill up here,' she said, wrapping the flounced muslin around her shoulders and holding it together with one hand at her neck, as if it were a cape. 'I want him to see this.' Her cheeks were flushed almost red. I wondered if she would be feverish if I touched her.

She let go of the coverlet and leaned forward as if looking at something. The coverlet slipped off her shoulders. 'Bring me a lantern,' she said, and fumbled with the satin edge of the blanket.

I wondered if I should try to wake her up. She was breathing fast and shallowly, and her cheeks were as red as fire. She clutched the edge of the blanket in a desperate pantomime of something.

I moved forward to take the blanket away from her before she tore it, and as I did she looked directly at me with the unseeing gaze of the sleeping, and let go of it.

'Annie?' I said softly, and she sighed and lay down. The coverlet was bunched behind her neck, and her head was at an awkward angle, and I gently eased the coverlet out from under and pulled the blanket up over her shoulders.

'I had a dream,' Annie said. She was looking at me and this time she saw me. Her cheeks were still flushed, though not as red as they had been.

'I know,' I said. I hung the coverlet over the end of the bed and sat down beside her. 'Do you want to tell me about it?'

She sat up, tucking the pillow up against the headboard and pulling the muslin coverlet up over her bent knees. 'I was standing on the porch of my house at night, looking down at the lawn. It was winter, I think, because it was cold, but there wasn't any snow, and the house was different. It was on a steep hill, and the lawn was a long way below me, at the bottom of the hill. I was looking down at the lawn, but I couldn't see it because it was too dark, but I could hear the sound of someone crying. It was a long way off, so I couldn't really be sure what I heard, and I kept squinting down at the lawn, trying to make out what was down there.

'I turned on the porch light, and that just made it worse. I couldn't see anything. So I turned it off again and stood there in the dark and just then somebody crashed into me and it was a Union soldier. He had a message for me, and I knew it would be good news, but I was afraid if I turned on the porch light to read it by, I wouldn't be able to see what was on the lawn.

'Then I saw a light in the sky, a long way off, and I thought, Oh, good, somebody on their side has turned a porch light on, but it wasn't like that, it bobbed and danced, and I thought, Somebody is bringing me a lantern to read the message by, and then the whole sky lit up with red and green, and I could see the bodies on the lawn.'

'Were they Union soldiers?' I asked.

'Yes,' she said, 'only they weren't wearing blue uniforms. Some of them were wearing long underwear, red and white, and some of them were naked, and I thought how cold they must be lying there without any clothes on. Do you know where we are?'

Oh, yes, I thought, I know where we are. I hadn't taken her anywhere near the battlefield all day, but she had been there anyway. And why had I thought the battles Lee had won would haunt him any less than the ones he had lost?

'They weren't wearing uniforms because the Confederates came down from Marye's Heights in the middle of the night and stole them off the dead bodies. After the battle of Fredericksburg.'

She leaned back against the pillows as if I had said something comforting. 'Tell me about the battle.'

'After Antietam, Lee retreated back into Virginia. It took forever for the Union army to make up its mind to follow him, and when they did it was at the worst possible place. In December, the Union army crossed the Rappahannock at Fredericksburg and tried to march across the plain southwest of town, but the Confederate army held Marye's Heights above the plain. They proved beyond a shadow of a doubt that you can't attack a defended ridge from an open plain.'

'And after the battle the wounded soldiers lay there crying for help on the plain?'

'Yes. It froze that night.'

'And the Confederate soldiers stole their clothes,' she said softly. 'What about the message?'

'A Union courier got lost in the dark the night before the battle and wandered up to a Confederate picket line. He was captured and the orders he was carrying were taken to Lee. That same night the aurora borealis shone, lighting up the whole sky with red and green. Both sides took it as a good omen.'

She sat a long time huddled under the coverlet. 'What time is it?' she asked.

'Eleven forty-five.'

She lay down. 'If this time is anything like the others, I shouldn't have any more dreams tonight. I usually don't have them after midnight.'

'Was this dream like the others, Annie?' I asked, thinking of the 'storm of dreams' Dr Stone had said followed abrupt discontinuation of a sedative.

'No,' she said. She had propped herself up on one elbow, and she was smiling. 'It was easier. Because you were here to tell me what it meant.' She yawned. 'Can I sleep late tomorrow?'

'Of course. The morning after a battle the soldiers always get to sleep late,' I said, which was a lie. The morning after the battle the soldiers were marched off to the next battle, and the next, till they came to the one that killed them.

I sat down in the green chair and picked up the galleys.

'You don't have to stay up, Jeff,' she said. 'I won't have any more dreams. You can go to bed.'

'I just thought I'd finish reading the chapter we were on,' I said. 'Don't worry about me. Go back to sleep.'

She was asleep almost instantly, but I kept on reading. Ben and Malachi made it out of their cornfield and into the dubious safety of the West Wood. Hooker opened fire on another cornfield with every battery he had, and nobody made it out of there. Ben's brother and the rest of Mansfield's Twelfth Corps got the order to hold the East Wood and, in the smoke and confusion, began firing at their own Union troops. When Mansfield tried to stop them he was hit in the chest by Confederate fire. It was a mortal wound, but he managed to dismount and lead his wounded horse to safety before he died.

CHAPTER SEVEN

D. H. Hill had three horses shot out from under him at Antietam. Lee rode Traveller through the whole battle, though he had trouble controlling him with his bandaged hands. When General Walker brought the last of his men across the ford into Virginia the following night, Lee was sitting on Traveller in midstream. 'How many divisions are left?' Lee asked, and when Walker told him he was the last except for some wagonloads of wounded that were right behind him, Lee said, 'Thank God!' It was Walker's impression that he had been sitting there all night.

Annie didn't have any more dreams. I dozed in the green chair until it was light outside and then went to bed and slept until after nine. Annie was still dead to the world, but Richard was up. He had already called Broun's house and left another message for me.

'It's obvious that you're projecting your hostility onto me as an authority figure, but of course Broun is the real object of your anger. You're superimposing your own revenge fantasy on Annie's emotional illness, but it's Broun who's your real enemy.'

He stopped long enough for me to say, 'You're the enemy, you bastard.'

'Your conscious mind can't acknowledge the rage you feel toward Broun for getting his name on the books you've researched, so your subconscious cloaks that rage by distorting Annie's neurotic dreams into Robert E. Lee's dreams. By so doing, your subconscious can declare war on Broun, as Lee declared war on Lincoln. It's a common phenomenon in neurotic patients.'

'How about drugging patients? Is that a common phenomenon in neurotic psychiatrists?'

Annie was standing in the doorway in her nightgown. She looked frightened. 'Who were you talking to, Jeff? Richard?'

'I wasn't talking to anybody,' I said, and held the phone out to her so she could listen. 'It's the answering machine. Richard doesn't know where we are, so he's trying to get you back this way, by remote psychoanalysis. You'll be glad to know I'm the one who's crazy today.' I put the phone back up to my ear. 'This may take a while. Broun's answering machine can hold three hours of messages. Why don't you get dressed and we'll go have breakfast. We've got to go see the vet at eleven.'

She nodded and disappeared into the other room. I listened to the rest of Richard's harangue, made sure Broun hadn't called in another message, and erased everything on the machine. Broun usually didn't call in to pick up his messages when he was out of town, He left messages for me as to where he could be reached and then let me get back to him with a list of the things that couldn't wait. I didn't think he'd pick up his messages this trip, especially when he thought I was there to do it, but I thought I'd better call the machine once a day to collect them and erase the tape just in case. I didn't want Broun hearing Richard's ravings.

Annie came and stood in the doorway again. 'You were friends, weren't you?' she said. 'Before all this?'

'We were roommates. I guess we were friends, but we were headed in different directions all along.' I picked up my jacket. 'He thought I should study something useful instead of history.'

'I'm sorry,' Annie said.

'About what? My studying history?' I grinned at her. 'It hasn't turned out to be all that useless.'

We went over to the coffee shop. It was crowded with people who looked like they were on their way to church. We had a different waitress from the one who had drenched us in coffee the night before, a pretty redhead not much older than Annie, but she came over immediately with the coffeepot, too. 'You two must be tourists,' she said when she saw the map of Virginia I'd brought along. She pulled two menus out from under her arm and handed them to us. 'Have you been out to the battlefield?'

'No,' Annie said. 'We haven't been out there yet.'

'Well, you've got to go. It's the only thing Fredericksburg's famous for.' She set the coffeepot down and fished an order pad out of her pocket. 'The National Park Service has it fixed up real nice. They've got an electric map and everything. Now, what'll you have? Eggs? Hotcakes?'

The waitress took our order, gave our still-full cups what she called a warmup, and went off to the kitchen.

'Did you say the appointment with the vet was at eleven?' Annie said.

'Yeah, but it's out of town so we'd better allow a little time to find it. You didn't have any other dreams last night, did you?'

She shook her head.

'Was the dream different from the other dreams? I mean, I know it was about Fredericksburg, but was it the same kind of dream as the others?'

She thought about it a minute. 'It was clearer than the other dreams. I don't know how to describe it exactly, but they make more sense.' She shook her head again. 'That's not it, exactly. I still don't have any idea where I am or what the things in the dream are until you tell me afterward, but it's as if I'm getting closer to understanding the dreams.'

'You mean what's causing them?'

'I don't know. It's … I can't explain it. They're getting clearer.' And more frightening, I thought, watching her face. Whatever it is that she thinks she's starting to understand is terrifying her.

The waitress brought our breakfast and more coffee. I waited till Annie was done with her eggs and then asked her, 'When do you usually have the dreams? You said last night you usually don't have them after midnight.'

'Between nine and midnight. That was why Richard was so worried that night at the reception, because it was after nine. I think he thought I might fall asleep on the loveseat or something, but I don't have narcolepsy. I just have bad dreams.'

'You said the Thorazine kept you from dreaming that afternoon after I took you home from Arlington. Do you have the dreams during the day, too?'

'When the dreams first got bad I thought maybe if I could stay awake past midnight, the dreams would leave me alone, and it worked for a while, but then I started dreaming as soon as I went to sleep, so then I tried staying up all night and sleeping during the day, but that didn't work either.'

'And that was two weeks ago?'

'Yes.'

'And you were on the Elavil then?'

'Yes. I'd been on it for a month and a half.'

'Did Richard think that was odd, that you were dreaming? Antidepressants are supposed to repress the dream cycle. Did Richard say anything about that?'

'He was a little worried at first, but he said it took the Elavil a while to work and my sleep record was better. I wasn't waking up so often, and I was getting a lot more rest.'

'What about when the dreams got worse … clearer?'

'He said that was a good sign, that whatever was causing the dreams was trying to break through, that my subconscious was determined to make itself heard.'

I had assumed that he had taken her off the Elavil because it wasn't working or was even making the dreams worse. If that wasn't the reason, what was? According to Annie, he hadn't even been worried about the dreams, but something had happened to frighten him so badly that he had given her Thorazine to try to stop them.

The waitress made a frontal assault on our coffee cups again, and Annie and I both tried unsuccessfully to hold her off. 'Maybe we'd better retreat before she drowns us in this stuff.' I looked at my watch. 'It's ten-fifteen. Why don't we go ahead and see if we can find this Dr Barton?'

'All right,' Annie said. She folded her napkin and laid it on the table.

'Were you on anything before you came to the Institute? You said your doctor sent you to the Institute. Did he have you on any sedatives or anything?'

We stood up. 'Phenobarbital,' she said, reaching for her coat.

'Did Richard know that?'

'Yes, he was upset about it. He said that nobody used barbiturates anymore, certainly not in cases of pleisomnia, that my treatment had been all wrong.'

'You didn't keep taking the phenobarbital, did you?'

'No.'

I handed Annie the map and got the directions the vet's wife had given me out of my wallet. South of town, she had said, past Hazel Run on the Massaponax road. A house with a porch.

All the houses had porches, and we meandered along at least three roads marked Massaponax before we found it. Dr Barton was back from rounds but just barely and he still had a few animals to look at, his wife told us. She was much younger than she had sounded on the phone, not much older than Annie. She told us we were welcome to go around back to the stable and talk to him there.

The vet was young, too, with a thin, boyish mustache, and he obviously had never had acromegaly. He was only about five foot eight. He was wearing a pocketed blue shirt, jeans, and a pair of high boots that made him look like a Union army officer.

'What can I do for you?' he said, looking at a sorrel mare with a bad foot.

'I doubt if you can do anything for me,' I said. 'I've made a mistake. I was looking for a Dr Barton who has acromegaly.'

'That was my father,' he said, picking up the mare's left hind foot. 'I told Mary I bet that was who you wanted to see when she told me you'd mentioned Dr Stone's name.' He put the foot down. 'Dad died of a heart attack this fall. What did you want to talk to him about?'

'I work for Thomas Broun.' The vet nodded as if he'd heard of him. 'He's doing a book on Abraham Lincoln. Lincoln had acromegaly.'

'I know,' he said. 'Dad was always interested in other people who'd had acromegaly, especially famous people. Edward the First, the pharaoh Akhenaten, but especially Lincoln. I think because in late years he got to look like

Lincoln. That happens, you know, with the acromegaly. They all get the big ears and nose and the splayed hands.'

He picked up each of the mare's feet one by one, laid his hand flat against the sole of it, and then set the foot back down so the mare would put her weight on it. When he got to the right forefoot, the mare held the foot above the ground for a minute and then set it down carefully. Annie sat down on a bale of hay and watched him.

'What Broun's really interested in is Lincoln's dreams,' I said.

'The boat dream, huh?' He picked up the forefoot, looked at it, and set it down again. This time the mare put it firmly on the ground. 'Dad was always fascinated by that.'

'Boat dream?'

'Yeah. Lincoln had this recurring dream.' He started on the mare's feet again, picking them up, setting them down. When he let go of the right forefoot, the mare put it down and then picked it up again and held it just above the ground. 'In the dream he was in a boat drifting toward a dark, hazy shore. He dreamed it before battles: Bull Run, Antietam, Gettysburg. He dreamed it the night before he was assassinated, too.'

I looked at Annie, worried about what effect all this talk about dreams might be having on her, but she looked more interested in the mare than in our conversation.

'Did your father ever mention having any dreams?'

He pulled a small curved knife out of his shirt pocket. 'About boats? I don't think so. Why?'

'Broun thinks Lincoln's dreams may have had something to do with his acromegaly. Did he ever mention the acromegaly causing him to dream a lot?'

'That's an interesting theory.' He thought a minute. 'I don't remember Dad ever mentioning any dreams. If you know anything about acromegaly, you know it produces headaches and depression. My father was a very unhappy man. He didn't talk much, especially about his acromegaly. He told me as much about his symptoms as this mare does. The only time I ever heard him talk about it was in connection with famous people like Lincoln or Akhenaten. Toward the end it became almost an obsession with him.'

He picked up the right front foot and began scraping away at the bottom of the hoof with the knife. 'Speaking of Akhenaten, the Egyptians were big on dreams,' he said. 'They wrote them down, hired soothsayers to interpret them, believed their dreams could predict the future. There might be something …' He brushed away the shavings and peered at the bottom of the foot. 'No, I doubt if there'd be anything on Akhenaten's dreams. The next pharaoh who came along, Ramses, wiped out just about every trace of him. Knocked down all his statues, scratched out his name wherever he could find it, burned everything.'

'Then how do they know he had acromegaly?'

'They don't,' he said. He poked at something on the hoof with the top of the knife and frowned. He let go of the foot and watched as the mare put her foot down. She put her weight on it with no hesitation. 'It was just a pet theory of Dad's. There are a couple of wall paintings and statues that Ramses missed. They show him as having elongated ears and a wide, flat nose, and what records there are comment on his height. One of the hieroglyphics also called him melancholy, which, like I said, is one of the symptoms of acromegaly.'

'Or of knowing the next pharaoh's going to do his best to make everybody forget you,' I said.

He grinned. 'Right. It's all just a game, guessing what diseases people back in history had. Or guessing what diseases people have now, for that matter.' He took hold of the mare's bridle and began walking her up and down past us, watching carefully to see which foot she favored.

'With animals it's really a guessing game. They can't tell you where it hurts or what they think they have. Like this mare here,' he said, still parading her in a slow circle. 'She's got a sore foot, probably a bruised sole or a prick from a horseshoe nail, but it could be laminitis or corns or something else altogether. I can't find the infection, so I can't tell. The only sure way of finding out is to let her alone till it's gotten really serious. Then the infection will be easy to find – the hoof will be hot to the touch, she won't be able to put any weight on it, and she'll have developed a lot of other symptoms. Only problem is, by then it could be too late to do her any good, especially if she's picked up a nail. I need to find it now.'

'What if you can't find it?' Annie said.

'Then I'll give her a tetanus shot and wait till I can, but I'll find it. The clues to what's going on are there. You just have to look a little harder to find them at this stage.' He stopped the mare and tied her bridle securely to a rail and picked up the right front foot again. 'With animals you either have too many symptoms or not enough, and one's as bad as the other. I had a bay in here last week had every symptom in the book and then some. Had to sort through a dozen diseases before I got the right one. But I love a good mystery, don't you?'

He scraped away at the caked dirt on the hoof, turning the knife blade on edge to get in close to the shoe. We weren't getting anywhere with all this, but the barn was warm and smelled of dry hay, and Annie looked as if she was thinking about the mare's sore foot and not about that other horse with its legs shot off. Dr Barton dug in with the knife, and the mare began to shake her head as if telling him to stop. Annie stood up and went over to her, taking hold of the bridle just under the mare's chin, and stroking her neck.

'Your father never talked about his dreams, not even in connection with Lincoln's boat dream?'

'Not to me. He moved to Georgia last year when he started having heart problems. Did you know high blood pressure and heart disease were connected to acromegaly?'

'No, I didn't.'

He stopped scraping and put the horse's foot down. 'Dad might have told my sister his dreams. She was always his favorite, and he used to talk to her more than to the rest of us. Would you like me to call her?'

'I'd appreciate it if you would,' I said, and wrote out our phone number at the inn. 'Ask her if he had any dreams. They don't have to be about boats.'

'Boats,' he said thoughtfully, folding up the piece of paper and sticking it in his pocket. The mare had tangled her mane in the bridle when she tossed her head. Annie pulled the forelock out from under it, smoothed it, and patted the mare's forehead. 'The Egyptians dreamed a lot about boats. Symbol of the passage to the world of the dead.'

We left the vet to the mystery of the sore foot and drove back to the inn. We had lunch at a McDonald's on the way back into town, and when we got back to the inn, Annie took a nap.

I called the answering machine. There was a jumble of messages from people who hadn't figured out Broun was gone yet, and Richard had left another message on the machine.

'I've been looking at the results of Annie's blood tests, and I think I've found the key to what's happening here,' he said in his Good Shrink voice. 'Her L-tryptophan levels are indicative of cryptomnesia.' He waited long enough for me to ask what cryptomnesia was. 'It occurs when the patient presents early memories as reality, something the patient saw or read in a book and the conscious mind has forgotten. The subconscious mind then reintegrates the material as reality. Bridey Murphy. Her memories of an earlier life in Ireland were stories her nurse had told her in a preverbal stage, and under hypnosis she presented them as a previous life.'

'Annie wasn't hypnotized,' I said. 'She was drugged.'

'She obviously had preverbal contact with someone who told her stories about the Civil War, or there's a possibility of more recent reading of Civil War novels. Maybe she read one of Broun's books. That would account for her immediate neurotic attachment to you. She's experiencing schizophrenic dissociation, and you represent Broun.'

So now it was cryptomnesia, and I represented Broun. This morning it had been a revenge fantasy and Broun had represented Annie's dreams. And before that it had been a psychotic break and a half-buried trauma and a murder in the orchard with a cap pistol, and who knew what it would be the next time Richard called, and never in all these calls a word about the Thorazine he had given her.

Did he honestly think he could talk me into bringing Annie back with all this psychiatric gibberish? Maybe he was the crazy one and all this talk about Annie's repressed guilt and my obsession and Lincoln's impending nervous breakdown was nothing but – what was the proper psychiatric term? – projection.

I called Broun at the number he had given me before he left for California. 'How's it going?' I asked. 'Did you get in to see your prophetic-dreams expert?'

'This morning. He told me time and space aren't real, that they only exist in the conscious part of our brain, and down in the subconscious there's no such thing as a space-time continuum. He said everything that's ever happened or is going to happen is already in our subconscious, and it comes out in dreams.' He talked the way he always had, as if we had never had that fight about California. 'Then he says most people have to wait for dreams to tell them what's going to happen, but *he* can tell me my future right now just by putting me to sleep and watching my rapid eye movements.'

'And what did you say?'

'I said I'd already dreamed I didn't give money to phony fortune-tellers, and since it had already happened there wasn't any way I could change it.'

'And what did he say?'

'I didn't wait to find out. I wish I could dream what was going to happen. Then I wouldn't get stuck listening to cock-and-bull stories like that. Where are you, at home?'

'No,' I said. 'I'm in Fredericksburg. The phone rang off the hook yesterday, and I decided I wasn't going to get any work done, so I came down here. I think I might stay awhile. At least until McLaws and Herndon figure out where I am. There isn't any snow here.'

'I won't tell a soul where you are, son. Let McLaws and Herndon talk to the answering machine. That's what the damned thing's for. How're you coming on the galleys?'

'Fine. I looked up your Dr Barton. He died last fall, but I talked to his son. He couldn't remember his father talking about any unusual dreams. He's going to call his sister and ask her. Oh, by the way, I've got another dream for your collection. Lincoln had a dream the night before he died. He told his Cabinet about it. He dreamed he was in a boat.'

'"A singular and indescribable vessel,"' Broun said. 'I know.'

'You knew about the boat dream?' I said. 'Then why didn't you tell me?'

There was a silence at the other end so long that had plenty of time to think of all the things we hadn't told each other in the last week. I wondered what would happen if I told him I thought the fortune-teller was right, and down in Annie's subconscious Lee was fighting the Civil War. Would he call that a cock-and-bull story, too?

'Are you all right?' he asked. 'Are you taking care of yourself?'

'I'm sleeping till noon every day,' I said, 'and don't worry about the galleys. I'm over halfway through the book already.'

'I'm not worried about the galleys,' he said.

After I hung up I went and woke Annie up. We drove down to Bowling Green for dinner. Annie didn't show any of the tension I'd seen the day before, and the color in her cheeks was back to normal. Even after we got back to the inn and were reading galleys up in her room, me in the green chair and she sitting cross-legged on the bed, she was relaxed and interested.

'Why don't you go ahead and go to bed, Jeff?' she said at a little after eleven. 'You didn't get much sleep last night. I don't think I'll have a dream.'

'Okay,' I said. 'Call me if you need me.'

I left the door of the room open and the light beside the bed on. I took off my shoes and settled down with the book I'd bought in Bowling Green. It was a pop history moment-by-moment account of the day Lincoln died, but it had a long description of the Cabinet meeting.

Lincoln had told his boat dream before the meeting started, while they were still waiting for Stanton. Grant said he was worried about Sherman, and Lincoln said not to worry, that he had had a sign, and told them his dream. He said he had had the same dream before every victory in the war and named Antietam and Gettysburg and Stone River.

Grant, who didn't believe in dreams, said Stone River wasn't his idea of a victory and a few more victories like that would have lost the war, and Lincoln said, 'It must relate to Sherman. I know of no other important event which is likely just now to occur.'

I looked at my watch. It was a quarter to twelve. I turned off the light. What if Grant had believed in dreams? Would he have been able to figure out where the danger lay in time to bring up reinforcements, to set up a line of defenses that would have stopped John Wilkes Booth?

He didn't believe in dreams. He knew a cock-and-bull story when he heard one, even when Lincoln was the one telling it. But I wondered if, afterwards, he ever dreamed that Cabinet meeting?

'My house is on fire,' Annie said.

I turned on the light. She was standing in the door in her white nightgown, holding the galleys. She came over to the bed and handed them to me. 'He's dead, isn't he?' she said, and the tears streamed down her unseeing face. 'Isn't he?'

CHAPTER EIGHT

Lee and Traveller were well matched. If Lee demanded more stamina and spirit than the average horse could give, Traveller had too much stamina and spirit for the average rider. He chafed at being reined in, had to be exercised strenuously, and had an uncomfortable, high trot. When Rob Lee had to ride him down to Fredericksburg for his father in 1862, he complained, 'I think I am safe in saying that I could have walked the distance with much less discomfort and fatigue.'

It took me almost an hour to get her back to bed and sleeping more or less peacefully. I had tried to wake her up, even though I had read someplace that you weren't supposed to wake sleepwalkers – or maybe that was one of Richard's theories – but I couldn't.

'Annie!' I said, and took hold of her hands. They were hot. 'Wake up, Annie!'

'Is he dead?' she said, the tears running down her face and under her chin.

Is he dead? Who? General Cobb? He had died at Fredericksburg, but I wasn't convinced we were still there. We could be anywhere. Armistead and Garnett had died at Gettysburg, A. P. Hill at Petersburg two weeks before the surrender. It could even be Lincoln.

'Who, Annie?'

Her nose was running from all the tears, but she didn't make any effort to wipe it. I led her gently by the hand into the bathroom and got a Kleenex. 'Tell me what's happening,' I said gently and wiped her reddened nose. 'Can you tell me, Annie?'

'My house is on fire.'

I dabbed clumsily at her cheeks with the wadded-up Kleenex. 'What does the house look like, Annie?' I asked, and wiped her nose again.

She stared at our reflections in the mirror. 'He's dead, isn't he?'

I walked her back to her own bed and covered her up. She had stopped crying, but her lashes were matted with tears. The Kleenex was a sodden wad, but I wiped her nose again with it and tucked her in.

I stood beside the bed for a while, thinking she would wake up, but she didn't. I reached for Freeman on the floor next to the green chair and tried to find a burning house. During the battle of Antietam, Longstreet had helped some women and children get their belongings out of a burning house in Sharpsburg, but Lee hadn't been there. In the weeks before the battle of Fredericksburg, most of the town had been burned down, but no one had been killed except for seventeen thousand soldiers.

'I had another dream,' Annie said, without any trace of tears in her voice. She sat up in the bed. 'My house was on fire.' She shook her head as if to contradict what she was saying. 'It was the same house as in the other dreams, but it wasn't my house, and it wasn't Arlington.'

'Whose house was it?'

'I don't know. We were standing under the apple tree watching it burn, and a rider handed me a message. I couldn't open it because I was wearing gloves, so I handed it to somebody who was standing beside me. It was the clerk here at the inn. He opened the message with one hand. There was something wrong with his other arm. When he opened the message, I saw it was a box of candles.'

I shut Freeman. I knew whose house was on fire now. 'One of Lee's aides risked his life to bring Lee a box of candles because he was having trouble reading the dispatches by the light of the campfire,' I said. 'It's the Chancellor house that's on fire. We're at Chancellorsville.'

'It isn't a box of candles, though,' Annie said, looking at me the way she had looked at her own reflection in the mirror. 'It's a message.'

'The message is about Stonewall Jackson,' I said. 'Lee's right-hand man. He was injured at the battle of Chancellorsville. He had his arm amputated.'

'I sent a message back to Jackson, didn't I?'

'Yes,' I said. I knew what was in that message, too. 'Give Jackson my affectionate regards,' Lee had written. 'Tell him to make haste and get well and come back to me as soon as he can. He has lost his left arm, but I have lost my right.'

Annie leaned back against the pillows, rubbing her wrist as if it hurt. 'But he's not going to get well, is he? He's going to die.'

'Yes,' I said.

She lay down immediately, docilely, as if she were a child who had promised to go to sleep after a bedtime story, and I went back into my room and got a blanket and brought it into Annie's room so I could spend the night in the green chair.

Jackson's doctors had predicted a speedy recovery, but he developed pneumonia and died nine days later. Toward the end he was delirious much of the time. 'Order A. P. Hill to prepare for action!' Jackson had said once. Lee had called out for Hill, too, when he lay dying of a heart attack seven years later. 'Tell Hill he must come up!' he had said clearly. I wondered if they had dreamed of the same battle and which one it was, and if Annie was doomed to dream it, too.

At five I gave up trying to sleep and went into my room and read galleys, leaving the door open in case Annie woke up again. Ben and Malachi spent the rest of the morning and most of a chapter trying to find their regiment, and Robert E. Lee found his son Rob. He was standing on a little knoll by the road when Rob's artillery unit came straggling past with the only gun they had left. They were filthy and exhausted, and Rob stopped in front of his father and said, 'General, are you going to send us in again?'

Robert E. Lee had his arm in a sling. A courier was holding Traveller because Lee's hands were too swollen for him to hang on to the reins, and all around them cornfields and woods were on fire, and Antietam Creek ran a rusty red.

'Yes, my son,' Lee said. 'You all must do what you can to help drive these people back.' He told them to take the best horses and sent them back into battle.

I had left Freeman on Annie's bed. I went in to get it. She was asleep on her stomach, one hand under her cheek, the other flung out across the book. I eased the book gently out from under her, and then went on sitting there, as if my presence could somehow protect her from the dreams.

She had made me promise to help her have the dreams. Well, I was helping, all right. She'd already had more dreams since she met me than she had ever had with Richard, drugs or no drugs, and there didn't seem to be anything I could do for her while she was having them. I couldn't even wake her up.

Sitting here wasn't helping her either. I needed to be awake and alert when she had the next dream, and I hadn't had any real sleep since we got to Fredericksburg. But I didn't want to get up and go in to bed. I don't know what I wanted. Maybe for Annie to wake up, to open her blue-gray eyes and look at me. Not at smoke and horses and fallen boys, but at me. To look at me and smile and say sleepily, 'You don't have to stay here with me,' so I could say, 'I want to.' And what did I want her to say to that? 'I'm glad you're here. I never have the dreams when you're here'?

Annie murmured something and turned her face ever so slightly against the pillow. There weren't any traces of tears left, though her nose was still red. Her hair had stuck to her cheek when the tears dried, and I brushed it back off her face. Her cheek felt warm to the touch. I laid my hand against it.

She frowned as if she were disturbed. I took my hand away. Her face softened at once. She sighed and turned onto her side, pulling her knees up, drawing into herself. Her breathing steadied.

I stood up, carefully, so as not to disturb her, and took Freeman into the other room and looked up Lee's insomnia. He had had trouble sleeping throughout the war. 'I fear I shall not sleep for thinking of the poor men,' he had written to his wife a week after Antietam. If he was ever able to get to sleep before midnight, his aides were under strict orders not to wake him up unless it was absolutely necessary. He had told them that to him one hour's sleep before midnight was worth two hours' after that time.

I fell asleep with the volume of Freeman still open on my chest and slept till after noon, and even though my sleep hadn't come before midnight, it was still worth its weight in gold. I felt better than I had since before the trip to West Virginia, and able to think clearly for the first time about this whole mess. I had promised I would help Annie have the dreams. There was only one way to do that, and that was to figure out what was causing them.

I checked on Annie, who was still asleep. I shaved and got dressed, took a sheet of Fredericksburg Inn stationery out of the chiffonier, and started making a list of the dreams. Arlington first, and then Antietam, Fredericksburg, Chancellorsville. The Lees had evacuated Arlington in May of 1861. I wasn't sure of the date of the letter from Markie Williams that told what had happened to Tom Tita the cat, but it was sometime in 1861. Antietam was September 1862, Fredericksburg December of the same year, and Chancellorsville May of 1863. That meant the dreams were in chronological order, though they were telescoped in some way. Annie had dreamed almost a year of the war in one week, though she had dreamed about Arlington for over a year, with it only gradually becoming clearer. And there were important battles during that period of time that Annie hadn't dreamed about at all.

I started another list on a second sheet of stationery, writing the dates of the dreams in one column and the drugs she had been taking when she had the dreams in a second column. The drugs had some connection with the dreams, though I didn't know what it was. They had not suppressed REM sleep or kept her from dreaming at all, even though they were supposed to.

It was when Annie was on the Elavil that her dreams had suddenly become clearer, and the phenobarbital her family doctor had had her on apparently hadn't worked at all to stop the Arlington dream. Thorazine had stopped the dreams, but she hadn't had the storm of dreams Dr Stone had predicted when she stopped taking it, and none of the dreams seemed to have any particular correlation with the drugs she was or wasn't taking, so maybe there wasn't a connection after all, and the timing of the dreams had more to do with when Lee managed to get a few hours of sleep than with the tranquilizers.

Annie was awake. I could hear her moving around. I folded up the lists and put them into my jeans pocket. I knocked on the half-open door and she opened it the rest of the way immediately.

'Have you been up forever?' she said, looking at her watch. She looked tired in spite of all the sleep. 'I couldn't believe it when I saw how late it was.'

'I could. I woke up starving to death. It's a good thing they serve breakfast all day at the coffee shop. What say we go get some?' I pulled on my coat. 'I want to go to the library this afternoon. I think I've got an idea of what's causing the dreams.'

I told her about Lee's insomnia at breakfast, and then we walked down to the library. I bought a notebook at the convenience store on the way. 'I should probably be doing research on Lincoln's dreams, too, in case the vet doesn't find anything out,' I said.

'I'll do that for you,' Annie said. 'What do you want me to look for?'

'Anything on his acromegaly, which won't be in the indexes because nobody knew what he had. Any references to his having headaches or bouts of depression. And anything you can find out about Willie's death.'

'Willie. That was his son that died during the war?' she asked.

I nodded. 'Yeah. He was Lincoln's favorite child. Lincoln could hardly stand it after he died.'

We went into the library and looked around for the biographies. I hadn't paid much attention to the library when I'd come here to look up Thorazine the day before yesterday, except to notice that it had been a school before it was a library, one of those square three-story buildings built in the early 1900s.

It could have been beautiful, with its high, sashed windows and oiled wooden floors, but it seemed almost determinedly drab. The hardwood floors had been covered with speckled tile and a carpet that looked like the Union army had marched over it. Stiff, patched shades had been pulled down over the windows so that the only light of any use was the sharp fluorescent light from tubes in the ceiling.

I'd spent a lot of time in libraries, and I usually preferred the old-fashioned ones with their dusty stacks to the modern plastic-and-plants 'multimedia resource centers,' but I would have been glad to see a little updating in here.

The room the biographies were in was off to the side and up a few steps, an old classroom probably, though the blackboards had been replaced by book-shelves. I put my notebook down on the scratched wooden table and went to see what they had in the Ls. There were exactly two books on Lincoln: Thomas's *Abraham Lincoln* and an ancient leather-bound book by someone whose name I didn't even recognize.

I handed them to Annie. 'We're in the South now. We're lucky they've got any books on him at all.'

She took the books back to the table, and I got down on all fours to see what they had on Lee. It might have been the South, but I didn't do much better. I went out to the desk, asked where the history section was, and got directed to a little alcove located a half-flight up from the reference section where I had found the drug compendium.

Since I was already there and I knew where Annie was, I took the opportunity to look up phenobarbital in the dated drug compendium. It said about what I expected it to, that it was a tranquilizer and worked by suppressing REM sleep. Barbiturates were addictive, especially when used over a long period of time, and maybe that was why Richard had been so upset about Annie's family doctor prescribing it, but phenobarbital was comparatively mild, and it didn't have nearly the number of contraindications and warnings that Elavil had had, let alone Thorazine.

I went up into the alcove. It was labeled 'Virginiana,' and was about as sparse as the biographies had been, which didn't make any sense. Fredericksburg was a major battle, and we were within shooting distance of Spotsylvania, Chancellorsville, and the Wilderness. This should be a main source library for those battles, at least, and, since researchers would inevitably come here, for the rest of the Civil War as well.

I gathered up what I could find on the three battles Annie had dreamed so far and took them back up to the biography room. The librarian, a sharpish-looking woman who would have been at home teaching school there in the old ruler-rapping days, gave me a suspicious glance but made no attempt to stop me.

Annie had the books open and had torn some pages out of my notebook to take notes on. She looked up and smiled when I came in and then bent back over the book, her light hair swinging forward across her cheeks. I sat down opposite her and tried to find out Lee's sleeping habits.

Lee's 'precious hours' of sleep between nine and midnight couldn't account for the dreams Annie had had late at night or during the day, but she had said that she'd started having those only after she began staying awake to avoid the dreams. And maybe Lee had tried to grab a few hours here and there to compensate for his sleepless nights.

Lee had 'slept little' the night before Antietam, and, according to General Walker, who had seen him sitting on Traveller in midstream when he took his division across, Lee had been there all night, supervising the retreat across the Potomac.

On the night before Fredericksburg, that same night that the aurora borealis lit up the sky and the Union messenger stumbled into Confederate lines, Lee had kept his staff up working all night. At dawn he had ridden out to inspect the pits dug by the work parties overnight. None of the books mentioned whether Lee had gotten some rest after the battle was over, though it was obvious from these accounts that he must have been ready to collapse with fatigue.

Dr Stone had said that when the body was deprived of REM sleep, it made it up with a vengeance. Was that what the dreams were? Had Lee, worn out from the strain of battle and a lack of sleep, experienced a storm of dreams?

I couldn't find the same clear-cut pattern with Chancellorsville. Jackson had been wounded on May second, and as soon as Lee found out about it, he wrote him, 'I would I were wounded in your stead.' The message of the amputation of his arm arrived on the night of the fourth. There was no mention of Lee's having insomnia that night, though it was hard to imagine him getting a good night's sleep after news like that. On the fifth, word came that Jackson was recovering, and he definitely slept well that night, under a fly-tent at Fairview.

On the morning of the seventh, Jackson began to get worse, and by afternoon he was lost in delirious dreams, calling out for A. P. Hill and telling the infantry to move up. 'Do your duty,' he told the doctor who was dosing him with mercury and opium. 'Prepare for action.' On Sunday he said clearly, out of the final dream of some battle, 'Let us cross over the river and rest under the trees,' and died.

Annie closed both the Lincoln books. 'Would they have anything else on Lincoln?' she asked.

'I don't know,' I said. 'They might have something in the reference section. It's downstairs.'

She nodded and left, taking her notes with her.

I started through the biographies of Lee, wishing I had brought Freeman with me. The first book was arranged so hopelessly I never even found Chancellorsville, let alone any references to Lee's insomnia, but the second one, so old the pages were edged in gilt, and written in indecipherably flowery language, said, 'When Lee received the dreadful news that the doctors' ministrations were to no avail and that Jackson was sinking fast, he turned to that last, best source of hope in times of trouble. All night he prayed fervently on his knees for Jackson's recovery.'

He had been up all one night praying and probably had slept badly three or four nights before that because of worrying about Jackson. There was definitely a pattern. During each of the events Annie had dreamed about, Lee had gone without sleep for several days in a row. Maybe when he did finally sleep, he experienced the storm of dreams that Dr Stone had described. Dr Stone had called them powerful, frightening dreams. Could they have been powerful enough to have blasted their way across a hundred years to Annie? And if they had, why was she having them one right after the other? Jackson had died five months after the battle of Fredericksburg.

I looked at my watch. It was four-thirty. I piled the books up and took them back downstairs. Annie was in the reference section with a large book spread open in front of her. They must have had something after all. I went up into the alcove and put the books back on the shelves where they belonged so they would be there if I needed them again and not on a cart guarded by that fierce-looking librarian, and found a book on Gettysburg.

It weighed a ton. I didn't try to carry it back up to the biographies room or even get it up onto a table. I just laid it open on the floor and bent over it, trying to see if the same pattern of lack of sleep persisted with Gettysburg. Gettysburg was the next big battle after Chancellorsville, but Annie wasn't dreaming all the battles. I needed to see if the same conditions for dreaming had occurred during that battle.

There was a full page of references to Lee in the index. I tried looking them up, keeping one hand in the index page and going down the two-column pages with a finger of my other hand, hoping Lee's name or the word *sleep* would jump out at me. At five-fifteen I gave up. It was in there, every word ever written about Gettysburg had to be in there, which was the whole problem. There was too much stuff to sort through, the way the vet's bay had had too many symptoms. Lee's insomnia was lost in the sheer volume of facts. I hefted the book back onto its shelf and went to look for Annie.

She wasn't in the magazine section. I looked along the stacks and found her finally back in the biographies room. She had let up one of the shades and was looking out the window in the direction of the Rappahannock.

'I think I've figured out what's causing the dreams,' I said.

She turned around. She looked tired, as if she had been up all night instead of a few hours.

'I think you were right when you said you were helping Lee sleep,' I said. 'I think that may be exactly what you're doing.'

We went out the arched green doors and down the cement steps. It must have rained while we were inside because the library's asphalt parking lot was covered with puddles, but the sky was as clear as when we went inside, paling to lavender with the evening. The air smelled like apple blossoms.

'You said he couldn't sleep,' I said. 'You were right. He apparently suffered from insomnia through the whole war, and during the battles he didn't sleep at all.' I explained my theory to her as we walked back to the inn, telling her about Dr Stone's storm of dreams and the pattern I'd discovered in her dreams.

'I still think the drugs you took are somehow connected to all this, but I haven't figured out how yet,' I said. 'You said your family doctor put you on phenobarbital. Did you notice any change in the dreams while you were on it?'

'No,' Annie said, looking in the direction of the inn two blocks away. The black cat was coming out to meet us, highstepping its way along the wet sidewalk.

'How long were you on the phenobarbital?' I asked.

The cat meowed a greeting that sounded like a complaint. Annie knelt to pick it up. 'Did you know that when Willie Lincoln had pneumonia he kept calling for the boy across the street?' she said. 'His name was Bud Taft. He came and held Willie's hand and sat with him the whole time, did you know that?'

'No, I didn't.'

'One night while Bud was with Willie, Lincoln came in and said, "Better go to bed, Bud," and Bud said, "If I go, he will call for me." '

The cat struggled to be let down. Annie put it back on the sidewalk, and it stalked off, offended. Half a block away, it sat down on the sidewalk and began to lick its white paws.

'You didn't happen to find out where Willie Lincoln was buried, did you?' I said.

'I thought he was buried at Arlington.'

'Nope. And I don't know where he *was* buried.' Annie looked at the cat. 'Maybe nobody knows,' she said.

When we came up even with the cat, it stood up and walked alongside us all the way back to the inn.

CHAPTER NINE

Lee's affection for Traveller was obvious. 'If I were an artist like you,' he wrote his cousin Markie Williams, 'I would draw a true picture of Traveller ... Such a picture would inspire a poet, whose genius could then depict his worth and describe his endurance of toil, hunger, thirst, heat, cold, and the dangers and sufferings through which he has passed. He could dilate on his sagacity and affection, and his invariable response to every wish of his rider. He might even imagine his thoughts through the long night marches and days of battle through which he has passed. But I am no artist.'

When Michael Miley took Lee's photograph, Lee insisted that he be mounted on Traveller, 'just as we went through the four years of war together.'

We went back to the inn after dinner and waited for Lee's aides to deliver some last message so that he could take off his boots and settle onto his camp cot and go to sleep.

Annie rechecked the galleys that I had read the night before, and I got out my trusty Freeman and started in on Gettysburg. It was impossible for me to believe that Lee wouldn't dream about this, the worst battle of the war, the end of the war really for the Confederacy, though Broun would fight me on that.

He claimed that Antietam was the decisive battle, that with the failure of Lee's push into Maryland the war was effectively over for the Confederacy, even though there were three more years of killing left and Lee knew it.

Whether it was or not, and, more important, whether Lee was aware of it, he certainly knew it at Gettysburg a year later, and if anything would have given him bad dreams, it was that misbegotten battle. The high-water mark of the Confederacy. Lee made it all the way into Pennsylvania before the Union army stopped him, and then for three days he unleashed one assault after another that made it look like he could win after all.

On the morning of the third day, Lee met with Longstreet outside a school-house. Longstreet didn't like Lee's plan of attack. Later Longstreet claimed he had said, 'It is my opinion that no fifteen thousand men ever arrayed for bat-tle can take that position,' and had considered the matter settled. Lee never blamed anybody but himself for the failure of Pickett's Charge, but when his aide Colonel Venable said bitterly that he'd distinctly heard Lee direct Long-street to send up Hood's division in support, Lee had said, 'I know! I know!'

Lee's plan was to send Pickett's men directly on a frontal assault at the Union center, and it almost worked. Pickett's men made it up to the famous bloody angle of a stone wall and held it for almost twenty minutes, without any support at all, in spite of the fact that this time it was Fredericksburg in reverse, Lee's men in an open field marching toward a defended ridge. But Longstreet didn't send up the supporting divisions, and they couldn't hold the wall. When the soldiers began to fall back, Lee rode down to meet them and send them back to Seminary Ridge, speaking encouragingly to nearly every man who passed.

'Try to reform your division in the rear of this hill,' he had told Pickett, and Pickett had said, 'General Lee, I have no division.'

Annie went to sleep around ten, the covers pulled up over her shoulders as if she were cold. I called the answering machine, and Richard gave me his new theory, this one about sexual guilt and repressed Oedipal attachments.

I had felt all along that these calls, these theories, were leading somewhere, that they were all part of a pitch to persuade me to bring Annie back, but now I was not so sure. The theories didn't fit together. Sometimes they even con-tradicted each other, and he jumped from one to another with the same quiet urgency of a man recounting a dream. He still used his Good Shrink voice, but, listening to him, I had the feeling that it was not me he was trying to convince, but himself.

'I talked to a Jungian psychiatrist today,' Broun said after Richard ran down. He pronounced Jung to rhyme with 'hung.' 'He's got a theory that our subconscious is really a storage bin for everything that's ever happened in the past. Jung's collective unconscious, only he says it's not just common racial memories, it's everything.'

He sounded excited, agitated. Maybe he *was* getting obsessed with Lin-coln's dreams. 'Dates, people, places. It's all down there, but people only dream bits and pieces of it, and even then something has to trigger the mem-ories. That's where Lincoln's acromegaly comes in. He says a hormonal imbalance can unlock the collective unconscious. I know, I know, this sounds like the fortune-teller, but I think he's on to something.'

I erased the messages, thinking about what he'd said. If a hormonal imbal-ance could unlock the collective unconscious, maybe a chemical imbalance could, too, and that was where the drugs came in. It would explain why the dreams had suddenly gotten clearer when Annie was on the Elavil. Maybe the phenobarbital had started to let down some kind of guard in the subconscious, and then the Elavil had completed the process, so that Lee's dreams came through loud and clear.

If that was the case, then the dreams would gradually lose their power and clarity now that Annie was off the drugs, and the best thing to do was to wait them out till the chemical balance in her brain was restored and the dreams faded away.

I shut off the lights and went back into Annie's room to wait it out with her, and was asleep in the chair within minutes. When I woke up it was three-thirty by the lighted dial of my watch. Annie was still sleeping peacefully, though she had flung most of the covers off. I thought, with the confused logic of the half-awake, that I must somehow have slept through her dream, but her breathing wasn't the heavy, almost drugged-sounding breathing she had after the dreams, and my next thought, even more confused, was that I had stopped the dreams simply by telling her what caused them, and went back to sleep.

I must have heard the door slam because when I woke up again I was already halfway to it, only barely glancing at the bed because I knew she wasn't there. I had it open and was out in the hall in time to hear the outside door close. The outside door that opened on the fire escape.

I ran to the end of the hall and pushed down on the metal bar. The bar gave, but the door wouldn't open. Annie must be pushing on it from the outside. Or be lying crumpled against it. 'Annie!' I shouted through the door, and then stopped. You weren't supposed to startle a sleepwalker. If they were somewhere dangerous, on a cliff or something, they might fall. I tore back down the hall, down the front stairs, and through the empty lobby to the front door. It was locked, but from the inside. I got it open and raced around to the side of the building.

Annie was standing at the top of the stairs in her white nightgown, looking like a ghost in the gray, indistinct light of dawn. The cat was sitting on the top step, watching her.

'Annie,' I said quietly from the bottom of the stairs, 'you're having another dream.'

She was looking toward the Rappahannock. Fog lay along the line of trees like a gray blanket. 'Goodbye, Katie,' she said with a catch in her voice. 'Promise you'll come back.'

'Stay there,' I said, 'I'm coming.' I started up the stairs, one hand on the railing and the other held out to catch her if she fell. 'What are you dreaming, Annie?'

She half-raised her hand in its full white sleeve as if to wave. 'I wish you didn't have to go,' she said, and then buried her face in her hand and began to cry. The cat watched her incuriously.

I stepped onto the landing and put my hand gently on her shoulder. 'Annie, can you wake up? You're having a bad dream.'

She took her hand away from her face and turned to me, her face alight. 'No tears at Arlington!' she said brightly, 'no tears,' and flung her arms around my neck and sobbed.

'Annie, don't cry!' I put my arms around her. Sobs shuddered through her. 'Honey, oh, don't cry!'

She clung tighter to me, shivering in the thin nightgown. I patted her back and reached behind me for the door with one hand. I was afraid it would be locked from the outside, and how would I ever get her down these narrow stairs and back inside the inn? The metal bar gave under the pressure of my hand and opened. 'Let's go inside, Annie,' I said. 'It's cold out here, honey. Let's go back to the room.'

She tightened her arms around me and pressed her face against my neck. 'I don't want you to leave,' she said, and lifted her tear-stained face up to mine, her face full of love and sorrow. Her eyes were wide open, but she wasn't looking at me. Whoever she was clinging to, begging them not to go, it wasn't me.

Her nightgown had come unbuttoned at the neck and was pulled away from the long curve of her throat. I could feel the uneven catch of her sobs through the thin cotton of the nightgown. 'Annie,' I said, and the pain in my voice brought her awake.

Her eyes focused on me, frightened or surprised. 'Where am I?' she said, and looked bewilderedly at the stairs and the fog-shrouded Rappahannock. 'Did I have another dream?'

'Yes,' I said, disengaging her hands gently from my neck. I stepped back and down a step, almost onto the cat. 'Do you remember it?'

'I was at Arlington,' she said. She looked down at her unbuttoned nightgown. 'What did I do? – when I was asleep?'

I shoved down the bar of the door and it opened. 'You did a little sleepwalking, that's all.' I motioned her through the door, standing back, not touching her. The cat stood up and sauntered after her, and I shut the door in its face and then jammed the door down into its lock position and followed Annie into the room.

She was standing with her head bent, buttoning up her nightgown. I locked the door and put the chain on, which was what I should have done in the first place. If I had, none of this would have happened.

'You said you were at Arlington in the dream,' I said. 'Was it the same dream as before?'

'No.' She took her blue robe off the bedpost and put it on. 'I was standing on the porch with the waitress from the coffee shop, the one with the red hair, and she was getting ready to leave.' She cinched the tie belt of the robe and sat down on the bed, holding the robe closed at the neck with one hand. 'We were waiting for the carriage. There were a lot of suitcases piled up on the porch. I didn't want her to go.'

'I got that much,' I said, thinking of her arms around my neck, of the beautiful curve of her throat. 'Why did you say, "No tears at Arlington"?'

'I didn't. He …' She frowned and looked past me. 'We were standing on the porch and then …' She leaned forward as if she were trying to reach something, though her hand remained fastened on the collar of her robe.

'Why don't we talk about this in the morning,' I said. I stood up and pushed the green chair over against the door. 'This probably won't stop you if you sleepwalk again, but it'll slow you down long enough for me to hear you.' I balanced the volume of Freeman on the arm. It would fall off if she tried to move the chair.

'Jeff,' she said, clutching the blue robe tight against her neck. 'I'm sorry I … about all this.'

I wanted to shout at her, 'I'm not Richard. I'd never take advantage of you while you were asleep, for God's sake,' but I wasn't sure that was the truth.

'There's nothing to be sorry about. You were dreaming,' I said, and went into my room and shut the door.

My collar was wet from Annie's tears. I took off my shirt and put on another one and then went over and stood by the window, waiting for it to get light and thinking about Richard. 'I wasn't trying to hit on her, it just happened,' he had said when I accused him of taking advantage of Annie. 'I was trying to help her.'

'That's no excuse,' I said out loud, and didn't know if I was talking to Richard or myself.

When it was light enough to read, I picked up volume one. I had left volume four, the one with the index in it, out on the chair for a sleepwalking alarm, but I didn't know what to look for anyway, except for the reference to Arlington. If the dream had really taken place there, then this dream was from before the war, which meant my carefully worked-out theory was shot to pieces and I could start over, and volume one was as good a place to start as any.

I read till eight-thirty and then went out my bedroom door and over to the coffee shop and had breakfast. The redheaded waitress was there. 'Your name wouldn't be Katie, would it?' I asked her when she refilled my coffee cup.

'No,' she said disapprovingly, as if she thought I was trying to flirt with her in Annie's absence. 'It's Margaret. Did you guys make it out to the battlefield yesterday?'

'No,' I said. Maybe we should have, I thought. Maybe then Annie would have dreamed about Fredericksburg again, and I would have known what to tell her when she woke up.

'We were standing on the porch at Arlington,' Annie had said. 'The waitress was leaving and I didn't want her to go.' Who could Lee have had visit that he wouldn't want to go home? I didn't know much about Lee's life outside the war. All the research I had done for Broun had been about specific battles, and I was not even sure what family and friends Lee had outside of his son Rob, whom he had sent back into battle at Antietam, and the cousin, Markie Williams, who had gone back through enemy lines to fetch the Lees' belongings from Arlington and found the cat.

Who would Lee have flung his arms around, have cried over? The answer was nobody. The men who had been in the war with Lee described him almost uniformly as 'grave and kind' and 'showing no sign of his emotions.' One of his biographers had nicknamed him 'the marble man,' and all of them said he was devoted solely to his duty. He never talked about what was troubling him, never wept, not even over Stonewall Jackson. When the war was over, he never spoke of it.

He had paid dearly for that self-control. He had died of a heart attack, the controlled man's disease, and he had had bad dreams about the war up to the very end. He had told Hill to come up when he was dying, and then, at the very end, said, 'Strike the tent.' But he hadn't cried or clung to his family, even on his deathbed.

What if this wasn't one of Lee's dreams at all? What if now that the barriers to the collective unconscious were down, Annie would start dreaming other people's dreams?

Annie came over at a little before ten, looking like she hadn't slept either. She was wearing a high-necked blouse buttoned all the way up.

'I don't have any idea what your dream was,' I said. I dog-eared the page I was on and shut the book. 'You're sure it was at Arlington?'

'Yes. I was standing on the porch. The cat was there, and the apple tree. Its leaves had turned. It must have been in the fall. I'm sure it was Arlington. I mean, it's always my house, the house I grew up in, but it stands for other houses.' She shook her head as if that weren't the right word. 'It feels like other houses. I think Lee must have to use the images I have in my mind to make the dreams out of, and then he makes them stand for other things. It's the same with the people. I think he must choose the person who's most like the person he knew …'

The redheaded waitress bustled over and took Annie's order, apologizing for not having seen her right away and filling both our coffee cups to the very brim.

'Like the waitress?' I said after she left.

'Yes. It was the waitress, but it wasn't her really.'

'You called her Katie. Do you know her last name or what her relationship to Lee was? Was she a friend of his, a relative?'

'No, she was a friend of …' She picked up her spoon and stirred her coffee.

'I just remembered something about the dream,' she said. 'That never happened before.'

'What?'

'The waitress ... Katie and I were standing on the porch saying goodbye, and I didn't want her to go. We were both crying, and laughing at the same time because neither of us had a handkerchief, and then all of a sudden I was out by the apple tree and walking up to the house. You know how sometimes in a dream you're one person and then you're somebody else, only you're still the first person, too? That's how this was. I was walking up from the apple orchard, too, and I was still on the porch saying goodbye to Katie. I had on my white nightgown, and she was in her waitress uniform, and we were both crying, and I went up on the porch and said to them, "No tears at Arlington!" and laughed, and gave Katie my big handkerchief to blow her nose on.'

'Do you know who the girl on the porch was?' I asked. 'The girl who was you?'

'No. But coming up from the apple orchard I was Lee.'

Well, at least the Pandora's box of the whole world's dreams hadn't been opened yet, and she was still dreaming Lee's dreams, even if I couldn't place this one. 'And so then this girl, whoever she is, flung her arms around Lee's neck and started to cry?'

'No.' She put her coffee cup down and stared into it. 'He ... I ... Lee came up on the porch,' she said slowly, 'and said, "No tears," and all of a sudden I felt that I knew what was causing the dreams.' She looked up at me. 'I was myself in the dream right then, not Lee or the girl in the white nightgown. I was myself. And I knew what was causing them. I knew why I was having the dreams.' She put her hand up to her mouth. Her eyes filled with tears. 'Poor man,' she said softly. 'Poor man.'

It had been Annie with her arms twined around my neck, after all, even though it wasn't me she clung to. 'Do you still know?' I said, wanting to reach across the table and comfort her, but not daring to even touch her. 'Do you remember what it was that was causing the dreams?'

She wiped her eyes with her paper napkin. 'No. I woke up and found myself hanging all over you. I was so ashamed that I'd been sleepwalking and that my nightgown was half off. I was afraid I'd tried to kiss you or something.'

You didn't try to kiss me, Annie, I thought. I wasn't even there. 'You didn't try to kiss me,' I said.

'And then when I tried to remember the dream, I couldn't ...' Her voice trailed off again the way it had the night before. After a minute she shook her head. 'Jeff, I think we should go back to Arlington.'

That one had come right out of left field. 'We can't go back,' I said, stammering in my surprise. 'Richard's there.'

'I know, but when I went there before, it helped.'

Helped her to dream the horrors of Antietam and Fredericksburg and Chancellorsville, I thought. I could see the look of terror on her face as she stood there in the snow, looking down at the bodies on the lawn. I didn't want to subject her to that again, even to solve the puzzle of the dreams.

'We're only going to be here a couple more days. I need to see the vet again and finish up my research at the library for Broun.' These were useless excuses. I could obviously call the vet from D.C., and the only research I'd done since I'd been here had been on Lee, not Lincoln, but Annie wasn't listening to me. She was leaning forward, as if she could almost reach out and touch the meaning of the dreams.

'The dreams have something to do with Arlington,' she said in that inflectionless voice she used to recite the dreams. 'And the yellow-haired soldier. And the cat. Nobody knows what happened to them.' She looked up at me. 'Did Lee have a daughter?'

'He had several, I think,' I said, relieved that she had changed the subject. 'I know he had at least one. Agnes, I think her name was.' I stood up. 'Go ahead and finish your breakfast. I'm going to go get my notebook and then we'll go to the library and see what we can find out about Agnes.'

I went back to the room and gathered up the two volumes of Freeman that were by my bed. Annie had left the chair close to the door. Volume four was on the seat. I pushed the chair back where it belonged so the maid wouldn't think we were trying to steal the furniture and picked up the book.

Annie was standing at the cash register talking to the redheaded waitress when I got back. I hoped she wasn't pitching the battlefield again.

'The weather's supposed to turn this afternoon,' the waitress said. 'Big cold front moving in.'

Good, I thought. Maybe we'll be snowed in here.

We walked down to the library. The librarian glared at me when I came in carrying my stack of books, as if she thought I'd taken them the day before without checking them out. Annie borrowed a piece of paper and a pen from me and said she was going back down to the reference section.

'I'll be in biographies, where we were yesterday,' I said.

I looked up 'Lee, daughters of.' He had had three other daughters besides Agnes: Mary, Ann, and Mildred. Since I had no way of knowing which one was in this dream, I used the only other clue I had. An hour into the index references under Arlington, I found what I was looking for.

In the fall of 1858, Katherine Stiles, a friend from Georgia, had come for a visit. When she got ready to leave, Lee had found her and his daughter Annie weeping together. 'No tears at Arlington!' he had told them. 'No tears!' His daughter Annie.

I looked up 'Lee, Annie Carter (Robert E. Lee, daughter of)' in the index and started going through the page references. On March second, 1862, Lee had written her: 'My Precious Annie, I think of you all, separately and collectively, in the busy hours of the night, and the recollection of each and every one whiles away the long night, in which my anxious thoughts drive away sleep. But I always feel that you and Agnes at those times are sound asleep, and that it is immaterial to either where the blockades are or what their progress is in the river.'

There it was, the connection I'd been looking for. I had tried to come up with all kinds of complicated rationales for why Annie was having the dreams – Richard's drugs and chemical imbalances and Dr Stone's storm of dreams. It had never occurred to me that Annie might simply be having the dreams because Lee had called out her name in his sleep.

The sharp-faced librarian was leaning over me. 'I see you brought your own books with you today,' she said in a voice with a surprisingly gentle tone and a marked Virginia accent. 'I'm afraid our Civil War materials are very limited. Most people do their research out at the National Park Service Library.'

'The Park Service?' I said.

'Yes. It's out at the Fredericksburg battlefield. When I saw you in here yesterday I wondered if you knew about it, but I didn't like to interrupt your work. All the main source materials are out there. Do you know how to get there?'

Yes. March across an open plain to a defended ridge. 'Yes. Thank you.' I gathered up my stack of Freeman. 'Do you happen to know when they're open?'

'Nine to five,' she said in that impossible Southern belle voice. 'The battlefield itself is open until dark, I believe.'

I went and found Annie, who was in the encyclopedias, surrounded by the *L*s. 'I found what I needed. Let's get out of here,' I said.

The librarian was standing at the front desk looking as forbidding as ever. I hustled Annie past without even telling her thank you, for fear she would say something to Annie about the battlefield, and suggested we walk downtown and get something to eat. 'I saw a drugstore on the way up that had a soda fountain, believe it or not,' I said.

'I'm not very hungry,' Annie said.

'Well, then something to drink. A lemonade or something.'

The drugstore did have a fountain, though it was pretty decrepit-looking. The faded pictures of ice cream and grilled cheese sandwiches and root beer floats looked like they'd been up since the Civil War, and there was nobody behind the counter. A balding pharmacist was filling prescriptions in a booth at the back, but he didn't look up, even when we sat down on two of the plastic stools.

'I'll go ask if the fountain's open,' I said and started toward the back, but before I got there the phone rang and he answered it. I waited for him to look up, reading the labels on the medicines. Half the rack was devoted to sleeping pills: Sominex, Nytol, Sleep-Eze. Richard would have felt right at home.

The pharmacist cupped his hand over the mouthpiece of the phone and whispered, 'Be right with you.'

I nodded and went back up to the front. Annie was looking at the rack of postcards next to the counter. I hoped to God they didn't have one of Arlington.

'The pharmacist said he'll wait on us as soon as he gets off the phone.' I leaned over her shoulder to see the postcard she was holding. It was a photograph of Lee's tomb at Lexington. The marble statue was of Lee asleep on his camp cot in his dress uniform and boots, with a blanket draped over him. One arm lay at his side, the other was folded across his chest. 'I think I know what's causing the dreams,' I said. 'The girls on the porch were Katherine Stiles and Annie Lee.'

She put the postcard back in the rack with infinite care. 'Annie Lee?'

'Lee's daughter. You were right about it being one of his daughters. Annie didn't want her friend to leave. Both girls were crying, and Lee told them, "No tears at Arlington."'

Annie sat down at the counter. 'No tears,' she said and put her hands on the volume of Freeman, one over the other.

'Don't you see what this means? The dreams aren't meant for you. Lee was thinking of his daughter, and through some freak of time, the message got sent to you by mistake. I don't know how. Maybe you heard your name being called down in the collective unconscious or something.'

'Mistake,' Annie said, and shook her head. 'He's trying to tell me something. That's what the paper on the soldier's sleeve is, only I can't read it. It's a message of some kind.'

'But not to you,' I said. 'You were right in more ways than one when you said they weren't your dreams. They belong to Annie Lee. Her father was sending them to her.'

'There are messages in all the dreams except this last one,' Annie said. 'There's the message that the Union soldier was carrying when he got captured at Fredericksburg, and the message about Jackson's arm being amputated. And Special Order 191.'

'And the reason you can't make out the messages is because they weren't meant for you. They were meant for Annie Lee. She'd recognize Katherine Stiles and she'd remember that day at Arlington and Tom Tita. She'd know what all of it meant. They're her dreams, Annie, not yours.'

The pharmacist came bustling up to wait on us and tell us a long and involved story about Lila who usually took care of the front for him but who had broken her foot. 'Messing around with horses at her age,' he said without explaining what she'd been doing. He stuck two paper cones into metal bases.

'She should have known better.' He squeezed lemons into the paper glasses. 'You folks tourists?'

'Sort of,' I said. 'We're here for a few days.'

He held the glasses under the soda water siphon one at a time, stirring the lemonades with a long-handled spoon. 'You been out to the cemetery yet?'

'Cemetery?' Annie said.

'The battlefield. It's a national cemetery now. Union soldiers. Confederates are buried over on Washington Avenue.' He scooped ice into the glasses.

'How far is it from here?' Annie said.

'Two miles maybe. You go down Caroline, that's this street, till you come to Lafayette Boulevard,' he said, drawing a map on the damp counter with his finger. 'That's US 3. Turn right on Lafayette and follow it all the way out to Sunken Road. You can't miss it.' The phone rang. The pharmacist plopped two lemon slices into the glasses, shoved them across the counter at us, and hurried back to answer it.

I peeled the paper off a straw and jabbed the ice in my lemonade with it. Did everybody in this whole damned town own stock in Fredericksburg battlefield? It's a great place to visit. Seventeen thousand dead. There's even an electric map, red lights for the mortally wounded soldiers, blue for the ones who froze to death. You can't miss it. Take US 3 to Sunken Road, where the bodies are lying ten deep in front of the stone wall.

Annie was still looking at the counter where the pharmacist had drawn the map. In a minute she would say, 'I want to go out to the battlefield, Jeff,' or worse, 'I think we should go to Arlington,' and what excuse was I going to come up with this time?

'Do you think they'd have any aspirin in those little tins?' Annie said. 'I didn't bring any with me today, and I've got kind of a headache.'

'Sure,' I said. I slid off the stool and went to the back to ask the pharmacist. He was still on the phone. 'You of all people should know I can't prescribe without a doctor's orders, Lila,' he said loudly. There was a long, frustrated pause, during which he stared at the phone.

I searched along the rack of medicine but didn't find any tins. I grabbed a bottle of a hundred and took it back up to Annie. 'Are you all right?' I broke the seal, dug out the wad of cotton, and shook two into her hand. She took them with a sip of lemonade. 'Do you want to go back to the inn?'

'Yes,' she said.

I went back to the pharmacist and handed him three ones, holding up the bottle of aspirin where he could see it. 'Especially not for you!' he shouted at Lila. 'With your heart condition?' I waited some more. He looked up, finally, and nodded at me.

Annie was standing by the door waiting for me, the four volumes of Freeman in her arms. 'Here. Let me take those,' I said, tucking them under my arm. I opened the door for her. 'Do you want me to go back to the inn and get the car?'

'No, I'm fine, Jeff, really.' She smiled wearily. 'I think Lee must be thinking about his daughter again.'

'I can go get the car,' I said, and then saw the blue Ford sedan let an elderly black woman out a block down and start toward us.

'Taxi!' I shouted, jumping out into the street as if I were trying to stop a runaway horse. 'Taxi!'

The taxi driver pulled over and opened the back door for us. He was at least sixty, with a huge cigar and a stubbly beard that looked even sharper and more disreputable than Broun's. I gave him the inn's address, and he pulled out into the street.

'You two tourists?' he said over his shoulder. 'You been out to the battle-field yet?'

CHAPTER TEN

Pickett's Charge was the worst moment of the war for Lee. In spite of his telling his men, 'Don't be discouraged,' he had to have known the war was lost with it. Generals Garnett and Armistead were dead, General Kemper was mortally wounded, and there had been over twenty thousand casualties in three days. Even if the army managed to retreat safely into Virginia, it would never have the strength again for a major offensive. The long retreat to the apple orchard was beginning.

That night, worn out, Lee had tried to dismount and been unable to. A cavalryman leaned forward to assist him, but before he could reach him, Lee had gotten down by himself and stood leaning against Traveller. 'Too bad!' he said. 'Too bad! Oh, too bad!'

Annie slept fitfully all afternoon, not dreaming but not getting any rest either. At six I drove to McDonald's and got hamburgers. She got up then, but she ate hardly anything, and afterwards she couldn't get back to sleep. She walked the length of the room, back and forth, like a penned animal.

'Do you want to read galleys?' I asked, remembering that she'd said they helped keep her mind off the dreams, but she shook her head and went on pacing, stopping now and then to lean against the window. She looked dead on her feet. Her eyes were shadowed with fatigue, and there was hardly any color in her face.

'Do you think the library would be open tonight?' she asked.

'It closed at six,' I said. 'We could go take in a movie. I could go get a paper and we could see what's on.'

'No, I ...' She went over to the bed and lay down. After a while she said sleepily, 'When does it open in the morning?'

'The library? Nine,' I said, wanting to ask her what she wanted at the library but afraid I'd wake her up. She seemed to be asleep already.

I read Freeman awhile. I didn't try to find out anything else about Annie Lee. There was no point. I had thought Annie would be glad we had finally found out why she was having the dreams, but she hadn't even acted like she cared. And the information hadn't helped her sleep.

When I got bored with Freeman, I picked up the galleys. Ben and Malachi ran into some of their own artillery and took cover behind it. I didn't remember that. In the last version I'd read, they'd gotten separated, with Ben ending up on an ambulance detail, but in this version they were clear across the valley from where they should have been. I wondered if this was the scene Broun had written that afternoon after I'd accused him of being obsessed with the Lincoln book.

'Shouldn't we ask somebody where our regiment is?' Ben asked.

Malachi pointed back across the cornfield to a road and a fence full of men. It wasn't so smoky down there, and Ben could see the sun glinting off their bayonets. 'They're clear the hell over there, mebbe, and how do you conjure we get to 'em? We got ourselves separated and we're gonna stay that way.'

Malachi shouted the whole speech, but toward the end of it Ben could only tell what he was saying by reading his lips. The noise of the guns was getting louder every minute, and the firings and the shells landing had stopped making separate sounds and were roaring, like thunder. Ben could only tell when the guns fired by the smoke.

'Come on!' Malachi said. Ben didn't hear that either, but they started to run, keeping their heads down as if to protect them from the noise.

They ran straight into one of the guns. Its barrel had exploded and there were men lying on their backs in a circle around it. A man wearing a straw hat, and a boy were trying to free the horses from the caisson. A lieutenant rode up and shouted, 'Pull those horses back!' and Ben wondered how he was able to make himself heard. 'You two there! Help him!' he said, pointing his sword at the boy, who was struggling with the reins.

The man wearing the straw hat had unbuckled the harnesses, but the horses had gotten themselves tangled in it. One of the girth straps was wrapped around the nearer horse's hind leg. The harder he strained the tighter it pulled.

Ben grabbed hold of the horse's dragging reins and tried to steady him. Malachi got alongside the horse and began to push him back against the caisson. The man in the straw hat reached under to cut the strap. The horse whinnied and reared up.

'Dang your hide, you crazy fool,' Malachi shouted at the horse. 'Do you want to get kilt?'

Ben stepped back out of the reach of the hoofs, grabbing for the reins. 'Hold still, dang ya!' Malachi shouted.

There was a terrible roar. It surprised Ben that he could hear it. Dirt and grass and pieces of metal flew up in front of the caisson, and the horse came down on its front feet, hard, and pitched sideways onto Malachi. Ben ran over to him. The horse's full weight was on his chest. 'Dang your hide, you ugly plug!' Malachi said. 'Get off 'n me.'

Ben got his hands under Malachi's shoulders and tried to pull him out, but he couldn't budge him. He stood up and called to the boy to come and help, but he couldn't see him anywhere. The man with the straw hat was bending over the tongue of the caisson, his arms swinging lazily back and forth.

'I allus hated horses,' Malachi said in a strong, clear voice that Ben didn't have any trouble hearing. 'Danged gray gelding bit me in the backside when I was a young 'un and I never trusted them since.'

Ben was still holding on to the reins. He stepped back and pulled on them, and the horse's head moved a little. Its neck looked impossibly long, lying there on the ground, like he had stretched it with his pulling. Ben tried again.

'Dang horse throwed a shoe and I got off to look at his hoof. No way he'd let me pick it up to look at it, so I bend over to see if mebbe he's split the hoof,' he said. A bubble of blood and mucus showed in his nose. He sniffed and went on talking. 'He takes a piece out of my britches and what's under 'em. I stood up to supper for two weeks.'

Ben dropped the reins and knelt down beside Malachi. He worked his hands under the horse's flank and tried to lift it up a little. 'Can you ease yourself out a ways?' he asked.

'You are allus lookin' behind you after a thing like that, but I never expected a durn horse to come at me from the side.' A larger bubble of blood came out of the corner of his mouth and trickled into his beard.

'Malachi?' Ben said, even though he knew he was dead. He stood up. The fighting had moved farther south, toward Sharpsburg. Ben could hear the individual guns easily now. He looked back down at Malachi. One of his boots was sticking out from under the horse's tail, and the other one was half under its leg. Ben knelt down and pulled the boot off. Malachi wasn't wearing socks, and there was a blue-black blister on the heel. Ben turned the boot upside down. He set the boot down next to Malachi and started to pull the other one off.

'You there!' a man on a horse said. It was the same lieutenant who'd told them to help pull the horses back. He waved his sword at Ben. 'Come away from there! What's your regiment?'

The boot came free, and Ben straightened up, holding it. 'I was looking ...'

'You were looking to get a new pair of boots. Get back to your regiment before I have you shot for looting!' He waved the sword close to Ben's middle.

Ben felt around the inside of the boot and pulled out a damp square of paper. 'You got no call to talk to me thataway,' he said. 'I was just trying to help.' He knelt down and tucked the paper in the pocket of Malachi's shirt and started down the hill toward the sound of shooting.

In the original version Ben had never found out what happened to Malachi. He had simply dropped out of sight, like how many soldiers at Antietam and Fredericksburg and Chancellorsville? 'Did he die?' I had asked Broun after reading the first draft.

'Die? Hell, no, an old vet like Malachi was too tough to die. He hightailed it to California after Gettysburg.'

Broun had rewritten the scene because he was furious with me, but what was he trying to communicate? Was he supposed to be Malachi, struggling with a recalcitrant research assistant who wouldn't cooperate even when it was for his own good, or was he supposed to be Ben, who was only trying to help and who got threatened with being shot as a looter for his pains? Broun had been angry with me that afternoon, but he'd been worried, too. He had asked me that afternoon if I was Richard's patient, if I was taking any medication. Maybe he had written this chapter to show me he was worried about me, that he only wanted to help.

I looked at my watch. It was eleven-thirty, eight-thirty in California, and God only knew what time it was in northern Virginia or Pennsylvania or wherever the hell Lee was tonight. Annie sighed in her sleep and turned over. I put the chain on the door and moved the chair over between it and the bed. I stood there awhile, watching her sleep, wishing I could help, and then went on reading.

Ben carried wounded soldiers off the field all afternoon. Ben's Union brother made it out of the East Wood and away from the Sunken Road before he was hit in the side. He lay still for a while in the hot sun and then crawled under a haystack and passed out. Around two-thirty an artillery shell set the haystack on fire, and he was burned alive.

'They can't possibly hold that position,' Annie said. She sat up and swung her feet over the side of the bed. 'I told him ...' She stood up.

I glanced at the door, even though I had just fastened the chain, and took a protective step toward it, but she sat down on the side of the bed and put her arms around the wooden poster at the head of the bed. 'My fault,' she said, so softly it was almost a sigh.

I tried to sit down next to her, but she pulled away, so I sat in the green chair and leaned forward, my hands between my knees. 'Annie!'

'I know! I know!' she said bitterly. She stood up again, one arm still wrapped around the bedpost. 'Where is he?' she asked, and turned to look at someone behind her. 'He was supposed to tell Hood to bring up his division.'

She took a stiff, sleepwalker's step toward the door to my room. 'Try to reform your men among the trees,' she said kindly, as if she were speaking to a child.

'Annie?' I said quietly, moving so I was between her and the door, wishing I had chained the outside door of my room, too. 'I know where we are. It's Pickett's Charge. Longstreet didn't send the reinforcements up.'

She looked straight at me. 'Don't be discouraged,' she said. There was no emotion in her voice at all, but the look on her face was the look she had had at Arlington, looking down the hill at the bodies on the lawn. 'It was my fault this time. Form your ranks again when you get under cover.'

It went on for half an hour like that. Sometimes she reached down, her hand almost touching the floor, and I thought she must be helping lift up a soldier who had fallen. Then I remembered that Lee had been on horseback. He had ridden Traveller down from his command post to meet the survivors and send them back to the safety of the woods. He must be reaching down to rest his hand on a private's shoulder, to give his soldiers some encouragement as they limped past. 'My fault,' Annie said softly, over and over. 'My fault.'

And I had wanted her to dream Gettysburg to prove my theory. 'It's not your fault,' I said.

I took her arm, gently, and led her back to the bed, and she sat down and put her arms around the post again. 'Too bad,' she said despairingly. 'Oh, too bad.'

She wouldn't let go of the post even after she was awake. 'I was under the apple tree watching the house,' she said calmly, but her arms were still wrapped around the turned wood. 'Only this time it wasn't an apple orchard. It was a forest.'

'The point of woods,' I said. 'At Gettysburg.'

'I knew it wasn't really an apple orchard and that they weren't really apple trees even though there were green apples on them. It was summer. It was so hot it was like an oven. I was wearing my gray coat, and I kept thinking I should take it off, but I couldn't because I had to tell all the soldiers who kept coming past to get under the trees. They were trying to get up over the railing onto the front porch and it wasn't a railing, it was more like a wall, but they couldn't and I couldn't see why they couldn't get onto the porch because of all the smoke and then they'd come back into the apple orchard, all bloody. I said, over and over, "This is my fault, this is my fault," to all of them as they came past.'

I sat beside her on the bed and told her what the dream meant, even though I was past believing I was helping her with my explanations any more than Richard had helped her with his theories and his sleeping pills.

She had told me that my explaining the dreams made them easier, but I had been doing that for a week, and the dreams had gotten steadily worse. Taking her to Arlington wasn't going to help, either, and I wasn't about to take her back within reach of Richard, but keeping her here in Fredericksburg wasn't much better. Sooner or later she would decide she wanted to go out to the battlefield. To find what? A whole new batch of dreams? Spotsylvania? Petersburg? The Wilderness, where the wounded were burned alive? There were all sorts of wonderful possibilities. The war was only half over.

'Promise me you won't try to stop me from having the dreams,' she had said that first day in Fredericksburg. And I had promised. Lee had made promises, too. 'I could have taken no other course,' he had written Markie Williams. But when he saw boys of sixteen cut down like stalks of corn, when he saw them barefoot and bleeding and dead on their feet, didn't he ever consider breaking his promise?

I felt suddenly too tired to even stand. I went back into my room, pushed the galleys off my bed onto the floor, and went to bed.

I slept till six-thirty. Three-thirty in California. Too early to call Broun. I went over to the coffee shop and read galleys, letting the redheaded waitress fill my coffee cup whenever it got halfway down, till it was a uniform, undrinkable temperature.

D. H. Hill's horse got its legs shot off. Ben found his regiment, and they marched south and east toward Sharpsburg. Lee tried to look through a lieutenant's telescope but couldn't because his hands were bandaged. A. P. Hill came riding up in a red wool shirt to save the day, and Ben got shot in the foot.

At nine I called Broun's hotel from the pay phone in the coffee shop. He had checked out.

I went back to the room and let myself in through my door. Annie was asleep, clutching her pillow the way she had the bedpost. I called the answering machine. 'You're probably wondering where I went,' Broun said. 'I'm in San Diego. At the Westgate. I came here to see an endocrinologist. The psychiatrist put me on to him. He's an expert on hormonal imbalances in the brain. Call me if you need anything, son.'

'I'm trying to,' I said. I called the Westgate in San Diego. A recorded voice asked who I was trying to call, and when I told it, it rang Broun's room. He wasn't there.

I wondered where he really was. He could be meeting with the endocrinologist, or standing in line at LAX, or be someplace else altogether, and his kind, gruff voice would still say, 'I'm in San Diego at the Westgate.' The plane to San Diego could have crashed and it still wouldn't have made any difference. That voice would still have talked to me. I wondered if that was what was happening here, if the dreams were some kind of prerecorded message left by Lee, and he wasn't there at all.

I went and got the car. Take Lafayette Boulevard to Sunken Road. You can't miss it. The pharmacist had been right about that. There were signs everywhere: highway signs for US 3, small brown National Park Service signs every block or so on Lafayette Boulevard, a big brown sign at the entrance, a 'Closed After Dark' sign next to the iron gates, Fredericksburg Historic Tour marker Number 24, a white 'National Cemetery' sign. Sunken Road was marked with a regular green-and-white street sign. I pulled into Sunken Road and parked across from the Visitors' Center. It was after nine, which meant the Visitors' Center and, presumably, the library were open, but I didn't go in. I went up the hill to see the graves.

It wasn't as bad as I had thought it would be. The hill was terraced into grassy shelves just wide enough for a row of graves, and at the top the carved headstones sloped down and away in neat rows toward a flag anchored with pyramids of decorative solid shot, but the hill wasn't even half as high as the hill at Arlington, hardly high enough to be called a ridge.

The plain below, where all the bodies had lain, was covered with grass and trees and criss-crossed with brick paths. Azaleas and ivy had been planted around the Visitors' Center. It looked like somebody's backyard.

Well, that was the kind of war the Civil War had been, wasn't it? A backyard war, fought in cornfields and on front porches and across rutted country lanes, a homey little war that had killed two hundred and four thousand boys and men outright and four hundred thousand more with dysentery and amputated arms and bilious fever. But in spite of the neat rows of graves stretching away like points on a radius, it didn't look like anybody had ever been killed here. And it didn't look like Arlington.

At the top of the hill I took the brick path that led along its edge to a large sign that turned out to be a painting of Lee looking through binoculars out over the battlefield. Next to it was a brick pillar with a speaker in it. I pushed the button for the know-nothing tourist's guided tour.

'At this spot on Marye's Heights,' the deep, authoritative voice said, 'General Robert E. Lee stood, commanding the Battle of Fredericksburg.' It sounded like Richard on the answering machine. I let the voice ramble on while I looked at the graves on the edge.

They were marked with granite squares maybe six inches across. There were two numbers on each square. The one nearest me read 243, and then a line, and below that the number 4. I scribbled the numbers down on a piece of paper so I could ask what they meant.

'Good morning,' a brown-hatted ranger said. He came up beside me, carrying a plastic trash sack. 'Did you need in to the Visitors' Center? I was out checking the grounds, so I locked it up, but I can go open it. We've been having problems with kids getting in at night.' He pulled a beer can out of the sack to show me and then dropped it back in. 'The first tour's at eleven. Are you looking for a particular grave?'

'No,' I said. 'I just wanted to see the battlefield from up here.'

'It's hard to imagine there was ever a battle here, isn't it? The artillery were all along this ridge, and there were sharpshooters down behind that stone wall, where the road is. It's not the original wall, by the way. General Robert E. Lee commanded the battle from up here,' he said with the enthusiasm of someone who's never been in a war. 'He watched the Union army coming up from the river there,' he pointed across the trees and roofs of Fredericksburg toward the Rappahannock, 'and he said, "It is well that war is so terrible, or we should grow too fond of it."'

'What do the numbers on the unmarked graves mean?'

'Those are the graves' registration numbers. After the war there were bodies buried all over this area from the battles of Fredericksburg and Spotsylvania and the Wilderness. When the battlefield was made into a national cemetery, quartermaster teams were sent around to disinter the bodies and rebury them here. The numbers tell where the bodies were found.'

I took out the piece of paper I'd written the numbers on and unfolded it. 'Can you tell me about this one?' I said. 'Two hundred forty-three, and under that there's a line and the number four.'

'Two hundred forty-three is the registration number. The four is the number of bodies.'

'The number of bodies?'

'That were found in the original grave. Or parts of bodies. It was hard to tell, sometimes, how many soldiers there really were. Some of the bodies had been buried for three years.'

Like Willie Lincoln, I thought irrelevantly. Maybe he had been buried in a field somewhere, and then a quartermaster's team had dug him up and sent him home with his father's body to Springfield.

'At Chancellorsville they found a grave full of arms and legs. They figured it must have been near a field hospital where they were doing amputations. And lots of times they'd buried horses along with the bodies.'

'How did they arrive at these numbers, then?'

'Skulls. It was a grisly business,' he said cheerfully. 'If you'd like to come down to the Visitors' Center, I can look up that grave number for you.'

'No,' I said. 'I think I'll stay up here awhile.'

'It is beautiful up here, isn't it?' he said. He tipped his broad-brimmed hat to me and went back along the brick path and down the hill, stopping once to pick up a scrap of paper by one of the graves.

It was beautiful up here. The spreading town with its blue and gray roofs and blossoming trees hid where the plain had been, and below, where the infantry had been cut down by the rifles behind the stone wall, there was a line of ragtag souvenir shops selling postcards and Confederate flags. There was no sign of the dead horses that had littered the field, the wounded Union soldiers taking cover behind them because there was no other cover. 'It is well that war is so terrible,' Lee had said, watching it, 'or we should grow too fond of it.'

Too fond of it. Was that what the dreams were all about? Was Lee so fond of it he couldn't let go of it, even in dreams? No, of course not. He had said that in the morning, when the plain was full of flags and bugle calls and sunlight glinting off the barrels of Springfield rifles.

That night the wounded had lain there where the souvenir shops and the Visitors' Center were now, freezing to death, and Lee's barefoot, threadbare soldiers had gone down the hill and over the stone wall that would have been black with blood and icy to the touch. Of course they had to put up a new one. The Confederates had gone down the hill and over the wall and taken their uniforms, with the names pinned to the sleeves, their boots with the names stuffed in the toes. And nobody, not even Lee, could have been fond of war at that point.

I could not possibly let Annie come out here. She had been here already in her dreams, had seen the bodies lying there on the cold ground, had seen the aurora borealis do its bloody dance in the northern sky, but she hadn't seen the rows of granite markers, and she hadn't seen the Roll of Honor or heard the ranger read the entries cheerfully, enthusiastically, not even aware of the horror of what he was saying. A lot of times they'd buried horses along with the bodies.

Maybe I couldn't stop the dreams, but I could protect her from this. And that meant getting her out of Fredericksburg, where well-meant waitresses and pharmacists and taxi drivers drew maps on drugstore counters in their eagerness to get us out here. I went down the hill and into the Visitors' Center.

The ranger was behind the information desk, emptying a metal wastebasket into the trash can. 'I found that grave number for you,' he said, brushing his hands together. He opened a thick, leather-bound book to a page he had marked with a scrap of paper. 'They're listed alphabetically by quartermaster team.'

He turned the book toward me, and I read down the fine-printed page. 'Found Wilderness battlefield. Three bodies. Found Charis farm, in cornfield. Two skulls. Found Chancellorsville battlefield. Two bodies.'

'Here it is,' the ranger said, twisting his body around so he could read the numbers. 'Two forty-three.' He pointed to a line near the bottom of the page. 'Found Lacey's farm, in apple orchard. Four skulls and parts.'

Found in apple orchard. Four skulls and parts. 'It has something to do with the soldier with his name pinned to his sleeve,' Annie had said, trying to get at the meaning of the dreams. But it wasn't one yellow-haired boy with his name too blurred to read.

It was so many it took them years to dig up all the bodies buried in cornfields and under apple trees and put them here, so many they couldn't bury them separately, they had to bury them all together under one marker.

'Do you know of any good tourist attractions away from Fredericksburg?' I said. 'Someplace we could go today? Say within a hundred miles of here.'

He pulled a brochure out from under the desk. 'The Wilderness battlefield is only …'

'Not the Wilderness. Not anything to do with the Civil War.'

He reached under the counter again, looking bewildered, and came up with a road map of Virginia. 'Well, there's Williamsburg, of course. It's about a hundred miles.' He spread out the map on the counter. 'Shenandoah National Park is about a hundred and twenty.' He pointed. 'It's got a lot of beautiful views and hiking trails. I don't know what the weather's like to the west, though. There's supposed to be a big front coming in.'

I leaned over the map. There was no way out of Fredericksburg. To the south, Sayler's Creek blocked our way to Richmond; to the north we would have to cross the Antietam. Chancellorsville and the Wilderness were between us and Shenandoah on US 3. But if we went south, not so far that we would run into Spotsylvania, and kept to the back roads till we were west of Culpepper, where the battle of Cedar Mountain had been fought, we might be able to do it.

'Is there anything else I can do for you?' the ranger asked eagerly. 'There's a guided tour at eleven.'

'No, thanks.' I folded up the map. 'How many unknown soldiers were there altogether?'

'Here, you mean? There are twelve thousand seven hundred and seventy buried in Fredericksburg National Cemetery,' he said as if it were a point of pride. 'They're all Union soldiers, of course.'

'How many altogether? In the whole war?'

'The whole war? Oh, I have no idea. I'm not even sure there's any way …' He took a pencil out of his pocket and began writing on the battlefield brochure. 'All right. We have twelve thousand seven hundred seventy here, and there are eleven hundred and seventy Confederate unknowns in the Confederate Cemetery, and then Spotsylvania.' He wrote down a figure and then reached under the counter again and brought up a stack of brochures. 'The Unknowns of the Civil War Memorial at Arlington has two thousand one hundred and eleven …' He shuffled through the brochures, turned one over. 'There are four thousand, a hundred and ten at Petersburg. Gettysburg has nine hundred and seventy-nine unknowns in the cemetery proper, but of course there are more graves on the battlefield. Most of the Confederate dead were moved to Richmond and Savannah and Charleston after the war and buried in mass graves there.'

He riffled through the brochures again. 'It all depended on who won the battles, of course. For the loser, over eighty percent would be unknown at any one battle.' He started adding up the figures. 'I'd say between a hundred and two hundred and fifty thousand unknown dead altogether, but if you want a more accurate number ...'

'Never mind,' I said, and got in the car and went to get Annie.

CHAPTER ELEVEN

Traveller only let Lee down once. It was on the march into Maryland, right before Antietam. Lee had been sitting on a log, holding Traveller's reins loosely in his hands. It was raining, and Lee was wearing a poncho and rubber overalls. Someone shouted, 'Yankee cavalry!' and Traveller started. Lee stood up to grab his bridle and tripped over the poncho. He caught himself on his hands. One of his wrists was broken and the other was severely sprained. At Antietam his hands were still in splints.

Annie wasn't at the inn or the coffee shop. The redheaded waitress, still disapproving, said she had told her to tell me she was at the library, and I thanked her with such obvious relief that she was probably convinced we had had some kind of lovers' quarrel.

Annie was in the reference section, the *L* encyclopedias spread out around her in a half-circle, most of them open to a picture of Lincoln's careworn face, but she wasn't looking at them. She was staring at the orange-painted bookcases across from her and not seeing them, thinking hard about something. I hoped the something wasn't Gettysburg.

'Good morning,' I said, sounding like the inanely cheerful park ranger. 'I didn't think you'd be up this early.'

She made a reflexively protective gesture toward the book in front of her, and then shut it before I could see the page it was open to.

'I want to go out and see the vet,' I said. 'Maybe he's heard from his sister.'

'All right.' She closed the other books and stacked them on top of the book in front of her. 'Let me just put these away.'

'I'll help you,' I said, and grabbed for the bottom three books before she could pile the others on top of them. The top two were encyclopedias. The bottom one was the drug compendium I had used to find out about Thorazine. 'Wnat are you looking up here?' I asked. 'Are you all right? You're not having any side effects from the Thorazine, are you?'

'I'm fine,' she said, turning away to put the other encyclopedias back on the shelves. 'I wanted to know if the Thorazine was causing the headaches I've been having, but it isn't. Did you go out to the battlefield this morning?'

'Yes,' I said, trying to keep my voice as casual as hers. 'They've got a reference library out there. That's why this library's so skimpy on Civil War-iana. Ready? Maybe we can catch the vet before he makes his rounds.'

We drove out and saw the vet. He was in the stable again, feeding some horses he was boarding. 'I'm afraid I don't have any information for you,' he said, forking a bundle of hay into one of the stalls. 'I haven't been able to get in touch with my sister yet, but I'm going to a conference on horse diseases in Richmond tomorrow, and I should be able to run down and see her then.'

I had been counting on his having already talked to her, so that I could say to Annie, 'Well we've done what we came to do. There's no point in sticking around here.'

'When will you be back?' I asked.

He stopped and leaned on the pitchfork. 'It lasts through the weekend. I'll probably come back Monday. Will you still be here?'

'If I'm not, I'll call you on Monday.' Annie was looking at me. 'We'll still be at the inn. You've got the number, don't you?'

'Yeah. Sorry you had to come all this way out here for nothing.' He filled a washtub with a hose. 'I looked through some of my dad's stuff on Akhenaten. There was nothing about him having dreams. Dad did have this one book on dreams and what the Egyptians believed about them, though. It was pretty interesting. They believed that dreams were messages from the gods or from the dead.'

'Messages?' Annie said. 'What kind of messages?'

'All kinds. Advice, warnings, blessings. The gods could tell you who you were going to marry, whether you should take a trip, if you were getting sick and with what. If you were getting a fever you dreamed about one thing, if you were catching cold you dreamed about something else. They had it all written down in this dream book, what everything meant.'

The vet's wife came to the door to tell him he was wanted on the phone.

'I'll call you when you get back from your conference,' I said.

'Is the horse all right?' Annie said. 'She didn't get lockjaw, did she?'

'What horse? Oh, the mare that was out here the other day? She's fine. Bruised sole, just like I thought.'

'Good,' Annie said. 'I'm glad.'

I headed back toward town the way we had come until the first fork in the road and then took the left-hand turn. Annie didn't seem to notice. She had rolled her window halfway down and was leaning back, her head against the seat. The breeze from the moving car ruffled her hair. Her face had the serious, almost wistful expression it had had in the library.

This road wasn't as pretty as the one we'd taken down to the vet's. It was lined with the debris that towns always have on their outskirts: storage units, car junkyards, old trailers with porches and dog kennels tacked on and a horse tethered out back.

'It's beautiful out here, isn't it?' I said to be saying something, anything to get her mind off whatever battlefield she was thinking about. 'The waitress said a cold front was supposed to be coming in, but I don't see any signs of it.'

I turned again, to the south, and ran right into the interstate.

'Is this the way we came?' Annie said when the six-lane road loomed up ahead.

'I thought I'd take the scenic route back,' I said, ignoring the I-95 sign and cutting over to US 1. 'I saw the cat this morning. It was sitting in front of the coffee shop. I think it was waiting for you. Have you been feeding it?'

'I gave it one of those little cream containers this morning,' she said. 'And some bacon. It looked hungry,' she added defensively.

'All cats look hungry,' I said, looking for road signs. I didn't want to turn west until we were past Spotsylvania. 'You realize you're stuck with him for life. Or at least until something better comes along. He'd desert you in a minute for somebody with a sardine.'

'Desert,' she said, looking out the window. We were passing a field with a haystack in it. 'They shot deserters, didn't they? In the war.'

And there we were, right back in it, in a war she didn't even call the Civil War anymore because it was so familiar to her, because she fought its battles every night.

'Not always,' I said. 'A lot of deserters got clean away. To California. Speaking of California, Broun's gone down to San Diego, so he'll be in California a few more days, and the vet won't have any information for us till Monday. Why don't we drive over to Shenandoah this afternoon? See the Blue Ridge Mountains? There's supposed to be a great place for fried chicken in Luray, be a nice change from the coffee shop. There's really no reason to stick around Fredericksburg.'

We were going to run into the interstate again if we went much farther north. I turned left at the next road. It was State Highway 208. The road to Spotsylvania. I turned north onto a gravel road, then made three more turns, going north and west, trying to get as far from Fredericksburg as I could.

'What about *The Duty Bound*?' she asked.

'The galleys? Broun and I can finish them after he comes home from California.'

'I think we should finish them,' she said. 'I'd like to know how it ends.'

'Fine. We'll finish them when we get back.' The road we were on jogged north and ran into a four-lane highway. I hoped I hadn't managed to run into the interstate again. I hadn't. It was US 3, and the towns in both directions were clearly marked with arrows. The Wilderness was that way, Chancellors-ville the other. Take your pick.

'Maybe it is a good idea,' Annie said, looking at the signs. 'To get away.'

'Great,' I said. I crossed the highway and went west at the next turn. 'We'll get some fresh air and some southern fried chicken, a little exercise. There are all kinds of hiking trails.'

'And no battlefields,' she said softly.

'You know what else is in that neck of the woods? Monticello. Thomas Jefferson's plantation. We could spend the night in Luray and then drive down the Skyline Drive tomorrow and see Monticello.'

We could drive down to Monticello, and while we were there that big front would come in, and we would have to go south to avoid it, into North Carolina and then Georgia and finally Florida, where there hadn't been any war.

'Monticello's a great place,' I said, turning again onto what looked like a paved road. After the first mile, the asphalt gave way to gravel. 'Jefferson made this great clock out of cannonballs. And curtains,' I added hastily. 'Jefferson made his own curtains.' The gravel turned into dirt, and the road became so deeply rutted I was going to high-center the car if I didn't turn around. I put the car in reverse.

There was barely room to turn in the narrow lane. On one side of the road the weeds grew up knee-high next to a ditch, and on the other was a thin stand of pines that had been planted almost to the edge of the road. I stretched my arm out over the back of Annie's seat and started to back carefully so I wouldn't end up in the ditch.

'The dreams all have messages,' Annie said.

'What?' I said, angry that something in this rutted lane, this pine woods, had made her think of the dreams again. I could no more get her out of the Civil War than I could get her out of the grave-filled circuit of Fredericksburg. I shifted into first again and killed the engine.

'I was thinking about what Dr Barton said about the Egyptians. He said they believed that dreams were messages from the dead.'

'I thought we weren't going to talk about the dreams again,' I said. I tried to start the car again and flooded it.

'Did you know that Abraham Lincoln dreamed about Willie after he died?' she said. I turned the ignition again, but Annie reached out to stop me. 'Willie's face came to comfort him in dreams, the book said. I think he's dead, Jeff. I think the dreams are messages from the dead.'

I took my hand away from the keys. So it hadn't been the sunken lane, the west wood after all.

'I thought you were right, that Lee was having the dreams during the Civil War and they were coming across time somehow, but yesterday, when I saw that postcard of his tomb at Lexington, I knew he was dead.' She was looking at me earnestly, her hand still on my arm. 'Richard told me that dreams help you work through the things that happened to you, that they're kind of a healing mechanism to help you get over grief and come to terms with the guilt you couldn't deal with any other way, only if there's too much guilt the dreams can't handle it. That's what he said was happening with me, but what if you had so much guilt and grief that you went on dreaming after you were dead?'

How many dreams would it take to heal Lee of Fredericksburg? Twelve thousand seven hundred and seventy? Lee's dreams weren't a 'healing mechanism.' They were a burial detail, and how many dreams would it take to bury all those boys at Gettysburg who staggered back from Pickett's Charge to collapse at Lee's feet, how many dreams to bury all the boys in the bloody angles and sunken roads of Lee's mind? Two hundred and fifty-eight thousand? A hundred years' worth?

'You told me Lee was a good man,' Annie said, 'and he is, Jeff, but he had to send all those boys back into battle, and they didn't have any shoes and no ammunition. He knew they'd be killed, but he had to send them in anyway. He had to send his own son Rob back in. How could he stand it, all those boys killed and nobody even knowing what happened to them? I think they still haunt him, after all these years, even though he's dead.'

'And so he haunts you.'

'No. It isn't like that. I think he's trying to atone.'

'By inflicting his nightmares on you?'

'He's not inflicting them on me. It isn't like that. I'm helping him sleep somehow. Even though he's dead.'

'And in the meantime, what are the dreams doing to you?'

She didn't answer.

'I'll tell you what they're doing. The dreams are getting worse, and they're going to go on getting worse until we do something.' She started to protest. 'Look, maybe you're right. Lee's dreaming in his tomb, and you're letting him get some sleep by having the dreams, in which case it won't matter where we go, the dreams will go right along with us. Only maybe not. Maybe it's the battlefield that's aggravating the dreams, and if we get away from it, the dreams will let up. The point is, you're not getting any sleep, you're not eating anything, and what good are you going to be to Lee if you pitch headlong down a flight of stairs some night?'

I started the car. 'I think we should go to Shenandoah, get some rest, eat some fried chicken, get away from the dreams for a while, and if we can't get away from them, try to ignore them. You're not deserting. You're just getting away for a little while. On furlough.' I was lying. If I managed to get her out of here I would never let her come back.

'Clean away,' Annie said, and I wondered if she knew I was lying, if she wanted to get away, too.

'We won't talk about the dreams, we won't think about the dreams, we'll go hiking and eat fried chicken and look at the Blue Ridge Mountains. All right?'

She sighed, a long, surrendering sigh. 'All right,' she said.

I drove back onto gravel, onto pavement, and out onto the road we had come up on. A mile up it turned into a county road, and a few miles after that onto a two-lane highway with a long, straight stretch of road.

It could have been summer. Some of the trees were already in full leaf, and it was unbelievably warm. There weren't any clouds at all in the sky, not even above the line of blue in the west where we could already see the Blue Ridge Mountains. I speeded up, anxious to put as much distance as I could between us and Fredericksburg. It was past lunchtime, but we would eat later, when we were closer to Shenandoah.

'This is more like it,' I said, resting my arm on the open window. 'I thought for a while there we were never going to see a highway again.' I had told Annie we weren't going to talk about the dreams, but that was easier said than done. The dreams were all we'd thought about for days. I couldn't talk about the battlefield, or Lee, or Lincoln either, who had been afflicted with bad dreams, too. And I could hardly tell her carefree college-days stories about my old roomie Richard.

'This is pretty country, isn't it?' I said, sounding more than ever like the park ranger. 'Broun and I got lost on a back road like that one time when I first came to work for him. He wanted me to take some pictures of the country around Antietam, but he was convinced I'd get lost, so he came with me and got us both stuck in a mud puddle. We had to walk out and get a tow truck. He wouldn't even let me do that by myself. He was like that the whole first year I worked for him.'

'Not letting you do anything?' Annie said. 'Why not?'

'I don't know. He'd never had a research assistant before, and I guess he was used to doing everything himself. He was just starting *The Duty Bound*, and there was tons of research to do on Antietam, but he insisted on doing it all, especially the stuff at the battlefield. I thought when we got there he'd let me do at least some of the legwork for him, but he wouldn't. He traipsed around the battlefield, taking notes like crazy, snapping pictures, stretching out flat on his back so he could get what he called the "soldier's eye view—"'

I stopped and glanced anxiously at Annie, but she was watching the scenery, still smiling. Her blonde hair was blowing in the wind, and she brushed it out of her face.

'He cut his foot wading across Antietam Creek,' I went on. 'On an old tin lid. It bled like crazy. His foot, not the lid. He had to have a tetanus shot and twelve stitches, and he still wouldn't let me take over.'

Outside of Remington, the two-lane highway connected with the state highway to Culpepper. I cut south again.

'So here he is, hobbling around, trying to run things—'

'Like Longstreet,' Annie said.

'And he announces he's going to Springfield. His publishers called and they want him to check the epigraph he used on the last book, so he's going all the way to Springfield to see what's written on Lincoln's tomb or some damn thing, and I blew up. I said, "What in the hell did you hire me for? You won't let me do anything, not even go look at some damned dead bodies."'

Oh, Richard would have a heyday with this conversation. 'Those are obviously Freudian slips,' he would say in his Good Shrink voice. 'The subconscious is speaking, bringing up subjects the conscious mind wants to avoid.'

'So did he let you go to Springfield for him?' Annie asked, looking like she was unaware of the slips, Freudian or otherwise. She had taken my advice to heart. She was relaxing, getting away, even though I didn't seem able to.

'He let me go to Springfield, but he kept calling me on the car phone on the trip out, reminding me to look at this and remember to ask that. He left messages at my motel and made me call every night and dictate my notes onto that damned answering machine of his. He just about drove me crazy. And then I don't know what happened. Maybe he decided he hadn't hired an incompetent idiot or something. He quit pestering me and let me do the research he'd sent me to do and from then on he let me do what he'd hired me to, which was to help him.'

I didn't know till I got to the end of that instructive little story that that was what it was. My subconscious was calling for attention, all right, banging on the door to be let out. 'He still does a lot of his own research,' I said, as if to convince myself that I hadn't just been lecturing Annie on the subject of letting me take over, letting me help her. I have your best interests at heart.

'Maybe he had trouble giving up the research because he loved it,' Annie said.

'Maybe,' I said, thinking of how excited he had sounded about Lincoln's dreams. 'He loves Lincoln anyway.'

'And you.'

'Yeah.'

'I came to see Broun the night of the reception,' she said. 'I made Richard come. I knew Broun knew all about the Civil War. I thought he might be able to tell me what the dreams meant.'

'Only Richard wouldn't let you near him, and you got stuck with me.'

'Not stuck,' she said, and smiled at me the way she had that night in the solarium, that sweet, sad smile. 'It's you that got stuck with me.'

'We're stuck with each other,' I said lightly. 'And with Lee. But not today. Today we're on leave. Are you hungry?'

'A little.'

'We'll stop for lunch the next town we come to. We just came through

Remington. There's a map in the glove compartment. You can see if there's a town coming up—'

'Stop the car,' Annie said. She had her hands on the edge of the half-open window and was looking back at what we had just passed. 'Stop the car!'

She was out of the car before I had even pulled halfway onto the shoulder. She grabbed for the door handle and was out of the car and running toward the road.

'Annie!' I shouted, fumbling with the door. I leaped out after her.

She was standing on the edge of the shoulder, looking at nothing in particular, a rail fence and a plowed field, off in the distance a house with a wide porch. Her hands were balled into fists at her sides. 'What is this place?' she demanded. 'I know this place.'

Damn it. Damn it. I had thought we would be safe coming this way, away from Chancellorsville and the Spotsylvania Courthouse and the Wilderness. I had brought her this way on purpose because I thought it was safe.

'Did you dream it?' I said, dreading the answer.

'I don't know,' she said. 'I have the feeling that I've been here before. Where are we?'

'I don't know,' I said. 'We just went through Remington.' I opened the car door and reached in for the map. The engine was still running. I switched it off. It couldn't be Culpepper. I had seen a sign for Culpepper in Remington. We were still at least ten miles east of it. I grabbed the map out of the glove compartment, snapped it open, and scanned the map, unable to find Remington.

We were only a few miles past Remington. The next town ... The next town was Brandy Station, two miles away. We were north of Brandy Station. There wasn't a monument symbol next to it on the map, or a cross, though there should have been. The whole damned state was a graveyard. That plowed field was probably full of yellow-haired boys and grizzled veterans and horses.

'I feel like I've been here before,' she said, and walked across the road. She didn't look in either direction, and I was not sure that for her there was even a road there. A blue car whipped around the curve and between us. It missed Annie by inches, lifting her skirt in the wind it made when it zoomed by. She didn't jump or step away from it, startled. She didn't even know it had been there.

I ran across the road to her. 'It's Brandy Station,' I said. 'There was a cavalry battle near here. Lee's son Rooney was wounded. Lee saw him being carried off the field. I'm sorry.' I took hold of her arm. 'I shouldn't have brought you here. Let's go back to the car and get out of here.'

She didn't move. She didn't resist me, either. She simply stood there, stock-still, in the middle of the road. 'Did he die?' she said.

'Rooney? I don't know. I don't think so. It was a leg injury.' I tugged at her arm. 'We can find out when we get to Luray.'

She shook her head. 'I want to go back to Fredericksburg.'

'Why? They'll have a library in Luray. We can look up Rooney there. He didn't die. I know he didn't die. He was at his father's funeral.'

Annie was staring at the plowed field as if she could see it all, Rooney on a litter, his leg torn open, the bandage soaked through with blood. 'None of Lee's sons were killed in the war,' I said.

'I have to go back,' she said. 'I can't desert him like that.'

I could hear a car coming, the low roar rising in pitch as it started to round the curve. 'Desert him?' I said angrily, and practically pushed her back across the road and into the car. 'You're not one of his soldiers, Annie. You didn't sign up for this war.'

A jeep roared past, straddling the center line. I came around and got in. I started the car and roared off the shoulder and onto the road, whipping around the rest of the curve at the same speed as the jeep, wanting us out of sight of the plowed field, out of sight of Rooney on a stretcher. 'I had no business bringing you here!'

'It's not your fault,' Annie said.

'Then whose fault is it? I take you to Fredericksburg. Fredericksburg, for God's sake, where they've got so many bodies they've got to bury them in groups! I read you a book about Antietam out loud! And then, just to make sure you dream about Brandy Station tonight, I bring you out here so you can see the battle for yourself. And I wonder why the dreams are getting worse!'

There was a billboard up ahead. VISIT MANASSAS NATIONAL BATTLEFIELD PARK. I pushed my foot down hard on the accelerator. 'Why don't we drive up to Manassas? And then tomorrow we'll run down to Richmond so you can dream the Seven Days battle. I was trying to get you the hell out of there to someplace that wasn't a goddamned battlefield!'

The truck in front of me put on its brake lights. I jammed on the brakes. Annie's hands came up hard against the dashboard.

'I was trying to help.'

'I know,' Annie said. 'I know you were trying to help.'

I slowed the car down to a sane speed. 'I was taking the back roads because I didn't want to run into the Wilderness. Did I hurt your hand?' I asked anxiously.

'No,' she said. She rubbed her wrist.

'We'll go to a doctor. In Luray. We'll have him look at your hand and then we'll—'

'It's no use, Jeff,' Annie said. 'I can't leave him. I have to see the dreams through to the end.'

I pulled the car over to the edge of the road and stopped. 'The end? What end? What if Lee goes on dreaming for a hundred years? What if he decides to dream the whole damn Civil War?' I said bitterly. 'Are you going to dream it for him?'

'If I have to.'

'Why? They're not your dreams. They're Lee's. He's the one who ordered all those boys back into battle. Let him dream them himself. Let his daughter Annie dream them for him, if she wants to, it's her father. But not you.'

'I have to.'

'Why?'

'Because I can't bear it,' she said, and started to cry. 'Poor man, poor man, I have to help him. I can't stand to see him suffer so.'

I took her hand in mine and rubbed the wrist gently. 'And I can't stand to see what they're doing to you,' I said. I brought her hand up to my chest and held it there. ' "I would that I were wounded in your stead," ' I said. 'Lee said that when they told him Stonewall Jackson had been wounded at Chancellorsville.'

She looked up at me, the tears running down her face. Her tears, not Lee's, not Lee's daughter's. And it was me she was looking at this time.

'I would, you know,' I said. 'If there was any way I could, I'd have the dreams for you.'

I listened to what I'd said and looked at her dear, tear-streaked face. 'Which is what you're trying to do, isn't it? Have the dreams for Lee, so he won't suffer?'

'Yes,' she said.

'All right,' I said. I let go of her hand and turned the car around. 'We'll find a place in Fredericksburg that has fried chicken. And we'll hope to God you don't dream about Brandy Station.'

She didn't. She dreamed about a chicken. And Annie Lee's grave.

CHAPTER TWELVE

At the battle of the Wilderness, Lee yelled to the Texas brigade to form a line of battle and then spurred Traveller through an opening between the guns and up to the front of the line to lead the attack. 'Go back, General Lee!' the soldiers shouted. 'Go back!' A sergeant grabbed hold of Traveller's bridle, and General Gregg rode up to head him off. The soldiers stopped in their attack and shouted, 'We won't go on unless you go back,' but Lee seemed not to hear them.

*

We read galleys after we got back, me in the green chair with my feet on the bed, Annie propped up against the pillows with the copyedited manuscript on her knees. Broun had written himself off the battlefield finally, and into a makeshift hospital near Winchester, where Ben had been taken with his wounded foot and was being nursed by a sixteen-year-old girl named Nelly.

In these chapters Broun introduced a lot of new characters: an over-worked, alcoholic surgeon who had been a horse doctor before the war, a battle-ax nurse named Mrs Macklin, a fast-talking private named Caleb who was all of fifteen.

Theoretically, it was a bad idea to bring in so many new characters so late in the book, but Broun didn't have any choice. Like Lee, he'd killed off every-body else, and now it was time to bring in the old men and the boys. And the women.

'Where'd you get shot?' (Annie read) *the boy in the bed next to Ben said. 'I got it in the foot.'*

'Me, too,' Ben, said and turned his head carefully to look at him. He was afraid if he moved too quickly he would pass out. He had passed out in the wagon. The ambulance detail had propped him up in the back of it with his arms over the sides, and he had watched blood drip from under the wagon onto the dirt road. He had had the idea it was all his blood, and after he had bled more than any one person could possibly bleed, he had fainted.

He had come to when they tried to get him up the stairs, but one of them, a big, mean-looking woman, had hit his foot against the bannister, and he had passed out again.

'I ain't shot bad,' the boy said proudly. He had a friendly, sunburned face. 'I'm goin' back soon's they let me. My name's Caleb. What's yours?'

Ben had tried to answer him, but then it was dark and there was the sound of a horse whinnying. Ben's heart pounded. 'Malachi?' he said.

'Promise me you'll hold my hand,' somebody said pitifully, and Ben was afraid he was the one who had said it, but the voice went on, 'Nothing bad can happen so long's you are holdin' it,' and Ben knew that wasn't true so he decided he must not be the one talking. The horse whinnied again, and Ben recognized it as a scream this time.

'I promise,' a girl's voice said, gravely, kindly, and then it was morning and the girl was standing over him saying, 'I've brought you your medicine. Can you sit up and take it?'

She was beautiful. She had light, fine hair pulled back into a bun. When she bent over, to set the brown bottle on a chair, Ben could see the part in her hair. She was wearing an apron and a gray dress that looked like it had faded from blue.

'Course I kin sit up for you,' the boy named Caleb said. He was sitting up on top of the covers. 'For you I could git up out of this bed and go dancing, but

would you dance with me? No. You're breaking my heart, Miss Nelly, you know that, don't you?'

'I do not think you are quite ready for dancing yet,' Nelly said, pouring the laudanum into a tin spoon. Caleb's leg was bandaged with heavy white strips of linen, but Ben could see that there wasn't a foot there at all. He wondered if he himself had a foot.

Ben gulped the laudanum down.

'I am willing to dance with you this very day,' Caleb said, grabbing for Nelly's hand. 'We shall push the beds back against the wall, Miss Nelly, and you,' he waved his hand at Ben, 'shall play us a jig tune.'

'Nelly! Come away from there!' a woman's voice said. She came and stood at the foot of the bed where Ben could see her. It was the woman who had hit his foot bringing him up the stairs.

'Have one of the others do that!' she barked. 'We got another wagonload coming in, and here you are flirting with the menfolks.' She glared at Caleb. 'You woke every soul in the house with your screaming last night.'

He grinned at her. 'I dreamed Miss Nelly wouldn't marry me,' he said.

'You can't marry Nelly,' Ben tried to say. 'I love her.'

Nelly set the bottle of laudanum down on the chair and went out of Ben's range of vision. Caleb swung his legs over the side of the bed and leaned across to pick up the bottle. 'I dreamed Miss Nelly said she wouldn't marry me and old Mrs Macklin said she would.' He winked at Ben. 'It was a nightmare, that's what it was.'

I watched Annie read, her head bent over the manuscript so I could see the part in her hair. 'It's the war,' Broun had said when I had refused to believe that Ben could fall in love with Nelly after only one day in the hospital. 'A spoonful of laudanum, and Ben will do anything for her,' I had said, and Broun had answered, 'People did things like that in a war, fell in love, sacrificed themselves.'

Maybe it was the war. We had been through a lot together – Fredericksburg and Chancellorsville and Brandy Station. I had explained her dreams to her, held her hand while she slept, dried her tears. All that was bound to produce feelings of camaraderie, affection. But I knew it wasn't true. I had loved her since the moment I saw her standing there in the solarium in her gray coat.

I insisted on finding a restaurant that served fried chicken, as if that had been why we intended to go to Shenandoah. Annie brought home a drumstick wrapped in a napkin for the cat.

'You'll kill it with kindness,' I told her. 'You're not supposed to feed them chicken bones,' but the cat was nowhere to be found. It had come out to the car when we got back in the afternoon, meowing reproaches, but now it wasn't on the outside steps or over in front of the coffee shop.

'He'll be back,' I said. 'Cats always come back.'

'Tom Tita didn't. He was locked in. He couldn't get out.'

'The cat isn't locked in. He's probably found some other pushover to feed him, that's all. You notice Tom Tita didn't try very hard to get out. He was perfectly happy in the attic with all those mice, and when Markie Williams let him out he didn't go racing back to Lee. He didn't even miss Lee as long as the Union soldiers would feed him.'

'Lee missed him,' she said. 'Cats don't have any sense of loyalty, do they?'

'Their first loyalty is to themselves. What good would it have done Tom Tita to follow Lee through the Civil War? He would just have gotten himself killed. And the Union soldiers took good care of him, the way somebody's taking good care of this cat right now.'

'You're right,' she said. 'Somebody's taking care of him, and he's fine,' but she stripped the meat off the drumstick and left it in a little pile at the bottom of the steps before we went in.

She went to bed at eight, and I tried to call Broun at the Westgate in San Diego again. There was no answer. I called the answering machine.

'I'm still in San Diego, Jeff,' Broun said. 'I didn't get in to see the endocrinologist. He was called out of town. I'm going to a place called Dreamtime while I wait for him to get back. Probably a bunch of quacks, but you never know.' I waited, thinking there'd be a message from Richard, but there wasn't.

Annie tapped lightly on my door. 'I had a dream about a chicken,' she said.

'Are you sure this is one of Lee's dreams and not just something you ate?' I asked her, giddy with relief that I hadn't inflicted Brandy Station on her.

'I'm sure,' she said. She leaned against the door. She was wearing the blue robe over her nightgown, and her eyes were bluer than I had ever seen them. Her short hair was tangled from sleeping on it. She looked beautiful. 'The chicken was on the porch of my house. She acted like she belonged there. Did Lee have a chicken?'

'He had a horse,' I said. 'He had a cat. I refuse to believe he had a chicken. It sounds to me like this dream is one of your own, brought on by that southern fried chicken we had for dinner. I told you I was giving you bad dreams.'

She went back to bed. I put the chain on the door and moved the chair over next to it, balanced the book on the arm. I corrected galleys for a while, read Freeman for a while, napped for a while, but I couldn't sleep in spite of the fact that I had had maybe three hours sleep in the last two nights. It was a good thing.

Annie got out of bed, put on her robe, and tied the belt, all so calmly I thought she was awake. She pushed the chair out of the way. The book thumped onto the carpeted floor, making less noise than I thought it should. She reached for the chain.

'Where are you going, Annie?' I said quietly.

'My fault,' she said. She unfastened the chain.

'It's not your fault. Let's go back to bed.' I hooked the chain and led her carefully back to bed, my hand barely touching her arm. She didn't resist at all. She stopped next to the bed and took off her robe.

'What happened to them?' she asked.

The chicken? Tom Tita? Or all those yellow-haired boys?

'We'll find them,' I said. She got into bed and lay down. I covered her up. Fifteen minutes later we went through the whole thing again. After I had her back in bed, I wedged the chair under the doorknob and waited.

It took half an hour that time, and then she stood up again, put her robe on, tied the belt, and tried to move the chair. It wouldn't budge. She turned and looked at me. 'What happened to them?' she said angrily, as if I had hidden them from her.

'We'll find them,' I said, and started back to the bed, my hand lightly on her arm, but halfway there she stopped and took two steps toward the windows.

'My fault,' she said softly. 'My fault.'

We were at Gettysburg again, in the woods that were like an oven, watching the soldiers struggle back from Pickett's Charge.

'My fault,' she whispered, took a few faltering steps forward, and sank down on her knees, her face in her hands.

'What is it, Annie?' I said, squatting beside her. 'Is it Gettysburg? Is it Pickett's Charge?'

She took her hands away from her face and sat back on her heels, staring blindly at whatever it was.

'Can you wake up, Annie? Can you tell me what you're dreaming?'

She stretched her hand out toward something on the floor in front of her and then drew it back. 'She's dead, isn't she?'

She knelt there for over an hour, me squatting beside her until my legs cramped and I had to switch positions, talking to her, trying to wake her up, trying to get her back to bed. In the end I picked her up and carried her, placing her arms around my neck so she wouldn't fall back, unfastening them when I had her in bed.

'What happened to them?' she asked when I covered her up.

'I don't know,' I said, 'but I'll find out. I promise.'

Five minutes later she stood up again, put on her robe, and went over to the door.

'Annie, you've got to wake up,' I said tiredly.

She stopped pushing on the chair, straightened up, looked at the door, at me. 'Did I do it again? Did I go outside?'

'You were trying your darnedest to,' I said. 'Where were you? Gettysburg?'

'No,' she said, sitting down in the chair. 'I was at Arlington again. It had snowed, like in the first dream, and I was looking for the cat. He was out under the apple tree, and I went out to get him, and I stepped on something. It was a Union soldier. He was lying face-down, with his rifle underneath him, and his name pinned to his sleeve.'

She was clutching the tie belt of her robe the way she had clutched the African violet in Broun's solarium that first night. 'I bent down to unpin the paper, but when I did, it wasn't a blue uniform sleeve, it was white. And then I saw it wasn't a dead soldier, it was a girl in a white nightgown, asleep under the apple tree.'

She didn't ask me where it was or what the dream meant. She sat for a while in the chair, looking toward the middle of the room as if she could still see the apple tree and the girl asleep under it.

'I'm sorry I was sleepwalking again, Jeff,' she said. 'Maybe you should tie me to the bed.' She took off her robe and lay down, her arms stiffly at her sides, as if she were willing herself not to walk in her sleep.

She lay that way the rest of the night. I didn't know if she was asleep. She didn't move when I picked up Freeman from where it had fallen on the floor and went into my room to get the other three volumes, when I locked the connecting door to my room and pulled the desk across it, or when I moved the lamp over by the green chair so I could read by its light.

There weren't very many index references to Annie Lee, in spite of her having been Lee's favorite daughter. I looked up the last one first. 'I have always promised myself to go, and I think if I am to accomplish it, I have no time to lose,' he had written his son Rooney in 1870. 'I wish to witness Annie's quiet sleep.' She had died during the war at White Sulphur Springs, North Carolina. She was twenty-three years old.

'He was a good man,' Annie had said. His soldiers loved him, his children loved him, and he had had to sacrifice them all to the war, even his favorite daughter. Annie Lee had died of a fever, but she was as much a casualty of the Civil War as any soldier, dying young and far away from home. At least Lee had had the comfort of knowing where she was buried. He had gone to visit her grave in 1870. 'I wish to witness Annie's quiet sleep.'

Poor man. When he had gotten the letter of her death, he had not shown any outward emotion. He had read the letter and then gone on answering his official correspondence with his aide. But when the aide had come back into the tent a few minutes later, he found Lee weeping.

It was four o'clock, one in California. I called Broun at the Westgate in San Diego, at the L.A. number. I called directory assistance and got the number for Dreamtime. There was no answer anywhere.

Just before dawn, Annie got out of bed and put on her blue robe. I put out a restraining hand, afraid she was sleepwalking again. She went over to the window. 'Did you find out what the dream meant?' she asked.

I told her about Annie Lee. 'She died in 1862,' I said. 'Right before Fredericksburg.'

'Willie Lincoln died in 1862. He was Lincoln's favorite son,' she said, hugging her arms to herself. 'What did she die of?'

'I don't know. A fever of some kind.'

'Poor man,' she said, and I wondered which man she meant, or if she would know if I asked her.

We spent the morning trying to sleep, gave up, and went to see the last tourist attraction in town, Hugh Mercer's apothecary shop. We looked at silver-plated pills and brown glass laudanum bottles and handwritten prescriptions for curing fevers.

We spent the rest of the day in the library. Annie took notes on Lincoln. I read Lee's letters and tried to find out what Annie had died from. Nobody seemed to know. I found the chicken, though. Its name was Little Hen. She had walked uninvited into Lee's tent one day, and Lee had kept her for over a year. She laid an egg under Lee's camp cot every day and sat on Traveller's back, which delighted the soldiers.

We looked for the cat after dinner, but it was nowhere to be found. The neat pile of chicken scraps Annie had left for it was still on the step. 'It's probably holed up someplace warm,' I said. 'It's supposed to turn cold tomorrow.' We went back to the room, and I barricaded the doors, as if I thought I could somehow keep the dreams out.

I needn't have bothered. Annie didn't sleepwalk. She lay quietly, and watching her I thought the dreams must not be as bad, though when she told me about them, they were worse than ever.

Her house was on fire and a rider handed her a message which she tried to open with one hand. The message was wrapped around three cigars, and she couldn't open it because her hands were bandaged. She handed it to the red-headed waitress and she couldn't open it either, there was something wrong with her arm, and it wasn't the waitress, it was a girl in a white nightgown and the message wasn't wrapped around cigars, it was a letter, and Annie was afraid to read it.

She dreamed she stood on the porch of Arlington and argued with Richard, who was wearing slippers. The vet was in the dream, too. He handed Richard a message, and Richard tore it into little pieces and threw them on the ground.

'Who is the vet?' she asked me.

'I don't know,' I said. 'Pickett maybe? Longstreet?'

'No,' she said bitterly. 'Richard is always Longstreet.'

She dreamed about Gettysburg, the retreating soldiers sometimes coming back into the orchard from a burning house, sometimes carrying a chicken in their arms. She tried to reform them under the apple tree, but she couldn't because Annie Lee was asleep under the tree.

There were no tears or sleepwalking during the dreams, and afterwards she recited her horrors to me gravely and I explained them as best I could, but she scarcely heard me. She seemed to be conserving all her strength for the dreams, lying perfectly still under the green-and-white coverlet. Her cheeks no longer burned, and when I touched her hands or her forehead, they were cold.

In the early hours of the morning I called the answering machine. Richard said, 'Annie's records show low levels of serotonin, which is indicative of a suicidal depression. The symbolism of her dream corroborates that. The rifle represents the desire to inflict harm, the dead soldier is obviously herself.'

'I was right about the Dreamtime thing,' Broun said. 'They were a bunch of quacks. Imaginative quacks, though. They said the dreams were warnings sent by Willie Lincoln to his dad, and when I asked them how Willie Lincoln happened to be sending messages, and why, if they knew what was going to happen, the rest of the dead didn't warn us of impending disaster, they came back with this theory that the dead normally sleep peacefully, but that Willie's rest had been disturbed when Lincoln dug him up.

'I'm flying up to Sacramento Wednesday to a sleep clinic there. I'll be home sometime Tuesday. I've got an autograph party Saturday in L.A. and an appointment on Monday. I hope you're doing okay on the galleys, son. I'm going to be impossible to get in touch with for the next few days.'

'I know,' I said.

I didn't get any sleep to speak of. 'Did you manage to get some sleep, Jeff?' Annie asked at breakfast. She looked as if she hadn't. Her face was pale and there were dark, bruised-looking shadows around her eyes. She sat stiffly in the booth, as if her back hurt, and occasionally rubbed her hand along her arm.

'Some. How about you?'

'I'll be all right,' she said, and handed me the stack of manuscript. She let the waitress pour her some coffee while she tried to find the place we'd left off.

'You know that big front they were talking about?' the waitress said. 'It got stalled over the Midwest for a few days, but now it's moving again. We're supposed to get six inches of snow tonight. Can you believe that? In April.'

'Where are we?' Annie said after she left.

'Page six-fifty-six,' I said. 'Where it starts, " 'No,' Nelly said." Page six-fifty-six.' I separated the manuscript into two piles, one only fifty or so pages thick. We were almost done, and what would we do then while we waited for the dreams?

'No,' Nelly said, (Annie read) *and Ben tried to come awake to help her, but it was like trying to roll out from under the horse that had fallen on Malachi.*

'He's dead,' Mrs Macklin said. She sounded impatient, as if Nelly had done something stupid.

'I know he's dead,' Nelly said, and the need in her voice brought Ben completely awake. He pushed himself up in the bed. Pain roared out from his ankle, and he opened and closed his mouth in little gasps, trying to keep from screaming, pinned down by the pain.

He turned his head and looked at Nelly. She was sitting on a wooden chair next to Caleb's bed. She was holding Caleb's hand, gently, as she had every night since he had been brought in. His fingers clung to hers, and his eyes were closed, but he didn't look like he was asleep. He must have been dead the whole night.

'You can't do anything for him,' Mrs Macklin said, and took hold of Nelly's wrist.

'Let go of her,' Ben said, and then had to breathe in and out rapidly again so the pain wouldn't overtake him. 'Leave her be.'

Mrs Macklin ignored him. 'Twenty men downstairs half-dead and you sit here,' she said accusingly. 'Let go of his hand.' Still holding Nelly by the wrist, she yanked her to standing, and Caleb's arm came up smartly, as if he were saluting.

'No,' Nelly said desperately, 'please,' and Ben lunged for Mrs Macklin, but he didn't make it. His foot got shot off again, worse than the first time, and he thought they must have had to cut it off at the knee.

When he opened his eyes to see, Nelly was still sitting beside the bed, but the boy's body was gone, and somebody had laid a gray blanket over the ticking.

'I'm sorry,' Ben said.

Nelly rubbed her wrist. It looked red and puffy. 'Do you know what he said to me yesterday?' she said. 'He said that as long as I was holding on to him he had beautiful dreams.' She rubbed at her wrist, making it redder.

'You done the best you could,' Ben said. 'He ain't dreaming no more now anyways,' and he wanted to take her hand and hold tight, but he knew he'd be shot again before he reached the edge of the bed.

'I broke my promise,' she said.

'My friend Toby Banks that I told you about promised his mama he'd come home without a scratch on him. Some promises they just ... you done the best you could. After he was,' he stopped and cast around for some way to say 'dead,' 'after he was passed on to glory, he couldn't feel whether you was holding on nohow.'

'Promise me you won't reenlist when your foot gets better,' she said.

'I promise,' he said, but she went on sitting by the bed, rubbing her wrist.

After a while Mrs Macklin came in and asked to look at Nelly's wrist. 'No,' Nelly said.

'It's all swollen,' Mrs Macklin said angrily. 'I'm a nurse. It's my duty to tend to …'

Nelly stood up, knocking the wooden chair over. 'Don't you talk to me about duty,' she said, cradling her arm like a baby against her, 'not when you wouldn't let me do mine.'

Annie stopped reading. 'I want to go to Arlington,' she said.

We had been through all this before. 'There's no reason to go to Arlington. We know what the dreams mean. Lee blamed himself for Annie's death. Maybe he thought it wouldn't have happened if Annie had been at home, if they hadn't had to leave Arlington. We even know what the message is. It's the letter telling him Annie's dead. There isn't any reason to go back to Arlington.'

'I have to …' She didn't finish what she was going to say. 'The dreams are going in circles. It's like when I kept dreaming about the cat, and then when we went out to Arlington, it helped.'

Helped who? I wondered. You or Lee? She was helping him have the dreams, helping him sleep in that marble tomb of his at Lexington, and what was he doing to her?

'I think he is trying to atone,' Annie had said. Lee had loved his daughter. Surely he wouldn't do anything to hurt Annie. I wished I could believe that. I wished I could believe this atonement of his didn't mean dragging Annie through the Civil War till both their hearts were broken.

'Look,' I said, 'you heard what the waitress said. The weather's supposed to get bad, and anyway the vet's not back from his conference. I think we should wait till we hear from him. That way we can finish the galleys, too. We can take them up to New York and stop at Arlington on the way.'

The waitress brought our eggs. 'It's snowing in Charleston,' she said. 'I just heard it on the radio.'

'See?' I said, as if that settled it.

Annie cut her ham up but didn't eat it. She just kept cutting it into smaller and smaller pieces. 'It isn't supposed to snow till tonight,' she said. 'You could call the vet from Broun's, Jeff. We could take the galleys with us and finish them in D.C.' She put the knife down and rubbed her wrist.

'Annie, you're not in any shape to go to Arlington or anywhere else. You haven't had any sleep for two days, and your wrist is obviously hurting.'

She stopped rubbing it. 'I'll be all right.'

'You could have sprained it when you hit it on the dashboard. Maybe we should go have a doctor look at it.'

'No,' she said and put it in her lap as if to hide it from me. 'It isn't sprained.'

'But it hurts. And you're exhausted. We're both too tired to think straight. I think the best thing for both of us to do is take some aspirin and try to get some sleep, and then we'll talk about Arlington.'

'All right,' she said and looked, I thought, relieved.

We went back to the inn, and Annie did what I'd told her to, even though she protested that her wrist really didn't hurt, took some aspirin and went straight to bed. I called Broun's West Coast agent. He would know where Broun was if anybody did, and I had meant what I said about our being too tired to think straight. Broun wouldn't be dead on his feet. He would know what to do, how to help.

His agent's call referral service told me he was in New York. When I said I was trying to get in touch with Broun, she gave me a number to call. It was the number of Broun's answering machine.

Broun hadn't left any new messages. Richard had. I fast-forwarded over it to see if Broun had left a hotel name or a number and found a call from Broun's agent. 'You've got to get the galleys in now,' she said. 'McLaws and Herndon is screaming bloody murder. They're not the only ones who've called. Everybody's looking for you. I got a call from a Dr Stone, head of the ...' there was a pause and a rustle while she looked at the message, 'head of the Sleep Institute. He called to say that he had checked out the Gordon thing for you, and –'

'The Gordon thing?' I said. Gordon? I didn't remember any Gordon.

'– that there was no clinical verification for Dr Gordon's theory that dreams can prefigure illness. You're supposed to call him for the results.'

I called Broun's agent and told her the galleys were almost done. 'You don't know how I can get in touch with Broun, do you?' I said. 'There are a few errors I want to check out with him before I turn in the galleys.'

'All I've got is his West Coast agent's number,' she said. 'If you do get in touch with him, have him call me. I've got a lot of messages for him. What's he doing out there?'

'He's working on a new book about Lincoln's dreams.'

'Oh, good,' she said. 'I was afraid he was still messing with *The Duty Bound*. Oh, and Jeff, there was a call for you. A Dr Richard Madison. He said it was urgent that he get in touch with you. I thought you were in California with Broun, so that's what I told him. I'm sorry.'

'That's okay. I've been hiding out trying to get the galleys done. When did he call?'

'Oh, gee, it was two or three days ago. He didn't leave a number. Shall I try to find him in the phone book?'

'No!' I said and then laughed, hoping it sounded apologetic and not unstrung. 'I've got to get these damn galleys in before I talk to anybody. If he calls back, I'm still in California, okay?'

'Okay.' There was a pause. I was so used to talking to the answering machine I almost punched in the erase code. 'Jeff, all these psychiatrists are just helping Broun with his research, right?'

'Yeah. He's trying to find out what caused Lincoln's dreams.'

'Oh, good,' she said. 'He had so much trouble with *The Duty Bound* I thought maybe … I've been worried about him.'

'He's fine. I'll have the galleys in to McLaws and Herndon by Monday.'

I went in to check on Annie. She was already asleep, one hand cradling the other. I wondered if I had done the right thing, trying to get her to sleep, or if I was only letting her in for more nightmares. I knew how Lee felt sending his son Rob back in at Antietam. I had told her I would try to get some sleep, too, but I doubted if I'd be able to. I was too worried about her. I took my shoes off and settled down in the green chair with the acknowledgments sheets for *The Duty Bound*.

'I'm going to the battlefield, Jeff,' Annie said, bending over me. She had on her gray coat. 'Go ahead and sleep.'

'Are they open at night?' I said. I sat up, spilling the acknowledgments everywhere. I had fallen asleep and she had dreamed about Fredericksburg again. 'I don't think they're open at night.'

'It's three o'clock,' she said, and picked up her purse and the room key. 'Go back to sleep.'

It was almost dark in the room. She had turned on the lamp by her bed. Three o'clock. I couldn't let her go out to the battlefield in the middle of the night. I had to get up and get dressed and go with her.

'I'll go with you,' I said, and bent over to put on my shoes. 'Wait for me.'

'Go back to sleep,' she said, and shut the door behind her.

I stood up, still convinced that it was three o'clock in the morning and surprised to find myself dressed. I must have slept through the afternoon and on into the night while Annie dreamed about Fredericksburg or worse. Asleep on duty. They shot soldiers for that.

I grabbed my coat and racketed down the outside stairs to the little parking lot, but the car was still there. She wasn't in it. I stood looking around the parking lot for a long, stupid minute, trying to think where she had gone and waking up to the fact that it was not the middle of the night.

It was getting dark out, and some cars had their lights on. The weather the waitress had predicted had come in. It was windy, and the sky was a gray blanket of cloud. The waitress was right, I thought, and would have given anything if she'd been hovering by my shoulder waiting to pour me a cup of coffee to wake me up.

And where was Annie? What if she hadn't gone out to the battlefield at all? What if she'd caught a bus to Arlington? What if she'd taken off altogether, afraid I was going to try to stop the dreams, afraid I was going to put Thorazine in her food like Richard?

Richard. He had called Broun's agent. Who else had he called? Nobody knows where we are, I thought desperately. But what if Annie had told Richard her second dream after all, and he had recognized it as Antietam? And when we weren't in Antietam, he had gone on to the next battle? Which was Fredericksburg.

I raced back up the stairs, across the hall, and down to the desk. 'Did you see a man in here, about my height, dressed like a doctor?'

The clerk grinned. 'You looking for Mrs Davis?' he said, emphasizing the *Mrs*. 'She asked us to call her a taxi.'

A taxi? She wasn't in a car with Richard, drugged and helpless, on her way back to Washington. She had taken a taxi to Arlington because I wouldn't take her. 'Did she say where she was going?'

'She didn't say anything to me,' he said, still grinning. 'When she called for the taxi, though, I heard her say she wanted to go out to Fredericksburg battlefield.'

I took the stairs two at a time, grabbed my car keys, and raced back out to the car and across town. But before I'd gone two blocks I knew I was too late.

Lincoln pardoned the sentries who fell asleep on duty, saying it was hard for farm boys to break their country habits. He wouldn't pardon me. I had let Annie go out to the battlefield by herself, and it was starting to snow.

CHAPTER THIRTEEN

Lee never forgot his love for horses, even at the end. One of his chief concerns that last week, while Five Forks fell and Sheridan cut off all hope of escape to the north, was with the starving mules and horses. He had had to give their rations of parched corn to the men.

The morning of the surrender Colonel John Haskell rode up 'like the wind' with news that Fitz Lee had learned of a road over which the army might still be able to escape. He had only one arm, and he couldn't get his horse stopped until he was nearly a hundred yards past Lee. 'What is it?' Lee cried, running up to the winded horse. 'Oh, why did you do it? You have killed your beautiful horse!'

The blue taxi was sitting just outside the National Park gates. I tore up the terraced slopes to the cemetery. I didn't even look for her in the Visitors' Center or on the brick paths. There was only one place she was going to be.

She was standing on Marye's Heights where Lee must have stood, the skirt of her gray coat whipping around her in the wind. It was snowing, stray angled flakes like rifle fire. Annie was holding a brochure but not looking at it. And what was she looking at? The flash and shine of sun on metal, the whipping of flags, the breathless hush before the men on the naked plain were cut to ribbons, the flags toppling one by one and the horses going down? Or the graves, terraced row on row below her?

I came up the last step, panting. 'Are you all right?' I said, and had to take a breath every other word.

'Yes,' she said, and smiled at me, her face grave and kind.

'You should have woken me up,' I said. 'I would have brought you out here.'

'You needed to get some sleep. I've been worried about you. You stay up with me all night and don't get any sleep.'

She turned and looked down the long terraced slope at the graves.

'They didn't build this cemetery until after the war,' I said, still having trouble getting my breath. 'It isn't like they buried the soldiers here after the battle. This wasn't made into a national cemetery until 1865. A lot of the soldiers buried here probably didn't even die in the war.'

She looked down at the brick path we were standing on. There were grave markers set into the path. She bent and swept snow off the granite square. 'This is where the unknowns are buried, isn't it?'

'None of these graves are Confederate dead,' I said. 'They're not even from the battle of Fredericksburg. The Confederate soldiers are all buried in the city cemetery.'

She stood up and looked at the brochure. 'This says there are over twelve thousand unknown soldiers buried here,' she said, 'but there aren't really, you know. There aren't any.'

I took the brochure away from her and pretended to read it. The snow was melting on it in big spots that blurred the ink.

'You said nobody knows what happened to the chicken, but it isn't true,' she said. 'I know what happened to it. It got killed. One of the soldiers wrung its neck for dinner.'

'You don't know that. Maybe it ran away into the woods and became a wild chicken. Maybe some little girl found it and kept it for a pet.'

'The brochure says nobody knows what happened to the soldier that's buried under this marker, but that isn't true either. After the war, when he didn't come back, the people who were waiting for him knew. His mother or his sweetheart or his daughter. They knew he was dead because he didn't come back.'

'Some of the soldiers just never went home after the war. Some of them lit out for California and the gold mines, and they wrote letters home that got lost in the mails, and they weren't dead after all.'

The wind had stopped and the snow was falling slowly, covering the numbers on the marker at our feet, burying the boys with their yellow hair and their outflung arms, blurring the charred pieces of paper they had pinned to their sleeves.

'What happens to Ben in *The Duty Bound*?' Annie asked.

I had no idea how Broun had ended the book. He had killed off Malachi and Toby and Caleb. Maybe he had an epidemic of typhoid in the last chapter and killed everybody else. 'I don't know,' I said.

'Does he die?'

'Die? Ben? He's the hero. Of course he doesn't die. He marries Nelly and they go back to Hillsboro and have ten kids and live happily ever after. Broun loves happy endings.'

The marker was completely covered with snow. You couldn't even tell it was there in the path.

'I'm sorry I got you into all this, Jeff,' she said, still looking at the marker. 'I needed your help. I didn't even think how it would be for you.' She looked up at me. 'I had another dream.'

'When? This afternoon? Is that why you came out here by yourself?'

'Last night,' she said. 'I didn't tell you.'

'Because you didn't want to wake me up?'

'Because I didn't want to have the dream. Because I already knew what it meant.'

'You don't have to tell me your dream,' I said. 'Let me take you back to the inn. It's starting to snow. You'll catch pneumonia.'

'Did you know that when Willie Lincoln had pneumonia, Bud Taft held his hand the whole time?'

'Annie ...'

'Bud fell asleep once, and Lincoln picked him up and carried him off to another room. He shouldn't have done that. Willie might have called for him.'

'Bud was only a little boy,' I said.

'Right before he died, Willie clutched Bud's hand and said his name.' She was still watching the snow sift down onto the graves. 'What happened to Lee after the war?'

'He lived for years. He became president of Washington College. Miley came out and took his picture, and tourists came and pulled hairs out of Traveller's tail. Lee said he looked like a plucked chicken. He took little girls for rides on Traveller and let them hang daisy chains on him. They lived for years.'

'I think the war is almost over,' she said. 'I think that's what my dream means.'

'Did you know Traveller saved Lee's life up here?' I said, sounding like a frantic tour guide. 'A shell burst and Traveller reared up on his hind legs or they'd both have been killed. The shell went right under them.'

She didn't even hear me.

'I was asleep,' she said, looking at the snow falling on the graves. 'In the dream. I was sleeping out under the apple tree in the bed I had when I was a little girl, only in the dream it had a green-and-white coverlet. I was asleep and the pharmacist came and woke me up and told me it was time to go and I got up and got dressed. I put on a dress with a red sash I had for Easter the year I was ten, and a blue cape. I knew I had to look as nice as possible, and at the last minute, when I was all dressed and they were all waiting for me, I stopped and made my bed. I asked the pharmacist to help me. He was getting dressed, too. He was putting his cuff links in, but he stopped to help me, and all the time we worked on the bed he was crying. "It's time to go," he said. The whole time I was dreaming I had the feeling it was Easter Sunday.'

She stopped and turned to look at me, expectantly, waiting for me to help her. And I could no more help her than Ben could keep them from taking away Caleb's body.

And what had I expected? I had brought her here to this town that was all graveyard and told her about other graveyards – Arlington and Chancellors-ville and Gettysburg – and, as if that weren't enough, I had read her a whole book on the subject of Duty, hundreds and hundreds of pages of people who had just signed up they didn't know why, of people who had had to see it through even though they hadn't counted on getting kilt.

Where had I thought it would lead, this road 'past the second Manassas, to Chancellorsville,' except here? I should have known from the beginning that to get her away from Arlington, to help her past Fredericksburg and Jackson's death, past even Gettysburg, was bound to lead to this, that all the roads Traveller carried Lee over had to converge here in an apple orchard near Appomattox Court House. She had dreamed about an apple orchard in the very first dream, an apple orchard and a house with a porch. I should have known then.

Lee had lost a third of his men at Sayler's Creek. The day after, April seventh, Grant wrote offering surrender terms. Sheridan was moving west and north to block Lee's retreat at Appomattox Station, and Meade had the rear guard under attack. The infantry wasn't strong enough to fight its way through. Its only chance was to try to escape to the west, into the moun-tains, slipping around the Union flank, and for the next two days they tried that.

At dawn on April ninth, Palm Sunday, they attempted to break out near Appomattox Station, but the attack failed. Lee met with his officers in an apple orchard outside Appomattox Court House and told them he had arranged to meet with General Grant. The surrender terms were signed in the house of Wilmer McLean, a man who had originally lived near Manassas Junction. After the second battle of Bull Run, he had moved to the little village of Appomattox Court House, 'where the sound of battle would never reach them.' The house was a two-story brick farmhouse. It had a covered wooden porch that ran the length of the building.

'We can't stay out here in this snow,' I said. 'It's getting dark. Why don't we go have some supper? Our waitress won't know what to do with herself if we're not there to have our coffee cups refilled.'

Annie's uncovered hair was getting wet. It curled up around her face.

'Please,' she said, and held her hand out to me, and she was as far away from me as Ben had been from Nelly, distanced not so much by the dead man between them as by his own pain.

Maybe Annie was right, and the dream meant the war was almost over. Maybe the dreams were almost over, too, and we could both go home together, paroled. At Appomattox Lee had gotten Grant to let the men keep their horses.

'It's not Easter,' I said, looking down across the graves, past the souvenir shops and the roofs and trees to the line of river, wondering if Lee had been thinking of Traveller when he asked Grant not to confiscate the horses. 'It's Palm Sunday.'

Lee had gotten up and dressed in his best, his dress uniform and a red sash and his blue military cape because, as he said, he was likely to be taken prisoner. 'There is nothing left for me to do but go and see General Grant,' he told his officers, 'and I would rather die a thousand deaths.' Lee asked advice of Longstreet and the other officers, and then mounted Traveller and rode to the McLean house. Along the way he saw Sam McGowan, his staff officer, struggling out of his muddy clothes and into a dress uniform, weeping like a child.

Annie and I went back down the hill, she holding my hand, the terraced steps already slippery, the graves hardly visible in the coming dark. The taxi was still there, its motor running and its windshield wipers going, the driver waiting patient as a horse.

I sent him home and took Annie to the coffee shop and told her about the last days before the surrender. Our waitress poured us cups of coffee that steamed the windows up so we couldn't see out into the snowy darkness.

'They say it's supposed to warm up tomorrow and turn into rain, but I don't believe it,' she told us. 'I hope you aren't going anywhere.'

'No,' I said, and wished it were true. 'We aren't going anywhere.'

I took Annie up to the room and put her to bed. 'I'll be right here,' I said, as if she were going away, and held her hand till she fell asleep. Then I finished the acknowledgments and went and stood by the window and waited.

She lay perfectly still under the coverlet, one hand resting on her chest, the other at her side, her cheeks pale as marble. After a long time, she sat up in the bed, the green-and-white sprigged muslin over her hunched knees like a crinoline, and put her hands over her face.

'What is it?' I asked. 'What did you dream?'

She looked up at me and tried to speak, her eyes full of tears.

'Did you dream about Appomattox?' I asked.

She nodded, looking straight ahead, the tears welling up, and she didn't have to tell me what she had dreamed. I knew.

They met in the parlor of the McLean house in the early afternoon. Grant told Lee that they'd met before in Mexico and that he would have known him anywhere. He apologized to Lee for being in a field uniform and muddy boots. He and Lee discussed the terms of surrender, Grant doing his best to 'let 'em up easy,' as Lincoln had ordered him to.

Lee told Grant that in the Confederate army the cavalry and artillery units owned their own horses, and asked that they be allowed to keep them since most of the men were small farmers and would need them for the spring planting. Arrangements were made to feed Lee's army from Union supplies. The terms of surrender were drawn up and signed.

When it was all over, Lee came out of the house and stood by Traveller while the orderly buckled the bridle. Lee slipped Traveller's forelock over the browband and smoothed it, absently patting the gray's forehead. Then he mounted the horse that had carried him from 'Fredericksburg, the last day at Chancellorsville, to Pennsylvania, at Gettysburg, and back to the Rappahannock' and rode back to the apple orchard to tell his men. 'Men, we have fought through the war together,' he told them, 'and I have done the best I could for you.'

The men, boys most of them, barefoot and hungry and dead on their feet, his men crowded around him, yelling out, 'We'll go on fightin' for you, General!' and 'I love you just as well as ever!' and 'Goodbye!,' but most of them couldn't speak at all and they reached out to touch Traveller's mane and side and flanks. Lee looked straight ahead, his face set, tears in his eyes, but Traveller tossed his head all down the line, as if the cheers were for him.

'It's all right,' I said. 'You won't dream anymore. The war's over.'

She held out her arms to me, and I took her and held her and never let her go.

CHAPTER FOURTEEN

Lee seemed to understand the need for surrender before any of his generals did. By the time they made it to the apple orchard, half of his army had been destroyed. Nothing was left of the infantry but a few brigades and Longstreet's and Gordon's corps, and none of them had had anything to eat in days. Yet, when he showed Grant's first letter of surrender terms to General Longstreet, Longstreet snapped, 'Not yet,' and when he asked Venable what kind of answer he should send, Venable said stiffly, 'I would not answer such a letter.' 'Ah, but it must be answered,' Lee said.

The last night before the surrender he slept, all alone, under an apple tree, holding on to Traveller's bridle.

We went on reading galleys in the coffee shop the next day as if nothing had happened and we would do this every morning for the rest of our lives. During the night the snow had turned to a cold rain.

'We should be able to finish them off this afternoon,' I said, 'and then tomorrow we can run them up to New York and hand them to the publishers. What's the weather like?' I asked our waitress.

'It's raining hard north of here. Some truckers in here were talking about flooding.'

Annie yawned. She looked beautiful, rested, her cheeks as pink as that first night when she had come to me for help. I took hold of her hand.

'Why don't you go back to bed?' I said. 'You've got a lot of catching up on sleep to do. I'll call McLaws and Herndon.' The waitress frowned. 'And the highway patrol.'

We went back up to the room. I called the answering machine to make sure Broun hadn't decided to come home. Broun had left a message. 'Pay dirt,' he said, sounding excited. 'I knew I was on the right track. The sleep clinic has some TB patients they've been studying because the fever makes them have more REM sleep. All of them dream about being buried alive. They say they can feel the cold wet dirt being shoveled in on them. The doctors say it's the night sweats, but I talked to them and some of them started having these dreams before they had any other symptoms.

'Not only that, but as the disease progresses the dreams get clearer and less symbolic and they dream their own symptoms, fevers and coughing and blood, and sometimes they dream about dying, being at their own funeral, being in the coffin. That's why Lincoln dreamed the coffin dream that last week. His acromegaly was getting worse.

'But here's the best part. One of the patients is this kid who was reading *Treasure Island*. I asked him about it and he said Robert Louis Stevenson was his hero because he had TB as a kid, too. He said Stevenson had dreamed about being buried alive, too. Robert Louis Stevenson dreamed the same dream over a hundred years ago!'

He didn't say where he was. He had an autograph party in L.A. on Saturday and an appointment with a neurologist on Monday. He would be home sometime Tuesday if he finished with the prodromic-dreams thing.

Broun's agent had left another message. 'I told McLaws and Herndon the galleys would be in Monday at the latest. If you can't reach Broun, they'll have to go in as is.'

Before she had even stopped talking, Richard said, 'You have to call me immediately.'

'The hell I do,' I said, and hung up. I took the galleys and went back into Annie's room. Annie was asleep, on top of the covers, her legs pulled up against her body. She was cradling her left arm in her right, as if it hurt. I took the folded-up blanket at the foot of the bed and put it over her.

There were only a few pages of *The Duty Bound* left to go. Mrs Macklin had broken Nelly's wrist trying to get her away from her dead private. The alcoholic surgeon had had to take time off from sawing at arms to set hers and put it in a sling. Mrs Macklin wanted her to go home. *'You can't do any good here,' she said.*

'You told me that once before,' Nelly said. 'You have your duty. I have mine,' and kept working as long as they had a hospital, which wasn't long. The armies swarmed around and past Winchester, and the hospital had to be moved and then dismantled and the soldiers too hurt to walk taken off in wagons. When Ben's unit marched past on its way to Fredericksburg, Ben went with them.

'No,' Nelly said when he told her he was going.

Annie sat up in the bed and screamed. I jerked as if I'd been shot. I dropped the galleys and stood up. My foot was asleep and I half-fell onto the bed. She screamed again and put up her hands to ward me off. I grabbed her wrists. 'Wake up, Annie. You're having a bad dream. Wake up!'

I could feel her heartbeat through her wrists, fast and light. 'No!' she said, and her voice was full of desperation. She tried to pull away from my grip.

'Annie, wake up! It's just a dream.'

'I'm so cold,' she said, and I thought for a minute she was awake. 'It got so cold. In the church.' She was shivering and her breath was coming in gasps, as if she had been running. 'The meeting took so long.'

What meeting? Not the meeting with Longstreet at Gettysburg. That was in a school, not a church. Dunker Church? Surely she wasn't going to dream Antietam, not now, when the dreams were supposed to be over.

'They couldn't decide … I finally said … so cold!' Her teeth were chattering. I let go of her wrists and wrapped the blanket around her shoulders. I pulled the sides of the coverlet up and over her legs.

'What were they meeting about?'

She tried to say something through her chattering teeth, closed her eyes, and turned on her side. She gasped and shifted, as if her arm hurt. She put her hand up to cradle her elbow and murmured something I could not make out. Then she turned again, still holding her arm, and said clearly, 'Tell Hill to come up.'

And now I knew what church she'd dreamed about. I shut my eyes.

She slept for another hour. I sat with her awhile and then went into the other room, hobbling on my still half-asleep foot, stripped the bed, and piled the blankets over her.

The phone rang. It was the vet's wife with a message. Dr Barton had called home from the horse-disease conference. He had two things he wanted to tell me. One was that he had gotten to talking about me with some of the other veterinarians at the convention, and one of them mentioned that he had just read an article about acromegaly in one of the science magazines. He thought I might be interested. She didn't know which magazine, she was just relaying the message.

The second thing was that he had finally gotten in touch with his sister. She didn't remember Dr Barton – she meant Dr Barton's father – ever saying anything about dreaming about coffins or boats, and she thought he would have mentioned it. He was very interested in dreams because of his study of the Egyptians. He had had a recurring dream for months before he died that he was convinced was warning him of his death. He had dreamed he was lying dead out under the apple tree in his backyard.

'What did he die of?' I asked. 'The acromegaly?'

'No,' the vet's wife said. 'He died of a heart attack.'

'What symptoms did he have? Before the heart attack?'

'Gosh, I don't know. He was living with Hank's sister, and we didn't see much of him. He complained of his arm hurting a lot, I know, because Hank's sister thought it was arthritis, but afterwards the doctor told her it was probably angina, and I remember he rubbed his wrist all the time.'

I thanked her for giving me the message and hung up the phone. Then I went and stood by the window, looking out at the Rappahannock. My precious Annie.

When Annie woke up, I said, as casually as I could, 'The weather's supposed to get worse tonight. Maybe we should go on up this afternoon.'

'I thought you said tomorrow,' she said.

'I did, but I don't want to get caught in a blizzard the way I did on my way back from West Virginia.'

She stood up, still cradling the arm. 'What about the galleys?'

'We can stop somewhere for lunch along the way and finish them off. There are only a few pages left.'

She was looking at the tangled heap of blankets. 'What happened?' she said. 'Did I have another dream?' She turned to me, her face innocent and trusting, as if this dream were like all the others and I would say it was Antietam or The Further Adventures of Little Hen. There was nothing in her face to show she had realized there was something terribly wrong, that with the surrender the dreams were supposed to be over. Over.

'I don't know,' I said. I pushed the blankets aside and laid her open suitcase on the bed. 'You muttered something about being cold a couple of times. It was cold in here. I put some more blankets on you and I wrapped you up in the bedspread.'

'I'm still a little cold,' she said, and shivered. She began taking things out of the closet and putting them in the suitcase, and I noticed that now that she was awake she was using both hands, but she moved a little stiffly, as if her back hurt.

'I'll go check us out downstairs,' I said.

'Wait a minute. What about Dr Barton? Weren't you going to wait till he got back?'

'He called,' I said. 'His sister said their father never mentioned any dreams.' I shut the door and went down the stairs, thinking how easy that had been, as easy as emptying a capsule into her food. For her own good.

I went across the street to the phone booth in the coffee shop and called the hospital. 'I have a friend who's sick,' I said, and then stopped. I would never get her to a hospital. They would want to know the name of her doctor, they would have a thousand forms and while I was filling them out she would call a taxi and disappear.

I called the Sleep Institute and asked for Dr Stone. 'I'm sorry,' the receptionist said. 'Dr Stone's in California. Can I take a message?' I called Broun's hotel in L.A. He had checked out. I asked the clerk whether Broun had mentioned where he was going, and he repeated, 'Mr Broun has checked out.'

He had checked out, and I didn't know where his autograph party was being held today or who the neurologist was he was going to see on Monday, and he wouldn't be home till Tuesday, which was three days from now.

Annie insisted on having lunch at the coffee shop so she could say goodbye to the redheaded waitress, but she was not there. Her little girl was sick, the manager told us. 'Tell her goodbye for me,' Annie said and went on reading galleys as if we were not now cut off from everyone, the rear guard destroyed at Sayler's Creek, Sheridan already at Appomattox Station, and Meade in the rear and coming up fast, Grant already writing the terms of surrender.

'No,' Nelly said when he told her, and he could hear the desperation in her voice, but this time he was the cause of it and there was nothing he could do. 'The army won't take you. You can't even march.'

'I'm walking pretty good,' Ben said. 'Mebbe they won't take me now, but there's a time when they will and be glad of me.'

'Why are you doing this?'

'I gotta. I don't know why. It's the same as when I signed up. I just gotta.'

'I will never know what happened to you,' she said.

'I been thinkin' on that,' he said. He pulled a piece of folded paper out of his shirt pocket. 'Friend of mine told me to put my name and my kin in my shoe, *but that didn't do no good. The boot was shot clean off and the paper with it. I want you should keep this.'*

'What good will that do?'

Ben thought of her sitting by Caleb's bed, holding his dead hand. 'After the war's over, you show them this paper and you point at one of them bodies and say, 'That's him,' and they'll put my name on a grave and write my kin, so's they'll know what happened to me.'

'All right,' she said.

After he was gone she opened up the paper and read it. 'Toby Banks,' it said. 'Big Sewell Mountain, Virginia.'

Annie stopped.

'I did have a dream,' she said. 'I remember it now. I think I was in our church, the Presbyterian church on Main Street back home, and they were taking up the collection, only it wasn't a church service. It was a meeting of some kind.'

A vestry meeting. At Grace Church.

'I don't remember very much of it. It wasn't like the other dreams.' Some of the panic came back in her face as she tried to remember. 'It was cold. I remember thinking I should have worn my other coat and wishing they'd stop arguing so I could go home.'

They had been arguing over a raise of fifty-five dollars for the minister. The meeting had gone on for three hours, and finally Lee had said, 'I will give that sum,' just so it could be over. Lee had only worn his military cape, and he walked home through the chilly rain.

The family was waiting for him at the tea table. He sat down heavily on the sofa, cradling his left arm, and his wife said, half-joking, 'Where have you been? You've kept us waiting a long time,' and asked him to say grace. He stood up and looked as though he were trying to say something, and then collapsed onto the sofa.

'What is it?' Annie said.

'It's probably Dunker Church at Antietam. Let's go.'

'I didn't say goodbye to the cat.' She insisted on going around to the outside steps. It wasn't there, and the scraps of chicken were half-buried in the snow. 'What if something happened to it, Jeff?' Annie said, rubbing her wrist.

'Nothing happened to it. It's holed up someplace nice and warm, in an attic full of mice maybe. There's no sense waiting around for it to come back. Come on. Let's go.'

She slept the whole way up as if she had been drugged. She didn't even wake up when I stopped at a filling station just outside Woodbridge. It was raining there, a chilly, autumn-feeling rain that might turn to snow any minute.

I went inside and called the answering machine again. 'Pay dirt,' Broun said. 'I knew I was on the right track.' I hadn't erased the messages. I listened to the whole message repeat itself, trying to pick up some clue to where Broun was.

Broun's agent said, 'I told McLaws and Herndon the galleys would be in by Monday at the latest. If you can't reach Broun, they'll have to go in as is.'

'You have to call me immediately,' Richard said. I had hung up on him before, but now I listened to the message hoping that Broun had called again to tell me where he was, afraid to fast-forward for fear I'd go right over it and miss it. 'I just got the test results back from the lab. There's a problem with the EKG. I don't know for sure what it is. Have you noticed any chest pains? Any pains in the wrist or the back or down the arm? If it's unstable we could be looking at a myocardial infarction anytime. You've got to come back immediately.' There were no more messages. The machine ran on to the end and then switched off by itself.

Broun's West Coast agent's number was busy. I bought a cup of coffee to go and went back out to the car. Annie was still asleep, curled up in the passenger seat with her left arm cradled against her body. Her short hair was brushed back off her flushed cheeks. I took the lid off the Styrofoam cup, put the cup between my knees, and started the car. Annie shifted slightly and brought her other arm up to support her left arm. 'Strike the tent,' she said.

I turned off the car. After a while I opened the door and poured the coffee out onto the ground and went back inside and called Richard.

CHAPTER FIFTEEN

After the surrender, Lee was offered the job of president of a little college in Lexington. He rode up on Traveller to arrange for a home for his family. 'He starts tomorrow,' his wife wrote, 'on horseback because he prefers it that way and besides, does not like to part even for a time from his beloved steed, the companion of many a hard-fought battle.'

In Lexington he rode Traveller every day, stopping to give rides to little girls and to talk to the students. Lucy Long, the mare that had been stolen, was found and bought back, and one of Lee's daughters would accompany him on the mare when he exercised Traveller. As time went on Traveller's hard trot fatigued him more and more, and when he went on a speaking tour, he took the train. 'Tell him I miss him dreadfully and have repented of our separation but once,' Lee wrote his wife, 'and that is the whole time since we parted.'

*

I took Annie to Broun's. 'We can take the galleys over to Federal Express later,' I said. 'This stuff's going to turn into snow if we go any farther north. I'm not driving up to New York tonight. I need to check for messages and look at the mail.'

I had told Richard to park several streets over so Annie wouldn't see the car, but the front door wasn't locked and Broun's Siamese was crouched on the bottom step. My first thought was that it had somehow gotten locked in when we left for Fredericksburg, but then I saw that the mail was neatly stacked on the hall table and that there was a jacket hanging over the bannister. Annie was standing in the door of the solarium with her gray coat and her gloves still on, and her left arm still cradled in her right, looking at the African violets. They had been watered – there was muddy water standing in puddles on the table.

'Is that you, Jeff?' Broun said, and came clattering down the stairs. He was wearing a black overcoat that looked like he'd slept in it. 'Thank God!' he said, and hugged me. His beard hadn't grown at all in the week we'd been gone, and the rough stubble scratched my ear. 'Are you all right? I called every motel in Fredericksburg, but nobody had you registered.' He pushed me out to arm's length and peered at me with his sharp little eyes. 'You got Richard's message then?'

'What message?' I said. I pulled away from him, and shrugged out of my coat. 'I'm fine, now that the damn galleys are finished. What a mess! Transposed chapters, missing chapters, the works. I finally called Annie here and talked her into coming down to help me finish them. You remember my boss, don't you, Annie?' I said. I draped my coat over the newel post. 'The man who is responsible for all our misery these last few days? Broun, you remember Annie?'

'Yes, of course,' Broun said, and shook hands with her.

'Hello,' she said gravely. I couldn't read her face at all.

'It's freezing out here in the hall,' I said. 'Didn't you turn the heat up? Let's go in the solarium.' I took Annie's arm and led her into the room. 'Good, it's warmer in here. Annie, let me take that wet coat.'

Broun came and stood in the doorway. 'Why didn't you tell me you were sick, Jeff?' he said. 'I thought there was something wrong that night you got in from Springfield. Why didn't you tell me you were having chest pains? I would have canceled my trip. Have you been to see a doctor?'

'The records from the family doctor show a problem with the EKG,' Richard had said. 'Have you noticed any chest pains?' Broun had thought the message was about me, had flown home to help me, but it was too late. I looked at Annie. She had taken her gloves off and had backed up until she was against the table that held the African violets. She stood there twisting her gloves and watching me, waiting to hear what I would say.

'I'm not the one who's sick,' I said. 'Annie is. I brought her home to put her in the hospital.' I took hold of her hands. 'I called Richard,' I said. 'He'll be here any time.'

She stood very still for a moment, as though she were going to speak, and then lurched forward, the way Lee had when Traveller bolted, the gloves still in her hands.

'You're suffering from angina,' I said. 'That's what's making your wrist hurt. Lee had angina all through the war, pains in his shoulder, along his arm, in his back. He died of a heart attack. The dreams are a warning. Like Lincoln's dreams. You've got to see a doctor.'

'And so you called Richard.'

'Yes.'

She sat down on the couch. 'You promised,' she said.

'That was before I knew the dreams were killing you. I'm doing this for your own good.'

'Like Richard,' she said, twisting the gloves in her lap.

I knelt beside her. 'Annie, listen to me, the dream you had this morning, it wasn't about Antietam. I lied to you. The meeting you dreamed was at Grace Church in Lexington. Lee went to that meeting and sat there all afternoon in the cold and then walked home in the rain and had a heart attack! I'm not going to let that happen to you!'

'I have to do this.' She twisted the gloves. 'I have to see it through. Please try to understand,' she said, gravely, kindly. 'I can't leave him. I promised to have his dreams. Poor man … I have to try and help him. I can't leave him. He's dying.'

'He's not dying, Annie!' I shouted. 'He's dead. He's been dead over a hundred years. You're holding on to the hand of a corpse. You can't do anything for him! Don't you see that?'

'I promised.'

'And I made some promises, too, but I'm damned if I'm going to let you die for the sake of a goddamned answering machine! That's what it is, some kind of biological prerecorded message that switches on when you're going to have a heart attack and leaves a message for you to call the doctor.'

'No, they're not,' Annie said. 'They're Lee's dreams.'

'Lee's dreams,' Broun said. He took hold of the door jamb and leaned against it as if he couldn't stand.

'They're prodromic dreams, Annie! They're caused by the angina!'

Broun took a step toward Annie. 'Are you having Robert E. Lee's dreams?' he said in a labored, uncertain voice, as if he could not get his breath.

'No,' I said.

'Yes,' Annie said.

Broun groped blindly behind him for a chair and sat down heavily. 'Lee's dreams,' he said.

'Annie, don't you understand?' I said. 'You're in danger. I have to get you to a hospital.'

'I can't. I promised.'

'What did you promise? To march up to the Bloody Angle and get yourself killed? You're not one of Lee's soldiers! His soldiers *had* to stay with him. They'd have been shot for deserting.'

'That isn't why they stayed,' Annie said.

It was true, barefoot and bleeding, they still hadn't deserted him, not even at the end. We'll go on fightin' for you, Marse Robert.

'Lee's soldiers knew when they signed up they could get killed. You didn't. You didn't sign up at all.'

'I did sign up,' Annie said. 'That day we went to Shenandoah. I realized then that I couldn't leave him, that I had to stay and help him have the dreams.'

'That day we went to Shenandoah you didn't know you had angina!'

'Yes, I did.' She put the gloves down on her lap. 'I figured it out that morning in the library. My wrist hurt, and I thought maybe it was a side effect of the drugs I'd been taking, so I looked it up. It said Elavil was contraindicated for patients with heart conditions.'

'Elavil?' I said stupidly.

'A year ago when I went to my doctor for the insomnia, he told me I had a minor heart condition.'

'Why didn't you tell me? I could have taken you to a doctor.'

'I couldn't go to a doctor.' She looked at me. 'The dreams are a symptom. If you cure the disease, the symptoms go away. And I can't leave him.'

'Why didn't you tell me?' I said again.

She didn't say anything. She sat with her hands in her lap.

'Because I would have tried to stop the dreams,' I said for her. Like I was doing now.

The doorbell rang. Broun put his hands on the arms of the chair and made a motion to get up, then sat down again watching Annie. She stood up. Her gloves fell to the floor, unnoticed. 'You promised,' she said.

'I'm doing this for your own good,' I said, and opened the door to Richard.

He didn't have a coat on. His sweater and jeans were wet clear through. His hair was wet, too, and he looked tired and worried, the way he had the night of the reception when he was still my old roommate, still my friend.

'Where is she?' he said, and swept past me into the solarium.

Annie had backed into the table holding the African violets and was standing there, her hands at her sides. She had knocked one of the violets over, and muddy water dripped off the edge of the table onto the floor.

'Thank God you're all right!' he said, and took hold of her wrist. 'I've called the hospital, and they'll have a room ready when we get there. Are you feeling any pain?'

'Yes,' she said, and looked across the room at me. Broun stood up.

'Where? In your arm?'

'No,' she said, still looking at me. 'Not in my arm.'

'Well, where then? Back, jaw, where? This is important!' he said angrily, but he didn't wait for her answer. He turned to look at Broun, and as he did he pulled Annie with him, her arm coming up smartly, like a corpse's.

'Call an ambulance,' he said.

'No,' Annie said, to Broun, not to me. 'Please.'

I had thought I could do it. She had already lived through that other surrender. I had not thought this one would be so bad. But that surrender had been different. Lincoln had told Grant to 'let 'em up easy,' and Grant had. He hadn't taken Lee prisoner at Appomattox. He hadn't even demanded Lee's sword. He had arranged for rations to be distributed to the men and for the officers to keep their horses, and then he had let Lee go.

I looked at Broun standing there in his black overcoat, his arms hanging at his sides as if he were overcome with fatigue or sorrow, and then back at Richard. I could have surrendered to Lincoln, I thought. I could have surrendered to Grant. But not to Longstreet. Not to Longstreet.

'Let go of her,' I said. Richard turned and looked at me. 'There's no need for an ambulance. We've already been to see a doctor. In Fredericksburg. Dr Barton.'

'What did he say? Why didn't he have her admitted to a hospital?'

'He did. He took her in and did an EKG on her and ran blood tests. He asked her if she'd been taking any drugs, and she told him Elavil.' I waited to see what effect that had on him.

'You didn't say anything about this on the phone.'

'Doctor Barton wanted to know why somebody had prescribed Elavil for a heart condition.'

Annie and Broun stood perfectly still, watching him. The room was so quiet I could hear the water from the African violet dripping onto the floor.

'A mild sedative was indicated for the patient's insomnia,' he said in his Good Shrink voice. 'The record from Annie's family doctor indicated nothing more than a functional heart murmur, and her EKG confirmed that. There were no symptoms of heart disease, and Elavil is only contraindicated in cases of maximum and long-term dosage. I prescribed a mild dose, monitored the patient carefully, and removed her from the drug immediately when it failed to have any effect on her symptoms.'

'Her symptoms,' I said. 'You mean the dreams?'

'Yes,' he said. He still didn't let go of Annie's wrist.

'I asked Dr Barton about the dreams,' I said. 'He said he didn't know what was causing them until he saw her blood tests this morning. They showed traces of Thorazine. He said the Thorazine was probably causing the dreams. He asked Annie who'd prescribed Thorazine for her, and she said nobody. She said she didn't know what he was talking about, that she'd never taken any Thorazine.'

'Thorazine was indicated,' he said. 'It's routinely prescribed in cases of sleep disorders.'

'Dr Barton said that Thorazine is prescribed for institutionalized mental patients, not for people with bad dreams.'

'That's what this is all about, isn't it? You still believe she's having Robert E. Lee's dreams.'

'Dr Barton said it was a crime for a doctor to give a patient a drug without this knowledge. He said a doctor could lose his license for that. Is that true, Richard? Could you lose your license?'

'You bastard,' my old roommate said, and let go of Annie's wrist. 'I was only trying to help you, Annie. I had a duty as a doctor.'

'Don't you talk to me about duty,' Annie said, cradling her arm like a baby against her, 'not when you wouldn't let me do mine.'

Broun made a sound. His face under the beard was deathly pale. He looked sick, like a writer who had just heard the words he wrote spoken in earnest.

'Call the ambulance,' Richard said to Broun.

'No,' Broun said. 'She's having Robert E. Lee's dreams.'

'You've convinced him, too, haven't you?' he said to me. 'You're all crazy, you know that?'

'Like Lincoln?' Broun said.

'Call an ambulance,' Richard said, and Broun turned and stumbled up the stairs.

'I told Annie I was going to prescribe Thorazine for her and informed her of its side effects,' the Good Shrink said. 'She took the first dose herself. Thorazine will sometimes temporarily impair the patient's short-term memory.'

'After the Civil War, Longstreet wrote long, involved explanations of how he hadn't let Lee down at Pickett's Charge,' I said, 'how it was all Lee's fault. But it didn't work. There were too many eyewitnesses.'

'Is this supposed to be something Robert E. Lee dreamed?'

'No,' I said. 'It's supposed to be a warning. I have two Thorazine capsules and all those messages you left on the answering machine on tape. You leave her alone or I'll send them to your boss, Dr Stone, at the Sleep Institute. I'll tell him you gave a patient Thorazine without her knowledge. I'll tell him you gave Elavil to a patient with a heart condition.'

Broun came down the stairs, carrying the answering machine. He had wrenched it out of the wall. The shredded ends of the wire dragged on the floor beside him.

'If you still want to call an ambulance, you'll have to use the phone next door, Richard,' I said, 'only I doubt if our neighbor will let you in. Not after she had you arrested once.'

'You bastard,' he said again. 'I'm not going to let you get away with this. I called you, did you know that? To tell you I had a patient who was having terrible dreams and I didn't know what to do. I called you and you weren't home.'

'Did you call me for help or were you trying to establish an alibi?' I said, but he had already slammed the door shut behind him.

I pulled my coat on. 'He may try to follow us,' I said. 'He's parked at least a block away. If we go right now, we can lose him.' I grabbed up Annie's gloves and thrust them at her.

'Do you have any money?' I said to Broun. He fumbled in his pockets and came up with a twenty and some change. 'Is that all?' I said, shouting at him as if I were trying to wake him up.

He reached into the inside pocket of the jacket that was still hanging over the bannister with his right hand, still holding the answering machine in the other, and pulled out a wad of bills. He handed it to me and then sat down heavily on the loveseat.

'Thank you,' I said. I snatched up Annie's suitcase and hustled her out the door. Broun didn't answer me. I could see him through the solarium window when I started the car, still sitting there cradling the answering machine against him, like a man asleep.

The rain was trying to turn into snow. I took side streets as far as Ohio Drive and then turned onto the Memorial Parkway. After we'd crossed the bridge, I looked behind me and then went on past the Washington Memorial Parkway exit.

'I'm not going to take you to the airport,' I said. 'Richard may not be that far behind us,' I went on hastily so she wouldn't think this was another trap and that I was taking her to a hospital. 'I'm going to take you to the Arlington Metro stop. You can take the Metro to the airport, if you want, or to the train station or the bus, and Richard won't have any idea where you've gone.' And neither will I, I thought.

Annie nodded without looking at me, her gloved hands clasped tightly in her lap. I pulled the car over next to the white stones that marked the entrance to the Metro station and stopped.

'I had a dream about you. On the way up today,' she said, still looking straight ahead. 'I was in my room at home, in bed, propped up against the pillows, and you came in and said, "I'll drive you to Fredericksburg," and I wanted to go with you, but I couldn't. I couldn't even answer you. I just shook my head.' She turned to me, her eyes filled with tears. 'It was the first time I ever dreamed about you. I've dreamed about Richard and Broun, but never you, Jeff. Who do you suppose you were? I was so glad to see you.'

'I don't know,' I said, though I had guessed almost from the beginning what part I played. 'Lee's doctor maybe? I would drive you to Fredericksburg, you know. Or anywhere at all.'

Would I? Knowing where the dreams were leading her, would I be able to take her there? Or would I call Richard again? I got out of the car and took her suitcase out of the trunk and put it on the top of the steps. I opened the door for her. She folded a piece of paper, put it in her pocket, and then got out.

I gave her Broun's money and all the cash I had. 'There's about five hundred here. That should get you home or wherever you want to go.'

'Thank you,' she said.

'This is the Blue Line. You can take it straight to the airport. If you want Amtrak, change to the Red Line at Metro Center and that'll take you to Union Station.'

She bent her head to fumble in her purse and put the money away. 'I won't know what happened to you,' I said. 'Promise me you'll go see a doctor.'

'After the war,' she said. She took the folded piece of paper out of her pocket and handed it to me.

I nodded. 'After the war.'

She reached up and brushed the hair off my forehead. 'I was so glad to see you,' she said. She picked her suitcase up in her left hand, put it down on the wet sidewalk and picked it up in her right, and went down the stairs.

I went out to the edge of the platform and stood there long enough for her to get away, holding the folded paper and looking up the hill toward Arlington House. It started to snow. I put the piece of paper in my coat pocket and went back home.

I didn't look at it until the next day for fear she had written the address of that house with the wide porch and the apple orchard, and that I, like Richard, would try to follow her.

It was still wet. I unfolded it carefully, so it wouldn't tear, and read it. She had written in blue proofreader's pencil, 'Tom Tita, Arlington House.'

CHAPTER SIXTEEN

Lee only lasted two weeks after the rainy afternoon in Grace Church. For most of that time he lay in silence or dozed. Outside it rained, and the rivers around Lexington rose till it was impossible for Rob to make it to his bedside. For several nights the aurora borealis lit up the sky, as it had at Fredericksburg. Lee talked very little, though he sometimes muttered in his dreams, but when the doctor told him, 'You must make haste to get well; Traveller has been standing so long in the stable that he needs exercise,' he only shook his head, unable to speak.

He died on the twelfth of October, saying, 'Strike the tent,' and then moving off to some old battle, leaving Traveller behind. Traveller walked in the funeral procession, his head bent, his saddle and bridle covered with black crepe. Then he was taken home to his stable to wait out the end. Did he dream of Lee? I wonder. Do horses dream?

When I got home, Broun was still sitting on the loveseat in the solarium. The Siamese had jumped up on his lap, and he had set the answering machine down on the loveseat beside him so he could pet the cat.

He stood up as soon as I came in, dumping the cat on the floor to come and put his arm around my shoulders. He didn't ask me what had happened, and because he didn't, because he didn't say, 'How could you let her go like that? She's sick. She needs a doctor,' I told him I had taken her to the Metro station, and then I told him everything else.

He didn't say, 'They're only dreams,' or tell me any of the theories he had picked up in California. He only said quietly, 'It was a terrible war, the Civil War. So many young people … I had no business going to California. Out on a wild goose chase after Lincoln's dreams when I should have been here.'

'It's not your fault,' I said, and went up to bed even though it was still early afternoon, and slept for two days. When I woke up, an electrician was there, fixing the wires on the answering machine, putting it back in the wall.

'In case she calls,' Broun said.

I took the galleys up to New York. When I got back, we started the Lincoln's dreams novel. I did Broun's legwork for him, drove him places, looked up obscure facts that didn't matter to anyone, and dreamed of Annie.

While we were in Fredericksburg, I had not had any dreams at all, as if Annie were dreaming enough for both of us, but now I dreamed nearly every night, and in the dreams Annie was fine. I dreamed that she had left a message on the answering machine. 'I'm fine,' she said. 'I didn't want you to worry.'

'Where are you?' I asked, even though I knew it was only a message, that she wasn't really there. I had never been able to break myself of the habit of replying to people who were not there, and if I could not, how did I think Annie could, Lee whispering to her night after night, telling her his dreams?

'I'm fine, Jeff,' she told me in the dream. 'They're taking good care of me.' It was not a message. It was really her on the phone, and she was fine, fine. She had gone home to that house with the wide porch and the apple tree and when she got there she had gone to see the doctor. 'I thought you were afraid they'd stop the dreams,' I said into the phone.

'I was, but then I thought about what you said about Tom Tita. What good would it have done for me to follow Lee through the Civil War? I would just have gotten myself killed. My first loyalty was to myself.'

'That was what you meant in the message,' I said, clutching the receiver. 'That was what you meant when you wrote Tom Tita's name.'

'Of course,' she said. 'What did you think the message meant?'

'That you were locked in. That you couldn't get out.'

'I'm fine,' she said. 'They're taking good care of me.'

We worked on the book all summer. In the fall, *The Duty Bound* came out, and we went to New York to promote the book. 'I'm glad to see Broun looking so well,' his agent told me at the McLaws and Herndon reception. 'I was afraid all that running around in California would be too much for him, but he looks wonderful. I also can't tell you how relieved I am to see that book in print,' she said, jabbing her finger at a stand-up display card of *The Duty Bound*. 'Did you know he called me after the galleys were in and wanted to change the ending? He wanted to have Ben and Nelly get married. Can you believe that?'

'When did he do that?' I asked.

'Oh, I don't know. After you brought the galleys up. Luckily, he called me first and not McLaws and Herndon. I managed to convince him it wouldn't work at all.'

'No, I suppose not.'

'Well, I mean, it was obvious from the very beginning she was in love with that boy who died, what was his name?'

We were in New York till after Christmas, doing autograph signings and talk shows. On the day we got home, while I was next door getting the Siamese cat back from Broun's neighbor, Broun had a heart attack. It was very small. There was hardly any damage. He was only in the hospital a week, and he seemed more upset about the fact that a battle-ax of a nurse had shaved his beard off than he did about the heart attack.

'Didn't you have any symptoms?' I demanded of him. He was lying in the hospital bed, propped up against the pillows.

'A little indigestion,' he said. 'Or what I thought was indigestion.'

'Didn't your arm hurt? Or your wrist?'

'No,' he said. 'I thought I'd eaten too much.'

'Didn't you dream anything?'

'I was awake when I had it, son,' he said gently.

'Before the attack,' I yelled. 'What did you dream about?'

Broun's doctor pulled me out into the hall. 'I know you're under a lot of stress, but so is he.' He looked at Broun's chart. 'And so am I. I don't want him having a third heart attack on me.'

'A third?' I said.

'Of course,' he said, still frowning at the chart. He looked up and saw the expression on my face. 'Why, the old son of a gun! He never told you, did he? It was three years ago,' he pulled back several pages on the chart, 'in September. September twenty-eighth. You were out of town, I think. He said he called you.'

Three years ago in September I had been in Springfield, looking at Lincoln's tomb and being driven crazy by Broun, and halfway through the trip the calls had stopped, the messages had stopped, and when I got home, he was willing to let me do his legwork for him.

'How bad was the first one?' I asked.

'Bad enough to scare him. He was convinced he was going to die. That's why I believed he'd told you.' He let the pages fall back and tucked the chart under his arm. 'Now, I'll agree he needs yelling at for not telling you, but as his doctor I'm not going to let you back in to see him unless you promise not to mention this heart attack thing to him until he's in better shape than he is right now. He must have had his reasons for not telling you about the heart attack.'

'Yeah,' I said.

I went back into the room and apologized for yelling at him. 'I didn't have any dreams before my heart attack,' Broun said. 'I didn't have any warning at all.'

'Annie did,' I said. 'The dreams were trying to warn her. Only she wouldn't listen.'

He leaned back against the pillows. 'If I'd dreamed I was in a boat before my heart attack, traveling toward a shadowy, indefinite shore, I wouldn't have listened either. If Lincoln was letting me dream his dreams for him, there is nothing on this earth I would let stop me. Not even somebody I loved.'

'Even if you ended up having a heart attack? Even if it killed you?'

'Even then,' he said softly. 'Maybe she's all right. Maybe she went to see a doctor when she got home, like she promised.'

Broun started back to work on the Lincoln book as soon as he was out of the hospital, in direct defiance of doctor's orders. 'I'm going to finish this damn book if it kills me,' he said, scratching at his unshaven chin. He was trying to grow another beard.

'Which it will at this rate,' I said. 'At least let me do the legwork for you.'

'Fine,' he said, and sent me to the White House to take notes on the purple-hung Guest Room where Willie Lincoln died and the stairs Lincoln had descended in his dream and the East Room, where Willie's coffin and then his father's had lain.

I was having a new dream now. In it, I dreamed I woke and heard the sound of crying, but when I went downstairs I couldn't see anyone. There was a guard standing at the door of the solarium, and I asked him, 'Who is dead in the White House?' but when he turned around to answer me, it wasn't the guard at all, it was Annie. She was wearing her gray coat, and she looked beautiful, fresh and rested.

'Are you all right?' I asked her. 'Did you go see a doctor?'

'A doctor?'

'A doctor,' I said urgently. 'The dreams were a warning.'

'I know. They were trying to warn us about Broun's heart attack, but we didn't understand them. We were looking at all the wrong clues.'

'Broun isn't going to have another heart attack, is he?'

She shook her head. 'The dreams have stopped.'

'And you're all right?'

She smiled at me, a sweet smile with no sadness in it. 'I'm fine.'

In April, Broun was hospitalized again with chest pains. 'I've been think-ing about what caused Annie's dreams,' he said, lying against the pillows. He was refusing to let the nurses near him for fear they might shave his beard, and he looked terrible, grubby and disreputable. 'Do you remember Dreamtime?'

'The quacks in San Diego?'

'Yes,' he said. 'Remember they had that theory that the dead sleep peace-fully until something disturbs them, like Willie Lincoln being dug up, and then they start dreaming. Well, what if something like that happened with Lee? What if they moved his body and that's what started him dreaming?'

'Lee's body hasn't been moved,' I said. 'It's still buried in the chapel at Lexington.'

'Maybe the dreams weren't because of the angina. Maybe they started because his body was disturbed some way. Was his daughter Annie's body moved?'

'No. She's still buried in North Carolina where she died.'

He lay silently for a while, glaring at the door whenever a nurse passed, and then said, 'They moved Lincoln's body. First they moved it to Springfield on the funeral train, stopping at every damned one-horse town and whistle stop along the way.' He pushed himself up against the pillows, and the line on the EKG screen behind his head spiked suddenly. 'And then there was that kidnap plot and the guard moved him out of the tomb and buried him in a passage of the Memorial Hall.'

'Annie didn't have Lincoln's dreams,' I said calmly, reasonably, watching the screen. 'They were Lee's dreams.'

'In 1901, they moved Lincoln back into the tomb again. He was moved four times altogether, not counting the funeral train.' The screen jerked in sharp, dangerous lines. 'What if those Dreamtime quacks were right, and all that jostling woke him up?'

'They weren't Lincoln's dreams,' I said. 'They were Lee's.'

'Maybe,' he said, sitting up with a motion that sent the EKG lines to the top of the screen. 'I want you to bring me some books.'

He asked for books the next three days, and by the end of the week he had half his library in his hospital room. 'I've got it all worked out,' he said. He was able to sit up by then without setting off the EKG. 'They were Lincoln's dreams.'

He had it all worked out. Lincoln had been the one who had dreams, not Lee, and their dreams wouldn't have been all that different. They would both have dreamed about Gettysburg and Appomattox. Lincoln had known about Special Order 191 before Lee did, and the cat didn't have to be Tom Tita, did it? It could have been one of Lincoln's kittens. Lincoln loved kittens. He had it all worked out.

'What if they were Lincoln's dreams?' I said when I couldn't take it anymore. 'What would that prove?'

'Lincoln tried to save Willie's pony from the burning stable. That's what the house on fire really is, not Chancellorsville.'

'They weren't Lincoln's dreams, damn it,' I shouted. 'They were Lee's.'

'I know,' he said quietly, and the EKG line above his head went right off the screen. 'I know they're not Lincoln's dreams.'

'Then why did you do all this?'

'Because then she'd be all right. If they were warnings from Lincoln, they wouldn't have been about apple orchards, they'd have been about boats. I thought if I could make them Lincoln's dreams, then that would mean she was all right.'

'He's in no shape to be upset,' Broun's doctor said. He had yanked me out into the hall again and down to an empty room. The EKG had set off an alarm at the nurses' station that brought everybody running.

'I know,' I said.

'You look as bad as he does,' he said. 'How are you sleeping?'

'I'm not,' I said. If I slept I dreamed about Annie. She was standing on the porch of Arlington with her arms around my neck, crying, and I kept saying over and over, 'I don't want you to leave.'

'Would you like me to prescribe something for you? To help you sleep?'

'What did you have in mind? Thorazine?'

He didn't get the joke. He pulled out a prescription pad. 'Who's your regular doctor?'

'I don't have one. Do you want my family doctor? He's in Connecticut.'

'I don't like to prescribe without seeing a patient's records.' He wrote busily on the prescription pad. 'I'll give you something mild for now and then wait till I have your records to put you on anything stronger. You don't have any health problems I should know about, do you? Diabetes, heart condition?'

'No.' I told him my doctor's name. 'How long will it take to get the records?'

'Depends. If they're computerized, we'll have them in a few days. If not, it could take several weeks. Why? Are you having that much trouble sleeping?'

'No,' I said and pocketed the prescription without looking at it. But Annie had been having trouble sleeping. She had been having so much trouble sleeping that Richard had put her on Elavil right away. He hadn't done an EKG. He had told me in that phone message that the EKG was just back from the lab, but EKGs didn't have to go to the lab. Broun's doctors read his as they came off the machine. He had said Annie's records showed a functional heart murmur, but how could they when it took two weeks to a month to get the records? Annie had told me he put her on Elavil right away. Richard hadn't done an EKG, and he hadn't waited for the records from her family doctor. The Elavil had made the dreams worse, but Richard hadn't taken her off the Elavil then. He had taken her off of it when her records came, when he saw she had a minor heart condition and he had had no business putting her on Elavil in the first place.

He had panicked and called me, only I wasn't there. I was in West Virginia. What if I had been there? Would he have told me the truth, that he had been so frantic with worry that he had made a terrible mistake, that when he had seen the dreams and what they did to Annie, all he could think about was stopping them and how the hell could he wait for the family doctor's records when they might take a month to get there? Or would he have used his Good Shrink voice on me even then?

Why had he put her on the Thorazine? To try to stop the dreams? Thorazine could have stopped a train, and it wasn't contraindicated. (*Note:* Sudden death apparently due to cardiac arrest, has been reported, but there is not sufficient evidence to establish a relationship between such deaths and the administration of the drug.) Or did he give it to her to keep her from going back to the Institute, from telling Dr Stone he'd given her a medicine that was explicitly contraindicated for heart patients? Why didn't Longstreet send his troops up at Pickett's Charge?

Lee never gave any indication after the war that he considered Longstreet's actions at Gettysburg as anything more than 'the error of a good soldier.' But after the battle, when Colonel Venable said bitterly, 'I heard you direct General Longstreet to send Hood's division up,' Lee had blamed him. And I blamed Richard. I'm trying to do my duty as a doctor. I have your best interests at heart.

I took the prescription out of my pocket and looked at it. Broun's doctor had written a prescription for Elavil.

In July Broun finally let his doctor perform the bypass he had been resisting. He came through it fine, jubilant because nobody had shaved his beard off while he was under the anesthetic, but he didn't show any interest in working on the Lincoln book.

He sent me to Springfield, complaining that he couldn't go any farther with the book till he knew where Willie Lincoln had been buried. I spent nearly a month there trying to find out, and then came back and started through the grave registries of the D.C. cemeteries. I had had the prescription for the Elavil filled while I was in Springfield. It stopped the dreams completely, repressing REM sleep the way it was supposed to.

Broun still wasn't doing any work on the book, even though Willie Lincoln's burial site was a fact he could add after he got it. He had me do a lot of research he never even bothered to look at, and in the fall he started having chest pains again.

In October he insisted I take him out to the Lincoln Memorial. 'I don't think this is a good idea,' I said. 'It has steps. You know you're supposed to take it easy on steps.'

He climbed the steps, shaking off my assistance, and went into the memorial to look at the statue of Lincoln. 'You know what theory nobody came up with in all that traipsing around California?' he said, looking at Lincoln sitting in the big marble chair with his too-big ears and wide nose and his too-long legs, his too-large hands resting on the marble armrests. 'That he was lying about the dreams.'

'Lying?' I said.

'He loved the Union,' he said. 'He would have done anything he could to save it, even if it meant trumping up some dream about a boat and a shadowy shore to keep the Cabinet off his back.' His words echoed in the cold room. 'He would have sacrificed his own son to save his precious Union.'

'He didn't sacrifice Willie,' I said. 'He loved Willie. He would never have done anything to hurt him. Willie died of typhoid.'

'He should have been home taking care of him instead of off gallivanting around some battlefield,' he said.

'What are you talking about?' I said. 'He wasn't off gallivanting. He was right there by Willie's side the whole time.'

'I never should have gone to California,' Broun said, still looking at Lincoln. 'I should have stayed home.'

'It isn't your fault,' I said.

Broun let me help him back down the stairs. At the bottom he turned and looked back up at the memorial. 'It's been over a year, hasn't it?'

'A year and a half,' I said.

I was almost out of the Elavil. I called Broun's doctor and asked him if I could refill the prescription. 'Is it helping you sleep?' he asked me. 'You're not having any side effects, are you?'

'No,' I said.

'Your records are here. I want to check them, and then if everything's okay I'll call it in for you. By the way, is Broun still interested in Lincoln's dreams?'

'I don't know.'

'Well, if he is, there's a paper by a psychiatrist he might be interested in, a Dr Madison. He has a theory that you can dream yourself into ulcers or asthma—'

'Or a heart attack?'

'Yeah. Interesting theory.' He read me the title of the paper and the journal he'd read it in. 'It says here Dr Madison's degree is from Duke University. You went to Duke, didn't you? Maybe you know him. Richard Madison?'

Longstreet became quite successful after the war, in spite of Southern criticism that the failure of Pickett's Charge had been his fault, becoming president of a cotton factory and then an ambassador to Turkey. He wrote articles and a book, and in them he defended his actions at Gettysburg until I think finally he convinced even himself that he had done the right thing and was not to blame for anything that had happened.

'No,' I said. 'I don't know him.' I started taking the Elavil two at a time.

After that trip to the Lincoln Memorial, Broun had put the Lincoln book aside, boxing up all the research and the rough draft and having me carry it up to the attic for him. I spent most of my time at the library. I was still trying to find out where Willie Lincoln was buried, even though Broun wasn't interested anymore. I checked all the grave registries in the towns around Washington and even called Arlington, thinking maybe Commander Meigs had buried Willie in the front lawn of Lee's house.

I ran out of Elavil again, but I didn't call the doctor back. I didn't dream very much, and when I did, Annie wasn't in the dreams. I dreamed of a place I'd never seen before, a place with green hills and white fences. For some reason, I thought it was in West Virginia.

In February I found out what had happened to Willie Lincoln. He had been buried at Oak Hill Cemetery in Georgetown, in a vault belonging to William Thomas Carroll, a clerk of the Supreme Court and a friend of the Lincolns.

The information was in a biography of Mary Todd Lincoln at the branch library, and when I read it, I slammed the book shut, grabbed it up, and went running out. Alarms clanged, and Kate ran out on the steps and shouted after me, 'Jeff, are you all right?' I didn't answer her. I leaped in the car and went tearing out to the cemetery.

The narrow roads between the graves were blocked with snow so deep most of the gravestones were buried, but I got out of the car and walked through the snow to the tomb and looked at it, as if I thought Willie was still there, as if I thought, disturbed out of his sleep, he would tell me where Annie was and what had happened to her.

But he wasn't there. He was in Springfield, lying beside his father. I had thought that finding his grave would tell me what had happened to Willie, but I already knew that, didn't I? It was the same thing that had happened to all of them – Ben and Tom Tita and Little Hen. They had died in the war. Willie's pony had been burned alive and Annie Lee had died of a fever, but they were Civil War dead, and they were all buried together at Fredericksburg, along with Stonewall Jackson's arm, under a numbered granite square no larger than a scrap of paper. I knew what had happened to all of them except Annie. And Traveller. So I walked back through the snow and went home and got out Freeman.

I knew that Traveller had outlived Lee because I remembered reading that he was part of Lee's funeral procession, but there was no mention of him after that in the last chapter of Freeman and nothing at all about him in Davis or even Robert E. Lee, Jr.'s recollections of his father.

I went downstairs to the solarium and found Sanborn's *Robert E. Lee*. I went back up to the study and sorted through the stacks of books Broun had piled on his desk and the leather chair, looking for any mention of Traveller. Pierson mentioned almost in passing that Traveller had been boarded out at a friend's farm because Mrs Lee was too ill to care for him. Lovesey's *Man and Horse* said he had 'lived on for two years, waiting faithfully for the master who would never come again.' Hinsdale said he was kept on at the stable Lee had built for him until he picked up a nail, contracted lockjaw, and had to be shot.

I looked at that for a while and then went back to the last chapter of Freeman, though I already knew everything there was to know: Traveller had had the misfortune to outlive the person he loved, he had waited for nearly two years, and where he had been those two years didn't matter any more than where Willie Lincoln had spent those last three years of the war, and then he had died. Freeman couldn't tell me any more than that, but I went back anyway, writing down the page numbers after 'Traveller' in the index as if they were the Roll of Honor numbers on some soldier's grave, because I couldn't face the idea that Freeman, who had loved Lee enough to write four volumes about him, would have forgotten Traveller, and he hadn't.

It was in one of the appendices in volume one. He wrote that Traveller had died of lockjaw and been buried on the grounds of Washington and Lee University. His bones had been disinterred by the Daughters of the Confederacy and put in the basement of the Lee Memorial Chapel. Near Lee's tomb.

In March I took Broun to see his doctor, and he got a clean bill of health.

'He told me I could do anything I wanted, climb stairs, write a book,' he said on the way home. 'I want to write a book about Robert E. Lee.' He waited to see what I would say.

'And Traveller,' I said.

'Of course Traveller.'

We started work on the new book. Broun sent me out to Arlington to take notes on the porch and the parlor and the attic where Tom Tita had been imprisoned. There was going to be a military funeral in the afternoon, and they had blocked off the drives. I had to park the car in the visitors' parking lot and walk up the hill. It was a warm day, the first one in over two months, and the snow that had fallen in February was just now starting to melt. The water ran in rivers along the curving drives.

Custis Walk was blocked off, too. I had to cut across the grass to get to Arlington House. I made it as far as the grave. The workmen had trampled the snow down till you could see the grass in places. They had used a backhoe to dig the grave, heaping dirty snow at the sides, and it was melting, too, and running across the grass and the snow in muddy rivulets.

The workmen had gone off to eat lunch or smoke a cigarette. They had left a metal clipboard lying under a tree on the far side of the grave, with a piece of paper clipped to it. It would have the name of who the grave was for written on it, and I wanted to walk over to the tree and read it, but I was afraid that I would not be able to get back, that the ground would give way, and I would step on all their mangled bodies.

'It has something to do with Arlington and the unknown soldier and a message,' Annie had said, trying to understand the dreams. 'I think he was trying to atone,' and I should have asked her, 'How is he trying to atone?' instead of shouting at her. Because of course the dreams were an atonement.

He was trying to warn her. His daughter Annie had died, and he hadn't been able to do anything to save her. He hadn't been able to save any of them, Stonewall Jackson or the ragged soldiers he had to keep sending back into battle, or the Confederacy. But he could save Annie. She reminded him of his daughter, and she was twenty-three years old. He was trying to warn her.

The dreams were terrifying, full of images of death and dying. They were meant to frighten her, to make her go see a doctor before it was too late, a warning as clear, as easy to interpret as Lincoln's dreams of himself in a coffin, only nobody saw it. Except Annie, and she wouldn't listen.

'It's the war,' Broun had said. 'People do things like that in a war, sacrifice themselves, fall in love.' They had been together night after night, through battle after heartbreaking battle. She was bound to fall in love with him, wasn't she? And then, even though she knew the dreams were a warning, even though the warnings got plainer and more terrifying, Lee willing even to dream Appomattox again, to dream his own death for her, to warn her, she couldn't leave him.

She had stayed with him to the end, as she had promised, and when the snow melted a little more I would be able to see her body, face-down, her arm flung out, still holding on to her Springfield rifle. I leaned against the backhoe, unable to stand.

I could see the square white subway entrances looking like gravestones and beyond them, across the river, the square white tomb of the Lincoln Memorial. I thought about the statue inside, Lincoln sitting with his long legs planted in front of him and his hands on the arms of the chair, looking like a man who has lost a child.

Lincoln had gone out to the cemetery in Georgetown and had the vault opened twice, trying, I think, to convince himself that Willie was really dead, but it hadn't helped. It hadn't helped, and he couldn't sleep, and his grief nearly drove him insane. Until finally, in Broun's words, Willie's face had come in dreams to comfort him. As Annie's face had come to comfort me, though she was dead.

Though she was dead.

It took me a long time to get back to the road, high-stepping like a cat among the snowy graves, and an even longer time to drive home. When I got there, Broun was in the solarium, watering his African violets.

I stood against the door, still in my coat, watching him spill water out of the already-full pots onto the table. He will never look like Lincoln. The heart attacks have aged and somehow saddened his face, and his beard, which has finally, after almost two years, grown in the way he wanted it, is nearly white. He looks like Lee.

I wondered why I had never noticed it before, why I had kept instead the image I had had of him the night of the reception, of someone sharp and disreputable and not to be trusted. He has been nothing but kind to me. And one snowy night he sold me to Annie, who was having someone else's dreams.

'Jeff'll take good care of her,' Broun had said, like a man trying to make a deal, 'won't you, Jeff?'

And I had said, 'I'll take good care of her. I promise.'

I think some part of me has blamed him for that all this time, in spite of the fact that he has been nothing but kind, loves me as much, I think, as

Lincoln loved Willie, is down here now not because the violets need watering, but because he wondered where I was, because he didn't know what had happened to me.

I have blamed him for something that wasn't even his fault. It was love at first sight for both of them, wasn't it? Didn't Lee call him 'my colt' even before he bought him?

I belonged to her from the minute I saw her standing there in her gray coat, and she took me, her faithful, following companion, from Fredericksburg to Chancellorsville and Gettysburg and finally to Appomattox, and then left me behind.

'I had no business sending you out there,' Broun says.

I cannot answer. I stand there by the door with my head down, winded, blown. Poor Traveller. Did he know that Lee was dead, or, poor dumb animal that he was, had he waited every day for two years for him to come back?

'What happened?' Broun says, alarmed. 'What's wrong?'

'I have picked up a nail.'

PASSAGE

In loving memory of Erik Felice, the Tinman

Grateful thanks to my editor Anne Groell, to my agent Ralph Vicinanza, to Doris Myers, and to Phyllis Giroux and Elizabeth A. Bancroft, M.D., who helped me with the medical details.

Writing this book turned out to be a near-death experience in itself, and I wouldn't have survived without the support of my daughter Cordelia, my long-suffering friends, the staff of Margie's Java Joint, and the above-and-beyond-the-call-of-duty help of my husband Courtney and my Indispensable Girl Friday Laura Norton.

I will remember it forever, the darkness and the cold.

– EDITH HAISMAN, A *Titanic* survivor

'What is it like down there, Charides?'
'Very dark.'
'And what of return?'
'All lies.'

– CALLIMACHUS

PART 1

'Shut up, shut up, I am working Cape Race.'

– Wireless message from the *Titanic*, cutting off an
ice warning the *Californian* was trying to send

1

'More light!'
    – GOETHE's last words

'I heard a noise,' Mrs Davenport said, 'And then I was moving through this tunnel.'

'Can you describe it?' Joanna asked, pushing the minitape recorder a little closer to her.

'The tunnel?' Mrs Davenport said, looking around her hospital room, as if for inspiration. 'Well, it was dark ...'

Joanna waited. Any question, even 'How dark was it?' could be a leading one when it came to interviewing people about their near-death experiences, and most people, when confronted with a silence, would talk to fill it, and all the interviewer had to do was wait. Not, however, Mrs Davenport. She stared at her IV stand for a while, and then looked inquiringly at Joanna.

'Is there anything else you can remember about the tunnel?' Joanna asked.

'No ...' Mrs Davenport said after a minute. 'It was dark.'

'Dark,' Joanna wrote down. She always took notes in case the tape ran out or something went wrong with the recorder, and so she could note the subject's manner and intonation. 'Closemouthed,' she wrote. 'Reluctant.' But sometimes the reluctant ones turned out to be the best subjects if you just had patience. 'You said you heard a noise,' Joanna said. 'Can you describe it?'

'A noise?' Mrs Davenport said vaguely.

If you just had the patience of Job, Joanna corrected. 'You said,' she repeated, consulting her notes, '"I heard a noise, and then I was moving through this tunnel." Did you hear the noise before you entered the tunnel?'

'No ...' Mrs Davenport said, frowning, '... yes. I'm not sure. It was a sort of ringing ...' She looked questioningly at Joanna. 'Or maybe a buzzing?' Joanna kept her face carefully impassive. An encouraging smile or a frown could be leading, too. 'A buzzing, I think,' Mrs Davenport said after a minute.

'Can you describe it?'

I should have had something to eat before I started this, Joanna thought. It was after twelve, and she hadn't had anything for breakfast except coffee and a Pop-Tart. But she had wanted to get to Mrs Davenport before Maurice

Mandrake did, and the longer the interval between the NDE and the interview, the more confabulation there was.

'Describe it?' Mrs Davenport said irritably. 'A *buzzing*.'

It was no use. She was going to have to ask more specific questions, leading or not, or she would never get anything out of her. 'Was the buzzing steady or intermittent?'

'Intermittent?' Mrs Davenport said, confused.

'Did it stop and start? Like someone buzzing to get into an apartment? Or was it a steady sound like the buzzing of a bee?'

Mrs Davenport stared at her IV stand some more. 'A bee,' she said finally.

'Was the buzzing loud or soft?'

'Loud,' she said, but uncertainly. 'It stopped.'

I'm not going to be able to use any of this, Joanna thought. 'What happened after it stopped?'

'It was dark,' Mrs Davenport said, 'and, then I saw a light at the end of the tunnel, and—'

Joanna's pager began to beep. Wonderful, she thought, fumbling to switch it off. This is all I need. She should have turned it off before she started, in spite of Mercy General's rule about keeping it on at all times. The only people who ever paged her were Vielle and Mr Mandrake, and it had ruined more than one NDE interview.

'Do you have to go?' Mrs Davenport asked.

'No. You saw a light—'

'If you have to go …'

'I don't,' Joanna said firmly, sticking the pager back in her pocket without looking at it. 'It's nothing. You saw a light. Can you describe it?'

'It was golden,' Mrs Davenport said promptly. Too promptly. And she looked smugly pleased, like a child who knows the answer.

'Golden,' Joanna said.

'Yes, and brighter than any light I'd ever seen, but it didn't hurt my eyes. It was warm and comforting, and as I looked into it I could see it was a being, an Angel of Light.'

'An Angel of Light,' Joanna said with a sinking feeling.

'Yes, and all around the angel were people I'd known who had died. My mother and my poor dear father and my uncle Alvin. He was in the navy in World War II. He was killed at Guadalcanal, and the Angel of Light said—'

'Before you went into the tunnel,' Joanna interrupted, 'did you have an out-of-body experience?'

'No,' she said, just as promptly. 'Mr Mandrake said people sometimes do, but all I had was the tunnel and the light.'

Mr Mandrake. Of course. She should have known. 'He interviewed me last night,' Mrs Davenport said. 'Do you know him?'

Oh, yes, Joanna thought.

'He's a famous author,' Mrs Davenport said. 'He wrote *The Light at the End of the Tunnel*. It was a best-seller, you know.'

'Yes, I know,' Joanna said.

'He's working on a new one,' Mrs Davenport said. '*Messages from the Other Side*. You know, you'd never know he was famous. He's so nice. He has a wonderful way of asking questions.'

He certainly does, Joanna thought. She'd heard him: 'When you went through the tunnel, you heard a buzzing sound, didn't you? Would you describe the light you saw at the end of the tunnel as golden? Even though it was brighter than anything you'd ever seen, it didn't hurt your eyes, did it? When did you meet the Angel of Light?' Leading wasn't even the word.

And smiling, nodding encouragingly at the answers he wanted. Pursing his lips, asking, 'Are you sure it wasn't more of a buzzing than a ringing?' Frowning, asking concernedly, 'And you don't remember hovering above the operating table? You're sure?'

They remembered it all for him, leaving their body and entering the tunnel and meeting Jesus, remembered the Light and the Life Review and the Meetings with Deceased Loved Ones. Conveniently forgetting the sights and sounds that didn't fit and conjuring up ones that did. And completely obliterating whatever had actually occurred.

It was bad enough having Moody's books out there and *Embraced by the Light* and all the other near-death-experience books and TV specials and magazine articles telling people what they should expect to see without having someone right here in Mercy General putting ideas in her subjects' heads.

'Mr Mandrake told me except for the out-of-body thing,' Mrs Davenport said proudly, 'my near-death experience was one of the best he'd ever taken.'

Taken is right, Joanna thought. There was no point in going on with this. 'Thank you, Mrs Davenport,' she said. 'I think I have enough.'

'But I haven't told you about the heavenly choir yet, or the Life Review,' Mrs Davenport, suddenly anything but reluctant, said. 'The Angel of Light made me look in this crystal, and it showed me all the things I'd ever done, both good and bad, my whole life.'

Which she will now proceed to tell me, Joanna thought. She sneaked her hand into her pocket and switched her pager back on. Beep, she willed it. Now.

'... and then the crystal showed me the time I got locked out of my car, and I looked all through my purse and my coat pockets for the key ...'

Now that Joanna wanted the beeper to go off, it remained stubbornly silent. She needed one with a button you could press to make it beep in emergencies. She wondered if RadioShack had one.

'... and then it showed my going into the hospital and my heart stopping,'

Mrs Davenport said, 'and then the light started to blink on and off, and the Angel handed me a telegram, just like the one we got when Alvin was killed, and I said, "Does this mean I'm dead?" and the Angel said, "No, it's a message telling you you must return to your earthly life." Are you getting all this down?'

'Yes,' Joanna said, writing, 'Cheeseburger, fries, large Coke.'

' "It is not your time yet," the Angel of Light said, and the next thing I knew I was back in the operating room.'

'If I don't get out of here soon,' Joanna wrote, 'the cafeteria will be closed, so please, somebody, page me.'

Her beeper finally, blessedly, went off during Mrs Davenport's description of the light as 'like shining prisms of diamonds and sapphires and rubies,' a verbatim quote from *The Light at the End of the Tunnel*. 'I'm sorry, I've got to go,' Joanna said, pulling the pager out of her pocket. 'It's an emergency.' She snatched up her recorder and switched it off.

'Where can I get in touch with you if I remember anything else about my NDE?'

'You can have me paged,' Joanna said, and fled. She didn't even check to see who was paging her till she was safely out of the room. It was a number she didn't recognize, from inside the hospital. She went down to the nurses' station to call it.

'Do you know whose number this is?' she asked Eileen, the charge nurse.

'Not offhand,' Eileen said. 'Is it Mr Mandrake's?'

'No, I've got Mr Mandrake's number,' Joanna said grimly. 'He managed to get to Mrs Davenport before I did. That's the third interview this week he's ruined.'

'You're kidding,' Eileen said sympathetically. She was still looking at the number on the pager. 'It might be Dr Wright's. He was here looking for you earlier.'

'Dr Wright?' Joanna said, frowning. The name didn't sound familiar. From force of habit, she said, 'Can you describe him?'

'Tall, young, blond—'

'Cute,' Tish, who'd just come up to the desk with a chart, said.

The description didn't fit anybody Joanna knew. 'Did he say what he wanted?'

Eileen shook her head. 'He asked me if you were the person doing NDE research.'

'Wonderful,' Joanna said. 'He probably wants to tell me how he went through a tunnel and saw a light, all his dead relatives, and Maurice Mandrake.'

'Do you think so?' Eileen said doubtfully. 'I mean, he's a doctor.'

'If only that were a guarantee against being a nutcase,' Joanna said. 'You know Dr Abrams from over at Mt Sinai? Last week he suckered me into

lunch by promising to talk to the hospital board about letting me do interviews over there, and then proceeded to tell me about *his* NDE, in which he
saw a tunnel, a light, and Moses, who told him to come back and read the
Torah out loud to people. Which he did. All the way through lunch.'

'You're kidding,' Eileen said.

'But this Dr Wright was *cute*,' Tish put in.

'Unfortunately, that's not a guarantee either,' Joanna said. 'I met a very cute
intern last week who told me he'd seen Elvis in his NDE.' She glanced at her
watch. The cafeteria would still be open, just barely. 'I'm going to lunch,' she
said. 'If Dr Wright shows up again, tell him it's Mr Mandrake he wants.'

She started down to the cafeteria in the main building, taking the service
stairs instead of the elevator to avoid running into either one of them. She
supposed Dr Wright was the one who had paged her earlier, when she was
talking to Mrs Davenport. On the other hand, it might have been Vielle, paging her to tell her about a patient who'd coded and might have had an NDE.
She'd better check. She went down to the ER.

It was jammed, as usual, wheelchairs everywhere, a boy with a hand
wrapped in a red-soaked dish towel sitting on an examining table, two women
talking rapidly and angrily in Spanish to the admitting nurse, someone in one
of the trauma rooms screaming obscenities in English at the top of her lungs.
Joanna worked her way through the tangle of IV poles and crash carts, looking for Vielle's blue scrubs and her black, worried-looking face. She always
looked worried in the ER, whether she was responding to a code or removing
a splinter, and Joanna often wondered what effect it had on her patients.

There she was, over by the station desk, reading a chart and looking worried. Joanna maneuvered past a wheelchair and a stack of blankets to get to
her. 'Did you try to page me?' she asked.

Vielle shook her blue-capped head. 'It's like a tomb down here. Literally. A
gunshot, two ODs, one AIDS-related pneumonia. All DOA, except one of
the overdoses.'

She put down the chart and motioned Joanna into one of the trauma
rooms. The examining table had been moved out and a bank of electrical
equipment moved in, amid a tangle of dangling wires and cables. 'What's
this?' Joanna asked.

'The communications room,' Vielle said, 'if it ever gets finished. So we can
be in constant contact with the ambulances and the chopper and give medical instructions to the paramedics on their way here. That way we'll know if
our patients are DOA before they get here. Or armed.' She pulled off her
surgical cap and shook out her tangle of narrow black braids. 'The overdose
who wasn't DOA tried to shoot one of the orderlies getting him on the examining table. He was on this new drug, rogue, that's making the rounds. Luckily
he'd taken too much, and died before he could pull the trigger.'

'You've got to put in a request to transfer to Peds,' Joanna said.

Vielle shuddered. 'Kids are even worse than druggers. Besides, if I transferred, who'd notify you of NDEs before Mandrake got hold of them?'

Joanna smiled. 'You *are* my only hope. By the way, do you happen to know a Dr Wright?'

'I've been looking for him for years,' Vielle said.

'Well, I don't think this is the one,' Joanna said. 'He wouldn't be one of the interns or residents in the ER, would he?'

'I don't know,' Vielle said. 'We get so many through here, I don't even bother to learn their names. I just call all of them "Stop that," or, "What do you think you're doing?" I'll check.' They went back out into the ER. Vielle grabbed a clipboard and drew her finger down a list. 'Nope. Are you sure he works here at Mercy General?'

'No,' Joanna said. 'But if he comes looking for me, I'm up on seven-west.'

'And what about if an NDEer shows up and *I* need to find you?'

Joanna grinned. 'I'm in the cafeteria.'

'I'll page you,' Vielle said. 'This afternoon should be busy.'

'Why?'

'Heart attack weather,' she said and, at Joanna's blank look, pointed toward the emergency room entrance. 'It's been snowing since nine this morning.'

Joanna looked wonderingly in the direction Vielle was pointing, though she couldn't see the outside windows from here. 'I've been in curtained patient rooms all morning,' she said. And in windowless offices and hallways and elevators.

'Slipping on the ice, shoveling snow, car accidents,' Vielle said. 'We should have lots of business. Do you have your pager turned on?'

'Yes, Mother,' Joanna said. 'I'm not one of your interns.' She waved goodbye to Vielle, and went up to first.

The cafeteria was, amazingly, still open. It had the shortest hours of any hospital cafeteria Joanna had ever seen, and she was always coming down for lunch to find its glass double doors locked and its red plastic chairs stacked on top of the Formica tables. But today it was open, even though a hairnetted worker was dismantling the salad bar and another one was putting away a stack of plates. Joanna snatched up a tray before they could take those away and started over to the hot-food line. And stopped short. Maurice Mandrake was over by the drinks machine, getting a cup of coffee. Nope, thought Joanna, not right now. I'm liable to kill him.

She turned on her heel and walked swiftly down the hall. She dived in the elevator, pushed 'Close Door,' and then hesitated with her finger above the floor buttons. She couldn't leave the hospital, she'd promised Vielle she'd be within reach. The vending-machine snack bar was over in the north wing, but she wasn't sure she had any money. She rummaged through the pockets of her cardigan sweater, but all she turned up besides her minirecorder was a pen, a dime, a release form, an assortment of used Kleenex, and a postcard of a tropical ocean at sunset with palm trees silhouetted blackly against the red sky and coral-pink water. Where had she gotten that? She turned it over. 'Having wonderful time. Wish you were here,' someone had written over an illegibly scrawled signature, and next to it, in Vielle's handwriting, *Pretty Woman, Remember the Titans, What Lies Beneath.* The list of movies Vielle had wanted her to get for their last Dish Night.

Unfortunately, she didn't also have the popcorn from their last Dish Night, and the cheapest thing in the vending machine was seventy-five cents. Her purse was up in her office, but Dr Wright might be camped outside, waiting for her.

Where else would have food? They had Ensure in Oncology, but she wasn't *that* hungry. Paula up on five-east, she thought. She always had a stash of M&M's, and besides, she should go see Carl Aspinall. She pressed the button for five.

She wondered how Coma Carl, which was what the nurses called him, was doing. He'd been in a semicomatose state ever since he'd been admitted two months ago with spinal meningitis. He was completely unresponsive part of the time, and part of the time his arms and legs twitched, and he murmured words. And sometimes he spoke perfectly clearly.

'But he's not having a near-death experience,' Guadalupe, one of his nurses, had said when Joanna had gotten permission from his wife to have the nurses write down everything he said. 'I mean, he's never coded.'

'The circumstances are similar,' Joanna had said. And he was one subject Maurice Mandrake couldn't get to.

Nothing could get to him, even though his wife and the nurses pretended he could hear them. The nurses were careful not to use the nickname Coma Carl or discuss his condition when they were in his room, and they encouraged Joanna to talk to him. 'There have been studies that show coma patients can hear what's said in their presence,' Paula had told her, offering her some M&M's.

But I don't believe it, Joanna thought, waiting for the elevator door to open on five. He doesn't hear anything. He's somewhere else altogether, beyond our reach.

The elevator door opened, and she went down the corridor to the nurses' station. Paula wasn't there. A strange nurse with blond hair and no hips was at the computer. 'Where's Paula?' Joanna asked.

'Out sick,' the pencil-thin nurse said warily. 'Can I help you, Dr …' She looked at the ID hanging around Joanna's neck. 'Lander?'

It was no use asking her for food. She looked like she'd never eaten an M&M in her life, and from the way she was staring at Joanna's body, like she didn't approve of Joanna's having done so either. 'No. Thanks,' Joanna said coolly, and realized she was still carrying the tray from the cafeteria. She must have had it the whole time in the elevator and never been aware of it.

'This needs to go back down to the kitchen,' she said briskly, and handed it to the nurse. 'I'm here to see Com— Mr Aspinall,' she said and started down the hall to Carl's room.

The door was open, and Guadalupe was on the far side of the bed, hanging up an IV bag. The chair Carl's wife usually occupied was empty. 'How's he doing today?' Joanna whispered, approaching the bed.

'Much better,' Guadalupe said cheerfully, and then in a whisper, 'His fever's back up.' She unhooked the empty IV bag and carried it over to the window. 'It's dark in here,' she said. 'Would you like some light, Carl?' She pulled the curtains open.

Vielle had been right. It was snowing. Big flakes out of a leaden gray sky. 'It's snowing, did you know that, Carl?' Guadalupe said.

No, Joanna thought, looking down at the man on the bed. His slack face under the oxygen tubes was pale and expressionless in the gray light from the window, his eyes not quite closed, a slit of white showing beneath the heavy lids, his mouth half-open.

'It looks cold out there,' Guadalupe said, going over to the computer. 'Is it building up on the streets yet?'

It took Joanna a moment to realize Guadalupe was talking to her and not Carl. 'I don't know,' she said, fighting the impulse to whisper so as not to disturb him. 'I came to work before it started.'

Guadalupe poked at icons on the screen, entering Carl's temperature and the starting of the new IV bag. 'Has he said anything this morning?' Joanna asked.

'Not a word,' Guadalupe said. 'I think he's boating on the lake again. He was humming earlier.'

'Humming?' Joanna said. 'Can you describe it?'

'You know, humming,' Guadalupe said. She came over to the bed and pulled the covers up over Carl's taped and tubed arm, over his chest. 'Like a tune, only I couldn't recognize it. There you are, all tucked in nice and warm,' she said and started for the door with her empty IV bag. 'You're lucky you're in here and not out in that snow, Carl,' and went out.

But he's not in here, Joanna thought. 'Where are you, Carl?' she asked. 'Are you boating on the lake?'

Boating on the lake was one of the scenarios the nurses had invented out of his murmurings. He made motions with his arms that might have been rowing, and at those times he was never agitated or cried out, which was why they thought it was something idyllic.

There were several scenarios: The Bataan Death March, during which he cried over and over, 'Water!', and Running for the Bus, and one each of the nurses had a different name for – Burned at the Stake and Vietcong Ambush and The Torments of Hell – during which he flailed wildly at the tangled covers, yanked out his IV. Once he had blacked Guadalupe's eye when she tried to restrain him. 'Blanked out,' he had screamed over and over, or possibly 'placket!' or 'black.' And once, in a tone of panicked dread, 'Cut the knot.'

'Maybe he thinks the IV lines are ropes,' Guadalupe, her eye swollen shut, had said helpfully when she gave Joanna a transcript of the episode.

'Maybe,' Joanna had said, but she didn't think so. He doesn't know the IV lines are there, she thought, or the snow or the nurses. He's a long way from here, seeing something different altogether. Like all the heart attack and car accident and hemorrhage patients she'd interviewed over the last two years, wading through the angels and tunnels and relatives they'd been programmed to see, listening for the offhand comment, the seemingly irrelevant detail that might give a clue as to what they had seen, where they had been.

'The light enveloped me, and I felt happy and warm and safe,' Lisa Andrews, whose heart had stopped during a C-section, had said, but she'd shivered as she said it, and then sat for a long time, gazing bleakly into the distance. And Jake Becker, who had fallen off a ledge while hiking in the Rockies, had said, trying to describe the tunnel, 'It was a long way away.'

'The tunnel was a long way away from you?' Joanna had asked.

'No,' Jake had said angrily. 'I was right there. In it. I'm talking about where *it* was. It was a long way away.'

Joanna went over to the window and looked out at the snow. It was coming down faster now, covering the cars in the visitors' parking lot. An elderly woman in a gray coat and a plastic rain bonnet was laboriously scraping snow off her windshield. Heart attack weather, Vielle had said. Car accident weather. Dying weather.

She pulled the curtains closed and went back over to the bed and sat down in the chair beside it. Carl wasn't going to speak, and the cafeteria would close in another ten minutes. She needed to go now if she ever wanted to eat. But she sat on, watching the monitors, with their shifting lines, shifting numbers, watching the almost imperceptible rise and fall of Carl's sunken chest, looking at the closed curtains with the snow falling silently beyond them.

She became aware of a faint sound. She looked at Carl, but he had not moved and his mouth was still half-open. She glanced at the monitors, but the sound was coming from the bed. Can you describe it? she thought automatically. A deep, even sound, like a foghorn, with long pauses between, and after each pause, a subtle change in pitch.

He's humming, she thought. She fumbled for her minirecorder and switched it on, holding it close to his mouth. 'Nmnmnmnm,' he droned, and then slightly lower, shorter, 'nmnm,' pause while he must be taking a breath, 'nmnmnm,' lower still. Definitely a tune, though she couldn't recognize it either, the spaces between the sounds were too long. But he was definitely humming.

Was he singing on a summer lake somewhere, while a pretty girl played a ukulele? Or was he humming along with Mrs Davenport's heavenly choir, standing in a warm, fuzzy light at the end of a tunnel? Or was he somewhere in the dark or the jungles of Vietnam, humming to himself to keep his fears at bay?

Her pager began abruptly to beep. 'Sorry,' she said, scrabbling to turn it off with her free hand. 'Sorry.' But Carl hummed on undisturbed, nmnm, nmnm, nmnm, nmnm, nm, nm. Oblivious. Unreachable.

The number showing on the pager was the ER. 'Sorry,' Joanna said again and switched off the recorder. 'I have to go.' She patted his hand, lying unmoving at his side. 'But I'll come see you again soon,' and she headed down to the ER.

'Heart attack,' Vielle said when she got there. 'Digging his car out of a ditch. Coded briefly in the ambulance.'

'Where is he?' Joanna said. 'Up in CICU?'

'No,' Vielle said. 'He's right here.'

'In the ER?' Joanna said, surprised. She never talked to patients in the ER, even though there were times she wished she could so she could interview them before Mr Mandrake did.

'He came back really fast after coding, and now he's refusing to be admitted till the cardiologist gets here,' Vielle said. 'We've paged him, but in the meantime the guy's driving everybody crazy. He did *not* have a heart attack. He works out at his health club three times a week.' She led Joanna across the central area toward the trauma rooms.

'Are you sure he's well enough to talk to me?' Joanna asked, following her.

'He keeps trying to get out of bed and demanding to talk to someone in charge,' Vielle said, sidling expertly between a supply cart and a portable X-ray machine. 'If you can distract him and keep him in bed till the cardiologist gets here, you'll be doing everybody a big favor. Including him. Listen, there's your subject now.'

'Why isn't my doctor here yet?' a man's baritone demanded from the end examining room. 'And where's Stephanie?' His voice sounded strong and alert for someone who'd just coded and been revived. Maybe he was right, and he hadn't had a heart attack at all. 'What do you mean, you haven't gotten in touch with her yet? She has a cell phone,' he shouted. 'Where's a phone? I'll call her myself.'

'You aren't supposed to get up, Mr Menotti,' a woman's voice said. 'You're all hooked up.'

Vielle opened the door and led Joanna into the room, where a nurse's aide was vainly trying to keep a young man from removing the electrodes pasted to his chest. A very young man, not more than thirty-five, and tan and well muscled. She could believe he worked out three times a week.

'Stop that,' Vielle said and pushed him back against the bed, which was at a forty-five-degree angle. 'You need to stay quiet. Your doctor will be here in a few minutes.'

'I have to get in touch with Stephanie,' he said. 'I don't need an IV.'

'Yes, you do,' Vielle said. 'Nina here will call her for you.' She looked at the heart monitor and then checked his pulse.

'I already tried,' the aide said. 'She isn't answering.'

'Well, try again,' Vielle said, and the aide scooted out. 'Mr Menotti, this is Dr Lander. I told you about her.' She pushed him firmly back against the bed. 'I'll let you two get acquainted.'

'Don't let him get up,' she mouthed silently to Joanna and went out.

'I'm glad you're here,' Mr Menotti said. 'You're a doctor, maybe you can talk some sense into them. They keep saying I had a heart attack, but I couldn't have. I work out three times a week.'

'I'm not a medical doctor. I'm a cognitive psychologist,' Joanna said, 'and I'd like to talk to you about your experience in the ambulance.' She pulled a release form out of her cardigan pocket and unfolded it. 'This is a standard release form, Mr Menotti—'

'Call me Greg,' he said. 'Mr Menotti's my father.'

'Greg,' she said.

'And what do I call you?' he asked and grinned. It was a very cute grin, if a little wolfish.

'Dr Lander,' she said dryly. She handed him the form. 'The release form says that you give your permission for—'

'If I sign it, will you tell me your first name?' he asked. 'And your phone number?'

'I thought your girlfriend was on her way here, Mr Menotti,' she said, handing him a pen.

'Greg,' he corrected her, trying to sit up again. Joanna leaped forward to hold the form so he could sign it without exerting himself.

'There you go, *Doctor*,' he said, handing her back the form and pen. 'Look, I'm thirty-four. Even if you're not a doctor, you know guys my age don't have heart attacks, right?'

Wrong, Joanna thought, and usually they aren't lucky enough to be revived after they code. 'The cardiologist will be here in a few minutes,' she said. 'In the meantime, why don't you tell me what happened?' She switched on the minirecorder.

'Okay,' he said. 'I was on my way back to the office from playing racquetball – I play racquetball twice a week, Stephanie and I go skiing on the weekends. That's why I moved out here from New York, for the skiing. I do downhill and cross-country, so you can see it's impossible for me to have had a heart attack.'

'You were on the way back to the office—' Joanna prompted.

'Yeah,' Greg said. 'It's snowing, and the road's really slick, and this idiot in a Jeep Cherokee tries to cut in front of me, and I end up in the ditch. I've got a shovel in the car, so I start digging myself out, and I don't know what happened then. I figure a piece of ice off a truck must have hit me in the head and knocked me out, because the next thing I know, there's a siren going, and I'm in an ambulance and a paramedic's sticking these ice-cold paddles on my chest.'

Of course, Joanna thought resignedly. I finally get a subject Maurice Mandrake hasn't already corrupted, and he doesn't remember anything. 'Can you remember anything at all between your – between being hit in the head and waking up in the ambulance?' Joanna asked hopefully. 'Anything you heard? Or saw?' but he was already shaking his head.

'It was like when I had my cruciate ligament operated on last year. I tore it playing softball,' he said. 'One minute the anesthesiologist was saying, "Breathe deeply," and the next I was in the recovery room. And in between, nothing, zip, nada.'

Oh, well, at least she was keeping him in bed until the cardiologist got there.

'I told the nurse when she said you wanted to talk to me that I couldn't have had a near-death experience because I wasn't anywhere near death,' he said. 'When you *do* talk to people who have died, what do they say? Do they tell you they saw tunnels and lights and angels like they say on TV?'

'Some of them,' Joanna said.

'Do you think they really did or that they just made it up?'

'I don't know,' she said. 'That's what I'm trying to find out.'

'I'll tell you what,' he said. 'If I ever *do* have a heart attack and have a near-death experience, you'll be the first one I'll call.'

'I'd appreciate that,' Joanna said.

'In which case, I'll need your phone number,' he said, and grinned the wolfish grin again.

'Well, well, well,' the cardiologist said, coming in with Vielle. 'What have we here?'

'*Not* a heart attack,' Greg said, trying to sit up. 'I work out—'

'Let's find out what's going on,' the cardiologist said. He turned to Joanna. 'Will you excuse us for a few minutes?'

'Of course,' Joanna said, gathering up her recorder. She went out into the ER. There was probably no reason to wait, Greg Menotti had said he hadn't experienced anything, but sometimes, on closer questioning, subjects did remember something. And he was clearly in denial. To admit he'd had an NDE would be to admit he'd had a heart attack.

'Why hasn't he been taken to CICU?' the cardiologist's voice, clearly talking to Vielle, said.

'You're not taking me anywhere till Stephanie gets here,' Greg said.

'She's on her way,' Vielle said. 'I got in touch with her. She'll be here in just a few minutes.'

'All right, let's have a listen to this heart of yours and see what's going on,' the cardiologist said. 'No, don't sit up. Just stay there. All right …'

There was a minute or so of silence, while the cardiologist listened to his heart, and then instructions that Joanna couldn't hear. 'Yes, sir,' Vielle said.

More murmured instructions. 'I want to see Stephanie as soon as she gets here,' Greg said.

'She can see you upstairs,' the cardiologist said. 'We're taking you up to CICU, Mr Menotti. It looks like you've had a myocardial infarction, and we need to—'

'This is ridiculous,' Greg said. 'I'm fine. I got knocked out by a piece of ice, is all. I didn't have a heart—' and then, abruptly, silence.

'Mr Menotti?' Vielle said. 'Greg?'

'He's coding,' the cardiologist said. 'Drop that bed and get a crash cart in here.' The buzz of the code alarm went off, and people converged on the room, running. Joanna backed out of the way.

'Start CPR,' the cardiologist said, and something else Joanna couldn't hear. The code alarm was still going, an intermittent ear-splitting buzz. Was it a buzzing or a ringing? Joanna thought irrelevantly. And then, wonderingly, that's the sound they're hearing before they go into the tunnel.

'Get those paddles over here,' the cardiologist said. 'And turn off that damned alarm.' The buzzing stopped. An IV pole clanked noisily. 'Ready for defib, clear,' the cardiologist said, and there was a different kind of buzz. 'Again. Clear.' A pause. 'One amp epi.'

'Too far away,' Greg Menotti's voice said, and Joanna let out her breath.

'He's back,' someone said, and someone else, 'Normal sinus rhythm.'

'She's too far away,' Greg said. 'She'll never get here in time.'

'Yes, she will,' Vielle said. 'Stephanie's already on her way. She'll be here in just a few minutes.'

There was another pause. Joanna strained to hear the reassuring beep of the monitor. 'What's the BP?' the cardiologist said.

'Fifty-eight,' but it was Greg Menotti's voice.

'Eighty over sixty,' another voice said.

'No,' Greg Menotti said angrily. 'Fifty-*eight*. She'll never get here in time.'

'She was just a few blocks away,' Vielle said. 'She's probably already pulling into the parking lot. Just hang on, Greg.'

'Fifty-eight,' Greg Menotti said, and a pretty blond in a blue parka came hurrying into the ER, the nurse's aide who'd been in the room before right behind her, saying, 'Ma'am? You need to wait in the waiting room. Ma'am, you can't go in there.'

The blond pushed into the room. 'Stephanie's here, Greg,' Joanna heard Vielle say. 'I told you she'd get here.'

'Greg, it's me, Stephanie,' the blond said tearfully. 'I'm here.'

Silence.

'Seventy over fifty,' Vielle said.

'I just left my cell phone in the car for a minute while I ran into the grocery store. I'm so sorry. I came as soon as I could.'

'Sixty over forty and dropping.'

'No,' Greg said weakly. 'Too far away for her to come.' And then the steady flatline whine of the heart monitor.

2

'Over Forked River. Course Lakehurst.'
> – Last wireless message of the *Hindenburg*

'Are you sure you told her I was looking for her?' Richard asked the charge nurse.

'I'm positive, Dr Wright,' she said. 'I gave her your number when she was here this morning.'

'And when was that?'

'About an hour ago,' she said. 'She was interviewing a patient.'

'And you don't know where she went from here?'

'No. I can give you her pager number.'

'I have her pager number,' Richard said. He had been trying her pager all morning and getting no response. 'I don't think she's wearing it.'

'Hospital regulations require all personnel to wear their pagers at all times,' she said disapprovingly and reached for a prescription pad as if to record the infraction.

Well, yes, he thought, and if she had it on, it would make his life a lot easier, but it was a ridiculous rule – he turned his own pager off half the time. You were constantly being interrupted otherwise. And if he got Dr Lander in trouble, she'd hardly be inclined to work with him.

'I'll try her pager again,' he said hastily. 'You said she was interviewing a patient. Which patient?'

'Mrs Davenport. In 314.'

'Thank you,' he said and went down the hall to 314. 'Mrs Davenport?' he said to a gray-haired woman in the bed. 'I'm looking for Dr Lander, and—'

'So am I,' Mrs Davenport said peevishly. 'I've been having her paged all afternoon.'

He was back to square one.

'She told me I could have the nurse page her if I remembered anything else about my near-death experience,' Mrs Davenport said, 'and I've been sitting here remembering all *sorts* of things, but she hasn't come.'

'And she didn't say where she was going after she interviewed you?'

'No. Her pager went off when I was right in the middle, and she had to hurry off.'

Her pager went off. So, at that point, at least, she had had it turned on. And if she had hurried off, it must have meant another patient. Someone who'd coded and been revived? Where would that be? In CICU? 'Thank you,' he said and started for the door.

'If you find her, tell her I've remembered I did have an out-of-body experience. It was like I was above the operating table, looking down. I could see the doctors and nurses working over me, and the doctor said, 'It's no use, she's gone,' and that's when I heard the buzzing noise and went into the tunnel. I—'

'I'll tell her,' Richard said, and went back out into the hall and down to the nurses' station.

'Mrs Davenport said Dr Lander was paged by someone while she was interviewing her,' he said to the nurse. 'Do you have a phone I can use? I need to call CICU.'

The nurse handed him a phone and turned pointedly away.

'Can you give me the extension for CICU?' he said. 'I—'

'It's 4502,' a cute blond nurse said, coming up to the nurses' station. 'Are you looking for Joanna Lander?'

'Yes,' he said gratefully. 'Do you know where she is?'

'No,' she said, looking up at him through her lashes, 'but I know where she might be. In Pediatrics. They called down earlier, looking for her.'

'Thanks,' he said, hanging up the phone. 'Can you tell me how to get to Peds? I'm new here.'

'I know,' she said, smiling coyly. 'You're Dr Wright, right? I'm Tish.'

'Tish, which floor is Peds on?' he asked. 'The elevators are that way, right?'

'Yes, but Peds is in the west wing. The easiest way to get there is to go over to Endocrinology,' she said, pointing in the other direction, 'take the stairs up to fifth, and cross over—' She stopped and smiled at him. 'I'd better show you. It's complicated.'

'I've already found that out,' he said. It had taken nearly half an hour and asking three different people to get from his office down to Medicine. 'You can't get there from here,' a pink-smocked aide had said to him. He'd thought she was kidding. Now he knew better.

'Eileen, I'm running up to Peds,' Tish called to the charge nurse, and led him down the hall. 'It's because Mercy General used to be South General and Mercy Lutheran and a nursing school, and when they merged, they didn't tear out anything. They just rigged it with all these walkways and connecting halls and stuff so it would work. Like doing a bypass or something.' She opened a door marked 'Hospital Personnel Only' and started up the stairs. 'These stairs go up to fourth, fifth, and sixth, but not seventh and eighth. If you want those floors, you have to go down that hall we were just in and use the service elevator. So how long have you been here?'

'Six weeks,' he said.

'*Six weeks?*' Tish said. 'Then how come we haven't met before? How come I haven't seen you at Happy Hour?'

'I haven't been able to find it,' he said. 'I'm lucky to find my office.'

Tish laughed a tinkling laugh. 'Everybody gets lost in Mercy General. The most anybody knows is how to get from the parking lot to the floor they work on and back,' she said, going ahead of him up the stairs. So I can see her legs, he thought. 'What kind of doctor are you?' she asked.

'A neurologist,' he said. 'I'm here conducting a research project.'

'*Really?*' she said eagerly. 'Do you need an assistant?'

I *need* a partner, he thought.

Tish opened a door marked '5,' and led him out into the hallway. 'What kind of project is it?' she asked. 'I really want to transfer out of Medicine.'

He wondered if she'd be as eager to transfer after he told her what the project was about. 'I'm investigating near-death experiences.'

'You're trying to prove there's life after death?' Tish asked.

'No,' he said grimly. 'This is *scientific* research. I'm investigating the physical causes of near-death experiences.'

'Really?' she said. 'What do you think causes them?'

'That's what I'm trying to find out,' he said. 'Temporal-lobe stimulation, for a start, and anoxia.'

'Oh,' she said, eager again. 'When you said near-death experiences, I thought you meant like what Mr Mandrake does. You know, believing in life after death and stuff.'

So does everybody, Richard thought bitterly, which is why it's so hard to get serious NDE research funded. Everyone thinks the field's full of channelers and cranks, and they're right. Mr Mandrake and his book, *The Light at the End of the Tunnel*, were prime examples. But what about Joanna Lander?

She had good credentials, an undergraduate degree from Emory and a doctorate in cognitive psychology from Stanford, but a degree, even a medical degree, wasn't a guarantee of sanity. Look at Dr Seagal. And Arthur Conan Doyle. Doyle had been a doctor. He'd invented Sherlock Holmes, for God's sake, the ultimate believer in science and the scientific method, and yet he'd believed in communicating with the dead *and* in fairies.

But Dr Lander had had articles in *The Psychology Quarterly Review* and *Nature*, and she had just the kind of experience in interviewing NDE subjects he needed.

'What do you know about Dr Lander?' he asked Tish.

'Not very much,' she said. 'I've only been in Medicine for a month. She and Mr Mandrake come around sometimes to interview patients.'

'Together?' he asked sharply.

'No, not usually. Usually he comes and then she comes later.'

To follow up? Or was she working independently? 'Does Dr Lander believe in "life after death and stuff," as you call it?' he asked.

'I don't know. I've never talked to her except about whether a patient can have visitors. She's sort of mousy,' she said. 'She wears glasses. I think your research sounds really interesting, so if you *do* need an assistant—'

'I'll keep you in mind,' he said. They had reached the end of the hall.

'I guess I'd better get back,' she said regretfully. 'You go down that hall,' she pointed to the left, 'and make a right. You'll see the walkway. Go through it, take a right and then a left, and you'll come to a bank of elevators. Take one down to fourth, turn right, and you're there. You can't get lost.'

'Thanks,' he said, hoping she was right.

'Anytime,' she said. She smiled up at him through her lashes. '*Very* nice meeting you, Dr Wright. If you want to go to Happy Hour, just call me, and I'll be glad to show you the way.'

A right to the walkway, and then a right and a left, he thought, starting down the hall, determined to get to Peds before Dr Lander left. Because once she did, he'd never find her, not in this rabbit warren. There were so many wings and connecting walkways and corridors that they could be on the same floor and never run into each other. For all he knew, she'd spent the day searching for him, too, or wandering lost in stairwells and tunnels.

He took the elevator and turned right and yes, there was Peds. He could tell by the charge nurse, who was wearing a smock covered with clowns and bunches of balloons.

'I'm looking for Dr Lander,' he said to her.

The nurse shook her head. 'We paged her earlier, but she hasn't come up yet.'

Shit. 'But she is coming?'

'Uh-huh,' a voice from down the hall piped, and a kid in a red plaid robe and bare feet appeared in the door of one of the rooms. The – boy? girl? he couldn't tell – looked about nine. He? she? had cropped dark blond hair, and there was a hospital gown under the plaid robe. Boy. Girls wore pink Barbie nightgowns, didn't they?

He decided not to risk guessing. 'Hi,' he said, walking over to the kid. 'What's your name?'

'Maisie,' she said. 'Who are you?'

'I'm Dr Wright,' he said. 'You know Dr Lander?'

Maisie nodded. 'She's coming to see me today.'

Good, Richard thought. I'll stay right here till she does.

'She comes to see me every time I'm in,' Maisie said. 'We're both interested in disasters.'

'Disasters?'

'Like the *Hindenburg*,' she said. 'Did you know there was a dog? It didn't die. It jumped out.'

'Really?' he said.

'It's in my book,' she said. 'Its name was Ulla.'

'Maisie,' a nurse – not the one who'd been at the desk – said. She came over to the door. 'You're not supposed to be out of bed.'

'*He* asked me where Joanna was,' Maisie said, pointing at Richard.

'Joanna Lander?' the nurse said. 'She hasn't been here today. And where are your slippers?' she said to Maisie. 'You. Into bed,' she said, not unkindly. 'Now.'

'I can still *talk* to him, right, though, Nurse Barbara?'

'For a little while,' Barbara said, walking Maisie into the room and helping her into the bed. She put the side up. 'I want you *resting*,' she said.

'Maybe I should—' Richard began.

'What's an Alsatian?' Maisie asked.

'An Alsatian?' Barbara said blankly.

'That's what Ulla was,' Maisie said, but to Richard. 'The dog on the *Hindenburg*.'

The nurse smiled at him, patted Maisie's foot under the covers, and said, '*Don't* get out of bed,' and went out.

'I think an Alsatian's a German shepherd,' Richard said.

'I'll bet it is,' Maisie said, 'because the *Hindenburg* was from Germany. It blew up while it was landing at Lakehurst. That's in New Jersey. I have a picture,' Maisie said, putting the side of the bed down and scrambling out and over to the closet. 'It's in my book.' She reached in a pink duffel bag – *there* was Barbie, on the side of the duffel bag – and hauled out a book with a picture of Mount St Helens on the cover and the title *Disasters of the Twentieth*

Century. 'Can you carry it over to the bed? I'm not supposed to carry heavy stuff.'

'You bet,' Richard said. He carried it over and laid it on the bed. Maisie opened it up, standing beside the bed. 'A girl and two little boys got burned. The girl died,' she said, short of breath. 'Ulla didn't die, though. See, here's a picture.'

He leaned over the book, expecting to see a picture of the dog, but it was a photo of the *Hindenburg*, sinking in flames. 'Joanna gave me this book,' Maisie said, turning pages. 'It's got all kinds of disasters. See, this is the Johnstown flood.'

He obediently looked at a photo of houses smashed against a bridge. A tree stuck out of the upstairs window of one of them. 'So, you and Dr Lander are good friends?'

She nodded, continuing to turn pages. 'She came to talk to me when I coded,' she said matter-of-factly, 'and that's when we found out we both liked disasters. She studies near-death experiences, you know.'

He nodded.

'I went into V-fib. I have cardiomyopathy,' she said casually. 'Do you know what that is?'

Yes, he thought. A badly damaged heart, unable to pump properly, likely to go into ventricular fibrillation. That accounted for the breathlessness.

'When I coded I heard this funny sound, and then I was in this tunnel,' Maisie said. 'Some people remember all kinds of stuff, like they saw Jesus and heaven, but I didn't. I couldn't see hardly anything because it was dark and all foggy in the tunnel. Mr Mandrake said there was a light at the end of the tunnel, but *I* didn't see any light. Joanna says you should only say what you saw, not what anybody else says you should see.'

'She's right,' Richard said. 'Mr Mandrake interviewed you, too?'

'*Uh-huh*,' Maisie said, and rolled her eyes. 'He asked me if I saw people waiting for me, and I said, "No," because I couldn't, and he said, "Try to remember." Joanna says you shouldn't do that because sometimes you make up things that didn't really happen. But Mr Mandrake says, "Try to remember. There's a light, isn't there, dear?" I *hate* it when people call me "dear."'

'Dr Lander doesn't do that?'

'No,' she said, her emphaticness making her breathe harder. 'She's *nice*.'

Well, there was a reference for you. Dr Lander clearly wasn't a researcher with a preset agenda. And she was obviously aware of the possibilities of post-NDE confabulation. *And* she had brought a book to a little girl, albeit a peculiar book for a child.

'Look,' Maisie said. 'This is the Great Molasses Flood. It happened in 1919.' She pointed to a grainy black-and-white photo of what looked like an oil slick. 'These huge tanks full of molasses – that's a kind of syrup,' she confided.

Richard nodded.

'These huge tanks broke and all the molasses poured out and drowned everybody. Twenty-one people. I don't know if any of them were little kids. It would be kind of funny to drown in syrup, don't you think?' she asked, beginning to wheeze.

'Didn't the nurse say you were supposed to stay in bed?' he said.

'I will in just a minute. What's your favorite disaster? Mine's the *Hindenburg*,' Maisie said, turning back to the photo of it, falling tail first, engulfed in flames. 'This one crew guy was up on the balloon part when it blew up and everybody else fell, but he hung on to the metal things.' She pointed to the metal framework visible among the flames.

'Struts,' Richard said.

'His hands all burned off, but he didn't let go. I need to tell Joanna about him when she comes.'

'Did she say when she was coming?' Richard asked.

She shrugged, bending over the picture, her nose practically touching it, as if she was looking for the hapless crewman amid the flames. Or the dog. 'I don't know if she knows I'm here yet. I told Nurse Barbara to page her. Sometimes she turns her pager off though, but she always comes to see me as soon as she finds out I'm here,' Maisie said, 'and I have lots more *Hindenburg* pictures to show you. See, here's the captain. He died. Did you know—'

He interrupted her. 'Maisie, I've got to go.'

'Wait, you can't go yet. I know she'll be here pretty soon. She always comes just as soon as—'

Barbara poked her head in the door. 'Dr Wright? There's a message for you.'

'See,' Maisie said as if that proved something.

'I thought I told you to get back in bed,' Barbara said, and Maisie hastily climbed up into it. 'Dr Wright, Tish Vanderbeck said to tell you that she'd gotten in touch with Dr Lander and asked her to come up to Medicine.'

'Thank you,' he said. 'Maisie, I've got to go meet Dr Lander. It was nice talking to you.'

'Wait, you can't go *yet*,' Maisie said. 'I haven't told you about the girl and the little boys.'

She looked genuinely distressed, but he didn't want to miss Dr Lander again. 'All right,' he said. 'One quick story and then I have to go.'

'Okay,' she said. 'Well, the people had to jump out because everything was on fire. The girl jumped, but the little boys were too scared to, and one of them, his hair caught on fire, so his mother *threw* him out. The crew guy was on fire, too, his hands, but he didn't let go.' She looked up innocently. 'What do you think that would be like? Being on fire?'

'I don't know,' Richard said, wondering if talking about such grisly things with such a sick little girl was a good idea. 'Terrible, I'd think.'

Maisie nodded. 'I think I'd let go. There was this other guy—'

Talk about letting go. 'Maisie, I *have* to go find Dr Lander. I don't want to miss her.'

'Wait! When you see Dr Lander, tell her I have something to tell her. About near-death experiences. Tell her I'm in Room 456.'

'I will,' he said and started out.

'It's about the crew guy who was up inside the balloon part of the *Hindenburg* when it exploded. He—'

At this rate, he would be here all day. 'I've got to go, Maisie,' he said and didn't wait for her to protest. He hurried back down the hall, turned left, and immediately got lost. He had to stop and ask an orderly how to get to the walkway.

'You go back down this hall, turn right, and go clear to the end of the hall,' the orderly said. 'Where are you trying to get?'

'Medicine,' Richard said.

'That's in the main building. The fastest way is to go down this hall and turn left till you come to a door marked "Staff." Through there there's a stairway. It'll take you down to second. You take the walkway and then cut through Radiology to the service elevator, and take it back up to third.'

Richard did, practically running down the last hallway, afraid Dr Lander would have come and gone. She wasn't there yet. 'Or at least I haven't seen her,' the charge nurse said. 'She might be in with Mrs Davenport.'

He went down to Mrs Davenport's room, but she wasn't there. 'I *wish* she'd get here,' Mrs Davenport said. 'I have *so* much to tell her and Mr Mandrake. While I was floating above my body, I heard the doctor say—'

'Mr Mandrake?' Richard said.

'Maurice Mandrake,' she said. 'He wrote *The Light at the End of the Tunnel*. He's going to be so excited that I've remembered—'

'I thought Dr Lander was interviewing you.'

'They both are. They work together, you know.'

'They *work* together?'

'Yes, I think so. They've both come in and interviewed me.'

That doesn't mean they work together, Richard thought.

'– although I have to say, she's not nearly as nice as Mr Mandrake. He's so interested in what you have to say.'

'Did she tell you they worked together?'

'Not exactly,' she said, looking confused. 'I assumed ... Mr Mandrake's writing a new book about messages from the Other Side.'

She didn't know for certain that they worked together, but if that was even a possibility ... Messages from the dead, for God's sake.

'Excuse me,' he said abruptly and walked out of the room, straight into a tall, gray-haired man in a pin-striped suit. 'Sorry,' Richard said, and started past, but the man held his arm.

'You're Dr Wright, aren't you?' he said, gripping Richard's hand in a confident handshake. 'I was just on my way up to see you. I want to discuss your research.'

Richard wondered who this was. A fellow researcher? No, the suit was too expensive, the hair too slick. A hospital board member.

'I intended to come see you after I saw Mrs Davenport, and here you are,' he said. 'I assume you've been in listening to her account of her NDE, or, as I prefer to call them, her NAE, near-afterlife experience, because that's what they are. A glimpse of the afterlife that awaits us, a message from beyond the grave.'

Maurice Mandrake, Richard thought. Shit. He should have recognized him from his book jacket photos. And paid more attention to where he was going.

'I'm delighted you've joined us here at Mercy General,' Mandrake said, 'and that science is finally acknowledging the existence of the afterlife. The science and medical establishments so often have closed minds when it comes to immortality. I'm delighted that you don't. Now, what exactly does your research entail?'

'I really can't talk now. I have an appointment,' Richard said, but Mandrake had no intention of letting him go.

'The fact that people who have had near-death experiences consistently report seeing the same things proves that they are not mere hallucinations.'

'Dr Wright?' the charge nurse called from her desk. 'Are you still looking for Dr Lander? We've located her.'

'Jo?' Mandrake said delightedly. 'Is that who your appointment's with? Lovely girl. She and I work together.'

Richard's heart sank. 'You work together?'

'Oh, yes. We've worked closely on a number of cases.'

I should have known, Richard thought.

'Of course, our *emphasis* is different,' Mandrake said. 'I am currently interested in the message aspect of the NAEs. And we have different interview methods,' he, added, frowning slightly. 'Were you supposed to meet Dr Lander here? She is often rather difficult to locate.'

'Dr Lander's not the person I have the appointment with,' Richard said. He turned to the charge nurse. 'No. I don't need to see her.'

Mandrake grabbed his hand again. 'Delighted to have met you, Dr Wright, and I'm looking forward to our working together.'

Over my dead body, Richard thought. And I won't be sending you any messages from beyond the grave.

'I must go see Mrs Davenport now,' Mandrake said, as if Richard were the one who had detained him, and left him standing there.

He should have known better. NDE researchers might collect data and do statistical samplings, might publish papers in *The Psychology Quarterly Review*, might even make a good impression on children, but it was all a blind. They were really latter-day spiritualists using pseudoscientific trappings to lend credibility to what was really religion. He started down the hall to the elevators.

'Dr Wright!' Tish called after him.

He turned around.

Tish said, 'Here she is,' and turned to hurry after a young woman in a skirt and cardigan sweater walking toward the nurses' station. 'Dr Lander,' she said as she caught up to her. 'Dr Wright wants to talk to you.'

Dr Lander said, 'Tell him I'm—'

'He's right *here*,' Tish said, waving him over. 'Dr Wright, I found her for you.'

Damn you, Tish, he thought, another minute and I would have been out of here. And now what am I supposed to tell Dr Lander I wanted her for?

He walked over. She was not, as Tish had said, mousy, although she did wear glasses, wire-rimmed ones that gave her face a piquant look. She had hazel eyes and brown hair that was pulled back with silver barrettes.

'Dr Lander,' he said. 'I—'

'Look, Dr Wright,' she said, putting her hand up to stop him. 'I'm sure you've had a fascinating near-death experience, but right now's not the time. I've had a very bad day, and I'm not the person you want to talk to anyway. You need to see Maurice Mandrake. I can give you his pager number.'

'He's in with Mrs Davenport,' Tish said helpfully.

'There, Tish will show you where he is. I'm sure he'll want to know all the details. Tish, take him in to Mr Mandrake.' She started past him.

'Don't bother, Tish,' he said, angered by her rudeness. 'I'm not interested in talking to Dr Lander's partner.'

'Partner?' Dr Lander wheeled to face him. 'Who told you I was his partner? Did *he* tell you that? First he steals all my subjects and *ruins* them and *now* he's telling people we work together! He has no right!' She stamped her foot. 'I do *not* work with Mr Mandrake!'

Richard grabbed her arm. 'Wait. Whoa. Time out. I think we need to start over.'

'Fine,' she said. 'I do *not* work with Maurice Mandrake. I am *attempting* to do legitimate scientific research on near-death experiences, but he is making it *absolutely* impossible—'

'And I've been *attempting* to contact you to talk to you about your research,' he said, extending his hand. 'Richard Wright. I'm doing a project on the neurological causes of the near-death experience.'

'Joanna Lander,' she said, shaking his hand. 'Look, I'm really sorry. I—'

He grinned. 'You've had a bad day.'

195

'Yes,' she said, and he was surprised by the bleakness of the look she gave him.

'You said this was a bad time to talk,' he said hastily. 'We don't have to do it right now. We could set up a meeting tomorrow, if that would be better.'

She nodded. 'Today just isn't – one of my subjects—' She recovered herself. 'Tomorrow would be good. What time?'

'Ten o'clock? Or we could meet for lunch. When is the cafeteria open?'

'Hardly ever,' she said, and smiled. 'Ten is fine. Where?'

'My lab's up on six-east,' he said. '602.'

'Tomorrow at ten,' she said, and started down the hall, but before she had gone five steps she had turned and begun walking back toward him.

'What—' he said.

'*Shh*,' she said, passing him. 'Maurice Mandrake,' she murmured, and pushed open a white door marked 'Staff Only.'

He glanced back, saw a pin-striped suit coming around the corner, and ducked in the door after her. It was a stairway, leading down.

'Sorry,' she said, starting down the gray-painted cement stairs, 'but I was afraid if I had to talk to him right then, I'd kill him.'

'I know the feeling,' Richard said, starting down the stairs after her. 'I already had one encounter today.'

'This'll take us down to first,' she said, already down to the landing, 'and then to the main elevators.' She stopped short, looking dismayed.

'What is it?' he said, coming down to where she was standing. A strip of yellow 'Do Not Cross' tape stretched across the stairway. Below it, the stairs gleamed with shiny, wet, pale blue paint.

3

'Oh, shit.'
> – Last words on majority of flight recorders
> recovered after plane crashes

'Maybe the paint's dried,' Dr Wright said, even though it was obviously still wet.

Joanna stooped and touched it. 'Nope,' she said, holding her finger up to show him the pale blue spot on the tip.

'And there's no other way out?'

'Back the way we came,' she said. 'Did Mr Mandrake happen to tell you where he was going?'

'Yes,' Richard said. 'In to see Mrs Davenport.'

'Oh, no, he'll be in there forever,' she said. 'Mrs Davenport's life review is longer than most people's lives. And it's been three hours since I saw her last. She's no doubt "remembered" all sorts of details in the meantime. And what she hasn't, Mr Mandrake will manufacture.'

'How did a nutcase like Mandrake get permission to do research in a reputable hospital like Mercy General anyway?' he asked.

'Money,' she said. 'He donated half the royalties of *The Light at the End of the Tunnel* to them. It's sold over twenty-five million copies.'

'Proving the adage that there's one born every minute.'

'And that people believe what they want to believe. Especially Esther Brightman.'

'Who's Esther Brightman?'

'The widow of Harold Brightman of Brightman Industries and the oldest member of Mercy General's board of trustees. And a devout disciple of Mandrake's, I think because she might cross over to the Other Side at any moment. She's donated even more money to Mercy General than Mandrake, *and* the entire Research Institute, and when she dies, they get the whole kit and caboodle. If she doesn't change her will in the meantime.'

'Which means allowing Mandrake to pollute the premises.'

She nodded. 'And any other project connected with NDEs. Which is what I'm doing here.'

He frowned. 'Isn't Mrs Brightman afraid legitimate scientific research might undermine the idea of life after death?'

She shook her head. 'She's convinced that the evidence will prove the existence of the afterlife, and that I'll come to see the light. I should be grateful to them. Most hospitals won't touch NDE research with a ten-foot pole. I'm not, however. Grateful. Especially right now.' She looked speculatively up at the door. 'We might be able to sneak past him while Mrs Davenport's telling him the riveting story of her third-grade spelling test.' She tiptoed up the stairs and opened the door a silent crack.

Mr Mandrake was standing in the hall, talking to Tish. 'Mrs Davenport and the others have been sent back as emissaries,' he said, 'to bring us word of what awaits us on the Other Side.'

Joanna eased the door shut carefully and went back down to where Dr Wright was standing. 'He's talking to Tish,' she whispered, 'telling her how NDEs are messages from the Other Side. And meanwhile, we're trapped on This Side.' She walked past him down to the landing. 'I don't know about you, but I can't stand the thought of having to listen to his theories of life after death. Not today. So I think I'll just wait here till he leaves.'

She went around the landing and sat down out of sight of the door above, her feet on the step above the yellow 'Do Not Cross' tape. 'Don't feel like you have to stay, Dr Wright. I'm sure you've got more important things—'

'I've already been caught once today by Mandrake,' he said. 'And I wanted to talk to you, remember? About working with me on my project. This looks like an ideal place. No noise, no interruptions – but it's not Dr Wright, not when we're stuck in a half-painted stairwell together. I'm Richard.' He extended his hand.

'Joanna,' she said, shaking it.

He sat down across the landing facing her. 'Tell me about your bad day, Joanna.'

She leaned her head back against the wall. 'A man died.'

'Somebody you were close to?'

She shook her head. 'I didn't even know him. I was interviewing him in the ER … he …' He was there one minute, she thought, and the next he was gone. And that wasn't just a figure of speech, a euphemism for death like 'passed away.' It was how it had felt. Looking at him lying there in the ER, the monitor wailing, the cardiologist and nurses frantically working over him, it hadn't felt like Greg Menotti had shut down or ceased to exist. It was as if he'd vanished.

'He'd had an NDE?' Richard asked.

'No. I don't know. He'd had a heart attack and coded in the ambulance, and he said he didn't remember anything, but while the doctor was examining him, he coded again, and he said, "Too far for her to come."' She looked up at Richard. 'The nurses thought he was talking about his girlfriend, but he wasn't, she was already there.' And he was somewhere else, Joanna thought. Like Coma Carl. Somewhere too far for her to come.

'How old was he?' Richard asked.

'Thirty-four.'

'And probably no prior damage,' he said angrily. 'If he'd survived another five minutes, they could have gotten him up to surgery, done a bypass, and given him ten, twenty, even fifty more years.' He leaned forward eagerly. 'That's why this research is so important. If we can figure out what happens in the brain when it's dying, then we can devise strategies for preventing unnecessary deaths like the one that happened this afternoon. And I believe the NDE's the key, that it's a survival mechanism—'

'Then you don't agree with Noyes and Linden that the NDE's a result of the human mind's inability to comprehend its own death?'

'No, and I don't agree with Dr Roth's theory that it's psychological detachment from fear. There's no evolutionary advantage to making dying easier or more pleasant. When the body's injured, the brain initiates a series of survival strategies. It shuts down blood to every part of the body that can do without it, it increases respiration rate to produce more oxygen, it concentrates blood where it's most needed—'

'And you think the NDE is one of those strategies?' Joanna asked.

He nodded. 'Most patients who've had NDEs were revived by paddles or norepinephrine, but some began breathing again on their own.'

'And you think the NDE was what revived them?'

'I think the neurochemical events causing the NDE revived them, and the NDE is a side effect of those events. And a clue to what they are and how they work. And if I can find that out, that knowledge could eventually be used to revive patients who've coded. Are you familiar with the new RIPT scan?'

Joanna shook her head. 'Is it similar to a PET scan?'

He nodded. 'They both measure brain activity, but the RIPT scan is exponentially faster and more detailed. Plus, it uses chemical tracers, not radioactive ones, so the number of scans per subject doesn't have to be limited. It simultaneously photographs the electrochemical activity in different subsections of the brain for a 3-D picture of neural activity in the working brain. Or the dying brain.'

'You mean you could theoretically take a picture of an NDE?'

'Not theoretically,' Richard said. 'I've—'

The door above them opened.

They both froze.

Above them a man's voice said, '– very productive session. Mrs Davenport has remembered experiencing the Command to Return and the Life Review while she was dead.'

'Oh, God,' Joanna whispered, 'It's Mr Mandrake.'

Richard craned his neck carefully around the corner.

'You're right,' he whispered back. 'He's holding the door partway open.'

'Can he see us from there?'

He shook his head.

'Then it's true?' a young woman's voice said from the door.

'That's Tish,' Joanna whispered.

Richard nodded, and they both sat there perfectly still, their heads turned toward the stairs and the door, listening alertly.

'Your whole life really does flash before you when you die?' Tish asked.

'Yes, the events of your life are shown to you in a panorama of images called the Life Review,' Mr Mandrake said. 'The Angel of Light leads the soul in its examination of its life and of the meaning of those events. I've just been with Mrs Davenport. The Angel showed her the events of her life and said, "See and understand."' Mandrake must have leaned against the door and opened it wider because his voice was suddenly louder. 'See and understand we shall,' he said. 'Not only shall we understand our own lives but life itself, the vast ocean of understanding and love that shall be ours when we reach eternity.'

Richard looked at Joanna. 'How long is he likely to go on like that?' he whispered.

'Eternally,' she whispered back.

'So you really believe there's an afterlife?' Tish asked.

Doesn't she have any patients to attend to? Joanna thought, exasperated. But this was Tish, to whom flirting was as natural as breathing. She couldn't help sending out spinnerets over any male, even Mr Mandrake. And Richard had obviously met her. Joanna wondered how he'd managed to get away.

'I don't think there's an afterlife,' Mr Mandrake said. 'I know it. I have scientific evidence it exists.'

'Really?' Tish said.

'I have *eyewitnesses*,' he said. 'My subjects report that the Other Side is a beautiful place, filled with golden light and the faces of loved ones.'

There was a pause. Maybe he's leaving, Joanna thought hopefully.

The door opened still farther, and someone started down the stairs. Richard shot to his feet and was across the landing in an instant, pulling Joanna to her feet, pressing them both flat against the wall, his arm across her, holding her against the wall. They waited, not breathing.

The door clicked shut, and footsteps clattered down the cement stairs toward them. He'd be down to the landing in another minute, and how were they going to explain their huddling here like a couple of children playing hide-and-seek? Joanna looked questioningly at Richard. He put his finger to his lips. The footsteps came closer.

'Mr Mandrake!' Tish's distant voice called, and they could hear the door open again. 'Mr Mandrake! You can't go down that way. It's wet.'

'Wet?' Mr Mandrake said.

'They've been painting all the stairwells.'

There was a pause. Richard's arm tightened against Joanna, and then there was a sound of footsteps going back up.

'Where were you going, Mr Mandrake?' Tish asked.

'Down to the ER.'

'Oh, then, you need to go over to Orthopedics and take the elevator. Here, let me show you the way.'

Another long pause, and the door clicked shut.

Richard leaned past Joanna to look up the stairs. 'He's gone.'

He took his arm away and turned to face Joanna. 'I was afraid he was going to insist on seeing for himself if the stairs were wet.'

'Are you kidding?' Joanna said. 'He's based his entire career on taking things on faith.'

Richard laughed and started up the stairs toward the door. 'I wouldn't do that if I were you,' she said. 'He's still out there.'

Richard stopped and looked down at her questioningly. 'He said he was going down to the ER.'

She shook her head. 'Not while he's got an audience.'

Richard opened the door cautiously and eased it shut again. 'You're right. He's telling Tish how the Angel of Light explained the mysteries of the universe to Mrs Davenport.'

'That'll take a month,' Joanna said. She slumped down resignedly on the step. 'You're a doctor. How long does it take for someone to starve to death?'

He looked surprised. 'You're hungry?'

She leaned her head back against the wall. 'I had a Pop-Tart for breakfast. About a million years ago.'

'You're kidding,' he said, rummaging in the pockets of his lab coat. 'Would you like an energy bar?'

'You have food?' she said wonderingly.

'The cafeteria's always closed when I try to eat there. Is it ever open?'

'No,' Joanna said.

'There don't seem to be any restaurants around here either.'

'There aren't,' Joanna said. 'Taco Pierre's is the closest, and it's ten blocks away.'

'Taco Pierre's?'

She nodded. 'Fast-food burritos and *E. coli*.'

'Umm,' he said. He pulled out an apple, polished it against his lapel, and held it out to her. 'Apple?'

She took it gratefully. 'First you save me from Mr Mandrake and then from starvation,' she said, taking a bite out of the apple. 'Whatever it is you want me to do, I'll do it.'

'Good,' he said, reaching in his other pocket. 'I want you to define the near-death experience for me.'

'Define?' she said around a mouthful of apple.

'The sensations. What people experience when they have an NDE.' He pulled out a foil-wrapped Nutri-Grain bar and handed it to her. 'Do they all experience the same thing, or is it different for each individual?'

'No,' she said, trying to tear the energy-bar wrapper open. 'There definitely seems to be a core experience, as Mr Mandrake calls it.' She bit the paper, still trying to tear it. 'Defining it's another matter.'

Richard took the energy bar away from her, tore it open, and handed it back to her.

'Thanks,' she said. 'The problem is Mr Mandrake's book and all the

201

near-death-experience stuff out there. They've told people what they should see, and sure enough, they all see it.'

He frowned. 'Then you don't think people actually see a tunnel and a light and a divine figure?'

She took a bite of energy bar. 'I didn't say that. NDEs didn't start with Mr Mandrake or this current crop of books. There are accounts dating all the way back to ancient Greece. In Plato's *Republic*, there's an account of a soldier named Er who died and traveled through passageways leading to the realms of the afterlife, where he saw spirits and something approaching heaven. The eighth-century *Tibetan Book of the Dead* talks about leaving the body, being suspended in a foggy void, and entering a realm of light. And most of the core elements seem to go way back.'

She took another bite. 'It's not that people don't see the tunnel and all the rest. It's just that it's so hard separating the wheat from the chaff. And there's tons of chaff. People tend to use NDEs to get attention. Or to stump for their belief in the paranormal. Twenty-two percent of people who claim they've had NDEs also claim to be clairvoyant or telekinetic, or to have had past-life regressions like Bridey Murphy. Fourteen percent claim they've been abducted by aliens.'

'So how *do* you separate the wheat from the chaff, as you call it?'

She shrugged. 'You look for body language. I had a patient last month who said, "When I looked at the light, I understood the secret of the universe," which, by the way, is a common comment, and when I asked her what it was, she said, "I promised Jesus I wouldn't tell," but as she said it, she put her hand out, as if reaching for something just out of her grasp,' Joanna said, demonstrating. 'And you look for experiences outside the standard imagery, for consistency. People tend to include many more specific details, some of them seemingly irrelevant, when they're describing what they've actually experienced than when they're describing what they think they should have seen.'

'And what have they actually experienced?' Richard asked.

'Well, there's definitely a sensation of darkness, and a sensation of light, usually in that order. There also seems to be a sound of some kind, though nobody seems to be able to describe it very well. Mr Mandrake says it's a buzzing—'

'– so all of his patients say it's a buzzing,' Richard said.

'Yes, but even they don't sound all that convinced,' Joanna said, remembering the uncertainty in Mrs Davenport's voice. 'And my subjects are all over the map. It's a click, it's a roar, it's a scraping sound, and it's a shriek.'

'But there definitely seems to be a sound?'

'Oh, yes, eighty-eight percent of my patients mentioned it. Without prompting.'

'What about the floating-above-your-body-on-the-operating-table?' Richard asked, pulling a box of raisins out of his pocket.

'Mr Mandrake claims sixty percent of his patients have an out-of-body experience, but only eleven percent of mine do. Seventy-five percent of mine mention feelings of peacefulness and warmth, and nearly fifty percent say they saw some kind of figure, usually religious, usually dressed in white, sometimes shining or radiating light.'

'Mandrake's Angel of Light,' Richard said.

She held out her hand, and he tipped some raisins into her palm. 'Mr Mandrake's brainwashees see an Angel of Light and their dead relatives, waiting to greet them on the Other Side, but for everyone else, it seems to be religion-specific. Christians see angels or Jesus unless they're Catholics, then they see the Virgin Mary. Hindus see Krishna or Vishnu, nonbelievers see relatives. Or Elvis.' She ate a raisin. 'That's what I mean about chaff. People bring so many biases from their own background, it's almost impossible to know what they actually saw.'

'What about children?' he asked. 'Don't they have fewer preconceived ideas?'

'Yes,' Joanna said, 'but they're also more apt to want to please the adult who's interviewing them, as proved by the nursery-school-abuse cases of the eighties. Children can be manipulated to say anything.'

'I don't know,' he said doubtfully. 'I met a little girl today who didn't look too influenceable. You know her. Maisie?'

'You talked to Maisie Nellis?' she said, and then frowned. 'I didn't know she was back in again.'

Richard nodded. 'She told me to tell you she has something important to tell you. We had quite a chat about the *Hindenburg*.'

She smiled. 'So that's the disaster of the week?'

He nodded. 'That and the Great Molasses Flood. Did you know that twenty-one people met a pancakelike death in 1919?'

'How long were you there?' she laughed. 'No, let me guess. Maisie's wonderful at thinking up excuses for why you have to stay just a little longer. She's one of the world's great stallers. And one of the world's great kids.'

He nodded. 'She told me she has cardiomyopathy and that she'd gone into V-fib.'

Joanna nodded. 'Viral endocarditis. They can't get her stabilized, and she keeps having reactions to the antiarrhythmia drugs. She's a walking disaster.'

'Hence the interest in the *Hindenburg*,' he said.

She nodded. 'I think it's a way of indirectly addressing her fears. Her mother won't let her talk about them directly, won't even acknowledge the possibility that Maisie might die,' she said. 'But more than that, I think Maisie's trying to make sense of her own situation by reading about other people who've had sudden, unaccountable, disastrous things happen to them.' She ate another raisin. 'Plus, children are always fascinated by death.

When I was Maisie's age, my favorite song was 'Poor Babes in the Wood,' about two children 'stolen away one bright summer's day' and left in the woods to die. My grandmother used to sing it to me, to my mother's horror. The elderly are fascinated by death, too.'

'Did they?' Richard asked curiously. 'Die? The babes in the wood?'

She nodded. 'After wandering around in the dark for several stanzas. "The moon did not shine and the stars gave no light,"' she recited. '"They wept and they sighed, and bitterly cried, and the poor little children, they lay down and died." After which the birds covered them with strawberry leaves.' She sighed nostalgically. 'I loved that song. I think because it had children in it. Most of Maisie's disasters involve children. Or dogs.'

Richard nodded. 'There was a dog on the *Hindenburg*. Named Ulla. It survived the crash.'

She wasn't listening. 'Did she say what she wanted to talk to me about?'

'Near-death experiences.'

'Oh, dear, I hope she didn't go into V-fib and code again.'

'I don't think so. She was up and around. The nurse had a hard time keeping her in bed.'

'I should go see her,' Joanna said, looking up the stairs.

She crept up them and opened the door a crack. '... an Angel of Light, with golden light radiating from him like sparkling diamonds,' Mr Mandrake was saying.

She eased the door shut. 'Still there.'

'Good,' Richard said, 'because I haven't had a chance to convince you to come work with me on my project yet, and you haven't finished telling me what people experience during an NDE. And we haven't had dessert yet.' He reached in his lab coat pocket and pulled out a package of peanut M&M's.

She shook her head. 'No, thanks. They'd just make me thirsty.'

'Oh, in that case,' he said. He reached in his right pocket. 'Mocha Frappuccino,' he said, pulling out a bottle and setting it on the step, and then pulling out another. 'Or ...' he read the label, 'mandarin green tea with ginseng.'

'You're amazing,' Joanna said, taking the Frappuccino. 'What else do you have in there? Champagne? Lobster thermidor? All I've got in my pockets is a postcard and my tape recorder and ...' she fumbled in her cardigan pockets, '... my pager – oops, which I'd better turn off. I don't want it going off and giving away our position to Mr Mandrake,' she switched it off, 'and three used Kleenexes.' She opened the Frappuccino. 'You wouldn't have a straw, would you?'

He pulled a paper-wrapped one out of his pocket. 'You said there's a sensation of darkness,' he said, handing it to her. 'Not a tunnel?'

She unwrapped the straw. 'The majority of them call it a tunnel, but that isn't what they describe. For some it seems to be a spinning vortex, for others a passage or hallway or narrow room. Several of my subjects have described darkness collapsing in around them.'

Richard nodded. 'The visual cortex shutting down.' He jerked a thumb up toward the door. 'What about the life review?'

'Only about a quarter of my subjects describe having one,' Joanna said, sipping her Frappuccino, 'but the flashing of your life before your eyes is a well-documented phenomenon in accidents. Mr Mandrake says the NDE, or near-afterlife experience, as he prefers to call it –'

'He told me,' Richard said, grimacing.

'– has ten core elements: out-of-body experience, sound, tunnel, light, dead relatives, Angel of Light, a feeling of peace and love, a life review, the bestowing of universal knowledge, and a command to return. Most of my subjects experience three or four of the elements, usually the sound, the tunnel, the light, and a sense that people or angels are present, though when they're questioned, they have trouble describing them.'

'That sounds like temporal-lobe stimulation,' he said. 'It can cause a feeling of being in a holy presence without any accompanying visual image. It can also cause flashbacks and assorted sounds, including voices, but so can carbon dioxide buildup, and certain endorphins. That's part of the problem – there are several physical processes that could cause the phenomena described in an NDE.'

'And Mr Mandrake will claim that the effects produced in the laboratory aren't the same as the ones the NDEer is experiencing. In his book Mr Mandrake says the lights and tunnel vision produced during anoxia experiments are completely unlike the ones his patients describe.'

'And without an objective standard, there's no way to disprove that,' Richard said. 'NDE accounts are not only subjective, they're hearsay.'

'And vague,' Joanna said. 'So your project is hoping to develop an objective standard?'

'No,' he said. 'I've got one. Three years ago I was using the RIPT scan to map brain activity. You ask the subject to count to five, what his favorite color is, what roses smell like, and locate the areas of synaptical activity. And in the middle of the experiment, one of the subjects coded.'

'Because of the scan?'

'No. The scan itself's no more dangerous than a CAT scan. Less, because there's no radiation involved. It was a massive coronary. Completely unrelated.'

'Did he die?' Joanna asked, thinking of Greg Menotti.

'Nope. The crash cart team revived him, he had a bypass, and he was fine.'

'And he'd had an NDE?'

Richard nodded. 'And we had a picture of it.' He reached in his lab coat pocket and pulled out an accordion-folded strip of paper. 'It was three minutes before the crash cart could get there. The RIPT scan was running the entire time.'

He shifted so he was sitting next to her and unfolded the long strip of pictures. They showed the same black cross-section of the brain she'd seen in PET scan photos, with areas colored in blue and green and red, but in sharper detail than she'd seen in the PET scan photos, and with rows and rows of coded data along either side.

'Red indicates the greatest level of activity and blue the lowest,' Richard said. He pointed to an orangish-red area on the pictures. 'This is the temporal lobe,' he said, 'and this,' pointing to a smaller splash of red, 'is the hippocampus.' He handed her the strip. 'You're looking at an NDE.'

Joanna stared at the splotches of orange and yellow and green in fascination. 'So it is a real thing.'

'That depends on what you mean by real,' he said. 'See this area where there's no activity? That's the visual cortex, and this and this are sensory areas, where outside information is processed. The brain isn't getting any data from outside. The only stimuli are coming from deep inside the brain, which is bad news for Mandrake's theory. If the patient were actually seeing a bright light or an angel, the visual cortex here and here,' he pointed, 'would be activated.'

Joanna stared at the dark blue areas. 'What did he see?' she asked. 'The man who coded.'

'Mr O'Reirdon,' Richard said. 'A tunnel, a light, and several scenes from his childhood, all in succession.'

'The life review,' Joanna murmured.

'My guess is that those images are what account for the activation here,' he said, pointing at yellow-green spots in a succession of the pictures. 'These are random firing of long-term-memory synapses.'

'Did he see a shining figure in white?' Joanna asked.

He shook his head. 'He felt a holy presence that told him to come back, and then he was on the table.'

He indicated a picture near the end of the strip. 'This is where he came out of the NDE state. You can see the radically different pattern. Activity drops off sharply in the temporal lobe and increases in the visual and auditory cortexes.'

Joanna wasn't listening. She was thinking, they always talk about going and coming back, as if it were a real place. NDEers all talked about it that way. They said, 'I came back to the ambulance then,' or, 'I went through the tunnel,' or, 'The whole time I was there, I felt so peaceful and safe.' And Greg Menotti had said, 'Too far away for her to come,' as if he were no longer in the ER but had gone somewhere else. *Far*. 'That far country from whose bourne no traveller returns,' Shakespeare had called death.

'The greatest level of activity is here,' Richard was saying, 'next to the Sylvian fissure in the anterior temporal lobe, which indicates the cause may be temporal-lobe stimulation. Temporal-lobe epileptics report voices, a divine presence, euphoria, and auras.'

'A number of my subjects describe auras surrounding the figures in white,' Joanna said, 'and light radiating from them. Several of them, when they talked about the light, spread their hands out as if to indicate rays.' She demonstrated.

'This is exactly the kind of information I need,' Richard said. 'I want you to come work with me on this project.'

'But I don't know how to read RIPT scans.'

'You don't have to. That's my department. I need you to tell me exactly the kind of thing you've been telling me—'

The door banged open, and a nurse clattered down the steps. Joanna and Richard both made a dive for the landing, but it was too late. She'd already seen them.

'Oh,' the nurse said, looking surprised and then interested. 'I didn't know anything was going on in here.' She gave Richard a winsome smile.

'You can't get through this way,' Joanna said. 'They painted the steps.'

She arched a speculative eyebrow. 'And you two are waiting for them to dry?'

'Yes,' Richard said.

'Is Mr Mandrake still up there?' Joanna asked. 'In the hall?'

'No,' she said, still smiling at Richard.

'Are you sure?' Joanna asked.

'The only thing in the hall is the supper cart.'

'Supper cart?' Joanna said. 'Good Lord, how late is it?' She glanced at her watch. 'Oh, my gosh, it's after six.'

The eyebrow again. 'Lost all track of time, did you? Well, have fun,' she said, and waved at Richard. She clattered up the stairs and out.

'I had no idea it was this late,' Joanna said, wadding up the energy-bar wrapper and sticking it in her pocket. She stood, gathering up the Frappuccino bottle and the apple core.

Richard ran up two stairs and turned, blocking her way. 'You can't go yet. You haven't agreed to work with me on the project.'

'But I already interview everyone who comes into the hospital,' Joanna said. 'I'd be glad to share my transcripts with you—'

'I'm not talking about those people. I want you to interview *my* volunteers. You're an expert at, as you said, separating the wheat from the chaff. That's what I want you to do: interview my subjects, separate out their actual experiences so I can see how it relates to their RIPT scan maps.'

'Their RIPT scan maps?' Joanna said, bewildered. 'I don't understand.

Very few people code in the hospital, and even if they do, you'd only have four to six minutes to get your scanner down to the ER, and—'

'No, no,' he said. 'You don't understand. I'm not observing NDEs. I'm manufacturing them.'

4

'I beg your pardon, monsieur. I did not mean to do it.'
— MARIE ANTOINETTE, after she had accidentally stepped
on the executioner's foot while mounting to the guillotine

'You manufacture NDEs? You mean, like in *Flatliners*?' Joanna blurted out, and then thought, you shouldn't have said that. You're alone in a stairwell with him, and he's clearly a nutcase.

'*Flatliners*?' Richard said, horrified. 'You mean that movie where they stopped people's hearts and then revived them before they were brain dead? Of course not. Manufacturing's the wrong word. I should have said simulating.'

'Simulating,' Joanna said, still wary.

'Yes, using a psychoactive drug called dithetamine. Wait, let me start at the beginning. Mr O'Reirdon coded, and we got his NDE on tape, so to speak, but, as you can imagine, I wasn't eager to publish that fact. Mr Mandrake's book had just come out, he was on all the talk shows claiming the afterlife was real, and I could just imagine what would happen if I showed up with photographic proof.' He moved his spread hand through the air, as if displaying a headline: ' "Scientist Says Near-Death Experience Real." '

'No, no,' Joanna said, ' "Scientist Takes Photo of Heaven," with an obviously faked picture of the pearly gates superimposed on a diagram of the brain.'

'Exactly,' Richard said, 'and besides, it didn't have anything to do with the mapping project I was working on. So I documented the scans and Mr O'Reirdon's NDE account and stuck them in a drawer. Then, two years later, I was reading about a study showing the effects of psychoactive drugs on temporal-lobe activity. There was a photo of a PET scan of a patient on dithetamine, and I thought, that looks familiar, and got out Mr O'Reirdon's scans. They showed the same pattern.'

'Dithetamine?' Joanna said.

'It's a drug similar to PCP,' Richard said, fumbling in his lab coat pockets, and Joanna wondered if he was going to come up with a vial full of the drug.

He pulled out a roll of spearmint Life Savers. 'After-dinner mint?' he said, offering Joanna the roll. She took one.

'It doesn't produce PCP's psychotic side effects,' Richard said, peeling back the paper covering the Life Savers, 'or its high, but it does cause hallucinations, and when I called the doctor who conducted the study and asked him to describe them, he said his subjects reported floating above their bodies and then entering a dark tunnel with a light at the end of it and a radiant being standing in the light. And I knew I was on to something.'

To be able to find out what happened after death was something people had always been fascinated with, as witness the popularity of spiritualism and Mr Mandrake's books. Nobody'd ever figured out a scientific way to do it, though, unless you counted Harry Houdini, whose attempt to communicate with his wife from beyond the grave had failed, and Lavoisier.

Sentenced to die on the guillotine, the great French chemist had proposed an experiment to prove or disprove the hypothesis that the beheaded retained consciousness after death. Lavoisier had said he would blink his eyes for as long as he retained consciousness, and he had. He had blinked twelve times.

But it might have been nothing more than a reflex action, like that of chickens running around with their heads cut off, and there had been no way to verify what had happened. Until now. 'So your project involves giving patients dithetamine and putting them under a RIPT scan,' Joanna said. 'And then interviewing them?'

'Yes, and they're reporting tunnels and lights and angels, all right, but I don't know if they're the same kind of phenomena NDEers experience, or if it's a totally different type of hallucination.'

'And that's what you'd want me for,' Joanna asked, 'to interview your subjects and tell you if I thought their accounts matched those of people who'd had an NDE?'

Richard nodded. 'And I'd want you to obtain a detailed account of what they've experienced. Their subjective experience is an indicator of which brain areas are being stimulated and which neurotransmitters are involved. I really need your NDE interviewing expertise on the project,' Richard said. 'The accounts I've been able to get from my subjects haven't been very enlightening.'

'Then they must be NDEs,' Joanna said. 'Unless Mr Mandrake's been telling them what to say, NDEers are notoriously vague, and if you try to press them for details, you run the risk of influencing their testimony.'

'Exactly,' Richard said, 'which is why I need you. You know how to ask questions that aren't leading, and you have experience with NDEs. Except for the core elements, I have no way of knowing how the dithetamine hallucinations compare to real NDEs. And I think it would be useful to you, too,' he said earnestly. 'You'd have the opportunity to interview subjects in a controlled environment.'

And without worrying about Mr Mandrake getting to them first, she thought.

'So what do you say?' Richard asked.

'I don't know,' Joanna said, rubbing her temple tiredly. 'It sounds wonderful but I'll have to think about it.'

'Sure. Of course,' he said. 'It's a lot to lay on you all at once, and I know you've had a hard day.'

Yes, she thought, and saw Greg Menotti's body lying there on the examining table, pale and cold. And uninhabited. Gone. 'You don't have to decide now,' Richard was saying. 'You'll want to see the setup, read my grant proposal. You don't have to make a decision tonight.'

'Good,' Joanna said, suddenly worn out. 'Because I don't think I can.' She stood up. 'You're right, it has been a hard day, and I've still got some interviews to transcribe before I go home. And I've got to go see Maisie—'

'I understand,' he said. 'You think about it tonight, and tomorrow I'll show you the setup. Okay?'

'Okay. Ten o'clock,' she said, and started up the stairs. 'And thank you for dinner. Your lab coat's the best restaurant around.'

She went cautiously to the top of the stairs, opened the door a crack, and peered out. The hall was empty. 'The coast is clear,' she said, and they went out into the hall.

'I'll see you at ten o'clock,' he said and smiled at her. 'Or call me if you have any questions.' He pulled a business card out of his lab coat pocket. He's like one of those clowns, she thought, who keep pulling handkerchiefs and bicycle horns and rabbits out of their pockets.

'I think we'd make a great team,' he said.

'I want to think about it,' she said. 'I'll let you know tomorrow.'

He nodded. 'I really want you to work with me. I think we could accomplish great things.' He started down the hall and then turned back, looking bewildered. 'How do I get back to my office?'

She laughed. 'Elevator up to seventh, go across the walkway, and take the stairs outside Magnetic Imaging back down to sixth.'

He grinned. 'You see? I can't do without you. You've got to say you'll do the project.'

She shook her head, smiling, and turned to go over to the west wing to see Maisie. And ran straight into Maurice Mandrake.

'I couldn't get you through your pager,' he said sternly. 'I assumed you were interviewing a patient. Is that where you're going now?'

'No,' Joanna said, continuing to walk.

'I heard someone who'd coded was brought into the ER this afternoon,' he said. 'Where is he?'

That's the question, Joanna thought. Where is he? 'He died,' she said.

'Died?'

'Yes. Right after they brought him in.'

'Pity,' Mr Mandrake said. 'Heart attack victims have the most detailed NDEs. Where are you going now?'

He must think she had another NDEer stashed somewhere. 'Home,' she said and walked determinedly away from him.

He caught up with her. 'I spoke with Mrs Davenport this afternoon. She's remembered a number of additional details about her NDE. She remembers a golden staircase, and at the top of it, two angels with shining white wings.'

'Really?' Joanna said, continuing to walk. There was a staff elevator at the end of the hall if she could just get away from him for a moment, which didn't seem likely.

'Standing between the angels was her uncle Alvin, wearing his white naval uniform,' Mr Mandrake said, 'which proves that the experience was real. Mrs Davenport had no way of knowing what he was wearing when he was killed at Guadalcanal.'

Except for family snapshots and every World War II movie ever made, Joanna thought, wondering whether Mr Mandrake intended to follow her all the way to wherever she was going. Apparently he was, which meant she didn't dare go see Maisie. Maisie could hold her own against Mr Mandrake, but he didn't know she was back in the hospital, and Joanna wanted to keep it that way.

'I'm anxious to tell Dr Wright about Mrs Davenport's experience,' he said. 'One of the nurses told me he is attempting to reproduce the NAE in the laboratory, which is, of course, impossible. Any number of researchers have tried, using sensory deprivation and drugs and sonic vibrations, but none of them have been able to reproduce the NAE because it is spiritual, not physical.'

Joanna looked down the hall at two women coming their way, hoping it was someone she knew, but they were clearly visitors. One of them was carrying a bouquet of tulips.

'The NAE cannot be explained by anoxia, endorphins, or randomly firing synapses, as I proved in my book, *The Light at the End of the Tunnel*,' Mr Mandrake said as they passed the visitors. 'The only explanation is that they have actually been to the Other Side. In my new book, I explore the many messages that—'

'Excuse me,' a voice from behind them said. It was the woman with the tulips. 'I couldn't help overhearing. You're Maurice Mandrake, aren't you? I just wanted to tell you—'

Joanna didn't hesitate. She said, 'I'll leave you two,' and darted around the corner to the stairs.

'I've read your book, and it gave me so much hope,' she heard the woman say as she opened the door. She darted down to second, sprinted through Radiology across the walkway to the west wing, and up the stairs to the fourth floor.

Maisie wasn't there. She must have been taken down for tests, Joanna thought, peeking in 456. The bed was unmade, the sheets pushed back where Maisie had gotten out of them. The TV was on, and on the screen an assortment of orphans was dancing up and down stairs. *Annie*.

Joanna started down to the nurses' station to find out when she'd be back, and then saw Maisie's mother coming down the hall, smiling. 'Were you looking for Maisie, Dr Lander?' she asked. 'She's down having an echocardiogram.'

'I just dropped by to see her, Mrs Nellis,' Joanna said. 'Would you tell her I'll come see her tomorrow?'

'I don't know if she'll be here tomorrow,' Mrs Nellis said. 'She's just in for follow-up tests. Dr Murrow will probably let her go home as soon as they're finished.'

'Oh?' Joanna said. 'How's she doing?'

'Really well,' Mrs Nellis said enthusiastically. 'This new antiarrhythmia drug's working wonderfully, much better than the one she was on before. I've seen enormous improvement. I think she may even be able to start back to school soon.'

'That's wonderful,' Joanna said. 'I'll miss her, but I'm glad she's doing so well. Tell her I'll come by and see her early tomorrow morning before she goes home.'

'I will,' Mrs Nellis said. She looked at her watch. 'I'd better get going. I need to go pick up something to eat, and I want to be here when Maisie gets back.' She hurried off toward the elevators.

I hope she's not counting on the cafeteria, Joanna thought, and started toward the stairs.

'Don't leave!' a voice shouted. She turned. It was Maisie, gesturing wildly from a wheelchair being pushed by a nurse. Joanna walked over to them.

'See?' Maisie was saying triumphantly to the nurse. 'I told you she always comes to see me as soon as she knows I'm here.' She turned to Joanna. 'Did Dr Wright tell you I had something to talk to you about?'

'Yes,' Joanna said, and to the nurse, 'I can take her back to her room.' The nurse shook her head. 'I've got to hook her up to the monitors, and see that she gets in bed and rests,' she said mock-fiercely to Maisie.

'I will,' Maisie said, 'only I've got to tell Joanna something first. About NDEs. I was reading this book about the *Hindenburg*,' she told Joanna as she was pushed to her room. 'It's really neat. Did you know they had a piano? Up in a balloon?'

The nurse pushed the wheelchair into the room and over next to the bed. 'It was an aluminum piano, but still!' Maisie said, bounding out of the wheelchair before the nurse could get the footrests flipped up. She dug in the drawer of the stand next to her bed. 'I bet it fell on somebody when the *Hindenburg* blew up.'

I'll bet it did, Joanna thought.

'Maisie,' the nurse said, holding the monitor wires and the tube of gel to attach the electrodes.

'Why don't you get into bed?' Joanna suggested, 'and I'll look for the book.'

'Not the book,' Maisie said, still digging. 'The paper. The piano weighed 397 pounds.'

'Maisie,' the nurse said firmly.

'Did you know there was a reporter there?' she said, matter-of-factly yanking her hospital gown up so the nurse could attach electrodes to her flat little-girl chest. 'He reported the whole thing. "Oh, this is terrible!" Ow! That's cold! "Oh, the humanity."'

She chattered on while the nurse checked the monitor, adjusted dials, and checked the readouts. It had nothing to do with NDEs, but Joanna hadn't really expected it to. Maisie had spent the better part of three years in hospitals – she knew exactly how to distract nurses, put off unpleasant procedures, and, above all, get people to stay and keep her company.

'All right, now don't get out of bed,' the nurse ordered. 'See that she rests,' she said to Joanna and went out.

'You heard what she said,' Joanna said, standing up. 'How about if I come see you tomorrow morning?'

'No,' Maisie said. 'You can't go yet. I haven't told you about the NDE thing yet. You know how I didn't see anything that time I almost died, and Mr Mandrake said I did, that everybody sees a tunnel and an angel. Well, they don't. This guy, he worked on the *Hindenburg*, and he was up inside the balloon part when it blew up, and everybody else fell off, but he didn't. He hung on to the metal struts and it was really hot. His hands got all burned into these black claws,' she demonstrated, 'and he wanted to let go, but he didn't. He squinched his eyes shut' – she demonstrated – 'and he saw all these different things.'

She unfolded the paper and handed it to Joanna. It was a Xerox of a page out of a book. 'I don't know if it was a real near-death experience or not because, if he was dead, he would have let go, wouldn't he? But he saw stuff like in one. Snow and a train and a whale flipping its tail up out of the ocean.'

She leaned forward, careful not to unhook her electrodes, and handed the folded paper to Joanna. 'I like the part the best when he's in the birdcage and he has to hang on with his feet like on a trapeze so he won't fall into the fire.'

Joanna unfolded the paper and read the account of what the crewman had seen: glittering white fields and the whale Maisie had described and then the sensation of a train going by. He had been surprised that it didn't stop, he had decided it must be an express, but that couldn't be right. There was no express to Bregenz.

Joanna looked up. 'I think you're right, Maisie,' she said. 'I think this was a near-death vision.'

'I know,' Maisie said. 'I figured it was when I read about him seeing the snow, because it's white like the light everybody says they see. Did you get to the part where the snow turns into flowers?'

'No,' Joanna said and began reading again. He had seen his grandmother, sitting by the fire, and then himself as a bird in a cage being thrown into it, and then the white fields again, but not of snow, of apple blossoms in fields stretching beneath him in endless heavenly meadows.

'Well, what do you think?' Maisie said impatiently.

I wish he were one of my interview subjects, Joanna thought. His account was full of details and, except for the mention of the heavenly meadows, devoid of the standard religious imagery and tunnels and brilliantly white lights. The kind of NDE account she dreamed of and hardly ever got.

'I think he was brave to keep hanging on, don't you?' Maisie said. 'With his hands hurting so bad and everything.'

'Yes,' Joanna said. 'Can I keep this?'

'That's what I made Nurse Barbara copy it for, so you could use it in your research.'

'Thank you,' Joanna said, and folded the paper up again.

'I don't think I could've,' Maisie said thoughtfully. 'I think I would've probably let go.'

Joanna stopped in the act of sticking the paper in her pocket. 'I'll bet you would've hung on,' she said.

Maisie looked seriously at her for a long minute, and then said, 'Did I help you with your research?'

'You did,' Joanna said. 'You can be my research assistant anytime.'

'I'm going to look for other ones,' she said. 'I'll bet lots of people in disasters had them, like during earthquakes and stuff.'

I'll bet they did, Joanna thought.

'I'll bet the people at Mount St Helens *really* had them.' She shoved the covers back and started to get out of bed.

'Not so fast,' Joanna said. 'You're all hooked up. You can only be my research assistant if you do what the nurses tell you. I mean it. You're supposed to be resting.'

'I was just getting my earthquake book,' Maisie said. 'It's on the windowsill. I can rest and read at the same time.'

I'll bet, Joanna thought, getting the book for her. 'You can read for fifteen minutes, that's it.'

'I promise,' Maisie said, already opening the book. 'I'll page you when I find some more.'

Joanna nodded. 'I'll see you later, kiddo,' she said, giving Maisie's foot under the covers a squeeze, and started for the door.

'Don't leave!' Maisie said, and when Joanna turned around, 'I have to show you this picture of the piano.'

'Okay. One picture,' Joanna said, 'and then I *have* to go.'

Three pictures of the piano and the smoking skeleton-like wreck of the *Hindenburg* later she finally succeeded in getting away from Maisie and back to her office. And at some point along the way, her second wind deserted her, and she felt utterly exhausted.

Too exhausted to water her Swedish ivy or listen to her voice messages, even though her answering machine was blinking in the double-time that meant it was full. She laid her turned-off pager on the desk, got her coat and gloves, and locked the office behind her.

'Oh, good, you haven't left yet,' Vielle said. Joanna turned around. Vielle was coming down the hall toward her, still in her dark blue scrubs and surgical cap.

'What are you doing up here?' Joanna asked. 'Please tell me it's not another NDE.'

'No, all quiet on the western front,' she said, pulling her surgical cap off and shaking out the tangle of narrow black braids. 'I came up to see if Dr Right ever found you, and to ask you what movies you wanted me to rent for Dish Night Thursday.'

Dish Night was their weekly movie rental night. 'I don't know,' Joanna said wearily. 'Nothing with dying in it.'

'I know,' Vielle said. 'I never got a chance to talk to you after – we worked on him for another twenty minutes, but it was no use. He was gone.'

Gone, Joanna thought. NDEers weren't the only ones who talked about going and coming back in regard to dying. Doctors and nurses did, too. The patient passed away. He passed over. He left a wife and two children. He passed on. Joanna's mother had told people her father 'slipped away,' and the minister at her mother's funeral had spoken of 'the dear departed' and 'those who have gone before us.' Gone where?

'It's always bad when they go like that, with no warning,' Vielle said, 'especially when they're as young as he was. I wanted to make sure you were okay.'

'I'm okay,' Joanna said. 'It's just – what do you think he meant, "It's too far for her to come"?'

'He was pretty far gone when his girlfriend arrived,' Vielle said. 'I don't think he realized she was there.'

No, Joanna thought, that wasn't it. 'He kept saying "fifty-eight." Why would he say that?'

Vielle shrugged. 'Who knows? Maybe he was echoing what the nurses were saying. His blood pressure was eighty over fifty.'

It was seventy over fifty, Joanna thought. 'Did the cell phone number of his girlfriend have a fifty-eight in it?'

'I don't remember. By the way, did Dr Right ever find you? Because if he didn't, I think you should stop trying to avoid him. I ran into Louisa Krepke on my way up here, and she said he's a neurologist, absolutely gorgeous, and single.'

'He found me,' Joanna said. 'He wants me to work on a research project with him. Studying NDEs.'

'And –?'

'And I don't know,' Joanna said wearily.

'He isn't cute? Louisa said he had blond hair and blue eyes.'

'No, he's cute. He—'

'Oh, no, please don't tell me he's one of those near-death nutcases.'

'He's not a nutcase,' Joanna said. 'He thinks NDEs are the side effect of a neurochemical survival mechanism. He's found a way to simulate them. He wants me to work with him, interviewing his subjects.'

'And you said yes, didn't you?'

Joanna shook her head. 'I said I'd think about it, but I don't know.'

'He doesn't want *you* to do this simulation stuff, does he?'

'No. All he wants me to do is consult, interview subjects, and tell him if their experiences match the NDE core experience.'

'So what's the problem?'

'I don't know … I'm so far behind in my own work. I have dozens of interviews I haven't transcribed. If I take on this project, when will I have time for my own NDE subjects?'

'Like Mrs Davenport, you mean?' Vielle said. 'You're right. Gorgeous guy, legit project, no Maurice Mandrake, no Mrs Davenport. Definitely sounds like a bad deal to me.'

'I know. You're right,' Joanna said, sighing. 'It sounds like a great project.'

It did. A chance to interview patients Mr Mandrake hadn't contaminated and to talk to them immediately after their experience. She almost never got the chance to do that. A patient ill enough to code was nearly always too ill to be interviewed right away, and the greater the gap, the more confabulation there was. Also, these would be subjects who were aware they were hallucinating. They should be much better interview subjects. So why wasn't she leaping at the chance?

Because it isn't really about NDEs, she thought. Dr Wright saw the NDE as a mere side effect, a – what had he said? – 'an indicator of which areas of the brain are being stimulated and which neurotransmitters are involved.'

It's more than that, Joanna thought. They're seeing something, experiencing something, and it's important. She felt sometimes, like this afternoon with Greg Menotti, or with Coma Carl, that they were speaking directly to her, trying to communicate something about what was happening to them, about dying, and that it was her duty to decipher what it was. But how could she explain that to Vielle or to Dr Wright, without sounding like one of Maurice Mandrake's nutcases?

'I told him I'd think about it,' Joanna said evasively. 'In the meantime, would you do something for me, Vielle? Would you check Greg Menotti's records and see if his girlfriend's phone number had a fifty-eight in it, or if there was some other number he might have been talking about, his own phone number or his Social Security number or something?'

Vielle said, 'ER records are—'

'Confidential. I know. I don't want to know what the number is, I just want to know if there was some reason he kept saying "fifty-eight."'

'Okay, but I doubt if it's anything,' Vielle said. 'He was probably trying to say, "I can't have had a heart attack. I did fifty-eight push-ups this morning."' She took Joanna's arm. 'I think you should do the project. What's the worst that could happen? He sees what a great interviewer you are, falls madly in love with you, you get married, have ten kids, and win the Nobel Prize. You know what I think? I think you're afraid.'

'Afraid?' Joanna echoed.

Vielle nodded. 'I think you like Dr Right, but you're afraid to take a chance. You're always telling me to take risks, and here you are, turning down a terrific opportunity.'

'I do not tell you to take risks,' Joanna said. 'I try to get you to avoid risks. It is the front down there in the ER, and if you don't transfer out—'

The elevator dinged. 'Saved by the bell,' Vielle said and stepped quickly into the elevator. 'This could be the chance of a lifetime. Take it,' she said. 'See you Thursday night. Nothing with dying in it. And remember,' she burst into song, '"You've got a lot of living to do!"'

'And no musicals,' Joanna said. 'Or dopey romances,' she added as the door closed on Vielle. Joanna pressed the 'up' button, shaking her head. Love, marriage, children, the Nobel Prize.

And then what? Boating on the lake? An Angel of Light? Wailing and gnashing of teeth? Or nothing at all? The brain cells started to die within moments of death. By the end of four to six minutes the damage was irreversible, and people brought back from death after that didn't talk about tunnels and life reviews. They didn't talk at all. Or feed themselves, or respond to light, or register any cortical activity at all on Richard's RIPT scans. Brain death.

But if the dying were facing annihilation, why didn't they say, 'It's over!' or, 'I'm shutting down'? Why didn't they say, like the witch in *The Wizard of Oz*, 'I'm melting, I'm melting'? Why did they say, 'It's beautiful over there,' and, 'I'm coming, Mother!' and, 'She's too far away. She'll never get here in time'? Why did they say 'placket' and 'fifty-eight'?

The elevator opened on fifth, and she walked across the walkway to the elevators on the other side. The Other Side. She wondered if this was how Mr Mandrake envisioned the NDE, as a walkway like this. It was obvious he thought of the Other Side as a Hallmark card version of this side, all angels and hugs and wishful thinking: everything will be all right, all will be forgiven, you won't be alone.

Whatever death is, Joanna thought, taking the elevator down to the parking lot, whether it's annihilation or afterlife, it's not what Mr Mandrake thinks it is.

She pushed open the door to the outside. It was still snowing. The cars in the parking lot were covered, and flakes drifted goldenly, silently down in the light from the sodium streetlights. She lifted her face to the falling snow and stood there, watching it.

And how about Dr Wright? Was dying what he thought it was – temporal lobe stimulation and a random flickering of synapses before they went out?

She turned and looked up at the east wing, where Coma Carl lay boating on the lake. I'm going to tell Dr Wright no, she thought, and started out to her car.

She should have worn boots this morning. She slipped on the slick snow, and snow filled her shoes, soaking her feet. Her car was completely covered. She swiped at the side window with her bare hand, hoping against hope it was just snow and not ice. No such luck. She unlocked the car, threw her bag in the backseat, and began rummaging for the scraper.

'Joanna?' a woman's voice said behind her.

Joanna backed out of the car and turned to face her. It was Barbara from Peds.

'I've got a message from Maisie Nellis,' Barbara said. 'She said to tell you she's back in and that she has something important to tell you.'

'I know,' Joanna said. 'I've already been up to see her. I understand she's doing really well.'

'Who told you that?'

'Her mother. She said Maisie was just in for tests, and the new antiarrhythmia drug was working wonders. It isn't?'

Barbara shook her head. 'She *is* in for tests, but it's because Dr Murrow thinks there's a lot more damage than showed up on the heart cath. He's trying to decide whether to put her on the transplant list or not.'

'Does her mother know that?'

'That depends on what you mean by knowing. You've heard of being in denial, haven't you? Well, Maisie's mother is Cleopatra, the Queen of Denial. And positive thinking. All Maisie has to do is rest and think happy thoughts, and she'll be up and around in no time. How did you get permission from her to interview Maisie about her NDE? She doesn't even let us use the term *heart condition*, let alone *death*.'

'I didn't. Her ex-husband was the one who signed the release,' Joanna said. 'A heart transplant? What are Maisie's chances?'

'Of surviving a transplant? Pretty good. Mercy's got a seventy-five percent survival rate, and the rejection stats keep improving all the time. The chances of keeping her alive till a nine-year-old's heart becomes available? Not nearly as good. Especially when they haven't found a way of controlling the atrial fib. She's already coded once,' she said. 'But you know that.'

Joanna nodded.

'Well, anyway, I just wanted you to know she was back in. She loves it when you visit her. God, it's cold out here! My feet are freezing!' she said and headed off toward her Honda.

Joanna found the scraper and started in on the front windshield. The wait for a heart was frequently over a year, even if you were moved to the top of the list, a year during which the damaged heart continued to deteriorate, dragging the lungs and the kidneys and the chances of survival down with it.

And that was for an adult heart. The wait for children was even longer, unless you were lucky. And lucky meant a child drowned in a swimming pool or killed in a car accident or frozen to death in a blizzard. Even then the heart had to be undamaged. And healthy. And a match. And the patient had to be still alive when it got there. Had to have not gone into V-fib again and died.

'If we can figure out how the dying process works,' Richard had said, 'that knowledge could eventually be used to revive patients who've coded.'

Joanna moved to the back windshield and began brushing snow off the window. Like the elderly woman she had seen from Coma Carl's window. Heart attack weather, Vielle had said. Dying weather. Disaster weather.

She went back into the hospital and asked the volunteer at the front desk if she could borrow the phone. She asked for Dr Wright's extension.

He wasn't there. 'Leave a message at the tone,' the message said. It beeped.

'All right,' Joanna said to the answering machine. 'I'll do it. I'll work with you on your project.'

5

'CQD CQD SOS SOS CQD SOS. Come at once. We have struck
a berg. CQD OM. Position 41° 40' N, 50° 14' W. CQD SOS.'
– Wireless message sent by the *Titanic* to the *Carpathia*

Richard checked his answering machine as soon as he got to work the next
morning to see if Joanna had called. 'You have twelve messages,' it said
reprovingly. Which was what you got for spending all day running around
the hospital looking for someone.

He started going through the messages, clicking to the next one as soon
as the caller had identified himself. Mrs Bendix, Mrs Brightman. 'I just
wanted to welcome you to Mercy General,' she said in an ancient, quavery
voice, 'and to tell you how delighted I am that you are researching near-death
experiences, or, rather, near-*life* experiences, for I feel sure your experiments
will convince you that what these patients are witnessing is the life and the
loved ones we will find again on the other side of the grave. Are you aware
that Maurice Mandrake is also at Mercy General? I presume you have read
The Light at the End of the Tunnel?'

'Oh, yes,' Richard said to the machine.

'We're extremely fortunate to have him here,' Mrs Brightman's message
continued. 'I feel sure you two will have a great deal to say to each other.'

'Not if there's a stairway handy,' he said and hit 'next message.' A Mr Edelman
from the National Association of Paranormal Experiences, Mr Wojakowski.

'Just double-checking about tomorrow,' Mr Wojakowski said. 'Tried to call
you before, but couldn't get through. Reminds me of these telephones we had
on the *Yorktown* for sending messages up to the bridge. You had to wind 'em
up with a crank kinda deal, and—'

Mr Wojakowski, once started on the *Yorktown*, could go on forever. Richard hit 'next message.' The grants office, telling him there was a form he hadn't
turned in. 'Wright?' a man's voice said. Peter Davis, his roommate when they
were interns. He never bothered to identify himself. 'I suppose you've heard,'
Davis said. 'I can't believe it about Fox, can you? This isn't some kind of virus,
is it? If so, you'd better get vaccinated. Or at least call and warn me before you
hit the star. Call me.'

He wondered what that was all about. The only Fox he knew was R. John
Foxx, a neuropsychologist who'd been conducting research on anoxia as the
cause of near-death experiences. Richard hit 'next message' again.

Someone from the International Paranormal Society. Mr Wojakowski again. 'Hiya, Doc. Hadn't heard from you, so I thought I'd try again. Wanted to make sure it's two o'clock tomorrow. Or fourteen bells, as we used to say on the *Yorktown*.'

Amelia Tanaka, saying, 'I may be a few minutes late, Dr Wright. I've got an anatomy exam, and last time it took the whole two hours. I'll be there as soon as I can.' Mr Suarez, wanting to reschedule his session for tomorrow. Davis again, even more incomprehensible than before. 'Forgot to tell you where. Seventeen. Under phantom,' followed by an unrecognizable tuneless humming. Housekeeping.

'Dr Wright?' Joanna's voice said. He leaned alertly toward the machine. 'This is Joanna Lander. A— Your machine is full,' the answering machine said.

'*No,*' Richard said. Damn Davis. Damn Mr Wojakowski, with his endless reminiscences of the *Yorktown*. The one message he really needed to hear –

He hit 'repeat' and played the message again. 'Dr Wright? This is Joanna Lander. A—' Was that sound at the end 'I,' as in, 'I'd love to work with you on your project.' Or a short 'a,' as in, 'After due consideration, I've decided to decline your offer'?

He listened to it again. 'Ah,' he decided. As in, 'Ah, forget it'? Or, 'All my life I've wanted a chance at a project like this'? There was no way to tell. He'd have to wait until ten o'clock and see if she showed up. Or try and locate her.

Or not, considering this hospital. That was all he needed, for her to be here waiting and looking at her watch, while he tried to find his way back from the west wing. He picked up the phone and paged her, just on the chance she had her pager switched on, and then hit 'repeat' again. There must have been something in her tone that would be a clue as to whether—

'All your messages have been erased,' the machine said. No! He dived at the machine, hit 'play.'

'You have zero messages.'

Richard grabbed for a prescription pad. 'Wojakowski,' he scribbled. 'Cartwright Chemical, Davis –' Who else? he thought, trying to reconstruct the messages in his mind. Mrs Brightman, and then somebody from Northwestern. Geneva Carlson? The phone rang. Richard snatched it up, hoping it was Joanna. 'Hello?'

'So, have you seen it?' Davis said.

'Seen what, Davis?'

'The star!'

'What star? You call and leave an undecipherable message—'

'Undecipherable?' Davis said, sounding offended. 'It was perfectly clear. I even told you what page the article was on.'

Not a star. The *Star*, the tabloid newspaper. 'What was the article about?' Richard asked.

'Foxx! He's gone nutcase and announced he's proved there's life after death. Wait a minute, I've got it here, let me read it to you ...' There was a thunking sound as he dropped the phone, and a rattle of paper. '"Dr R. John Foxx, a respected scientist in the field of near-death research, said, 'When I began my research into near-death experiences, I was convinced they were hallucinations caused by oxygen deprivation, but after exhaustive research, I've concluded they are a preview of the afterlife. Heaven is real. God is real. I have spoken to Him.'"'

'Oh, my God,' Richard murmured.

'He's leaving medicine to open the Eternal Life Institute,' Davis said. 'So, my question is, is this something that happens to everybody who does NDE research? I mean, first Seagal claims he's located the soul in the temporal lobe and has photos of it leaving the body, and now Foxx.'

'Seagal was always crazy,' Richard said.

'But Foxx wasn't,' Davis said. 'What if it's some kind of virus that infects everybody who studies NDEs and makes them go wacko? How do I know you won't suddenly announce that a picture of the Virgin Mary appeared to you on the RIPT scan screen?'

'Trust me, I won't.'

'Well, if you do,' Davis said, 'call me first, before you call the *Star*. I've always wanted to be that friend they interview, the one who says, "No, I never noticed anything unusual about him. He was always quiet, well mannered, something of a loner." Speaking of which, any babes on the horizon?'

'No,' Richard said, thinking of Joanna. He glanced at the clock on the wall. It was after ten. Whatever the cut-off 'A—' in her message had meant, it wasn't acceptance. She'd probably read the *Star* and decided working with anybody on near-death research was too risky. It was too bad. He had really looked forward to working with her. I should have offered her something more substantial than an energy bar, he thought.

'No cute little nurses, huh?' Davis said. 'That's because you're in the wrong specialty. I got 'em lined up out the door.' Knowing Davis, he probably did. 'Of course, there's another explanation.'

'For having women lined up out the door?' Richard said.

'No,' Davis said, 'for everybody associated with NDE research suddenly becoming true believers. Maybe it's all true, the tunnel and heaven and the soul, and there really *is* an afterlife.' He began humming again, the same weird nontune as he had hummed on the answering machine.

'What *is* that ungodly sound supposed to be? *The Twilight Zone*?'

Davis snorted. 'It's the theme from *The X-Files*. It's a possibility, you know.

The NDEers are right, and when we die we end up surrounded by Precious Moments figurines. In which case, I for one am not going.'

'Me neither,' Richard said, laughing.

'And I'd appreciate you calling and warning me so I can get started on immortality research right away.'

'I will,' Richard promised. There was a knock on the door. Richard looked up eagerly. 'Gotta go,' he said, hung up, and hurried across the lab to open the door.

'Ah, Dr Wright,' Mr Mandrake said, coming into the lab, 'I was hoping you'd be here. We didn't have a chance to talk yesterday.'

Richard resisted the impulse to look wildly around for an exit. 'I'm afraid now isn't a good time—'

Mr Mandrake walked over to the RIPT scan. 'Is this what you hope to capture the NAE with?' he asked, peering underneath its arch-shaped dome. 'You won't be able to, you know. The NAE can't be photographed.'

Like ghosts? Richard thought. And UFOs?

'Any number of researchers have already tried to find a physical cause that can explain the NAE, you know,' he said. 'Carbon-dioxide buildup, endorphins, random firing of synapses.' He gave the RIPT scan a dismissive tap and walked over to the EEG. 'There are a number of NAE phenomena that science cannot explain.'

Name one, Richard thought.

'How do you explain the fact that every person who has experienced the NAE says that it was not a dream, that it really happened?'

Subjective experience is hardly proof of anything, Richard thought.

'And how could endorphins or CO_2 buildup confer knowledge on the subject experiencing the NAE?' Mr Mandrake asked. 'Knowledge that scientists agree the subject could not have attained by normal means?'

What scientists? Richard thought. Dr Foxx? Dr Seagal?

'A number of my subjects have reported seeing a relative on the Other Side whom they thought was alive and being surprised to see them there,' Mandrake said. 'When the subjects returned, they telephoned family members and were informed that the relative had just died. In each of these cases, there was no way the subject could have known about the relative's death in advance.'

'Do you have a list of their names?' Richard asked.

'It would be highly unprofessional for me to release the names of the subjects of my studies,' Mr Mandrake said disapprovingly, 'but there have been numerous documented instances of the phenomenon.'

'Really?' Richard said. 'In which journals?'

'The scientific establishment is unfortunately extremely narrow-minded when it comes to publishing the results of near-death research,' Mr Mandrake said stiffly. 'Except for a few brave pioneers like Dr Seagal and Dr Lander, they cannot see the greater realities which lie around them.'

At the mention of Joanna's name, Richard glanced at the clock again. Ten-thirty.

' "There are more things in heaven and earth, Horatio, than are dreamt of in your philosophy," ' Mr Mandrake said. 'There have also been numerous cases of returned NAEers displaying paranormal gifts. One of my subjects—'

'This really isn't a good time,' Richard said. 'I have a phone call I need to make, so if you'll excuse me—' He picked up the phone.

'Of course,' Mr Mandrake said. 'I must go see Mrs Davenport. I'll be eager to discuss your findings with you.'

He exited. Richard started to put the phone down and then picked it up again and began punching in Amelia Tanaka's number as Mr Mandrake reappeared. 'I wanted you to have a copy of *The Light at the End of the Tunnel*,' he said, reaching for Richard's pen. 'No, no, don't let me interrupt your call.' He waved to Richard to keep dialing. 'It's Wright with a *W* isn't it?'

'Yes,' Richard said, punching in the rest of the number. It began to ring. Mandrake scrawled something on the title page. 'Ms Tanaka?' Richard said into the phone. 'This is Dr Wright.'

Mr Mandrake shut the book and handed it to Richard. 'I think you'll find it useful,' he said and started out.

'Just returning your call, Ms Tanaka,' Richard said to the continued ringing. 'Yes. Eleven o'clock.' And I hope you're passing your anatomy exam, he thought. 'Right. No, that won't be a problem.'

Mr Mandrake went out, shutting the door behind him. Richard hung up the phone and looked at the clock. Ten forty-five. Joanna definitely wasn't coming.

He opened the book to see what Mandrake had written. 'To aid you in your journey,' it read, 'into death and beyond.' Is that supposed to be a threat? Richard wondered.

There was a knock on the door. No doubt Mandrake, back to tell him some other reason CO_2 buildup couldn't cause an NDE. He snatched up the phone again and called, 'Yes, come in.'

Joanna opened the door. 'I'm sorry I'm late – oh, you're on the phone.'

'No, I'm not,' he said and hung up. 'Come in, come in.'

'I *am* sorry I'm late,' she said. 'Did you get my message?'

'No.'

'Oh, well, I left you a message, but I fully intended to be here at ten to talk to you.' She's not going to do it, he thought. She just came to tell me she's not interested. 'But I had to go see Maisie, and I had trouble getting away from her.' She shook her head, smiling. 'As usual.'

'She still talking about the *Hindenburg*?' he asked. It was only delaying the inevitable, but maybe if they talked, she'd change her mind.

She nodded. 'Did you know a number of children who'd come to the airfield to meet their parents saw them plunge burning to their deaths?'

'I was not aware of that,' Richard said. 'She really goes for the gory details, doesn't she? Is that what she wanted to see you about?'

'No,' Joanna said. 'She found me an account of an NDE connected to the *Hindenburg*, and I needed to ask her about it. I wanted to know if the account of it was secondhand and if it was written at the time or sometime after.'

'Did Maisie know?'

She shook her head. 'Her books didn't say anything about the circumstances, or the name of the crewman, but she said she'd try to find out.'

'And this NDE was a crewman on the *Hindenburg*? He coded during the crash and had an NDE?'

'No, a vision,' Joanna said. 'He had it while he was hanging on to the metal framework up inside the burning Zeppelin.'

'But he saw a tunnel and angels?'

'No, a whale and a birdcage. It doesn't have any of the standard imagery, but that's why it's interesting. It predates Moody and company, so the imagery hasn't been contaminated, and yet there are definite correspondences to the typical NDE. He hears a sound – the scream of tearing metal – and sees his grandmother and a dazzling white light that he interprets as snowfields. And there are a number of images that parallel the life review. It could be really useful, but I don't want to get my hopes up until I know how and when he gave his account. It could all be confabulation, especially if he gave the account several weeks or months after the crash.

'Anyway,' she said, pushing her glasses up on her nose, 'getting away from Maisie took a while, and then, as I was on my way here, I saw Mr Mandrake headed for your lab.'

And you ducked into the nearest stairway, Richard thought. 'What did he want?' she asked. 'Did he try and pump you about your project?'

'No. He was more interested in telling me why it was doomed to fail.'

'Which speech was it? His "Mere science cannot explain the NAE" speech, his "If it looks real, that proves it's real" rant, or the "more things in heaven and earth" speech?'

'All of the above,' Richard said. 'He told me there were documented cases of people receiving knowledge during NDEs they couldn't have known otherwise.'

She nodded. 'One of the people waiting to greet them is Aunt Ethel, and when they're revived they call Minnesota and discover that, in fact, Aunt Ethel was just killed in a car accident.'

'So there *are* cases?'

She shook her head. 'Those stories have been around since the days of the Victorian spiritualists, but there's no documentation. They're all either third-hand – somebody knew somebody who told him it had happened to his Aunt Ethel – or the whole thing was conveniently reported *after* the call from Minnesota reporting the death, and last names are always conveniently left out 'for the privacy of the subjects,' so there's no way to verify or disprove the story. Plus, no one ever bothers to report seeing someone on the Other Side who later turns out *not* to be dead. Did Mr Mandrake mention W. T. Stead?'

'No. Who's that?'

'A famous spiritualist and psychic who wasn't all that psychic, as it turned out, or he'd never have booked passage on the *Titanic*. Every other psychic and medium in the business later claimed they'd had visions or premonitions of his death, but not one of them thought to mention it until after the sinking hit the front page, with Stead listed among the lost. And the last person who spoke to Stead reported that when he was told the ship had hit an iceberg, he said, "I suppose it's nothing much."' She frowned. 'Mr Mandrake didn't ask you about your project?'

'He looked at the RIPT scan and the EEG, but he didn't ask any questions. Why? Should he have?'

She was still frowning. 'He spends half his time snooping around trying to find out who my patients are so he can get to them first. He didn't ask you *anything*?'

'No. When he first came in, he said he wanted to discuss the project, but then he launched into how physical explanations couldn't account for the NDE, and from there to the narrow-mindedness of the scientific establishment. Except for brave pioneers like you and Dr Seagal.'

'You didn't tell him we were going to be working together, did you?' Joanna asked.

'No,' he said, trying not to show the sudden uprush of delight he felt. 'Are we?'

'Yes,' she said. 'Didn't you get my message?'

'No, my answering machine—'

'Oh, well, I said yes, I'd like to work with you on your project. Actually, I think I said, "All right, I'll do it," or something equally cryptic. I left the message last night.'

Not, 'Ah, forget it.' 'All right.' 'Great,' he said, and grinned. 'I'm delighted. It's going to be great working together.'

'I want to keep interviewing patients who come into the hospital, too,' she said, 'unless you think that's a bad idea.'

'No, the more data we have on actual NDEs, the more we'll be able to tell how ours compare. I only schedule one or two sessions a day, because of the time it takes to analyze the scans. I'm sure we can work around your schedule.'

'I'd appreciate that.'

'Great,' he said. 'I'll talk to the grants office this afternoon about making it official.'

She nodded. 'Great. Only don't tell Mr Mandrake. The longer we can keep it from him, the less time I'll have to spend trying to avoid him. So,' she smiled at him, 'you want to show me the setup?'

'I'll do better than that. I've got one of my volunteers coming in in about,' he glanced at the clock. A quarter past eleven. 'Any time now. In the meantime,' he led her over to the console, 'this is the scan console. The images show up here,' he said, pointing to the bank of monitors above the console. 'This is the brain in a normal working state,' he said, typing instructions onto the keyboard, and the screen lit up with an orange, yellow, and blue image. He typed some more. 'And this is the brain in a REM-sleep dreaming state. See how the prefrontal cortex – that's the area of waking thought and reality-testing – and the sensory-input areas show almost no activity. And this,' he typed again, 'is the brain in an NDE-state, or at least what I hope is an NDE-state.'

Joanna pushed her glasses up on her nose and peered at the screen. 'It looks similar to the dream state.'

'Yes, but there's no activity at all in the prefrontal cortex and increased activity in the anterior lobe, here,' he said, pointing to the red areas, 'and in the hippocampus and amygdala.'

'And those are the long-term memories?' she asked, pointing to a scattering of pinpoint red and orange in the frontal cortex.

'Yes.' He blanked out the screens and called up Mr O'Reirdon's scan. 'This is the template scan,' he said, typing, 'and this is the scan from Mr Wojakowski's first session.' He superimposed them on a third screen. 'You can see the pattern, except for the activity in the frontal cortex, is similar, but not identical. Which is one of the reasons I need you on the project.'

He went over to the scan and put his hand on the arch-shaped dome. 'And this is the RIPT scan. The subject lies down here,' he indicated the examining table, 'under the scan, and then it's positioned above the head. The tracer and then a short-term sedative and the dithetamine are fed in through an IV, and blood samples are taken before, during, and after the NDE. I have a nurse assist. I've been using a floater.'

Joanna was looking thoughtfully at the arch-shaped opening. 'Problem?' Richard asked.

She nodded. 'It looks like a tunnel. Is there a way to cover it, put something in front of it till the subject is in place? You want to eliminate any possible physical explanations for the vision.'

'Sure. Can do.'

She was looking up at the ceiling. 'Do you need that overhead light during the procedure?'

'No,' he said, 'but the subject's eyes are covered.'

'With what?'

'A black sleep mask,' he said. He got one out of the cabinet to show her. 'They also wear headphones, through which white noise is fed.'

'Good,' she said, 'but I also think we should mask the light. Garland's explanation for the bright light NDEers see is that it's the light above the operating table, and the reason it's blindingly bright is because their pupils are dilated.'

Richard looked happily at her. 'This is exactly the kind of thing I was hoping you'd help me with. I'll get some black paper over it right away. We're going to make a great team.'

Joanna smiled back at him, then walked over and looked at the gunmetal-gray supply cabinet and the tall wooden glass-doored medicine cupboard, left over from an earlier hospital era, her hands on her hips. 'Is there anything else you want changed?' Richard asked.

'No,' she said. 'Added.' She reached in her cardigan pocket and pulled out an object wrapped loosely in newspaper. 'This is our tennis shoe.'

'Tennis shoe?' Richard said, looking at the newspaper-wrapped object. It was clearly not big enough to be a shoe, unless it was a child's.

'Hasn't Mr Mandrake told you about the shoe yet?' she said. 'I'm surprised. He tells everybody how the shoe is scientific proof of the reality of NDEs. Even more than Aunt Ethel.'

She stuck the newspaper-wrapped object back in her pocket and went over to his desk. 'A woman named Maria coded during an operation.' She pulled his chair out. 'Afterward, she reported floating above her body on the examining table, and she described the procedures they were doing to her in highly accurate detail.'

'A number of patients have done that,' he said. 'Described the intubation and the paddles. But couldn't they have gotten that information from previous hospital visits?'

'Or from an episode of *ER*,' Joanna said dryly. 'Maria described something else, though, and it constitutes the "scientific proof" Mr Mandrake's always referring to.' She pushed the chair over in front of the gunmetal cabinet. 'Maria said that when she was up near the ceiling, she saw a shoe on a ledge outside the window, a red tennis shoe.' She stepped up on the chair, looked at the top of the cabinet, frowning, and stepped back down. 'The shoe wasn't visible from any other part of the room, but when the doctor went up to the next floor and leaned all the way out of the window, there it was.'

'Which proved that the soul had actually left the body and was hovering above it,' Richard said.

'And, by extension, that everything the subject experiences in an NDE is real and not just a hallucination.' She dragged the chair over to the wooden medicine cupboard and stepped up on it. 'Pretty convincing, huh? The only problem is, it never happened. When researchers tried to verify it, it turned out there was no such event, no such patient, no such hospital.'

She withdrew the newspaper-wrapped object from her pocket. 'Of course, even if it had been a true story, it wouldn't have proved anything. The shoe could have been visible from some other part of the hospital, or the patient or the NDE researcher could have put it there. If and when a subject tells us he saw this,' she said, holding up the object, 'I'll consider the possibility that he really was out of his body.'

'What is it?' Richard asked.

'Something no one's likely to guess,' she said, leaning forward on tiptoe and stretching up to place it on top of the cupboard. 'Including you. If you don't know, you can't accidentally communicate the knowledge to anyone.' She wadded up the newspaper and stepped back down. 'I'll give you a clue,' she said, dropping the crumpled paper into his hand. 'It's not a shoe.' She turned and looked speculatively at the clock on the wall.

'Do you want the clock taken down, too?'

'No, although it might be a good idea to move it to where the subject can't see it. The fewer objects the subject has to confabulate about, the better. Actually, I was wondering about your subject. What time did you say she'd be here?'

'She was scheduled for eleven, and she called to say she had an exam and would be a few minutes late. She's a premed student,' he said, glancing at the clock. 'But I expected her by now.'

'Your subject pool is premed students?'

'No, just Ms Tanaka,' he said. 'The other volunteers are all—'

'Volunteers?' she said. 'You're using volunteers? How did you describe the project in your call for volunteers?'

'Neurological research. I've got a copy right here,' he said, going over to his desk.

'Did it mention NDEs?'

'No,' he said, rummaging through the stacks of papers. 'I told them what the project entailed when they came in for screening.'

'What kind of screening?'

'A physical and a psych profile.' He found the call for volunteers and handed it to her. 'And I asked them what they knew about near-death experiences and if they'd ever had one. None of them had.'

'And you've sent some of them under already?'

'Yes. Mrs Bendix has been under once, and Mr Wojakowski and Ms Tanaka, that's the one who's coming in today, have been under twice.'

'Did you take all the applications at once and then bring them in for screenings?'

He shook his head. 'I started the screenings right away so I wouldn't have to wait to begin the sessions. Why?'

There was a rapid knock on the door, and Amelia Tanaka swept in. 'I am *so* sorry I'm late,' she said, dropping her backpack on the floor and yanking off her wool gloves. She jammed them in her pockets. 'You got my message, didn't you, that I was going to be?'

Her long, straight black hair was flecked with snow. She shook it out. 'The anatomy exam was *horrible*,' she said, securing it with a clip. 'I didn't make it through half the questions.' She unzipped her coat. 'Half the things he'd never even mentioned in class. "Where is the vestigial fold of Marshall?" *I* don't know. I said in the pericardium, but it could just as well be in the liver, for all I know.' She stripped off her coat, dumped it on top of the backpack, and came over to them. 'And then it snowed the whole way over here—'

She seemed suddenly to become aware of Joanna. 'Oh, hi,' she said, and looked questioningly at Richard.

'I want you to meet Dr Lander, Ms Tanaka,' he said.

'Amelia,' she corrected. 'But it's going to be mud if I did as bad as I think I did on that exam.'

'Hi, Amelia,' Joanna said.

'Dr Lander's going to be working with me on the project,' Richard said. 'She'll be conducting the interviews.'

'You're not going to ask questions like "Where is the vestigial fold of Marshall?" are you?' Amelia asked.

'No.' Joanna grinned. 'I'm just going to ask you what you've seen and heard, and today I'd like to ask you a few questions about yourself, so I can get to know you.'

'Sure,' Amelia said. 'Did you want to do that now or after I get ready for the session?'

'Why don't you get ready first?' Joanna said, and Amelia turned expectantly to Richard. He opened the gunmetal supply cupboard and handed her a pile of folded clothing. She disappeared into a small room at the back.

Richard waited till she'd shut the door and then asked Joanna, 'What were you going to say before Ms Tanaka came in? About the screenings?'

'Can I see your list of volunteers?' she asked.

'Sure,' he said and rummaged through the papers on his desk again. 'Here it is. They've all been approved, but I haven't scheduled them all yet.'

He handed it to Joanna, and she sat down on the chair she'd stood on to put the 'shoe' on top of the medicine cupboard and ran her finger down the names. 'Well, at least this explains why Mr Mandrake didn't try to pump you about your project. He didn't have to.'

'What do you mean?' Richard said. He came around behind her to look at the list.

'I mean, one of your volunteers is a subject of Mr Mandrake's, there's another one I think probably is, and this one,' she said, pointing at Dvorjak, A., 'has CAS, compulsive attention syndrome. It's a form of incomplete personality disorder. They invent NDEs to get attention.'

'How do you *invent* an NDE?'

'Over half of the so-called NDEs in Mandrake's book, which I see you have a copy of here, aren't really NDEs at all. Visions during childbirth and surgery, blackouts, even fainting episodes qualify if the person experiences the standard tunnel, light, angels. Amy Dvorjak specializes in blackouts, which, conveniently, don't have any external symptoms so you can't prove they didn't happen. She's had twenty-three.'

'Twenty-three!'

Joanna nodded. 'Even Mr Mandrake doesn't believe her anymore, and he believes everything anybody tells him.'

He grabbed the list away from her and crossed out 'Dvorjak, A.'.

'Which ones are Mandrake's subjects?'

She looked ruefully at him. 'You're not going to want to hear this. One of them's May Bendix.'

'Mrs Bendix!' he said. 'Are you sure?'

Joanna nodded. 'She's one of Mandrake's favorite subjects. She's even in his book.'

'She said she didn't even know what a near-death experience was,' he said, outraged. 'I can't believe this!'

'I think before we send anybody else under, I'd better check the rest of the names on this list,' Joanna said.

He glanced at the door of the dressing room. 'I'll tell Amelia the scan's down and we can't do a session today.'

Joanna nodded. 'I'd also like to interview her, and the rest of the subjects, after I've checked to see whether they have any connections to Mr Mandrake or the near-death community.'

'Right,' he said. 'Wait, you said there was another one you thought might be connected to Mandrake. Which one?'

'This one,' she said, pointing at the name on the list. 'Thomas Suarez. He called me last week and told me he'd had an NDE. I suggested he call Mr Mandrake.'

'I thought you said you tried to get to subjects before Mandrake could corrupt them.'

'I do. Usually,' she said. 'But Mr Suarez is part of that fourteen percent who also believe they've been abducted by a UFO.'

6

'Hey, where the hell are the parachutes?'
– Question asked by GLENN MILLER as he boarded
the plane to Paris, to which Colonel Baesell replied,
'What's the matter, Miller, do you want to live forever?'

When Joanna checked the rest of the list against the membership of the Society for Near-Death Studies, she turned up two more names. 'Which makes five,' she told Richard.

'All spies of Mandrake's?' Richard said, outraged.

'No, not necessarily. Bendix and Dvorjak are both perfectly capable of signing up on their own. True Believers are constantly on the lookout for anything that might validate their beliefs.'

'But how could they have found out about it?'

'This is Mercy General,' Joanna said. 'Otherwise known as Gossip General. Or someone in the first set of interviews may have notified the others of what your research was about. NDEers have quite a network – organizations, the Internet – and it's common knowledge that the Institute does NDE research. Mr Mandrake may not know anything about this.'

'You don't seriously believe that, do you?'

'No.'

'I still think we should report him to the board.'

'That won't do any good,' she said, 'not with Mrs Brightman on the board. And the last thing you need is a confrontation with him. We need to—'

'– hide down stairways?'

'If necessary,' she said. 'And make sure none of the other volunteers are connected to Mandrake or the near-death community.'

'Or are raving lunatics,' he said. 'I still can't believe the psych profile didn't pick them up.'

'Believing in the afterlife isn't a mental illness,' Joanna said. 'A number of major religions have been doing it for centuries.'

'What about Mr Suarez's UFOs?'

'Mentally competent people believe all kinds of goofy things,' she said. 'That's why I want to interview them as soon as I've finished checking for near-death connections.' She spent the rest of the afternoon doing that and printed out the International Society for the Advancement of Spiritualism and the Paranormal Society membership lists to take home.

Mr Mandrake had left three messages on her answering machine saying he wanted to talk to her, so she went a roundabout way down to the parking lot, across the fifth-floor walkway to the west wing, down to third, back across the walkway, and through Oncology to the patient elevator.

A middle-aged man and woman were standing waiting for the elevator. 'You go on,' the man was saying to the woman. 'There's no reason for both of us to stay.'

The woman nodded, and Joanna noticed her eyes were red-rimmed. 'You'll call me if there's any change?'

'I promise,' the man said. 'You get some rest. And eat something. You haven't had anything all day.'

The woman's shoulders slumped. 'All right.'

The elevator dinged, and the door opened. The woman pecked the man on the cheek and stepped into the elevator. Joanna followed her. She pressed 'G,' and the door started to close. 'Wait! Do you have my cell phone number?' the woman called through the closing door.

The man nodded. '329-6058,' he said, and the door closed.

Five-eight, Joanna thought. Fifty-eight. She'd thought Greg Menotti might have been trying to tell them a phone number, but when people recited their phone numbers, they said the individual digits. They didn't with addresses. They said, 'I live at twenty-one fifteen Pearl Street.' She wondered what Greg Menotti's address had been.

She leaned forward and pressed two, and when the elevator reached second, she got out, went down to the visitors' lounge, and looked up his address in the phone book: 1903 South Wyandotte, and his phone number was 771-0642. Not even a five or an eight, let alone a fifty-eight. The address he was trying to say could have been his girlfriend's, of course, or his parents'. But it wasn't, Joanna thought. He had been trying to tell her something critical. And what critical piece of information had the number fifty-eight in it?

She shut the phone book and went back down the hall to the elevator. A nurse's aide passed her, carrying a Styrofoam cup, and stopped to ask a nurse, 'What room did you say he was in?'

'Two fifty-eight.'

Could Greg Menotti have known someone here in the hospital and been trying to tell them to go get them? That didn't make any sense. He would have mentioned that before, when he was demanding they contact his girlfriend. What other kinds of rooms had numbers? An office? An apartment?

Joanna rode down to the parking lot. Fifty-eight. A safety deposit box number? A date? No, he was too young to have been born in 1958. She got in her car. Fifty-eight wasn't the number of anything famous, like thirteen or 666. She drove out of the parking lot and down Colorado Boulevard. The car ahead of her had a purple neon light around the license plate. 'WV-58.' Joanna glanced at the gas station on the right. 'Unleaded,' the sign read. '1.58.99.'

A frisson of superstitious fear passed up Joanna's spine and raised the hairs on the back of her neck. It's that movie Vielle and I rented, the one about the plane crash with all the omens in it. *Final Destination.*

She grinned. 'What it really was was a heightened awareness of something that had been present in her surroundings all along. The number fifty-eight had always been there, just like every other number, but her brain had been put on alert to look for it, like a hiker cautioned to watch for snakes. That was what superstition was, an attempt to make sense of random data and random events – stars and bumps on the head and numbers.

It doesn't mean anything, she told herself. You're assigning meaning where there isn't any. But when she got home, she got on the Net and ran a search engine on the number fifty-eight. It turned up several obituaries – 'Elbert Hodgins, aged fifty-eight' – one U.S. highway and fourteen state highways, and three books on Amazon.com: *Russian-American Cold War Policy from 1946–58, Adrift on the Fifty-eighth Parallel*, and *Better in Bed: 58 Ways to Improve Your Sex Life.*

Which doesn't exactly add up to *The Twilight Zone*, Joanna thought, amused, and started through the Paranormal Society membership list. Amelia wasn't a member, and neither were any of the other volunteers, but when she went through the ISAS list, she found the name of a volunteer, and when she checked the NDE Web site the next morning, she found two more, which left them with eight subjects. Before she'd even interviewed anyone.

'I am so sorry,' she told Richard. 'My goal was to make sure you didn't get any ringers, not to decimate your project.'

'I'll tell you what would have decimated my project, to have one of my subjects show up in Mandrake's book. Or on the cover of the *Star*,' he said. 'You were right. I shouldn't report Mandrake to the board. I should punch him out.'

'We don't have time,' Joanna said. 'We've got to screen the subjects we've got left and line up additional ones. How long will the approval process take?'

'Four to six weeks to get clearance from the board and the projects committee. It took five and a half weeks for the paperwork on this group to go through.'

'Then we'd better put out another call immediately,' Joanna said, 'and I'll get started on these interviews. I'm about ready to talk to Amelia Tanaka. She looks good. I haven't found anything questionable except maybe the fact that she says she's twenty-four and she's still a premed student, but my gut instincts say she's not a nutcase.'

'Gut instincts,' Richard said. He grinned at her. 'I didn't think scientists had gut instincts.'

'Sure they do. They just don't rely on them. Evidence,' she said, waving the ISAS membership list, 'that's the ticket. Outside confirmation. Which is why I'm calling her references and why I want to interview her. But if it goes okay, I don't see any reason why you shouldn't go ahead as planned with her.'

She went back to her office and called Amelia's references and then Amelia and set up an interview. It took some doing. Amelia had classes and labs, and she really needed to study for this biochem exam she had coming up. Joanna finally got her to agree to one o'clock the next day.

She was pleased that rescheduling her had been so difficult. Her very lack of eagerness was evidence that she wasn't a True Believer. Joanna checked her name against the Theosophical Society's membership list and then started through the files of the other seven volunteers.

They looked promising. Ms Coffey was a data systems manager, Mr Sage a welder, Mrs Haighton a community volunteer, Mr Pearsall an insurance agent. None of their names, nor Ronald Kelso's or Edward Wojakowski's, showed up on any of the NDE sites. The only one she was worried about was Mrs Troudtheim, who didn't live in Denver.

'She lives out on the eastern plains,' she told Richard the next day, 'near Deer Trail. The fact that she'd drive all that way – how far is it? sixty miles? – to be in a research project is a bit suspicious, but everything else about her checks out, and all the others look fine.' She looked at the clock. It said a quarter to one. 'Amelia Tanaka should be here in a few minutes.'

'Good,' he said. 'If you don't turn up anything negative, I'd like to proceed with a session. I told the nurse to be on standby.'

There was a knock on the door. 'She's early,' Joanna said, and went over to answer the door.

It was a short elderly man with faded red hair receding from a freckled forehead. 'Is Doc Wright here?' he asked, leaning past Joanna to see into the lab. He spied Richard. 'Hiya, Doc. I thought I'd stop by and check to see when my next session was. I'm one of Doc Wright's guinea pigs.'

'Dr Lander, this is Ed Wojakowski,' Richard said, coming over to the door. 'Mr Wojakowski, Dr Lander's going to be working with me on the project.'

'Call me Ed. Mr Wojakowski's my dad.' He winked at her.

Joanna thought of Greg Menotti having made the same joke. She wondered how old Mr Wojakowski was. He looked at least seventy, and the project had specified volunteers aged twenty-one to sixty-five.

'I knew a Joanna once,' Mr Wojakowski said, 'back when I was in the navy, during World War II.'

World War II and the navy again, Joanna thought. First Mrs Davenport and now Mr Wojakowski. Did that mean she'd talked to him? Or had Mr Mandrake talked to both of them? She hoped not – at this rate they'd be out of subjects in no time.

'She worked at the USO canteen in Honolulu,' Mr Wojakowski was saying. 'Nice-looking girl, not as pretty as you, though. Me and Stinky Johannson sneaked her on board one night to show her our Wildcat, and—'

'We haven't scheduled your next session yet,' Richard said.

'Oh, okay, Doc,' Mr Wojakowski said. 'Just thought I'd check.'

'Since you're here,' Joanna said, 'would you mind if I asked you a few questions?' She turned to Richard. 'Ms Tanaka won't be here for another fifteen minutes.'

'Sure,' Richard said, but he looked doubtful.

'Or we could schedule it for later.'

'No, now's fine,' Richard said, and she wondered if she'd misread him. 'Do you have time to answer a few questions, Mr Wojakowski?'

'Ed,' he corrected. 'You bet I got time. Now that I'm retired I got all the time in the world.'

'Yes, well,' Richard said, looking doubtful again, 'we've got another interview scheduled for one.'

'I gotcha, Doc,' Mr Wojakowski said. 'Keep it short and sweet.' He turned back to Joanna. 'Whaddya wanta know, Doc?'

Joanna looked at Richard, uncertain whether he really wanted her to proceed, but he nodded, so she offered Mr Wojakowski a chair, thinking, We have to establish some kind of code for situations like this. 'I just want to find out a little bit about you, Mr Wojakowski, get to know you, since we're going to be working together,' Joanna said, sitting down opposite him. 'Your background, why you volunteered for the project.' She switched the recorder on.

'My background, huh? Well, I'll tell ya, I'm an old navy man. Served on the USS *Yorktown*. Best ship in WWII till the Japs sank her. Sorry,' he said at her look, 'that's what we called 'em back then. The enemy, the Japanese.'

But she hadn't been thinking about his use of the offensive word *Japs*. She'd been calculating his age. If he'd been in World War II, he had to be nearly eighty. 'You say you served on the *Yorktown*?' she said, looking at his file. Name. Address. Social Security number. Why wasn't his age listed? 'That was a battleship, wasn't it?' she said, stalling for time.

'Battleship!' he snorted. 'Aircraft carrier. Best damn one in the Pacific. Sank four carriers at the Battle of Midway before a Jap sub got her. Torpedo. Got a destroyer that was standing in the way, too. The *Hammann*. Went down just like that. Dead before she even knew it. Two minutes. All hands.'

She still couldn't find his age. Allergies to medications. Health history.

He'd marked 'no' to everything from high blood pressure to diabetes, and he looked spry and alert, but if he was eighty –

'... took the *Yorktown* a lot longer to sink,' he was saying. 'Two whole days. Terrible thing to watch.'

Work history, references, person to contact in case of emergency, but no birthdate. By design?

'... the order to abandon ship, and the sailors all took off their shoes and lined them up on the deck. Hundreds and hundreds of pairs of shoes—'

'Mr Wojakowski, I can't find—'

'Ed,' he corrected, and then, as if he knew what she was going to ask next, 'I joined the navy when I was thirteen. Lied about my age. Told 'em the hospital where they had my birth certificate had burned down. Not that they were checking things like that right after Pearl.' He looked challengingly at her. 'You're way too young to know what Pearl Harbor is, I s'pose.'

'The Japanese surprise attack on Pearl Harbor?'

'Surprise? Thunderbolt, is more like it. The U.S. of A. just sitting there, mindin' her own business, and blam! No declaration of war, no warning, no nothin'. I'll never forget it. It was a Sunday, and I was reading the funny papers. "The Katzenjammer Kids," I can still see it. I look up, and in comes the lady from two doors down, all out of breath, and says, "The Japs just bombed Pearl Harbor!" Well, none of us even knew where Pearl Harbor was, except my kid sister. She'd seen it in a newsreel at the movies the night before. *Desperadoes*, that's what was playing. Randolph Scott. And the very next day, I went downtown to the navy recruiting center and signed up.'

He paused momentarily for breath, and Joanna said quickly, 'Mr – Ed, what made you volunteer for the project? How did you find out about it?'

'Saw a notice in the recreation center at Aspen Gardens. That's where I live. And then when I came in and talked to the doc, I thought it sounded interesting.'

'Had you ever been involved in a research study here at the hospital before?'

'Nope. They put up notices all the time. Most of them you have to have some special thing wrong with you – hernias or can't see good or something, and I didn't, so I couldn't be in 'em.'

'You said the project sounded interesting,' Joanna said. 'Can you be more specific? Were you interested in near-death experiences?'

'I'd seen shows about 'em on TV.'

'And that was why you wanted to participate in the project?'

He shook his head. 'I had more than enough near-death experiences in the war.' He winked. 'Tunnels and lights, let me tell you, they're nothing compared to seeing a Zero coming at you, and the machine gun you're supposed to be firing jams. Those damned 1.1 millimeters, they were always sticking, and you had to have a gunner's mate crawl underneath 'em with a hammer and unjam 'em. I remember one time Straight Holecek, we called him Straight 'cause he was always drawing to inside straights, well, anyway, he—'

No wonder Richard had been reluctant to have her question Mr Wojakowski with Amelia coming in a few minutes. He'd moved around to stand behind Mr Wojakowski. She glanced up at him, and he grinned at her.

'… and just then a Zero dived straight at us, and Straight gives a yelp and drops his hammer right on my foot, and—'

'So if it wasn't NDEs you were interested in, what was it about the project that interested you?' Joanna asked.

'I told you I served on the *Yorktown*,' he said, 'and let me tell you, she was a great ship. Brand-new and bright as a button, and real bunks to sleep in. She even had a soda fountain. You could go in there and order a chocolate malted or a cherry phosphate, just like the drugstore back home.' He smiled reminiscently. 'Well, after we hit Rabaul, they put Old Yorky, that's what we called her, on patrol duty down in the Coral Sea, and for six weeks we just sat there, playing acey-deucey and bettin' on whose toenails'd grow the fastest.'

Joanna wondered what this had to do with why he had volunteered. She had a sneaking suspicion there was no connection at all, that he simply used any opening anybody gave him to talk about the war, and if she didn't stop him, he'd go right on through the Battle of Midway.

'Mr Wojakowski,' she said. 'You were going to tell me why you volunteered for this project.'

'I am,' he said. 'Well, so anyway, we're sitting there twiddling our thumbs, and by the end of a week we were bored as hell and couldn't *wait* for the Japs to dive-bomb us. At least it'd be something to do. Speaking of dive-bombing, did I ever tell you about what Jo-Jo Powers did at Coral Sea? The first time out his squadron doesn't hit anything, all their torpedoes miss, and so he's getting ready for his second run, and he says, "I'm going to hit that flight deck if I have to lay my bomb on it myself," and –'

'Mr Wojakowski,' Joanna said firmly. 'Your reason for volunteering.'

'You ever been over to Aspen Gardens?'

She shook her head.

'You're lucky. It's just like being on patrol duty in the Coral Sea, only without the acey-deucey. So I thought I'd come on over and do something interesting.'

Which was an excellent reason. 'Have you ever had a near-death experience yourself, Mr Wojakowski?'

'Not till the doc put me in that doughnut thing all hooked up like Frankenstein. I'd always thought that tunnel and light and seeing Jesus stuff was all a bunch of hooey, but, sure enough, there I was in a tunnel. No Jesus, though. I still say that's a bunch of hooey. I saw too much stuff in the war to put much stock in religion. One time, at Coral Sea—'

She let him ramble on, satisfied that he wasn't one of Mr Mandrake's spies. It was clear the real reason he'd volunteered was to have somebody new to tell his war stories to. And if Mr Mandrake tries to pump him, it'll serve him right, she thought, smiling to herself. He'll get the whole history of the war in the Pacific. And if Amelia didn't get here soon, she would, too. She glanced at the clock. It was nearly two. Where was she?

Joanna's pager beeped. 'Excuse me,' Joanna said and made a point of pulling it out of her pocket and looking at it. 'I'm sorry,' she said. 'I've got a call I've got to take.'

'Sure, Doc,' he said, looking disappointed. 'Those are great little gizmos. Wish we'd had 'em back in WWII. It sure woulda helped the time we—'

'We'll call you as soon as we've finished setting up the schedule,' Joanna said, escorting him firmly across the lab to the door with him still talking. She opened the door. 'We should know in a day or two.'

'Anytime's fine. I got all the time in the world,' he said, and Joanna felt suddenly remorseful.

'Ed,' she said, 'you never finished telling me about the dive-bomber, the one who said he'd hit the flight deck if he had to lay the bomb on there himself. What happened to him?'

'You mean Jo-Jo?' he asked. 'Well, I'll tell ya. He said he'd sink that carrier if it was the last thing he ever did, and he did it, too. It was a sight to see, him coming in straight at the *Shokaku*, his tail on fire, Zeroes all around him. But he did just what he said he was gonna do, laid that bomb right on her flight deck, even though he couldn't'ta been more than two hundred feet above that deck when he dropped it, and then, wham! his bomber crashed into the ocean.'

'Oh –' Joanna said.

'But he did it, even if he was already dead when that bomb went off. He still did it.'

7

'On board the *Pacific* from Liverpool to N.Y. – Confusion on board – Icebergs around us on every side. I know I cannot escape. I write the cause of our loss that friends may not live in suspense. The finder will please get it published. Wm. Graham.'

– Message found in a bottle, 1856

It took another twenty minutes and two more stories about the *Yorktown* to get rid of Mr Wojakowski. 'My gosh,' Joanna said, leaning against the door she had finally managed to shut behind him, 'he's harder to get away from than Maisie.'

'Do you think he's one of Mandrake's?' Richard asked.

'No, if he were a True Believer, we'd have heard *all* about it. He'll actually make a very good subject if I can just keep him away from the topic of the USS *Yorktown*. He's got an eye and an ear for detail, and he talks.'

Richard grinned. 'You can say that again. Are you sure that's an advantage?'

'*Yes*. There's nothing worse than a subject who answers in monosyllables, or just sits there. I'll take talkative any day.'

'Then I can schedule him?'

'Yes, but I'd do it right before another subject's session. Otherwise, we'll never get him turned off.' She went over to the desk and put down Mr Wojakowski's file. 'I kept hoping Amelia Tanaka would come in and provide a good cutoff point. She was supposed to be here by now. Is she usually late?'

'Always,' Richard said, 'but she usually calls.'

'Oh, maybe she did,' Joanna said, pulling her pager out. 'I gave her my pager number.' She hastily called the switchboard and asked for her messages.

'Amelia Tanaka said she'd be late, she'll be there by two,' the switchboard operator said. 'And Nurse Howard wants you to call her.' That was Vielle, and she must not be calling about an NDE. When it was someone who'd coded, she simply left a message for Joanna to come to the ER.

She's found out what Greg Menotti meant by 'fifty-eight,' Joanna thought. She glanced at the clock. It was one-forty. 'I'm running down to the ER,' she told Richard, hanging up the phone. 'Amelia will be here at two. I'll be back before then.'

'What is it?' he asked. 'An NDE?'

'No,' she said, 'I just have to find out something from Vielle.' What fifty-eight means.

And it's probably nothing, she told herself, hurrying down the steps to fifth. Vielle will probably tell me Greg Menotti was trying to say something perfectly ordinary, like, 'Try Stephanie's office. The address is 1658 Grant.' Or, 'I can't be having a heart attack. I did fifty-eight laps at my health club this morning.'

But he wasn't, she thought, crossing the walkway to the main building and the elevator. He wasn't talking about laps or phone numbers. He was talking about something else. He was trying to tell us something important.

She took the elevator down to first and ran down the stairs and along the hall to the ER. Vielle was at the central desk, making entries on a chart. Joanna hurried over to her. 'You found out what it meant, didn't you?' she said. 'What was he trying to say?'

'Who?' Vielle said blankly. 'What are you talking about?'

'Greg Menotti. The heart attack patient who coded on Tuesday.'

'Oh, right,' Vielle said, 'the myocardial infarction who kept saying, "fifty-nine."'

'Fifty-eight,' Joanna said.

'Right. I'm sorry. I was going to check his girlfriend's phone number,' she said, pushing her elasticized cap back off her forehead. 'I forgot all about it.' She looked past Joanna. 'I'll check on it this afternoon, I promise. Is that why you came down here?'

'No,' Joanna said. 'You called me, remember?'

'Oh, right,' Vielle said, looking uncomfortable. 'You weren't there.' She busied herself with the chart again.

'Well?' Joanna said. 'What did you want to talk to me about?'

'Nothing. I don't remember. It was probably about Dish Night. Do you know how hard it is to come up with movies that don't have any deaths in them? Even comedies. *Shakespeare in Love, Sleepless in Seattle, Four Weddings and a Funeral.* I spent an hour and a half in Blockbuster last night, looking for something death-free.'

And you are clearly trying to change the subject, Joanna thought. Why? And what had she called about? Something she had obviously changed her mind about telling her.

'You can't even find *kids'* movies,' Vielle was rattling on. 'Cinderella's father, Bambi's mother, the Wicked Witch of the West – what is it, Nina?' she said to an aide who had come up, and that was odd, too. Vielle usually shouted at aides who interrupted her.

'Mrs Edwards at the desk said to give this to you,' Nina said, handing a blown-up photograph to Vielle. It was a picture of a blond, tattooed teenager in a knitted cap, obviously a mug shot since there was a long string of numbers along the bottom.

'You didn't have another shooting, did you?' Joanna asked.

'No,' Vielle said defensively. 'It's been quiet as a church in here all day.

Nothing but sprained ankles and paper cuts. Why did Mrs Edwards say to give this to me?' she asked Nina.

'The police said if this guy comes in, you're supposed to call them, he shot a guy in the leg with a nail gun—'

'Thank you, Nina,' Vielle said, handing her back the paper. 'Go show it to Dr Thayer.'

'If the guy he shot shows up, you're supposed to call them, too,' Nina said. 'They're both gang members—'

'*Thank* you, Nina.'

As soon as Nina was gone, Joanna said, 'A nail gun! Vielle, when are you going to transfer out of here? It's dangerous—'

'I know, I know, you've told me before,' she said, looking past Joanna. 'Oops, gotta go.' She started toward the front of the ER, where two men were holding a pasty-faced woman up by the armpits.

'Vielle—'

'See you tomorrow night at Dish Night,' Vielle said, breaking into a trot.

Too late. The woman vomited all over the floor and the two men. One of the men let go and jumped backward out of the line of fire, and the woman slid sideways onto the floor. Vielle, her worried look back, caught her before she fell.

There was no point in waiting around. The woman was obviously going to take some time, and it was already nearly two. And what could she say if she did stay? 'Vielle, why did you really call me? And don't tell me it was about Bambi's mother!'

Joanna went back upstairs. Amelia still wasn't there. 'Did you find out what you needed to know?' Richard asked.

'No,' Joanna said. In more ways than one.

'By the way, Vielle—'

There was a knock on the door, and Amelia swept in, exclaiming, 'I am *so* sorry I'm late. Can you believe my professors *all* decided to give an exam the same week?' She divested herself of her backpack, gloves, and coat with the same speed as she had two days before, talking the entire time. 'I know I blew it. I hate biochem!'

Her long black hair was twisted up into the messy-looking topknot all the college students were wearing these days. She shook it out and twisted it up again into an even messier knot. 'I got a D, I know it,' she said, securing it with a large gold plastic clip. 'Do you want me to go get undressed, Dr Wright?'

'Not yet,' he said. 'Dr Lander needs to ask you some questions first.'

'Amelia,' Joanna said, indicating one of the three chairs. She sat down herself, and Richard came around and took the other one. 'You're a premed student, is that right?'

Amelia plopped down in the third. 'Not after the biochem exam I just took. It was even worse than anatomy. I was premed. Now I'm dead meat.'

Joanna wrote down 'premed.' 'And you're how old?'

'Twenty-four,' Amelia said. 'I know, that's old to still be in premed. I got a BA in music theater before I decided I didn't want to be an actress.'

An actress. Good at playing roles. At fooling people. 'Why did you decide you didn't want to be an actress?'

'I realized the only parts I was ever going to get were Tuptim and Miss Saigon, and I was never going to get to play Marian the librarian or *Annie Get Your Gun*, so I decided to go to medical school instead. At least doctors can always get parts.' She grinned up at Joanna. 'You know, kidneys, gallbladders, livers.'

A joke, which True Believers hardly ever told. If there was any characteristic NDE nuts and ESPers and UFO abductees had in common it was a complete lack of a sense of humor. And Amelia also had a knowledge of science and a willingness to volunteer information that indicated she had nothing to hide. I believe we have a winner, Joanna thought. 'Can you tell me why you volunteered for the project?' she asked.

Amelia glanced guiltily at Richard. 'Why I volunteered?' she said and looked away. 'Well …'

Just when you thought it was safe to go back in the water, Joanna thought.

'You said you were interested in neurology,' Richard said. Don't give her an out, Joanna thought, glaring at him.

'I *am* interested in neurology,' Amelia said. 'It's what I want to go into, but what I didn't tell you,' she twisted her hands in her lap, 'is that I didn't volunteer on my own.'

Here it comes, Joanna thought, Mr Mandrake told her to. Or worse, the voices in her head.

'My psych professor is really big on the idea of premeds being patients ourselves, so that when we become doctors we can empathize with our patients,' Amelia said, looking at her hands. 'He gives extra credit for participating in a research project, and I really need the points. I'm doing terrible in psych.' She looked apologetically at Richard. 'I didn't tell you because I was afraid you wouldn't take me.'

Take you? Joanna thought. I only wish there were a dozen more like you. Students volunteering for extra credit were perfect. They had no agenda and no particular interest in the subject, which made it unlikely they'd read Mandrake's book or the other NDE books. 'Your professor assigned you to the project?' Joanna asked.

'No,' Amelia said and glanced guiltily at Richard again. 'We picked whatever project we were interested in.'

'And you were interested in NDEs?' Joanna asked, her heart sinking.

'No, I didn't know it was about NDEs when I signed up.' She began the hand-twisting again. 'I thought it would probably be one of those memory experiments. Not that I wanted it to be,' she said, flushing, 'this is a lot more interesting.'

She glanced over at Richard again, and it hit Joanna. 'I'll need a copy of your class schedule so we can set up a good session time, Amelia,' she said.

Richard was looking questioningly at her. Joanna ignored him. 'Will tomorrow at eleven fit your schedule, Amelia?' she asked.

'Yes,' Amelia said eagerly. 'I can even stay this afternoon and do one, if you want.'

'Great,' Joanna said. 'Why don't you go get undressed?' She stood up, still avoiding Richard's eye, and started over to the examining table.

'I know where everything is,' Amelia said, grabbed the pile of clothing off the table, and disappeared into the dressing room.

'Are you sure this is a good idea?' Richard said as soon as the door shut behind her. 'Did you see her reaction when you asked her why she volunteered for the project? She got really upset. I don't think she was telling the truth.'

'She wasn't,' Joanna said. 'Do you need me to help set things up?'

'If she was lying, how can you be sure she isn't one of Mandrake's ringers?'

'Because it was a peripheral lie,' Joanna said, 'lying for a personal reason that has nothing to do with the matter at hand, the kind of lie that always gets people in trouble in murder mysteries.' She smiled at him. 'She's not a True Believer. The personality profile's wrong, and so was her account of her first NDE. Her references check out, and her interview confirms what I thought when I first met her. She's exactly what she seems to be: a premed student doing this for extra credit.'

'Okay,' he said. 'Great. Let's get started. I'll go get Nurse Hawley.' He left the lab. After a moment, Amelia emerged from the dressing room with a hospital gown on over her jeans and the sleep mask dangling from her neck. She looked around questioningly.

'Dr Wright's gone to get the assisting nurse,' Joanna said.

'Oh, good,' Amelia said, coming over to her. 'I didn't want to tell you with him around. I didn't tell you the truth before. About why I picked this project.'

Don't lead, Joanna thought, especially not when you think you know the answer. Amelia ducked her head, the way she had before. 'The real reason I picked it was because of Dr Wright. I thought he was cute. That doesn't disqualify me from being a volunteer, does it?'

'No,' Joanna said. She'd thought that's what it was. 'He is cute.'

'I *know*,' Amelia said. 'I couldn't believe how adorable—' She cut off abruptly, and both of them turned to look at the door.

'Nurse Hawley wasn't there,' Richard said, coming in. 'I'll have to page her.' He went over to the phone. 'I need to hire a nurse to assist.' He dialed the switchboard.

'While we're waiting, Amelia,' Joanna said, 'why don't you tell me what you saw during your first session?'

'The first time I went under?' Amelia asked, and Joanna wondered if her use of that phrase was significant. 'The first time all I saw was a bright light,' she said. 'It was so bright I couldn't really see anything. The second time I went under it wasn't as bright, and in it I could see people.'

'Can you be more specific?'

'Not really. I mean, I couldn't really see them, because of the light, but I knew they were there.'

'How many people?' Joanna asked.

'Three,' Amelia said, squinting as if she were envisioning the scene. 'No, four.'

'And what were they doing?'

'Nothing,' Amelia said. 'Just standing there waiting.'

'Waiting?'

'Yes. Waiting for me, I think. Watching.'

Watching and waiting were not the same thing. 'Were there any feelings associated with what you saw?' Joanna asked.

'Yes, I felt warm and ...' She hesitated. '... peaceful.'

Warm and *peaceful* were words frequently used by NDEers to describe the feeling they'd experienced, also *safe* and *surrounded by love*, feelings also associated with the release of endorphins.

'Can you think of any other words to describe the feeling?'

'Yes,' Amelia said, but then was silent for several seconds. 'Serene,' she said finally, but her inflection at the end of the word rose, as if it were a question. 'Cozy,' she said with more certainty, 'like being in front of a fire. Or wrapped up in a blanket.' She smiled as if remembering the feeling.

'What happened after you saw the figures in the light?'

Joanna asked. 'Nothing. That's all I remember, just the light and them standing there waiting.'

Richard came over, looking irritated. 'Nurse Hawley isn't answering her pager,' he said. 'We'll have to do it without her. Amelia, you can go ahead and get up on the table.'

Amelia hopped onto the examining table and lay down on her back. 'Oh, good,' she said, 'you covered up that light. It kept blinding me.'

Richard shot Joanna an approving glance and then picked up an oxygen indicator and clipped it onto Amelia's finger. 'We continuously monitor pulse and BP.'

He stepped back to the console and typed in something. The monitors above the terminal lit up. Changing readouts appeared on the lower right screen. Oxygen levels 98 percent, pulse 67. He went back over to the table. 'Amelia, I'm going to put the electrodes on now.'

'Okay,' Amelia said.

Richard pulled the neck of the hospital gown down and attached electrodes to her chest. 'These monitor heart rate and rhythm,' he said to Joanna. He attached a blood pressure cuff to Amelia's arm. 'Okay,' he said to her. 'It's time for you to put on your sleep mask.'

'Okay,' she said, raising her head slightly as she positioned the mask over her eyes, and then lying back down. Richard began attaching electrodes to her temples and her scalp. 'Wait!' She tried to sit up.

'What is it?' Joanna said. 'Is something wrong?'

'Yes,' Amelia said. She felt blindly for her hair clip with her left hand, took it out, and shook out her long hair. 'Sorry, it was digging into the back of my head,' she said, lying back down. 'I didn't unhook anything, did I?'

'You're fine,' Richard said, reattaching the electrodes to her temples. He began attaching smaller ones along her scalp.

Joanna looked at her, lying there with her black hair fanned out around her pale face. She looks like Sleeping Beauty, she thought, and wondered if Sleeping Beauty had had visions during her hundred years of being in a coma. And if she had, of what? Tunnels and lights, or a boat on a lake? A middle-aged nurse came bustling in. 'I'm sorry I'm late. I was with a patient.'

'You can start a saline IV,' Richard said, lifting the sides of Amelia's sleep mask to stick electrodes at the corners of her eyes. 'These electrodes record eye movements during the period when the subject's in REM sleep.'

The nurse had tied a piece of rubber tubing around Amelia's arm and was expertly probing for a vein. Richard raised Amelia's other arm and placed a two-inch-thick piece of foam under it. To reduce external stimuli, Joanna thought, watching him place them under her knees, her legs.

'Is the IV in?' Richard asked the nurse. 'Okay, start the tracers.' He leaned over Amelia. 'Do you hurt anywhere? Anything pinch? Pull? Ache?'

'Nope,' Amelia said, smiling blindly up at him. 'I'm fine.'

'Good,' he said. He picked up a pair of headphones, plugged them into a jack, and put them on. He listened for a moment and then took them off and brought them over to Amelia. 'We're ready to start,' he said. 'I'm going to put the headphones on you now. You ready?'

'Can I have a blanket?' Amelia asked. 'I always get cold.'

Cold? Joanna wondered. She had said she felt warm and cozy. Joanna thought back to Lisa Andrews, shivering as she said she felt warm and safe.

'When do you get cold, Amelia?' she asked.

'Afterward. When I wake up, I'm freezing.'

'Body temperature drops when you're lying down,' Nurse Hawley said, and Joanna could have throttled her.

'Do you wake up and then get cold, or are you already cold when you wake up?' Joanna asked.

'I don't know. After, I think,' but there was that same questioning inflection in her voice.

Richard spread a white cotton blanket over Amelia's body, leaving the arm with the IV uncovered. 'How's that?' he asked her.

'Good.'

'Okay, I'm putting your headphones on,' he said to her. He placed them over her ears upside down, the headband under her chin. So they don't obstruct the scan, Joanna thought.

'White noise is being fed through the headphones,' Richard said to Joanna. 'It masks any stray inner-ear noises along with any outside sound. Amelia?' he said loudly. No answer. 'Okay,' he said, stepping around Joanna to take down the cardboard screen in front of the scan. 'You ready?'

'Yes,' Joanna said, but looking down at Amelia, lying still and silent under the white blanket, her black hair splayed out around her head, she felt a shiver of anxiety. 'You're sure this procedure is safe?'

'I'm sure,' Richard said. 'And you don't have to whisper. Amelia can't hear you. It's perfectly safe.'

That's what the passengers on the *Hindenburg* thought, Joanna thought. And Mr O'Reirdon had coded in the middle of a scan. 'But what if something did go wrong while Amelia's under?'

'There's a program that continuously monitors the vitals readouts and the RIPT scan images,' Richard said. 'Any abnormality in brain function or heart activity triggers a computer alarm that automatically stops the dithetamine and administers norepinephrine. If it's a serious problem, the computer's hooked up to the code alarm for a crash cart team.'

'On this floor?' Joanna asked, thinking of a crash cart trying to find its way up from five-west.

'On this floor,' Richard reassured her. 'In this wing. But we won't need it. The procedure's perfectly safe, and the subjects are continuously monitored during and after the session.'

'I think I should tell you nothing's happening,' Amelia said, her voice with the too-loud emphasis of nonhearing.

Richard raised one headphone an inch, said, 'Coming right up,' and replaced it carefully over her ear. 'You think there's some other precaution we should be taking?' he asked Joanna.

Yes, Joanna thought. 'No.'

'Okay, then, let's do it,' he said. 'Nurse, start the zalepam. I put the subjects into non-REM sleep first,' he explained to Joanna, 'though it's possible for them to achieve an NDE-state without.'

Nurse Hawley began the feed. Richard positioned himself in front of the console. After a minute, Amelia's hands relaxed, the fingers splaying out a little from the position they had consciously held. Her face, half-hidden by the sleep mask, the electrodes, seemed to relax, too, the lips parting slightly, her breathing becoming lighter. Joanna glanced at the readouts. Amelia's pulse had risen slightly and her brainwaves were shallower.

'See how the activity shifts from the motor and sensory cortexes to the inner brain,' he said, pointing to the screens. 'She's in non-REM sleep. Okay, now I'm starting the dithetamine. Watch.' He pointed to the scan image again, where the color in the anterior temporal lobe was deepening from yellow to red and changing shape. 'The temporal lobe's taking on the characteristic pattern of the NDE,' he said, and, as the temporal lobe flared to red, 'And we have liftoff.'

'She's experiencing an NDE?' Joanna looked up at the image and then back down at Amelia. 'Right now?'

He nodded. 'She should be looking at the light,' he said, 'and feeling warm and peaceful.'

Joanna looked at Amelia. There was no indication that she was experiencing a tunnel or a bright light, and no sense, as Joanna had felt with Coma Carl or Greg Menotti, of Amelia's being somewhere far away, out of reach. She simply looked asleep, her lips still slightly parted, her face relaxed, giving no clue of what she was experiencing.

Joanna looked up at the screen, but its bright blotches of blue and red and yellow told her no more than Amelia's expression.

Richard had said her brain activity and vital signs were being monitored and an alarm would go off at any change in her blood pressure or brain function, but what if it didn't show up on the monitors? Fourteen percent of NDEers reported having frightening experiences, devils and monsters and suffocating darkness. What if something terrifying was happening to Amelia right now and she had no way to tell them?

But she didn't look terrified. In fact, she was smiling slightly, as if she were seeing something pleasant. Angels? Heavenly choirs? 'How long does the NDE last?' Joanna asked.

'It depends,' Richard said, busy at the console. 'Mr O'Reirdon's NDE lasted three minutes, but there's no physical reason they can't go ten to fifteen minutes.'

But four to six minutes causes brain death, Joanna thought, still unable to shake the feeling that this was an actual NDE and not a simulation.

'Theoretically, it could last as long as dithetamine's being fed in,' he said, 'but half the time, the— damn!'

'What? Is something wrong?' Joanna asked, glancing anxiously at the monitors and then at Amelia.

'She came out of the NDE spontaneously,' Richard said. 'I don't know if it's a problem with the dosage or if it's related to the NDE. It's one of the things we need to find out, what's kicking them out of the NDE-state and back into consciousness.'

'She's awake?'

'No,' Richard said, taking another look at the monitors. 'She's back in non-REM sleep.'

Joanna looked down at Amelia. Her hands still lay limply on the foam. The pleased half-smile remained. 'If the NDE is causing it,' Richard said, 'it may be the same mechanism that causes patients experiencing an NDE to revive, and if that's the case—'

There was a sound. 'Shh,' Joanna said, and bent over Amelia.

'Is she awake?' Richard said, looking at the screens. 'She shouldn't be. The pattern shows her in non-REM sleep.'

'*Shh*,' Joanna said and bent close to Amelia's mouth.

'Oh, no,' Amelia murmured, and her voice was hoarse and despairing. 'Oh, no, oh, no, oh, no.'

8

'To die would be an awfully big adventure.'
  – Last words of Broadway producer CHARLES FROHMAN,
    quoting from his close friend James Barrie's *Peter Pan*
      just before he went down on the *Lusitania*

Amelia Tanaka had no memory of anything negative in her NDE. 'It was just like the last time,' she told Joanna. 'There was a light, and this wonderful feeling.'

'Can you describe it?'

'The feeling?' Amelia said dreamily. 'Calm ... safe. I felt enveloped in love.'

You didn't sound enveloped in love, Joanna thought. You sounded terrified. 'Did you have that feeling the entire time?'

'Yes.'

Joanna gave up on that for the moment. 'Can you describe the light?'

'It was beautiful,' Amelia said. 'It was bright, but it didn't hurt my eyes.'

'What color was it?'

'White. Like a lamp, only really bright,' she said, and this time she squinted, as if it *had* hurt to look at it, in spite of what she had said.

'Was the light there all the time?'

'No, not at first, not till after they opened the door.'

Richard looked sharply at Joanna. I'm going to have to tell him he can't be present at these interviews, she thought. 'Where was the door?' she asked impassively.

'At the end of … I don't know,' Amelia said, frowning. 'I was in a hall, or a tunnel, or …' She shook her head.

Joanna waited, giving her time to say something else. When she didn't, Joanna said, 'You said, "They opened the door." Can you be more specific?'

'Um, I didn't actually see anybody open the door,' Amelia said. 'It was dark, and then all of a sudden, there was a light, like when somebody opens a door at night and the light spills in. I thought …' She squinted again and then shook her head. 'There was a light.'

'Did you hear anything?'

She shook her head, and then said, 'There was a sound at the very beginning.'

'Can you describe it?'

'It was a …' A ringing or a buzzing, Joanna thought resignedly. 'I can't really describe it,' Amelia said. 'I heard a sound, and then I was in this hall and the door opened and I saw the light. It was very real.'

'How did it feel real?'

'It wasn't like a dream. I was really there,' but when Joanna pressed her about tactile sensations and sensory involvement, she turned vague again. 'The light was all around me. I felt warm and … nice.'

'What about before the light? When you were in the dark place?'

Amelia smiled. 'Peaceful.'

'Were you aware of the temperature?'

'No, not at all.'

You just said you felt warm, Joanna thought, but she didn't say it. She switched the questioning to the door and the people in white, and then, after several minutes, brought the conversation back to feelings, but Amelia merely repeated that she had felt calm, nice, warm. 'The warmth surrounded me, like the light,' she said, 'and then Dr Wright was removing my headphones and asking me how I was feeling.'

When Joanna told her she was finished asking questions, Amelia said eagerly, 'When do I get to go under again?' and later, after she'd gotten dressed, she asked again, 'When's my next session?' She shouldered her backpack. 'This is a lot more fun than biochem.'

'Joanna, you were great,' Richard said as soon as Amelia was gone. 'I can't believe how much you got out of her.'

'I didn't find out why she said, "Oh, no, oh, no, oh, no." '

'That may have been part of the waking process and not the NDE,' he said. 'Mr Wojakowski said something the first time he came out of the dithetamine.'

'What?' Joanna demanded.

'I don't remember,' Richard said. 'Knowing him, it probably had something to do with the *Yorktown*.'

'When he said it, did he sound frightened?'

'I don't think so. I don't remember. The nurse might. Her name is in the session transcripts. It couldn't have been part of the NDE, you know. Speech isn't possible in the NDE state. The outer brain, including the speech cortex, is essentially shut down.'

But it could be Amelia's memory of the NDE immediately after she was revived, Joanna thought. A memory much different from the NDE she reported.

Richard said, 'What I'm really interested in is, how does her account compare with the subjects you've interviewed?'

'She had three of the ten core elements: the sound, the light, and the feeling of peace.'

'And the tunnel,' Richard said.

Joanna shook her head. 'Too vague. She couldn't describe either the darkness or the tunnel-slash-hall, and she didn't even mention it till I asked her if the light had been there all along. There may simply have been a blank space there between the sound and the light, and she was confabulating something to fill it.'

'But if you don't count the tunnel because she couldn't describe it, what about the sound?' Richard asked. 'She couldn't describe that either.'

'*Nobody* is able to describe the sound with any certainty,' Joanna said. 'Most of them can't describe it at all, and the ones who can say it's a ringing the first time you ask them and a whoosh the next, or a scream or a scraping sound or a thud. Or all three. Mr Steinhorst described it as someone whispering, and then, the second time I asked him, as a whole supermarket shelf of canned goods crashing down. I don't think they have any idea what they heard.'

'Do they have the same inconsistency describing what they've seen?'

'Yes and no. They're more consistent, but unless they've been coached by Mr Mandrake, they tend to use vague, general terms. The light is "bright," the place they're in is "beautiful." They hardly ever use specific sensory words or colors, with the exception of "white" and "golden." '

'That might indicate that the language cortex is only marginally involved,' he said, making a note of that. 'Which could cause their vagueness in describing the sound, too.'

She shook her head. 'They're not the same. When they describe what they've seen, they're vague, but they know what they've seen, even if they have trouble describing it. But with the sound, they don't seem to have any idea what they've heard. I get the idea they're just guessing.'

'You said she had three of the ten core elements,' Richard said. 'Do most subjects have all ten?'

'Only Mr Mandrake's,' she said. 'Most of my interview subjects have had between two and five. Some only had one. Or none,' she said, thinking of Maisie seeing fog and nothing else. 'The three Amelia had, plus the sense of people or "beings" being present, are the most common.'

'Was there anything you saw that indicated it wasn't an NDE? You seemed concerned about Amelia's sounding frightened. Is fear an indication it's not an NDE?'

'No, twenty percent of the experiences I've recorded have had a negative element, such as feeling fear or anxiety or a sense of impending doom.'

'Understandable under the circumstances,' Richard said.

Joanna grinned. 'Eleven percent report a completely negative experience – a gray, empty void or frightening figures. I've only had one who experienced a traditional hell – flames, smoke, demons.' She frowned. 'But Amelia said she didn't feel anything negative. And usually if they report a negative feeling, they don't also report feelings of peacefulness or warmth.'

'That's interesting,' Richard said. 'It might mean that in some NDEs, the endorphin levels are lower and can't completely mask anxious feelings. I want to look at the activity in Amelia's endorphin receptor sites,' he said, going over to the console. 'Was there anything else that made you think this wasn't an NDE?'

'No, there weren't any anomalous elements and nothing that indicated it was some other type of experience – a superimposed vision or a dream. In fact, her insistence that it wasn't a dream is a common phenomenon among NDEers. Nearly all of my subjects say something to the effect that it's real and become quite agitated if you suggest it might have been a dream or a vision. I can remember Mr Farquahar shouting, "I was there! It was real! I *know*!"'

'So you definitely think it was an NDE?' Richard said.

'I think so, yes. Her account sounded just like the revived patients I've interviewed.'

'It wasn't too close, was it?' he asked. 'You don't think she could be a spy for Mandrake and have faked it?'

She laughed. 'If she were one of Mandrake's spies, she'd have had all ten elements and brought back a message from the Other Side, telling us there are things science can't explain.' She stood up. 'I'd better get this transcribed before it gets cold. And I've still got to set up interviews with the other three volunteers,' she said. She gathered up the files. 'I'll be in my office if you need me. Otherwise, I'll see you tomorrow.'

'Tomorrow?' he said, surprised.

'Yes. Why? Was there something else you needed me for this afternoon?'

'No,' he said, frowning. 'No. I'm going to look at the receptor sites and then check Amelia's readouts to see what endorphins were present.'

Joanna went back to her office to transcribe the interview, but first she needed to call the rest of the volunteers. She set up interviews with Mr Sage, Ms Coffey, and Mrs Troudtheim, calling Mrs Haighton, who was apparently never home, in between. Vielle called at four. 'Can you come over early?' she asked. 'Say, at six-thirty?'

'I guess,' Joanna said. 'Look, if you want to get to bed early, we can make this another night.'

'No,' Vielle said. 'I just want to talk to you about something.'

'What?' Joanna said suspiciously. 'That nail-gunner didn't show up and shoot somebody, did he?'

'No. The nail-gunnee showed up, though, and you should have seen the police officer they sent over to arrest him. Gorgeous! Six foot three, and looks just like Denzel Washington. Unfortunately, I was cleaning pus out of an infected toe and didn't get to meet him.'

'Is Denzel what you wanted to talk to me about?' Joanna asked, amused.

'Oops, gotta go. Van rollover. Wouldn't you know it? Right as I'm supposed to get off.'

'If you're going to be late,' Joanna began, 'we could—'

'Six-thirty. And can you pick up some cream cheese?' she said and hung up.

And what was that all about? Dish Night was completely informal. Half the time they didn't start the movies till halfway through the evening, so if Vielle wanted to talk, they could do it anytime. And earlier she'd done everything she could to avoid talking.

She's found out what Greg Menotti was talking about, and it's something terrible, Joanna thought, so terrible she couldn't tell me in the ER.

But when she'd asked her, she'd genuinely seemed to have forgotten about him. She's transferring out of the ER, Joanna thought. Oh, now she was letting her imagination completely run away from her.

She typed up Amelia's account of her NDE with annotations. When she got to the 'oh, no's' on the tape, she stopped, rewound, and listened to it two more times. Fear, and despair, and something else. Joanna rewound again, and pressed 'play.' 'Oh, no, oh, no, oh, no.' Knowledge, Joanna thought, like someone has just told her something she can't bear to hear.

She went back to the lab, got Mr Wojakowski's file from Richard, and looked up the name of the nurse who'd assisted at Mr Wojakowski's session. Ann Collins. It wasn't anybody Joanna knew. She called the hospital operator and found out what floor she was subbing on, but she'd gone off-shift at three. 'You have several messages,' the operator said sternly.

'Sorry,' Joanna said. 'What are they? I think there's something wrong with my pager.' The operator told her. Mr Mandrake, of course, and Mrs Davenport, and Maisie. 'She said to tell you she'd found out something important about ...' she hesitated, 'the Hildebrand?'

'The *Hindenburg*,' Joanna said. She looked at her watch. It was after five. If she went to see Maisie now, she was likely to get caught, and she still hadn't transcribed her conclusions. She'd better finish the account first, and run by Maisie's room on her way out.

Just before she left, she tried Mrs Haighton one more time, and, amazingly, got an answer. 'This is her housekeeper. Mrs Haighton's at her Symphony Guild board. Is this Victoria? She said to tell you she'll be late to the meeting tomorrow because she has an Opera Colorado meeting.'

'I'm not Victoria,' Joanna said, and asked her to tell Mrs Haighton to please call her tomorrow, gathered up her coat and bag, and started down to see Maisie. As she got out of the elevator next to the walkway on fifth, she saw Mr Mandrake down the hall, expounding on the afterlife to a patient in a wheelchair. She stepped hastily back in the elevator, punched three, and took the third-floor walkway instead, cutting through Medicine and the Burn Unit, and up the service stairs to fourth.

Maisie was lying back against her pillows, reading *Peter Pan*. All very innocent, but there was an air of secretiveness, of hurried movement about the scene, as if she would have caught Maisie turning somersaults or swinging from the traction bars above her bed if she'd gotten there a moment earlier. 'You rang, kiddo?' Joanna said, and Maisie instantly shut the book and sat up.

'Hi,' she said happily. 'I knew you'd come. Nurse Barbara didn't want to page you, but I told her you'd want to know this right away. You know the guy on the *Hindenburg* who had the NDE?'

'Yes. Did you find out his name?'

'Not yet,' Maisie said, 'but I figured out a way to. The librarian at my school, Ms Sutterly, always brings me books to read, so the next time she comes I'm going to ask her if she can look it up. She's really good at finding things out.'

And you're really good at thinking up reasons to get me down here, Joanna thought.

'Wasn't that a good idea?' Maisie said.

'Yes. When you find out from her, you can have me paged.' And not before, she added silently. She started for the door.

'Wait, you can't go yet,' Maisie said. 'You just got here. I've got a whole bunch of stuff to tell you.'

'Two minutes,' Joanna said, 'and then I have to go.'

'Are you going out on a date?'

'No, I'm going to Dish Night.'

'Dish Night? What's that?'

Joanna explained how she and Vielle got together to eat popcorn and watch movies. 'So I've really got to go,' she said, patting Maisie's feet through the covers. 'Bye, kiddo. I'll come see you tomorrow, and you can tell me all about the *Hindenburg*.'

'*Not* the *Hindenburg*,' Maisie said. 'I don't like it anymore.'

Joanna looked at her, surprised. 'How come?' Was it possible a disaster had gotten too grisly even for her?

'It was boring.'

'So what are you reading now?' Joanna asked, leaning over to pick up Maisie's discarded book. '*Peter Pan*. Good book, huh?'

Maisie shrugged. 'I think the part where Tinkerbell almost dies and they save her just by everybody believing in fairies is stupid.'

I can imagine, Joanna thought.

'I like the part where Peter Pan says to die would be an awfully big adventure, though,' she said. 'Did you know there were a whole bunch of babies on the *Lusitania*?'

'The *Lusitania*? You mean the ship that got torpedoed by the Germans in World War I?'

'Yes,' Maisie said happily. She reached under the covers and pulled out an enormous book with a tornado on the cover. Which explained the sensation of abruptly checked movement Joanna had felt when she walked in. 'There were all these babies on the ship,' Maisie said, opening the book. 'They tied lifejackets to their bassinets, but it didn't do any good. The babies still all drowned.'

Well, so much for the 'too grisly' theory. 'This is Dean and Willie,' Maisie said, showing Joanna a picture of two little boys in white sailor suits. 'They drowned, too. And here's the funerals.' Joanna looked dutifully at the photo of a phalanx of priests in white surplices officiating over rows of coffins.

'One of the *Lusitania* stewards kept saying everything was all right, that they weren't sinking, and there was nothing to worry about,' Maisie said. 'He shouldn't have done that, should he?'

'No, not if the ship was sinking.'

'I *hate* when people lie. You know that dog named Ulla on the *Hindenburg*?'

'The German shepherd?'

Maisie nodded. 'He didn't get saved. The mom and dad just said he did. He got *burned up*, and the mom and dad got another German shepherd and told their kids it was Ulla. So they wouldn't feel bad.' She looked belligerently at Joanna. 'I don't think parents should lie to their kids about dying, do you?'

'No,' Joanna said, afraid of where this was going, of what Maisie would ask next. 'I don't.'

'There was a poodle on the *Lusitania*,' Maisie said, and showed her a picture of it and of bodies washed onto the shore, of the *Lusitania* foundering helplessly in the water, smoke and fire all around.

'I've really got to go, Maisie,' Joanna said. 'I told my friend I'd bring some cream cheese, and I've got to stop at the store on the way.'

'Cream cheese?' Maisie said. 'I thought you said you ate popcorn.'

'We usually do,' Joanna said, wondering again what Vielle was up to and what she wanted to talk about that made it necessary for her to come early. 'But this time we're eating cream cheese, and I've got to go pick it up.' She started out.

'Wait!' Maisie yelped. 'I have to tell you about Helen first.'

'Helen?'

'This little girl on the *Lusitania*,' Maisie said, and hurried on before Joanna could stop her, 'she looked all over for her mom, but she couldn't find her anywhere, so she ran up to this man, and said, "Please, mister, will you take me with you?" and he said, "Stay right there, Helen," and ran to get her a lifejacket.'

And he never saw her again, Joanna thought, knowing the type of story Maisie usually told. But, surprisingly, Maisie was saying, '... and he ran back and tied the lifejacket on her and then he picked her up and took her to look for a lifeboat, but it was already going down the side.' Maisie paused dramatically. 'So what do you think he did?'

He tried to save her, but he couldn't, Joanna thought, looking at Maisie. And she drowned. 'I don't know,' Joanna said.

'He threw Helen into the boat,' Maisie said triumphantly, 'and then he jumped in, too, and they both got saved.'

'I like that story,' Joanna said.

'Me, too,' Maisie said, ''cause he saved her. And he didn't tell her everything would be all right.'

'Sometimes people do that because they hope things will be all right,' Joanna said, 'or because they're afraid the person will be frightened or sad if they know the truth. I think that's probably why the parents lied to their children about Ulla, because they wanted to protect them.'

'They still shouldn't've,' Maisie said, her jaw set. 'People should tell you the truth, even if it's bad. Shouldn't they?'

'Yes,' Joanna said and waited, holding her breath for the question that was coming, but Maisie merely said, 'Will you put my book away first? It goes in my duffel bag. So my room won't be all messy.' And so your mother won't catch you with it, Joanna thought. She took the book over to the closet, stuck it in the pink duffel bag, and handed Maisie back *Peter Pan*.

And just in time. Maisie's mother appeared in the door with a huge pink teddy bear and a beaming smile. 'How's my Maisie-Daisy? Dr Lander, doesn't she look wonderful?' She handed Maisie the teddy bear. 'So, what have you two been talking about?'

'Dogs,' Maisie said.

9

'Mildred, why aren't my clothes laid out? I've got a seven o'clock call.'

– Last words of BERT LAHR

It was six-forty-five before Joanna made it to Vielle's. 'What happened to you?' Vielle said. 'I said six-thirty.'

'I got caught by Maisie. And her mother,' Joanna said, taking off her coat. 'She wanted to tell me how well Maisie's doing.'

'And is she?'

'No.'

Vielle nodded. 'Barbara told me they put her on the transplant list. It's too bad. She's a great kid.'

'She is,' Joanna said and took her coat into the bedroom.

'Did you bring the cream cheese?' Vielle called from the kitchen.

Joanna brought it in to her. 'What are you making?'

'This luscious dip,' Vielle said, leaning over a cookbook with a knife in her hand. 'It's got deviled ham in it. And chiles.' She glanced at the clock. 'Listen, the reason I wanted you to come over early was so we'd have a chance to talk before Dr Wright gets here. So how are you two getting along?'

'You invited Richard to Dish Night?' Joanna said. 'No wonder he looked at me funny when I told him I'd see him tomorrow.'

'Richard, huh? So you two are on a first-name basis already?'

'We're not—' A thought struck her. 'That's what you called from the ER about, wasn't it? And why you were acting so peculiar.'

'I *called* to tell you I couldn't find any movies that didn't have death in them and did you have any suggestions,' Vielle said, opening the refrigerator and getting out a bunch of green onions, 'and you weren't there, so I told him some of us were getting together for munchies and a movie and did he want to drop by.'

'Some of us!' Joanna said. 'And when he gets here, and it's you and me, you don't think he'll realize you've been matchmaking? Or were you planning to hand me the deviled ham dip and duck out the back door? I can't believe you did this.'

'Don't you like him?'

'I hardly know him. We only started working together two days ago.'

Vielle shook the bunch of onions at her. 'And you'll never get a chance to know him once the nurses of Mercy General get their claws into him. Do you know who asked me if he was single this afternoon? Tish Vanderbeck. You don't see her waiting around because she "hardly knows him." If you don't watch it, you'll get stuck with somebody like Harvey.'

'Harvey? Who's Harvey?'

'The driver for Fairhill Mortuaries. He asks me out every time he comes to pick up a body.'

'Is he nice?'

'He tells me embalming stories. Did you know they really like carbon monoxide poisoning over at Fairhill because it turns the corpses a pretty rose-pink, in contrast to the usual gray? He imparted that little gem Tuesday and then asked me out for sushi.'

Tuesday. The day Greg Menotti died. She wondered if his was the body Harvey had picked up. 'Did you find out if there was a fifty-eight in Greg Menotti's health insurance number?'

'Greg Menotti?' Vielle said as if she'd never heard the name before, and then, 'Oh, right. Yes, I checked. No fifty-eights. I checked his address, office, home and cell phone numbers, health insurance number—'

'His Social Security number?' Joanna asked.

She nodded. 'His license number was on the paramedic's report. I checked that, too. Ditto his girlfriend's address and phone numbers. Nothing.' She bent over to get a cutting board out of the cupboard. 'Like I told you, people in extremis say things that don't make any sense. I had a guy who kept calling, 'Lucille,' and we all thought it was his wife. Turns out it was his dog.'

'Then it did mean something,' Joanna said.

'That one did, but a lot of them don't. A head trauma last week kept saying, 'camel,' which obviously wasn't his wife or his cat.'

'What was it?'

'We didn't get a chance to ask him,' Vielle said tersely, 'but my guess is, it didn't mean anything. People like your infarction aren't getting enough oxygen, they're disoriented, and they're not making any sense.'

She was right. When he was dying, the author Tom Dooley had told his friend to go ahead to the airport and save him a seat on the plane, and prima ballerina Anna Pavlova had ordered her doctors to get her swan costume ready.

'Back to Dr Wright,' Vielle said. 'I'm not saying you have to marry the guy.

All we're doing is putting an option on him. They do it in Hollywood all the time.' She laid the onions in a row on the board. 'You option the screenplay, it doesn't necessarily mean you're going to make a movie out of it, but later on, if you decide you do want to, somebody else hasn't snapped it up in the meantime.'

'Dr Wright is not a screenplay.'

'It was a simile.'

Joanna shook her head at her. 'Metaphor. A simile is a direct comparison using *like* or *as*. A metaphor is indirect. My English teacher spent my whole senior year drilling the difference into me.' She stopped, staring at the cutting board.

'Your English teacher should have spent time on more important things,' Vielle said, 'like teaching you that when Mr Right, or Dr Wright, comes along, you have to—'

The doorbell rang. 'He's here,' Vielle said, but Joanna didn't hear her. For an instant, standing there watching Vielle chop green onions, she had had the feeling, out of nowhere, that she knew what Greg Menotti had been talking about, that she knew what 'fifty-eight' meant.

It must have been what she or Vielle had said. They had been talking about Dr Wright, and—

'Come on in,' Vielle said from the living room. 'Joanna's in the kitchen. Sorry about the knife. I'm in the middle of making dip.'

Something about optioning a screenplay. No. It stayed tantalizingly there at the edge of her memory, just out of reach.

'Look who's here,' Vielle said, leading Richard into the kitchen. 'I believe you two know each other.'

'I'm sorry I'm late,' Richard said, handing Vielle a six-pack of Coke. 'I got caught by Mandrake on my way out. Oh, and Joanna, I think I've got a nurse lined up to assist. Tish Vanderbeck. She works on third.'

Behind him, Vielle mouthed, 'What did I tell you? Tell him no.' Joanna ignored her.

'She says she knows you,' Richard said.

'I do know her,' Joanna said. 'She'll be great. What did Mandrake want?'

'He wanted to know if—'

'Stop!' Vielle said, brandishing the knife. 'This is Dish Night. No talking about work or the hospital allowed.'

'Oh,' Richard said. 'Sorry. I didn't know there were rules. This isn't like *Fight Club*, is it?'

'No,' Joanna laughed.

Behind him, Vielle made an 'okay' sign and mouthed, 'Mr Right.'

'It isn't a club at all. Vielle and I got to talking one day and discovered we both liked discussing movies.'

'As opposed to bitching about the patients and the doctors and the cafeteria's never being open,' Vielle said.

'It isn't, is it?' Richard said. 'It's closed every time I go down there.'

Vielle held up a warning finger. 'Rule Number One.'

'So we decided to get together once a week and watch a double feature,' Joanna said.

'And eat,' Vielle said, taking a package of hot dogs out of the refrigerator. 'Rule Number Two, only concession-stand foods allowed – popcorn, Jujubees—'

'Deviled ham dip,' Joanna said.

Vielle glared at her. 'Rule Number Three, you have to stay for the entire double feature—'

'But you don't have to pay any attention to it,' Joanna said. 'You're allowed to talk during the movie and make rude comments *about* the movie or about movies in general.'

Vielle nodded. '*Dances with Wolves* was good for all of the above.'

'Rule Number Four, no movies with Sylvester Stallone in them, no Woody Allen movies, and no *Titanic*. This is a *Titanic*-free zone.'

'And why is it called Dish Night?' Richard asked. 'I thought Rule Number One was no gossiping.'

'It is,' Vielle said. 'The reason it's called Dish Night is—'

'Because my grandmother used to tell me about going to the movies in the thirties,' Joanna said quickly, 'when they used to have Dish Night and raffle off a set of dishes, and this is an old-fashioned night at the movies. Vielle, where are the movies?'

'Right here.' She handed them to Joanna. 'And because we're a couple of dishes. Or at least Joanna is. Why don't you two go start the movie? I've got to finish my dip.' She pushed them into the living room.

And could you be more obvious? Joanna thought. 'I want to apologize for my idiot friend,' Joanna said. 'And for the mix-up this afternoon. She forgot to tell me you were coming.'

He grinned at her. 'I figured that out.'

Joanna glanced toward the kitchen. 'What did Mr Mandrake want?'

'He said he'd heard I had a new partner,' Richard said.

'Good old Gossip General,' Joanna said, shaking her head. 'Did he know it was me?'

'I don't think so. He—'

'Rule Number One,' Vielle shouted from the kitchen.

Joanna called back, 'Which movie do you want to watch first? *A Will to Win* or' – she looked at the second box – '*Lady and the Tramp*?'

'You said something with no deaths in it,' Vielle shouted.

'Is that a rule, too?' Richard asked.

'No,' Joanna said, turning on the TV. An ad for Carnival Cruise Lines was on. A couple stood on deck, leaning over the railing. 'What did Mandrake say?'

Richard grinned. 'He came in when I was working on the scans, which, by the way, did show that Amelia Tanaka had a lower level of activity at the endorphin receptor sites, and said he'd heard I had a new partner, and he hoped I hadn't made a final decision yet because he had several excellent people he could recommend.'

'I'll bet,' Joanna said, sticking *A Will to Win* in the VCR and fast-forwarding through the previews to the opening credits. She hit 'pause.'

'He also said he hoped the partner I chose wouldn't be "narrow-minded" and "biased toward traditional, so-called scientific interpretations of the NDE,"' Richard said, 'but would be "open to nonrationalist possibilities."'

Joanna laughed.

'Well, you obviously can't be talking about work,' Vielle said, appearing with two cans of Coke. She handed them to them. 'What's wrong with the movie?'

'Nothing,' Joanna said. 'We were waiting for you.'

'Go ahead and start it,' Vielle said. 'I'll be right in. Sit *down.*'

They sat down on the couch. Joanna picked up the remote and unpaused the video, and they watched as a family gathered around the bedside of an old man. A nurse stood next to the bed, taking his pulse. 'I've gathered you all here because I'm dying,' the old man said.

'Hey, Vielle,' Joanna called, 'I thought this was supposed to be a death-free movie.'

'It is,' Vielle said, appearing in the door with the knife and a can of chiles. 'Isn't it?'

Joanna pointed to the screen, where the old man was clutching his chest and gasping, 'My pills!'

'Oh, my God,' Vielle said, coming around the couch for a closer look. 'The Blockbuster clerk told me this was a comedy.'

'It is,' Richard said. 'I've seen a preview. The old man dies without telling them where he's hidden his will, and all the heirs race around trying to find it.'

The old man began to gasp and wheeze. 'Have to … tell you …' he choked out, and everyone, including the nurse, leaned forward. '… my will …'

'This would never happen,' Vielle said. 'They'd have called 911 by now, and the whole bunch of them would be enacting this little scene in the middle of my ER.'

'Oh, that's right, you work in the ER,' Richard said to Vielle. 'I heard about the incident this afternoon.'

'What incident?' Joanna asked sharply.

'You're breaking Dish Night Rule Number One,' Vielle said. 'No discussing work.'

Joanna turned to Richard. 'What did you hear?'

'Just that a woman high on this new drug rogue came in and was waving a razor around,' Richard said.

'A *razor*,' Joanna said. 'Vielle, you have got to—'

'Finish making my dip.' She waved the knife at them. 'Go on. Watch the movie. I'll be right back.' She disappeared.

'Excuse me for a minute,' Joanna said and followed her into the kitchen. 'Why didn't you tell me about it?' she demanded.

'It's Dish Night,' Vielle said, stirring chiles into the dip. 'Besides, it was nothing. Nobody got hurt.'

'Vielle—'

'I know, I know, I've got to get out of there. Do you think we need a knife, or should we just dip?'

'We don't need a knife,' Joanna said, giving up. Vielle handed her the plate of crackers and picked up the dip, and they went back into the living room.

'What'd we miss?' Vielle asked, setting the dip on the coffee table.

'Nothing,' Richard said. 'I paused it.' He picked up the remote and pointed it at the screen.

'I've gathered … you here …' the old man, lying against his multiple pillows, gasped. '… Don't have long to live …' The family leaned forward like a pack of vultures. 'Made a new will … hid it in … the …' He flung his arms out and fell back peacefully against the pillows, his eyes closed. The family exchanged glances.

'Is he gone?' one of the women said, sniffing phonily and dabbing at her eyes with a lace handkerchief.

'Movie dying,' Vielle sniffed, dipping a cracker in the deviled ham dip. It broke off.

'Movie dying?' Richard asked, scooping up dip with a cracker. It broke off, too.

'Meaning totally unrealistic,' Joanna said. 'Like movie parking, where the hero is always able to find a parking place right in front of the store or the police station.'

'Or movie lighting,' Vielle said, digging cracker pieces out of the dip.

'Let me guess,' Richard said. 'Being able to see in the middle of a cave in the middle of the night.'

'We should add a new category for this kind of thing,' Joanna said, gesturing at the screen, where the relatives were bickering across the old man's body. 'I mean, why do people in movies always say things like, "The secret is – argggghh!" Or "The murderer is—" Bang! You'd think, if they had something that important to communicate, they'd say that first, that they wouldn't say, "The will is in the oak tree," they'd say, "Oak tree! Will! It's in there!" If I were dying, I'd say the important part first, so I wouldn't run the risk of going "… argghh!" before I managed to get it out.'

'No, you wouldn't,' Vielle said, 'because you wouldn't be saying something like that in the first place. They only talk about secrets and clues in the movies. In the six years I've been in the ER, I've never had a patient whose last words were about a will or who the murderer is. And that includes murder victims.'

'What are their last words?' Richard asked curiously.

'Obscenities, a lot of them, unfortunately,' Vielle said. 'Also, "My side hurts," "I can't breathe," "Turn me over."'

Joanna nodded. 'That's what Walt Whitman said to his nurse. And Robert Kennedy said, "Don't lift me."'

Vielle explained, 'As if talking to patients about their NDEs isn't bad enough, in her spare time Joanna researches famous people's last words.'

'I wanted to know if there are similarities between what they say and what people report in their NDEs,' Joanna explained.

'And are there?' Richard asked.

'Sometimes. Thomas Edison's last words were "It's beautiful over there," but he was sitting by a window. He may just have been looking at the view. Or maybe not. John Wayne said, "Did you see that flash of light?" But Vielle's right. Mostly they say things like "My head hurts."'

'Or, "I don't feel good,"' Vielle said, 'or, "I can't sleep," or, "I'm cold."'

Joanna thought of Amelia Tanaka asking for a blanket. 'Do they ever say, "Oh, no, oh, no, oh, no"?' she asked.

Vielle nodded. 'A lot of them, and a *lot* of them ask for ice,' she said, taking a swig of Coke, 'or water.'

Joanna nodded. 'General Grant asked for water, and so did Marie Curie. And Lenin.'

'That's funny,' Richard said. 'You'd expect Lenin's last words to be "Workers, arise!" or something.'

Vielle shook her head. 'The eternal verities aren't what's on people's minds when they're dying. They're much more concerned with the matter at hand.'

'"Put your hands on my shoulders and don't struggle,"' Joanna murmured.

'Who said that?' Richard asked.

'W. S. Gilbert. You know, of Gilbert and Sullivan. *Pirates of Penzance*. He died saving a young girl from drowning. I've always thought that if I could choose, that's how I'd like to die.'

'By drowning?' Vielle said. 'No, you don't want to drown. That's a terrible way to die, trust me.'

'Gilbert didn't drown,' Joanna said. 'He had a heart attack. I meant, I'd like to die saving somebody else's life.'

'I want to die in my sleep,' Vielle said. 'Massive aneurysm. At home. How about you, Dr Wright?'

'I don't want to die at all,' Richard said, and they all laughed.

'Unfortunately, that's not an option,' Vielle sighed, breaking off another cracker in the stiff dip. 'We all die sooner or later, and we don't get to choose the method. We have to take what we get. We had an old man in the ER this afternoon, final stages of diabetes, both feet amputated, blind, kidney failure, his whole body coming apart. His last words were, as you might expect, "Leave me alone."'

'Those were Princess Di's last words, too,' Joanna said.

'I thought she asked someone to take care of her sons,' Richard said.

'I think I'd believe the first one,' Vielle said. '"Tell Laura I love her" is for romantic movies like *Titanic*. The patients we get in the ER hardly ever have messages for anybody. They're too busy concentrating on what's happening to *them*, although I suppose Joanna knows of some famous people who sent last messages to their loved ones. Right, Joanna?'

Joanna wasn't listening. As Vielle was talking she'd had it again, that teasing sense that she knew what 'fifty-eight' meant. 'Right, Joanna?'

'Oh. Yes. Tchaikovsky and Queen Victoria and P. T. Barnum. Anne Brontë said, "Take courage, Charlotte, take courage." This dip is not a dip. We do need a knife after all,' she said and escaped into the kitchen.

What had they been talking about that had triggered the feeling? Princess Di? Diabetes? No, it must have been something that echoed their earlier conversation. Joanna took a table knife out of the silverware drawer and then stood there with it in her hand, trying to reconstruct the scene in her head. They'd been talking about movie options, and—

'Can't you find the knives?' Vielle called from the living room. 'They're in the top drawer next to the dishwasher.'

'I know,' Joanna said. 'I'll be there in a minute.' Could there be a movie with the number fifty-eight in the title? Or a song? Vielle had mentioned 'Tell Laura I love her—'

'Joanna,' Vielle called, 'you're missing the movie!'

This was ridiculous. Greg Menotti hadn't been trying to say anything. He'd been echoing the nurse's reciting of his blood pressure, and she had only thought it meant something because of a fifty-eight in her memory, a fifty-eight their conversation had triggered. A line from a movie or a number out of her past, her grandmother's address, her high school locker number—

High school. It had something to do with high school—

'Joanna!' Vielle called.

'If you don't get in here,' Richard said, 'our last words are going to be "Joanna, we're starv— ... argghh!"'

Something about high school and— It was no use. Whatever it was, was gone. She took the knife into the living room and handed it to Richard. 'You're saying it wrong. Important words first. Like this. "Starving we argghh!"'

They all spread deviled ham dip on their crackers. 'Maybe the best plan would be to decide in advance what you wanted your last words to be and then memorize them, so you'd be ready,' Joanna said.

'Like what?' Richard said.

'I don't know,' Joanna said. 'Words of wisdom or something.'

'Like "A penny saved is a penny earned"?' Vielle said. 'I'd rather have "My side hurts."'

'How about "So here it is at last, the distinguished thing"?' Joanna suggested. 'That's what Henry James said right before he died.'

'No, wait,' Richard said. 'I've got it.' He spread his arms for dramatic effect. '"There are more things in heaven and earth, Horatio, than are dreamt of in your philosophy."'

10

'Water! Water!'
— Last words of CAPTAIN LEHMANN,
captain of the *Hindenburg*, dying of burns

'He definitely likes you,' Vielle said when she called between patients the next morning. 'Now aren't you glad I invited him to Dish Night?'

'Vielle, I'm busy—' Joanna said.

'He's handsome, smart, funny. But that means there's going to be a lot of competition out there, so you're going to have to really go after him. And the first thing you've got to do is stop him from hiring Tish.'

'It's too late,' Joanna said. 'He hired her this morning.'

'And you *let* him?' Vielle squealed. 'She flirts with everything that moves. *What* were you thinking?'

That, unlike Karen Goebel, who had been the only other applicant, Tish wasn't a spy for Mr Mandrake. And that since Tish's chief goal was pursuing Richard, she probably wouldn't endanger her chances with him by blabbing to Mr Mandrake. And she was a very good nurse.

'I can't believe you let him hire her!' Vielle said.

'Did you call for some reason, Vielle?' Joanna asked. 'Because if you didn't, I have background checks to run, I've got to interview the rest of our volunteers, and Maisie's been calling me all morning wanting me to come see her.'

And I need to try to remember what triggered that feeling of knowing what 'fifty-eight' meant last night.

'You just answered the question I called to ask you,' Vielle said. 'You don't have time.'

'For what? An NDE subject? Did somebody come into the ER?'

'Yes. A Mrs Woollam. They've already taken her upstairs. I tried to page you, but you weren't answering. I thought if I had you paged over the intercom, Mr Mandrake would descend—'

'– "like a wolf on the fold,"' Joanna said, and stopped. There was that sensation again, that feeling of knowing what Greg Menotti had been talking about. What was the rest of that quote? 'Something something purple and gold.'

'Joanna?' Vielle said. 'Are you still there?'

'Yes. Sorry. What did you say her name was?'

'Mrs Woollam. And, listen, she's not just an ordinary NDEer. She's a sudden deather.'

'Sudden deather?'

'Her heart tends to fibrillate suddenly and stop pumping. Luckily it also tends to start up again with a shot of epi and one good shock from the paddles, but she's coded eight times in the past year. We're talking experienced.'

'Why haven't I met her before?' Joanna said.

'The last time she was at Mercy General was before you came,' Vielle said. 'They usually take her to Porter's. Her doctor just switched HMOs, though, so now they're bringing her here. She says she's had an NDE all but one time she coded.'

Someone who'd had several NDEs and could compare and contrast them. It sounded perfect. 'Where did they take her?'

'CICU,' Vielle said. 'They took her up about ten minutes ago.' And it would be another fifteen before they got her settled and allowed visitors in. Joanna looked at her watch. Mr Kelso would be here in ten minutes. She'd have to wait till after his interview, and the one after that, with Ms Coffey, by which time Mr Mandrake would have convinced her she'd seen an Angel of Light and had a life review, but it couldn't be helped.

'I'll go see her as soon as I can,' she promised Vielle. 'I'm sorry about my pager, but Mr Mandrake keeps calling me. He says he's got something urgent to discuss with me. I'm afraid it means he's found out about my working on the project.'

'He had to find out sooner or later. But maybe he'll be so busy descending on you, he won't find out about Mrs Woollam,' she said and hung up.

Descending like a wolf on the fold. 'And his cohorts were gleaming in purple and gold.' That was the line. But where on earth had it come from? And what did it have to do with anything, let alone Greg Menotti's murmuring, 'Fifty-eight'?

There wasn't time to worry about it. She needed to look over Ronald Kelso's file and get to the lab in case, unlike Amelia Tanaka, he was on time.

He was, and neatly dressed, in slacks, a shirt, and a tie. 'I work at Hollywood Video,' he said when Joanna asked him to tell her a little about himself, 'but I'm studying to be a computer programmer. I'm taking classes at Metro Technical College.'

'Can you tell me why you volunteered for this project?' Joanna asked.

'I want to know death.'

'Know death?' Richard said, turning faintly green.

'How did you know the project involved near-death experiences?' Joanna asked.

'One of the people in my chat room told me it did.'

'Who?' Richard asked.

'I don't know. His on-line name is Osiris.' He leaned forward eagerly. 'People in our society don't understand death. They won't even talk about it. They just pretend it's not there, that it's not going to happen to them, and when *you* try to talk about it, they look at you like you're crazy. Have you ever seen the movie *Harold and Maude*?'

'Yes,' Joanna said.

'It's my favorite movie of all time. I've seen it probably a hundred times, especially the scene where he hangs himself.'

Joanna said, 'And so you think this project …'

'Will give me the chance to experience death firsthand, to look it in the face and find out what it's really like.'

'We haven't finalized our participant list yet,' Joanna said, showing him to the door. 'We'll let you know.'

'I can't believe it,' Richard said after she'd shut the door. 'Another one! And he looked perfectly normal.'

'He probably is,' Joanna said. '*Harold and Maude*'s a really good movie, and he didn't say anything that wasn't true. People in our society *don't* want to talk about death. They *do* pretend it's not there and it's not going to happen to them.'

'You're not seriously suggesting we should accept him into the project?' Richard said.

'No,' Joanna said. 'He's a little too fascinated by the subject matter, and his comments about the hanging scene were rather disturbing. *And* we've got a rule about movies with death in them.' She grinned at him.

'This isn't funny,' Richard said. 'How many volunteers are left on the list? Three?'

'Four,' Joanna said. 'Ms Coffey's next. She'll be here at ten.'

'The data systems manager,' Richard said, cheering up. 'Great. She's got an MBA and works for Colotech.'

That isn't any guarantee, Joanna thought, although she had to agree with Richard. MBAs weren't usually the *Harold and Maude* type, and Ms Coffey looked extremely promising when she arrived. She was dressed in a stylish black suit, and her sleek haircut, her makeup, were the image of Corporate Woman. When Joanna asked her to tell her a little bit about herself, she opened her Corporate Woman day planner and pulled out a folded sheet of cream-colored vellum. 'I know you have my application,' she said, 'but I thought a résumé might be useful, too.' She smiled and handed it to Richard.

'Why did you volunteer for the project?' Joanna asked.

'As you can see on my résumé –' Ms Coffey said and pulled out another folded sheet. She smiled. 'I brought an extra one, just in case. In my job, details really matter.' She handed the résumé to Joanna. 'As you can see, under "Service,"' she pointed out the place, 'I do a lot of work with the community. Last year I participated in a sleep study at University Hospital.' She smiled warmly at Richard. 'And when Dr Wright described the project, I thought it sounded interesting.'

'Have you ever had a near-death experience?' Joanna asked.

'You mean where I nearly died and then experienced a tunnel and a light? No.'

'What about an out-of-body experience?' Joanna asked.

'Where people imagine they actually leave their bodies?' she said, frowning skeptically. *'No.'*

'Are you familiar with the works of Maurice Mandrake?' Joanna asked, watching her closely, but there wasn't even a flicker of recognition as she shook her sleekly coiffed head.

Richard fidgeted, trying to catch Joanna's eye. He was obviously convinced, and there wasn't anything suspicious in Ms Coffey's background. 'If we asked you to participate in the project,' Joanna asked, 'when would you be available?'

'Wednesday mornings and Thursday afternoons,' Ms Coffey said, 'but Mondays would be the best for me. My psychic powers are strongest on days governed by the moon goddess. Because of the sympathetic harmonic vibrations.'

'We'll let you know,' Joanna said. Ms Coffey gave them each a copy of her business card. 'My home and office numbers are there, and my cell phone number. Or you can contact me via e-mail.'

'Or via telepathy. My God!' Richard exploded as soon as the door was safely shut behind her. 'Are they all crazy?'

I hope not, Joanna thought and pulled out Mrs Troudtheim's file. She made a note to ask her why she'd volunteered to drive all the way from Deer Trail to participate in a research project and hoped there was a rational answer. Rural Colorado tended to have more than its share of UFO abductees and cattle mutilation conspiracy theorists.

'Oh, but I'm not driving,' she told Joanna. 'I have to have a whole bunch of dental work done, and you never know about the weather this time of year so I'm staying with my son till it's all done. But you know how it is, living with your kids. I thought participating in a study was a way to get out of my daughter-in-law's hair once in a while. And I hate just sitting around doing nothing.'

Apparently. 'Do you mind if I crochet while we talk?' she had asked Joanna at the beginning of the interview and, when Joanna said she didn't, had pulled out yarn and a half-finished orange-and-yellow-green Afghan and begun working on it with work-weathered hands.

Joanna asked her about Deer Trail and her life on the ranch. Mrs Troudtheim's answers were comfortable and matter-of-fact, and when Joanna asked her to describe the ranch, she was impressed with the detailed and vivid picture she gave of the land and cattle. If she participated in the project, she would be a good observer. Joanna was also impressed with her friendly, comfortable manner and her open face.

'You told Dr Wright you've never had a near-death experience,' Joanna said, consulting her notes. 'Have you ever known anyone who had one?'

'No,' Mrs Troudtheim said, looping the yarn around the crochet hook and pulling it through the edge of the Afghan, 'the day before my aunt died, she said she saw her sister – that was my mother – standing at the foot of the bed, dressed in a long white dress. My mother had been dead for several years, but my aunt said she saw her standing there, plain as day, and that she knew she'd come for her. She died the next day.'

'And what did you think of that?' Joanna asked.

'Oh, I don't know,' she said, pulling out a length of yarn thoughtfully. 'The doctor had her on pretty heavy medication. And I can't see my mother in a long dress. She hated draggy skirts. People sometimes see what they want to see.'

But I'll bet you don't, Joanna thought, and asked her what times she had available.

'She's the most promising subject yet,' she told Richard after Mrs Troudtheim had crammed the Afghan back in her tote bag and departed. 'She reminds me of my relatives in Kansas, tough and kind and realistic, the type who can survive anything and probably have. I think she'll be perfect for the project. I was especially impressed with her observational skills.'

'Except that she's obviously color-blind. Did you see that Afghan?' Richard asked, shuddering.

'You obviously have never been to Kansas,' Joanna said. 'That one wasn't half bad.'

'Whatever you say,' Richard said.

Joanna grinned. 'I say she'll make an excellent subject.'

'I'd settle for just a subject.'

Me, too, Joanna thought, relieved that she had finally found someone she could okay. She looked at the schedule. Mr Sage was next, and then Mr Pearsall, but not until one-thirty. If Mr Sage's interview didn't take too long, she should be able to get down to see Mrs Woollam. There wouldn't be time for a full interview, but she could at least run down and meet her, get her to sign a waiver, and set up an interview for this afternoon. If Mr Sage wasn't long-winded.

He wasn't. In fact, she had trouble getting anything out of him. Mr Sage gave brief, bitten-off answers to everything she asked, which worried Joanna a little. She wondered how forthcoming he would be about what he'd seen in the NDE. But he wasn't a psychic, or overly interested in death. And he had the best answer yet for why he had volunteered for the project: 'My wife made me.'

'What's your opinion of near-death experiences?' Joanna asked him.

'I don't know,' he said. 'I never thought much about them.' Good, Joanna thought, and asked him about his schedule.

'He was awfully silent,' Richard fretted after he'd left.

'He'll be fine. People vary in their descriptive powers.' She stood up. 'Richard, I'm going to go—' she began, and her pager went off.

She had already gotten in trouble with Vielle today by not answering it – she'd better at least see who it was. She called the operator, who gave her Maisie's number. 'She said it's an emergency and you need to call her immediately. I, for one, would appreciate it if you did,' the operator said. 'She's been calling all morning, pestering me to page you on the intercom.'

'Okay,' Joanna laughed, and did.

'You have to come down right now!' an agitated Maisie said. 'Ms Sutterly found out about the crewman on the *Hindenburg* like you wanted, and you have to come down so I can tell you.'

'I can't right now, Maisie,' Joanna said. 'I have an appointment—'

'But I'm going *home*, and if you don't come right away it'll be too late! I'll already be *gone*!'

She sounded genuinely upset. 'Okay, I'll be right down,' Joanna said. 'I can only stay a couple of minutes,' she added, though there was no chance she'd get away in time to go see Mrs Woollam. She'd have to wait till this afternoon.

'I'm going down to tell Maisie good-bye,' she said to Richard. 'She's going home.'

'What about the interview with Mr Pearsall?'

'If I'm not back when he gets here, page me,' she said, waving her pager at him to show him she had it, and ran down to fifth and over to the walkway, but it was blocked with a sawhorse and more yellow tape.

'They're laying new tile,' a lab tech heading the other way said. 'Are you trying to get to the west wing? You have to either take the elevator up to seventh or down to the third-floor walkway.'

Joanna started back toward the elevators and saw Mr Mandrake coming toward her. There was nowhere to go, no stairway she could duck into, not even an open door, and, anyway, he had already seen her. 'Hello, Mr Mandrake,' she said, trying not to look like a cornered rabbit.

'I'm glad I ran in to you,' he said. 'I've been trying to reach you all morning.'

'This isn't a good time,' Joanna said, looking pointedly at her watch. 'I have an appointment.'

'With an NDE patient?' he asked, instantly interested.

'No,' Joanna said, grateful that at least he hadn't caught her going in to see Mrs Woollam. Or Maisie. 'A meeting, and I'm late already.'

'This will only take a moment,' he said, planting himself in front of her. 'I have two matters I need to speak with you about. First, Mrs Davenport informed me you haven't been back to take down the rest of her NDE. She has remembered additional details about the manner of her return. The Angel of Light—'

'– gave her a telegram telling her she had to return. I know,' Joanna said. 'She already told me about it.'

'No, no, she's remembered a great deal more. The telegram was only the beginning. The Angel told her she was to be a messenger, and as He raised His shining hand ...' Mr Mandrake raised *his* hand in a sweeping gesture to illustrate, '... the mysteries of life and death were revealed to her, and she understood All. She's very anxious to share the knowledge she was given with you.'

I'll bet, Joanna thought.

'When you hear what she has learned, there will be no doubt in your mind that Mrs Davenport has truly brought back news from the Other Side.'

'Mr Mandrake—'

'The second thing I wanted to talk to you about was, I don't know if you're aware of this, but there is a new researcher here at the hospital whose intent is to undermine the credibility of our near-death research. His name is Dr Wright. He claims to be able to reproduce the NAE in the laboratory through the administration of drugs. Of course that's impossible. The NAE is a spiritual reality, not a drug hallucination, but people are gullible. They may well believe his claims, particularly when he cloaks them in the trappings of technology and science.'

'I have to go,' Joanna said and started toward the elevator, but Mr Mandrake went right along with her.

'I'm very concerned about the effect of this so-called research on our studies. I tried to communicate my concerns to him, but he was extremely unresponsive. He has a partner, or so I understand, although I haven't met him, and I'm hoping he will be more cooperative. That's where you come in.'

'Come in?' Joanna said, reaching the elevator. She pushed the button.

'I haven't been able to discover who this partner is. I want you to find out.'

The elevator pinged its arrival. Joanna waited for the door to open. 'I already know.'

'You do?' he said, clearly surprised. 'Who is it? Who's his new partner?'

Joanna stepped in the elevator, pressed the 'door-close' button, and waited till it was already sliding shut. 'I am,' she said.

She almost wished she could have seen the look on his face before the door closed, but then she wouldn't have gotten away. You had no business doing that, she thought, going up to seventh and across to the west wing. Now he'll never give you any peace. But he and his network of spies would have found out soon anyway, and if she hadn't told him, he would have accused her of intentionally deceiving him. Now, of course, he would accuse her of being gullible. Her, gullible!

She cut through CICU and took the service elevator down to Peds. Maisie was sitting on the side of her bed, dressed in a pink jumper with butterfly-shaped pockets. Which she must detest, Joanna thought. 'You rang, kiddo?' Joanna said, and then saw Maisie's mother was in the room, busily stuffing Maisie's robe and slippers in a plastic hospital carry bag.

'Dr Murrow was *so* happy with her progress on the inderone, he told us she could go home a day earlier,' she told Joanna brightly. She opened the closet door and picked up Maisie's Barbie duffel bag.

Joanna glanced at Maisie, but she seemed unconcerned. 'Dr Murrow also said Maisie could start thinking about going back to school,' Mrs Nellis said. She laid the duffel bag on the chair. 'I'll give you two a chance to chat. I need to talk to Dr Murrow about getting Maisie on an experimental ACE-blocker before we leave.'

As soon as she went out, Maisie said, 'I was afraid I was going to already be gone,' and pulled a folded piece of paper out of a patch pocket and handed it to Joanna. Joanna unfolded it. It said, 'Joseph Leibrecht. 1968.'

Maisie said, 'Ms Sutterly said the guy who wrote the book went to Germany and interviewed this Leibrecht guy when he was writing the book. In 1968. Can you use it? His NDE?'

She couldn't possibly. The *Hindenburg* had crashed in 1937, over thirty years before. Events remembered from that long ago would inevitably be distorted, details forgotten and added, blanks filled in with confabulations. It was virtually useless, but she hated to disappoint Maisie. 'You bet,' she started to say, and realized Maisie was waiting, breath held, for her answer, as if it were some sort of test.

'I'm afraid I can't,' Joanna said. 'NDE interviews need to be done right after the experience, or people forget things.'

'Or make up things,' Maisie said.

'That's right,' Joanna said. 'I'm sorry.'

'That's okay,' Maisie said, not upset at all. In fact, she was grinning.

Joanna grinned back. 'So you're going home? Are you happy about that?'

She nodded. 'Ms Sutterly took my books for me,' she said, with a significant look at the duffel bag.

'Good. So how's the *Lusitania*?'

'I'm not interested in it anymore,' she said. 'It didn't take very long to sink. Have you ever been to a circus?'

She would never get used to Maisie's sudden conversational shifts. 'Yes,' she said, 'when I was a little girl.'

'Was it fun? Were there clowns?'

'Yes and yes,' Joanna said, thinking, even Mrs Nellis would approve of this conversation. 'I remember one clown who had a red nose and baggy pants, and he pulled a big polka-dot handkerchief out of his pocket to blow his nose with, but it was tied to a big red handkerchief, and that was tied to a blue one and a green one and a yellow one, and he just kept pulling and pulling and pulling handkerchiefs out of his pocket, looking for the end.'

'I bet that was funny,' Maisie said. 'Do you know what a Victory garden is?'

'A Victory garden?' Joanna asked, lost again. 'I'm not sure. I know what one kind is. During World War II, people planted gardens to grow food for the army. And the navy,' she added, thinking of Mr Wojakowski, 'to help win the war, and they were called Victory gardens. Is that the kind you mean?'

'I think so,' she said. 'There was this circus in Hartford, that's in Connecticut, and the tent caught fire and they all burned to death.'

I might have known, Joanna thought.

'One hundred and sixty-eight people died,' Maisie said. 'I'd show you the picture except I don't have my books. I'll bring them next time I come to the hospital.'

'How do you know there'll be a next time? Your mother says you're really doing well,' Joanna nearly said, and then bit it back. 'How did the fire start?' she asked instead.

Maisie shrugged her thin shoulders. 'Nobody knows. It just happened.'

It just happened, Joanna thought. A cigarette, a spark, in sawdust or canvas and, just like that, one hundred and sixty-eight people dead. And probably most of them children, Joanna thought, knowing circuses. And Maisie.

'Lots of kids died,' Maisie said, as if reading her mind. 'Do you think it hurts to die? In a fire, I mean.'

'I don't know,' Joanna said, well aware of what she was really answering.

'Probably only for a little while. Most of them probably died of smoke inhalation. I think the worst part would be the being afraid.'

'Me, too,' Maisie said. 'When I coded, it only hurt for a minute. I wasn't afraid either.' She looked at Joanna seriously. 'Do you think that's what NDEs are for, to keep you from being afraid?'

'That's what Dr Wright and I are trying to find out.'

'What do you think happens after that, after the NDE?' Joanna had known this was coming, ever since their conversation about Ulla. She glanced at the door, wishing Maisie's mother would magically appear with a wheelchair and happy thoughts.

'I want to know,' Maisie said. 'The truth.'

'The truth is, I don't know,' Joanna said. 'I think probably nothing. When the heart stops beating, the body quits sending oxygen to the brain, and the brain cells start to die, and when they die, you can't think anymore, and it's like going to sleep or switching a light off.'

'Like shutting down C-3PO,' Maisie said eagerly.

'Yes, just like that,' Joanna said, thinking that if this conversation was upsetting or frightening Maisie she certainly wasn't showing it.

'Would it be dark?' Maisie asked.

'No. It wouldn't be anything.'

'And you don't even know you're dead,' Maisie said.

'No,' Joanna said, 'you don't even know you're dead,' and for some reason thought of Lavoisier.

'How come you said probably?' Maisie asked. 'You said probably nothing happens.'

'Because nobody knows for sure,' she said. 'No dead person's ever come back to tell us what death is like.'

'Mr Mandrake says he knows,' Maisie said, making a face. 'When he came to see me that time I coded, he said he knows exactly what happens after you die.'

'Well, he doesn't.'

Maisie nodded sagely. 'He says all the people you know who've died are there waiting for you, and then you all go to heaven. I think that's what he *wants* to be true. Just because you want something to be true doesn't make it true. Like with Tinkerbell.'

'No, it doesn't,' Joanna said. 'But just because you want something to be true doesn't make it *not* true either.'

'So there might be a heaven,' Maisie said.

'There might,' Joanna said. 'Nobody knows.'

'Except people who've died,' Maisie said. 'And they can't tell us.' No, Joanna thought, they can't tell us. In spite of Richard's and my best efforts.

'So everybody has to find out for themself,' Maisie said, 'and nobody gets to go with you. Do they?'

No, Joanna thought. I wish I could, kiddo. I hate to think of you having to go through it by yourself. But everybody has to die alone, no matter what Mr Mandrake says. 'No,' she said.

'Unless it's a disaster,' Maisie said. 'Then a whole bunch of people die all together. Like the Hartford circus fire. They couldn't get out because the animal cages, you know, for the lions and tigers, were in the way, and everybody kept pushing and they all got smushed to death except for the ones who had smoke …' She frowned, groping for the word.

'Inhalation,' Joanna said.

'All set,' Maisie's mother said gaily, coming in with a wheelchair. 'As soon as the nurse brings in your release form, we can go.' She began helping Maisie into the wheelchair.

'I've got to go, too,' Joanna said. 'Good-bye, kiddo. Be good.' She started back to the lab. Barbara was in the nurses' station, filling out paperwork. Joanna looked back down the hall to make sure Maisie and her mother were still in Maisie's room, and then said to Barbara, 'Maisie's mother said she's doing better. Is she?'

'That depends on how you define "better,"' Barbara said. 'Her basic condition hasn't changed, but her heart function's up slightly, and the inderone seems to be working to stabilize her heart rhythm, though I don't know how long they can keep her on it. The side effects are pretty bad – liver damage, kidney damage, but, yeah, her mother was telling the truth for a change. She is doing better.'

'Good,' Joanna said, relieved. 'You haven't seen Mr Mandrake on the floor, have you?'

'No,' Barbara said.

'Even better,' Joanna said. She slapped the counter of the nurses' station with both hands. 'See you later.'

'Oh, good, you're still here,' Maisie's mother said, coming up to the nurses' station. 'I just wanted to thank you for spending so much time with Maisie. She loves visitors, but so many of them insist on talking about depressing things, illness and … they just upset her. But she loves to have you come. I don't know what you two find to talk about, but she's always so cheered up after your visits.'

11

'Jesus … Jesus … Jesus …'
— JOAN OF ARC's last words, in the flames

Joanna didn't get down to see Mrs Woollam until after three. Mr Pearsall had arrived late, and his interview (which went fine) had been interrupted by a phone call from Mrs Haighton, who was apparently calling from her crafts fair, because she kept shouting asides to people named Ashley and Felicia who were apparently hanging things.

'This week is impossible,' she told Joanna, 'but next week – just a minute, let me get my calendar – might just be possible – no, it's too high on that end.'

Mr Pearsall was waiting patiently, and Joanna knew the appropriate thing to do was to tell Mrs Haighton to call back later, but she had the feeling that if she did, she'd never hear from her again. 'What times do you have available next Monday?' Joanna asked her, smiling apologetically at Mr Pearsall.

'Monday, let me see – it needs to drape more – no, the afternoon won't work, and, let's see, what's in the morning? I have an AAUW meeting at ten. Would eleven forty-five work for you?'

'Yes,' Joanna said, even though she already had Mrs Troudtheim scheduled for eleven. Even taking Mrs Troudtheim's oral surgery appointments into account, she could reschedule Mrs Troudtheim easier than Mrs Haighton. 'Eleven forty-five will be fine.'

'Eleven forty-five,' Mrs Haighton said. 'Oh, no, I was looking at Wednesday, not Monday. I can't do it Monday after all.'

'What about Tuesday?'

Joanna spent the next ten minutes listening to a litany of Mrs Haighton's meetings, in between instructions to Felicia, before finally agreeing to sandwich Joanna in Friday between her library board and her yoga class. 'Although I was almost sure I had something else that day.'

Joanna hung up before she had a chance to remember what it was and went back to questioning Mr Pearsall, who had never had surgery, let alone been near death. 'I've never even had my appendix out, or my tonsils. Neither has anyone else in my family. My father's seventy-four and never been sick a day in his life.'

Mr Pearsall had never met Mr Mandrake or read his books, and when Joanna asked him whether he believed in spiritualism, he said, looking faintly scandalized, 'This is *medical* research, isn't it?'

'Yes,' Joanna said and let him go.

There was still the schedule to set up, though, and she had to tell Richard about her encounter with Mr Mandrake. 'He thinks you're trying to debunk his research,' she said.

'I am,' he said. 'What did he think about your working with me?'

'I escaped before he could tell me,' Joanna said. 'I imagine he'll try to talk me out of it. If he can catch me,' she added. 'I'm going down to the cardiac care unit to interview an NDEer. If Mr Mandrake calls, tell him I went to see Maisie.'

'I thought she went home,' he said.

'She did,' Joanna said, and went down to the cardiac care unit, only to find Mrs Woollam had already been moved out of cardiac care and into a regular room.

Her watch said four-sixteen by the time she got down to her room. Mrs Woollam had been in over seven hours. Mr Mandrake had had time not only to ruin her for interview purposes, but to turn her into another Mrs Davenport. Unless Mrs Woollam couldn't have visitors, in which case she wouldn't be able to see her either.

But yes, Mrs Woollam could have visitors, Luann said. She was doing fine. They were just keeping her a couple of days for observation. 'Has Mr Mandrake been in to see her?' Joanna asked.

'He tried,' Luann said, 'Mrs Woollam threw him out.'

'Threw him out?'

Luann grinned. 'She's one tough cookie. Go on in.'

Joanna rapped gently on the open door. 'Mrs Woollam?' she said timidly.

'Come in,' a soft voice said, and Joanna found herself looking at a frail old woman not much bigger than Maisie. Her white hair was as fine and insubstantial as the fluff on a dandelion, and Mrs Woollam herself looked like she might blow away in the first breeze. She certainly didn't look capable of throwing anyone out, least of all the immovable Mr Mandrake. She was sitting up in bed, hooked with an array of wires to a bank of monitors. She was reading a book with a white cover, which she reached over and put in the nightstand drawer as soon as she saw Joanna.

'I'm Joanna Lander,' Joanna said. 'I—'

'Vielle's friend,' Mrs Woollam said. 'She told me about you.' She smiled. 'Vielle's a wonderful nurse. Any friend of hers is a friend of mine.' She dimpled again, a smile of incredible sweetness. 'She tells me you're studying near-death experiences.'

'Yes,' Joanna said. She pulled a release form out of her pocket, explained it, and gave her a chance to look it over.

'I don't always experience the same thing,' Mrs Woollam said, pen poised above the release form, 'and I've never floated above my body or seen angels, so if that's what you're looking for—'

'I'm not looking for anything,' Joanna said. 'I'd just like you to tell me what you experienced.'

'Good,' she said. She signed the release form in a spidery hand. 'Maurice Mandrake was determined to have me see a tunnel and an Angel of Light the last time I was here. Dreadful man. You don't work with him, do you?'

'No,' Joanna said, 'no matter what he might tell you.'

'Good. Do you know what he told me?' Mrs Woollam asked indignantly. 'That near-death experiences are messages from the dead.'

'You don't think they are?'

'Of course not. That's not the sort of message the dead send to the living.'

Oh, no, Joanna thought. 'What kind of messages do they send?' she asked carefully.

'Messages of love and forgiveness, because so often we cannot forgive ourselves,' she said. 'Messages only our hearts can hear.' She handed Joanna the release form and her pen. 'Now, what did you want to ask me? I *have* been in a tunnel, though I didn't tell Mr Mandrake that.'

'What sort of tunnel?' Joanna asked.

'It was too dark to see exactly what it was, but I know it was smaller than a railway tunnel. I've been in a tunnel twice, the first time and the second to last time.'

'The same tunnel?' Joanna asked.

'No, one was narrower and its floor was more uneven. I had to hold on to the walls to keep from falling.'

'What about the other times?' Joanna asked, wishing Mrs Woollam didn't have a heart condition and wasn't nearly eighty. She would make a wonderful volunteer.

'I was in a dark place. Not a tunnel. Outside, in a dark, open …' she looked past Joanna, 'there was nothing around for miles on any side …'

'You were in this dark place all the other times?' Joanna asked.

'Yes. No, once I was in a garden.'

Maisie never told me why she wanted to know what a Victory garden was, Joanna thought suddenly.

'I was sitting in a white chair in a beautiful, beautiful garden,' Mrs Woollam said longingly.

Gardens were a common NDE experience. 'Can you describe it?'

'There were vines,' Mrs Woollam said, looking around at the walls of her room, 'and trees.'

'What kind of trees?' Joanna prompted.

'Palm trees,' Mrs Woollam said.

Vineyards and palm trees. Standard religious imagery. 'Do you remember anything else about the garden?'

'No, only sitting there,' she said, 'waiting for something.'

'For what?'

'I don't know,' she said, shaking her white head. 'That was the first time my heart stopped. That was nearly two years ago. I don't remember it very well.'

'What about this last time?' Joanna asked.

'I was standing at the foot of a beautiful staircase, looking up at it.'

'Can you describe it?'

'It looked like this,' Mrs Woollam said, reaching into her nightstand for her book. Joanna saw to her dismay that it was a Bible. Mrs Woollam leafed through the tissue-thin pages to a colored plate and held it out for Joanna to see. It was a picture of a broad golden staircase, with angels standing on each step and at the top a rayed light in which could be seen the outline of a figure with outstretched arms.

I should have known it was too good to be true, Joanna thought. 'The staircase looked just like this?' she said.

'Yes, except it curved up,' she said. 'And the light at the top of the stairs was sparkling, like diamonds.'

And sapphires and rubies, Joanna thought.

'But there weren't any angels, no matter what Mr Mandrake said. He kept trying to convince me that what I was seeing was heaven.'

'And you don't think it was?' Joanna said.

'I don't know,' Mrs Woollam said. 'They might all be heaven – the tunnel and the garden and the dark open place.' She took back the Bible and turned to another page. 'John 14, verse 2, "In my Father's house are many mansions." Or they might be something else.'

'Sorry to interrupt, ladies,' Luann said, 'but it's time to take you,' she nodded at Mrs Woollam, 'downstairs.'

'Heart cath?' Mrs Woollam said, closing her Bible.

'Uh-huh,' Luann said. Her beeper went off. 'Sorry,' she said, pulling it out of her pocket and glaring at it. 'I'll be right back.' She went out.

'You said what you saw in your NDEs might be something else,' Joanna said. 'What did you mean? What do you think they might be?'

'I don't know. Sometimes …' Her voice trailed off. 'But I know that whatever it is, Jesus will be there with me.' She opened her Bible again. 'Isaiah 43, verse 2, "When thou passest through the waters, I will be with thee. When thou walkest through the fire, thou shalt not be burned."'

Luann came back in, looking frazzled.

'I'd like to come talk with you again,' Joanna told Mrs Woollam. 'May I?'

'If I'm still here,' Mrs Woollam said, and twinkled. 'The HMO keeps cutting the amount of time the hospital can keep me. I'd like to talk to you, too.

I'd like to know what you think these experiences are and what you think about death.'

I think the more I find out the less I know, Joanna thought, heading back upstairs. She wished she didn't still have two or more hours of transcribing tapes ahead of her. She couldn't leave them till tomorrow, not with a full schedule of sessions, and she was already a week behind. She went into her office, took a tape out of the shoe box she kept her untranscribed tapes in, and turned on the computer.

'Oh, good, you're back,' Richard said, sticking his head in the door. 'I had to reschedule Mr Sage's first session to this afternoon. This shouldn't take long. Tish has already got him prepped.'

Richard was wrong. It took forever. Not because Mr Sage had lots to relate, however. Getting him to say anything at all was like pulling teeth. 'You say it was dark,' Joanna asked after fifteen minutes of questioning. 'Could you see anything?'

'When?'

'When you were in the dark.'

'No. I told you, it was dark.'

'Was it dark the whole time?'

'No,' followed by an interminable pause while Joanna waited for him to add something.

'After it was dark, what happened?' she asked.

'Happened?'

'Yes. You said it wasn't dark the whole time ...'

'It wasn't.'

'Was it light part of the time?'

'Yeah.'

'Can you describe the light?'

He shrugged. 'A light.'

She didn't do any better when she asked him what feelings he'd had during the NDE. 'Feelings?' he repeated as if he had never heard the word before.

'Did you feel happy, sad, worried, excited, calm, warm, cold?'

The shrug again. 'Would you say you felt good or bad?' she asked.

'When?'

'*In the dark,*' Joanna said, gritting her teeth.

'Good or bad about what?' And so on, for over an hour.

'Boy,' Richard said when Mr Sage had taken his silent leave, 'when you said people vary in their descriptive powers, you weren't kidding.'

'Well, at least we established that it was dark, and then light,' Joanna said, shaking her head.

They were alone in the lab. Tish had stayed till halfway through the interrogation and then left, saying to Richard, 'I'm going over to Happy Hour at the Rio Grande with a bunch of people, if you're interested. Either of you,' she'd added as an afterthought.

'I'm sorry I couldn't get anything out of him about what he was feeling, if he was feeling,' Joanna said. 'I don't think he had any negative feelings. He didn't respond when I asked him if he'd felt worried or afraid.'

'He didn't respond at all,' Richard said, going over to the console, 'but at least we've got another set of scans to look at.' He began typing in numbers. 'I want to compare his endorphin levels with Amelia Tanaka's.'

And so much for Happy Hour at the Rio Grande, Joanna thought, but it was just as well. She had Mr Sage's account, such as it was, to type up, and all the other tapes she hadn't transcribed yet. She went back to her office.

Her answering machine was blinking. Don't let it be Mr Mandrake, she thought, and hit 'play.' 'This is Maurice Mandrake,' the machine said. 'I just wanted to tell you how delighted I am you're working with Dr Wright. I'm sure you will be an excellent influence. When can you meet with me to plan strategies?'

There were messages from Mrs Haighton and Ann Collins, the nurse who had assisted at Mr Wojakowski's session, asking Joanna to call them. And play another round of telephone tag, Joanna thought wearily, but she called them both back. Neither one was there. She left a message on both answering machines, and then sat down at her computer and transcribed Mr Sage's account.

It only took five minutes. She popped out the tape and stuck another one in. 'It was …,' an interminable pause, '… dark …,' another one, '… I think …' Mrs Davenport. 'I was in …,' very long pause, '… a kind of …' very, very long pause, and then her voice rising questioningly, '… tunnel?' This was ridiculous. She could put the tape on fast-forward and still type faster than Mrs Davenport was speaking. And why not? she thought, reaching for the recorder. Even if she had to rewind to get it all, it would be an improvement on this.

It didn't work. When she hit 'fast-forward,' it produced a high-pitched squeal. She tried hitting 'fast-forward' and 'play' at the same time. The 'fast-forward' button clicked off and there was a deafening whine. A man's voice said, 'Turn off that damned alarm.'

A sudden silence, then the same voice saying, 'Let me see a rhythm strip.'

Greg Menotti coding, Joanna thought, I must have left the recorder on; she reached to hit 'rewind.'

'She's too far away,' Greg said, his voice distant and despairing, and Joanna took her finger off the 'rewind' button and listened. 'She'll never get here in time.'

Joanna grabbed the shoe box of untranscribed tapes and rummaged through them as the tape played, looking at the dates. February twenty-fifth, December ninth.

'She'll be here in just a few minutes,' Vielle's voice said from the tape, and the cardiologist's, 'What's the BP?' January twenty-third, March – here it was. 'Eighty over sixty,' the nurse said, and Joanna hit 'rewind,' let it run, hit 'play.' 'Fifty-eight,' Greg said, and Joanna stopped the tape. She popped it out of the recorder, stuck the other one in, fast-forwarded to the middle.

'It was beautiful,' Amelia Tanaka said. Too far. Joanna rewound, listened, rewound again, hit 'play.'

'She's coming out of it,' Richard's voice said. Joanna leaned forward. 'Oh, no,' Amelia said, 'oh, no, oh, no, oh, no.'

Joanna played it twice, then popped the tape out and the other one back in, even though she already knew what it would sound like, already knew why Amelia's voice had been so troubled. She had heard it before. 'Too far for her to come,' Greg had said, and his voice had held the same terror, the same despair.

She hit 'rewind' and played it again, but she was already certain. She had heard the identical tone twice today, the first time reading the Bible, 'When thou passest through the waters, I will be with thee. When thou walkest through the fire, thou shalt not be burned.'

And if she had gotten Mrs Woollam's voice on tape, all three voices would have sounded exactly the same. Just like Maisie's, saying, 'Do you think it hurts?'

12

'Why, man, they couldn't hit an elephant at this dist—'
— American Civil War general JOHN SEDGWICK's last
words, at the Battle of Spotsylvania Courthouse

Mr Wojakowski was right on time the next morning. 'That's one thing they teach you in the navy, being on time,' he told Richard and launched into a story about GeeGaw Rawlins, a perennially tardy gunner's mate. 'Killed at Iwo. Tracer bullet right through the eye,' he finished cheerfully and trotted off into the dressing room to put on his hospital gown.

Richard called up his scans from Mr Wojakowski's last session. He hadn't had a chance to look at the endorphin levels in them yet. He'd spent the last two days analyzing Amelia Tanaka's scans from her two previous sessions for endorphin activity. As he'd expected, the level of activity was significantly lower for her most recent session, and fewer receptor sites were involved, even though she'd received the same dose of dithetamine. Did subjects develop a resistance to the drug's effects after repeated exposures?

He split the screen and did a side-by-side of Mr Wojakowski's sessions, looking for a decrease of endorphin activity in the second one, but, if anything, it had increased. He did a superimpose and looked at the receptor sites.

'Hi,' Tish said, coming in. 'I missed you last night at Happy Hour.'

'Did you see Dr Lander on your way in?' he asked her, and when Tish shook her head, he said, 'I'll go get her.'

Joanna was just coming out of her office. 'I'm sorry,' she said breathlessly. 'I was trying to schedule Mrs Haighton's interview, but she's never home. I do nothing but talk to her housekeeper. I'm seriously thinking of asking *her* to come in and interview. Speaking of which, I put out a new call for volunteers, with new wording and a different contact phone number that Mrs Bendix and her buddies won't recognize.'

They went into the lab. Mr Wojakowski was lying on the examining table, watching Tish start the IV. 'Hiya, Doc,' he said, and to Joanna, 'I plan to find out what that sound is for ya this time, Doc,' he said to her.

'Can you do that?' Joanna asked, sounding interested.

'I don't know,' he said, and winked at her. 'You never know if you don't try. Olie Jorgenson used to say that. He was the supply officer on the *Yorktown*. Always figuring out ways to break the rules. This one time the captain—'

'We're ready to start,' Richard said. 'Tish, can you put on Mr Wojakowski's headphones and his mask?' and caught Joanna grinning at him.

Blinded and with white noise coming through his headphones, Mr Wojakowski was much easier to deal with. Next time he would have to tell Tish to put them on first. 'Ready?' Richard said, told Tish to start the sedative and then the dithetamine, and went back to the console to watch the scans.

Mr Wojakowski went into the NDE-state almost immediately, and Richard watched the orange-and-red flare of activity in the temporal lobe, the hippocampus, the random firings in the frontal cortex. He focused in on the endorphin receptor sites. No decrease there. All the sites that had been activated in the previous sessions were orange or red, and there were several new ones.

Mr Wojakowski's session lasted three minutes. 'I pinned that noise down for ya, Doc,' he said to Joanna as soon as the monitoring period was over and Tish had removed his electrodes.

'You did?'

'I told ya I would,' he said. 'It reminds me of the time—'

'Start at the beginning,' Joanna interrupted, helping him sit up.

'Okay, I'm lying there with my eyes closed, and all of a sudden I hear a sound, and I stop and listen hard, I'm in the tunnel trying to think what it reminds me of, and after a minute it comes to me. It sounds like the time my wing got shot up, at the Battle of the Coral Sea. Did I ever tell you about that?' he said. 'We were going after the *Shoho*, and a Zero came after me—'

'And the noise you heard in the tunnel sounded like a plane's wing being hit with bullets? Can you describe the sound?' Joanna asked hastily, trying to stop him, but he was already well launched on his story.

'My copilot and my gunner both bought it in the attack, and my left wing's all shot up. I'm trying to nurse her back to the *Yorktown*, but I'm low on gas, and when I finally spot her, there are Zeroes everywhere, and the Old Yorky's got a fire in her stern. Well, hell, I don't have enough gas to come in on, let alone take on a bunch of Zeroes, and I'm trying to figure out how I'm going to land when, blam!' He clapped his age-freckled hands together sharply. 'The *Yorktown* takes one right down the middle, and I stop worrying about how I'm going to land because in a couple of minutes, there isn't going to be a carrier to land on. Smoke's pouring out of her midsection, and she's starting to list, so I get as far away as I can and ditch her in the water, and when I make it ashore on Malakula the next day, the natives tell me they heard the Japs saying she sank during the night.'

'I thought you said the *Yorktown* sank at Midway,' Joanna said.

'She did. She hadn't sunk. She'd limped back to Pearl for repairs, but I didn't know that. That was some deal, I'll tell you. She goes limping in, leaking oil like a sieve, and they put her in dry dock and—'

Oh, no, Richard thought, he's off on another story. He looked at Joanna, trying to signal her to ask another question, but her eyes were on Mr Wojakowski.

' – says, "How long to fix her?" and the harbormaster says, "Six months, maybe eight," and the captain says, "You got three days."' Mr Wojakowski slapped his knee in glee. 'Three days!'

'And did they fix her in three days?' Joanna asked.

'You bet they did. Fixed her bulkheads and welded her boilers and sent her off to Midway. Raised her from the dead in three days flat. Hell, those Japs looked like they'd seen a ghost when she showed up and sank three of their carriers.'

He slapped his knee again. 'But I didn't know any of that then. I thought she was sunk for sure, and so was I. The Japs were already on Malakula. I talked the natives into smuggling me across to Vanikalo, but the Jap navy was landing on all those islands, so I swiped a dugout canoe and some coconuts, and set out for Port Moresby. I figured dying at sea's better than being caught by Japs. And that's just about what I did. I ran out of food and water, and sharks started circling, and I was thinking, I'm done for, when I see something on the horizon.'

He leaned forward, pointing past Joanna. 'It's a ship, and at first I think I'm seeing things, but it keeps coming, and as it gets closer, I see it's got an island.

I can see the masts and the antennas on it. Well, the only thing with an island like that is an aircraft carrier, and if it's a Jap carrier I better get the hell out of there. I try to make out if there's a rising sun on her flag, but I can't tell, the sun's right behind her island, and I can't see a damn thing except that she's coming straight at me. And then I see her hull number, CV-5, and I know it's the *Yorktown*, risen up right out of the grave. I knew right then nothing and nobody could sink her.'

'But she sank at the Battle of Midway, didn't she?' Joanna asked.

He glared at her. 'Not before she sank three carriers and won the war, she didn't.'

'I'm sorry,' Joanna said. 'I didn't mean—'

'It's okay,' Mr Wojakowski said. 'All ships sink sooner or later. But not that day. Not that day. That day she looked like she was going to stay afloat forever. I never seen a more beautiful sight in my life.' He gazed past them, remembering, his freckled face alight.

'I thought she was sunk, that I was never going to see her again. I thought I was done for, and here she was, plowing through the water toward me, her flags flying and every sailor on board leaning over the railing of the flight deck, all in their dress whites, waving their hats in the air and hollerin' for me to come aboard. It was the best day of my life!' He beamed at Joanna, and then at Richard. 'The best damned day of my life!'

It took Joanna another ten minutes to get Mr Wojakowski back on track enough to tell them the tunnel was really a passageway and that there was a door at the end of it, with a bright light and people dressed in white when he opened it. 'The light kept bouncing off 'em till I couldn't see a damn thing.'

Joanna asked him how he'd felt during the NDE. 'Felt? I don't know that I felt anything. I was too busy looking at things. It was like when the Japs hit us that first time at Coral Sea. I remember thinking I should be scared outta my pants, only I wasn't. Mac McTavish was standing next to me, and—' It took all of Joanna's skill and another ten minutes to stop him from going off into another story, and they never did get an answer.

'Sorry,' she apologized after Mr Wojakowski finally left. 'I didn't want to risk asking him again.'

'It's too bad his account of his NDE couldn't be as colorful as that story about the *Yorktown* rescuing him,' Richard said.

'He actually told us quite a bit,' Joanna said. 'His being reminded of being attacked by Zeroes indicates he did feel some fear, even though he said he didn't.'

'He was also reminded of the best damned day of his life,' Richard said. 'He commented that the light was brighter than last time. Did Amelia Tanaka say anything about comparative brightnesses or radiance in her NDEs?'

'I don't remember. I can check her accounts,' she said and stood up as if to go to her office.

'I don't need it right now,' he said. 'I was just wondering, Mr Wojakowski's endorphin levels were elevated this time, and I thought they might be producing the effect of the light.'

'"… shiny white stuff the light kept bouncing off of,"' Joanna read from her notes. 'That isn't what struck me about his account. What struck me was that he opened the door.'

'Opened the door?' Richard said, wondering what was extraordinary about that.

'Yes, it's the first time I've heard of an NDEer acting with volition. Every account I've heard has been a passive vision, with the NDEer seeing and experiencing things or being acted upon by other figures, but Mr Wojakowski not only opened the door, he also stopped and listened purposely to the sound.' She started for the door. 'I'll check on the brightness.'

She came back in less than an hour to report that there was nothing in Amelia's accounts about comparative brightness, 'so I called her and asked her, and she said the light was much brighter her first session. I also asked her about the feeling of warmth and love she'd described, and she said that was present in all three sessions and strongest in the first. Of course, you have to keep in mind that over ten days have passed since her first session, and four since her last one, so her memory may not be reliable.'

But it matched the scans, which showed a much higher level of endorphin activity in the first session than the second, and the neurotransmitter analysis confirmed it. Higher levels of both beta- and alpha-endorphins in the first. Not only that, but NPK was present in the first and not the second.

He compared it with the scans they'd just gotten of Mr Wojakowski. Both NPK and beta-endorphins, and in greater amounts than either of Amelia's. When Joanna came in for Mrs Troudtheim's session, he asked her if she could check the NDE interviews she'd done over the past two years for bright lights and warm feelings.

She'd already started. 'There does seem to be a correlation,' she said. 'It's hard to tell from secondhand accounts, especially since *bright* is a subjective word, but the subjects who describe the feeling as "enveloping me in love and peace," or, "overwhelming me in a sense of safety," also report a very bright light, and sometimes nothing but a light, as if the glare were so bright they couldn't see anything else.'

'"I couldn't see a damn thing,"' Richard said, quoting Mr Wojakowski. 'Interesting. We'll have to see what Mrs Troudtheim says on the subject.'

But Mrs Troudtheim didn't say anything. And she wasn't 'our best observer yet,' as Joanna said right before Tish started the dithetamine. She was instead a huge disappointment.

Not that she wasn't every bit as sensible and matter-of-fact as Joanna had predicted. She undressed and climbed on the examining table with no fuss, repositioned the sleep mask herself when it didn't fully cover her eyes, and recounted what she'd experienced with a clear precision.

The problem was, there was no experience to recount. She didn't enter the NDE-state at all. Instead, after five minutes in non-REM sleep, the scan pattern shifted abruptly to that of a waking brain. 'What happened?' Richard said to Tish. 'Is Mrs Troudtheim all right?'

Joanna looked down at Mrs Troudtheim, alarmed, and Tish said, 'Vitals normal.'

'She's awake,' Richard started to say, and Mrs Troudtheim's voice cut across his with, 'Are you ready to start?'

It developed, on Joanna's close questioning of her, that she had nodded off for a moment and 'awoke' to feel Tish's hand on her wrist, taking her pulse. 'I'm so sorry,' she said. 'I'll try to stay awake next time.'

'Do you remember the point at which you feel asleep?' Joanna asked.

'No, I was lying there, and it was so quiet and dark …' she said, clearly making an effort to remember. 'I don't know what came over me. I don't usually doze off like that.'

'Did the quality of the silence or the dark change at any point?' Joanna pressed. 'Did something wake you up? A sound?' But it was no use. Mrs Troudtheim had told her everything she remembered.

'I'll be happy to try it again, and this time I promise to stay awake,' she said.

Richard explained to her that they couldn't send her under again so soon. 'This doesn't disqualify me, does it?' she said worriedly.

'Not at all,' Richard said. 'There's usually some trouble getting the dosage right at first. I'd like to schedule you for another session this week. Can you come in day after tomorrow?' That would give him time to look at the scans and the data and see what the problem was. It was probably simply that Mrs Troudtheim required a higher dosage to achieve an NDE-state. It was too bad, though. He could have used another set of scans for comparing the endorphin sites.

'I just thought of something,' Joanna said after Mrs Troudtheim left. 'She had oral surgery the day before yesterday. Could the anesthetic she's getting for her oral surgery be interfering with the dithetamine?'

'It shouldn't be,' he said, but he had Joanna call and ask her what she was getting, which turned out to be short-term novocaine and nitrous oxide, neither of which should have stayed in her system for more than a few hours, but he checked her neurotransmitter analysis anyway and then called up Mr Wojakowski's, and then Mr O'Reirdon's.

He spent the rest of the day analyzing them for endorphins. Both showed the presence of beta-endorphins. Alpha-endorphins were present in Mr Wojakowski's, but not Mr O'Reirdon's. Tish came back at five to collect a scarf she'd forgotten and to ask him if he wanted to go to dinner at Conrad's, 'a bunch of us are going,' but he wanted to go over the rest of the analyses before Amelia's session, so he told her no.

'All work and no play,' Tish said, and then, coming closer to look at the screens, 'What do you see in those things anyway?'

Good question. There was no NPK in Mr O'Reirdon's analysis either, and when he checked Mr Sage's, he didn't show any, and no alpha-endorphins. He did, however, show the presence of dimorphine. And high levels of beta-endorphins, which must be the key.

He did some research. In laboratory experiments, beta-endorphins had been shown to produce feelings of warmth and euphoria and sensations of light and floating. He called up the scan of Amelia's third session again, the one after she had uttered the famous 'oh, no,' and looked at the beta-endorphin receptor sites. As he'd expected, they showed lower levels of activity. The majority of the sites registered yellow rather than red, and two were yellow-green. In addition, several receptor sites for cortisol, a fear-pro-ducing neurochemical, were lit.

Could Mrs Troudtheim need a higher dosage of dithetamine to generate those endorphins? He went over her analysis, but her waking and non-REM sleep endorphin levels were within the normal range and her scans on enter-ing non-REM sleep looked identical to both Amelia Tanaka's and Mr Wojakowski's. When Joanna asked him the next day if he'd found out what had gone wrong, he said, 'Not a clue.'

'I still haven't been able to get in touch with Mrs Haighton,' Joanna reported. 'She was at the Women's Networking Seminar or the Women's Investment Club, I forget which. And there's a problem with Mr Pearsall. He couldn't come in tomorrow or Thursday, so I scheduled him for today after Amelia.'

'Good,' he said. If Mr Pearsall's NDE showed the same beta-endorphin levels—

'Sorry I'm late,' Tish said, coming in. 'I was at Happy Hour till after mid-night. You should've been there, Dr Wright.'

'Umm,' Richard said, and to Joanna, 'Have any of your subjects used the word *floating* to describe the out-of-body experience?'

'Nearly all of them,' she said. 'Or *hovering*.'

'Do you know if there's a correlation between out-of-body experiences and a blindingly bright light?'

'No, I can check.'

'Hi, Dr Wright,' Amelia said, coming in. She shrugged out of her backpack. 'I'm sorry I'm late. Again.'

Tish handed her a folded gown. 'I'm Tish,' she said. 'I'm going to be prep-ping you today.'

Amelia ignored her. 'I got a B-plus on that biochem exam, Dr Wright!' she said. 'And an A on my enzyme analysis.'

'Great,' Richard said. 'Why don't you go get dressed, and we'll get this show on the road,' and went over to the console to look at the scans again while Tish prepped Amelia and started the IV, and then went over to the examining table.

'All set?' he asked Amelia.

She nodded. 'Can I have a blanket first, though? I'm always *so* cold afterward.'

'Were you just as cold both times?' Joanna asked. 'Or were you colder one time than the other?'

Amelia considered that. 'I was colder last time, I think.'

Which might mean that was an effect of lower endorphin levels, too, rather than lowered body temp. Richard had the nurse start the feed and then went back over to the console to watch Amelia's NDE. Both the intensity of activity and the number of sites were greater this time, so the variation must not be due to a developed resistance.

He looked over at the examining table. Joanna, who had looked anxious at the beginning of the session, had relaxed, and Amelia's face had the same Mona Lisa smile as during previous sessions.

Richard kept her under for four minutes. When she came out, there were no frightened murmurs, and, as he had expected, Amelia described the light as being brighter and 'sort of shining out,' spreading her hands in a feathering motion to indicate rays. Definitely endorphin-generated.

'Did you have a warm, safe feeling?' he asked, and felt a sharp kick to his ankle.

'Can you describe the feelings you had during the NDE?' Joanna asked, her face impassive.

'I felt warm and safe just like Dr Wright said,' Amelia said, smiling at him, and he knew Joanna would accuse him of leading, but Amelia mentioned the warmth and the light several more times as she recounted what she'd seen, and when Joanna asked her, poker-faced, if she'd experienced anything that frightened her, her answer was a definite no.

What she had seen was a long, dark room 'like a hallway,' with an open door at the end of it, and people standing behind the door. 'Did you recognize the people?' Joanna asked, and there was a pause before Amelia shook her head. 'They were dressed in white,' she offered.

'What happened then?' Joanna asked.

Amelia pulled the blanket closer around her shoulders. 'They just stood there,' she said.

Joanna wasn't able to get much more out of her except that she had heard a sound (which she couldn't identify) as she entered the hallway, and that just before that, she had had a momentary sensation of floating.

Definitely the beta-endorphins, Richard thought. He needed to look at the neurotransmitter analysis and the bloodwork, but if they were both higher than Amelia's two previous sessions, then possibly all the core elements were endorphin-generated. Which would mean that the NDE might be what Noyes and Linden had thought – a protective mechanism to shield the brain from the traumatic emotions of dying and not a survival mechanism after all.

If the endorphin levels consistently matched, and if increased levels produced more core elements. He needed more data to prove either of those premises, which meant sending Amelia under again as soon as possible, but scheduling her for another session turned out to be almost as difficult as scheduling Mrs Haighton for an interview.

'I've got a really big anatomy test coming up next week,' Amelia said, smiling apologetically at Richard. 'Could we do it after next week?'

'I'd really like to schedule it earlier than that,' Richard said.

'Okay, Dr Wright,' Amelia said, smiling at him, 'but I want you to know you're the only person I'd do this for, and if I flunk anatomy, it'll be your fault.'

By the time they'd worked out a time, Mr Pearsall had arrived. After what had happened the day before, he was a little worried about Mr Pearsall's being able to achieve the NDE-state, but he not only achieved it, he was right on the mark. His scan matched the standard nearly as closely as Tanaka's, and in the interview afterward, he reported five core elements, including an out-of-body experience.

'I was lying on the table, waiting for you and the doctor to start,' he told Joanna. 'I couldn't see anything, of course, because of the mask and my eyes being closed, and then all of a sudden I could. I was up above the table, and I could see everything, the nurse checking my blood pressure, and you, holding a little tape recorder up to my mouth, and the doctor over at the computer. There were colored patterns on the screens, and they kept changing, from yellow to orange and from blue to green.'

'You said you were above the table,' Joanna said. 'Can you be more specific?'

'I was all the way up next to the ceiling,' Pearsall said. 'I could see the tops of the windows and the cabinets.' But not what Joanna put up on top of the medicine cupboard, Richard thought, and everything else he described he's looking at right now or could have seen when he came into the room.

He was impressed all over again at Joanna's savvy. He shuddered to think what would have happened if he hadn't asked her to work with him. Headlines in the *Star*: 'Scientists Prove Life After Death Real,' with a testimonial from Mr Mandrake and sidebar interviews with Dr Foxx and Ms Coffey the moon psychic. And no funding again ever, even from Mercy General. No credibility.

Joanna gave credibility to the project just by being on it. Sitting there in her cardigan sweater and wire-rimmed glasses, she was an island of sanity and sense in a field full of cranks and nutcases. He would never pick up the *Star* and find she'd decided the Other Side was real. And she wasn't just sensible, she was intelligent, and an amazing interviewer. Without seeming to do anything at all, she elicited much more information than he'd been able to.

'What happened then?' she was asking Mr Pearsall.

'I heard a sound, and then I was in a dark place,' Mr Pearsall said.

'Can you describe the sound?' Joanna asked.

'It was a sort of … rumbling, like a truck going by … or a clattering.'

Or bullets hitting the wing of a Wildcat, Richard thought, wondering what the sound was that they all had so much trouble identifying it. Was it a completely alien sound?

'And when I got to the end of the tunnel, there was a gate barring the way. I wanted to get through, but I couldn't,' Mr Pearsall said, but without any anxiety in his voice, and when Joanna asked him to describe the light, he said, 'It was brighter than anything I've ever seen, and it made me feel peaceful and warm and safe.'

But when Richard reviewed the scans, fewer than half of the beta-endorphin sites were activated, and those showed either green or blue, the lowest level of activity, and there were only trace levels of the beta-endorphins and NPK. There were high levels of alpha-endorphins, though, and of GABA, an endorphin inhibitor.

He called up the analysis of Amelia's most recent set of scans. No beta-endorphins, no NPK, low levels of alpha-endorphins.

And the cortisol level was off the charts.

13

'This is funny.'
   – DOC HOLLIDAY's last words

If Joanna had any illusions about subjects in a controlled experiment being easier to interview than patients, the next two weeks stripped her of them. She couldn't get Mr Sage to talk, she couldn't get Mr Wojakowski to shut up, and Mrs Troudtheim, in spite of Richard's attempts to adjust her dosage, still hadn't had an NDE.

'I don't know what's wrong,' Richard said disgustedly after the third try. 'I thought the problem might be the sedative, since she wakes up, so I raised the dosage last time, and this time I used dipral instead of zalepam, but nothing.'

'Could Mrs Troudtheim be one of those people who simply don't have

NDEs?' Joanna asked. 'Forty percent of patients who've coded and been revived don't remember anything at all.'

'No, that's not it,' Richard said.

'How do you know?'

'Because we've only got five volunteers,' he said. 'I'm going to check her cortisol levels. Maybe the dosage is still too low.'

But that just made it worse. When Joanna came into the lab for Amelia's next session, he asked abruptly, 'Didn't you tell me your subjects frequently say the NDE isn't a dream?'

'Yes,' Joanna said. 'It was one of the things that surprised me when I first started interviewing. One of Mandrake's big arguments for the reality of the NDE was that all of his subjects said it was real. Of course, subjective experience isn't proof of anything, as I've tried to tell him, and I assumed he'd coached his NDEers into making the comment anyway. But when I started interviewing, I found he wasn't exaggerating: nearly all of them volunteer that their experience was real, "not like a dream."'

'And have you been able to get them to be more specific?' Richard asked.

'Do you have any food?' Joanna asked. 'I spent my entire lunch trying to track down Mrs Haighton.'

'Sure,' Richard said, reaching in his pockets. 'Let's see, V8 juice, trail mix, cheese-and-peanut-butter crackers ... and an orange. Take your pick.'

'No, to answer your question,' Joanna said, ripping the crackers' cellophane. 'They just keep repeating that it feels real. I think it may be because the NDE doesn't have incongruities and discontinuities.'

'Discontinuities?'

'Yes, you know,' Joanna said, 'you're in your pajamas taking a final for a class you never had, and then suddenly you're in Paris, which is somehow south of Denver and on the seacoast. Dreams are full of places and times that shift with no transition, juxtapositions of things and people from different times and places, inconsistencies.' She took a swig of V8. 'None of my NDEers ever report any of those things. The NDE seems to proceed in a logical, linear fashion.'

She ate a cracker and then said, 'There also seems to be a much longer retention of an NDE. The memory of a dream fades very quickly, usually within a few minutes of waking up, but NDEers retain their memories for days, sometimes years. Why all these dream questions?'

'Because when I checked Mrs Troudtheim's cortisol levels against the template, I noticed the acetylcholine levels matched those of REM sleep, and when I checked the other subjects, they had similarly high levels.'

'So you think the NDE is similar to a dream, in spite of what they say?'

'No, because there's no corresponding drop in norepinephrine, which there would be in dreaming. I don't know what to think. There's no consistency in endorphin levels, and I found levels of cortisol in all of Mr Wojakowski's NDEs, in spite of the fact that he says he doesn't feel any fear.'

'But he does talk a lot about Zeroes and people being killed,' Joanna said. 'I found them in Amelia's most recent NDE, too. I have no idea what's going on.'

Joanna didn't either. Amelia's session yesterday had been her most euphoric so far. When Joanna'd asked her to describe her feelings, she'd beamed at Richard, and said happily, 'Warm, safe, wonderful!'

None of the others had showed any signs of anxiety either. Joanna had finally managed to get in touch with Ann Collins, the nurse who'd attended the session at which Mr Wojakowski had murmured something while coming out. 'He said, "Battle stations!"' Ann reported, which somehow wasn't a surprise and, when Joanna asked how he had sounded when he said it, had said, 'Excited, jubilant.'

So cortisol didn't explain Amelia's saying, 'Oh, no.' Or Greg Menotti's 'fifty-eight,' the meaning of which still nagged at her. After her second visit to see Mrs Woollam (a very short one because she had been scheduled for a chest X-ray), Joanna had even gone to the hospital chapel, gotten a Bible, and looked up Psalm 58, but it was about the sins of the wicked, who were going to be melted away 'as waters which run continually.'

Joanna had spent a few guilty minutes flipping through the rest of the Bible and discovered that most chapters didn't have a verse 58, and the ones that did tended to say something like, 'The gates of Babylon shall be burned with fire, and the people shall labor in vain, and the folk in the fire,' which wasn't exactly helpful. Especially the part about laboring in vain.

But even though the answer wasn't in the Bible, it was somewhere. The feeling that she knew what it meant persisted, and sometimes, listening to Mr Sage's interminable pauses or ducking into an elevator to get away from Mr Mandrake, she felt she almost had it. That if she just had an uninterrupted half-hour to concentrate, she could get it.

But there were no half-hours. Mrs Haighton called to say Thursday wouldn't work, and Vielle, and Maisie, to tell Joanna she was back in the hospital. 'I went into A-fib again,' she said matter-of-factly. 'I've been here a whole day. Don't you ever answer your pages?'

No, Joanna thought. They were always from Mr Mandrake, trying to find out from her who their subjects were and what they'd experienced.

'I need to see you right away,' Maisie said. 'I'm in the same room as before.'

Joanna promised she'd be down right after Mr Sage's session. He saw a tunnel (dark), a light (bright), and some people (maybe), which it took an hour and a half to get out of him. It was a positive pleasure to talk to Maisie.

'You never told me why you wanted to know what a Victory garden was,' Joanna said, trying not to look appalled at Maisie's badly puffed face. Fluid retention, Joanna thought. A bad sign.

'Oh,' Maisie said, 'because Emmett Kelly, he's this clown who has a really sad face and raggedy clothes, I've got a picture – it's the big red book with the volcano,' she said. 'It's in my Barbie bag.'

'I see Ms Sutterly brought your books,' Joanna said, looking through the bag. *100 Worst Disasters Ever*, with the *Hindenburg* crashing in flames on the cover, *Disasters of the World*, with a world map dotted with red flags, *Great Disasters*, with a black-and-white photo of the San Francisco earthquake. Here it was. *Disasters of the Twentieth Century*, with a garish red-and-black painting of a volcano.

'What's this?' Joanna asked, bringing it over to the bed. 'Pompeii?'

'Pompeii's the city,' Maisie corrected her. 'Mount Vesuvius is the volcano. But this is Mount Pelee. It killed thirty thousand people in like two minutes.' She opened the book and began turning pages filled with photos and maps and newspaper headlines. The Triangle Shirtwaist Factory fire, the sinking of the *Morro Castle*, the Galveston hurricane.

'Here it is,' Maisie said, wheezing a little. With the mere effort of turning pages? Maisie showed Joanna a double-page spread of photos. The one at the top was of Emmett Kelly, with his white-painted downturned mouth, his battered hat and enormous flopping shoes, running toward the circus tent with a bucket of water. There was a look of horror and desperation on his face, visible even under the clown makeup, but Maisie seemed blissfully unaware of it.

'Emmett Kelly helped get all of these little kids out of the fire,' she said, 'and there was this one little girl, he saved her, and after he got her out of the tent, he said, "Go over there in the Victory garden and wait for your mother." So she'd be out of the way.'

'Oh,' Joanna said, 'and you thought that was some sort of special place they had at circuses back then?'

'No,' Maisie said. 'I thought a victory was a kind of vegetable.' She pushed the book around so the other half of the double page was facing Joanna and pointed at a man in a tall bandleader's hat, waving a baton. 'That's the bandleader. When the fire started, he made the band play 'The Stars and Stripes Forever.' Do you know how that goes?'

'Yes.' Joanna hummed a few bars for her.

'Oh, I know that song,' Maisie said. 'That's the duck song, "Be kind to your web-footed friends." If you're at a circus and you hear that song, you need to get out of there fast. It means there's a fire or a lion loose or something.'

'I didn't know that.'

Maisie nodded wisely. 'It's like a signal. Whenever the band plays it, all the circus people know to come 'cause there's an emergency. Like when some-body codes. How come Emmett Kelly's clothes are all raggedy?'

Joanna explained he was supposed to look like a tramp and then, because her humming 'The Stars and Stripes Forever' had reminded her of Coma Carl's humming, went up to see him for a few minutes.

His wife said he was having a good day, which meant he hadn't yanked out his IV in his flailings and hadn't been ambushed by the Vietcong, but Joanna thought he looked much thinner. When she went out to the nurses' station, Guadalupe gave her an index card of his murmurings, saying, 'He hasn't said much lately.'

'Does he still row on the lake?' Joanna asked.

'No,' Guadalupe said.

Joanna looked at the card. 'No,' he had said. '... have to ... male ... patches ...,' and underneath, scrawled in a different hand, 'red.'

Joanna transcribed the words, entering them onto Carl's computer file along with 'water' and 'oh, grand' and Guadalupe's comments about his movements. Looking through it, she realized she hadn't transcribed his hum-ming. It must be on one of the dozens of tapes piled in a shoe box she hadn't gotten to yet and wouldn't any time soon. The project tapes took precedence, and conducting interviews, and scheduling. And rescheduling.

Mrs Haighton couldn't come on Friday – this time it was the Art Museum Gala – and Amelia needed to reschedule, too. She had another big exam com-ing up, and her professor had scheduled a review session she couldn't miss, and no, she couldn't do it Thursday either. She had a test in statistics that day.

'How many exams do they have in college these days?' Richard exploded when Joanna told him. 'I thought midterms were over. What's going on? Has she gotten a new boyfriend?'

It's more likely she's given up on you ever noticing her, Joanna thought, because although Amelia was increasingly perky and smiling, Richard was totally preoccupied with his failure to get Mrs Troudtheim under. 'I don't know what else to try,' he told Joanna, exasperated.

The worst part of Mrs Troudtheim was that if they'd had a full slate of vol-unteers he'd simply have declared her nonviable and gone on to other subjects. But there were no other subjects to go on to. Joanna was obviously never going to get Mrs Haighton in for an interview, let alone a session, and Mr Pearsall had called to say that his father, the one who had never been sick a day in his life, had had a stroke, and that he was flying out to Ohio and didn't know when he would be back. Which left Mr Sage the Silent, the increasingly hard-to-get Amelia Tanaka, and Mr Wojakowski. At least he was available. And more than eager to talk.

'I was in the tunnel,' he said, beginning his fifth account. They were alone in the lab. Richard, eager to get his bloodwork analyzed, or maybe unwilling to listen to another of Mr Wojakowski's rambling stories, had taken the blood down to the lab himself.

'It was dark, I couldn't see anything, but I wasn't scared. I had a kind of peaceful feeling, like when you know something's going to happen, but you don't know what, and you don't know when. Like the day they bombed Pearl.' I knew he'd find a way to work the *Yorktown* into this, Joanna thought. 'I can still remember that morning. It was a Sunday –'

Joanna nodded, wondering if she should try to get him back on track, or if that would just send him veering off on some other story. He usually did eventually work his way back to the question she'd asked. She leaned her chin on her hand and prepared to wait.

'I'm coming back from shore leave in Virginia Beach – the *Yorktown* was in Norfolk – and I saw this sailor up on the island –' He fished in his pocket and brought out the tattered picture of the *Yorktown*. 'That's the island,' he said, pointing at the tall tower in the middle of the ship. It had three cross-barred masts that Joanna assumed were radio or radar antennae, and an assortment of ladders.

'See, that's the radar mast, and there's the bridge,' Mr Wojakowski said, pointing to them. 'So, anyway, he looks like he's going to break his neck, he's coming down off the island so fast, and he's got a paper clutched in his right hand.'

He folded up the picture and put it carefully back in his wallet. 'I should've known something was up – the only thing up that ladder was the radio shack – but I didn't even think about that. I just stood there, waiting to see if he broke his neck, and when he didn't, I went on down belowdecks to change out of my civvies, and then I heard 'em announcing over the PA that the Japs had bombed Pearl Harbor, and I knew what he must've been carrying was a telegram.' He shook his head at his own slowness. 'I had that same kind of feeling in the tunnel, waiting for something to happen, and not knowing what or when.'

He looked expectantly at Joanna, but she wasn't listening. She was trying to remember what he'd said that first day, when she'd asked him about his age. He had told her he'd signed up the day after Pearl Harbor, she was sure of it.

'Some of the guys didn't believe it, even when they heard it over the PA,' Mr Wojakowski said. 'Woody Pikeman comes in and says, "Who's the wiseguy?" meaning the PA announcement. "The Emperor Hirohito," I says.'

'Mr Wojakowski,' Joanna said, 'I just remembered a meeting I have to be at.' She stood up and switched off the minirecorder. 'If you don't mind—'

'Sure, Doc,' he said. 'You want me to come back later?'

'Yes. No. I don't know how long the meeting will take.' She scooped up the recorder and her notebook.

'I've got lots more to tell you,' he said.

'I'll call you and set up another time for us to finish your account,' she said firmly.

'Anytime, Doc,' he said, and ambled out. As soon as he was gone, she picked up the phone, intending to page Richard, and then changed her mind. She needed to check the transcripts before she made an accusation.

She set the receiver down and stood there with her hand on it, trying to remember exactly what Mr Wojakowski had said about enlisting. She had only half-listened to his rambling war stories, but she was positive he'd said he'd enlisted the day after Pearl. None of them had even known where Pearl Harbor was, except his kid sister, who'd seen a newsreel at the movies the night before.

She went down to her office. She hadn't transcribed that account yet. She rummaged through the shoe box till she found the right tape, stuck it in the recorder and fast-forwarded to the middle. 'Well, after we hit Rabaul ...' Too far. She rewound. 'Dead before she ever knew it ...' Forward again. '... The funny papers.' Here it was: '... in comes the lady from two doors down, all out of breath, and says, "The Japs just bombed Pearl Harbor!"'

Joanna skipped forward. Kid sister, newsreel, *Desperadoes*. 'And the very next day, I went downtown to the navy recruiting center and signed up.'

She put her hand to her mouth, thinking, Oh, my God, he made it up. But which one? Or had he made up both versions? Or all of it? It didn't matter. If even part of his account were concocted, it meant his descriptions of his NDEs were useless.

Unless he'd told her the story about signing up after Pearl Harbor to cover up his real age. She'd thought that first time she saw him that he had to be nearly eighty. He might have made up the story to hide his age and then, in the heat of describing the NDE, forgotten and told her the truth. If it was only a matter of lying about his age, everything else he'd told them might be true.

But how could they be sure? She thought about his other stories, the soda fountain, the *Hammann* sinking with all hands in two minutes flat, his joyous rescue by the miraculously resurrected *Yorktown*, flags flying, sailors waving their white hats in the air. They had all sounded completely credible. But so had both accounts of December seventh, 1941.

She needed some kind of outside confirmation. She could call the library and ask them where the *Yorktown* had been on December seventh, but that wouldn't prove Mr Wojakowski had been there. She supposed she could call the Department of Veteran Affairs or the navy and find out if an Edward Wojakowski had served on the *Yorktown*, but that would take time, and probably bureaucratic red tape. She needed to find out now, before Richard sent him under again.

She leafed through the transcripts, looking for something that might be independently verifiable. The dive-bomber – what was his name? Here it was, Jo-Jo Powers – who had crashed putting his bomb on the flight deck? No, that might have been in a book, or a movie. There was a movie called *Midway*, wasn't there? She remembered seeing it in the action section at Blockbuster. So, none of the Midway stuff. What about his ditching of his plane in the Coral Sea? That story was full of facts that should be independently verifiable – dates and events and place names.

She scrolled through the transcripts, looking for the account of the rescue. Here it was. He had ditched his plane in the Coral Sea, swum to Malakula, been smuggled by friendly natives to another island, set out in a dugout canoe for Port Moresby. The *Yorktown*, meanwhile, had limped back to Pearl Harbor for repairs, been refitted in three days, and then sailed straight to Midway.

She needed a map. Who would have one here in the hospital? Maisie, she thought, remembering the map on the cover of one of her disaster books, and scribbled down the details. Coral Sea, Malakula, Vanikalo. She scribbled down the dates, too, on the off-chance that the sinking of the *Yorktown* counted as a disaster, and ran down to fourth.

Maisie was lying propped against pillows, glaring at a video. 'Pollyanna,' she told Joanna disgustedly. 'All she does is tell people to be glad about stuff. It is *so* sickening.' She pointed the remote at Hayley Mills, wearing a white dress and a big blue sash, and switched it off.

'She falls out of a tree later,' Joanna said.

'Really?' Maisie said, perking up. 'Do you want to hear a neat thing about the Hartford circus fire? The Flying Wallendas, they were this acrobat family, they were up on the high wire, and they heard the band play the duck song, and—'

'Not right now,' Joanna said. 'Maisie, I need a map of the islands in the Pacific Ocean. Do you have one in one of your disaster books?'

'Uh-huh,' she said, starting to get out of bed.

'You stay there,' Joanna said. 'I'll get it. Do you know which book it's in?'

'I think *Best Disasters of All Time*,' Maisie said. 'In the part about Krakatoa. It's the one with the *Andrea Doria* on the cover.'

Joanna pulled it out of the bag and brought it over to the bed, and Maisie began searching through it. 'Krakatoa was the biggest volcano ever. It made these red sunsets all over the world. *Blood* red. Here it is.'

Joanna leaned over her shoulder. There was a map, all right, but it was no more than a pale blue square with the outlines of India and Australia in black and a red star labeled 'Krakatoa.' 'You had a book with a map on the cover,' Joanna said.

'Yeah, *Disasters of the World*,' Maisie said. 'But it's not a very good one either.' She kicked off the covers. 'I think there's one in *Earthquakes and Volcanoes.*'

'Maisie,' Joanna protested, but Maisie had already gotten out of bed and extracted the book from the pile.

'It blew the whole island apart. Krakatoa,' she said, flipping through the book. 'It made this *huge* noise, like a whole bunch of cannons.' Maisie turned pages. 'I *knew* there was one,' she said triumphantly and dumped the book on the bed. 'See? There's Krakatoa.'

And there were Hawaii and the Solomon Islands and the Marshalls, scattered across an expanse of blue. 'Do you see Midway Island anywhere?' Joanna asked, bending over the map.

Maisie pointed eagerly. 'Right there. In the middle.' Of course. That's why it was called Midway Island. And there was Pearl Harbor. Where was Malakula? She peered closer, trying to read the tiny print. Necker Island and Nikoa and Kaula, and a bunch of unnamed dots. It would be no proof of anything if Malakula wasn't on the map. There were dozens of minuscule islands between Midway and Hawaii.

'What are you looking for?' Maisie demanded, breathing hard.

Joanna looked at her. Her lips were lavender. 'Back in bed,' Joanna ordered, pulling back the covers.

'I want to help you look.'

'You can look in bed.'

Maisie dutifully clambered in and lay back against the pillows. 'What are you looking for?' she repeated.

'An island named Malakula,' Joanna said, laying the open book on Maisie's knees so they could both see it. 'And the Coral Sea.'

'The Coral Sea ...' Maisie murmured, poring over the map, her short hair swinging forward over her puffy cheeks. They had less color than the last time Joanna had seen her, and there were violet smudges under her eyes. It was easy to forget just how sick she was.

'*Here* it is,' Maisie cried.

'Malakula?' Joanna asked, following Maisie's finger.

'No. The Coral Sea.'

Joanna's heart sank. The Coral Sea was all the way down by Australia. There was no way Mr Wojakowski could have covered it in a native dugout. Or in a motorboat, for that matter. It was hundreds – no, thousands, she corrected, looking at the map's scale – of miles away.

He had made it up – the coconuts and the jammed machine guns and the Katzenjammer Kids. Maybe there's an explanation, she thought, bending over the map again. Maybe he meant another island, with a name like Malakula. Marakei. Or Maleolap. But neither of those was any closer to

Midway than Malakula, and Midway was the only island for hundreds of miles in every direction that began with an M. But you said yourself there were dozens of unnamed islands. And it's been sixty years since World War II. Maybe he got the names mixed up. I need to talk to Mr Wojakowski, she thought.

She closed the book and stood up. 'Thank you. You were a lot of help. You're a very good researcher.'

'You can't go yet,' Maisie said. 'I have to tell you about the people at the circus. They all tried to go out the main entrance, but they couldn't, 'cause of the animal run, and the Wallendas—'

'Maisie, I really have to go,' Joanna said.

'I know, but I have to tell you this one thing. The Flying Wallendas and everybody tried to get them to go out the performers' entrance, but—'

'I promise I'll come back so you can tell me all about the tent and the Flying Wallendas. Okay?' She started for the door.

'Okay,' Maisie said. 'Does she die?'

Joanna stopped cold. 'Who?'

'Pollyanna. When she falls out of the tree.'

'No,' Joanna said. She came back around the bed, picked up the remote, and turned the TV back on. She hit 'play.' 'It's a Disney movie.'

'Oh,' Maisie said, disappointed.

'But she hurts her back and can't walk,' Joanna said. She handed Maisie the remote. 'And she's very crabby about it.'

'Oh, good,' Maisie said. 'Did somebody have an NDE about the Coral Sea?'

'No more questions,' Joanna said firmly. 'Watch your movie,' and went back up to her office to listen to the tape again. He had definitely said Malakula and the Coral Sea. She called him and left a message for him to come in at three, and then went through the transcripts again, looking for some definitive discrepancy that would make the interview unnecessary. And, reading through his accounts, she became more and more convinced there had to be some mistake.

The naval terms – hatches, islands, flight decks – and the gratuitous details – not just a canoe, but a dugout, not just a soda fountain, but one that made cherry phosphates. Surely he couldn't have made up the Katzenjammer Kids and the neighbor lady two doors down and the newsreel about Pearl Harbor. He had even known the name of the movie that was playing.

But he couldn't have been on the *Yorktown and* in his hometown when Pearl Harbor was bombed. And the Norfolk story was full of believable details, too, from the PA system to Woody Pikeman asking, 'Who's the wiseguy?' I have to talk to Richard, she thought.

The phone rang. She picked it up, hoping it was him. It was Mrs Haighton. 'I got your message,' she said. 'I'm afraid neither Tuesday nor Thursday will work. I've got a hospital board meeting Tuesday, and Thursday's my afternoon to volunteer at the crisis center.'

We've got a crisis right here, Joanna thought. 'How would Wednesday afternoon work?' she said. 'Two? Four? Or we could do this in the evening.'

'Oh, no, evenings are even worse,' she said and launched into a litany of board and organizing committee meetings.

'Earlier then,' Joanna said doggedly. 'I really need to schedule you this week, if possible. It's important.' But this week was absolutely impossible. Maybe next week. No, that was the Women's Center fundraiser. The week after.

And by then we'll have no volunteers at all, Joanna thought. She printed out the transcripts, and took them and the tapes to the lab to show Richard. 'Hiya, Doc,' Mr Wojakowski said. He was standing outside the door in the exact spot where she'd left him.

'What are you doing here?' Joanna asked, turning hastily away to open the door so he couldn't see the stricken expression on her face.

'I figured I'd stick around till you got done with your meeting,' he said, following her into the lab. 'I remembered what you said about talking about the stuff you saw while it was still fresh in your mind, and I didn't have anyplace to go, so I thought, I'll just wait till she comes back, so we can get it all down before my memory gets mixed up.' He sat down in the chair and leaned forward, his ruddy face eager, smiling, waiting for her to begin asking questions, and she thought again, there must be some mistake.

But how could she find out what it was? She couldn't ask him directly, 'Why did you tell me two different stories about where you were when Pearl Harbor was bombed?' or, 'Do you have any proof you served on the *Yorktown?*' Not with him sitting there, his face eager and open.

'I was telling you about the peaceful feeling I had in the tunnel, like something was going to happen,' he said, 'so I walked a little ways till I come to a door, and all of a sudden there was this bright light, and I mean bright. The only time I ever saw something that bright was when a bomb from an Aichi-99 went right through the hangar deck and blew up Repair 5. She took three hits that day.'

'Was that at the Battle of the Coral Sea?' Joanna asked, feeling like a traitor, like a Nazi grilling a spy, trying to trap him into a mistake, an inconsistency. And if he told her a different version this time, named a different island, a different kind of canoe, what would it prove? Only that his memory was fuzzy. The Battle of the Coral Sea had happened sixty years ago, and confabulations multiplied over time.

'One of the depth charges hit her in the port-side oil tanks,' Mr Wojakowski was saying, 'and oil was gushing out of her side. She woulda bled to death if we hadn'ta gotten her back to Pearl when we did. Boy, were we glad to see Diamond Head—'

'You went with the *Yorktown* back to Pearl Harbor?' Joanna blurted.

'Yep,' Mr Wojakowski said, 'and helped patch her up myself. We worked straight through, welding her boilers and patching up her hull. I worked on the crew fixing her watertight doors. We worked seventy-eight hours straight and were still working on 'em when we left Oahu. I tell ya, I was so tired when we got done, I slept all the way back to Midway.'

14

'Mother never reached me. If … anything happens … you must be prepared. Remember the message: Rosabelle, believe. When you hear those words … know it is Houdini speaking …'
– HARRY HOUDINI's words to his wife on his deathbed, promising to communicate with her from the afterlife

'He made the whole thing up?' Richard said. 'Even being on the *Yorktown*?'

'I don't know,' Joanna said, pacing back and forth, her hands jammed in her cardigan pockets. 'All I know is that he couldn't have been in Pearl Harbor repairing the *Yorktown* and adrift at sea thousands of miles away at the same time.'

'But does it have to mean he's lying?' Richard said. 'Couldn't it just be a memory lapse? He's sixty-five, after all, and the war was over fifty years ago. He may have forgotten exactly where he was at a given time.'

'How do you forget being shot down and losing your copilot and your gunner? You heard him tell that story. It was the best damned day of his life.'

'Are you sure he said he was in Pearl Harbor while the ship was being repaired?' Richard asked. 'Maybe he was just speaking generally –' but she was shaking her head violently.

'He also told me he was on board the *Yorktown* when he heard Pearl Harbor was bombed,' she said, '*and* that he was reading the funny papers back home. "The Katzenjammer Kids,"' she added bitterly. 'You can't tell me he doesn't remember where he was when he heard about Pearl Harbor. An entire *generation* remembers where it was when it heard about Pearl Harbor!'

'But why would he lie about something like that?'

'I don't *know*,' she said unhappily. 'Maybe he's trying to impress us. Maybe he's listened to so many war stories over the years he's gotten them all confused. Or maybe it's more serious than that, Alzheimer's, or a stroke. All I know is—'

'That we can't use him,' Richard said. 'Shit.'

Joanna nodded. 'I went back and checked the transcripts and then the tapes. They're full of discrepancies. According to Mr Wojakowksi, he was' – she pulled a piece of paper from her pocket and read from it – 'a pilot, a gunner's mate, a pharmacist's mate on burial detail, a semaphore flagman, and an airplane mechanic. I also checked the movie he said was playing the Saturday night before Pearl Harbor was bombed. *The Desperadoes* wasn't made until 1943.'

She wadded up the paper. 'I feel so stupid I didn't catch this sooner. Being able to tell whether people are telling the truth or confabulating is what I do for a living, but I honestly thought – his body language, the irrelevant details …' She shook her head wonderingly. 'I am *so* sorry. You hired me to spot this kind of thing, and I was completely fooled.'

'At least you caught it when you did.' He looked at her. 'Do you think he lied about what he saw in his NDEs, too?' and, at the look on Joanna's face, 'Don't worry, I know he has to go. I just wondered.'

'I don't know,' Joanna said, shaking her head, 'and there's no way to tell without outside confirmation. Some of the stories he told about the *Yorktown* were true. I checked them out before I came to talk to you. There really was a Jo-Jo Powers who 'laid his bomb right on the flight deck' and was killed doing it, and they really did repair the *Yorktown* and get it back to Midway in time for the battle. It was what saved the day, because the Japanese navy thought it had been sunk.'

'But there's no way to get outside confirmation on an NDE,' Richard finished. 'Except the scans, which can't tell us what the subject saw.'

'I am *so* sorry,' Joanna said. 'All I've done since I joined this project is decimate your subject list, and then, when I should have caught—'

'You did catch it,' Richard said. 'That's the important thing. *And* you caught it in time, before we published any results. Don't worry about it. We've still got five subjects. That's more than enough—' He stopped at her expression.

'We only have four,' she said unhappily. 'Mr Pearsall called. His father died, and he has to stay in Ohio to arrange the funeral and settle his affairs.'

Four. And that was including Mr Sage, who even Joanna couldn't get anything out of. And Mrs Troudtheim.

'What about Mrs Haighton?' he said. 'Have you been able to set up an interview yet?'

She shook her head. 'She keeps rescheduling. I don't think we should count on her. We're just one item on her very long list of social activities. How's the authorization on the new volunteers coming?'

'Slowly. Records said six more weeks,' he said, '*if* the board votes to continue the project.'

'What do you mean?' Joanna said. 'I thought you had funding for six months.'

'I did,' he said. 'I got a call from the head of the institute this morning. It seems Mrs Brightman has been telling everyone what high hopes she has for the project, that we've already found indications of supernatural phenomena.'

'Mr Mandrake,' Joanna said through gritted teeth.

'Bingo,' he said. 'So now the head of the institute wants a progress report that he can use to reassure the board we're doing legitimate scientific research.'

'Didn't you tell him—?'

'What? That half our subject list turned out to be cranks, plants, and psychics? That there's something wrong with the process that keeps our best subject from responding?' he said bitterly. 'Or did you want me to tell him about the imaginative Mr Wojakowski? I didn't know about him when the head called.'

'How long do we have?' Joanna said. 'Before we have to file this progress report?'

'Six weeks,' he said. 'Oddly enough.'

'You've got Amelia's scans,' she said, 'and Mr Sage's, and one set of Mr Pearsall's. Maybe it won't take him very long to settle his father's affairs.'

'Right, and, having just buried his father, he would definitely be an impartial observer,' Richard said, and then felt ashamed of himself. It wasn't Joanna's fault. He was the one who'd approved a list of unreliable people.

'I'm sorry.' He raked his hand through his hair. 'I just … maybe I should go under.'

'*What?*' Joanna said. 'You can't.'

'Why not? One, it would give us one more set of scans and one more account for comparison. I'd have to be at least as good an observer as Mr Sage,' he said, ticking reasons off on his fingers. 'Two, I'm not a spy or a crank. And three, I could go under right now, today, instead of waiting for authorization.'

'Why wouldn't you have to be authorized?'

'Because it's my project, so it would qualify as self-experimentation. Like Louis Pasteur. Or Dr Werner Forssmann—'

'Or Dr Jekyll,' Joanna said. 'Talk about something that would jeopardize the credibility of the project. Dr Foxx experimented on himself, didn't he?'

'I am not going to suddenly announce I've found the soul,' Richard said, 'and there's a long, legitimate tradition of self-experimentation – Walter Reed, Jean Borel, the transplant researcher, J. S. Haldane. All of them experimented on themselves for precisely the same reason, because they couldn't find willing, qualified subjects.'

'But who would supervise the console? You'd have to train someone to monitor the dosage and the scans. Tish can't do it.'

'You could—' he started.

'I *won't* do it,' she said. 'What if something went wrong? It's a terrible idea.'

'It's better than sitting around for the next six weeks trying to pry two words out of Mr Sage and waiting for our funding to be cut,' he said. 'Or do you have a better idea?'

'No,' she said unhappily. 'Yes. You could send me under.'

'You?' he said, astounded.

'Yes. If one of us is going to go under, I'm the logical choice. One, I don't need authorization either, since I'm part of the project. Two, I'm not going to see a bright light and assume it's Jesus. Three, Mr Mandrake can't convert me,' she said, ticking off reasons just like he had. 'Four, I'm not indispensable during sessions like you are. All I do is hold my tape recorder. I can just as easily turn it on before I go under. Or Tish could turn it on. Or you.'

'But what about afterward? The interview—'

'Five,' she tapped her thumb, 'I don't need to be interviewed. I already know what you want to know. And I'm sure I can do better than "It was dark," or "I felt peaceful." I could describe what I saw, the sensations I was feeling.'

'You could be more specific,' he said thoughtfully. It was a tempting idea. Instead of prying answers out of untrained observers, Joanna would know what to look for, how to describe it. She would be able to tell him whether what she saw was a superimposed vision or a hallucination and what subjects meant when they insisted it wasn't a dream.

More than that, she'd recognize the sensations for what they were. She'd know that certain effects were due to temporal-lobe stimulation or endorphins, and she could provide valuable information about the processes causing the sensations. She would know—

And that was just the problem. 'It won't work,' he said. 'You said yourself a subject shouldn't have preconceptions about what he was going to experience. You've interviewed over a hundred people. You've read all the books. How do you know your experience wouldn't be totally shaped by them?'

'It's a possibility,' she said. 'On the other hand, I'd have the advantage of being on guard. If I found myself in a dark enclosed space I wouldn't automatically assume it was a tunnel, and if I saw a figure radiating light, I *definitely* wouldn't assume it was an angel. I'd look at it – really look at it – and then tell you what I saw, without waiting for you to ask.'

Richard held his hands up in surrender. 'You've convinced me. If one of us were going under, you'd be the best one,' he said, 'but neither of us is going under. We still have four volunteers left, and what we should be doing is concentrating on how to make them more effective.'

'Or present,' Joanna said.

'Exactly. I want you to call Mrs Haighton and get her in here for a session.'

'I haven't even interviewed her yet,' Joanna said doubtfully.

'Do it over the phone if you have to. Tell her how much we need her. In the meantime, I'll work on Mrs Troudtheim.'

'What about Mr Sage?'

'We'll get a crowbar,' he said and grinned at her.

Joanna left to call Mrs Haighton, and he went back to comparing Mrs Troudtheim's data with the scans of the other subjects just prior to the NDE-state, looking for differences, but they were identical. Joanna had said some patients didn't have NDEs. He wondered which ones.

He went down to her office to ask her. She was just coming out, wearing her coat. 'Where are you going?' he asked her.

'To the Wilshire Country Club,' she said in an affected, aristocratic voice. 'I couldn't get Mrs Haighton on the phone, but her housekeeper told me she was setting up for the Junior Guild Spring Fling, whatever that is, so I'm going to see if I can catch her there.'

'Spring Fling?' Richard said. 'It's the middle of winter.'

'I know,' Joanna said, pulling on her gloves. 'Vielle called. She says it's snowing outside. I'll be back in time for Mrs Troudtheim's session.' She started walking toward the elevator.

'Wait a minute,' Richard said. 'I need to ask you a question about patients who have NDEs versus patients who don't. Is there a pattern to it?'

'Not a reliable one,' she said, pressing the 'down' button. 'NDEs mostly occur in certain types of death – heart attacks, drownings, car accidents, childbirth complications – but that may be just because patients with those sorts of traumas are more likely to be revived than patients with, say, a stroke or traumatic internal injuries.' The elevator opened.

'And the patients who don't have NDEs tend to have coded from other causes?'

She nodded. 'But of course we don't know if they didn't have an NDE, or if they had one but simply didn't remember it,' she said, and got in the elevator. 'Remember, before techniques for recording REM sleep, it was thought that certain people didn't dream.'

The door shut. Heart attacks, drownings, car accidents, Richard thought, staring blindly at the door. All traumatic events, with a high level of epinephrine. And cortisol.

He went back to the lab and called up Mrs Troudtheim's analysis and looked at the cortisol level. It was high, but no higher than Amelia Tanaka's during her fourth session, the one in which she had been under nearly five minutes. The epinephrine was slightly lower, but no lower than Mr Sage's, and he'd had no trouble achieving an NDE-state, even if he was maddeningly vague about describing it.

Maybe the problem was a lack of receptor sites. He brought up Mrs Troudtheim's scans and started through them, focusing on the hippocampus. Yellow activity along the hippocampus edges, where there were large numbers of cortisol receptor sites. He went forward through the frames and then backward, mapping the areas of activity. The anterior hippocampus went from yellow to orange and then red. He clicked back another single frame, looking at the edges and then at the epinephrine receptor sites in the—

He stared at the screen, clicked on 'stop,' made it go back three frames, and then forward again to the same frame, and stared at the screen again. He clicked on 'side-by-side,' and called up the standard and then Amelia Tanaka's scan.

There was no mistaking it. 'Well, at least I know it's not insufficient epinephrine,' he muttered. Because what he was looking at was unmistakably the brain in an NDE-state.

He did a superimpose with Mr O'Reirdon's scan to make sure, but it was already obvious. Mrs Troudtheim had had an NDE.

The pattern only lasted a single frame, but it changed the whole nature of the problem. He had been focused on what was preventing Mrs Troudtheim from achieving the NDE-state, but she had had one. The problem was that she hadn't been able to sustain it. Why not? Why had she immediately bounced out of it and into a waking state? And had this happened before?

He began mapping the NDE frame, looking for anomalies that might explain the NDE's nonsustainability. Nothing. It showed the same red-level activity in the right anterior temporal lobe, the amygdala, and the hippocampus, the same random scattering of orange- and yellow-level activity in the frontal cortex.

Joanna came back, her hair windblown and her cheeks pink from the cold and handed him an orange-and-yellow-green crocheted thing in a small clay pot. 'From the Spring Fling,' she said.

'What is it?' he said, turning the pot around.

'A marigold. A crocheted marigold. I thought of you as soon as I saw it. I know how fond you are of orange and vile green.'

'Did you see Mrs Haighton?'

'Yes, *and* interviewed her, and she's fine, no secret supernatural beliefs, *and* she's scheduled to come in Thursday afternoon. I know, that's Mr Sage's slot, but between the Philharmonic Guild and the charity fashion show, it was the only time she was available, so I decided it was worth moving him. I'm going to call him now.'

'Wait a minute,' Richard said. 'I want to show you something.' He showed her the side-by-side of the standard and Mrs Troudtheim's NDE frame.

'She had an NDE?' Joanna said. 'Do you think she's lying to us about not remembering it?'

That idea hadn't occurred to him. 'No,' he said. 'It only lasted a tenth of a second, if that. I doubt if she's even aware it happened. If she is, it's probably only as a flicker of light. Or darkness. But it changes the nature of the problem. She's achieving the NDE-state, but something's short-circuiting it. I've got to find out what that something is.'

He worked on doing just that the rest of the day and the next morning. He mapped the frames before and after the NDE, and then went back over the scans of Mrs Troudtheim's other sessions. He found an identical pattern in her second set of scans. There were none in the other sessions, but the RIPT images were a hundredth of a second apart. If the NDE-state was shorter than that, it would only show up part of the time, and the frames immediately succeeding the two NDE frames were identical to frames in the others.

He mapped them. They didn't match those of the other subjects. They showed sharply decreased acetylcholine and elevated norepinephrine, both consistent with arousal. Mrs Troudtheim was right. She'd jerked awake. When he compared them with the other subjects' arousal frames, the levels were identical.

He looked at the other neurotransmitters. High cortisol, no alpha- or beta-endorphins, traces of carnosine, amiglycine, and theta-asparcine. Carnosine was a variety of peptide, but he'd never heard of amiglycine or theta-asparcine. He'd need to talk to a neurotransmitter expert. He called Dr Jamison, who had an office up on eighth, and made an appointment to see her, but she wasn't much help. 'Amiglycine is present in the anterior pituitary gland. It acts as an inhibitor. Theta-asparcine is an endorphin that seems to primarily be involved in digestion.'

Digestion, Richard thought. Wonderful.

'It's been produced artificially,' she said helpfully. 'I think someone did a study on it recently. I'll see if I can find it. It may have other functions. Endorphins frequently have multiple functions.'

And maybe one of them is inhibiting NDEs, Richard thought, going back to the lab, but when he looked at the other NDEs, theta-asparcine was present in one of Mr Sage's and two of Amelia Tanaka's, and he didn't find any other anomalies in the neurotransmitter analysis or the bloodwork that might explain its instability.

He spent the next two days going over the scans again, but to no avail. When Mrs Troudtheim arrived the next day, he still had no idea what the problem was.

She oohed and ahhed over the crocheted marigold. 'Well, isn't that the cutest thing?' she said to Joanna. 'You don't have the pattern, do you?'

'Sorry, I don't,' Joanna said. 'I bought it at a bazaar.'

'I'll bet I could take a pattern off it,' Mrs Troudtheim said, leaning over the console to examine the yarn flowers. 'This is just double crochet with a shell stitch—'

'You can take it home with you if you like,' Richard said, handing her the pot.

'Are you *sure?*' Mrs Troudtheim said.

'I'm sure. Keep it as long as you like. You can have it.'

'Well, how nice,' she said, pleased. 'Look, Tish, isn't it the cutest thing?'

Tish oohed and ahhed, too, and they all examined the petals. Maybe the problem's nothing but simple anxiety, Richard thought, and talking like this will calm her down to the point where she can sustain the NDE, but it didn't. She was in the NDE for the space of a single, perfect frame, and then wide awake.

'I feel so embarrassed that I can't do this,' she said. 'I don't know what my problem is.'

I don't either, Richard thought, looking at the scans after she left with her crocheted marigold. The NDE frame was a dead-on match for Mr O'Reirdon's.

Joanna came in. 'Mrs Haighton just called,' she said. 'She can't come Thursday after all. Emergency Friends of the Ballet meeting.'

'Did you reschedule her?'

'Yes,' she said. 'For Friday after next. Listen, I've been thinking about what we talked about, and there's another reason you should send me under. It would make me a better interviewer. The accounts are all so vague, even from good observers like Amelia Tanaka, and I think the reason is that I simply don't know what to ask. It's like if you were asking someone to describe a painting without knowing whether it was a Monet or a Salvador Dalí. No, worse, it's like if you were trying to get them to describe a painting without ever having *seen* a painting yourself. Right now I have no idea what they're experiencing. They all say it's not a dream, that it's real. What does that mean?

'If I went under and *saw* that painting for myself, I'd know. I'd know if dark meant dark as in Carlsbad Caverns or the hospital parking lot at nine o'clock at night. I'd know if peaceful meant "tranquil" or "anesthetized." And I'd know what they're experiencing that they're not even mentioning because they don't realize it's important, and I don't know how to ask them about it. I think you should do it. I think you should send me under.'

He shook his head. 'I haven't given up on Mrs Troudtheim yet, and we've still got Amelia Tanaka. We do still have Amelia Tanaka?'

She nodded. 'At eleven.'

'That means I'd better get things set up.' He turned his attention back to the console. 'I want to lower the dosage again. The lack of detail you're worried about may not have anything to do with your questions. It may be due to endorphin levels, and if it is, it's simply a question of finding the right level, and even Mr Sage will turn into a fountain of observation.'

'And if it doesn't? What then?'

'We'll deal with that when it happens. Right now, you need to call Tish and tell her to get up here. Amelia will be here any minute.'

'There's plenty of time,' Joanna said. 'Amelia's always late. She won't be here for at least fifteen minutes.'

But she came in right on time, carrying her backpack. Richard shot Joanna a triumphant look. 'Go ahead and get ready, Amelia,' he said, and started over to the console.

'Can I talk to you a minute, Dr Wright, Dr Lander?' she said, and he saw that she hadn't made a move to shed her backpack or coat.

'Sure,' he said.

'The thing is, my biochem professor is really piling it on, and I'm getting totally swamped ...'

'And you need to reschedule? That's not a problem,' Richard said, trying not to show his disappointment. 'What time will work for you?' he said. 'Thursday?'

She shook her head. 'It isn't just biochem. It's all my classes. My anatomy prof's giving a test a week, and my genetics class – there's so much home-work, and the labs are getting a lot harder. My biochem lab –' She stopped, an odd look on her face, and then went on. 'I need the extra psych credit and all, but it won't do me any good if I don't pass the class. Or all my classes.' She took a deep breath. 'I think the best thing is for me just to drop out, and for you to find somebody else.'

Somebody else, he thought desperately. There isn't anybody else. 'I'm sure that won't be necessary,' he said, avoiding looking at Joanna. 'I'm positive we can work something out. How about if we cut your sessions down to one a week? Or if next week is bad, we could skip it altogether,' but Amelia was already shaking her head.

'It isn't just next week,' Amelia said uncomfortably. 'It's every week. I just have too much going on.'

'I'll be honest with you,' he said. 'I'm short on subjects, and you're one of my best observers. I really need you in the project.'

For a moment he thought, from the look Amelia gave him, that he had swayed her, but then she shook her head again. 'I just can't—'

'Is it because of the project?' Joanna asked, and Richard looked at her in surprise. 'Did something happen during one of your sessions? Is that why you want to quit?'

'No, of course not,' Amelia said, turning to smile at Richard. 'The project's really interesting, and I *love* working with you, with both of you,' she added, glancing briefly at Joanna. 'It isn't the project at all. I'm just so worried about my classes. Like in psychology—'

'I understand,' Richard said, 'and, trust me, the last thing I want you to do is fail psychology, but I also don't want to lose you. That's why I'm so determined to work something out.'

'Oh, Dr Wright,' Amelia said.

'What about weekends?' he said, pressing his advantage. 'We could schedule sessions on Saturday morning, if that's better for you. Or Sunday. You just tell us what would work for you and we'll do it.' He smiled at her. 'It would really help me out.'

She bit her lip, and looked at him uncertainly.

'Or evenings. We could schedule sessions at night if that's better.'

'No,' Amelia said, and her chin went up. 'I've made up my mind about this. It's no use trying to change it. I want out of the project.'

15

'Adieu, my friends! I go to glory!'
    – ISADORA DUNCAN's last words, spoken as she got into a
        roadster and flung her long scarf around her neck in a
        dramatic gesture. When the car pulled away, the scarf
        caught in the spokes of the wheel and strangled her.

Vielle had a fit.

'What do you mean, he's sending you under?' she said when Joanna went down to the ER to talk to her about Dish Night. 'That wasn't part of the deal. He was supposed to send volunteers under, and you were supposed to interview them afterward.'

'There've been complications,' Joanna said.

'What kind of complications?'

'Some of the subjects turned out to be unsuitable,' Joanna said, thinking, That's putting it mildly, 'and two have quit, and we can't get approval on a new set of volunteers for at least six weeks, so—'

'So Dr Right, or should I say, Dr Frankenstein, decides to experiment on you,' Vielle said.

'Experiment on –? I can't believe I'm hearing this! You were the one pushing me to work with Richard in the first place.'

'*Work* with,' Vielle said, 'conduct experiments with, go out for Happy Hour after work with, not become a human guinea pig of. I can't believe he'd let you do something so dangerous.'

'It's *not* dangerous,' Joanna said. 'You weren't upset about his subjects undergoing the procedure.'

'They volunteered.'

'So did I. This was my idea, not Richard's. And the procedure's perfectly safe.'

'There's no such thing,' Vielle said.

'Richard's done over twenty sessions without any adverse effects.'

'Really? Then how come you can't hang on to your volunteers?'

'Their quitting didn't have anything to do with the project,' Joanna said. 'And dithetamine's been used in dozens of experiments with no side effects.'

'Yes, well, and people take aspirin every day without side effects, and get their teeth cleaned, and take penicillin, and then one day they show up in the ER in anaphylactic shock. Or cardiac arrest. There are side effects to everything.'

'But—'

Vielle cut her off. 'And even if there aren't any side effects, you're taking a drug that mimics a near-death experience, right?'

'Yes—'

'So what if it does such a good job of convincing the brain that it's dying that the body takes the hint?'

'It doesn't work like that,' Joanna said.

'How do you know? I thought you told me one of the theories was that the near-death experience served as a shut-down mechanism for the body.'

'There's been no indication of that in our experiments,' Joanna said. 'In fact, the opposite may be true, that the NDE's a survival mechanism. That's what we're trying to find out. Why are you so upset about this?'

'Because interviewing patients and discussing death at Dish Night is one thing. Doing it's a whole different matter. Trust me, I see death every day, and the best survival mechanism is staying as far away from it as possible.'

'I won't be "doing it." I'm not going to be having a real near-death experience. I'm going to be having a simulation of one.'

'Which produces a brain scan identical to the real thing,' Vielle said. 'What if something goes wrong? What if the light at the end of the tunnel turns out to be an oncoming train?'

Joanna laughed. 'I'm more worried that I'll see an Angel of Light who'll tell me Mr Mandrake was right, and the Other Side is actually real. Don't *worry*,' she said seriously. 'I'll be fine. And I'm finally going to get to see what I've only been hearing about secondhand.' She hugged Vielle. 'I have to get back. We're doing a session at eleven.'

'With you?' Vielle demanded.

'No, with Mrs Troudtheim.' She didn't tell Vielle she was scheduled for the afternoon. It would just upset her. 'The *reason* I came down here was to check with you about Dish Night and see what movies you wanted me to rent.

'*Coma*,' she said. 'This girl gets killed in the first scene because she's convinced nothing can go wrong on the operating table.'

Joanna ignored that. 'Will Thursday work, or are you going out with Harvey the Scintillating Conversationalist?'

'Are you kidding? He was in here this morning, explaining the intricacies of embalming. Thursday's fine – just a minute,' she said, and then to the aide who'd come over, looking upset, 'What is it, Nina?'

'The guy in Trauma Room Two's acting really funny,' Nina said. 'I think maybe he's on rogue.'

'I'll be there in a minute,' Vielle said and turned back to Joanna.

'Rogue?' Joanna said. 'You mentioned that before –'

'It's the latest variety of PCP,' Nina said, 'and it's really scary. Psychotic hallucinations plus violent episodes.'

'I said I'd be right there, Nina,' Vielle said coolly.

'Okay. It started in L.A.,' Nina went on chattily. 'Attacks on ER personnel out there have increased twenty-five percent, and now it's here. Last week a nurse over at Swedish—'

'Nina!' Vielle said dangerously. 'I said I'd be there in a minute.'

'Yes, ma'am,' Nina said, cowed, and went off toward the front.

Joanna waited till she was out of earshot, and then said, 'Attacks on ER personnel up twenty-five percent, and you're lecturing me on doing something dangerous?'

'All right,' Vielle said, putting her hands up. 'Truce. But I still think you're crazy.'

'It's mutual,' Joanna said, and at Vielle's skeptical expression, 'I'll be fine. There's nothing to worry about.'

But, lying on the examining table that afternoon, looking up at the masked overhead light and waiting for Tish to start the IV, Joanna felt a dull ache of anxiety. It's the nervousness patients always feel, she thought. It comes from having a hospital gown on and your glasses off. And from lying flat on your back, waiting for a nurse to do things to you.

And not just any nurse. Tish, who had said, when Joanna emerged from the dressing room, 'How did you manage to talk Dr Wright into sending *you* under?'

Joanna had wondered, considering Vielle's out-of-left-field reaction, if Tish would suddenly voice all kinds of objections, too, and she did, but not the kind Joanna expected.

'How come you get to do this, and I don't?' she had asked, as if Joanna had talked Richard into taking her to Happy Hour. Joanna explained as best she could from her supine and nearsighted position. 'Oh, right, I forgot, you're a doctor, and I'm only a lowly nurse,' Tish said and began slapping electrodes on Joanna's chest.

She would have thought Tish would like the prospect of having Joanna absent and Richard all to herself for the duration of the session. I *should* be nervous, she thought. Tish is liable to start flirting with Richard and forget all about me. Or she'll decide this is a good time to get rid of the competition once and for all, and pull the plug.

But there was no plug to be pulled. Even if the two of them went off to Conrad's and left her lying there, she would simply wake up when the dithetamine wore off. Or kick out of her NDE like Mrs Troudtheim.

Which was something else to worry about. What if she, like Mrs Troudtheim, proved unable to achieve an NDE-state? Mrs Troudtheim had kicked out again this last session, even faster than before, in spite of the fact that Richard had adjusted the dosage.

'I don't know what else to try,' Richard had said, looking at her scans after the session. 'Maybe you're right, and she's one of those forty percent who don't have NDEs.'

What if I'm one of them, too? Joanna worried. What would they do then? 'Relax,' Tish snapped, raising her knee to put the pad under it. 'You're stiff as a board.' She shoved a pad under Joanna's left arm and came around the table to do the other side.

Joanna consciously tried to relax, breathing slowly in and then releasing the breath, willing her arms, her legs, to lie limply. Relax. Let go. She stared at the blacked-out light fixture. Without warning, Tish wrapped a rubber tube around her upper arm and twisted a knot in it. She jerked her head around to look at what Tish was doing. 'Relax!' Tish ordered, and began poking around the inside of her elbow, looking for a vein.

If nothing else, I'll know a lot more about how to treat our subjects, Joanna thought. They need to be told everything that's going to happen. They need to be told, 'I'm going to start the IV now. Small poke,' Joanna thought.

Tish didn't say anything. She swabbed Joanna's arm, jabbed in the needle, attached the IV line, all without a word. She disappeared out of Joanna's field of vision, and Joanna felt the sleep mask being placed over her eyes and something icy on her forehead. 'What are you doing?' she asked involuntarily.

'Attaching the electrodes to your scalp,' Tish said, irritated. 'They say doctors make the worst patients, and they're right. Re*lax!*'

Joanna resolved to give Mr Sage and Mrs Troudtheim a running account of every procedure the next time they went under. And they shouldn't be left lying on the table for long periods of time with no idea what's going on, she thought, straining to hear voices or footsteps or *something*. She wondered if Tish and Richard had gone off to Happy Hour. No, she would have heard the door shut. Could Tish have put the headphones on her without her realizing it?

'All ready?' Richard's voice said abruptly in her left ear, and she groped blindly for his arm. 'You're sure you want to do this?' Richard said worriedly, and the anxiety in his voice made hers vanish completely.

'I'm positive,' she said, and smiled in what she hoped was his direction. 'I'm determined to solve the mystery of the ringing or the buzzing once and for all.'

'All right,' he said. 'You may not see much. It sometimes takes a couple of tries to get the dosage right.'

'I know.'

'You're sure about this?'

'I'm sure,' she said, and was. 'Let's get this show on the road.' She let go of his arm.

'Okay,' he said, and someone – Richard? Tish? – fitted the headphones over her ears. Joanna relaxed into the white-noise silence and the darkness, waiting for the sedative to take effect. She breathed in deeply. In. Out. In. Out. It isn't working, she thought, and heard a sound.

Tish didn't get the headphones on properly, she thought. 'Richard,' she started to say, and realized she wasn't in the lab. She was in a narrow space. She could feel walls on either side of her. A coffin, she thought, but it was too wide for that, and she was standing up. She looked down at her body, but she couldn't see anything, the space was completely dark. She raised her hand in front of her face, but she couldn't see it either, or feel the movement of her arm.

I can't see because of the sleep mask, she thought, and tried to take it off, but she wasn't wearing it. She was wearing her glasses. She felt her forehead. There were no electrodes on her scalp, no headphones. She felt her arm. No IV.

I'm in the NDE, she thought, in the tunnel, but that wasn't right either. It wasn't a tunnel. It was a passage. Can you be more specific? she asked silently, and looked around her at the darkness.

It's narrow, she thought, with no idea how she knew that. Or that there were walls on either side, that there weren't walls in front of or behind her, and that there was a low ceiling. She stared up at the unseeable ceiling, as if willing her eyes to adjust, but the darkness remained absolute. And how do you know it's not the roof of a tunnel?

She looked down at the floor, which she could not see either, and tapped her foot tentatively against it. The floor – if it was a floor – felt hard and smooth, like tile or wood, but her foot made no sound.

Maybe I'm barefoot, she thought. Paul McCartney was barefoot on that Beatles album cover, that's how you knew he was dead. But Joanna couldn't feel the floor against her skin, the way she would if she were barefoot. Maybe I don't have feet. Or maybe I can't hear. Her patients had talked about the Angel of Light talking to them, 'but in thoughts, not words.' Perhaps the NDE was only visual.

But she remembered hearing a sound as she came through. She turned her head, trying to remember it. It had been a loud sound. She had heard it distinctly right after she came through. Or had it been as she was coming through? No, she had been in the lab, and then, abruptly, she was here.

As she thought it, she had the sudden feeling that she knew where 'here' was, that it was somewhere familiar. No, that was the wrong word. Somewhere she recognized, even though the passage was completely dark.

It's a place, she thought, a real place. I know where this is, and light poured into the passage ahead of her. She turned to look at it. It filled the corridor, blindingly bright, and she thought, now I'll see where I am, but the light was too dazzling. It was like trying to look directly into headlights. You couldn't see anything.

Headlights. 'What if the light at the end of the tunnel turns out to be an oncoming train?' Vielle had said. Joanna looked instinctively down at her feet for railroad tracks, but the light came from all directions, the glare as intense from below as from ahead of her, so bright she had to close her eyes against the pain of the brightness.

No wonder her subjects had squinted. It was like someone turning on the light in the middle of the night, or shining a flashlight in your face. But neither one, because the light was golden.

Her patients said that, too – 'it was golden' – and when she had said, 'It wasn't white?' they had said, irritated, 'No, it was white and golden.' Now she knew what they meant. The light *was* white, but not the greenish-white of a fluorescent light, the searing blue-white of an arc light. It had a golden cast, like candlelight, only much, much brighter.

She put her hand up to shade her eyes. The light, though it was all around, came from the end of the passage. Where somebody opened a door, she thought. The light's coming from outside, from beyond the door.

She began to walk toward the end of the passage, squinting against the light, and as she walked, it seemed to dim a little. No, that wasn't right, the brightness stayed the same, but now she could almost make out a figure outlined in the light. A figure in white.

Mr Mandrake's Angel of Light, she thought, walking toward it, but the figure did not grow clearer. She wasn't sure there was really a figure at all, or whether it was just a trick of the light.

She squinted, trying to see, and was back in the lab. 'I did it,' she said, but no sound came out, and she thought, I must be in the non-REM state, and fell asleep.

She woke to Richard calling her from a long distance away. That's what Greg Menotti meant by 'Too far away,' she thought. I must still be near where the NDE was.

'Joanna?' Richard said, much closer, and she opened her eyes. Richard was bending over her, and she thought, Vielle's right, he really is cute, and fell asleep again.

'She's awake,' Tish said. 'Should I stop recording?' She was holding the recorder, and Joanna thought, Oh, God, I hope I didn't say he was cute out loud.

'Did I say anything?' she asked.

Richard leaned over her, grinning. 'You won't believe what you said.'

Oh, no, Joanna thought. 'What?'

'You said, "It was dark," ' Tish volunteered.

'Like every other NDEer,' Richard said.

'It *was* dark,' Joanna said, trying to sit up. 'It was pitch-black, like in a cave, only it wasn't a cave, or a tunnel. It was a passageway.'

'Don't sit up,' Richard said, 'and don't try to talk till the effect of the sedative's worn off.'

Joanna lay back down. 'No, I want to describe it before I forget. Is the recorder going?' she asked Tish.

'It's on,' Tish said, handing it to Richard. He put it close to her mouth.

'I was in the lab, and then I was in a tunnel,' Joanna said.

'Nothing in between?' Richard said. 'No sensation of leaving the body or hovering above it?'

'You're not supposed to lead the subject,' Joanna said reprovingly. 'No, I just found myself in the passage.'

'You keep saying "passage," ' Richard said. 'What do you mean? An underground passage?'

'You're leading again,' Joanna said. 'No, not an underground passage. And not one of the passageways the Greek soldier Er took to the realms of the afterlife. It was some kind of corridor or hallway, and there was a door at the end of it.' She described the passage and the light and the dimly seen figure.

Tish took Joanna's pulse and entered it on the chart. 'It felt like an actual experience in an actual place,' Joanna said. 'It wasn't a dream or a superimposed vision. There was no sense of what I was seeing being imposed on where I really was like Saint Paul on the road to Damascus or Bernadette in the cave at Lourdes, where even though you're seeing a blinding light or the Virgin Mary, you're still aware of where you are. I had no awareness of being in the lab, of lying on the table.' Tish wrapped the blood pressure cuff around her arm. 'It felt like I was really there, that it was a real place.'

'Do you know what kind of place it was?' Richard asked.

'No, but I had the feeling that I knew where I was.'

'You recognized it?'

'Yes. No,' she said. 'I had the *feeling* that I recognized it, but I can't –' She shook her head, frustrated. No wonder her subjects ended up shrugging lamely.

Tish checked her pulse again and then began peeling the electrodes off her scalp.

'I recognized the place,' Joanna said, 'but—'

'But at the same time you knew you'd never been there?' Richard said. 'You had a sensation of déjà vu, of experiencing something new and feeling you've experienced it before?'

'No,' she said, trying to remember the fleeting feeling. It had felt familiar, no, not familiar, yet she had had the feeling that she recognized it. 'Maybe. It might have been déjà vu,' she said doubtfully.

'That's a strong indicator of temporal-lobe involvement,' he said and couldn't keep the excitement out of his voice. 'The feeling of déjà vu's been definitively located within the temporal lobe.'

Tish finished removing the IV and put away the equipment. 'Do you need me for anything?' she asked.

'I don't think so,' Richard said absently. 'Temporal-lobe involvement … you didn't have an out-of-body experience?'

'Leading,' Joanna said. 'No. I was in the lab and then in the tunnel, with nothing in between.'

'Did you feel –?' He broke off and started again. 'What feelings did you experience?'

'The light didn't make me feel warm and safe, or loved. I felt … calm. I guess you could describe it as peaceful, but it was really more just … calm. I wasn't frightened.'

'Interesting,' Richard said. 'Did you feel detached? Did it feel like you were separated from what was happening, that what was happening was unreal, dreamlike?'

'It wasn't a dream,' Joanna said firmly.

'If you don't need me for anything, I'm going to go,' Tish said, and they both looked at her, surprised she was still there. 'Do you need me tomorrow?'

'I don't know yet,' Richard said. 'I think so. I'll call you, Tish, thanks,' and turned expectantly back to Joanna. 'How was it different from a dream?'

'It … dreams feel real while you're having them, and then when you wake up, you realize they weren't. But the NDE still feels real even now. That's something nearly all of my subjects have said, that what they experienced was real. I didn't know what that meant, but they're right. It doesn't feel like the memory of a dream. It feels like the memory of something that actually happened.'

'Can you be more specific?'

Joanna grinned. 'It – I could move in a normal way. There was no floating or moving swiftly through the tunnel like some of my subjects have described, and there were no dreamlike discontinuities or incongruities. It felt like it was really happening.'

318

'And you said you sensed the presence of someone in the light.'

She nodded. 'I thought I could see someone, but the light was too bright.'

'The sensation of a presence is a temporal-lobe effect, too,' he said. 'I'd been assuming the light and peaceful feeling were endorphin-generated, but maybe it's the temporal lobe that's causing … I want to look at your scans.'

Joanna nodded and started to get down off the examining table. 'Wait,' Richard said. 'We're not done yet. You still haven't answered the big question.'

'The big question?' Joanna asked. 'Do you mean, was what I saw real? Was it heaven? Or the doorway to the Other Side?'

'No. The *big* question,' he said, and grinned. 'You said you heard a sound. Well? Was it a ringing or a buzzing?'

'It …' she said, and stopped, bewildered. 'I have no idea. I know I heard it. I was in the tunnel …'

'Was it loud or soft?'

Loud, she thought. She had heard it quite clearly. But, trying to remember it now, she found she couldn't reconstruct it at all, or even identify the type of noise it had been. A ringing? A buzzing? A horrible crash, like a whole stack of canned goods crashing down, as Mr Steinhorst had described it?

'Has the memory of it faded?' Richard asked.

She considered that. It must have, because she couldn't recall it, but the rest of the NDE was as crystal-clear as when she was having it, and she remembered thinking she had heard the sound and turning in its direction to identify it. So she hadn't known what it was even during the NDE.

'Joanna?' Richard prompted.

'No, it's not that I've forgotten it, I don't think. I can't remember it. No, that's not right either. I'm sorry,' she said, defeated. 'I'm no better than Mr Sage.'

'Are you kidding?' Richard said. 'You're wonderful. I should have sent you under to begin with and to hell with the other subjects. You've given me more detail than all of them put together, and this is just the first time. I want to send you under again as soon as possible, which means as soon as the dithetamine's out of your system. It takes about twelve hours. How about tomorrow afternoon?'

'Great,' Joanna said. 'I can't wait.'

And it was true. She wanted nothing more than to go back there and figure out what the sound was, where the place was. There hadn't been anything dangerous or frightening about it at all. So why, when Richard asked her, had she felt a sudden sense of dread?

And had Amelia Tanaka had it, too? Was that why she had quit?

16

'Even in the valley of the shadow of death, two and
two do not make six.'
— Words of TOLSTOY on his deathbed,
on being urged to return to the fold
of the Russian Orthodox Church

'It's a residual effect of the dithetamine,' Richard said when Joanna told him about the dread she felt.

'Or a warning that something bad's going to happen if you go under again,' Vielle said when she came over for Dish Night.

'Nothing bad is going to happen,' Joanna said, taking a packet of popcorn out of the box. 'Look at me. I'm fine. My body didn't get confused when it saw the tunnel and the light and trigger some dying process. They didn't have trouble bringing me out of it. Nothing happened.'

'So you did see a tunnel and a light?' Vielle asked curiously. 'Was Mandrake there?'

'No,' Joanna said, laughing. 'No, no Mr Mandrake and no Angel of Light.' She told Vielle about the passage and the light coming from behind the door. 'I didn't have an out-of-body experience either, or a life review, at least not this time.' She opened the refrigerator. 'What do you want to drink? I've got Coke, ginger ale, and ... ginger ale.'

'Coke,' Vielle said. 'What do you mean, "this time"? You're not going under again, are you?'

'Of course,' Joanna said, reaching into the refrigerator for two Cokes.

'But what about this feeling of dread you had? What if it was trying to tell you there's something terrible waiting behind that door?'

'I didn't have the feeling when I looked at the door,' Joanna said, handing Vielle her Coke. 'I didn't have it during the NDE at all, not until nearly an hour afterward.'

'When Dr Right asked you to go under again.'

'Yes, but only for a few seconds, and I didn't have it when he set up a time for the session,' Joanna said. 'Richard showed me the cortisol in my readouts. The levels were definitely elevated, and cortisol frequently remains in the system after a return to the waking state. It's what causes that frightened feeling you can't shake after a nightmare.'

'But what if the cortisol's elevated because of what you saw? You said the tunnel looked familiar. What if the dread comes from your recognizing it? What if it comes from your knowing what's waiting behind that door?'

The microwave beeped. Saved by the bell, Joanna thought, and took her time tearing the bag open, finding a bowl, pouring the popcorn in.

'What if—?' Vielle said.

'Rule Number One,' Joanna said. She took the popcorn into the living room. 'What movies did you bring?'

'*Flatliners*,' Vielle said. 'It's about a bunch of medical students who mess with near-death experiences with tragic results. They think they're going to see angels, but they start having terrible—'

'I know what it's about,' Joanna said. 'I can't believe you—'

'Julia Roberts is in it,' Vielle said innocently. 'Dr Right said he liked Julia Roberts. Or is the ban on dying still on?'

Joanna ignored that. 'Richard isn't coming,' she said. 'He's meeting with Dr Jamison.'

Vielle's eyes narrowed. 'Dr Jamison? Male or female?'

'Female. She's an expert on neurotransmitters.'

'I'll bet,' Vielle said. 'And I'll bet they had to meet at night. Where? At Happy Hour? Honestly, first Tish and now this. If you don't take an option on him soon, Dr Right is going to be Dr Out of Circulation.'

'Yes, Mother,' Joanna said. She picked up the other video. What else had Vielle brought? *Altered States*?

'It's *The Pelican Brief*,' Vielle said, taking it away from her and sticking it in the VCR. 'Also with Julia Roberts. You should have told me Dr Right wasn't coming. At least it's got Denzel Washington in it.' She hit 'play.'

At least it wasn't *Flatliners*.

'Have you seen it?' Vielle said, settling down on the couch. 'It's about a young woman who gets in over her head because she doesn't pay attention to the warning signals.'

'I only had the feeling of dread once, for about ten seconds,' Joanna said. 'I haven't had it since.'

And she didn't have it again, not even when she lay down on the table the next afternoon and Tish began putting the electrodes on her, not even when Richard said, 'All ready?' All she felt was eagerness. She was determined to identify the sound this time, and to see what was behind the door. And to figure out what the place was and why it looked so familiar. Not familiar, that was the wrong word, and not déjà—

There was a sound, and Joanna was back in the passage. In the same place, Joanna thought, even though it was pitch-black, and saw the light. It was still blinding, but instead of a radiating blur, it was a narrow band of gold along the side and underneath the door.

The door seemed much farther away than it had the last time, and the passage impossibly long, or maybe that was because the door was only open an inch or so. The light that came from it lit the first few feet of the floor and walls, and she could make out shapes in the darkness even closer than that. Doors lined both sides of the hall at even intervals, like in a hotel.

Not a hotel, she thought. What else had long halls lined with doors? Mercy General? No, it wasn't a hospital either. Patients' doors were nearly always open. These were all closed, and the hall was narrower than a hospital corridor.

And she had obviously been in hospitals. I've never been here before, she thought. So what else had long, narrow halls lined with doors that she would recognize without ever having been there? Versailles? No, it had mirrors, didn't it? A mansion?

' "In my Father's house are many mansions," ' Mrs Woollam had told her, but she had meant a heavenly mansion. A palace? That seemed to ring a bell, although a palace would have carpeting, wouldn't it, not wooden floors? And she could see the floor in the little pool of light from under the door. It was made of long, narrow varnished boards. Impossibly long. Like the passage, she thought, but when she began walking toward the door, it was not nearly as far away as she'd thought.

It's the floor, she thought, stopping halfway to the door. There's something about it that makes the hall look longer than it is, or something about the way the floor looks as it meets the door. She squinted at the place where they met, and as she did, the light seemed to waver, becoming dimmer, then brighter, then obscured again, flickering. No, moving.

No, the light wasn't moving. Something in front of it was. There was someone, or something, behind the door, walking, blocking the light as it moved. 'What if it's something terrible?' Vielle had said. A tiger, pacing back and forth.

No one has *ever* mentioned a tiger in his NDE, she told herself. It's a person walking back and forth, and she thought she heard a murmur of voices. She moved forward, keeping her eyes on the line of light, straining to hear.

'What's happened?' a woman said, and the pattern of light shifted, as if the woman had taken a step toward the door.

Joanna moved closer. 'I'm sure it's nothing,' a man's voice said.

More shadows as they walked between her and the light. 'It's so cold,' the woman said.

'I'll get you a blanket,' Richard said, and wrapped the blanket around her shoulders.

'No, not me. The woman,' Joanna said and realized she was in the lab.

She opened her eyes. Her sleep mask was off, and her headphones, and Tish was spreading the white cotton blanket over her. Richard's face appeared above her. 'Did you see the same thing this time?' he asked.

'Don't lead,' Joanna said. 'Where's the recorder?'

'Right here,' Richard said and switched it on. 'What did you see this time?'

'It was the same place as before. It's a hallway, with doors along the sides and a door at the end.' She told him about the hall seeming longer than it was and about the voices. 'The woman said, "What's happened?" and the man said, "I'm sure it's nothing," and then the woman, I think it was the same one, said, "It's so cold."'

'Are you sure you heard the woman say it?' Richard asked, and then explained, 'You said, "It's so cold," five minutes after the NDE, while you were in non-REM sleep.'

'That's why I brought you the blanket,' Tish said.

'No, I'm sure she said it,' Joanna said. 'I must have repeated it afterward. I didn't have any reason to say it. I wasn't cold.'

'You're shivering,' Tish said.

'No, I'm not –' Joanna began, and realized her teeth were chattering. Amelia gets cold, too, she thought.

'You weren't cold during the NDE?' Richard asked.

'No, it wasn't cold in the passage.'

'You said the woman said it was,' Tish pointed out.

'But she was outside,' Joanna said.

'You saw what was beyond the door?' Richard asked.

'No, I ...' she said, and stopped, wondering how she knew the people were outside. The door hadn't looked like an outside door, and she had not seen anything except shadows. 'I don't know why I think they were outside. It's just a feeling.'

'You say it wasn't cold in the passage. Was it warm?'

'No,' Joanna said. 'I didn't notice anything about the temperature. And when I saw the light I didn't feel the warmth and love other NDEers have described. I felt anxiety at what might be behind the door, and otherwise, nothing.'

'Did you feel detached, as if you were observing yourself?'

'No,' she said definitely. 'I was there, experiencing the hallway and the light under the door and the voices. The vision is very convincing. It feels totally real.'

'And you experienced voices, but you didn't see anyone?'

'Not unless you count the shadows of their feet from under the door.'

Richard was busily taking notes. 'Okay, tunnel, light, voices. Out-of-body experience?'

'No.'

'What about the sound? Did you hear it this time?'

'The *sound*,' Joanna said, disgusted. 'I fully intended to listen to it and identify it, and then when I got there I forgot all about it in trying to remember where I knew the hallway from.'

'You experienced the déjà vu again?'

'It's not déjà vu,' she said. 'I've had that sensation, where it feels like you've been somewhere or done something before, even though you know you haven't. This wasn't like that. I felt ...' She paused. '... I knew I'd never been there before, but ... I recognized it.'

'You recognized it?' Tish asked curiously. 'Where was it?'

'I don't know,' Joanna said, frustrated. 'I felt I could almost ...' She reached out her hand, as if to grab at the knowledge. One of my patients made a gesture just like that, she thought. I need to find her account and see what she was talking about.

'Do you still have the feeling?' Richard was asking.

'No.'

'Sound, tunnel, light, voices, sense of recognition,' he said, ticking them off. 'What about a command to return?'

'No, no one ordered me to return. They didn't even know I was there.'

'It's still five of the core elements,' Richard said, looking happy. 'I think if I adjust the dosage, we may get all ten. And this feeling of recognition is very interesting.'

Joanna's teeth had begun to chatter again. 'Can we finish this after I get dressed?' she asked. 'I'm freezing to death. Are you finished monitoring me, Tish?'

Tish nodded, and Joanna slid off the table and padded across the lab to the dressing room, holding the blanket tightly around her. She went into the dressing room, shut the door, and reached for her blouse. As she did, she caught sight of her image in the mirror on the door, and the feeling of recognition hit her again. I know, I know where it is, she thought.

The feeling only lasted for an instant. In the time it took for her to turn and face the mirror straight on, it faded to nothing, and she was left staring at her image, wondering what it was that had triggered it. The blanket or the door?

As soon as she was dressed, she told Richard about it. 'Could it have been the mirror itself?' he said, looking at the mirror on the door. 'Did you see a mirror in your NDE? Or a reflection of something?'

'Leading,' Joanna said. 'No.'

'But it was the same feeling of déjà vu?'

'It's *not* déjà vu. I've never been there, but I knew where it was. It was like knowing you were in Paris because you recognized the Eiffel Tower, even though you've never been there before. Except that I can't place it,' she finished lamely.

'Do you still have the feeling?'

'No, it just sort of flashes past.'

'Interesting. I want you to tell me if the feeling recurs,' he said.

'Or if I figure out where it is,' she said, and spent the remainder of the afternoon and evening trying to place it. Something to do with a blanket and a wooden floor. And a palace. No, not a palace, but something with the word *palace* in it. The Palace Hotel? But it wasn't a hotel. The Palace Theater?

She got exactly nowhere. It's the watched-pot syndrome, she thought, driving to work the next morning, and decided to *not* think about it in the hope the elusive memory would kick spontaneously forward. She focused on transcribing her account and on helping prep Mrs Troudtheim, who kicked out immediately with no memory of having had an NDE. 'It was the same as last time,' she said. 'I was lying there in the dark, trying not to fall asleep, but I guess I must have. I'm so sorry. I even took a nap this morning so I wouldn't.'

'You were lying there in the dark,' Joanna said. 'Did the darkness change at any point? Grow darker? Or take on a different quality?'

'No.'

'You say you fell asleep. Do you have any memory of being asleep?'

'No. I was just lying there, and then I sort of jerked awake.'

'Did something wake you? A movement? A sound?'

'No.'

'Nice try,' Richard said after Mrs Troudtheim had left, 'but it's no use. She doesn't remember.'

And neither do I, Joanna thought, typing up Mrs Troudtheim's non-transcript. Not thinking about the tunnel hadn't worked any better than trying to place the passage.

She did a global search on 'floor' and then 'blanket,' neither of which turned up any matches. She tried, 'It's so cold.' Nothing. She ran it again on 'cold,' and this time there were a number of hits. Most were vague references to feelings the subject had had in the tunnel or on returning, and a couple were in Joanna's notes. 'During interview subject repeatedly asked me if I thought room was cold,' and, 'Subject seemed cold, put on robe, then stuck hands up inside sleeves.'

All of which was very interesting, but it didn't tell her where the tunnel was, and when Richard told her he wanted to send her under the next day, her first thought was, 'Maybe when I see it again, I'll know.' Her second was, 'But first I'm going to identify that sound if it kills me,' and she held that thought through Tish's attaching the electrodes, starting the IV, adjusting the sleep mask.

'The sound,' she murmured to herself as Tish put on her headphones. 'First identify the sound, then the hallway.'

There was a sound, and she was in the passage. The line of light where the floor met the door still looked oddly distant, but she knew she must be closer to the door than the last time. She could clearly hear the sound of voices beyond the door.

The sound! She had intended to listen for the sound, and she had forgotten again. She whirled to look back down the dark tunnel. It was a sound that – what? She clearly remembered hearing something, but what was it? 'Was it a ringing or a buzzing?' she said, frustrated, and her voice sounded shockingly loud in the tunnel. She looked back toward the door and the light, half-expecting the voices to have stopped in surprise, but they continued to talk.

'I'm sure it's nothing,' the man said, and Joanna wondered if he was talking about her.

'Should we send someone to find out?' another man's voice said. Maybe their voices are what I heard coming through, Joanna thought, and knew they weren't. They hadn't started till halfway through the last time, and the first time she hadn't heard anything. After the sound stopped, the passage had been absolutely silent.

And it was a *sound*, she thought, not voices. A sound like … She could not call up any memory of it at all. But it came from down here, she thought, and started back along the passage. It came from the end of—

And she was back in the lab. Oh, no, she thought, I've kicked out, just like Mrs Troudtheim.

'I'm sorry' she said, but Tish ignored her and went on taking off the head-phones and detaching the electrodes as if nothing catastrophic had happened.

'Is she awake?' Richard asked from over at the console, and he didn't sound upset either.

'Did you change the dosage?' she asked, groping for the edge of the examining table so she could pull herself to a sitting position.

'Why?' Richard said, appearing above her. 'Was your experience different?'

'No, but when I went back to—'

'Wait,' he said, fumbling in his pocket for her minirecorder. 'From the beginning.'

She stared up at him uncomprehendingly. 'Didn't I kick out?'

'Kick out?' he said. 'No. Didn't you experience an NDE this time?'

'Yes, I was in the passage,' she said, and he held the recorder up to her mouth, 'and I turned around to see where the sound came from. I was determined this time to identify it, and I started back down the passage toward it, and—'

'Did you?' Richard cut in. 'Identify it?'

'No,' she said. 'It's so odd. I know I hear it, but when I try to reconstruct it, I can't.'

'Because it's a strange sound you've never heard before?'

'No, that's not it. It's like when you wake up in the middle of the night, and you know something awakened you, but you can't hear it now, and you didn't really hear it because you were asleep, so you don't know if it was a branch scraping against the window or the cat knocking something off the counter. That's what this feels like.'

'So you think the sound is something you hear before you go into the NDE-state?'

Joanna considered that. 'I'm not sure. Maybe.' She looked thoughtfully at him. 'When the patient I was interviewing in the ER coded and a nurse pushed the code alarm, I remember thinking that maybe that was what people were hearing in their NDEs. It was a sort of cross between a ringing and a buzzing.'

'There's no code alarm in here,' Tish said. Richard looked at her in surprise, as if he'd forgotten she was there. 'She wouldn't have been able to hear a code alarm, anyway, if there had been one,' Tish said. 'She was wearing headphones, remember?'

'She's right,' Joanna said. 'It can't be an outside sound. It's ...'

'And you said none of the patients you interviewed were able to describe the sound either,' Richard said.

'Not with any degree of confidence,' Joanna said, 'or consistency, and now I feel guilty I was so impatient with them.'

'As soon as you finish your account, I want to take a look at the superior auditory cortex,' he said.

'That *is* my account,' Joanna said. 'I turned around to see where the sound came from and started back down the passage, and I was back in the lab. That's why I asked you if I'd kicked out of the NDE.'

Richard had put down the recorder in his surprise. 'How long were you in the tunnel?'

'I don't know,' Joanna said. 'However long it takes to turn around and take a couple of steps.'

'How long were you there the time before?'

'I don't know, several minutes. Longer than the first time.'

Richard was already over at the console, calling up the scans. 'Normal time?' he asked, and when she looked blank, he said, 'Was there any sense of time dilation, of time being slowed down or speeded up?'

'No,' she said. 'Why?'

'Because you were in the NDE-state the first two times a little over two minutes,' he said, calling up arrays of numbers, 'and this time nearly five.' He looked over at her. 'Have you ever asked your patients how long their NDEs lasted?'

'No,' Joanna said. 'It never occurred to me.' She had always assumed they were experiencing the NDE in what Richard called normal time. Some of them had talked about moving rapidly through the tunnel, and she had asked what they meant by 'rapidly' to see if they were attempting to describe some sort of speeded-up sense of time, but she had never thought to ask how long they'd stared at the light or how long the life review had taken. She'd simply assumed that the duration of the NDEs matched the length of the activities they'd described. And it had never occurred to her to compare their subjective experience with the length of time they'd been clinically dead.

'What about at the end of your NDE?' Richard asked. 'Was there time dilation as you were going back down the tunnel?'

'I didn't go back down the tunnel,' she said. 'I started to, and then all of a sudden I was back in the lab. It wasn't like the other times I've returned. It was much more ... abrupt,' she said, trying to think of a way to describe it, but Richard was back on the subject of time dilation.

'You didn't experience time dilation the other times either?'

'No.' I need to ask Mrs Woollam if the duration of her NDEs varies, she thought. And Maisie. Maisie'd said she'd only seen fog, and Joanna had assumed from that that her NDE had only lasted a few seconds. Now she wondered.

'Look at this,' Richard said, staring at the console screen. 'The duration of Amelia Tanaka's NDE-state varies as much as four minutes.'

Tish went over to stand next to him and look interestedly at the screens. 'Maybe it's like time in a dream. You can dream whole *days* between the time your alarm goes off and when you wake up a few seconds later,' she said. 'I had a dream like that the other morning. I dreamed I went to Happy Hour at the Rio Grande and then up skiing at Breckenridge and it all happened in the two seconds between the guy on the radio saying, "It's six o'clock," and, "More snow predicted for the Rocky Mountain area today,"' but Richard didn't hear her. He went on typing, totally absorbed.

'Can I get dressed now?' Joanna asked, but he didn't hear that either. 'I'm getting dressed now,' she said, slid off the examining table, and went into the dressing room.

Richard was still at the console, staring intently at the images, when she came out. Tish was putting on her coat. 'I'm leaving,' she said disgustedly. 'Not that he'd notice. If you can get through to him, tell him if he wants me here before two tomorrow to give me a call.' She looked wistfully at him. 'At least I know it's not me. He doesn't know you exist either.' Tish pulled on her coat. 'There are more things in life –'

Than are dreamt of in your philosophy, Horatio, Joanna thought.

'– than just work, you know,' Tish finished. She pulled on her gloves. 'Happy Hour's at Rimaldi's tonight, if you want to ditch Doctor-All-Work-and-No-Play.'

'Thanks,' Joanna said, smiling, 'but I've got to get my NDE recorded while it's still fresh in my mind.'

Tish shrugged. 'There'd better be more things in death than work,' she said, zipping up her coat, 'or *I'm* not going. 'Bye, Dr Wright,' she called gaily on her way out.

Richard didn't even look up. 'Mr Sage's NDEs vary by two minutes and fifteen seconds,' he said. 'I'd been assuming there was a direct correlation between real time and the subjective time of the NDE, but if there's not ...'

If there's not, then maybe brain death doesn't occur in four to six minutes, Joanna thought. Maybe it's shorter. Or longer.

'Can you check for references to time dilation in your interviews?' Richard asked.

'Yes,' she said, but there aren't any, she thought. If time had seemed to slow down or speed up, they wouldn't have said it wasn't a dream, that it felt real.

And it did feel real, she thought, going back to her office to record her account. It had seemed like it was happening in real time, in a real place. Which you're no closer to identifying than you were.

And no closer to identifying the sound, which meant it only took her a few minutes to record her entire NDE. She described the voices and what they'd said, her turning around, starting back –

I wonder if that was what ended the NDE, she thought, and started through the transcripts, looking specifically at the endings. A number of them described their return as 'abrupt' or 'sudden.' 'I felt like I was being pulled back to my body,' Ms Ankrum had said, and Mr Zamora had described the end of his NDE as 'like somebody picked me up by the scruff of the neck and threw me out.'

Neither of them had mentioned the tunnel as being the way back, but Ms Irwin had said, 'Jesus told me, "Your time is not yet fulfilled," and I found myself in the tunnel again,' and nearly a dozen had said they'd reentered the tunnel. 'The spirit pointed to the light and said, "Dost thee choose death?" and then he pointed at the tunnel and said, "Or dost thee choose life? Choose thee well."' Why does every spirit and religious figure and dead relative speak in that stilted, quasi-religious manner, a cross between the Old Testament and Obi-Wan Kenobi? Joanna thought.

She made a list of the references to show Richard, wishing she'd gone to Happy Hour, where there would at least be nachos or something to eat. She hadn't had any lunch because of the session. She opened her desk drawer, looking for a stray candy bar or an apple, but all she found was half a stick of gum so old it broke when she pulled the foil off.

She should have ransacked Richard's lab coat pockets before she left the lab. He'd never have noticed, she thought, and had the feeling again of almost, almost knowing where the tunnel was. She sat perfectly still, trying to hold on to the feeling, but it was already gone. What had triggered it? Something about stealing food from Richard's lab coat supply. Or could it have been the gum? And what famous place had she never been to that featured wooden floors, blankets, and ancient gum?

It's hunger, she thought. Starving people are prone to mirages, aren't they?

But Richard had told her to tell him if the feeling recurred, so she went up to the lab and reported it to him.

'You don't have to steal, you know,' he said, producing a package of Cheetos, a pear, and a bottle of milk from his pockets. 'You can just ask.'

'It wasn't the food,' she said, opening the milk. 'It was the idea that you were so intent on what you were doing that you wouldn't know I was taking it.'

'Do you have the feeling now?'

'No.'

'I think it might be the temporal lobe.' He went over to the console. 'I've been looking at your scans. Tell me again about the sound. You heard it, but you can't identify it?'

She nodded, biting into the pear.

'I think that may be because it's not occurring. Look at this,' he said, pointing to a blue area on the scan. 'There's no activity in the auditory cortex. I'd been assuming there was an actual auditory stimulus from within the brain, but I think it may be a temporal-lobe stimulus instead.'

'Which means what?'

'Which means you can't identify the sound because you're not hearing it. You're only experiencing a sensation of having heard something, with no sound to attach it to.'

But I did hear it, Joanna thought.

'Temporal-lobe stimulation would explain why there's so much variation in description. Patients have a feeling they heard a sound, so they simply confabulate one out of whatever sound they heard last.'

Like the ringing of the code alarm, Joanna thought, or the hum of the heart monitor going flatline.

'It might also explain some of the other core elements, too,' Richard said. 'I've been assuming the NDE was endorphin-generated, but maybe ...' He began typing. 'Light, voices, time dilation, even déjà vu, are also effects of temporal-lobe stimulation.'

'It wasn't déjà vu,' Joanna said, but Richard was already lost in the scans, so she ate her Cheetos and went down to ask Mrs Woollam about the duration of her NDEs and the manner of her return.

'I was standing there looking up at the staircase,' Mrs Woollam, even more fragile-looking in a white knitted bed jacket, said, 'and then I was in the ambulance.'

'You weren't doing anything?' Joanna asked. 'Like walking back down the tunnel? You were just standing there?'

'Yes. I heard a voice, and I knew I had to go back, and there I was.'

'What did the voice say?'

'It wasn't a voice exactly. It was more a feeling, inside, that I had to go back, that it wasn't my time.' She chuckled. 'You'd think it would be, wouldn't you, as old as I am? But you never know. There was a girl in the room with me at Porter's last time. A young girl, she couldn't have been more than twenty, with appendicitis. Well, appendectomies aren't anything. They did them back when *I* was a girl. But the day after her operation, she died. You never know when your time will come to go.' Mrs Woollam had opened her Bible and was leafing through the tissue-thin pages. She found the passage and read, ' "For none may know the hour of his coming." '

'I thought that verse referred to Christ, not death,' Joanna said.

'It does,' Mrs Woollam said, 'but when death comes, Jesus will be there, too. That was why He came to earth, to die, so that we would not have to go through it alone. He will help us face it, no matter how frightening it is.'

'Do you think it will be frightening?' Joanna asked, and felt the sense of dread again.

'Of course,' Mrs Woollam said. 'I know Mr Mandrake says there's nothing to fear, that it's all angels and joyous reunions and light.' She shook her white head in annoyance. 'He was here again yesterday, did you know that? Talking all sorts of nonsense. He said, "You will be in the Light. What is there to fear?" Well, I'll tell you,' Mrs Woollam said spiritedly. 'Leaving behind the world and your body and all your loved ones. How can that not be frightening, even if you are going to heaven?'

And how do you know there is a heaven? Joanna thought. How do you know there isn't a tiger behind the door, or something worse? and remembered Amelia's voice, full of knowledge and terror: 'Oh, no, oh, no, oh, no.'

'Of course I will be afraid,' Mrs Woollam said. 'Even Jesus was afraid. "Let this cup pass from me," he said in the garden, and on the cross, he cried out, *"Eloi, eloi, lama sabacthani."* That means, "My God, my God, why hast thou forsaken me?" '

She opened her Bible and leafed through the pages. The skin on her hands was as thin as the gilt-edged pages. 'Even in the Psalms, it doesn't say, "Yea, though I walk through the valley of the shadow of death, I will not fear it." It says,' and Mrs Woollam's voice changed, becoming softer and somehow bleaker, as if she were really walking through the valley, ' "Yea, though I walk through the valley of the shadow of death, I will fear no evil." '

She closed the Bible and held it to her birdlike chest like a shield. 'Because Jesus will be with me. "And, lo, I am with you always," he said, "even unto the end of the world." '

She smiled at Joanna. 'But you didn't come to be preached to. You came to ask me about my NDEs. What else do you want to know?'

'The other times you had NDEs,' Joanna asked, 'was the return the same?'

'Except for one time. That time I was in the tunnel and then all of a sudden, I was back on the floor by the phone.'

'On the floor?'

'Yes. The paramedics hadn't gotten there yet.'

'And the transition was fast?'

'Yes,' Mrs Woollam said. She opened her Bible again, and for a moment Joanna thought she was going to read her a Scripture, like, 'in the twinkling of an eye we shall all be changed,' but instead she held the Bible up and closed it with a sudden slap. 'Like that.'

'She described it as abrupt, like a book slamming shut,' Joanna told Richard the next day while they were waiting for Mr Sage, 'and Mrs Davenport described her return as sudden, too.'

'Mrs Davenport?' Richard said disbelievingly.

'I know, I know,' Joanna said, 'she'll say anything Mr Mandrake wants her to. But he's not interested in returns, and the word *sudden* occurs several times in her account. And in both cases, their hearts spontaneously started beating again, without medical intervention.'

'What about your other interviews?' Richard asked. 'Is there a correlation between the means of revival and the manner of return?'

'I'll check as soon as we're done with Mr Sage,' she said.

'Ask him about time dilation,' Richard said, 'and his return,' and Joanna dutifully did, but it didn't yield much. After twenty minutes of struggling with time dilation, she gave up and asked, 'Can you describe how you woke up? Was it fast or slow?'

'I don't know,' Mr Sage said. 'Just waking up.'

'Waking up like when your alarm clock goes off?' she asked, and Richard shot her a questioning glance.

I know I'm leading, she thought. I've given up all hope of getting anything out of him *without* leading. 'Like when your alarm clock goes off,' she repeated, 'or like on a Saturday morning, where you wake up gradually?'

'I work Saturdays,' Mr Sage said.

It was a relief to go back to her office and look for abrupt returns, even though there didn't seem to be a clear correlation between them and spontaneous revival. 'Abraham said, "Return!"' Mr Sameshima had said, 'and wham! just like that I was back on the operating table,' but when she checked his file, they had used the paddles on him four times. Ms Kantz, on the other hand, who had begun breathing on her own after a car accident, said, 'I drifted for a long time in this sort of cloudy space.'

At four, Joanna compiled what she had. While it was printing out, she listened to her messages. Vielle, wanting to know if she'd made any progress with Dr Wright yet. Mr Wojakowski, wanting to know if they needed him. Mrs Haighton, saying she needed to reschedule, she had an emergency Spring Frolic meeting. Mr Mandrake. She fast-forwarded through that one. Guadalupe. 'Call me when you get the chance.'

She probably wants to know whether I'm still interested in Coma Carl, Joanna thought. I haven't been to see him in days.

She ran the list up to Richard, who barely glanced up from the scans, and then went down to see Guadalupe. She was in Carl's room, entering his vitals on the computer screen. Joanna looked over at the bed. It was at a forty-five-degree slant, and Carl, propped on all sides with pillows, looked like he might slide down to the foot of it at any moment. A clear plastic oxygen mask covered his nose and mouth.

'How's he doing?' Joanna asked Guadalupe, forcing herself to speak in a normal tone.

'Not great,' Guadalupe whispered. 'He's been having a little congestion the last two days.'

'Pneumonia?' Joanna whispered.

'Not yet,' Guadalupe said, moving to check his IVs. There were two more bags on the stand than last time.

'Where's his wife?' Joanna asked.

'She left to get something to eat,' Guadalupe said, punching numbers on the IV stand. 'She hadn't eaten all day, and the cafeteria was closed when she went down. Honestly, why do they even bother *having* a cafeteria?'

Joanna looked at Carl, lying still and silent on the slanting bed. She wondered if he could hear them, if he knew his wife had left and Joanna was there, or if he was in a beautiful, beautiful garden, like Mrs Woollam. Or in a dark hallway with doors on either side.

'Has he said anything?' she asked Guadalupe.

'Not today. He said a few words on Pam's shift yesterday, but she said she had trouble making it out because of the mask.' Guadalupe reached in her pocket for a slip of paper and handed it to Joanna.

Carl moaned again and muttered something. Joanna went over closer to the bed. 'What is it, Carl?' she said and took his limp hand.

His fingers moved as she picked up his hand, and she was so surprised, she nearly dropped it. He heard me, she thought, he's trying to communicate with me, and then realized that wasn't it. 'He's shivering,' she said to Guadalupe.

'He's been doing that for the past couple of days,' Guadalupe said. 'His temp's normal.'

Joanna went over to the heating vent on the wall and put her hand up to it to see if any air was coming out. It was, faintly warm. 'Is there a thermostat in here?' she asked.

'No,' Guadalupe said, and started out, saying as she went, 'You're right. It does feel chilly in here. I'll get him another blanket.'

Joanna sat down by the bed and read the slip of paper Guadalupe had given her. There were only a few words on it: 'water' and 'cold? code?' with question marks after them, and 'oh grand' again.

Carl whimpered, and his foot kicked out weakly. Shaking something off? Climbing into something? He murmured something unintelligible, and his mask fogged up. Joanna leaned close to him. 'Her,' Carl murmured. 'Hurry,' he said, his head coming up off the pillow. 'Haftoo –'

'Have to what, Carl?' Joanna asked, taking his hand again. 'Have to what?' but he had subsided against the pile of pillows, shivering. Joanna pulled the bedspread up over his unresisting body, wondering what had happened to Guadalupe and the blanket, and then stood there, holding his hand in both of hers. Have to. Water. Oh, grand.

There was a sudden difference in the room, a silence. Joanna looked, alarmed, at Carl, afraid he had stopped breathing, but he hadn't. She could see the shallow rise and fall of his chest, the faint fogging of the oxygen mask.

But something had changed. What? The monitors were all working, and if there had been some change in Carl's vitals, they would have started beeping. She looked around the room at the computer, the IV stand, the heater. She put her hands in front of the vent. No air was coming out.

The heater shut off, she thought, and then, What I heard wasn't a sound. It was the silence afterward. That was what I heard in the tunnel. That's why I can't describe it. Because it wasn't a sound. It was the silence after something shut off, she thought, and almost, almost had it.

'Here we go, Carl, a nice toasty blanket,' Guadalupe said, unfolding a blue square. 'I warmed it up for you in the microwave.' She stopped and stared at Joanna's face, her clenched fists. 'What's wrong?'

I almost had it and now it's gone again, Joanna thought, that's what's wrong. 'I was just trying to remember something,' she said, making her hands unclench.

She watched Guadalupe lay the blanket over Carl, watched her tuck it around his shoulders. Something to do with a blanket and a heater. No, not a heater, she thought, in spite of the blanket, in spite of the woman's saying, 'It's so cold.' It was something else, something to do with high school, and ransacking the pockets of Richard's lab coat, and a place she had never been. A place that was right on the tip of her mind.

I know, I *know* what it is, she thought, and the feeling of dread returned, stronger than before.

17

'And in my dream an angel with white wings came to me, smiling.'
– From PAUL GAUGUIN's last notes,
published after his death

'Interesting,' Richard said when Joanna told him about the episode of the heater. 'Describe the feeling again.'

'It's a …' she searched for the right word, '… a conviction that I know where the hallway in my NDE is.'

'You're not talking about a flashback, are you? You don't find yourself there again?'

'No. And, no, it's not déjà vu,' she said, anticipating his next question. 'I know I've never been there before.'

'How about *jamais vu?* That's the feeling that you're in a strange place even though you've been there many times? It's a temporal-lobe phenomenon, too.'

'No,' she said patiently. 'It's a place I know I've never been, but I recognize it. I know what it is, but I just can't think of it. It's like,' she pushed her glasses up on her nose, trying to think of a parallel, 'okay, it's like, one day I was at the movies with Vielle, and I saw this woman buying popcorn. I *knew* I'd seen her somewhere, but I couldn't place her. I had the feeling it was something negative, so I didn't want to go up to her and ask her, and I spent the whole movie trying to think whether she worked at the hospital or lived in my apartment building or had been a patient. It's that feeling.' She looked expectantly at Richard.

'Who was she?'

'One of Mr Mandrake's cronies,' she said, and grinned. 'Three-fourths of the way through the movie, Meg Ryan had her palm read, and I thought, "That's where I know her from. She's a friend of Mr Mandrake's," and Vielle and I sneaked out before the credits.'

Richard looked thoughtful. 'And you think the heater going off was the same kind of trigger as the palm reading.'

'Yes, except it didn't work. All three times I've felt like the answer was just out of reach –' She realized she was starting to make the clutching gesture again and stopped herself. 'But I couldn't get it.'

'When the feeling occurred, did you experience any nausea?'

'No.'

'Unusual taste or smell?'

'No.'

'Partial images?'

'Partial images?' she asked.

'Like when you're trying to think of someone's name, and you remember that it begins with a T.'

She knew what he meant. When Meg Ryan held her palm out to the fortune-teller, she had had a sudden memory of Mr Mandrake calling to her from down the hall. 'No.'

He nodded vigorously. 'I didn't think so. I think what you're experiencing is a sense of incipient knowledge, a feeling of significance. It's a visceral sensation of possessing knowledge coupled with an inability to state what the content of that knowledge is. It's an effect of temporal-lobe stimulation, which turns on a significance signal in the limbic system, but without any content attached to it.'

'Like the sound,' Joanna said.

'Exactly. I'll bet you both it and this feeling of recognizing the tunnel are temporal-lobe effects.'

'But I know—'

He nodded. 'There's an intense feeling of knowing. The person experiencing it will state definitely that he understands the nature of God or the cosmos, but when he's asked to elaborate, he can't. It's a common symptom in temporal-lobe epileptics.'

'And NDEers,' Joanna said. 'Over twenty percent of them believe they were given special knowledge or an insight into the nature of the cosmos.'

'But they can't articulate it, right?'

'No,' she said, remembering an interview with a Mrs Kelly. 'The angel said, "Look at the light,"' Mrs Kelly had said, 'and as I did I understood the meaning of the universe.'

Joanna had waited, minirecorder running, pencil poised. 'Which is?' she'd asked finally, and then, when Mrs Kelly looked blank, 'What is the meaning of the universe?'

'No one who hasn't experienced it could possibly understand,' Mrs Kelly had said haughtily. 'It would be like trying to explain light to a blind man,' but Joanna could still remember the frantic, frightened look on her face. She hadn't had a clue.

'But the knowledge NDEers feel they have is metaphysical,' Joanna said to Richard. 'This feeling has nothing to do with religion or the nature of the cosmos.'

'I know, but in a subject with a scientific background, that sense of cosmic awareness might take another, secular form.'

'Like thinking I recognize the location of the tunnel.'

He nodded. 'And attributing significance to random items, like the blanket and the heater, which is also a common phenomenon. What you're interpreting as recognition is really just temporal-lobe overstimulation.'

'You're wrong. I do know what it is. I just can't ...'

'Exactly,' Richard said. 'You can't tell me what it is because it's an emotion, not actual knowledge. Feeling without content.'

Richard's theory made sense. It explained why, in spite of repeated incidents, she was no closer to an answer, and why the stimuli seemed so unrelated – a blanket, a heater shutting off, Richard's lab coat, a floor that looked wrong. And something to do with high school, she thought, don't forget that.

'But it feels so real ...'

'That's because it's the same neurotransmitters as are present when the brain experiences an actual insight,' Richard said. 'If you have another incident, document everything you can about it. Circumstances, accompanying symptoms—'

'And if next time I actually figure out what it is?' she asked.

He grinned. 'Then it wasn't temporal-lobe stimulation. But I'm betting it is. It would account for the presence of such varied endorphins, and nearly all the core elements are also temporal-lobe symptoms – sounds, voices, light, feelings of ineffability and warmth ...'

It wasn't warm, Joanna thought stubbornly, it was cold. And I do know where it is. And the next time I have an incident, I'll figure it out.

But there were no more incidents. It was as if being told their cause had cured her. And it was just as well. Joanna was too busy the next three days to even catch her breath, let alone remember anything. There was a sudden rash of patients coding and being revived. Mrs Jacobson, whom she'd interviewed six weeks ago, was brought in in cardiac arrest, and there were two unrelated asthma attacks.

Joanna listened to them describe the tunnel (dark), the light (bright), and the sound they'd heard (they couldn't). The only thing they were agreed on was that the NDE felt like it had really happened. 'I was *there*,' Mr Darby said almost violently. 'It was *real*. I *know* it.'

In between interviews, she left messages for Mrs Haighton to call her and searched the transcripts for instances of incipient knowledge or ineffability and for hypersignificance. A number of NDEers talked about having returned to earth to fulfill a mission, though none of them were able to articulate exactly what the mission was. 'It's a *mission*,' Mr Edwards had said vehemently. 'Topic upsets him,' Joanna had written in her notes.

Instances of hypersignificance were rarer. Miss Hodges had said, 'Now when I look at a flower or a bird, it *means* so much more,' but that might just have been a heightened appreciation of life, and none of the subjects had talked about *almost* knowing the key to the universe. All of them, as near as she could tell, were convinced they were already in possession of the knowledge, not that it was just out of reach.

She did a global search on 'elusive', but it didn't turn up anything, and she had to abandon 'tip of the tongue' in midsearch because the ICU called with two more heart attacks, and while she was interviewing the second one, Vielle paged her with an anaphylactic shock.

Joanna went up to see him immediately, but not soon enough. 'I went straight into a tunnel', he said the minute she entered the room. 'Why didn't I leave my body first and float up by the ceiling? I thought that was supposed to happen first.'

Uh-oh, she thought. 'Has Mr Mandrake been in to see you, Mr Funderburk?'

'He just left', Mr Funderburk said. 'He told me people leave their bodies and hover above them, looking down on the doctors working on them.'

'Some people have an out-of-body experience and some don't', Joanna said. 'Everyone's NDE is different.'

'Mr Mandrake said everyone had an out-of-body experience, a tunnel, a light', he said, ticking them off on his fingers, 'relatives, an angel, a life review, and a command to return.'

Why am I even bothering? Joanna thought, but she took out her minirecorder, switched it on, and asked, 'Can you describe what you experienced, Mr Funderburk?'

He had experienced, predictably, a tunnel, a light, relatives, an angel, a life review, and a command to return.

'Did your surroundings seem familiar to you?'

'No, should they have?' he said, as if he'd been cheated of something else. 'Mr Mandrake didn't say anything about that.'

'Tell me about your return, Mr Funderburk.'

'You have to have the life review first', he said.

'Okay, tell me about the life review.'

But he was extremely vague about both its form and its content. 'It's a review', he said. 'Of your life. And then the angel commanded me to return, and I did.'

'Can you describe your return?'

'I returned.'

She was starting to appreciate Mr Sage. 'During your NDE, do you remember hearing anything?'

'No. Mr Mandrake said there was supposed to be a sound when I went into the tunnel, but I didn't get that either', he said, sounding exactly like someone complaining that dessert was supposed to come with the meal, it said so in the menu.

The other interviews went better, though neither of them contributed much in the way of detail about the manner of their return or the sound.

Ms Isakson couldn't describe the sound at all. 'Are you certain it was a sound?' Joanna asked.

'What do you mean?' Ms Isakson asked.

'Could it have been the silence after a sound had stopped that you heard instead of the sound itself?' Joanna asked, knowing it was a leading question, but unable to think of any other way to ask what she needed to know, and her suggestion had no effect on Ms Isakson.

'No, it was definitely a sound. I heard it when I first entered the tunnel. It was a tapping sound. Or a whine. I don't really remember because I was so happy to see my mother.' Tears came to her eyes. 'She looked so well and happy, not like the last time I'd seen her. She got so thin there at the end, and so yellow.'

A classic comment. NDEers always described their dead relatives as looking healthier than they had on their deathbeds, with the weight or limbs or faculties they'd lost in life restored.

'She was standing there in the light, holding out her arms to me,' Ms Isakson said.

'Can you describe the light?' Joanna asked.

'It was beautiful,' she said, looking up and opening her hands out. 'All spangled.'

'Can you describe the tunnel?'

'It was pretty dark,' she said hesitantly. 'It reminded me of a hallway. Sort of.'

'You say it reminded you. Did it seem familiar to you?'

'No,' she said promptly. Well, that was that, Joanna thought. She glanced over her notes, trying to think what she'd forgotten to ask her about.

'I had the feeling,' Ms Isakson said thoughtfully, 'that wherever it was, it was a long way away.' She's right, Joanna thought, remembering the passage. It is a long way away. That's what Greg Menotti meant when he said it was too far for his girlfriend to come.

I lied to Richard, Joanna thought. I told him I'd only had three incidents, but there were four. She'd forgotten about Greg's murmuring, 'Fifty-eight.' When he'd said it, she'd had the same feeling that she almost knew what he was talking about. And that can't have been temporal-lobe overstimulation, she thought. I hadn't even gone under then. I hadn't even met Richard.

'Thank you for your input,' she said to Ms Isakson, switching off the minirecorder. She stuck her notebook and Ms Isakson's waiver in her pocket, said good-bye, and walked out of the room. And into Mr Mandrake.

'Dr Lander,' he said, looking surprised to see her and vexed that she had actually beaten him to a patient. 'You were in seeing Ms Isakson?'

'Yes, we've just finished,' she said and started quickly down the hall.

'Wait,' he said, cutting off her escape. 'I have several things I've been wanting to discuss with you.'

Please don't let him have found out I've been going under, Joanna prayed, looking longingly at the elevators at the end of the hall, but he had her pinned between a supply cart and the open door of Ms Isakson's room.

'I'm curious to know how your and Dr Wright's research is progressing,' he said.

I'll bet you are, she thought, especially now that you've lost all your spies.

'I must confess, I was disappointed when you told me you were working with Dr Wright. If I had known you were interested in collaboration, I'd have asked you to assist me, but it had always been my impression you preferred to work alone.'

The elevator dinged faintly, and Joanna looked down the hall at it, praying, Let someone I know get off. Anyone. Even Mr Wojakowski.

'And to have chosen such a dubious project! Attempting to reproduce a metaphysical experience through physical means!'

The elevator opened and a portly man carrying a large potted mum got out.

'All any of these so-called experiments has been able to produce is a few lights or a sensation of floating. In not one has anyone seen angels or the spirits of the departed. Have you seen Mrs Davenport?'

Is she departed? Joanna thought, startled, and then amused. That's all I need, she thought, to see Mrs Davenport standing at the end of the tunnel.

Mr Mandrake was waiting for her answer. 'Is Mrs Davenport still in the hospital?' Joanna asked. 'I assumed she'd gone home.'

He shook his head. 'She's developed several symptoms the causes of which the doctors have been unable to find, and has had to stay for additional tests,' he said. 'As a result, I've been able to interview her several times, and each time she has remembered additional details about her experience.'

I'll bet, Joanna thought, leaning her head back against the wall.

'I know your view that interviews should be conducted as soon as possible after the event,' he said, 'but I have found that patients' memories improve over time. Only yesterday Mrs Davenport remembered that the Angel of Light had raised his hand and said, "Behold," and she saw that Death was not Death, but only a passage.'

'A passage?' Joanna said, and was instantly sorry, but Mr Mandrake didn't seem to notice.

'A passage to the Other Side,' he said, 'which was revealed to Mrs Davenport in all its glory. And as she gazed at the beauties of the next life, the secrets of past and future were revealed to her, and she understood the secrets of the cosmos.'

'Did she say what those secrets were?'

'She said mere words were incapable of expressing them,' Mr Mandrake said, looking irritated. 'Can Dr Wright produce a revelation like that in his laboratory? Of course not. Such a revelation could have come only from God.'

Or the temporal lobe, Joanna thought. He's right. These are all temporal-lobe symptoms.

'"There are more things in heaven and earth, Horatio, than are dreamt of in your philosophy,"' Mr Mandrake intoned, and Joanna decided that was as good an exit line as any.

'I have another patient to see,' she said, 'on six-west.' She squeezed past him, and walked down to the elevator. When it came, she pushed eight, and, as soon as it had gone up a floor, five. That should keep Mr Mandrake busy for a while, she thought, getting off on five. And, she hoped, away from poor Ms Isakson. She started for the stairs.

'Hey, Doc,' a voice behind her called.

It's my own fault, she thought. Be careful what you ask for. 'What are you doing here, Mr Wojakowski?' she said, trying to smile.

'Friend of mine fell and broke his hip,' he said cheerfully. 'One minute he's walking to ceramics class, and the next he's flat on his back. Reminds me of that time at Coral Sea when a depth charge hit us. Me and Bud Roop were down on the hangar deck repairing the magneto on a Wildcat when it hit, and one of the props flew off and took half of Bud's head with it. Bam!' He made a slashing motion across his forehead. 'Went down just like that. One minute he's alive, chewing gum and talking away to me – he always chewed gum, Blackjack gum, haven't seen it in years – and the next, half his head's gone. He never even knew what hit him.' He shook his head. 'Not a bad way to go though, I guess. Better than my friend in there.' He jerked a thumb back in the direction of the hall. 'Cancer, congestive heart failure, and now this hip thing. I'd take a Jap bomb any day over that, but you don't get to choose how you go, do you?'

'No,' Joanna said.

'Well, anyway, I'm glad I ran into you,' Mr Wojakowski said, brightening. 'I been trying to get ahold of you and ask you about that schedule.'

'I know, Mr Wojakowski. The thing is—'

''Cause I've got a problem. I told this friend of mine over at Aspen Gardens I'd sign up for this hearing study with him. It was before I signed up for yours, and I forgot I'd told him, so here I am signed up for two things at the same time. Yours is a heck of a lot more interesting, and I ain't really hard of hearing, except for a little ringing in one ear. I've had it ever since Coral Sea, when this bomb hit just forward of the Number Two elevator and—'

'But you did sign up for it first,' Joanna said, deciding she couldn't wait for an opening. 'The hearing study has to take precedence.'

'I don't wanta let you down.'

'You're not.'

'Helluva thing, letting a friend down. Did I ever tell you about the time Ratsy Fogle told Art Blazaukas he'd take mess duty for him so Art could go see this native gal over on Maui?'

'Yes,' Joanna told him, but to no avail. She had to listen to the whole story, and the one about Jo-Jo Powers, before he finally let her go.

She went straight to her office and stayed there, looking up examples of ineffable revelations and all-encompassing wisdom until it was time for her session, and then took the list to the lab.

Richard was at the console, looking at scans. 'Where have you been?' he asked without taking his eyes from the screen.

'Discussing philosophy with Mr Mandrake,' she said. She handed him the transcripts and went in to get her hospital gown on. The sight of herself in the mirror reminded her that she hadn't told Richard about the Greg Menotti incident, and as soon as she came out, she said, 'Richard, you asked me if I had had any other incidents besides the—'

'Hello, all,' Tish said, coming in, waving a piece of paper. 'Word from on high.' She handed the paper to Richard.

'What's this?' he asked.

'It was on your door,' she said.

'"Attention, all hospital personnel,"' Richard read aloud. '"Because of a recent series of drug-related events in the ER—"' He looked up. 'What events?'

'Two shootings and a stabbing,' Joanna said.

'And an attack with an IV pole,' Tish added, attaching electrode cords to the monitor.

'"– of drug-related events in the ER,"' Richard continued, '"all personnel are advised to take the following precautions: One. Be alert to your surroundings."'

'Oh, that'll help a lot when a hopped-up gangbanger is brandishing a semi-automatic,' Tish said.

'"Two. Do not make sudden movements. Three. Note all available exits."'

'Four. Do not work in the ER,' Joanna said.

'No kidding,' Tish said, setting out the IV equipment. 'The board decided to hire one more security guard. I think they should have hired about ten. I'm ready for you, Joanna.' Joanna got on the table and lay down. Tish began placing the pads under her lower back and legs. '"Four,"' Richard said, still reading. '"Do not attempt to engage or disarm the patient. Five,"' he wadded the memo into a ball and lobbed it into the trash.

'Jenni Lyons told me she's put in a transfer to Aurora Memorial,' Tish said, knotting the rubber tubing around Joanna's arm. 'She says at least they've got a metal detector.' She poked the inside of Joanna's elbow with her finger, trying to find a vein.

I have to get Vielle out of there, Joanna thought while Tish attached the electrodes, put on the headphones.

I have to convince her to transfer before something happens, she thought, and was in the tunnel, but much farther away from the door than she had been before, and this time the door was open. It spilled golden light half the length of the passage.

She couldn't see shadows or movements in it, as she had before, or hear any voices. She stood still, listening for their murmur, and then thought, You did it again. You forgot to listen for the sound.

But it wasn't a sound, or, rather, a cessation of sound. It was a *feeling* of having heard a sound brought on by the temporal lobe. There was no actual sound.

But standing there in the tunnel, she was sure there had been. A sound like – what? A roar. Or something falling. She felt a strong impulse to turn around and look back down the dark passage as if that would help her identify it, to go back down the passage toward it.

No, she thought, holding carefully still, not even turning her head, it'll send you back to the lab. Don't do that. Not until you've seen what lies beyond the door, and began walking toward it.

The light seemed to grow brighter as she approached it, illuminating the walls and the wooden floor, which still gave a look of impossible length to the corridor. The walls were white, and so were the doors, and as she neared the end of the corridor, she could see they had numbers on them.

What if one of them's fifty-eight? she thought, clenched her fists at her sides, and went on. 'C8,' the doors read, the letters and numbers in gold, 'C10, C12.' The light continued to grow brighter.

She had expected it to become unbearably bright as she got closer, but it didn't, and as she came nearer the open door, she could make out shapes in it. Figures in white robes, radiating golden light.

Angels.

18

'I dread the journey greatly.'
> – MARY TODD LINCOLN, in a letter written
> shortly before her death

Joanna's first thought was: Angels! Mr Mandrake will be furious.

Her second thought was, No, not angels. People. The light came from behind them, around them, outlining them in golden light so that it seemed to radiate from them, from their white robes. And they weren't robes. They were white dresses with skirts that trailed the floor. Old-fashioned dresses.

The dead relatives, Joanna thought, but they weren't gathered around the door, waiting to welcome her to the Other Side. They milled about, or stood in little groups of two or three, murmuring quietly to each other. Joanna moved closer to the door, trying to make out what they were saying.

'What's happened?' a young woman in a long, high-necked dress asked. Her hair hung down her back nearly to her waist.

A long-dead relative, Joanna thought, trying to see past her to the man she was speaking to. He spoke, and his voice was too low for Joanna to hear. She squinted at the light surrounding him, as if it would make his voice clearer, and saw that he was wearing a white jacket and had a pleasant face. An unfamiliar face. And so was the woman's. Joanna had never seen either of them before.

The young woman said something else to the man, who bowed from the waist, and walked over to two people standing together, a man and a woman. The other woman was in white, too, but her hair was piled on top of her head. Her hands were white, too, and when she placed her hand on the gentleman's arm, it flashed, sparkling. The man had a trimmed white beard that looked like something from an old photo album, and so did the woman's hair, but their faces were unfamiliar. If they're dead relatives, Joanna thought, they must be someone else's.

The woman with her hair down her back spoke to the bearded man. Joanna took another step forward, nearly up to the door, trying to hear. The bearded man said, 'I'm sure it's nothing.'

Joanna shot an anxious glance back down the passageway. That was what he'd said the last time, and then the woman had said, 'It's so cold,' and the NDE had ended. If she was going to test her theory that the passageway was the way back, that going back down the tunnel would end the NDE, she needed to do it now, before the NDE ended on its own, but she wanted to stay and hear what they were talking about.

It's a clue to where this is, she thought, hesitating, poised on one foot, ready to run, trying to decide. Like Cinderella at the ball, with the clock striking midnight, she thought, and then, looking at the women again in their long white dresses, that's what this must be, a ball. That's why the woman's hand on the bearded man's arm was white, because she was wearing white gloves, and the sparkling flash when she moved her hand was jewels in a bracelet. And the young man was dressed in a white dinner jacket. She shaded her eyes against the light, trying to see what the man with the white beard was wearing.

'It's so cold,' the young woman said, and Joanna gave her one last, frustrated glance, then turned and ran down the passageway.

And into the lab. 'I want to hear about your return,' Richard said as soon as Tish had finished monitoring her and removed the electrodes and the IV.

'Was it –?' he said and then clamped his lips shut. 'Tell me about your return.'

She told him what she'd done. 'Why? Did it look different on the scans?'

'Radically,' he said, pleased, and started over to the console, as if he were finished.

'Wait, you have to hear about the rest of the NDE,' Joanna said. 'I saw another one of the core elements this time. Angels.'

'Angels?' Tish said. 'Really?'

'No,' Joanna said, 'but figures dressed all in white, or "snowy raiment," as Mr Mandrake would say.'

'Did they have wings?' Tish asked.

'No,' Joanna said. 'They weren't angels. They were people. They were dressed in long white robes, and there was light all around them,' Joanna said. 'I'd always assumed that people saw what they thought were angels and then gave them the traditional white robes and haloes because that was what they'd learned angels looked like in Sunday school. But now I wonder if it isn't the other way around, that they see the white robes and the light surrounding them, and that's what makes them think they're angels.'

'Did they speak to you?' Tish asked.

'No, they didn't seem to know I was there,' Joanna said. She told Richard what the woman had said.

'You could hear them talking,' he said.

'Yes,' she said, 'and it wasn't the telepathic communication some NDEers report. They were speaking, and I could hear some of what they said, and some I couldn't, because they were too far away.'

'Or because it lacked content,' Richard said, 'like the noise or the feeling of recognition.'

No, Joanna thought, typing her account into the computer that afternoon, because I don't know what they said, and I *know* where the tunnel is. I'm sure of it.

Someplace with numbers on the doors and a door at the end, where people stood, milling around in white dresses. A party? A wedding? That would explain the preponderance of white. But why would they keep asking, 'What's happened?' Had the groom jilted the bride? And why would the men be in white, too? When was the last time you saw a bunch of men and women dressed in white, standing around complaining about the cold?

During a hospital fire drill, she thought. Hospitals are full of people wearing white, and that was where nearly all patients experienced their NDEs. The vast majority of them had their NDEs in an ER, surrounded by doctors and nurses and a buzzing code alarm and a resident, leaning over the unconscious patient, shining a light in their eyes, asking, 'What happened to him?' It made perfect sense.

Except that the ER staff didn't wear white, they wore green or blue or pink scrubs, and the trauma rooms weren't numbered C8, C10, C12. C. What did C stand for?

Confabulation, she thought. Stop thinking about it. Get busy, which turned out to be easier than she thought. The torrent of NDEs continued for several days, and Joanna dutifully interviewed every one, though they didn't prove all that useful. They were uniformly unable to describe what they'd experienced, as if ineffability had infected every aspect of their NDE: the length of time they'd been there, the manner of their return, the things they'd seen, including angels.

'They looked like angels,' Mr Torres said irritably when Joanna asked him to describe the figures he'd seen standing in the light, and when she asked him if he could be more specific, 'Haven't you ever seen an angel?'

I need to talk to someone intelligent, Joanna thought, and went down to the ER, but they were swamped. 'Head-on between a church bus and a semi,' Vielle said briefly and ran off to meet a gurney being brought in by the paramedics. 'I'll call you.'

'Forget about this one,' the resident said. 'She's DOA.'

Dead on arrival. Arrival where? Joanna wondered, and went up to see Mrs Woollam. She'd promised her she'd visit again, and she wanted to ask her if she'd ever seen people in the garden or on the staircase.

Mrs Woollam wasn't there, and it was obvious she hadn't been taken somewhere for tests. The bed was crisply made up, with a blanket folded across the foot and a folded hospital gown lying on top of it. Her insurance must have run out, Joanna thought, disappointed, and walked down to the nurses' station. 'Did you move Mrs Woollam to another room, or did she go home?' she asked a nurse she didn't know.

The nurse looked up, startled, and then reassured at the sight of Joanna's hospital ID, and Joanna knew instantly what she was going to say. 'Mrs Woollam died early this morning.'

I hope she wasn't afraid, Joanna thought, remembering her clutching her Bible to her frail chest like a shield. 'She went very quietly, while she was reading her Bible,' the nurse was saying. 'She had such a peaceful expression.'

Good, Joanna thought, and hoped she was in the beautiful, beautiful garden. She went back to the door of the room and stood there, imagining Mrs Woollam lying there, her white hair spread out against the pillow, the Bible lying open where it had fallen from her frail hands.

I hope it's all true, Joanna thought, the light and the angels and the shining figure of Christ. For her sake, I hope it's all true, and went back up to the lab. But Richard was busy working on Mrs Troudtheim's scans, and there were all those tapes to be transcribed and two NDEers she hadn't interviewed. She got some blank tapes from her office and went down to see Ms Pekish.

She was almost as uncommunicative as Mr Sage, which was actually a blessing. The effort to get answers out of her kept her from thinking about Mrs Woollam, alone somewhere in the dark. Not alone, she corrected herself. Mrs Woollam had been sure Jesus would be with her.

'And then I saw my life,' Ms Pekish said.

'Can you be more specific?' Joanna asked.

Ms Pekish frowned in concentration. 'Things that happened.'

'Can you tell me what some of those events were?'

She shook her head. 'It all happened pretty fast.'

She was equally vague when it came to describing the light, and she wouldn't even venture a guess as to the sound. Ms Grant, at least, did. 'It sounded like music,' she said, her thin face uplifted as if she were hearing it right then. 'Heavenly music.'

Ms Grant had coded during stem cell replacement therapy for her lung cancer. She was bald and had the drawn, concentration-camp look of late-stage cancer. Joanna was surprised she was willing to talk about her experience, but when Joanna handed her the release form – her last one, she needed to pick up some more from the office – she signed it eagerly.

'It was beautiful there,' she said before Joanna could ask her anything. 'There was light all around me, and I felt no fear, just peace.'

She had obviously had the classic kind of positive NDE Mr Mandrake claimed proved there was a heaven, and Joanna couldn't help being glad.

'I was standing in a doorway,' Ms Grant said, 'and beyond it I could see a beautiful place, all white and gold and sparkling lights. I wanted to go there, but I couldn't. A voice said, "You are not allowed on this side."'

That was classic, too. NDEers frequently talked about wanting to 'cross over' and being told they couldn't, or being stopped by a barrier – a gate or a threshold of some kind. Mrs Jarvis, the first NDEer she had ever interviewed, had told her, 'I knew the bridge divided the land of the living from the land of the dead,' and Mr Olivetti had said, 'I knew if I went through that gate, I could never come back.'

'And then I was back here,' Ms Grant said, indicating her hospital bed, 'and they were working on me.'

'You said you heard music,' Joanna said. 'Can you be more specific? Voices? Instruments?'

'No voices,' Ms Grant said, 'just music. Beautiful, beautiful music.'

'When did you hear it?'

'It was there the whole time, till the very end,' Ms Grant said, 'all around me, like the light and the feeling of peace.'

'I think that's everything,' Joanna said and shut her notebook. She reached to turn off the recorder.

'What have other people said they saw?' Ms Grant asked.

Joanna looked up, wondering if she had another Mr Funderburk on her hands, determined to get everything she was entitled to. 'I don't usually—'

'Have they seen a place like that, white and gold and full of lights?' Ms Grant asked, and her voice was more agitated than eager. Joanna glanced at the IV bags, thinking, I need to check and see what drugs she's on.

'Have they?' Ms Grant insisted.

'Yes, some subjects have talked about seeing a beautiful place,' Joanna said carefully.

'Do they say what happens next if you don't come back?' she asked, and it wasn't agitation in her voice, it was fear. Joanna wondered if she should call the nurse. 'Does anybody ever talk about bad things happening to them there?'

'Did you see something that frightened you?' Joanna asked.

'No,' she said, and then, as if Joanna's question had reassured her, 'No. It was all beautiful. The light and the music and the feeling of peace. I didn't feel any fear at all while I was there, just calmness and peace.'

And, afterward, dread, Joanna thought, on her way back up to her office. 'And how can we not be afraid of death?' Mrs Woollam had said. Joanna pushed open the door to the third-floor walkway to the main building. It was dark out, the wide windows reflecting blackness. What time was it, anyway? She glanced at her watch. Six-thirty, and she still had all these NDEs to write up.

The glassed-in walkway was freezing. She pulled her cardigan around her and started across the walkway.

She stopped. Something about the walkway reminded her of the tunnel. What? Not the sound of a heater shutting off, since it obviously hadn't been on in here all day, and anyway, there was a low hum from the hospital's generating plant across the way.

And this feeling wasn't the overwhelming sense of knowing she had had before. It was less intense, like seeing someone who reminded you of someone else. The walkway's like the tunnel, she thought, but how? The walkway was wider and higher than the hallway and the hallway was lined with doors, not windows.

It's something about the floor, Joanna thought, suddenly certain. But this one was nothing at all like the floor in the tunnel. It was tiled in nondescript gray tiles speckled with pink and yellow.

It's not this walkway, she thought, squinting at the tiles, but it's a walkway here in the hospital, a walkway I've been in. But none of the walkways had a wooden floor. The one on second was carpeted, and the ones that led over to the east wing were tiled, too. Only the Sloper Institute building was old enough that it had wooden floors, but the basement walkway that led under the street to it was all concrete.

But it's one of them, she thought, hurrying the rest of the way across the walkway, through the door, and down the corridor to the elevator. It was just opening, and empty. She pressed 'two' and leaned back against the wall, her eyes closed, trying to remember which one it was, trying to visualize their floors. The third-floor walkway had beige tile and was lower by half a step than the corridors at either end. The carpet in the second-floor walkway was blue, no, blue-green –

I shouldn't be doing this, Joanna thought, opening her eyes, I should go straight up to the lab. Richard said if I had the feeling of significance again to go right to the lab so he could capture it on the RIPT. She reached forward to press the button for six, and then let her hand fall. The numbers above the door blinked 'two,' and she walked quickly down the corridor to the walkway. She knew instantly, looking at the well-worn carpet, which was dark plum, that it wasn't the right one either.

Yes, well, and you knew the carpet was blue-green, too, she thought, retracing her steps, and how do you know that this compulsion to find out isn't the result of temporal-lobe stimulation? But when the elevator came, she pressed 'three' and got out at third to go look at the west-wing walkway.

This part of the hospital was all newly carpeted in heather gray, with color-coded lines showing the way to outpatient surgery and the urology clinic and X-ray, down the length of the long hallway. 'Just follow the yellow brick road,' she'd heard a nurse tell a patient one day when she was taking a shortcut up to Coma Carl's. She followed the red line – how appropriate! – to outpatient surgery and turned left, hoping the recarpeting hadn't extended as far as the walkway.

It hadn't, but the painting had. The half-open door to the walkway was blocked off not only by yellow crime-scene tape, but also by two orange traffic cones, and, when she sidled around them to look through the door, its entire length was swathed in plastic drop cloths. 'You can't get through that way,' a passing orderly told her. 'You have to go up to fifth and over.'

Good old Mercy General, Joanna thought. You can't get there from here. The nearest elevator was all the way down at the end of outpatient surgery. She took the stairs instead, hoping she didn't encounter any more paint or tape. She didn't, and, amazingly, Maintenance wasn't doing both walkways at the same time.

She opened the door and went in. She knew before she'd come five steps that it wasn't this one either. The floor was tiled with alternating black and white squares, like a checkerboard, and the angle where they met at the bottom of the door was perfectly square. But so was the one in the tunnel, she thought, stepping back to look at the end of the walkway. It didn't curve. Why did I think it curved? Perspective caused the rows of black and white tiles to seem to narrow at the far end, making the walkway appear longer than it was. Like the tunnel? It had seemed impossibly long, but could that have been some trick of perspective?

She squatted down, squinting at the place where the door and the tiles met. Was it something about the wooden boards as the perspective narrowed them that made the floor look curved? No, not curved—

'Lose something?' someone said, standing over her.

She looked up. It was Barbara. 'Just my mind,' Joanna said and stood up, dusting off her hands. 'What are you doing over here?'

Barbara held out two cans of Pepsi and a Snickers bar. 'The vending machines in our wing are all out. This is dinner. I'm glad I ran into you. I wanted to tell you Maisie Nellis went into V-fib again this afternoon—'

'Is she all right?' Joanna cut in.

Barbara nodded, and Joanna's heart started beating again. 'She was only out a few seconds, and it doesn't look like there was any major damage. I left a message on your answering machine.'

'I haven't been in my office since early this morning.'

'I figured as much,' Barbara said. 'I'd have paged you if it looked bad.'

I had my pager off, Joanna thought guiltily.

'Anyway, Maisie's up in CICU, and she wants to see you. I have to get back,' she said, twisting the hand holding the two Pepsis around so she could see her watch.

'I'll come with you,' Joanna said, pushing the walkway door open for her. 'Can she have visitors?'

'If she's still awake.'

'What time is it?' Joanna said, looking at her watch as they started down the hall. A quarter to nine. She'd been stalking obsessively around the hospital for nearly two hours, oblivious to everything and everybody, while Maisie –

The feeling of nearly knowing washed over her abruptly, almost sickeningly, and she glanced instinctively at the floor, at the end of the hall, but there was no door there, only a bank of telephones. And that wasn't it. It was something to do with what she'd just been thinking, about her being oblivious to what was happening, and having her pager off, and—

'Are you all right?' Barbara said, looking at her worriedly, and she realized she'd stopped short, her hand to her stomach. 'Maisie's okay, really. I didn't mean to scare you like that. I know how attached you are to her. She's fine. She was regaling Paula with stories about Mount Vesuvius when I left. I'll bet you didn't have dinner either. Here.' Barbara popped open one of the Pepsis and handed it to her. 'Your blood sugar's probably even lower than mine. That cafeteria should be taken out and shot.'

It was gone, as suddenly as it had come, and if she went straight up to the lab right now, the traces would surely show up on her RIPT, it had been so strong. But she had already let Maisie down once today. She wasn't about to do it again.

She took a grateful swig of the Pepsi. 'You're right,' she said. 'I haven't had anything since this morning.' She immediately felt better. And maybe it was just low blood sugar, she thought as they went down to Peds, combined with worry over Maisie.

And there was certainly reason to worry. 'The doctors can't keep her stabilized,' Barbara told her in the elevator. 'They've put her on stronger and stronger antiarrhythmics, which all have serious liver and kidney side effects, but nothing seems to be working. Except in Mrs Nellis's mind, where everything's wonderful, Maisie's getting better every day, and her coding is just a little blip. That's what she called it,' she said disgustedly. 'A little blip.'

Which on the *Yorktown* would have meant a Japanese Zero, Joanna said silently, thinking of Mr Wojakowski. Or a torpedo.

She went up to the CICU. Maisie was asleep, an oxygen line under her nose, electrodes hooked to her chest, her IV hooked to almost as many bags as Ms Grant's had been. Joanna tiptoed a few inches into the partly darkened room and stood there watching her a few minutes. And there was no need to wonder where the sense of dread came from this time. Because it was one thing to simulate dying and another altogether to be staring it in the face.

What did you see, kiddo, when you coded? Joanna asked her silently. A partly opened door, and people in white, saying, 'What's happened?' Saying, 'It's so cold'? I hope you saw a beautiful place, Joanna thought, all golden and white, with heavenly music playing, like Ms Grant. No, not like Ms Grant. Like Mrs Woollam. A garden, all green and white.

Joanna stood in the dark a long time, and then went back up to her office, telling Barbara, 'I'll be around at least till eleven. Page me,' and typed in interviews until after midnight, waiting for her pager to go off, for the phone to ring.

But in the morning Maisie was as chirpy as ever. 'I get to go back to my regular room tomorrow. I hate these oxygen things,' she told Joanna. 'They don't stay in your nose at all. Where were you yesterday? I thought you said you were supposed to tell what you saw in your NDE right away so you wouldn't forget or confabulate stuff.'

'What did you see?' Joanna asked.

'Nothing,' Maisie said disgustedly. 'Just fog, like last time. Only it was a little thinner. I still couldn't see anything, though. But I heard something.'

'What was it?'

Maisie scrunched her face into an expression of concentration. 'I think it was a boom.'

'A boom.'

'Yeah, like a volcano erupting or a bomb or something. *Boom!*' she shouted, flinging her hands out.

'Careful,' Joanna said, looking at the IV in Maisie's arm.

Maisie glanced casually at it. 'It was a big boom.'

'You said you *think* it was a boom,' Joanna said. 'What do you mean?'

'I couldn't exactly hear it,' Maisie said. 'There was this noise, and then I was in this foggy place, but when I tried to think about what kind of a sound it was, I couldn't exactly remember. I'm pretty sure it was a boom, though.'

Like a volcano erupting, Joanna thought, and she just happened to be reading about Mount Vesuvius right before she coded. But Maisie was still a better subject than anyone else she'd interviewed lately. 'What happened then?'

'*Nothing,*' Maisie said. 'Just fog, and then I was back in my room.'

'Can you tell me about coming back? What was it like?'

'Fast,' Maisie said. 'One second I was looking around trying to see what was in the fog, and the next I was back, just like that, and the crash team guy was rubbing the paddles together and saying, "Clear." I'm glad I came back when I did. I *hate* it when they do the paddles.'

'They didn't shock you?' Joanna asked, thinking, I need to ask Barbara.

'No, I know 'cause the guy said, "Good girl, you came back on your own."'

'You said you were looking around at the fog,' Joanna said. 'Can you tell me exactly what you did?'

'I sort of turned in a circle. Do you want me to show you?' she asked and began pushing the covers back.

'No, you're all hooked up. Here,' she said, grabbing a pink teddy bear, 'show me with this.'

Maisie obligingly turned the bear in a circle on the covers. 'I was standing there,' she said, holding the bear so it was facing her, 'and I looked all around,' she turned the bear in a circle till it was facing away from her, 'and then I was back.'

She was facing back down the tunnel when she returned, Joanna thought.

If it was a tunnel. 'Did you walk this way before you came back?' she asked, demonstrating with the bear.

'Hunh-unh, 'cause I didn't know what might be in there.'

A tiger, Joanna thought. 'What did you think might be in there?'

'I don't know,' Maisie said, lying tiredly back against the pillows, and that was her cue.

She switched the recorder off and stood up. 'Time for you to rest, kiddo.'

'Wait, you can't leave yet,' Maisie said. 'I haven't told you about the fog, what it looked like. Or Mount St Helens.'

'Mount St Helens?' Joanna said. 'I thought you were reading about Mount Vesuvius.'

'They're *both* volcanoes,' Maisie said. 'Did you know at Mount St Helens this guy lived right up on the volcano, and they kept telling him he couldn't stay there, it was going to blow up, but he wouldn't listen to them? When it erupted, they couldn't even find his body.'

I need to tell Vielle that story, Joanna thought. 'Okay, you told me about Mount St Helens,' she said. 'Now it's time for you to rest. Barbara said I wasn't supposed to tire you out.'

'But I haven't told you about Mount Vesuvius. There were all these earthquakes and then they stopped, and *then*, about one o'clock, there was all this smoke and it got all dark, and the people didn't know what happened, and then all this ash and rocks started falling down, and the people got under these long porch things—'

'Colonnades,' Joanna said.

'Colonnades, but it didn't help, and then –'

'You can tell me later,' Joanna said.

'– and they all tried to grab their stuff and run out of the city. This one lady had a golden bracelet, and—'

'You can *tell* me later. *After* you rest. Put your oxygen cannula on,' and Joanna made it to the door.

But not out. 'When are you coming?' Maisie demanded.

'This afternoon,' she said, 'I promise,' and went up to her office.

Halfway there she ran into Tish. 'I asked Dr Wright if we could move your session up to one, and he said to ask you,' she said. 'I've got a dentist appointment.'

Or a hot date, Joanna thought. 'Sure,' she said. 'Is he in the lab?'

'No, he was just leaving to go see Dr Jamison,' Tish said, 'but he said he'd be back by noon. Doesn't it drive you crazy that he's so oblivious?'

Oblivious, Joanna thought. Something about being oblivious to something terrible that was happening.

'Of course it doesn't drive you crazy,' Tish said disgustedly, 'because you're exactly the same. Did you hear anything I just said?'

'Yes,' Joanna said. 'One o'clock.'

'And he said to ask you if you'd been able to reach Mrs Haighton yet,' Tish said.

Mrs Haighton. 'I'll go try her right now,' Joanna said and went on to her office to spend what was left of the morning leaving fruitless messages for Mrs Haighton and staring at her Swedish ivy, trying to remember where she'd seen the tunnel.

Something about being oblivious, and Richard's lab coat and the way the floor met the bottom of the door. And cohorts gleaming in purple and gold. And high school. It had wooden floors, she thought. She saw in her mind's eye the long second-floor hall, the waxed wooden floor. There was a door at the end of that hall, she thought. The assistant principal's office, where Ricky Inman spent half his time. And was that what she was remembering – a memory from high school? Complete with a nice authority-figure judgment image?

It made sense. Those halls were long and lined with numbered doors. The lab coat could be the one the chemistry teacher – what was his name? Mr Hobert – wore, the sound could be the passing bell, which sounded like both a ringing and a buzzing, and the door to the assistant principal's office –

But it wasn't a door to an office. The door in the tunnel opened onto the outside. I need to open that door and see what's outside it, Joanna thought. When I do, I'll know where it is.

And at one-fifteen, lying sleepily under the headphones and the sleep mask and waiting for the dithetamine to work, she thought, The door, the answer lies through the door –

And was in the tunnel. The door was shut. Only a knife-blade-thin line of light showed at the bottom of the door. Joanna had to feel her way along the pitch-black tunnel toward it, her hand on one wall.

The line of light was too narrow for any shadows, and she could not hear even a murmuring of voices. The tunnel was utterly silent, like Coma Carl's room after the heater shut off. No, not a heater. Some other quiet, steady sound you didn't notice till it had stopped.

'– stopped,' a voice said softly from beyond the door, and Joanna waited, listening.

Silence. Joanna stood there in the darkness a long minute, and then began feeling her way toward the door again, thinking, What if it's locked? But it wasn't locked. The knob turned easily, and she pulled the door open onto a blast of brilliant light. It hit her with an almost physical force, and she reeled back, her hand up to shield her face.

'What's happened?' a woman's frightened voice said, and Joanna thought for a moment she meant the light and that it had burst on all of them like a bomb when Joanna opened the door.

'I'm sure it's nothing, miss,' a man's voice said. As Joanna's eyes adjusted, she could see the man in the white jacket. He was talking to the woman with her hair down her back.

'I heard the oddest noise,' she said.

Noise, Joanna thought. Then it was a sound, after all.

The white-jacketed man said something, but Joanna couldn't hear what it was, or what the woman answered. She moved forward, up to the door, and instantly she could see the people more clearly. The young woman had a coat on over her white dress, and the man's white jacket had gold buttons down the front. The woman in the white gloves was wearing a short white fur cape.

'Yes, miss,' the man said, and Joanna thought, He's a servant. And that white jacket is a uniform.

'It sounded like a cloth being torn,' the young woman said and walked over to the man with the white beard. 'Did you hear it?'

'No,' he said, and the woman with the piled-up hair inquired, 'Do you suppose there's been an accident?' She had her white-gloved hand at her throat, holding her fur cape closed, as if she were cold, and Joanna thought, That's because they're outside, and tried to look around at their surroundings, but the light was behind them, and she couldn't see anything except the white wall against which they stood. She looked down at the floor they were standing on. It was wooden, like the floor in the hallway, but unwaxed. Some sort of porch, Joanna thought, or patio.

'It's so cold,' the young woman said, pulling her coat more tightly around her. No wonder she's cold, Joanna thought, looking at her dress under the open coat. It was made of thin muslin, much too thin for this weather, and hung full and straight to her feet like a nightgown.

'I shall see what's happened,' the bearded man said. He was in evening clothes, with a stiff-fronted white shirt and a white bow tie. He jerked his chin imperiously at the servant, and he hurried over.

'Yes, sir?' he said.

'What has happened? Why have we stopped?'

'I don't know, sir. It may be some sort of mechanical difficulty. I'm sure there's nothing to be alarmed about.'

'Go and find Mr Briarley,' the bearded man said. 'He'll be able to tell us.'

'Yes, sir,' the servant said. He disappeared into the light.

'Mr Briarley will be able to explain things,' the bearded man said to the ladies. 'In the meantime, you ladies should go back inside where it's warmer.'

Yes, Joanna thought, back inside where it's warmer, and was back in the lab, with Tish working reproachfully over her. 'You were under *forever*,' Tish said, taking her blood pressure. She entered Joanna's vitals on the chart, removed her electrodes, took out her IV, looking at her watch every few minutes.

'Okay,' she said finally. 'You can sit up.'

355

Richard came over. 'There definitely was a noise,' Joanna told him. 'One of the women heard it. She said it sounded like cloth tearing.'

'Can you put the rest of this stuff away?' Tish said, stowing the IV equipment. 'I'm already late.'

'Yes,' Richard said. 'What about duration? How long were you there?'

'Ten minutes maybe,' Joanna said, 'while the people outside the door talked, and it *was* outside. The man with the white beard said, "You ladies need to go back inside." They talked about the noise and then the bearded man told the servant to go find out what had happened.'

'The servant?' Richard asked.

'I'm off,' Tish said. 'What time tomorrow?'

'Ten,' Richard said, and Tish went out. 'One of them was a servant?'

'Yes,' Joanna said. 'I could see the gold buttons on his uniform and the embroidery on the woman's white dress, only it wasn't a dress. It was a nightgown. She had a coat on over it ...' She frowned, remembering the woman pulling it tighter around her. 'No, not a coat, a blanket, because –'

She stopped suddenly, breathing hard. 'Oh, my God,' she said. 'I know what it is.'

PART 2

'Do you think death could possibly be a boat?'
                                    – TOM STOPPARD, *Rosencrantz and
                                              Guildenstern Are Dead*

19

'Vancouver! Vancouver! This is it!'
— Last radio message from vulcanologist DAVE
JOHNSTON on Mount St Helens

'You know what it is?' Richard said blankly, thinking, Joanna can't possibly know. Temporal-lobe feelings of recognition were just that, feelings, with no content behind them. But she clearly thought she knew. Her voice was full of suppressed excitement.

'It all fits,' she said, 'the floor and the cold and the blanket, even the feeling that I shouldn't have shut off my pager, that something terrible had happened I should have known about. It all fits.' She looked up at Richard with a radiant expression. 'I told you I recognized it but had never been there, and I was right. I told you I knew what it was.'

He was almost afraid to say, 'Well, what is it?' When he did, she would look bewildered or angry, or both, the way she had for the last two weeks whenever he'd asked her. It was amazing how strong the conviction of knowledge was with temporal-lobe stimulation, even in someone like Joanna who understood what was causing it, who knew it was artificially induced.

'I told you the sound wasn't a sound,' she said, 'that it was something shutting off, and it was. That was what woke them up, the engines shutting off. Hardly anyone heard the collision. And they went outside on deck to see what had happened—'

'On deck?'

'Yes, and it was bitterly cold. Most of them had just thrown a coat or a blanket on over their nightclothes. It was after midnight and they'd already gone to bed. But not the woman with the piled-up hair. She and her husband must still have been up. They were wearing evening clothes,' she said thoughtfully, as if she were puzzling all this out as she spoke. 'That's why she was wearing white gloves.'

'Joanna —'

'The third-floor walkway is recessed, with a step at the end that makes it look like it's curving up,' she said. 'And your lab coat.'

'Joanna, you're not making any sense —'

'But it *does* make sense,' she said. 'A stoker came up behind Jack Phillips

359

and tried to steal his lifejacket right off him, and he didn't notice. He was so intent on sending the SOSs, and—'

'SOS? Lifejackets?' Richard said. 'What are you talking about, Joanna?'

'What it is,' she said. 'I told you I knew what it was, and I did.'

'And what was it?'

'I knew the word *palace* had something to do with it. That's what they called it, a floating palace.'

'What they called what?'

'The *Titanic*.'

He was so surprised by the answer, by any answer, that he simply gaped at her for a moment.

'I told you it was someplace I recognized but had never been,' she said. 'The *Titanic*.'

'Yes. It's not a hall, it's a passageway, and the door's the door that opens out onto the deck. After the *Titanic* hit the iceberg, they stopped the engines to see how much damage had been done, and the passengers went out on deck to see what had happened. The cold should have been a clue. The temperature had dropped nearly twelve degrees during the evening because of the ice. I should have realized what it was when the woman in the nightgown said, "It's so cold."'

The *Titanic*. And he had called her an island of sanity. He had told Davis there was no way she would ever turn into R. John Foxx.

'It all fits,' she said eagerly. 'The feeling I had in the walkway of being oblivious while something terrible was happening. That was the *Californian*. It turned its wireless off for the night five minutes before the *Titanic* sent its first SOS, and then sat there, fifteen miles away all night, completely unaware that the *Titanic* was sinking.'

Davis had said that everybody who studied NDEs went wacko sooner or later. Maybe he was right. Maybe it was some sort of infectious insanity. But surely not Joanna, who saw right through Mandrake and his manipulations, who knew the NDE was a physical process. There must be some mistake. 'Let me get this straight,' he said. 'You're saying you were there? On board the *Titanic*?'

'Yes,' Joanna said eagerly. 'In one of the stateroom passages. I don't know which one. I think it may have been in second class because of the wooden floor – it was the curve of the deck that made the passage look longer than it was. First class would have been carpeted, but the people outside on the deck looked like first-class passengers, so it might have been in first class. The woman with the piled-up hair was wearing jewels, and white gloves. I wonder who she was,' she murmured. 'She might have been Mrs Allison.'

'And who were you?' Richard asked angrily. 'Lady Astor?'

'What?' Joanna said blankly.

'Who exactly were you in this previous life?' Richard said. 'The Unsink-able Molly Brown?'

'Previous life?' Joanna said as if she had no idea what he was talking about.

'Were you Shirley MacLaine? Wait, don't tell me,' he said, holding up a warning hand. 'You were Bridey Murphy, and she came over from Ireland on the *Titanic*.'

'Bridey *Murphy*?' Joanna said, and her chin went up defiantly. 'You think I'm making this up?'

'I don't know what you're doing. *You* said you were on the *Titanic*.'

'I was.'

'Who else was on board? Harry Houdini? Elvis?'

She stared at him. 'I can't believe this—'

'*You* can't believe this? I can't believe that you're sitting here telling me you had some past-life regression!'

'Past-life—'

'"You should send me under," you said. "I'll be an impartial scientific obser-ver. I won't fall prey to thinking I see Angels of Light." Oh, no, you saw something even better! Do you have any idea what Mandrake will do when he gets hold of this, not to mention the tabloids? I can see the headlines now.' He swept his hand across the air. '"Near-Death Scientist Says She Went Down on *Titanic*."'

'If you'd just listen – I didn't say it was a past-life regression.'

'Oh? What was it?' he said nastily. 'A time machine? Or were you tele-ported there by aliens? I believe that first day I met you, you said that fourteen percent of all NDEers also believed they'd been abducted by UFOs. What you should have told me was that you were part of that fourteen percent.'

'I don't have to listen to this,' she said and flung herself off the examining table, clutching at the back of her hospital gown, and stomped, stocking-footed, over to the dressing room.

He started after her. 'I should have stuck with Mr Wojakowski, the com-pulsive liar,' he said. 'At least the only ship he was on was the *Yorktown*.'

'Fine,' she said, and slammed the door in his face.

She opened it again immediately and came out, buttoning her blouse, yanking on her cardigan. 'Mr Mandrake's the one you should have asked to be your partner,' she said, pushing past him. 'You two would make a perfect couple. You both want to hear what fits your preconceived theories and noth-ing else.'

She halted at the door. 'For your information, it wasn't time travel or a past-life regression. It wasn't the *Titanic*. It was – oh, what's the use? You won't listen anyway.' She yanked the door open. 'I'll tell Mr Mandrake you're looking for a new partner.'

It wasn't the *Titanic*? 'Wait –' he said, but the door had already slammed behind her.

He wrenched it open. She was already at the elevators. 'Joanna, wait!' he shouted and sprinted down the hall after her.

The elevator dinged. 'Wait!' he shouted. 'Joanna!'

She didn't so much as glance at him. The doors slid apart, and she stepped on. She must have pushed the 'door close' button because the doors immediately began to slide shut.

'Joanna, wait!' He forced the doors apart and shoved onto the elevator. The doors closed behind him. 'I want to talk to you.'

'Well, I don't want to talk to you,' she said. She reached for the 'door open' button.

He blocked her from reaching it. The elevator started down. 'What did you mean, it wasn't a past-life regression?'

'Why are you asking me? I'm Bridey Murphy, remember?' She made another try for the buttons, and he grabbed the red emergency button and turned it. An unbelievably loud alarm went off, and the elevator lurched to a stop.

Joanna looked at him disbelievingly. 'You're crazy, you know that?' she shouted over the alarm. 'And you accuse me of being a nutcase!'

'I'm sorry,' he shouted back. 'I jumped to conclusions, but what am I supposed to do when you tell me you've been on board the *Titanic*?'

'You're supposed to let me at least finish my sentence,' she shouted. 'Turn that off.'

'Will you come back to the lab with me?'

She glared at him. The alarm seemed to be getting louder by the minute. 'I promise I won't jump to conclusions,' he bellowed over it. 'Please.'

She nodded reluctantly. 'Just stop that thing!' she yelled, her hands over her ears.

He nodded and pushed the emergency button. It kept ringing. He pushed 'door open.' Nothing. He twisted the emergency button again, and then the floor buttons, one after the other. Nothing. He tried turning the emergency button the other way, but that only seemed to make the alarm louder. If that were possible.

Joanna reached past him to press the 'door open' button again, and the elevator moved upward, though the ringing still didn't stop. Richard yanked at the emergency button again, and the noise abruptly shut off, leaving an echoing ringing in his ears.

'Whoa, was it a ringing or a buzzing?' he said, hoping she'd smile.

She didn't. She pressed 'six,' and the doors slid open. Richard had half-expected a crowd of anxious rescuers, or at least *someone* who'd come out to see what all the noise was, but the hall was empty. Joanna stalked off the elevator and down to the lab ahead of him, her chin in the air. Inside, she turned to face him, her arms folded across her chest.

'Do you realize we could have been trapped in there forever,' Richard said, trying to break the ice, 'and nobody would ever have come to rescue us?'

Nothing.

'Look,' he said. 'I'm sorry I flew off the handle like that. It's just that—'

'– you thought I'd turned into one of Mr Mandrake's nutcases,' she said. 'How could you *think* that?'

'Because people do it all the time. Perfectly rational people who suddenly announce they've seen the light and start spouting nonsense. Look at Seagal. Look at Foxx.'

'But you *knew* me,' she said.

'Like you knew Mr Wojakowski?'

'Touché,' she said quietly. 'But when he told me about being on the *Yorktown* during Pearl Harbor, I didn't just accuse him. I checked my facts first. I got outside confirmation. You didn't even listen to what I was trying to tell you.'

'I'm listening now,' he said.

Her chin shot up again. 'Are you?'

'Yes,' he said seriously. He indicated a chair, and she sat down, looking wary. He sat down, too, and bent forward, his hands between his knees. 'Shoot.'

'All right.' She pushed her glasses up on her nose. 'It was the *Titanic* ...' He must have tensed involuntarily, because she said, 'I thought you said you were going to listen.'

'I am. It was the *Titanic*.'

'But it didn't feel like I was in 1912, or like I was seeing the ship that night. It wasn't like that.'

'What was it like?'

She got the thoughtful, inward look she had had when she was trying to identify the noise. 'It was the *Titanic*, but not the *Titanic*. I knew I wasn't on board the actual ship, that what I was seeing wasn't an event from that night. But, at the same time, it *was* the *Titanic*.'

'It didn't feel real?' Richard asked. 'Was it a superimposed vision?'

'No,' she said. 'The vision was substantial and three-dimensional, just like the other times. The illusion that you're really in that place is complete. I was really there in the passage and standing on the deck, only ...' She seemed to draw into herself. 'It was as if there was something else behind it, some deeper reality ...' She looked curiously at him. 'But why would I see the *Titanic*?'

'I don't think you did,' he said. 'I think you confabulated it. You didn't recognize it as the *Titanic* during the NDE. You concluded that afterward while you were giving your account. You're familiar with the process. Your conscious mind ...'

'No,' Joanna said. 'I recognized it in the passage that very first time. I told you. I knew I recognized it but that I'd never been there. And if it was a confabulation, why would I confabulate the *Titanic*, of all things? Confabulations are the result of expectations and influences. I've never heard of anyone seeing the *Titanic* in his or her NDE. If I confabulated it, why didn't I see an Angel of Light or a golden stairway?'

'There are a couple of possibilities. Come over here a minute,' he said, standing up and going over to the console. He called up four images from her NDE. 'Look at this,' he said, pointing to a scattering of orange, red, and yellow points in the frontal cortex of each scan. 'Those are random neural firings in the area of the frontal cortex devoted to long-term memory. One of those firings may have been a memory of the *Titanic*.'

'But it wasn't just one memory, it was dozens of memories. The engines stopping and the passage and the passengers standing outside on the deck –'

'Which may all be confabulations growing out of that memory, the sensations of sound, light, and figures in white you were experiencing, and the same sort of persistence of meaning that causes dreams to be a coherent story rather than a series of separate images.'

She didn't look convinced. 'But why would a *Titanic* neuron fire, out of all the – how many are there? Millions, billions of memories?'

'That's what random means,' Richard said, 'and your remembering something about the *Titanic* wouldn't be that statistically unlikely.'

Now Joanna was looking at him like he was crazy. 'It wouldn't?'

'No. After all, it's a disaster, and you spend a lot of time talking to Maisie about disasters.'

Joanna shook her head. 'But not the *Titanic*. I don't think I've ever heard Maisie mention the *Titanic*.'

'She talked about the *Lusitania*, and I'll bet you anything there are pictures of the *Titanic* in those books of hers,' Richard said. 'The day I met her she turned every single page, looking for some photo. You could have seen that picture of the *Titanic* half out of the water,' but Joanna was shaking her head.

'If it was Maisie, I'd have been more likely to have seen Pompeii, and that isn't where the memory's from.'

That's interesting, Richard thought. 'You know the source of the memory?'

She got that odd, inward look again. 'No. But I know it wasn't Mr Wojakowski or Maisie. And it wasn't random.'

'How do you know?'

'Because ... I don't know,' she said, defeated. 'It doesn't feel random. It feels like it came from something.'

'It might have,' Richard said. 'Frequently accessed long-term memories have stronger neuronal pathways than the average memory, which makes them easier to retrieve.'

'But the *Titanic*'s not a frequently accessed memory. I haven't thought of it since—'

'The movie came out?' Richard said. 'That's the most obvious source. It even has a scene at the end where the old woman sees herself on the *Titanic* in a white dress surrounded by a halo of light. You saw the movie—'

'Five years ago,' Joanna said, 'and I didn't even like it.'

'Liking wouldn't have anything to do with it,' Richard said, 'and there are references to the *Titanic* everywhere – TV specials, books. I heard that godawful song of Celine Dion's on my way to the hospital this morning, and I know for a fact you've accessed *Titanic*-related memories twice recently.'

'When?' she demanded.

'The day I met you, you told me about the spiritualist – what was his name? Stead? – going down on the *Titanic*, and that night at Vielle's, you said Dish Night was a *Titanic*-free zone, so the neural pathway would have been not only recent, but reinforced. Your memory of the scene in the movie where the engines stopped and the passengers went out on deck to see what had happened—'

She was already shaking her head. 'That scene, with them standing around out on the deck, wearing nightgowns and evening clothes, wasn't in *Titanic*.'

'All right, then a book or—'

'No,' she said, but less certainly, 'I don't think it was a book.'

'Or a conversation –' but she was already shaking her head.

'Not a conversation. The memory came from somewhere else.'

'Where?'

'I don't know. You say my seeing the *Titanic* is determined by the random firing of a synapse –'

'And temporal-lobe stimulation.'

'But nearly all the NDEers conclude they're seeing heaven. If random firings were determining the content, wouldn't they be reporting a whole variety of places and experiences?'

'Not necessarily,' Richard said. 'The firing of the synapses may be too weak in most cases to produce an image. Or the sense of cosmic significance may override any other images.'

'Then why didn't it in mine?'

'Because you were on guard against those interpretations. As you said when you were trying to talk me into letting you go under, when you saw a radiant figure, you wouldn't automatically assume it was an Angel of Light.'

'But why would I assume it was the *Titanic*, of all things? Why not a railroad tunnel? Just last week Vielle said, "What if the light at the end of the tunnel's an oncoming train?" And I live in Colorado. There are dozens of tunnels in the mountains. One of them would have been the logical association, not a ship. I've never even been on a ship.'

'You're thinking logical explanations,' Richard said, 'but these synapse firings are random –'

Joanna was shaking her head again. 'It doesn't feel random. I have this feeling that I saw the *Titanic* for a reason, that it means something.'

And here we are, Richard thought, right back at the temporal lobe and the sense of significance. 'This feeling,' he said, 'can you describe it?'

'It has to do with where the memory that triggered the image of the *Titanic* came from,' she said. 'I have this strong feeling that I know where the memory came from, and that if I could just remember –'

'But you can't?'

'No, it's right ...' her hand reached out, as if trying to grasp something, '... on the tip –' She stopped and yanked her hand back to her side. 'You don't think that means anything either, do you?' she said angrily. 'You think it's temporal-lobe stimulation again.'

'It would explain why you can't remember where you got the memory,' he said mildly. 'Are you having the feeling now? That you know where the memory came from?'

'Yes.'

'Get on the table,' he said, going rapidly over to the supply cabinet. 'I want to see if we can catch this on the scan.' He got out a syringe.

'Do you want me to get undressed?'

'No, and I'm not going to bother with an IV, since all I'm going to inject is the marker,' Richard said, filling the syringe. 'Take off your sweater and roll up your sleeve.'

Joanna took off her cardigan and got up on the table, unbuttoning the cuff of her blouse and pushing the sleeve up.

He began positioning the RIPT scan. 'You had a feeling of recognition in the first three scans, and in this one you recognized the *Titanic*. Those two things may have nothing to do with each other.'

'What do you mean, nothing to do with each other?'

He swabbed the inside of her elbow with alcohol and injected the marker. 'The feeling of recognition you experienced in the walkway and when the heater shut off may have been just that, a feeling, triggered by random stimuli, and unrelated to your recognition of the *Titanic*.'

'But they weren't random,' she said, flushing. 'They all fit, your lab coat and the cold and the—'

'Those could apply to any number of situations.'

'Name one,' Joanna said.

'You yourself said the people you saw could have been at a party or a ball.'

'The woman was in her nightgown!'

'You *concluded* it was a nightgown after you realized it was the *Titanic*.

Earlier, you said it was an old-fashioned dress. You originally thought it was an angel's robe. Lie down.'

'But what about the curving floor,' she said, lying down on the examining table, 'and your lab coat, and—?'

'Don't talk,' he said, moving the scan into position. He walked over to the console. 'All right,' he said, starting the scan. 'I want you to count to five in your head.'

He looked up at the image on the scans. 'Now, I want you to visualize the tunnel. Think about what you saw.'

A number of frontal-cortex sites lit up, indicating a variety of sources for the memory, both auditory and visual, which might be why Joanna couldn't remember whether she'd heard or read something about the engines stopping and the passengers going out on deck to see what had happened.

Or seen it in the movie, he thought. He still considered that the most likely possibility, in spite of Joanna's protests. The movie had been an enormous hit, and for over a year it had been impossible to turn around without being bombarded with information about it – books, CDs, newspaper articles, TV specials. And a few years before that the same thing had happened with the discovery of the wreck. It was impossible not to know something about the *Titanic*, and Joanna obviously did. She not only knew that there'd been carpets in the first-class passageways, but that the wireless operator had been Jack Phillips. 'All right, now, Joanna, concentrate on the source of the memory,' he said and looked up at the temporal-lobe area on the screen, expecting it to light up.

It did, a vivid orange-red. He asked her several more questions and then shut off the scan. 'You can get up now,' he said and started graphing the scans.

Joanna came over to the console, rolling down her sleeve. 'I still haven't recorded my NDE.' She pulled on her cardigan. 'I'll be in my office.'

'Don't you want to see your feeling of significance?' He called the scan up. 'There it is,' he said, pointing to the temporal lobe. 'That's why you feel seeing the *Titanic* isn't random.'

She looked at it glumly, her hands jammed in her lab coat pockets, as he showed her the areas of activity.

'But the feeling that I know where the memory came from is so strong ...' she murmured.

'Like the feeling you had in the dressing room and the walkway,' Richard said.

'Yes,' she admitted.

He pointed at the red-orange temporal lobe. 'Your mind is simply trying to make sense of an irrational feeling by giving it an object, in this case the source of the memory, but it's only a feeling.'

She looked like she was going to contradict him, but all she said was, 'I still haven't recorded my account.' She picked up her recorder.

'When you write it up—'

'I know,' Joanna said. 'Don't let it fall into enemy hands.'

'Mandrake would—'

'I know,' she said. 'Have a field day with this.'

She started out of the lab. At the door she turned and looked back at the scan. 'I think I liked it better when you were accusing me of being Bridey Murphy,' she said ruefully and went out.

20

'I scorn to answer you such a question!'
— QUEEN ELIZABETH I, on being asked on her
deathbed by Sir Robert Cecil if she had seen any spirits

Richard's wrong, Joanna thought, opening the door to her office. It isn't a content-free feeling. The memory didn't come from the movie, and it's not the first thing my long-term memory happened to stumble over. It's the *Titanic* for a reason.

And no doubt he'll be down here in a minute to tell me my thinking that is yet another symptom of temporal-lobe stimulation, and show me a scan that proves it. I don't want to see it, she thought, and I don't want to hear another lecture on what will happen if Mr Mandrake finds out about this. I'll record my account somewhere else.

She yanked her door shut, locked it, and walked quickly down the hall to the stairs. She would go record her account in the cafeteria, if it was open, or in one of the nurses' lounges. Anywhere where I don't have to listen to him telling me the *Titanic* was a random synapse, she thought, clattering down the stairs. It's not random. I'm seeing the *Titanic* for a reason. I know it.

And could hear Mr Darby's voice insisting, 'I was *there*. It was real. I *know* it.' She sounded just like him. And that's why you don't want to talk to Richard, she thought, because you know he's right.

He's *not* right, she thought stubbornly. I *know* the memory isn't from the movie.

Yes, and Mr Viraldi *knew* he'd seen Elvis, Mr Suarez *knew* he'd been abducted by aliens, Bridey Murphy *knew* she'd lived a previous life in Ireland. Her psychiatrist had been certain Bridey's memories were proof of reincarnation, even though it had later been proved they'd been concocted out of folk songs and half-remembered stories her nanny'd told her, and that subjects under hypnosis could be talked into all sorts of false memories. And how do you know this isn't the same thing? How do you know the memory isn't from the movie, like Richard said?

But that scene isn't in the movie, she thought, and knew it very well might be. Memory had been proved notoriously unreliable in study after study, and she and Vielle had had more than one argument about what was and wasn't in various movies. After they'd watched *A Perfect Murder* at Dish Night, Vielle had been convinced that Gwyneth Paltrow had stabbed Michael Douglas to death with a meat thermometer instead of shooting him. Joanna had had to rent the video again and show her the ending to prove it to her. A scene with the passengers standing around asking the steward what had happened might very well be in *Titanic*, and she'd simply forgotten it. And there was a simple way to prove it, one way or the other. Watch the movie.

But Richard was already convinced her NDE had been influenced by the movie. If she watched it, her memory of her NDE would be hopelessly contaminated by its images, and so would any future NDEs she might have. And no matter what she saw in them, Richard would claim the memory came from the movie.

I need to have somebody else watch it and see if the scene's there, she thought. But who? Vielle would have a fit if she told her she'd seen the *Titanic*. She'd be convinced it was a warning from the subconscious about going under.

Maisie? She was a disaster expert, but, as Joanna had told Richard, she'd never heard her so much as mention the *Titanic*, and, anyway, it was unlikely Maisie's mother would allow her to see the movie. Quite apart from the 'negative subject matter,' there was a nude scene and sex in the backseat of a Renault.

Tish? No, Joanna couldn't trust her to keep her mouth shut, and Richard was right, Mr Mandrake would have a field day if he found out about this, which eliminated anybody connected with Gossip General.

It would have to be Vielle, who, she hoped, wouldn't ask too many questions. Joanna went down to the basement, past the morgue, and across to the ER.

It was jammed, as usual, with drugged and dangerous-looking people, though there didn't seem to be any rogue-ravers on the premises at the moment. The new security guard was looking bored in a chair by the door. Joanna worked her way through the mess to Vielle, who was handing a patient on a gurney over to two orderlies. 'She goes up to four-west,' Vielle said to them. 'Do you know how to get there?'

The orderlies nodded uncertainly. Vielle gave them complicated instructions, laid the chart on the patient's stomach, then turned to Joanna. 'You're too late,' Vielle said. 'We had a patient who coded twice. You just missed him.'

'He died?'

'No, he's fine,' Vielle said. 'It would have been a case of natural selection if he'd died, though. He electrocuted himself taking down his Christmas lights.'

'His Christmas lights?' Joanna said. 'It's February.'

'He said it was the first day it hadn't snowed.'

'I thought Christmas lights were shielded.'

'They are. Except when you walk your ladder straight into a power line. Your metal ladder.' She grinned at Joanna. 'He's up in CICU – a little fried, but able to talk. You better get up there fast, though. Maurice Mandrake was just down here, looking for you, and I saw him talking to Christmas Lights Guy's doctor.'

'Mr Mandrake was looking for me?' Joanna asked. That was all she needed.

'Yeah. He said if I saw you, I was to tell you he was going up to your office. That was before Christmas Lights Guy, though, but if he did go up to your office, you might be able to beat him to the CICU.' She walked away.

Joanna followed her. 'I didn't come down to see if anyone'd coded,' she said. 'Vielle, you remember the movie *Titanic*. Was there a scene in it where people were standing on deck trying to find out what had happened?'

'All I remember about *Titanic* was the two of them wading around in ice-cold water for two hours and not getting hypothermia. Do you know how long they really would have lasted in water that cold? About five minutes.'

'I know, I know,' Joanna said. 'Try to remember. People standing out on deck, wondering what's happened.'

'There's that scene where the iceberg scrapes by, and people are out on the deck, throwing snowballs—'

'No, no,' Joanna said impatiently. 'These people didn't know they'd been hit by an iceberg. They were just standing there, some of them still in their night-clothes. The engines' stopping woke them up, and they went out on deck to see what had happened. Do you remember a scene like that?'

Vielle shook her head. 'Sorry.'

'I've got a favor to ask,' Joanna said. 'Could you rent the video and see if there's a scene like that in it?'

'Wouldn't it be easier to rent it yourself? You're the one who knows what you're looking for. If you want, we can watch it at Dish Night, so long as you fast-forward through that stupid 'king of the world' scene.'

'No,' Joanna said. 'Look, I'll pay for the rental and your gas. I just need you to see if the scene's in there.' She fumbled in her cardigan pocket.

'You can pay for the videos on Dish Night,' Vielle said, eyes narrowing. 'What's this all about? It has something to do with your project, doesn't it? Don't tell me one of your subjects found themselves on the *Titanic*.'

'Shh,' Joanna said, glancing anxiously around. She had had no business asking Vielle where people could hear her.

'That's it, isn't it?' Vielle said, dropping her voice. 'One of your NDE subjects saw the *Titanic* when he went through the tunnel.'

'No, of course not,' Joanna said. 'This is something Richard and I were talking about.' Well, it's true, she thought defensively. We *did* talk about it, and Vielle asked me if my subjects had seen it, not if *I'd* seen it. And besides, it wasn't the *Titanic.*

'Something you and Richard were talking about, huh?' Vielle said, her whole manner changing. 'Well, at least you're discussing something other than RIPT scans and endorphin levels, though why you picked *Titanic*, I don't know.'

Joanna forced herself to smile and not look around to see if anyone else had heard them.

'Surely there are better movies you two could fight over,' Vielle said. 'I thought you hated the movie. When I wanted to rent it, you had a fit about how some officer hadn't shot himself—'

'Officer Murdoch,' Joanna said. Vielle was right. She *had* had a fit. The movie was full of historical inaccuracies. Not only was there no proof that Officer Murdoch had shot a passenger and then killed himself, but the movie had made Officer Lightoller look like a coward instead of the hero he'd been, unlashing the collapsible lifeboats on top of the officers' quarters, keeping overturned Collapsible B afloat all night –

The memory can't have come from the movie, she thought, because I already knew about the *Titanic* when I saw the movie. 'Everyone knows about the *Titanic,*' Richard had said, but he was talking about the basic facts. Everyone knew it had sunk, they knew about the iceberg and the lack of lifeboats, and the band playing 'Nearer, My God, to Thee' as the ship went down. Not about Murdoch. Or Collapsible B.

'Why don't you just rent the movie, invite him over, and make some of my special deviled ham dip –?'

'It involves our memories of the movie,' Joanna said evasively. 'So if you could rent it and see if there's a scene like that in it, I'd appreciate it. You don't have to watch the whole movie, just the part right after the iceberg.'

'Anything to help this romance along. Tell me again what I'm looking for.'

'People standing out on deck, wondering what's happened and asking the steward why they've stopped, some of them in evening clothes and some of them looking like they just got out of bed. And not frightened or shouting, not trying to get up to the Boat Deck, just standing there.'

'Got it,' Vielle said. 'I don't remember anything like that in the movie.'

I don't either, Joanna thought. 'Can you watch it tonight?'

'No,' Vielle said. 'It'll have to be tomorrow.'

'Why?'

'Oh, there's a stupid meeting tonight,' Vielle said carelessly.

'What about?'

'I don't know. ER safety or something. Apparently they didn't think their memo was enough, so now they're going to subject us to a seminar. "Be alert to your surroundings. Avoid sudden movements." I wonder if that includes jerking awake after you've nodded off during the seminar.'

'Don't make jokes,' Joanna said. 'The ER is dangerous. You *have* to ask for a transfer out of here.'

'Can't,' Vielle said breezily. 'I'm too busy watching videos for my friends.'

'I'm serious,' Joanna said. 'You're going to get killed one of these days if you stay down here. I think you should—'

'Yes, Mother,' Vielle said. 'Now, what am I looking for again? People standing in the hall in their PJs talking about hearing the engines shut off?'

'Out on deck. Not in the passages. How soon do you think you can find out?'

'As soon as I can get out of here tomorrow night, get to Blockbuster, and fast-forward through the first two hours of Leo and Kate hanging out over the railing and saying lines like, "I'm so lucky to be on this ship,"' Vielle said, miming sticking a finger down her throat. 'Eight o'clock?'

Eight o'clock tomorrow, Joanna thought, wishing it were sooner. 'Call me as soon as you find out.'

'You're sure one of your volunteers didn't see the *Titanic*?' Vielle said, looking worried.

'I'm sure. Where did you say Christmas Lights Guy was?'

'CICU.'

'CICU,' Joanna said and left before Vielle could ask any more questions. She didn't have any intention of interviewing Christmas Lights Guy till she had this figured out. She'd just asked where he was to get Vielle off the subject of the *Titanic*, though if she wanted to get his NDE she really needed to do it now, get it recorded before he'd confabulated the—

I haven't recorded mine, she thought, appalled. She'd been so distracted by wanting to prove the images hadn't come from the movie, she'd forgotten where she'd been going in the first place. And all this speculation about where the memory came from and what it meant would be useless if her NDE wasn't documented.

I need to get it down now, she thought, before any more time goes by, and ran up to first to the cafeteria. Halfway there, Lucille from CICU stopped her in the corridor. 'Did Maurice Mandrake find you?' she asked. 'He was looking for you.'

'Where did you see him?' Joanna asked.

'Up in CICU. He came up to interview a patient.'

Of course, Joanna thought, and there goes Christmas Lights Guy. But at least if he was up there, he wasn't in the cafeteria. She thanked Lucille and went on down. The cafeteria was closed.

Of course. Joanna yanked on the locked double doors and then stood looking through them at the red plastic chairs upended on the Formica tables, trying to think where else she could go. Not her office, obviously, and not the doctors' lounge. She couldn't run the risk of anyone overhearing her talking about the *Titanic*. The visitors' lounge in outpatient surgery was usually empty this time of day, but she'd have to go through three corridors and two walkways to get there, increasing the risk of running into Mr Mandrake.

I need someplace deserted where Mr Mandrake won't think to look for me, Joanna thought, which was where? My car, she thought, and fumbled in her cardigan pocket for her car keys. She didn't have them. The only key she had was to her office. Her car keys were in her bag in the drawer of her desk, and her car was locked. And it was too cold to sit on the hood.

The stairway, she thought, remembering the blocked-off stairwell she and Richard had sat in the day they met. But surely they were finished painting it by now, and people were using it again. Still, it was comparatively private and out of the way.

And warmer than the parking lot, Joanna thought, taking the service elevator up to third. And if she sat in the middle of the landing, where she could see both doors, she could hear people coming in plenty of time to stop recording, so she wouldn't be overheard.

The elevator door opened. Joanna leaned out cautiously, looking for signs of Mr Mandrake, but there was no one in the corridor. She walked down the hall and across the walkway, turned the corner, and started through Medicine.

'... and then my uncle Alvin said, "Come," ' a woman's voice said from the half-open door of one of the rooms, 'and he stretched out his hand to me and said, "There is naught to fear from death." '

Oh, no, Joanna thought, stopping short of the door. She had thought Mrs Davenport would have been discharged by now. What HMO did she have that would let her stay in the hospital this long? More important, who was she talking to, Mr Mandrake? And would he suddenly emerge from the room?

But another woman's voice – a nurse? Mrs Davenport's hapless room-mate? – said breathlessly, 'And then what happened?'

'Light came from his hand, and it sparkled like diamonds and sapphires and rubies.'

Mrs Davenport was in full cry now, and, Joanna hoped, was looking at her audience and not at the door. She tiptoed quickly past and down toward the door marked 'Staff Only.'

'And he took my hand and led me to a beautiful, beautiful garden,' Mrs Davenport said, 'and I knew what I was seeing wasn't a dream or a hallucination, it was real. I was actually seeing the Other Side. And do you know what Alvin said then?'

Joanna didn't wait to hear. She opened the stairwell door and ducked in. Nothing had changed since the last time she'd been in there. The yellow 'Do Not Cross' tape still stretched between the railings, and below it, the pale blue steps still looked shiny and wet.

They weren't, she determined with a careful finger. The paint was long since dry, but that didn't matter. People obviously thought the stairway was still blocked, which meant she'd have it all to herself. She positioned herself on the left side of the landing, where she could see the door, and switched on her recorder.

'NDE account, Joanna Lander, session four, February 25,' she said and then stopped, staring at the pale blue steps, thinking about the collapsibles.

She had already known about them when she saw the movie, and about Lightoller and Murdoch. And Lorraine Allison, she thought. She remembered ranting, 'Why didn't they tell the stories of the *real* people who died on the *Titanic*, like John Jacob Astor and Lorraine Allison?' and Vielle asking, 'Who was Lorraine Allison?' and her telling her, 'She was six years old and the only first-class child to die, and her story's a lot more interesting than dopey Jack and Rose's!'

She had known about Lorraine Allison before the movie, so the memory couldn't have come from *Titanic*, or from Maisie's disaster books. It had to come from something earlier. A book, no, it wasn't something she'd read, though there was a book involved somehow. Something someone had read to her, or said.

And what they had said was connected to why she was seeing the *Titanic* instead of a railroad tunnel or a hospital walkway. And it was important.

This was getting her nowhere. Record your account, she told herself. Describe what you saw and heard. She switched the recorder on and started again. 'I was in the passage. It was dark.' She described the unheard sound, the light under the door, the people. 'The bearded gentleman was in evening dress, with a long formal coat and a white tie and vest, and the woman had long white gloves and a beaded cream-colored dress.' And you have just described Kate Winslet's gown, she told herself, clicking the recorder off. You're starting to confabulate.

She rewound to 'the woman' and started again. 'She was wearing a long white gown or robe and a sparkling light seemed to come from her hand. She said, "Do you suppose there's been an accident?" and then the steward came up –

No, that wasn't right. The steward had been talking to the woman in the nightgown. She'd said, 'I heard the oddest noise,' and he'd said, 'Yes, ma'am,' and then the bearded man had come over, but that wasn't right either, because the woman in the white gloves had been standing there, too …

She clicked off the recorder and pressed her fingers to her forehead, trying to remember where the bearded man had been standing, what the steward had said.

The woman in the nightgown had spoken to the steward and then gone over to the bearded man and said, 'Did you hear it?' And the bearded man had said, 'I shall see what's happened,' and motioned the steward to come over. 'What's happened? Why have we stopped?' he asked the steward, and the steward said there was nothing to be alarmed about, and the bearded man said, 'Go find Mr Briarley. He will know what's going on.'

'Mr Briarley,' she said. Her English teacher her senior year of high school.

She could see him standing in front of the blackboard in his gray tweed vest and bow tie, an eyebrow cocked ironically, hear him saying, 'Well, Mr Inman, can you tell us what happens in "The Rime of the Ancient Mariner"?' No answer. 'Ms Lander? Mr Kennedy? *Anyone?*' Still nothing. 'What's that?' Mr Briarley putting his hand behind his ear, listening, and then shaking his head. 'I thought it was an answer, but it was only the band, playing "Nearer, My God, to Thee."'

And how could she have forgotten that? Forgotten Mr Briarley, who had talked about the *Titanic* constantly in class, who'd used it as a metaphor for everything. 'Water up to the boilers,' he had written on an essay of hers, 'Putting the women off in boats.' He was always telling them stories about the loading of the lifeboats and the lights going out, reading them long passages about the band and the *Californian* and the passengers. 'I knew I hadn't read it,' Joanna said out loud. 'I heard Mr Briarley say it.'

And he held the answer. He had said something about the *Titanic*, something in English class, and – 'I have to find him,' Joanna said, jamming her recorder in her pocket. 'I have to ask him what he said.'

She ran up the stairs to the nurses' station. 'I need a phone book,' she said breathlessly.

'White or yellow pages?' Eileen asked. 'Are you okay?'

'I'm fine,' Joanna said. 'White.'

Eileen set the heavy phone book on the counter, and Joanna flipped rapidly through the B's, trying to remember Mr Briarley's first name. She wasn't sure she'd ever heard it. He'd simply been Mr Briarley, like all her teachers. Bo, Br—

A buzzer sounded. Eileen reached to turn it off. 'Patient calling,' she said. 'Are you sure you're okay?'

'I'm fine,' Joanna murmured, running her finger down the list of Br's. Braun. Brazelton.

'Okay,' Eileen said, 'just stick the phone book on the desk,' and went off to answer the patient's call.

Breen. Brentwood. Joanna hoped there weren't dozens of Briarleys. Brethauer. She needn't have worried. There weren't any. The list went straight from Brian to Briceno. He probably has an unlisted number, she thought, to keep students from making prank calls. I'll have to talk to him at school.

She glanced at her watch. Three o'clock. School got out at three-fifteen, or at least it had when she was in high school, but the teachers had been required to stay till at least four. If she hurried, she might make it there by then. She shut the phone book and started quickly down the hall toward the elevator, fumbling for her car keys as she walked.

She didn't have them. They were up in her office, where Mr Mandrake, and probably Richard, lay in wait. I'll have to borrow a car, she thought and ran back to the nurses' station to ask Eileen, but she wasn't there, and there wasn't time to look for her. She'd have to borrow Vielle's. She started back toward the elevator.

'Oh, good, Dr Lander,' a familiar voice said, and Joanna looked up in horror to see Mrs Davenport heading toward her in an orange-and-yellow-and-electric-blue-splotched robe. 'You're just the person I wanted to see.'

21

'Turn up the lights. I don't want to go home in the dark.'
– Last words of O. HENRY (WILLIAM SYDNEY PORTER)

This is what you get for not watching where you're going, Joanna thought. 'Be alert to your surroundings,' the hospital memo on protecting yourself from rogue-crazed ER patients had said. Joanna should have paid attention to it.

'I've remembered more details of my NDE,' Mrs Davenport said, planting her multicolored self squarely between Joanna and the elevator. She looks just like an RIPT scan in that robe, Joanna thought. 'After the Angel of Light showed me the crystal, my uncle Alvin led me over to a shimmering gray curtain, and when he drew it aside, I could see the operating room and all the doctors working over my lifeless body, and—'

'Mrs Davenport,' Joanna interrupted, 'I have an appointment—'

'– and Alvin said, "Here on the Other Side we know everything that happens on Earth,"' Mrs Davenport went on as if Joanna hadn't spoken, '"and we use that knowledge to protect and guide the living."'

'I have to be on the other side of town by four,' Joanna said, looking point-edly at her watch.

'"All you have to do is listen, and we will speak to you," Alvin said, and he was right,' Mrs Davenport said. 'Just the other day he told me where my pearl earring that I'd lost was.'

I wonder if he can tell me how to get away from his niece, Joanna thought. 'I wish I could stay, Mrs Davenport, but I *have* to go.'

'And two nights ago, in the middle of the night, I heard him say, "Wake up," and when I looked at the time, it was 3 A.M.'

Mrs Davenport was never going to let her go. She was simply going to have to walk around her. She did. Mrs Davenport followed her, still talking. 'And then I heard him say, just like he was there in the room, "Turn on the TV," and I did, and do you know what was on?'

A Ronco infomercial? Joanna thought. She hit the elevator 'down' button. 'A show on paranormal experiences,' Mrs Davenport said, 'which is proof that those who have passed over are in communication with us.'

The elevator opened and Joanna practically jumped in, praying Mrs Dav-enport wouldn't follow her. 'And just this morning I heard Alvin say—'

The closing elevator door cut her off before she could communicate Alvin's message. Joanna hit 'G' and, as soon as the elevator opened, sprinted over to the ER, praying nobody had coded and Vielle was in the middle of trying to revive him.

Nobody had, and Vielle wasn't. She was yelling at an intern. 'Who gave you authorization to do that?' she was saying.

'I ... I ... nobody,' the intern stammered. 'In medical school ...'

'You're not in medical school,' Vielle snapped. 'You're in my ER.'

'I know, but he was –' He stopped and looked hopefully at Joanna as if she might rescue him.

'Sorry,' Joanna said to Vielle. 'Can I borrow your car?'

'Sure,' Vielle said promptly, and to the intern, 'Stay right there. And don't touch *anything*.' She started across the ER. 'My keys are in my locker. What happened? Died, huh?'

'Who?' Joanna said, following her into the ER lounge, and realized belatedly that Vielle meant her car. 'No. My car's fine.'

Wrong answer. Vielle turned, her hand already on the locker combination, and frowned at her. 'Then what do you need mine for? This doesn't have any-thing to do with the *Titanic* scene you asked me about, does it?'

'I just don't want to go up to my office to get my keys. Mr Mandrake's got it staked out,' she said evasively, 'and I don't want to see him.'

'I don't blame you,' Vielle said and turned back to the combination. 'What time will you be back?' she asked, digging in her purse and coming up with the keys. She dropped them in Joanna's hand. 'I get off at seven.'

'Where's your car?'

'North side, second or third row, I don't remember,' Vielle said. 'Where are you going?'

'I'll be back in an hour or so,' Joanna said and hurried out to the parking lot.

Vielle's car was in the fourth row, at the very end, and it was three-thirty before Joanna located it and headed south to Englewood. He'll be gone by the time I get there, she thought, but Mr Briarley had always stayed later than the rest of the teachers, and even if he wasn't there, she could get a phone number and an address from the people in the office. And places called up all sorts of memories – just standing in her old English classroom might be enough to jog her memory. It was something he said in a lecture, she thought, turning west on Hampden, or read out loud to us.

It looked like it could snow any minute. Joanna parked as close as possible to the door that led to the English classrooms, and went up to the door. It was locked. A computer-printed sign taped to the glass said, 'No visitors allowed in building without authorization. Please check in at main office.' A diagram with arrows indicated how to get there, which entailed tramping all the way around the building.

They had done a lot of adding on since Joanna had been here. She rounded a long wing with a new auditorium at the end and came, finally, to the front door. Next to it were the words 'Dry Creek High School', and a pouncing tiger with purple-and-gold stripes.

Purple and gold, Joanna thought, and suddenly remembered Sarah Dix and Lisa Meinecke in their cheerleader outfits coming in late in the middle of class and Mr Briarley putting his textbook down on the desk and saying, 'Where's the Assyrian?'

'Assyrian?' Lisa and Sarah had said, looking bewilderedly at each other.

'Your cohort. "The Assyrian came down like the wolf on the fold,"' Mr Briarley had said, pointing at their short skirts with the purple-and-gold pleats. '"And his cohorts were gleaming in purple and gold."'

I *knew* it had something to do with high school, Joanna thought triumphantly. Richard's wrong. It isn't contentless. It *means* something, and Mr Briarley knows what it is. She opened one of the double doors and walked through it into a gold-carpeted lobby, with wide wood-and-steel stairs leading up and down to three different levels. And a metal detector.

A uniformed security guard was standing next to it, reading *Clear and Present Danger*. He put the paperback down as soon as Joanna came in and switched on the detector. 'Can you tell me where I can find the office?' she asked.

He nodded and indicated her bag. She handed it to him, thinking the ER could use a setup like this, and then tried to imagine the ambulance crew trying to get a metal gurney through it. All right, maybe not a metal detector, but something.

The guard unzipped the compartments of her bag, poked through them, and handed the bag back to her. 'I'm looking for a teacher I had when I went to school here,' she said. 'Mr Briarley?'

The guard motioned her through the detector. 'Up those steps and to the left,' he said, pointing, and picked up his paperback.

The office of Mr Briarley? Joanna wondered, going up the stairs, but of course he had meant the office. The wide, glass-fronted space wasn't anything like the cramped cubbyhole of a principal's office she remembered, but there was a large sign taped to the glass that said, 'All visitors must obtain a visitor's pass upon entering the building.'

Joanna went in. 'Can I help you?' the middle-aged woman seated at a terminal said.

'I'm looking for Mr Briarley,' Joanna said, and at the woman's uncomprehending look, 'He teaches here.'

The woman came over to the counter and consulted a laminated list. 'We don't have any faculty members by that name.'

Joanna hadn't even considered that possibility. 'Do you know if he moved? Or retired?'

The woman shook her head. 'I've only worked here a year. You might check with the administration office.'

'And where is that?'

'4522 Bannock Street,' she said. 'But they close at four.'

Joanna looked at the clock on the wall behind the woman's head. It said five to four. 'What about a teacher who would have been here when he was?' Joanna said, wracking her brain trying to think of her other teachers' names. 'Is Mr Hobert still here? Or Miss Husted?' she asked. What was the name of the PE teacher, the one everybody hated? A color. Mr Green? Mr Black? 'What about Mr Black?'

The woman consulted her list. 'No. Sorry.'

'An English teacher then. Mr Briarley taught senior English. Who teaches that class now?'

'Ms Forrestal, but she's already left for the day.'

'Can you give me her home number?'

'We're not allowed to give out that information. I'd suggest you contact the administration offices. They open at ten,' she said and walked back over to her terminal.

'Thank you,' Joanna said and went out into the hall. Now what? she thought, walking back toward the stairs. The administration office was closed till tomorrow at ten, and they would only tell her the same thing, that they weren't allowed to give out that information.

She started down the stairs toward the lobby. The guard, deep in his thriller, didn't look up. She would have to come back tomorrow, during school, and see Ms Forrestal – if the office would give her a visitor's pass. And there was no guarantee that Ms Forrestal would have Mr Briarley's address. Or be willing to give it to her. I need to just go up and down the halls and talk to teachers till I find someone who knew him, Joanna thought.

She stopped, her hand on the railing, and looked across at the guard. He still hadn't seen her. She retreated silently back up the stairs, wishing the office didn't have such a large expanse of window, but the woman she'd talked to was bent over her terminal, typing something in. Joanna sped past the windows and into the stairwell at the far end. This is ridiculous, she thought, racing up the stairs. You're going to get yourself expelled. Or worse, she amended, remembering the security guard's shoulder holster.

But when she paused for breath at the top of the stairs, there was no sound of shouts and cries, or even of following footsteps. She stepped out into the corridor. The English classrooms had been at the north end of the school, on the second floor. She went up to second at the first opportunity and started along the hall, looking for something, anything familiar.

The high school had apparently employed the same architects as Mercy General. It was a maze of locker-lined halls and connecting walkways, and they all looked exactly alike except for the posters on the walls. And even the posters had changed radically. No posters with cut-out hearts advertising the Valentine Dance or the Sophomore Class Bake Sale. They all announced rape hot lines or listed the warning signs of anorexia and suicide. 'Do you know someone at risk?' several of them asked.

Most of the classroom doors were shut. She leaned into the ones that were open, but didn't see anyone inside. The corridor made an abrupt ninety-degree turn, past a drunk-driving poster that proclaimed, 'You can save a life!,' went up four steps, and zigzagged again. Joanna had no idea where she was, and there was no one she could ask directions of. The hallways were deserted.

That's because they can't get in, Joanna thought, trying the locked class-room doors, peering in through the squares of glass in the doors. The hallway ended in a stairwell with a pale blue banner that asked, 'Need Help?' Joanna flipped a mental coin, went down, and found herself outside what must be the band room. There was a battered-looking upright piano inside, sur-rounded by a semicircle of chairs and music stands. A tuba stood propped against the wall.

'Excuse me,' Joanna said to the stout, balding man stacking sheet music on top of the piano. He wasn't anyone she knew, but he was the right age to have been here when Mr Briarley was, and he was cheerful-looking. 'I'm looking for Mr Briarley. He used to teach English here. I was wondering if you might know how I can get in touch with him, Mr –'

'Crenshaw. Do you have a visitor's pass?' he said, looking pointedly at the lapel of her cardigan.

'No,' Joanna said, and added hastily, 'You see, I had Mr Briarley for senior English. He was my favorite teacher, and I wanted to—'

'No one is allowed in the building without a visitor's pass,' Mr Crenshaw said, still looking sternly at her chest. 'It's school policy.'

'I only—' Joanna began, but he was already holding the door open.

'You have no business being here. You need to go back to the office and sign in. Go down this hall,' he said, pointing, 'and turn right, down the stairs, and then right again.' He ushered her out the door. 'I don't want to have to call Security.' He watched her all the way to the end of the hall, his arms crossed over his chest, making sure she turned right.

He was right about one thing. She had no business being here. It was a wild goose chase. Mr Briarley wasn't here, and it was becoming obvious why he had left. She could imagine what his response to visitors' passes and metal detectors would have been.

She turned right and went down the hall, but there weren't any stairs, just a hallway that led off at right angles in both directions. Mr Crenshaw had said right. She went right. It ended in an outside door marked 'Emergency Exit Only. Alarm Will Sound.' She went back and took the left-hand fork, wondering what time they locked the front doors.

The place was a labyrinth, the kind you could get lost in forever. She began to long for another Mr Crenshaw to order her back to the office. She would ask him to go with her to show her the way. But there was nobody in any of these classrooms. All the doors were locked up tight.

This hall was deadending, too. There was a glass-fronted room at the end of it. The assistant principal's office? No, his office had been midway down a hall. The library, she thought, recognizing it even though it had a sign saying 'Media Resource Center.' Banks of terminals stood where the study tables had been, and she couldn't see any books at all, but it was still the same library. And that meant she was at the south end of the building, as far from the English classrooms as it was possible to be.

But at least it was something familiar, and the doors were open. She took off her cardigan and draped it over her arm with a sleeve showing, so the librarian might conclude her visitor's badge was pinned to it, and went in.

The librarian was younger than Joanna, but at least her eyes didn't dart immediately to Joanna's chest. 'We're just closing up,' she said. 'Can I help you?'

'I doubt it,' Joanna said, thinking, I should just ask for directions back to the office. And a map. 'I'm looking for Mr Briarley. He used to teach senior English here.'

'Oh, yeah, Mr Briarley,' the librarian said. 'My husband went to school here. He had him. He *hated* him.'

'Do you know where I could find him?'

'Gosh, no,' she said. 'He wasn't here when I came. I think I remember somebody saying that he'd died.'

Died. That had somehow never occurred to her, which was ridiculous, considering she spent her whole life dealing with death. 'Are you sure?'

'Just a minute,' the librarian said, walking toward the stacks. 'Myra? Didn't you tell me Mr Briarley had died? The English teacher?'

A gray-haired woman emerged from the stacks, a pile of books pressed against her chest. 'Mr Briarley? No. He retired.'

'Do you know how I could get in touch with him?' Joanna asked. 'Is there anybody who might know his address?' but the old woman was already shaking her head.

'Everybody who would have known him's gone, too. The district offered an early-retirement bonus three years ago, and everybody who had over twenty years took it.'

'And that was when Mr Briarley retired? Three years ago?'

'No, longer than that. I don't know when.'

'Well, thank you,' Joanna said. She reached in her bag for her card and handed it to the woman. 'If you think of anybody who might know how I could find him, I can be reached at this number.'

'I doubt if there's anybody,' Myra said, pocketing the card without even looking at it.

Joanna went over to the door. The young librarian was already locking up. She turned the key to let Joanna out. 'Any luck?'

Joanna shook her head.

'He used to live over by DU. My husband pointed out his house to me one time.'

Joanna's pager began to beep. Not *now*, she thought, digging in her bag for it. She scrambled to turn it off. 'Your husband showed you where Mr Briarley's house was?'

She nodded, grinning. 'He and a bunch of his friends had egged it the night before graduation.'

'Do you remember the address?' Joanna said eagerly.

'No. I don't remember the name of the street either. It was next to the park with the observatory.'

'Do you remember what the house looked like?'

'Green,' the librarian said, squinting in thought. 'Or white with green trim, I don't remember. There was a weeping willow in the front yard. It was on the west side, I think.'

'*Thank* you,' Joanna said and went out the door. The librarian started to shut it behind her. 'Oh, wait,' she said, putting her hand on the doorjamb. 'One more quick question. Does an alarm go off if you open the outside doors?'

'No,' the librarian said, bewildered, and Joanna took off down the hall and went out the first door she came to. It was still snowing, and she was, of course, on the opposite side of the building from her car, but she didn't care. She knew where Mr Briarley lived. Over by DU. The park with the observatory. She didn't know the name of the street either, but she knew the park, and the observatory could be seen from Evans.

She drove to University and turned north. A house with green on it and a weeping willow in front. Unless they had painted the house. Or the willow had died. Or Mr Briarley had. 'I remember somebody saying he had died,' the librarian had said, and just because Myra hadn't told her that, didn't mean she hadn't heard it from somebody else. He had been middle-aged when Joanna had him, and more than ten years had gone by. And he might have retired early because he was ill. Or he could have gotten ill and died in the years since.

Or moved away, she thought, turning east onto Evans and looking down side streets for the park. This area had been upper middle class a few years ago, but now a lot of the houses had been turned into apartments. There were 'Apt. for Rent' signs in nearly every yard. For all she knew, the park wasn't even there anymore.

No, there it was, and the domed observatory still stood at the end of it, but the house on the corner had a 'To Let' sign and parked out in front was a rusted Cadillac.

She hadn't seen the park in time to turn. She drove on to the next street, turned south, and drove back, looking for a willow tree and wishing she'd asked the librarian whether the house had been on the end of the block or in the middle.

A green house with a willow tree. That meant it was probably a one-story brick with a crab apple out front. Or had belonged to some other teacher. 'My husband *hated* him!' the librarian had said, which didn't sound like Mr Briarley. He could be sarcastic, and his tests had been notoriously difficult, but nobody had hated him. Even Ricky Inman, whose smart mouth had gotten him in trouble at least twice per class period, had loved him. It was Mr Brown they'd hated.

Mr Brown, that was the name of the PE teacher, not Mr Black. No wonder the woman in the office had never heard of him. And that proved just how unreliable memory could be. The house the librarian's husband had pointed out to her might be across from a warehouse or a Starbucks and flanked by fir trees.

She turned onto Fillmore. Mr Brown. If the house didn't pan out, she could see if Mr Brown was still at the high school. He had said he'd never retire, that they'd have to carry him out feet first. He would definitely still be there.

And so was the house. It stood in the middle of the block, a three-story house with a wide porch. Joanna pulled the car over to the curb and stopped. The house was pale green, and that was definitely a weeping willow out front. It looked like a white fountain under its coating of snow.

But that doesn't mean Mr Briarley still lives here, she thought, getting out and going up the sidewalk. And that was obviously the case. There was a bicycle on the porch, and when she rang the bell, a girl in jeans and a thin flannel shirt over a tank top appeared in the door. She was barefoot and had short, fair hair like Maisie's.

Mr Briarley hadn't been married. 'Ms Austen is correct in her comment regarding people's assumptions about bachelors,' he had said when they read *Pride and Prejudice*, 'but let me assure you that many men, including myself, are *not* in want of a wife. They move your books so that you cannot find them.' And anyway, this girl was far too young to be his wife, or anyone's wife, for that matter. She looked about seventeen.

'Can I help you?' the girl said warily. She had a fragile prettiness, but she was too thin. Her collarbones showed sharply above the tank top.

'Does Mr Briarley live here?' Joanna asked, even though it was obvious he didn't.

'Yes,' the girl said.

'Oh … oh,' Joanna said, stammering in her surprise. 'I – I'm a former student of his.' She'd realized in the course of saying this that the girl had made no motion to open the door, that in fact she was holding on to it as if Joanna were a salesman and she intended to shut it on her at any minute.

'My name's Joanna Lander,' Joanna said. 'Mr Briarley was my high school English teacher. Could I talk to him for a few minutes?'

'I don't know …' the girl said uncertainly. 'Is it something I could help you with?'

'No,' Joanna said. 'He was my teacher for senior English, and I need to ask him a couple of questions about the class.'

'Questions?'

'Yes. Oh, not about the grade I got on my term paper or anything. It's too late for that,' she laughed, knowing she sounded like an idiot. 'I work at Mercy General Hospital, and—'

'Did my mother send you?'

'Your mother?' Joanna said blankly. 'No, as I said, I had Mr Briarley as a teacher. I went to the school to find out if he was still teaching, and one of the librarians told me where he lived. I do have the right house, don't I? The Mr Briarley I'm looking for taught English at Dry Creek High School?'

'Yes,' the girl said, 'but I'm afraid he can't—'

'Is there somebody at the door?' a man's voice called from the depths of the house.

'Yes, Uncle Pat,' the girl shouted back, and Joanna thought, This can't possibly be the right Mr Briarley. She couldn't imagine his being anyone's uncle, let alone Uncle Pat.

'Who is it?' the voice said, and this time she recognized the voice. It was Mr Briarley. Uncle Pat.

'Is it Kevin?' Mr Briarley called.

'No, Uncle Pat. It's not Kevin,' the girl said, and to Joanna, 'I'm afraid this isn't a good—'

'Tell him to come in,' he said, and Mr Briarley appeared in the door. He looked exactly the same, his hair still dark with a little gray at the temples, his eyebrows still arched sardonically. Joanna would have sworn he was wearing the exact same gray tweed vest.

The girl opened the door farther. 'Uncle Pat, this is—'

'Joanna Lander. I'm an ex-student of yours,' Joanna said, sticking out her hand. 'I don't expect you to remember me. I had you for senior English twelve years ago. Second period,' she added irrelevantly.

'I have an excellent memory,' he said. 'Kit, where are your manners? Don't make Ms Lander stand out in the cold. Open the door.'

Kit opened the door all the way, and Joanna stepped into the narrow hallway. 'Come into my library,' Mr Briarley said, and led the way into a room that looked exactly like Joanna would have expected. Three entire walls were covered with books from floor to ceiling, and on the fourth, between the windows, hung engravings of Westminster Abbey and the Globe Theater. There was a mahogany desk and two dark red leather chairs, both piled with books, and there were books stacked on the end tables, on the wide window-sill, on the floor.

Kit scurried to move the books off one of the chairs and motioned Joanna to sit down. She did, and he sat down opposite her. Kit stood next to his chair, still looking wary.

Now that Joanna had had a chance to look at Kit, she wondered if she were as young as she'd first thought. There were faint bluish shadows under her eyes, and unhappy lines around her mouth. Behind her, on one of the bookcases, was a picture of her carrying a stack of books and standing in front of University Hall at DU, and one of her and a young man. The Kevin Mr Briarley had thought was at the door? Kit looked twenty pounds healthier in both photos and considerably happier. What had happened since they were taken? Anorexia? Drugs? And was that why she was living here? Somehow she couldn't see Mr Briarley as a rehab counselor, but then again, she couldn't imagine him as being anyone's uncle, and there had been her odd, sharp reaction when Joanna had said she worked at Mercy General.

'I really appreciate this,' Joanna began. 'I would have called but I didn't have your phone number. I went over to the high school, hoping you still taught there, and they told me you'd retired. When did you retire?'

'Five years ago,' Kit volunteered.

He glared at her. 'Kit,' he said, 'don't just stand there. Offer our guest some—'

'Tea,' Kit said, too eagerly. 'Ms Lander, can I get you a cup of tea? Or coffee?'

'Oh, no, nothing,' Joanna said.

'Tea,' Mr Briarley said firmly. ' "And sometimes counsel take," ' he quoted, ' "and sometimes tea." '

'*The Rape of the Lock*,' Joanna said, delighted that she remembered. 'Alexander Pope. I remember your reading him out loud to us,' Joanna said. 'And "The Rime of the Ancient Mariner" by Coleridge. That was my favorite. "Water, water everywhere, and all the boards did shrink –" ' she said and paused, expecting him to say the next two lines.

'Coleridge,' he muttered, 'overrated Romantic,' and then turned abruptly to Kit and snapped, 'Where's my tea?'

It was the tone used to a servant. Joanna looked at him, and then at Kit, in surprise, but Kit merely said, 'I'll get it right away,' and started for the door.

'And I want the water boiled,' Mr Briarley snapped, 'not heated to luke-warm in that ridiculous—'

'Microwave,' Kit said. 'Yes, Uncle Pat.'

'And don't take all day, Kit. *Kit*,' he repeated contemptuously, turning to Joanna. 'What sort of a name is that? It's a label for a box full of first-aid bandages, not a name for a person.'

What was going on here? Joanna wondered. Had she walked in on an argument? She remembered Kit's reluctance to let her in. She glanced up at her, expecting her to look sullen or angry, but she looked wary, or worried, the way she had when she opened the door, her reactions all wrong for the situation.

'Go on, *Kit*,' Mr Briarley said, emphasizing the name nastily. 'I want to speak with my student.'

'I'll only be a minute,' Kit said with a last worried glance at Joanna and disappeared.

I hope that doesn't mean he'll turn on me now, Joanna thought, but when she turned back to Mr Briarley, he was smiling benignly at her. 'Now then,' he said. 'What can I do for you? You said you'd been to the high school –?'

'Yes, looking for you,' Joanna said.

'I don't teach there anymore,' he said in an odd, uncertain tone, as if he were trying to convince himself. ' "Neither fish nor fowl, neither out nor in." '

He must miss it, she thought. 'It looked so different, I hardly recognized it. I don't know if you remember the class I was in, Ricky Inman was in it, and Candy Simons—'

'Of course I remember,' he said, almost belligerently.

'Good, because I need to ask you about something you said in class about—'

'The tea will only be a minute,' Kit said, appearing in the doorway with a tray. She'd slid her feet into a pair of flip-flops. Joanna cleared a stack of books off the little table, and Kit set the tray down. 'I brought the cups and saucers, and the sugar,' she added unnecessarily.

Mr Briarley looked the tray over irritably. 'You didn't bring any—'

'Spoons,' Kit said, darting out to the kitchen. 'I forgot the napkins, too.'

'And the milk,' Mr Briarley called after her. 'How difficult is it to make a cup of tea? I was wrong,' he said to her as she came back, carrying a pitcher and the silverware. 'The name Kit suits you admirably. As in *mess* kit. Don't you agree?' he asked Joanna.

This was not the way Joanna remembered Mr Briarley as being at all. He had been sarcastic, yes, and sometimes even cutting, but never spiteful. He would never have humiliated Ricky Inman the way he had just done Kit.

'Here's the tea,' Kit said, coming in again with a teapot. 'You take milk and sugar, don't you, Uncle Pat?' she asked, already adding them. She handed the cup to him.

Joanna was afraid he would complain about the amount, or, after she'd taken a sip from the cup Kit handed her, the temperature. In spite of Mr Briarley's snapped orders, it was obvious Kit had used the microwave. The tea was barely lukewarm. But he seemed to have lost interest in the tea. And in Kit's shortcomings, and her name. He leaned back in his chair, the cup and saucer on his knee, and gazed pensively at the rows of books.

'It was so nice of you to come visit Uncle Pat,' Kit said, taking the half-drunk cup from her as if the visit were over.

'I didn't just come to visit,' Joanna said to Mr Briarley. 'I came to ask you about something you talked about in English class, something you taught—'

'I taught a good many things,' he said. 'The definition of an adverb, the number of metric feet in blank verse, the difference between assonance and alliteration –' Mr Briarley said. 'You will have to be more specific.'

Joanna smiled. 'This was something about the *Titanic*.'

'The *Titanic*?' Kit said sharply.

'Yes, I don't know if you read it out of a book or if it was in a lecture you gave,' Joanna said. 'I work at Mercy General Hospital—'

'Hospital?' he said. The teacup clattered on the saucer.

'Yes. I'm working on a project that involves memory, and –' She could tell by the look on his face that she was explaining herself badly. 'I'm working with a neurologist who—'

'I have an excellent memory,' Mr Briarley said, glaring at Kit as if holding her responsible for Joanna's being here.

'I'm sure it is,' Joanna said. 'In fact, that's what I'm counting on. I've forgotten something you taught us or read to us, and I'm hoping you remember what it was. It was about the *Titanic*. One of the parts I remember was about people standing out on deck after the collision. They were in their nightclothes, and they didn't know what had happened. They'd been awakened by the engines stopping.' She leaned forward, holding her cup and saucer. 'Do you remember talking about that? Or reading something to the class about it?'

'I *remember*,' he said contemptuously, 'that I scarcely had time to teach Dickens and Shakespeare, let alone a book about the *Titanic*.'

'I don't know that it was a book,' Joanna said. 'It might have been an essay, or a lesson—'

'A lesson? On what? The onomatopoeia of the iceberg scraping along the side? Or an exercise diagramming the passengers' drowning cries? What on earth does a shipwreck have to do with the teaching of English literature?'

'B-but you talked about it all the time in class,' Joanna stammered, 'about the band and Lorraine Allison and the *Californian*—'

'I realize, of course, that nowadays English classes teach everything but English – rope-skipping rhymes and Navajo tribal chants and deconstructionist drivel. Why not maritime disasters?'

'Uncle Pat,' Kit said, but he didn't even hear her.

'Perhaps the *Titanic* and Toni Morrison constitute what is taught nowadays, but in *my* classes I taught Wordsworth and Shakespeare.'

'Uncle Pat—'

'You asked me when I retired,' he said. 'I'll tell you when. When I could no longer bear to cast my pearls of English literature before my swinish students, when I could no longer tolerate their appalling grammar and their stupid questions.'

Joanna's cheeks flushed with anger. Was this how he'd been the last few years he'd taught? If so, she could see why they'd egged his house. She set her cup and saucer down and stood up. 'I'm sorry to have bothered you,' she said stiffly.

'I'll see you out,' Kit said, standing up, too, and looking distressed.

'No, thank you, I can find my own way out.' She started for the door.

'Perhaps if you had paid more attention in class, Ms Lander,' she heard him say as she went out the door, 'you would not have found it necessary to—'

She shut the door behind her, and walked blindly out to her car, some part of her mind that wasn't furious registering that it was late, that the afternoon light was fading. She opened the door of the car, fumbling for Vielle's keys.

'Wait!'

Joanna looked up. Kit was on the porch. She ran down the steps, the tails of her flannel shirt flapping behind her. 'Don't leave! Please!' She caught up to Joanna. 'Please. I wanted to explain.' She put her hand on the open car door. 'I'm so sorry about what happened just now. This was all my fault. I shouldn't have –' She stopped to catch her breath. 'I don't want you to think –'

'I had no right to come barging in without calling like that,' Joanna said. 'He had every right to be angry with me.'

Kit shook her head. 'It wasn't you Uncle Pat was angry at.'

'Well, he gave a pretty good imitation of it,' Joanna said. 'It's all right. I'm sure it's very irritating to have ex-students bothering him and asking him about—'

'You don't understand. He didn't know what you were talking about. He suffers from Alzheimer's disease. He's got severe memory loss. He—'

'Alzheimer's?' Joanna said blankly.

'Yes. He didn't know who you were. He thought you were a doctor – he's afraid he'll have to go into a nursing home. That's why he was so angry, because he thought I'd asked you to come examine him.'

'Alzheimer's,' Joanna said, trying to take this in. 'He has Alzheimer's disease?'

Kit nodded. 'The anger's part of the disease. He uses it to cover the fact that he can't remember. I didn't think that would happen. He was having a good day, and … I am so sorry.'

Kit's hesitation when Joanna had said she wanted to ask Mr Briarley a few questions, her finishing of his sentences, the alarm he'd shown at the mention of the word *hospital*. Alzheimer's. 'But he was able to quote *The Rape of the Lock*,' Joanna said, and remembered he hadn't continued with the quotation from 'The Rime of the Ancient Mariner.' 'How bad is it?'

'It varies,' Kit said. 'Sometimes he only has trouble remembering a few words, other days it's pretty bad.'

Pretty bad. That was hardly the word. Alzheimer's was a form of death by inches as the person lost his memory, his ability to speak, his control of bodily functions, descending into paranoia and darkness. She remembered one of her NDE subjects whose husband had suffered from Alzheimer's. In the middle of the subject's interview, he had stood up suddenly and said in a frightened voice, 'What's that stranger doing in my house? Who are you? What do you want?' and Joanna had started to try to explain, but he hadn't been talking to her. He'd been talking to his wife of forty years.

'And you live with him?' Joanna asked. 'You take care of him?'

She nodded. That was why he retired, Joanna thought suddenly, and not because the district offered an early-retirement bonus. Because he could no longer teach. She remembered him in class, reeling off pages and pages of *Macbeth* and 'The Rime of the Ancient Mariner' from memory. Dates and plots and poetic meters. Conjunctions, couplets, quotations. *The Briarley Anthology of English Literature*, Ricky Inman had called him. Unable to remember the word for 'spoons.'

'I didn't want you to think he's the way he was in there,' Kit said, shivering. She had to be freezing in that tank top and those flip-flops.

'You'd better get back inside,' Joanna said. 'You'll catch your death.'

'I'm okay,' she said, her teeth chattering. 'I wanted to tell you not to give up, that sometimes he remembers things out of the blue, and other times he'll answer a question you asked days, even weeks before, as if his mind had been searching for the memory all that time and finally found it. So he still might remember. You said it was something to do with the *Titanic*?'

'Yes,' Joanna said. 'He said something, or he read something out loud –'

Kit nodded. 'He is – was – a huge *Titanic* buff. If he remembers, or says anything about it, I'll call you. I can reach you at Mercy General, right?'

'I'll give you the number,' Joanna said. She fumbled in her bag for her pen and something to write on. 'I've got an answering machine. Just leave a message.' She scribbled her number and handed it to Kit, 'and I'll call you back – or is that a problem?'

'No,' Kit said. 'If he answers, just tell him you want to talk to me.' She told her the number.

'And I should ask for Kit?' Joanna asked. 'Or is your name Katherine?'

'It's Kit. Kit Gardiner. I was named after Kit Marlowe, Uncle Pat's favorite writer. He was the one who picked my name.'

And he's forgotten that, Joanna thought, appalled. 'I'll call you if he says anything about the *Titanic*,' Kit said, sticking the paper in her jeans pocket.

'I'd appreciate that.'

'Kit,' Mr Briarley said, appearing at the door, 'where have you put my *Tragical History of Dr Faustus*?' He came out onto the porch.

'I'll find it, Uncle Pat,' Kit called, and took off for the porch, hugging the flannel shirt to her thin form. 'I'll call you.'

'Thank you,' Joanna said.

'I've told you not to move my books,' Mr Briarley said. 'I can never find them.'

Kit ran back up the walk. Joanna got in the car, watching Kit run up onto the porch, watching her take Mr Briarley's arm and lead him inside. She put the car in gear and pulled away from the curb. She drove two blocks and then pulled the car over and turned it off and sat there with her hands on the steering wheel, staring blindly out at the fading winter light.

He didn't know what he'd said about the *Titanic*. The memory was gone, as lost as if he had died. And he *had* died, was dying, syllable by syllable, a memory at a time, Coleridge and sarcasm and the word for sugar. And the name of his own niece, whom he had christened.

It had to be torture, forgetting the poems and the people that had made up your life, and torture for Kit, too, watching it happen. And the fact that he couldn't remember a lecture about the *Titanic* was the least important aspect of the tragedy she'd just witnessed. But it wasn't because of Kit or Mr Briarley that she put her hands to her face, it wasn't their loss she sat in the cold car and mourned in the fading light. It was her own.

He couldn't tell her what he had said about the *Titanic*. He didn't know. He didn't remember. And it was important. It was the key.

22

'You go first. You have children waiting for you.'
– Last words of EDITH EVANS to
Mrs John Murray Brown

I should go back to the hospital, Joanna thought, I still haven't finished my account, but she continued to sit in the parked car, thinking about Mr Briarley. Kit had said he sometimes remembered things he hadn't been able to the day before. Maybe if she continued to ask him what it was he'd said ...

Don't be ridiculous, she thought. He has Alzheimer's. The neurotransmitters have shut down and the brain cells are deteriorating and dying, and his memory along with them, and if you ever wanted proof that there isn't an afterlife, all you have to do is look at a patient in the final stages of Alzheimer's, when he's not only forgotten his own niece and the word for sugar, but all words, and how to talk, how to eat, who he is. The soul not only doesn't survive death, with Alzheimer's, it doesn't even survive life. The Mr Briarley who knew what he'd said in class that day was dead. He could no more tell her what she needed to know than Greg Menotti.

And I do need to know, she thought. What he said in class is the reason I saw the *Titanic*. And the reason's important. It has something to do with the nature of the NDE.

What had he said? She could see him, perched on the edge of his desk, with the textbook in his hand. Somebody had said something, and he had shut the book with a snap, and said ... what? She squinted through the windshield at the darkening gray sky, trying to remember. Focusing on extraneous details sometimes triggered memories. What was on the blackboard? Where were you sitting?

The second row, Joanna thought, by the window, and it was foggy out. So foggy Mr Briarley had to ask Ricky Inman, who sat by the light switch, to turn on the overhead lights, and then Ricky said something, and he shut the book with a snap, and—

No, not foggy, overcast. But fog had something to do with it. Or had she confabulated that from Maisie's having seen fog? Or from some other day in class? And how many times had Mr Briarley perched on the edge of his desk and slapped a book shut for emphasis? It was gray, overcast. Or snowy, and Mr Briarley said something –

It was no use. She couldn't remember. All right, then, who could? Who else had been in that class? Not Ricky Inman. He'd never paid attention in the first place. Candy Simons? No, the only thing she'd paid attention to was her appearance. Joanna could remember her sitting in the desk in front of her, combing her blond tresses and putting on her makeup in the mirror she'd propped against her textbook.

Who else had been in that class? She'd lost her yearbook in the move to grad school. The high school library would have one, *if* she could get past security to get up there, but if this afternoon was any indication, even if she did find out who'd been in the class, the school wouldn't be willing to give out any information regarding their whereabouts, and she'd been very bad about keeping in touch. The only person from high school she ever saw was Kerri Jakes, and that only because she worked at Mercy General, in outpatient surgery, but Kerri had had English fifth period. She might remember who else had been in second period, though.

I'll call her when I get home, Joanna thought. There was no point in going back to the hospital now. It must be after five. She glanced at her watch. Good Lord, seven-thirty. She'd been sitting here for hours. Vielle would have a fit. She'd tell her she could have gotten hypothermia sitting there without a coat on in a freezing car –

In *her* freezing car. This is Vielle's car, Joanna thought, horrified. I promised to have it back hours ago. She started the car and pulled out into traffic. Vielle had finished her shift at seven and was probably trying to page her right now.

She fumbled to get her pager out of her pocket and switched it back on. She had forgotten about someone paging her while she was in the high school library, she had been so eager to hear the young librarian's directions. It had probably been Vielle, wanting to know where her car was. And what reason could she give her for being over three hours late? My English teacher can't remember something he said when I was in high school, and it's the end of the world?

Maybe there'll have been a five-car pileup, and Vielle will be too busy to ask me where I've been, Joanna thought, pulling into the hospital parking lot, but there were only the usual suspects in the ER waiting room: a Hispanic teenager holding an icebag to his eye, a homeless man muttering to himself, a five-year-old boy holding his stomach, his mother sitting next to him, holding an emesis basin and looking worried. At least Vielle wasn't standing by the door, tapping her foot in impatience. Maybe she'd caught a ride home with someone.

Joanna went over to the admitting desk and asked the nurse, 'Is Nurse Howard still here?'

She shook her head. 'She's at the meeting.'

'What meeting?' Joanna started to ask and then remembered. The meeting about ER safety. 'How long do you think it will last?'

'I don't know,' the admitting nurse said. 'The staff was pretty upset. After that last rogue incident—'

'Rogue incident?' Joanna said. 'I thought it was a gangbanger.'

'Gangbanger? No,' the nurse said, looking puzzled. 'Oh, you mean the nail gun thing. Then you didn't hear about this last incident.'

'No,' Joanna said.

'Well,' the nurse said, glancing at the Hispanic man and the mother and then leaning forward confidentially, 'this guy comes in, scared to death and talking about the Vietcong and Phnom Penh, and everybody thinks they've got a 'Nam junkie or maybe post-traumatic stress syndrome, and the next thing you know he's gotten a bloody syringe from someplace and is screaming that he's gonna take us all with him. This rogue stuff is bad news, a lot worse than angel dust.'

'When did this happen?'

'Tuesday. I would've thought Vielle would have told you.'

'So would I,' Joanna said grimly. Of course Vielle hadn't told her. She'd known exactly what Joanna would have said. Would say, as soon as she saw her.

'You borrowed her car, right?' the nurse was saying. 'Vielle said to just leave the keys here at the desk.'

I'll bet she did, Joanna thought, handing the keys over, but she was nonetheless grateful that she didn't have to face her tonight. She went up to the lab. The door was shut and locked. Good, she thought. I won't have to deal with Richard till tomorrow either.

The answering machine was blinking insistently. She hesitated and then hit 'play.' 'You have eighteen messages,' it said. She hit 'stop.' She pulled the minirecorder out of her pocket. She really should record the rest of her account tonight, before any more time elapsed, but she felt too emotionally drained. I'll do it in the morning, she thought, gathered up her coat, bag, and keys, and locked her office.

'Oh, good, you're still here,' Richard said, coming down the hall. 'I was afraid you'd gone home. I have something to show you.'

More scans, Joanna thought.

'I tried to page you earlier,' he said. 'Where were you?'

'I had to go see someone,' she said. 'You tried to page me?'

He nodded. 'I had some questions to ask you, and I wanted to let you know Maisie called.'

'Maisie?' Joanna said. She'd promised to go see her, and then her NDE and the fight and Mr Briarley had driven it out of her head. 'Is she all right?' she asked urgently.

'She sounded fine when I talked to her,' Richard said, 'at three. And four. And four-thirty. And six. Did you know the inhabitants of Pompeii were suffocated by ash and poisonous gases? With, I might add, very impressive sound effects.'

'I can imagine,' Joanna said, smiling. 'I need to go see her.' She glanced at her watch. Eight o'clock. It was late, but she'd better at least go say hi, or Maisie might insist on waiting up for her. 'I don't suppose she'd be willing to wait till tomorrow morning, would she?'

'I doubt it. She said she'd been trying to page you all afternoon.'

That's who paged me when I was in the library, Joanna thought, and felt a flash of guilt and fear, like the one she'd felt in the walkway with Barbara. Like the one the captain of the *Californian* must have felt when he realized the *Titanic* had gone down.

'She told me to tell you that you were supposed to come see her immediately,' Richard said, 'that she had something important to tell you.'

'Did she say what it was?'

'No. My guess would be that it has something to do with Mount Vesuvius. Did you know the archaeologists found the body of a dog? It had struggled all the way to the end of its chain before it died, trying to stay on top of the falling ash.'

'You'd think somebody would have unchained it instead of just leaving it there with a volcano erupting,' Joanna said.

'Maisie thought so, too,' he said. 'She was pretty incensed about it, also that it didn't have a dog tag.'

'A dog tag?' Joanna said, frowning.

'So we'd know what its name was,' he said. 'I told her its name was Fido, that all Roman dogs were named Fido.'

'Did she believe you?'

'Are you kidding? This is Maisie we're talking about.'

Joanna nodded. 'I'd better go at least check in with her so she won't think I've forgotten her.' She rubbed her forehead tiredly. She was getting a headache, probably because she hadn't had anything to eat for hours. I'll stop by for a minute, and then I'm going home, she thought.

'Before you go see Maisie, I want to show you something,' Richard said. He led the way up to the lab. 'You were right about the *Titanic*. It wasn't a random memory.'

'It wasn't?'

'No,' he said, stopping at the door and unlocking it. 'I've just been up conferring with Dr Jamison. After you left, I got to thinking about what you said about the NDEs not being varied enough to support a theory of randomness,' he opened the door and switched on the lights, 'and I decided I should take another look at the synapse firings in the frontal cortex.' He walked over to the console and switched it on. 'And when I did, I noticed something interesting.' He began typing in commands. 'Are you familiar with Dr Lambert Oswell's work?'

Joanna shook her head.

'He's done extensive research on long-term memory, mapping L+R patterns,' Richard said. 'When you ask a subject a straightforward question, like, "Who won the Battle of Midway?" you get a fairly simple L+R pattern.'

'Unless you're Mr Wojakowski,' Joanna said, 'in which case it reminds you of a story.'

Richard grinned. 'Or a whole novel. Anyway,' he said, typing, 'the pattern looks like this.' He called up a series of scans. 'See how the neural firings very quickly become localized? That's the mind zeroing in on the target, as Mr Wojakowski would say. Now, no two people would have the same pattern for "Who won the Battle of Midway?" because not only is there no particular storage location for a given memory, but the same memory may be stored in any number of categories: World War II, islands, Pacific Ocean, or words beginning with M, to name just a few. The pattern's not even always the same for a given question. Oswell asked identical questions at intervals of three months and got different L+R patterns each time. *But*,' he said, 'he was able to come up with mathematical formulas for the patterns that make it possible for us to tell if a pattern is an L+R or something else.'

He typed some more, and the right-hand scan disappeared and was replaced by another one. 'The pattern's different, and so is the formula, for a question like "What is the *Yorktown*?"'

Or, 'What was it Mr Briarley said that day in class?' Joanna thought, watching the neural pathways wink on and off, red to green, yellow to blue, blossoming like fireworks and then fading out. He had been sitting on the edge of his desk, talking about what? *Macbeth*? Subjunctive clauses? 'The Rime of the Ancient Mariner'?

'If I ask a question like "What is the *Yorktown*?" – assuming you're not Mr Wojakowski – the L+R pattern involves the selection and discarding of possibilities and is much more complex. It's also broader, since it's searching through a whole variety of memories for the information. Is it a place? A battle? The name of a movie? A racehorse? The pattern has a much higher degree of apparent randomness.'

Joanna squinted at the screen, trying to follow what he was saying, her headache getting worse by the minute. 'And that's what the pattern in the scans resembles?'

'No,' he said. 'However, Dr Jamison reminded me that Dr Oswell also did a series of experiments on image interpretation. He showed his subjects an abstract—'

'Do you have any food?' Joanna interrupted.

Richard turned and looked at her.

'I'm sorry,' she said, 'but I didn't get any dinner. Or lunch, now that I think of it, and I thought maybe you—'

'Sure.' He was already reaching in his pockets. 'Let's see, I've got a Mars bar,' he said, examining the items as he pulled them out, '… some cashews … Listen, we could go get some real dinner if you'd rather. I don't suppose the cafeteria's open at this hour?'

'The cafeteria's never open.'

'We could run to Taco Pierre's.'

'No, I've still got to go see Maisie,' she said, taking the Mars bar. 'This is fine. You were saying?'

'Oh, yeah, well, in a separate series of experiments, Oswell showed subjects a scene in which objects and shapes were kept intentionally vague and abstract.'

'Like a Rorschach,' Joanna said.

'Like a Rorschach,' Richard said. 'The subjects were asked, "What is this a picture of?" Here's an orange.' He handed it to her. 'In most cases the pattern was similar to that of the open-ended L+R with increased activity in the memory cortex, and the subjects described the pattern as being … Skittles … and a package of cheese crackers with peanut butter. Nothing to drink, though, so maybe peanut butter's a bad idea. I could get you a Coke from the vending machine –'

'I'm fine,' Joanna said, peeling the orange. 'They described the pattern as being?'

'Just what you'd expect,' Richard said. 'A big white oblong object on a blue background with a round blob of pink off to the right. However, in some instances, the subjects answered, "It's Antarctica. There's the ice and the sky. And there's the sun setting." In those cases, the subject had searched through long-term memory to find a scenario that explained not only the separate images, but a metaphor for all the shapes and colors the subject was seeing.'

A metaphor. Something about a metaphor. That's what triggered the feeling at Dish Night, Joanna thought, Vielle's saying something about a metaphor. No, Vielle had called optioning Richard a simile, and she had corrected her, had told her a simile was a comparison using 'like' or 'as' while a metaphor was a direct comparison. Mr Briarley taught me that, she thought, and tried to remember exactly what he had said. Something about fog.

'… with an abstract scene, the scans showed an entirely different pattern,' Richard said, 'one that was much more scattered and chaotic –'

Fog. Ricky Inman, she thought, asking Mr Briarley about a poem. 'I don't get it,' he'd said, rocking back in his chair. 'How can fog come on little cat feet?'

And Mr Briarley, picking up an eraser as if he were going to throw it and sweeping it across the blackboard in wide strokes, searching for a stub of chalk, printing the words in short strokes. She could hear the tap of chalk against slate as he printed the words. 'Metaphor. [Tap.] A direct or implied comparison. [Tap.] "This is a nightmare." [Tap.] As opposed to simile. [Tap.] "Silent as death." [Tap.] Does that help, Mr Inman?'

And Ricky, rocking so far back he threatened to overbalance, saying, 'I still don't get it. Fog doesn't have feet.'

'The mathematical formula for the frontal-cortical activity is identical,' Richard said. 'Your mind was clearly searching through long-term memory for a unifying image that would explain all the sensations you were experiencing – the sound, the tunnel, the light, figures in white. And, as you said, it all fit. The *Titanic* was that unifying image.'

'And that's why I saw it,' Joanna said, 'because it was the best match for the stimuli out of all the images in my long-term memory.'

'Yes,' Richard said. 'The pattern—'

'What about Mercy General? Or Pompeii?'

'Pompeii?' he said blankly.

'Mercy General fits all the stimuli – long dark walkways, figures in white, buzzing code alarms – and so does Pompeii. The people wore white togas, the sky was pitch-black from ashfall,' she said, ticking the reasons off on her fingers, 'it had long covered colonnades like tunnels, the volcano's erupting made a loud, hard-to-describe sound, and Maisie talked to me about it not two hours before I went under.'

'There may be more than one suitable image in long-term, and the one that happens to be accessed first is chosen,' Richard said. 'That wouldn't necessarily be the most recent memory. Remember, acetylcholine levels are elevated, which increases the brain's ability to access memories and see associations. Or the brain may only be able to access memories in certain areas. Some areas may be blocked or shut down.'

Like Mr Briarley's memory, Joanna thought. 'That isn't why I saw the *Titanic*,' she said. 'I know where the memory came from.'

'You do?' Richard said warily.

He's still afraid I'm going to turn into Bridey Murphy at any moment, she thought. 'Yes. It came from my high school English teacher, Mr Briarley.'

'Your high school – when did you figure this out?'

'This afternoon.' She told him about recording her account and remembering that the steward had said Mr Briarley's name. 'And I remembered he'd talked about the *Titanic* in class.'

Richard looked delighted. 'That fits right in with the mind's attempting to unify everything into a single scenario, including the source of the memory. Your mind did an L+R, searching for a unifying image that would explain the outline of figures in a light and an auditory-cortex stimulus, and—'

She shook her head. 'That isn't why I saw it. There's something else, something to do with something Mr Briarley said in class.'

'Which was?'

'I don't know,' she had to admit. 'I can't remember. But I know—'

'– that it means something,' Richard finished. He was looking at her with that maddening superior expression.

Joanna glared at him. 'You think this is the temporal lobe again, but I told you I recognized the passage, and I did, and I told you I knew the memory wasn't from the movie, and it wasn't, and now—'

'Now you know the *Titanic* wasn't chosen for a unifying image because it fit the stimuli,' Richard said.

'Exactly. I was right the other times, and—'

'And when you discovered what the passage was, the feeling of almost knowing should have disappeared, but it didn't, did it? It transferred to the source of the memory and now to Mr Briarley's words. And if you're able to remember his words, the feeling will transfer to another object.'

Was that true? Joanna wondered. If Kit called right now and said, 'I asked Uncle Pat again, and he said what he said was ...' and told her, would she transfer the feeling to something else?

'How the feeling of significance factors into the choice of scenario is one of the things I want to explore,' Richard said. 'Also, does the scenario remain the same, or does it change depending on the stimuli, or the initial stimulus?'

'The initial stimulus? I thought you said—'

'That the unifying memory fit all the stimuli? I did, but the initial stimulus may be what determines the choice of one suitable image over another. That would explain why religious images are so prevalent. If the initial stimulus was a floating feeling, there would be very few suitable memories, except for angels.'

'Or Peter Pan.'

Richard ignored that. 'You didn't have an out-of-body experience. Your initial stimulus was auditory.'

So I saw a ship that sank nearly a hundred years ago, Joanna thought.

'If the initial stimulus changes, does the unifying image change? That's one of the things I want to explore the next time you go under.'

'Go under?' Joanna said. He wanted to send her under again. To the *Titanic*.

'Yes, I'd like to schedule you as soon as possible.' He called up the schedule. 'Mrs Troudtheim's scheduled for one. We could do yours at three, or would you rather switch with Mrs Troudtheim and do yours at one?'

One, Joanna thought. It's already gone down by three.

'Joanna?' Richard said. 'Which one will work better for you? Or is morning better? Joanna?'

'One,' she said. 'I might need to go see Maisie in the morning if I can't get in to see her tonight.'

'Which you'd better go do,' Richard said, glancing at the clock, which said eight-thirty. 'Okay, I'll call Mrs Troudtheim and reschedule. I hope she doesn't have a dental appointment. And if you have any time – tomorrow, not tonight – I'd like you to go through your interviews and see if there's a correlation between initial stimulus and subsequent scenario.'

There isn't, she thought, going down to Maisie's. That isn't what the connection is. It's something else. But the only way to prove that was to get hard evidence, which meant finding out what Mr Briarley had said.

But how? Even if Mr Briarley didn't have Alzheimer's, he probably wouldn't have remembered a stray remark he'd made in class over ten years ago, and his students were even less likely to. If she could find them. If she could even remember who they were. I need to call Kerri, she thought again. But first she needed to go see Maisie, who she hoped wasn't asleep.

She wasn't. She was lying back against her phalanx of pillows, looking bored. Her mother sat in a chair next to the bed, reading aloud from a yellow-bound book: ' *"Oh, don't be such a gloomy-gus, Uncle Hiram," Dolly said. "Things will work out all right in the end. You just have to have faith,"* ' Mrs Nellis read. ' *"You're right, Dolly," Uncle Hiram said, "even if you are a little slip of a girl. I shouldn't give up. Where there's a will—"* '

Maisie looked up. 'I knew you'd come,' she said. She turned to her mother. 'I told you she would.' She turned back to Joanna, her cheeks pink with excitement. 'I told her you promised you'd come.'

'You're right, I did promise, and I'm sorry I'm so late,' Joanna said. 'Something came up …'

'I *told* you something happened,' Maisie said to her mother, 'or she'd have been here. You said she probably forgot.'

I did forget, Joanna thought, and even worse, shut my pager off and was out of touch for hours, hours during which something could have happened to you.

'I told Maisie you were very busy,' Mrs Nellis said, 'and that you would come and see her when you could. It was so nice of you to drop by with all the other things you have to do.'

And dropping by was clearly all it could be with Maisie's mother in the room. She said, 'I was wondering if it would be all right if I came back tomorrow morning, Maisie?'

'Yes,' Maisie said promptly. 'If you stay a really long time.'

'Maisie!' Mrs Nellis said, shocked. 'Dr Lander is *very* busy. She has a great many patients to see. She can't—'

'I promise I'll come and stay as long as you want,' Joanna said.

'Good,' Maisie said, and added meaningfully, ''cause I have lots of stuff to tell you about.'

'She certainly does,' Mrs Nellis said. 'Dr Murrow's got her on a new anti-arrhythmia drug, and she's doing *much* better. She's completely stabilized, and her lungs are sounding better, too. Which reminds me, sweetie pie, you haven't done your breathing exercises this evening.' She laid the book down on the bed and went over to the counter next to the sink to get the plastic inhalation tube.

'I'll be here first thing tomorrow morning,' Joanna said, looking at the book. Written in curly green letters was the title, *Legends and Lessons*.

Legends and Lessons. Her English textbook had had a title like that, *Something and Something*. She had a sudden image of Mr Briarley sitting on the corner of his desk, holding it up and reading from it. She could see the title in gold letters. Something and Something. *Poems and Pleasures* or *Adventures and Allegories* or *Catastrophes and Calamities*. No, that was Maisie's disaster book.

'When tomorrow morning?' Maisie was asking.

'Ten o'clock,' Joanna said. Something about a trip. *Journeys and Jottings. Tales and Travels*.

'That's not first thing in the morning,' Maisie said.

'Sugarplum, Dr Lander is very, very busy –'

V. It began with a V. Verses. No, not Verses, but something like that. Vases. Voices.

'Dr Murrow says he wants you to get the ball above eighty, that's this line, five times,' Mrs Nellis was saying, indicating a blue line on the plastic cylinder, 'and I *know* you can do it.'

Maisie obediently put the mouthpiece in her mouth. 'I'll see you tomorrow, kiddo,' Joanna said and hurried out of the room and down to her car. V. What else began with a V? Victorians. Vignettes. *Voices and Vignettes*. No, that didn't sound right either, but it definitely began with a V.

She got in her car and pulled out of the parking lot. The windshield immediately fogged up. She switched on the heater and slid the bar to 'defrost,' peering through the foggy window at the traffic. Vantage. Mount Vesuvius. Visions. *Voices and Visions*. No, that sounded like one of Mr Mandrake's books.

She stopped at a stoplight, waiting for it to turn green. What color had the book been? Red? No, blue. Blue with gold letters. Or purple. Purple and gold. You're confabulating, she thought. It wasn't purple. It was blue, with—

The car behind her honked, and she looked up, startled. The light had turned green. She stepped on the gas, stalled the car, and fumbled to get it into gear. The car behind her honked again. You're not only confabulating, you aren't paying attention to what you're doing, she thought, turning the key in the ignition. The car finally started, though not before the car behind her had roared around her, dangerously close, the driver shaking his fist. And not, Joanna hoped, a loaded gun.

Stay alert to your surroundings, she thought, and tried to concentrate on her driving, but the picture of Mr Briarley, sitting on the corner of his desk, kept intruding. He was holding the book up. It was blue, with gold letters, and there was a picture of a ship on the cover, its bow cutting sharply through the water, throwing up spray. She could see it clearly. And how did she know that wasn't a confabulation? Or maybe it was the other way around, and she'd confabulated the *Titanic* from the ship on the cover of her textbook.

But it wasn't that kind of ship. It was a sailing ship, with billowing white sails. Mr Briarley had shut the book with a clap, as if he'd finished reading something aloud. And if it was from a story or a poem, it wouldn't matter that Mr Briarley had no memory of it. She could simply find it in the book. If she could find the book.

They wouldn't still be teaching from it. It had been out of date when she'd had it, and, as Mr Briarley said, they taught a whole new curriculum now, but Mr Briarley might have a teacher's edition. From the looks of those overflowing bookshelves, he hadn't ever thrown a book away. But he wouldn't remember where it was.

Kit might, though, or might be able to look through the bookshelves and find it, if Joanna told her what it looked like. I know it had a sailing ship on a blue background, she thought, and it was called ... She squinted, trying to see the gilt letters, and found herself sitting at another green light, staring at the 7-Eleven across the street. 'Marlboros,' the sign read. '$19.58 a carton.'

Luckily, there was no one behind her this time, or coming across, because she managed to stall the car again halfway through the intersection. This is a good way to get yourself killed, she told herself, starting it and pulling through the intersection, and then you won't have to wonder what Greg Menotti was trying to tell you and why you saw the *Titanic*. You'll be able to find out firsthand.

She forced herself to focus on the road, the lights, the traffic, the rest of the way home. She turned onto her street, past the local Burger King. 'X-Men Action Figures,' the marquee read. 'Collect All 58.' Could he have been trying to tell her a page number? She could see Mr Briarley, picking up the blue book, opening it. 'All right, class, open your textbooks to page fifty-eight.'

Stop it, Joanna told herself, pulling into her parking space and getting out of the car. Richard's right. You are turning into Bridey Murphy. Or Mr Mandrake. You need to go upstairs, take a bath, watch the news, and let your right temporal lobe cool down, because that's what this obsession with *Tales and Travels*, or whatever it's called, is, a symptom of temporal-lobe stimulation.

She opened the door and flicked on the lights. And if you did call and get her to find *Verses and Victorians*, it wouldn't solve anything. Because even if there were a story about the *Titanic*'s engines stopping on page fifty-eight, the feeling of significance would just transfer itself to something else.

Besides, it's too late to call. You'd upset Mr Briarley, and Kit has enough to deal with already. And the person you need to call is Vielle. You need to thank her for letting you borrow her car and apologize for taking so long to bring it back and ask her what she wants you to rent for Dish Night on Friday. And not *The Sixth Sense*.

Joanna picked up the phone and punched in the number. 'Hello, Kit, this is Joanna Lander,' she said when Kit answered. 'Does your uncle still have the textbooks he used when he taught?'

23

'Nothing in the world can endure forever.'
— Words found scratched on a wall at Pompeii

Joanna called Kerri Jakes and then went straight to see Maisie as soon as she got to the hospital the next morning. She'd told her ten, but she didn't want to get sidetracked and forget again, and she also wanted to get there before Maisie's mother did.

And Kit said she'd call as soon as she found the textbook, Joanna thought, crossing the walkway and taking the stairs up to Peds, and I might have to go get it. Or go see someone who had English second period. She'd had to leave a message for Kerri – mornings were outpatient surgery's busiest times – and she hadn't wanted to play telephone tag, so she'd asked her about second period and the book, hoping she remembered the title. She hoped that when she got back from seeing Maisie, Kerri or Kit would have called. Although I don't know how Kit could be expected to find it with the pathetic description I gave her, Joanna thought.

But Kit had acted like her calling was the most normal thing in the world (and maybe it was, considering what she must be living with) and had immediately asked what year Joanna had been a senior, how big the book was, how thick. 'And you think the title is *Something and Something*,' she'd said. 'Beginning with a V.'

'I think so,' Joanna had said. 'I'm sorry I'm giving you so little to go on.'

'Are you kidding?' Kit had said. 'I'm an expert at figuring out things people can't remember. This may take a while. Uncle Pat's got a *lot* of books. They used to be organized, but—'

'You're sure you don't mind doing this?' Joanna had asked.

'I'm delighted I can help,' Kit had said and actually sounded like she was.

'Is that Kevin on the phone?' Mr Briarley's voice said in the background. 'Tell him I'm delighted. And congratulations.'

'I'll call you tomorrow,' Kit said.

Joanna wasn't sure it would be that soon, considering how many books were in that house and how many of them were blue. If it was blue. This morning she wasn't so sure. It seemed like the book Candy 'Rapunzel' Simons had propped her hair-combing mirror against had been red. You're confabulating, she told herself sternly, and ran up the stairs to Peds. The breakfast cart was still in the hall, and a skinny black orderly was loading empty trays onto it. Joanna waved at him and went in to see Maisie.

Her breakfast tray of scrambled eggs and toast and a glass of juice was still on the bed table pulled across her lap. 'Hi, kiddo,' Joanna said, coming in. 'What's up?'

'I'm eating breakfast,' Maisie said, which was an exaggeration. Two mouse-like bites had been nibbled out of the piece of toast she was holding, and the eggs and juice looked untouched.

'I see,' Joanna said, pulling a chair over to the bed and sitting down. 'So, tell me all about Pompeii.'

'Well,' Maisie said, putting down her toast, 'the people tried to run away from the volcano, and some of them almost made it. There was this one mother who had two little girls and a baby that made it almost all the way to the gate. It's in my big blue book.'

Joanna obediently went over to the closet and got *Catastrophes and Calamities* out of the Barbie duffel bag. She handed it to Maisie, who pushed the bed table away and opened the book. 'Here it is,' she said, turning to a page with a garish painting of a volcano spewing red and black on one page and a black-and-white photo on the other. Maisie put her finger on the photo and pushed it over toward Joanna.

It wasn't a black-and-white photo. It only looked that way because it was a group of plaster casts that looked as though they were made out of the gray ash themselves. They lay where they had fallen, the mother still clutching the baby in her arms, the two girls still clutching her hem.

'This is the servant,' Maisie said, pointing to a curled-up figure lying near them. 'He was trying to help them get out.' She took the book back. 'Lots of little kids got trampled,' she said, flipping through the pages. 'There was this one –' She looked up sharply, clapped the book shut, and shoved it under the covers. She was just pulling the bed table toward her when Barbara came in.

'Good morning, ladies.' Barbara came over to look disapprovingly at Maisie's uneaten breakfast. 'Didn't like the eggs, huh? Would you like some cereal?'

'I'm not very hungry,' Maisie said.

'You need to eat something,' Barbara said. 'How about some oatmeal?'

Maisie made a face. 'I don't like oatmeal. Can't I eat it later? I have to tell Dr Lander something important.'

'Which can wait till after you finish breakfast,' Joanna said, immediately standing up and starting for the door.

'No, wait!' Maisie yelped. 'I'll eat it.' She picked up the triangle of toast and took another mouselike nibble. 'I can eat while I'm talking to Dr Lander, can't I?'

'*If* you eat,' Barbara said firmly. She turned to Joanna. 'Half the eggs, a whole piece of toast, and all the juice.'

Joanna nodded. 'Got it.'

'I'll be back to check,' Barbara said. 'And no hiding things in your napkin.' She went out.

Maisie immediately pushed the bed table away and leaned over to open the drawer of the nightstand. 'Whoa,' Joanna protested. 'You heard what Barbara said.'

'I *know*,' Maisie said, 'but I have to get something.' She reached in the drawer and pulled out a folded piece of lined tablet paper like the one she'd written the *Hindenburg* crewman's name on and handed it to Joanna.

'What's this?' Joanna asked.

'My NDE,' Maisie said. 'I wrote the rest of it down after you left so I wouldn't forget anything.'

Joanna unfolded the sheet. 'The fog was gray-colored,' Maisie had written in her laboring round cursive, 'and dark, like at night or if somebody turns out the lights. I was in this long narrow place with real tall walls.'

'I probably forgot some stuff,' Maisie said.

'Eat,' Joanna said. She pushed the bed table over in front of her and continued to read. Maisie picked up her fork and poked listlessly at her eggs.

'If you're not going to eat, I guess I'll have to come back another time,' Joanna said.

Maisie immediately scooped up a forkful of eggs and popped it in her mouth. Joanna watched until she'd chewed, swallowed, and taken a sip of her apple juice, and then sat down on the chair and read through the rest of the NDE. 'I don't know if there was a ceiling. It kind of felt like the place I was in was outside, but I don't know for sure. It kind of felt like inside and outside at the same time.'

'The walls were tall?' Joanna asked.

Maisie nodded. 'They went up really high on both sides.' She raised both arms to demonstrate. 'I thought some more about the coming-back part. It was different from the other time. That time it wasn't as fast. I wrote that down.'

Joanna nodded. 'Can I take this paper with me?'

'Sure,' Maisie said, and Joanna folded it up and stuck it in her pocket. 'But you can't go yet, I have lots more stuff to tell you.'

'Then eat,' Joanna said, pointing at the eggs.

Maisie picked up her fork. 'They're cold.'

'Whose fault is that?'

'Did you know they found eggs when they dug up Pompeii?' Maisie said. 'They got covered up by the ash and turned into stone.'

'Four bites,' Joanna said, her arms folded. '*And* the juice.'

'Okay,' Maisie said and plodded through four minuscule bites, chewing laboriously.

'And the juice.'

'I am. I have to open the straw first.'

The Queen of Stallers, Joanna thought. She leaned back in the chair and watched Maisie peel the paper, stick the straw in the juice, sip daintily, waiting her out. Finally, Maisie finished, slurping to prove it was empty. 'You know the dog that was chained up, and they don't know its name 'cause it didn't have a dog tag?' she asked. 'Well, there was a little girl like that.'

'In Pompeii?'

'*No*,' Maisie said indignantly. 'In the Hartford circus fire. She was nine years old. Anyway, that's what they think, nobody knows, 'cause they don't know who she was. She died from the smoke. She wasn't burned at all, and they put her picture in the paper and on the radio and everything. But nobody ever came to get her.'

'Ever?' Joanna said. Someone would have had to identify her eventually. A child couldn't just disappear without anyone noticing, but Maisie was shaking her blond head.

'Hunh-unh. They had this big room where they put all the bodies, and the mothers and fathers came and identified them, but nobody ever did her. And they didn't know her name, so they had to give her a number.'

Joanna was suddenly afraid to ask. Not fifty-eight, she thought. Don't tell me it's fifty-eight.

'1565,' Maisie said, ''cause that was the number of her body. She should have had a name tag or put her name in her clothes or something, like Mr Astor.'

'Who?' Joanna said, sitting up straight.

'John Jacob Astor. He was on the *Titanic*. His face got all smashed in when one of the smokestack things fell on him, so they couldn't tell who he was, but he had his initials inside of his shirt' – she reached around to the back of her hospital gown and grasped the neck of it to demonstrate – 'J. J. A., so they were able to figure it out.'

'You know about the *Titanic*, Maisie?' Joanna asked.

'Of *course*,' she said. 'It's like the best disaster that ever happened. *Lots* of children died.'

'I never heard you talk about it.'

'That's 'cause I read about it before, when I was in the other hospital. I wanted to see the movie, but my mother wouldn't let me watch the video because it had …' she leaned forward and dropped her voice to a whisper, 'S-E-X in it. But this girl Ashley who had her appendix out said it didn't, just naked people. She said it was really cool, especially when the ship went up in the air and everything started falling down, all the dishes and furniture and pianos and stuff, with this big enormous crash. Did you know the *Titanic* had *five* pianos?'

'Maisie—' Joanna said, sorry she had brought this up.

'I know *all* about it,' Maisie said, oblivious. 'They had all these dogs. A Pekingese and an Airedale and a Pomeranian and this really cute little French bulldog, and their owners would take them for walks on the deck, only most of the time they had to be kept in this kennel down in the hold, except for this little tiny dog Frou-Frou, he got to stay in the cabin –'

'Maisie—' Joanna said, but Maisie didn't even hear her.

'– and after it hit the iceberg, this passenger, I don't know his name, went down to the kennel and –'

'Maisie—'

'– let out all the dogs,' Maisie finished. 'They all still drowned, though.'

'You can't tell me about the *Titanic*,' Joanna said. 'I'm doing some research—'

'Do you want me to help you?' Maisie said eagerly. 'Ms Sutterly could bring me some books, and I know lots of stuff already. It didn't really hit the iceberg, it just sort of scraped along the side. It wasn't even a very bad cut, but the watertight compartments—'

She had to put a stop to this. 'Dr Wright told me they found the body of a dog in Pompeii,' she said.

'Yeah,' Maisie said. She told her about the chain and it trying to climb on top of the ash. 'Dr Wright told me all the Pompeii dogs were named Fido, but I don't think so. How would they know to come when their master called if they all had the same name?'

'I think Dr Wright was kidding,' Joanna said. 'Did you know Fido means "faithful" in Latin?'

'No,' Maisie said, appeased. 'That would have been a good name for this one dog they found.' She pulled the book out from under the covers and began flipping through it till she found another of the photos. 'It was trying to save this little girl.' She showed the picture to Joanna. The plaster casts of the long-muzzled dog and the little girl lay huddled against a wall, their limbs tangled together. 'But he couldn't. They both died.'

She took the book back. 'It didn't have any dog tags either,' she said and then suddenly lunged for her book again.

Joanna looked toward the door. Maisie raised the blankets to stick the book under them, and then stopped and laid it back on the bed as the black orderly came in. 'Hi, Eugene,' she said, picking up her tray and handing it to him.

'Hi, Eugene,' Joanna said. 'You have to leave the tray. Maisie's supposed to finish her eggs.'

'He's supposed to take all the trays back at the same time,' Maisie said.

'No, that's all right,' Eugene said, setting the tray back down. 'I can come back for it later.' He winked at Joanna.

'Thanks,' Joanna said. Eugene went out. Joanna stood up. 'I've got to go, too.'

'You can't. You promised you'd stay as long as I wanted. I have to show you this one picture.'

She showed her at least twenty pictures before she finally let Joanna go – excavated ruins, reconstructed Roman baths, a gold bracelet, a silver mirror, paintings of people in white togas running terrified from a red-and-gold-spewing volcano, of people cowering in ash-darkened colonnades. And if I don't see Vesuvius this time, Joanna thought, going back up to her office, then Richard's theory's got to be wrong.

She unlocked her office, went in, and checked her answering machine. The light was blinking almost hysterically. 'You have twenty-three messages,' it said when she pressed the button. And all from Mr Mandrake and none from Kit or Kerri Jakes, she thought, hitting 'play.'

Not all. Three were from Maisie, one from Richard, and four from Vielle, all trying to find her yesterday afternoon. 'Hi, you remember you've got my car, don't you?' Vielle's last one began. 'I'm leaving now. When you get back, just leave my keys with the admitting nurse. I think I'll rent *Gone in Sixty Seconds* or *Grand Theft Auto* for our next Dish Night.'

There was a pause, and then Vielle gasped, 'Oh, my God, you won't believe who just walked in. Do you remember that cute police officer who came in to tell us about the nail gunner, the one who looks just like Denzel Washington? Well, he's here, and it looks like he's going to be at the meeting. Officer Right, here I come!'

Joanna grinned and hit 'delete' and 'next message.'

'Hi, this is Kerri Jakes. Do I remember the name of our high school English textbook? Are you kidding? I barely remember high school. What do you need to know for? Don't tell me you didn't really graduate and they're making you take senior English over. Anyway, no, I don't remember the name of the book, and the only one I remember being in second period was Ricky Inman because I had this awful crush on him, and I used to hang around Mr Briarley's door before third period, waiting for him to come out.'

Kerri was right. She didn't remember high school. Joanna hit 'next message.' 'This is Elspeth Haighton. I'm trying to reach Dr Lander. The session we set up won't work. I have a Junior League meeting that day. Please call me and reschedule.'

Fat chance, Joanna thought, but she dialed Mrs Haighton's number. It was busy. How can it be busy? Joanna thought, she's never home, and went back to listening to messages.

There were three in a row from Mr Mandrake, all beginning, 'You never answer your pages, Dr Lander,' and wanting to talk to her about some astonishing new details Mrs Davenport had remembered, 'which are so vivid and authentic that they cannot fail to convince you that what is being experienced during the NDE is, in fact, real.'

But it's not, Joanna thought, even though he's right about the details being vivid and authentic. She could see the lace insets on the young woman's nightgown, the frightened expression on her face, the filigreed light sconces in the passage. But it wasn't the actual *Titanic*, in spite of the reality of the vision. It was something else.

'... not only Mrs Davenport's uncle Alvin, but the spirits of Julius Caesar and Joan of Arc, waiting to welcome her to the Other Side,' Mr Mandrake was saying.

Joanna erased him, and went on through the rest of the messages, jotting them down and promptly forgetting them, except the one from Mr Wojakowski, who had ostensibly called to tell her the hearing research was going to last eight weeks and after that he'd be available for the project again, but really to tell her the story of the *Yorktown*'s sinking and the men lining their shoes up along the deck all over again. That one she didn't jot down. She deleted it and hit 'next message,' wondering how long before she got to the end of the messages.

'This is Kit Gardiner. I'm trying to reach Joanna Lander,' Kit's voice said. 'I think I've found the book.'

In the background, Mr Briarley's voice said, 'Joanna? Bride,' and then he must have moved away from the phone because Joanna only caught part of what he said. '– wasn't ... the key ...'

'It's blue with gold lettering, and it's called *Voyages and Voices*,' Kit continued. 'Does that ring a bell?'

It didn't, but the title did begin with a V, like Joanna had remembered.

'I'm pretty sure it's the right one. It has a ship on the cover. Uncle Pat,' Kit dropped her voice, 'usually takes a nap from eleven to one, so that would be a good time.'

' "The bride hath paced into the hall," ' Mr Briarley's voice said. ' "Red as a rose is she." Have you seen my grade book, Kit?'

'I'd better go,' Kit said. ''Bye.' The machine beeped the end of the message.

Joanna glanced at her watch. Eleven-thirty. She grabbed up her bag, keys, and coat and went up to the lab. Richard was at the console, his chin in his hand, staring at scans. 'I have something I need to check on,' she said. 'I'll be back by one.'

He nodded without turning around, and she went out and down to the elevator. 'Wait!' Richard called, sprinting after her, and she thought, watching him come toward her, He really is cute. 'I wanted to talk to you before Tish gets here. I don't think we should talk about the *Titanic* in front of her. If you see the *Titanic*, which I don't think you will,' he said. 'I'm increasing the dosage, which should change the temporal-lobe stimuli, particularly the initial stimulus, and I think it will produce a totally different L+R pattern.'

'But just in case I do see it, you want me to record my account in my office.'

'Or on the other side of the lab. I know you need to record it as soon as possible after the NDE,' he said and looked sheepish. 'It's not that I think Tish would go tell Mr Mandrake, but –'

'Loose lips sink ships,' Joanna said.

'In this case, literally,' Richard said, grinning. 'You said you'll be back by one?'

Joanna nodded.

'Great,' he said, starting back to the lab. 'Did you have a chance to look at those multiple NDEs?'

'Not yet,' she said, pushing the 'down' button. 'I'll start them as soon as I get back. Oh, and Mrs Haighton called. She can't come Thursday.'

'I knew it was too good to be true,' he said. 'See you at one.' He nodded, waving good-bye to her over his shoulder. The elevator opened. Joanna stepped in. And found herself face to face with Vielle. She was in her scrubs and surgical cap and was wearing sterile booties over her shoes.

This is what you get for not taking the back way, Joanna thought. 'Vielle, what are you doing up here?' she said. 'You haven't had another incident, have you?'

'Incident?'

'Yes, you know, crazy druggie on rogue trying to stab people. Like the last incident, which you neglected to tell me about. Vielle, you have got to transfer out of—'

'I know, I know,' Vielle said, waving her hand dismissively. 'You'll have to lecture me some other time. I'm on break. I have to get back, and I came up here to tell you three things. Are you going down?' she asked, looking at Joanna's coat and bag.

She obviously was. 'Yes,' she said and pushed 'G.' 'What three things?'

'One,' Vielle said, 'tomorrow night will work for Dish Night if it will work for you and Richard. Two, Dr Jamison was down in the ER the other day – she's working with one of the interns on some project – and you don't have anything to worry about. She's sixty if she's a day. And three, I found out what you asked me about.'

'About Dr Jamison?' Joanna said, confused.

'No, about the movie. You asked me if there was a scene in it with people out on deck after the engines stopped? There's not. There's a scene where people are sticking their heads out of their cabins and the stewards are telling them to go up to the Boat Deck and there's another scene where Kate Winslet's mother and her creepy fiancé are standing around in lifejackets next to the Grand Staircase waiting for their lifeboat to be called.'

'But I thought you said your meeting went till eleven-thirty,' Joanna said, confused. Vielle surely hadn't gone out after the meeting and rented the video.

'It did,' Vielle said. 'I would've called you last night and told you, but it was so late. There's a scene out on deck where passengers are playing with pieces of ice, and one where they're letting the steam off, and it's so deafening nobody can hear anything, but Heidi says she doesn't remember anything with people just standing around not knowing what happened.'

'Heidi?' Joanna said sharply.

'Yeah, during one of the potty breaks at the meeting I saw Heidi Schlagel. She's an LPN, works graveyard, but she used to work the three-to-eleven, and she has the world's biggest crush on Leonardo DiCaprio. She used to drive us all crazy talking about *Titanic*. She saw it about fifty times. I figured if anybody knew the answer to your question, it'd be Heidi, and she did,' Vielle said, smiling, and obviously pleased at having been so clever.

'I asked *you* to rent the video,' Joanna said, glancing anxiously at the floor indicator, hoping no one got on in the middle of this.

'I know,' Vielle said, looking surprised, 'but I knew I wouldn't be able to watch it till tonight, and you sounded like you needed it right away.'

If Mr Mandrake got hold of this – 'I told you not to tell anyone.'

Vielle frowned. 'I didn't tell her what I wanted it for. I didn't even mention your name. She thinks I'm the one who wanted to know.'

'But what if she saw you talking to me?'

'What?' Vielle said, amazement in her voice. 'You sound completely paranoid. I told you, Heidi works graveyard, and even if she did hear us, she wouldn't think anything about it. She assumes *everyone* spends their time discussing *Titanic*. When I told her I had a question about it, I had to listen to a whole spiel on how wonderful *Leo*,' she said the word in a schoolgirl squeal, 'was in *The Beach*, and how the critics don't appreciate him, before I even got to ask it. And after I got my answer, she spent the rest of the break telling me how the Grand Staircase was an *exact* replica of the one on the *Titanic*, clock and skylight and all. Trust me, I don't think she even remembered I'd asked a question, she was so glad to find somebody who'd let her talk about it.'

I hope so, Joanna thought, but how many people had heard them talking? Gossip General –

'I don't understand why a bet between you and Richard has to be a state secret anyway, but if you're worried about it, I can ask Heidi not to say anything about—'

'No!' Joanna said. If Heidi wasn't suspicious, this would definitely make her suspicious, and if she already was, it would make it worse. 'No, that's okay, it doesn't matter,' she said, trying to sound casual. 'I'm just worried that now every time you see her you'll be subjected to how wonderful Leo is.' She tried to smile. 'Did you make any headway with Officer Right at the meeting?'

'I didn't get a chance to,' Vielle said. 'I'd been kind of hoping you wouldn't bring my car back from wherever you went, and I could talk him into giving me a ride home. Speaking of which, where did you take off to in such a hurry?'

'So my bringing your car back ruined your plan?' Joanna asked. 'If I'd known –'

'It wasn't your fault. He left before the break. Where did you go?' The elevator opened on the ground floor. 'And where are you going now?'

'I've got an errand to run,' Joanna said. And the last thing she wanted to do was walk all the way to the ER with Vielle, on her way to the parking lot, and give her a chance to grill her. 'I just remembered, I wanted second,' Joanna said, pressing 'two.' 'Tomorrow's fine for Dish Night for me,' she said, wishing the door would close. 'I'll ask Richard if he can come.'

Vielle stopped the closing door with her hand. 'Are you all right? Yesterday you—'

'I'm fine,' Joanna said. 'Just awfully busy. There've been so many NDEs –'

'Is that where you went in such a hurry yesterday? To interview an NDEer?' Vielle asked, and the door alarm began, blessedly, to buzz.

'Is it your turn or mine to rent the movies?' Joanna shouted over the sound.

'Yours,' Vielle said and reluctantly let go of the door. 'You still haven't—'

The door began to close. 'I'll try to get something with Denzel Washington in it. What was the one about the Civil War called?'

'*Glory.*'

'*Glory,*' Joanna said and watched the door shut in Vielle's worried face.

24

'Wait till I have finished my problem.'
       – Last words of ARCHIMEDES, to the Roman
       soldier who ordered him to follow him

The streets were nearly as empty of traffic as they had been the night before. Joanna made it over to Mr Briarley's in less than fifteen minutes. Now, if only the book Kit had found was it.

It wasn't. She knew as soon as Kit, barefoot and wearing a white spaghetti-strap top and jeans, led her into the library, explaining in a hushed voice, 'Uncle Pat just lay down,' and showed her the book.

It should have been the right one. It had a blue cover, gold lettering, a graceful clipper ship in full sail, its prow cutting sharply through blue-green waves, everything Joanna had described. But it wasn't the book.

'It wasn't a clipper ship.' Joanna squinted at the cover. 'It was one of those ships like Sir Francis Drake had, a caravel,' she said, the word suddenly coming to her from somewhere deep in long-term memory, 'and it was smaller. I'm sorry.' She shook her head apologetically. 'It's exactly what I told you, I know.'

'If it's not the right one, it's not the right one,' Kit said philosophically. She waved her hand around at the rows of books lining the library. 'I have only just begun to look. The book was smaller?' she asked, pointing at *Voyages and Voices*.

'No, the book's the right size, but I remember the picture as smaller.'

'What about the color? Was it light or dark blue?'

'Dark, I think,' Joanna said. 'I'm not sure. I'm sorry I'm being so vague. I'd know it if I saw it.'

Kit nodded, putting the book back on the shelf. 'I called the high school this morning on the off-chance they were still using the same book in their English classes, but I couldn't get them to give me any information. You'd have thought I was trying to steal highly classified documents or something.'

Joanna nodded, remembering the woman in the office. 'I didn't mean for you to go to all this trouble.'

'Oh, I don't mind,' Kit said cheerfully. 'It gives me something to think about besides – it's kind of fun,' she amended, 'a sort of treasure hunt.'

'Well, I really appreciate it,' Joanna said, moving toward the door. 'And if I remember anything more specific, I'll call you.'

'Oh, you're not leaving yet, are you?' Kit said, and sounded just like Maisie. 'I was hoping you'd have time to stay for a cup of tea.'

Joanna glanced at her watch. 'I have to be back by one,' she said doubtfully.

'It'll only take a minute to heat up the water,' Kit said, leading the way down the hall past the stairs to the kitchen. 'I made cookies this – oh, no!'

'What is it?' Joanna said, trying to see past Kit into the kitchen.

'I thought he was asleep,' Kit said as if she hadn't heard Joanna and hurried back past her through the hall and up the stairs. 'Excuse me a minute. I'll be right back.'

Joanna looked into the kitchen, afraid of what she might see. An empty plate with some crumbs sat on the table. Next to it was a skillet and two saucepans, and, on the red-and-white tiled floor, more pans and lids and muffin tins, cookie sheets, pie tins, and a big roasting pan.

Kit pattered back down the stairs. 'I'm sorry,' she said, her voice matter-of-fact now. She went into the kitchen and began to pick up the pans. 'He *is* asleep now. He must have come down while we were in the other room.' She stacked two small saucepans inside a larger one and stuck them down in a cupboard next to the sink. 'Taking things out of drawers and cupboards is a common behavior with Alzheimer's,' she said, putting a skillet away.

And a nightmare for the people who live with them, Joanna thought. 'Can I help?' she asked.

'No, I've got it,' Kit said, taking the lid off a Dutch oven and pulling out two books. She reached up and set them on the table. 'Sit down. I'll start the tea.'

She got two mugs out of an upper cupboard, filled them with water, and stuck them in the microwave, punching in the code. 'The problem is he's sleeping less and less,' she said, setting sugar and teabags on the table. 'He used to sleep a couple of hours during the day,' she got out two spoons, 'but now it's hardly any, even at night. Now, the question is,' she said, looking around the room, her hands on her hips, 'where did he put the cookies?' She looked in the refrigerator, the freezer, the wastebasket.

'Would he have eaten them?' Joanna asked, thinking, I can't believe we're talking about Mr Briarley, who knew all about Dylan Thomas and Henry the Eighth's wives and Restoration drama, like this.

'He doesn't usually take food,' Kit said. 'He has almost no appetite.' She opened drawers one after the other, and then stood looking speculatively around the kitchen. 'There's usually a logic in what he does and says, even though sometimes it's hard to figure out the connection.'

She walked swiftly over to the oven and opened it. 'Ah, here we are,' she said, pulling out the top rack, on which sat the cookies, arranged in neat rows on the wire rack. She grabbed the cookie plate and began putting the cookies on it. 'Luckily, it wasn't the dishwasher,' she said, setting the plate on the table. The microwave dinged, and Kit took the mugs out and handed one to Joanna and sat down opposite her.

'How long has Mr Bri— your uncle been like this?' Joanna asked.

'Taking things out of the cupboards, or the Alzheimer's? The cupboards, only a couple of months. The Alzheimer's was diagnosed five years ago, but I started noticing things two years before that.'

That surprised Joanna. She'd thought from what Kit said before that she'd moved in with her uncle when they'd found out he had Alzheimer's, but apparently she'd been living with him before that. While she went to school? she wondered, remembering the photo of Kit in front of University Hall. DU was only a few blocks from here.

'The memory loss probably started several years before that,' Kit was saying, dipping her teabag. 'It takes a while for symptoms to develop, and Alzheimer's patients learn to cover really well.'

Joanna thought about Mr Briarley muttering, 'Coleridge. Overrated Romantic,' the day before. She wondered if he even remembered who Coleridge was.

'I don't know how much you know about the disease,' Kit said, offering Joanna a cookie. 'The first symptoms are little things, forgetting appointments, misplacing things – Uncle Pat kept losing his grade book and a couple of times he forgot a faculty meeting – the kind of things you put down to age or stress.' She put sugar in her tea and stirred it. 'It was funny, you mentioning the *Titanic* yesterday, because that was how I realized there was something really wrong. I went to see the movie, which, having listened to Uncle Pat talk about the disaster for years, I *hated*.'

'I did, too,' Joanna said.

'Oh, good, then you know what I mean. Well, anyway, I came home and told Uncle Pat how the movie made everyone look like cowards, even Lightoller and Molly Brown, and how they'd gotten all kinds of facts wrong – like Murdoch shooting a passenger! – and he was furious, just like I knew he would be. He said he was going to write a stinging letter to James Cameron in the morning, and when I went up to bed, he had all his *Titanic* books out, looking things up so he could quote them exactly.'

She took a sip of tea. 'The next morning I asked him if he'd written the letter yet,' she said, and all the despair of Amelia Tanaka and Greg Menotti was in her voice. 'He didn't have any memory of the letter or our conversation, not even of my having gone to the movie. He didn't even know who Lightoller was.'

And yesterday I came blundering in, Joanna thought, not only talking about the *Titanic*, but asking Mr Briarley if he remembered what he'd said in class. 'Kit, I am so sorry,' she said. 'If I'd known—'

'Oh, no, it's okay. I just wanted you to know that was why I acted so peculiar yesterday, asking you if my mother had sent you and everything. My mother and I have a difference of opinion regarding Uncle Pat's care. She's always sending people over to try to talk me into putting him into a care facility. She thinks taking care of him is too much for me.'

I can see why she thinks that, Joanna thought, looking at Kit's painfully thin collarbones, her shadowed eyes. She had said Mr Briarley wasn't sleeping. Joanna would bet she wasn't either.

'I know Uncle Pat will have to be institutionalized someday,' Kit said, 'but I want him to be able to stay here as long as he can. He was very kind to me, and – anyway, when you said you worked at Mercy General, I assumed – what *do* you do at Mercy General?' she asked curiously.

'I'm a cognitive psychologist,' Joanna said and wondered if she should let it go at that, but Kit reminded her of Maisie in more ways than one, and Maisie hated not being told the truth. 'I'm working on a research project involving near-death experiences,' she said. 'You know, the tunnel-and-light phenomenon?'

Kit nodded. 'I read *The Light at the End of the Tunnel*. My cousin made me read it after –' She stopped, her cheeks red with anger or embarrassment.

And what could be worse than discovering your uncle had Alzheimer's? Joanna thought. Having your cousin comfort you by inflicting Maurice Mandrake on you.

'You don't work with Mr Mandrake, do you?' Kit asked challengingly.

'*No,*' Joanna said.

'Good. I thought it was a horrible book. "Don't worry, the dead aren't really dead, and they aren't really gone. They can still send messages to you from the Other Side."'

'I know. I work with Dr Wright. He's a neurologist. We're trying to figure out what near-death experiences are and why the dying brain experiences them.'

'The dying brain?' Kit said. 'Does that mean everyone has them? I thought they were something only a few people had.'

'No, about sixty percent of revived patients report having a near-death experience, and those are concentrated in certain kinds of deaths – heart attacks, hemorrhaging, trauma.'

'You mean like car accidents?' Kit asked.

'Yes, and stabbings, industrial accidents, shootings. Of course there's no way to tell how many people who aren't revived have them.'

'But they're pleasant, for the ones who do have them, I mean?' Kit said. 'They're not frightening?'

Joanna thought of the young woman, standing out on deck, asking the steward, 'What's happened?' her voice filled with fear. And Amelia, saying, 'Oh, no, oh, no, oh, no.'

'*Are* they frightening?' Kit asked. 'Uncle Pat has hallucinations sometimes. He sees people standing at the foot of his bed or in the door.'

In the door. Joanna would have to tell Richard that. Alzheimer's was caused by a malfunctioning of neurochemicals. Maybe there was a connection.

'… and sometimes the things he's saying seem to indicate he's reliving past events,' Kit was saying.

L+R, Joanna thought. 'Most people who've had near-death experiences report feeling warm and safe and loved,' she said reassuringly. 'Dr Wright's found evidence of elevated endorphin levels, which supports that.'

'Good,' Kit said and then shook her head. 'Uncle Pat's are almost always upsetting or frightening things. It's like he can't forget them and can't remember them at the same time, and he goes over and over them. It's like he's trying to make sense of them, even though his memory of them is gone.' She put her hands over her face for a moment. 'The books say not to confront him or contradict him, but not to go along with the hallucination either, which is hard.'

'It sounds like it's all hard,' Joanna said.

Kit smiled wryly. 'I thought a sudden death was the worst thing that could possibly happen, and now it's obvious it's not.' She sat up. 'I'm sorry, you don't want to hear all this. I didn't mean to go on like that. It's just that I hardly ever get to talk to anybody about this, and when I do, I –' She made a face. 'I obviously need to get out more.'

'You should come to Dish Night tomorrow night,' Joanna said impulsively.

'Dish Night?'

'Yes. It's not an organized event or anything, just a casual get-together. Dr Wright comes, and my friend Vielle – you'd love her. We get together and watch movies on video and eat and talk. Mostly talk. We use it as a safety valve, and it sounds like you could use one, too. Do you like movies?'

'Yes. I haven't seen one in a long time. Uncle Pat confuses what's happening on the screen with reality. That's a common occurrence with Alzheimer's patients, too. It would be wonderful to watch a movie, but …' She shook her head. 'Thanks, but I'm afraid I can't.'

'Is it because you don't have anyone to stay with him?'

'Oh, no, my mother comes over when I have to go to the grocery store, but –' She was looking at the pan cupboard, and Joanna could guess what she was thinking. If Mr Briarley took all the pans out again, her mother would use it as ammunition for putting Mr Briarley in a care facility.

'Have you ever used Eldercare?' Joanna asked. 'Mercy General has a program where the caregivers come to your home. They're very good. I know one of the people who works with the program. I'd be glad to call her.'

'But if Dish Night is tomorrow night?'

'They have a twelve-hour emergency program,' Joanna said. 'They know the people who call them are usually at the end of their rope. They have care-givers specifically trained in Alzheimer's,' she said, but Kit was already shaking her head.

'They sound wonderful, but I'm always afraid something will happen while I'm gone, and if I call home to check, that can upset him,' she said. 'So thank you for inviting me, but I'd better not.'

'You should get a pager,' Joanna said, pulling hers out of her pocket to show her. 'Or a cell phone. That way they could reach you wherever you are.' Unless she left it in the car while she ran into the grocery store, like Greg Menotti's girlfriend.

'A cell phone,' Kit said. 'I hadn't thought of that. I'll have to see … you think they could come by tomorrow night?'

Joanna nodded. 'If you want to come, I could pick you up.'

'I don't know … can I call you tomorrow and let you know?'

'Sure,' Joanna said.

'Or sooner, if I find the book. If Uncle Pat stays asleep for a while, I'll go down to the basement and start in on those books –'

'Oh, you made cookies,' Mr Briarley said, coming into the kitchen.

'I thought you were lying down, Uncle Pat,' Kit said.

'I was, but I heard voices, and I thought Kevin was here. Oh, hello,' he said to Joanna.

'Hello, Mr Briarley,' she said.

'Would you like a cup of tea?' Kit asked, reaching for a china cup and saucer.

'No, I'm rather tired. I think I'll go lie down. It was nice meeting you,' he said to Joanna, and started down the hall.

'Be right back,' Kit said and darted after him.

Joanna could hear them starting up the stairs, and then Mr Briarley's voice saying, 'They know it when they see it. It is the very mirror image.'

I'd better think about getting back, Joanna thought, and looked at her watch. It said twelve-thirty. 'Oh, my gosh,' she said and started putting on her coat. She went out to the foot of the stairs. 'Kit,' she called up the narrow wooden stairs, her hand on the railing. 'I've got to go. I'll call you tomorrow about Dish Night.'

Kit appeared at the head of the stairs. 'Okay,' she said. 'I'll call you if I find the book.'

Joanna opened the front door. As she let herself out, she heard Mr Briarley say, 'Aren't you going to go say good-bye to Kevin?'

Was there a Kevin, Joanna wondered, driving back to the hospital as fast as the traffic would allow, or was he one of the hallucinations Kit had talked about? She remembered the picture of Kit and a blond young man in the library. Had he been unwilling or unable to cope with the day-in, day-out nightmare of caring for an Alzheimer's patient, or had Kit simply given him up, as she had apparently given up movies, her education, her freedom?

And how did she end up as his caregiver? Joanna wondered, gunning her car through a yellow light. Her mother would seem to be the logical choice to take care of him, and she was obviously worried about what it was doing to Kit. 'As well she should be,' Joanna muttered.

She roared into the hospital parking lot. There was some mystery here, but, whatever it was, she didn't have time to solve it now. She needed to get upstairs. It was ten to one. She didn't even have time to take the back route. She'd have to take the main elevator, and please, don't let me run into Mr Mandrake.

Her luck was in. She made it up to sixth without seeing a soul she knew and skidded into the lab, already taking off her coat. Richard was at the console, Tish over by the examining table, hooking a bag of saline to the IV stand. '... found this new place for Happy Hour,' Joanna heard her say as she came in.

'Sorry I'm late,' Joanna said. 'I found out something interesting. Mr Briarley' – Richard shot her a warning glance and nodded in Tish's direction, but Joanna ignored him – 'has Alzheimer's, and his niece says he has hallucinations where he sees people around his bed or standing in the door.'

'Interesting,' Richard said. 'Alzheimer's is caused by a lack of acetylcholine, though, not elevated levels. Did she say if he had any of the other NDE elements?'

'She said he seemed to be reliving past events.'

'The life review,' Richard said. 'I wonder—'

'Can we get going?' Tish asked. 'I have an eye appointment.'

Dentist appointment, Joanna corrected, going into the dressing room. She put on her hospital gown, went over to the examining table, got up on it, and lay down. Tish began placing the foam cushions under her arms and legs. 'Do you like Tommy Lee Jones?' she said, looking at Richard. 'He's got a new movie out I'm dying to see.' She moved to Joanna's other side and began attaching the electrodes.

Richard came over. 'You ready?' he asked Joanna. She nodded, hindered by the electrodes. 'I've adjusted the dosage, and I'm going to increase the time spent in non-REM sleep,' he said. 'We shall see what we shall see.'

Which was what? Joanna wondered, watching Tish start the IV. 'I loved him in *Volcano*,' Tish said, taping it in place. 'Did you see it?'

No, but at this rate, I might, Joanna thought. She could see the wall clock from where she lay, even though Richard had moved it. It said five to one. We need to take it down altogether, she thought.

'I loved that scene in the subway tunnel,' Tish said, covering Joanna's eyes with the black mask and beginning to attach the electrodes. 'Where they could see this light at the end, and they didn't know what it was, and then they realized it was molten lava, and it was heading right for them. And the part where the lava caught the guy and—'

At that point Tish mercifully put the headphones on her, and Joanna lay, waiting for Richard to come over and lift the earphone and ask her if she was ready.

Ready for what? she wondered. A fall of ash? Tommy Lee Jones? Vesuvius erupted at one o'clock, she thought, and was in the tunnel.

The passage was silent, as if a loud sound had just stopped. The light shone, blinding gold, from the open door. If it's Vesuvius, just put your hand over your mouth and nose and run back into the tunnel, she told herself, starting toward the door. But it wasn't Vesuvius, or an oncoming train, or the walkway down on third, and she had known it from the moment she came through. It was the *Titanic*, and through the open door she could see the woman in the white nightgown talking earnestly to the woman with the white gloves.

'I'm sure there's nothing to worry about, Edith,' the woman with the white gloves said.

'Go and find Mr Briarley,' the bearded man said to the steward. 'He'll be able to tell us.'

'Yes, sir,' the steward said.

'We'll be in our cabin.'

'Yes, sir,' the steward said and started into the light.

Joanna tried to see where he was going, but the glare was too bright. She moved forward, trying to see, and then stopped. I need to cross the threshold, she thought, and felt the sense of dread again.

'A voice said, "You are not allowed on this side,"' Ms Grant had said, and Mr Olivetti, 'I knew if I went through that gate, I could never come back.' What if, once out on the deck, she couldn't return? Or what if Vielle was right, and the NDE was some kind of death process that crossing the threshold set in motion?

It's not, Joanna thought. They're both wrong, and so is Mr Mandrake. The NDE isn't a gateway to the Other Side. It's something else, and I have to find out what it is. But when she came up even with the door, she halted again and looked down at the floor. Light spilled onto it, and the line between the waxed wood of the passageway and the unvarnished boards of the deck was sharply marked.

Joanna put her hand to her chest, as if to quiet her heart. '"To die will be an awfully big adventure,"' she said and stepped across the threshold and out onto the deck.

25

'Now we can cross the shifting sands.'

— Last words of L. FRANK BAUM

'Mr Briarley will be able to explain things,' the bearded man said to the women. None of them had turned to look at Joanna when she came out onto the deck. She wondered if they could see her.

'In the meantime,' the bearded man said, 'you ladies should go back inside where it's warmer.'

The young woman nodded, clutching her coat to her. 'It's so cold.'

The steward had disappeared into the light. Joanna started through the group of people, trying to see where he had gone, past the young woman and a stout white-haired man in tweeds.

'What do they say is the trouble?' the stout man asked a taller man in a black overcoat as Joanna edged by him.

'What are you doing here?' the bearded man said loudly.

Joanna jumped and looked back at him, startled, but he wasn't talking to her. He was addressing a young man in a grubby-looking sweater and a soft cap.

'You shouldn't be here,' the bearded man said sternly. 'This area is restricted.'

'Sorry,' the young man said, looking around nervously. 'I heard a noise and came over to investigate.'

So did I, Joanna thought, and walked toward the light. As she got closer, she saw it was radiating from a lamp on the white-painted metal wall. One of the deck lights, Joanna thought, and it must still be very early. Toward the end, the lights had begun to dim and glow red because the engineers couldn't keep the dynamos going.

And then they went out, Joanna thought. But this light was reassuringly bright, so bright she couldn't see anything through its radiance, even when she shielded her eyes. She would have to walk past it to be able to see anything.

She paused again, the way she had at the threshold, her hand to her chest, and then walked down the deck in the direction the steward had gone and into the light, through it, beyond it.

She had been wrong. It wasn't outside, in spite of the biting cold. The deck was glassed in, with long, wide, white-framed windows that stretched the length of the deck. Joanna went over to them and looked out, but the glass refleeted the light so she couldn't see anything but the reflection of the white wall and the empty deck. Joanna turned and looked back at the door to the passage. It yawned blackly.

The passengers must have gone back inside. The bearded man had told the steward, 'We'll be in our cabin,' and the women had complained about being cold. They must have gone back to their staterooms, Joanna thought, and started after them, back toward the passage.

Toward the tunnel. Don't, she thought. You don't want to go back yet, not till you've found out why you're seeing the *Titanic*, not till you've found out what the connection is. Don't even look at it. Remember what happened to Orpheus, she thought, and turned forcibly away from the door.

'But what if I can't find it when I'm ready to go back?' she said out loud, and her voice echoed hollowly in the enclosed deck. She wished she'd brought some breadcrumbs with her, or a ball of Mrs Troudtheim's yarn. You'll just have to keep track of where you go, she thought, and not stay too long. You have a little over two and a half hours. Or four to six minutes.

But this wasn't a real NDE. This was a simulation, and she only had till Richard stopped giving her dithetamine, which might be any minute. So you need to get going.

She started down the deck. The steward had disappeared, and the long deck was empty except for deck chairs and low, white-painted lockers with the word *Lifejackets* stenciled on the lid. At intervals, shuffleboard courts were painted on the deck.

Far down the deck, she caught a glimpse of the steward's white jacket as he emerged from a door and started on down the deck. His white coat flickered to brightness as he passed one of the deck lights and then disappeared into the shadows between, like a light blinking on and off.

Joanna walked faster, trying to catch up with him, but he was already opening another door. She hurried down the deck to where he'd gone in, searching the inside wall for a door, but the wall was blank, though it seemed to Joanna she had already walked past the spot where he had disappeared.

No, here it was, a white metal door. Joanna reached for it, wondering what would happen. Would she be able to open it, or would her hand go through it like a ghost's?

Neither. Her hand closed firmly on the handle and pulled, but it was locked. She tried again, with both hands, and then gave up and started down the deck again. There was another door a few yards past the first one, and another farther on, but they were both locked when Joanna tried them.

The deck began to bend inward, following the line of the ship, and become narrower. Farther down, directly under a deck light, was a door. She hurried down to it and pulled on the handle.

It gave under her hand, and she started in and then stopped and looked back down the deck the way she had come. She couldn't see the passage because of the curve of the deck, and she hesitated, wondering if she should go back and check to make sure the door was still open, and then opened the door and went in.

She was in some sort of lobby. There were rugs on the polished wooden floor and high-backed benches against the walls. In the center was a straight wooden staircase with carved banisters. Joanna went over to it and leaned over the polished railing. She could see the stairs going down to the next deck and the one below that, receding into darkness.

She looked up, trying to see to the top of the stairs, but it was dark up there, too, and there was no sign of the steward. She hesitated, her hand on the railing, trying to decide which way to go. Not down, she thought, not on the *Titanic*, and started up the stairs.

At the top was another flight of stairs, narrower, steeper, and another lobby, this one much more elegant. The rugs on the floor were Persian, and paintings hung on the wallpapered walls. Off to the right was a pair of doors inset with beveled glass. Through the glass, Joanna could see a large rose-carpeted room filled with tables set for dinner.

The First-Class Dining Saloon, Joanna thought and tried to open the double doors, but they were locked. She couldn't see anyone inside and no waiters moving among the white-linen-draped tables. Each table had flowers and a small rose-silk shaded lamp on it, and the silver and crystal and china glittered pinkly in its glow.

There were rose lamps on the walls, too, which were paneled in some pale, fawn-colored wood, and a lamp on the top of the grand piano. The piano was made of the same pale wood, only highly polished. Its angled top glittered goldenly in the light from the crystal chandelier overhead. A gilt birdcage stood in front of it, though from this distance Joanna couldn't make out whether there was a bird in it or not. Had there been birds on the *Titanic*? Maisie hadn't mentioned any.

A narrow wooden stairway led up past the windows of the dining saloon, and there was another flight above that. Joanna climbed up. The stairs ended at a door with a porthole in it. It must lead to the deck outside, she thought, but when she looked through the porthole, she couldn't see anything but darkness. She opened the door.

She still couldn't see anything. The sudden coldness told her she was out-side, but she couldn't feel any wind on her face, not even a breeze. It was utterly still that night, she thought. Mr Briarley had talked about that in class, about how the survivors had all commented how still the water had been, without any waves at all.

She stared into the darkness, her hand on the door, waiting for her eyes to adjust. Maybe it's like the passage, she thought, and there's no light for them to adjust to, but after what seemed like a very long time, she began to make out shapes. Railings, and a horn-shaped vent, and, looming above her on the right, a tall, massive shape.

One of the funnels, she thought, looking up at its black shape against the blacker sky. She was in a little area bounded by railings. At first she thought the railings completely enclosed it, but after a minute she saw a little metal staircase, four steps leading up to a higher deck.

She started toward it, letting go of the door. It began to swing shut. Joanna grabbed for the handle and then stood there, unwilling to let it shut. She looked around the little deck, but she couldn't see anything on the deck to prop the door open with, and she didn't dare shut it in case it locked.

She transferred the handle to her other hand, bent down, and took off her shoe. She wedged it in the door, closed it carefully, and walked over to the stairway. She climbed the steps, holding on to both railings, and started along the upper deck. This had to be the Boat Deck. There were the giant funnels, four of them, looming above, and the thick cables of the rigging, the cargo cranes. But where were the lifeboats? She couldn't see them. They should be all along the deck.

What if they're already gone? she thought, and felt a stab of panic. But they couldn't be. Collapsible A hadn't gone until two-fifteen, when the bow was already underwater and the slant of the deck was so bad they had had to cut the ropes and float her off, and the deck here was still level.

And even after the boats had gone, there had been people on the Boat Deck, the Strauses and the Allisons, and all the men who hadn't been allowed in the boats, all the steerage passengers who'd found their way up from below-decks too late.

And the band, Joanna thought. They'd been on the Boat Deck, playing ragtime and waltzes the whole time they were loading the boats, and then 'Nearer, My God, to Thee.' They had been on deck playing till the very end.

So it can't be after the boats have gone, Joanna thought, because there was no one on the darkened deck. No one at all, and no sound, except for the uneven patter and tap of Joanna's bare foot and remaining shoe.

The stretch of deck ended abruptly in a low white structure with a latticed roof. Next to it, a set of metal stairs, longer than the first one, led down through a cut-out roof to a covered deck. Joanna climbed down, looking back as she did to memorize the route she'd come so she could retrace it, and then turned around.

And there were the boats. They hung in their white metal davits, suspended from pulleys and thick bundles of ropes, and Captain Smith must not have given the order for the boats to be lowered yet. They were still shrouded in their canvas covers.

But there should still be officers on the deck. Captain Smith had sent two of the officers to investigate the damage, but he'd stayed on the bridge with the other officers till they returned, and some of the passengers had come up to see what had happened. And there were always officers on watch, and passengers walking around the deck. It had never been completely deserted like this.

Maybe it's not the *Titanic*, maybe it's the *Mary Celeste*, Joanna thought, and then, jamming her hands in her pockets, The ship's not deserted. It's just too cold for them to be out here. They're all inside.

That had to be it. She could see her breath, and her bare foot was freezing. They were inside. Far up ahead, she could see light coming from a line of windows. It shone out in a golden square onto the deck. That's where they are, she thought, and walked toward it, past a long, low, white building. 'Officers' Quarters,' a sign on the door said.

That's where they stored the collapsibles, Joanna thought, and looked up at the flat roof, trying to see the lifeboats, but it was too dark, she couldn't make them out.

And if this was the officers' quarters, the lights ahead were from the wheelhouse, and the bridge. She walked on till she was standing in the light that shone out on the deck. There were steps leading up. Passengers aren't allowed on the bridge, Joanna thought, and climbed up.

The bridge was deserted. The huge wooden wheel stood in the center, in front of the windows. Beyond it were two large metal drums with knobbed levers. The boiler room and engine room telegraphs. They had writing on them: Astern. Ahead. Full. Dead Slow. Stop. The levers on both were at Dead Slow.

Joanna walked between them to the windows and looked out, but she couldn't see anything but darkness. It was utterly black. No wonder they couldn't see the iceberg, she thought, peering forward into the darkness. You can't even see where the water meets the sky. It had been a dark moonless night, she remembered Mr Briarley saying, so dark the stars came right down to the horizon. But she couldn't see any stars either, only black, blank darkness.

'No time for that,' a man's voice said below her and off to the side.

Joanna looked through the side window of the bridge, but she couldn't see anyone. She ran back to the head of the steps. Two men were below her, one in the dark blue uniform of an officer, the other in sailor's whites.

'The captain wants you to set up the Morse lamp,' the officer said. 'Over here.'

As he spoke, the two men moved off, and Joanna scrambled down the ladder after them, straining to see where they'd gone in the darkness.

'The Morse lamp?' the sailor said, his voice registering disbelief. 'To use it on what?'

'On that,' the officer said. They were over by the railing, and the officer was pointing into the blackness. She could see the sailor, both hands on the railing, lean far over it, his neck extended. 'What? I don't see anything.'

'The light,' the officer said, pointing again. 'There.'

The *Californian*, Joanna thought. They're signaling the *Californian*. She looked out across the darkness. She couldn't see any sign of a light, just featureless blackness, but the sailor must have seen it because he said, 'I doubt if she'll be able to see us at this distance. They need to use the wireless.'

'They are. They can't raise her. Do you have the key?'

'It's in the …' Joanna lost the last word as he turned away. They started across the deck in front of the bridge, and Joanna followed them, but this part of the deck was littered with coiled ropes and chains, and by the time she'd picked her way through them, the two men had disappeared.

Joanna hesitated, trying to decide which way they'd gone, and, after a minute, the men came back across the deck past her and over to the railing, the sailor carrying an old-fashioned lantern.

He hoisted it up onto the forecastle railing. The officer struck a match and reached inside the lantern. Yellow light flared. The sailor shifted the lantern, so it sat at an angle, and slid a piece of metal down in front of the glass, obscuring the light. A shutter, Joanna thought. It made a scraping noise as he slid it down. 'What do you want me to send?' he asked.

The officer shook his head. 'Mayday. SOS. Help. I don't know, anything that'll work.'

The sailor pulled the shutter up, and the light flared out again. Down, up, down, the shutter scraping along the glass as he raised and lowered it. Up, down, up.

Joanna stared out across the darkness, looking for an answering flicker, a light, but there was nothing, not even a glimmer. And no sound except the scrape of the lantern. Down, up, down. Scrape, scrape. She moved away from the men a little, listening for the lap of water, but there was no sound of water slapping the bow, no breeze. Because we've stopped, she thought, because we're dead in the water.

'She's not responding,' the sailor said, lowering the shutter. 'Are you sure it's a light and not just a star?'

'It better not be a star,' the officer said. 'We're taking on water.'

The sailor's hand jerked on the lantern, making the light flicker. 'Isn't anyone coming?'

'The *Baltic*, but she's over two hundred miles away.'

'What about the *Frankfurt*?'

'She's not answering,' the officer said, and the sailor began signaling again, the light flaring on, off, on, the shutter scraping like fingernails on a blackboard.

'I'm not getting anything,' he said. 'How long do you want me to do this?'

'Till you get through to her.'

The Morse lamp went on sending. Light, dark, scrape, scrape. 'Sir?' a voice called, off to Joanna's left, and an officer ran past Joanna and up to the men.

He saluted smartly. 'I was just below, sir. Boiler rooms five and six and the mail room's flooded, and there's water coming in on D Deck.'

D Deck. She was on C Deck. That was why the staterooms were numbered C8, C10, C12. But she had come up three flights, and the deck below this was the Promenade Deck. Was that A Deck, or was this? If this was, that would make the Promenade B Deck, and the one with her passage in it –

She took off running, the sound of the Morse lamp steadily scraping, down, up, down, reaching all the way down the deck. And please let the door be open, she prayed, racing up the metal stairs. Still let my shoe be in it.

It was, and there was no time to retrieve it. She flung the door open and was down the stairs. One flight. Two. Past the dining room, with its glittering crystal and piano. Three. Please let it not be flooded, she prayed, and pushed through the door.

The deck was dry, but because of the curve, she couldn't see all the way to the passage. She ran past the locked doors, around the curve. And there it was, the black rectangle of the passage door, still open, still above water. She pelted toward it, her bare foot slapping an awkward rhythm with her remaining shoe as she ran.

Down the deck, which was still – thank God – dry, past the deck chairs, her reflection flickering in the glass of the windows as she sped past. Past the light. Into the passage, and into darkness.

And more darkness. What happened? Joanna thought, panic clutching at her. Why didn't I go back? And realized she was back, her sleep mask still on, the IV tugging at the inside crease of her elbow, white noise playing in her ears. 'Tish?' she said and pulled the headphone down off her ear with her left hand.

'... pulse just spiked,' Tish was saying. 'Pulse 95, BP 130 over 90. Wait, she's awake.'

'Good,' Richard said, and she could hear his footsteps as he came over to the examining table. She felt Tish removing the electrodes along her scalp, and then the sleep mask was off, and she was looking up at Richard.

'Well?' he said.

She shook her head against the pillow. 'I didn't have a different vision, like you expected,' she said, and tried to sit up. 'It was—'

'Stay put,' he said, putting a hand on her shoulder.

'But I need to tell you,' Joanna said, lying back, 'it was definitely—'

'Hang on,' Richard said. 'Don't say anything until I get the recorder started.' He began pushing buttons randomly on the minirecorder. The tape feed popped open. He took the tape out and examined both sides. What was he doing? He'd watched her put a new tape in right before they started. 'Tish, can you get Joanna a blanket?' he said. 'She's shivering.'

No, I'm not, Joanna thought, and realized he was stalling until Tish moved away so she wouldn't hear what she said.

'Sure,' Tish said, and went over to the supply cabinet.

'Tell me what you saw,' Richard said as soon as she was out of earshot.

'The *Titanic*.'

'You're sure? You had the same vision as last time? The passage and the people milling around beyond the door?'

'Yes, but this time I went out on deck, and –' She stopped as Tish came back with the blanket.

'I'm going to wait on recording the account till after you've done monitoring her,' Richard said to Tish. 'Go ahead and finish unhooking the electrodes.' He went back over to the console without another look at Joanna and started going through the scans. And what would he say when Tish left? Joanna wondered, watching Tish spread the blanket over her legs and pull it up to cover her shoulders. Would he accuse her of being Bridey Murphy again for seeing the *Titanic*?

I can't help it, she thought. It *was* the *Titanic*. She went over the NDE in her mind again while Tish unhooked the electrodes and checked her pulse and BP so she wouldn't forget any of the details – the stairway, the First-Class Dining Saloon, the door to the Boat Deck –

I left my shoe in the door, she thought, and sat up. It's still on the ship.

'Whoa, what are you doing?' Tish said.

'I –' Joanna said, and stared at her navy-stockinged feet sticking out below the blanket. But I was barefoot, she thought.

'I haven't got your IV out yet,' Tish said, and Joanna obediently lay back down. It had felt so real. She could remember her bare foot on the icy deck, could remember taking her shoe off and wedging it in – She started to laugh.

'What's so funny?' Tish asked, taping a piece of cotton over the site of the needle.

'My shoe –'

'They're in the dressing room,' Tish said, 'but you're not going anywhere yet. I need to take your vitals one more time.' She did and then said, 'So what's so hilarious about your shoes?'

Nothing, Joanna thought. They weren't what I was wearing.

'Come on, tell me, what's the joke?' Tish said.

I can't, Joanna thought, you wouldn't understand. Because the shoe she'd left behind, wedged in the door, was a red tennis shoe, just like the one the patient had supposedly seen outside on the ledge when she floated up above the operating table.

Tish was still waiting for her to explain what was so funny. 'Nothing, I'm sorry,' Joanna said. 'I think I'm still a little disoriented,' and lay still while Tish took the foam cushions out from under her arms and legs. I need to tell Richard about this, she thought. I wonder if this counts as an out-of-body experience.

But Richard wasn't interested in which core elements she'd had or what she'd seen. He was only interested in whether or not she'd seen the *Titanic*.

'You had the same vision this time?' he asked as soon as Tish was gone.

'No,' Joanna said, sitting up. 'Not the exact same vision.' Richard looked both pleased and relieved. 'But it was still the same place, and it is the *Titanic*.'

'How do you know?'

Joanna told him about the dining room and the Boat Deck. 'It had to be the *Titanic*. They were signaling the *Californian* with a Morse lantern.'

'Dr Wright?' Tish said from the door. Joanna wondered how long she'd been standing there. 'I forgot to ask you before I left, are you interested?'

'In what?' Richard asked.

'Seeing Tommy Lee Jones's new movie.'

'Oh,' he said, and it was clear from his tone that he had no idea at all what she was talking about. 'Uh, no, Joanna and I have to go over her account, and I have to analyze the scans. It'll probably be pretty late.'

'It doesn't have to be tonight,' she said, and then, before he could give her another excuse, 'I'll talk to you about it tomorrow.'

'Tomorrow?'

'Yes. Mr Sage. At ten?'

'Oh, yes,' he said. 'Right. Mr Sage. See you then.'

'Wait,' Joanna said. 'What about Mrs Troudtheim? Doesn't she have a session at three?'

'She called and canceled,' Richard said.

'While you were under,' Tish added helpfully.

'She said she thinks she's coming down with the flu and she'll call and reschedule when she's feeling better,' Richard said; and to Tish, still lingering in the door, 'Tomorrow at ten.'

Tish left, and he turned back to Joanna. 'Did they say it was the *Californian* they were signaling?'

'No, but they said they were taking on water and that the *Baltic* and the *Frankfurt* were coming. And the dining room had to be the First-Class Dining Saloon –'

'Tell me about the beginning. Was it the same?'

'Yes,' she said, 'except for the young man in the sweater.' She told him about the bearded man telling him the area was restricted and the young man replying that he'd heard a noise and come to investigate.

'But the noise was the same?'

'Yes,' Joanna said.

'And the passage, and the door? And the light?'

'Yes,' Joanna said, puzzled.

'And the unifying image was the same,' he murmured. 'Come here,' he said. 'I want to show you something.'

Joanna wrapped the blanket around her shoulders, slid down off the examining table, and followed him over to the console. He'd already called up her scans.

'This is the NDE you just experienced,' he said, and typed rapidly. All the areas went black except the frontal cortex. 'What you're looking at now is the long-term-memory activity.' He typed some more. 'This is fast-forward,' he said, and the scans shifted rapidly, small scattered areas winking on and off, orange, red, and then back to blue, exploding across the screen like fireworks in a complex pattern.

'Okay,' he said, freezing the screen and putting another scan up beside it, 'this is Tuesday's NDE.' He went through the same process. 'Now I'm going to superimpose the two,' he said and did. 'Today's is the darker shades, Tuesday's is the lighter.'

Joanna watched the colors blink on and off, blue to orange, then red and back to blue-green, lighting randomly and going out again in different spots, at different speeds. 'They don't look anything like each other.'

'Exactly,' Richard said. 'The L+R is completely different, which should indicate a completely different experience and a completely different memory as a unifying image. There's not a single point of congruity, and yet you say you experienced the same images and the same central image.' He stared at the screen. 'Maybe the frontal-cortex activity is random, after all, and it's the temporal lobe that's dictating the experience.'

He turned to her. 'I'd like you to record as detailed an account as possible. Put down exactly what you saw and heard.' He stared at the scans. 'When you had patients who'd coded more than once, did they have the same NDE each time?'

'No,' Joanna said. 'Mrs Woollam saw a garden one time, and a stairway, and a dark, open place. She did see that more than once, and she said she had been in a tunnel twice.'

He nodded. 'Have you had other patients with more than one NDE?'

'Yes,' she said, trying to remember. 'I'll have to look up their accounts.'

'I'd like to have a list of them with what they saw each time, especially if it was the same thing.' He went back to looking at the screens. 'There's got to be a clue in here somewhere as to why you're still seeing the *Titanic*.'

There is, Joanna thought, but it's not in the scans. It's in something Mr Briarley said in class, or read to us out of a blue book with a caravel on it, and wondered if Kit had found the book yet.

That was hardly likely. She'd only had a few hours to look, and Joanna hadn't exactly given her helpful clues, but she checked her answering machine anyway. Mr Mandrake had called, and Guadalupe. 'Do you still want us to write down what Carl Aspinall says?' her voice asked.

Yes, Joanna thought, feeling guilty. She hadn't been over to five-east in nearly two weeks. Guadalupe probably thought she'd forgotten all about him. She thought about running down right then, but it had already been over an hour since she'd come out of the NDE. She'd better get her account down before she forgot anything. Oh, and she'd promised to contact Eldercare and put them in touch with Kit.

She did, and then recorded her account, putting it directly on the computer to save time. She printed it out and ran it up to Richard, who was on the phone, then went down to talk to Guadalupe, taking the stairs down to fifth and cutting through Pathology to the walkway.

The painters had been here, too. The walkway doors were swathed in yellow 'Do Not Cross' tape, and someone had jammed a metal bar through the door handles for good measure. She would have to go down to third, which meant going straight past Mrs Davenport's room. An unacceptable risk.

She went down to second, crossed the walkway, and took the service elevator up to fifth. And ran into the painters themselves, working on the hallway ceiling. 'You can't come through here,' the nearest one said, pointing off to her left with a paint roller. 'You need to go down to fourth and take the visitors' stairs.' Which would take her through Peds and right past Maisie's, but better Maisie than Mrs Davenport, and maybe she was watching one of her videos and wouldn't notice.

Fat chance. 'Joanna!' Maisie called the second she started past the door, and when Joanna leaned in and said, 'Hi, kiddo,' she said breathlessly, 'I've got something to show you.'

The fluid retention was back. Her arms and legs were swollen, and her face was puffy.

'I can only stay a minute,' she said. 'I have to go see a patient.'

'It'll just take a minute,' Maisie said, hauling books out from under her covers. 'I had Ms Sutterly bring me a whole bunch of *Titanic* books. Look!' She held up a large picture book. On the cover was the familiar picture of the *Titanic*, its stern out of the water, propellers dripping and unlikely smoke still coming out of her funnels, poised for the final plunge, her lights still blazing.

'Did you know the band played right up till the very end?' Maisie asked.

'Yes,' Joanna said, thinking, I never should have mentioned the *Titanic* to her. 'They played "Nearer, My God, to Thee."'

'Huh-*unh*,' Maisie said. 'Nobody knows for sure what they played. Some people think it was "Nearer, My God, to Thee," and some people think it was this other song, "Autumn." But nobody knows for sure, 'cause they all died.'

430

'Your teacher brought you all these books?' Joanna asked to change the subject.

'Uh-huh,' Maisie said, digging under the covers again. 'She brought me a lot more, but some of them were little-kids' books. Did you know there's a *Titanic* ABC book?' she said, disgusted.

'No,' Joanna said, glad that it was possible to offend even Maisie's sensibilities. She wondered what the letters stood for. I is for Iceberg? L is for Lorraine Allison? D is for Drowning?

'Do you know what they had for F?' Maisie said contemptuously. 'First-Class Dining Saloon.'

'What should they have had?' Joanna said, almost afraid to ask.

Maisie gave her a withering look. 'F is for *French bulldog*. You know, the one I told you about. Did you know there was this little girl who played with it on the Promenade Deck all the time?'

'Maisie—'

'There's a *Titanic* pop-up book, too,' Maisie said. 'I made Ms Sutterly take those back to the library, but these have lots of stuff in them, so now if you need me to help with your research, I can,' she said, still breathless. With the exertion of digging for the books? Or with something else? Not only was she retaining fluid, but her lips looked bluer than usual, and when she inhaled, Joanna could hear a faint catch, like the beginning of a wheeze. She's getting worse, Joanna thought, watching her leaf through the book.

'So, do you want me to look up something for you?' Maisie said.

'I think right now I want you to just read about the *Titanic*, so when I have questions, you'll be ready to answer them. And I want you resting and doing everything the doctors and nurses tell you.' She began stacking up the books. 'Where do you want these?'

'In my Barbie bag in the closet,' she said, 'except for this one.' She grabbed a tall red book called *The Child's Titanic*.

Joanna put the rest in the pink duffel bag and shoved it out of sight on the side of the closet. 'Now I've got to go see my patient,' she said. 'I'll come see you soon, kiddo,' and started out of the room.

'Wait!' Maisie said before she'd taken two steps. 'I have to ask you something.' She paused for breath, and Joanna heard the wheezing catch in her breath again. 'What happens if your bracelet gets too tight?' She held out her puffy wrist with the plastic ID bracelet on it.

'Barbara will just cut it off and make a bigger one,' Joanna said. Was she worried about getting puffier? The bracelet wasn't even snug, let alone pressing into the flesh.

'What if after they cut it off something bad happens,' Maisie said, 'like a disaster, and they can't put another one on?'

Had she been thinking about the abandoned gold bracelet they'd found in the ruins of Pompeii? 'There won't be a disaster,' Joanna started to say, and then decided not to. 'I'll tell Barbara if she has to cut this one off, she should put the new one on first,' she said. 'All right?'

'Did you know the firemen go visit her grave every year?' Maisie said.

'Who?'

'The little girl,' Maisie said, as if it were obvious. 'From the Hartford circus fire. They go put flowers on it every year. Do you think maybe her mother died?'

'I don't know,' Joanna said. The mother's dying in the fire, too, would explain why no one had come forward to identify the little girl, but all the other bodies had been identified, and if someone had identified the mother, why not the child? 'I don't know.'

'The firemen buried her in the cemetery, and every year they go put flowers on her grave,' Maisie said. 'They put up a tombstone and everything. It says "Little Miss 1565" on it and the year she died and stuff, but it's not the same as a name.'

'No,' Joanna said. 'It's not.'

'I mean, at least all the little kids on the *Titanic*, they knew who they were, Lorraine Allison and Beatrice Sandstrom and Nina Harper and – is Sigrid a boy or a girl?'

'A girl.'

'And Sigrid Anderson. Of course they didn't have tombstones, but if they did—'

'Maisie—'

'Can you put in a video?' Maisie said, lying back against the pillows.

'Sure. Which one? *Winnie the Pooh*?' Joanna said, reading out titles. '*The Wizard of Oz*? *Alice in Wonderland*?'

'*The Wizard of Oz*,' Maisie said.

'That's a good one,' Joanna said, sliding it in and pushing 'play.'

Maisie nodded. 'I like the tornado.' Of course, Joanna thought. What was I thinking?

'And the part where the hourglass is running out,' Maisie said, 'and they don't have much time left.'

26

'See you in the morning.'
    – Last words of JOHN JACOB ASTOR to his bride,
        as he put her into one of the *Titanic*'s lifeboats

Joanna didn't make it up to Coma Carl's. By the time she escaped from Maisie's room – Maisie insisted on telling her a few choice details about the 1953 Waco, Texas, tornado first – it was four.

Guadalupe will already have gone home, Joanna thought. It was just as well. She wanted to talk to Barbara and ask her about Maisie's condition and find out what all this talk about her hospital wristband was about. But Barbara was in with a three-year-old boy with advanced leukemia, trying unsuccessfully to get an IV started.

Joanna went back up to her office and spent the rest of the afternoon working on the list of people who'd had more than one NDE. They seemed to be split evenly between people who'd seen radically different scenes and people who'd seen the same thing each time. Mr Tabb had seen by turns an opening with a light coming through it and 'bright figures beyond,' a stairway, a reddish darkness, and a feeling of intense warmth, while Ms Burton, a brittle diabetic who'd coded four separate times, had had the exact same vision each time, 'which is how I know it's real.'

It seemed to Joanna that its always being exactly the same thing would more likely be proof that it was a prerecorded experience, played over and over again by the brain like a record stuck in a groove. She wished she'd asked Ms Burton exactly what she meant by 'real,' wished she'd asked all of her patients if it had seemed like an actual place, if it seemed to them like they had really gone there.

Because that was how it felt, even though Joanna knew intellectually that it was a hallucination and that she hadn't gone anywhere, that she had really been lying on an examining table in her stocking feet while Tish monitored her blood pressure and flirted with Richard. But it *felt* as real, as three-dimensional, as her office with its Swedish ivy and shoe box full of interviews she hadn't transcribed yet.

Joanna went over Ms Burton's separate accounts, and they did in fact seem to have been exactly the same, but Mr Rutledge's varied slightly from NDE to NDE, even though he said his were the same, too.

She found Mrs Woollam's two interviews. Joanna had told Richard she'd been in the tunnel twice, but Mrs Woollam had said she didn't think it was the same one, that the second time the tunnel had been narrower and the floor more uneven. Apparently the 'dark, open place' she'd been in the remaining four times had been the same place, but, looking at Mrs Woollam's account, Joanna wondered. She had said it was too dark to see anything. The same went for Maisie's fog. And several people who'd been completely blinded by the light.

Joanna worked till after seven, compiling a partial list, and then put on her coat and took the list to the lab. Richard was still there, staring at the scans, his chin in his hands. When she gave him the list, he barely grunted an acknowledgment.

'We're having Dish Night tomorrow night. Can you come?'

'Sure,' he said, and turned back to the scans.

Well, it's not exactly wild enthusiasm, Joanna thought, going out into the hall, but at least he didn't turn me down. Down the hall, the elevator dinged, and Joanna ran to catch it. It opened, and Mr Mandrake stepped out. 'Oh, good, Dr Lander,' he said. 'I'm glad you're still here. I've been trying to reach you for two days.' He pursed his lips.

'Mr Mandrake, I'm afraid this isn't a good time to talk,' she said, knowing it was hopeless. She was obviously on her way home, so she couldn't claim she had an appointment. A date? No, he'd simply say, 'This will only take a few minutes.'

'This will only take a few minutes,' he said. 'I wanted to ask you about these NDEs of yours.'

He knew she'd been under! How had he found out? Tish? She'd been upset that Richard wouldn't go out with her. Had she told another nurse about the scene and accidentally revealed that Joanna was the subject, and then the nurse had spread it through the rest of Gossip General? Or had Heidi seen her and Vielle talking and somehow figured it out, and he knew about the *Titanic*, too? 'NDEs of mine?' she said, glancing anxiously toward the door of the lab.

'And of Dr Wright, of course,' Mr Mandrake said. 'That is, assuming that you have succeeded in producing these so-called NDE simulations with your subjects. Have you?'

'Yes,' Joanna said in her relief that he didn't know, and was instantly sorry.

'And the subjects have experienced the tunnel, the light, and the dead waiting for them?'

Yes, Joanna thought, and the Boat Deck and a Morse lamp and a red tennis shoe. 'The NDEs have varied,' she said.

'Which means they haven't experienced those things. As I expected. Have they experienced the Life Review and the Revelation of the Mysteries of the Cosmos?'

'No.'

'And the Bestowing of Powers?'

'Bestowing of Powers?' Joanna said. That was a new one.

'Yes, many of my subjects display enhanced paranormal abilities after their return: clairvoyance, telepathy, communications from the dead. I don't suppose any of your subjects have evidenced such abilities?'

No, Joanna thought, because if they had, I'd be using them to send a telepathic message to Richard to come and save me.

'I take it your silence means they haven't, which is not surprising. No laboratory stimulation of the brain could do any more than create physical sensations and the NDE is not physical, it is spiritual. It shows us the world that lies beyond death, the Reality beyond reality, and a number of my subjects have been in touch with that reality. Mrs Davenport ...'

Maybe I do have telepathic powers, Joanna thought. I knew we'd get around to Mrs Davenport sooner or later.

'... received a message from her great-grandmother last night, a message she knew to be authentic. Do you know what that message was?'

' "Rosabelle, believe?" ' Joanna said.

Mr Mandrake glared at her.

'She said, "There is no fear here," ' Mr Mandrake intoned, ' "and no regret." Have any of your subjects spoken to the dead? Of course not, because these so-called simulations of the NDE are just that, mere physical imitations. Mrs Davenport has also received messages from a number of ...'

Joanna looked longingly at the door, and Richard, impossibly, emerged with an armful of scan printouts and file folders. 'Oh, Dr Lander, there you are,' he said, bending to lock the lab door. 'I was afraid you'd forgotten.'

'Forgotten?' Joanna said.

'Our meeting.'

'Oh, our meeting,' Joanna said, clapping her hand over her mouth, 'with Dr Tabb. I did forget. You're lucky you caught me. I was just on my way home. I'm sorry, Mr Mandrake. Dr Wright and I have a meeting –'

'Ten minutes ago,' Richard said, looking pointedly at his watch. 'And you know how Dr Tabb is about punctuality.' He took Joanna's arm.

Mr Mandrake pursed his lips. 'This is extremely—'

'We're late. If you'll excuse us,' Richard said to Mandrake. He led Joanna rapidly toward the stairs and through the door.

'*Thank* you,' Joanna said, racketing down the stairs beside him. 'In another minute he'd have had me going down to see Mrs Davenport, who is now receiving messages from the dead. How did you know we were out there?'

'Telepathy,' he said, grinning. 'And Mandrake's piercing voice. Who's Dr Tabb?'

'*Mr* Tabb is a patient I interviewed two years ago. I didn't want to name a real doctor for fear he'd go try to get information out of him.'

'Well, hopefully he'll spend the next few days searching for Dr Tabb instead of paging us.' They'd reached the bottom of the stairs. 'Which way are we least likely to run into him?'

'This way,' Joanna said, leading him through the oncology ward to a service elevator. 'I can get out to the parking lot from here,' she said, 'oh, but you can't go back to the lab, can you? Not if we're supposed to be in a meeting.'

'That's okay. I wanted to talk to you anyway. Shall we go get something to eat?'

'That'd be great,' Joanna said, feeling inordinately pleased, 'but I'd imagine the cafeteria's closed.'

It was. 'Is it ever open?' Richard asked as they stared through the locked glass doors.

'No,' Joanna said. 'What now? You don't have any food in your lab coat, do you?'

He made a search and came up with a Mountain Dew and half a Hostess cupcake. 'I need to restock,' he said. 'How does Taco Pierre's sound? Oh, wait,' he rummaged through his pockets again, 'I don't have my keys.'

'I've got mine,' Joanna said, 'but you don't have a coat.'

'Taco Pierre's has hot sauce, and your car does have a heater, doesn't it?'

'It does,' Joanna said.

She cranked it all the way up to high as soon as they got in and handed him her mittens, but he was shivering by the time they got to Taco Pierre's, and he ordered two coffees with his tacos. 'One for each hand,' he explained, and picked up six packets of extra hot sauce on the way to the table.

The dining area was littered with taco wrappings and straw papers. Joanna had to wipe off their table with a napkin before they sat down. 'Somebody has *got* to open a restaurant closer to the hospital,' Richard said.

'A *nice* restaurant,' Joanna whispered, smiling at him. The place was a mess, the blond, tattooed kid behind the counter looked like the mug shot of the nail gunnee, and it wasn't exactly a romantic setting, but it was warm, and deserted. And it's a date of sorts, Joanna thought, Vielle will be so pleased, and felt pleased herself, taking a bite of a Tater Torro that had been fried at least a week ago. 'At least it's warm in here,' she said.

'And the coffee's cold. So what did Mandrake have to say? I missed the first part.'

She told him while they ate. 'And now Mrs Davenport's receiving messages from the dead.' She sipped thoughtfully at her Coke. 'I wonder if they're in code.'

'In code?' Richard asked, drinking his cold coffee.

'Yes, like the message Houdini promised to try and send his wife after he died,' Joanna said, taking a bite of taco.

' "Rosabelle, believe," he told her, but the message was really "Rosabelle answer, tell, pray-answer, look, tell, answer-answer, tell." The words stood for the letters in "believe." It was the code they'd used in their old mind-reading act.'

'Did he succeed?'

'No, and if anybody could have gotten a message through, it was Houdini,' Joanna said, taking a drink of her Coke, 'though doubtless in a couple of days Mrs Davenport will announce that she's spoken to him personally and he's told her,' she affected a sepulchral voice, '"There is no fear here, and no regret."'

'"And no daring underwater escapes,"' Richard said in the same ghostly tone. 'Why does the afterlife always sound like the most boring place imaginable?'

'Boring might be good,' Joanna said, thinking of the empty darkness beyond the bridge, of the officer saying, 'There's water on D Deck.'

'You mean as opposed to the *Titanic*,' Richard said, as if he were telepathic. He crumpled up the papers his burrito had been wrapped in. He took the tray over to the trash. 'Actually, that's what I wanted to talk to you about.' He rummaged through the file folders on the seat next to him and pulled out the transcript of her NDE. 'You keep saying it's the *Titanic*,' he said. 'How do you know it is?'

So much for this being a date, Joanna thought. 'I'm not claiming it's the actual *Titanic*,' she said patiently. 'I explained that before. It isn't the historical ship that went down in 1912. It's – I don't know – some sort of *Titanic* of the mind.'

'I know,' Richard said. 'That's not what I'm asking. How do you know what you're seeing is the *Titanic*?'

'How do I know it is?' she said. 'I heard the engines stop and saw the passengers out on deck. I saw them signaling the *Californian*.'

'Correction,' Richard said, looking through her stapled account, 'you saw them signaling something. No mention was made of the *Californian*. You assumed that.' He took a sip of coffee. 'There's no mention by any of these people you saw of an iceberg or a collision. In fact, the steward says he thinks it was a mechanical problem.'

'But the young woman in the nightgown heard it,' Joanna said.

Richard shook his head. 'She heard a sound like a cloth tearing. That could be any number of things.'

'Like what?'

'A collision, an explosion, the mechanical problem the steward described. Did you see anything that identified the *Titanic* by name? Something with SS *Titanic* written on it?'

'RMS,' Joanna corrected. 'She was a royal mail ship.'

'All right, with RMS *Titanic* on it.' He flipped through the stapled pages of her account. She could see that a number of lines had been marked with yellow highlighter. 'You said you saw the lifeboats. Was there a name on the side of them?'

'They had canvas covers over them,' Joanna said, trying to remember if she'd seen the *Titanic*'s name anywhere. Had the steward's white jacket had an insignia on it? Or the officer's cap? She couldn't remember. What else would have had an insignia on it, or the *Titanic*'s name?

The life preservers, she thought, trying to remember if she'd seen one on the Boat Deck. No, but it seemed like one had been on the inside wall of the deck just outside the passage next to the deck light, with RMS *Titanic* stenciled on it in red.

You're confabulating, she told herself sharply. That's an image from the movie, and if it was next to the deck light, you wouldn't have been able to see it for the glare. 'No,' she said, 'I didn't see anything with *Titanic* on it.'

'I didn't think so,' he said. 'I'm not sure it is the *Titanic*. I've been going over your transcript.' He turned to a page halfway through, heavily marked in yellow, and read, ' "Isn't anyone coming?" "The *Baltic*, but she's over two hundred miles away." "What about the *Frankfurt?*" ' He looked at her. 'It was the *Carpathia* who came to her aid. And, as you say yourself in your account,' he said, looking back through the pages, 'the *Californian* was the ship that didn't answer, not the *Frankfurt*.'

'But they would have radioed more than one ship,' Joanna said. 'They said both ships were too far away to help. They might have been two out of a dozen they tried to reach.'

'There's also the staircase. I *know*,' he said, putting up his hands defensively, 'you said the memory didn't come from the movie, but one thing the movie did show was the staircase outside the dining room, with the fancy winding stairs and the big skylight –'

'The Grand Staircase,' Joanna murmured. He was right. The stairs leading down to the First-Class Dining Saloon had been marble, with filigreed gold and wrought-iron balustrades and a bronze cherub on the newel post, holding an electric torch, and at the head of the stairs a huge clock, with two bronze figures placing a laurel wreath atop the clock face. Honour and Glory Crowning Time.

I must have been on another staircase, she thought, but there wouldn't have been two stairways next to the First-Class Dining Saloon, would there? And there was the empty deck and the deserted bridge. 'So, what do you think?' Joanna asked. 'That I'm seeing some other ship?'

'I think it's possible. Nothing you've described would eliminate it from being the *Lusitania*, for instance.'

'Except that the *Lusitania* sank in broad daylight. And nobody stands around calmly asking what's happened when a torpedo hits them.'

'Or some other ship you've heard about from Maisie,' he continued imperturbably. 'Or from Mr Wojakowski.'

'The *Yorktown* was an aircraft carrier,' Joanna said. 'This was an ocean liner. I saw the funnels.'

'Correction,' he said, consulting the account again. 'You saw a large black looming shape. The central island of an aircraft carrier would be a large black looming shape, wouldn't—' and looked up at the kid from behind the counter, who was standing over them.

'We're closin',' he said and continued to stand there, his tattooed arms folded across his chest while Richard disposed of his coffee cup, and Joanna put on her coat.

They went out into the freezing darkness. It had started to snow while they were inside, a wet, sleety snow. 'How long did Vielle say the passengers could survive before they got hypothermia?' Richard asked, blowing on his hands.

'It wasn't an aircraft carrier,' Joanna said, starting the car and heading back to the hospital. 'Aircraft carriers have flat decks, and they don't have dining saloons with crystal chandeliers and grand pianos.'

'And this ship doesn't have a Grand Staircase,' he said, 'which makes me think it's an amalgam of ships and ship imagery stored in your long-term memory. You said yourself it might be the *Mary Celeste*.'

'The *Mary Celeste* was a sailing ship,' she said, but he was right. There were discrepancies. The deck had been empty and deserted, and there had been no one on the bridge.

She pulled into the parking lot. 'Where's your car parked? Oh, wait, you've got to go get your coat.'

'Yeah, and I want to look at your scans again.'

Joanna pulled around by the north entrance and stopped. 'Thanks for rescuing me from the clutches of the Evil One,' she said.

'I hope he isn't still crouched outside the lab, waiting.'

'I hope Mrs Davenport isn't really telepathic.'

Richard laughed and got out, and then leaned back in. 'You said before you know it's the *Titanic*. Is this sense of conviction you have the same as the one you had when you first recognized the passage as being on the *Titanic*?'

I know where this is going, Joanna thought wearily. 'Yes.'

He nodded. 'That could be it. The temporal lobe rather than a memory out of long-term is what's producing the spurious feeling that it's the *Titanic*.' He slapped the roof of the car. 'I'm freezing. Good night. See you in the morning.' He shut the car door.

I hope you succumb to hypothermia, Joanna thought as she drove away. It isn't a spurious feeling. It's the *Titanic*.

The phone was ringing when she got home. It's probably Mr Mandrake, she thought, leaving his fourteenth message. She let the answering machine pick up. 'Hi, this is Kit Gardiner—'

Joanna snatched up the phone. 'I'm here, Kit, sorry, I just walked in the door.'

'I know it's late,' Kit said, 'but I found something. Not the textbook,' she hastened to add. 'You said you were trying to remember something Uncle Pat said about the *Titanic*. Well, this afternoon I found all his *Titanic* books, and I thought what you were trying to remember might be in one of them and I wondered if you were interested in looking at them. Or I could look it up for you, if you like. You said it was something about the engines stopping and passengers being out on deck in their nightclothes.'

'Yes,' Joanna said. 'Listen, Kit, could you look up something else for me, too? I need to know what the First-Class Dining Saloon on the *Titanic* looked like.'

'Sure, I'll be glad to look it up. Anything else?'

'Yes,' Joanna said, trying to think what would prove the ship was the *Titanic*. 'I need you to find out if they used a Morse lamp to signal the *Californian* that night. And the names of the ships they contacted by wireless. If that's not too much.'

'It's not,' Kit said cheerfully. 'When do you need it? Would tomorrow night be soon enough? If your invitation to Dish Night still holds. I decided I'd like to try to come, after all. You were right about the Eldercare program. They *are* willing to come on short notice.'

'Great,' Joanna said. 'Can I pick you up?'

'That would be wonderful. I can't tell you how much I appreciate this,' Kit said, as if Joanna were the one searching for textbooks and looking up facts instead of her. 'What time?'

'Dish Night starts at seven,' Joanna said. 'I'll pick you up at six-thirty.'

'Great,' Kit said, 'I'll see y—'

There was a sudden, earsplitting sound. 'Oh, my gosh!' Kit said. 'Can you hang on a minute?'

'Is everything okay?' Joanna said, but the only sound was the high-pitched ringing. Or buzzing, Joanna thought, wondering if she should hang up so that Kit could call 911. Or if she should hang up and call it herself.

'It's all right, Uncle Pat,' she heard Kit's faint voice say calmly in the background, 'everything's fine,' but the sound didn't shut off. I wonder what's making it, Joanna thought. It sounded like a cross between a teakettle's shrill whistle and a code alarm. Or how the funnels on the *Titanic* must have sounded, she thought, blowing off steam in a deafening roar, and wondered if that, and not the engines stopping, was the sound she'd heard in the passage.

'Most of them didn't hear it at all,' Mr Briarley said suddenly into the phone. He must have come into the library while Kit was trying to deal with whatever was making the sound.

'Mr Briarley?' Joanna said.

'Yes. Who's this?'

'Joanna Lander.'

'Joanna Lander,' he repeated, no recognition at all in his voice.

'I'm an ex-student of yours. From Dry Creek High School.'

'High school,' he said. There was a soft clunk, like he'd laid the phone down, but apparently he hadn't because after a few seconds he said, 'It was the sudden ceasing of the engines' vibration. Jack Thayer heard it, and the Ryersons, and Colonel Gracie, and they all went out on deck to see what had happened.'

He's telling me about the engines stopping on the *Titanic*, Joanna thought, clutching the phone. Kit said he sometimes remembers things the next day.

'No one seemed to know,' Mr Briarley said. 'Howard Case thought they'd dropped a propeller. One of the stewards said it was a minor mechanical problem. No one thought it was serious ...' He paused, as if waiting for her to say something.

'Mr Briarley,' Joanna said, her heart beating painfully, 'what did you say about the *Titanic* that day in class?'

27

'I sometimes think what a grand thing it will be to say to oneself, "Death is over now; there is not *that* experience to be faced again."'
– CHARLES DODGSON (LEWIS CARROLL),
shortly before his death

For a long moment all Joanna could hear was the high-pitched scream going on and on, and then Mr Briarley said, 'They speak to us.' Joanna waited, not understanding, but afraid if she interrupted his train of thought she'd destroy it. 'Boring, dusty artifacts. That's what literature *is*,' he said, and then, impatiently, 'Yes, Mr Inman, this will be on the final. *Everything* is on the final,' and the scream abruptly cut off.

That's definitely what I'm hearing in the passage, Joanna thought irrelevantly, listening to the ringing silence. It's definitely a sound cutting off. 'Mr Briarley,' she said, 'can you remember what you said in class that day?'

'Remember?' he said vaguely. There was a long, breathing pause, and then he said, in a tone full of sorrow and despair, 'I shall remember it forever.'

I had no business asking him, Joanna thought. 'I'm sorry,' she murmured. 'I—'

'Who is this?' Mr Briarley demanded. 'Are you a friend of Kevin's?'

'I'm an ex-student of yours, Mr Briarley. Joanna Lander.'

'Then you'll sit on this side,' he said, and in the background she could hear Kit say, 'Don't hang up, Uncle Pat. It's for me.'

'I don't know who it is,' Mr Briarley said grumpily. 'People don't give you their names,' and the sound of the phone being handed over.

'Sorry,' Kit said. 'Uncle Pat somehow got the kitchen smoke alarm down and the alarm button stuck, and I couldn't get it shut off. You said you'll be here at six-thirty?'

'Yes. Kit—'

'Oops, gotta go. 'Bye,' Kit said and hung up.

Joanna stood there, staring at the receiver. 'I shall remember it forever,' Mr Briarley had said, but it wasn't true. He couldn't remember it, and neither could she. She felt suddenly bone-tired.

She put the phone down. Her answering machine was blinking. She hit the 'play' button. 'You have one message,' the machine said. 'Vielle here. Did you remember to pick up the videos?'

'No,' Joanna said aloud, 'I'll do it in the morning,' and went to bed. But Blockbuster didn't open till eleven, she found out on her way to work the next morning. Isn't anything ever open? she wondered, staring at the locked doors and wondering when she was going to be able to get back.

It would have to be this afternoon. Mr Sage's session was at ten, and it usually took a half hour for his session and at least two hours to pry his account out of him. That meant twelve-thirty, and then she had to transcribe his account. At least that won't take long, she thought. But she also needed to finish the list of multiple NDEs for Richard and try to get in touch with Mrs Haighton. And talk to Guadalupe. And tell Vielle she'd invited Kit to Dish Night.

She did that as soon as she got to work, hoping Vielle would be busy so she couldn't interrogate her again. She was. The ER was jammed. 'Spring has sprung!' Vielle said, and when Joanna looked confused, remembering the sleet she'd just driven to work in, explained, 'Flu season, in force. Fevers, de-hydration, projectile vomiting – you'd better get out of here.'

'You, too,' Joanna said. 'I just came to tell you I invited someone to Dish Night.'

'Oh, please tell me it's Officer Denzel!'

'It's not,' Joanna said. 'It's the niece of my high school English teacher. That's who I went to see the other day when I borrowed your car. Mr Briarley,' Joanna said, wondering how she was going to explain why she'd gone to see him. 'He has Alzheimer's.'

'Alzheimer's,' Vielle said, shaking her head sympathetically. 'Didn't he have a Do Not Resuscitate order? His relatives should definitely get one for him if this happens again. We get last-stage Alzheimer's patients in here, and reviving them isn't a kindness,' Vielle said, and Joanna realized Vielle thought that Mr Briarley had coded and been revived, and that she'd gone over to record his NDE.

Maybe I can let her go on thinking that, Joanna thought, but Kit might say something. And Vielle's your best friend. You have no business lying to your best friend. But she couldn't tell her the truth. If she so much as mentioned the *Titanic* –

'Remember when we were talking the other night about the best way to die?' Vielle was saying. 'Well, Alzheimer's has got to be the worst, forgetting everything you ever knew or loved or were, and knowing it's happening. Was he a good teacher?'

'Yes,' Joanna said. 'He used to recite pages and pages of Keats and Shakespeare, and his tests were incredibly hard.'

'He sounds like a real gem,' Vielle said sarcastically.

'He *was*. He had this dry sense of humor, and he knew everything, all about literature and writers and history. He was always telling us the most fascinating things. Did you know Charles Lamb's sister stabbed their mother to death one night at the dinner table with a table knife?'

'It sounds like you paid a lot more attention in English class than I did,' Vielle said.

But not enough, Joanna thought, not enough, because I can't remember what he said about the *Titanic*. 'He knew everything. That's why I went to see him,' Joanna said, hoping Vielle wouldn't ask her to be more specific. 'I didn't know he had Alzheimer's, and I met his niece, and I had to invite her. She's his full-time caregiver and she never gets out, the only time she leaves the house is to go to the grocery store, and they never have any visitors –'

'Gilbert and Sullivan try to rescue another drowning victim,' Vielle murmured.

'I'm not – well, all right, maybe I am, but she's very nice, you'll like her.'

'So that was why you tore off like that in my car and were gone for over four hours,' Vielle said skeptically. 'To ask your old English teacher a question? About Charles Lamb's sister?'

'No,' Joanna said. 'Is there any particular video you want me to get for tonight? Besides *Glory*?'

'How about *Meet Joe Black*?' Vielle said. 'About a woman who falls so much in love with Death she nearly ends up dying.'

'I'll get a comedy,' Joanna said and went up to see Guadalupe, who wasn't there.

'She's out today,' an unfamiliar nurse at the charge desk said. 'She's got this flu that's going around.'

443

'Oh,' Joanna said. 'Well, will you tell her when she comes back that, yes, I'm still interested in having the nurses write down what Mr Aspinall says.'

'I'll leave a note for her,' the nurse said, grabbing a pad of Post-it notes. 'Still interested … nurses … write down …' she said, writing, and looked up. 'Are you sure you mean Mr Aspinall? He –'

'Yes, I'm aware he's in a coma,' Joanna said. 'Guadalupe will know what the message means.'

She watched the nurse finish writing the message and stick it in Guadalupe's box and then went down to Coma Carl's room. His wife was sitting next to his bed, reading aloud from a paperback. ' " *We got him now,' Buck drawled, reining in his horse,"* ' she read. ' " *He can't get through thataway. Even an Apache tracker'd get lost in among them canyons.'* " '

Joanna looked at Carl. In the week since she'd seen him he'd clearly gone downhill. His chest and his face both looked more sunken than before, and grayer. The number of bags on his IV stand had multiplied, and so had the number of monitors.

'Dr Lander!' Mrs Aspinall said, surprised and pleased. She closed the book.

'I just thought I'd stop in for a moment and see how Mr Aspinall was doing,' Joanna said.

'He's holding his own,' Mrs Aspinall said, and Joanna wondered if she was as much in denial as Maisie's mother, but it was obvious from looking at her that she wasn't. She'd lost weight, too, and strain was apparent in her face. 'Carl?' Mrs Aspinall said, leaning forward to touch his arm. 'Carl, Dr Lander's here to see you.'

'Hello, Carl,' Joanna said.

Mrs Aspinall laid the book, which had a picture of a galloping horse and rider on the cover, on the nightstand. 'I've been reading aloud to Carl,' she said. 'The nurses say he can hear my voice. Do you think that's true?'

No, Joanna thought, remembering the silence of the Boat Deck, the darkness beyond the railing. Even if Tish had taken the headphones off and Richard had shouted in her ear, she couldn't have heard them.

'Sometimes I think he does hear me,' Mrs Aspinall said, 'but other times he seems so … Still, it can't hurt,' she said, smiling up at Joanna.

'And it may help,' Joanna said. 'Some patients have reported being aware of the presence of their loved ones while they were in a coma.'

'I hope so.' Mrs Aspinall clasped his unresisting hand. 'I hope he knows I'm here, and that I'd do anything for him,' she said fiercely, 'anything.'

Joanna thought of Maisie. 'I know,' she said, and Mrs Aspinall looked embarrassed, as if she had forgotten Joanna was there.

'It's so kind of you to come see Carl,' she said and picked up the book again.

'It was nice to see you, Mrs Aspinall,' Joanna said, and, even though she was convinced he was somewhere he couldn't hear her, 'You hang in there, Carl.'

She went back up to her office, also using the back way and opening the door of the stairway a crack before she came out. Mr Mandrake wasn't there, but he'd left three more messages on her answering machine. There was also one from Mrs Troudtheim saying she wasn't getting the flu after all and when did they want her to come in, but none from Kit.

She'd been half-hoping she'd hear from her, though she'd said tonight, and if there had been a message from her, it would most likely have been her canceling because Mr Briarley was having a bad day. But she'd hoped Kit would call and say, 'The *Titanic* contacted the *Baltic* and the *Frankfurt,*' or 'The dining saloon had pink lamps and a rose carpet,' so she could convince Richard it *was* the *Titanic*, and not an amalgam.

Because it was. It wasn't just an assortment of ship-related images dredged up out of long-term memory. There was a reason it was the *Titanic*. Mr Briarley had slapped the book shut and dropped it on the desk and said ... Joanna stared at the answering machine, trying to remember. It was foggy out, she thought, and had a sudden image of a snowy, sunny day, the light from the icicles flashing, glittering ...

You're confabulating, she told herself sternly. Maybe she should take a different tack, not try to remember that particular incident, but what she knew about the *Titanic*, and maybe that would trigger the memory.

All right. She knew about the ship going full speed ahead, even though there had been dozens of ice messages, and about the men calmly playing bridge in the first-class smoking room after the boats had gone, about Mrs Straus, who'd refused to leave her husband, and Benjamin Guggenheim, who'd gone below and put on tails and a white waistcoat. 'We've dressed in our best,' he'd said, 'and are prepared to go down like gentlemen.' And about the *Californian*, who hadn't seen the Morse-lamp messages the *Titanic* was sending, hadn't understood that the rockets it saw were distress signals –

'Dr Lander?' Tish said, knocking on the door. 'Dr Wright said to tell you he's ready to begin the session.'

'He is?' Joanna said, glancing at her watch. Good God, it was nearly ten.

'Sorry,' she said, 'be right there,' and scrambled to collect her minirecorder, a new tape, and her notebook. 'Is Mr Sage here?'

'Yes,' Tish said. 'Talkative, as usual.'

Joanna grinned, shut the door, and locked it, just in case Mr Mandrake came snooping around. They started back toward the lab.

'But at least Mr Sage doesn't have his head in RIPT scans like some people I could name,' Tish said sarcastically, 'and he actually listens to you when you talk to him. The reason I came to get you,' she said, leaning confidentially toward Joanna, 'was to tell you I've given up on Dr Wright. He's all yours.'

'He doesn't listen to me either,' Joanna said, thinking of their conversation at Taco Pierre's.

'That's because he spends all his time thinking about NDEs. And I mean *all* his time. Do you know what he said when I told him I'd rented that Tommy Lee Jones movie that we'd talked about?'

That *you* talked about, Joanna thought.

'And that I'd bought steaks and made a salad? He said he can't, that he's busy tonight. Probably staring at his scans.'

This is probably not a good time to tell her about Dish Night, Joanna thought.

'He's completely obsessed with those scans. If he doesn't watch it, he'll start believing NDEs are real, like Mr Mandrake.'

'Somehow I can't see that happening,' Joanna said and went in the lab. Richard was at the console, staring at the scans, his hand up to his chin. 'See?' Tish mouthed to Joanna.

Joanna went over to the examining table, where Mr Sage was sitting, his hospital gown on. 'Good morning, Mr Sage,' she said. 'How are you this morning?'

Mr Sage thought about it a good forty seconds. 'Okay,' he said. Tish gave Joanna a significant look.

At least his account won't take long to record, Joanna thought, watching Tish prep Mr Sage. Ten minutes for the session and another fifteen to pry out of him the fact that it was dark.

She was wrong. After two minutes and forty seconds in non-REM sleep, he went into the NDE-state. And stayed there.

After ten minutes, Richard asked, 'How long was he under last time?'

'Two minutes, nineteen seconds,' Joanna said.

'Tish, how do his vitals look?'

'Fine,' Tish said. 'Pulse 65, BP 110 over 70.'

A minute later, Richard asked, 'What about his vitals now?'

'The same,' Tish said. 'Pulse 65, BP 110 over 70. Is he in non-REM sleep?'

'No,' Richard said, sounding bemused. 'He's still in the NDE-state. Let's stop the dithetamine.'

Tish did, but it didn't change anything. Ten minutes later, Mr Sage was still in the NDE-state. 'Is there a problem?'

'No,' Richard said. 'His EKG's fine, his vitals are fine, and the scan patterns aren't showing any abnormalities. He's just having a long NDE.'

Joanna looked down at Mr Sage. What if he can't find the passage, or the tunnel, or the whatever it is where he is, back? she thought. What if he forgot to wedge his tennis shoe in whatever door or gate or barrier he went through, and it swung shut behind him and locked?

At twenty-eight minutes and fourteen seconds, Richard said, 'All right, that's long enough,' and told Tish to administer the norepinephrine and bring him out. 'One good thing,' he said, watching the scans finally shift to the non-REM and then the waking pattern. 'Mr Sage should have plenty to tell us.'

But he was as noncommunicative as ever. 'It was dark …' he said, pausing forever between phrases, 'and then there was a light … and then it was dark again.'

'Were you there longer this time?' Joanna asked.

'Longer?'

I honestly think he's dimwitted, Joanna thought. 'Yes,' she said patiently. 'Did it feel like more time had passed?'

'When?'

'In the dark,' Joanna said, and when he looked confused, 'or in the light.'

'No.'

'Were you in the same place?'

'Place?'

She tried for nearly two and a half hours to get something, anything, out of him, to no avail.

At least his account won't take long to type up, she thought, and I can run over to Blockbuster, but when she ran the transcript up to Richard, he asked for any and all references to elapsed time in her NDE interviews and any information on the actual time, if documented, of the clinical death. That took all afternoon. Halfway through writing it up, Richard knocked on her door. 'I don't think I'm going to be able to make it to Dish Night tonight,' he said. 'I'm not done analyzing Mr Sage's scans, and I've still got the neuro-transmitter analysis to go.'

'What time is it?' Joanna asked, glancing at her watch. 'Oh, my gosh, it's a quarter to six,' she said, hitting 'save' and grabbing her coat. She was supposed to pick up Kit at six-thirty. And she still hadn't gotten the videos.

'Tell Vielle I'm sorry. Maybe next time,' Richard said as she searched for her keys.

'I will,' she said and took off for Blockbuster. All right now, she told herself, skidding into the parking lot, just go in, grab a couple of movies, and go get Kit. Easier said than done. *Glory* was checked out, and so was *Jumpin' Jack Flash*, and when she browsed the aisles, the first movie she picked up was a Woody Allen, the second starred Kevin Costner, and everything else seemed to have been made by demolitions experts.

'Are you finding everything?' a short kid in a blue-and-yellow shirt said.

No, she thought. Do you know where the Grand Staircase is? Or why I'm seeing the *Titanic*? 'Can you suggest a good comedy?' she said.

'You bet,' he said, striding purposefully down the New Releases aisle and picking up a box with a photo of Robin Williams made up as a clown on the cover. '*Die Laughing*,' he said. 'It's about a man who's dying of a heart condition.'

Joanna shook her head. 'Or how about this? *Missing Link*. It's a comedy about a man with amnesia who doesn't know who he is or what his name is –'

'What about Julia Roberts?' Joanna said. 'Do you have anything with Julia Roberts in it?'

'Yeah, sure,' he said and walked over to the drama section. '*Dying Young*. Julia Roberts and Campbell Scott. It's about a young woman who's a caregiver for a man dying of leukemia –'

'I meant a Julia Roberts *comedy*,' Joanna said desperately.

He frowned. 'Her new one's all checked out. How about *Runaway Bride*?'

'Great,' she said, snatching the blue-and-yellow box from him, and when he started to walk away, 'Nobody dies in this, do they? Or loses their memory?'

He shook his head.

'Great,' she said and began rummaging for her Blockbuster card. She knew Dish Night was supposed to be a double feature, but there was no way she could live through another round of this. One would have to do.

There was also no time. She'd promised she'd pick up Kit at six-thirty, and it was already twenty-five after. She took *Runaway Bride* from the out-stretched hand of the short kid and ran, hoping her being late wouldn't give Kit time to change her mind about going, but Kit met her at the door with her coat on. 'Hi, come on in,' she said. 'I'm almost ready to go.'

'Where are you going?' Mr Briarley called sharply from the library.

'I'm going out, Uncle Pat,' Kit called back. 'With Joanna. We're going to watch a movie.'

'I'm sorry,' Joanna whispered. 'Should I have waited for you in the car?'

Kit shook her head. 'I tried sneaking out a couple of times so he wouldn't see me leave,' she whispered back, 'but it just made it worse. Come on in. I just need to tell the caregiver something. I found the answers to some of your questions.'

She led the way into the library. Mr Briarley was sitting in his dark red leather chair, reading a book. He didn't look up when they came in.

A gray-haired woman in a shirtwaist was sitting on the couch. She reminded Joanna of Mrs Troudtheim. She had the same friendly, no-nonsense, 'I can survive anything' manner, and she even had a tote bag full of olive-green-and-bright-purple yarn. What is it with crocheting? Joanna wondered. Do people automatically go color-blind when they learn to crochet?

'Now, you have my cell phone number,' Kit said to her. 'I borrowed my cousin's till I can get one of my own,' she explained to Joanna.

'Right here,' Mrs Gray said, patting the breast pocket of her dress.

'Do you want Vielle's number, too?' Joanna asked Kit, and, when she nodded, recited it to Mrs Gray.

'And you'll call me if there's anything?' Kit said anxiously. 'Anything at all?'

'I'll call you,' Mrs Gray said, pulling out her crocheting. 'Now, you go have a nice time, and don't worry. I've got things under control here.'

'Go?' Mr Briarley said, shutting his book and marking the place with his thumb. 'Where are you going?'

'I'm going out, Uncle Pat,' Kit said. 'I'm going to watch a movie. With Joanna, Joanna Lander,' she said, presenting Joanna to him.

He gave no sign of recognition. 'She was a student of yours at Dry Creek,' Kit said. 'We're going to go watch a movie.'

Joanna thought of the steward, repeatedly starting off down the deck, of the young woman in the nightgown, saying over and over again, 'It's so cold.' Was that what having Alzheimer's was like, being trapped in a hallucination, in a dream, repeating the same lines, the same actions, over and over again? And how about Kit? She was trapped, too, in an endlessly repeating nightmare, though you couldn't tell by the quiet, loving way she answered him, patted his arm.

'What about Kevin?' he asked. 'Isn't he going with you?'

'No, Uncle Pat.' She turned to Joanna. 'Ready? Oh, wait, I had a book I wanted to show you before we go,' she said, and ran upstairs.

At the word *go*, Joanna looked apprehensively at Mr Briarley, but he had returned to his book. Kit reappeared, carrying two textbooks. 'I don't think either of these is it,' she said, handing them to Joanna, 'but since you're here –'

Neither of them was it. Joanna knew as soon as she saw them. 'Well, it was worth a try,' Kit said, ran them back upstairs, and came down again, cell phone in hand. 'Okay. I'm ready. Good-bye, Uncle Pat.' She kissed him on the cheek.

' "The Rime of the Ancient Mariner" is not, contrary to the way it is popularly taught, a poem about similes and alliteration and onomatopoeia,' Mr Briarley said, as if he were lecturing to her second-period class. 'Neither is it about albatrosses and oddly spelled words. It is a poem about death and despair. And resurrection.' He stood up, walked to the window, and pulled the curtain aside to look out. 'Where's Kevin? He should be here by now.'

Kit went over and led him back to his chair. He sat down. 'I'll be back soon,' she said.

He looked up innocently. 'Where are you going?'

'I'm going out with Joanna. We're going to go watch a movie,' she said and held her cell phone up to show Mrs Gray, who was contentedly crocheting. 'Call me,' she said.

'Does that happen every time you go out?' Joanna asked as they got in the car.

'Pretty much,' Kit said, turning on her cell phone. 'This was such a great idea. Now I won't worry that Mrs Gray's trying to reach me and I don't know it.'

Like the *Californian*, Joanna thought, wondering how to broach the subject of the questions Kit had said she'd found the answers to. If she asked her now, on the way over, it would sound like she'd only invited Kit to Dish Night to get information out of her. But if she waited, Kit might bring it up in the middle of the movie, with Vielle right there, and Vielle was already suspicious.

It had better be now. But at least lead up to it, Joanna thought. 'I'm so glad you decided to come, Kit,' she said.

'So am I,' Kit said, reaching in the pocket of her coat and pulling out a folded sheet of paper. 'Okay, the Morse lamp,' she said. 'They did use one on the *Titanic*, to signal the *Californian*. It was on the port bridge wing, which, according to the map in *The Illustrated Titanic*, was just in front of the bridge and off to the left. I had to look that up,' she said, smiling. 'I never can remember which is port and which is starboard. Port is left as you're facing the bow. Starboard's right.'

In front of the bridge and off to the left. That was where the two men had stood, signaling with the lantern. 'Did it say what the Morse lamp looked like?'

Kit shook her head. 'Unfortunately, even though it's called *The Illustrated Titanic*, there was no illustration, and no description. I'll keep looking. Now, about the ships she tried to contact, I'm not sure I've got them all. The stuff about the wireless is scattered all over the place, and half the books don't have indexes, so I don't know if this is all of them, but the ones I have are ...' she peered at the paper in the light from the passing streetlights, '... the *Virginian*, the *Carpathia* – that's the one that picked up the survivors – the *Burma*, and the *Olympic*.'

The *Virginian*, the *Carpathia*, the *Burma*, and the *Olympic*. Not the *Baltic* or the *Frankfurt*. But Kit had said the information about the wireless was scattered all over the place, and the *Titanic* could have signaled dozens of ships. The books might only mention those that were close enough to help or had responded. The officer had said the *Frankfurt* wasn't answering.

'And of course the *Californian*,' Kit said, 'but you said "contacted," and they were never able to contact her. Did you know her wireless operator shut down his wireless and went to bed five minutes before the *Titanic* sent her first SOS?'

Joanna laughed.

'What is it?' Kit asked. 'Did I say something funny?'

'You just remind me of somebody, a little girl I know who's always beginning her sentences with "Did you know?"'

'A patient of yours?' Kit asked.

'Sort of,' Joanna said. 'Were you able to find out anything about the first-class dining room?'

'First-Class Dining Saloon,' Kit corrected. 'Yes, there was tons of stuff. It was ...' she consulted her notes by the light of the streetlights again, '"a sumptuous dining room patterned after England's Haddon Hall and decorated in the Jacobean style." '

Jacobean. Joanna had no idea what Jacobean furniture looked like. She pulled into the parking lot of Vielle's apartment complex. 'Now, I have to warn you,' she said, shutting off her headlights. 'We have a rule against talking about work at Dish Night, so you'll have to tell me about the rest of this on the way back.'

'Okay,' Kit said. 'Just let me finish this part about the dining saloon.' Joanna nodded and switched on the overhead light. 'It was located in the center of the ship, on the saloon deck, next to the Grand Staircase. It was one hundred and fourteen feet long and was capable of seating five hundred passengers at a time. It was painted white and had two rows of white pillars down the middle. The chairs and tables were dark oak, and the chairs were upholstered in dark green velvet with headrests embroidered in fleurs-de-lis.' Kit folded up the paper and stuck it back in the pocket of her coat. 'I'll tell you what I found out about the engines stopping on the way back,' she said, but that wouldn't be necessary.

Richard was right. It wasn't the *Titanic*.

28

'SOS. Come at once – big list – ten miles south Head Old Kinsale – SOS …'
           – Wireless message from the *Lusitania*

Vielle had a fit about Joanna's having brought Kit. 'Are you out of your mind?' she whispered when Kit took the popcorn into the living room. 'Letting her near Richard? Did you *look* at her? She's beautiful, and guys really go for the fragile, helpless type. If he gets one look at her, you can kiss your chances with Dr Right good-bye.'

'Richard's not coming,' Joanna said. 'We had a problem with the session this afternoon, and he needed to—'

'What kind of problem?' Vielle demanded. 'And whose session? Yours?'

'Dish Night Rule Number One, no talking about work,' Joanna said. 'I've already warned Kit about that.'

'Is that why you brought her?' Vielle asked. 'So I couldn't ask you about the project? Or about why you're so interested all of a sudden in a movie neither of us liked? Or why you don't want to watch it –?' She broke off as Kit came in the kitchen with her cell phone, studying the buttons on it.

'How can you tell if it's on and not just on standby?' she asked.

Vielle looked at it. 'It's on,' she pronounced. 'Did you want to call and check on your uncle?'

'No, that's okay,' Kit said. 'Mrs Gray has your number. I'm just a little nervous. He gets disoriented sometimes when I'm not there.' She turned to Joanna. 'Sorry. I know we're not supposed to discuss things like that at Dish Night. What are we supposed to discuss?'

'Movies,' Joanna said, 'or, rather, movie. I had a little difficulty at Blockbuster. They didn't have *Glory*. Or *Jumpin' Jack Flash*.' She handed the video to Vielle. 'It's a comedy. With Julia Roberts.'

'*Runaway Bride*,' Vielle said, reading the box.

'*Bride*?' Kit echoed.

'Have you already seen it?' Vielle asked.

'No,' Kit said, but in a tone that made Joanna wonder if she had and was lying to protect their feelings. Her cheeks had gone very pink. 'I haven't seen any movies at all the last few years, and I loved Julia Roberts in *Pretty Woman*. And *Flatliners*.'

'Except that in *Flatliners* she needlessly risks her life,' Vielle said, looking at Joanna.

'And ends up with Kiefer Sutherland,' Joanna said lightly. 'I thought Kevin Bacon was a lot cuter.' She took the video away from Vielle. 'This one's got Richard Gere in it.' She stuck it in the VCR and turned on the TV. 'So let's get this show on the road. Kit doesn't want to be gone too long,' and the cell phone rang.

Kit dived for it. 'Hello?' she said anxiously, and to Joanna and Vielle, 'It's Mrs Gray.'

'You can take it in the bedroom if you want,' Vielle said, and Kit nodded gratefully. Vielle led her in and shut the door behind her.

'Oh, I hope Mr Briarley hasn't gotten so upset she has to go home,' Joanna said. 'She was looking forward to this so much.'

'Don't change the subject,' Vielle said. 'You said there was a problem with the session today? Who with?'

'Not me,' Joanna said, and Vielle immediately looked relieved. 'And I shouldn't have said "problem." Nothing went wrong.' She looked at the bedroom door.

'And what about *your* sessions?' Vielle asked. 'Are you telling me nothing went wrong with them either?'

'What do you mean?'

'I mean, you come racing down to the ER white as a ghost and demand to know whether there's an engine-stopping scene in *Titanic*, and then when I find out for you, you're not even interested, you're just afraid I might have told somebody. And then Barbara from Peds tells me she saw you in the walkway up on fifth the night before and you looked like you'd just seen a ghost.'

Of course. Good old Gossip General, and this was exactly why she couldn't tell Vielle. Because there was no such thing as a secret at Mercy General. 'Did she also tell you I'd just found out Maisie Nellis had coded again?'

'She told me she was worried about you. *I'm* worried about you. It's the project, isn't it? You're seeing things in your NDEs. You're seeing the *Titanic*, aren't you?'

No, Joanna thought, apparently not. 'No. I'm not seeing the *Titanic*.'

'Then what are you seeing?'

'I don't know,' Joanna said. 'It's—'

The door opened, and Kit came out, all smiles. 'Mrs Gray just wanted to call to try the phone out, so I'd know it was working, and to tell me how Uncle Pat was doing.'

'How is he doing?' Joanna asked.

'Not too bad. He keeps looking out the window for me and asking her where I am.'

I would have thought someone so much like Mrs Troudtheim would have enough sense not to tell her that, Joanna thought. It will only worry her, and it must have shown in her face because Kit said, 'If she'd told me everything was fine, I wouldn't have believed her. I want her to tell me the truth.'

She sounds just like Maisie, Joanna thought, and, as they settled in to watch *Runaway Bride*, She looks like her, too, with her short blond hair and thin arms and shoulders. But it was more than that. She also had Maisie's courage, her charm, her earnestness. She watched the movie as attentively as if Mr Briarley would be giving one of his notorious finals on it.

Joanna, on the other hand, found her mind wandering. If it wasn't the *Titanic*, what was it? An amalgam of ships and ship-related images, Richard had said. *What* ship-related images? She'd grown up in a completely land-locked state. She'd never been on a ship in her life.

She tried to concentrate on the movie. Richard Gere was being introduced to a gaggle of giggling women. 'I'm Betty Trout,' one of them said, and Joanna thought, Betty Peterson. She sat next to me in second period. And she had been an A student. She would definitely remember the name of their text-book. She might even remember what it was that Mr Briarley had said. But it's not the *Titanic*, so he isn't why you're seeing it.

'It's not fair,' Vielle said.

'What isn't?' Joanna said, jolted out of her reverie.

'That,' Vielle said, gesturing at the screen where Richard Gere was kissing Julia Roberts. 'She has five gorgeous guys to choose from and I can't even find *one*, unless you count Harvey the embalming expert.'

Kit stopped with a handful of popcorn halfway to her mouth. 'Embalming expert?'

'Yes, and a scintillating conversationalist,' Vielle said. 'Did you know Ajax is the best thing to use to get teeth shiny and white?'

'Ajax?' Kit put the handful of popcorn down on a napkin.

'Rule Number Eighteen,' Joanna said. 'No discussing embalming techniques at Dish Night.' She reached for some popcorn. 'What about Officer Denzel? This police officer Vielle met who looks like Denzel Washington,' she explained to Kit.

'And who she can't think of a way to meet again,' Vielle said. 'Maybe I'll get lucky, and another rogue-raver will shoot up the ER,' and immediately looked sorry she'd said it.

'Vielle works in the ER,' Joanna explained to Kit, 'the most dangerous place in the hospital. I keep telling her she needs to transfer out –'

'And I keep telling *her* she has no business playing *Flatliners*,' Vielle said, pointing at Joanna.

'Flatliners?'

'She means the research project I'm working with Dr Wright on, but it's nothing like *Flatliners*,' Joanna said.

'Except that you're having near-death experiences,' Vielle said.

'They're drug-induced hallucinations, and they're perfectly safe,' Joanna said. 'Unlike working in the ER where people get shot and stabbed –'

'Rule Number One,' Vielle said, rewinding to the kissing scene. 'No talking about work at Dish Night. Isn't that right, *Joanna*?'

'Right. Which of Julia's wedding dresses do you like the best, Kit?' Joanna asked, changing the subject.

'I don't know,' Kit said, leaning forward to make sure the cell phone was still on. 'They're all pretty.'

'The one with the train,' Vielle said. 'I definitely want a dress with a train. And a *big* wedding, with all the trimmings. Bridesmaids, flowers, the works. Do police officers get married in their uniforms?'

'You're thinking of the military,' Kit said.

'And counting your chickens before they're hatched,' Joanna said. 'She hasn't even found out his name yet, let alone gotten him to the altar, and a lot can happen in between, right, Kit?'

'I think I'd better call and make sure my uncle's okay,' Kit said, standing up.

'I thought you said calling upset him,' Joanna said.

'I know,' she said uncertainly.

'Do you want me to take you home?'

'No, that's okay,' she said and sat back down. 'I'm sure he's okay. And Mrs Gray said she'd call if there was a problem.' But as soon as they finished the movie, she insisted on leaving. 'This has been great, but I think I'd better not stay too long,' she said. 'It's tempting fate.'

'I hope you'll come again,' Vielle said. 'We promise next time we won't talk about work.'

'Or embalming,' Joanna said, and Kit smiled, but when they got in the car, Kit said seriously, 'I have a question to ask you.'

'About embalming?' Joanna said, starting the car.

'No,' Kit said. 'About your research project. If that's okay. I mean, I know you have a rule about discussing work.'

'Which we obviously don't follow,' Joanna said, pulling out of the parking lot. 'And, besides, Dish Night's officially over.' She turned onto the street and started toward Kit's. She explained the way the project worked. 'It's not *Flatliners*, if that's what you were going to ask.'

'No,' Kit said. She was silent for almost the length of a block, and then, as Joanna stopped at a light, said, 'What does the *Titanic* have to do with your project? Do you think it's what you're seeing when you have these near-death experiences?'

You don't have to tell her, Joanna thought. *You can tell her the results of the project are confidential. But, like Maisie, she'd already figured it out, and, like Maisie, she deserved a straight answer.*

She wished Kit had asked the question the way Vielle had, so she could say no. But I do *think it's what I'm seeing, in spite of the First-Class Dining Saloon being the wrong colors, in spite of the officer naming the wrong ships. And it has something to do with what Mr Briarley said. He, and Kit, are my only chance of finding out what.*

'Yes, I think I'm seeing the *Titanic*,' she said, and Kit sucked in her breath. 'But I don't know for sure, and if I read about the *Titanic* to find out –'

'You won't be able to tell if reading about it is what made you see it. The *Titanic*,' she murmured. 'How terrible.'

'It's not really,' Joanna said. 'The visions are very strange. They feel utterly real, but at the same time, you know they're not.' She looked at Kit. 'You're afraid of what this means in regard to your uncle's hallucinations, aren't you?' she asked. 'This isn't the vision the malfunctioning brain normally produces. It seems to be peculiar to me. Most people have a warm, fuzzy feeling and see lights and angels. That's why I came to ask Mr Briarley what he'd said in class, because I think my mind saw some connection between that and what was happening in the NDE, and that connection is what triggered this particular vision.'

'But Uncle Pat was a *Titanic* expert. Wouldn't he have made the same connection?'

'Not necessarily.' Joanna explained about the acetylcholine, and the brain's increased associative abilities. 'Dr Wright thinks it's a combination of random images out of my long-term memory, but I'm convinced there's a reason for the vision, that the *Titanic* stands for something.' She looked at Kit. 'If you don't want to be involved with this anymore, I completely understand. I sound crazy even to myself when I try to explain it, and I had no business asking you. Or bothering Mr Briarley.'

It was a relief to have told her, even if Kit did say, 'I'd rather not be involved,' or look at her as if she were an NDE nutcase.

But she did neither. She said, 'Uncle Pat would have loved to help you if he could, and since he can't, I want to. Speaking of which, I still haven't told you about the engines stopping. I think I found the thing you mean. It's in Walter Lord's *A Night to Remember.* The passengers noticed that the hum of the engines had stopped, and they went out on deck to see – wait,' she said, fumbling in the pocket of her coat. 'I brought the book with me so I could read you the part –'

She pulled out a paperback book, and Joanna switched on the overhead light and then looked anxiously toward the house, wondering if Mr Briarley would see the car and Kit, haloed in the light.

'Here it is … "wandered aimlessly about or stood by the rail, staring into the empty night for some clue to the trouble,"' Kit read, and Joanna looked at the book.

It was an ancient paperback, dog-eared and tattered, with the same picture of the *Titanic* that had been in Maisie's book: the stern rising out of the water, the boats in the foreground full of people with blankets around their shoulders, watching in horror, the picture that was on every book about the *Titanic,* except that this one was in red, like a scene out of hell: the sea blood red, the ship burgundy, the enormous funnels black-red.

She had seen Mr Briarley brandishing the book dozens of times, making a point, reading a passage. It was as familiar as her sophomore English textbook had been. But that wasn't why she stared at it. It had been there, in Mr Briarley's hand, that day. He had shut it with a snap and dropped it on the desk. It hadn't been the textbook, after all. It was *A Night to Remember.*

But the textbook had been there, too. She could see its blue cover and gold lettering, and a paperback didn't make a snapping sound when you shut it, didn't make a thud when you let it drop. But it was still the book.

'"… their dress was an odd mixture of bathrobes, evening clothes,"' Kit read, '"fur coats, turtle-neck sweaters—"'

'Kit,' Joanna interrupted, 'was the First-Class Dining Saloon the only dining room on board?' No, of course it wasn't, there had to be second-class and steerage dining rooms, too, but the silver and crystal, the piano had to be first-class. 'I mean, the only first-class dining room?'

'No,' Kit said. 'There were several smaller restaurants. The Palm Court, the Verandah Cafe—'

'What about stairways? Would there have been more than one?'

'Passenger stairways or crew stairways?'

'Passenger,' Joanna said.

'I know there were at least two,' Kit said, turning to the back of the paperback, 'and maybe – rats, this is one of those books that doesn't have an index. I can run inside, and—'

'No, that's okay,' Joanna said. 'I don't need to know this second. You can call me when you find out.'

'You want to know how many staircases and how many dining rooms?'

'Yes,' Joanna said. 'Specifically, I want to know if there was a dining room with light wood paneling, a rose carpet, and rose-upholstered chairs.'

'And you want to know the other ships the *Titanic* tried to contact,' Kit said.

Joanna nodded. They'll turn out to be the *Baltic* and the *Frankfurt*, she thought, scarcely hearing Kit's thanks and good night. I need to see if Betty Peterson's in the phone book, and if she's not, tomorrow I'll look on the Net.

She was in the phone book, and still living in Englewood, and when Joanna called her from the office the next morning, she sounded overjoyed to hear from her. Joanna asked her if she remembered the name of their textbook. 'I should,' Betty said. 'It was blue, I remember, with gold lettering, and the title began with an M. And there was an "and" in it. M Something and Something.'

But when Joanna asked her about the *Titanic*, she said, 'All I remember about that class is that Mr Briarley made me redo the footnotes on my term paper *four* times. Why don't you ask him?'

Joanna explained about him having Alzheimer's. 'Oh, yes, that's right,' Betty said, 'I remember hearing about that. How sad.'

'Can you remember who else was in that class with us?' Joanna asked.

'Gosh, in that class …' Betty said, considering. 'Ricky Inman. Did you know he's a stockbroker now? Can you imagine?' Joanna couldn't. 'John Ferguson, no, he's in Japan. Melissa Taylor?'

Melissa Taylor was a possibility. 'What about Candy Simons?' Joanna asked. 'The one we called Rapunzel because she was always combing her hair. Do you know where she is?'

'Oh, Joanna,' Betty said, sounding shocked. 'I guess you didn't know. She died two years ago. Of ovarian cancer.'

'No,' Joanna said, thinking of Candy, endlessly combing her long blond hair. Her hair would have come out during the chemo, she thought, appalled.

Betty chattered on, talking about various students, none of whom had been in second-period English, and about herself. She worked for a computer company, was married, had three children. 'I can't believe you're not married yet,' she said, sounding just like Vielle, and Joanna told her she had to go and gave her her number, 'in case you remember anything else.'

'I will,' Betty promised. 'Oh, wait. I do remember something about the book. It had a picture of Queen Elizabeth on it in one of those ruff things.'

Queen Elizabeth? Not a ship? 'Are you certain?' Joanna asked.

'Positive. The reason I know is I remember Ricky Inman drawing glasses and a mustache on her.'

Joanna vaguely remembered that, too, but she also remembered a ship. So did Melissa Taylor, whom Joanna called after lunch. Which proved what? That memory is extremely unreliable, Joanna thought.

Her pager went off, and when she called the hospital switchboard, it was Vielle, saying, 'I have a you-know-what for you.' An NDE or another series of questions? Probably both, Joanna thought, and decided to call her instead of running down to the ER, so she could hang up if Vielle started grilling her. But first she needed to call Mrs Haighton. Her housekeeper said she was at a fundraiser for the Denver Theater Guild.

Joanna called the ER. The phone rang a long time. I'm going to have to go down there after all and talk to her, Joanna thought, and was about to hang up when a man answered. One of the interns, Joanna thought, to whom Vielle will say, 'What do you think you're doing?' in a moment and snatch the phone away from him. 'This is Dr Lander,' Joanna said. 'Is Vielle there?'

'Vielle?' the young man said in a tone of blank surprise. Definitely one of the interns.

'Yes, Vielle Howard. Can I speak to her, please?'

'I … just a minute …' Joanna could hear a muffled conversation in the background and then another voice, a woman's, came on the line. 'Who is this?' the woman asked.

'Joanna Lander. I'm trying to reach Vielle Howard. She left me a message to call her.'

'Dr Lander, hi. Vielle's not here. She said if you called to tell you she went home sick.'

'Home sick?' Vielle never went home sick, even when she was on her last legs. 'Is she okay? Is it this flu that's going around?'

'She said to tell you she'll call you later.'

'Did she say anything about this message she left me?' Joanna asked, though it was unlikely she would have left a message about an NDE with Mr Mandrake snooping around constantly.

And she hadn't. 'No, nothing about a message. Just that she'd call you,' the woman said and hung up.

Joanna hoped Vielle hadn't tried to call her to see if she could give her a ride home while she was on the phone with Mrs Haighton. She called her at home, but there was no answer. She's got the phone turned down so it won't disturb her, Joanna told herself, but it worried her. Vielle had to be practically at death's door for her to have gone home, which meant she was probably too sick to drive.

Joanna called down to the ER again to find out if somebody had driven Vielle home and when she'd left, but no one answered. Joanna wished Mrs Troudtheim wasn't scheduled. She'd run over to Vielle's to check on her. Hopefully, Mrs Troudtheim's session wouldn't take long.

It didn't. Mrs Troudtheim kicked out after only one frame and remembered nothing. As soon as she left the lab with her crocheting, Joanna called Vielle again. This time the phone was busy. 'She probably took the phone off the hook,' Tish said. 'If it's the same flu my roommate had, it hits you like a ton of bricks. It doesn't last all that long, but, boy, while it does, you wish you were dead.'

Not exactly reassuring, Joanna thought, and tried again. This time Vielle answered. 'Hi, it's me,' Joanna said. 'Spring has sprung, huh?'

'What?' Vielle said blankly.

'The ER told me you'd gone home with the flu. Did you call me to give you a ride home? If so, I am really sorry. I was on the phone, trying to schedule a subject interview.'

'No,' Vielle said. She sounded exhausted to the point of tears. 'I didn't call you.'

'How did you get home?' she asked, and when Vielle didn't answer, 'You didn't drive yourself home, did you?'

'No. Somebody at the hospital gave me a ride.'

'Good. I'm going to come over,' she said. 'Is there anything you want me to bring you? 7Up? Chicken noodle soup?'

'No,' Vielle said. 'I don't want you to come over. I'm fine.'

'Are you sure? I could at least fluff your pillows and make you some tea.'

'No. I don't want you getting the flu, too. I'm fine. I just decided to stay home for once and get over it instead of ignoring it and ending up really sick. As soon as I hang up, I'm going straight to bed.'

'Good idea,' Joanna said. 'Do you need me to do anything here at the hospital? Take any messages down to the ER for you?'

'No. They already know I'm going to be out for a few days.'

'Okay. I'll stop by in the morning to see if you need anything.'

'No,' Vielle said adamantly. 'I'm going to turn the doorbell and the phone off, and try to get some sleep.'

'Okay,' Joanna said doubtfully. 'Call me if you need anything. I'll have my pager on, I promise. And take care of yourself. This flu is supposed to be a real doozy. I don't want *you* having a near-death experience.'

'No,' Vielle said, and the exhaustion was back in her voice.

'Okay, you get some rest. I'll talk to you tomorrow.'

'I'll call you,' Vielle said.

As soon as she hung up, Joanna realized she'd forgotten to ask Vielle about the you-know-what she'd originally called about. She considered calling her back, but the last thing Vielle needed to be worrying about was somebody else's NDE, and anyway, several hours had passed. Mr Mandrake had probably gotten to whoever it was by now. Joanna called Kit instead and told her she might have been exposed to the flu.

'If I was, it was still worth it. It was so great to get out for a little while,' Kit said. 'I found out the answer to one of the questions you asked me last night. The dining room you described – light wood paneling, rose curtains, grand piano – is the À La Carte Restaurant. Here, let me read you the description. "In the sumptuous À La Carte Restaurant, pale walnut paneling contrasts beautifully with the rich Rose du Barry carpet. The chairs are covered in rose Aubusson tapestry."'

'Where was it on the ship?'

'On the Promenade Deck, all the way aft,' Kit said. 'That's toward the back of the ship.'

'The stern,' Joanna could hear Mr Briarley say in the background.

'Right, the stern,' Kit said. 'It was next to the second-class stairway. There were definitely two staircases, and I think there may have been three, but I can't tell for sure. One book mentions an aft stairway and another one a rear stairway. I can't tell if they're both referring to the same thing. I do know the Grand Staircase was in the middle of the ship.' And I intend to find it, Joanna thought.

She called Vielle in the morning, but Vielle had apparently taken the phone off the hook like she'd said she was going to. There was no answer, and no messages on her answering machine when she got to work. I should have swung by, she thought, getting dressed to go under. If there was still no message after the session, she would.

'The switchboard just called,' Richard said when she came out of the dressing room. 'Tish is out. She went home yesterday afternoon with the flu.'

'Does this mean I can't go under?' Joanna asked. Good. She'd be able to run over to Vielle's and make sure she was all right.

'They're sending a sub up,' Richard said, 'as soon as they can find one. The switchboard says a ton of people are out. How do *you* feel?'

'Fine.'

'Good. I'm raising the dosage this time. That will increase the amount of stimulation in the temporal lobe and alter the endorphin levels. That will alter the stimuli, which should produce a different unifying image.'

It won't, Joanna thought as the sub nurse, a stolid sixtyish woman, put the headphones on her and pulled the sleep mask down over her eyes without a word. It can't, because it's the *Titanic*, and I'm going to prove it. I'm going to find the Grand Staircase, she thought, and was in the passage, looking toward the door. It was half-shut, light coming from around the edges, and the voices from beyond it were muffled.

'... noise ...' she heard a man's voice say.

'What ... sound ...?' a woman's voice asked anxiously, and Joanna recognized it as that of the young woman in the nightgown. She pushed open the door.

The young woman was talking to the young man who'd come over to this side to investigate. 'You said you heard a noise,' she said, clutching the white sleeve of his sweater. 'Did it sound like something crashing down?'

'No,' the young man said. 'It sounded like a child's cry.'

Joanna looked over at the inside wall. There *was* a life preserver hanging next to the deck light, but she couldn't read what it said. The stout man in tweeds was standing in the way. She started toward him.

The stout man said, turning to his friend, 'What do they say is the trouble?'

Joanna strained to hear what his friend answered, but he spoke too softly, and he couldn't have said, 'We've struck an iceberg,' because the stout man sat down in a deck chair and opened his book, but at least he had moved from in front of the life preserver. She put up her hand, shielding her eyes from the glare, and tried to read the lettering.

She had been wrong. There was no lettering around the white ring of the life preserver, and no lettering on the backs of the deck chairs, or the metal lockers, or the doors. But one of them has to lead to the Grand Staircase, she thought, walking along the deck, trying each one.

The first two were locked. The third opened on a bare lightbulb and a metal stairway leading down. A crew stairway, Joanna thought, and tried the next one.

It was locked, too, but the one after that opened onto a darkened wooden staircase. It was wider than the one she'd climbed up before. The railings and newel posts were more elaborately carved, and rose-colored carpeting covered the stairs.

But the stairs should be marble, she thought, and why is it dark? There were light sconces on the wall, but no switch that she could see. She walked over to the railing and looked up. Far above, several decks up, she thought she caught a glimpse of gray. The skylight? Or the steward's white jacket? Or something else? There was only one way to find out. Joanna put her hand on the railing and started up the stairs.

It grew progressively darker as she climbed, so that she could barely see the steps in front of her, and nothing of what she was passing. The First-Class Dining Saloon should be here, she thought, rounding the landing. No, that was down on the Saloon Deck, but the cherub should be here, and the clock with Honour and Glory Crowning Time, and the skylight.

The skylight was there, a dark gray dome above her head as she started up the third flight. She could see its wrought-iron ribs, darker between the curves of darkened glass, but there was no cherub. The newel post was carved wood in the shape of a basket of fruit. There was a clock at the top of the stairs, but it was a square wooden one. Yet this had to be the Grand Staircase. There wouldn't be two elaborate skylights on one ship. What if Richard's right, and it is an amalgam? she thought, and opened the door at the head of the stairs.

She was back on the Boat Deck and it was still deserted and dark. There wasn't even a light on the bridge. She peered toward the bow, trying to make out the flicker of the Morse lamp or catch the scrape of the lantern shutter, but the deck was utterly silent. The boats, off to her right, still hung in their davits, shrouded in canvas.

The boats should have the name of the ship on them, she thought, and tried to raise the canvas on the nearest one, but it was lashed down tightly, the ropes knotted into fist-sized bundles. She couldn't budge the canvas at all.

She walked along the line of boats, trying to find one whose canvas was looser, but they were all as immovable as the first one. She crossed to the other side of the deck. There was a light on this side. From the bridge? No, closer than that. An open door in the near end of the building that housed the officers' quarters. Joanna went over to it and looked in.

It was some sort of gymnasium. There were Indian clubs and medicine balls stacked against the inside wall and pieces of exercise equipment scattered around the red-and-white tile floor: a mechanical horse and a rowing machine and a tall black weight-lifting apparatus, the same shape and size as a guillotine. A punching bag hung from the ceiling.

Against the right-hand wall stood a line of stationary bicycles. A young man in a T-shirt and gray sweatpants was riding the middle bicycle, pedaling furiously. On the wall in front of him was a large clock face with numbers and red and blue arrows pointing to them.

The young man had pedaled till both arrows were on the final number. He gave a final burst of effort, bent forward over the handlebars. The red-and-blue numbers swung up to zero, and he stopped pedaling and raised his fists, like a runner after a race. He dismounted and bent to pick up a towel, and she saw his face. 'Oh,' she said and sucked in her breath.

It was Greg Menotti.

29

'I am dying, but without expectation of a speedy release. Is it not strange that very recently by-gone images, and scenes of early life, have stolen into my mind …?'
– From a letter written by SAMUEL TAYLOR COLERIDGE

'I know you,' Greg Menotti said, dabbing at his face with a towel. He walked over to where she was standing. 'Don't I?'

'I'm …' Joanna said, and for one horrible moment could not think of her name, '… Joanna Lander,' and then remembered he had known her as Dr Lander. 'Dr Lander.'

'Dr Lander?' he said, clearly still trying to place her. 'You look so familiar … oh, wait, I remember you. You were the one who asked me all those questions that day I got hit on the head. You wouldn't give me your phone number. So what are you doing here? Did you change your mind?'

'Hit on the head?'

'Yeah, by a piece of ice a semi threw off. I was shoveling my car out of a ditch, and it knocked me unconscious, and they took me to the ER, and then you came and asked me a lot of questions about tunnels and lights and angels,' he said. 'Don't tell me you don't remember.'

'No,' Joanna said slowly. 'I remember.'

'I kept trying to tell that to the ER people, but they insisted I'd had a heart attack.' He shook his head, amused. 'So is that why you came back? You decided you'd give me your phone number after all?'

'No,' Joanna said, thinking, He doesn't know he's dead. 'I came to find out the name of this ship.'

'Ship?' he said blankly. 'What do you mean, ship? This is a health club. I work out here three times a week. Haven't you been here before? Here, let me show you around.' He took her arm and led her over to the stationary bicycles. 'See this dial? This blue arrow measures distance traveled and this red one measures your speed.'

He led her over to what looked like one of those mechanical bulls they had in bars, only with an uncomfortable-looking hump. 'This is a mechanical camel, and over there's the rowing machine. Excellent cardiovascular exercise. There's also a squash court, a swimming pool, a massage room –'

Joanna was looking at the stack of Indian clubs and medicine balls. They should have 'Property of' and the name of the ship on them. She disengaged her arm from Greg's grip and went over to look at them. She picked up a medicine ball. It was almost too heavy to lift, but Greg took it easily out of her hands and tossed it against the wall. It rebounded with a loud thud.

Joanna bent and looked at the other medicine ball and then the Indian clubs, but there was no name on any of them. And Greg doesn't even know he's on a ship, let alone which ship, she thought. 'Greg,' she said. 'Have you heard anything?'

He tossed the medicine ball again. 'Heard anything?'

'Yes,' she said.

'Like what?' Thud.

'Like engines stopping?' she said. 'Or a collision?' Leading, she thought, waiting for his answer.

'A collision? No, thank goodness. Especially since it was one of those Ford Explorers. They're huge.' He tossed the medicine ball again. 'No, just a bump on the head, but it must have really knocked me out cold because the paramedics thought I'd had a heart attack. I told them, "I can't have had a heart attack—" '

'I work out three times a week at my health club,' Joanna said and then was sorry because Greg stopped, clutching the heavy medicine ball to his chest, and looked at her fearfully. He went over to the rowing machine, sat down, and began pulling the oars toward him with strong, steady strokes.

'Greg –' Joanna said, and caught a flicker of movement in the corner of her eye. She ran over to the door. The steward. He was walking toward the bridge with a folded note in his hand.

Joanna hurried after him. He walked past the officers' quarters and turned into an unlit corridor. Joanna followed him, around a corner, down a short, narrow passage, around another corner. Like a maze, Joanna thought. Down another passage, and out onto the other side of the deck. There were boats on this side, too. Was that where the officer was going, to uncover the boats?

No. He knocked on a door and opened it. Golden light spilled out onto the deck, and she could hear the murmur of voices. 'You may never get another chance,' the officer said, and reemerged, laughing, and walked down the deck toward the stern, obviously headed for the stairs. Joanna followed him, stopping as she passed to look in the still-open door.

A blond man in a white shirt sat with his back to the door, hunched over a table, tapping steadily on a telegraph key. His coat was slung over the back of his chair and he was wearing headphones, old-fashioned ones with a band around the back of his head as well as over the top. Above his head, a blue spark jumped the gap between two metal struts, flickering and snapping as he tapped the key.

This is the wireless room, Joanna thought, forgetting all about the officer. And the man was Jack Phillips, busily sending out messages. Not SOSs yet, Joanna thought, looking at the blue spark, dancing merrily above the wireless operator's head, and remembering the officer's laughter. And Jack wasn't wearing his lifejacket yet.

These must be passenger messages he was sending, the backlog that had built up over the weekend. Joanna remembered Mr Briarley telling the class that the wireless was such a novelty the passengers all wanted to send one, and Jack Phillips had been so busy the night of the collision that, when the *Californian* had tried to cut in with an ice message, he had cut them off, he had told them to shut up, that he was working the relay station, Cape Race.

And SOSs were simple. Three dots, three dashes, three dots. She remembered Mr Briarley telling them that was why SOS had been chosen for the distress call, because it was so simple, anyone could send it. These messages weren't simple. 'Having wonderful time,' Joanna thought, listening to the complicated tapping. 'Wish you were here.'

She leaned forward, trying to hear the pattern, trying to decipher the message, but he was tapping too fast for her to be able to separate out the dots from the dashes, and the buzzing from the spark overhead interrupted her concentration.

She walked up closer behind him, and as she did, she could hear a low murmur. He's saying the letters as he taps them out, she thought. 'C,' he said, making a rapid series of taps, 'Q … D … C … Q … D.' Not a word. A code? The call letters of the *Titanic*?

There was a thud from somewhere out on deck. Greg Menotti, Joanna thought, throwing the medicine ball against the wall of the gymnasium, and glanced behind her. Jack Phillips didn't look up or pause in his sending.

He can't hear with his headphones on, Joanna thought, any more than I can hear Richard or Tish with my headphones on, and when the *Titanic* was sinking, he had been so intent on sending he hadn't even noticed the stoker sneaking up behind him, attempting to steal his lifejacket. Joanna took another step closer, trying to hear his murmurings over the heavy thuds. 'Q … D …'

Thud. It was impossible to hear the tapping with this thudding going on. She went outside on deck to tell Greg to stop, but the sound wasn't coming from the gymnasium, it was coming from the stairway.

Joanna opened the door to the stairwell and went in. Thud. The sound was coming from below. She leaned over the railing and looked down but she couldn't see past the first turning of the stairs. 'Hang on!' a man's voice said. Joanna recognized it as the voice of the officer who had ordered the sailor to use the Morse lamp. 'What do you think you're doing?'

There was no answer except a thud and then another one. Joanna went down to the first landing. A man in a dark blue uniform was dragging something heavy up the stairs. It looked like a body.

465

The officer was at the bottom of the flight and climbing up toward the man, looking angry. 'You can't bring that up here.'

'It's the only way up that's not flooded,' the man in the uniform said, and dragged the body up one step, then another, till he was only five steps below Joanna. It wasn't a body. It was a big canvas sack with a crest stenciled on it. A mailbag, Joanna thought.

'There's water all over the mail room,' the man, who must be a postal clerk, said. He opened the neck of the bag, reached in, and pulled out a handful of sodden letters. 'Look at that!' he said, waving them in the face of the officer. 'Ruined!' He brandished them at Joanna. She flinched back. 'How'm I supposed to deliver that?' he demanded. He jammed it back in the bag, cinched the neck shut, humped the mailbag up over another step.

'Then you'll have to bring it up some other way,' the officer said, stepping in front of him. 'You'll ruin the floors.' He pointed down at the carpet. Where the bag had rested, the rose carpet was wet.

'Can't be helped,' the postal clerk said, heaving the bag up another step. 'It's got to get through. I have to get it into the boats. Give me a hand here,' he said to Joanna, but she was looking down at the wet carpet. The water had soaked into it, staining its rose a dark, disturbing red, like blood.

'How bad is it?' the officer asked.

'All the way up to the saloon deck,' the postal clerk said. 'She doesn't have much longer.'

'What does he mean, she doesn't have much longer?' Greg Menotti said from behind her. She turned around. He was on the step above her, watching the postal clerk hoist the mailbag up another step. 'Why is he doing that?'

'Because she's sinking,' the postal clerk said, and to Joanna, 'You'd better get into a boat, miss.'

'Which deck is the Saloon Deck?' Joanna asked him. 'Is it C Deck?'

'What does he mean, sinking?' Greg said. 'This isn't a ship. It's a health club.' He took hold of Joanna's arm. 'I thought you wanted to see the rest of the facilities.'

'There isn't time,' Joanna said, trying to free her arm. 'Is the Saloon Deck C Deck?'

'You have to make time,' Greg said, pulling her up the stairs. 'Your health is the most important thing there is. We've got a full program of squash, racquetball, tennis –'

He was going too fast. She lost her balance and nearly fell. 'Steady, looks like you could use some stair-walking exercise,' he said, pulling her to her feet, but she couldn't get her balance. The stair was angled oddly, her foot kept sliding off it –

Oh, God, she thought, it's beginning to list. 'I have to go,' she said, tugging frantically to free her arm from Greg's hand. 'The Saloon Deck—'

'I work out here three times a week,' he said, remorselessly gripping her arm. 'A regular exercise regimen is essential to—'

Joanna wrenched free and ran toward the stairs, stumbling, her arms out for balance, and pushed open the door to the stairway. The mail clerk had dragged the mailbag nearly all the way to the top of the stairs. Joanna ran past him down the steps, skirting the dark, wet stain where the mailbag had lain.

'You shouldn't run without warming up first,' Greg called after her. 'You'll get a charley—' The door closed on his voice and she fled down the stairs, around the landings, her hand skimming the polished oak railings as she ran. Down and down, not counting landings or decks or doors, running blindly, blindly, out the door, down the deck, yanking the door open and plunging into the passage, into the dark and the dark –

And the dark. I'm still in the passage, Joanna thought desperately, and heard Richard say, 'You need to remove the sleep mask.'

She opened her eyes and blinked in surprise at a total stranger. It took her another panicked minute to remember that Tish was out with the flu and this was the sub nurse. 'Just rest. Don't try to talk,' Richard said, and began explaining the post-session procedures to the nurse. He doesn't want me to say it's the *Titanic* in front of her, she thought.

But it wasn't the *Titanic*. The staircase was all wrong and so was the gymnasium. The *Titanic* had had one. She remembered Mr Briarley talking about it, telling them how opulent the ship had been, but it would hardly have been up on the Boat Deck. And, even though the *Titanic* had been a royal mail ship, they wouldn't have dragged sacks of mail up from the mail room. Fifteen hundred people had drowned that night. They would hardly have been worried about the mail. And Greg Menotti obviously wasn't on the *Titanic*, Joanna thought, frustrated.

Not half as frustrated as Richard, however. 'You saw the *Titanic* again!' he said when the nurse had finished monitoring her vitals and left, and Joanna had told him. 'How could you have? Look at these scans.' He'd dragged her over to the console. 'The pattern of temporal-lobe activity is completely different, and the acetylcholine level is much higher than before.'

'That looks the same,' Joanna said, pointing at a red-orange patch in the hippocampus.

'It is, and so's the activity in the amygdala. They're the same in all the NDEs, but they don't have anything to do with producing images.'

'Was the pattern in long-term completely different, too?' Joanna asked, looking at the shifting reds and blues and yellows.

'No,' he admitted. 'The last few scans match, although they don't fit any of the L+R formulas. Was the ending of your NDE the same as last time?'

'No,' she said. She told him about the flight down the stairs and into the passage. 'It was the same passage, but this time the door was shut and I had to run a lot farther before I was back in the lab.'

'You say the same passage? Do you mean it looked the same?'

'No,' Joanna said. 'I mean it's the same passage. It's in the same place, it always opens onto the same part of the deck,' she said. 'It's a real place. The doors always open on the same stairways, the Boat Deck's always the same number of flights up, the lifeboats and the officers' quarters and the bridge are always in the same relationship to each other.'

'You said this time there was a gymnasium,' Richard said skeptically.

'It was always there, but the door was shut before. It's not like a dream where things shift around and you're in one place and then another with no transition in between. It's a *real* place.'

'Real,' he said, and all the wariness and skepticism were back in his face. In a minute he'd accuse her of being Bridey Murphy again.

'I don't mean real,' she said, defeated. 'I mean three-dimensional. I mean linear.'

He was shaking his head. 'There's no activation of the spatial cortex areas. What about the beginning? Was it the same?'

'No,' she said. 'I came through a little later this time, after the young man came over to investigate the noise.'

'But the people and what they said were the same?'

'Basically.'

'Basically,' he muttered, staring at the screens. 'Even though the temporal-lobe and L+R patterns are completely different. What were you thinking about just before you went into non-REM sleep? Maybe your conscious mind is influencing what you see.'

'The *Titanic*,' Joanna admitted, and Richard looked encouraged. 'But last time I was thinking about Pompeii, and the first three times I obviously couldn't have been thinking about the *Titanic*, and it's been the same place every time.'

'And you hear the same sound as you go through,' Richard said thoughtfully and began to type, absorbed.

Joanna went down to her office to transcribe her account and check on Vielle. There was no answer, but she had seven new messages. Joanna listened to them, fast-forwarding as soon as she'd established it wasn't Vielle. Records. Maisie. Guadalupe.

She must not have gotten the message I left for her, Joanna thought. And she must be back at work, and Tish was right about this flu not lasting long. Maybe Vielle's back, too, and that's why she's not answering. She hit 'next message.' Mr Mandrake. She hit 'delete.' Betty Peterson.

'I found out the title,' Betty's voice said, and Joanna pulled back the finger she had poised over the 'next message' button and listened to the message.

'You'll never guess how!' Betty said. 'Last night I dug out my old high school yearbook to see who else was in that class with us, and I was going through the section with our pictures – and, oh, my God, the hair! the clothes! – and as I'm looking through them, I saw that Nadine Swartheimer – do you remember Nadine? Wild hair that stuck out all over and Birkenstocks, even in the dead of winter? – well, anyway, she'd signed her picture, and there it was! But that's not all. I found out something else. You need to call me. 'Bye.'

I don't believe it, Joanna thought. After all that, she didn't tell me the name of the book, and now I'll have to call her back, and we'll probably play telephone tag for a week. How did Betty ever get straight A's?

She'd have to call her, but not until she'd finished checking to see if Vielle had called. She went rapidly through the rest of the messages. Mr Mandrake again. Delete. Someone named Leonard Fanshawe.

But not Vielle. Joanna tried her again, but there was still no answer. I think I'd better go down to the ER and see if she's back and, if she's not, go check on her, Joanna thought, and gathered up her coat, keys, and purse, but just as she was starting out the door, the phone rang. Joanna let the answering machine pick up. 'Hi,' Vielle said, and Joanna snatched up the receiver.

'How *are* you?' she said.

'Better,' Vielle said, and she sounded better. Her voice was stronger and steadier than the day before. 'I'm still going to stay at home for a couple of days, and, no, I don't need you to bring me anything. I don't want you getting this.'

'Okay,' Joanna said, 'although I've already been exposed. Tish has it, and so does Guadalupe.'

'Well, you're not going to get it from me. I'm locking my door, and I'm not letting you in. So don't even think about coming over.'

'All right,' Joanna promised, 'but you have to promise to call me and tell me how you're doing and if you need anything,' and, before Vielle could protest, 'I can leave it outside your door.'

'I promise I'll check in,' Vielle said and started to hang up.

'Oh, wait,' Joanna said. 'What about the you-know-what?'

'The what?'

'I don't know. That was what you called it. You left a message that I was supposed to call you, that you had a you-know-what for me. Yesterday. Before you went home sick. You paged me.'

'Oh,' Vielle said finally. 'Yes. A patient came in with a gall bladder attack and happened to mention he'd had an NDE a couple of years ago. We admitted him for surgery.' Joanna wondered if that was the Leonard Fanshawe who had called her, but Vielle said, 'His name's Eduardo Ortiz.'

'Who else was there when he mentioned it?' Joanna asked, thinking of Mr Mandrake.

'Just me,' Vielle said. 'I thought he was a good bet since he wasn't admitted for anything life-threatening, so he'd be flying below Mr Mandrake's radar.'

Joanna thought so, too. As soon as she got off the phone, she called the switchboard and got his room number, and then called the surgical floor. 'He had surgery this morning, and he's still out,' the nurse said.

'When does he go home?' Joanna asked.

The nurse checked. 'Tomorrow.' Which is what's wrong with HMOs, Joanna thought. They're not in the hospital long enough to tell anyone they've even *had* a near-death experience, let alone describe it. The nurse had thought Mr Ortiz would probably wake up around noon, which would give Joanna plenty of time to record and transcribe her NDE.

She did both and then took the transcript to Richard, who was glaring at the screens. 'How's it going?' she asked, handing him the transcript.

'Terrible. I thought maybe the initial stimulus was what was determining the unifying image, and that was why you continued to see the *Titanic*, even though the stimuli were different, but in this last NDE there was no activity in the superior auditory cortex at all.' He raked his hand through his hair. 'I just don't have enough data. Have you been able to reschedule Mrs Haighton yet?'

'No.'

'And you haven't heard from Mr Pearsall about when he's coming back?'

She shook her head.

'Then I've got to find out what's aborting Mrs Troudtheim's NDE-state and fix it. We need her.'

'I'll call Mr Pearsall and Mrs Haighton,' Joanna said. And go find her at the Spring Fling, or wherever she is, and drag her back here myself, she thought, going back to her office to call, but the housekeeper didn't know where she was.

'Some kind of meeting,' she said. 'She has so many I get them confused.' And there was no answer at Mr Pearsall's number.

Joanna made a note to try them both again and then listened to the messages she'd fast-forwarded through before. Guadalupe wanted Joanna to call her. Maisie had something important to tell her. Leonard Fanshawe said, 'I understand you're interested in near-death experiences. I had one six months ago, and since then I have discovered I have unusual powers: telekinesis, clairvoyance, distance-viewing, and teleportation. I would very much like to talk with you about this,' and gave his number.

Joanna called him and gave him Mr Mandrake's number. Then she called Mr Pearsall again. No answer. She called Betty Peterson. Her line was busy.

She printed out a file copy of the transcript and then sat there staring at the screen, trying to make sense of it. It *was* the *Titanic*, she was sure of it, in spite of the staircase and the mailbag and the lack of activity in the auditory cortex.

She called Kit to ask her what the call letters of the *Titanic* had been and what deck the gymnasium had been on. And whether it had a mechanical camel. I surely wouldn't have confabulated a detail that specific, she thought, punching in Kit's number, and then remembered Mr Wojakowski and 'The Katzenjammer Kids.'

Kit's line was busy. Joanna looked at her watch. It was eleven-thirty. She decided to take a chance on Mr Ortiz's having come out of the anesthetic early, and went down to the surgical ward. He was awake, but the surgeon was in with him. 'And then we've got to do his post-op check,' the nurse subbing for Patricia said. 'It'll be about twenty minutes.'

Twenty minutes. Not long enough to go back up to her office and get anything useful done. She could go see Maisie – Peds was just two floors up and actually in the same wing – but the likelihood of getting away from Maisie in under an hour was nonexistent. I'll go see Guadalupe instead, Joanna thought, and headed for the elevator.

A pair of nurses Joanna didn't know were waiting for it, their heads together, talking. '... and she said, that's it, I'm not coming to work in that ER one more day,' one of the nurses said, and the other said, 'I don't blame her.' Vielle should be listening to this, Joanna thought, and the elevator door opened.

Mr Mandrake was inside. '... evidence which will prove to the skeptic that the near-death experience is real,' he was saying to a man with a copy of *The Light at the End of the Tunnel.* 'No so-called "rational" explanation is possible.'

All his attention was on the man, and the two nurses, still gossiping, shielded her for the moment. '... just a flesh wound, thank God,' one of them said, 'but still.'

Mr Mandrake hadn't seen her yet. Joanna turned and walked rapidly away, her head averted. I'll go see Guadalupe later, she thought. I'll go down and pick up the release forms instead.

'Joanna Lander,' Mr Mandrake said.

Oh, no, he'd seen her. She kept walking, resisting the impulse to look back and see if he was following her.

'... a colleague of mine,' he said.

He hadn't seen her. He was just talking about her. 'She's working on a project that will confirm my findings.'

A *colleague* of mine, Joanna fumed, walking faster. It would almost be worth it to turn around and go tell the man she was *not* Mr Mandrake's colleague and their project proved no such thing.

Almost, she thought and ducked into a stairway. It only went down one flight, but at least she had gotten away from Mr Mandrake. She could take the service elevator up to the fifth-floor walkway. No, she'd have to go through Medicine. She didn't want to take the risk of running into Mrs Davenport.

Talk about out of the frying pan into the fire. She'd better take the walkway on second.

She went down the stairs and along a corridor full of offices. It was usually deserted, but not today. A group of elderly people were sitting in the hall on plastic chairs, playing cards. One of them stood up as soon as he saw Joanna and waved his cards at her. 'Hiya, Doc,' he said.

30

'Come as quickly as possible, old man. Engine room filled up to the boilers.'
     – Wireless message from the *Titanic* to the *Carpathia*

This is not my day, Joanna thought. 'Mr Wojakowski,' she said. 'What are you doing here?'

'Ed,' he corrected. He cocked his thumb at the door behind him. 'This is that hearing project I told you about.' He leaned toward her confidentially. 'I gotta say, Doc, your project was a hell of a lot more interesting than this thing. All we do is sit around with headphones on and raise our hands if we hear a beep.'

Joanna looked at the cardplayers. 'And play acey-deucey?'

'Naw, none of them were ever in the navy. All they know how to play is hearts. I been trying to talk 'em into poker, but they're all too cheap. Say, I heard one of the docs down in the ER got shot. You know anything about that?'

That must be what the two nurses by the elevator had been gossiping about. 'No.'

'I hope it's nothing serious. Did I ever tell you about the time on the *Yorktown* when I got shot right in the – well, it ain't polite to say where – and I start yelping and Big Bunion Pakigian says—'

'Mr Wojakowski?' a lab-coated technician with a clipboard said from the door.

'Be right there,' Mr Wojakowski said. 'Well, anyway, Doc, you see you don't go getting shot. And if you need me on your project, you just go ahead and schedule me. Like I say, all we do's sit around. I got plenty of time to do your project and this one both.'

'Mr *Wojakowski*,' the technician said disapprovingly.

Mr Wojakowski leaned close to Joanna and whispered, '4-F.' Joanna had to laugh. The technician looked even crabbier. 'See ya, Doc,' Mr Wojakowski said jauntily, handed his cards to one of the volunteers, and disappeared through the door.

She looked at her watch and went back up to the surgical ward. Mr Ortiz's door was shut. 'One of his drains came out,' the sub nurse told her. 'It'll be another twenty minutes at least.'

Joanna thanked her and went up to see Maisie. Mrs Nellis was just coming out of the room, smiling brightly. 'Maisie's on a new drug and it's working wonders. She's stabilized, and it's completely eliminated the fluid-retention problem. If this keeps up, I'll be able to take her home before you know it.'

She was right. Maisie's arms and legs weren't as puffy, but, because the swelling had gone down, you could see how pitifully thin she'd gotten. Her hospital ID bracelet dangled loosely from her birdlike wrist. At least she can stop worrying about them having to cut it off, Joanna thought.

'I've been reading about the *Titanic* so I'd be ready to help you with your research,' Maisie said eagerly, reaching immediately in the bedside drawer for her tablet and pencil. 'So, what do you want me to look up?'

'Are you sure you shouldn't be resting?' Joanna asked. 'I just saw your mom, and she said you'd just started on a new drug.'

'It's *not* new,' Maisie said. 'It's nadolal, the same one I was on before I was on the amiodipril.'

The one that couldn't keep her stabilized, Joanna thought. The one she was on when she coded.

'And all I *do* is rest. Looking up stuff doesn't make me tired. It's a lot more fun than watching stupid videos.' She waved her hand at the TV, where *Winnie the Pooh* was playing soundlessly.

'All right. I need to know the names of all the ships the *Titanic* sent SOSs to,' Joanna said. 'That should be safe, and, according to Kit, time-consuming.'

Maisie frowned at her. 'You don't send SOSs *to* anybody. You just send them out and hope somebody hears you.'

'That's what I meant,' Joanna said, 'the names of the ships the *Titanic*'s wireless contacted.'

Maisie wrote 'ships' in her childish round hand. 'I bet there's a lot of them 'cause the wireless operator kept sending right up till it sank.'

'Maisie—'

'His name was Jack Phillips, and the captain told him he could stop. "At a time like this, it's every man for himself," he said, but he just kept on sending.'

'Maisie,' Joanna said seriously, 'if you're going to help me, you can't tell me things about the *Titanic*, just the answers to my questions. Not anything else. It's important. Do you understand?'

'Uh-huh,' Maisie said. 'Because of confabulation, right?'

She is entirely too smart, Joanna thought. 'Yes. Telling me things could contaminate the project. Do you think you can do that? Just tell me the answers and nothing else?'

'Uh-huh. Can I tell you stuff not about the *Titanic*?'

'Of course,' Joanna said. 'Is that why you called me, because you had something to tell me?'

'Well, ask you, really,' Maisie said, and Joanna braced herself. 'What if Mercy General burned down?'

And where did *this* come from? Joanna wondered. 'The alarms would go off, and we'd get all the patients outside,' Joanna said. 'And there's a sprinkler system that comes on automatically.'

'No, I know that,' Maisie said. 'I mean, what about their ID bracelets? They're plastic. If the hospital burned up, they'd melt and nobody would know who they *are*.'

The hospital bracelet again. This has to do with Little Miss 1565, Joanna thought. Maisie's afraid she'll die and no one will identify her. But everyone in the hospital knew her, she was surrounded by family and friends. Why was she worried about that? Was she taking a small and manageable worry and making it stand for the things that were really worrying her, a metaphor for fears she was too frightened to face? Like loss of identity?

Which is the thing everyone's afraid of when it comes to death, Joanna thought. Not judgment or separation or the fires of hell, but the idea of not existing. That's why everyone likes Mr Mandrake's Other Side, Joanna thought. It isn't because it promises light and warm, fuzzy feelings. It's because it promises that, even though the heart has stopped and the body shut down, you won't suffer the fate of Little Miss 1565. That the people gathered at the gate will know who you are, and so will you.

'Your doctor ID would burn right up, too,' Maisie was saying. She pointed at Joanna's hospital ID hanging from its woven lanyard. 'They should be metal.'

Like dog tags, Joanna thought.

'So, what else do you want me to find out?' Maisie said, as if the matter had been settled. 'Do you want me to write down the wireless messages he sent to the different ships?'

'No, just the name of the ships,' Joanna said and then thought of something. 'And the call letters of the *Titanic*.'

'I don't have to look that up. I already know. It's MGY, because—' she said, and then stopped.

'Because why?' Joanna asked, but Maisie didn't answer. She folded her arms and stared belligerently at Joanna.

'Maisie?' she asked. 'What's the matter?'

'You *told* me I was supposed to tell you the answer and not anything else.'

'You're right, I did. That's just what I wanted.' Only what I really wanted was the call letters to be CQD, not MGY.

'Okay, what else?' Maisie said.

'That's all, just the call letters and the names of the ships,' Joanna said.

'That's hardly anything,' Maisie protested. 'It'll take me about five minutes. Don't you have anything else you want me to find out?'

It was tempting to ask her about the Morse lamp. She'd have the answer more promptly even than Kit, and Joanna knew Maisie could keep a secret. She was a master at it. But she also wouldn't be able to resist saying, 'Did you know …?' 'I need to know about the *Carpathia*,' Joanna said, deciding. The *Carpathia* hadn't shown up on the scene until well after the *Titanic* had gone down, so information about it couldn't contaminate her NDEs, and there was a ton of information on the *Carpathia*. It should keep Maisie occupied for days.

'Car-pa-thia,' Maisie said, writing it down. 'What do you need to know?'

'Everything,' Joanna told her. 'Where it was, when it found out the *Titanic* was in trouble and what it did, and how it picked up the survivors.'

'And who they were,' Maisie said, writing busily. 'I know who one of them was. Mr Ismay.' Her tone conveyed contempt. 'He was the owner guy, but he didn't even try to save people, he just climbed in one of the lifeboats even though the men weren't supposed to, it was supposed to be women and children first, and saved himself, the big coward. Everybody else was really brave, though, like—'

'Maisie,' Joanna warned. 'Only the answers I asked for.'

'Okay,' Maisie said. 'Can I tell you what Molly Brown said to Mr Ismay? She was on the *Carpathia* when she said it.'

'All right,' Joanna said, thinking, Maybe I should have picked the *Californian*. It didn't have any contact with the *Titanic* at all. 'What did Molly Brown say?'

'She went up to Mr Ismay,' Maisie said, putting her hands on her hips, 'and said, "Where I come from, we'd string you up on the nearest pine tree." And I think they should've. The big coward.'

'Maybe he was afraid,' Joanna said, thinking of her own panicked flight down the slanting stairs and into the passage.

'Well, of *course* he was afraid,' Maisie said. 'He still should have tried to save Lorrai—' She bit off the word. 'I was going to say somebody's name,' she said virtuously, 'but you said just the answer, so I didn't.'

'Good girl,' Joanna said, looking at her watch. It was nearly two. 'I have to go.' She stood up.

'I'll page you when I find out stuff,' Maisie said, pulling *The Child's Titanic* out from under the covers.

'No,' Joanna said, envisioning Maisie paging her every fifteen minutes. 'Don't page me till you know all the ships.'

'Okay,' Maisie said, opening her book, and, amazingly, didn't try to stop Joanna from leaving.

I need to get down to see Mr Ortiz, she thought, going through Peds, but instead she went back down to the hearing center. The group of volunteers had dwindled to four, but Mr Wojakowski was still there. Joanna had the feeling he stayed for the company even when he was no longer needed.

'Well, hiya, Doc,' he said when he saw her, sounding genuinely surprised and pleased, and she wondered, ashamed, if he realized how she tried to avoid him.

I have no business asking him a favor, she thought, but this was for Maisie, and if he didn't know, he could just say so. And how can he know? she thought. He probably wasn't even *in* the navy. He made all this up, remember?

'Ed, you were in the navy. Do you know where I could get a set of dog tags made? It's for a friend of mine.'

'Well, now, that's a tough one,' he said, taking off his baseball cap and scratching his head. 'During the war you got 'em when you signed up. They stamped 'em out with a hand press, looked like a cross between a typewriter and a credit card machine, and hung 'em around your neck straight out of the showers, before they even issued you your uniform. I says to the CO, "Don't we need pants more'n dog tags?" and he says, "You might get killed before you get your pants on and we'd need to know who you are," and Fritz Kraut-hammer says, "Hell, if I'm killed without pants on, I don't *want* anybody to know who I am!" Fritz was a card. One time—'

'Do you know where I could get dog tags nowadays? They wouldn't have to be real ones.'

'You used to be able to get 'em made at the dime store or the train station.' He scratched his head again. 'I'll have to give it some thought. What would you want on 'em?'

'Just a name,' she said, taking her notebook out of her cardigan pocket. 'And it wouldn't have to look like dog tags. Just a name tag on a chain that goes around the neck. Metal,' she added. She printed Maisie's name, tore the sheet out of the notebook, and handed it to Mr Wojakowski.

'I'll ask around,' he said doubtfully. 'You sometimes can find stuff you never thought you could. Did I ever tell you about the time I had to ditch my Wildcat and ended up on Malakula?'

Yes, Joanna thought, but she had just asked him a favor. She owed him one, and she knew what it was like when no one would listen to your stories, or believe you. So she sat down on one of the plastic chairs and listened to the whole thing: the escape in a dugout canoe, the drifting at sea for days, the *Yorktown* steaming up, flags flying, sailors hallooing, to save him, 'just like Jesus Christ Himself, raised from the dead,' and she had to admit that, true or not, it was a great story.

Mr Wojakowski walked Joanna to the elevator. 'I'll see what I can do about these dog tags. How soon do you need 'em?'

'Soon,' Joanna said, thinking of Maisie's thin wrist, her blue lips.

'It's too bad Chick Upchurch isn't still around. Did I ever tell you about Chick? Machinist's mate on the Old Yorky, and he could make anything, and I do mean anything,' Mr Wojakowski said, and she had to practically shut his hand in the elevator to get away from him, though he didn't seem put out.

Neither did Mr Ortiz, even though he had three drains in him, two of which had already had to be replaced. 'I don't care. I feel better than I have in two years,' he said. 'They should've thought of this before.'

He was happy to talk to Joanna. 'It's still as real to me today as it was two years ago,' he said, and described it for her in detail: floating near the ceiling of the operating room, tunnel, light, the Virgin Mary radiating light, dead relatives waiting to welcome him to heaven.

Maybe Mr Mandrake's right, Joanna thought, listening to him describe his life review, and what I'm seeing isn't a real NDE at all. Certainly no one else has seen a postal clerk dragging a sack of wet mail up a carpeted staircase.

'And then I had this feeling like it was time to go back,' Mr Ortiz said, 'and I went back down the tunnel, and at the end of it was the operating room.'

'Can you be more specific?' Joanna said. 'About the feeling?'

'It was like a tug,' he said, but the gesture he made with his hand was of a shove. 'I can't describe it.'

Joanna consulted her notes. 'Can you tell me how the Virgin Mary looked?'

'She was dressed in white. She had this light radiating from her,' he said, and this time the gesture matched his words, 'like diamonds.' She asked him several more questions and then shut off the recorder and thanked him for his time.

'I'm not really all that interested in near-death experiences,' he said. 'My real interest is in dreams. Is your project involved with dream imagery at all?'

'No,' Joanna said and stood up.

Mr Ortiz nodded. 'Most scientists are too hidebound and narrow-minded to believe in dreams. Analyzing the images in your dreams can cure cancer, did you know that?'

'No.'

Mr Ortiz nodded wisely. 'If you dream of a shark, that means cancer. A rope means death. If you want to tell me one of your dreams, I can analyze it right now.'

'I have an appointment,' Joanna said, and escaped.

Is everybody a nutcase? she wondered, going back up to her office. Dream imagery. But once in her office, going over the transcripts of the multiple NDEs, she began wondering if dream imagery might be the key. Not Mr Ortiz's brand, of course, where images were assigned arbitrary meanings: a snake means sex, a book means an unexpected visitor. That was only a kind of glorified fortune-telling.

And Freudian dream analysis wasn't much better. It tried to reduce everything to basic sexual desires and fears when dreaming was actually much more complex. Some imagery in dreams was lifted directly from the events of the day before, some from underlying worries and concerns, some from outside stimuli, like an alarm clock, and some from the neurochemicals generated during REM sleep, most particularly acetylcholine, which Richard had said was elevated during NDEs.

It was acetylcholine that made connections between the inputted data and long-term memory, connections the dreaming mind expressed sometimes directly and sometimes symbolically, so that the alarm clock's ringing was transformed into a siren or a scream, and it, the Pop-Tart you had for breakfast, and the patient you were worried about all became incorporated into a single dream narrative. And it was possible, taking all those things into consideration, to analyze the content of the dream. Which was what Richard had been doing when he'd said the acetylcholine made the *Titanic* as likely an association as a hospital walkway, but he had been talking about the NDE as a whole, not the individual images within it.

Joanna hadn't thought of analyzing those in terms of dream imagery, partly because the NDE didn't feel like a dream and partly because some of the imagery – the light and the tunnel – was obviously direct manifestations of the stimuli. But that didn't mean all of them were. What if some of them were symbolic interpretations of what was happening in the NDE?

Could that be why she kept remembering Mr Briarley's lecture on metaphors, because the images in the NDE were metaphors? She had focused all her attention on trying to find out what Mr Briarley had said, but maybe the connection was in the NDE itself, hidden in what she was seeing and hearing.

She called up the transcript of her last time under and began going through it line by line. Some things were obviously direct representations of temporal-lobe stimuli. The lights from the Morse lamp and the deck lights and the light spilling out from the gymnasium and bridge obviously were, and she wondered if all the instances of white clothing – gloves, nightgown, steward's white jacket – weren't, too.

Some of the images were clearly taken directly from the *Titanic* – the lifeboats, the passengers out on deck, the deck chairs – and still others from her waking life – Greg Menotti and the red sneaker, and maybe even the blanket, though that could also be from the illustration on the cover of *A Night to Remember*.

Which left the details that couldn't be attributed to the *Titanic* or the temporal lobe and therefore might be significant: Jack Phillips's tapping out CQD instead of MGY, the mail clerk dragging the wet sack of mail up the stairs, the stairs themselves, similar to the Grand Staircase and yet lacking the cherub and Honour and Glory, the location of the gymnasium, the mechanical camel. If they were symbols, they were much more subtle ones than 'snake equals sex.'

If they were symbols. There was no point in trying to decipher them if in fact they were something that had come from her memories of the *Titanic*. She needed to have Kit find out. She made a list of things she needed to know and then called Kit. Mr Briarley answered. 'Do you have a hall pass?' he demanded, and when she told him she needed to speak to Kit, ' "He cut a rope from a broken spar and bound her to the mast." '

Kit came on the line. 'Sorry,' she said. 'He's been doing "The Wreck of the Hesperus" all morning. I thought it might be a clue, but it's Longfellow, so he would have taught it in junior English, not senior.'

' "Oh, father! I hear the church-bells ring, oh, say, what may it be?" " ' Mr Briarley said in the background. ' " "'Tis a fog-bell on a rock-bound coast!' and he steered for the open sea." '

'I need you to look up some things,' Joanna said. 'If it's not too much trouble.'

'I told you,' Kit said. 'I want to help.'

Joanna read her the list. When she got to the mechanical camel, Kit said, 'I know that one. Yes, there's a photo of it in one of the books.'

'Do you know what deck the gymnasium was on?'

'Yes, the—'

'They say the dead can't speak,' Mr Briarley said, 'but they can!'

'It was on the Boat Deck,' Kit said. 'I found that when I was looking for the Morse lamp.'

All right, scratch the gymnasium. She read her the rest of the list. 'I'll work on these tonight,' Kit said. 'Oh, and I found out about the staircases. There were three of them. The rear one was the second-class stairway. It was all the way in the stern, next to the À La Carte Restaurant. The aft stairway was midway between it and the Grand Staircase. It's described as a less elegant version of the Grand Staircase, with its own skylight and the same gold-and-wrought-iron balustrades.'

And scratch the stairway, Joanna thought, going back to the transcript after they hung up. She must have stored every single thing Mr Briarley had ever said about the *Titanic* in long-term memory. Who says we don't remember what we learned in high school?

She transcribed Mr Ortiz's NDE and then called Vielle, but the line was busy. She called her again when she got home and managed to wake her up. 'I'm sorry,' Joanna said. 'You sound like you're feeling better.'

'I am,' Vielle said.

'Will you be back at work tomorrow?'

'No,' Vielle said. 'I'm still pretty wobbly.' And she must be, Joanna thought after she hung up. Or groggy, because she hadn't said a word about the dangers of going under.

Tish was still out the next day, too, and nursing subs were impossible to get. 'Do you know what they said when I called and asked for a sub?' Richard said when Joanna got to work. '"Spring has sprung." So I rescheduled Mr Sage for tomorrow. It's supposed to be a twenty-four-hour bug, isn't it?'

'I don't know. Vielle's already been out a couple of days,' Joanna said, thinking it was just as well they'd had to cancel. She needed to finish the list of people who'd had more than one NDE, and she wanted to go over her earlier NDEs and analyze them for possible clues.

She spent all morning in the office doing just that and ignoring the blinking light on her answering machine. At lunchtime she went down to the lab and foraged some lunch from the lab coat pockets of Richard, who had spent the morning like she had, staring at a computer screen. 'How's it going?' she asked him, taking the Butterfinger he gave her.

'Terrible,' he said, leaning back from the screen. 'I still haven't found anything to explain why Mrs Troudtheim keeps kicking out. Or why you felt the fear you describe. Only a few cortisol receptors were activated.'

'I felt the fear I describe because I was on the *Titanic* and D Deck was underwater, and I was afraid I couldn't get back.'

'You're still having the feeling that what you're seeing is the *Titanic*, huh?'

'Yes, and it's not just a feeling,' she said. 'The places I described to you were on the *Titanic*, and the reason the stairway didn't have marble steps and a cherub was because it wasn't the Grand Staircase. It was the second-class staircase, and it was right where it was supposed to be, next to the À La Carte Restaurant. That's the dining room I saw, and it *did* have walnut paneling and rose-colored chairs and—'

'How do you know this?' Richard said, sitting forward, and then, accusingly, 'Have you been reading about the *Titanic*? No wonder you keep seeing it.'

'No, of course I haven't been reading about it,' she said. 'I know that would contaminate the NDE. I asked someone—'

'*Asked* someone?' he said, coming up out of his chair. 'At Mercy General? My God, if Mandrake—'

'It's no one who works here,' Joanna said hastily. 'I asked a friend with no connection to the hospital, and I specifically asked her not to volunteer any information, just to confirm whether the things I've seen were on the *Titanic*. And they were, the gymnasium with the mechanical camel and the wireless room and –'

He was giving her his Bridey Murphy look again. 'What are you saying? That there's no possible way you could know all these details, so what you're seeing is real?'

'No, of course not.'

'You said you were afraid you couldn't get back –'

'That's because it feels like it's a real place, like it's really happening, but I know it's not,' she added hastily, 'and Mr Briarley talked about the *Titanic* all the time. Every one of the details I'm talking about could have come from him or the movie or *A Night to Remember*.'

He visibly relaxed. 'So what are you trying to tell me?'

'I'm trying to tell you it's the *Titanic*, not an amalgam or the first image the L+R happened to find that fit all the stimuli. It's the *Titanic* for a reason. It has something to do with what the NDE is, with how it works.'

'But you don't know what the reason is,' Richard said. 'Does everything you're seeing match the *Titanic*?'

'No. There should have been people on the Boat Deck uncovering the boats, and the bridge shouldn't have been empty, and the call letters the wireless operator was sending weren't right.'

'And you still haven't seen or heard the name *Titanic* or any reference to an iceberg. Or have you?'

'No, but I think those discrepancies and omissions may be a clue to deciphering the NDE.' She told him her dream-imagery theory. 'I think the details that don't fit may be symbolic.'

He nodded as if that were the answer he'd expected. And here it comes, she thought.

She was right. 'Your conscious mind has confabulated a rationale to justify the sense of significance,' he said. 'The fact that it's so elaborate, even to explaining details that don't belong in the scenario, has to mean temporal-lobe stimulation is central to the NDE. The feeling you're having that there's a connection—'

'I know, I know. Never mind,' she said. 'The feeling I'm having is a sense of incipient knowledge, it's a feeling of significance, and it's all right there in the scans. I just have one question.'

'What is it?'

'What would the scans look like if it wasn't just a temporal-lobe sensation, if there really was a connection? Would they look any different? Never mind.' There was no way she was going to convince him until she had the connection in her hands and could show it to him.

She couldn't do that till she went under again, but she could at least try to decipher what she'd already seen. She broke her NDEs down into individual images and drew a map of the routes she'd taken and of the Boat Deck, marking the wireless room and the bridge and the place where the sailor had stood, working the Morse lamp, and then made a second list for Kit. Was there a grand piano in the À La Carte Restaurant? A birdcage? Was C Deck enclosed in glass or open? Did the *Titanic* have a squash court?

In the late afternoon – or at least she thought it was late afternoon; when she glanced at her watch, it was nearly six – someone knocked on her door. Mr Mandrake, she thought, and glanced at the bottom of the door to see if the light showed under it.

The knock came again. 'It's Ed Wojakowski, Doc. I got your dog tags for ya.' She opened the door. 'They're not the real thing,' he said, handing her a chain with a metal tag. Maisie's name was engraved on it in neat letters. 'It's really one of those medical alert things, but you said metal and a neck chain, and it's got those.'

'It's perfect,' Joanna said, turning the tag over, expecting to see the red medical alert symbol, but it was plain silver.

'I filed the medical stuff off,' he said, looking very pleased with himself. 'I asked around like I told you I would, but nobody'd seen one of them dog tag machines in years, and then I went to get a prescription filled and there this was. Tags made while you wait.'

'*Thank* you,' Joanna said. 'How much do I owe you?'

He looked insulted. 'Glad to do it,' he said. 'Reminds me of the time when I was on the *Yorktown* and me and Bucky Parteri needed to get us a couple of leave passes so we could go see these WACs on Lanai. Well, we asked around, but the captain and the shore patrol were really cracking down, so then we thought, What about getting somebody to make us a couple, and ...'

It was a long story, some of it no doubt derived from real events and some symbolic. Joanna didn't try to sort out which. She waited for something resembling a break in the action and said, 'I'd love to hear the rest of this, but I really should take this to Maisie.'

He agreed. 'Tell her hi for me. I wish they were the real thing, like the ones I had in the navy. Did I ever tell you how I fell overboard and lost 'em? We were on our way back to Pearl—'

It was after eight by the time Joanna got away from Mr Wojakowski, and Maisie was asleep. 'I'll bring them by in the morning,' she told Barbara. 'How's she doing?'

'They had to take her off the amiodipril.'

'I know. Maisie told me they'd put her back on nadolal.'

Barbara nodded. 'They're out of new drugs to try. That's why her mother fought so hard to get her into the clinical trials of amiodipril. They're talking about putting her on a new ACE-blocker, but it has really severe side effects, and she's already pretty weakened.'

'And a heart?'

'Pray for a school bus accident,' she said. 'Sorry. It's been a long day, and I think I'm getting the flu. She's doing fine right now, and who knows, maybe there'll be a miracle.'

'Maybe,' Joanna said and went back upstairs to go over her NDEs with a fine-tooth comb, looking for clues, till after eleven.

She didn't find any, and in the morning when she went back to see her, Maisie was down having a heart cath. 'She's staying out of A-fib so far,' Barbara reported. 'She said if you came by, to give you this.' She handed Joanna a sheet of paper from a tablet repeatedly folded into a tight packet.

Joanna waited to unfold it till she was back in her office. Written on it in pencil was a list of ships: *Carpathia, Burma, Olympic, Frankfurt, Mount Temple, Baltic.* I must really have paid attention in class, she thought, though, even hearing the names, she had no memory of Mr Briarley having talked about them in class.

Which doesn't mean he didn't, she thought. And there were examples of people recalling books and movies almost verbatim. The phenomenon was called cryptomnesia. Which was what it had been determined Bridey Murphy had, Joanna thought wryly.

'We've got a problem,' Richard said as soon as she walked in.

'Tish is still out?'

'No, she's back, but Mr Sage just called to cancel.'

'Has he got the flu, too?'

'This is Mr Sage,' Richard said irritably. 'It took me ten minutes to get the fact that he was *canceling* out of him. So, can I send you under?'

'Sure,' Joanna said. 'What time?'

'I told Tish eleven.'

She nodded and went back to her office. Kit had called. 'The gymnasium was on the Boat Deck,' her message said, 'on the starboard side just aft of the officers' quarters. The Marconi shack was on the port side even with the officers' quarters.'

Everything Mr Briarley had ever said. Did that include his showing them a map of the Boat Deck? She couldn't remember, but he might have. Maisie's disaster books were full of maps and diagrams: the route Amelia Earhart's plane had taken, the ruins of Pompeii, the layout of the *Hindenburg's* gondola.

Joanna called Kit. The line was busy. She called Maisie. 'Maisie, you said MGY were the call letters for the *Titanic*, and then you started to say something else. What was it?'

'You said I wasn't supposed to talk about anything except what you asked.'

'I know. That still goes, except for this one thing. What were you going to say?'

'That I knew it was MGY because of the message the *Titanic* sent. "MGY CQD PB. Come at once. We have struck a berg." CQD means "help," ' Maisie explained.

'I thought the *Titanic* sent SOSs.'

'It did, but – are you sure it's okay to tell you this?'

'I'm sure,' Joanna said.

'Well, first it sent CQDs, and then Harold Bride, that was the other wireless guy, said, kind of laughing, "Let's send SOS. That's the new distress code, and it may be your last chance to send it." '

31

'Well, it can't be helped.'
        – Last words of GEORGE C. ATCHESON, aide to general
        MacArthur, when he saw that the plane carrying himself
              and twelve others was going to crash into the Pacific

The entire time they were prepping Joanna, Tish chattered about how sick she'd been. 'I thought I was going to die,' she said, sounding not at all unhappy about it. 'I ached all over, and I was so dizzy.' She attached the electrodes to Joanna's chest. 'I practically passed out on the way down to my car,' she said, fitting the sleep mask over Joanna's eyes, 'and this doctor who was in the elevator with me had to drive me home. His name's Ted.'

Well, no wonder she's so chipper, Joanna thought, wishing Tish would hurry up and put the headphones on. She wanted to focus on what she was going to do and where she was going to go when she got on board.

If she got on board. Richard had announced he was decreasing the dosage, 'which will decrease the amount of temporal-lobe stimulation. That should lessen the intensity of the sense of significance, which should allow a different unifying image.'

No, it won't, Joanna thought, because that's not what it is. There's a connection, and I'm going to find out what. But first I have to make sure it's not an amalgam.

'Ted insisted on going inside with me and getting me settled before he left,' Tish was saying, holding the headphones, ready to put them on. 'He's new here. He's an obstetrician, and,' she bent over Joanna and whispered, 'he's really cute, his hair's a little darker blond than Dr Wright's, and he has gray—'

'Tish, is Joanna ready?' Richard called from the console.

'Just about.' She dropped her voice again, 'Gray eyes and *no* scans,' and blessedly, put on the headphones.

All right, Joanna thought, I'm going to try to find the Grand Staircase, and if that fails, the First-Class Dining Saloon. The green velvet fleur-de-lis'd chairs would prove it was the *Titanic*, and there might also be menus or a bill-of-fare with RMS *Titanic* on it. But the À La Carte Restaurant was locked, she thought. What if the dining saloon is, too? And she was in the passage.

It was dry, and level, and there were only a few people outside the door. It must be earlier, Joanna thought, but when she stepped over the threshold, the young woman had changed out of her nightgown and into a red coat and a fur stole made of red-fox heads with sharp noses and shiny black glass eyes. The woman with the piled-up hair was wearing a coat, too, and a lifejacket.

'It's so cold,' the young woman said, shivering. 'Shouldn't we go up to the Boat Deck?'

Joanna hoped they would. Then she would know where the door to the Grand Staircase was. But the bearded man shook his head and said, 'I have sent the steward to find out what is happening. Until then, I think it best that we remain here.'

'Yes, Edith,' the other woman said, putting a white-gloved hand on the young woman's arm, 'we'll ask the steward to light a fire,' and they turned to go back into the passage.

Joanna stepped out of their way and out into the middle of the deck. The Grand Staircase should be in the middle of the ship or slightly forward, which meant she needed to go toward the bow. She wondered if she could, or whether any movement in that direction would take her back to the lab.

I'll have to risk it, she thought, looking toward the bow. There was another deck light that way, shining with a blinding brilliance she couldn't see past. She shielded her eyes and walked into it.

And into a wall. It extended all the way to the windows with no doors in it. Now what? she thought. I'll have to access the Grand Staircase from one of the other decks, and remembered there was an entrance to it from the Boat Deck. The band had stood just inside the doors to it while they played.

She ran down the deck to the aft staircase. It was locked, but the door to the second-class stairway wasn't. She ran up the three flights to the Boat Deck. Her red tennis shoe was still in the door, wedging it open. She left it there and walked toward the bow, trying every door. They were all locked, even the one to the wireless shack. She went around to the gymnasium.

Greg Menotti was just coming out, dressed in a white Nike sweatshirt and dark blue sweatpants, a water bottle strapped to his leg. 'Greg,' she said. 'Do you know where the Grand Staircase is?'

'Grand Staircase?' he said. 'You mean the main staircase? It's over here.' He jogged over to the aft stairway, Joanna in his wake.

'No, not that one,' she said breathlessly. 'The Grand Staircase. It has marble steps and a bronze cherub.'

He was shaking his head. 'You're really out of shape, you know that?' he said. 'How often do you jog?'

'You haven't seen any other stairways? What about on the other decks? Did you see any other stairways there?'

'On the other floors, you mean? No. 'Bye. I've got six more laps to do.' He jogged off toward the stern, his white sweatshirt bobbing in and out of shadow.

What now? She was sure there was an entrance to the Grand Staircase from the Boat Deck. Heidi had said Kate Winslet's mother and the creepy boyfriend had stood at the foot of its stairs waiting for their boat to be called, so all she had to do was find it. But the only doors left to try were those to the officers' quarters.

She tried them anyway. They were all locked, too, except for the last one. It was a closet, with piles of blankets. Maybe they have the *Titanic*'s name on them, she thought, and shook one out, but it was a featureless gray, and when she put it back, she saw, high up on a shelf, the Morse lantern the sailor had propped on the bow.

The name would be on the bow, Joanna thought, and ran out onto the forecastle and over to the railing. She grasped the rail with both hands and leaned far out, trying to see the side of the ship below her, but it was too dark to see it. She looked out at the horizon, searching for the *Californian*'s light and then down at the blackness below. There's nothing down there, she thought, nothing out there. Not just no light. Nothing. And if it goes down –

She began to run, past the bridge, past the officers' quarters, past the life-boats, thinking, Please let my shoe still be there, please let the door to the passage be open, and was all the way down the stairs past the À La Carte Restaurant before she was able to stop herself, grabbing on to the polished railing as if it were a lifeline, forcing herself to stand still, to think.

'You can't go back yet,' she said aloud, her hands gripping the stair rail. 'You have to find out for sure if it's the *Titanic*.' And the deck's not listing yet, the stairs are still dry. There's plenty of time. And there has to be an entrance to the Grand Staircase from the Promenade Deck.

She forced herself to walk back up the stairs to the restaurant and along the passage. It ended in a door, and she opened it and went out on the Prom-enade Deck. It was dark, but there was light coming from windows farther along. Stained-glass windows. They shone in patterns of red and yellow, blue and green, on the wooden deck. She walked down to them and looked in the windows.

It was a bar of some sort. It was dimly lit and smoky, and over against one wall, she could see a mirrored mahogany bar with ranks of liquor bottles and glittering glasses. At one of the tables a man in evening dress with a dark mus-tache sat, dealing out a hand of cards. He dealt them one at a time, facedown, and then picked them up, stared at them, arranged his hand, stared at them again. After a while he shuffled his hand into the deck, and dealt another hand.

I could go ask him what the name of the ship is, Joanna thought. Unlike Greg Menotti, he looked like he had no illusions about where he was and what he was doing here, but something in his face made her drop her hand from the door and leave him there, dealing, shuffling, dealing again.

There was no one in the next room, which was even more elegant than the bar. The walls and the white pillars were decorated with gold filigree, and the chairs and sofas were upholstered in gold brocade. Yellow-silk-shaded lamps stood next to the chairs and on small tables, casting a golden light over the whole room. Books lay on the tables and stood in glassed-in bookcases lining both end walls.

The ship's library, Joanna thought, or some sort of writing room. On the far wall, next to the deck windows, was a row of desks. They had lamps, too, and neatly arranged pens and envelopes and cream-colored writing paper. The name of the ship will be on the stationery, Joanna thought.

She pushed open the beveled-glass door and walked in and across to the nearest desk. Too late, she saw the room wasn't deserted after all. A man sat at the last writing desk, bent earnestly over a letter. She could see his graying hair and the white sleeve of his shirt as he dipped his pen in the ink bottle, wrote, dipped it again.

She hesitated, but he hadn't looked up as she came across the room. He dipped his pen in the ink again, poised it above the paper again. Joanna tip-toed to the nearest desk. The envelopes and writing paper lay in cubbyholes. She reached to pull out a sheet of the paper.

'Do you have a hall pass, Ms Lander?' the man said sternly, and Joanna wheeled.

'Mr Briarley!' she gasped.

'Joanna Lander,' Mr Briarley said, smiling broadly. 'I had no idea you were here!' He stood up and started toward her, knocking against the desk as he did. The ink bottle wobbled, and the pen rolled off onto the gold carpet. He steadied the ink bottle and then clasped her hand in both of his. 'How delightful! Sit down, sit down,' he said, pulling a chair over from one of the other desks. 'I had no idea you were on board.'

'You remember me?' Joanna said.

'I remember all my students,' he said, 'even though there were hordes of them, gleaming in purple and gold. You were in second period. You were fond of "The Rime of the Ancient Mariner," as I recall. "Alone, alone, all, all alone, alone on a wide, wide sea." And you never asked, "Will this be on the final?"'

'That was because I knew what you'd say,' Joanna smiled. 'You always said, "It will *all* be on the final."'

'And so it will,' Mr Briarley said. 'Knowing that did not stop Ricky Inman from asking, however. Tell me, does he still rock back in his chair and overbalance?'

'I don't know,' Joanna said, laughing. 'He's a stockbroker these days.'

'And you?' Mr Brairley asked. 'Let me see, as I recall, you intended to major in psychology.'

'I did,' Joanna said, thinking joyfully, He remembers. This is the old Mr Briarley, the way he ought to be, funny and acerbic and smart, and this is the conversation we ought to have had that day at the house. 'I'm at Mercy General now. I'm working on a research project involving near-death experiences.'

'Which would explain why you were not on the passenger list,' he said. 'I was certain I hadn't seen your name. Near-death experiences. Accounts of those who have returned to tell the tale. "The times have been that, when the brains were out, the man would die, and there an end, but now they rise again." And what have you learned from these voyages to "the country from whose bourn no traveler returns"?'

'I—' Joanna said, and, across the library, the door opened, and the steward came in.

He walked quickly up to them. 'I beg your pardon, miss,' he said to Joanna and turned to Mr Briarley. 'If I might speak to you a moment, sir.'

'Of course,' Mr Briarley said. The two men went over by the bookcases, and the steward began speaking in a low, urgent voice. Joanna caught the words 'requested me to ask you' and 'know what happened.'

'Tell them …' Mr Briarley said, and Joanna stepped forward, trying to hear. As she did, her hand brushed against the desk and knocked the ink bottle over. Ink splashed onto the floor, soaking darkly into the carpet. Joanna bent to right the bottle, reaching in her pocket for a Kleenex.

'Yes, sir, thank you, sir,' the steward said. 'I'll tell them. They will be much relieved.'

The steward went out, and Mr Briarley came back over to the desk where Joanna knelt, blotting up the spilled ink.

'Never mind,' he said, taking her arm to raise her gently to standing. 'It doesn't matter. Come, sit down, and in a moment we'll go have tea,' he said, sitting down at the desk again. 'I must just finish writing a note first.' He picked up the pen and began to write.

Joanna had forgotten that she'd come in here to look for the *Titanic*'s name on the stationery. She looked down at the note he was writing, hoping the letter would be faceup so she could see the letterhead, but it wasn't a letter. It was a postcard.

'I was writing a message to my niece,' Mr Briarley said. There was no printed letterhead on the postcard, only three lines for the address and the words 'Dear Kit.'

'Have you met my niece?' he asked and, before she could answer, said, 'You'd like her. She was named after Kit Marlowe. "Is this the face that launched a thousand ships?" Though I doubt he meant this one. And, "Honour is purchased by the deeds we do. It is not won until some honourable deed is done." Did he manage to win it? I wonder. There is always less time than we imagine. Time that in his case ended abruptly in an inn in Deptford.'

'I know,' Joanna said.

Mr Briarley looked pleased. 'You remember that from class?'

'No, I saw the movie. *Shakespeare in Love*,' she said. 'With Gwyneth Paltrow.' I can't believe we're having this conversation, she thought. 'Vielle and I rented it.'

'Stabbed to death,' Mr Briarley said. 'A quick way to die, though not as quick perhaps as he imagined. Or as serene, though he may have had some idea. "Pray for me!" Faust says, "and what noise soever ye hear, come not unto me, for nothing can rescue me." Though that's not always true. And, at any rate, there is still time for tea, though it is a pity I didn't know of your being on board sooner. We would have had time to talk of many things, "of shoes and ships –"' He stood up and took his coat off the back of the chair and put it on. 'And time to solve the mysteries of the universe. Well, it can't be helped, and there should still be time for tea, at least.'

He picked up the postcard and slid it inside his jacket, too quickly for Joanna to get more than a glimpse of a hand-colored photo of a ship and pale blue ocean, pale blue sky, on the other side. 'I have an errand to run first,' he said, 'and then we'll go to the À La Carte Restaurant. No, perhaps it had better be the Palm Court. It's farther aft.' He looked at his watch. 'Yes, definitely the Palm Court, but I must take this to the post office first.'

'The post office?' Joanna said, thinking of the mail clerk, dragging the wet canvas bag up the stairs. 'No, wait, Mr Briarley,' but he was already out the door of the library.

She ran after him out onto the deck. 'Mr Briarley!' she called, but he was disappearing through another door. 'You can't go down to the mail room,' she shouted, opening it and running down the curving marble steps to the bronze statue at its foot. 'It's already underwater,' she said, and stopped, staring at the statue.

It was a cherub, with wings and curly hair, holding aloft a golden torch. I knew there was an entrance on the Promenade Deck, Joanna thought. Because there was no mistaking this was the Grand Staircase. And no mistaking what ship she was on.

She turned and looked back up at the head of the stairs, and there was the bronze clock flanked by two angels with long robes and wings. Honour and Glory Crowning Time. Joanna craned her neck to look up at the skylight.

The curved glass was the same milky-gold color as in the one above the aft staircase, but this one was much larger, and in the center hung a crystal chandelier, light radiating from it like glittering diamond prisms. 'It *is* the *Titanic*,' Joanna said, and turned back to Mr Briarley.

He wasn't there. While she'd been looking at the skylight, he'd vanished. Which way had he gone? She ran down to the bottom of the stairs to look over the railing at the decks below. 'Mr Briarley!' she shouted, but he wasn't on the stairs, and as she leaned forward, trying to see into the darkness, she heard a door off to the left slam. She ran in the direction of the sound, down a long, brightly lit corridor carpeted in red toward the door that was just closing.

'Mr Briarley!' she called, opening the door. Beyond it, the corridor widened and made a turn, and there was another stairway, and on the deck below, the sound of another door closing. Joanna pattered down the stairs. Next to the stairway was a small room with a red-and-white-striped pole. The barber shop, and next to it, on the corner, a teller's window with a gold-lettered sign above it: 'Purser's Office.' The post office must be somewhere nearby.

Between the barber shop and the purser's was a door. There was no sign on it, but when Joanna put her hand on it, it opened easily. Inside, red-and-black cloth-covered wires crossed and recrossed on a large wooden board, and coming from somewhere – the headphones, lying in front of the board – was an insistent ringing.

The ship's switchboard, Joanna thought, hurrying past the purser's and around the corner. This passage wasn't lit, and after the bright lights of the stairway, she couldn't see anything. She took a few tentative steps in. 'Why, this is my passage,' she said.

'What did she say?' Richard asked sharply.

' "Passed away," ' Tish said. 'I think she's awake.'

'She can't be,' Richard said, and Joanna felt her sleep mask being removed.

She opened her eyes. 'I am,' she said, 'but I didn't say "passed away." I said "passageway." I went in by mistake. I didn't realize it was my passage.' She tried to sit up. 'It was the other end of it. I was –'

'Lie still,' Tish said, wrapping a blood pressure cuff around Joanna's arm. 'I haven't even taken your vitals yet.'

'I wouldn't have gone in it if I'd realized—'

'Lie *still*,' Tish said. Joanna obeyed, waiting for Tish to finish monitoring her and begin unhooking the electrodes and the IV.

'Do you think it was because of the lowered dosage?' Tish asked, untaping the IV needle and sliding it out.

'I don't know,' Richard said. 'It was well above the threshold level.'

'What happened?' Joanna asked, twisting her head around to see Richard.

490

'You kicked out,' Tish said. 'Just like Mrs Troudtheim.'

'Kicked out?' Joanna said, bewildered. 'But I couldn't have. I was all over the –' She looked at Tish. 'I was all over. I was there a long time.'

Richard helped her to a sitting position. 'How long?'

'I don't know,' Joanna said, trying to think. She'd gone up to the Boat Deck and talked to Greg Menotti and then had the conversation with Mr Briarley. How long had that taken? And then they'd walked down to the Grand Staircase –

'Oh, I have something to tell you,' she said. 'About what I saw. It's definitely the ... what we discussed before.'

'How long?' he repeated as if he hadn't heard her.

'An hour at least.'

'An *hour*?' Tish blurted.

'You have a continuous memory of events?' Richard asked. 'Not fragmented flashes?'

'No. It was just like the other times. Everything happened in sequence.'

'What about time dilation?'

She shook her head. 'Nothing was speeded up or slowed down. It all happened in real time.' Only obviously it hadn't. 'How long was I under?'

'Eight seconds,' Richard said. 'How long was it compared to the other times?'

'Longer,' she said promptly.

'Then that and Mr Sage's NDE confirm there's no correlation between subjective time and elapsed time,' he said, and Joanna thought suddenly of Lavoisier. How long had he really been conscious? And how much time had elapsed for him between each blink?

'Was it a complete NDE or did it cut off in the middle?' Richard was asking.

'Both,' Joanna said, wishing Tish would finish unhooking her so she could explain. 'I was trying to find Mr Briarley. He was going to the post office, and I was trying to catch up with him, and I started down this passage –'

'Post office?' Tish said. 'I thought you were supposed to see heaven.'

'– and I didn't realize till I was already in it that it was the same one, and then it was too late. I was already back in the lab.'

'So the ending was different?' Richard said eagerly.

'Yes and no. I came back through the same passage, but it was more sudden than the other times. There was more of an abrupt cutoff.'

Richard went over to the console and typed rapidly, and then looked up at the screen. 'Just what I thought. Your last scan is a dead-on match for Mrs Troudtheim's.' He began typing again. 'I need you to get your account recorded and transcribed as soon as possible.'

'I will,' Joanna said, 'and I want to talk to you about what I saw.'

He nodded absently, staring at the screens. Joanna gave up and went into the dressing room, pulled on her blouse and jacket and put on her shoes, and then came back out. Richard was still typing. Tish was winding up the monitor cords. She was nearly done putting things away. I'll wait till she's gone and then tell him about the Grand Staircase, Joanna thought, and pulled a chair over to the far corner of the lab, sat down, and switched the recorder on.

Of course he'll probably say I confabulated it from the conversation we had, she thought, and began recording. 'Joanna Lander, session six, March 2. I heard a noise, and I was in the passage,' she said softly into it. She described her attempts to find the Grand Staircase, her fruitless conversation with Greg Menotti, her going out onto the Promenade Deck. 'I walked along the deck to where the light from the bar –' she said, and thought of something.

She had said an hour, and it had definitely seemed that long, but an hour after the collision the ship would have had a definite list. Maybe there had been time dilation, after all, or maybe that was another discrepancy that meant something.

I need to tell Richard that, she thought, and looked over at the console. He was taking papers out of the printer. 'Joanna,' he said, 'I want to show these readouts to Dr Jamison and see what she thinks,' and walked out before she could turn off her recorder.

She had half stood up. She sat down again, frustrated, and began recording where she'd left off, describing the man dealing out cards, the library, seeing the man at the writing desk. 'And when he looked up, I saw it was Mr Briarley, my high school English teacher, but it wasn't the Mr Briarley I'd seen five days ago. He remembered my name and which class I was in, and he looked well and happy –'

Well and happy. 'My mother looked well and happy,' Ms Isakson had said, 'not like the last time I'd seen her. She got so thin there at the end, and so yellow,' and Joanna had thought, That's how NDEers always describe their dead relatives, with their limbs *and their faculties restored*.

Mr Briarley remembered who Kit had been named for, he had been able to quote 'The Rime of the Ancient Mariner.'

He's dead, she thought, and a current of fear ran through her. He died. That's why I saw him on board. The stories Mr Mandrake told me about seeing someone in an NDE and then finding out they'd died are true.

No, they aren't, Joanna thought, glaring at the recorder in her hand. You know perfectly well that none of those cases were documented, that the subjects never even mentioned having seen the person until after they'd had outside confirmation of the death, like those mediums who claimed they'd 'seen' W. T. Stead at two-twenty on the night the *Titanic* went down. Not a single one had come forward with their claim until after they'd seen Stead's name listed among the lost. Those stories aren't true. Mr Briarley's not dead. You saw him because you were thinking about him, because you were worrying about him. Then why didn't I see Vielle? Or Maisie? And why *did* I see Greg Menotti?

Because he's dead, she thought, the dead are who's on board, and felt the shiver of fear again. I have to find out. I have to call Kit.

But if she called, and something had happened to Mr Briarley, she'd be in exactly the same situation as Mr Mandrake's NDEers. She'd have no proof she hadn't had advance knowledge of his death, that she hadn't talked to Kit first and then confabulated Mr Briarley's presence in the library.

I have to tell Richard about my NDE first, before I call Kit, she thought, but there was no telling when he'd be back. She could try to find him, but even if she did, he hadn't been with her the whole time. For all he knew, she might have received a call from Kit while he was out of the lab.

Tish could attest to the fact that she hadn't left the lab, or received or made any calls, but Richard didn't want her to know about the *Titanic*. He's right, Joanna thought. If Mr Mandrake were to find out about this ... she could see the *Star* headlines already: 'I See Dead People! Scientist Receives Message from Afterlife.'

But there was no one else who could prove she hadn't known about Mr Briarley's death. And if I don't hurry, I won't have Tish either, she thought, looking over at where Tish was setting up for Mr Sage's session. In another five minutes, she'd be ready to leave.

Joanna bit her lip, trying to decide what to do, and then switched on the recorder and began speaking quickly, describing everything she could remember about how Mr Briarley had looked and what he'd said. 'There is always less time than we imagine,' he'd said, and ' "whatsoever noise ye hear, come not unto me, for nothing can rescue me." '

He was trying to tell you he was dead, she thought, and had to force herself not to stand up and go over to the phone, to finish recording the account. 'All this time Mr Briarley's being there seemed perfectly normal,' she said into the recorder, 'but when—'

'Did you say something?' Tish asked from over by the examining table.

'No, I'm just recording my account,' Joanna said.

'Oh. Is there anything else you need me to do, or can I go to lunch now?'

'No, I need you to do something for me,' Joanna said.

'Oh,' Tish said, disappointed. 'What is it? Because it's already one and the cafeteria –'

Probably closed at twelve forty-five, Joanna thought, and if you leave, there goes my documentation. 'I need you to witness something,' she said.

'Witness something? You mean, like a will?'

'No, not a will,' Joanna said. 'A statement of fact. But before you do, I need to finish recording my account of my NDE, so it'll be a few minutes.'

'Can't I go and come back?'

'No,' Joanna said. 'I need you here. I'm going to want you to witness the fact that I didn't leave the room or make or receive any phone calls.'

She switched the recorder back on and began to talk rapidly into it. '– but when I came out of the NDE-state and began recording my account, I experienced an overpowering feeling that his being there meant that he was dead,' she said, trying not to be distracted by the sight of Tish standing in the middle of the lab, tapping her foot and looking at her watch every few seconds. 'As far as I am aware, Mr Briarley – Tish, you don't have to watch me.' Tish shrugged, went over to the dressing room door, and began applying lipstick in the mirror on the inside of the door.

'As far as I am aware, Mr Briarley is alive,' Joanna said. 'I saw him five days ago and spoke with him on the phone yesterday, and, so far as I know, he was in good health, with the exception of his Alzheimer's, and uninjured. I have had no communication with him or regarding him since then. End of Joanna Lander's account. Completed at 1:08 P.M.'

She popped the tape out of the recorder. 'Okay,' she said to Tish, who was applying mascara, and went over to Richard's desk. She reached to switch on the computer and then thought better of it – there shouldn't be any possibility of outside input, including e-mail – and grabbed a piece of paper. Tish came over to the desk, her bag already over her arm, obviously in a hurry to leave. Which is good, Joanna thought. She won't ask a lot of questions.

Joanna wrote, 'I was in the presence of J. Lander from the beginning of the procedure to the completion of the recording of her account. At no time did J. Lander leave the laboratory or have any communication with anyone outside it,' and pushed the paper across the desk to Tish. 'I need you to sign and date this, and put the time,' she said, handing her a pen.

Tish read the affidavit. 'What's this for?' she said. 'I'm not providing you an alibi for a crime, am I?'

'No,' Joanna said. 'I just need you to document when and where my NDE account was written.'

'You never asked me to document any of the others,' Tish said suspiciously.

'Dr Wright usually documents them,' Joanna lied. She looked pointedly at her watch. 'It's one-fifteen.'

'It is?' Tish said anxiously and signed the paper. 'Is that all you need?'

'No,' Joanna said, holding up the tape. 'This is the tape of my account.' She wrapped it in another sheet of paper and taped the ends closed. 'I need you to sign across the tape and date it.'

'All this for an NDE where you see the *post office*?' Tish said. 'If I ever have an NDE, I certainly hope it has something more exciting in it than the post office.'

No, you don't, Joanna thought. She handed Tish the pen. 'It's one-seventeen.'

Tish looked at her watch and then signed it. 'Is *that* it?'

'No, one more thing,' Joanna said, picking up the phone. 'I want you to witness me making this phone call.' She punched in Kit's number, hoping, for the first time, that Mr Briarley would answer the phone, and wondering what she'd say if he didn't. 'Hi, we're performing a little experiment here. Is your Uncle Pat alive?'

Tish was tapping her foot again. And what if no one answered? She obviously wouldn't be willing to stick around while Joanna attempted to call –

'Hello?' a woman's voice, not Kit's, answered. 'Hello?'

I dialed the wrong number, Joanna thought. 'Is … I'm trying to reach Kit Gardiner,' she stammered. 'Is she there?'

'No,' the woman said. 'This is Mrs Gray, the Eldercaregiver.'

'Is Mr Briarley there?'

'No,' Mrs Gray said. 'They just left for the emergency room.'

32

MISSION CONTROL: *Challenger*, go at throttle up.
CHALLENGER: Roger, go at throttle up. (static)

(Pause)

MISSION CONTROL: Flight controllers here are looking very carefully at the situation. Obviously a major malfunction.

'Emergency room,' Joanna said numbly. Mr Briarley's dead, and I knew it, even though there was no way I could have known. She jammed down the phone and started for the door.

'Where are you going?' Tish said. 'I thought you wanted me to witness your phone call.'

Joanna stopped, staring at her blankly.

'So, do you want me to sign something saying who you called and what you said?' Tish asked.

'No,' Joanna managed to say. 'You can leave now.'

'Okay,' Tish said doubtfully. 'I thought that was why you wanted me to stay, to witness it.'

To witness it. To attest to the fact that she couldn't have known he was dead beforehand. Dead. And himself again, no longer struggling to remember his niece or the word for 'tea.' Well and happy, with his memory restored. On the Other Side.

'Dr Lander?' Tish asked, looking anxiously at her. 'Are you okay?'

No, Joanna thought. They're real. They're not a hallucination. 'I'm fine. Go on, Tish. I know you wanted to get to lunch.'

Tish nodded. 'The cute new obstetrician I told you about hasn't figured out when the cafeteria's open,' she said, digging through her tote bag. 'I brought a whole bunch of quarters for the vending machines. *Where* is that coin purse? I'll admit Doritos and Skittles aren't very romantic, but since there aren't any restaurants around here – Oh, good, here it is.' She brought out a red polka-dotted coin purse and stuck it in her pocket. 'Somebody really needs to open one across the street,' she said, starting for the door. 'They'd make a killing,' and was finally gone.

Joanna forced herself to wait till she heard the ding and whoosh of the elevator, then raced out of the lab and down to the ER. It can't be true, she thought, tearing down the stairs. The mediums were fakes, and Mrs Davenport's a moron. There wasn't a shred of truth to any of their claims. It couldn't be true. But there wasn't any other way she could have known. No one had discussed it while she was under. Richard and Tish didn't even know Mr Briarley, and if Kit had called and left her a message, Richard would have mentioned it as soon as she came out.

Joanna burst through the side door to the ER and stood there, panting. She couldn't see Kit anywhere, or paramedics or the crash team. Over by the ambulance doors a security guard straightened from leaning against the wall and looked at her. You have to act normal, she thought, and tried to slow her breathing, calm her expression, look like she was just down here looking for someone.

She tried to spot the aide – what was her name, Nina? – that Vielle was always yelling at, or the gangly intern, but the flu had apparently taken its toll. She didn't recognize a soul, and she couldn't just march into the trauma rooms, particularly not with the security guard eyeing her, although he had apparently seen her lanyard and ID and decided she was on staff and belonged here. He had gone back to leaning against the wall.

She still couldn't go barging into trauma rooms. She'd have to ask the admissions nurse. She pushed her way across the ER and out to the admissions desk. 'I'm looking for Patrick Briarley,' she said urgently to the admissions nurse, whom she didn't recognize. 'His niece, Kit Gardiner, would have brought him in.'

'Briarley?' the nurse said, typing in his name and looking for several moments at the screen. 'You're too late.'

Too late. I knew that, Joanna thought. I saw him on the Other Side. I can document it.

'He just left,' the nurse said.

'Left?' The word made no sense.

The nurse looked defensive. 'There was nothing on his record about him staying until you arrived, Dr –?' she said, trying to read Joanna's ID badge. 'Do you want his home number? I'd call it for you, but I don't think they're there yet. They *just* left, not five minutes ago.'

'For upstairs?' He hadn't died, after all. The crash team had managed to revive him. 'He's been admitted?'

'For a cut thumb?' the nurse said.

A cut thumb? Not a stroke or a heart attack. A cut thumb. He wasn't dead. She had frightened herself like a superstitious child, spooked by shadows.

'You say he was cut,' Joanna said. 'How badly?'

'You'll have to talk to the resident on duty,' the nurse said, staring suspiciously at Joanna's ID badge. 'Dr Carroll. That's who treated him.'

Joanna turned and walked purposefully into the ER, wishing it were an intern instead of a resident who'd treated him. They talked freely about patients and treatments to anybody who asked them. Vielle was always drilling patient confidentiality into them. 'At least by the time they're residents, they've learned that,' she'd told Joanna, 'even if they haven't learned anything else.'

She'd have to ask one of the nurse's aides. Oh, good, Nina was here after all, over by the instrument sterilizer. She walked over to her. 'Nina, I need –'

Nina jumped and dropped a pair of forceps. 'Oh, Dr Lander, what are you doing down here?' she said, looking nervously around. 'If you're looking for Nurse Howard, she's not here.'

'I know. It's you I need to talk to. Who assisted Dr Carroll with the patient who was just in with a cut thumb? Mr Briarley?'

'Mr Briarley?' Nina said, sounding relieved for some reason, but, instead of answering, she motioned Joanna into the communications room. It was still unfinished, the radio console trailing wires, and boxes everywhere. Nina pulled the door shut. 'So we can talk without all that noise.'

There hadn't been all that much noise, but maybe Nina had had patient confidentiality drilled into her, too. 'Who assisted Dr Carroll in bandaging Mr Briarley's cut thumb?' Joanna asked.

'Nobody,' Nina said. 'It wasn't a bad enough cut for stitches. Dr Carroll just butterflied it and then put a bandage on it because his niece said otherwise he'd forget what the butterfly was for and pull it off.'

Mr Briarley cut his thumb. He was here in the ER having it bandaged while I was seeing him on the *Titanic*, and the feeling that he was dead came from the temporal lobe, not the Other Side. And if the feeling, no, the *conviction*, that Mr Briarley was dead was false, what about the conviction that the *Titanic* was somehow the key to NDEs?

'... funny old guy,' Nina was saying. 'He kept saying, "Who would have thought the old man would have had so much blood in him?" and something about the ocean.'

'"Will all great Neptune's ocean wash this blood clean from my hand?"' Joanna said.

'Yeah, that's it,' Nina said. 'Is that from something?'

'*Macbeth*,' Joanna said. She could remember him acting out scenes for them, with a ruler for a sword. '"Present fears are less than horrible imaginings."'

Horrible imaginings. What an appropriate quotation to remember. That was exactly what she'd been indulging in. 'Lady Macbeth suffers from a lack of imagination,' he'd said in class, 'and Macbeth from too much, hearing voices and seeing ghosts.'

'Is there a phone in the waiting room?' she asked Nina abruptly.

'Sure,' Nina said, 'but I can bring you one.'

She went out. Joanna could hear a woman's voice saying plaintively, 'You don't understand, the British are com—' before Nina shut the door behind her.

She was back immediately with a cordless phone. 'There'll be phones in here if they ever get this thing done,' she said, handing it to Joanna.

'Thanks,' Joanna said and didn't wait for Nina to leave to punch in the number. The line was busy. Joanna hit 'end' and then 'redial.'

'I have to warn them!' the same woman's voice said, loud even through the door, and rising ominously. 'One if by land, two if by sea!'

'Uh-oh,' Nina said, leaning out the door to look. 'It sounds like another nutcase just came in. I hope it's just a schizo and not somebody on rogue. After what happened –' She stopped, looking nervous. 'What I mean is, they're so out of it, they don't even know what they're doing. They look at you, and they don't even see you. It's like they're in this whole other place.'

Joanna wasn't listening. The phone was ringing.

'Nina!' a man's voice called. 'John! I need some assistance here. Stat.'

'I gotta go,' Nina said, looking out the door. Three rings. Four.

'I'm fine!' the woman shrieked. 'You don't understand, I saw the signal! It was *real*!'

'Nina! Get out here! Guard!'

'Just leave the phone on the station desk when you're done.' Nina went out, shutting the door behind her. Six rings. Seven.

'Hello,' Mr Briarley said.

Relief flooded over Joanna. 'Mr Briarley?'

'Yes. Who's calling?'

'I … it's Joanna Lander,' she stammered. 'I—'

'Oh, yes, Ms Lander. Did you wish to speak to Kit?'

'Yes.'

'I'll get her. Kit!' she heard him call. 'It's Joanna Lander,' and Kit came on the line.

'Oh, hi, Joanna. Look, I'm afraid I haven't had time to look for the book or find out the things you asked about. Uncle Pat cut his thumb, and—'

'I know,' Joanna said. 'Is he all right?'

'He's fine, though I was really scared when I saw all that blood. I didn't know a cut thumb could bleed like that.'

' "Their hands and faces were all badg'd with blood," ' Mr Briarley's voice said in the background.

'Luckily, Mrs Gray was here,' Kit said. 'She bandaged it up till I could get him to the ER.'

'How did he do it?'

'A juice glass broke, and he was trying to pick up the pieces,' Kit said, and Joanna wondered if that was the whole story, or if he had been dismantling the kitchen again.

'But he's okay?'

'He's fine,' Kit said. 'I was worried the emergency room might upset him, but it's one of his good days.' She laughed. 'He kept quoting *Macbeth* to the staff.'

' "So were their daggers, which unwip'd we found," ' Mr Briarley said, ' "unmannerly breech'd with blood." '

He was fine. Not only fine, but having a good day.

'Who's that on the phone?' Mr Briarley said. 'Is it Kevin?'

'I'd better go,' Kit said.

'If it's Kevin, tell him the assignment is 'The Wreck of the Hesperus.' Pages 169 to 180. Tell him it will be on the final.'

'I'm glad he's all right,' Joanna said.

' " "Oh, father! I see a gleaming light," " ' Mr Briarley said. ' " "Oh, say, what may it be?" " '

And so much for the good day, Joanna thought.

'I'll call you as soon as I find the book,' Kit said and hung up.

He wasn't dead. She had outside confirmation. Then why did she still have the feeling? It persisted, in spite of the relief she'd felt hearing Mr Briarley's voice, in spite of the fact that people didn't die of cut thumbs. Maybe it's a message of some kind, a premonition.

There was a sudden shriek from outside in the ER, and a clattering crash. 'Mrs Rosen,' Nina said, exasperated, 'the British aren't coming!'

'They *are*!' the woman said, her voice rising ominously. 'I saw the light!'

The feeling's a message, all right, Joanna thought, a message that you're starting to sound just as crazy as that woman out there. Richard was right. You are turning into Bridey Murphy.

It wasn't a premonition, or precognition, or proof that Mr Briarley was dead. It was a contentless feeling, brought on by temporal-lobe stimulation. And what about the feeling that the *Titanic* is the key to the NDE? Doesn't this prove it's purely chemical, too?

499

'No,' she said stubbornly to the radio control board and the dangling wires. 'It means something, and I'm going to find out what.' Which meant calling Betty Peterson back and going over the NDE accounts line by line, looking for clues.

Nina had asked her to take the phone back to the station desk. She picked it up and opened the door. The British are coming! woman had stopped screaming. Joanna leaned out the door to see if she was still out there.

She wasn't, and Joanna couldn't see Nina anywhere. The security guard was still lounging against the wall, and scrubs-clad nurses were moving routinely between the trauma rooms. Halfway down the row a young man in a lab coat and running shoes – Dr Carroll? – stood, earnestly reading a chart.

But there was no telling when the next rogue-raver or gun-waving gang-banger might show up. Joanna started for the side door, keeping a sharp eye out for anyone who looked dangerous. At least Vielle isn't here, she thought, walking between two heart monitors. And maybe a few days away from the ER had given her a new perspective. Joanna went over to the station desk and set the phone down. The door of Trauma Room 2 opened, and an orderly came out, talking to a black nurse in a surgical cap and dark blue –

'Vielle!' Joanna said. She started across the crowded space toward them. 'What are you doing here?'

Vielle had turned at the sound of her name. As she caught sight of Joanna, she grabbed compulsively at her right arm and cradled it close to her body as if protecting it.

'I thought you weren't coming back till next week,' Joanna said. 'What made you change –?' and saw what Vielle was protecting. No, hiding. It was a bandage, and it covered half her forearm.

'What happened?' Joanna said blankly.

'Didn't you hear about Vielle getting shot?' the orderly asked.

'Shot?'

'This guy comes in, waving a gun around,' the orderly said, 'and he says, "Where the—"'

'Don't you have work to do?' Vielle said sharply. 'The bed in Four needs to be stripped. And mop the floor,' but she was looking at Joanna.

Joanna couldn't take her eyes off Vielle's bandaged arm. 'You didn't have the flu,' she said numbly. 'You got shot.'

'Joanna –'

'You could have gotten killed.'

Vielle shook her capped head. 'It's just a flesh wound. It—'

'They told me you went home with the flu. Where were you? Up in the ICU?'

'No, of course not,' Vielle said. 'The bullet barely creased the skin. I didn't even have to have stitches.'

'That's why you wouldn't let me come over. You said you didn't want me to catch the flu, but it was because you didn't want me to know you'd been shot.'

'Joanna –'

'You told me you were going to stay home and get over it,' Joanna said. 'Did you, or was that a lie, too, and you were back at work the next day because you couldn't wait to let them take another shot at you?'

'I didn't tell you because I knew you'd be upset,' Vielle said, 'and I didn't see any point in—'

'Upset? *Upset?*' Joanna said furiously, and Dr Carroll and one of the nurses turned around to look at them. The security guard began to lumber to his feet. 'Why should I be upset, just because my best friend has been *shot*?'

'Keep your voice down,' Vielle hissed, looking anxiously toward the security guard. 'This is exactly why I didn't tell you, because I knew you'd overreact –'

'*Overreact?*'

'Problem, Nurse Howard?' the security guard said, heading toward them, his hand on his gun.

'No,' Vielle said, 'no problem.'

'Yes,' Joanna said to him, 'where were you when the guy was waving a gun around?' She turned back to Vielle. 'When exactly did you plan to tell me? Or did you plan to? If he'd shot you through the heart, would you have told me then?' and flung herself across the ER.

'Joanna –' Vielle called after her.

She pushed through the side door. Behind her, she heard Vielle say, 'Cover for me. I'll be back in a few minutes. Joanna, wait –'

Joanna ignored her and headed down the hallway.

'Joanna, please!' Vielle caught up to her just before she reached the stairs. 'Don't be angry,' she said, clutching at Joanna's arm with her left hand. 'The reason I didn't tell you was—'

'Because you knew what I'd say,' Joanna said. 'You're right. I would have said it. Did you really expect me to stand idly by and watch my best friend get killed?'

'It was just a scratch,' Vielle protested. 'He wasn't shooting at me. I don't even think he knew he had a gun. He was on rogue –'

'On rogue,' Joanna said, 'which has caused a twenty-five percent increase in emergency room casualties.'

'You don't understand,' Vielle said. 'I was as much to blame as he was. I should have seen he was too far gone to reason with. I thought I could calm him down, and I took hold of his arm. The first thing the hospital memo said was, "Do not attempt to engage the patient." I had no business—'

'You have no business working in the ER,' Joanna cut in. 'How many more warnings do you need? This is about as plain as it gets. You've got to get out of there.'

'I can't. We're shorthanded as it is. Two of our nurses are out with the flu, and the bad publicity means we can't get subs. Look, it won't happen again. They've hired an additional security guard. He starts tomorrow, and the hospital is talking about putting in a metal detector.'

'The hospital that responded to the last shooting by putting out a *memo*? Vielle, listen to me. You've got to transfer out now.'

Vielle was looking at her with an odd expression. 'All right,' she said.

Joanna blinked. 'You'll ask for a transfer?'

'I'll make you a deal. I'll transfer out of the ER, and you tell Richard you can't be his guinea pig anymore.'

Joanna stared at her. 'Quit the project? Why?'

'You said you couldn't stand idly by and watch your best friend get killed? Well, neither can I. I'm worried about you.'

'Worried about *me*?' Joanna said. 'You're the one with a bandage on her arm. You're the one who—'

'*You're* the one who's got shadows under her eyes practically down to her knees,' Vielle said. 'Have you looked in a mirror lately?'

'I'm fine,' Joanna said.

'That's what the woman in there just said, the one who keeps screaming, "The British are coming!"; the one who doesn't realize she's crazy. You're nervous as a cat, you space out when people are talking to you. When you came down to the ER just now, you looked—'

'You *saw* me?' Joanna said, outraged all over again. 'What were you doing, *hiding* from me? You were,' she said, suddenly remembering Nina looking anxiously around and then hustling her into the communications room. 'You waited till you thought I'd gone to come out.'

'Don't change the subject,' Vielle snapped. 'You looked white as a ghost. You still look white as a ghost.'

'And how am I supposed to look? I just found out my best friend was shot by a lunatic.'

Stalemate. They stood there, bristling like a pair of dogs for a long minute, then Vielle said patiently, 'You're overwrought, you're losing weight –'

'I've been busy,' Joanna said defensively. 'The cafeteria's always closed –'

'The cafeteria has nothing to do with your disappearing for hours, jumping if anybody talks to you. You know who you're acting like?'

'Julia Roberts in *Flatliners*?' Joanna said sarcastically.

'Julia Roberts in *Mary Reilly*. She had shadows under her eyes, too, and she nearly got herself killed because she refused to stop working for Dr Jekyll.'

'Richard's not Mr Hyde.'

'*Richard* wouldn't notice if you fell over unless it showed up on one of those scans of his. You have to tell him you can't go under anymore.'

'I can't,' Joanna said.

'Why not?'

Because it *means* something, Joanna thought. Because it's important. 'Richard doesn't have any other subjects,' she said, 'except Mr Sage, and he's useless. The progress report is due in two weeks, and if we don't discover how the NDE works soon –' She broke off and started again. 'If it's a survival mechanism, it could be used to revive patients who've coded, and the key is the images I'm seeing in my NDEs. I have to figure out what they mean.'

Vielle was regarding her solemnly. 'This is about Maisie Nellis,' she said wonderingly. 'You think you're going to make some big discovery about NDEs that'll bring back patients whose hearts have given out. That's why you joined the project in the first place, not because you could find out firsthand what NDEs were like or because Dr Wright was Dr Right. You did it because you thought you could save Maisie from drowning.'

'I don't—'

'Nurse Howard,' Nina called, leaning her head out the side door. 'Nurse Gilbert wants to talk to you.'

'Tell her I'll be there in a minute,' Vielle said.

Nina's head disappeared and then popped out again. 'Where's the fiber-optic gastroenterology scope?'

'Examining Room Two,' Vielle said, 'lefthand side of the cabinet above the sink,' and Nina disappeared again.

Vielle turned back to Joanna. 'When I first started in the ER,' she said, 'I thought if I just worked long and hard enough, I could fix everything, I could save everybody's life.' She smiled wryly. 'You can't. You're only human.'

'You still have to try,' Joanna said.

'Even if it means risking your own health? And don't tell me about want-ing to die like Sullivan or Gilbert, whichever one it was, because, trust me, dying isn't something you want to do. I work with death every day in there. It's something to avoid at all costs.'

'Then why are you still working in there?'

Nina leaned out again. 'It's locked.'

'The key's in the station desk. Top drawer, right side.'

'And Stan wants to know if he's supposed to work a double shift tonight.'

Vielle sighed. 'Tell him to ask Mr Avila in Ops. He'll know what's happening.'

He'll know what's happening. 'Ask Mr Briarley,' the bearded gentleman had told the steward. 'He'll know what's happening.' He was right. The Mr Briarley on board had remembered Ricky Inman and 'The Rime of the Ancient Mariner.'

He'd remember what he had said in class. I should have asked him there in the writing room, Joanna thought. He would have been able to tell me, and then, with a shock of comprehension, That's why he was there. Not because he was dead. Because he knew the answer.

'Well, then ask *her* where Mr Avila is,' Vielle was saying.

I have to get Richard to send me under again, Joanna thought, so I can ask Mr Briarley what he said.

'All right,' Vielle was saying resignedly. 'I'll be right there.' She turned to Joanna. 'What say we both quit right now and walk out that door?' She pointed to the door that led to the parking lot. 'We get in my car and go someplace where it never snows and there aren't any Ninas.'

'Or rogue-ravers.'

'Or sick people.'

'Or Mrs Davenports.'

Vielle smiled. 'And the cafeteria's open twenty-four hours a day.'

'You've just described Mr Mandrake's Other Side.' Joanna grinned.

'Except for the Mrs Davenport part,' Vielle said. 'Can you imagine how awful that would be? You die and go through the tunnel, and there, waiting for you in the light, is Mrs Davenport. Can you imagine anything worse than that?'

Yes, Joanna thought.

'I'd settle for just no snow,' Vielle said. 'How about this? We go to Hollywood and get jobs as film consultants. I tell them why people can't survive in twenty-eight-degree water, and you tell them what John Belushi's last words were. We've got the credentials. All those Dish Nights.'

Nina leaned her head out the door again. 'Dr Carroll said to tell you we've got incoming. A three-car crash on I-70.'

'Coming,' Vielle said and started toward the door. She put her hand on it. 'Think about it, okay?'

'About Hollywood?'

'About quitting. I really am worried about you, you know.'

'Ditto,' Joanna said.

'Or, if you won't quit, about taking a couple of weeks off to catch up on your sleep and get any excess dithetamine out of your system. Promise me you'll think about it.'

'I promise,' Joanna said, but as soon as Vielle had gone into the ER, she tore up the stairs, across the walkway, and up to the lab to talk Richard into sending her under right away.

33

'Everything has gone wrong, my girl.'
            – Novelist ARNOLD BENNETT's last words

Richard wasn't there. Which was just as well, Joanna thought, catching sight of herself in the dressing-room-door mirror. Tish had left it open after her makeup session, and Joanna's reflection looked wild-eyed and disheveled, like someone escaping from Pompeii.

If Richard saw me like this, he'd never send me under again, she thought. And he had to. She had to ask Mr Briarley what the connection was.

The affidavit and the sealed tape she'd had Tish sign were both on Richard's desk where she'd left them. She picked them up. She could tear up the affidavit and unseal the tape, and Richard would never have to know about it. If Tish said anything, she could say she just wanted the fact that she'd recorded her NDE immediately after her session documented.

But then she was as bad as Vielle. Worse, she thought, because this is a scientific experiment, and Richard can't possibly come up with a theory without all the data. You have to tell him. But she didn't have to look like a nutcase while she was doing it. She combed her hair and put on some lipstick so she wouldn't look so pale, and then stood there trying to think of a way to explain it to Richard, but the image of Vielle and a kid brandishing a gun kept intruding. If he'd waved it a little more to the right, if it had ricocheted a little differently –

Richard came in, and walked straight to the console. 'I think we may finally have something. Your readouts aren't identical, but they show at least one of the same neurotransmitters as Mrs Troudtheim's, and I need to check the cortisol numbers, but I think they're the same, too. Have you written up your NDE yet? If you have, I need a copy. I'm meeting with Dr Jamison at two-thirty, and –' he stopped. 'My God, what's wrong? Are you all right?'

'No,' she said. 'Vielle got shot.'

'Shot?' he said. 'Good God, is she okay?'

She nodded. 'It was only a flesh wound.'

'My God! When did this happen?'

'Three days ago,' Joanna said, and burst into tears.

He was across the lab in two steps, his arms around her. 'What happened?'

She told him through her tears. 'She didn't tell me because she knew what I'd say.'

'I don't blame you,' he said. 'She's got to transfer out of there. It's getting ridiculously dangerous.'

'I know, but she won't,' she said, wiping at her tears with her hand. 'She says they're too shorthanded.'

He reached in his lab coat pocket and pulled out a package of Kleenex, which made her laugh. 'I'm sorry to cry all over you,' she said.

'Anytime,' he said. 'You doing okay now?'

She nodded and blew her nose. 'I just keep thinking about what might have happened –'

'I know. Look, let me call Dr Jamison and cancel our meeting, and you and I go get something to eat.'

It sounded wonderful, but if she went out with him, she was liable to blurt out what had happened with Mr Briarley just like she'd blurted out the news about Vielle, and, worse, try to explain her conviction that Mr Briarley could tell her the reason she was seeing the *Titanic*, and he'd decide she was too distraught or unstable to go under again.

And she had to go under again, had to ask Mr Briarley, 'What did you say in class that day? What does the *Titanic* have to do with NDEs?'

'No, I'm okay now, really,' she said. 'I don't want to take you away from what you're doing, especially if you're on to something, and I need to go transcribe my account.' She picked up the sealed tape and quickly stuck it in her cardigan pocket. 'You said you needed it by two-thirty?'

'Actually, all I need is the very end,' he said. 'You said you came back through the same passage, but it was in a different place?'

'No.' She explained about following Mr Briarley, opening the door to the passage, realizing it was the same one. 'The passage is always in the same location. Everything is. It's a real place. I mean,' she said at his look, 'it feels like a real place.'

'And the return was sudden?'

'Yes, like someone slapping a book shut –' she said. 'I just thought of something. Mrs Woollam said one of her returns was like that, and I think it was a time when she revived on her own.'

'I'd like to see her account, too,' Richard said. 'You're sure you're okay?'

'I'm fine,' she said. 'Thank you for the Kleenex. And the shoulder.'

He grinned. 'As I said, anytime,' and went back over to the console.

She stood there a minute, looking at his blond head bent over the keyboard, wanting to tell him everything, and then said, 'When do you think you'll send me under again?'

'Tomorrow, if possible. I'd like to do another session at this lower dosage and see if it's a factor. And see how the scans compare.'

'I'll call Tish,' Joanna said and went to her office, cut the taped and signed paper off the tape, and began typing up the transcript.

Listening to the tape was like experiencing it all over again: leaning over the bow, looking down at the side of the ship, gazing down into nothingness, seeing Mr Briarley in the library. 'Have you met my niece?' Joanna typed, and thought, He didn't remember that. She looked back over the conversation. He'd greeted her as if he hadn't seen her since high school. There'd been no mention of having seen her just a few days before.

Because he didn't remember those things, she thought. It wasn't a whole and healthy Mr Briarley she'd seen, but the old Mr Briarley, whom she'd had in second period, the part of Mr Briarley that had died. 'Dying in pieces,' Vielle had said. And her acetylcholine-enhanced mind had given the idea concrete form. No wonder she had been convinced he was dead. Part of him was, and maybe that, and not his holding the key to the connection, was why she'd seen him on the *Titanic*. In which case he wouldn't be able to tell her what the connection was and what the NDE was.

He has to, she thought, and continued going through the account, looking for clues. ' "And what noise soever ye hear, come not unto me, for nothing can rescue me," ' she typed, and, 'I must take this to the post office first.'

She stared at the screen, her chin in her hands. When he'd said that, she'd assumed he meant the mail room. That was why she'd run after him, because the mail room was flooded. But she was almost sure he'd said 'post office,' and, now that she thought about it, it was unlikely that passengers would have been allowed all the way down on G Deck. More likely, they would have handed their letters to a steward or dropped them in a mailbox or a mail slot. But Mr Briarley had said 'post office,' and he'd disappeared into one of the passages on C Deck, and the other rooms Joanna had seen – the À La Carte Restaurant and the lounge and the gymnasium – had all existed.

She called Kit. 'I need to know if there was a post office on the *Titanic*, and if so, where it was.'

'You don't mean the mail room?' Kit said. 'I found out about it and the mail, by the way.'

'No, this would have been a post office for the passengers,' Joanna said.

'Post ... office ... for ... passengers,' Kit said, obviously writing it down. 'Anything else?'

Yes, but this was the one she needed before she went under again so she could find Mr Briarley, and if she gave Kit the other rooms to find and a list of quotations to look up, she might not find out about the post office in time.

'No, that's all,' she said. 'Now, what about the mail?'

'The mail clerks did drag the mail up to the Boat Deck,' Kit said. 'The mail room was in the bow, so it was one of the first things to flood, and the mail clerks carried the sacks of first-class and registered mail up to try to save it.'

But the mail was already ruined, Joanna thought, remembering the sodden, dripping bag, the dark stain on the stairs. 'Did it say which staircase they used?' she asked.

'No, do you want me to try to find that out?'

'The post office is more important,' she said.

She hung up and called Tish, who wasn't available till Thursday. 'They've got me subbing in Medicine till then. This flu,' she explained. Thursday. Two days till she could ask Mr Briarley what the connection was. At least there'd be enough time for Kit to locate the post office.

'... and why didn't you tell me Vielle Howard had been shot?' Tish was asking. 'I just found out.'

I just found out, too, Joanna thought. 'I assumed you already knew,' she lied.

'Is she okay?'

'It was just a flesh wound,' Joanna said. She hung up and finished transcribing the account. She considered leaving off the last paragraph, but it was part of the data. She compromised by adding, 'Upon checking, I found Mr Briarley to be alive and in good health except for his Alzheimer's, thus providing a documented instance which contradicts Mr Mandrake's claims of extrasensory perception.'

She printed out the transcript and fished in her pockets for a paper clip to put on it. She came up instead with Maisie's dog tags. Which I never did deliver, she thought, and decided to run down as soon as she'd taken the account to Richard.

He wasn't there. Good, she thought, and ran down to four-west. 'Oh, good,' Barbara said. 'Maisie will be glad to see you. She's having a rough day.'

'I'm in A-fib again,' Maisie said disgustedly, lying back against the pillows. She was wearing an oxygen mask, which she pulled off as soon as Joanna came into the room. 'They're trying to get me converted. Did Barbara give you the list?'

'Yes,' Joanna said. 'Put your oxygen mask back on.'

'There might be some more ships. I didn't look in *Catastrophes and Calamities* yet.'

'Put your—'

'*Okay,*' Maisie said and put the mask over her mouth and nose. It immediately fogged up.

'You don't need to look up any more ships,' Joanna said. 'I found out what I needed to know.'

'I'll look up –' Maisie said, her voice muffled by the mask. She took it off again. 'I'll look up the *Carpathia* stuff tonight,' she said and popped it back on.

'I don't want you doing anything till you're out of A-fib,' Joanna said, and then brightly, 'I've got a surprise for you,' and could tell from Maisie's face she sounded just like her mother. 'I brought you something.' She fished the necklace out of her pocket and held it up by the chain. 'This is—'

'Dog tags,' Maisie said, beaming. 'In case the hospital burns down. Will you put them on me?'

'You bet,' Joanna said and took hold of Maisie's thin shoulders to pull her forward a little. It was like handling a sparrow. She put the necklace on over her head, careful of Maisie's oxygen tubes and her IV lines, and arranged it on her chest. 'A friend of mine, Mr Wojakowski, made it for you.'

Barbara came in. 'Look what Joanna gave me.' Maisie held them out for Barbara to admire. 'Dog tags! Aren't they cool?'

'You always know just what will make her feel better,' Barbara said, walking Joanna out, but it wasn't true. She hadn't done anything. Maisie was still as frail as a bird and getting frailer, and she was no closer to knowing anything about NDEs than she had been when she'd sat listening to Mrs Davenport for hours. She wasn't even any closer to knowing what Mr Briarley had said in class, or even the name of the textbook.

That at least she could do something about. She called Betty Peterson again, but the line was busy. Waiting to try again, she started through her messages. Mr Mandrake, Mr Mandrake, Mr Ortiz, wanting to tell her a dream he'd had the night before. Guadalupe. She must not have gotten the note Joanna had left with the sub nurse.

She went up to four-west. As soon as Guadalupe saw her, she handed her a sheet of paper with a single line typed on it: '... (unintelligible) ... smoke ... (unintelligible).'

'You didn't get my message?' Joanna asked. 'That I wanted you to keep writing down what Coma Carl said?'

'I got it, and that's everything he said,' Guadalupe said. 'He's pretty much stopped talking.'

'When did this happen?' Joanna asked.

'It's been a gradual falling off,' Guadalupe said. 'He would murmur at wider and wider separated intervals, and it got harder and harder to hear him.'

As if he were getting farther and farther away, Joanna thought.

'By the time I sent you that message he'd pretty much stopped altogether, except for a few unintelligible words,' she said. 'That's really why I called you that day, to ask you if you wanted to call it off.'

Call it off. Joanna thought of the wireless operator in the Marconi shack, hunched over the telegraph key, tirelessly sending.

'He hasn't said anything for nearly a week.'

'Can I see him?' Joanna asked. 'Is his wife in with him?'

Guadalupe shook her head. 'She went out to the airport. His brother's coming in. Sure, go on in.'

There were three more bags hanging from the IV stand and two more monitors. The IV monitor began to beep, and a nurse Joanna didn't know bustled in to check his IV lines. 'You can talk to him,' she said to Joanna.

And say what? 'My best friend was shot by a rogue-raver?' 'This little girl I know is dying?' 'The *Titanic*'s going down?'

Mrs Aspinall came in, accompanied by a tall, bluff man. 'Oh, hello, Dr Lander,' she said and went over to the bed and took Carl's bruised and battered hand. 'Carl,' she said, 'Martin's here.'

'Hello, Carl,' Martin said, 'I got here as soon as I could,' and Joanna almost expected Carl to stir, in spite of the mask and the feeding tube, and murmur, 'Too far for him to come,' but he didn't. He lay, gray and silent in the bed, and Joanna was suddenly too tired to do anything but go home and go to bed.

On the way there, it occurred to her with a kind of horror that she might be catching the flu. Richard won't let me go under if I'm sick, she thought, but in the morning she felt much better, and when she got to work, there was a message from Betty Peterson on her answering machine. 'I just realized I never told you the name of the book: *Mazes and Mirrors*.'

Mazes and Mirrors. Joanna could instantly see the title in her mind's eye, lettered in gold across a blue cover, though oddly, the name didn't conjure up the rest of the cover. Joanna squinted, trying to envision a ship under the title and then Queen Elizabeth with a mustache and glasses, but neither seemed right. It will probably turn out to be Windsor Castle, Joanna thought. But at least we know the title.

'I told you it began with an M,' Betty's voice was saying. 'And there it was, in the margin, next to Nadine's picture. Just a minute, let me read it to you. I've got it right here.' There was a pause, and her voice continued, ' "Betty, just think, no more of Mr Briarley's boring stories about the *Titanic* and no more *Mazes and Mirrors*! Your pal in second period, Nadine." You still need to call me, though. I talked to my little sister and she told me this thing about Mr Briarley. Oh, and I called Blake Dirkson. He was the year ahead of us. He couldn't remember the name of the book either, but he said it had one of those quill pens and a bottle of ink on the cover. He smoked a lot of pot in high school, though, so I don't know. Anyway, call me. 'Bye.'

A quill pen and a bottle of ink? Oddly, that seemed vaguely familiar, too. We're all confabulating, she thought. She called Betty, but the line was busy again. Which isn't a surprise, Joanna thought, considering how long she talks when she's just leaving a message, and called Kit.

'*Mazes and Mirrors*,' Kit said. 'Great. That'll make it a lot easier.'

'She says she thinks she remembers a picture of Queen Elizabeth in a ruff on the cover, or a quill pen and a bottle of ink. I still think it's a ship, but it could be one of the others.'

'I'll get right on it,' Kit said. 'I haven't been able to find out anything on a post office, but I'm still looking.'

And if she couldn't locate the post office, how else could Joanna find Mr Briarley? He'd mentioned the Palm Court. She needed to ask Kit where it was and what deck it was on, although the easiest way to find him would probably be just to follow the steward when the bearded man asked him to go find Mr Briarley.

Richard stuck his head in the door. 'I just wondered if you'd finished typing up your account,' he said, 'and if you were feeling better.'

'Yes,' she said, handing him the transcript and Mrs Woollam's. 'Tish can come tomorrow at two. How are things coming with Mrs Troudtheim?'

'We isolated three neurotransmitters that were present in both of your exit scans and all of Mrs Troudtheim's: LHRH, theta-asparcine, and DABA. LHRH was also present in the template scan, so it's probably not the culprit, but the DABA may be a possibility. It's an endorphin inhibitor, and Dr Jamison thinks beta-endorphins, rather than being just a side effect, may be a factor in sustaining the NDE-state, and that the DABA may be inhibiting them.' He waved the transcripts at her. 'Thanks. Tomorrow at two.'

The phone rang. Richard said, 'I'll talk to you later,' and Joanna picked it up, thinking, too late, It's probably Mr Mandrake.

'I can't believe it's really you,' Betty Peterson said. 'I've been trying to reach you for days. Did you find out whatever it was you needed to find out?'

'Find out?'

'From *Mazes and Mirrors*.'

'Oh. No, not yet,' Joanna said.

'Wasn't that the luckiest thing, finding it in my yearbook like that? I guess it's a good thing Nadine hated Mr Briarley, isn't it?'

'You said you had something to tell me about Mr Briarley,' Joanna said. 'Something your sister told you.'

'Oh, yes. I called her right after you called me to see if maybe she knew the name of the book. She was three years behind us, but I thought maybe they might have had the same textbook. I mean, our history books were ancient. They said John F. Kennedy was president.'

It was like talking to one of her NDEers. 'Did she know it?' Joanna asked to get her back on track.

'No, but she told me this awful story, and since you said you'd gone to see Mr Briarley I thought I should tell you. Did you meet his niece? Her name's Kathy or Katie or something.'

'Kit,' Joanna said.

'Kit,' Betty said. 'Well, she was supposed to get married, she was having this big wedding, and Mr Briarley was supposed to give her away. My little sister said he talked about it constantly in class, even more than he used to talk about the *Titanic*. I guess she was his favorite niece, and then her fiancé – my sister told me his name, but I don't remember it –'

'Kevin,' Joanna said, thinking, I was right. He wasn't willing to take on the responsibility of an Alzheimer's patient. He left Kit at the altar.

'Kevin, that's right. Well, anyway, the morning of the wedding, he went to pick up some film, and this kid ran a red light and plowed right into him.'

It was so different from what she had thought Betty was going to say that for a minute Joanna couldn't take it in.

'Killed him instantly,' Betty said. 'It was awful, and I guess Mr Briarley was the one who had to tell her. My little sister says she thinks that was what caused his Alzheimer's, that he's just trying to forget.'

One small part of her mind thought, That's ridiculous, that isn't what causes Alzheimer's, but she didn't say it, couldn't say it. Belated understanding pounded at her, memories of words that she hadn't comprehended, that she'd misinterpreted, thudding like the medicine ball hitting the gymnasium wall.

Kit asking her if people in car accidents had NDEs, if they were pleasant. 'They're not frightening, are they?' she'd said. And 'My aunt made me read *The Light at the End of the Tunnel* after –' and, 'Uncle Pat was very kind to me,' saying, 'Sometimes he relives past events.'

She should have seen it. Kit's thinness, her shadowed eyes, the photo of her and the blond young man, smiling, and Mr Briarley saying, 'Kevin should be here by now,' quoting, ' "The bride hath paced into the hall." '

Oh, my God, Joanna thought, horrified, I made her watch *Runaway Bride*!

'My sister knew this girl who was there and she said it was just tragic,' Betty was saying. 'I guess she was already in her wedding dress and everything.'

Did it have a train? Joanna wondered, feeling sick. 'Which wedding dress do you like the best?' she'd asked Kit. 'I want a big wedding, with all the trimmings,' Vielle had said.

'And since you said you'd gone over to see Mr Briarley, I thought you should know so you wouldn't put your foot in it.'

Put my foot in it, Joanna thought. She had sat there in the kitchen, casually discussing near-death experiences, blithely telling Kit heaven was a hallucination of the dying brain.

I have to call Kit, she thought, I have to tell her how sorry I am, and hung up unceremoniously on the still-chattering Betty. She punched in Kit's number and then hung up and went to see her instead.

I was going to rescue her, she thought. I was going to play W. S. Gilbert and save her from drowning, so I invited her over to Vielle's to discuss weddings and watch a movie with no less than five of them in it. She remembered Kit's intentness watching it, as if she were afraid there was going to be a test, but the movie itself was the test. No, wrong word. Ordeal. Trial by fire.

I couldn't have done worse if I'd tried, she thought, getting out of the car and going up the walk. And what do I say to her now? I'm sorry I tortured you, I was too stupid to put two and two together?

She didn't have to say anything. Kit said, looking like she'd just been arrested for a crime, 'How'd you find out?' She opened the door, shivering in a halter top, capri pants, and no shoes, and to Joanna she looked even thinner and more drawn, or was that only because now she knew?

'Why didn't you tell us that night?' Joanna said. 'I mean, *Runaway Bride!*'

'Rule Number One of Dish Night,' Kit said. 'No discussion of work. It was all right. One of the things that was so terrible was the way everybody tiptoed around me. Still tiptoes around me.' She smiled wryly. 'My cousin got married last summer, and nobody told me. I found out by accident. Which, I suppose, is how you found out.'

Joanna nodded. 'Betty Peterson told me. The one who found out the title of the book. Her little sister told her.'

'And I should have told you,' Kit said. 'It was just so nice having somebody treat me like a person instead of a ...'

Disaster victim, Joanna thought, and realized why Kit had reminded her so much of Maisie.

'You have no idea the things people do to you trying to comfort you,' Kit said. 'They say, "You'll fall in love again," and, "At least he didn't suffer." How do you know? I wanted to ask them. How do you know he didn't suffer?'

I told her I saw the *Titanic*, Joanna thought, feeling sick. I introduced the possibility that Kevin didn't die instantly, that he experienced something terrible, something terrifying.

'My aunt Julia kept saying, "God never sends us more than we can bear,"' Kit was saying, 'and, "You need to be thankful it was quick." Well, it was. So quick I didn't even get to say good-bye.'

And so you get to say good-bye to Mr Briarley instead, Joanna thought. An endless, agonizing good-bye.

'The only one who didn't say any of those things was Uncle Pat. He was wonderful. He didn't try to tell me it was going to be all right or that Kevin was in a better place or that I'd get over it. He didn't tell me any lies at all. He took me in, talked to me about Coleridge and Kevin and Shakespeare, made me tea, made me finish college. He saved my life,' she said, staring blindly toward the library, 'and then when he got sick ... My mother thinks I'm in denial, that I believe I can save him, or that I'm punishing myself somehow ... He doesn't say those things on purpose, you know. He ... I think he has a fragmented memory of Kevin and something bad happening and a wedding, and he keeps trying to put it together in his mind, even though most of the pieces are missing.'

Like me, Joanna thought, trying to remember what Mr Briarley said, trying to piece together the connection.

'I know I can't save him,' Kit said. 'I know he'll have to go into a nursing facility eventually, but –'

'You have to try,' Joanna said, and Kit smiled suddenly at her.

'I have to try. He saved my life. I want to stay with him as long as I can.' And keep the lights on, Joanna thought, so the passengers don't panic.

'And I want to help you,' Kit said. 'I still haven't been able to find anything about a post office, but—'

'No,' Joanna said. 'Absolutely not. I've already made you watch *Runaway Bride*. I'm not going to force you to do research on a disaster.'

'I want to,' Kit said. 'I love the idea of actually being able to *help* someone for a change. And it's an appropriate disaster.'

'Appropriate?'

She nodded. 'There were eight honeymoon couples on the *Titanic*. Most of them didn't get a chance to say good-bye either.' She smiled sadly. 'They didn't realize they were never going to see each other again. Some of the men even made jokes as the boats were lowered. They laughed and said, "Put the brides and grooms in first," and, "We won't let you back on the ship without a pass." '

'And did they? Let the brides and grooms get in the boats first?'

'Two of them,' Kit said. She stood up abruptly, got several typed sheets out of a drawer, and handed them to Joanna. 'Here's everything I could find on the engines stopping and what various passengers and crew heard when the iceberg hit.'

Joanna paged through it. 'It sounded like a wave striking the ship.'

'… a little jar …'

'It was as if the ship had rolled over a thousand marbles.' That sounded familiar. Had Mr Briarley mentioned it?

'I thought, We're landing. How funny!'

'Now, about this post office,' Kit said, all business. 'I haven't been able to find anything except the mail room down on G Deck. Are you sure there was a post office? Any letters the passengers wrote wouldn't have been delivered till the ship reached New York, anyway, so wouldn't they just have waited till they docked to mail them? Did you see a post office?'

'No,' Joanna said and started to add, 'Mr Briarley said he was going there,' but stopped herself. She'd inflicted enough pain on Kit without telling her she'd seen her uncle just like he used to be.

'Well, I'll keep looking. Anything else?' Kit asked, and her expression made it a plea.

'Yes,' Joanna said, and Kit flashed her that sudden smile again. So much like Maisie. 'I need …' What? 'I need to know if there was anyone on board named Edith.'

'Edith Evans,' Kit said. 'I remember Uncle Pat talking about her. She gave up her place in the boat to the mother of two children.'

And died, Joanna said silently, and thought of the young woman saying anxiously, 'Shouldn't we go up to the Boat Deck?' I know why I saw her,

Joanna thought. She died just like W. S. Gilbert. But when Kit said she'd see if there were any other Ediths on board, Joanna didn't stop her. She seemed so eager to, as she said, actually *help* someone.

She's right, Joanna thought, going out to her car, it's terrible standing there watching Mr Briarley, watching Coma Carl, watching Maisie, unable to help, unable to stop their slow declines. That's why I have to find Mr Briarley and ask him what he said in class.

She glanced at her watch. Oh, God, her session was in less than twenty minutes. She dashed back to the hospital and ran up to her office. Tish was waiting at the door. 'You're late,' she said, 'and I want to be out of here on time, so try to have another of those eight-second sessions, okay?'

'You've got a hot date with the obstetrician?' Joanna asked, walking her up to the lab.

'No, I'm working. Half the hospital's out with the flu, and I might as well get some overtime. It's not as if I have anything else to do.'

'The obstetrician didn't work out?'

'I don't want to talk about it.'

Richard wasn't in the lab. 'He's upstairs with Dr Jamison,' Tish said. 'He said for me to go ahead and get you prepped, and he'll be right down.'

Joanna put on her hospital gown and got up on the table. 'What is it with all these guys who are obsessed with their work?' Tish asked, fitting the foam pads under her. 'The obstetrician's just as bad as Dr Wright. He spends all *his* time looking at ultrasounds. I don't think it's healthy. Someday they're liable to just snap.'

She started the IV and hooked up the electrodes, chattering on as she did so. Joanna tried to ignore her. She needed to focus on finding Mr Briarley. Locate the steward as soon as you go through, she told herself, and stick close to him. Don't let him out of your sight.

Richard came in. 'Sorry,' he said, 'I was talking to Dr Jamison. All set?' he asked Tish. She nodded. 'How about you?' he asked Joanna.

'All set.' He put her sleep mask on. Don't look back at the passage, Joanna thought. Look straight ahead. Find the steward.

'Okay, Tish,' Richard said, 'start the sedative.' He began fitting the head-phones over her ears.

See where the steward goes, Joanna said silently, follow him up the stairs, and thought suddenly of the mail clerk hauling the wet canvas sack up the stairs, of the dark, wet stain on the carpet, the listing deck –

'Wait!' she said, and felt the headphones being lifted off. 'Richard –'

'What is it?' she heard Richard say. 'You're shivering. Do you want a blanket? Tish, go get Joanna a blanket.'

She could hear Tish moving away. 'Richard,' she said, groping blindly for his hand, 'if it starts to sink, promise me you'll come and get me.'

34

'I shall hear in heaven.'
— BEETHOVEN's last words

I shouldn't have said that, Joanna thought before it was even out of her mouth. Now he'll never send me under. Maybe I just thought it and didn't say it, she thought, but he'd already pulled her sleep mask down and was asking her if she was okay.

'Sorry,' she said and smiled up at him. She wondered if she could pretend she had been making a joke. No, not the way she'd gripped his arm. 'I guess I got a little disoriented there. Did Tish start the sedative?' she asked, knowing full well she hadn't.

'No,' Richard said, frowning.

'I must have dozed off on my own then. I haven't gotten much sleep the last couple of nights, what with worrying about Vielle –' No, don't say that either. 'You know that state of near-sleep where you feel like you're falling and then you jerk awake? That's what it felt like. Sorry,' she said again and flashed him a smile that rivaled Maisie's mother's. 'I didn't mean to make you think I'd turned into a nutcase.'

Tish was back, spreading the blanket over Joanna's legs, her shoulders. 'Thanks, Tish,' Joanna said, looking at Richard. 'That's much better. I'm all set now. Shall we get this show on the road?'

Richard was still frowning. He went over to the console and typed busily for a few minutes, but whatever he saw must have reassured him, because he said, 'Okay, Tish, start the sedative.'

Joanna pulled the sleep mask up over her eyes before he could change his mind, thinking, Don't say anything, don't do anything stupid, and was in the passage.

The door was open, and beyond it she could see the people milling about on deck. She hurried down the passage and out onto the deck, looking for the steward. She couldn't see him for the crowd. There were a lot more people than there had been, and several of them were wearing lifejackets.

It's later than it was, Joanna thought anxiously, and the steward's already gone. She looked down at the deck to see if it had a list, and it seemed like it did, but only a slight one, and when she looked up again, she saw the young woman. She was still in her nightgown, and the stout man in tweeds was still there, standing on the far side of the crowd and talking to his friend.

Joanna craned her neck to see over their heads and down the deck, looking for a glimpse of the steward's white coat moving in and out of the deck lights, but the length of the deck was empty. 'Go and find Mr Briarley,' a man's voice said, and there was the bearded man, talking to the steward. Joanna squeezed through the crowd, toward them.

'He'll know what's happening,' the bearded man said.

'Yes, sir,' the steward said and turned to go.

Joanna squeezed between the young woman and the young man in the sweater and started to edge past the stout man. 'What's happened?' he said.

'Iceberg,' his friend said. And there's your proof that it's the *Titanic*, Richard, Joanna thought, sidling past him.

'Icebergs,' the stout man said, nodding. 'Well, I don't suppose it's anything much,' and Joanna turned and stared at him, thinking, It's W. T. Stead, the spiritualist.

'Aren't you going up to the Boat Deck?' his friend asked.

'No. I believe I'll read a bit,' W. T. Stead said and walked over to one of the deck chairs. He sat down on it and opened his book.

'You ladies should go back inside where it's warmer,' the bearded man said, and Joanna whirled, but the steward had already disappeared.

He couldn't have. Only a few seconds had passed. He hadn't had time to walk the length of the deck, or even to the aft staircase. Where had he gone? She ran down the deck, trying doors. The second one opened on a narrow stairwell with latticed metal steps. One of the crew stairways. She started up it, but the stairs only went up one deck and then stopped, and the door at the top was locked. She ran back down and on to the next door.

It looked just like the door to the crew stairway, but when she opened it, she was in a wide space with a carpeted floor and marble stairs. The Grand Staircase. Which led to the Promenade Deck and the library, and if Mr Briarley wasn't there, the Palm Court was on the same deck. But what if he wasn't either place? He had said he was going to the post office, and she had no idea where that was.

But you do know where the library is, she thought, so check that first and then the Palm Court. She ran up the slightly tilting stairs, past the cherub, past Honour and Glory, up to the Promenade Deck and along the deck to the frosted glass doors of the library.

Mr Briarley was there, sitting not at the desk under the window, but at a small table near the glassed-in bookcases. He was writing earnestly, the yellow-shaded lamp making a circle of golden light on the white paper of the postcard, the white cuffs of his formal shirt.

'Mr Briar –' she called, and saw it wasn't him. It was the mustached man she had seen carefully dealing out cards in the lounge. She threaded her way through the gold tapestry chairs to him.

He didn't look up as she approached. He continued to write, dipping his pen into the ink bottle, lifting it out, scrawling a word, dipping it again. Joanna looked down at his letter. It wasn't written on a sheet of *Titanic* stationery. The paper was a torn sheet from an appointment book, the edge ragged along one side. He had scrawled across the middle of the page: 'If saved, inform my sister Mrs F. J. Adams of Findlay, Ohio. Lost. J. H. Rogers.'

'Mr Rogers,' Joanna said, 'there was a man in here at that desk.' She pointed at the desk. 'He was writing a note to his niece. Did you see where he went?'

The man blotted the letter carefully.

'Please. It's important. He was in here before, writing a postcard to his niece.'

He folded the note neatly in quarters and scrawled something on the outside. 'Mr Rogers,' Joanna said desperately and reached for his arm.

He shook his head. 'Not Mr Rogers,' he said, as though that was who she'd said she was looking for. 'Sorry.' He slid the note in his inside coat pocket and stood up. 'I'm needed on the Boat Deck,' he said. 'You should get into one of the boats, miss,' and strode across the room and through the door to the Grand Staircase.

'Then can you tell me where the Palm Court is?' Joanna asked, pursuing him through the door and up the stairs, but he had already disappeared out onto the Boat Deck, and she couldn't see which way he had gone in the darkness. The only light was from the open door of the gymnasium. Joanna looked in, but he wasn't there, and neither was Greg Menotti. The bicycles and the rowing machine and the gullotine-like weight-lifting apparatus stood motionless on the red-and-white tile floor.

She would have to find the Palm Court herself. It would have to have been on the Promenade Deck or the Bridge Deck, and all the way aft, which meant she should take the second-class stairway, and she started toward it, but as she passed the aft stairway, she thought she heard voices. She went inside and leaned over the railing, listening. She couldn't hear them, but above her, coming down the steps, was a thumping sound. The mail clerk, Joanna thought, and looked up the stairs.

It was Greg Menotti, dressed in swim trunks and backless beach sandals that flapped loudly against his heels at every step. He had a towel draped over his shoulders. 'Just heading for the swimming pool,' he said. 'Care to join me? The water's rather cold, but that's good for the circulation.'

'I'm looking for Mr Briarley,' Joanna said. 'He's tall, and he's wearing a gray tweed vest. Have you seen him?'

'No.' He started down the stairs.

Joanna ran down the steps in front of him to block his way. 'There's no time for swimming. You have to help me find Mr Briarley. It's important.'

'I want to get down there early,' he said, sidestepping her. 'I'm scheduled to play squash at two-fifteen –'

'No,' she said, stepping in front of him again. 'You have to help me. It's important. Mr Briarley knows why it's the *Titanic*.'

'The *Titanic*?' Greg said, and there was a flicker of fear in his eyes.

'Yes. The *Titanic*. And it's going down. You have to help me find him.' A man passed them, heading rapidly down the stairs. Joanna glanced at him, wondering if it was the steward, but it was an older man in a gray tweed vest and – 'Mr Briarley!' Joanna cried.

'It can't be the *Titanic*,' Greg said. 'I work out three times a week.'

Mr Briarley was already a flight and a half below her. She ran down after him, counting the decks as she went. B Deck. C. D. 'There's water coming in on D Deck,' the officer on the Boat Deck had said. She looked anxiously down at the carpet for the dark red stain of water.

E Deck. Below her, a door opened. She rounded the landing just in time to see it close. F Deck. She opened the door. Mr Briarley was already halfway down the passage. 'Mr Briarley!' she called.

She started after him. And ran straight into the steward. 'I'm sorry, miss. This area is restricted.'

'But I need to speak to Mr Briarley,' she said, looking anxiously past him.

The steward turned and looked, but Mr Briarley was already out of sight. 'Mr Briarley?' he said, frowning, and she saw that it was a different steward from the one the bearded man had sent to find Mr Briarley.

'He's my –' she said, and stopped. He's my – what? My high school English teacher? Did they even have high schools in 1912?

'I'll escort you back to your cabin, miss,' he said.

'Wait,' she said. 'Where does that passage lead?'

'To the boiler rooms, miss, but passengers aren't allowed in—'

'Captain Smith told me I had permission to go see –' What was in the boiler room? '– the ship's telegraph,' she said at random. 'I'm terribly interested in modern communications.'

'Only crew are allowed in the boiler rooms,' the steward said, and put a firm hand on her arm. 'I'll escort you back up to your stateroom.'

'Please,' Joanna said. 'You don't understand. It's important—'

'I'm sorry to interrupt,' a voice said, and Joanna jerked around. 'Mr Briarley!' she said, relieved.

'Ms Lander,' he said disapprovingly. 'What are you doing down here?'

'I need to talk to you,' she said. 'It's about –' but he was shaking his head.

'I'm afraid we won't be able to have tea in the Palm Court, after all. Something has come up.' He pulled the steward aside and spoke rapidly to him.

Joanna couldn't hear what either one said, but after a couple of sentences, Mr Briarley snorted in disgust. 'What's the quickest way there?' he demanded.

'Back up to E Deck and down Scotland Road to the stairs next to the elevators,' he said, and Mr Briarley immediately started back down the passage toward the stairway.

'Mr Briarley!' Joanna dashed after him. 'I need to talk to you,' she said, catching up.

'What is it?' he said, starting back up the stairs. It reminded her of times she'd caught up to him between classes, on his way to the office, and danced along at his side, asking him how many pages an assignment had to be.

'I need to know what you said in class,' Joanna said.

'You know I never give hints of what's going to be on the final,' Mr Briarley said, reaching the top of the flight of stairs.

'I don't need to know it for the final,' Joanna said. 'You said something in class—'

'I said a good many things in class,' Mr Briarley said, reaching the top of the flight of stairs. 'Can you be more specific?' He pushed open a door and started down a passage. They must still be in the crew section. The walls were painted gray, and there were pipes running along the ceiling.

'You were talking about the *Titanic*,' Joanna said, 'and you closed *Mazes and Mirrors* and dropped it on the desk, and then you said something about the *Titanic*.'

'Mazes,' Mr Briarley said thoughtfully, turning another corner. He yanked a metal door open. 'After you.' He bowed, and Joanna went ahead of him through the door and into another passage. This one was painted a shiny white and stretched endlessly into the distance. Mr Briarley set off down it at a rapid pace.

'And whatever it was,' Joanna said, 'when I experienced my first NDE, my subconscious saw a connection, and that's why I'm here.'

'Instead of in a tunnel with a light at the end of it,' Mr Briarley said. He stopped and looked bleakly down the long passage and then turned and looked at her. 'And you want me to tell you the connection?'

'Yes,' Joanna said.

'Connection. Fascinating word. From the Greek, "to send." But you must know the connection already,' he said to her, 'or how could you have made it?'

'I *don't* know it,' she said. 'My conscious mind's forgotten it.'

'Forgotten it? You should have paid more attention in class, Ms Lander,' he said severely and began walking again. 'I suppose you've forgotten what onomatopoeia is, too,' he said, 'and alliteration. And a metaphor.'

'Mr Briarley, please! This is important.'

'Indeed it is. Well?' he said and looked out over the passage as if it were a classroom. 'What is a metaphor? Anyone?'

'A metaphor is a figure of speech that likens two objects.'

'Wrong, and wrong again,' he said. 'The likeness is already there. The metaphor only sees it. And it is not a mere figure of speech. It is the very essence of our minds as we seek to make sense of our surroundings, our experiences, ourselves, seeing similarities, parallels, connections. We cannot help it. Even as the mind fails, it goes on trying to make sense of what is happening to it.'

'That's what I'm trying to do, Mr Briarley,' Joanna said. 'Make sense of what's happening to me. And what you said in class is the connection. It was about the *Titanic* –' she prompted.

'There are so many connections,' he said, frowning. 'The *Titanic* symbolizes so many, many things. Promethean arrogance, for instance,' he said, striding tirelessly along the passage, 'man challenging Fate and losing.' Joanna trotted beside him, trying to listen and keep up with him. 'Or Frankensteinian hubris, man putting his faith in science and technology and getting his comeuppance from Nature for it.'

The passage was endless. Joanna kept her eyes fixed on the door at the far end. 'Or the futility of human endeavor. "Look on my works, ye mighty, and despair,"' he quoted. '"Ozymandias." Percy Bysshe Shelley. Who also ended up at the bottom of the ocean.'

Water, in a narrow, uneven line, was trickling down the middle of the shiny floor from the end of the passage. 'Mr Briarley,' Joanna said, tugging on the sleeve of his shirt, 'look. Water.'

'Ah, yes,' he said, not even slackening his pace. 'Water is a symbol, too.' The thin line of water was growing wider as they neared the end of the passage, becoming two, then three rivulets. 'The crossing of water has been a symbol of death since ancient times,' Mr Briarley said, stepping easily between the rivulets. 'The Egyptians journeyed to the Land of the Dead in a golden boat.'

They were nearly to the end of the passage. He's going to open the door, Joanna thought, frightened, but at the last minute he turned and went down a dry metal stairway at the side. 'Aeneas is rowed across the Styx to the underworld by the boatman Charon,' he said, his voice echoing in the stairwell as Joanna rattled down after him, 'and Frodo sets sail for the Blessed Realm.'

He reached the bottom and started off down a passage. Joanna saw with relief that the floor was dry, though how was that possible, when there was water on the deck above? She looked anxiously up at the low ceiling overhead. Mr Briarley, unconcerned, was discussing 'In Memoriam.' 'Tennyson's dead friend sets sail over an unknown sea, to a still more unknown shore.' He opened a door. 'And, of course, there's the River Jordan. After you, Ms Lander,' he said, bowing, and Joanna stepped across the threshold. And into six inches of water.

The entire floor was awash. Letters, packages, postcards floated in the ankle-deep water, the ink on the addresses blurring, running down the envelopes in streaks like tears. On the far side of the room a mail clerk in a dark blue uniform and cap was bending in front of a wooden rack of pigeonholes, taking letters, already wet, out of the lowest row and moving them up to the top row.

It won't do any good, Joanna thought. The whole room will be underwater in a few minutes. 'Mr Briarley, we all need to get out of here,' she said, but Mr Briarley, oblivious, was splashing across the room to the mail clerk, pulling a folded piece of paper from his gray tweed vest pocket, and handing it to him.

The mail clerk shifted the stack of mail to one hand so he could unfold the note. He read it, nodded, and handed Mr Briarley the sodden mail. Then he reached inside the neck of his uniform and pulled out a ring of iron keys on a chain. He lifted the chain and the keys from over his head and handed them to Mr Briarley, taking back the mail.

'Which one is it?' Mr Briarley asked, but the mail clerk had already begun sorting again, putting the unreadable letters into the pigeonholes.

Mr Briarley waded back across the mail room, out the door, and down the passage, the chain swinging from his hand. He started up the stairs. 'Where are we going now?' Joanna asked, clambering after him.

'That is the question,' Mr Briarley said. 'To Hades or heaven? Or to the pharaohs' Hall of Judgment?' He reached the top of the steps and turned back down Scotland Road, where the water was now a stream flowing down the center of the tiled floor. 'And in which boat?' he asked. 'Charon's ferry?' He led her around to the metal stairway and past it, to an elevator with a brass folding grille across it. 'Or King Arthur's funeral barge?'

He pushed the grille open. 'After you,' he said, bowing. Joanna stepped in, and he got in after her and pulled the grille across. 'Frodo boarded an elven ship at the Grey Havens.' He pushed an ivory button labeled 'up.' The elevator rumbled upward. 'And the dead in *Outward Bound* found themselves on an ocean liner much like this one.'

The elevator jerked to a halt, and Mr Briarley shoved the grille open and strode out ahead of Joanna toward the doors that led out on deck. 'And then, of course there's the Ancient Mariner's ship. ' " 'There was a ship,' quoth he," ' he said, and pushed the doors open. They were on the Boat Deck. She could see the lights from the wireless room and the bridge ahead.

'It's fitting that that was your favorite poem,' Mr Briarley said, walking purposefully past the lifeboats toward the wireless room. 'It has icebergs in it, you know. "And ice, mast-high, came floating by, as green as emerald." '

'Is that the connection?' Joanna asked. 'Is that what you were reading that day?'

He didn't answer. He had stopped outside the wireless room, in front of a padlocked metal locker, and was taking the ring of keys from around his neck. 'Is it?' Joanna said, clutching at his sleeve.

He knelt in front of the locker. 'No,' he said, trying the long-barreled keys one after the other in the padlock, 'though it would be appropriate. Ships figure heavily in it, and water.' He inserted a key. It didn't fit. He tried another. 'And death. "Four times fifty living men, they dropped down one by one."' It didn't fit. He tried another. 'The universality of death, is that the symbol you're looking for?'

The key fit. He opened the locker, pulled out a wooden box, and carried it across to the railing. 'Certainly that was the *Titanic*. Astors and Irish immigrants, stokers and schoolteachers, perishing together in the icy water.'

He opened the box, squatted down, pulled out a cardboard cylinder and stood it against the railing, and then stood up again. 'Children and debutantes and professional cardsharps, all equally helpless, equally doomed.'

He patted the pockets of his gray vest as if he were looking for something. 'Unless, of course, you were in steerage, where your chances of perishing were somewhat more than equal.' He pulled a book of matches out of his pocket. 'In which case – step back.'

'What?'

'Step back,' he said, and put out his hand to push her away. He knelt, striking the match as he did so, holding it to the bottom of the cylinder.

In the last split second before he lit the fuse, she thought, The rockets! He's setting off the distress rockets! and a stream of flame shot up and burst into a shower of white sparks. Joanna craned her neck, looking up at the falling white stars, and as she did, she had the feeling that it was important, that she was close to the meaning.

'Would you like me to do that for you, sir?' a man's voice said, and Joanna looked down and saw an officer in a white uniform standing next to Mr Briarley.

'Thank you.' Mr Briarley handed over the matches to the officer and walked rapidly down the deck to the staircase.

Joanna ran after him. 'Mr Briarley! Wait!' She caught up with him on the second landing. 'In which case, what?'

'In which case,' he said, hurrying down the carpeted stairs, 'the meaning of the *Titanic* becomes a political one. The evils of a class-structured society, or of plutocracy, or the repression of women.'

'It wasn't political,' Joanna said. 'It was something important.'

'Important,' he said, reaching the bottom of the stairs. He strode across the foyer to a door and opened it. 'After you,' he said, bowing, and she stepped through.

And saw too late that it was the passage she had come through in. 'No, wait, you haven't –' she said, and was back in the lab.

Not yet, she thought. I almost had it. Something about the rockets, about Mr Briarley –

'Joanna?' Richard was saying above her. 'Joanna?'

She opened her eyes. Tish had already taken her IV out and was checking her vitals. 'Did I kick out again?'

'No,' Richard said, and he looked as worried as Vielle did in the ER. 'Are you all right?'

I said something coming out, she thought. I made him promise he'd come and get me again.

'I'm fine,' she said brightly. 'How long was I under?'

'Four minutes and ten seconds,' Tish said, lifting her arm up to remove the foam pads.

'Were you frightened during your NDE?'

Leading, she thought irrelevantly. I asked him to come and get me again. He thinks I think it's real, and he won't send me under again, and he has to. I almost had it.

'Frightened?' she said, smiling. 'Why? Did I say something?'

'Yes,' Tish volunteered. ' "Elevator." '

'Elevator?' Joanna said, relieved and surprised. Why had she said 'elevator' when it was the rockets –?

'You have the most boring NDEs,' Tish said, standing over her and look-ing at her watch as she waited out the monitoring period. 'First a post office and now an elevator? Don't you ever see anything exciting?'

She checked Joanna's pulse and blood pressure one last time, noting them on the chart, and then said to Richard, 'Can I leave now? I need to go see somebody before Mr Sage comes at three.'

He nodded and, as soon as she was out of the room, asked again, 'Were you afraid during your NDE?'

'Why?' Joanna asked. 'Did I sound frightened when I said "elevator"?'

'No, but your scans showed an extremely high level of cortisol. What hap-pened during your NDE?'

'I saw Mr Briarley again.' She told him about the trip to the mail room, the rockets, the elevator. 'And when he opened the door I stepped through it before I realized it was the passage,' she said. 'That's why I was afraid I'd kicked out, because it felt the same as last time.'

'And you didn't feel any fear?'

'I did when I saw the water in Scotland Road and when I saw the mail room was awash,' she said, trying to remember. She had been so intent on finding Mr Briarley and asking him what the NDE meant, she hadn't felt much fear, certainly not when compared to what she'd felt when she'd looked at the stain from the mailbag, when she'd looked over the side of the ship down into nothingness.

'Was my cortisol higher than the last two times?' she asked.

'I haven't looked at the neurotransmitter analysis yet, but going by the scans, yes. You were more frightened those times?'

She thought of her panicked flight down the stairs, along the deck, into the passage. 'Yes.'

'I was afraid of that,' he said and went over to the console.

Joanna dressed quickly. 'I'm going to go record my account,' she said, 'I'll be back at three,' and hurried down to her office before he could ask her anything else. She needed to think about the NDE before she lost the feeling of almost, almost knowing the answer. It was something about the rockets, and Mr Briarley setting them off.

She went through the scene again, trying to remember Mr Briarley's exact words. 'Step back,' he had said, and the rocket had shot up and burst into white stars –

She recorded the scene and then went back to the beginning and did the whole NDE, trying to hold on to the feeling. Something about the rockets, though they weren't a discrepancy, unless the ones she'd seen were different from the ones on the *Titanic*.

She called Kit and asked her what the emergency rockets had looked like. 'White fireworks,' Kit said. 'I remember Uncle Pat saying white was the color of the international distress signal, and there was a scene of them being fired in the movie.'

Of course. She remembered it. The officer had leaned the cylinder against the railing. 'Anything else?' Kit asked.

'Yes. I want to know if there was something called Scotland Road on the ship. It would have been a long passage down on' – she tried to think which deck it was on – 'E or F Deck. And also whether there was a library on board. It would have been on the Promenade Deck, next to a bar. And anything about what the rockets looked like and where they were kept.'

'Scotland Road, library, rockets. Okay,' Kit said. 'Oh, and if you have a minute, I've got a list of Ediths who were on board. I've found four. I'm not sure that's all. The crew are only listed by an initial and a last name, and some of the passengers are only down as Mrs Somebody.'

'How many were lost? Of the four?'

'Only Edith Evans.'

Joanna went back to the NDE. Not the rockets, but something in that part of the NDE. The elevator? That was definitely a discrepancy. They hadn't had elevators in 1912, and even if they had, they wouldn't have had one on board a ship. And she had murmured, 'Elevator,' when she was coming out.

She called Kit again. The phone was busy. She glanced at her watch. A quarter past two. Not enough time to run over there before Mr Sage's session. But she needed to know *now*, before she lost the feeling. It would have to be Maisie.

She ran upstairs, hoping Maisie wasn't down for tests. She was lying in bed, listlessly watching *Winnie the Pooh*. As soon as she saw Joanna, she pushed herself up higher against the pillows and said, 'I found out about the *Carpathia*.'

'Good,' Joanna said. 'I need to ask you something. Did the *Titanic* have an elevator?'

'Yeah,' Maisie said. 'Don't you remember, in the movie, they were running away from the bad guy and they got in the elevator and went down?'

'I thought your mother hadn't let you see *Titanic*.'

'I didn't. My friend that I told you about that saw it, she told me about that part,' she said, and it was a very convincing story, even though Joanna didn't believe it for a minute.

'Did your friend tell you what the elevator looked like?'

'Yeah,' Maisie said. 'It had one of those accordion things across it that you pull.' She demonstrated.

The grille. So the *Titanic* had had an elevator, and it wasn't a discrepancy. She could imagine what Richard would say when he found out. She'd have to hope when she did her account, there was some other discrepancy in her NDE, and she'd better go do that now, before she forgot what Mr Briarley said. 'I gotta go, kiddo,' she said, patting the covers over Maisie's knees.

'You *can't*,' Maisie said. 'I haven't told you about the *Carpathia* yet. And I have to ask you a question. How fast do ships go?'

'How fast?' The *Titanic* had been going much too fast for the ice warnings, she knew that, but how fast was that? 'I don't know.'

''Cause in my book it said the *Carpathia* came really fast, but this other book said it was fifty-eight miles away –'

'Fifty-eight?' Joanna said. 'The *Carpathia* was *fifty-eight* miles away?'

'Yeah,' Maisie said. 'And it took her three hours to get there. The *Titanic* had already sunk *ages* before. So I don't think it could've been very fast 'cause fifty-eight miles isn't very far to come.'

35

'I believe it's death.'
— Dying words of TCHAIKOVSKY

'What's wrong?' Maisie asked, looking at Joanna alertly. 'Are you okay?'

'Nothing's wrong,' Joanna said. 'You're right. Fifty-eight miles doesn't sound all that far. How far away was the *Californian*?' Fifty-eight miles. That day in the ER, he was talking about the *Carpathia*.

'You looked really funny when I told you how far away it was,' Maisie said. 'Did one of your near-death people see the *Carpathia*?'

'No. How far away was the *Californian*?'

'It was really close,' she said, still looking suspicious. 'It saw their rockets and everything, it could have saved them probably, only it turned off its wireless, so it didn't hear any of their SOSs, and it didn't even know what happened till the next morning.'

Joanna wasn't listening. He was trying to tell me the *Carpathia* was too far away, that it would never get there in time.

'I don't think they should've done that,' Maisie said. 'Turned off their wireless. Do you?'

'No,' Joanna said. That's why Greg's words haunted me so, why I kept feeling I knew what they meant. They meant he was on the *Titanic*.

'It was *really* close,' Maisie said. 'I mean, the people on the *Titanic* saw its lights. They told the lifeboats to try to row to it.'

'I need to go,' Joanna said, and stood up.

'I won't talk about the *Titanic* anymore, I promise. I'll just talk about the Hartford circus fire, okay?' Maisie went on rapidly. 'The people tried to get out the main entrance, but the cage for the lions and tigers was in the way and they got all jammed up against it, and the ringmaster kept trying to tell them to go out the performers' entrance – that's where all the clowns and acrobats and stuff come in when it's time for their acts – but they just kept trying to go out the way they came in.'

She'd convinced herself the *Titanic* wasn't real, that it was a symbol for something, an image her mind had chosen because of something Mr Briarley had said. But what if it wasn't?

'The thing was, they didn't have to go out the entrances,' Maisie said. 'They could have just lifted up the tent and crawled under it.'

The mail room, the aft staircase, Scotland Road, were all in the right place. They all looked exactly the way they really had, even the red-and-blue arrows on the stationary bicycles. Because you were really there. Because it was really the *Titanic*.

But how can it be? Joanna thought desperately. The NDE isn't a doorway into an afterlife or another time. It's a chemical hallucination. It's an amalgam of images out of long-term memory. But Greg had said, 'Fifty-eight,' and it wasn't an address, it wasn't a blood pressure reading. It was miles, and he had been talking about the *Carpathia*.

I have to get out of here, Joanna thought. I have to get somewhere where I can think about this. She started blindly for the door.

'You can't go *yet*,' Maisie pleaded. 'I haven't told you about the band yet.'

'I have to,' Joanna said, desperate, and like the answer to a prayer, her pager went off. 'See? They're paging me.'

'You can call them on my phone if you want,' Maisie said. 'It might not be your patient. Or it might be them saying they have to go down to Radiology so you don't need to come right now.'

Joanna shook her head. 'I have to go, and you need to—'

'*Rest,*' Maisie said mockingly. 'I hate resting. Can't I do some research? Please? It doesn't make me tired at all, and I promise I won't—'

'All right,' Joanna said, and Maisie immediately leaned over and got her tablet and pencil out. 'I need you to' – she cast about for something harmless –' make a list of all the wireless messages the *Titanic* sent.'

'You said you just wanted the names of the *ships.*'

'I did,' Joanna said, trying not to sound as desperate as she felt, 'but now I want to know what the messages were.'

'Okay. What else?'

What else? 'And where the swimming pool was.'

'Swimming pool? On a *ship*?'

'Yes. I want to know what deck it was on.' While Maisie was writing it down, she made it to the door.

'All the wireless messages or just the ones calling for help?' Maisie asked.

'Just the ones calling for help. Now I *have* to answer my page,' she said and went out. And since it was impossible to get anything past Maisie, she walked down to the nurses' station and called the switchboard to see who'd paged her.

'You have four messages,' the operator said. 'Mr Mandrake wants you to call him, it's very important. Dr Wright wants you to call him about Mr Sage's session. Vielle Howard wants you to call her when you have time, she's in the ER, and Kit Gardiner wants you to call her right away. She says it's urgent. Do you want me to connect you with Mr Mandrake's office?'

'No,' Joanna said and pressed down the button to break the connection. She didn't want to be connected with anyone, least of all Mr Mandrake. But not Vielle either, or Richard – oh, God, Richard! What would he say if she told him Greg Menotti had been on the *Titanic*?

I have to get somewhere where I can think about all this, she thought, and started to put down the receiver, and then thought, Kit said it was urgent. What if Mr Briarley had hurt himself again? She dialed Kit's number. 'Hi, Kit?'

'I am so glad you called,' Kit said. 'I've got it!'

'Got it?'

'The book! *Mazes and Mirrors.* I'm sure it's the right one,' she said excitedly. 'It has a homework assignment in it dated 14 October 1987. You'll never guess where I found it. Inside the pressure cooker. I think that was why Uncle Pat kept taking everything out of the cupboards. I can't wait for you to see it. Can you come over this afternoon?'

No, Joanna thought. Not until I've figured this out. 'I'm pretty busy,' she said.

'Oh,' Kit said, sounding disappointed. 'I'd bring it over to the hospital, but Uncle Pat's having a bad day –'

'No, I don't want you to have to do that. I'll come by tonight,' she said and hung up quickly. She'd call Kit later and make some excuse for why she couldn't come.

I can't come because I've been traveling back in time to a sinking ship, she thought wildly. Or how about, I can't come because I've turned into an NDE nutcase?

'Oh, Dr Lander, you *are* here,' a nurse's aide she vaguely recognized said. 'Mr Mandrake's looking for you. Barbara said you weren't on the floor, and that's what I told him.'

Bless Barbara, Joanna thought, looking anxiously in the direction of the elevator. 'When was he here?' she asked.

'About ten minutes ago. He said if I saw you, to tell you to call him immediately, that he'd found proof that near-death experiences are real.'

So have I, Joanna thought bleakly. 'Did he say where he was going?' she asked the aide.

'Hunh-unh. I can page him,' she said, reaching for the phone.

'No! That's okay,' Joanna said. 'It'll be faster just to go up to his office,' she said, and started toward the door to the stairs.

'Those stairs don't go up to seventh,' the aide called after her.

'Shortcut,' Joanna said, pushing open the door.

'Oh,' the aide nodded, and Joanna made her escape. But to where? she thought, clattering down the steps. She couldn't go back to her office or the lab, and with him roaming the halls, nowhere was safe. And I cannot, *cannot* stand to see him right now, she thought, and listen to him prattling on about heaven and happily ever after.

She ran down the steps to third and then stopped, her hand on the door. To get to the parking lot from here, she'd have to take the walkway and go through Medicine and past Mrs Davenport, and Mr Wojakowski was on second.

She let go of the door and ran all the way down to first and outside. A taxi, she thought, there are always taxis out front. If I've got money, she thought, fumbling in her pocket. She came up with two dollars, a quarter, and three pennies. She ran down to the basement, past the morgue, and outside.

It was freezing and the leaden sky looked like it might snow any minute. She pulled her cardigan close and hurried past the generating plant and around to the front. There was a single battered-looking Yellow Cab directly in front of the glass lobby doors. Joanna ducked into the backseat. 'Where to?' the cabbie asked.

Joanna leaned forward. 'The hospital parking lot,' she said.

'Is this some kind of joke?' he said, peering at her in the rearview mirror.

'No. I need you to take me to my car. It's parked there.'

He squinted at her as if she were a nutcase. Well, and wasn't she? Fleeing Mr Mandrake as if he were a monster instead of a nuisance? Believing the unbelievable? 'I intended to walk over to my car,' she said, 'but it's too cold.'

The explanation made no sense, and she waited for him to say, 'Why don't you go back inside and walk across?' but he grunted, 'Two-buck minimum,' put the car in gear, and pulled out of the driveway. And why shouldn't he believe her explanation? She believed she and Greg Menotti had been transported back to the *Titanic*. The cabbie tapped the meter. 'Two-ten,' he said.

Joanna handed him all her money, said, 'Thank you. You saved my life,' and walked out to her car, half-expecting Mr Mandrake to be standing next to it, waiting for her.

He wasn't. Or at the parking lot gate. She turned south on Colorado Boulevard, west on Sixth Avenue, south again on University, as if she were a character in a Sylvester Stallone movie, trying to throw the bad guy off the track. A fire truck roared toward her, sirens wailing and honking, and she pulled off to the side of the street, and then just sat there, gripping the steering wheel with both hands and staring into space.

Greg Menotti had been on the *Titanic*. She had seen him there, she had assumed that he was there, that Mr Briarley was there, because she had constructed them out of memory and wishful thinking. But what if the *Titanic* was real, and they were really there, Mr Briarley caught in some hideous limbo between two worlds, part of him already dead, and the place you went after you died wasn't heaven but back in time to the decks of the *Titanic*?

You can't believe this, she thought, and realized she didn't. It made no sense, not even if the NDE was a spiritual experience. Heaven, the Elysian Fields, Hades, Valhalla, even Mr Mandrake's Hallmark Card Other Side, were more logical than this. Why, even if the dead were sent back in time in a bizarre sort of reverse reincarnation, would they be sent to the *Titanic*? Was it some kind of punishment? Or were the dead supposed to be sunk in the depths of the Atlantic, and the *Titanic* just happened to be in the way?

And it isn't the *Titanic*, she thought. She had never once, even in that first rush of recognition, thought it was the actual ocean liner. It was something else, for which the *Titanic* was only the metaphor, not just for her, but, hard as it was to believe, for Greg Menotti, too. And how could it be?

Maybe he went to Dry Creek High School and heard Mr Briarley give the same lecture. No, she remembered him saying he had just moved out here from New York.

All right, then, maybe he was a *Titanic* buff, just like Mr Briarley. Are you kidding? she thought. He worked out at a health club three times a week. But, as Richard had said, movies and books and TV specials about the *Titanic* were everywhere, any one of them could have mentioned the *Carpathia's* being fifty-eight miles away –

If it *was* fifty-eight miles away. You only have Maisie's word for it, and you heard her, she said the *Titanic* had sunk hours before the *Carpathia* got there. She could have been exaggerating, or gotten the number wrong, it could have been fifty-seven miles away, or sixty, and you're getting yourself into a state for nothing, like that night you kept seeing fifty-eight on license plates and McDonald's signs.

No, she thought, staring blindly through the windshield at the snow that was beginning to fall, it was fifty-eight. She had known the minute she heard Maisie say it. Like you knew Mr Briarley was dead, and went tearing down to the ER? she asked herself. Outside confirmation. You need to at least double-check your facts, make Maisie show you the book, or ask Kit.

Kit. She had asked her to come over and look at the textbook. She could ask her to look it up, to verify it. It would only take a few minutes.

She started the car and pulled out from the curb, and realized that she was nearly there. In her panicked flight she had driven almost all the way to DU. She drove the rest of the way to Mr Briarley's, thinking, I won't even have to explain. I'll tell her I came over to look at the book. I'll pretend this is just another piece of information I need.

Only after she was on the porch, had rung the bell and was standing there shivering in her cardigan, did she remember that Kit had said Mr Briarley was having a bad day. I shouldn't have come, she thought, but Kit had already opened the door.

She was wearing jeans and a lace midriff top and a pair of ballet slippers. It must really be cold, Joanna thought irrelevantly. She's actually wearing shoes.

'Hi!' Kit said, her face lighting up. 'I thought you said you couldn't come today.'

'I was able to get away after all,' Joanna said. 'I hope this isn't a bad time.'

'No, it's great!' Kit said. 'I can't wait to show you the book. I knew it was the right one the minute I saw it. You know how sometimes you just *know*? And you know how you said different people thought it had different things on the cover. Well, they were *all* right. Geez, it's cold out here,' she said and shivered in her midriff top. She opened the door wide. 'How come you're not wearing a coat?'

Joanna had no idea how to answer that, but Kit didn't seem to require an answer. 'Let me go get the book,' she said, and went into the library. She was back out in less than a minute, quietly closing the door behind her. 'Uncle Pat's dozing,' she whispered, motioning Joanna to follow her down the hall to the kitchen. 'He'll wake up again in a few minutes. I want to let him sleep if he can. He had a bad night last night.'

A bad night. He had dismantled the kitchen again, more completely than before. Dishes and silverware were everywhere, and the entire contents of the refrigerator sat on the floor. A full roll of paper towels was draped over, under, among the canisters and cookie sheets and china. A smashed bottle of ketchup lay on the counter, leaking red into the sink. A dustpan of broken glass sat on the table, and the wastebasket was nearly full of it.

'Uncle Pat was looking for the book,' Kit said, taking two teacups off a tottering stack. 'I think he must have had a vague memory of having put it somewhere in the kitchen, and that's why he kept doing this.'

She stepped over a head of lettuce to the sink to fill the two cups. 'I'm so glad you were able to come over. I'm positive this time it's the right book. It's blue, just like you said, and it's got all the things you said it had on it.' She put the cups in the microwave and punched buttons. 'They're inside these gray panels that I think are supposed to be mirrors –'

Mazes and Mirrors, Joanna thought, and could see the mirrors, set at an angle, with different pictures in each one – a bottle of ink and a quill pen, and Queen Elizabeth, whom Ricky Inman had drawn a mustache and glasses on, and the carved prow of the caravel, plowing through the blue water.

Kit said, looking under a pile of potholders, 'One of them has a ship, just like you said, and a—'

'– castle and a crown on a red velvet pillow,' Joanna said. 'It's definitely the right one.'

'Oh, good!' Kit clapped her hands. 'Now, if I can do as good a job finding the teabags ...' She looked under an unsteady tower of cereal boxes and spices.

'How far away was the *Carpathia* from the *Titanic*?' Joanna said.

'The ship that came to the *Titanic*'s aid?' Kit asked. 'I don't know. I'll look it up.' She set a tin of cinnamon down and started for the door, stepping over a broiler pan, a jar of olives, and a carton of eggs. 'Be right back.'

She pattered down the hall and up the stairs and back down almost immediately, carrying a stack of books. 'I checked on Uncle Pat. He's still asleep,' she said, clearing a space on the table to set the books down. 'Let's see,' she said, opening the top book to the index. 'Carpathia, *Carpathia*. Here it is, fifty-eight miles.'

'Are you sure?' Joanna said. And of course she was sure. You knew it the minute Maisie said it. You were kidding yourself that you needed outside confirmation.

'It's right here,' Kit said. ' "Fifty-eight miles southwest of the *Titanic* when she received its first SOS," ' she read, ' "the *Carpathia* came at full steam, but arrived too late to take passengers off the ship." ' She closed the book to look at the cover. 'That's *The Titanic: Symbol for Our Time*. Do you want me to double-check it in something else?'

'No,' Joanna said. 'No.'

'What is it? Are you all right, Joanna?'

'No.'

'This has something to do with your NDE,' Kit said anxiously, 'doesn't it?'

'No,' Joanna said. 'With somebody else's.'

She told her about Greg Menotti's last words, and the nagging feeling that she should know what they meant, about Maisie telling her. 'He was talking about the *Carpathia*,' she said.

'And so you think that means he was seeing the *Titanic* in his NDE, too?'

'Yes. But why would he see the same imagery I saw?' Joanna asked. 'The RIPT scans show that the NDEs get their imagery from long-term memory. Those memory patterns are different for every subject. So why would the two of us have identical NDEs? Why would he see the *Titanic*?'

'Are you sure he did?' Kit said. 'I mean, fifty-eight could mean lots of different things. Addresses, PIN numbers – how old was he?'

'Thirty-four,' Joanna said. 'It wasn't his blood pressure or his cell phone number or his locker combination. It was miles. He said, "Too far for her to come." He was talking about the *Carpathia*. I'm sure of it. He was on board the *Titanic*, just like I was.'

'Or – there's another possibility, you know,' Kit said thoughtfully. 'You said he had the same NDE as you. Maybe that's not right. Maybe it's the other way around.'

'The other way around?' Joanna said. 'What do you mean?'

'Remember how you told me everybody sees tunnels and lights and relatives because that's what they've been programmed to expect? And how Mr Mandrake influences all of his subjects to see the Angel of Light?'

Joanna nodded, unable to see where this was going.

'Well, what if, when you heard this patient say, "Fifty-eight," your subconscious connected it to the *Titanic*, because of all the stories Uncle Pat told you, and that was why when you went under, you saw the *Titanic*? Because he'd influenced you. He could have been talking about anything, but you connected it to the *Carpathia*.'

It made perfect sense. She had been steeled against seeing the relatives and angels and life reviews everyone else reported. But that didn't mean she hadn't had expectations. She'd spent the last two years watching her subjects' expressions, and their body language, trying to find out what their near-death experiences were like. 'Oh, no, oh, no, oh, no,' Amelia had said, and Mrs Woollam had held her Bible to her frail chest and said, 'How can it not be frightening?'

And during the period right before she'd gone under, she had been thinking about Greg Menotti, worrying over what he'd said, trying to make sense of it. She had thought 'fifty-eight' sounded familiar. Her subconscious mind must have remembered that was how far away the *Carpathia* had been and triggered the other memories, triggered the NDE and the reference to Mr Briarley, and it wasn't the engines stopping that was the connection she'd been trying to remember, it was Mr Briarley saying, 'The *Carpathia* was fifty-eight miles away, too far for her to come in time.'

'That has to be it,' Joanna said. 'It makes perfect sense.'

'But how does the book fit into it?' Kit asked. 'I'll bet it has a poem or something in it about the *Carpathia* and if it does, that will prove it,' she said excitedly. 'This is just like a detective story.' She put down the book and began threading her way through the pans and groceries. 'I'll go get it.'

'I don't want you to disturb Mr Bri—'

'I'll be quiet. Be right back,' she said and went down the hall.

Joanna picked up *The Titanic: Symbol for Our Time* and looked at the picture of the half-sinking ship with a rocket bursting above it. If Greg Menotti had been the influence for her NDE, then that would explain why he was in it. And Mr Briarley –

'Oh, no!' Kit said from the study, and Joanna stood up quickly, knocking her knee against the table leg as she did. A stack of plates slid toward the edge, and a half-dozen dinner knives went onto the floor with a clatter.

Joanna dived for the plates and moved them back from the edge. 'What's wrong?' she called to Kit, maneuvering the maze of pans and salad-dressing bottles between her and the door.

There was no answer. 'Kit! Are you okay?' Joanna called, pelting down the hall, thinking, Mr Briarley's dead. 'What happened?'

Kit was standing arms akimbo over Mr Briarley, and he wasn't dead. He was awake and staring dully ahead, slumped in the dark red leather chair, his hands loosely folded in his lap. Joanna saw with a pang that his gray tweed vest was buttoned wrong. Looking at him, Joanna realized that this, and not the disaster in the kitchen, was what Kit had meant when she said he was having a bad day.

'It's not there,' Kit said disgustedly.

'What isn't?' Joanna said.

'*Mazes and Mirrors*,' Kit said. She knelt down in front of Mr Briarley. 'Uncle Pat, did you take the book?'

He didn't answer, or even give any indication he'd heard her, or knew she was there. He stared dully at the opposite side of the room.

'Where did you put it, Uncle Pat?' Kit asked, and when there was no answer, she straightened. 'He's hidden it again. He can't have been awake more than five minutes. He was still asleep when I brought the books about the *Titanic* down.'

'Where did you leave it?' Joanna asked.

'Right *here*,' Kit said, pointing to an empty space at the end of a bookshelf.

'I thought he wouldn't notice it in the bookcase. I should never have left it in here. I should have put it upstairs with the *Titanic* books.'

'It doesn't matter,' Joanna said, worried that Kit seemed so upset. 'The book was an excuse. I really came to ask you about the *Carpathia*, to find out why Greg Menotti saw the *Titanic* when he was dying –'

'It *does* matter,' Kit said, nearly in tears. 'I should have known not to leave it in here. Yesterday, I found him hiding my boots in the clothes hamper – wait a minute! I just had an idea!' She ran up the stairs.

'Can I help?' Joanna called after her.

'No, you'd better stay there with him,' she said. 'There's no telling what he'll hide next!'

Joanna went back in the library, though Mr Briarley didn't look like he would move from his chair, let alone sneak out of the room to hide things. He looked as still, as senseless, as Coma Carl, and Joanna felt suddenly embarrassed to be looking at him, as if she had broken into a house when no one was home. She turned and stared at the bookcases.

If he had taken the book out of one bookcase, he might have put it in another. She scanned the books lying along the tops of the shelves first and then along the ranks of shelved volumes, looking for something thick, with a textbook binding. And here it was, sandwiched in between *Bleak House* and *Spoon River Anthology*. She called up to Kit, 'I've foun—' then stopped, looking at it.

'You found it?' Kit said from the top of the stairs.

'No,' Joanna shouted up to her. 'Sorry, it's the other one, the one that wasn't right.'

The one that wasn't right, she thought, looking down at the clipper ship and the blue background and the orange lettering. It wasn't right, even though it fit all the criteria.

And neither was Kit's theory. It was logical, it fit all the circumstances, but even if they found *Mazes and Mirrors* and it had a poem about the *Carpathia*, a poem with an introduction that explained in italics, 'On the night the *Titanic* sank, the steamer *Carpathia* was fifty-eight miles away, too far away for her to come to the liner's rescue ...' it still wouldn't make it the right one.

I didn't see the *Titanic* because of Greg's dying words, she thought. It was because of something Mr Briarley said in class. And she would know it when she heard it, the way Kit had known when she found the right book, the way she had known that the sound she'd heard was the stopping of the engines.

Joanna went over to Mr Briarley's chair. 'Mr Briarley,' she said, kneeling next to the arm of the chair. 'You said something in class about the *Titanic*, about what it meant. What was it? Can you remember?'

Mr Briarley continued to stare dully at the opposite wall.

'I know it's hard for you to remember,' Joanna said gently, 'but this is really important. It was something about the *Titanic*. You shut the book, and you said,' she hit the leather arm of the chair, trying to make the memory come, '*something*. About the *Titanic*. It was foggy out, and you were holding a book …'

Joanna shut her eyes, trying to remember if he had been holding *Mazes and Mirrors* or the tattered paperback of *A Night to Remember*. 'Please try to remember what you said, Mr Briarley,' she whispered. 'Please. It's important.'

There was no response at all.

He's too far away to hear me, Joanna thought. Where are you, Mr Briarley? Standing in the mail room, ankle-deep in water, asking the clerk for the key? Or in the library, trying to scrawl Kit a message?

Or nowhere, the brain cells that held awareness and comprehension and identity destroyed by the plaque of Alzheimer's, the synapses that held the memory of that foggy afternoon sunk without a trace? 'You don't remember,' she said hopelessly and stood up. 'It's all right. Don't worry about it.'

She put *Voyages and Voices* back on the shelf and searched carefully along the rest of the shelves, even though it was useless. Because *Mazes and Mirrors* didn't have anything about the *Titanic* in it. She had remembered it not because of a poem or an essay, but because Mr Briarley had been holding it when he made the speech that was the trigger. And that was why, when Betty had told her the title, she had felt that shock of recognition. Because it was the cover she remembered, the cover she was looking at when he said the critical words.

She finished the bookshelves and started through the books piled in the window seat. She wondered if the window seat lifted up, if Mr Briarley could have put the textbook inside.

'What else would he see?' Mr Briarley said from his chair.

'What?' Joanna said, startled into answering. He had sat up and was looking at the side of the chair where she had knelt.

'Who can tell me what a metaphor is?' he asked, scanning the room. His class, she thought. He's seeing his English class.

'Ms Lander?' he said, his gaze coming back to the space next to his chair. 'Can you define a metaphor?'

Joanna glanced toward the stairs, wondering if she should call Kit.

'A metaphor is an implied or direct comparison of two things that are alike in some way,' he said. 'Death is a journey, a voyage, a passage. And yes, I know, Mr Inman, you never saw fog with feet. That is because most things are only alike in one or two ways. Like a cat, the fog is silent, mysterious. On the other hand, it does not eat fish or, as you have pointed out, Mr Inman, have feet.' Mr Briarley stood up and walked over to the library table, sat down on the edge of it.

Joanna held her breath.

'Usually there are only a few points of comparison, but sometimes, sometimes, the two things are mirror images. Have you never wondered why I would spend valuable class time on a shipwreck?' Mr Briarley said. 'Have you never wondered why, after all these years, all those books and movies and plays, people are still fascinated?'

He's talking about the *Titanic*, Joanna thought. He remembers. She sank down on the window seat, waiting.

'They know it when they see it,' he said. 'They recognize it instantly, though they have never seen it before. And cannot take their eyes off it.'

He was talking in riddles, in tangles of memory and metaphor, and it might mean no more than his asking her why she didn't have a hall pass, but she sat silently on the window seat, afraid to move, afraid even to breathe.

'They tell themselves that isn't what it is, that it's a morality play or a comedy of errors,' Mr Briarley said. 'They say it looks like class warfare or technological arrogance or the vengeance of a wrathful God, but they're lying to themselves. They know, they know what it looks like. And so did he.'

'That's why he saw it,' Mr Briarley said, and Joanna realized what he was talking about. He hadn't heard her when she knelt next to his chair and asked him to remember. He had heard her before, talking to Kit, asking her why Greg Menotti had seen the *Titanic*, and he had spent the past fifteen minutes searching patiently through the passages of his blocked and damaged brain, trying to find the answer.

' "I shall never forget it," ' he murmured. 'Edith said that,' and, as if she had asked, 'Edith Haisman. She said, "I shall never forget it, the darkness and the cold," but she wasn't talking about the *Titanic*. And the forward lookout, who saw it first – who gave the warning – hanged himself from a lamppost. Because he knew what it really was. He knew it as soon as he saw it, knew –'

'I can't find it anywhere,' Kit said, and Joanna could hear her pattering down the stairs.

No, Joanna thought, pressing herself against the back of the window seat as she had against the stairwell wall that day she and Richard had hidden from Mr Mandrake.

'It wasn't in the clothes hamper or under the mattress or behind the radiator,' Kit said, halfway down, two-thirds.

Don't, Joanna prayed. Not now –

'Wait!' Kit said, only a few steps from the bottom. 'I just thought of something. I know someplace else,' and ran back up.

Mr Briarley looked after her, his head cocked as if listening for her voice, and then slumped back into his chair again. Joanna waited, but Kit's voice, all unintending, had broken the spell, and he had sunk back into unawareness.

What does it look like, Mr Briarley? Joanna nearly asked, but she was afraid of breaking the connection that might still be there in his mind. Wait, she thought, listening anxiously for Kit. Don't lead. Wait.

'I kept losing my grade book,' Mr Briarley said, and his voice had changed. It was introspective, even gentle. 'And I couldn't remember the names of Lear's daughters. Ice warnings. But I didn't listen to them. "Getting old," I told myself. "Typical absentminded professor." Very few of the passengers even heard the collision, you know. It was the engines stopping that woke them up.'

Joanna's heart beat painfully. Wait.

'I told myself there was nothing to worry about,' he said. 'Modern medicine had made the ship unsinkable, and the lights were still on, the decks were still comparatively level. But inside ...'

He stared ahead blindly for a moment and then went on. 'The perfect metaphor,' he said, 'looming up suddenly out of nowhere in the middle of your maiden voyage, unseen until it is nearly upon you, unavoidable even when you try to swerve, unexpected even though there have been warnings all along. Literature, literature is a warning,' he said, and then waveringly, ' "No, no, my dream was lengthened after life." Shakespeare wrote that, trying to warn us of what's coming. "I passed, methought, the melancholy flood, With that sour ferryman which poets write of, Unto the kingdom of perpetual night." ' He looked out over the library as if it were a classroom. 'Can anyone tell me what that means?'

Above them, Kit slammed a drawer shut, and Mr Briarley said, as if the sound had been a question, 'Nothing can save you, not youth or beauty or wealth, not intelligence or power or courage. You are all alone, in the middle of an ocean, with the lights going out.'

Above, Kit shut a door, pattered into the hall. She would be down any minute. There was no time to wait.

'Why did he see the *Titanic* when he was dying?' Joanna asked, and Mr Briarley turned and looked at her in surprise.

'He didn't,' he said. 'He saw death.'

Death. 'And it looked like the *Titanic*,' Joanna said.

'And it looked like the *Titanic*.'

Kit appeared in the door. 'I heard you talking,' she said. 'Did you find it?'

36

'7 A.M. sailing today Thursday on *Titanic* on her maiden trip, to New York, her first trip on the Atlantic. Goodbye. Love, P. D.'
— Postcard sent by PATRICK DOOLEY to
Mary Tonnery from Queenstown

Joanna wasn't even sure of how she got back to the hospital. She had wanted only to get away, to escape what Mr Briarley had told her, and what she might tell Kit.

'What's wrong?' Kit had said after one look at her face. 'What's happened?'

'Nothing,' Joanna had said, trying to keep the knowledge out of her face. 'I didn't find the textbook.' Kit had come into the library and was standing in front of the banked pictures, so that the photo of Kevin smiled over her shoulder. I can't tell her, Joanna had thought. I can't let her find out. 'I have to go,' she'd said and gone out into the hall.

'Uncle Pat didn't say something, did he?' Kit had said anxiously, following her to the door. 'He sometimes says terrible things, but he doesn't mean them. They're part of his illness. He doesn't even know he says them.'

'No,' she'd said, trying to smile reassuringly. 'He didn't say anything terrible.' Only the truth. The terrible, terrible truth.

There was no question of its being true, even though, listening to him, she had felt no sudden 'Eureka!,' no epiphany, only a feeling of dread. A sinking feeling, she thought, and her lips twisted. How appropriate. What had Mr Briarley called it? The very mirror image of death.

Which was why it had resonated down through the years. All disasters — Maisie's *Hindenburg* and Pompeii and the Hartford circus fire — had some of the attributes of death, its suddenness or its panic or its horror, but the *Titanic* had them all: courage and destruction and casualness and a dreadful confluence of coincidence and culpability, terror and gallantry and despair.

The tragedy of the *Titanic* was both sudden and slow — the impact with the iceberg as unexpected as a car accident, as a stroke. But it was also endless, the passengers sitting quietly on deck chairs after all the boats were gone or playing bridge in the smoking room, like patients in nursing homes, in the oncology ward, waiting forever to die.

All the attributes. The injury that seemed minor at first — a lump, a shadow on the X rays, a cough — nothing to worry about. Modern medicine has made the ship nearly unsinkable, and the captain surely knows what to do.

She thought of Greg Menotti, protesting that he went to the health club every day even as the killing pain clamped his chest. Of Maisie's mother, insisting the new drug was stabilizing Maisie's arrhythmia. Of the men on the *Titanic* leaning over the railing and laughing down to the women in the boats: 'We'll see you at breakfast,' and, 'You'll need a pass to get back on, ladies.'

Denial, and then worry. The doctor's scheduled an exploratory, the CAT scan shows progressive degeneration of cortical nerve cells, the deck is starting to list. But there's still no indication that it's really serious. There's certainly no need for your brother to come, no need to put on a lifejacket or draw up a will, not with the decks still lit and the band still playing.

More denial, and then a frantic rush for the lifeboats, for chemotherapy, for a clinic in Mexico, and then, with the boats all gone, good-byes and a desperate clinging to deck chairs, religion, positive thinking, Mr Mandrake's books, a light at the end of the tunnel. But nothing works, nothing holds, because the whole ship is coming apart, breaking up, crashing – that's why they call it a crash cart, Joanna thought suddenly – the body's crashing, going under, going down, and the *Titanic* isn't just a mirror image of dying, but of what happened to the body, because it didn't die all at once any more than the person did, but by stages, the breathing coming to a stop, and then the heart and the blood in the veins, one watertight compartment after another flooding and spilling over into the next: cerebral cortex, medulla, brain stem, all faltering and flickering out, and in their final moments seeing their own end. The ship going down by the head.

But taking forever to sink, the eyes' pupils dilating even as they dulled in a doomed effort to keep the lights on. Some cells surviving for hours, the liver still metabolizing, the bones still manufacturing marrow like stokers down below in the engine room still working to fire the boilers, to keep the dynamos going, unaware that the ship has already foundered. Sinking slowly at first and then faster, the body growing darker by degrees, and colder.

'I shall never forget it, the darkness and the cold,' Joanna thought, shivering. She was sitting in her car in the hospital parking lot, her hands numb on the steering wheel. She wondered how long she had sat there, staring unseeing at the hospital, at the gray sky.

A long time. It was getting dark out, the gray of the sky deepening, closing in, and lights had come on in nearly all the hospital windows. At some point she must have turned off the engine because the car was icy. She couldn't feel her feet. You'll catch your death, she thought, and got out of the car and went into the hospital. It was bright inside, the fluorescents making her squint as she opened the door. At the far end of the hall, framed in the blinding light, she could see a woman in a white coat and a white knitted cap and a man in a dark suit.

Mr Mandrake, Joanna thought. She had forgotten all about him.

'But he's going to be all right, isn't he?' the woman asked, a quaver in her voice.

'We're doing everything we can,' the man said.

A doctor, not Mr Mandrake, but Joanna ducked into the nearest stairway anyway and started up to the lab.

'We're doing everything we can,' the doctor had said, but there wasn't anything anybody could do. Only now that all hope of it was gone, did Joanna realize how badly she had wanted the NDE to be a physical phenomenon, a survival mechanism, how badly she had wanted to present Richard triumphantly with the solution to the puzzle. How badly she had wanted to tell Maisie, 'We've got a new treatment.'

But that had always been wildly unlikely. Medical discoveries and actual treatments were years, sometimes decades, apart, and the person who had inspired the research hardly ever benefited from it. She, of all people, should know that. After the *Titanic*, legislation had been passed shifting the shipping lanes farther south, mandating twenty-four-hour wireless operation, requiring lifeboats for everyone on board. All too late, too late for the fifteen hundred lost souls.

And even if the NDE had been a survival mechanism, there had been no guarantee that a treatment could have been developed from it. But it wasn't. It wasn't any kind of evolutionary defense mechanism at all, and her persistent feeling that it was, that she was on the verge of some significant medical discovery, had been wishful thinking, confabulation, chemically induced.

It wasn't a defense of the body against death. It was the reverse. It was coming face to face with death with no defenses at all, recognizing it in all its horror. And no wonder Mr Mandrake and Mrs Davenport and all the rest had opted for lights and relatives and angels. The real thing was too terrible to contemplate.

She had arrived at the sixth floor. She put her hand out to open the stairway door and then let it drop. I can't do this, she thought. There was no way she could stand by and watch Richard intentionally send Mr Sage under. Into the mirror image of death.

But if she told him that, he'd ask her what was wrong. And she couldn't tell him. He'd be convinced she'd turned into a nutcase, like Seagal and Foxx. He'd accuse her of having been converted by Mr Mandrake.

I'll make some excuse, she thought. I'll tell him … but she couldn't let him see her. Like Kit, he would take one look at her face and ask, 'What's wrong? What's happened?' She would have to call him from her office. I'll tell him I have a headache and am going home, she thought, heading back down the stairs. I'll tell him we have to reschedule.

There was a scrawled note taped to her office door. 'Mr Sage had to cancel,'

Joanna read and felt a rush of relief. 'He has the flu. Went to see Dr [unintelligible] over at St Anthony's ...'

The rest of the note was illegible. She couldn't make out what Richard had gone over to St Anthony's about, or whether he was the one who had gone. Mr Sage might have been the one who'd gone to see Dr [unintelligible] about his flu. The only word she could make out was 'Richard,' scrawled at the bottom of it. But it didn't matter. All that mattered was that she'd had a reprieve.

Down the hall behind her, the elevator dinged. Richard, she thought, or Mr Mandrake. She fumbled for her keys, got them out. She could hear the elevator doors swoosh open. She got her key in the lock, turned it, put her hand on the knob.

'Joanna,' Vielle called, and there was nothing for it but to turn around, smile, hope all Vielle wanted was to discuss Dish Night.

No such luck. 'Are you all right?' Vielle asked. She was wearing the worried expression she always had in the ER. 'Did something happen? I saw you leaving the hospital in a taxi. I called to you, but you didn't hear me, I guess. Where were you going?'

Joanna looked anxiously down the hall. They shouldn't stay out here talking. 'I went over to Kit's,' she said, opening the door and going into her office.

'In a *taxi*?' Vielle said, right behind her. 'Did your car break down? You could have borrowed mine.'

'Mr Mandrake was after me,' Joanna said and tried to smile lightly. 'He had the parking lot staked out.'

Vielle appeared to accept that. 'How come you went over to Kit's?'

'I had to pick up a book,' Joanna said. Which she clearly didn't have with her.

'I got worried about you when I saw you weren't wearing a coat,' Vielle said.

'I told you, Mr Mandrake was after me. I couldn't even go back to my office to get my bag. It's getting so he stalks me constantly. We're going to have to start holding Dish Night underground,' she said, trying to change the subject. 'Speaking of which, what night do you want to have it?'

It didn't work. 'Are you sure you're okay?' Vielle said. 'The last couple of weeks you've seemed so distracted.'

'I have been,' Joanna said. 'My best friend's still working in the ER, even though a drug-crazed maniac nearly shot her arm off.' She looked pointedly at Vielle's bandaged arm. 'How'd it go today? Any attempted murders?'

'Okay, okay,' Vielle said, raising her hands in a gesture of surrender. 'How about tomorrow night? For Dish Night? You tell Richard, and I'll call Kit.'

And Kit and Vielle will compare notes, will ask me why I left in such a hurry and what Mr Briarley said. 'I can't,' Joanna said. 'I'm swamped with interviews I've got to transcribe.' She sat down at her desk and switched on her computer to make the point. 'There's no way I'm going to get home before ten any night this week. How about Saturday?'

'Perfect. That way I can tell Harvey the Ghoul I'm busy. Did you know morticians inject mastic compounds in the corpse's cheeks to make him look healthier?'

'Saturday then?' Joanna asked, picking up a tape and sticking it in her minirecorder.

'Well, I'll let you get busy,' Vielle said, looking worried again. 'I just wanted to make sure nothing was wrong.' At the door she turned. 'I know this dithetamine is supposed to be harmless, but everything has side effects, even aspirin. Have you told Richard about – whatever it is that's been worrying you?'

I can't tell Richard, Joanna thought. I can't tell anybody, not even you. Especially not you. You deal with people dying every day. How could you bear it if you knew what happened to them afterward? She looked brightly up at Vielle. 'There's nothing worrying me,' she said, 'except how I'm going to get all these tapes transcribed.'

'I'd better let you get started on them then,' Vielle said, and smiled at her. 'I just worry, you know.'

'I know,' Joanna said, and as she went out the door, 'Vielle –'

But Vielle had already turned and was pulling the door sharply to behind her. 'Mr Mandrake just got off the elevator,' she whispered. 'Lock the door and shut off your lights,' and ducked out, shutting the door behind her.

Joanna dived for the light switch and then the lock. 'She's not here,' she could hear Vielle say. 'I was just leaving her a note.'

'Do you know when she'll be back?' Mr Mandrake's voice said.

'I sure don't.'

'I have something very important to tell her, and she *does not* answer her pages,' Mr Mandrake said disapprovingly. 'Did you say you left her a note? I think I'd better leave her one, too.'

There were shuffling sounds, as if Vielle were trying to block his getting to the door, and then the knob rattled.

'I must've accidentally locked it when I shut it,' Vielle said. 'Sorry,' and then, from farther down the hall, 'I'll tell her you want to see her,' and the faint ding of the elevator.

Joanna stood by the door, listening for the sound of Mr Mandrake's breathing, afraid to turn on the light for fear he was still waiting out there, ready to pounce, and then, after a while felt her way over to her desk and sat down, trying to think what to do.

I'll have to quit the project, she thought, make up some excuse, tell Richard I'm too busy, the project's interfering with my own work. Quit and go back to – what? Interviewing people who had coded, knowing what she knew? Talking to Maisie, who was going to die before she got a new heart? To Kit, whose fiancé had gone down on the *Titanic*, whose uncle was trapped on it, sending up rockets no one could see? I can't, she thought. She would have to leave the hospital altogether, go someplace else, get away. Like Ismay, she thought, sneaking off in a lifeboat. Leaving the women and children to drown. 'He was *such* a big coward,' Maisie had said contemptuously, and Maisie certainly knew something about courage. She had been looking death squarely in the face for a long time and had never tried to run away.

Only because she can't, Joanna thought, but that was a lie. Look at Mr Mandrake and Mrs Davenport. And Maisie's own mother. And Amelia.

That's why Amelia quit, Joanna thought, and it was like another revelation. She had thought at the time Amelia's story of being worried about her grades wasn't the whole truth, but she had assumed her quitting had had something to do with her crush on Richard. But it hadn't. Amelia had recognized death, had murmured, 'Oh, no, oh, no, oh, no,' and resigned from the project.

But Amelia was only twenty-two. She was only a volunteer, not a partner. She hadn't signed on to try and find out what NDEs were, and then, when she found out, panicked, lost her nerve, bolted for the nearest lifeboat. '"Where I come from, we'd string you up on the nearest pine tree,"' Joanna murmured.

But even if she stayed, even if she told Richard, what would that accomplish? Richard wouldn't believe her. He'd think she'd turned into Bridey Murphy. He'd tell her she was having temporal-lobe delusions.

All right then, make him believe you, she thought, and went over to the door, cracking her knee on the file cabinet, and switched on the light. Prove your theory. Collect evidence. Get outside confirmation. Starting with Amelia Tanaka.

Joanna called Amelia that night and again the next morning, and asked her to come in. 'I'm not in the project anymore,' she said, and Joanna thought she was going to hang up on her.

'I know you're not,' Joanna said quickly. 'I just have a few questions I need to ask you about your sessions for our records. It'll only take a few minutes.'

'I'm really busy right now. I have three tests this week, and my biochem project's due. I won't have any time till after the end of the semester,' Amelia said, and this time did hang up.

And did Joanna really need any more proof than that? Fear and reluctance had been in every word. Joanna went and got Amelia's file out of the cabinet. On the questionnaire, Joanna had made her list not only her address but her class schedule, complete with buildings and room numbers. She had biochem tomorrow afternoon from one to two-forty.

One o'clock tomorrow. And until then … Joanna stuck Amelia's disk in the computer and started through her transcript, looking for clues. There weren't any. Warmth, peace, a bright light, nothing at all about water or an up-curving floor or people standing out on the deck.

No, wait. She had said, when Joanna asked her if the light had been there all the time, '… not till after they opened the door.' Later, she had amended it to, 'I just assumed somebody had opened a door because of the way the light spilled in,' but Joanna wondered if the first version was the true one.

She read the rest of it. When she had asked Amelia her feelings, she had said, 'Calm, quiet,' which might be a reference to the engines stopping, and she had complained after each session of being cold. All of which proved exactly nothing, except that you could find anything you tried to look for in an NDE, just like Mr Mandrake.

She took out Amelia's disk, put in one of last year's interviews, printed out half a dozen files, and started through them with a yellow marker, highlighting words and phrases. 'I was lying in the ambulance, and all of a sudden I was out of my body. It was like there was a porthole in my body, and my soul just shot out of it.' Joanna highlighted the word *porthole* in yellow.

'I felt like I was going on a long voyage.'

'… light all around,' Kathie Holbeck had said, looking up at the ceiling, and spread her hands out like a flower opening. Or a rocket going off. Ms Isakson had done that, too. Joanna looked up her file. 'All spangled,' she'd said. Like the starburst of a rocket.

'My father was there, and I was so glad to see him. He was killed in the Solomons. On a PT boat.'

Joanna tapped her marker thoughtfully on that one, thinking about Mr Wojakowski and all his *Yorktown* stories. Could he have been reminded of them because he'd been on a ship?

Mr Wojakowski wasn't reminded of anything, she thought. He made it all up. And even if he had been, it was hardly the sort of proof she could offer to Richard. She continued through the transcripts:

'I heard a sound, but it was funny, like not really a sound at all, you know what I mean?'

'It sounded exactly like something rolling over a whole bunch of marbles.' Marbles. She found Kit's notes of the engines stopping. And there it was. 'It was as if the ship had rolled over a thousand marbles,' passenger Ella White had said when asked what the iceberg sounded like.

Joanna started through the transcripts again. 'I was traveling through the tunnel, very fast, but smooth, like being in an elevator.'

'I knew I was crossing the River Jordan.'

She hadn't lied to Vielle when she'd said she wouldn't get home before ten. At half-past nine she was still only halfway through the set of interviews. She shut the computer off, pulled on her coat, and then sat down, still in her coat, and switched it on again.

She saved all of her interviews from the past two years onto a single file and then typed in 'water' and hit 'global search' and 'display,' and watched them come up.

'I felt like I was floating in the water.'

'The light was warm and glimmery, like being underwater.'

'... being at the lake' (this from Pauline Underhill's description of her life review), 'where we used to go when I was little. I was in our old rowboat, and it was leaking, the water was coming in the side ...'

Rowing on the lake, Joanna thought, and called up Coma Carl's file, with its long list of isolated words and (unintelligible)s.

'Water,' and 'placket' or 'blanked out' or 'black.' Or 'blanket,' Joanna thought. She read through the rest of his file. 'Dark' and 'patches' and 'cut the rope.' Cut the rope. The men up on top of the officers' quarters, trying to cut the collapsibles loose as the water came up over the bow. She read on. 'Water ... cold? code? ... oh, grand.' The Grand Staircase.

She quit at one o'clock, went home, and read *The Light at the End of the Tunnel* till she fell asleep, dog-earing pages that had NDEs that mentioned 'water' and 'voyage' and 'darkness.'

In the morning, she went to see Coma Carl, hoping he might have begun talking again, but he had a feeding tube in and an oxygen mask. 'He's not having a very good day,' Mrs Aspinall whispered, which was putting it mildly. He was a corpselike gray, and his thin chest, his skeletal arms and legs, seemed to be sinking into the bed, into death itself.

'They can't seem to keep his temperature down,' Mrs Aspinall said, sounding near tears. She looked terrible, too. Dark gray shadows under her eyes and a general look of exhaustion. A pillow and a hospital blanket were stacked neatly on the windowsill, which meant that she was sleeping in the room. And getting no sleep at all.

'You look tired,' Joanna said. 'Would you like to go get a cup of coffee, or lie down in the waiting room? I'll sit with him.'

'No, he might ... no,' Mrs Aspinall said. 'I'm fine. Thank you, though. It's very kind of you.' She looked at Carl. 'He's stopped talking. Of course, he can't talk with the feeding tube in, but he doesn't even try to make sounds anymore. He just lies there,' her voice broke, 'so still in the bed.'

But he's not in the bed, Joanna thought, and remembered standing beside his bed the day she'd met Richard, thinking he was somewhere far away. She wondered where. At the foot of the Grand Staircase, waiting for his boat to be called? Or in one of the lifeboats, rowing against the darkness and the cold?

She moved around to the side of the bed. 'Carl,' she said, and covered his poor, battered hand with hers. 'I came to see how you were doing,' she said, and then stopped, unable to think of anything at all to say. 'Get well'? He obviously wasn't going to. 'The doctor says you're doing fine'?

Maisie had said, 'I think people should tell you the truth even when it's bad.' Or even when they're too far away to hear you. 'Your wife's here,' Joanna said. 'The nurses are taking really good care of you. We all want you to come back to us.'

Behind her, Mrs Aspinall was fumbling in her purse for a Kleenex. Joanna leaned over and kissed him on his papery cheek. 'Don't be afraid,' she whispered, and went back up to her office and started through the transcripts again.

'I don't think it was the same tunnel,' Mrs Woollam had said. 'It was narrow, and the floor was uneven, so I had trouble walking.' And she had seen a stairway, and a dark open space with nothing around for miles.

But she had also seen a garden, 'green and white, with vines all around.' And there was Maisie, who hadn't seen lights or people dressed in white, but fog.

At half-past one, Joanna left for the university to see Amelia, leaving plenty of time to find the building and the room, remembering what a nightmare parking usually was, but the bad weather must have kept a lot of the students home. She found a parking place in the very first row.

Movie parking, she thought, I'll have to tell Vielle. But Vielle would ask, 'What were you doing at the university?' And if I told her, Joanna thought, she'd accuse me of stalking Amelia. Which is what I'm doing, she thought, standing outside the door of the classroom, waiting for her to come out. Amelia quit the project, and she made it plain she didn't want to talk to me. I have no right to be here.

But when Amelia came out, toting her backpack, pulling on her mittens, Joanna went up to her and said, 'Amelia? Is there somewhere we can talk for a few minutes?' before she could bolt. Which, after a terrified glance at Joanna, she had looked like she was going to do, taking a caged glance around as if trying to find a stairway to duck into. That's what I look like whenever I see Mr Mandrake, Joanna thought, and wondered if Amelia put her in the same category. Was that a possibility, that Amelia had quit not because she had seen something that frightened her, but because she thought of the project as pseudoscience?

That might be it, because, when they got to the cafeteria, which was, astonishingly, open in the middle of the afternoon, and Joanna asked Amelia if she could get her a Coke or coffee, Amelia said, 'I have a class in a few minutes,' which Joanna knew was a blatant lie.

'This will only take a few minutes,' Joanna said, opening a notebook. 'I just need to complete your exit interview,' which sounded, she hoped, official and required. 'You were with the project how long?'

'Four weeks,' Amelia said.

Joanna wrote that down. 'Reason for quitting?'

'I told you, my classes are really hard this semester. I just didn't have time.'

'Okay,' Joanna said, as if consulting a list of questions. 'The first session you had that I was there, that would be your third session, you said that you felt a sense of warmth and peace.'

'Yes,' she said, but this time there was no half-smile as she remembered. Her hands clenched.

'And your last session you said you could see more clearly, that you saw people standing in the light, but you couldn't make them out.'

'No, the light was too bright.'

'Could you see anything of your surroundings?'

'No,' she said, and her hands clenched again. She seemed to become aware of it and laid them in her lap.

'How did you feel during that fourth session?'

'I told you, I had a feeling of peace. Look, are there any more questions? I have a class I have to get to.'

'Yes,' Joanna said. 'Were your classes the only reason you quit?'

'I *told* you—'

'I got the idea that you might have seen something in that last session that frightened you. Did you?'

'No,' Amelia said, and stood up. 'I told you, I've got really hard classes this semester. Is that all?'

'I need you to sign this,' Joanna said, and pushed the paper and a pen at her. Amelia bent over the form, her long black hair swinging forward over her face. 'If you did see something frightening, I need you to tell me. It's important.'

Amelia straightened. 'All I saw was a light,' she said. She handed Joanna back the pen with an air of finality and picked up her backpack. 'I felt warm and peaceful.' She slung the heavy backpack onto her shoulders and looked challengingly at Joanna. 'There wasn't anything frightening about it at all.'

Which proved exactly nothing, Joanna thought, watching her make her way out of the crowded cafeteria, except that she didn't want to talk to me. It certainly didn't prove that she had seen the *Titanic*. But she had. And she was terrified at the prospect of being sent under again, which was why she had quit.

But it was scarcely proof, and neither was a scattering of words and phrases in her interviews. 'The word *silver* appears in the interviews, too,' she could hear Richard saying. 'That doesn't mean they saw the *Hindenburg*.' He was right. Even the Devil could quote Scripture, and sifting through interviews and taking only the parts that fit your theory was Mr Mandrake's modus operandi, not a reputable scientist's, especially when there were things that didn't fit at all, like Mrs Woollam's garden and Maisie's fog.

I need evidence, she thought. The testimony of witnesses, but there weren't any – except herself – and Richard had already rejected that. Amelia refused to testify, Mrs Troudtheim refused even to go under, and Carl Aspinall was in a coma. There was Mr Briarley, but why on earth would Richard believe the ramblings of an Alzheimer's patient, even if she could get Mr Briarley to repeat them? There must be some outside confirmation she could get, like the facts about Midway and the Coral Sea that she had used to prove Mr Wojakowski was lying.

As if she had conjured him up, or, worse, was hallucinating, she saw Mr Wojakowski coming toward her across the cafeteria, carrying his baseball cap in his hand and smiling broadly. 'Hiya, Doc, what are you doing here?' he said. 'Ain't you supposed to be at the hospital?'

'What am *I* doing here?' Joanna said. 'What are *you* doing here?'

'Art show,' he said and grimaced. 'Damn modern stuff made out of wires and toilet seats. Aspen Gardens brought a bunch of us over in a van to see it.' He waved his cap in the direction of the serving line, where Joanna saw several blue-haired ladies getting coffee. 'Did you get that schedule worked out yet?'

'No,' Joanna said. 'Not yet.'

'I figured that. I been calling you and the doc all week. I was starting to feel like Norm Pichette. Thought I was going to have to get me a machine gun.'

Joanna looked at him, startled, but he was grinning amiably at her.

'I guess I never told you about how he got accidentally left behind when we abandoned the *Yorktown*. He was down in sick bay, and when he wakes up, there's nobody on board but him and George Weise, who's got a skull fracture and who's out cold. Well, everybody's already been transferred to the *Hammann* and the *Hughes*.'

He can't be making it up, Joanna thought all over again. Not with all these details. Part of it has to be true.

'He calls over to us, but we can't hear him, we're too far away. Well, he tries everything – he hollers and waves his arms.' Mr Wojakowski demonstrated, waving his arms over his head like a semaphore. 'He even gets a stew pot out of the galley and bangs on it, but we're too far away and there's too much going on. So there he is, on a ship that's going down and no way to get a message to anybody.'

'Mr Wojakowski –' she said, but he was off again.

'So what does he do? He takes a machine gun and fires it into the water. We're too far away to hear it, but Meatball Fratelli sees the splashes in the water and shouts, 'Sub!' and everybody looks, but we can't figure out what it is. It's not a sub, and it doesn't act like a depth charge, and then I look up, and there he is, standing on the port catwalk. Pretty smart of him, huh, figuring out a way to get a message to us like that?'

'Mr Wojakowski, I have a question I need to ask you.'

'Ed.'

Why am I asking this? she thought. It will just remind him of another *Yorktown* story, and even if he did answer it, Richard would hardly believe someone who was a compulsive liar.

'Go ahead, Doc, shoot,' Mr Wojakowski said.

'Mr Wo— Ed,' she said, 'during your interviews, you talked a lot about World War II. Was there something in your NDEs that made you think of your war experiences?'

'On the *Yorktown*, you mean?' He took off his baseball cap and scratched his freckled head. 'Not that I can think of.'

The one time I want him to come up with a story, she thought, and he lets me down.

'Nothing in particular, Doc,' he said. 'Sorry.'

'That's okay,' she said and gathered up her belongings. 'I just wondered.'

He put his baseball cap back on. 'You mean besides that I was on a ship, right?'

37

'I must go in, the fog is rising.'
– EMILY DICKINSON's last words

'You were on a ship?' Joanna said carefully. 'what ship?'

'I don't know,' Mr Wojakowski said. 'Not the *Yorktown*. I knew every inch of her, and this was an alleyway I'd never seen before. And the door wasn't like the ones we had. It was more like the door you'd see on the captain's cabin. Which reminds me of the time I went to ask the captain somethin', and who do I see coming out of his cabin but Stinkpot Malone. Now, Stinky can't be up to anything but no good, he's the biggest stool pigeon in the whole U.S. Navy, and that's going some. So, anyway, Stinky sees me and he says—'

'What makes you think it was a ship?' Joanna cut in.

'You ever been on board?' he said. 'Once you have, you can't mistake that feeling for anything else. You'd know it even if you was blindfolded and had earplugs on. Which, come to think of it, I guess I was.'

'But you couldn't tell what ship?'

'Nope,' he said. 'It was a navy ship, that's all I know, 'cause I could see sailors outside the door.'

'You could see sailors?'

'People, anyway. I thought they were sailors. The light was too bright to make out much, but I could see they had their dress whites on, so I figured they must be sailors.'

A ship, and people outside the door, dressed all in white.

'You said it felt like you were at sea. Were the engines going?'

'The engines?' he said, surprised. 'No,' and the blue-haired ladies came up, looking determined.

'The van is waiting, Edward,' one of them said, glaring at Joanna.

'Be right with you,' Mr Wojakowksi said. 'You gals go on. I gotta say good-bye to my girlfriend here.' He winked at Joanna. The ladies moved off a few steps and then stood there, waiting impatiently. 'What other questions you got, Doc?'

'Why didn't you tell me this before?'

'Well, I'll tell ya, I didn't want to just yammer on like Edgewise Eggleton. Did I ever tell you about him? We called him that 'cause when you were around him you couldn't ever get a word in edgewise, and—'

'You'd better go,' Joanna said, indicating the ladies, who looked like they were about to have a stroke. 'You don't want the van to go without you.'

'I'd never hear the end of it,' he said and sighed. 'You call me as soon as you get that schedule set, Doc. I can come in anytime.' He sauntered over to the women and then came back. 'I just got to thinking. It might've been the *Franklin*. I don't know how she went down, though.'

'Went down?'

'No, come to think of it, it couldn'ta been the *Hammann*, because her back got broken. And not the *Wasp* because she went belly up, and the *Lexington* was clear over on her side, and this ship, whatever she was, was going down by the head.'

And there it was, her outside confirmation. It wouldn't convince Richard. It wouldn't convince anyone, not with Mr Wojakowski's record, but it was still evidence that she was on the right track. And where there was some evidence, there was more. She just had to find it.

She drove back to the hospital and spent the rest of the day and all of the next barricaded in her office, going through the transcripts. She switched her pager off, but kept the phone on and let the answering machine pick up, mostly so she could keep track of Mr Mandrake.

He called at two-hour intervals, becoming more and more irritated that he couldn't corner her. 'If you can't make time to return my calls,' he huffed and puffed, 'you should at least go hear what Mrs Davenport has to say about the visions she's been having. They prove beyond a shadow of a doubt that messages can be sent from beyond the grave.'

Joanna erased the message, taped black paper along the bottom of the door so light couldn't be seen from the outside, and went back to reading transcripts:

'I was traveling down through a long, sloping tunnel.'

'The feeling was warm, like being wrapped in a blanket.'

'A woman and a little girl were standing in the doorway, and I knew it must be my mother and my little sister who died when she was six, even though it didn't really look like them. The little girl took my hand and led me into a beautiful garden.'

The garden again. Joanna did a global search. 'I was in a sort of garden.' 'Elijah was standing in the Garden of Eden.' 'Beyond the doorway I could see a garden.'

Gladys Meers had been the most specific. 'There were trees all around, and white trellises with vines growing up them. "Pray be seated," the angel said, and I sat down in a white wicker chair, the kind they have on patios.'

There couldn't possibly have been a garden on the *Titanic*, Joanna thought, and wished she could believe that, but it had had a swimming pool, it had had a Turkish bath. Maybe it had had a garden, too.

She called Kit, but the line was busy. She printed out the list of garden references and then went to see Maisie. She was lying in bed, watching TV, but her shallow breathing and flaring nostrils gave her away. She just jumped into bed, Joanna thought, wondering what book she'd just hidden, and then saw that there were wires leading under her Barbie pajama top to the heart monitor.

'I didn't find out the wireless messages yet,' Maisie said when she saw Joanna. She pointed her remote at the TV and turned it off. 'I'm in A-fib again. I'm not supposed to read even. I found out two.' She took a couple of panting breaths before she went on. 'They're in the drawer,' turning her head to indicate the nightstand. 'I'll look up the others as soon as I feel better.'

Joanna opened the drawer and took out Maisie's tablet. On the first page was written, 'Sinking. Cannot hear for noise of steam.' And under it, 'Come quick. Our engine-room flooded up to the boilers.'

Like you, Joanna thought, and tried not to think of Maisie on the listing decks of the *Titanic*, on the slanting steps of the Grand Staircase. But she saw fog, Joanna thought, and the night the *Titanic* sank, it was clear. And if there wasn't a garden on the *Titanic*, then Mr Briarley's wrong.

'Maisie,' she said. 'Did the *Titanic* have a garden?'

'A garden?' Maisie said, incredulous. 'On a ship?'

'Or something that looked like a garden, with flowers and trees,' but Maisie was shaking her head. And if there were one, Joanna thought, she would have known about it.

'I never heard of a garden,' Maisie said. 'I bet if there was, though, there'd be a picture of it in my *Titanic Picture Book*.' She pushed the covers off and sat up.

'No,' Joanna said. 'No looking things up till you're out of A-fib.'

'But—'

'Promise me, or I'll fire you as my research assistant.'

'*Okay,*' Maisie said grudgingly. 'I promise,' and, at Joanna's skeptical look, 'Cross my heart.'

Which isn't worth a damn, Joanna thought. 'You get some rest, kiddo,' she said, picking up the remote and switching it on, 'and I'll come see you soon.'

'You can't go yet,' Maisie said. 'I haven't told you this neat thing I found out about the *Mackay-Bennett.*'

'Okay,' she said. 'Two minutes, and then you have to rest. What's the *Mackay-Bennett*?'

'It was this ship they sent out to pick up the bodies.'

'I thought the bodies all sank,' Joanna said.

'I did, too, but some of them were wearing lifejackets, so they floated.' She laid her head back against the pillows, arms outstretched, mouth open in a grotesque imitation of a floating corpse. 'And they were afraid people on other ships would see them, so they sent the *Mackay-Bennett* out to get them. It had all these coffins and a minister. What's an embalmer?'

'It's a person who prepares bodies for burial. To keep them from spoiling.'

'Oh,' Maisie said. 'Well, they had an embalmer, and all this ice. That was to keep them from spoiling, too, right?'

'Yes,' Joanna said. 'Okay, your two minutes are up.' She stood up.

'*No,*' Maisie said. 'I haven't told you the thing yet. One of the bodies was this little boy who nobody knew who he was, and nobody came to claim him, so the captain and the guys on the *Mackay-Bennett* had a funeral for him and a little white coffin and they put up a headstone to "The Unknown Child Whose Remains were Recovered after the Disaster to the *Titanic.*"'

'Just like Little Miss 1565,' Joanna said.

'*No,*' Maisie said, "cause this one they found out who he was.' She wrapped her hand around her dog tags, as if it were a rosary. 'Gosta Paulsson,' she said. 'That was his name. Gosta Paulsson.' Joanna ended up sitting with Maisie till her mother came in, bubbling with cheer.

'The nurses say you're doing *much* better,' Joanna heard her say as she scooted out of the room. 'I brought you a brand-new video. *Rebecca of Sunnybrook Farm.*'

Joanna went back to her office, feeling relieved. There wasn't a garden on the *Titanic*, and no fog, and Maisie wasn't the only NDEer to have seen fog. It was listed as a separate NDE category in one of the books, *Entranced by the Light*. She read the section. 'A number of patients describe being in an open, undefined, foggy space. Some say it is dark, like fog at night, others that it is light. Nearly all describe it as being a cold and frightening place. This is clearly Purgatory, and those who see it can be described as nonreligious or unsaved.'

Joanna closed the book with a slap and did a global search of 'fog,' and scrolled down through the references. 'It was cold,' Paul Smetzer had said, 'and there was so much fog I couldn't see my hand in front of my face.'

Paul Smetzer. That name rang a bell. She called up his file and read the full account. Oh, yes, Paul. '... I couldn't see my hand in front of my face. Of course, if I was dead, I guess I wouldn't have had a hand, would I? Or a face, for that matter.'

Paul Smetzer, the Ricky Inman of NDEers. He had also told her he'd seen an angel, 'almost as cute as you,' and asked her if it was true there wasn't any sex in heaven, 'because if it is, I told her, I want to go to the other place.'

His remarks could be discounted, but he wasn't the only one who had mentioned fog: 'There were people standing there, but I couldn't see who they were because of the fog.' 'No, it was dark' (this in response to Joanna's asking Ray Gomez to describe the tunnel), 'and all blurry, like fog or something.' 'I was floating in a kind of fog.'

And there definitely hadn't been any fog that night. Just to make sure, Joanna called Kit, but her number was still busy. She printed out the list of fog references to take home and began gathering up her things.

The phone rang. 'Hi, it's Richard,' he said to the answering machine. 'I just wanted to tell you Mrs Troudtheim's coming in at four tomorrow if that will—'

She picked up the phone. 'Hi, I'm here.'

'Oh, I thought you'd gone home,' he said. 'I came by earlier and didn't see any light under your door.'

'Nope, I'm still here. I've been working on the backlog of transcripts,' she said, which was at least partly true. 'I thought you weren't going to send Mrs Troudtheim under again until you'd figured out why she keeps kicking out.'

'I wasn't, but when I told Dr Jamison about the DABA, she suggested I go talk to Dr Friedman over at St Anthony's. He's worked extensively with DABA and artificial DABA surrogates. He said DABA alone couldn't inhibit endorphins, but combined with cortisol, it definitely could.'

'And inhibiting the endorphins would kick her out?'

'I don't know yet. I asked him about theta-asparcine, too, but it's not an inhibitor. His specialty's inhibitors, so he didn't know much about it. He said he thought it had a regulatory function and that an artificial surrogate's been produced. I need to do some more research, but not till I've checked Mrs Troudtheim's NDEs to see if cortisol's been present in all of them. If it has, there are a number of ways to counteract the cortisol and keep her under. So I'll see you tomorrow at four o'clock.'

Four o'clock. And by that time, she should know one way or the other. Or maybe sooner, if she could reach Kit. She called her again, and as soon as she got home, slightly worried, and at fifteen-minute intervals till she finally got through.

'Oh, I'm so glad you called,' Kit said. 'I wanted to apologize for leaving the book where Uncle Pat could find it. I don't blame you for walking out like that.'

'That wasn't the reason –' Joanna said, but Kit wasn't listening.

'It was an unbelievably stupid thing to do,' she said. 'I mean, he'd hidden it once. He'd obviously try to hide it again. I don't blame you for being mad.'

'I'm not mad –' Joanna said.

'Well, you should be,' Kit said. 'I still haven't found it, and I've looked absolutely everywhere. Down behind the radiators, inside—'

'Actually, I didn't call about the textbook,' Joanna said.

'Oh, of course, you want to know about the questions you asked. There was no library as such, but there was a Reading and Writing Room on the Promenade Deck that had bookshelves and writing tables, and it was right next to the First-Class Lounge, which did have a bar. And, yes, Scotland Road was a crew passage on E Deck that ran nearly the whole length of the ship. It—'

'I need to know something else. Do you know if it was foggy that night?'

'No,' Kit said promptly. 'It was perfectly clear. And very still. One of the survivors described the water as being like a lake. That's why they didn't see the waves hitting the iceberg.'

'And there couldn't have been fog later on? After they hit?'

'I don't think so,' she said just as promptly. 'All the survivors said it was the clearest night they'd ever seen. It was so clear the stars came right down to the horizon. Do you want me to find out?'

'No, that's okay. Thanks,' Joanna said. 'You told me what I wanted to know.' What I already knew, she thought after she hung up, and that, combined with the frequent image of the garden, meant that Mr Briarley was wrong.

No, not wrong about why she'd seen the *Titanic*. He was right, it was the mirror image of death. Wrong only in that everyone, thank God, was not doomed to see it, and maybe Kit was right, and Greg Menotti had been talking about something completely different from the *Carpathia*.

I hope so, she thought, going up to her office the next morning. I hope so.

Her answering machine was blinking hysterically. She took off her coat and hit 'play.' Richard, saying, 'Tish had a conflict at four. I've moved Mrs Troudtheim up to two. Call me if that won't work.'

Leonard Fanshawe. Mr Mandrake. 'I've just heard from a very reliable source that you are now a subject in Dr Wright's project.'

Oh, no, Joanna thought. That's all I need.

'I am eager to discuss your experience with you to determine whether in fact it is an authentic NDE. I doubt whether it is.'

I hope you're right, Joanna thought, deleting the rest of his message. The phone rang. And if you think I'm going to pick it up, Mr Mandrake, you're crazy, she thought.

The answering machine clicked on. 'You need to come right away,' Maisie's breathless voice said. 'I need you to see something.'

Joanna picked up the phone. 'I'm here, Maisie. What do you need me to come see?'

'I looked in the … *Titanic Picture Book*.' she said and paused to take another breath, 'and—'

'Are you still in A-fib?' Joanna demanded.

'Yes, but … I'm feeling lots better,' she said.

'I told you you weren't supposed to look anything up till you were out of A-fib.'

'I only looked in one book,' she protested, 'but I don't know if it's really … a garden, so you need to come.'

'If what isn't a garden?'

'The Verandah Cafe,' Maisie said. 'It's got flowers and trees and vines on … these things I don't know the name of, they're white and they crisscross –'

Trellises, Joanna thought. 'Tell me what the chairs look like,' she said, calling up Gladys Meers's file.

'They're white and made of little tiny … I don't know,' Maisie said, frustrated. 'You need to come look.'

'I can't come right now,' Joanna said. 'Little tiny what?'

'Long, round things. Like a basket.'

Wicker. The word was right there on the screen. 'There were trees all around, and white trellises with vines growing up on them. I sat down in a white wicker chair, the kind they have on patios.'

'Are there trees?' Joanna asked, calling up Mrs Woollam's file.

'Yes,' Maisie said, and Joanna already knew what she was going to say. 'Palm trees, but you need to come *see* it.'

Not a heavenly garden. The Verandah Cafe. On the *Titanic*.

'Can you come this morning?' Maisie was asking.

No, Mrs Troudtheim's coming at two. I have to find out for sure there wasn't any fog. 'I'm too busy to come this morning,' she said.

'You have to come right after lunch then. I found out all the wireless messages. You said to tell you when I had the whole list done, and you'd come.'

'I'll come this afternoon.'

'Right after lunch?'

'Right after lunch.'

'You promise? Cross your heart?'

'Cross my heart,' Joanna said and hung up. She called up the list of fog references again, looking for clues. 'I was up on the ceiling, looking down at the operating table, and I saw the doctor put these flat things on my chest, like ping-pong paddles, and then I couldn't see more, because it got foggy,' Mr James had reported, and Mrs Katzenbaum had said, 'The tunnel was dark, but at the end of it was this golden light, all fuzzy like there was smoke or fog or something in the way.'

Smoke. Coma Carl had said something about smoke, too. What if it wasn't fog, but smoke? Or steam? The *Titanic* had been a steamship. 'Sinking. Cannot hear for noise of steam,' the telegram Maisie had written down said.

But that steam would have gone up out of the funnels. It wouldn't have been on the decks. What about smoke? Could fires have broken out on board as the ship tilted? Burning coal from the boilers sliding out onto the floor of the boiler room, or a candle toppling over onto a tablecloth in the First-Class Dining Saloon?

She called Kit, but the line was still busy. Maisie would know if there'd been a fire, especially in light of her interest in the Hartford circus fire, and it wasn't as if she were asking about fog. Who are you kidding? Joanna thought. She'll see the connection instantly.

She tried Kit again. Mr Briarley answered. 'Mr Briarley, I need to speak to Kit,' Joanna told him.

'She's not here,' he said. 'She's at the church. They're all over at the church. Except for Kevin. I don't know where he is.'

This is what Kit meant when she said he said terrible things, Joanna thought. I thought she was talking about obscenities.

'"All alone, so Heav'n has willed, we die,"' he said. 'Kevin went to pick up film. Kit sent him. I don't know why she didn't think of it earlier.'

They are obscenities, Joanna thought, and then, Kit can't hear this. 'Tell her I called. Good-bye,' she said and started to hang up, but it was too late. Kit was already on the line.

'Hi. Who is this?' she said in her cheerful voice. 'Oh, hi, Joanna, did you forget something?'

Maybe she didn't hear him, Joanna thought, maybe she just came down the stairs and saw him holding the phone, and knew it wasn't true, that she had heard every word. And how many times? Dozens? Hundreds?

'Joanna?' Kit said. 'Was there something else you wanted to know about the *Titanic*?'

'Yes,' Joanna said, trying to sound as calm as Kit. 'Do you know if there were fires on board?'

'You mean accidental fires or regular fires?' Kit said.

'Regular fires?'

'I mean, like the fires in the boilers and the fireplaces.'

'There were fireplaces on the *Titanic*?' Joanna said and then remembered the woman with the piled-up hair saying, 'We'll ask the steward to light a fire.'

'Yeah,' Kit said, 'in the smoking room, I think, and some of the first-class cabins.' Started because the passengers had gotten cold out on deck, Joanna thought, and then left burning when they went up to the Boat Deck, and,

557

when the deck began to list, the wood and ashes sliding out onto the carpet, catching the curtains, filling the cabin with smoke.

'Is that the kind of fire you meant?' Kit was asking.

'I don't know what I mean,' Joanna said. 'I'm looking for any kind of fire that might have produced a lot of smoke. Or steam.'

'I remember Uncle Pat talking about a fire in one of the boiler rooms,' Kit said, 'in the coal bin. It had been smoldering since they left port, but I don't think there was any smoke. Or steam, you said?'

'Yes.'

'I was just thinking of that scene in the movie where there's that deafening blast, and steam swirls around everybody on the Boat Deck. I'll see what I can find. Did you call before and get a busy signal?'

'Yes,' Joanna admitted.

'I was afraid of that. Uncle Pat's started taking the phone off the hook. I keep checking it, but—'

' " "Oh, father, I hear the sound of guns," " ' she heard Mr Briarley say.

'I'll call you as soon as I find anything,' Kit said.

'I need the information as soon as –'

' " "Oh, say, what may it be?" " ' Mr Briarley said.

'– as soon as possible,' Joanna finished, and Kit said okay, but Joanna wasn't sure she'd really heard her because of Mr Briarley, declaiming in the background, ' " "Some ship in distress that cannot live." " They *speak* to us!'

Joanna hung up the phone and then stared at it, thinking about the possibility of the fog being steam. But none of the NDEers had said anything about the fog swirling, or moving at all, and Maisie had said she'd been inside, not out on the Boat Deck.

Or had she? She called up the first interview she'd had with Maisie. 'I was inside this place, I think it was a tunnel, only I couldn't see 'cause it was dark and all foggy,' she'd said, and she'd talked about walls that went up on either side of her. 'They were really tall. The top was so high I couldn't see it.'

No room had high ceilings on a ship, even a luxurious one like the *Titanic*. She must have been out on the Boat Deck, and the noise she'd heard was the funnels letting off steam. She had said a roar. But there was nothing on the Boat Deck that was narrow with high walls on either side. On the other hand, smoke had a distinctive smell. Steam didn't.

Joanna typed in 'steam' and 'mist' and 'swirling' and ran global searches on each of them, wishing Kit would call back. At eleven, she did. 'Hi,' she said excitedly, 'I've got it.'

Joanna gripped the phone. 'There was a fire on the *Titanic*?'

'A fire?' Kit said blankly. 'Oh, no, I haven't found anything yet. The only reference in any of the indexes was to the fires in the boilers and the stokers working to put them out before the water reached them and caused an explosion. Nothing about smoke either, but I'm still looking. That isn't why I called. I found the book!'

Now it was Joanna's turn to answer blankly. 'The book?'

'*Mirrors and Mazes*! Finally. I've been turning the house upside down. The kitchen looks as bad as it did when Uncle Pat dismantled it. You'll never guess where it was. In the refrigerator. The crisper drawer, so it's sort of damp and chilly, but at least I've got it, and I put it in a safe place, so Uncle Pat can't hide it again. Can you come over? I can fix you lunch.'

'No, I'm busy. I …' I already know what the *Titanic* is. I don't need the book anymore. I need proof.

'I'm not sure when I'll be able to get over. Things are crazy around here.'

'I can bring it to the hospital,' Kit said. 'Eldercare is supposed to come over this evening, but I could call and see if they can change to this afternoon.'

'No,' Joanna said, and tried to put more enthusiasm in her voice. 'I'll come get it.'

'Great,' Kit said. 'I can't wait for you to see if the connection's in it. I'll bake cookies.'

'Oh, don't go to any trouble. I don't know exactly when—'

'It's no trouble. I've already got all the ingredients out anyway,' Kit said. 'And the heat from the oven will help dry out the book. I'll see you this afternoon,' she said, and hung up before Joanna could remind her to call her if she found any fires.

She won't, Joanna thought, because there weren't any. If there had been a fire, it would definitely have been in the movie with Hollywood's penchant for special effects, and the one she had envisioned, the burning logs sliding out of the fireplace as the ship tilted, catching the carpet on fire, would have been put out almost immediately by the encroaching water. It has to have been steam, she thought, but Mrs Katzenbaum had said smoke, and so had Coma Carl.

The phone rang. It's Kit calling back, Joanna thought. She reached for it and then pulled her hand back and let the answering machine click on. And a good thing, too. It was Mr Mandrake.

'I cannot understand why I haven't heard from you. I have paged you and been by your office numerous times,' he said, his voice vibrating with irritation. 'I have evidence …'

Evidence, Joanna thought contemptuously. What? Something else Mrs Davenport's remembered to order for you? Leading questions? Data twisted to fit your theory, with the facts that don't fit left out?

And what do you call what you have? How is your evidence any different from Mr Mandrake's? So you've got dozens of references to the *Titanic*. It doesn't prove anything except that you can find proof of anything you want if you look hard enough. Because it's still all subjective, no matter what percent of the accounts are consistent. There isn't any outside verification. I need a red tennis shoe, she thought, or a map of the South Pacific.

And how am I supposed to get that? Mr Wojakowski's a compulsive liar, Mr Briarley can't remember, Amelia Tanaka refuses to talk, Coma Carl – 'Coma Carl,' she said out loud. She wasn't the only one who had heard him. Guadalupe had, too, and his wife. If there was something in his ramblings that pointed clearly to the *Titanic* –

She called up his file again. He had said, 'smoke' and 'ohhh … grand,' but neither were definitive. She scrolled down the screen. 'Water … have to …' Guadalupe had written, '… gone …' The boats are gone?

Someone knocked on the door. Mr Mandrake, Joanna thought, and froze. 'Joanna?' Richard called. 'Are you in there?'

'Just a minute,' she said. She cleared the screen, laid Mr Wojakowski's file on top of the transcripts, and opened the door.

'Hi,' Richard said, 'I just wanted to tell you I'm going to be out of the lab for a while. I'll be up in Dr Jamison's office on eighth if you need me for anything. I'm hoping she'll be able to look at Mrs Troudtheim's scans and see something I can't.'

'Cortisol wasn't present in Mrs Troudtheim's other NDEs?' Joanna said, leaning against the door so he wouldn't come in.

'No, it was there in spades.' He raked his hand through his hair. 'Unfortunately, it and DABA were also present in one of Amelia Tanaka's, two of yours, and three of Mr Sage's, including his record-breaking twenty-eight-minute one.'

'So you're not going to send Mrs Troudtheim under?' Joanna asked hopefully.

'No, I've still got a couple of other ideas. One's the theta-asparcine.'

'I thought you said it wasn't an inhibitor?'

'It's not, but it might abort the NDE some other way. And you kicked out when I lowered the dosage. That may mean Mrs Troudtheim's NDE threshold is higher than normal, so I'm going to raise the dosage and see if that keeps her in. That's why I came down. I wanted to make sure two o'clock would work for you. I'm meeting with Dr Jamison at one, but I'll be back in plenty of time, and I told Tish to be here at one-thirty in case Mrs Troudtheim shows up early. So,' he said, slapping the doorjamb with the flat of his hand. 'See you at two o'clock.'

'Yes,' she said, 'I should be finished by then,' and some of the regret in her voice must have come through because he leaned back in and said, 'You know what? We've both been working way too hard. What do you say, when this is all over, we go out to dinner. Not Taco Pierre's. A real restaurant.'

When this is all over. 'I'd like that,' Joanna said.

'So would I,' he said, and smiled at her. 'I've missed you these last few days.'

'Me, too,' Joanna said.

'Oh, and I'd keep your door shut if I were you. Mandrake was just up in the lab looking for you. I told him you were in the cafeteria.'

'*Thank* you,' Joanna said.

' "There are more things in heaven and earth, Horatio, than are dreamt of in your philosophy," ' he intoned, grinning, and disappeared into the elevator.

Joanna shut and locked the door and went back to searching through Guadalupe's reports. '... have to ... can't ... patches ...' Patches?

I need to look at Guadalupe's actual notes, Joanna thought, and got out the sheaf of prescription-pad forms and scraps of paper that Guadalupe had jotted them down on. The first one, written on the back of a patient menu form, said, 'Vietcong POW again. No intelligible words. Pulled IV out.' '... smoke ...' The next one, on a sheet from a prescription pad, said, '... can't ... two ...' Or 'too,' as in 'too far for her to come'? Or was he trying to say 'have to ...' again? Have to what?

Most of them were short. 'Boating on the lake' or 'mumbled a lot. Nothing intelligible,' or the ominous 'very quiet all day.' Here was a long one, on the back of a pharmaceutical-company ad. 'Nothing I could make out on my shift yesterday. Sub on the three-to-eleven and Paula forgot to tell her, so no record of that shift. I asked her today if he said anything, and she said no, just humming. She couldn't make out the tune either, but said it sounded like a hymn.'

A hymn. Coma Carl droning, long, long, short, short, long. She flipped back to the computer and typed in 'humming,' looking for her own notes. 'Long, long, short, short,' she had written. 'Descending scale.'

'Hmmm, hmmm, hm, hm, hm, hmm,' she hummed, trying it out. 'Half note, half note, quarter note ...'

'Nearer, My God, to Thee.'

On tape. Outside confirmation. She leaped up and grabbed the box of tapes. It was on the day she'd met Richard, when was that? January the ninth. She clattered through the pile of tapes, looking for the date. Here it was. She jammed it in the recorder and hit 'play.'

'It was dark ...' Mrs Davenport droned. She fast-forwarded. 'And then I saw myself at my eighth birthday party. I was playing Pin the Tail on the Donkey, and ...' Fast-forward. '... my wedding ...' Fast-forward. 'And the angel handed me a telegram.'

She fast-forwarded again, too far, there was only silence. She rewound, and here it was. Coma Carl humming, agonizingly slowly. She played it through, making notations on a memo pad, lines for the length of the note, arrows for pitch – long, long, the pitch dropping with each note, short, long – wishing she could read music. Did the tune of 'Nearer, My God, to Thee' go up or down?

She hummed the opening bars, trying to stretch the notes out to match

Coma Carl's glacial humming, but it was no good. The tune could have been anything. I need to speed it up, she thought. She rewound to the beginning and then fast-forwarded, but it was just a whir, and there was no way on her little recorder to control the speed.

I need a fancy stereo, she thought, and tried to think who might have one. Kit? If she had one, Joanna could go listen to the tape and pick up the book at the same time, but she couldn't remember any stereo equipment in Mr Briarley's library, not even a record player. Kit might have one up in her room, though. She called Kit, but the line was busy.

All right, who here in the hospital? Maisie's tape player was a pink plastic affair, probably worse than her minirecorder. Vielle? No, all they had in the lounge in the ER was an eight-track player, 'because nobody's been in here long enough to listen to any music since 1974,' Vielle had complained one hectic night.

She squinted at the minirecorder, trying to remember where she'd seen a tape recorder. In one of the offices, where they listened to music while they were working. Billing or Personnel. Records, she decided. She snapped the tape out of the minirecorder, jammed it in her pocket, and ran down to Records.

And her memory had been accurate. On the far wall, above the cubicles, was a bank of sophisticated-looking stereo equipment. But first she would have to get past the woman at the front desk, who looked solid and dedicated to following the rules. Almost before Joanna had gotten her name out, the woman had swiveled so she was facing a rack of printed papers and was holding her arm up in preparation for grabbing the appropriate form.

'I don't think there's a form for what I need ... Zaneta,' Joanna said, reading the name off the sign on the woman's desk. 'I need a tape recorder that can play a tape at different speeds,' but Zaneta had already swiveled back to face her.

'This is Records,' Zaneta said. 'You want Equipment next door.'

'No, I don't want to requisition a tape recorder. I just want to borrow yours for a couple of minutes to listen to a tape,' she said, pulling the tape out of her pocket to illustrate. 'My recorder doesn't have a fast-forward that lets me control the speed, and I need—'

'Do you work here?' Zaneta said.

'Yes, my name's Joanna Lander,' she said. 'I work with Dr Wright up in research,' and Zaneta swiveled to face her computer terminal. 'All I want—'

'Lander?' Zaneta asked, typing. 'L-a-n-d-e-r?'

'Yes,' Joanna said. 'I need to transcribe this tape, but a section of it needs to be listened to at a faster speed, and I wondered if I could –'

Joanna's beeper went off. No, she thought, and reached in her pocket to turn it off, but Zaneta was already pushing the phone toward her. 'You're being paged,' she said severely.

Joanna gave up. Please don't let it be Mr Mandrake, she prayed, and called the operator.

'Call the fourth floor nurses' station, stat,' the operator said. 'Extension 428.'

Fourth floor. Coma Carl, she thought, and realized she had known this call was coming.

Zaneta was pushing a memo pad and pencil toward her. Joanna ignored it and punched in the extension. Guadalupe answered. 'What is it, Guadalupe?' Joanna said. 'Is it Coma Carl?'

'Yes, I've been trying to reach you. You haven't seen Mrs Aspinall, have you? We can't find her anywhere,' and her stunned and shaken voice told Joanna all she needed to know.

'When did he die?' she said, thinking of him, all alone out there in a lifeboat, humming.

'Die?' Guadalupe said in that same stunned voice. 'He didn't. He's awake.'

38

'... Morse ... Indian ...'
— The only two distinct words in the last
sentence HENRY DAVID THOREAU spoke

Guadalupe was at the nurses' station, talking on the phone, when Joanna arrived. 'Is he really awake?' Joanna asked, leaning over the counter.

Guadalupe put a hand up, signaling her to wait. 'Yes. I'm trying to reach Dr Cherikov,' she said into the receiver. 'Well, can I speak to his nurse? It's important.' She cupped her hand over the mouthpiece. 'Yes, he's really awake,' she said to Joanna, 'and wouldn't you know it, we can't find his doctor. Or his wife. You didn't happen to see Mrs Aspinall on your way up here, did you?'

'No,' Joanna said. 'Have you tried the cafeteria?'

'I've got an aide checking,' Guadalupe said. 'Mrs Aspinall's been here day and night for two weeks, and she always tells us when she's leaving. Except today. How long does it take to call his nurse to the phone?' she said impatiently.

'Has Carl said anything?' Joanna asked.

'He asked to see his wife,' Guadalupe said. 'And he said he was hungry, but we can't give him anything to eat because we don't have any orders, and we can't find his doctor. He isn't answering his page.'

'Has he said anything about the coma?'

She shook her head. 'Most coma patients – yes,' she said into the phone. 'This is Guadalupe Santos over at Mercy General. I need to talk to Dr Cherikov. It's urgent. It's about his patient Carl Aspinall.' There was a pause. 'No,' Guadalupe said, and her tone made Joanna think the nurse had asked if he'd died, like she had. 'He's conscious.'

She cupped her hand over the receiver again and said to Joanna, 'Paula went in to check his vitals about half an hour ago. She opened the curtains, and he said, "It isn't dark." Scared her half to death – I've been *trying* his pager,' she said into the phone. 'Do you know where he went?'

She turned back to Joanna. 'Most patients have very fuzzy memories of the time they spent in a semicomatose state, if that.'

And those memories will only get fuzzier with every moment that passes, Joanna thought, glancing in the direction of his room. I need to get in there now. 'Can he have visitors?' she asked.

Guadalupe frowned. 'I don't know who's in with – yes,' she said into the phone. 'Harvest?' She grabbed a pen and jotted something down on a prescription pad. 'Please have him call me as soon as he gets back.'

She hung up. 'Dr Cherikov is at lunch,' she said disgustedly, reaching for a phone book. 'At the Harvest or Sfuzzi's. He has them both written down on his calendar.' She began searching through the phone book. 'Carl's wife probably went to lunch, too. Harvest, Harvest.'

Joanna glanced toward his room again. She had to get in there and talk to him before his wife and Dr Cherikov descended, but if they had somebody in there with him, and surely they did, a patient who'd just regained consciousness would hardly be left alone –

The elevator dinged, and Guadalupe and Joanna both looked down at where a nurse's aide was emerging from the open doors. 'Did you find her?' Guadalupe asked.

The aide walked toward them, shaking her head. 'She wasn't in the cafeteria. What about paging her?'

Guadalupe shook her head. 'We don't want to scare her half to death. We just want to get her up here.' She picked up the phone.

'What about the chapel?' Joanna asked.

'Corinne's checking it,' Guadalupe said. She punched in a phone number, looking back and forth from it to the phone book. 'Did you check the gift shop?' she asked the aide.

The aide nodded. 'And the vending machines.'

'Did you check – This is Nurse Santos at Mercy General. I'm trying to locate Dr Anton Cherikov. He's having lunch there.' Pause. 'No, I can't page him.' Pause. 'Well, would you please look? It's an emergency.' She cupped her hand over the receiver again. 'Did you check the solarium?' she said to the aide.

Neither of them was paying any attention to Joanna. She stepped away from the nurses' station and, when Guadalupe glanced up, pointed to her watch and waved slightly. 'I've checked everywhere,' the aide said. 'I'll bet she went home.'

'We've already called,' Guadalupe said. 'She's not there. I left a message.'

'Won't that scare her, too?' the aide asked.

Joanna walked rapidly down the hall, on past Carl's room, till she was out of sight of the nurses' station. She stopped, waited. 'You're sure he's not there?' Guadalupe said, and there was the sound of a phone being hung up, and a brief silence. 'How do you spell Sfuzzi's?'

'Sfuzzi's? I don't know. What is it?'

'A restaurant.'

More silence. Joanna came quietly back up the hall till she could see the nurses' station. Guadalupe and the aide were both bent over the counter, looking at the open phone book. Joanna ducked quickly, silently across the hall to Carl's room.

All I need is a minute, she thought, looking in the door. There wasn't a nurse in the room. She slipped in. All I need is to ask him whether he was on the *Titanic*, she thought, pulling the door nearly shut. Before he forgets, before –

'Hello,' a voice said from the bed. She turned and looked at the grayhaired man sitting up in the bed, wearing blue pajamas. 'Who are you?' he asked.

For a long, heart-pounding minute, she thought, I've sneaked in the wrong room, and how am I going to explain this to Guadalupe? How am I going to explain this to Richard?

'Did they find my wife?' the man asked, and she saw, like one of those trick pictures shifting suddenly into focus, that it was Coma Carl.

It was not that he looked like a different person. It was that he looked like a person where before he had been an empty shell. His concave chest, his thin arms looked filled out, as if he had gained weight, even though that was impossible, and his face, covered with the same gray stubble, looked occupied, like a house where the owners have suddenly come home. His gray-brown hair, which the aides had kept neatly combed back off his forehead, was parted on the side and fell almost boyishly over his forehead, and his eyes, which she had always thought were gray through the half-open slits, were dark brown.

She was gaping at him like an idiot. 'I …' she said, trying to remember what he had asked her.

'Are you one of my doctors?' he asked, looking at her lab coat.

'No,' she said. 'I'm Joanna Lander. Do you remember me, Mr Aspinall?'

He shook his head. 'I don't remember very much,' he said. His voice was different, too, still hoarse, but much stronger, deeper than his murmurings. 'I was in a coma, you know.'

'I know,' she said, nodding. 'That's what I'd like to talk to you about. What you remember. I'd just like to ask you a few questions, if that's all right.'

It isn't all right, she told herself. You need a waiver. The one his wife signed was only good when he was unconscious. You need to have him sign a release form. This is completely against protocol. But there wasn't time to write one out, to explain it to him. The doctor or his wife could arrive any minute.

Joanna pulled a chair over to the bed, glancing anxiously at the door as it banged against the IV pole, and sat down. 'Can you tell me what you remember, Mr Aspinall?'

'I remember coming to the hospital,' he said. 'Alicia drove me.'

Joanna reached carefully into her cardigan pocket for her minirecorder. It wasn't there. I left it in my office, she thought, when I took the tape down to Records.

'I had a terrible headache,' he said. 'I couldn't see to drive.'

Joanna fished in her pocket for something to write with, but she didn't even have one of those release forms she hadn't had him sign. At least she had a pen. She glanced surreptitiously around the room, looking for something to write on, a menu, an envelope, anything. Guadalupe had taken the chart out with her, and there was nothing on the bedstand.

'She was going to take me to the doctor, but my headache kept getting worse –'

Joanna reached in the wastebasket and pulled out a discarded get-well card with a picture of a bluebird on the front. The bluebird had a letter in its mouth. 'This get-well message is winging its way straight to you,' the card said on the inside. Joanna turned it over. There was nothing on the back.

'– so she brought me to the emergency room instead, and then …' Carl's voice trailed away and he stared straight ahead of him. 'It was dark.'

Dark, Joanna thought, and her hand shook as she wrote the word.

'Alicia hates driving at night,' he said, 'but she had to. It was so cold.' He reached back and touched his neck, tenderly, as if it still hurt. 'I remember the doctor saying I had spinal meningitis, and then I remember them putting me in a wheelchair, and then I remember the nurse opening the curtains, and I was surprised it wasn't dark.' He smiled across at Joanna. 'And that's pretty much it.'

It was Greg Menotti all over again. 'Do you remember anything between the wheelchair and the curtains?' Joanna asked.

'No,' he said. 'Not between.'

'What about dreams?' Joanna asked. 'Coma patients sometimes dream.'

'Dreams,' he said thoughtfully, 'no,' and there was no defensiveness in his voice, no avoiding of her eyes. He said it quite matter-of-factly.

And that was that. He didn't remember. And she should thank him, tell him to get some rest, get out of here before she was caught redhanded and waiverless by Guadalupe. But she didn't get up. 'What about sounds?'

He shook his head.

'Or voices, Carl?' she said, reverting to his first name without thinking. 'Do you remember hearing any voices?'

He had started to shake his head again, but he stopped and stared at her. 'I remember your voice,' he said. 'You said you were sorry.'

'I'm sorry,' she had said, apologizing for her beeper going off, for having to leave.

'There were voices calling my name,' he said, 'saying I was in a coma, saying my fever was up.'

That was us, Joanna thought, whispering about his condition, calling him Coma Carl. Guadalupe was right, he *could* hear us, and felt ashamed of herself.

'Were you here?' he said, looking slowly around the hospital room.

'Yes,' she said. 'I used to come and sit with you.'

'I could hear your voice,' he said, as if there were something about that that he couldn't understand. 'So it must have been a dream. I was really here, the whole time.' He looked up at her. 'It didn't feel like a dream.'

'What didn't?'

He didn't answer. 'Could you hear me?' he asked.

'Sometimes,' she said carefully. 'Sometimes you hummed, and once you said, "Oh, grand." '

He nodded. 'If you heard me, it must have just been a dream.'

It took all her willpower not to blurt out, 'Was "grand" the Grand Staircase? What were you humming?' Not to say, 'You were on the *Titanic*, weren't you? Weren't you?'

'If you heard me, I couldn't really have been there,' he said eagerly.

'Why not?' she asked.

'Because it was too far –' He stopped and looked at the door.

Too far for her to come. She said urgently, 'Too far for what?' and the door opened.

'Hi,' a lab technician said, coming in with a metal basket of tubes and needles. 'No, don't get up,' he said to Joanna, who'd jerked guiltily to her feet. 'I can do it from this side.' He set the basket on the table over the bed. 'Don't let me interrupt you two,' he said, putting on gloves. 'I just need to take some blood.' He tied a strip of rubber around Carl's arm.

Joanna knew she should say, 'Oh, that's okay,' and chat with him while he drew the blood, but she was afraid if she did, Carl would lose the tenuous thread of memory.

'Too far for what?' she asked, but Carl wasn't listening. He was looking fearfully at the needle the technician had pulled out.

'This will just be a little sting,' the technician said reassuringly, but Carl's face had already lost its frightened look.

'It's a needle,' he said, in the same wondering tone as when he'd asked her if she'd been here in the room, and extended his arm so the technician could insert the needle, attach it to the glass tube. Carl's dark blood flowed into the tube.

The technician deftly filled the tube, pulled the needle out, pressed cotton to it. 'There,' he said, putting a strip of tape over it. 'That wasn't so bad, was it?'

'No.' Carl turned to look at the IV in his other arm.

'Okay, you're all set. See you later,' the technician said, the glass basket clanking as he went out.

He hadn't shut the door all the way. Joanna got up and started over to close it. 'It was just the IV,' Carl said, looking curiously at the clear narrow tubing dangling from the IV bag. 'I thought it was a rattler.'

Joanna stopped. 'Rattler?'

'In the canyon,' Carl said, and Joanna sat down again, greeting card and pen in hand.

'I was hiding from them,' Carl said. 'I knew they were out there, waiting to ambush me. I'd caught a glimpse of one of them at the end of the canyon.' He squinted as he said it, bringing his hand up as if to shade his eyes. 'I tried climbing up the rocks, but they were crawling with rattlers. They were all around,' his voice rose in fear, 'rattling. I wonder what that was,' he said in a totally different tone of voice. 'The rattling.' He looked around the hospital room. 'The heater, maybe? When you were in here, did it make a rattling sound?'

'You were in a canyon?' she said, trying to take in what he was telling her.

'In Arizona,' he said. 'In a long, narrow canyon.'

Joanna listened, still trying to take it in, taking notes almost automatically. In Arizona. In a canyon.

'It had had a stream in it,' Carl said, 'but it was all dried up. Because of the fever. It was dark, because the walls were so high and steep, and I couldn't see them, but I knew they were out there, waiting.'

The rattlers? 'Who was up there waiting?'

'They were,' he said fearfully. 'A whole band of them, arrows and knives and tomahawks! I tried to outride them, but they shot me in the arm,' he said, grabbing at his arm as if he were trying to pull an arrow out. 'They –' His shoulders jerked, and his face contorted. The arm connected to the IV came up, as if fending off an attack. 'They killed Cody. I found his body in the desert. They'd scalped him. His head was all red,' Carl said. 'Like the canyon. Like the mesas.' His fists clenched and unclenched compulsively. 'All red.'

'Who did that?' Joanna asked. 'Who killed Cody?' and he looked at her as if the answer were obvious.

'The Apaches.'

Apaches. Not patches. Apaches. He hadn't been on the *Titanic*. He'd been in Arizona. She'd been wrong about the *Titanic* being universal. But he had said, 'Oh, grand.' He had made rowing motions with his hands. And just now he had said, 'It was too far –'

'You were in Arizona,' she began, intending to ask, 'Do you remember being anywhere else?'

'*No!*' he shouted, shaking his head vehemently. 'It *wasn't* Arizona. I thought it was, because of the red sandstone. But it wasn't.'

'Where was it?' Joanna asked.

'Someplace else. I was really here, though, the whole time,' he said as if to reassure himself. 'It was just a dream.'

'Did you have other dreams?' she asked. 'Were you other places besides Arizona?'

'There wasn't any other place,' he said simply.

'You said, "Oh, grand."'

He nodded. 'I could see telegraph poles off in the distance. I thought they must be next to a railroad line. I thought if I could reach it before the train came through –' he said, as if that were an explanation.

'I don't understand.'

'I thought I could catch the Rio Grande. But there weren't any tracks. Just the telegraph wires. But I could still send a message. I could climb one of the poles and send a message.'

She was only half-listening. Rio Grande. Not Grand Staircase. Rio Grande.

'… and it was too far to ride on horseback,' Carl was saying, staring straight ahead, 'but I had to get it through.' As he spoke, he jogged gently up and down, his arms bent as if he were holding on to reins.

This is what Guadalupe thought was rowing, Joanna thought, even though it didn't look like rowing. It looked like what it was, Carl riding a horse. He wasn't humming, 'Nearer, My God, to Thee,' she thought. It was probably 'Home on the Range.'

And Mrs Woollam had been in a garden. Mrs Davenport had seen an angel. But she had wanted it to be a woman in a nightdress. She had wanted it to be the Verandah Café and the Grand Staircase. To fit her theory. So she had twisted the evidence to fit, ignored the discrepancies, led the witnesses, and believed what she wanted to. Just like Mr Mandrake.

She had been so set on her idea she'd refused to accept the truth – that Carl had gotten his desert, his Apaches, from the Westerns his wife read to him, incorporating them into the red expanse of his coma the way she'd incorporated Mr Briarley's *Titanic* stories into hers. Because they happened to be there in long-term memory.

And the imagery meant nothing. It wasn't universal. It was as random, as pointless, as Mr Bendix's seeing Elvis. And the feeling of something significant, something important, came from an overstimulated temporal lobe.

And meanwhile, she had bullied Amelia Tanaka, she had harassed a man just out of a coma and possibly endangered his health, breaking rules right and left. Acting like a nutcase.

'… before it got dark,' Carl was saying, 'but when I got closer, I saw the Apaches were already there.'

Joanna put the bluebird greeting card and the pen in her pocket and stood up. 'I should go,' she said. Before Guadalupe catches me in here. Before the review board finds out you didn't sign a waiver. Before anyone finds out how I've acted. She patted the covers. 'You need to get some sleep.'

'Are you leaving?' he said, and his hand lunged for her wrist like a striking snake. 'Don't leave.' He gripped it tightly. 'I'm afraid I'll go back there, and it's getting dark back there. It's getting redder.'

'It's all right, Carl,' Joanna said soothingly. 'It was just a dream.'

'No. It was a real place. Arizona. I knew it was, because of the mesas. But it wasn't. And it was. I can't explain it.'

'You knew Arizona was a symbol for something else.'

'Yes,' he said, and she thought, It *does* mean something. The NDE isn't just random synapses firing, random associations. 'What was it a symbol for, Carl?' she asked, and waited, breath held, for his answer.

'They scalped Cody. Took the top of his skull right off, and I could see his brain. It was all red,' he said. 'I had to get out, before it got dark. I had to get the mail through.'

The mail. The letters floating in the ankle-deep water of the mail room, the names on their envelopes blurred and unreadable, and the mail clerk putting them onto higher and higher racks, dragging them up the carpeted stairs.

'The mail?' Joanna asked, her chest tight.

'For the Pony Express,' he said. 'Cody was the regular rider, but they killed him, and I didn't have any way to get the mail through. It was too far to ride on a horse, and the Apaches had cut the wires.'

And the *Carpathia* was too far away, Joanna thought. The *Californian* wasn't answering. She thought of Mr Briarley writing a postcard to Kit, sending up rockets, trying to send out messages. And none of them getting through.

'The mesa was a long way,' Carl was saying, 'and I was afraid there wouldn't be anything up there to make a fire with.'

'A fire?' Joanna said, thinking of Maisie.

'For the smoke signal. I got the idea from the Apaches. You hold the blanket down over the fire and then yank it back, and the smoke goes up.' He pulled back on an imaginary blanket, his hands holding its imaginary sides, a sharp backward motion with both hands. Like rowing. Like rowing.

'I didn't know any Apache,' he said. 'All I knew was Morse code.'

The sailor working the Morse lamp, and Jack Phillips, bent tirelessly over the wireless key, tapping out CQD, SOS – 'SOS,' she said. 'You sent an SOS.'

'And as soon as I did, the nurse was opening the curtains and I was back here.'

'You were back here,' Joanna said, remembering Mr Edwards saying, 'The light started to flash, and I knew I had to go back, and all of a sudden I was in the operating room.' Remembering Mrs Woollam saying, 'I was in the tunnel, and then all of a sudden I was back on the floor by the phone.' Remembering Richard saying, 'Something just kicks them out.'

Out in the hall, a voice said excitedly, 'We found her!'

Joanna glanced at the door, the half-open door she had forgotten to shut. 'Finally,' Guadalupe's voice said, and then, 'Where were you? We've been looking all over for you.'

Looking all over. The steward, heading up the aft staircase to the Promenade Deck, checking the smoking room, the gymnasium, looking for Mr Briarley. And Mr Briarley, running down to G Deck, along Scotland Road, into the mail room, looking for the key. The key.

'Oh, my God!' Joanna breathed. 'I know what it is!' She put her hand up to her mouth. 'I remember what Mr Briarley said!'

39

'Well, Wiley's got her warmed up. Let's go.'
   – Last radio broadcast by WILL ROGERS before the
   plane crash in which he and Wiley Post were killed

'What?' Carl said, alarmed. 'What do you mean, you know what it is?' but Joanna didn't hear him.

I have to tell Richard, she thought. I have to tell him I've figured it out.

She stood up. 'You're not leaving, are you?' Carl said, reaching for her wrist again. 'You know what what is? What Arizona is?'

'He's sitting up talking,' Guadalupe's voice said out in the hall.

They're coming this way, Joanna thought. She stood up and jammed the scribbled-on greeting card in her pocket. 'Your wife's here,' she said, and hurried toward the door before Carl could protest.

And how was she going to explain her being here? she wondered, peering out the door. Mrs Aspinall was standing next to the nurses' station, Guadalupe and the aide bent comfortingly over her. 'You shouldn't cry *now*,' the aide was saying, 'it's all over.'

'I don't want him to see me like this,' Mrs Aspinall said tearfully, dabbing at her eyes.

'I'll get you a Kleenex,' Guadalupe said, disappearing around the corner of the nurses' station.

Joanna didn't hesitate. She bolted out the door, across the hall, and into the waiting room, and just in time. Guadalupe reappeared with the Kleenex, Mrs Aspinall blew her nose, and all three of them started toward Carl's room.

There was no one in the waiting room. Joanna leaned against the door, waiting for them to go into the room. It's an SOS, Joanna thought, belated understanding pouring in like seawater through the gash in the *Titanic's* side. That's what the NDE is. It's the dying brain sending out a call for help, a distress signal, tapping out Morse-code messages to the nervous system: 'Come at once. We have struck a berg.'

Transmitting signals to the brain's neurotransmitters, trying to find one that could kick lungs that were no longer breathing into action, trying to find one that could jump-start a heart that was no longer beating. Trying to find the right one.

And sometimes it succeeded, reviving patients who were clinically dead, bringing them back abruptly, miraculously. Like Mr O'Reirdon. Like Mrs Woollam. Because the message got through.

'Carl, oh, Carl!' Mrs Aspinall said tearfully. 'You're all right!'

Joanna looked down the hall. Mrs Aspinall and Guadalupe had gone into the room, and the aide was headed back toward the elevators, carrying a piece of equipment.

Joanna waited till she'd gone into the elevator, and then ran down to the nurses' station. She grabbed up the phone receiver from behind the counter, leaning over it to punch in the lab's number. If Guadalupe caught her out here, she'd just think she'd gone and then come back.

If Carl hasn't blabbed, she thought, listening to the phone ring. 'Answer, Richard,' she murmured. 'Answer.'

Answer. That was what the NDE was doing, too, punching in numbers and listening to the phone ring, trying to get through, hoping someone would answer on the other end. And if Richard knows it's an SOS, she thought, he'll be able to figure out what the other end is.

And no wonder her mind, trying to make sense of it, had fastened on to the *Titanic*. It was the perfect metaphor. The SOS sent five minutes after the *Californian's* wireless operator had gone to bed, the Morse lamp, the rockets, the screams for help from the water. And above all, Phillips sitting in the wireless room, faithfully tapping out, 'SOS, CQD,' tapping out, 'We are flooded up to the boilers,' sending out calls for help to the very end.

Richard wasn't answering. He's sitting at the console, she thought, staring at Mrs Troudtheim's scan, trying to figure out the problem. 'It's not a problem, Richard,' she murmured. 'It's the answer.' And it made evolutionary sense, just like he had predicted it would. The NDE wasn't cushioning the body from trauma, wasn't setting a death program in motion. It was trying to stop it.

The answering machine clicked on. 'This is Dr Wright's office. If you wish to leave –' his voice said, but Joanna had already jammed the phone down and was pelting up the stairs to the lab.

Richard wasn't there. The door was locked, so he intended to be gone for longer than a few minutes. She unlocked it and went in, and then stood there, staring around the deserted lab, trying to think where he might have gone. Down to the cafeteria for lunch? she thought, and glanced at the clock. It was a quarter to one. The cafeteria might actually be open this time of day.

He said he had an appointment, she thought, and tried to remember his words when he was in her office. He'd said, 'I'm going to be out of the lab for a while.' Where?

Dr Jamison, she thought, what Richard had said clicking in suddenly. She walked rapidly over to the phone and called the switchboard. 'Get me Dr Jamison's office,' and listened to another droning ring.

Doesn't anybody answer their phones? Joanna thought. No, and the brain kept calling and calling, trying first one number and then, when there was no answer, another. Dialing and redialing, punching in code after code, trying to connect.

She depressed the receiver button and called the switchboard again. 'Where's Dr Jamison's office? What floor?'

'I'll have to look that up,' the operator said, and, after a maddening minute, '841.'

'Thanks,' Joanna said and started to hang up, then thought better of it. 'I want you to page her for me,' she said.

'Do you want her to call the lab?'

'No. My pager. And I want you to page Dr Wright, too,' she said, reaching in her pocket to switch her pager on, thinking with a sudden sinking feeling, He won't have his turned on either.

She hung up. Room 841 was in the west wing. The shortest way would be to go down to fifth and take the walkway across. No, they were painting the walkway on fifth. Down to the walkway on third. She scribbled a note: 'Went to find you. Page me,' dropped it on his desk, and ran out, slamming the door behind her, not even taking the time to lock it, hitting the elevator button again and again, willing it to open, willing it not to stop on fifth, or fourth.

When the elevator opened on third, she ran down the hall, across the walkway, and through Medicine to the other walkway. Don't let Mrs Davenport be out taking a constitutional, she thought, glancing nervously at the door to her room. I don't have time to listen to her latest confabulations.

Joanna pressed close to the other wall and hurried past the half-open door, past the sunroom, past the nurses' station.

'Hey, Doc!' a voice called behind her. 'Doc!' Mr Wojakowski. She kept going, acting as if she hadn't heard him. Down to the end of the hall. Around the corner. Into the walkway.

The walkway door opened behind her. 'Doc!' Mr Wojakowski called, panting. 'Doc Lander! Wait up!' and there was nothing to do but turn around.

'I *thought* that was you, Doc,' he said, beaming. 'I saw you back there and tried to catch you as you went past, but you were going like you'd just heard 'em sound "Battle Stations." Where you headin' in such a hurry?'

'I'm looking for Dr Wright. I have to find him right away,' she said.

'I haven't seen him,' he said cheerfully. 'I came to visit a friend of mine.' He nodded his head back in the direction of Medicine. 'Had a stroke. Bad one, too. One whole side paralyzed, can't talk. Happened while he was square dancing. Fell over right in the middle of a dosey-doh –'

'I'm sorry to hear that,' Joanna said, glancing toward the end of the walkway. 'I wish I could stay and talk. I—'

'You know who you remind me of? Ace Willey. He was a midshipman on the *Yorktown*, and he was *always* in a hurry. "Where the hell do you think you're going in such a hurry?" I used to say to him. "You're on a damned *ship*." Well, one day, he's hurrying across the hangar deck, and he steps into an open hatch and—'

'Mr Wojakowski, I'd love to hear the rest of your story, but I've got to go. I have to find Dr Wright.' She took off across the walkway, looking determinedly ahead.

'Wait up, Doc.' He caught up to her as she reached the door. 'I had something I wanted to ask you.'

She pushed open the door. 'Mr Wojakowski, I—'

'Ed.'

'Ed,' she said, not stopping. 'I'm sorry, but I just don't have time to talk.'

'I just wanted to know if you'd ever got that schedule of yours figured out,' he said, panting to keep up with her.

'No,' Joanna said, rounding the corner and coming, finally, to the elevators. She pushed the button, praying, Please don't take forever. 'We'll let you know as soon as we do.'

'Good. Just give me a call,' he said. 'I can do it just about anytime.'

The elevator finally, blessedly opened and Joanna stepped in. For one awful moment she thought he intended to follow her, but he had just stepped up to the elevator's edge. 'So anyway, Ace wasn't looking where he was going, and he stepped in an open hatch and fell two full decks. Broke both legs. Spent the next year and a half in a hospital on Oahu.'

Joanna pushed 'eight' and the door started slowly, slowly to close. '"So where did all your hurrying get you?" I asked him,' he said as the door slid shut. 'You shoulda seen him, all hung up in traction and two plaster casts that went all the way up to his—'

He was still talking when the elevator door snicked shut. And probably *still* talking, Joanna thought, stepping out of the elevator on eight and looking for the room signs.

'830–850,' one of them said, pointing to the hall on the left. She started down it, looking for 841. Two Hispanic men in white coveralls stood down by the end, leaning over a cluster of buckets, mixing paint.

All of the doors in the hall were open except 841. Joanna knocked on it, banging progressively harder when no one answered. She tried the door. It was locked. 'Do you know where Dr Jamison is?' she called down to the painters.

They both shook their heads and went back to pouring paint from one bucket to another. Joanna frowned at the door, frustrated. Where were they? Had they gone someplace else to talk? To the cafeteria, maybe?

She walked down to the painters, who both straightened up, as if expecting to be lectured by her. 'Did either of you see Dr Jamison leave?' Joanna asked. They shook their heads again, with a timidity that made her wonder if either of them spoke English.

'Señor –' she began, and a young man stuck his head out of the door next to Dr Jamison's office and said, 'You're looking for Dr Jamison? She had to go see somebody in the ER.'

'Thank you,' Joanna said. 'Do you know if Dr Wright was with her?'

He shook his head. 'I just got back from lunch and saw her note.'

'Her note?'

'On the door,' he said, leaning around his door to point at Dr Jamison's. 'Oh,' he said when he saw it wasn't there. 'Somebody must have taken it down.'

Richard. He'd seen the note, pocketed it, gone down to the ER after her. Or the painters had taken it down. She considered asking them, then discarded the idea. 'Can I use your phone for a second?' she asked the young man.

'Sure,' he said, opening the door farther to let her in.

She dialed the lab, listened to the ring till the answering machine clicked on, and hung up. 'Thanks,' she said, and started back for the elevators, trying to think what the fastest way down to the ER was. Back down to third, take the walkway to main, and the elevators down to first, she thought, pushing the button for the elevator. I should have punched the button when I got off. It might be here by now.

She pushed the button again, thinking of Mr Briarley pressing the ivory-and-gold button over and over and over, of him smacking *A Night to Remember* against his desk the same way, over and over and over – 'Literature is a message!' he'd shouted, whacking the paperback for emphasis.

And that was the lecture she'd been trying to remember, the lecture that came welling up out of her long-term memory now when she no longer needed it, when she'd already figured out what the NDE was. 'It's a message!' he'd thundered, and she could see Ricky Inman cowering in his seat. She could see it all, the snow – not fog but snow – falling outside the windows and the words 'The Rime of the Ancient Mariner' on the board and Mr Briarley in his gray tweed vest, hitting the red-and-white paperback against his desk, shouting, 'What do you think these poems and novels and plays are? Boring, dusty artifacts? They're *not*!' Smack. 'They're messages, just like the *Titanic* sent!' Smack. 'Samuel Taylor Coleridge, John Milton, William Shakespeare, they're tapping out messages to you!'

He shook *A Night to Remember* at them. 'They say the dead can't speak, but they can! The people in this book died over sixty years ago, in the middle of the ocean, with no one around them for miles, but they still speak to you. They still send us messages – about love and courage and death! That's what history is, and science, and art. That's what *literature* is. It's the people who went before us, tapping out messages from the past, from beyond the grave, trying to tell us about life and death! Listen to them!'

She had listened. And remembered. And over ten years later, while she was experiencing an NDE, Mr Briarley had spoken to her out of the past, trying to tell her the NDE was a message.

The elevator opened, and she stepped in. On second thought, she'd better not risk third. Mr Wojakowski might still be standing outside the door of the elevator, waiting to finish his story about Ace Willey. She'd better go down to second, cut through Radiology, and take the service elevator. She punched the button for 'two.'

I'm doing what the brain does during an NDE, she thought, watching the floor numbers descend. Racing around, taking roundabout routes when there's no direct way through, trying one thing, and then, when that doesn't work, trying another. Asking Mr Briarley for the answer, and then when he couldn't help her, trying to find the textbook, looking through transcripts, asking Kit, asking Maisie.

Just like in Carl's coma – heading first for the railroad tracks, then, when the wires were cut, trying to get to the mesas. Images of searching and not finding, of lines down and doors locked and passages blocked. Images of the dying brain.

And images of hurrying because there's not any time. Brain death occurs in four to six minutes, and the mail room's already flooded, the elevator's not working, it's already getting dark.

Images generated by endorphins and electrical impulses, frantically sending out SOSs, desperately reaching out for something to latch on to, like Coma Carl grabbing for her wrist. And the rest of it, the tunnels and relatives and Angels of Light, the gardens and slanting decks and sandstone deserts are nothing more than side effects, she thought, taking the hall that led to Surgery, passing a nurse she didn't recognize, the desperate efforts of the conscious mind to keep up with what it's experiencing, to make sense of sensations it can't understand, searching through its long-term memories for its own connections, its own metaphors.

How could I not have recognized the metaphor? she thought. And ran straight into Mr Mandrake.

'Dr Lander. Just the person I wanted to see,' he said sternly. 'I have been searching all over for you. You never answer your pages.'

'This really isn't a good time, Mr Mandrake,' she said, sidestepping to go around him. 'I'm –' but he'd taken a firm grip on her arm.

'This will only take a few minutes,' he said smoothly, steering her over to the side of the hallway. 'Now that you've become one of Dr Wright's subjects, I'm sure you've realized that his lab-produced hallucinations bear no resemblance to authentic NAEs. Or, if you, through some fluke, *have* experienced a true NAE, then you *know* that it is real, that what you are seeing is the afterlife that awaits—'

'I don't have time to discuss this with you right now,' Joanna said and started to walk rapidly away.

He darted in front of her. 'That's exactly the issue. You don't have time to discuss your findings with me. All of your time is taken up with Dr Wright's project, which can't possibly lead to anything useful.'

That's what you think, Joanna thought.

'Because the physical aspects are completely insignificant,' Mr Mandrake was saying. 'It is the supernatural aspects that matter. The NDE is a spiritual experience through which the Angel of Light is trying to tell us about the world that awaits us after death. It is a message—'

Joanna laughed, a spurt of delight that escaped in spite of her.

'I see nothing funny –' Mr Mandrake said, drawing himself up.

'I'm sorry,' Joanna said, trying to suppress it. 'It's just that you're right. It *is* a message.'

He stared at her, speechless. 'Well, I'm glad you've finally realized –' he said after a moment.

'I should have listened to you in the first place, Mr Mandrake,' she said giddily. 'It was all right there in your book. Telegrams, rockets, lights – did you know that white is the international color for a distress signal?'

'Distress –?' he said, frowning uncertainly.

'It just never occurred to me that *you*, of all people … But you were right.' She grasped his sleeves. 'The NDE is a message. It's an SOS. It's a call for help.'

She squeezed his arms. 'And you're wrong about Richard's research not leading anywhere. It's going to save Maisie. It's going to work miracles!' she said, and left him standing there, gaping after her, not even attempting to follow.

But she didn't take any chances. Instead of the service elevator, she ducked down the nearest stairway to second and out into the chilly parking lot, so she wouldn't run into anyone else. It was snowing again, and she hugged her arms to her chest as she ran across the parking lot to the side door of Main.

And her luck was against her. Maisie's nurse Barbara was scraping ice off her back window. 'Joanna!' she called, 'Maisie wants to see you!' and started over to her, scraper in hand.

'I know. I'll be up this afternoon,' she called back, and hurried on.

And who will I run into in here? she wondered, pushing open the side door and starting down the stairs. Kit? Mrs Davenport? Everyone I've ever known? But there was no one in the stairwell, and no yellow tape stretched across the landing. She took the last few stairs and the hall leading down to the ER at a run.

She pushed the side door open and stood there for a moment, looking for Richard. She couldn't see him, or Dr Jamison, but there was Vielle, standing with one of the interns outside one of the trauma rooms with a young man, no, a boy. He wasn't as tall as Vielle, and the maroon jacket he was wearing was two sizes too big for him. An Avalanche jacket. Joanna could see the swooping blue-and-white logo on the back of it.

He didn't look like an emergency. He stood there talking to Vielle and the intern with no sign of injury Joanna could see, at least from the back, and whatever his problem was, even if somebody'd shot him with a nail gun, it could wait a minute because she had to find out where Richard was. She plunged across the ER, calling, 'Vielle!'

None of them looked up. A resident, still with his stethoscope on, turned and looked irritably at her over the chart he was reading, but the intern and Vielle continued to watch the boy, who was still talking earnestly to them. Joanna wondered what about. Vielle was frowning, and the intern's face was stiff with disapproval. Good, Joanna thought, sidling past a supply cart. They won't care if I interrupt them.

'Vielle, have you seen Dr Wright?' she said, nearly up to them now, but they still didn't look up.

'I have to get out of here,' the boy was saying with quiet intensity. 'They're going to close the lid.'

'No, they aren't,' Vielle said soothingly. 'I think you should—'

Joanna ran up behind the boy. 'You say that because you're the embalmer,' he said angrily. 'I know what you're trying to do.'

'Vielle, I'm sorry to interrupt, but I'm looking for—'

The boy whirled to face her, his arm coming up to strike her as he turned, and she knew, watching his panicked, desperate face, that he had moved suddenly. But it didn't seem sudden.

It happened slowly, slowly, the intern rearing backward, his mouth opening in alarm, the boy's maroon sleeve coming around and up, the satin catching the light from the fluorescents overhead, Vielle's arm, still in its white bandage, reaching forward to grab at his sleeve. They all moved slowly, stickily, as if they were mired in molasses.

The Great Molasses Flood, Joanna thought. But time dilation was caused by the surge of adrenaline that accompanied trauma. And this wasn't a trauma situation.

But time dilation was what it had to be, because she had plenty of time to see it all: the intern's face, nearly as frantic as the teenager's, turning to call the security guard, who was already lumbering to his feet. Vielle's hand, not reaching for his maroon sleeve, reaching for his hand.

To hear it all: Vielle's voice, coated with syrup, too, shouting, 'Joanna! Don't –!' The chart the resident was holding clattering to the floor. An alarm going off.

She had time to wonder if the time dilation might be some kind of side effect of the dithetamine. Time to think, I have to tell Richard. But if it wasn't a trauma situation, why was the guard, still lumbering to his feet, reaching for his gun?

Time to think, The boy must have a knife. He was holding a knife on them when I came in. That's why they didn't look up when I called, that's why they didn't see me till it was too late. That's what Vielle grabbed for.

Time to think, I *told* her the ER was an accident waiting to happen.

Time, finally, for the fact to penetrate: He has a knife, though she still didn't feel any fear. That's the endorphins, she thought, cushioning the mind against pain, against panic, so she could think clearly.

He has a knife, she thought calmly, and looked down at her blouse, down at his striking hand, but even though time was moving even more slowly than the security guard, she was too late. She couldn't see the knife.

Because it had already gone in.

40

'This is terrible! This is the worst of the worst catastrophes in the world … the frame is crashing to the ground, not quite to the mooring mast … oh, the humanity!'

– Radio reporter HERB MORRISON, broadcasting the crash of the *Hindenburg*

There was blood everywhere, which didn't make any sense because where the knife had gone in, there was hardly any, just a little ooze of dark red. 'We've got an emergency here!' the intern shouted, reaching out to keep Joanna from falling, but she had already fallen. She was lying on the tile floor, and Vielle was kneeling next to her, and there was blood all over her cardigan, all over the hand Vielle was holding.

Vielle grabbed for the knife, Joanna thought. He must have stabbed her hand. 'Are you hurt?' she asked Vielle.

'No,' Vielle said, but Joanna thought she must be, because there was a kind of sob in her throat.

'We've got a stab wound here,' the intern said to the resident. Good, they'll take care of it, Joanna thought, but the resident didn't even glance at Vielle. He looked at the little line of oozing blood in Joanna's chest and then turned and started putting on a pair of latex gloves. 'Get her on the table,' he said, pulling the glove down over his palm, 'and get me a cross match. What's her BP?'

'Ninety over sixty,' someone said, she couldn't see who. There were all kinds of people around her, hooking things up and drawing blood. How funny, Joanna thought. Why do they need more blood? There's already more than enough.

'Get a cardiac surgeon down here,' the resident snapped, 'and get me two more units of blood. Vielle, go get some direct pressure on that hand of yours,' and Joanna was afraid Vielle would leave and let go of her hand, but she continued to kneel next to Joanna.

'Don't try to move, honey,' she said, looking worried. 'Just lie still.' Joanna had always wondered whether Vielle's worried expression frightened her patients, but it didn't. It was comforting.

I wonder why, she thought, and tried to see what it was in her face that was reassuring, but she couldn't see it. She could only see the top of Vielle's head and the resident's, both in their green scrub caps, and the top of the security guard's head, standing over the boy in the Avalanche jacket. The boy lay sprawled on his face on the tile floor, and she could see the blue-and-white logo on the back of the maroon jacket, and maroon under the boy's face, too, where the guard had shot him.

The top of the guard's head was bald and shiny, reflecting the overhead fluorescent light as Joanna looked down on it. 'Just hang on, Joanna!' Vielle said, holding her hand, which was funny, because Joanna was up here, and Vielle was down there.

But she was down there, too. They all were, the intern and the resident and she couldn't tell who else because all she could see was the tops of their heads, as they worked over her, taking her blood pressure and hooking up IVs. 'Seventy-five over fifty,' one of them said.

'She's bleeding out. It must have hit the aorta,' someone else said, she couldn't see who, he was too far below her.

I'm up near the ceiling, Joanna thought. She would be able to look down and see the ledge outside. She wondered if there was a red tennis shoe on it, and then thought, I'm having an out-of-body experience. Finally. I have to tell Richard.

Richard, she thought with a kind of panic. I have to tell Richard the NDE's an SOS.

'Clear,' the resident said, and then, 'Where the hell is that surgeon? Did you page him?'

Not Carson, Richard, Joanna thought, looking at the resident, and now she could see his face, not at all worried, calm and impassive, and that was comforting, too.

'Page Richard. It's important,' she said, but nothing came out, her lips had not moved, and a nurse was trying to put something in her mouth, trying to force it down her throat.

'No,' she said, twisting her head to get away from her, looking for Vielle.

'I'm right here, honey,' Vielle said, holding Joanna's hand, and somebody must have bandaged her hand, it was white, and so bright she could hardly look at it.

'Page Richard,' Joanna said, but she couldn't tell if Vielle had heard her. There was a funny beeping sound. One of the nurses must have hit the code alarm. 'Page Richard and tell him I found out what the NDE is. It's an SOS,' she said, louder, but the beeping was drowning out her voice.

'What the hell is that?' the resident said, doing something to her chest.

'Her pager,' Vielle said.

'Well, shut the damn thing off.'

It's Richard, Joanna thought. I told him to page me. Tell him the NDE's a distress signal. Tell him he has to figure out the code. For Maisie, she tried to say, but now there was another sound drowning her out. A ringing. A buzzing. 'He's in the lab.'

'Sixty over forty,' the nurse said.

'She's bleeding out,' the resident said.

'Hang on, Joanna,' Vielle said, holding tight to her hand. 'Stay with me,' but she wasn't there. She was on the *Titanic*.

But not in the passageway. On the Grand Staircase. And a crush of passengers was all around her, jammed onto the stairs, dressed in dinner jackets and dressing gowns and lifejackets. They were pushing up the marble stairs, carrying her along with them. To the Boat Deck, Joanna thought. They're all trying to get up to the Boat Deck.

'I have to get back down to C Deck,' Joanna said, trying to turn around, but people were jammed next to her, around her, behind her, wedging her so she couldn't move. 'I have to tell Richard I found out the secret,' she said to them. 'I have to get back to the passage.'

No one heard her, they continued to push her up the white marble stairs. She looked over at the gilt-and-wrought-iron banisters, thinking, If I could reach the railing and hold on to it, I could work my way back down, against the crowd.

With a great effort, she turned sideways, struggling to move her arm, her torso, and set out across the flow of passengers toward the railing like someone wading through deep water. She reached it, grabbing for it as if it were a life preserver. But this was worse. People were using the railing to push themselves along as they climbed, they refused to let go to let Joanna pass. They shoved upward as if she weren't even there, carrying suitcases and steamer rugs, pushing Joanna back against the step she was on, nearly knocking her down.

'Just let me –' she said to a woman carrying a Pekingese and a furled umbrella, and stepped toward the middle of the step, trying to get out of the woman's way. She raised her arm, trying to reach around –

The umbrella caught her sharply in the ribs, and she gasped and grabbed for her side. She let go of the railing, and the crowd swept her up past the cherub, past the angels of Honour and Glory Crowning Time, through the etched-glass doors, and out onto the Boat Deck.

Joanna stood there a moment, holding her side, as they poured past her, and then started back through the crowd to the doors. 'Excuse me,' she said, squeezing past the uniformed man in the door, and saw it was the clerk from the mail room. He had a canvas mail sack over his shoulder, and it was dripping on the flowered carpet of the foyer. She stepped back, looking down at the carpet, at the dark drops.

'You'd better get into a boat, miss,' the clerk said kindly.

'I can't. I have to go back the way I came,' she said, trying to get past him without stepping in the damp spot, without touching the dripping sack. 'I have to tell Richard what I found out.'

He nodded solemnly. 'The mail must go through. But you can't go down that way. It's blocked.'

'Blocked?'

'Yes, miss. There are people coming up. You'll need to take the aft staircase, miss.' He pointed up the Boat Deck. 'Do you know where it is?'

'Yes,' Joanna said, and ran toward the stern, past the band getting out its instruments, setting up its music stands. The violinist set his black case on top of the upright piano and snapped the latches open.

' "Alexander's Ragtime Band," ' the conductor said, and the bass viol player sorted through a sheaf of sheet music, looking for it.

Past Lifeboat Number 9, where a young man was saying good-bye to a young woman in a white dress and a veil. 'It's all right, little girl,' he said. 'You go, and I'll stay awhile.' Past Number 11, where the mustached man she had seen in the writing room and in the lounge, dealing out hand after hand of cards, was lifting two children into the boat. Past Number 13, where an officer was calling, 'Anyone else to go in this boat? Any more women and children?'

Joanna shook her head and hurried past. And into a man in a denim shirt and suspenders. 'No need to panic, folks,' he said, herding people toward the bow. 'Just walk slowly. Don't run. Plenty of time.'

Joanna backed away from him. And into the officer. He took her arm. 'You need to get into a boat, miss,' he said, leading her back toward Number 13. 'There isn't much time.'

'No,' she said, but he was gripping her arm tightly, he was propelling her over to the davits.

'Wait for this young lady,' he called to the crewman in the boat.

'No,' Joanna said, 'you don't understand. I have to—'

'There's nothing to be afraid of,' he said, and his grip on her arm was like iron, it was cutting off her circulation. 'It's perfectly safe.'

'No!' She wrenched free of him and ran down the deck, past the officer, as if he were still chasing her, past the band and into the foyer of the Grand Staircase, thinking, The elevator. The elevator will be faster.

She pushed the gold-and-ivory button. 'Come on, come on,' she said, and pushed it again, but the arrow above the door didn't move. She abandoned it and ran over to the head of the staircase, down the stairs to B Deck, C Deck, thinking, What if it's blocked like he said?

It wasn't. It was clear. 'Again. Clear,' the resident said, and Joanna was in the emergency room and Vielle was holding her hand.

'I've got a pulse.'

'Vielle,' Joanna said, but Vielle wasn't looking at her, she was looking at the aide who had come out in the hall that day they had the fight, she was telling her, 'If he doesn't answer his page, go get him. He's in 602.'

'Vielle, tell Richard the NDE's a distress call the dying brain sends out,' Joanna tried to say, but there was something in her mouth, choking her.

'He's coming, Joanna,' Vielle said, holding tight to her hand. 'Just hang on.'

'If Richard doesn't get here in time, tell him the NDE's a distress signal. It's important,' Joanna tried to say around the choking thing in her throat. They've intubated me, she thought, panicked, and tried to pull it out, but it wasn't an airway, it was blood. She was coughing it up and out of her, gallons and gallons of blood. 'Who would have thought the old man to have had so much blood in him?' It was pouring out of her, and all over Vielle and the resident and the nurse, choking her, drowning her.

'Help,' she cried, 'I have to tell Richard. It's an SOS,' but it wasn't Vielle, it was the man with the mustache and she was back on the Boat Deck. The band was playing 'Goodnight, Irene,' and the officer was loading Number 4.

'I want you to do something for me when you reach New York,' the mustached man was saying to Joanna, putting something in her hand.

She looked down at it. It was a note, written in a childish round cursive. 'If saved,' it read, 'please inform my sister Mrs F. J. Adams of Findlay, Ohio. Lost. J. H. Rogers.'

'Please see that my sister gets this,' he said, closing her fingers over the note. 'Tell her it's from me.'

'But I'm not going to –' Joanna said, but he had already melted into the crowd, and the officer was headed toward her, calling, 'Miss! Miss!' She jammed the note into her pocket and ran down the deck toward the aft staircase, darting between couples, past a pair of cheerleaders in purple-and-gold pleated skirts, between families saying good-bye.

'But he's going to be all right, isn't he?' a woman in a white coat and white knitted cap said to an officer.

The officer looked pityingly at her. 'We're doing everything we can.'

Joanna pushed past the woman, but the way to the aft staircase was mobbed with people in kerchiefs and cloth caps, fighting to get into the boats, and sailors trying to free the boats, trying to lower them. 'You can't get through this way!' the sailor who had worked the Morse lamp called to her. He jerked his thumb back toward the stern. 'Try the second-class stairway,' and she turned and ran past the empty davits of the boats that had already been lowered, to the second-class stairway.

The door to the second-class stairway was standing open, her red tennis shoe lying on its side on the threshold. Joanna leaped over it and pelted down the stairs, past the À La Carte Restaurant, down the next flight, around the landing. And stopped.

Two steps below the landing, tied to the railings on either side, stretched a strip of yellow tape. 'Crime Scene,' it said. 'Do Not Cross.' And below it, submerging the stairs, pale blue, shiny as paint, the water.

'It's underwater,' Joanna said, and sat down, holding on to the railing for support. 'The passage is underwater.'

Maybe it's just the stairway, she thought, maybe it hasn't reached the passage, but of course it had. The second-class stairway was all the way in the stern, and the ship was going down by the head. And below the tape water was pouring in everywhere, drowning the mail room and Scotland Road and the swimming pool, the squash court and the staterooms and the glass-enclosed deck. And the way out, the way back.

There has to be another way out, Joanna thought, staring blindly at the pale blue water. The Apaches cut the wires, but Carl was still able to get the mail through. There has to be another way out. The lifeboats! she thought, and scrambled to her feet, tore up the stairs and back along the Boat Deck.

The boats were gone, the deck deserted except for the band, which had finished 'Goodnight, Irene.' They were searching through their music for the next piece, arranging the sheet music on their stands.

Joanna ran to the railing and leaned far over it, trying to see the lifeboat the sailor had been loading. It was miles below her, almost to the water. She couldn't make out anything in the darkness but the pale gleam of the sailor's white uniform. It was too far for her to jump, but maybe not too far for them to hear her. 'Hello!' she called down, cupping her hand around her mouth. 'Ahoy! Can you hear me?'

There was no movement of the white uniform, no sound. 'I need you to deliver a message for me,' she shouted, but the band had struck up a waltz, and her voice was lost in the sound of the violin, of the piano.

They can't hear me, she thought. She needed to drop a message down to them. She fumbled in her pockets for a pen and paper. She came up with the mustached man's note, but no pen, not even a stub of pencil. 'Just a minute!' she called down to the boat. 'Hang on!' and ran down the deck to the aft staircase and down to the writing room on the Promenade Deck, praying, 'Don't let it be flooded, don't let it be flooded.'

It wasn't. The Reading and Writing Room sat empty, the yellow-shaded lamps still burning on the writing desks. Joanna grabbed a sheet of stationery out of the rack, dipped a pen in the inkwell, and scribbled, 'Richard, the NDE is a distress signal the brain sends as it's dying –'

'What's going on?' a voice said. Joanna looked up. It was Greg Menotti. He was wearing jogging shorts and a Nike T-shirt. 'Somebody told me the ship's sinking,' he said, laughing.

'It is,' Joanna said, writing, '– and you have to find out what neurotransmitter it's trying to activate.' She scrawled her name at the bottom, snatched up the sheet of paper, and ran out onto the deck.

'What do you mean?' Greg said, jogging up beside her. 'It's unsinkable.'

She leaned over the railing into the darkness. 'Ahoy!' she called, waving the sheet of paper. 'Lifeboat!'

No answer. No gleam of white. Only the fathomless blackness.

She flung herself away from the railing and along the deck to the first-class lounge.

'But it can't be sinking,' Greg said, sprinting after her.

She yanked open the stained-glass door of the lounge. 'If it's sinking,' Greg said, 'we'd better get in one of the boats.'

She ran over to the mirrored mahogany bar. 'The boats are all gone.'

'They can't all be gone,' he said, panting, holding his arm. 'There has to be a way off this ship.'

'There isn't,' she said, grabbing a bottle of wine off the bar.

He snatched at the wrist of her hand holding the bottle. 'I work out at the health club three times a week!'

'It doesn't matter. The *Titanic* had sixteen watertight compartments, she had the latest safety features, and it didn't matter. An iceberg gashed her side and –' she said, and remembered her blouse and the little ooze of blood.

'It doesn't look like a very bad cut,' Maisie had said, scrutinizing the diagram of the *Titanic*. And it wasn't, but belowdecks, inside, water was pouring into the watertight compartments, spilling over into the engine room and the chest cavity and the lungs. 'How bad is it?' Captain Smith asked, and the architect shook his head. 'It's nicked the aorta.'

'What is it?' Greg asked, letting go of her wrist. 'What's the matter?'

'Nothing,' she said, thinking, You have to get the message to Richard. 'I need something to open the wine bottle with.'

'There isn't time. We have to get up to the Boat Deck,' he said, and his face was furious, frantic, like the face of the boy in the Avalanche jacket, whirling toward her …

'I have to do this first,' Joanna said, and began opening drawers, digging through silverware.

'I found this,' Greg said, and held out a knife to her. A knife. He had had a knife. But when she looked down, she hadn't been able to see it. Because it had already gone in. 'We've got a stab wound here,' the resident had said. 'Get a cross match.' But it was too late. Belowdecks it was roaring out, into the staterooms and staircases, putting out the boiler fires, flooding the passages. Flooding everything.

'Give it to me,' Greg said and wrenched the wine bottle out of her hand. He pried the cork out with the point of the knife, clumsily. The wine spilled on the flowered carpet, dark red, soaking into the carpet and her cardigan and Vielle's scrubs.

'We've got a stab wound here,' the resident had said to Vielle, but it wasn't Vielle's blood, it was hers. She sank against the bar, holding her side.

Greg was bending over her, holding the open bottle out. 'Now can we go up to the Boat Deck?' he said.

The boats are all gone, she thought, staring dully at the bottle. There's no way off the ship. 'I'm going,' Greg said, and put the bottle in her helpless hand. 'There have to be boats on the other side. They can't all be gone.'

But they are, Joanna thought, watching him run out. Because I'm the ship that's going down. I'm dying, she thought wonderingly, he killed me before I could tell Richard, and remembered why she had wanted the bottle.

She had wanted to send a message, but it was impossible. The dead couldn't send messages from the Other Side, in spite of what Mr Mandrake said, in spite of Mrs Davenport's psychic telegrams. It was too far. But Joanna stood up and poured the wine out onto the carpet, looking steadily at the dark, spreading stain. She folded the sheet of White Star stationery into narrow pleats and put it in the bottle, tamping the cork down and then prying it out again and putting in the note to Mr Rogers's sister, too.

She climbed back up the aft staircase to the Boat Deck, holding on to the railing with her free hand because the stairs had begun to slant, and walked over to the railing and threw the bottle in, flinging it far out so it wouldn't catch on one of the lower decks, straining to hear the splash. But none came, and though she stood on tiptoe and leaned far out over the rail, peering into the black void, she could not see the water below, or the light from the *Californian*, only darkness.

'SOS,' Joanna murmured. 'SOS.'

41

'Oh, Christ, come quickly!'
— Last words of a FRANCISCAN NUN,
drowned in the wreck of the *Deutschland*

Richard called up the neurotransmitter analysis for Joanna's first session and scanned through the list. No theta-asparcine, and there hadn't been any in any of Mr Sage's NDEs either.

He called up her second session. None there either. Theta-asparcine wasn't an endorphin inhibitor, but it might affect the L+R or the temporal-lobe stimulation. Dr Jamison had said she had a paper on recent theta-asparcine research findings. He wondered if she was back from her errand, whatever it was.

He glanced at his watch. Nearly two. Unless Dr Jamison called in the next fifteen minutes, he wouldn't be able to meet with her until after Mrs Troudtheim's session, and he'd wanted to find out if there was a possibility that it was the theta-asparcine and not the dithetamine dosage that was interrupting Mrs Troudtheim's NDEs.

He called up the third session and stared at the screen, frustrated. There it was, big as life, theta-asparcine, and Joanna had been in the NDE-state for – he checked the exact time – three minutes and eleven seconds.

Which puts me right back at square one, he thought, and there was no point in going through Joanna's other sessions. He called up her and Mrs Troudtheim's analyses again, looking for some other difference he might have missed, but every other neurotransmitter was present in other scans, including the cortisol.

Could the cortisol alone be aborting the NDE-state? It was present in other sessions, but only Amelia Tanaka's had shown similar high levels, and if Mrs Troudtheim's NDE-state threshold was lower, less cortisol might be needed to interfere with the endorphins. He'd ask Dr Jamison.

And where was she? And where was Joanna? Tish would be here any minute to set up, and he had hoped Joanna would come before Tish did, so he could ask her about her most recent account. She'd said she'd experienced a feeling that Mr Briarley was dead, which was obviously another manifestation of the sense of significance, but there had only been midlevel temporal-lobe activation in the area of the Sylvian fissures.

He looked at his watch again. Maybe he should call Dr Jamison. She had said she'd page him when she got back to her office.

He thought, You turned your pager off so Mandrake couldn't page you, and no wonder you haven't heard from Dr Jamison. He pulled the pager out of his lab coat pocket and switched it on. It immediately began to beep. He went over to the phone to call the switchboard.

'Dr Wright!' a voice said from the door, and a young Hispanic woman in pink scrubs burst into the room. 'Are you Dr Wright?' she said, breathing hard and holding her side. There was blood on her scrubs.

'Yes,' he said, slamming down the phone and hurrying over to her. 'What is it? Are you hurt?'

She shook her head. 'I ran –' she said, panting. 'I'm Nina. Nurse Howard – there's an emergency. You've got to come down to the ER.'

Vielle's been hurt, he thought. 'Did Dr Lander send you?'

She shook her head, still trying to catch her breath. 'Dr Lander, she – Nurse Howard sent me. You need to come right away!'

Maisie, he thought. She's coded again. 'Is this about Maisie Nellis?'

'No!' she said, frustrated. 'It's Dr Lander! Nurse Howard said to tell you it's an emergency.'

He gripped her shoulders. 'What about Dr Lander? Is she hurt?' Nina gave a kind of whimper. 'You said the ER?' Richard said and was out the door and over to the elevator, punching and repunching the 'down' button.

'This guy came into the ER,' Nina said, following him, 'and he must have been on rogue because all of a sudden, he pulled a knife –'

Richard punched the elevator button again, again. He glanced up at the floor lights above the door. It was on first. He took off running for the stairs with Nina on his heels, clutching her side. '– and I don't know what happened then,' she said, 'it was all so fast.'

'Is Dr Lander badly hurt?' Richard demanded, plunging down the stairs.

'I don't know. There was all this blood. The security guard shot the guy.'

Down the stairs, through the walkway, across Medicine.

'Nurse Howard said to page you, and I did, but you didn't answer, so then she said go get you. I came as fast as I could, but I went to the wrong wing –'

A metal ladder straddled the hallway, yellow tape barring the way in front of it.

'We can't go this way,' Nina said. Richard burst through the tape and ran under the ladder and down the hall, sidestepping paint buckets and trampling the plastic drops.

'You're not supposed to walk under a ladder,' Nina yammered right behind him. 'It's bad luck.' Into the service stairs, down to first, along the hall. And what if they'd already taken Joanna upstairs to ICU?

He burst through the side door, into the ER. Police everywhere, and the sounds of sirens in the distance, coming closer. Two black officers by the door, another officer talking to a man in pink scrubs, two more kneeling on the floor over by the desk, next to a body.

Not Joanna's, Richard prayed. Not Joanna's. She's in one of the trauma rooms, he thought, and started across the ER. A security guard raised his gun, and a police officer stepped in front of Richard. 'No one's allowed in here.'

'He's Dr Wright. Nurse Howard sent for him,' Nina said. The officer nodded and stepped back, and Nina led the way quickly across the floor and into a trauma room. She pushed open the door.

He didn't know what he'd expected to see. Joanna, sitting on an examining table, having her arm stitched up, turning her head to smile sheepishly at him as he came in. Or noise, activity, nurses hanging bags of blood, inserting tubes, doctors barking orders. And Vielle, stepping away from the examining table to explain Joanna's condition, saying, 'She's going to be fine.'

Not this. Not a dozen people in blood-spattered scrubs, blood-covered gloves, standing back from the table, stunned and silent, none of them saying anything, no sound at all except the flatline whine of the heart monitor.

Not the resident, handing the paddles back to a nurse and shaking his head, and Vielle, clinging to Joanna's limp white hand, saying, her voice rising sobbingly, 'No, she can't be! Hit her again!' Calm, professional Vielle sobbing, 'Do something! Do something!'

The resident pulled his mask down. 'It's no use. We couldn't save her.'

Couldn't save her, Richard thought, and finally, finally looked at Joanna. She lay with her hair fanned out around her head, like Amelia Tanaka's, but her brown hair was matted with blood, and there was blood on her mouth, on her neck, on her chest, blood everywhere. It stood out black-red against her white skin.

An airway had been inserted in her mouth, and there was blood on that, too. Her eyes were open, staring at nothing.

'I brought Dr Wright,' Nina said inanely into the silence, and the resident turned to look at him, his face solemn.

'I am so sorry, Dr Wright,' he said. 'I'm afraid she's gone.'

'Gone,' Richard repeated stupidly. The resident was right. She was gone. The body lying there, with its white, white skin and its unseeing eyes, was empty, abandoned. Joanna had gone.

Gone. Through a tunnel and into the passage, where a golden light shone from under a door. And passengers milled around out on deck in their night-clothes, wondering what had happened. And the mail room was already inches deep in water, the boiler rooms already full, and water was coming in on D Deck, the decks beginning to list, beginning to slant. 'If the boat sinks,' Joanna had said, unseeing behind her sleep mask, reaching blindly for his hand, 'promise you'll come and get me.'

'It's real,' she'd said. 'You don't understand. It's a real place.' A real place, with staircases and writing rooms and gymnasiums. And terror. And a way back, if it wasn't blocked, if he could get to her in time.

'Start CPR,' Richard said, and Vielle let go of Joanna's hand and moved forward as if to comfort him. 'Vielle, don't let them unhook anything!' he said, and, to the others, 'Start CPR. Keep shocking her,' and took off running.

'Richard!' Vielle called after him, but he was already through the door, down the hall, up the stairs. Four minutes. He had four minutes, six at the outside, and why the hell couldn't Mercy General have stairways that went more than two flights, why the hell didn't it have walkways at every floor?

He sprinted across the third-floor walkway, thinking, What's the fastest way up to the lab? Joanna would know. Joanna! He shoved open the doors like a runner breasting a tape and raced through Medicine. Not the elevator. There's no time to wait for an elevator. I have four minutes. Four minutes.

He clattered up the service stairs, rounding the landing. Fourth. It would take at least two minutes for the dithetamine to take effect, even using an IV push. There isn't time, he thought. But once he was under, time wasn't a factor. Joanna had explored the entire ship in eight seconds. Joanna – Fifth. Thirty seconds for Tish to find a vein, another thirty for her to start the IV and inject the dithetamine. What if Tish wasn't there? There was no time to find her, no time to –

He burst through the door to sixth, raced down the hall. Tish had to be there. Mrs Troudtheim's session was scheduled for two. She had to be there. 'Tish!' he shouted and flung open the door to the lab. 'Tish!'

Tish looked up from where she was hanging the bag of saline. 'You need to call the ER. They've been calling every two minutes,' she said. 'And there's a message for you from Dr Lander. You turned your pager off again, didn't –' She stopped when she saw his face. 'What is it? What's wrong?'

'Start an IV,' he said, striding over to the medicine cupboard. 'Saline and dithetamine.'

'But Joanna isn't here,' Tish said. 'I checked her office, and she's not there.'

'She coded,' he said, grabbing a vial of dithetamine and a syringe.

'Joanna coded?' Tish said blankly, coming over to the cupboard. 'What do you mean? Was she in a car accident?'

'She was stabbed,' he said, filling the syringe.

'Stabbed? Is she okay?'

'I told you, she *coded*,' he said. He walked rapidly back to the examining table. 'We're going to have to use an IV push!'

Tish looked at him blankly. 'An IV push? But – how can she go under if she –' she stopped, horrified. 'She didn't *die*, did she, and you're going to record her NDE?'

'She didn't die, and she's not going to,' he said. He wrenched off his lab coat and flung it over a chair. 'Because I'm going after her.'

'I don't understand,' Tish said bewilderedly. 'What do you mean, you're going after her?'

'I mean, I'm going to go get her. I'm going to bring her back.' He rolled up his sleeve.

'But you said the NDEs weren't real,' she said, looking frightened. 'You said they were hallucinations. You said they were caused by the temporal lobe.'

'I said a lot of things,' he said, laying his arm flat on the examining table with the hand palm-up. 'Start an IV.'

'But—'

'*Start the IV*,' he said fiercely, and Tish picked up the length of tubing and wrapped it around his upper arm. He made a fist, and she began probing for a vein.

'Hurry!' he said. 'We've only got four minutes.' Tish pushed the needle in, clipped it to the IV line, adjusted the feed. She began taping down the needle. 'You can do that later,' he snapped. 'Start the dithetamine. IV push.'

'Dr Wright, I don't think it's a good idea to do this while you're so upset,' Tish said. 'Why don't I call Dr Everett or somebody, and—'

'Because there's no time,' Richard said. 'Never mind. I'll do it myself.' He grabbed the syringe with his free hand and injected it into the line. 'Start the white noise,' he said and reached for the headphones.

'Dr Wright –' Tish said uncertainly and then went over to the amplifier.

Richard picked up the headphones and looked around for the sleep mask. He couldn't see it anywhere, and there was no time to look for it. He put on the headphones and lay down. 'Put the cushions under my arms and legs,' he said, unable to tell if Tish could hear him. He couldn't hear anything through the headphones. 'Put the –' he began, but she must have heard him. She was lifting his left arm and sliding the cushion under it and then under the other.

She placed the cushions under his legs and then wrapped a blood pressure cuff around his arm. 'Don't bother with that,' Richard said, but Tish wasn't listening to him. She was putting electrodes to his scalp.

'I don't need an EEG,' he said, but she didn't look up, he was trying to talk to the top of her head. 'Tish!' he shouted, and realized he was too far away for her to hear him. He was above her, above the examining table on which he lay, his arm hooked to an IV. He was drifting slowly up to the ceiling. He looked across to the top of the medicine cupboard. It was polished and bare, except for a glint of silver at the very back. He drifted closer, trying to see.

The silver object was tucked all the way back in the corner, where Joanna had put it, behind the raised edge of the cupboard. Out of sight except for someone having an out-of-body experience. He drifted still closer. It was a toy tin zeppelin.

Of course, he thought. The *Hindenburg*. I'll have to tell Joanna I saw it. But she wouldn't believe him. She would think he had climbed up on a chair to see what it was. Joanna would –

'Joanna!' he said, abruptly remembering. This was an out-of-body experience. But there wasn't any time for it. 'Send me through!' he shouted down to Tish. 'Send me into the tunnel!'

He continued to float slowly upward, wafting slowly back and forth, like the *Hindenburg* drifting in its moorings. 'Hurry!' he shouted, and looked down at Tish. She had found the sleep mask and was placing it over his eyes. He lay stiffly under the RIPT scan, his hands clenched tightly at his sides.

'Let go!' he shouted. The noise echoed loudly, reverberating as if he were in an enclosed space, and then stopped, and everything went dark.

I'm in the passage, he thought. He put out his hand in the pitch blackness and felt hardness, paint. The wall of the passage. There should be a light at the end of it, he thought, straining to see. Nothing. No light at all. It must be very late, after the lights had gone out. When had they gone out? Only a few minutes before the end.

It's because she's going down, he thought. Because there are only four minutes left. 'Joanna!' he called. 'Where are you?'

There was no answer. He fumbled for a book of matches in his lab coat pockets, but they were empty. He reached in his pants pocket. The pager. He drew it out. It was turned off. He fumbled for the switch in the darkness and turned it on. The face lit up – Joanna's number – but the LED numbers gave no light.

He began to grope his way along the corridor, feeling his way with a hand on each wall, trying to hurry. Because there's no time. But if it were that late, then the ship should be at a sharp angle, so tilted that he'd be having trouble standing, and he wasn't. The floor felt perfectly level.

'Joanna!' he called again, and saw a light ahead of him. It was a thin line of white, from under a door, and that must be what he had heard – the sound of the door slamming shut. He groped his way toward the door and felt for the doorknob, thinking, Don't let it be locked, don't let it be locked. He found the rectangular metal plate, found the knob, turned it. And opened the door onto another corridor. A brightly lit corridor, so bright it was almost blinding, and he shielded his eyes and stood there, blinking.

This wasn't the passage Joanna had come through. Hers had opened onto the outside, onto a window-lined deck. This was an inside passage, with a series of shut doors and light sconces on the walls between them. The lights had not gone out. They shone strongly all along the corridor, and the wooden floor was dry and perfectly level. It must be much earlier, before anyone realized it was sinking, and maybe the sound he'd heard was the same one Joanna had heard – the iceberg scraping along the side – and it had sounded different because he was in a different part of the ship.

Which part? Second class? The brass light sconces were elaborate enough for it to be first class, but the walls were unadorned, and there were no windows, no portholes. It must be an interior corridor, or belowdecks. Steerage?

Where *was* it? On C Deck, she had said. But where was C Deck? Above this? Below it? Did they count the decks down from the top or up from the bottom?

He remembered Joanna talking about climbing up to the Boat Deck. How many decks had she said she'd climbed? He couldn't remember. I should have paid more attention, he thought, starting down the passage at a run. I should have listened to her when she said it was real.

Because it was real. She had tried to tell him. She had said she saw colors, heard sounds, felt staircase railings under her hand, had tried to describe the reality of the ship, but he had been convinced it was a hallucination, that it was something happening in long-term memory and the temporal lobe, even when she'd tried to tell him, even when she'd said, 'It's a real place.'

I should have listened to her, he thought, looking for a stairway, or a door to the outside. I should have told her where I was going. I shouldn't have turned off my pager.

All the doors were shut, locked. 'Hey!' he shouted, banging on them, rattling the old-fashioned knobs. 'Anybody there?'

The third door opened under his hand. Inside, a man wearing headphones was sitting bent over a wireless key, listening. Dot-dash-dot-dot, he wrote on a pad. 'Hey!' Richard said. 'How do I get to C Deck?'

The man didn't look up.

'C Deck,' Richard said, coming to stand over him. 'Which deck is this I'm on now?'

The man went on writing, his face intent on the key, dash-dash-dot-dash-dot-dot-dot –

SOS, Richard thought. Of course. He's calling for help. When had they sent the first SOS? Not until after midnight.

'What time is it?' Richard asked him loudly. 'How long have you been sending?'

A gray-haired woman appeared in the door, in a high-collared blouse and a long black skirt. 'You're not supposed to be here,' she said, her hand on the doorjamb.

'I'm looking for—'

'How did you get in here?' she interrupted sternly. 'Unauthorized persons are not allowed in this part of—'

'I'm looking for Joanna Lander,' he said. 'I have to find her.'

'Yes, sir, I know, sir,' she said, leading him out of the wireless room, 'but this part of—'

'You don't understand. It's urgent. She's in danger. She'd be on C Deck. Or on the Boat Deck –'

'I know, sir,' she said, and her voice had, surprisingly, softened. 'If you'll just come with me, sir.' She led him back down the passage the way they'd come, her hand gently on his arm.

'Her passage is on C Deck,' he said. 'It opens onto the deck.'

'Yes, sir.' She opened a door and led him down a flight of stairs.

'She's about five foot six,' he said. 'Brown hair, glasses. She was wearing a cardigan sweater and –' He stopped. He didn't know what else. A skirt? Pants? He tried to envision the heap of clothes at the end of the table, but he couldn't tell what they were for the blood, the blood. 'I have to find her immediately.'

'Yes, sir,' she said, and continued to walk slowly, sedately down the corridor.

'You don't understand!' he said. 'It's urgent! She—'

'I understand that you're upset, sir,' she said, but didn't quicken her pace.

'She's in danger!'

The woman nodded and walked him slowly down the hall and around a corner.

Bong! He looked up, alarmed. It was a clock, a large wooden wall clock with Roman numerals and a pendulum. A quarter to two. And the *Titanic* had gone down at 2:20.

'You don't understand!' he said, clutching the woman's arms and shaking her. 'There's no *time*! I have to find her and get her off. Just tell me how to get to C Deck!'

Her eyes widened and filled with tears. 'If you'll just come this way, sir,' she said pleadingly. '*Please*, sir.'

'There's no time!' he said. 'I'll find her myself!' and ran down the passage and through the door at the end of it. And into a mass of jostling, gesturing people.

The Boat Deck, he thought, but this was an inside room, too, with large double doors along one side. Everyone was pushing toward those doors. The Boat Deck must lie beyond them, and they were waiting here for their chance to board. He stretched his neck, trying to see over the top hats of the men, the feathered hats of the women, looking for Joanna's bare head. He couldn't see her.

Joanna had said the passengers out on the deck had had no idea what was happening, but these people obviously did. They looked frightened, the men's faces strained and worried, the women's eyes rimmed with red. A young girl clung to an elderly man, sobbing helplessly into a black-edged handkerchief. 'There, there,' the old man said. 'We must not give up hope.' Did that mean all the boats were already gone? When had they launched the last one? Not until the very end, Joanna had said, but it couldn't be the very end. The deck wasn't slanting at all.

If he could get through the crowd. He pushed forward, looking for Joanna, craning his neck, trying to see over the sea of hats, trying to move forward, but the crowd was packed in tightly, and as he tried to push in, they blocked his way.

'Excuse me,' he said, shoving past a young man in a brown coat and hat. He had a newspaper under his arm. At a time like this, Richard thought. 'I have to get through. I'm looking for someone.'

'What was her name?' the young man asked, taking a leather notebook out of his pocket. 'Was she traveling first class?'

'She's on C Deck.'

'C Deck,' the young man said, jotting it down. 'Traveling alone?'

'Yes,' Richard said. 'Traveling alone.'

'Name?' he asked, taking more notes.

'Joanna Lander,' he said. 'Please. I have to get through. I have to find her.'

'She may very well have gotten into one of the boats,' the young man said.

'No,' Richard said. 'She can't get out that way. She has to go back down to C Deck to the passage,' but the young man wasn't listening. He had looked up toward the double doors. So had everyone else. The double doors opened, and someone must have come through because everyone looked at the doors expectantly. A hush fell, and the young girl who had been sobbing straight-ened up and clutched the elderly man's hand.

Richard pushed forward, elbowing his way past a middle-aged couple, a young woman with a baby, two teenaged boys, till he could see the man who'd emerged from the doors. He wore spectacles and was wearing a black frock coat and a black vest. He was carrying a sheaf of papers. He stepped up onto something – a dais? – and raised his hands to quiet the already quiet crowd. Who was this? The captain? One of the officers? Then why wasn't he in uniform?

'I know you are all anxious for news,' the man said, putting on the pincenez. 'We do not as yet have a full list of survivors.'

What?

'We are currently in wireless contact with the *Carpathia*, and as soon as we have a complete list—'

'No!' Richard said.

'Get hold of yourself,' the young man said, grasping his shoulder. 'She may have been in one of the boats.'

'No!' Richard yelled. He wrenched the newspaper out from under the young man's arm and yanked it open. '*Titanic* Lost,' it said. 'A thousand souls feared drowned.'

He pushed forward to the spectacled man in the black frock coat. 'What day is this?' he asked furiously. The gray-haired woman was headed toward him, a man with a medical bag behind her. Richard grabbed the spectacled man's black lapels. 'What *day* is this?'

'April eighteenth,' the man said nervously. 'I can assure you the White Star Line deeply regrets—'

'Sir,' the gray-haired woman said, and the man with the medical bag took his arm. 'You're distraught. I think perhaps you'd better lie down.'

'No!' he shouted, and it was a roar, a scream. '*No!*'

The doctor reached for his arm, and he leaped away through the crowd, shoving at their shoulders, pushing them out of his way. He thrust his way toward the door and through it and took off running down the corridor. Four minutes. And how much time, how much time had he wasted already, he thought as he ran, his heart pounding, too stupid to know where he was, to see that this was the White Star Line offices?

The clock at the foot of the stairs was striking the hour. Richard ran past it and started up the stairs, and an alarm went off somewhere, like a fire bell or a code alarm, clanging, buzzing, over the clock, still striking the hour.

He raced up the rest of the stairs, past the room where the wireless oper-ator sat, taking down the incoming taps of the key. From the *Carpathia*, not the *Titanic*. He should have seen that, should have known the *Titanic* would be sending, not receiving, and that the Marconi room was on the wrong deck. Should have seen instantly that this was a building, not a ship, and gone back, made Tish send him under again.

He rounded the corner, panting, and raced for the door, grabbed the doorknob, twisted it. It was locked. He rattled the doorknob, kicked at the door, hit at it with his fist.

It opened, and he burst through it into the dark corridor. And into the lab.

'Tish!' he called, yanking to get the headphones off, but there weren't any headphones. And no sleep mask, because he could see the light. It was killingly bright. I should have covered it with thicker black paper, he thought, and tried to sit up. He couldn't. He was bound with ropes. 'Tish!'

'Oh, Dr Wright!' Tish said, coming between him and the light. She was haloed in it and rays of dazzling light seemed to come from her. 'Thank God you're all right!'

'You have to send me under again,' he said. 'It was the wrong place, and the wrong time. She wasn't there.'

'Just lie still,' Tish said.

'You don't understand,' he said, and tried to sit up again. 'She's on the *Titanic*! I have to go get her before it goes down!'

'There, there,' Tish said, pushing him back down. 'You're still under the influence of the drug. You need to lie still until it wears off.'

'There's no time,' he said. 'Irreversible brain death occurs in four to six minutes. You have to send me back right now. And up the dosage of dithetamine.'

Tish just stood there, haloed in light.

'Now! Before it's too late!' he shouted, and saw that she was clutching a black-edged handkerchief, too, and her eyes were red-rimmed.

I'm not really back in the lab, he thought. This is still part of the NDE, and twisted around to see where the passage was.

'Don't, Dr Wright, you'll pull out your IV,' Tish said. 'You're still on a saline drip. When you didn't come out, I stopped the dithetamine –' She reached for the site.

He clapped a hand over the IV. 'Restart it now!' he shouted, and managed, finally, to heave himself to a sitting position. They had not been ropes, they were electrodes, hooked up to the EEG and EKG monitors, and this *was* the lab. The handkerchief Tish was holding was a sodden Kleenex.

'*Now*, Tish!' he shouted, 'or I'll do it myself!' but he had sat up too fast, he felt dizzy and cold. 'Tish, please! You don't understand. We're nearly out of time! You have to send me back under before it's too late!'

But she just stood there, haloed in light, turning the lump of tissue over and over in her hands. 'But you still didn't come out, even after I stopped the dithetamine, and I didn't know whether to administer norepinephrine or not. Your vitals were normal, and that one time Mr Sage was under for –'

He turned sharply and looked at the clock, but Joanna had moved it so it couldn't be seen from the far wall. 'Tish,' he said, 'how long was I under?' and waited with dread for the answer.

'I am so sorry, Dr Wright. Mrs Troudtheim told me when she came ...' She twisted the sodden Kleenex in her hands. 'She was so upset. We all loved Dr Lander—'

'How long was I under?' he repeated dully.

'I don't know. I can't read the scans, so I didn't know if you were in the NDE-state or if you'd come out and were in non-REM sleep –'

'How long was I under, Tish?' he said, but he already knew the answer. He had heard the clock striking in the corridor of the White Star Line offices, chiming the hours. 'Tell me.'

'Two hours,' Tish said, and started to cry.

PART 3

'There's another act coming after this. I reckon you can guess what that's about.'

– THORNTON WILDER, *Our Town*

42

'Nobody has heard the *Titanic* for about two hours.'
– Wireless message from the *La Provence* to the *Celtic*

That night Richard had gone back to his lab – even though work was impossible, unthinkable – because the police had said they might want him to make a statement and because he couldn't think of anywhere else to go. The ER had been cordoned off into a crime scene, with all the emergency patients shunted off to Swedish and St Luke's, and the doctors' lounge and the hallways and the cafeteria were full of people asking him, 'How are you holding up?' and, 'Where the hell were the security guards? I've been saying for the last three years that ER was an accident waiting to happen. Why didn't they have a metal detector?' and, 'Have they determined the cause of death?' All questions he had no idea how to answer.

She died of drowning, he wanted to tell them. She went down on the *Titanic*.

At one point – the first night? the next day? – he had gone down to the morgue. 'Oh, man, I'm sorry,' the attendant had said, shamefaced. 'They took her over to University.'

For the autopsy, Richard thought. When a crime was involved, they didn't do it at Mercy General. They sent the body over to the forensic pathologist at University Hospital.

'Maybe you could ...' the attendant began. Go over there, Richard thought, but the attendant didn't finish, and Richard knew he was sorry he'd spoken, that he was thinking of the Y-shaped incision in the chest, the ribs and breastbone removed, the heart pulled out, weighed, dissected. Joanna's heart.

'It's all right,' Richard said. 'I just wanted –'

Wanted – what? To convince himself that she was safely there, swathed in a plastic sheet in a metal drawer, safely dead. Instead of still on the *Titanic*, clinging to the railing on the slanting deck, waiting to drown.

'Why don't you go home and try to get some sleep, Dr Wright?' the attendant had said gently, and Richard had nodded and turned, and then just stood there stupidly, staring at the wall.

'How do I get out of here?' he had said finally.

'You go down this hall and take a right,' the attendant had said, pointing, and it was like a knife going in. You take that hallway down. There's a stairway.

You take the stairs up to seventh and go across the walkway to Surgery. Joanna, pointing. There's a hall on the right. You take that to the elevators and that'll take you down to Personnel. Him, disbelieving. Isn't there a shortcut I could take? Joanna, laughing, That *is* the shortcut.

The attendant had taken his arm. 'Here, I'll walk you up,' he said. He had led him back up to the first floor, supporting Richard's arm as if Richard were an old woman, down a hall and up a stairway and into the lobby.

And it must have been during the day because Mr Wojakowski was there, waiting for the elevator, his freckled face beaming. 'Mornin', Doc,' he'd said, bustling over to them. 'Say, did Joanna Lander ever find you?'

Beside him, the attendant gasped, his grip tightening on Richard's arm, but Mr Wojakowski, oblivious, swept on. 'I saw her up in Medicine,' he said, 'and she was – Say,' he said, looking at the attendant and then back at Richard, 'say, Doc, are you okay?'

The attendant pulled him off to one side, whispering, and Richard watched his face go white and abruptly old, the freckles standing out starkly against his skin. 'Hell, if I'd known, I wouldn't of – How'd it happen?'

The attendant whispered some more, and the elevator opened on emptiness. Richard stared into it.

'I want to tell him I didn't have any idea –' Mr Wojakowski said, looking anxiously in Richard's direction.

'Not now,' the attendant said and led Mr Wojakowski by the arm into the elevator, and then stood there like a bouncer, arms folded, till it closed.

He came back over to Richard. 'Are you okay, Dr Wright?' he said, taking possession of Richard's arm again. 'Do you want me to call somebody?'

Yes, Richard thought. The *Carpathia*. The *Californian*. But their wireless is turned off. The captain's gone to bed.

'You're sure there's nobody I can call? Girlfriend? Somebody you work with?'

'No.'

'Well, I don't think it's a good idea for you to be driving right now, man,' he'd said. 'Is there someplace here you could lie down?'

'Yes,' Richard had said, and gone back up to the lab. He'd slept on the floor, wrapped in the blanket he'd covered Amelia Tanaka, covered Joanna with, his pager next to him, turned on, as if it were not too late, as if what had happened were somehow reversible.

He wondered if the wireless operator on the *Californian* had done that, leaning endlessly over the key, headphones on, listening for other messages, hoping for a second chance. Or if, after two days, the operator had switched it off again, the way he did, unable to stand the questions, the condolences.

The resident who'd tried to save Joanna had called, and three reporters, and Tish. 'I've decided to go back to Medicine,' she said. 'In light of everything that's happened ... I've put in a formal transfer request. I'll need your signature.'

In light of everything that's happened.

'I'll be glad to show my replacement the lab procedures, of course.' She hesitated. 'I haven't told anybody about ... I don't want to get you in trouble with the hospital for going under like that. I wouldn't want you to lose your funding, and I know you reacted out of panic and weren't responsible for what you were doing –'

Responsible. I left Joanna on the *Titanic*, he thought, I left Joanna to drown.

'Dr Wright?' Tish was saying. 'Are you still there?'

'Yes.'

'I think it might be a good idea for you to talk to somebody,' she said. 'There's a really good doctor on staff here. Dr Ainsworth. She's a psychiatrist who specializes in cases like this.'

Like what? he wondered. Cases of abandonment? Of betrayal? He thought of Tish, standing over him, tears running down her mascara-stained cheeks. 'I'm sorry I frightened you,' he said into the phone.

'I know,' Tish said, and her voice quavered. 'I couldn't bring you out of it ...' Her voice broke. 'I thought you were dead.'

'Tish,' he said, but she'd recovered herself.

'Dr Ainsworth's extension is 308,' she said steadily. 'She specializes in post-traumatic stress disorders. I really think you should call her.'

Richard lasted two days with the pager on. Carla from Oncology called to tell him about a wonderful book called *Dealing with Tragedy in the Work-place*, and Dr Ainsworth, and a police officer. 'I just need to ask you a few questions,' he said. 'Just for the record. Were you there when the incident occurred?'

'No,' Richard said, 'I wasn't there.' I was in the White Star offices in New York, too stupid to tell the difference between an office building and a ship, too late to be of any use.

'Oh, sorry,' the police officer said. 'I'd been told you witnessed the murder.'

'No,' Richard said.

The officer hung up, and Richard unplugged the phone. And turned his pager off. But that only made it worse. When they couldn't get him on the phone, they came. Eileen from Medicine, to bring him a wonderful book called *The Healing Help Book*, and Maureen from Radiology with *Nine Steps to Recovering from Personal Tragedy*, and Dr Jamison.

She had a book, too. *The Idiots' Guide to Mourning*? Richard wondered, but it was a medical journal. 'This is that study I called you about,' she said. 'I've found concentrating on your work is the best way to get through a loss.' She tried to hand him the journal. 'It's the article by Barstow and Skal. They did a study of aspartate endorphins, and theta-asparcine—'

'The project's canceled.'

Her face went maddeningly sympathetic. 'I understand how you feel, but in a week or two –'

She left the journal on the desk. Richard shut the door behind her, but that didn't stop anyone either. Tara from Ob-Gyn knocked timidly and then opened the door as if he were one of her patients, and the resident who'd been on duty in the ER didn't knock at all.

'I thought you'd want to know the results of the autopsy,' and Richard wondered for one long, awful moment if he would say, 'They found water in her lungs.'

'The cause of death was acute hemorrhage leading to hypovolemic shock,' the resident said. 'It was just bad luck that the knife happened to hit the aorta. Ninety-nine times out of a hundred, the knife would have hit a rib, or, at the very worst, punctured a lung. Talk about being in the wrong place at the wrong time.'

He flipped up a sheet. 'She bled out in under two minutes. There wasn't anything anybody could've done.' I could have kept my pager on, Richard thought. I could have gone under two minutes earlier. In time to make it to the *Titanic*.

'We got the results on Calinga, too,' he said.

Calinga? That must be the teenager. He'd never heard his name.

'Enough rogue to kill an elephant.' The resident shook his head. 'Sixteen years old.' He slapped the file shut. 'Well, anyway, I thought you'd want to know Dr Lander didn't suffer.' He started for the door. 'She would have lost consciousness in under a minute. She probably didn't even have time to realize what had happened.'

That afternoon Vielle came up. 'I came …' she said and then hesitated.

'To bring me a copy of *The Dummies' Guide to Grieving*?' Richard said bitterly.

'I know,' she said. 'Dr Chaffey gave me a copy of *Coping with the Death of a Colleague*. A colleague!' She looked like she hadn't been home either. She was still wearing the same rumpled dark blue scrubs and surgical cap. Her eyes were red and swollen, with maroon smudges under them, like bruises, and her hand and her arm were both bandaged. 'You keep thinking it can't get any worse, and then it does,' she said.

'I know,' he said and pulled out a chair for her.

She sank down onto it. 'I came because … I keep seeing her there in the ER, I keep thinking about what she must have been going through those last few … There was this guy in the ER who'd had a myocardial infarction. Joanna interviewed him, and right before he died, he said, 'Too far away for her to come,' and Joanna said he was trying to tell her something, she kept talking about it, and then she …' She looked up at Richard. 'I know this'll sound like I'm crazy, and I guess I am a little. I keep seeing her running up to me and him whirling around, and the knife –' she said, and he realized that, rumpled as they were, they couldn't be the same scrubs. Those were covered with blood.

'I just stood there,' Vielle said, staring blindly ahead of her. 'I didn't do *any-thing*. I should have—'

'What?' Richard said. 'Tried to stop him? He was on rogue.'

'I could have warned her,' she said. 'If I'd shouted at her, told her not to come any closer … I didn't even see her till she was right next to him. I was looking at the knife he was holding, and by the time I saw her … she just walked right into it.'

And why didn't she see what was going on? he wondered. Why hadn't she noticed the charged silence, the frightened expressions on their faces?

Vielle blew her nose. 'Anyway, I keep going over everything in my mind, what she … and I have to ask you, even if it does sound crazy. When Joanna underwent the NDE experiments, what did she see?'

He stared at her.

'Did she see the *Titanic*?' she asked, and before he could answer, she rushed on tearfully, 'The reason I'm asking is, she asked me all these questions about the movie, about this one scene, and when I asked her why we didn't just rent it and watch it again, she said she couldn't, and then yesterday Kit told me Joanna was having her do all this research on the *Titanic*, and she'd seemed so preoccupied and worried these last few weeks … Is that what she saw in her NDE? The *Titanic*?'

'Yes,' he said, and watched her face go rigid with horror.

'I knew it,' she whispered. 'Oh, God, I just stood there. I—'

'It wasn't your fault,' he said. 'It was mine.'

'You don't understand,' she said, anguished. 'She wanted me to transfer up to Peds.' She stood up. 'She said the ER was dangerous. Dangerous!'

He reached for her hand. 'Vielle, listen to me. It wasn't your fault. I had my pager turned off. I –'

She shook his hand off angrily. 'She wouldn't even have been in the ER if I'd listened to her. She came down there to talk to me about Dish Night, about a stupid *movie*!' she said, and flung herself out of the room and down the hall.

'Vielle, wait!' he said and started after her, but she'd already disappeared into the elevator.

He punched the 'down' button impatiently, and the other elevator opened.

'Oh, good,' a middle-aged woman in a green dress said. 'I was coming to see you. I'm Sally Zimmerman from Surgery. I just wanted to drop this by.' She held out a book. The orange-and-yellow cover read *Eight Great Grief Helps*. 'It's really helpful,' she said. 'It has all kinds of mourning exercises and closure activities.'

'You keep thinking it can't get any worse,' Richard murmured.

'That's in there, too,' she said, taking the book back from him and thumbing through it. 'Here it is. "How to Raise Your Hope Quotient."'

The next day Mr Wojakowski came. 'I'm sorry I went on about Joanna like that,' he said. 'Nobody'd told me what happened.' He shook his head. 'Gone just like that! You never get used to it. One minute they're standing next to you on the gunnery deck and the next, gone! Bucky Tobias, my bunkmate. Nineteen years old. "Think the Japs know where we are?" he said to me, and ten seconds later, wham! half the deck's gone and nothing left! I heard he was on drugs,' he said, and for a moment Richard thought he was talking about his bunkmate on the *Yorktown*.

'Sixteen years old,' Mr Wojakowski said. 'Damned waste. I still can't believe it.' He shook his head. 'I just saw her that day up in Medicine looking for you.'

'Looking for me?' Richard said and felt a pain in his side, like a knife going in.

'Yeah, and whatever it was she was trying to find you for, it musta been important. She practically ran me over. "Did somebody call battle stations?" I asked her, she was movin' so fast.'

'When was this?' Richard demanded.

'Monday morning. I was over here seeing a friend of mine – had a stroke square dancing – after I did my hearing-research-sitting-around.'

'What time did you see her?'

'Let's see,' he said, scratching his cheek, 'Musta been around thirteen hundred hours. I came up right after I was done in the arthritis center, and that goes from eleven to twelve forty-five.'

One o'clock, Richard thought. She must have been on her way down to the ER. 'And she told you she was looking for me?'

'Yeah, she said she had to find you right away, so she didn't have time to talk.'

Joanna hadn't been looking for Vielle. She had been looking for him. He had to tell her, so she wouldn't go on thinking it was her fault. It was the least he could do.

'Just wanted you to know how bad I feel,' Mr Wojakowski said, picking up his hat. 'She was a great little gal. Reminded me of a navy nurse I dated in Honolulu. Pretty as a picture. Killed off Tarawa. Japs sank the transport she was being shipped home on.'

As soon as Mr Wojakowski left, he plugged in the phone and called the ER. Vielle wasn't there. He had her paged, and then sat there by the phone, waiting for her to call. She didn't, but Mrs Brightman did. And his old roommate.

'I was just watching CNN,' Davis said, without preamble. 'What the hell kind of hospital are you working in? Did you know this Lander person?'

'Yes,' Richard said.

'But you're all right?' Davis asked, and it was more a statement than a question.

Richard wondered what Davis would say if he said, 'No.' If he said, 'The NDEs aren't temporal-lobe hallucinations. They're real.' He already knew. 'You can't seriously believe that!' And 'First Foxx and now you? I *knew* it was a virus!' and 'Have you called the *Star* yet? Make them pay you for an exclusive, at least. You're going to need the money now that you're going to be out of a job.'

'I'm all right,' Richard said.

'You're sure?' Davis asked, and sounded really concerned.

'Yes,' Richard said, and went down to the ER to talk to Vielle. The crime scene tape had been removed, but there were cops at all the doors. They checked Richard's ID badge against a computer list before they let him in. Vielle was at the station desk, writing up a chart with her bandaged hand.

'It wasn't your fault,' he said. 'She wasn't looking for you that day to ask you about Dish Night. She was looking for me.'

'For you?' she said blankly. 'But you weren't—'

'I'd told her I was going to go talk to Dr Jamison.'

'And Dr Jamison had just been down here,' she said, and he could see the relief in her face, as if a load had been lifted off her.

'When she asked you about the movie *Titanic*, did she say what she was trying to –' he said, and saw she wasn't listening. She had glanced up, toward the door, and gone suddenly stock-still. He looked over at the door.

Joanna was standing in it. Richard's heart began to beat frantically, like a trapped bird battering its wings against the bars. She wasn't dead. It was all, all, the blood and the flatline and the White Star Line offices, a dream, it had only felt real because of elevated acetylcholine levels and temporal-lobe stimulation.

'Joanna,' he breathed, and took a step toward her.

'I'm June Wexler, Joanna Lander's sister,' the woman at the door said, and it was like hearing the news all over again. She's dead, he thought, and finally believed it. She's been dead three days.

'I'm glad I found the two of you together,' Joanna's sister said, pushing her glasses up on her nose. 'I understand you both worked with Joanna. I was wondering if I could talk to you about her.'

Her voice sounded like Joanna's, too, but somehow harsher. That's from crying, he thought, looking at her reddened eyes, the Kleenex in her hands.

'I hadn't talked to her in several months, and ...' She dabbed at her eyes with a Kleenex. 'We always think there'll be plenty of time, and then suddenly there isn't any time at all ... I was wondering if you knew whether she had been saved?' she said, and Richard wondered if she had somehow found out that he'd gone after her and failed.

'Saved?' Vielle said.

'Accepted the Lord Jesus Christ as her personal savior,' Joanna's sister said.

'I'd tried several times to bring her to the Lord, but each time Satan hardened her heart against me.'

'Satan,' Vielle said.

'Yes. I tried to witness to her, to tell her of the destruction that awaits the unrepentant, of God's judgment and the fire that shall never be quenched.' She dabbed at her eyes again.

Richard gazed at her. She didn't look like Joanna at all. It was only a trick of hair color, of the glasses.

'I continued to pray that, in working with you,' she said to Richard, 'and in speaking with people who had seen Christ face to face, she might come to believe.'

Richard realized after a moment that she was talking about near-death experiences.

'Did she?' she asked. 'Tell you that she had been saved?'

'No,' Vielle snapped.

'And you're sure she didn't change her mind at the last minute?' She turned to Vielle. 'They told me you were with her when she died. Did she say anything?'

Richard expected her to say 'no' again, but instead she hesitated a fraction of a second before she said, 'The knife slashed the aorta. Joanna lost consciousness almost immediately.'

'But even if it was in the last second,' Joanna's sister said. 'It's never too late for Jesus to forgive you for your sins, even if it's with your last breath that you beg that forgiveness. Did she?' Joanna's sister said eagerly. 'Say anything?'

'No,' Vielle said.

She's lying, Richard thought. She did say something.

'Are you sure?' Joanna's sister persisted. 'I've read about near-death experiences. I know they see Jesus waiting to welcome them into heaven, and "they that have seen have believed." Surely even Joanna's heart wasn't so hardened that she wouldn't repent when she saw the fate that awaited her.'

'I'm sure,' Vielle said stonily. 'She didn't say anything.'

'Then there's no hope,' Joanna's sister said, dabbing at her eyes, 'and she is in hell.'

'Joanna?' Vielle said, outraged. 'How dare you –!'

'It is not I who have condemned her, but God,' Joanna's sister said. 'For is it not written, "But they that do not believe shall be cast into outer darkness, and there will be weeping and gnashing of teeth"?'

'Get out,' Vielle said.

Joanna's sister looked at Richard, as if expecting support. He wondered how he could have ever thought she looked like Joanna. 'I will pray for you both,' she said, and walked away.

'Don't you *dare*,' Vielle shouted after her, and one of the police officers over by the door looked up alertly. 'You *arrogant, wicked*, holier-than-thou—'

'What did Joanna say?' Richard cut in.

Vielle turned and looked at him, the anger dying out of her face. 'Richard –'

'She *did* say something, didn't she? What?'

'I can't believe she'd come in here like that,' Vielle said. 'That bitch! I'll tell you who the Lord casts into outer darkness. So-called Christians like her.'

'What did Joanna say?'

'Joanna told me she and her sister weren't all that close,' Vielle said, walking over to the station. 'Light-years apart is more like it.' She picked up a chart. 'How sweet, kind, sensible Joanna could even *have* a sister like that is beyond—'

Richard caught her arm. 'What did she say?'

'Look, I've got patients to see. We're completely behind.'

'It's what you came up to the lab to see me about, isn't it? You said the guy who coded said, "Too far away to come," and that you'd been thinking about what she must have been going through those last moments. It was because of what Joanna said, wasn't it?' He gripped her arm. *'What did she say?'*

The police officer at the door started toward them, his hand on his gun.

'Richard –'

'It's important. Tell me.'

'She said, "Tell Richard –"' She paused, looking down at the chart.

Richard waited, afraid to speak.

She stared blindly down at the chart, and then looked up again, looking like Tish had in the lab. '"Tell Richard it's,"' she said, and swallowed hard, '"SOS. SOS."'

43

'For God's sake, take care of our people …'
— Last entry in ROBERT FALCON SCOTT's diary,
found with his body in the Antarctic

'Did you *page* Joanna?' Maisie asked her mother.

'Yes,' her mother said, busily straightening the things on Maisie's bed tray. 'Would you like some juice? Or a Popsicle?'

'*When* did you page her? Yesterday?'

'She probably has lots of things to do. How about some Jell-O?'

'She said she was coming on Thursday, and she didn't come Thursday *or* yesterday,' Maisie persisted. 'Are you *sure* Nurse Barbara paged her?'

'I'm sure,' her mother said, taking the top off the water pitcher and peering in. 'Guess who Nurse Barbara said's supposed to come and visit the floor tomorrow afternoon? A clown!'

'Like Emmett Kelly?' Maisie said, perking up.

'Emmett Kelly?' her mother said, surprised. 'Now, how do you know about Emmett Kelly?'

'He was in one of my videos,' Maisie said. 'One of the Disney ones. I don't remember which one. About the circus.'

'This clown does magic tricks,' her mother said. 'Won't that be fun?'

'Dr Lander told me about this clown who pulled a handkerchief out of his pocket, and it was hooked to another one and another one and another one,' Maisie said. 'Maybe she got busy and forgot. Maybe you need to call her.'

'If she's busy, we shouldn't bother her. Look, I brought you some new videos. *The Best Summer* and *The Parent Trap*. Which one would you like to watch?'

'She always comes when she says she will,' Maisie said. 'Even if she's really busy. Maybe she's sick. Nurse Amy was out with the flu.'

'You're supposed to be thinking positive thoughts, not worrying,' her mother said, putting *The Best Summer* in the VCR. 'Remember what Dr Murrow said. You've got to work on getting ready for your new heart.' She switched on the TV, picked up Maisie's water pitcher, and took it over to the sink. 'Which means no worrying.' She dumped the water and ice rattlingly into the sink and started for the door, holding the pitcher. 'I'll be right back. I'm going to ask them for some ice.'

'Ask them if they paged her,' Maisie called after her. 'Tell them I found out the stuff she asked me to.'

Her mother stopped halfway out the door. 'What stuff?'

'Just some stuff we were talking about when she came to see me.'

'It's very nice of the hospital staff to come visit you, but you have to remember they have jobs, and those have to come first.'

'But this was about her job,' Maisie started to say, but if she did, her mother would want to know what Joanna had asked her, so she didn't. She just said, 'Ask them if they paged her,' and when her mother came back in, carrying the pitcher and a can of juice, she said, 'Did you ask them?'

'Look, pineapple juice,' her mother said, popping the tab on the can of juice and holding it out to her. 'Your favorite.'

'Did you?' Maisie asked.

'Yes,' her mother said, setting the juice down on Maisie's bedtable. 'The nurses said she got a new job, and she moved. Do you want a straw?'

'*Where* did she move?'

'I don't know,' her mother said, unwrapping the straw.

'She wouldn't move without telling me,' Maisie said.

'She probably didn't have time. The nurses said she had to start her job right away.' She handed Maisie her juice. 'They told me she said to tell you good-bye, and that she wanted you to think happy thoughts and do what Dr Murrow tells you.' She turned up the TV. 'Now rest and watch your movie. It's about a little girl who's getting well. Just like you.' She handed Maisie the remote. 'I'll be back when you have your dinner,' she said, kissed her good-bye, and left.

After a minute, Maisie got out of bed, tiptoed to the door, and peeked down the hall. Her mother was at the nurses' station, talking to Barbara and the other nurse. She got back in bed, sitting on the edge where she could scramble under the covers if she heard anybody coming, and watched the first part of *The Best Summer*.

The little girl in the movie was in a wheelchair. She had a big bow in her hair and a shawl over her knees and looked very sad. 'You'll never get well looking like that,' the little girl's doctor said. 'It takes smiles to get well.'

'I haven't any smiles,' the little girl said.

'You must take one of my happy pills,' the doctor said, and pulled a puppy out from behind his back.

'Oh, a puppy!' the little girl cried. 'The darling! What is his name?'

'Ulla,' Maisie said, and got out of bed to check to see if her mother was still there.

She was gone. Maisie clicked off the TV and set the remote on the floor half under the bed. Then she got into bed and arranged the covers neatly. She waited awhile till she wasn't breathing so hard and then hit the nurse's call button.

It took a long time for the nurse to come. When she did, it was Barbara.

She was glad. Nurse Amy was always in a hurry. 'What do you need, honey?' Barbara asked.

'I dropped my remote,' Maisie said, pointing at the floor, and then, as Barbara stooped to pick up the remote, 'My mother said Dr Lander moved away.'

Barbara stayed bent down, looking for the remote. Maisie wondered if she had put it too far under the bed, it took her so long to answer.

'Yes, that's right,' she said finally.

'Is she already gone?' Maisie asked.

'Yes,' Barbara said, and her voice sounded funny from being under the bed. 'She's gone.'

'Are you sure?'

'Yes,' Barbara said. She stood up and switched on the TV. 'Which channel were you watching?' she asked without turning around.

'A video,' Maisie said. 'Maybe she isn't gone yet. I mean, don't people have to pack all their clothes and rent their apartments and stuff before they move?'

Barbara hit 'play.' The puppy was licking the face of the little girl in the wheelchair. The little girl was giggling. Barbara handed the remote to Maisie. 'All right now?' she asked, patting the covers over Maisie's knees.

'Maybe she isn't gone yet,' Maisie said. 'She's still getting ready to go, and then she'll come back and tell everybody good-bye.'

'No,' Barbara said, 'she left,' and went out before Maisie could ask her anything else.

Maisie lay there watching *The Best Summer*. The little girl got out of her wheelchair and walked with old-fashioned-looking crutches. 'You were right. You told me all it took to get well was smiles,' she told the doctor.

I'll bet the nurses forgot to page Joanna, Maisie thought, and she was so busy packing she didn't even think about the wireless messages the *Titanic* sent. I'll bet when she gets to wherever she moved to, she'll remember. She pushed the call button again, and when Barbara came in, she said, 'Where did Joanna move to?'

Barbara looked angry, like she was going to tell Maisie not to ring the call button so much, but she didn't. She reached over Maisie's head and flicked it off. 'Back east.'

'Back east where?'

'I don't know, New Jersey,' Barbara said and went out.

New Jersey was where the *Hindenburg* crashed. Maisie wondered if Joanna had gone there to interview the crewman who had had the near-death experience.

But he lived in Germany. Maybe she had found out about somebody else on the *Hindenburg* who'd had a near-death experience, and that was why she'd left in such a hurry. She'll call me as soon as she gets there, Maisie thought.

She wondered how long it took to get to New Jersey. She didn't think she'd better use the nurse's call button again. She waited till Eugene brought in her supper tray and asked him, 'How long does it take to get to New Jersey, Eugene?'

Eugene grinned at her. 'You plannin' to fly the coop?'

'No,' she said. 'To drive there, how many days would it take?'

'Oh, you're *drivin*',' he said. 'Ain't you a little young to be drivin'?'

'I'm serious, Eugene,' Maisie said. 'How many days would it take?'

'I dunno,' he said, 'three, maybe four. Depends on how fast you drive. You strike me as one a' them speedy drivers! You better watch out the police don't stop you and ask to see your license!'

Maisie figured it would probably take Joanna four days if she was moving all her stuff, but she had already left. When? Yesterday or Thursday? If she had left on Thursday, she might call the day after tomorrow.

When her mom came back right before supper, she asked her, 'Do you know when Joanna left?'

'No,' her mom said. 'Did you watch *The Best Summer*? I brought you another video, *The Secret Garden*.'

Maisie decided she had probably left yesterday. So she'll probably call Saturday, she thought, and I'd better find out as much as I can about the wireless messages so I'll have lots to tell her. She looked through her *Titanic* books again and wrote down the ones they sent before the iceberg, just in case Joanna decided she wanted them, too, and waited for her to call.

But she didn't call on Saturday, or on Sunday. She's probably busy interviewing the *Hindenburg* person, Maisie thought, watching the video of *The Secret Garden*. There was a little boy in a wheelchair in this one, and a little girl who was very crabby. Maisie liked her.

The little girl kept hearing funny noises, like somebody crying. When she asked the people in the house about it, they told her they didn't hear anything and tried to change the subject, so she went upstairs and looked for herself. She found the little boy in the wheelchair and started taking him outside without telling anybody.

I'll bet he gets well, too, Maisie thought disgustedly, and fell asleep. When she woke up, the little girl was writing her uncle a letter. 'Where shall I send it?' she asked the maid, and the maid told her the address.

When Barbara came in to take her blood pressure, Maisie waited until she'd taken the stethoscope off and then asked, 'Do you know Dr Lander's address?'

'Her address?' Barbara asked, putting the stethoscope back around her neck.

'The address of where she moved to.'

Barbara peeled the blood pressure cuff off Maisie's arm and put it in the basket on the wall. 'Maisie –' she said and then just stood there.

'What?' Maisie said.

'I forgot the thermometer,' she said, feeling in her pockets. 'I'll be right back.'

'But did she? Leave an address?'

'No,' Barbara said, and just stood there, like she had before. 'I don't know where she is.'

But I'll bet Dr Wright does, Maisie thought. They were working on a project. Joanna had to tell him the address of where she was going. She thought about asking Barbara to page him, but she remembered Joanna saying he sometimes turned his pager off, so she called the hospital switchboard herself.

'Can you give me Dr Wright's number?' she asked the operator, trying to sound like her mother.

'Dr Richard Wright?'

'Uh-huh,' Maisie said. 'I mean, yes.'

'I'll connect you,' the operator said.

'No, I want –' Maisie said, but the operator had already connected her. The phone was busy.

Maisie waited till nighttime, when the evening operator would be on, and tried again. This time she said, 'Dr Wright's number, please.'

'Dr Wright has gone home,' the operator said.

'I *know*,' Maisie said. 'I need his number so I can call him tomorrow. To make an appointment,' she added.

'An appointment?' the operator said doubtfully, but gave her the number. Maisie called it, just in case he hadn't gone home, but nobody answered. Nobody answered the next day either, even though she called every half hour.

She would have to go see him. She called the operator again and asked where Dr Wright's office was. '602,' the operator told her, which was good. She would have to take the elevator, but her room was 422, so his office should be right above it, and she wouldn't have to walk very far.

The hard part would be getting down to the elevator without anybody seeing her. The little girl in *The Secret Garden* had gone at night, but Dr Wright wouldn't be in his office then, and she couldn't do it in the morning because that was when they made the bed and helped her take her shower and brought the library cart around. And at two o'clock her mother came.

She would have to do it after they picked up the lunch trays. As soon as they made her bed, she went over to the closet and got her clothes and put them under the covers. She laid one of the *Titanic* books open on top of the lump it made so it wouldn't show, and then lay down and rested so she would have enough energy for the walking.

She ate a lot of her lunch, too, and Eugene, when he came in to pick up the tray, said, 'Awright! That's what I like to see! You keep eatin' like that, and you'll be out of this place in *no time!*'

She had put on her pants and socks before lunch. As soon as he took her tray out, she put on her shoes and turtleneck. She put her robe on over her clothes, pulled the covers up, and lay down, catching her breath and listening.

The little boy in 420 started crying. Footsteps came down the hall and went in the room.

She'd better turn on the TV so the nurses would think she was watching a video and wouldn't come in to see what she was doing. She got the remote off the bed table, rewound *The Secret Garden*, and hit 'play.'

The crying stopped. After a few minutes footsteps came out of the room and went back toward the nurses' station. On the TV, the little girl was sneaking up a long winding staircase. Maisie got out of bed, and took off her robe. She stuck it under the covers and tiptoed to the door. There was nobody in the hall, and she couldn't see Barbara or anybody in the nurses' station. She snuck really fast to the elevators, pushed the button, and then stood inside the door of the waiting room till the elevator light blinked on. The elevator door opened, and she darted across and pushed 'six.'

Her heart was pounding really hard, but it was partly because she was scared that somebody would see her before the door shut. 'Come on!' she whispered, and it finally shut, really slow, and the elevator started going up.

Okay. Now all she had to do was find 602. When the elevator opened, she got out and looked around. There were lots of doors, but none of them had numbers on them. TTY-TDD, a sign on one of them said.

She walked down the hall. LHS, the doors said, and OT, but no numbers. A lady carrying a clipboard came out of a door marked PT. She stopped when she saw Maisie, and frowned, and for a minute Maisie was afraid she knew she was a patient. The lady came over to her, holding the clipboard against her chest. 'Are you looking for somebody, honey?' she asked.

'Yes,' Maisie said, trying to sound very certain and businesslike. 'Dr Wright.'

'He's in the east wing,' the lady said. 'Do you know how to get there?'

Maisie shook her head.

'You need to go back down to fifth and take a right, and you'll see a sign that says 'Human Resources.' You go through that door, and it'll take you to the east wing.'

Is it real far? Maisie wanted to ask, but she was afraid the lady would ask her where she had come from, so she said, 'Thank you very much,' and went back to the elevator, walking fast so the lady wouldn't know she was a patient.

She rested in the elevator and then got out and turned right, like the woman said, and walked down the hall. The sign was a long way down the hall. Her heart started to beat real hard. She stopped and rested a minute, but a man came out of one of the doors, carrying a tray full of blood tubes, so she had to start walking again.

The door to the walkway was heavy. She had to push really hard on the handle to get it to open. Inside was a straight gray hallway. Maisie didn't know how long it was, but it was way farther than she was supposed to walk. Maybe she'd better not go down it. But it was a long way back to the elevators, too, and after she found Dr Wright and he told her Joanna's address, she could tell him he needed to take her back, and he could get a wheelchair or something. And she could walk really slow.

She started down the hallway. It was a funny hallway. It didn't have any windows or doors or anything, and no railings along the side to hang on to like in the rest of the hospital. She put one hand on the wall, but it wasn't as good, you got a lot tireder than with a railing.

'I think I'd better rest for a little while,' she said, and sat down with her back against the wall, but it didn't help. She still couldn't get her breath, and the lights on the wall kept swimming around in a funny way. 'I don't feel good,' she said, and lay down on the floor.

There was a loud noise, and the lights flared into brightness and then went nearly all the way out, turning a dark red. Like the lights on the *Titanic*, Maisie thought, right before they went out. I hope these don't go out, or the hall'll be really dark. But it wasn't the hall. It was the tunnel she had been in before. She could sense the tall, straight walls on either side of her.

This is an NDE, she thought, and sat up off the tile floor. Only it wasn't tile. It felt funny. She wished it weren't so dark, and she could see it. She had to look at everything so she could tell it to Joanna.

And listen to everything, she thought, remembering the sound before the lights turned red. It had been a boom, or a loud clap. Or maybe an explosion. She couldn't remember exactly. I should have been listening, she thought. I'm supposed to report on what I saw.

Her heart had stopped pounding, and she didn't feel dizzy anymore. She stood up and started walking along the tunnel between the high, straight walls. It was dark and foggy, like before, and really warm. She turned and looked back. It was dark and foggy both ways.

'*I told* Mr Mandrake there wasn't any light,' she said, and right then a light flickered at the end of the tunnel. It was red, like the lights in the hall had been, and wobbly, like somebody running carrying a lantern or something, and that must be what it was, because she could see people running toward her, though she couldn't see who they were because of the fog.

'Hurry!' they shouted. 'This way! Call a code! Now!'

They ran past her. She peered at them as they went past, trying to see their faces through the fog. Mr Mandrake said they were supposed to be people you knew who'd died, like your grandma, but Maisie didn't know any of them. 'Get that cart over here,' one of the ladies said to her as she ran past. She had on a white dress and white gloves. 'Stat!'

'Clear,' a man said. He was wearing a suit, like Dr Murrow always wore. 'Again. Clear.'

'Do you know who she is?' the lady with the white gloves said.

'My name's Maisie,' she tried to say, but they weren't listening. They just kept on running past.

'She must be a patient,' the man said. 'Do you know who she is?' he said to somebody else.

'It's on my dog tags,' Maisie said.

'What's she doing up here?' the man said. 'Clear.'

The light flared brightly, like an explosion, and she was back in the hallway and a bunch of nurses and doctors were kneeling over her. 'Awwll *riight*!' the man said.

'I've got a pulse,' one of the nurses said, and another one asked, 'Can you hear me, honey?'

'I had a near-death experience,' Maisie said, trying to sit up. 'I was in a tunnel, and—'

'There, there, lie down,' the nurse said, just like Auntie Em in *The Wizard of Oz*. 'Don't try to move. We're going to take care of you.'

Maisie nodded. They put her on a gurney and put a blanket over her, and when they did, she saw she wasn't wearing her turtleneck anymore, and she reached for her dog tags, afraid they'd taken those off of her, too. That was the one bad thing about dog tags, people could take them off of you.

'Just lie still,' the nurse said, holding her arm, and Maisie saw they were starting an IV and hanging a bag of saline on a hook above her. Her other arm was under the blanket. She reached up real slowly across her chest till she could feel the chain. Good, she still had them on.

'What's your name, honey?' the nurse starting the IV said.

'Maisie Nellis,' she said, even though it was right there on her hospital bracelet and her dog tags. What good was having I.D. stuff if people didn't read them? 'You need to tell Dr Wright to call Dr Lander,' she said. 'You need to tell him—'

'Don't try to talk, Maisie,' the nurse said. 'Is Dr Lander your doctor?'

'No,' Maisie said. 'She—'

'Is Dr Wright your doctor?'

'*No*,' Maisie said. 'He knows Dr Lander. They're working on a project together.'

Another nurse came up. 'She's from Peds. Viral endocarditis. Dr Murrow's on his way up.'

'Jesus,' the man who had shouted, 'Awwll riight!' said, and somebody else she couldn't see, 'There'll be hell to pay for somebody for this.'

At the same time, the nurse who'd started her IV said, 'Ready,' and they started to wheel her really fast back down the hall the way she'd come.

'No, wait!' Maisie said. 'You need to tell Dr Wright to call Dr Lander first. He's in the other wing. Tell him to tell her I didn't just see fog this time, I saw all kinds of stuff. A light and people and a lady in a white dress –'

The nurses looked at each other above her head. 'Just lie still,' the nurse who'd done her IV said. 'You're going to be fine.'

'You just had a bad dream,' the other one said.

'It *wasn't* a dream,' Maisie said. 'It was an NDE. You have to tell Dr Wright to call her.'

The first nurse patted her hand. 'I'll tell her.'

'*No*,' Maisie said. 'She moved away to New Jersey. You have to tell *Dr Wright* to tell her.'

'I'll tell him,' the nurse said. 'Now just lie still and rest. We're going to take care of you.'

'Promise,' Maisie said.

'I promise,' the nurse said.

Now she'll call for sure, Maisie thought happily. She'll call as soon as she hears I had a near-death experience.

But she didn't.

44

'It is another thing to die than people have imagined.'
                                    – Last words of ST BONIFACE, as boiling
                                          lead was poured into his mouth

Joanna stood at the railing a long time, looking out at the darkness, and then went over to the deck chairs and sat down.

She clasped her hands around her knees and looked down the Boat Deck. It was deserted, the deck lamps making pools of yellow light, illuminating the empty lifeboat davits, the deck chairs lined up against the wall of the wheel-house and the gymnasium. There was no sign of the officers who had been loading the boats, or of J. H. Rogers, or the band. Or of Greg Menotti.

Well, of course not. ' "All alone, so Heav'n has will'd, we die," ' Mr Briarley had said, reading aloud from *Mazes and Mirrors*, and Mrs Woollam had said, 'Death is something each one of us must go through by ourselves.'

' "Alone, alone, all all alone, alone on the wide wide sea," ' Joanna said, and her voice sounded weak and self-pitying in the silence. Don't be such a baby, she told herself. You were the one who said you wanted to find out about death. Well, now you're going to. Firsthand. 'To die will be an awfully big adventure,' she said firmly, but her voice still sounded shaky and uncertain.

It was very quiet on the deck, and somehow peaceful. 'Like waiting, and not waiting,' Mr Wojakowski had said, talking about the days before World War II. Knowing it was coming, waiting for it to start.

She wondered if there was something she was supposed to do. Benjamin Guggenheim and his valet had gone below and changed into formal evening dress, but the staterooms were already underwater. And you can't do anything, she thought. You're dead. You'll never do anything again. You're not even here. You're in the ER, on the examining table where you died, with a sheet over your face, and you're not capable of doing anything at all.

'Except thinking,' she said out loud to the silent Boat Deck, 'except knowing what's happening to you,' and she remembered Lavoisier, who had still been conscious after he had been beheaded, who had blinked his eyes twelve times, knowing, *knowing*, she thought, horror rising in her throat, that he was dead.

But only for a few seconds, she thought, and wondered how long twelve blinks took. 'Bud Roop went down, bam! just like that,' Mr Wojakowski had said. 'He never even knew what hit him. Died instantly.' Only it wasn't instant. Brain death took four to six minutes, and Richard believed there was no correlation between time in the NDE and actual time. That time she had explored the entire ship, she had only been under for a few seconds. 'I could be here for hours,' she said, her voice rising.

But you've already been here a long time, she told herself. You went down to the writing room and the First-Class Dining Saloon. You've already been here a long time, and the brain cells are dying, the synapses being shut down one by one. Soon there won't be enough of them to sustain the central unifying image, and it will start to break down. And in four to six minutes, all the cells will be dead, and you won't be capable of memory, or thought, or fear, and there won't be anything. Nothing. Not even silence or darkness, or the awareness of them. Nothing.

'Nothing,' she said, her hands gripping the hard wooden arms of the deck chair. You won't know it's nothing, she told herself. There's nothing to be afraid of. You'll be unconscious, oblivious, asleep.

'"To sleep, perchance to dream,"' Joanna murmured, but there was no possibility of dreaming. There were no synapses to dream with, no acetylcholine, no serotonin. Nothing. 'You won't exist,' she told herself. 'You won't be there.'

Not there. Not anywhere. And no wonder people loved Mr Mandrake's book – it wasn't the relatives and the Angels of Light they loved – it was the reassurance that they still existed, that there was *something*, anything, after death. Even hell, or the *Titanic*, was better than nothing.

But the *Titanic*'s sinking, she thought, and the panic rose like vomit in her throat. Her heart began to pound. I'm afraid, she thought, and that proves the NDE isn't an endorphin cushion. She looked at her palm, clammy and damp, and pressed it to her chest. Her heart was beating fast, her breathing shallow – all the symptoms of fear. She pressed two fingers to her wrist and took her pulse. Ninety-five. She reached in her pocket for a pen and paper to note it down so she could tell Richard.

So she could tell Richard. 'You still don't believe it,' she thought, and put her hand to her side. 'You still can't accept that you're dead.'

'It's impossible for the human mind to comprehend its own death,' she had blithely told Richard, and imagined that that would be a comfort, a protection against the horrible knowledge of destruction. But it wasn't. It was a taunt and a tease, beckoning tantalizingly just out of reach, like the light of the *Californian*, promising rescue even after the boats were all gone and the lights were going out.

'Hope springs eternal' isn't a saying of Pollyanna's, it's a threat, Joanna thought, and wondered, horrified, if Lavoisier had been signaling for help, dot dot dot, dash dash dash, dot dot dot. He had blinked twelve times. SOS. SOS.

Hope isn't a protection, it's a punishment, Joanna thought. And this is hell. But it couldn't be, because the sign above the gate to hell read, 'Abandon hope, all ye who enter here.' But that was an order, not a statement, and maybe that was the true torture of hell, not fire and brimstone, and damnation was continuing to hope even as the stern began to rise out of the water, as the flames, or the lava, or the train overtook you, that there was still a way out, that you might somehow be saved at the last minute. Just like in the movies.

And it was sometimes true, she thought, you were sometimes able to summon the cavalry. 'That's what I was trying to tell Richard,' she said, and remembered trying to move her lips as Vielle's worried face leaned over her, trying to hear, her hand holding tight to hers.

I didn't say good-bye to Vielle, Joanna thought. She'll think it was her fault. 'It was my fault, Vielle,' she said as if Vielle could hear her. 'I didn't stay alert to my surroundings. I was too busy working Cape Race. I didn't even see it coming.'

'I didn't say good-bye to anyone,' she said, and stood up hastily as though there were still time to do it. Kit. She'd left Kit without a word. Kit, whose fiancé and uncle had already left her. 'I didn't even say good-bye to Richard,' she said. Or Maisie.

Maisie. She had promised Maisie she would come see her. She'll be waiting, Joanna thought, the dread filling her chest, and Barbara will come in and tell her that I died. She had taken a step forward on the deck as if to stop Barbara, but she could not stop anyone from doing anything, and she had been wrong about the punishment of the dead – it was not hope or oblivion, but remembering broken promises and neglected good-byes and not being able to rectify them. 'Oh, Maisie,' Joanna said, and sat back down on the edge of the deck chair. She put her head in her hands.

'Are you supposed to be out here, Ms Lander?' a stern voice said. 'Where is your hall pass?'

She looked up. Mr Briarley was standing over her in his gray tweed vest. 'Mr Briarley … what?' she choked out. 'Why are you here? Did you die, too?'

'Did I die?' He pondered the question. 'Is this multiple choice? "Neither fish nor fowl, neither out nor in."' He smiled at her and then said seriously, 'What are you doing out here alone?'

'I was trying to send a message,' she said, looking over at the darkness beyond the railing.

'Did it get through?'

No, she thought, remembering Vielle's worried voice saying, 'Shh, honey, don't try to talk,' and her own, choking on the blood pouring out of her lungs, out of her throat, the resident's voice cutting across them, shouting, 'Clear. Again. Clear,' and behind it, above it, around it, the code alarm, drowning out everything, everything.

No, she thought, Vielle didn't hear me, didn't understand, didn't tell Richard, and the knowledge was worse than realizing she was dead, worse even than Barbara telling Maisie she'd died. Worse than anything. 'No,' she said numbly. 'It didn't get through.'

'I know,' he said, looking out past the railing, 'I know. I try sometimes. But it's too far,' and put his hand on her shoulder. She laid her own hand over his, and they stayed like that for a minute, and then Mr Briarley pulled his hand free and gave hers a brisk pat. 'It's freezing out here.' He pulled her to standing. 'Come along,' he said, and started off down the deck.

'Where are we going?' Joanna said, trying to catch up to him.

'The first-class smoking room,' he called over his shoulder. 'It's rather smoky, I'm afraid, as its name would indicate, but it's farther astern, and secondhand smoke is something we no longer have to worry about.'

Joanna caught up with him. 'Why are we going there?'

'That's one of the blessings of death, not having to be afraid of dying,' he went on as if he hadn't heard her. 'Having died by one means, you have eliminated all the others. As Carlyle wrote –' He glanced sternly at Joanna. 'You do remember Thomas Carlyle? British author of –? He will be on the final.'

'*The French Revolution*,' Joanna said, thinking of Lavoisier beheaded, blinking.

'*Very* good,' Mr Briarley said, slackening his pace momentarily. 'He also wrote, "The crash of the whole solar and stellar systems could only kill you once."'

He walked rapidly along the deck, as he had before on Scotland Road, so that Joanna nearly had to run to keep up with him. It was hard work. Joanna couldn't see that the deck was slanting, but it must be. It felt oddly uncertain, and Joanna stubbed her toe against the wooden boards several times.

'I was always afraid of dying in a plane crash,' Mr Briarley said. 'And of being beheaded, I suppose because of its connection to English literature. Sydney Carton and Raleigh and Sir Thomas More. More told the executioner, "I'll see to my going up, and you shall see to my coming down." Witty to the last.'

He shook his head. 'I also feared dying of a heart attack, though in retrospect I see that any of the three would have been a blessing. All of them quick, nearly painless, and the mind functioning fully to the very end.' He opened the door to the Grand Staircase. The band was at the head of the stairs, playing a Gilbert and Sullivan song. 'You no longer need fear volcanoes or Zeppelin crashes or torpedoes. Or drowning,' he said and started down the curving steps.

It can't be the end yet, Joanna thought, stopping to look at the band. They aren't playing 'Nearer, My God, to Thee.' Or 'Autumn,' she thought, and then, wonderingly, Now I'll find out which one they played.

'Come along,' Mr Briarley said from below. 'They're waiting.'

She started down the steps. 'Who is?'

Mr Briarley was standing in a shadow just above the first landing, and below him the steps curved down into darkness. And water. 'Who's waiting for me?' she said, coming down cautiously.

'There are all sorts of death you no longer have to fear,' Mr Briarley said. 'Drug overdoses. Gunshot wounds –'

Gunshot wounds. The teenager with the knife, lying dead on the emergency room floor. Dead. Joanna stopped, holding on to the railing. 'Is everyone here?' she asked breathlessly. 'Everyone who's died? On the ship?'

'Everyone?' Mr Briarley said. 'The *Titanic* was a great disaster, but she carried only two thousand souls. That's only a fraction of those who die every day,' he said and continued down the steps.

'That isn't what I meant,' she said, and thought, I meant, is he here, somewhere belowdecks, waiting? 'I meant, are the people who died when I did here?' she said aloud. 'In Mercy General?'

Mr Briarley stopped just above the landing and looked up at her. 'We're only going as far down as the Promenade Deck,' he said and pointed at the wide door leading out.

Joanna clutched the railing. 'Were you telling the truth when you said we can't die more than once?'

He nodded. '"After the first death, there is no other."' He went down the last two steps and across to the door. 'Dylan Thomas. "A Refusal to Mourn the Death, by Fire, of a Child –"' he said and, still talking, went out the door.

'What do you mean, the death of a child?' Joanna said. She let go of the railing and ran down the stairs after him. 'What do you mean, by fire?'

Mr Briarley was already walking rapidly along the Promenade Deck. 'The line "there is no other" has a double meaning. It alludes to the event of another's death awakening us to our own mortality, and to the Resurrection, but it can also be taken literally. There is no other. Having had our first death, we cannot be killed by lightning or by heart disease—'

'Is Maisie here?' Joanna said.

'By tuberculosis or kidney failure, by Ebola fever or ventricular fibrillation.'

'Did Maisie die?' Joanna said desperately. 'When Barbara told her I'd been killed? Did she go into V-fib?'

'You no longer need fear the gallows,' Mr Briarley said. It was colder down here, even though this part of the Promenade Deck was glassed in. Joanna shivered. 'Nor the guillotine.' He touched his neck gingerly. 'Nor strychnine poisoning. Nor a massive stroke –' and *she was in a dark hallway, groping her way toward the phone that was ringing wildly, wrestling one arm into her robe, feeling for the light switch, and for the phone, nearly knocking the receiver off, her heart jangling, knowing what she was going to hear, 'It's your father –'*

'What was that?' Joanna said. She was flattened against one of the windows, staring into her frightened reflection.

'What was what?' Mr Briarley said irritably from halfway down the deck.

'Something just happened,' she said, afraid to move for fear it would happen again. 'A memory or a ...'

'It's the cold,' Mr Briarley said. 'Come along, it's warmer in the smoking room. There's a fire.'

'A fire?' Joanna said. Smoke and a fire. The death of a child by fire. She turned away from the windows and caught up to him. 'Please tell me Maisie isn't here.'

'Fire's another death you don't have to fear,' Mr Briarley said. 'Nasty, lingering death. Joan of Arc, Archbishop Cranmer, Little Miss – Ah, here we are,' he said, and stopped in front of a dark wooden door.

45

'No lying in state anywhere … a simple service … no speaking … the body not embalmed …'
— Part of FDR's instructions for his funeral, which were not found until afterward and which had been completely disregarded

Joanna's funeral wasn't till Tuesday. Vielle came up to tell him. 'The sister doesn't trust any of the local ministers to conduct the service. She insists on bringing in her own hellfire-and-damnation specialist from Wisconsin.'

'Tuesday,' Richard said. It seemed an eon away.

'At ten.' She gave him the address of the funeral home. 'I just wanted to let you know. I've got to get back down to the ER,' but she didn't leave.

She lingered by the door, cradling her bandaged hand and looking unhappy, and then said, 'What Joanna said — it might not have meant anything. People say all kinds of crazy things. I remember one old man who kept muttering, "The cashews are loose." And sometimes you think they're trying to tell you one thing, and they're actually trying to say something else. I had an ischemia patient one time who said, "Water," over and over, but when we'd try to give her a drink of water, she'd push it away. She was actually saying, "Walter."'

'And — what?' Richard asked bitterly. 'Joanna was really saying "Suez"? Or "soy sauce"? You and I both know what she was trying to say. She was calling for help. She was trying to tell me she was on the *Titanic*.'

He unplugged the EKG monitor. 'That was what she'd come running down to the ER to tell me,' he said, winding up the cord, 'in such a hurry she ran straight into a knife. That it wasn't a hallucination. That it was really the *Titanic*.'

'But how could it be? Near-death experiences are a phenomenon of the dying brain.'

'I don't know,' he said, and sat down and put his head in his hands. 'I don't know.'

Vielle went away, but late that afternoon, or maybe the next day, she came again. 'I talked to Patty Messner,' she said. 'She ran into Joanna just as she came through the door of the ER, and she asked if Dr Jamison was there. She said, "I have to find Dr Wright. Do you know where he is?"'

He must still have been harboring some hope that something, someone else had brought Joanna to the ER, because as she spoke, it was like hearing Tish telling him Joanna was dead all over again. He wondered numbly why Vielle had come up all this way to tell him that.

'Patty said Joanna was in a hurry, that she was out of breath. I think you're wrong,' Vielle said. 'About what she was coming to tell you.'

She paused, waiting for him to ask why, and then, when he didn't, went on. 'When I got shot, I didn't tell Joanna because I knew what she'd say. She was always telling me I should transfer out of the ER, that I was going to get hurt. The last thing I wanted was for her to find out.' She looked expectantly at him.

'And Joanna knew I'd accuse her of turning into a nutcase if she told me it was the *Titanic*, is that the point you're trying to make?' Richard asked.

'The point I'm trying to make is, I avoided Joanna for days so she wouldn't see my bandage,' Vielle said. 'The last thing Joanna would have done if it was really the *Titanic* was to have gone looking for you all over the hospital. Don't you see?' she said earnestly. 'What she'd found out must have been something good, something she thought you'd be happy about.'

It was a nice try. It even made sense, up to a point. 'She was in such a hurry she almost ran me over,' Mr Wojakowski had said. And maybe she had been coming to tell him 'something good,' something one of her NDEers had told her, but whatever it was, it had been overwhelmed by the reality of what was happening to her, the panic and terror of being trapped on board. 'SOS,' she had called, and there was no mistaking what that meant, in spite of Vielle's well-meaning rationalizations. It meant, 'I am on the *Titanic*. We are going down.'

'I think you should try to find out what it was, the thing she was coming to tell you,' Vielle said and went away, this time for good.

But any number of other people came, bearing books and advice. Mrs Dirksen from Personnel, proffering a copy of *Seven Mourning Strategies*. 'It's not healthy to sit here all by yourself. You need to get out and be with people, try not to think about it.'

And Ann Collins with *Words of Comfort for Trying Times*: 'God never sends you more than you can bear.' And somebody from Personnel Relations with a flyer for a Coping with Post-Trauma Stress Workshop the hospital had scheduled for Wednesday.

And a fragile-looking young woman with short blond hair. Her frailness, her youth were somehow the last straw, and when she stammered, 'I'm ... I was a friend of Joanna Lander's. My name's Kit Gardiner, and I came—'

He cut in angrily. '– to tell me it isn't my fault, there was nothing I could do? Or at least it was quick and she didn't suffer? Or how about God tempers the wind to the shorn lamb? Or maybe all of the above?'

'No,' she said. 'I came to bring you this book. It—'

'Oh, of course, a book,' he said viciously. 'The answer to everything. What's this one? *Five Easy Steps to Forgetting*?'

He didn't know what he'd expected. That she would look hurt and surprised, tears welling up in her eyes, that she would slam the book down and tell him to go to hell?

She did neither. She looked quietly at him, no trace of tears in her eyes, and then, in a conversational tone, said, 'I slapped my aunt Martha. When my fiancé died. She told me God needed him in heaven, and I hauled off and slapped her, a sixty-year-old woman. They said I was half out of my mind with grief, that I didn't know what I was doing, but it wasn't true. People say unbelievable things to you. They deserve slapping.'

He stared at her in relief. 'They –'

'– tell you you'll get over it,' Kit said. 'I know. And that it's unhealthy to be so upset. And that you shouldn't blame yourself, it wasn't your fault –'

'– there was nothing anybody could have done,' he said. 'But that's a lie. If I'd gotten there earlier, if I'd had my pager on –' He stopped, suddenly afraid she'd say, 'You couldn't have known,' but she didn't.

She said, 'They all told me it wasn't my fault. Except Uncle Pat.' She stopped, looking down at the book she held, and then went on, 'It's a terrible thing to be told it isn't your fault when you know it is. Look,' she said, and started for the door. 'I'll come some other time. You've got enough to deal with right now.'

'No, wait,' he said. 'I'm sorry I was so rude. It's just that—'

'I know. My mother says it's because they don't know *what* to say, that they're just trying to comfort you, but Uncle Pat says ... said that's no excuse for them telling you stupid things like you'll get over it.' She looked up at him. 'You don't, you know. Ever. They tell you you'll feel better, too. That isn't true either.'

Her words should have been depressing, but oddly, they were comforting. '"You think things can't get any worse,"' he said, quoting Vielle, '"and then they do."'

Kit nodded. 'I found this book Joanna had asked me for, the day she was killed,' she said. 'I called and offered to bring it to her, but she said no, she'd pick it up later on.'

And if you'd brought the book over to her, she might not have been down in the ER when the teenager pulled his knife, Richard thought, marveling at how everyone found some way to blame himself. If only the lookouts had seen the iceberg five minutes earlier, if only the *Californian*'s wireless officer hadn't gone to bed, if only the *Carpathia* had been closer. It was amazing how much guilt and blame and 'if only's' there were to go around.

But the fact remained, they were going too fast, they didn't have enough lifeboats, he had turned his pager off. 'It was my fault, not yours,' he started to say, but she was still talking.

'I'd been looking for the book for her for weeks, and then when I found it, it was too late to be of any help to her. She wanted so much to find out what caused near-death experiences, how they worked. That's why I brought the book to you. She didn't get a chance to finish what she started, but maybe it'll help you in your research.' She held the book out to him.

He didn't take it. 'I've shut the research project down,' he said. And now she would say, 'You only think you feel that way now.'

She didn't. 'It's the textbook they used in Joanna's English class,' she said as if he hadn't spoken. 'My uncle was her English teacher in high school. Joanna asked me to look for it. She thought there might be something in it that made her NDEs take the form of the *Titanic*.' She held the book out.

'I don't need it,' he said. 'I already know the answer.'

'I talked to Vielle,' she said. 'She told me about your theory, that you think she was really on the *Titanic*.'

'Not think,' he said. 'Know.'

'Joanna didn't think she was. She thought the *Titanic* was a symbol for something else. She was trying to find out what. That's why she needed the book.' She laid it down on the examining table between them. 'She was convinced something Uncle Pat had said in his English class had triggered the image of the *Titanic*, but he has Alzheimer's and couldn't remember, so she asked me to help her. She was convinced there was some connection between it and the nature of the near-death experience, and that the book would help her find out why she was seeing the *Titanic*.'

'I know why she was seeing it. Because it was real. I have outside verification.'

'You mean because she said, "SOS"? That could mean lots of—'

'No.'

'Then what?'

'Because I went after her.'

She stared at him for a long minute. 'After her? What do you mean?'

'I mean, I went under to try to save her.' He gestured at the RIPT scan, at the examining table between them. 'I self-induced an NDE and went after her to try to bring her back.'

'You went after her,' she said, struggling to understand. 'Onto the *Titanic*?'

'No,' he said bitterly. 'I was too late for that.'

'I don't understand.'

'There are apparently several varieties of hell. Mine was to stand in a crowd in the White Star office and listen to an official read the names of the passengers who'd been lost.'

'You were there?'

'I was there. It really happened. She went down on the *Titanic*. And she called to me for help. And I came too late.' He had said it finally, and getting it all out, sharing, venting, was supposed to make you feel better, wasn't it, according to *Eight Great Grief Helps*? It didn't.

And now that it was out, Kit would say – what? 'You left her to *drown*?' or, 'I am *so* sorry,' or, 'You don't know what you're saying. You're half out of your mind with grief'?

None of the above. She said, 'How do you know? That you were really in the White Star office?'

'I *know*. It was a real place,' he said, and knew he sounded just like Mr Mandrake's nutcases, swearing they'd seen Jesus, but Kit only nodded.

'Joanna said it felt real,' she said, 'not like a dream. She said it was a very convincing hallucination.'

She was offering him a way out, just like, 'It wasn't your fault,' and, 'There's a reason for everything,' only this one was even better: it was only acetylcholine and random synapses and confabulation. He had conjured the White Star office out of Joanna's NDE accounts and the movie, created a unifying image out of panic and grief and temporal-lobe stimulation.

It almost worked. Except that Joanna, dying, had called out to him for help: 'SOS. SOS.' 'No thanks,' he said and handed her back the book.

And now she would say, 'You owe it to Joanna to continue your research. It's what she would have wanted.'

But she didn't. She said, 'Okay,' and put the book in her bag and then walked over to his desk and wrote on a pad. 'Here's my phone number if you decide you need it.'

She walked to the door, opened it, and then turned around. 'I don't know who else to tell this to,' she said. 'Joanna saved my life. My uncle ... living with someone ...' She stopped and tried again. 'I was going under, and she got me to go out, she convinced me to use Eldercare, she invited me to Dish Night. She told me,' she took a ragged breath, 'she wished she could die saving somebody's life. And she did. She saved mine.'

She left then, but the head of the board came, to remind him of the Coping with Post-Trauma Stress Workshop, and Nurse Hawley with *Practical Mourning Management*, and an elderly volunteer with a copy of the *Book of Mormon*. And on Tuesday, Eileen and two other nurses from three-west, to take him to the funeral. 'We won't take no for an answer,' they said. 'It's not good to be alone at a time like this.'

He supposed Tish had put them up to it, but although he had finally slept, he still felt bone-tired and unable to concentrate, unable to think of an excuse they would accept. And maybe this was a good idea, he thought, climbing into the cramped Geo. He wasn't sure he was in any shape to drive.

'I still can't believe she's dead,' one of the nurses said as soon as they had pulled out of the parking lot.

'At least she didn't suffer,' the other one said. 'What was she doing down in the ER, anyway?'

'Have you thought about grief counseling, Richard?' Eileen asked.

'I've got a great book you should read,' the first nurse volunteered. 'It's called *The Grief Workbook*, and it's got all these neat depression exercises.'

There was a crowd at the church, mostly people from the hospital, looking odd out of their lab coats and scrubs. He saw Mr Wojakowski and Mrs Troudtheim. Joanna's sister stood by the door of the narthex, flanked by two little girls. He wondered if Maisie would be there, and then remembered that her mother relentlessly shielded her from 'negative experiences.'

'Look, there's the cute policeman who took all of our statements,' one of the nurses said, pointing to a tall black man in a dark gray suit.

'I don't see Tish anywhere,' the other one said, craning her neck.

'She isn't coming,' the nurse said. 'She said she hates funerals.'

'So do I,' the other one said.

'It isn't a funeral,' Eileen said. 'It's a memorial service.'

'What's the difference?' the first nurse asked.

'There's no body. The family's having a private graveside service later.'

But when they came into the sanctuary, there was a bronze casket at the front, with half of its lid raised and a blanket of white mums and carnations on the other half. 'We don't have to file past and look at her, do we?' the shorter nurse asked.

'Well, *I'm* not,' Eileen said and slid into a pew. The other two nurses sat down next to her. Richard stood a moment looking at the casket, his fists clenched, and then walked up the aisle. When he got to the casket, he stood there a long moment, afraid to look down, afraid Joanna's terror and her panic might be reflected in her face, but there was no sign of it.

She lay with her head on an ivory satin pillow, her hair arranged around her head in unfamiliar curls. The dress she was wearing was unfamiliar, too, high-necked, with lace ruffles, and around her neck was a silver cross. Her white hands lay folded across her chest, hiding the slashed aorta, the Y incision.

A gray-haired woman had come up beside him. 'Doesn't she look natural?' she said. Natural. The mortician had set her glasses high on the bridge of her nose, and put rouge on her white cheeks, dark red lipstick on her bloodless lips. Joanna had never worn lipstick that color in her life. In her life.

'She looks so peaceful,' the gray-haired woman said, and he looked earnestly into Joanna's face, hoping it was true, but it wasn't. Her ashen, made-up face held no expression at all.

He continued to stand there, looking blindly down at her, and after a minute Eileen came up and led him back to the pew. He sat down. The nurse who had recommended *Ten Steps* reached across Eileen and handed him a pamphlet. It was titled 'Four Tips for Getting Through the Funeral.' The organist began playing.

Kit came in, leading a tall, graying man. Vielle was with them. They sat down several rows ahead. 'Who's getting married?' the man said, and Kit bent toward him, whispering, and no wonder she hadn't been shocked by what he'd told her. She witnessed horrors every day.

And the funeral was one of them. A soloist sang, 'On Jordan's Banks I Stand,' and then the minister preached a sermon on the necessity of being saved 'while there is yet time, for none knows the day or the hour when we will suddenly come face to face with God's judgment.

'As it says in the Holy Scriptures,' he intoned, 'when that judgment comes, those who have confessed their sins and taken Jesus Christ as their personal savior shall enter life eternal, but those who have not accepted Him shall go away into everlasting punishment. Now, will you please turn to Hymn 458 in your hymnals?'

Hymn 458 was 'Nearer, My God, to Thee.' I can't stand this, Richard thought, looking wildly around for a way out, but there was a whole row of people on either side.

The minister brought down his hands in a broad gesture. 'You may be seated. And now, Joanna's colleague and dear friend would like to say a few words about her life,' he said and nodded at Mandrake. Mandrake stood up, holding a sheaf of papers, and started for the front. As he came near the casket, he turned to smile comfortingly at Joanna's sister.

And if Richard had needed any proof that Joanna wasn't there, that she was oceans, years away, trapped on the *Titanic*, this was it.

Because if she'd been there, even though she was dead, she would never have lain there passively on the shirred satin, eyes closed, hands composed, with Mandrake coming. She would have been out of the casket and sprinting for the choir loft, making a dash for the side door, saying the way she had that first day, 'If I talk to him I'm liable to kill him.'

She didn't move. Mandrake went up to the casket, looked down at her, still with that disgusting smile, and bent to kiss her forehead. Richard must have made a sound, must have made a move to stand up, because Eileen reached over and put a hand on his arm, grasping it firmly, holding him down.

Mandrake walked to the pulpit and then stood there, his hands on the sides of the pulpit, smiling oilily at the congregation. 'I was Joanna Lander's friend,' he said, 'perhaps her best friend.'

Richard looked ahead at Vielle. Kit had her hand clasped firmly in Vielle's.

'I say that,' Mandrake said, 'because I not only worked with her, as many of you did, but because I shared a common goal with her, a common passion. Both of us had devoted our lives to discovering the mystery of Death, a mystery that is a mystery to her no longer.' He smiled gently in the direction of the casket. 'Of course we all have our faults. Joanna was always in a hurry.'

Yeah, trying to get away from you.

'She was also sometimes too skeptical,' he said, and chuckled as if it were an amusing shortcoming. 'Skepticism is an excellent quality ...'

How would you know?

'But Joanna often carried it to extremes and refused to believe the evidence that was so plainly before her, evidence that Death was not the end.' He smiled at the congregation. 'You may have read my book, *The Light at the End of the Tunnel*.'

'I don't believe it,' Eileen muttered next to him. 'He's plugging his book at a funeral.'

'If you've read it, you know that Death need hold no fears, that even though dying may seem painful, terrifying, to those of us left behind, it is not. For our loved ones await us, and an Angel of Light. We know that from the mouths of those who have seen that light, seen those loved ones, from the message they have brought back from the Other Side.'

He cast a sickly smile in the direction of the casket. 'Joanna didn't believe that. She was a skeptic – she believed near-death experiences were hallucinations, caused by endorphins or lack of oxygen,' he waved them away with his hand. 'Which is why her testimony, *the testimony of a skeptic*, is so compelling.'

He paused dramatically. 'I heard Joanna's last words. She spoke them to me only moments before her death, as she was on her way down to that fateful encounter. Joanna was heading down a hallway to the elevator that would take her down to the emergency room. And do you know what she did?' He paused expectantly.

She looked frantically around for a stairway, Richard thought, for a way out.

'I'll tell you what she did,' Mandrake said. 'She stopped me and said, "Mr Mandrake, I wanted to tell you, you were right about the near-death experience. It was a message from the Other Side." '

' "You have seen what lies on the Other Side then?" I asked her, and I could see the answer in her face, radiant with joy. She was a skeptic no longer. "You were right, Mr Mandrake," she said. "It was a message from the Other Side." What more proof do we need of the afterlife that awaits us? Joanna herself has told us, with her last breath, her last words.'

Her last words, Richard thought. 'Why do people in movies always say things like "The murderer is ... Bang!" ' Joanna had said at Dish Night. 'You'd think, if they had something that important to communicate, they'd say it first.'

'Joanna used her last words to send a message from the Other Side,' Mr

Mandrake said. 'How can we fail to heed that message? I for one intend to as I complete my new book, *Messages from the Other Side*.'

' "You're doing it wrong," ' she had said. ' "Important words first." ' ' "Tell Richard … SOS." '

'Joanna had only a few minutes to live,' Mandrake said, 'and how did she choose to spend it? By sharing her vision of the afterlife with us.'

'She didn't think it was the *Titanic*,' Kit had said. 'She said she wished she could die saving somebody's life.'

Mandrake must have finished. The organ was playing 'Shall We Gather at the River?' and people were starting to file out. Richard followed them into the aisle, and then stood there, staring at Joanna's casket.

'I don't think that was what she was trying to tell you,' Vielle had said. 'I think she was trying to tell you something good.'

People filed out past him, talking about the flowers, the solo, the casket. 'She can't be gone,' Nina sobbed to a gangly resident, 'I can't believe it.'

'I can't believe it about fox, can you?' Davis's message on the answering machine had said. 'Warn me before it hits the star,' and Richard hadn't understood the message at all. 'She kept saying, "Water," ' Vielle had said. 'She was really saying, "Walter." '

The minister laid a hand on his arm. 'Do you wish to say good-bye to the departed?' he whispered. 'They're about to close the casket.' Richard looked up the aisle. Two men in black suits stood by the casket, hands folded in front of them.

'There'll be a luncheon in the fellowship hall downstairs,' the minister said. 'We hope you'll stay.' He gave Richard's arm a gentle squeeze and walked up the aisle, nodding to the men as he went. They began moving the spray of flowers.

'The best plan would be to decide in advance what you wanted your last words to be and then memorize them, so you'd be ready,' Joanna had said.

The two men lowered the casket lid.

'Whatever it was must've been important,' Mr Wojakowski had said. 'She was in such a hurry to tell you, she almost ran me down.'

'Are you all right?' Eileen said, coming rapidly up the aisle to him.

The men fastened the casket lid shut and began shifting the blanket of flowers so it lay in the center.

'Look, we're all going to go over to Santeramo's and get a pizza,' Eileen said, taking his arm and leading him out of the sanctuary and over to the other two nurses. 'Why don't you come with us?'

'No,' he said, looking around for Kit and Vielle. He couldn't see them.

'It'd do you good,' the nurse who had given him the pamphlet said. 'It'd get your mind off it.'

'You need to eat something,' the other nurse said.

'I need to get back to the hospital. Vielle's giving me a ride back,' he said firmly and set out through the crowd to find her and Kit.

The minister and Joanna's sister were standing with Mandrake. '– just acknowledging there's an afterlife isn't enough,' Joanna's sister was saying stubbornly to Mandrake. 'You have to confess your sins before you can be saved.'

He couldn't see Vielle anywhere, or Kit. They must have left, or else gone downstairs to the fellowship hall. He started across to the basement steps and ran into Mr Wojakowski, holding forth to a circle of elderly ladies. 'Hiya, Doc,' he said. 'Sad, sad thing. I've seen a lot of funerals. On the *Yorktown*, they—'

'When you saw Joanna, that last day,' Richard said, 'did she say what she wanted to tell me?'

'Nope. She was in too big a hurry. She didn't even hear me the first coupla times I yelled at her. 'Did somebody call battle stations?' I asked her. At Midway, they'd call battle stations, and boy, did everybody scramble for their tin hats, 'cause they knew in about five minutes all hell'd be breaking loose. They'd run up those gangways so fast they didn't even take time to put on their pants, scared as rabbits –'

'Joanna was scared?' Richard asked. 'She seemed frightened, upset?'

'Joanna? Hell, no. She looked like my bunkmate Frankie Cocelli used to look during a battle. Little skinny guy, looked like you could snap him in two, but not afraid of anything. "Let me at 'em!" he'd shout when the sirens went, and go tearing off like he couldn't wait to get shot at. Did, too. Did I ever tell you how he got it? This Jap Zero—'

'And that's how Joanna looked?' Richard persisted. 'Eager? Excited?'

'Yeah. She said she had to go find you, that she had something important to tell you.'

'But she didn't say what?'

'Nope. So anyway, this Zero—'

Richard spotted Vielle, just inside the door. 'Excuse me,' he said and edged his way through the crowd to her. 'I've been looking for you,' he said.

'I was outside with Kit. She had to take her uncle home,' Vielle said. 'He kept asking her who'd died, over and over.' She shook her head. 'Poor man. Or maybe he's the lucky one. At least he won't remember this funeral.'

'I need to talk to you,' Richard said. 'I need to know exactly what Joanna said to you in the ER.'

'If you're worried about what Mandrake said, forget it. He's lying,' Vielle said. 'Joanna never voluntarily said two words to him in her life, let alone that NDEs were a message from the Other Side.'

'I know that,' he said impatiently. 'I need to know what she said to you.'

'There's no point in torturing yourself over—'

'The exact words. It's important.'

She looked curiously at him. 'Did something happen?'

'That's what I'm trying to find out. What did she say? Exactly.'

'She said, "Tell Richard," ' Vielle said, squinting in her effort to remember. ' "It's …" The resident was trying to start an airway, and she waved him away. And then, "SOS. SOS." '

He grabbed a pen out of his pocket and scribbled the words on the order of service. ' "Tell Richard … it's … SOS, SOS," ' he said. 'Is that all?'

'Yes. No. Just before that, she grabbed for my hand and said, "Important." ' Important.

'Are you okay?' Vielle said.

'Yeah,' he said, staring at the order of service. Tell Richard it's … what? What had she been trying to tell him when they interrupted her to put the airway in?

'Look, I don't think it's a good idea for you to be alone right now,' Vielle said, 'especially after that travesty of a funeral.' She glared across the room at Mandrake and Joanna's sister. 'Some of us from the ER are going to go get something to eat. Why don't you come with us?'

'No,' he said. 'I've got to get back to the hospital.' He walked quickly out into the parking lot and caught a ride with Mrs Dirksen from Personnel.

'Wasn't that a beautiful sermon?' she asked him. 'I loved the music.'

'Umm,' Richard said, not listening. Tell Richard it's … Important. She had been trying to tell him something. Something important.

But what if he was confabulating? Manipulating her words so he didn't have to face the fact that she had called out to him for help? 'The problem with NDEs is, there's no way to obtain outside confirmation,' Joanna had said.

'And Mr Mandrake's eulogy was just wonderful,' Mrs Dirksen said. She pulled into the hospital parking lot. 'Didn't you think so?'

'Thanks for the ride,' Richard said and dashed up the shortcut to the lab.

He pushed a chair over against the cabinet, climbed up on it, and reached his arm over the edge, feeling far back. There was nothing there. He patted around the top of the cabinet with the flat of his hand and then reached all the way back to the wall and swept his hand along the edge.

It was a piece of cardboard. He scooted it forward with his fingers till he could pick it up. It was a postcard of a tropical sunset, garish pink and red and gold, with palm trees silhouetted against the bright orange ocean. He turned it over, half afraid of what it would say, but it wasn't Joanna's handwriting.

Up at the top someone had written in a clear, spiky hand, one under the other, *Pretty Woman, Remember the Titans, What Lies Beneath.* The other hand, not Joanna's either, was a barely legible scrawl. He couldn't read the signature, and he had a hard time reading the message. 'Having a wonderful time,' it said. 'Wish you were here.'

A message from the dead.

He got down off the chair, plugged in the phone, and found Kit Gardiner's number. 'Kit,' he said when she answered. 'I need you to come to the hospital. And bring the book.'

46

'Tell me if anything was ever done.'

> – Line repeated over and over in
> LEONARDO DA VINCI's notebooks

They met in the cafeteria. Richard had called Vielle as soon as he hung up with Kit, and she had suggested it as being closer to the ER in case she was paged. 'If it's open,' she had added. 'Which I doubt.'

Amazingly, though, it was. Joanna would never believe this, Richard thought, and it was the first thought of her that didn't feel like a punch in the stomach.

The cafeteria was nearly empty. Because everyone assumes it's closed, Richard thought, going through the deserted line for his coffee, but Vielle said, filling a paper cup with Coke, 'Everybody's at the Coping with Post-Trauma Stress Workshop.' They paid a put-out-looking cashier in a pink uniform and sat down at the table in the far corner where Kit was already waiting.

'So,' Vielle said, setting her Coke down. 'Where do we start?'

'We reconstruct Joanna's movements that day,' Richard said. 'The last time I saw her was in her office. She was transcribing interviews. I went to tell her I was going to meet with Dr Jamison at one, but that I'd be back in time for Mrs Troudtheim's session. That was at eleven-thirty. At a little after one she told Mr Wojakowski she had something important to tell me, so important it couldn't wait till I got back to the lab, even though I'd told her I'd be back before two.'

'I talked to her on the phone around eleven-thirty, too,' Kit said. 'It must have been either right before or right after you saw her. I called to tell her I'd found the book she asked me to look for.'

'And how did she seem?' Richard asked.

'Busy,' Kit said. 'Distracted.'

'But not excited?' Vielle put in.

Kit shook her head.

'Mr Wojakowski says that when he saw her she was in a hurry, very excited,'

Richard said. 'And Diane Tollafson saw her then, too, going down the stairs to the ER, which leaves us with an hour and a half.'

Vielle shook her head. 'An hour. I talked to Susy Coplis. She says she saw Joanna getting into an elevator at ten to one, also in a hurry.'

'And excited?' Richard asked.

Vielle shook her head. 'She only saw Joanna from the back, but Susy was headed for the same elevator, and she was in a hurry, too, because she was late getting back from lunch, but Joanna was in so much of a hurry that by the time Susy got to the elevator, the doors had already closed.'

'Did she see which floor Joanna was going to?'

'*Yes,*' Vielle said, pleased, 'because she had to stand there and wait for it to come back. She said it went straight up to eight.'

'What's on eight?' Kit asked.

'Dr Jamison's office,' Richard said. 'She obviously went up there looking for me and found the note Dr Jamison had left on her door, saying she'd gone down to the ER, and assumed I'd gone there, too.'

'So that she was on her way there when she ran into Mr Wojakowski,' Kit put in.

'Yes,' Richard said. 'What floor was Susy on when she saw her?'

'Three-west,' Vielle said.

'The ICU's in the west wing, isn't it?' Richard asked, and when Vielle nodded, 'Did you call Joanna with any patients who'd coded that morning?'

'No, we didn't have any codes in the ER that day ... that morning,' Vielle corrected herself, and Richard knew she was thinking of the code alarm buzzing as they worked over Joanna.

He said rapidly, 'But a patient could have coded after they were sent upstairs? Did you have any coronaries that morning? Or strokes?'

'I don't remember. I'll check to see if we had any life-threatenings,' she said, jotting it down. 'And I'll find out if anyone coded in the ICU or CICU that day. If they did, one of the nurses might have phoned her.'

'And when she interviewed them they told her something,' Kit said.

'Yes,' Richard said. 'Is there a way to find out who coded that day, and not just in the ICU and CICU?' he asked Vielle.

She nodded. 'Couldn't Joanna also have talked to a patient she'd interviewed before,' Kit asked, 'and they told her something new? Or she found something in the transcript and went to ask them about it? You said she was transcribing interviews when you saw her.'

Richard nodded. He asked Vielle, 'Do you know if any of her previous subjects are still in the hospital?'

'Mrs Davenport,' Vielle said, but Richard doubted very much if Joanna would have voluntarily gone to see Mrs Davenport, or believed anything she had to say if she had. Who else had she mentioned? Mrs Woollam. No, Mrs

Woollam had died. He would have to check her transcripts for their names. It was unlikely any of the ones she'd interviewed in recent weeks were still in the hospital in this age of HMOs, but he made a note to check the transcripts for their names.

'We've still got an hour unaccounted for,' Richard said. 'Vielle, you haven't found anyone else who saw Joanna during that time?'

'Not yet,' Vielle said.

'What about Maurice Mandrake?' Kit asked. Richard and Vielle both turned to look at her.

'At the funeral, he said he talked to Joanna.'

'He was lying,' they both said together.

'I know he lied about what Joanna said,' Kit said, 'but isn't there a possibility he was telling the truth about having seen her?'

'She's right,' Vielle said. 'Joanna might have run into him accidentally, and if that's the case, he might be able to tell us which part of the hospital she was in and which direction she was headed.'

Away from Mandrake as fast as she could, Richard thought. 'Okay,' he said.

'Joanna might have found something in the transcripts,' Vielle said, 'and gone to ask someone about it, but couldn't she have just found something in them and gone to look for you, in which case the answer would be in the transcripts?'

Richard shook his head. 'She would have gone to the lab and then up to Dr Jamison's office on eighth, not down to three-west.'

'Oh, that's right,' Vielle said. 'Wait, Kit said she'd called and told Joanna she'd found a book. Joanna could have started over there to get it and gone down to the parking lot and then thought of something she'd seen in the transcripts. No, that wouldn't have taken her to the west wing either.'

'And she told me she didn't think she could come get the book till after work.'

'She might have changed her mind,' Vielle said, but Kit was shaking her head again.

'She didn't show any interest in the book at all,' Kit said. 'The first time I found it she was excited, she said she'd come right over. This time I got the idea she didn't even care.'

'What did she say?' Richard asked. 'Her exact words?'

'She said she was really busy, and she didn't know when she'd be able to get over,' Kit said slowly, trying to remember. 'She said, "Things are really crazy around here," but she didn't sound like that, like she was harassed and busy.'

'How *did* she sound?' Richard asked.

'Distracted,' Kit said. 'When I first told her about the book, I got the idea she didn't know what I was talking about. She sounded … distant, worried. Definitely not excited or happy.'

'And she didn't say why she was busy or what she was working on?'

'No,' Kit said, but she had hesitated before answering, she wasn't looking at him.

'She said something,' he said. 'We have to hear it, even if it's bad. What did she say?'

Kit tamped down the straw in her Coke. 'She asked me if I'd found out if there were any fires on the *Titanic*.'

'Fires?' Vielle said incredulously. 'The *Titanic* hit an iceberg, it didn't burn down.'

'I know,' Kit said, 'but she wanted to know if there had been any fires on board after it hit the iceberg.'

'Were there?' Richard asked curiously.

'Yes and no,' Kit said. 'There had been a fire smoldering in the coal in Boiler Room 6 since before the ship sailed, and there were fireplaces in the first-class lounge and the smoking room, but no other fires.'

'You said she asked you if you'd found this out?' Richard said. 'Had she asked you about a fire before?'

Kit nodded. 'The day I found the book,' she said. 'The first time, I mean. I'd found the book four days before, but when she came over to get it, my uncle had hidden it again.'

'And she asked you about the fires then?'

'Yes.'

And four days later she was still on the same track, Richard thought. Whatever it was.

'That was the day I saw her getting into a taxi,' Vielle said. 'She looked like she was in a desperate hurry, and she didn't have her coat on or her purse. Kit, did she have a coat on when she came to see you?'

'No, just a cardigan,' Kit said, 'but she didn't come in a taxi. She had her car.'

'And she asked you about fires on the *Titanic*?' Richard asked.

'Yes, and I said I didn't know of any, but I said I'd check.'

'And you're sure she came in her own car and not a taxi?' Vielle said.

'Yes, because she left in such a hurry. When I came downstairs from look-ing for the book, she said she had to go, and went out and got into her car without even saying good-bye. I thought she was upset because my uncle had said something to her – he does sometimes, he can't help himself, it's the illness – or because I couldn't find the book –'

Vielle was shaking her head. 'She was already upset when I saw her,' she said. 'I wonder where she was going in that taxi? What time did she come to your house?'

'Two o'clock,' Kit said.

'Are you sure?' Vielle asked, frowning.

'Yes. I was surprised to see her. She'd said she didn't think she'd be over till later on that afternoon. Why?'

'Because it was a quarter after one when she got in the taxi,' Vielle said, 'and she would have had to go wherever she went, come back, get her own car, and drive to your house, which is how far from the hospital?'

'Twenty minutes,' Kit said.

'Twenty minutes, by two o'clock,' Vielle finished her sentence. 'Which means wherever she was going in that taxi could only have been a few blocks away. What's a few blocks from the hospital?'

'What are you getting at, Vielle?' Richard asked. 'You think she found out whatever it was four days ago instead of the day she was killed?'

'Or part of it,' Vielle said, 'and then she spent the next three days trying to find out the other part, or trying to prove what she'd discovered. And it had something to do with a fire on the *Titanic*.'

'But there wasn't a fire on the *Titanic*,' Kit said, 'at least not the kind she wanted. When I told her about Boiler Room 6, she asked me if it had caused a lot of smoke, and when I said no, she asked me if there had been any other fires. And she wasn't excited. She seemed worried and upset. Was she excited when you saw her getting into the taxi, Vielle?'

'No,' Vielle conceded. 'I saw her that night after she got back, and she looked like she'd just had bad news. I was worried about her. I was afraid the project was making her sick.'

And four days later, excited and happy, she had run down to her death in her eagerness to tell him something.

'Are you finished with this?' a voice said. Richard turned around. The cafeteria lady was standing there, pointing grimly at his coffee.

He nodded, and she snatched it and the Coke cups off the table and wiped at the table with a gray rag. 'You need to finish up. We close in ten minutes,' she said, and went over to stand pointedly by the door.

'We need more time,' Vielle said.

Richard shook his head. 'What we need is more data. We need to find out where she went in the hospital.'

'And in that taxi,' Vielle said.

Richard nodded. 'We need to find out what she was doing on three-west, what she was looking for in the transcripts –'

'And what happened between her and my uncle while I was upstairs,' Kit said.

'Will he remember?' Richard asked.

'I don't know,' Kit said. 'Sometimes a direct question, if it's casual enough – I'll try.'

'I want you to go through the textbook, too,' Richard said, 'and see if you can find anything in it about the *Titanic*.'

'But she'd lost interest in the textbook,' Kit said.

'Maybe, or maybe she'd remembered what was in it and no longer needed it,' Richard said. 'And see what else you can find out about a fire. The ship was listing. Maybe a candle in one of the cabins fell over and caught the curtains on fire.'

'I'll talk to the staff,' Vielle said, 'and see if anybody coded that day, and if anybody else saw Joanna. And I'll try to find the driver of the taxi she took.'

'And I'll go through the transcripts,' Richard said.

'No,' Kit said, and he looked at her in surprise. 'I can go through the transcripts. You've got to keep working on your research.'

'Finding out what she said is more important –' Richard began.

She shook her head violently. 'There's only one thing Joanna could have had to tell you that was so important it couldn't wait, and that was that she'd figured out what the NDE is, and how it works.'

'How it –?' Richard said. 'But Joanna couldn't read the scans or interpret the neurotransmitter data—'

Kit cut him off. 'Maybe not the actual mechanics of the NDE, but the essence of it, the connection. She was determined to find out what my uncle said in class about the *Titanic*. She was convinced it was the key to the NDE, to how it worked. That was why she wanted the textbook, because she thought it might help her remember,' she said, and her earnestness reminded him of Joanna, saying, 'The *Titanic* means something. I know it.' And he had said, 'It's a contentless feeling. It's caused by the temporal lobe.'

'You think she discovered the connection?' Richard asked.

Kit nodded. 'It's the only thing that would have made her try so hard to tell you when she …' Kit faltered. 'She has to have remembered the connection. Maybe she found something in the transcripts, or someone she talked to said something that clicked, but whatever it was, it had something to do with the NDEs and the scans, so you have to keep working on them.'

'All right,' he said. 'And I'll talk to Mrs Davenport. What else?'

'You need to check her messages,' Vielle said. 'Someone might have called her. People who'd had NDEs were always calling her.'

Richard wrote down 'answering machine' and 'switchboard.' 'We'll meet again – when?' he asked. 'Friday? Does that give everybody time?'

Kit and Vielle both nodded. 'Same time, same place?' Vielle asked.

'We're closed on Fridays,' the cafeteria lady called over from the door. She tapped her watch. 'Five minutes.'

'In the lab,' Richard said, pushing his chair under the table. 'Or, if anybody finds out anything before then, we call and set up something sooner.'

The cafeteria lady was holding the door open. They filed through it under her disapproving eye. 'Do you want to come up to Joanna's office with me and get the transcripts now?' Richard asked Kit.

'I can't,' she said with an anxious glance at her watch. 'The Eldercare person can only stay until four. I'll come get them tomorrow morning. Will ten work?'

'Sure,' he said.

'I'll see you then,' she said and hurried toward the elevator.

'And I've got to get back to the ER,' Vielle said. 'I'll call you if I find anybody else who saw Joanna.'

She started for the stairs. Halfway there, she stopped, said, 'Damn!' and came back toward Richard.

'What's the matter?' he said.

'I keep forgetting I can't get there from here,' she said, exasperated. 'They're painting the whole first floor. It's completely blocked off.' She walked past him and headed for the elevator. 'I've got to go up to second and take the service elevator down.'

And that was exactly the problem, he thought, looking after her. Half the hospital's stairs and walkways were blocked off at any given time, and even when they weren't, it was nearly impossible to get from one part of Mercy General to another. And Joanna had had Mandrake on her tail. She might have ducked into an elevator or down a hall to avoid him, or taken a shortcut to avoid a blocked-off walkway. Which meant her having been seen on three-west didn't mean a thing. Unless we've got a map of Mercy General, and not just a map. A map of Mercy General that day. Which meant talking to Maintenance.

He went down to the basement and talked to a man named Podell, who clearly thought Richard was there to complain about something and who eventually reluctantly produced a work schedule. 'They may not have been painting those when it says, though,' he said helpfully.

But it was a start. Richard copied the schedule down and stuck it in his pocket. 'Do you have a map?'

Podell stared incredulously at him. 'Of Mercy General?'

Richard settled for asking Podell the quickest way to get up to three-west, and carefully writing his instructions down, then going up to Medicine to see Mrs Davenport. She wasn't there – she was out having a CAT scan. Richard asked how long she would be and then how to get to eighth, writing those instructions down, too, and drawing the beginnings of a rudimentary map of the halls and elevators as he went.

He did the same thing on eighth, opening doors to various linen closets and storage rooms, and when he found a stairway, following it as far down as it would go. By the time he went back to the lab, the paper was a maze of crisscrossing lines and squares. He put them on the computer, sketching in floors and the walkways, marking the routes he'd taken and the ones he knew, and outlining the sections he needed to fill in.

All of which was an elaborate form of stalling, so he wouldn't have to go into Joanna's office and get the transcripts. But Kit would be there in the morning to pick them up, and it had to be done sooner or later. He got the keys, and went down to her office.

He hadn't been in it since she died. He stood outside, bracing himself, for several minutes, before he unlocked the door and went in. Her computer was still on. Books and stacks of transcripts were heaped on either side of it, with a shoe box full of tumbled tapes on top. Joanna's minirecorder lay next to it, the tape bay open as if she had just popped a tape out. The message light on her answering machine was flashing.

It was impossible not to imagine, looking at the office, that she had not simply stepped out for a second. That she would not be right back, appearing in the doorway, breathless, saying, 'I'm sorry I'm late. Did you get my message?'

But the messages on the machine were a week old, the plant on top of the file cabinet was withered and brown, and he would have to figure out the message himself. Unless whomever she'd gone to see had called her, and she'd listened to the message and then not erased it. He went over to the answering machine and stood there, his finger poised above the 'play' button, bracing himself for the sound of her voice. But her voice wouldn't be on it, only the voices of the people leaving the messages and, he hoped, a clue. He hit 'play.'

Mr Mandrake with a long tirade about Joanna never returning his calls. Mr Wojakowski. Mrs Haighton's housekeeper, relaying the message that Mrs Haighton couldn't come Wednesday, she had a PEO meeting and would have to reschedule. Mr Mandrake again, trying to convince her to go see Mrs Davenport, who had 'overwhelming proof of psychic powers she was granted by the Angel of – machine full. No more messages can be recorded.'

He called the hospital switchboard. All pages were confidential, the operator told him, which under other circumstances would have struck him as funny, and, anyway, no permanent record was kept of the pages.

He hung up and started through the transcripts piled on the desk.

Phrases and words were highlighted in yellow. 'I felt happy and peaceful,' a Mr Sanderson had said, 'as though I had come to the end of a long voyage and was finally home.' The word 'voyage' was highlighted, and elsewhere in the transcript, 'water' and 'cold,' which both made sense, and 'glory,' which didn't. In the next transcript, 'cold' was highlighted again, and 'passage' and 'a sound like something ripping.' In the next, 'darkness' and 'smoke' and one entire sentence: 'I was standing at the bottom of a beautiful stairway going up as far as I could see, and I knew it led to heaven.'

Or the Boat Deck, Richard thought. Joanna had clearly been pursuing a connection with the *Titanic*. Every word and phrase she'd marked, with the exception of 'glory,' was *Titanic*-related. And 'smoke.' No, 'smoke' could relate to possible fires on the *Titanic*. Had she seen one? But she hadn't mentioned a fire in any of her accounts. Or had she? The last two times she'd gone under he'd scarcely listened to her accounts, he'd been so wrapped up in why she'd kicked out. Could there be something in one of them that had triggered the discovery, whatever it was? And made her go tearing off in such a hurry that she'd left the computer on and forgotten her minirecorder?

But she'd had her last session four days before she died. And gone tearing off somewhere in a taxi, looking upset, had showed up at Kit's an hour later without her coat and then left abruptly.

That's it, he thought, there was something in that NDE, and began going through the stack of transcripts, looking for Joanna's. They weren't there, and when he called up her files, neither of her last two accounts were on it. They must still be on the tapes.

He started sorting through them, but a third of them weren't labeled, and those that were, were in some kind of code. He would have to take them home and play them. He dumped all the tapes back into the shoe box and carried them, Joanna's minirecorder, and the computer disks down to the lab and then went back for the transcripts.

It took him two trips. He debated taking the plant, but it looked too far gone to be saved. He shut and locked the door, carried the transcripts down to the lab, stacked them on the examining table, and started down to see Mrs Davenport. Halfway to the elevator, he turned around, walked back to the lab for a beaker of water, and went back to Joanna's office to water the plant.

47

'Yes, lost.'
        – SHOLOM ALEICHEM, after the last card game
        he played on his deathbed, on being told he lost

'The first-class smoking room,' Mr Briarley said and led Joanna into a wide, red-carpeted room. It was paneled in dark wood, with deep red leather chairs. At the far end, near a blazing fireplace, sat a group of people around a table, playing cards.

Joanna could not make out who they were because of the bluish haze of smoke that hung in the room, but she could see that they were all adults. Maisie's not here, she thought, relieved, and then, these must be the first-class passengers who sat playing bridge as the *Titanic* was going down, Colonel Butt and Arthur Ryerson and –

But there were women at the table, too, and the people weren't playing bridge. They were playing poker. She could see the red chips stacked in piles in front of the players and scattered in the middle. And the table wasn't one of the oak ones of the smoking room. It was one of the cafeteria's Formica-topped tables.

Mr Briarley led her across the oak-paneled room toward them. The players looked up and saw them, and one of them laid down his cards and came to meet them. It was Greg Menotti, dressed in sweatpants and a white nylon jacket. 'Where have you been?' he demanded. 'There weren't any lifeboats on the other side. Are there some in second-class?'

'You've met Mr Menotti, of course,' Mr Briarley said, leading Joanna past him and on over to the table.

'I call,' a man in a white waistcoat said, fanning his cards out in front of him, and Joanna saw it was the mustached man who had given her the note. He began raking in a quantity of red chips.

Mr Briarley said, 'Ms Lander, may I introduce –' and the man let go of the chips and stood up, pulling on a dinner jacket.

'J. H. Rogers,' Joanna said. 'I put your message in a bottle and threw it over the side.'

He shook his head. He knows it didn't reach his sister, she thought. 'I'm sorry, Mr Rogers,' she said, and he shook his head again.

'Not J. H. Rogers,' Mr Briarley Whispered in her ear. 'Jay Yates. Professional gambler working the White Star liners under a variety of aliases.'

'You were the one who worked so hard loading the boats,' Joanna said. 'You were a hero.'

'Loading the boats?' Greg Menotti said, pushing himself between Joanna and Yates. 'Where are the others?'

'Others?' Yates said, bewildered.

'The other boats,' Greg insisted.

'There aren't any others,' one of the women said, and Joanna saw it was the woman who'd been out on deck in her nightgown. She was wearing her red coat and the fox fur stole.

'Miss Edith Evans,' Mr Briarley whispered to Joanna. 'She gave up her place in the last lifeboat to a woman with two children.'

'It can't have been the last one!' Greg said. 'There have to be others!' He whirled to face Yates again. 'You were loading the boats. What did they say about them? There were some down in second class, weren't there? Weren't there?'

Yates frowned. 'I remember there was some mention of lowering the boats to the Promenade Deck and loading them from there,' he said.

'But when they got there, the windows were shut,' Mr Briarley said, 'and they had to send everyone back up to the Boat Deck,' but Greg had already run out, pushing his way through the door to the Promenade Deck.

'Greg!' Joanna called after him and turned to Mr Briarley. 'Shouldn't we –?' but he was sitting down at the table, and Yates was pulling out a chair for her.

She sat down and looked around the table. W. T. Stead sat on her left, intent on his cards, which he had laid out in front of him on the table like a tarot hand and was turning over one by one. 'You know Mr Stead,' Mr Briarley said.

Stead glanced impatiently at Joanna, nodded curtly, and went back to turning the cards. 'And everyone else I think you know,' Mr Briarley said, waving his hand around the table.

No, I don't, Joanna thought, but as Mr Briarley introduced them, she realized they were NDE patients she had interviewed: Mr Funderburk, who had been so upset that he had not had an out-of-body experience, and bald, emaciated Ms Grant, who had been so afraid. 'And finally,' Mr Briarley said, indicating a frail, white-haired woman, 'Mrs Woollam.'

Oh, no, Joanna thought, not Mrs Woollam. She didn't deserve to be here. She was supposed to be in a beautiful, beautiful garden with Jesus. But the garden's the Verandah Café, Joanna thought. 'Oh, Mrs Woollam,' she said.

' "Yea, though I walk through the valley of the shadow of death," ' Mrs Woollam said, ' "I will fear no evil," ' but as she spoke, she pressed her Bible to her thin chest fearfully.

'Is that what this is?' Ms Grant said anxiously. 'The valley of the shadow of death?'

'No,' Mr Funderburk said firmly. 'That's nothing like this. I've been there. There's a tunnel, and at the end of it, there's a light. And a Life Review.' He looked skeptically around the smoking room. 'I don't know *what* this is.'

'It's five-card draw,' Yates said. He swept up the cards Stead had been turning over and shuffled them into the deck. 'Aces high,' he said, and began to deal the cards.

Joanna picked hers up as he dealt them. A five. An eight. 'If it isn't the valley of the shadow of death,' Ms Grant said, looking at Joanna, 'what is it?'

'I don't know,' Joanna said.

'*Really?*' Mr Stead said, arching an eyebrow at her. 'I was given to understand you were an expert on the phenomena of dying.'

'No,' Joanna said. 'I thought I was, but I didn't know anything.' And neither do you, she thought. Nobody knows anything.

'In that case,' Stead said, '*I* will explain. There is nothing to fear, Ms Grant. Death is not an end, but a transition. We are but sailing to the Other Side, where wait the spirits of our dear departed. They will greet us on that farther shore, where all is peace and knowledge.'

'And a Life Review,' Mr Funderburk said.

'And we shall understand all mysteries,' Stead said and picked up his cards.

'Are they right?' Ms Grant said. She was gazing hopefully at Joanna, and so was Mrs Woollam. So was Yates.

Joanna glanced at Mr Briarley, but his face was carefully impassive, like it had been in English class, offering no clue to what the answer was, no help at all. 'Are they?' Edith Evans said quietly, and Joanna thought suddenly of Maisie asking, 'Will it hurt?' and of her saying, 'People should tell the truth, even if it's bad.'

'No,' Joanna said, and a sigh went around the table, though of relief or despair she couldn't tell. 'This isn't real. It's all a hallucination. The dying mind—'

'A hallucination?' Mr Stead said, arching an eyebrow at her. 'Are you saying that this fire, this table, these cards –' he said, plucking two from his hand and pushing them across the table toward Yates. 'Two,' he said, and Yates dealt him a pair. He picked them up, arranged them in his hand. '– that these cards –' he fanned them out, face up, 'are not real, and we only imagine that we see them?' He stood up and went over to the fire. 'We only imagine we feel this fire's warmth?' he said, spreading his hands out to the flames. 'Or are we part of the hallucination as well?'

I don't know, Joanna thought.

' "All alone, so Heav'n has will'd, we die," ' Mr Briarley murmured beside her. She looked at him, wondering what he was, what they all were. Confabulations? Snatches of memory and sound and color, flickering randomly? Or metaphors? Symbols of her fear and faith and denial?

'The mind tries to make sense of whatever it experiences,' she said, trying to explain. To whom? To Edith Evans and Jay Yates, who had died ninety years ago? Or to herself? 'The mind can't help it. It keeps doing it even when what it's experiencing is a systems failure. The brain's shutting down and synapses are firing randomly as the cells die, but the mind keeps trying to make sense of it, even though it can't.'

Mrs Woollam was praying, her lips moving silently. Edith Evans had her chin up proudly, bravely. 'It looks for associations from long-term memory, for metaphors to explain what's happening,' Joanna said, 'and since the body's damaged and its systems are slowly going under, it confabulates the *Titanic*.'

'The very image and mirror of Death,' Mr Briarley said.

'But it isn't real,' Joanna said. 'It only seems real.'

'The sinking,' Ms Grant said fearfully. 'Will that seem real?'

'The soul cannot sink,' Stead said sternly. 'It is immortal, and if this,' he waved his arm to include the cards, the fireplace, the entire room, 'is, as Miss Lander says, a *symbol*, what else can it symbolize but the ship of the soul, eternal, indestructible?' He smiled at Ms Grant. 'Such a ship shall never sink.'

Joanna thought of Mr Wojakowski saying earnestly, 'All ships sink sooner or later.'

'Will we confabulate the sinking?' Ms Grant repeated, and it was Joanna she was looking at.

Yes, Joanna thought, afraid. 'I don't know,' she said. 'This is all just a metaphor for what the mind's experiencing, and as the experience changes, as the brain shuts down and the synapses start firing more and more erratically, and –' She thought of what had happened to her on the way down here, memories flaring up like a match and then going out.

'And what?' Ms Grant said frightenedly. 'What will happen?'

'Nothing,' Joanna said. 'As the cells die, there'll no longer be enough to hold the unifying image together, and the *Titanic* will fade, or come apart. It's already happening. This table is a table from Mercy General, and you –' She broke off and began again. '– and just now, on the stairs, I wasn't on the *Titanic*. I was in the hallway of my apartment the night my father died. And before, on the Boat Deck, I saw two cheerleaders from my high school. That will happen more and more, till the image of the *Titanic* breaks up completely.'

'And if it doesn't?' Ms Grant said.

'What happened on the *Titanic*?' Edith asked. 'After the boats were gone?'

Joanna looked at Mr Briarley, but he was busy sorting the cards in his hand. 'Her bow went under and she began to list to port,' she said. 'The water came up over the forward well deck and the A Deck companionway. The lights …' she faltered.

'The lights went out,' Edith Evans said.

'Do you think that will be part of the metaphor?' Ms Grant said fearfully. 'The lights going out?'

How can it not be? Joanna thought. This *is* the lights going out, one by one, memory by memory, sensation by sensation, telephone calls and birthday presents and Dish Night, peanut M&M's and snow and sitting perched on Maisie's bed, looking at pictures of the Johnstown flood.

'What happens then?' Edith asked. 'After the lights go out?'

The stern rises into the sky, Joanna thought, rearing up like a drowning swimmer, like a dying soul, and we go down into darkness.

'Death is only an illusion,' Stead said. He poked at the fire. 'A snare of science and unbelief.' He flung the poker into the fire, sending up sprays of ash and sparks. 'There are more things in heaven and earth, Ms Lander, than are dreamt of in your philosophy,' he said, and stalked out of the room.

'What happens then?' Ms Grant asked fearfully.

They take you to the morgue, Joanna thought, and cut your chest open in a Y to measure the knife wound, to determine the cause of death. And then they take you to the mortuary and inject embalming fluid into your veins and mastic compounds into your cheeks and brush your teeth with Ajax. And bury you in the ground.

'What happens then?' Edith said. 'After the lights go out?'

They were all looking at her, waiting for her answer. 'She sinks,' Joanna said.

There was a silence, and then Mrs Woollam said, '"When you pass through the waters, I will be with you, for I am the Lord your God."' She took a quavering breath. 'The important thing is to trust in Jesus.'

'And behave well,' Edith said, her chin up.

'And play the hand you're dealt,' Yates said.

'Yes, so we should,' Joanna said, and picked up the rest of her cards. A two. A six. An ace.

'How many cards do you want?' Yates asked her.

'Two,' she said, and pushed two of her cards at Yates. He dealt her two more, and she knew what they were before she even picked them up.

'I'll open for a hundred,' Mr Funderburk said.

'I'll see your hundred and raise you a hundred,' Edith said. The others, even Mr Stead, even Mrs Woollam, made their bets.

'I'll see you,' Joanna said to them all, 'and raise you everything I've got.' She pushed her stack of red chips to the center.

'When the end comes,' Edith said, reaching over to take Yates's hand. 'When it comes, what should we do?'

You've already done it, Joanna thought, looking enviously at them, all those mothers, all those children, you gave up your place and your life and saved them.

'The end can't come yet,' Mr Funderburk said. 'There is supposed to be a Life Review first.'

And this is it, Joanna thought, looking at Edith, at Yates, this is the Life Review, knowing you failed where others succeeded. Being tried in the balance and found wanting. Maisie, she thought despairingly. Maisie is the important thing. And I didn't do it.

'I call,' Yates said, and Joanna laid down her hand.

'Two pair,' she said. 'Aces and eights.' The dead man's hand.

The doors banged open and Greg stormed in. 'Half of C Deck's underwater,' he announced, 'and the whole First-Class Dining Saloon.'

Ms Grant stood up, wringing her hands. 'How long before the end, do you think?'

'I don't know,' Joanna said. 'Irreversible brain death occurs in four to six minutes, but synapses continue to fire for several minutes after that –'

'It's been longer than that,' Ms Grant said hopefully. 'Maybe—'

Joanna shook her head. 'Time doesn't—'

'The last regular lifeboat was launched at 1:55 A.M.,' Mr Briarley said. 'The lights went out at 2:15, and five minutes later the ship went down. That means there was approximately twenty minutes betwee—'

'*Regular* lifeboats?' Greg Menotti said. 'What do you mean, regular lifeboats?'

'Time doesn't what?' Ms Grant asked.

'There were also four collapsible boats with canvas sides,' Mr Briarley said, 'but only two of them were launched. Collapsible A was washed off the deck and swamped, and Collapsible B capsized. The men who managed to climb aboard her bottom had to—'

'Where are they?' Greg said to Joanna.

'Greg –' Joanna said.

'Time doesn't what?'

Greg grabbed her arm and yanked her to her feet, knocking cards and poker chips onto the floor. 'Where did they keep the collapsibles?'

'On the roof of the officers' quarters,' Mr Briarley said.

'Where are the officers' quarters?' Greg demanded.

'You don't understand,' Joanna said. 'This isn't the *Titanic*. It's a metaphor. We—'

Greg's grip tightened viciously on her arm. 'Where are the officers' quarters? Which deck?'

'Even if they *are* there,' Joanna said, 'it's too late. You had a heart attack. You d—'

'*Which deck?*'

'The Boat Deck,' Joanna said.

'Where on the Boat Deck?'

'On the starboard side,' Joanna said. 'Between the wheelhouse and the wire—' The wireless shack. Where Jack Phillips had kept sending out SOSs long after the boats were gone. Where he had kept sending out signals to the very end.

'Between the wheelhouse and the what?' Greg demanded, but she had already wrenched free of his arm, was already running.

48

'Hold tight!'
– KARL WALLENDA's last words

Mrs Davenport told Richard she had spoken to Joanna only yesterday. 'She has a message for you,' Mrs Davenport said. 'She said to tell you she is happy and doesn't want you to mourn her, because Death is not the end. It is only a passage to the Other Side.'

'I need to know when the last time you saw her on *this* side was,' Richard insisted. 'Did you see her on the day she was killed?'

'*She* was not killed,' Mrs Davenport said. 'Only her body. Her spirit lives eternally.'

I'm wasting my time here. Mrs Davenport doesn't know anything, Richard thought. But too much was at stake to turn on his heel and walk out. 'Did you see her on the day her *body* was killed?' Richard asked.

'Yes,' Mrs Davenport said. 'I saw her walking toward a bright light, and in the light was an angel, extending his hand to her, leading her to the light, and I knew then that she had crossed over, and I was glad, for there is no fear or sorrow or loneliness on the Other Side, only happiness.'

'Mrs Davenport,' Richard said, and her psychic powers must have told her his patience was at an end.

'I did not see her in her earthly body that day,' she said. 'I hadn't seen her for several weeks, even though I'd paged her a number of times.' She smiled beatifically. 'Now I speak with her nearly every day. She said to tell you that you cannot find the truth of death, or life, through science. Instead, you must seek the light.'

'Did she also say, "Rosabelle, believe"?' Richard asked.

'Yes, now that you mention it, I do remember her saying that,' Mrs Davenport said eagerly. 'She said, "Tell Richard, 'Rosabelle, believe.'" What does it mean?'

That you're just as in touch with the Other Side as all those bogus spiritualists Houdini's wife consulted, Richard thought. 'I have to go,' he said.

'Oh, but you can't,' Mrs Davenport said. 'You have to tell me what "Rosabelle, believe" means. Is it some kind of secret code? What does it mean?'

'It means it isn't Joanna you've been getting messages from, it's Houdini,' he said.

'*Really?*' Mrs Davenport said, thrilled. 'You know, I had a feeling it was. Oh, I must tell Mr Mandrake.'

Richard escaped while she was reaching for the phone, and went back up to the lab and science. He called up Amelia Tanaka's scans, and then, after a moment, deleted the command. The secret, if there was one, lay in something Joanna had experienced, something Joanna had seen. He called up Joanna's.

Her scan appeared on the screen, a pattern of purple and green and blue. Telling him something. 'Is it some kind of secret code?' Mrs Davenport had asked. It was, and like Houdini's mind-reading code, it had to be deciphered a little at a time. He began going through her scans, analyzing the patterns grid by grid, mapping the areas of activity, the receptors, the neurotransmitters.

The last time he'd talked to Joanna, he'd told her about the presence of DABA in her and Mrs Troudtheim's scans. Could she have discovered something about –? But she didn't know anything about inhibitors, and DABA was present in other NDEs.

Still, it was a place to start. He checked for its presence in each of Joanna's sessions. It was present in high levels in her last three sessions and at trace levels in her first one. He went through Mr Sage's scans. No DABA at all, but high levels in all but one of Amelia Tanaka's, and trace levels in the template scan. Wonderful.

He started through each session's data, graphing the neurotransmitters. Cortisol in 60 percent, beta-endorphins in 80 percent, enkephalin in 30 percent. And a long list of neurotransmitters present in only one blood panel: taurine, neurotensin, tryptamine, AMP, glycine, adenosine, and every endorphin and peptide in the book.

All right, combinations of neurotransmitters, he thought, and started looking for endorphins in tandem, but there weren't any. It's totally random, he thought at ten-thirty, grabbed a stack of transcripts to read through, and went home.

But the answer wasn't in Ms Kobald's 'The angel touched my brow, and I knew Death was only the beginning,' or in Mr Stockhausen's 'Brigham Young was standing in the light, surrounded by the elders.' It lay in the *Titanic*.

He looked at his watch. Eleven-thirty. The Tattered Cover and Barnes and Noble would both be closed. Who would have books on the *Titanic*? Kit. She had said Joanna had asked her to find out about fires and fog, and Mr Briarley had been an expert on the *Titanic*.

Richard picked up the phone and then put it down again. It was too late to call her, but as soon as he got to the hospital the next morning, he got her on the phone and said, 'When you come to pick up the transcripts, can you bring me an account of the sinking of the *Titanic*?'

'Yes, but I've got a problem. Eldercare can't send anyone over till this afternoon, and I really wanted to get started on the transcripts.'

'I could bring them over to your house,' Richard offered.

'No, I don't want you to have to do that. Look, I can bring Uncle Pat with me, I just can't leave him in the car by himself. Could you meet us in the parking lot at ten with the transcripts?'

'Sure,' he said, but, looking at the transcripts, he knew there was no way he could get them all down to the parking lot in one trip. He needed a box. He went down to Supplies to get one.

They didn't have any. 'Records might have one,' the pretty clerk said, smiling winsomely at Richard. 'They go through a lot of computer paper.'

He went over to Records and told an imperative-looking woman with 'Zaneta' on her nametag, 'I need a box –' but she had already swiveled in her chair to a rack of forms.

'A box of what?' she said, her hand poised to pluck the correct form from its slot.

'Just a box. An empty box,' and amazingly, she handed him a requisition form.

'Fill out the size and number of boxes you need,' she said, pointing to a square on the form, 'and your office number. It'll take a week to ten days.'

'All I want is an empty computer box,' he said, and his pager went off. He switched it off. Zaneta pushed the phone toward him.

'I'll call from my office,' he said and went down the hall and out a back door to the Dumpsters, found an empty IV-packs box, and took it back upstairs. Back in the lab, he filled it with the transcripts, keeping a close eye on the clock, and started down to the parking lot. At the elevator, he remembered he hadn't answered his page, and lugged the heavy box all the way back to the lab on the off-chance it was Vielle who had called.

It wasn't. It was Mrs Haighton, asking if she could reschedule. He didn't call her. He glanced at his watch and started down again, glad he already knew the quickest route to the parking lot and thinking he needed to add it to his map. Kit's car was already pulled up next to the handicapped entrance, its motor running, when he got there. 'Sorry I'm late,' Richard said, leaning in the window Kit rolled down.

'Do you have an excuse from your first-period teacher?' a man's voice demanded, and Richard looked across her at the graying man he'd seen at the funeral. Joanna's Mr Briarley.

'Don't just stand there,' Mr Briarley said. 'Sit down. We're on page fifty-eight, "The Rime of the Ancient Mariner."'

'Uncle Pat,' Kit said, laying her hand on his arm, 'this is Richard Wright. He—'

'I know who he is,' Mr Briarley said. 'When are you going to marry this niece of mine?'

'Richard's just a friend, Uncle Pat,' Kit said. 'I need to talk to him for a minute. You just stay here, all right?'

' "It is an ancient Mariner, and he stoppeth one of three," ' Mr Briarley said. ' " 'By thy long grey beard and glittering eye, Now wherefore stopp'st thou me? The Bridegroom's doors are opened wide, And I am next of kin.' " ' His hand scrabbled at his door, looking for the handle.

'No, you stay here,' Kit said, reaching across him and pushing the door lock down. 'I'll just be a minute. I have to put something in the trunk. You stay here.'

Mr Briarley let his hand drop into his lap. 'That's what history is, and science, and art,' he said waveringly. 'That's what literature is.'

'I'll be right back,' Kit said, opening the door. Richard stepped back, and Kit got out and went around to the back of the car to open the trunk. 'What did Mrs Davenport say?' she asked.

'A lot of nonsense,' Richard said.

'Had Joanna been to see her?' Kit pulled the trunk lid up.

'No.' He set the heavy box in the trunk. 'What about the textbook? Did you find anything?'

' "The Rime of the Ancient Mariner," ' she said ruefully, 'but nothing about the *Titanic*.' She shut the trunk and came around to open the back door. She leaned in and came up with a stack of books. 'Here's the stuff on the *Titanic*,' she said, handing them to him. 'I've got more if you need them.'

'These should keep me busy for a while,' he said, looking at the books.

'Ditto,' Kit said, gesturing toward the trunk. She got back in the car and started it. 'I'll call you if I find anything.'

' "He holds him with his skinny hand," ' Mr Briarley said. ' " "There was a ship," quoth he." '

'A ship?' Richard said.

Kit switched off the ignition and turned to face Mr Briarley. 'Uncle Pat,' she said, 'did you and Joanna talk about a ship?'

'Joanna?' he said vaguely.

'Joanna Lander,' Kit said gently. 'She was a student of yours. She came to see you. She asked you what you said in class. About the *Titanic*? Do you remember?'

'Of course I remember,' Mr Briarley said gruffly.

'What did you tell Joanna?' Kit asked, and Richard waited for his answer, afraid to move, afraid to breathe.

'Joanna,' he said, staring at the windshield. ' "Red as a rose was she." ' He turned and looked at Richard. 'It's a metaphor,' he said. 'You need to know it for the final.'

And that was that. Dead end. Try something else, Richard thought, carrying the books back up to the lab. He started in on the scans, comparing the frontal-cortex patterns with the presence of different neurotransmitters and then with the core elements, looking for correspondences.

There weren't any, but when he graphed the NDEs for length, he saw that Joanna had awakened spontaneously after her third session, and that was one in which theta-asparcine was present. *I wonder if that's the one where she turned and started back down the passageway*, he thought.

It was. He checked the accounts of the other two with theta-asparcine. The one where she had kicked out and the one where she had stepped from the elevator into the passage. But not the one where she had run headlong down the stairs and into the passage. And she had been under for nearly four minutes in the one with the elevator.

He worked until twelve-thirty and then went down to the cafeteria, got a sandwich, and started through the books Kit had given him. He checked their indexes for the entry 'elevator,' not really expecting to find it, and he didn't. He was going to have to read the books.

He started with a coffee-table book called *The Titanic in Color*, with detailed drawings of the smoking lounge, the gymnasium, the Grand Staircase. 'At the head of the William-and-Mary-style staircase was a large clock carved to represent Honour and Glory Crowning Time.' Glory, which Joanna had underlined. But no sign of an elevator.

The Untold Titanic didn't mention one either. It concentrated on the area belowdecks and the crew, hardly any of whom had survived: the officers who'd loaded the boats, the wireless operator, the engineers who had stayed at their posts, working to keep the dynamos for the wireless and the lights going till the very end. Assistant Engineer Harvey, who'd gone back into a flooded boiler room to rescue a crewman with a broken leg. And all the firemen and trimmers and postal clerks who'd stayed at their posts long after they'd been released from duty.

Richard read till he couldn't stand it anymore and then went down to the ER to see if Vielle had found anyone else who'd seen Joanna. 'Nobody,' she said, bandaging a little girl's elbow. 'I talked to a taxi driver who picked up a woman without a coat, but he couldn't remember what she looked like, so it may not have been Joanna.'

'Did he say where he took her?'

She shook her head. 'They're not supposed to give out that information except to the police. There's a guy on the force I'm going to call to see if he can help.'

Richard went back upstairs through the main building, noting down the locations of the elevators and stairways as he did. When he got back to the lab, Kit was waiting outside the door. 'What are you doing here?' he asked.

'I found something,' she said, 'and I was going to call you, but the Eldercare person came – I forgot to call them back this morning and tell them not to come – so I thought it would be easier if I showed you.'

He unlocked the door, and they went inside.

'I found a couple of odd transcripts. Most of them are in a question-and-answer form,' she handed him three stapled sheets, 'but this one's a monologue, and the name on it, Joseph Leibrecht, isn't on her interview list.'

Joseph Leibrecht. The name sounded familiar. He looked at the transcript. A whale, apple blossoms. 'This isn't an interview,' he said. 'It's an account of the NDE a crewman on the *Hindenburg* had.' He wondered what it was doing in with the transcripts. He thought she'd said it had been recorded too long after the fact to be useful, but she had highlighted the words *sea* and *fire*. The fire again.

'You said you found a couple of odd transcripts?' he asked Kit.

'Yes, I made a list of patients Joanna interviewed during the last few months, and there's one who comes up several times.'

'What's his name?' Richard asked, grabbing for a pencil.

'Well, that's just it,' Kit said, taking a transcript out of her bag. 'The name on the transcript is Carl, but I don't know if that's a first or a last name. All the other patients are listed by a first initial and a last name, and the transcripts are different from the others, too.' She pointed to a section. 'The other ones are all in the form of questions and answers, but this one's just phrases and single words, and it doesn't make a lot of sense.'

Richard looked at the line she was pointing at. 'Half? ... red ... patches ...' it read. 'When were these interviews, or whatever they were?' he asked.

Kit consulted her list. 'The first one's dated December fourth, and the last one's the eighteenth of this month.'

'Then whoever he is, there's a chance he was still in the hospital that day,' Richard said.

'Or she,' Kit said. 'If Carl's the last name, it might be a woman.'

'You're right,' Richard said and picked up the phone. 'Let's see if Vielle knows who it is.' He dialed the ER, expecting he wouldn't be able to get through and would have to page her, but a nurse's aide answered and said she'd get her, and after a short interval, Vielle came on the line. 'Did you ever hear Joanna mention a patient named Carl?' he asked her.

'Yes,' Vielle said, 'but that can't be who she went to see.'

'Why not?'

'Because he wasn't in a position to tell her anything. He was in a coma.' A coma. 'He muttered things sometimes,' Vielle explained, 'and she had the nurses write down what he said.'

And that explained the disjointed words and phrases, the question marks after the words. They represented a nurse's best guess at what Carl had mumbled. 'Did you talk to your friend on the police force?'

'No,' she said, 'but I talked to the crash team coordinator, and there were no codes that morning, so if she went to see an NDEer, it must have been one she'd interviewed befo— what?' she said to someone else, and then, 'Shooting accident, gotta go.' She hung up.

'Dead end,' Richard said, putting down the receiver. 'Carl's in a coma.'

'Oh,' Kit said, disappointed. 'Well, anyway, here are the names of the patients.' She started to hand the list to him and then took it back. 'And one of them …' she ran her finger down the list, 'mentioned fog. I thought that might be the source of her asking me if it had been foggy the night of the *Titanic*.' She found the name. 'Maisie Nellis.'

Maisie.

'I think I know where Joanna went,' he said, starting for the door, and then stopped. He didn't even know if Maisie was still in the hospital. 'Hang on,' he said to Kit and picked up the phone and called the switchboard operator. 'Do you have a Maisie Nellis listed as a patient?' he asked her.

'Yes—'

'Thanks,' he said and jammed the receiver down. 'Come on, Kit,' he said.

He told her about Maisie on the way down to four-west. 'She told me she'd seen fog in her NDE the first day I met her, and Joanna told me she saw fog in her second NDE, too.' They reached Peds.

The door to 422 was standing open. 'Maisie?' he said, leaning in. The room was empty, the bed stripped, and folded sheets and a pillow at the foot of it. The tops of the nightstand and the bed table had been cleaned off, and the door to the closet stood open on emptiness.

She's dead, he thought, and it was like Joanna all over again. Maisie's dead, and I didn't even know it was happening.

'Hi,' a woman's voice said, and he turned around. It was Barbara. 'I saw you go past and figured you were looking for Maisie,' she said. 'She's been moved. Up to CICU. She coded again, and this time there was quite a bit of damage. She's been moved to the top of the transplant list.'

'The top of the list,' he said. 'She gets the next available heart?'

'She gets the next available heart that's the right size and the right blood type. Luckily Maisie's Type A, so either a Type A or a Type O will work, but you know what a shortage of donors there is, particularly of children.'

'How long before a heart's likely to become available?' Kit asked.

'There's no way to tell,' Barbara said. 'Hopefully, no more than a few weeks. Days would be better.'

'How's her mother taking all this?' Richard asked.

Barbara stiffened. 'Mrs Nellis –' she started angrily and then stopped herself and said, 'It's possible to carry anything to extremes, even positive thinking.'

'Can Maisie have visitors?' Richard asked.

Barbara nodded. 'She's pretty weak, but I'm sure she'd love to see you. She asked about you the other day.'

'Do you know if Joanna was down here to see Maisie on the day she was killed?' he asked.

'I don't know. I wasn't on that day. I know she'd been down to see her or called her or something the day before because Maisie was all busy looking up something for her in her disaster books.'

'You don't know what it was, do you?'

'No,' Barbara said. 'Something about the *Titanic*. That was Maisie's latest craze. Do you know how to get to CICU?' She gave them complicated instructions, which Richard jotted down for his map, and they started toward the elevator.

'Dr Wright, wait,' Barbara said, hurrying after them. 'There's something you need to know. Maisie doesn't –' she said, and then stopped.

'Maisie doesn't what?'

She bit her lip. 'Nothing. Forget it. I was just going to warn you she looks pretty bad. This last episode –' she stopped again.

'Then maybe I shouldn't—'

'No. I think seeing you is just what she needs. She'll be overjoyed.' But she wasn't. Maisie lay wan and uninterested against her pillows, a daunting array of monitors and machines crowded around her, nearly filling the room. Her TV was on, and the remote lay on the bed close to her hand, but she wasn't watching the screen, she was staring at the wall below it. Her breath came in short, shallow pants.

There were at least six bags hanging from the IV pole. The tubing ran down to her foot, and when he looked at her hand, he could see why. It looked like she had been in a fight, the whole back of it covered in overlapping purple and green and black bruises. A metal ID tag hung around her neck.

'Hi, Maisie,' Richard said, trying not to let any of the horror he felt into his voice. 'Remember me? Dr Wright?'

'Uh-huh,' she said, but there was no enthusiasm in her voice.

'I've got somebody I want you to meet,' he said. 'Maisie, this is Kit. She's a friend of mine.'

'Hi, Maisie,' Kit said.

'Hi,' Maisie said dully.

'I told Kit you're an expert on disasters,' Richard said. He turned to Kit. 'Maisie knows all about the *Hindenburg* and the Hartford circus fire and the Great Molasses Flood.'

'The Great Molasses Flood?' Kit said to Maisie. 'What's that?'

'A big flood,' Maisie said in that same flat, uninterested tone. 'Of molasses.'

He wondered if this was what Barbara had started to warn him about. If it was, he could see why she had changed her mind. He would never have believed it, that Maisie, no matter how sick she was, could be reduced to this dull, passive state. No, not passive. Flattened.

'Did people die?' Kit was asking Maisie. 'In the Great Molasses Flood?'

'People always die,' Maisie said. 'That's what a disaster is, people dying.'

'Dr Wright told me you were friends with Dr Lander,' Kit said.

'She came to see me sometimes,' Maisie said, and her eyes strayed to the TV.

'She was a friend of mine, too,' Kit said. 'When was the last time Dr Lander came to see you, Maisie?'

'I don't remember,' Maisie said, her eyes on the screen.

'It's important, Maisie,' Kit said, reaching for the remote. She clicked off the TV. 'We think Dr Lander found out something important, but we don't know what. We're trying to find out where she was and who she talked to—'

'Why don't you write and ask her?' Maisie said.

'Write and ask her?' Richard said blankly.

Maisie looked at him. 'Didn't she leave you a forwarding address either?'

'A forwarding address?'

'When she moved to New Jersey.'

'Moved to –? Maisie, didn't anybody tell you?' Richard blurted.

'Tell me what?' Maisie asked. She pushed herself to a sitting position. The line on her heart monitor began to spike. Richard looked appealingly across the bed at Kit.

'Something happened to Joanna, didn't it?' Maisie said, her voice rising. '*Didn't* it?'

Her mother, trying to protect her, had told her Joanna had moved away, had kept Barbara and the other nurses from telling her the truth. And now he had – Behind her head the line on her heart monitor was zigzagging sharply. What if he told her, and she went into V-fib from the shock of it? She had already coded twice.

'You *have* to tell me,' Maisie said, but that wasn't true. The heart monitor was setting off alarms in the nurses' station. In a minute a nurse would be down here to shoo them out, to quiet her down, and he wouldn't have to be the one to tell her. 'Please,' Maisie said, and Kit nodded at him.

'Joanna didn't move away, Maisie,' he said gently. 'She died.'

Maisie gaped at him, her mouth open, her eyes wide with shock, not even moving. Behind her on the screen of the monitor, the green line spiked, and then collapsed. I've done it, Richard thought. I've killed her.

'I *knew* it,' Maisie said. 'That's why she didn't come to see me after I coded.' She smiled, a radiant smile. 'I *knew* she wouldn't just move away and not come and tell me good-bye,' she said happily. 'I *knew* it.'

49

'The executioner is, I believe, an expert, and my neck is very slender. Oh, God, have pity on my soul, oh, God, have pity on my soul ...'

– ANNE BOLEYN's last words, spoken just
before her beheading

Joanna tore back along the Promenade Deck. Let the wireless operator still be there, she prayed as she ran. Let him still be sending.

The slant of the deck had gotten worse while she was in the smoking room, and the ship had begun to list. She had to put her hand out to keep from falling against the windows as she ran. Don't let the stairs be underwater, she thought, and then, There was a crew stairway near the aft staircase, and began trying doors.

Locked. The second one opened on a tangle of ropes that fell forward onto the deck. The next was locked. Where *is* it? she thought, yanking on the doorknob, and the door came abruptly open on a metal stairway.

It wasn't the one she'd seen before. It was narrower, steeper, and the stairs were open, the rungs made of metal latticework. The other stairway had had doors on each deck, but this one was open. She could see, looking below her through the latticed steps, that it went all the way down. What if *he's* down there? Joanna thought, her hand still gripping the doorknob.

Joanna looked back down the Promenade Deck. Greg Menotti was halfway down the deck, running hard, his arms and legs pumping. 'You have to show me where the collapsibles are,' he shouted, and Joanna darted inside the stairway. The door swung shut with a click, and she fled up the steps, her feet clattering loudly on the metal stairs.

They tilted forward, so that her feet kept sliding backward off them. She needed to hang on to the metal railing, but she couldn't. She looked down at her hands. She was carrying a cafeteria tray. You've carried it all the way up to Peds without even knowing it, she thought, and tried to give it to the nurse with no hips, but she wasn't in Peds, she was on the stairs, and Greg was coming. You have to let go of it, she thought, and dropped the tray, and it fell through the stairs, hitting the stairs below and falling again, down and down, deck after deck after deck.

Joanna grabbed on to the metal side railing with both hands. It was sharp, so sharp it cut into her palms, and wet. She looked up. Water was trickling down from somewhere above. It's too late, Joanna thought, the railing cutting into her hands like a knife. It's going down.

But Jack Phillips had continued sending to the very end, even after the bow was underwater, even after the captain had told him it was every man for himself. Joanna released her left hand from the railing and began climbing again, staggering a little with the awkward angle of the steps, hitting her hips against the *table, knocking her Kool-Aid over, her mother saying, 'Oh, Joanna,' and reaching for the glass and a towel at the same time, soaking up the Kool-Aid, the towel turning red, redder, soaking through, and Vielle saying, 'Hurry! The movie's starting,' handing her the tub of popcorn, and Joanna feeling her way along the dark passage, unable to see anything, afraid the movie had already started, hoping it was only the coming attractions, seeing light ahead, flickering, golden, like a fire ...* she was on her knees, her fingers tangled in the metal latticework of the step above her. *No*, she thought, not yet, I have to send the message, and pulled herself to her feet. She started up the steps.

There was a sound, and she braced herself against going into the darkness, into the tunnel again. The sound came again from below, echoing, metallic. He's on the stairs, Joanna thought. He's coming up them. She looked down through the open steps, but it wasn't him, it was Greg Menotti starting up the stairs.

Hurry, she thought, and scrambled up the last of the steps, through the door, and was out on the Boat Deck, running, past the air shaft, past the raised roof of the Grand Staircase. Behind her, a door slammed. Hurry, hurry, she thought, and raced past the empty lifeboat davits. The light was still on in the wireless room. She could see it under the door up ahead. The wireless operator kept sending till the power failed, she thought, he kept—

The tail of her cardigan caught, yanking her backward. She fell awkwardly onto one knee. 'Where are the—?' Greg demanded, and there was a sudden, deafening roar of steam. Smoke swirled around them, and she thought, Maybe I can escape in the fog, but when she tried, he grabbed for her wrist, his other hand clutching a fold of her cardigan.

He yanked her to her feet. 'The collapsibles,' he shouted over the roar of the steam. 'Where are they?'

'On top of the officers' quarters,' Joanna said. She pointed with her pinioned hand in the direction of the bow. 'Down there.'

He pushed her ahead of him, her wrist twisted behind her back. 'Show me,' he said. He half-walked, half-shoved her past the funnel, past the wireless shack.

'I have to send a message,' Joanna said, her eyes on the light under the door of the wireless shack. 'It's important.'

'The important thing is getting off this ship before it goes down,' he said, pushing her forward.

He's not real, Joanna thought, willing him to disappear. He's a confabulation, a metaphor, a misfiring. I've invented him out of my own desperation to make sense of what's happening, out of my own panic and denial. He isn't really here. He died six weeks ago. He can't do anything to anybody. But even though she squeezed her eyes shut and tried to see his lifeless body in the ER, his fingers still dug into her wrist, his hand still propelled her roughly forward, past the chart room to the officers' quarters.

'They would have been there,' Joanna said, pointing with her chin at the flat roof above them.

'Where?' he said, looking up. 'It's too dark. I can't see.'

'These are the officers' quarters. They were stored on top,' she said. 'But they aren't there. This isn't the *Titanic*, it's –'

He climbed onto a deck chair, still grasping her wrist, pulling her up after him onto the chair, onto a windlass. He reached across to a stanchion, stretching, and let go of her wrist. Joanna didn't wait. She jumped down off the windlass, off the deck chair, and ran for the wireless shack.

The door was shut, and on it was a large poster. 'Do you know someone at risk?' it read. 'You can save a life.'

She pushed the door open, praying, Please let him still be there, please let him still be sending.

He was. He sat bent over the wireless key, his coat off, his headphones on over his blond hair, his finger jabbing fiercely at the telegraph key. The blue spark leaped between the poles of the dynamo. It's still working, she thought, a wave of relief washing over her. 'I have to send a message,' she said breathlessly. 'It's important.'

Jack Phillips didn't glance up, didn't pause in his steady tapping. He can't hear me, she thought, because of the headphones. 'Jack,' she said, touching his shoulder. He turned impatiently, pulling one of the headphones away from his ear. 'Mr Phil—' she said and stopped, staring.

50

> 'We are 157–337 running north and south. Wait listening on 6210.'
> – Last radio message from AMELIA
> EARHART and FRED NOONAN

Maisie insisted on hearing everything. 'How did she die?' she asked Richard. 'In a disaster?'

'No,' Richard said.

'She was stabbed by a man on drugs in the ER,' Kit said, and Maisie nodded in confirmation, as if they had said yes, in a disaster. And wasn't it? Unexpected, undeserved death, caused by being in the wrong place at the wrong time. How was it different from being in Pompeii when Mount Vesuvius blew? Or on the *Lusitania*?

'Did he stab her lots of times?' Maisie was asking.

Richard looked worriedly at the door. The CICU nurse had already been in once and demanded to know what they were doing. 'I felt funny before,' Maisie had said smoothly, 'but then Dr Wright and Ms Gardiner came to see me and made me feel better.'

It was true. She even looked better, though Richard couldn't have said quite how. Her eyes were still shadowed, her lips still faintly blue, but the strength was back in her voice, and the interest. 'Did the crash team work on her?' she asked. 'Did they use the paddles?'

'They did everything they could to save her,' Richard said, and there was no point in using layman's terms with an expert like Maisie, 'but the knife had sliced the aorta. She died of acute hemorrhage.'

Maisie nodded knowingly. 'What happened to the one who stabbed her?'

'The police killed him,' Kit said.

'Good.' Maisie leaned back against her pillows, and then sat up again. 'You said Joanna found out something important. What?'

'We don't know,' Richard said. He explained about Joanna telling Mr Wojakowski she had something important to tell him, about her trying to tell them something when she was dying.

'Was it about the *Titanic*?' Maisie asked.

Richard looked across the bed at Kit. 'What makes you say that?'

'She was always asking me about the *Titanic*. Was it about a wireless message?'

'Why?' Richard said, afraid to ask.

'She asked me to look up about the wireless messages the last time she came to see me,' Maisie said.

'When was that?' Richard asked. He started to say, 'She died on the fourteenth,' and could hear Joanna saying, Don't lead, don't lead.

'Umm,' Maisie said, screwing her face in thought. 'She asked me to look up the messages, and it took a long time because my mom was here a lot and I went into A-fib a couple of times and had to have all these tests. And then she came and asked me was there a garden on the *Titanic*, and I had to look that up—'

'A garden?' Kit asked. 'There was a list of garden references in her patients' NDEs,' she said to Richard.

'Was there a garden?' Richard asked Maisie.

'Kind of. There was a picture of the Verandah Cafe in one of my books, and it looked like a garden. You know, with flowers and vines and trees and stuff. I called her and told her she should come look at it and that I had the wireless messages all done.'

'Was that the same day she came and asked you about the garden?'

'No, she asked me the day before, and when I called her, she said she couldn't come, she was too busy, and she promised she'd come later, but she didn't. I thought she forgot, but she didn't.' She looked up at Richard. 'I don't know exactly what day it was. You can ask Nurse Barbara. I bet she'll know.'

There was no need to. Whoever Joanna had been to see the day she died, it wasn't Maisie. 'When did you call her, Maisie?' Richard asked. 'What time of day?'

'Right after my mom left to go see her lawyer. I think nine o'clock.'

Nine o'clock, and she had told Maisie the same thing she'd told Kit, that she was busy, that she'd come see her later.

'Did she say when she was going to come see you?' Richard asked.

'She said right after lunch.'

'And when is lunch?' Kit asked.

'Eleven-thirty.'

Joanna had intended to go see Maisie and then hadn't. That confirmed that something had happened, but not what. 'Did she say what she was busy working on?'

'I think the *Titanic* wireless messages, 'cause she asked me to find out what ones they sent.'

Richard and Kit looked at each other. 'Did she say why she wanted to know that?'

Maisie shook her head. 'She just said to write them down, so I did.' She reached over to the nightstand, and the line on her heart monitor began to jump.

'Here, let me,' Kit said hastily, coming around the bed. Maisie lay back against her pillow, and the line steadied. Kit opened the drawer. 'I don't see it,' she said.

'It's inside the *Secret Garden* box,' Maisie said. Kit picked up the video, slid the tape out, looked in the box and then shook it. A tightly folded piece of paper fell out.

Kit handed it to Maisie, who unfolded it carefully. 'Okay, the first one – I listed them by the times they sent them,' she explained. 'The first one was at five after twelve. The last one was at two-ten. It sank at two-twenty.' She stopped to take a breath. 'Okay, so the first one said, "CQD," that means, "all stations distress,"' another breath, '"MGY," that means the *Titanic*,' yet another breath, 'and then where they are.' She handed it to Richard.

He stared blankly at the first message on the page, printed in Maisie's childish hand. 'CQD. CQD. MGY 41.46N, 50.14W. CQD. MGY.'

'The *Titanic* didn't use SOS as its distress signal?' he asked, hope roaring up in him.

'Joanna asked me that, too,' Maisie said. 'They did later on.' She leaned forward to take the paper from him. 'Here it is,' she showed him the place, '"MGY SOS," at twelve-fifteen.'

SOS. Had Joanna seen the wireless operator tapping out one of those messages and wanted outside confirmation? Or was she trying to find out something else, and the clue was here, in Maisie's list? But it couldn't be, because Joanna had never seen it. 'Maisie,' he asked, 'when you called Joanna, did you tell her about the messages you'd found?'

'No,' Maisie said. 'I just told her I'd found them out. I showed her two of them before.'

'Which two?' Richard asked, handing her back the list.

'This one,' she said, pointing, 'and this one.'

'"Come quick. Our engine-room flooded up to the boilers." And "Sinking. Cannot hear for steam."' Joanna had asked Kit about steam and fires on the *Titanic* that might have caused smoke.

'Had she asked you other things about the *Titanic*?' Kit asked.

'Yeah, she asked me did it have an elevator and a swimming pool. And about the *Carpathia*.'

An elderly nurse poked her head in the door. 'It's been five minutes.' Richard nodded. Kit stood up.

'No, you can't go *yet*,' Maisie said and set the monitor zigzagging jerkily. 'You haven't told me what you think she found out or how you're going to figure it out. *Please*, Nurse Lucille,' she appealed to the nurse, 'just two more minutes, and then I'll rest, I promise.' She lay obediently back against the pillows as if to prove it. 'I'll drink my Ensure.'

'All right,' Lucille said, defeated. 'Two more minutes, and that's *all.*' She went out.

As soon as she was gone, Maisie sat up. 'Okay, tell me,' she said. 'You think she went to see somebody and they told her something, don't you? That's why you came to see me, because you thought it was me, right? But it wasn't. *I* bet it was one of her NDE people, so the first thing we've gotta do –'

'We?' Richard said. 'You aren't doing anything except resting.'

'But I could –' Maisie stopped short and slumped back against the pillows.

'Maisie?' he said, glancing anxiously at Kit, who had looked at the monitor and then back at Maisie. Maisie was watching the door.

Lucille came in with a small can with a straw in it. She set it on the tray across Maisie's bed. 'All of it,' she said.

'This is *vanilla,*' Maisie said. 'Don't you have any chocolate?'

'All of it,' Lucille said and walked out.

'I *hate* vanilla,' Maisie muttered, and pushed the can to one side. 'I bet Mr Mandrake knows who all the NDE people are. We could go ask—'

'You aren't going anywhere, Maisie. I mean it,' Richard said, 'you're not going to do anything except rest and get strong so you'll be ready for your new heart. Kit and I will find out who Joanna was talking to.'

'I *wouldn't* be doing anything,' Maisie said, appealing to Kit. 'Just asking people when they come to do stuff if they saw her talking to anybody, the guy who empties the wastebasket and stuff. I wouldn't even get out of bed.' She looked at Richard. '*Please.* Joanna said I was really good at finding stuff out.'

And you fully intend to go ahead whether I give you permission or not, he thought. He wondered how Joanna would have handled her, and then realized he knew. She had put her to work looking up wireless messages and Pacific islands. 'All right,' he said, looking at Kit, who nodded, 'you can help, but you have to promise you'll rest –'

'And do everything your nurses tell you,' Kit said.

'I will,' Maisie said meekly.

'We mean it,' Richard said. 'You're just to ask questions. You're not to *do* anything or go anywhere.'

'They won't let me anyway,' Maisie said disgustedly, and Richard wondered what the story behind that was. 'I promise. I'll just ask questions.'

'All right,' Richard said. 'The time we're looking for is after eleven and before twelve-fifteen.' Maisie started to reach over to the nightstand, and Kit leaped to get a pencil and tablet for her.

'Eleven and twelve-fifteen,' Maisie said, writing them down. 'Do you want me to page you when I find out?'

Richard smiled. 'You can just call me,' he said. He fished one of his cards out of the pocket of his lab coat.

'What if you're not there?'

'You can leave a message on my answering machine,' he said, and, at her skeptical look, 'I promise I'll come the minute I get the message.' He looked at his watch.

'We'd better go,' Kit said, standing up. 'It's been two minutes.'

'You *can't* go yet. I don't have *your* number,' Maisie said. 'In case Dr Wright's answering machine doesn't work.'

The master staller at work. She wrote down Kit's number and then Vielle's. 'But you're not to call the ER,' Richard said sternly. 'They're very busy. You call me.'

'I will,' Maisie said meekly.

'Now, you drink your Ensure and rest,' Richard said, and they started for the door.

'You know what this is just like?' Maisie said.

'What?'

'It's just like the *Titanic*. They had to figure out what happened to the people, only they were dead, so they had to talk to other people and find out what they did and who saw them and stuff.'

Piecing together the tragedy, bit by bit, conversations and glimpses and last words. 'Joanna was crazy about you, you know,' Richard said, and Maisie nodded solemnly.

'I *knew* she wouldn't just go off and leave me.'

'Are you going to be all right, Maisie?' Kit asked.

'Uh-huh,' Maisie said. 'It's almost time for the magazine lady to come. She goes all over the hospital giving people magazines. I bet she might have seen Joanna. Kit, can you fluff up my pillows before you go?'

It took them another five minutes and Lucille's finally coming in to get away. 'You're right,' Kit said as they waited for the elevator. 'She's quite a kid.'

'How did you know I should tell her about Joanna?' Richard asked her.

'She looked just like my uncle Pat the day he got the diagnosis,' she said, staring at the closed elevator door. 'There are worse things than death.'

'Like letting someone down.'

Kit looked up at him. 'We're not going to let Joanna down. We're going to decipher her message.'

But how exactly? By piecing together bits and pieces and conversations. Kit brought him the list of garden references she'd found in among the transcripts and another one headed 'Abrupt NDE Returns.'

'That's from several weeks ago. I've already seen it,' he told Kit, but when he looked at it again, he noticed Amelia Tanaka's name on the list, and when he checked her account against that session's scans, he found she'd come out of the NDE-state on her own, and that theta-asparcine was present.

He went through all of her NDEs and then started on Mr Sage's. Testimony was of no use with Mr Sage, but when Richard checked the scans, he found that he'd gone straight from the NDE-state to waking twice. Both times theta-asparcine had been present. But it wasn't present in Mr Pearsall's NDEs, or Mr O'Reirdon's.

He worked on the scans until his eyes began to burn, and then walked over to the west wing and mapped the rest of the floors, asking assorted nurses and orderlies, 'How can I get up to eight-east from here?' and, 'What's the quickest way down to the ER?', jotting down the answers, and adding the routes to his map.

In between, he pored over Maisie's list of wireless messages. They were almost unbearable to read, a litany of increasing disaster and desperation: 'We are on the ice.' 'We are putting the women off in boats.' 'Require immediate assistance.' 'Sinking fast.' 'SOS. SOS. SOS.'

There was a clue here somewhere, a connection. Joanna had had a reason for asking Maisie to look them up, but he was as dense as the ships replying to the *Titanic*'s SOSs had been. 'What is the matter with you?' the *Olympic* had asked, and then unbelievably, 'Are you steering south to meet us?' The *Frankfurt* had been so clueless that the wireless operator had snapped at him, 'You fool, stand by and keep out!' and even the *Carpathia*'s operator had asked, 'Should I tell my captain?' Thick-headed fools, all of them, unable to figure out a perfectly simple message. Like me, he thought.

Vielle called. 'I found somebody else who saw Joanna. Wanda Rosso. She's a radiologist. She says she saw Joanna on four-west around eleven-thirty.'

'Where on four-west?' Richard asked, calling up the map of Mercy General.

'She was getting into an elevator.'

There were two banks of patient elevators and two service elevators on four-west. 'Which elevator?' he asked.

'She didn't say,' Vielle said. 'I assume the one by the walkway.'

'Ask her,' Richard said. 'Did this Wanda know in which direction Joanna was going?'

'She couldn't remember,' Vielle said. 'She thinks she remembers the "down" arrow being lit, but she's not sure. I asked her if Joanna looked excited or happy, and she said she didn't notice anything except that she seemed to be in a hurry because she kept looking up at the floor numbers and tapping her foot.'

In a hurry, and going somewhere in the west wing. But where? Third was Orthopedics, which didn't seem likely, and below that it was all administrative offices. And this Wanda had said she wasn't sure which arrow was lit. Fourth was Peds, and she hadn't gone to see Maisie. Sixth was cardiac care, a possibility as far as NDEers were concerned, but Joanna hadn't taken her minirecorder with her.

'Did she say if Joanna had a notebook with her?'

'No.'

'Did you find out about the tape?' he asked. 'Do the police have it?'

'No,' Vielle said, and there was an odd change in her voice. 'Her clothes were disposed of.'

'Disposed of?' he said. 'Are you sure? It was evidence.'

'There's no case,' Vielle said. 'The suspect's dead, and there were eye-witnesses, so there was no reason to keep it.'

'But they wouldn't have disposed of the things in her pockets,' he said. 'They'd have returned them to her next of kin. Maybe her sister has the tape. And listen, I've been thinking, there may be notes, too. Joanna always took notes when she did interviews, and we know she didn't have her recorder with her. There may be a notebook, or a piece of paper –'

'It was all disposed of,' Vielle said, and her voice was clipped, definite. 'In the contaminated-waste bin.'

'The contaminated-waste bi—?' he said and then realized what Vielle had been trying to tell him without coming out and saying it. Joanna's clothes had been soaked in blood, and anything in her cardigan pockets would have been drenched, too. Ruined. Unreadable.

'I'm sorry,' Vielle said. 'I still haven't found the taxi driver, but I've got a couple of leads. I'll call you as soon as I've got anything.'

'Yeah,' he said, and went back to the *Titanic*, looking up 'À La Carte Restaurant,' 'gymnasium,' 'First-Class Dining Saloon.' Jim Farrell, a young Irish immigrant, had rounded up four young girls he'd promised to look after and led them all the way from steerage, through the First-Class Dining Saloon and a maze of passages and decks and stairwells to the Boat Deck, and then stepped back, unable to go in the boat himself.

He looked up 'Boat Deck.' Archibald Butt and Colonel Gracie and a gambler named J. H. Rogers had loaded boat after boat, handing babies and children down as the boats were lowered along the side.

Maisie didn't call, which surprised him. He hadn't really thought she'd be able to find out what Vielle, with all her staff connections, couldn't, but he hadn't expected that to stop her from calling him. But there were no messages on his answering machine, no urgent pages. He wondered if she was all right. She had seemed to take the news about Joanna's death in stride, but with kids, it was hard to tell, and it sometimes took bad news a while to sink in.

When she still hadn't called by the next afternoon, Richard ran over to see her. She wasn't there – she was out having an echocardiogram – but the nurse (not the one who'd shooed them out of the room) assured him she was doing fine. 'She's cheered up a lot these last few days,' she said, smiling. 'We've really had to sit on her to see that she stays in bed.'

'Tell her Dr Wright said hi, okay? And that I'll come see her later,' he said, took a few steps toward the elevator and then turned back, looking appropriately confused. 'I need to get down to the ER,' he said. 'What's the easiest way to get there?'

He repeated the process with a nurse and two orderlies, getting three completely different answers, and went back to the lab to add them to the map. He had all of Main and the west wing done and the top four floors of the east wing, and the map was starting to look as complicated as his diagrams of the scans, and just as intelligible.

Joanna had left her office and gone down to two-west and then later had gone up to Dr Jamison's office, and, from there, down to the ER. And in between? He had no idea. All he could deduce for sure was that it hadn't been anything on four-west, since she had been heading down – or up – from there, and that she had probably come down to four-west from her office and taken the walkway across. If she had in fact been coming from her office, if she hadn't gone somewhere else first.

He worked on the map awhile and then listed the neurotransmitters present in the theta-asparcine scans, looking for commonalities. There weren't any. But there was a connection somewhere. Joanna had seen it, and the answer lay somewhere in the scans or the transcripts or her NDEs. Or Joseph Leibrecht's, he thought, and read the crewman's account that Kit had left. He had seen a whale and a bird in a cage and apple blossoms.

Richard went back to the scans, trying to determine if there was any similarity among the non-theta-asparcine scans. There wasn't. He fished the journal Dr Jamison had left out of the mess on his desk and read the article on theta-asparcine. An artificial version had been produced and was being tested to determine its function, which was still not known.

It has something to do with NDEs, he thought. But what? Was it an inhibitor, after all? Or was its presence a side effect of the temporal-lobe stimulation or the acetylcholine?

He worked till he could justify going home, and then called Kit, who hadn't found anything either. 'It definitely has something to do with the *Titanic*, though,' she said, sounding tired. 'All the words she's highlighted relate to it.'

'Is that Ms Lander?' Mr Briarley said in the background. 'This is the second time she's been late for class.'

'It's Dr Wright, Uncle Pat,' Kit said patiently.

'Tell her the answer is C, the very mirror image.'

'I will,' Kit said, and to Richard, 'I'm sorry. What I was saying was that everything she's marked – "elevator" and "glory" and "stairway" – are things she described seeing on the *Titanic* during her NDEs.'

'Are there any highlighted references to wireless messages?' he asked.

'No,' she said, 'even though the word *message* is in nearly every transcript. I've gotta go. Have you heard from Maisie?'

'Not yet,' he said, and started in on the *Titanic* again, looking for clues. But all he found were more horror stories: the postal clerks going down for more sacks of mail and being trapped by water belowdecks; the steerage passengers being kept in the hold while two crew members led small groups up the second-class staircase to C Deck, through the third-class lounge, across the well deck, into the passage that led to first class and up the Grand Staircase to the Boat Deck; Captain Smith swimming toward one of the boats with a baby in his arms and then disappearing.

Richard didn't hear from Maisie the next day either, or the next. Vielle called to say that she'd checked with Wanda Rosso, and it *had* been the patient elevators next to the walkway. 'And she says, now that she's had a chance to think about it, she definitely remembers seeing Joanna press the "down" button.'

I'll bet, he thought, shaking his head. A classic case of confabulation, of filling in a memory that wasn't there with images of other times, other elevators, and of no use at all. 'And you haven't found anybody else in the west wing who saw her?' he asked.

'I haven't had a chance to talk to them. I'm still working on the taxicab thing,' she said and hung up.

All right then, he'd go ask. But nobody else on four-west, or third, or sixth, remembered seeing her. He did find out something. Fifth was completely blocked off for renovation and had been since January. A sign just outside the elevator said the arthritis clinic had been temporarily moved to the second floor of the Brightman Building.

He went back to the lab and marked it on the map, grateful he could eliminate *something*. And at least they had narrowed the place she'd been going to the west wing. Unless she'd been going down to second to the walkway to Main.

He gave up and went back to the scans. He did a series of superimposes of the scans in which theta-asparcine was present, looking for pattern similarities. There weren't any, which meant the theta-asparcine was just a side effect. Or the product of a randomly fired synapse.

And Kit had said, 'It definitely has something to do with the *Titanic*.' The answer was somewhere in the pile of books. He sat down, pulled *The Tragic End of the Titanic* out of the pile, and began to read, his head propped on his hand.

'Accounts of those left on board after the last boats were gone are, of course, sketchy,' he read, 'though all agree there was no panic. Men leaned against the railing or sat on deck chairs, smoking and talking quietly. Father Thomas Byles moved among the steerage passengers, praying and offering absolution. The deck began to list heavily, and the lights dimmed to a reddish –'

Richard slapped the book shut and went back over to the mind-numbing monotony of mapping the scans. He graphed the levels of cortisol and acetylcholine, and then got on the Net and did a search on theta-asparcine. There were only two articles. The first was a study of its presence in heart patients, which—

Someone knocked on the door. He turned around, hoping it was Kit, or Vielle, but it wasn't. It was a woman in a dressy pink suit and high heels. Could this be Mrs Haighton, he wondered, finally here, several eons too late, for her first session?

'Dr Wright?' the woman said. 'I'm Mrs Nellis, Maisie's mother.'

Oh, this is all I need, he thought tiredly. Here it comes. I had no business telling Maisie Joanna died, it's terribly important for her to have only upbeat, cheerful experiences. Positive thinking is so important.

'Maisie's told me so much about you,' Mrs Nellis said. 'I appreciate your taking the time to visit her. It's hard to keep her spirits up, here in the hospital, and your visit cheered her up no end.'

'I like Maisie,' he said warily. 'She's a great kid.'

Mrs Nellis nodded. She was still smiling, but the smile was a little strained.

'She's all right, isn't she?' Richard said. 'Nothing's happened to her?'

'No, oh, no,' Mrs Nellis said. 'She's doing *extremely* well. This new ACE-blocker she's on is working wonders. She tells me you're a research neurologist.'

He was surprised. He had had no idea Maisie knew anything about him except that he was a friend of Joanna's. And what was all this about? If she was going to lecture him over having told Maisie about Joanna, he wished she'd stop smiling and get it over with. 'Yes, that's right,' he said, and, to give her the opening she was apparently looking for, 'I'm researching near-death experiences.'

'So I was told,' she said. 'I understand you believe near-death experiences may actually be some sort of survival mechanism. I also understand that you hope to use your research to develop a technique for reviving patients who've coded, a treatment for bringing them back.'

Who had she been talking to? Joanna would never have told her anything like that, especially knowing her tendency to unbridled optimism, and neither would Maisie. Mandrake? Hardly. Who then? Tish? One of the subjects? It didn't matter. He had to stop this before it went any further. 'Mrs Nellis, my research is only in the very preliminary stages,' he said. 'It's not even clear yet what the near-death experience is or what causes it, let alone how it works.'

'But when you *do* find out how it works,' she persisted, 'and when you *do* develop a treatment, it could help patients who've coded. Like Maisie.'

'No – Mrs Nellis –' he said, feeling like someone trying to stop a runaway train. 'At some point in the far-distant future, the information that we're gathering might possibly be put to some practical use, but what that use might be, or whether, in fact, it will even turn out that—'

'I understand,' she said. 'I know how uncertain and time-consuming medical research is, but I also know that scientific breakthroughs happen all the time. Look at penicillin. And cloning. Amazing new treatments are being developed every day.'

Not a runaway train, a pyroclastic flow, he thought, seeing Maisie's photo of Mount St Helens in his mind's eye, the black cloud roaring unstoppably down the mountain, flattening everything in its path, and wondered if that was where Maisie had gotten her original interest in disasters. 'Even if there were a breakthrough in understanding near-death experiences,' he said, knowing it was useless, 'it wouldn't necessarily result in a medical application, and even if it did, there would have to be experiments, tests, clinical trials –'

'I understand,' she said.

No, you don't, he thought. You don't understand a thing I've said. 'Even if there were a treatment, which there's *not*, there has to be hospital approval and clearance by the research institute's board –'

'I know there will be obstacles,' she said. 'When amiodipril was approved for clinical trials, it took *months* to even get Maisie on the waiting list, but my lawyer's very good at overcoming obstacles.'

I can imagine, Richard thought.

'That's why it's critical to have Maisie in your project now, so all the problems can be worked out in advance. Of course, it's all just precautionary. Maisie's doing *extremely* well on the ACE-blocker. She's completely stabilized, and she may not even need the treatment. But if she does, I want everything to be in place. That's why I came to see you as soon as Maisie told me about your coding cure. If she's in your project, she'll already be approved and the paperwork all completed when the treatment becomes available, and there won't be any unnecessary delays in administering it,' she said, but he had stopped listening at 'as soon as Maisie told me.'

Maisie had told her mother? That he could bring people back from the dead? Where would she have gotten an idea like that? The only person she would ever have talked to about the project was Joanna, and Joanna had always been completely honest with her. She would never have given her false hopes.

And even if she had told Maisie there was a miracle cure (which Richard refused to believe), Maisie wouldn't have believed it. Not hardheaded Maisie, who wore dog tags around her neck so they would know who she was if she died while she was down having tests. If the *Hindenburg* and the Hartford circus fire and the *Lusitania* had taught Maisie anything, it was that there weren't any last-minute rescues. Her mother might believe in miracle cures, but Maisie didn't. And even if she did, she wouldn't have told her mother, of all people.

Joanna had said Maisie never told her mother anything. She hid her books from her, her interest in disasters, even the fact that he'd told her about Joanna's death, and her mother only allowed upbeat discussions. She would never even have let Maisie bring up the subject of coding. Something else must have happened. Maisie must have accidentally mentioned his name, and, to cover, so her mother wouldn't find out he'd been there telling her about Joanna, she'd said something about the project, and her mother had confabulated it, through her powers of positive thinking, into a miracle cure.

'You'll need a copy of her medical history,' Mrs Nellis said, busily planning. 'I'll pick up the project application from Records. Maisie will be so pleased. She was so excited when she was telling me about your project. The possibility of coding again's really worried her, I know. I told her her doctors won't let anything happen to her, but she's been fretting about it.'

But she had coded twice without a quiver. And she had known about the transplant when he and Kit saw her and hadn't seemed frightened. Her only thought had been to help them find out where Joanna had gone.

'Of course I realize a cure for coding will be tremendously in demand, and that there will be many patients competing for it. That's another reason I want Maisie in on the project at this stage,' Mrs Nellis said. 'I'll talk to my lawyer about arranging a waiver for participation by a minor. I'm on my way there now, and I'll ask him about any other possible obstacles.'

Why would Maisie have told her? She had to know she'd take even a casual mention of a possible treatment and turn it into an accomplished fact. So why had she told her? She had to have known she'd do exactly what she had done, come roaring up to the lab and –

That's it, he thought. That's why Maisie told her. So she'd come up here. So she'd insist on my going to see Maisie. Maisie's found out where Joanna was, he thought, and this is her way of telling me. But why hadn't she just called? Or had him paged?

'I'll need to talk to Maisie before I make any decisions regarding the project,' he said.

'Of course. I'll notify the CICU. Maisie doesn't have a phone in her room, but I'll tell the sector nurse to let you speak to her.' Maisie doesn't have a phone, he thought, and she couldn't get anyone to carry a message for her. This is her way of paging me.

'... and if you have any trouble getting through, just have the CICU call me,' she said. 'I'll go straight down there from here and have you put on the approved visitors list, and after I've seen my lawyer, I'll talk to Records about the application process. And I'll leave *you* to work on your project. I *know* your breakthrough's going to happen soon!' she said, smiled brightly, and was gone.

He waited till he heard the elevator ding, then grabbed his lab coat and his name tag, picked up an official-looking clipboard for good measure, and took off for the CICU, taking the stairs to seventh and crossing the walkway, thinking, All those hours of mapping paid off. I can get anywhere in this hospital in five minutes flat.

He ran up the stairs to sixth and down the hall to CICU, where a volunteer at a desk guarded the door. She glanced briefly at his name tag and smiled. He strode through the ward to Maisie's room. The nurse at the desk outside her door stood up. 'Can I help you?' she asked, moving so she was blocking the door.

'I'm Dr Wright,' Richard said. 'I'm here to see Maisie Nellis.'

'Oh, yes, Mrs Nellis said you'd be down,' she said and led the way into the room. Maisie was lying against her pillows, watching TV. 'Dr Wright's here to see you,' the nurse said, moving around behind the bed to look at her IVs. She pushed a button on the IV stand.

'Hi,' Maisie said listlessly, and looked back up at the TV. What if I'm wrong, and she wasn't trying to send a message? Richard thought, watching her. What if I confabulated the whole thing?

The nurse straightened the IV line, pushed the button again, and went out, pulling the door nearly shut behind her. 'Well, it's about time,' Maisie said, pushing herself up to sit. 'What *took* you so long?'

51

'Nearer, my God, to thee.'
  – Last words of US President WILLIAM MCKINLEY,
                              after being shot by an assassin

Joanna stared at the wireless operator's blond hair, at his young, open face. The face that had laughed happily at her from the photo in Mr Briarley's library. 'You're Kit's fiancé,' she said.

'You know Kit?' Kevin said, yanking the earphones off. 'She's not here, is she?' He leaped up, gripped Joanna's shoulders. 'Tell me she's not here.'

'No,' Joanna said hastily. 'She's fine. She's –' but he had already sat back down, was already sending again.

'I have to get a message to her,' he said, tapping out the code. 'I have to tell her I'm sorry. It was my fault, I didn't watch where I was going.'

'Neither did I,' Joanna said.

'I have to get the message to her that I love her,' Kevin said, his forefinger relentlessly tapping out the code. 'I didn't tell her. I didn't even say good-bye.' He picked up the headphones and held the earpiece to his ear. 'There isn't any answer,' he said. 'It's too far.'

'No, it isn't,' Joanna said, kneeling beside him, her hand on his arm. 'The message got through. She knows you loved her. She understands you couldn't say good-bye.'

'And she'll be all right?' he asked anxiously. 'I left her all alone.'

'She's not alone. She's got Vielle, and Richard.'

'Richard?' he said. An expression of pain crossed his face and was replaced by something sadder. 'I was afraid she'd be alone. I was afraid it was too far for the message to get through,' and laid the headphones down on the table.

'It wasn't,' Joanna said, still kneeling by him. 'It isn't. And I have to get a message through. It's important. Please.'

He nodded, put his finger on the key. 'What do you want to say?'

Good-bye, Joanna thought. I'm sorry. I love you. She glanced at the spark. It wavered, dimmed. 'Tell Richard the NDE's a distress signal from the brain to all the body's systems. Tell him it –' she said, and was yanked brutally to her feet.

'The collapsibles weren't there,' Greg growled, his hands gripping her shoulders. 'Where are they?' He shook her. 'Where *are* they?'

'You don't understand,' Joanna said, looking frantically back at Kevin. 'I have to send a –'

But Greg had let go of her, had grabbed Kevin's arm. 'That's a wireless!' he said. 'You're sending out SOSs! There are ships coming to save us, aren't there? Aren't there?'

Kevin shook his head. 'The *Carpathia*'s coming. But she's fifty-eight miles from here. She won't make it in time. It's too far for her to come.'

Joanna sucked in her breath.

'What do you mean, too far for her to come?' Greg said, and Joanna understood finally what it was she had heard in his voice in the ER. She had thought it was despair, but it wasn't. It was disbelief and fury. 'Fifty-eight?' Greg said, jerking Kevin around to face him. 'There has to be something closer than that. Who else are you sending to?'

'The *Virginian*, the *Olympic*, the *Mount Temple*,' Kevin said, 'but none of them are close enough to help. The *Olympic*'s over five hundred miles away.'

'Then send the SOS to somebody else,' Greg said and pushed Kevin down into the chair. 'Send it to somebody closer. What about that ship whose light everybody saw?'

'She doesn't answer.'

'She *has* to answer,' Greg said, and jammed Kevin's hand down onto the key. 'Send it. SOS. SOS.'

Kevin glanced at Joanna and then bent forward and began to tap out the message. Dot-dot-dot. Dash-dash-dash. Above his head, the blue spark arced, flickered, disappeared, arced again.

It's fading, Joanna thought, and pushed forward between them. 'No! It's too late for SOSs. Tell Richard *it's* an SOS, tell him Mrs Troudtheim's NDEs are the key.'

'Keep sending SOS!' Greg said, his hand snaking out to fasten on Joanna's wrist. 'You, show me where they keep the lifejackets.'

She called to Kevin, 'You have to get the message through to Richard. Tell him it's a code, that the neurotransmitters—' but Greg had already pushed her out of the wireless room, onto the deck.

'Where are the lifejackets?' he demanded. 'We have to stay afloat till the ship gets here! Where did they keep them?'

'I don't know,' Joanna said helplessly, looking back at the door of the wireless room. Light radiated from it, golden, peaceful, and in the light Kevin sat, his golden head bent over the wireless key, the spark above his head like a halo. Please, Joanna prayed. Let it get through.

'Where did they *keep* them?' Greg's fingers cut into her wrists.

'In a chest next to the officers' quarters,' Joanna said, 'but they won't help. There aren't any ships coming –' but he was already pushing her down the slanting deck toward the bow. Ahead, Joanna could hear a gentle, slopping sound, like water, like blood.

'Show me where the chest is – *so I can see what I'm doing!' the resident saying, and Joanna flinching away from the scissors, afraid he had a knife, a knife! Vielle saying, 'Hang on, honey. Close your eyes,' and the lights going off, the room suddenly dark, and then a door opening somewhere on light, on singing, 'Happy birthday to you!,' the candles on the cake flaring into brightness, and her father saying, 'Blow them out!,' and her, leaning far forward, her cheeks puffed with air, blowing, and the candles flickering red and going out, the deck lights dimming, glowing red, and then coming on again, but not as bright, not as bright.*

Joanna was sprawled over a white metal chest. 'What was that?' Greg said, on his hands and knees by the railing. 'What's happening?' His voice was afraid.

Joanna stood up. 'The unifying image is breaking up,' she said. 'The synapses are firing haphazardly.'

'We have to get our lifejackets on!' Greg said, scrambling wildly to his feet. He wrenched the chest open, hauled out a lifejacket and thrust it at her. 'We have to get off the ship!'

Joanna looked steadily at him. 'We can't.'

He tossed the lifejacket at her feet, snatched up another one, began putting it on. 'Why not?' he said, fumbling with the ties.

She looked at him with infinite pity. 'Because we're the ship.'

He stopped, his hands still clutching the trailing ties, and looked fearfully at her. 'You died, Greg, and so did I, in the ER. You had a massive heart attack.'

'I work out at the health club every day,' he said.

She shook her head. 'It doesn't matter. We hit an iceberg and we sank, and all this' – she waved her hand at the deck, the empty davits, the darkness – 'is a metaphor for what's really happening, the sensory neurons shutting down, the synapses failing to arc.' The poor, mortally wounded mind reflexively connecting sensations and images in spite of itself, trying to make sense of death even as it died.

He stared at her, his face slack with hopelessness. 'But if that's true, if that's *true*,' he said, and his voice was an angry sob, 'what are we supposed to *do*?'

Why is everyone always asking me? Joanna thought. I don't *know*. Trust in Jesus. Behave well. Play the hand you're dealt. Try to remember what's important. Try not to be afraid. 'I don't know,' she said, infinitely sorry for him, for herself, for everyone. 'Look, it's too late to save ourselves, but there's still a chance we can save Maisie. If we could get a message through –'

'Maisie?' he shouted, his voice filled with fury and contempt. 'We have to save ourselves. It's every man for himself.' He yanked the ties into a knot.

'There aren't enough lifeboats for everyone, are there?' he said. 'That's why you don't want to tell me where they are, because you're afraid I'll steal your place. They're down belowdecks, aren't they?'

'No!' Joanna said. 'There's nothing down there except water!' And darkness. And a boy with a knife.

'Don't go down there!' Joanna said, reaching out for him, but he was already past her, already to the door. 'Greg!' She raced after him.

He yanked the door open on darkness, on destruction. 'Wait!' Joanna called. 'Kevin! Mr Briarley! Help! SOS!'

There was a sound of footsteps, of people running from the stern. 'Hurry!' she said, and turned toward the sound. 'You have to help me. Greg's—'

It was a squat, white dog with batlike ears, padding down the deck toward her, trailing a leather leash. It's the French bulldog, Joanna thought, the one Maisie felt so bad about. 'Here, boy!' she called, squatting down, but the dog ignored her, trotting past with the frantic, single-minded look of a lost dog trying to get to its master.

'Wait!' Joanna said and ran after it, grabbing for the end of the leash. She caught the little dog up in her arms. 'There, there,' she said. 'It's all right.' It looked up at her with its bulging brown eyes, panting hard. 'Don't be afraid,' she said. 'I've got—'

There was a sound. Joanna looked up. Greg stood on the top step of the crew stairway, looking down into the darkness. He took a step down. 'Don't go down there!' Joanna cried. She thrust the little dog under her arm and ran toward the door. 'Wait!' she cried, but the door had already shut behind him. 'Wait!'

She grabbed the doorknob with her free hand. It wouldn't turn. She hastily set the dog down, looping the end of the leash over her wrist, and tried the doorknob again. It was locked. 'Greg!' she shouted through it. 'Open the door!'

She put her whole weight against the door and pushed. 'Open the door!'

Pounding on the glass of the door, shouting, 'What kind of hospital cafeteria is this?' Beating so hard the glass rattled, the cardboard sign that said '11 A.M. to 1 P.M.' shook, trying to make the woman inside look up from setting out the dishes of red Jell-O, shouting, 'It's not even one yet!' pointing to her watch in proof, but when she looked at it, it didn't say ten to one, it said twenty past two.

She was on her knees, holding on to one of the empty lifeboat davits. The little bulldog huddled at her feet, looking up at her, shivering. His leash trailed behind him on the slanting deck. *I let go of it,* she thought in horror. *I can't let go of it.*

She wrapped the leash tightly around her wrist twice, and clutched it in her fist. She scooped the little dog up in her arms, staggering against the rail as she straightened. The deck was slanting steeply now. 'I've got to get a life-jacket on you,' she said and set off with the dog in her arms, climbing the hill of the deck, trying to avoid the deck chairs that were sliding down, the birdcages, the crash carts.

I'm in the wrong wing, she thought, *I have to get to the Boat Deck,* and heard the band. 'The band was on the Boat Deck,' Joanna said, and climbed toward the sound.

The musicians had wedged the piano into the angle of the Grand Staircase and the funnel. They stood in front of it, their violins held to their chests like shields. As Joanna reached them, the bandleader raised his baton, and the musicians tucked their violins under their chins, raised their bows, began to play. Joanna waited, the bulldog pressed against her, but it was a ragtime tune, sprightly, jagged.

'It's not the end yet,' Joanna said to the dog, climbing past them, past the first-class lounge. 'We still have time, it isn't over till they play "Nearer, My God, to Thee."'

And here was the chest. Joanna rolled an IV pole out of the way, and a gurney, trailing a white sheet, and grabbed a lifejacket. She stood the little dog on the white chest to put the lifejacket on him, wrapping it around his squat body and pulling his front legs through the armholes. She reached for the dangling ties, clutched – '*"Come, let me clutch thee!"' Mr Briarley intoned from* Macbeth. *'"I have thee not, and yet I see thee still. Art thou a dagger of the mind …?"' Ricky Inman tilted back and forth in his chair, Joanna watching him, fascinated, waiting for him to overbalance. '"… a false creation, proceeding from the oppressed brain?"' and Ricky toppled over backward, grabbing at the wall, at the light switch, as he went over, Mr Briarley saying, as the light went out, 'Exactly, Mr Inman, "put out the light and then put out the light,"' and the whole class laughing, but it wasn't funny, it was dark. 'It was dark,' Mrs Davenport said, pausing between every word, Joanna, bored, uncaring, asking, 'Can you describe it?' and Mr Briarley answering, '"The sun did not shine and the stars gave no light."'*

She was clinging to the deck railing, her body half over the side. She had let go of the bulldog again, and it scrabbled at her legs, whimpering, sliding away from her down the steep deck.

She caught it up against her chest and groped her way toward the support in the middle of the deck, hanging on to the railing as long as she could and then letting go and half-sliding, half-falling toward the safety of the wooden pillar. The deck lights dimmed down to nothing and came on again, dull red.

'The visual cortex is shutting down,' Joanna said, and lurched for the pillar. She wrapped the leash around her wrist, struggling to bind them to the pillar without letting go of the leash. A crash cart slid past them, picking up speed. A tiger, its striped fur red and black in the dimming light, loped by.

Joanna passed the leash around her waist, the dog, the pillar, and tied it in a knot. 'This way I won't let go of you. Like "The Wreck of the Hesperus,"' she said and wished Mr Briarley were here. '"He cut a rope from a broken spar, and bound her to the mast,"' she recited, but when she said the next line, it didn't come out right. '"And when they were dead,"' she recited, '"the robins so red, gathered strawberry leaves and over them spread."'

The ship was beginning to overbalance, like Ricky Inman going over in his chair. The bulldog, between her chest and the pillar, looked up at her with wild, frightened eyes. 'Don't be afraid,' she whispered. 'It can't last much longer.'

Snow began to fall, large gray-white flakes drifting down onto the deck like apple blossoms, like ash. Joanna looked up, half-expecting to see Vesuvius above them. A sailor, all in white, ran past, dragging landing chocks behind him, shouting, 'Zeroes at oh-nine hundred!' The band stopped, paused, began to play.

'This is it,' Joanna whispered, '"Nearer, My God, to Thee."' But that wasn't the tune. 'Well, at least some good has come out of this,' she said to the dog, trying to smile. 'We've solved the mystery of whether they were playing "Nearer, My God, to Thee," or "Autumn."' But it wasn't 'Autumn' either. It wasn't a hymn at all. It was 'The Stars and Stripes Forever.'

'Oh, Maisie,' she murmured.

An Apache galloped past, brandishing a knife. Water began to pour from the lifeboat davits, from the railings, from the chest. 'This is the worst of the worst catastrophes in the world!' a reporter on the roof of the officers' quarters sobbed into a microphone. 'It's a terrific crash, ladies and gentlemen, the smoke and the flames now! Oh, the humanity!' The code alarm began to scream.

Joanna looked up. The stern of the ship reared above her, suspended against the blackness. She hugged the dog against her and tried to shield its head. The lights went out, blinked on dull red, went off, came on again. Like Morse code. Like Lavoisier.

There was a horrible rending sound, and everything began to fall, deck chairs and the grand piano and the giant funnels, violins and Indian clubs and playing cards, postcards and pomegranates and dishes and Dish Night, transcripts and trellises and telegrams. Books toppled out of their shelves, *Mirrors and Mazes* and *The Titanic ABC* and *The Light at the End of the Tunnel*. The davits broke loose from their moorings, and the mechanical camel, and the weight machine, looking more than ever like a guillotine. The stanchions fell, and the engine room telegraph, set now on 'stop', and scans and sleep masks and shortcuts, arteries, ancient mariners, minirecorders, metaphors, dog tags, heating vents, knives, neurons, night.

They crashed down on Joanna and the little bulldog with a rending, deafening roar, and in the last moment before it reached them, she realized she had been wrong about the noise she had heard when she came through. It was not the sound of the engines stopping or of the code alarm buzzing, of the iceberg slashing into the ship's side, but the sound of her whole life crashing, crashing, crashing down on her.

52

'Stand by.'
  – Wireless message from the
    Frankfurt to the *Titanic*

'I've been trying to call you since *Wednesday*,' Maisie said disgustedly to Richard. She reached for her remote and turned down the sound on *The Sound of Music*. 'But they don't let you have phones in your room in here, you have to tell the sector nurse and she makes the call *for* you, she dials it and everything, and they don't allow cell phones either 'cause of people's pacemakers, you might scramble their signals and they'd go into V-fib or something,' she said, a little like a runaway train herself, 'so I asked Nurse Lucille to call you, and she said, "What for?" and I couldn't say the real reason 'cause I'm not supposed to know about Joanna. We need to have a code for next time.'

'All right, we'll work one out,' Richard said. 'You found out who Joanna had been to see?'

'Yes. So, anyway, I told her to tell you I needed to see you, and I said you weren't a visitor, you were a doctor, but she still wouldn't call you.'

She paused to get her breath, wheezing a little, and then started up again. 'So I asked her to call Ms Sutterly to bring me my books, because she's not a visitor, I have to have my books so I can do my homework. I thought when she came I could secretly hand her this note with your phone number on it, but Nurse Lucille said "Family members only." It's like a *prison*.'

'So you told your mother I'd discovered a cure for coding?' Richard said.

She nodded. 'I got the idea watching *The Parent Trap*, the part where they fool the mom. I couldn't think of anything else,' she said defensively. 'I figured she'd *make* you come see me if she thought you'd figured out a way to bring people back after they coded. And she did.' She sobered. 'I know you don't really know how to do that. Are you mad?'

'No. I should have come to see you earlier when you didn't call. I came a couple of days ago, but you were out having tests.'

She nodded. 'An echocardiogram. Again. I tried the whole time I was down there to get somebody to page you, but nobody would. They said pages were for hospital business only.'

'But you got the message to me,' Richard said. 'That's the important thing. And you found out where Joanna was and who she talked to.'

She nodded emphatically. 'That was even harder than getting the message to you 'cause I couldn't *go* anywhere or call anybody, and I knew if I asked the nurses, they'd ask me what I wanted to know for, so I asked Eugene. He's the guy who brings the menu things. When I was down in Peds, Eugene brought the menu things down there, too, so I figured he did all the floors and saw lots of people.'

'And he saw Joanna?' Richard said, trying to get Maisie to the point.

'No,' Maisie said. 'I had to talk really hard to get Eugene to ask them if they saw Joanna. He didn't want to. He said patients were always trying to get him to do stuff he wasn't supposed to, like extra cookies on their tray and sneak in pizza and stuff, and he could lose his job if he did it, and I told him I wasn't asking him to *bring* me anything, just ask some questions, and I was really sick, I had to have a heart transplant and everything, and if he wouldn't do it, I'd have to ask them myself, and I'd probably code.'

Maisie Machiavelli. 'So he said he'd ask them.'

'Yes, and one of the tray people saw her in the west wing, going up the stairs to the fifth floor really in a hurry.'

The fifth floor. What was on five?

'I made Eugene talk to all the orderlies and stuff who worked on the fifth floor, but nobody else had seen her. And then I got to thinking about there being a walkway on the fifth floor and maybe she was going up to it.'

'How did you know there was a walkway on the fifth floor?'

'Oh, you know,' Maisie said evasively, her eyes straying to the TV screen, where the von Trapp children were sticking a frog in Maria's pocket. 'They sometimes take me for tests and stuff. *Anyway*, I thought she might have been going over to the east wing, so I told Eugene to ask all the tray people who worked over there, but nobody'd seen her, so I tried to think who else besides nurses and tray people are usually out in the halls, like the guys who mop and run the vacuum thing.'

'Is that who told you who Joanna talked to?'

'No,' Maisie said, 'So, anyway, Eugene told me one of the orderlies saw Joanna going down to the ER, but that wasn't any good, you already knew she did that, but I wrote his name down anyway in case you wanted to talk to him.' She reached over to the bedstand, pulled out a folded sheet of paper like the one she'd written the wireless messages on, and unfolded it. He could see two names written on it. 'Bob Yancey,' Maisie said.

'Is the name of the person Joanna talked to on there?' Richard asked, leaning forward to see the other name.

Maisie snatched the paper out of his reach. 'I'm getting to that part,' she said, folding it up. 'So, anyway, then this lady in the CICU went into V-fib, she had a quadruple bypass, and the chaplain came, and I thought, I'll bet he goes to see all the really sick people, he came to see me one time when I coded, so if the person Joanna went to see had had an NDE, *he* might have seen her.'

The chaplain. Of course. Richard hadn't even thought of him. 'The chaplain saw her?'

'I'm *getting* to that part.' And it was obvious he was going to have to hear the whole story of how she'd found out before she told him what he wanted to know.

'So I was going to ask Eugene to ask him to come and see me, but when the meal thing came, it wasn't him, it was this other guy, and when I asked him where Eugene was, he said, "He be taking a few days off," really madlike, so I said, "He didn't get fired, did he?" and he said, "No, and he don't plan on it and I don't neither, so don't go askin' me to play detective," and he wouldn't even listen when I said all I wanted was to talk to the chaplain, he just put down the meal thing and left. So then I tried to think of a way to get the chaplain to come see me. I thought about telling the sector nurse I was worried about heaven and stuff, but I figured she'd tell my mom and my mom would get all upset. I figured I could pretend to be in A-fib if I couldn't think of anything else –'

A-fib! I've created a monster, he thought.

'– but while I was trying to decide, the guy came in to draw blood, and he fastens the rubber tube thing around my arm and goes, "Are you the one who's asking around about Joanna Lander?" and I go, "Yes, did you see her?" and he says he saw her in the room with this patient and he knows the name and his room and everything, because of them having to write it on those little tube things.' She handed over the paper triumphantly.

Richard unfolded it. 'Room 508,' it read. 'Carl Aspinall.'

'He said he was in a coma,' Maisie said.

Richard's heart sank.

'What's the matter?'

He looked at her eager, expectant face. She'd tried so hard and succeeded where the rest of them had failed. It seemed cruel to disappoint her, no matter what Joanna had said about always telling her the truth. 'What's wrong?' she asked. 'Isn't he the one?'

'No,' Richard said. 'I already know about Carl. Joanna had the nurses write down words he said while he was unconscious. Joanna was probably there to talk to the nurses.'

'Hunh-*unh*,' Maisie said. 'Carl was talking to her. The blood guy said so. He said he was really surprised he was awake, and the nurses told him he just came out of his coma that morning all of a sudden, and everybody said it was a miracle.'

Came out of his coma. And told Joanna what he'd seen, told her something that gave her the key – Room 508. Richard reached for his cell phone, remembered he'd left it at the desk outside. 'Thanks,' he said, starting for the door. 'I need to go talk to him.'

'He's not here,' Maisie said. 'He went home, the blood guy said. Last week.'

He'd have to call Records, see if he could talk them into giving him an address, and if not, talk to his nurses. 'I've gotta go, Maisie,' he said. 'I need to find out where he lives.'

'3348 South Jackson Way,' Maisie said promptly, 'but he's not there. He went up to his cabin in the mountains.'

'Did the blood guy tell you that?'

'No. Eugene.' She reached over to the bedstand and extracted another sheet of paper. 'Here's how to get there.'

He read the instructions. The cabin was just outside of Timberline. 'You're a miracle worker, Maisie,' he said, sticking the paper in his pocket. 'I owe you one.' He started out the door.

'You can't go *yet*,' Maisie said. 'You haven't told me if you want me to keep on looking for people who saw Joanna.'

No, Richard thought. This is the one. It made perfect sense. Carl Aspinall had come out of his coma and told Joanna something about what he'd seen that had clicked with Joanna's own experiences, something that had made her realize what the NDE was, how it worked.

Maisie was waiting expectantly. 'You've already found the person I was looking for,' he said. 'And you're supposed to be resting. You rest and watch your video.'

'I *hate The Sound of Music*.' She flounced back against the pillow. 'It's so *sweet*. The only good part is where the nuns play that trick on the Nazi guys so they can escape.'

'Maisie –'

'And what if he isn't the guy you're looking for?' she said. 'Or he goes into a coma again? Or dies?'

He gave in. 'All right, you can keep looking, but no asking Eugene to do anything that will get him fired. And *no* faking A-fib. I'll come see you as soon as I get back from seeing him.'

'Are you going to take Kit with you?' she asked.

'No. Why?'

'She's nice,' Maisie said, looking up at the TV, where Captain von Trapp was singing to Maria. 'I just think she'd be good at asking questions. You have to come and tell me what he said right away.'

'I will,' he said and went back to the lab to call Carl Aspinall, but there was no number listed for the mountain cabin. They must have a cell phone, Richard thought, they surely wouldn't have taken off for the mountains a week after being released from the hospital without any way to get in touch, but the cell phone number was unlisted.

He would have to go there, which was just as well. If he called, he ran the risk of being told Aspinall was too ill to see him, of having Mrs Aspinall say, 'How would next week be?' He couldn't wait till next week or even till tomorrow, not when he was this close. He called Kit. He doubted if she'd be able to find someone to watch her uncle on such short notice so she could go with him, but he could at least get Carl's transcripts from her. He wanted to look at them before he interviewed Carl.

Kit's line was busy. He looked at his watch. It was after two, and Timberline was a good hour and a half into the mountains. He tried Kit's number again. Still busy. He'd have to go without the transcripts.

He grabbed his keys and started out the door and then stopped. He was doing just what Joanna had done, taking off without telling anyone where he was going. He called the ER and asked to speak to Vielle. 'She can't come to the phone,' the intern or whoever it was said. 'We've got a real mess down here. Twenty-car pileup on I-70. Fog.'

You had to take I-70 west to get to Timberline. 'Where?' Richard asked.

'Out east by Bennett,' the intern said. 'Can I give her a message?'

'Yes,' Richard said. 'Tell her I'm on my way to interview Carl Aspinall. *Carl*,' Richard said. He spelled it and then *Aspinall* slowly. 'Tell her I'll call her as soon as I get back.'

'Sure thing,' the intern said. 'Drive carefully.'

Richard hung up and tried Kit one more time. Mr Briarley answered the phone. 'Who's calling?' he demanded.

'Richard Wright,' he said. 'May I speak to Kit?'

'He's dead. He was stabbed to death in a tavern in Deptford.'

'It's for me, Uncle Pat,' Kit's voice said, and a woman's voice said, 'I'm sorry. He asked me for a cup of tea, and –'

He didn't hear the rest of it. Kit came on the line and, amazingly, already had someone there to watch her uncle. 'I was going to go to the library to see what I could find on a fire on the *Titanic*,' she said.

'What else would they see?' Richard could hear Mr Briarley say in the background. 'It is the very mirror image.'

'How long can the caregiver stay?' Richard asked.

'Till six,' Kit said. 'You found the person Joanna went to see, didn't you?'

'Yes. I want you to go with me to see him. Can you?'

'Yes!'

'Good. Bring the Coma Carl transcripts.'

'Metaphors are not just figures of speech,' Mr Briarley said.

'I'd better go,' Kit said and told him her address. 'I'll see you in a few minutes.'

Mr Briarley said, 'They are the essence and pattern of our mind.'

Richard hung up, stuck the cell phone in his pocket, and started for the parking lot. Almost to the elevators a young man in a suit intercepted him. 'Dr Wright?' he said, sticking out his hand. 'I'm glad I caught you. I'm Hughes Dutton of Daniels, Dutton, and Walsh, Mrs Nellis's lawyer.'

I should have taken the stairs, Richard thought. 'I really can't talk now,' he said. 'I'm going—'

'This will only take a minute,' Mr Dutton said, opening his jacket and pulling out a Palm Pilot. 'I'm negotiating approval of this coding treatment you've developed and I just need to clarify a few details. Is it classified as a medical procedure or a drug?'

'Neither,' Richard said. 'There *is* no treatment. I tried to explain that to Mrs Nellis but she wouldn't listen. My research into the near-death experience is in the very preliminary stages. It's purely theoretical.'

The lawyer scribbled on his Palm Pilot. 'Treatment in predevelopment phase.'

He's as bad as Maisie's mother, Richard thought. 'It's not in the predevelopment phase. There is no treatment, and even if there were, it would never be approved for experimental use on a child –'

'In ordinary circumstances, I'd agree with you, but where the treatment involved would be utilized in a postcode situation, there are several options, the least problematical of which is to classify the treatment as a postmortem experimental procedure.'

He's talking about Maisie, Richard thought, gritting his teeth. 'I have to go,' he said, going around the lawyer and toward the elevators. 'I was supposed to meet someone –'

'I'll ride down with you,' the lawyer said, leaning past him to press the 'down' button. 'Since the patient is technically deceased, the same legal permissions as those required for organ harvesting could be used.' The elevator arrived, and Richard and the lawyer stepped in. 'What floor?'

'G,' Richard said.

'Mercy General unfortunately has a policy forbidding experimentation on the just-deceased, though since it was intended to prevent interns practicing such procedures as femoral artery catheterizations, we can argue that your treatment doesn't fall under the ban. Our second option is an Extreme Measures order, which demands that every possible measure be taken to save the life of the patient.'

The elevator opened on G. The lawyer followed Richard out. 'An EM order is legally riskier, but it has the advantage of allowing the procedure to be done earlier than a postmortem would. At this point I'm pursuing all options,' he said and stepped back inside as the door began to close.

Thank God, Richard thought, heading for his car at a lope. I thought he was going to go with me. He debated calling Kit to tell her he'd be late, but he didn't want to take the time to find a phone, and if Mr Briarley answered again, it would take longer than driving over there, especially if traffic cooperated.

It didn't. There was fog, just as the intern had said, and traffic had slowed to a crawl. It was three-twenty by the time he got there.

And it will take another half an hour to get away from Mr Briarley, he thought, but Kit came out with the transcripts as soon as he pulled up. 'I brought my cell phone,' she said as he pulled away from the curb. 'So who is it?'

'You won't believe this,' he said, turning onto Evans. He told her about Carl Aspinall as he drove down to Santa Fe and picked up I-25. 'Aspinall must have told her what he'd experienced while in the coma, and something about it, or something combined with words he muttered while he was unconscious, provided the key.'

'Do you think he'll know what that something was?' Kit asked.

'I don't know. I'm hoping Joanna said something, shouted "Eureka!" and then explained why she was excited. If she didn't, we'll have to hope we see the connection, too. Why don't you read the transcripts out loud?'

Kit nodded and started through Joanna's notes. Richard turned onto I-70 and headed west. The fog thinned a little toward Golden and then closed in again as they began to climb into the foothills. The cars ahead of them disappeared, and so did the rocky slopes on either side. Twenty-car pileup, Richard thought. He turned his headlights on and slowed down.

'"... half ..."' Kit read, '"... to ... (unintelligible) ... fire ... make ..."' She glanced up. 'Where are we?' she said, looking out at the shrouded landscape.

'I-70, going up toward Timberline,' Richard said, handing her Maisie's page of directions. 'Aspinall and his wife are staying at their mountain cabin. Which exit do I take?'

She consulted the directions. 'This one,' she said, pointing at a green sign, barely visible through the fog. 'And then north on 58.' They both leaned forward, straining to see the signs and make the turn onto Highway 58, and then Kit went back to reading. '"… water … oh, grand (unintelligible) … smoke –"' She stopped, staring out at the fog.

'Is that all?' Richard asked.

'No,' she said, 'I was just thinking, maybe the smoke is the clue.'

'I thought you weren't able to find any fires on the *Titanic* that night.'

'I wasn't,' she said, 'but that's just it. Everything else Joanna saw – the mail clerks dragging sacks of mail up to the Boat Deck and the passengers milling around on deck and the rockets – all really happened, and her descriptions of the gymnasium and the Grand Staircase and the writing room could have been taken straight from Uncle Pat's books.'

'But not the smoke.'

'No, not the smoke, or the fog, or whatever it was she saw. It doesn't fit, and maybe in trying to find out why it didn't, she found out the answer. In science, isn't it the piece that doesn't fit that leads to the breakthrough?'

'Yes,' he said. 'Or maybe she was trying to prove it didn't fit, because that would prove it wasn't really the *Titanic*. Maybe that's why she asked you all those questions about the mail room and the First-Class Dining Saloon, because she was hoping her description wouldn't match.'

'But then why didn't she write down what she saw? If she was trying to prove discrepancies, she'd have wanted to document them, but there's no mention of smoke or a fire or fog anywhere in her accounts, taped or written. And it's in Maisie's account, and Ms Schuster's. I think it's the key.'

'Well, we'll know in a few minutes,' Richard said, pointing at a sign barely visible in the fog: 'Timberline 8 mi.'

The fog grew steadily thicker and the road twistier. Richard had to devote all his attention to seeing the center line. '"… water …"' Kit read, '"… no … blanked out …," and then two words with question marks after them, "cold? code?"'

'Tunnel,' Richard said.

'Tunnel?' Kit said. 'How do you get "tunnel" out of "cold" and "code"?'

'Tunnel,' he repeated, and pointed. The arched mouth of a tunnel loomed ahead, black in the formless fog.

'Oh, a *tunnel*,' Kit said, and they drove into it.

It was dark, which meant it must be a short one. The longer tunnels, like the Eisenhower and the ones in Glenwood Canyon, were lit with gold sodium-vapor lights. This one was pitch-black beyond the range of their headlights, and foggy.

'Why would I have seen the *Titanic*, of all things?' Joanna had said. 'I live in Colorado. There are dozens of tunnels in the mountains.'

And she was right, he thought. A tunnel like this was the obvious association. The narrow sides, the feeling of swift forward motion, the darkness. The tunnel must curve, because he couldn't see the end, couldn't see the light.

The light. There was no sensation of having driven around a curve, but he must have, because there was the mouth of the tunnel, blindingly bright and nearly upon them. Richard squinted against the sudden whiteness.

'A mountain tunnel would have been the logical association,' Joanna had said. The feeling of opening out into light, into space, the blinding brightness of eyes adjusting from blackness to daylight, no, brighter than that. Brilliant, dazzling. It's too bright, Richard thought and felt a stab of fear. Why is it so bright?

Beside him, Kit put up her hand to shade her eyes, and the movement looked defensive, as if she were shielding herself from a blow. Where are we? Richard thought, and was out of the tunnel and into another world. Blue sky and glittering snow and white, pine-covered slopes.

'What happened to the fog?' Kit asked wonderingly.

'We must have climbed above it,' Richard said, though there had been no sensation of climbing either, but at the next curve in the road, they could see the white layer of cloud below them, blanketing the canyon.

'Heaven,' Kit murmured, and Richard knew she was thinking the same thing he was.

'Everything except the ringing or buzzing sound,' he said, and Kit's cell phone rang.

'Mrs Gray, is everything all right?' Kit said anxiously. It must be the Eldercare person. 'Oh. In the cupboard above the sink, behind the oatmeal. I hope.' Kit punched 'end.' 'She couldn't find the sugar,' she said to Richard, looking relieved. She picked up the transcripts. 'I'd better finish reading these. We're almost there.'

'Correction, we are there,' Richard said, pointing at a sign that said Timberline. He turned onto a narrow, snowy road, and then a narrower, snowier one, and stopped in front of an elaborately rustic-looking chalet.

'I can't believe it,' Kit said as they walked up to the door. 'We're going to find out what Joanna was trying to tell us.'

A woman met them at the door, looking surprised and a little wary.

'Mrs Aspinall?' Richard said, wondering suddenly how to explain their mission here without sounding crazy. 'I'm Dr Wright. This is Ms Gardiner. We're from Mercy General. We—'

'Oh, come in,' she said, opening the door wide. 'How nice of you to come all this way! Carl's in the family room. He'll be so pleased to see you.' She took Richard's coat and hung it up. 'Dr Cherikov was here yesterday.' She took Kit's coat. 'All his doctors have been so nice, coming to check on him.'

'Mrs Aspinall –' Richard began, but she was already leading them down a long, pine-paneled hall, telling them about Carl's condition.

'He's making wonderful progress, especially now that we're up here. He's stopped having the nightmares –'

'Mrs Aspinall,' Richard said uncomfortably. 'I'm afraid there's been a mis-understanding. I'm not one of Mr Aspinall's doctors.'

Mrs Aspinall stopped in mid-hall and turned to face them. 'But you said you were from Mercy General.'

'We are,' Richard said. 'We were friends of Joanna Lander's. She was my partner on a research project.'

'Oh,' Mrs Aspinall said. She hesitated, as if she were going to show them the door, and then led them on down to the door at the end of the hall. It wasn't the family room. It was a decidedly unrustic kitchen. 'Would you like some tea?'

'No, thanks,' Richard said. 'Mrs Aspinall, the reason we came—'

'I was so sorry to hear of Dr Lander's death,' Mrs Aspinall said. 'She was so kind to Carl and to me. She used to come and sit with Carl so I could go get something to eat.' She shook her head sadly. 'Such a terrible tragedy! There's so much violence everywhere these days. It upset Carl terribly.'

Good, at least he knows, Richard thought, and we won't walk into a hor-nets' nest the way we did with Maisie, but he asked, just in case. 'You told your husband about her death?'

'I wasn't going to. He was still so fragile, and he didn't know her.' She smiled apologetically. 'It's so hard for me to remember that all the people who cared for him all those weeks and who I know so well are total strangers to him.'

Richard and Kit looked at each other across the table. 'But Carl heard the nurses talking,' Mrs Aspinall went on, 'and when Guadalupe came into the room, he could see she'd been crying, and he knew something was wrong. He was convinced I was keeping something from him about his illness, so I ended up having to tell him.'

'Mrs Aspinall,' Richard said, 'the day Dr Lander died, she was on the track of something important, something to do with the project we were working on. We're talking to everyone she saw that day, which is why we're here. We'd like—'

Mrs Aspinall was shaking her head. 'I didn't see her that day. The nurses told me she'd been in two days before to see him, but I wasn't there. The last time I saw her was at least a week before that, so I'm afraid I can't help you. I'm sorry.'

'Actually, it's your husband we want to talk to,' Richard said.

'Carl?' she said, bewildered. 'But he never even met Joanna. I don't think you understand, my husband was in a semicomatose state until—'

'– the morning of the day Joanna died,' Richard said. 'She had a conversa-tion with him that morning, just after he regained consciousness.'

'Are you sure? Carl didn't say anything about talking to her,' she said and then frowned, 'but he *was* dreadfully upset when I told him about her. I thought it was because he'd been so close to death himself, that he was so frightened of it, but … when could she have seen him? I came as soon as they told me he was awake, and I was with him the rest of the day.'

'At eleven-thirty,' Richard said, hoping he was right.

'Oh,' Mrs Aspinall said, nodding. 'That was just before I got there.' And just after Carl regained consciousness, Richard thought, when his vision would have been fresh in his memory.

'But I still don't understand,' Mrs Aspinall said. 'You say she was on the track of something regarding your research project? Why would she have told Carl about it?'

'We think—' Richard began.

There was a sudden loud banging from the next room, like someone hammering. 'That's Carl,' Mrs Aspinall said apologetically. 'He thumps his walking stick when he needs something. I brought a bell up, but I haven't been able to find it.' The pounding started again, heavy, rhythmic thumps. 'If you'll excuse me,' Mrs Aspinall said, standing up, 'I'll be right back.' She went out of the room.

The thumps continued a moment and then stopped, and they could hear a man's voice saying querulously, 'Who's here? I heard a car in the driveway.'

'Some people from the hospital,' she said, 'but you don't have to see them if you don't feel up to it, I can tell them to come back when you're feeling stronger.'

Kit shot an anxious glance at Richard. 'I feel fine,' the man's voice said. 'Dr Cherikov said I was making excellent progress.'

'You are, but I don't want you to overdo. You were very ill.'

Richard couldn't hear his answer, but Mrs Aspinall reappeared. 'If you could keep your visit short,' she said. 'He tires easily. This conversation you think Dr Lander and Carl had, what did—?'

Whump, the walking stick thumped, louder than before. 'We're coming,' Mrs Aspinall said, and led Kit and Richard into a pine-paneled room with a fireplace and wide windows looking out on a calendar view: snow-covered peaks, pine trees, an ice-bound mountain stream. The TV was on, and Richard looked toward the chair in front of it, expecting to see an invalid in a bathrobe with a blanket over his knees, but the chair was empty, and the only person in the room was a tanned, healthy-looking man in a white polo shirt and khaki pants, standing over by the window, looking out. The doctor? Richard wondered, and then noticed the gnarled walking stick the man held. Dr Cherikov was right, he was making excellent progress.

Mrs Aspinall walked rapidly to a thermostat on the wall, turned up the heat, and went over to the fireplace. 'Brr, it's so cold in here,' she said, taking a remote off the mantel and pointing it at the fireplace. A fire flamed up.

'Carl,' Mrs Aspinall said, walking over to the chair. She picked up another remote and muted the TV. 'This is Dr Wright and Ms Gardiner.'

'How do you do, Dr Wright?' Carl said, coming forward to shake hands. He looked just as healthy close up. His face was tanned, and his grip when he shook hands with Richard was strong. Except for the dark bruises and puncture marks on the back of his hand, Richard wouldn't have believed he'd been in the hospital only three weeks ago, let alone in a coma. 'Were you one of the doctors who stuck all those needles and wires and tubes in me?' Carl asked. 'Or have we met before? I keep meeting people who know me, and I don't know them from Adam.'

'No,' Richard said. 'We've never met. I'm—'

'And I *know* I've never met you,' Carl said, stepping past him to shake hands with Kit. 'I definitely would have remembered that.'

'How do you do, Mr Aspinall?' Kit said, smiling. 'How are you feeling?'

'Fine. Fit as a fiddle,' he said. 'Good as new.'

'Sit down, sit down,' Mrs Aspinall said, motioning them toward the couch. They sat down, and so did Carl, leaning his walking stick against the arm of his chair. Mrs Aspinall remained standing. Standing guard, Richard thought.

'Mr Aspinall,' he said, 'we won't take much of your time. We just want to ask you a few questions about Joanna Lander.'

'Do you remember Dr Lander, Carl?' Mrs Aspinall asked. 'I've told you about so many people, I know it's confusing –'

Don't lead, Richard thought, and looked anxiously at Carl, but he was nodding. 'Joanna,' he said. 'She came to see me. The day I …' His voice trailed off and he looked past them out the window at the icy stream.

At the water, Richard thought. It flowed dark and clear, half under and half over a thin film of ice.

'The day you regained consciousness?' Kit prompted.

'Yes. She died,' Carl said, and then after a moment, 'didn't she?'

'Yes,' Richard said. 'She was killed later that same day.'

'I thought so,' Carl said. 'I get it confused sometimes, what really happened and what …' his voice trailed off again.

'Dr Cherikov said you'd be a little confused at first,' Mrs Aspinall said, 'because of all the medications.'

'That's right. The medications,' he said. 'Are you doing something in Joanna's memory?' he asked. 'A charity fund or something? I'd like to contribute.'

'No,' Richard said, 'that isn't why we came –'

'There *is* something we're trying to do for Joanna,' Kit said earnestly, 'and we need your help. We think Joanna found out something important that day about the research she and Dr Wright were doing. We're trying to find out what it was. We think she may have said something to someone about it.'

'And you think she said something to me?' Carl said, already shaking his head. 'She didn't say anything about a discovery –'

'No, we don't think she said anything *directly*,' Kit said hastily. 'But we thought if we could talk to the people she talked to that day, there might be a clue of some kind.' That's why I brought you along, Richard thought, looking at her gratefully. 'Can you tell us what you talked about, Carl?'

'Talked about?' He looked past them again at the dark water. His hands fidgeted on the arms of the chair.

'Yes,' Kit was saying. 'Can you tell us what you and Joanna talked about?'

'Are you sure you're up to this, Carl?' Mrs Aspinall asked anxiously, stepping between them. 'I'm sure Dr Wright and Ms Gardiner would understand if—'

'I'm fine,' he said. 'Stop fussing. Why don't you go make us some tea?'

'They said they didn't want any—'

'Well, *I* do,' he said. 'Go make me a cup of tea and stop fussing over me like a mother hen.'

Mrs Aspinall left, still looking anxious, and Carl smiled at Kit and said, 'Now what were we discussing?'

'What you and Joanna talked about,' Kit said.

'Nothing very important,' he said. 'She asked me how I felt. She told me she was glad to see I was awake and said I should get well. And that's what I've been doing, resting, getting my strength back, doing what Dr Cherikov says. Focus on the present, Dr Cherikov says. Don't think about what's past. That's over and done with. Think about getting well.'

'You mentioned being in the coma,' Richard said. 'Did Joanna ask you what happened while you were in the coma? About having dreams?'

'They weren't dreams.'

Richard's heart leaped. 'What were they?' he asked, his voice and face carefully impassive.

Mr Aspinall looked toward the door, as if willing his wife to come back. 'Mr Aspinall, this is important,' Richard said. 'Joanna tried to tell us something as she was dying. We think it has something to do with something you told her, something about what you saw when you were in the coma,' but Carl had stopped listening.

'I thought she died instantly,' he said accusingly. 'The nurses told me she died instantly.'

Richard looked at him in surprise. What was going on here?

'You said she talked to you,' Carl said, his voice rising. 'You said she tried to tell you something.'

'She did, but she didn't live long enough to tell us. She died almost instantly.'

'There wasn't anything anyone could have done,' Kit said.

He ignored her. 'How did she die?'

Richard looked at Kit. She looked as bewildered as he felt. He wondered if they should call Mrs Aspinall, but if they did, it would be an end to the interview. 'How did she die?' Carl demanded.

'She was stabbed by a patient on drugs,' Richard said.

'Stabbed?' Carl said, and his hands clenched uncontrollably in his lap. 'With what?'

'A knife,' Richard said, and, surprisingly, the answer was the right one. Carl's fists unclenched and he leaned back into his chair. 'And she died almost instantly,' he murmured. 'She was only there a few minutes.'

'Where, Carl?' Richard said. 'Where were you when you were in the coma?'

Carl's hands clenched again, and his eyes strayed to the muted TV. Like Maisie's when she didn't want to talk. 'You said it wasn't a dream,' Richard said, leaning forward to put himself between Carl and the TV. 'What was it? Was it a place?'

'A place,' he said and looked past them, at the dark, icy stream. What was he seeing, staring out at it? The water, creeping up the deck? Or roaring in through the injured side?

'You said Joanna was only there a few minutes,' Richard said. 'Where? What were you afraid she'd been stabbed with?'

Carl's fists tightened, the skin between the bruises white. His face under the tan had gone white, too. It looked sodden, like something pulled out of the water. 'Where were you, Carl?' Richard repeated.

'Richard –' Kit said and put a restraining hand on his arm.

'Where were you?'

'I –' Carl said and took a wavering breath. 'It –' This is it, Richard thought. He's going to tell us.

Brring. The sound of the cell phone exploded into the silence like a bomb.

No! Richard thought, watching Kit scramble to get it out of her bag. Not now.

'I'm sorry,' Kit said, trying to shut off the ringing. 'I didn't know this was on.'

'Quite all right,' Carl said. His color had come back.

He looks like somebody who's just heard the bugle call of the cavalry coming to rescue him, Richard thought. 'Go ahead,' Carl said. 'Take your call.'

Kit sent Richard an agonized glance and put the phone to her ear. 'Hello?'

It will be Mrs Gray, wanting to know where the sugar is, Richard thought. Or the mustard.

'Oh, hello, Vielle,' Kit said. 'Yes, he's here.' She handed Richard the cell phone.

'Excuse me,' Richard said and walked over to the fireplace. 'Vielle –'

'What's going on? I got this garbled message from one of the interns. Honestly, you'd think they could deliver a simple message –'

693

'I can't talk now,' Richard said, his hand over the receiver. 'I'll call you back.'

'You'll never get through,' Vielle said. 'It's a total disaster here. The fog—'

Richard switched the phone off. 'Good-bye,' he said to the dial tone and handed the phone back to Kit. 'Sorry,' he said, turning to Carl.

'Perfectly all right,' Carl said. 'Where were we? Oh, yes, you were asking me what I remember of my coma, and I'm afraid the answer is, nothing at all.'

Damn you, Vielle, Richard thought. He was going to tell us. 'The last thing I remember is my wife putting me in the car to go to the hospital,' Carl said. His hands on the arms of the chair were relaxed, steady. 'She was having trouble getting my seat belt on, and the next thing I know this nurse I never saw before is opening the curtains, and this friend of yours comes in and talks to me for a few minutes, maybe five minutes at the most. She asked me how I was and we chatted a little, and then she stood up and said she had to go.' He smiled at Kit again.

'What did you chat about?' Richard said.

'I don't really remember.' Carl shrugged. 'I'm afraid there's a lot I don't remember about that first couple of days. The medications. I suppose that must be true for the dreams I had while I was in the coma, too.'

'You said they weren't dreams,' Richard said.

'Did I?' Carl said easily. 'I meant I didn't remember having any dreams.'

You're lying, Richard thought.

'Here's your tea, Carl,' Mrs Aspinall said, coming into the room. She handed him the mug. 'And after you drink it, I think you should lie down. You look pale.' She laid her hand on his forehead. 'And it feels like you've got a fever. I'm sure Dr Wright and Ms Gardiner will understand.'

'Sorry I couldn't help you,' Carl said and turned to his wife. 'You're right, I am tired. I think I will lie down.'

'I'll show Dr Wright and Ms Gardiner out,' Mrs Aspinall said, 'and then I'll come back and get you settled.'

They stood up. 'If you remember anything,' Kit said, 'please call us.'

'I doubt if I'll remember anything,' Carl said. 'Dr Cherikov said the more time has passed, the less I'll remember about the whole thing.'

'Which is good,' Mrs Aspinall said. 'You need to forget about what's past and concentrate on the present, and the future. Isn't that right, Dr Wright? I want to thank you for coming.'

End of interview. Mrs Aspinall led them quickly down the hall to the front door and helped them into their coats, obviously anxious to get rid of them so she could get back to her husband. 'It was so nice of you to come all this way,' she said, opening the door.

They went out onto the porch. 'I'm sorry my husband couldn't be more help,' she said.

'Maybe *you* can help us,' Richard said. 'Your husband told Joanna something that put her on the right track. Something he remembered from his coma.'

'He told you, he doesn't remember. His memory of his time in the hospital's very hazy –'

'But he might have said something to you,' Kit said, 'after he woke up. Made some reference to what he saw or—'

Richard interrupted. 'Your husband said the things he saw weren't dreams,' Richard said. 'Did he say what they were?'

Mrs Aspinall looked uncertainly down the hall toward the family room. 'Please,' Kit said. 'Your husband's the only one who can help us. It's so important.'

'What's important is my husband's recovery,' Mrs Aspinall said. 'He's still very weak. His nerves – I don't think you understand what a terrible ordeal he's been through. He was this close to death. I couldn't bear to lose him again. I have to think of his welfare –'

'You said Joanna was kind to you –' Richard said.

'She was,' Mrs Aspinall said, and took her hand off the door.

'Did he say anything about where he was?' Richard said rapidly. 'Did he mention a Grand Staircase?'

The loud thump of the walking stick sounded suddenly from the end of the hall. 'My husband's calling,' Mrs Aspinall said. 'I have to go get him settled for his nap.'

'He said, "She was only there for a few minutes," and the idea of her having been in the same place obviously frightened him,' Richard said over the thumping. 'Did he say where he was or why it was frightening?'

'I have to go.'

'Wait,' Richard said, fumbling in his pocket. 'Here's my card. That's my pager number. If you or your husband happen to remember anything –'

'I'll call you. Thank you again for coming all this way,' she said politely, and shut the door in their faces.

53

'V ... V ...'

– Last wireless message from the *Titanic*,
heard faintly by the *Virginian*

Joanna sank.

She was suddenly in water and darkness. She couldn't see, the rain on the windshield was suddenly a downpour, so heavy the wipers couldn't keep up. She flicked them to high, but it was no use, the rain was turning to sleet, to ice. She was going to have to pull off the road, but she couldn't even see the shoulder, she couldn't feel the bottom. Her toes stretched desperately down, trying to feel sand, her head going under. Under. Flailing and gulping for air, swallowing, choking. Drowning.

'Drowning's the worst way to die,' Vielle had said, but they were all terrible. Heart attack and kidney failure and beheading, drug overdoses and nicked aortas and being crushed by a falling smokestack. Joanna looked up, trying to see the *Titanic*, but there was only water above her. And darkness.

She reached up for the surface, but it was too far above her, and after a while she let her arms fall, and she fell. Her hair fanned out around her like Amelia Tanaka's had, lying on the examining table, her dead hands drifting limp and open in the dark water.

I let go of the French bulldog, she thought, and knew that she could not have held on to him or on to his memory, or on to the memory of Ulla or the dog at Pompeii, struggling against its chain, or of the *Titanic* passenger letting the dogs out of their cages, because the falling was itself a letting go, and as she fell, she forgot not only the dog but the meaning of the word *dog* and of *sugar* and *sorrow*.

They fell away from her like snow, like ash, memories of saying, 'Can you be more specific?' and eating buttered popcorn, of standing in the third-floor walkway, looking out at the fog, and sitting next to Mrs Woollam's bed, listening to her read passages from the Bible, 'When thou passest through the waters, I will be with thee,' and 'Rosabelle, remember,' and 'Put your hands on my shoulders and don't struggle.'

Names fell away from her in drifting tatters, the names of her patients and of her best friend in third grade, of the movie star Vielle's police officer had looked like and the capital of Wyoming. The names of the neurotransmitters and the days of the week and the core elements of the NDE.

The tunnel, she thought, trying to remember them, and the light, and the one Mr – what was his name? – she had forgotten – was so insistent about. The Life Review. 'There's *supposed* to be a Life Review,' he had said, but he was wrong. It was not a review but a jettisoning, events and happenings and knowledge being tossed overboard one by one: numbers and dates and faces, the taste of Tater Torros, and the smell of crayons, Indian red and gold and sea green, the combination of her junior high locker and her Blockbuster password and the best way to get from Medicine to ICU.

Code alarms and Victory gardens and scraping snow off her windshield, and somewhere a fire, burning out of control, sending up billows of black acrid smoke. And the smell of fresh paint, the sound of Amelia Tanaka's voice, saying, 'I was in a tunnel.' A tunnel, Joanna thought, looking down at the water she was sinking into, the narrowing darkness.

But there was no light at the end of this tunnel, and no angels, no loved ones, and even if there were, she would have forgotten them, fathers and grandmothers and Candy Simons. Would have left the memory of all of them, relatives and friends, living and dead, behind in the water. Guadalupe and Coleridge and Julia Roberts. Ricky Inman and Mrs Haighton and Lavoisier.

She had been falling a very long time. I can't fall forever, she thought. The *Titanic* hadn't fallen forever. It had come finally down to the bottom of the sea and settled into the soft mud, surrounded by chamber pots and chandeliers and shoes.

Will I be surrounded by shoes, too? she wondered, and could see them in the darkness: the red tennis shoe, jammed in the door, and Emmett Kelly's huge, flapping clown shoes and the tiny shoe in the Monopoly game, and the abandoned shoes of the sailors, lined up along the deck of the *Yorktown*. The *Yorktown* had come to rest, too, and the *Lusitania* and the *Hindenburg*, and Jay Yates and Lorraine Allison and Little Miss 1565, having forgotten everything, even their names. Rest in peace.

What was the Latin for 'Rest in peace'? *'Eloi, eloi, lama sabacthani,'* she thought, but that wasn't right. That was the Latin for something else. She had forgotten the Latin for 'Rest in peace' and the words to 'Nearer, My God, to Thee' and 'The Wreck of the Hesperus' and 'The Sound of Music.'

Everything she had learned by heart fell away from her, line after line, unraveling into the dark water like tape from a broken Blockbuster video, 'The Assyrian came down like the wolf on the fold,' and 'At a time like this, it's every man for himself.' 'Houston, we have a problem,' and 'Oh, don't you remember, a long time ago, there were two little children whose names I don't know.'

The words trailed away into the water, carrying memory with them, of

697

trailing electrode wires and lifejacket ties and yellow 'Do Not Cross' tape. And yellow Afghan yarn, yellow sneakers like the ones Whoopi Goldberg wore in *Jumpin' Jack Flash*, Jack in the Beanstalk, Jack Phillips.

And that was important. There was something important about Jack Phillips. Something about a lab coat, or a blanket. Or a heater, shutting off. They're shutting off, she thought, the receptors and transmitters and neurons, and this is just a symbol for it, a … but she had forgotten the word for metaphor. And for disaster. And for death.

Had forgotten the taste of Cheetos and the color of blood and the number fifty-eight, forgotten Mercy General and mercy everlasting, Zeppelins and kissing, her dress size, her first apartment, where she'd put her car keys, the answer to number fifteen on Mr Briarley's final, the sound in the tunnel and her 1040 form.

My taxes. I didn't send in my 1040. They're due April fifteenth, she thought, and remembered that the *Titanic* had gone down on the night of the fourteenth. All those people, she thought, they didn't file their income tax returns either. No, that was wrong. They didn't have income tax back then. That was why they were all so rich. But there were other things they hadn't done that they had intended to do: meet friends at the dock in New York, send a telegram announcing their safe arrival, marry, have children, win the Nobel Prize.

I never learned to play the piano, Joanna thought. I didn't tell Mr Wojakowski we couldn't use him in the project, and now he'll pester Richard. I didn't transcribe Mr Sage's NDE.

It doesn't matter, she thought. But I didn't pay the gas bill, she thought. I forgot to water my Swedish ivy. I didn't get the book from Kit. I promised I'd go pick it up. I promised I'd go see Maisie.

Maisie! she thought in horror. I didn't tell Richard, I have to tell him, but could not remember what it was she had wanted to tell him. Something about the *Titanic*. No, not the *Titanic*. Mr Briarley had been wrong, it wasn't about the *Titanic*. It was something about Indians. And the Rio Grande. And a dog. Something about a dog.

No, that wasn't right either. Fog, she thought, and remembered standing in the walkway, looking out at fog. It was cold and diffuse, like the water, like death. It blotted out everything, memory and duty and desire. Let it go, she thought, staring at nothingness. It's not important. Let it go.

Progress reports and delivering the mail and regret. They aren't important. Nothing's important. Not proving it's the *Titanic* or having a hall pass or avoiding Mr Mandrake. None of it matters. Not Mr Wojakowski or Mrs Haighton's never returning my calls or Maisie.

That's a lie, she thought. Maisie does matter. I have to find Richard. I have to tell him. 'Richard, listen,' she cried, but her mouth, her throat, her lungs, were full of water.

She kicked frantically, reaching up with her cupped hands, her arms. I have to tell him, she thought, clutching at the water as if it were the railing of a staircase, trying to pull herself up hand over hand. I have to get the message through. For Maisie.

She willed herself upward, kicking, stroking with her arms, trying to reach the surface.

And continued to fall.

54

'My God, My God, why hast thou forsaken me?'
– JESUS' last words from the cross

'Boy, just like Ismay,' Maisie said when they told her what had happened with Carl. 'How crummy!'

Leave it to Maisie to sum things up. Richard wondered if, clambering into the lifeboat, Ismay's hands had been as white and clenched as Carl Aspinall's, his face as sodden-looking.

'So what do we do now?' Vielle asked. She had called them on the way back, demanding to know what they'd found out, and Richard, unable to stand the prospect of telling it twice, had told her to meet them in Maisie's room.

'We could talk to the lab technician who saw Carl and Joanna,' Richard said. 'He may have heard what they were saying.'

'He didn't,' Maisie said. 'I asked him. He said they stopped talking when he came in the room.'

'He may have overheard something as he was coming in,' Richard said, 'or leaving. Or he may have seen someone else going in. If there was a lab tech in the room taking blood, there may have been other staff going in to take tests,' he said with a confidence he didn't feel. 'Or nurses. Who was the one Mrs Aspinall mentioned?'

'Guadalupe,' Kit said.

'I'll talk to Guadalupe and the rest of the staff on five-east. Vielle, you keep looking for people who might have seen Joanna in the hallways, and don't limit it to the professional staff. Talk to the volunteers and the kitchen help.'

'That's supposed to be *my* job!' Maisie said, outraged.

'Your job is to rest and get strong so you'll be ready for your new heart,' Richard said.

Maisie flung herself back against the pillows. 'That's no *fair*! I was the one who found out about Mr Aspinall. Besides,' she said, 'if I don't have anything to do or think about, I'll start worrying about my heart and how much the operation will hurt, and dying and stuff, and I might code.'

She was good, he had to admit that. 'All right,' he said sternly, 'you can help Vielle,' and she immediately said, 'I had another idea who to ask, Vielle. The painter guys. I bet they see a lot of people. And the breathing therapy lady. Should I page you when I think of other people?'

'No paging Vielle all the time,' Richard jumped in. 'She works in the ER, which is very busy. She'll come see you when she can, and when she does, no stalling.' He turned to Vielle. 'If Maisie finds out something, she's not going to tell you the whole story of *how* she found out, because she knows you have to get back to the ER.'

'But—' Maisie said.

'Promise,' Richard said. 'Cross your heart.'

'*Okay,*' she said grudgingly. She smiled at Vielle. 'I'll talk to the lady who empties the wastebaskets and the guy who runs the dust vacuum thing,' she said. 'And rest,' she added hastily.

'And drink your Ensure,' Richard said.

'What if nobody else was in the room and heard them?' Maisie asked.

'Maybe Mrs Aspinall will change her mind,' Kit said.

'That's right,' Richard said, though he didn't believe it for a moment. Her only concern was her husband, and his only concern was survival. And nothing, nothing could make him go back there, not even to save Joanna.

'But what if she doesn't change her mind?' Maisie said.

'Then we have to hope the lab technician knows something,' Richard said. 'Do you know his name, Maisie?'

'Yeah,' Maisie said. 'I saw it on his badge thing when he bent over to stick the needle in my IV line, and—'

'Maisie,' Richard said sternly. 'No stalling. You promised.'

'I promised *Vielle,*' Maisie said, and at his look, '*Okay.* Rudy Wenck. But what if he doesn't know anything?'

'Then we'll find somebody who did,' he said.

'But what if there isn't anybody?' Maisie persisted. 'What if nobody else heard them talking?'

I don't know, he thought. I don't know. 'We'll cross that bridge when we come to it,' he said cheerfully, thinking, You sound just like Maisie's mother.

And speak of the devil. Here she was, standing in the doorway with a yellow stuffed duck, a beribboned video-shaped package, and a blindingly bright smile. 'Dr Wright!' Mrs Nellis said. 'And Ms Gardiner. Just the people I needed to see.' She beamed at Vielle. 'I don't believe we've met.'

'This is Nurse Howard,' Richard said.

'She works in the ER,' Maisie said.

'We were just leaving.' Kit and Vielle took the cue and started for the door.

'Oh, but you can't go yet, Dr Wright,' Mrs Nellis said.

Well, now he knew where Maisie had gotten it from. He nodded at Kit and Vielle to keep going and said, 'I'm afraid I've got a meeting.'

'This will only take a minute,' Mrs Nellis said, setting the present and duck on the foot of the bed. She began rummaging through her purse. 'I've got the project release forms and the minor-child permissions for you, all signed and notarized.' She pulled out a manila envelope and handed it to Richard. 'My lawyer is working on a living will and resuscitation orders. Has he talked to you?'

'Yes,' Richard said. 'I really have to go.'

'Can I open my present now?' Maisie piped up, and Mrs Nellis, moment-arily distracted, moved to get her the package.

Good girl, Richard thought, and ducked out, but not fast enough. Mrs Nellis caught him just outside the door. 'I wanted to ask you about Nurse Howard,' she said eagerly. 'You said she worked in the ER, and I assume that means she's an expert on coding procedures. Is she working with you on the treatment? Does that mean you've had a breakthrough?'

'No,' Richard said.

'But you're getting close, right?'

'Mommy, come here!' Maisie said excitedly. 'I can't get my video open!' Mrs Nellis glanced toward the room, and then back at Richard, hesitating. 'Mommy! I want to watch it right away!'

'Excuse me,' Mrs Nellis said and hurried into the room. Richard didn't hesitate. He hotfooted it down the hall. Behind him he could hear Mrs Nellis asking, 'You like your video, sunbeam?' and Maisie saying, 'I love it! *Heidi* is my favoritest movie in the whole world!'

Kit and Vielle were waiting for him outside the CICU. 'We thought we were going to have to send the cavalry in after you,' Kit said.

'No, Maisie rescued me. At considerable sacrifice to herself.'

'So, what's the plan?' Vielle asked.

'Kit, I want you to go through Carl Aspinall's transcripts again and see if there's anything in them about a sword or ...' He cast around, trying to think of what else you could be stabbed with. '... a letter-opener or something. And then see if there's any reference to a stabbing the night of the *Titanic*. Vielle, see if you can find out who all was on four-east that day. I'll talk to Rudy Wenck.'

'I thought Maisie said he didn't remember hearing anything,' Vielle said.

'She did,' Richard said, 'but one thing I learned from Joanna is that people remember more than they think they do. And he has to have heard or seen *something*.'

But Rudy Wenck, even when pressed, didn't remember anything. 'He was scared of my drawing blood, that's all I remember, like I was trying to kill him or something. He seemed kind of out of it.'

'Can you be more specific?' Richard asked.

'No, just, you know, kind of wild-eyed and scared.'

'Did he say anything?'

'No.'

'What about Dr Lander? Did she say anything?'

'Yeah, she asked me if I wanted her to move, and I said, no, I could do it from that side.'

'Did she say anything else?'

'To me?'

'Or to Mr Aspinall, anything at all.'

He shrugged. 'She might have. I wasn't really listening.'

'If you could try to remember,' Richard said, 'it's very important.'

He shook his head. 'People are always talking when I'm in the room. I've learned to just shut it out.'

Guadalupe was even less helpful. 'I didn't know Joanna had even been in to see him,' she said.

'But you saw her on the floor that day?' Richard asked.

She nodded. 'I'd paged her because we couldn't find Mr Aspinall's wife and I thought Joanna might know where she was. She didn't, but she came up to the floor, and I talked to her for a couple of minutes. She asked about Mr Aspinall's condition, and she suggested a couple of places his wife might be, and then I assumed she left.'

'But you didn't see her leave?'

'No. Things were so crazy right then. We didn't expect Co— Mr Aspinall to regain consciousness. He'd been steadily sinking for several days, and then suddenly, he popped awake and we all started running around trying to find his wife and his doctor, so it's entirely possible Joanna was here. Why is it important?'

He explained. 'Did Mr Aspinall say anything to you about what he experienced while he was in the coma?'

'No. I asked him, because he'd flailed around so much –'

Drowning, Richard thought. He was drowning.

'– and he'd cry out. Mostly it was after we'd had to do something, like redo his IV, and I wondered if he was aware of what we were doing, but he said, no, there wasn't anybody else there, he was all alone.'

'Did he say where "there" was?'

She shook her head. 'Just talking about it seemed to upset him. I asked him if he'd had bad dreams – a lot of our coma patients remember dreaming – but he said no.'

Because it wasn't a dream, Richard thought.

'Have you tried talking to Mr Aspinall?' Guadalupe asked.

'He says he doesn't remember anything.'

She nodded. 'He was on a lot of drugs, which can really mess up your memory, and comas are funny. Some patients remember hearing voices and being aware of being moved or intubated, and then others can't remember anything.'

And some of them remember and won't tell, Richard thought bitterly, going through the list of people Vielle had come up with who'd been on four-east that day. They didn't know anything either. 'I was working the other end of the floor that day,' Linda Hermosa said, 'and we had all these subs because of the flu.'

'Subs?' Richard asked. 'Do you remember who they were?'

She didn't, and neither did the nurse's aides he questioned, but one of them said, 'I remember one was really old and she must have worked on five-east because she kept yelling at me and saying, "That isn't the way we do it up on fifth." I don't think she worked that end of the floor, though.'

Richard went up to fifth and gave the charge nurse his sketchy description. 'Oh, Mrs Hobbs,' she said, 'yes, she's a retired LPN who subs sometimes when they can't get anyone else.' She didn't know her number. 'Personnel takes care of all that.'

Richard thanked her and started down to Personnel. And what if Mrs Hobbs, who didn't sound promising, hadn't been in Carl's room either? What if, as Maisie said, there wasn't anybody who'd heard them talking? It was entirely possible that Joanna had taken advantage of the general chaos to speak to Carl alone before his memory of his hallucinations faded and then gone off to find him and said nothing to anybody along the way. What then?

There has to be somebody, he thought, crossing the walkway to the west wing. He turned down the hall toward the elevators. The center one pinged, and a man with a Palm Pilot stepped out.

Shit. Maisie's mother's lawyer. The last person he wanted to see. He turned sharply around and walked quickly back down the hall, wishing he'd finished mapping this part of the hospital. Then at least he'd know where the stairways were.

There was one at the very end of the hall. He ducked into it and clattered down the stairs. It only went as far down as third, but at least he knew where the elevators were on third. He opened the door and started down the hall.

'Last night I had another vision,' a woman's voice said, coming down the intersecting corridor toward him. 'This time I saw my uncle Alvin standing at the foot of my bed, as real as you or I.'

Shit. He'd been wrong about Mrs Nellis's lawyer being the last person in the world he wanted to see. That honor belonged to Mrs Davenport, and she was coming this way. Richard looked at the elevators, gauging the distance to

703

them, and then at the floor numbers above their doors. Both of them were on eight. Shit. He turned around and headed for the nurses' station.

'He was wearing his white sailor's uniform, and a radiant light came from him,' Mrs Davenport's voice said. 'And do you know what he said, Mr Mandrake?'

Mandrake, too. Shit, shit, shit. Richard looked desperately around for an escape route, a stairway, a laundry chute, anything. Even a linen closet. But there was nothing except patient rooms.

'He said, "Coming home,"' Mrs Davenport's voice said, coming closer. 'Just those two words. "Coming home." What can that mean, Mr Mandrake?'

'He was sending you a message from the Other Side, telling you that the dead haven't gone away,' Mandrake's voice said, 'that they are here with us, helping us, protecting us, speaking to us. All we have to do is listen –'

They were rounding the corner. Richard ducked through an unmarked door. A stairway. Great. And let's hope this goes all the way down to the basement, he thought, rounding the landing, so I can take the –

He stopped. Two steps below the landing, yellow 'Do Not Cross' tape stretched across the stairs, and, below it, pale blue steps shone wetly, though they could not possibly be wet. They had been painted over two months ago.

He wondered what had happened. Had the painters forgotten this stairway, or been unable to find it again in Mercy General's maze of walkways and corridors and cul-de-sacs? And the techs and nurses, seeing the tape, thought it was still blocked and had found other routes, other shortcuts?

They must have, because the painted steps below the yellow tape were shiny and untouched, not a footprint on them, and the stairwell still smelled of paint. It was obvious no one had been in here since the day he and Joanna had ducked in here, hiding from Mandrake, since the day she'd sat on the steps eating his energy bar and complaining about the cafeteria never being open, and he'd tried to talk her into working with him on the project and she'd asked if it was dangerous, and he'd said, 'No, it's perfectly safe –'

He had suddenly no strength in his legs. He groped for the round metal railing and sat down on the third step above the landing, where they had sat, where he had plied Joanna with apples and bottled cappuccino.

'The dead haven't gone away,' Mr Mandrake had said, and if that were true, if Joanna were anywhere, it would be here, in the embalmed and empty air of this stairwell where no one had been in two months, where nothing had disturbed the echoes of her voice.

He wished suddenly that Mr Mandrake were right, that Joanna would appear to him, standing on the pale blue steps, radiating light, and saying, 'I'm sorry I wasn't able to tell you what I'd found out. I was as bad as all those people in the movies. How were you supposed to know what "SOS" meant?

I'm surprised you didn't say, "Can you be more specific?"' He could almost see her, pushing her glasses up on her nose, laughing at him.

Almost.

And that was what made people believe in angels and put frauds like Mandrake on the best-seller list, that desire to believe. But it didn't bring them back. And it wasn't the presence of the dead that haunted people, that made them imagine they saw them standing there in their NDEs. It was their absence. In places where they should have been.

Because Joanna wasn't here, even in this place, where they had stood side by side, flattened against the wall, his arm stretched across her beating heart. There was nothing here, not even dust. She's dead, he thought, and it was like coming face to face with it all over again.

He had somehow managed to deny it, in all his running around, making maps, graphing scans, questioning nurse's aides, and he wondered now if that had been the point, if their obsession with Joanna's last words had simply been another form of denial, their own private Grief Coping Strategies Seminar?

Because if they could decipher Joanna's last words, it would make up for their having failed to save her. It would give the story a different ending. And how was that different from what Mandrake was trying to do?

He wondered suddenly if he had been just as deluded, if Joanna had murmured a few disjointed, delirious words, and he and Kit and Vielle had confabulated them into a message because it gave them something to think about, something to do besides grieving, besides giving way to despair, and Joanna's words meant nothing at all.

No. 'You *were* trying to tell me something,' he said to her, even though she wasn't there. 'I know you were.'

But she hadn't succeeded. The machine had clicked off before she could finish. He thought of the message she had left on his answering machine. 'A –' she had said, and he had played it over and over again, trying to decipher what she had started to say, but it was no use. There had been too many possibilities and not enough information. Like now, he thought, and knew, in spite of what he'd told Kit, that they would never find out.

In the movies they always found out who the murderer was, even though the victim died before she could tell them. In the movies, they always deciphered the message, solved the mystery, saved the girl. In the movies.

And maybe on the Other Side. But not on this side. On this side they never did find out what caused the Hartford circus fire or whether there was a bomb on the *Hindenburg*. On this side the doctor couldn't stop the bleeding, help didn't come in time, the message was too torn and stained to read.

'If anybody could have gotten a message through,' Joanna had said at Taco Pierre's that night, 'it was Houdini.' But that wasn't true. If anybody could have gotten a message through, it was Joanna. She had tried, even when she was choking on her own blood, even when she should have been unconscious. If she could have come from where she was – in the grave or on the foundering decks of the *Titanic* or on the Other Side – to tell him her message, she would have.

But she couldn't. Because she wasn't anywhere. She's gone, he thought, and buried his face in his hands.

He sat there a long time. His beeper went off once, startling in the silence, and he pulled it immediately out of his pocket, praying that it was Mrs Aspinall calling to tell him Carl had changed his mind, but it was only Vielle, paging him to call her so she could report that she'd found another sub who'd worked the wrong end of the floor that day, or that she'd narrowed the cab Joanna had taken down to Yellow and Shamrock.

That wasn't fair. Vielle had tried her best. They'd all tried their best. There were just too many pieces missing. The answer lay somewhere in the transcripts or the *Titanic* or the scans or English literature, but Joanna couldn't tell them where, and Mr Briarley, if he had ever known, could not remember. And Carl refused to tell.

And he, Richard, couldn't figure it out. It was time to admit that. Time to face facts, pack it in, put on evening clothes and admit defeat.

Joanna would surely understand. She had watched the crash team trying CPR, norepinephrine, saline, paddles, one after the other. And she had been on the *Titanic*, which was all about trying and failing. The lookout hadn't seen the iceberg in time, the *Californian* hadn't heard the SOSs, hadn't seen the Morse lamp's signal, hadn't understood the rockets. Assistant Engineer Harvey and the man he'd gone back to save had both drowned.

If there was any lesson to be learned from the *Titanic*, it was that attempts failed, rescue arrived too late, messages didn't get through, and he knew, even as he thought it, that it wasn't true.

The lesson of the *Titanic* was that people kept on trying even when they knew it was hopeless – tapping out SOSs, cutting the collapsibles free, going belowdecks and bringing the mail up, letting the dogs loose – all of them determined to save something, someone, even though they knew they couldn't save themselves.

You can't give up, Richard thought. Jack Phillips didn't. Joanna didn't.

'All right,' he said, and though he didn't know it, his voice sounded just like Joanna's on the answering machine.

He stood up. All right. Get Mrs Hobbs's number from Personnel. Find out who else was a patient on five-east that day. Find out who visited them. Go over the scans again, and the transcripts. Talk to Vielle. Talk to Bob Yancey. Go down trying.

He switched his pager back on and walked up the stairs, put out his hand to push the door open, and then ran back down to the landing. He tore the yellow tape free, ripping the trailing ends off the railing.

He carried the tangle of tape upstairs and out to the nurses' station. A nurse was on the phone, her back to him. 'The stairway down to second's open. The paint's dry,' he said, dumping the mass of tape on the counter. 'Is Maurice Mandrake still in with Mrs Davenport?'

'Hang on,' the nurse said into the phone. She half-turned and nodded at Richard.

'Thanks,' he said, and started down the hall toward the elevator.

'No, wait, Dr Wright –' the nurse called, her hand over the mouthpiece, '– I didn't realize it was you –' He came back to the nurses' station. 'Someone from the ER called looking for you. I didn't realize you were on the floor or I would have come looking for you. It was just a few minutes ago –'

'Was it Vielle Howard?' he cut in.

'Yes, I think so. I asked the other nurses, but they didn't think you'd been—'

'Did she say she wanted me to call her or come down to the ER?'

'She said there was someone waiting for you in your lab.'

'Man or woman?'

'Man,' the nurse said.

Carl Aspinall, he thought, and sprinted for the elevator. He changed his mind. He must have thought about what Kit said.

But when he got up to sixth, it wasn't Carl standing outside the lab door. It was Mr Pearsall.

55

'A little while and I will be gone from among you, whither I cannot tell. From nowhere we came, into nowhere we go. What is life? It is a flash of a firefly in the night.'
            – Last words of CROWFOOT, a Blackfoot Indian chief

There were fireflies. They winked on and off in the darkness around her. I'm in Kansas, Joanna thought. This must be part of the Life Review. And she must be getting near the end of it if she was remembering her childhood, visiting her relatives in Kansas, running around in the dark with her cousins, a Mason jar in one hand to catch the fireflies in, and the brass lid in the other, ready to clap it on when you'd caught one, the grass wet against her ankles, the rich, sweet scent of peonies filling the evening air.

But it wasn't evening – it was night. And no matter how late they had been allowed to stay up, it had never gotten completely dark like this. There had always been a bluish-purple cast to the sky, and even after the stars came out, you could still see the outlines of the houses, of the arching cottonwoods, against it. You could still see the grownups on the dark porch, and each other.

She could not see the grass that she was sitting on, or the house, or her own hand, which she held up in front of her face. It was utterly black, in spite of the fireflies. 'The moon did not shine,' she said out loud, 'and the stars gave no light.'

The stars. They were stars, shining clearly, steadily, in the black sky, and why had she thought they were fireflies? They were obviously stars, and they came down all the way, sharp and sparkling, to the horizon. The survivors of the *Titanic* had all remarked on that, how the stars hadn't dimmed near the horizon, but had shone all the way down to the water.

The water. I have survived the sinking, she thought. I am floating on something from the *Titanic*, a deck chair. But deck chairs were slatted. The surface below her was wide and smooth. A piano. The grand piano in the À La Carte Restaurant.

But pianos didn't float. In the movie *The Piano*, it had sunk like a stone, dragging her down with it into the cold, disintegrating water. Maybe it's the aluminum piano on the *Hindenburg*, she thought. That only weighed 397 pounds.

It would still sink, she thought. And maybe it was sinking. 'All ships sink sooner or later,' Mr Wojakowski had said, and maybe this was sinking very slowly, because the ocean was so still. The survivors had all said the water was as smooth as glass that night, so still the stars' reflections had been scarcely distorted at all.

Joanna reached her hand down over the edge of the piano, feeling for the keyboard and then for the water below it, and as she did, she realized she was holding on to something with her other hand, holding it tight against her in the crook of her arm.

The little French bulldog, she thought, I must have held on to it when I fell, though she remembered letting go of everything, everything in the water, though she remembered her open hands drifting emptily in the darkness.

The lifejacket, she thought, and felt for its dangling ties but could not find them. She bent over the little dog, trying to see it. It was too dark, but she could feel its silky head, feel its small body against her side. It did not move. 'Are you all right, little dog?' she asked, bending closer to hear the sound of its panting, the beating of its little heart, but she could not hear anything.

Maybe it drowned, she thought anxiously, but as she thought that, it pressed itself closer against her side. 'You're all right,' she said. 'Maisie will be so glad.'

Maisie, she thought, and remembered struggling up through the obliterating darkness, struggling to keep from forgetting until the message was sent. 'As soon as we're rescued,' she said to the little bulldog, 'I have to send Richard a message.'

She looked out at the darkness. The *Carpathia* would be here in two hours. She scanned the horizon, looking for its lights, but there were only stars. She looked up at them, trying to find the Big Dipper. The *Carpathia* had come up from the southwest. If she could find the Big Dipper, she could follow the handle to the North Star and tell which direction it would come from.

They had looked for the Big Dipper, those summer nights in Kansas. They had run around in the cool grass, trying to catch fireflies in their cupped hands, and when a car turned down the street, they had called out, 'Automobile!' and flopped down flat on their backs in the grass, motionless in the sweep of its headlights. Playing dead. And even after the car had passed, they had lain there, looking up at the stars, pointing out the constellations. 'There's the Big Dipper,' they had said, pointing. 'There's the Milky Way. There's the Dog Star.'

There were no constellations. Joanna craned her neck, trying to find the pattern of the Archer, the long spilled splash of the Milky Way down the center of the sky. But there were only stars. And they sparkled brightly, clearly, all the way down to the water, which was so still she couldn't hear it lapping against the sides of the piano, so still the stars' reflections were not distorted at all. They sparkled steadily, clearly, as if they were not reflections at all, as if there were sky below her instead of water.

She hugged the dog to her. 'I don't think we're in Kansas anymore, Toto,' she said, and pulled her feet up under her, away from the edge.

They were not in the Atlantic, and the thing they huddled on was not a piano. It was something else, an examining table, or a drawer in the morgue. Or a metaphor for the shipwrecked survivors of her consciousness, floating on the wreckage of her body, for her final synapses flickering out like stars, like fireflies.

And the Atlantic was a metaphor for someplace else. The River Styx or the River Jordan or Mr Mandrake's Other Side. No, not an Other Side, Joanna thought. It's someplace else altogether, with no connection to the world.

'The far country,' she thought, but that was not right either. It was not a country. It was a place so far away it was not even a place. A place so far away the *Carpathia* could not ever come, so far away there was no possibility of being rescued, of getting back. And from which nothing was ever heard, in spite of what Maurice Mandrake said, in spite of the messages he claimed he had had from the dead.

And even the last words of the dying were not messages at all, but only useless echoes of the living. Useless lies. 'I will never leave you,' they said, and left forever. 'I won't forget you,' they said, and then forgot everything in the dark, disintegrating water. 'We will be together again,' and that was the biggest lie of all. There were no fathers waiting on the shining shore. No prophets, no elders, no Angels of Light. No light at all. And they would never be together. She would never see them again, or be able to tell them where she had gone.

I left without saying good-bye, she thought, and felt a stab of pain, like a knife in the ribs. 'Good-bye!' she shouted, but her voice didn't carry across the water. 'Good-bye, Vielle!' she shouted, 'Good-bye, Kit! Good-bye, Richard!' trying to make them out, but they were too far away. Too far even for her to remember Richard's face, or Maisie's –

Maisie, she thought, and knew why she had thought the stars were fireflies. Morse-code bugs, they had called them back in Kansas. Winking on, winking off, sending coded messages in the dark. 'I have to get the message to Richard,' she said, and stood up on the piano, setting it rocking wildly. 'Richard!' she called, cupping her hands to her mouth like a megaphone, 'the NDE's the brain's way of signaling for help!'

It was too far. It would never reach him. Houdini, calling out, 'Rosabelle, answer, tell, pray!' to his wife across the void, could not make himself heard. And neither could she. 'It's an SOS!' Joanna called, but softly. 'An SOS.'

The little French bulldog was whimpering at her feet, frightened at being left alone. Joanna sat back down and reached for it, unable to find it at first in the dark, putting both arms around it, pulling it close. 'It's no use,' she said, stroking the silky head she could not see. 'It will never reach them.'

The little dog whimpered, heartbroken, a sound like a child's crying. 'It's all right,' Joanna said, even though it wasn't. 'Don't cry, I'm here. I'm here.'

I am here. 'Where are you?' The fireflies, trapped in a Mason jar, caught in cupped hands from which no light could escape, went on sending messages, on and off, on and off, even though it was no use. And Jack Phillips, even though the *Carpathia* was too far away, even though there were no other ships to hear, had kept on sending, tapping out SOS, SOS, till the very end.

'SOS,' she called, willing her thoughts to Richard and Kit and Vielle like wireless messages, through the nothingness, through the vast, dark distances of death. 'Good-bye. It's all right. Don't grieve.' The little bulldog quieted and slept, curled against her, but she continued to stroke its soft head. 'Don't cry,' she said, willing Maisie to hear, willing Richard to listen. 'It's an SOS.'

It will never reach them, she thought, but she sat on in the dark, holding tight to the little dog, surrounded by stars, sending out signals of love and pity and hope. The messages of the dead.

56

'Coming hard.'
> – Wireless message from the *Carpathia* to the *Titanic*

'Mr Pearsall,' Richard said, unable to keep the disappointment out of his voice. 'What are you doing here?'

'I wondered if you still needed me for your project,' he said. 'I just got back from Indiana. I had to stay a lot longer than I thought I was going to. My father died,' he had to clear his throat before he went on, 'and I had to settle his estate. I just got back yesterday.' He cleared his throat again. 'I heard about Dr Lander. I'm really sorry.'

That's what Carl Aspinall said, Richard thought bitterly.

'It's hard to believe,' Mr Pearsall said, clutching his hat in both hands. 'One minute they're there, and the next … I always thought near-death experiences were some kind of hallucination, but now I don't know. Right before my dad went, he said – he'd had a stroke and had trouble talking, he just sort of mumbled, but he said this as plain as day – "Well, what do you know!" '

Richard straightened alertly. 'Did he say anything else?'

Mr Pearsall shook his head. Of course, Richard thought.

'He said it like he'd just figured something important out,' Mr Pearsall said, shaking his head again. 'I'd like to know what it was.'

So would I, Richard thought.

'That's why I thought if you still needed volunteers, I could—'

'The project's been suspended.'

Mr Pearsall nodded as if that was the answer he'd expected. 'If you start it up again, I'd be glad to—'

'I'll give you a call,' Richard said, showing him out. He shut the door and went over to his desk and the tapes, but he'd scarcely gotten started when someone knocked. And this won't be Carl Aspinall either, he thought.

It was Amelia Tanaka. 'Amelia,' he said. 'What are you doing here?'

She stopped just inside the door and stood there, her coat and backpack on. Like the day she'd come to tell them she was quitting. 'I came …' Amelia said, and took a deep breath. 'Dr Lander came to see me at the university.'

That's where she went in the taxi, Richard thought, and wanted to ask her what day that was, but Amelia was having enough difficulty. He didn't want to throw her off.

'I didn't tell the truth about why I quit,' Amelia said. 'Dr Lander asked me if it was because I experienced something upsetting, and I told her no, but that wasn't true. I did, and I was so scared I couldn't face going under again, but then I heard she died, and I got to thinking about it happening to her, only she didn't have a choice, she couldn't back out.'

The words tumbled helplessly out of her, like tears. 'I got to thinking about what a coward I'd been. She was always so nice to me. Once, when I asked her to do something for me, she did, and I –' She broke off, blushing. 'She said it was important, my telling her what I saw. I shouldn't have lied. I should have told her. How can I be a doctor, if I let my fear –?' She looked up at Richard. 'It's too late to tell her, but she said it was important, and you're her partner –'

'It is important,' Richard said. 'Here, take your coat off and sit down.'

She shook her head. 'I can't stay. I've got an anatomy makeup lab.' She laughed shakily. 'I shouldn't even have taken the time to come over here, but I had to tell you –'

'Okay,' Richard said, 'you don't have to take your coat off, but at least sit down,' but she shook her head.

And she'll bolt if you push her, Richard thought. 'What did you see that frightened you, Amelia?'

'The ...' She bit her lip. 'Have you ever had a scary dream that, when you tried to explain it, there wasn't anything scary in it, like a slasher or –' She stopped, looking appalled. 'I didn't mean to say that. Honest, I –'

'You didn't see any murderers or monsters,' Richard prompted, 'but you were frightened anyway –'

'Yes,' Amelia said. 'I was in the tunnel, like I had been the times before, only this time I realized it wasn't a tunnel, it was ...' She glanced longingly at the door.

Richard stepped sideways, easing himself between her and the door. 'What was it?' he asked, even though he already knew what it was. And she was right, there was nothing inherently frightening in the sight of people in old-fashioned clothes standing outside a door, in the sound of engines shutting down. 'What's happened?' Lawrence Beesley had asked his steward, and the steward had said, 'I don't suppose it's much,' and Beesley had gone back to bed, not frightened at all.

'What was it, Amelia?' Richard said.

'I ... it sounds so crazy, you'll think ...'

That you're Bridey Murphy? he thought, like I did Joanna. He said, 'Whatever it is, I'll believe you.'

'I know,' she said. 'All right.' She took a deep breath. 'I have biochem this semester. The class is in the daytime, but the lab's at night, on Tuesdays and Thursdays, in this old room. It's long and narrow, with these dark wooden cabinets along the walls that they keep the chemicals in, so it looks like a tunnel.'

A long, narrow room with tall cupboards on either side. He wondered what it really was. The dispensary? He'd have to ask Kit where the dispensary on the *Titanic* was.

'It was the lab final,' Amelia said. 'We were supposed to do this enzyme reaction, but I couldn't get it to work, and it was really late. They'd already turned the lights off and were waiting for me to finish.'

'Who was?' Richard asked, thinking, lab final? Enzyme reaction?

'My professors,' Amelia said, and he could hear fear in her voice. 'They were standing out in the hall, waiting. I could see them standing outside the door in their white lab coats, waiting to see if I passed the final.'

The biochem final and professors in lab coats. She's had weeks to rationalize what she saw, he thought, to confabulate it into something that makes sense. Or at least more sense than the *Titanic*. 'When did you realize it was the biochem lab you'd been in?' he asked.

She looked at him, bewildered. 'What do you mean?'

'Was it a few days after your session or more recently?'

'It was right then,' Amelia said, 'when I was having the NDE. I didn't tell you and Dr Lander because I was afraid you'd make me go under again. I said I saw the same things I'd seen before, the door and the light and the happy, peaceful feeling, but I didn't. I saw the lab.'

It wasn't the *Titanic*, Richard thought. She didn't see the *Titanic*.

'It wasn't really the lab, though,' Amelia said, 'because the cabinets aren't really locked, like they were in the NDE, and it wasn't my biochem professor, it was Dr Eldritch from anatomy and this director I had when I was majoring in musical theater. And I was so frightened.'

'Of what?' Richard asked.

'Of failing,' she said, and he could hear the fear in her voice. 'Of the final.'

She wasn't on the *Titanic*, he thought, trying to take this in. She was in her biochem lab. 'What happened then?' he managed to ask.

'I started to look for the key. I had to find it. I had to get into the cabinet and find the right chemical. I looked under the lab tables and in all the drawers,' she said, her voice tightening, 'but it was dark, I couldn't see –'

The connection wasn't the *Titanic*. And that was what Joanna had realized when she talked to Carl Aspinall.

'– and the labels on the drawers didn't make any sense,' Amelia was saying. 'There were letters on them, but they weren't words, they were just letters and numbers, all strung together, like code. And I was so frightened ... and then I was back in the lab, so I guess I found it and I guess I passed. I don't know what grade I got.' She laughed embarrassedly. 'I told you it sounded crazy.'

'No,' he said. 'No, you've been very helpful.'

She nodded, unconvinced. 'I have to go to my anatomy lab, but –' she took another deep breath '– if you want me to, I'll go under again. I owe it to Dr Lander.'

'That may not be necessary,' he said, and, as soon as she was gone, called Carl Aspinall.

He was afraid Mrs Aspinall would be the one to answer the phone, but she didn't, and when Carl said, 'Hello, Aspinalls' residence,' Richard said, 'Mr Aspinall, this is Dr Wright. No, wait, don't hang up. I understand that you don't want to talk about your experience. I just want you to answer one question. Did your experience take place on the *Titanic*?'

'The *Titanic*?' Carl said, and the astonishment in his voice told Richard all he wanted to know.

He hadn't been on the *Titanic*. And that was the revelation that had sent Joanna on her plunge down to the ER. It wasn't what he'd told her about his NDE, it was the fact that he hadn't seen the *Titanic*, and Joanna, realizing that that wasn't the connection, that she had been on the wrong track, had seen what the real answer was, and run to tell him.

He had to make sure. He called Maisie. 'When you had your NDEs, Maisie, were you on a ship?' he asked her when the nurse finally let him talk to her.

'A *ship*?' she said, and he could see the face she was making. '*No.*'

'How do you know?'

'Because I know,' Maisie said. 'It didn't feel *anything* like a ship.'

'What did it feel like?'

'I don't know,' she said thoughtfully. 'I told Joanna I thought it was inside, but I think it was outside, too. Someplace both inside and outside,' and the carefulness of her answer convinced him more than anything else that if she'd been on a ship she would have known it, and the answer lay elsewhere.

But where? It had to lie somewhere in the NDEs, in some common thread they all shared, even though neither Amelia's nor Maisie's, nor, presumably, Carl Aspinall's, were anything like Joanna's. 'But it has to be there,' he told Kit on the phone, 'because as soon as Joanna realized Carl hadn't been on the *Titanic*, she knew what it was.'

'And it has to be something that's in all of them,' Kit said. 'Did you record what Amelia said just now?'

'No,' he said. 'She was too nervous. I've transcribed everything I remember, though.'

'What about your own?' Kit said. 'Have you transcribed it?'

'My own?' he said blankly. 'But it was—'

'Related to the *Titanic*,' she said. 'I know, but there might be a clue in it. I think you're right. I think there's got to be a common thread, and the more NDEs we have, the more apt we are to find it.'

She was right. He wondered if, if he called Carl Aspinall back and explained that his nightmares, whatever they were, were purely subjective, if he'd be willing to talk to him. He doubted it.

Which left Amelia's NDE, and his own, and Maisie's. And the vision of the crewman on the *Hindenburg*. He made a list of the elements in each of them. Joseph Leibrecht had seen snow fields, whales, a train, a bird in a cage, and his grandmother, and heard church bells and the scream of tearing metal. Amelia had seen enzymes, lab drawers, and her professors. Joanna had seen stairways and stationary bicycles, and he hadn't seen any of the above.

Joseph's was clearly dreamlike, with disconnected images rapidly succeeding one another, and completely unlike Joanna's. Amelia's was somewhere in between. There were no time or image jumps, but there were logic gaps, whereas in his own –

He realized he didn't know whether there were incongruities, except for the toy Zeppelin, in his own or not. He'd assumed it was real, that Joanna's were real, and later, going through Kit's uncle's books, he'd focused on the *Titanic* itself.

He hauled the books out again. People had in fact gathered at the White Star offices and at *The New York Times* building, but not inside. They had milled around in the streets outside, waiting for news from the *Carpathia*. When it finally came, there had been no public reading of the list of survivors. A list had been posted at the *Times* – Mary Marvin's mother, there with her son-in-law's mother, had yelped joyfully when she located her daughter's name on it, and then stopped, aghast, when she realized Daniel's wasn't next to it – but for the most part, relatives had gone into the White Star building one by one to inquire. John Jacob Astor's son had come back out immediately, his face buried in his hands.

And there hadn't been a wireless room in the White Star building. There had been one at the *Times*, but it was up on the roof. The wireless operator had put the deciphered messages in a box attached to a rope, shaken the rope against the metal walls of the shaft to signal the reporters below, and dropped the box down the shaft.

Which told him what? That he hadn't really been in the White Star offices? He already knew that. That he'd confabulated his NDE out of images from the movies and Joanna's NDEs. But not why. Not what the connection was.

He listed all the elements – his pager, the woman in the high-necked blouse speaking into the telephone, the man bent over the wireless, the clock on the wall, the stairs, the man with the newspaper under his arm – and then called Amelia and asked her to come over. 'Are you sending me under again?' she asked, and he could hear the fear in her voice.

'No,' he said. 'We just need to ask you some questions. Will tomorrow morning at nine work?'

'No, I have a psych test.' She's making excuses, he thought, like she did that last time Joanna tried to schedule her before she quit, but after a pause, she said, 'Would eleven o'clock work?' and, amazingly, showed up on time.

He had asked Vielle to sit in on the session. 'Amelia, we want you to tell us everything you can remember about your NDEs, starting with the first one,' he said, and Vielle switched on Joanna's minirecorder.

Amelia nodded. 'I promised you I'd do anything you asked,' she said and launched into a detailed account, made even more detailed by his and Vielle's questions.

'How many of your professors were in the office?' Vielle asked her.

'Four,' Amelia said. 'Dr Eldritch and my director and Mrs Ashley, my high school English teacher, and my freshman chem lab professor. He wasn't really a professor. He was a graduate student. I hated him. If you asked him a question, all he'd say was, "It's something you need to figure out yourself." '

'Your English teacher was there?' Richard asked, thinking of Mr Briarley.

Amelia nodded. 'I didn't really have her, though. She died a month after school started.'

Vielle grilled her about the labels on the chemical bottles. 'You know how in formulas, the numbers are below the line?' Amelia said. 'These were all in a row.'

'Can you remember what any of the letters were?' Vielle asked.

She couldn't. 'Do you remember anything else that wasn't right?' Vielle asked.

Amelia stared into space. 'The coldness,' she said finally. 'It's always hot in that room. It has these old-fashioned heating vents. But in my NDE, it was freezing, like they'd left a door open somewhere.'

'Joanna talked about it being cold, too,' Vielle said after Amelia was gone. 'Did Joseph Leibrecht?'

'He talked about seeing snow fields,' Richard said, 'but he also talked about a boiling sea and being tossed in a fire. And there was nothing hot *or* cold in my NDE.'

'You and Amelia were both looking for something,' Vielle offered.

'Joanna was, too,' Richard said, 'but Joseph Leibrecht wasn't.'

'What about her English teacher being someone who'd died?'

He shook his head. 'That's one of the core elements.'

'There's no chance you can convince Carl Aspinall to talk to you?' she asked.

'They're not answering their phone.'

Vielle nodded wisely. 'Caller ID. I don't suppose it's worth driving up there again?'

No, he thought, and that wasn't where the answer lay anyway. It lay with Mr Briarley, and he couldn't get it out of him either. 'It's something you need to figure out for yourself,' the graduate assistant had said.

'Could you send Amelia under again?' Vielle asked as he walked her to the door of the lab.

'Maybe,' he said, 'although the chances are she'll have a repeat of the same unifying image.'

'Oh, good, you're here,' a voice said, and Maisie's mother came in, dressed in a sunny yellow suit. 'Is this a bad time?'

'I was just leaving. I'll work on it some more and call you,' Vielle said and scooted out.

'I didn't mean to interrupt,' Maisie's mother said. 'Here.' She handed him a small black box.

'What's this?' he asked. It looked like a very small Palm Pilot.

'Your pager. You said a problem with implementing your procedure was that the window of opportunity was too short, only four to six minutes, you said.'

What I said was that irreversible brain death occurs in four to six minutes, he thought, but she can't even bring herself to say the words or to admit that what she wants me to do is bring Maisie back from the dead.

'This pager solves that problem,' she said, looking pleased as punch.

'I already have a pager,' he said. And even if this one went off the second Maisie coded, he would still have to get to a phone and find out where she was. If anyone was bothering to answer the phone during an emergency.

'It isn't an ordinary pager,' Mrs Nellis said. 'It's a locational device. Maisie has one of these, and so do each of her doctors and nurses, and, in the case of a coding situation, they've been instructed to hit this button immediately,' she pointed to a red button on the end of the box, 'and your pager will beep. It has a distinctive beep, so you won't confuse it with your own pager.'

It probably plays 'Put On a Happy Face,' he thought.

'As soon as you hear it beep,' Mrs Nellis flowed on, 'you press *this* button,' she indicated a black button on the side, 'and the location in the hospital the signal was sent from will appear on this screen. It will say "Cardiac Intensive Care Unit" or "west wing, fourth floor" or wherever. Maisie will be in her room in the CICU most of the time, of course, but, as you said, she might be down for tests, or,' she crossed her fingers coyly, 'in the OR, getting prepped for her new heart, and this way you'll know exactly where she is. I wanted one that would also plot where you were and map out the shortest route, but the computer engineer who designed this said the technology didn't exist yet.'

'The technology for reviving patients who've coded doesn't exist yet either, Mrs Nellis,' he said, trying to give her back the pager.

'But it will,' she said confidently, 'and when it does, you won't have to worry about the problem of locating her. I realize there's still the problem of reaching her quickly, but I've got another programmer working on that.'

And I know the shortest route, Richard thought. I have the whole map of the hospital in my head, all the stairs, all the shortcuts. I could get to Maisie in time, if I had a way to revive her. If I knew what Joanna was trying to tell me.

'Of course, this is really just a precaution. Maisie's doctors expect her to get a heart any day now, and she's doing really well, they're *so* pleased with her numbers. *Now*,' she said, putting the pager firmly in his hand, 'I knew you'd want to see it in action, so Maisie's going to activate her pager at two-ten so you can hear the beep and see how the locator screen works.'

'Two-ten?' Richard said.

'Yes, I suggested two o'clock so you'd know for certain it was a drill, but she insisted on two-ten. I have no idea why.'

I do, Richard thought. It's a code. She's found out something.

'They sometimes take her down for tests at two, and she may be thinking if she were somewhere other than her room, it would provide a better test. She's such an intelligent child.'

That she is, Richard thought. 'And where am I supposed to be at two-ten?'

'You're not,' she said. 'That's the point. Wherever you are, the pager will beep you and tell you where she is. Unfortunately, I have to meet with my lawyer at one-thirty, so I won't be there, but Maisie can probably answer any questions you have.'

Let's hope so, he thought, watching Mrs Nellis go down to the elevator. Maisie must have found someone else who'd seen Joanna in the elevator or one of the hallways. Or, if he was lucky, in the room with Carl Aspinall. Mrs Nellis stepped in the elevator. Richard waited for the door to close and then took off for the CICU.

'I was worried you wouldn't be able to figure it out,' Maisie said when he walked in her room. 'I thought maybe I should have said two-twenty, when it went down, instead of when they sent the last wireless message.'

'What did you find out?' Richard asked.

'Eugene talked to this orderly who saw Joanna that day. On two-east. He said he saw her talking to Mr Mandrake.'

Mandrake. Then he really had seen her, he hadn't just invented the incident for his self-serving eulogy. He must have waylaid her as she was on her way up to see Dr Jamison.

'Well?' Maisie was demanding.

Richard shook his head. 'Joanna may have run into Mandrake, but she wouldn't have told him anything. Did this orderly hear what Mandrake said?'

Maisie shook her head. 'I asked Eugene. He said he was too far away, but Mr Mandrake said a whole bunch of stuff, and so did she. He said she was laughing.'

'Laughing? With Mandrake?'

'I know,' Maisie said, making a face. 'I don't think he's very funny either. But that's what Eugene said he said.'

What Eugene said he said. It was a third-hand, no, fourth-hand, story, from someone too far away to overhear, and the chance that Joanna would have revealed anything substantive to Mandrake was nil, but Richard had promised Joanna he'd go down trying.

And you couldn't go much lower than this. 'I've been expecting you to call,' Mandrake said when Richard phoned him from the CICU's front desk. 'Mrs Davenport told me she'd spoken with you about the messages she's been receiving.'

I can't do this, Richard thought, and almost hung up the phone. It's betraying Joanna. She wouldn't care, he thought suddenly. All she cared about was getting the message through to me. 'I want to come see you,' he said. 'Are you in your office?'

'Yes, but I'm afraid I have several appointments this afternoon, and my publisher –' There was a pause, presumably while he checked his schedule. 'Would two o'clock ... no, I have a meeting ... and my publicist's coming at three ... would one o'clock work?'

'One o'clock,' Richard said and hung up, thinking, Hopefully in the next hour and a half the answer will come to me, and I won't have to talk to him at all.

He started through Joanna's transcripts again, making a list of everything they contained – swimming pool, Scotland Road, mail room, key – the key. What was the key? – rockets, gymnasium, mechanical bicycles, wireless shack, sacks of mail – looking for common elements with his and Amelia Tanaka's. They had both talked about doors and bottles, a bottle of chemicals in Amelia's and of ink in Joanna's, but there hadn't been any bottles in his. A key? He had had to turn the key to open the door to the hallway, Mr Briarley had gone to the mailroom to get the key to the locker that contained the rockets, the sailor who'd operated the Morse lamp had said something about a key, and Amelia, in talking about the catalyst, had said, 'I had to find the key.'

That's pushing it, he thought, and Joseph Leibrecht hadn't said anything about a key. And *key* wasn't one of the words highlighted on the transcripts.

All right then, how about the words that were? Water? There was no water in either his or Amelia's NDEs, and no fog. Time, he thought, remembering the clock on the wall of the White Star corridor. Amelia had been worried about finishing her final in time, and Joseph Leibrecht had mentioned hearing a church bell ring and knowing it was six o'clock. And the *Titanic* was all about running out of time.

And speaking of time, what time was it? Ten to one. Just enough time to go ask Vielle what similarities she'd found in the transcripts and then get over to Mandrake's office.

He went down to third. The walkway had a big sandwich board with 'Closed for Repairs' on it. They must have run out of yellow tape, he thought.

He'd have to go down to the basement and outside. He started back down the hallway. The pager in his pocket began to beep, a high-pitched, urgent ringing. Maisie's drill, he thought, pulling it out of his pocket. He pressed the red button. 'Six-west,' it said, and under it, the time: 12:58.

Six-west. What's she doing down there? he thought, and then, the readout sinking in, 12:58. 'She said two-ten,' he said and took off running, up to third, across the walkway, up the service stairs.

He made it up to sixth in three minutes and nineteen seconds and flung himself, out of breath, against the nurses' station. 'Quick. Maisie Nellis. Where is she?'

'Down there, second door,' the surprised nurse said, and it still didn't occur to him, tearing down the hall, that the nurse wouldn't have been just standing there in an emergency, that there was no code alarm blaring.

He burst into the room, where Maisie lay quietly on a gurney, looking at her pager.

'Did you talk to Mr Mandrake yet?' she asked eagerly.

'How – could – I?' he said, between panting breaths. 'You paged – me. What's the idea?' He slumped into a chair next to the wall.

'The drill,' she said.

'The *drill* was supposed to be at two-ten, not twelve-fifty-eight.'

'The two-ten was a *code*,' she said. 'They brought me here for some tests, and I thought it was a good idea to do the pager when you didn't know where I was, to see if it worked or not.'

'Well, it worked,' Richard said, 'so no more drills. I only want you paging me in a real emergency. Understand?'

'But shouldn't we practice a few times?' she said, looking longingly at the pager. 'So you could get faster?'

I was fast enough, he thought. I got here in under four minutes, from a point in the hospital almost as far away as there is. I made it in time. And had no way to save her when I got here. 'No,' he said. 'You page me if you code, and only if you code.'

'What if I think I'm going to code and then it turns out I don't?'

'Then it had better not also turn out that you just wanted to see me to tell me about the Hartford circus fire. I mean it.'

'Okay,' she said reluctantly.

'Okay.' He looked at his watch. One-ten. 'I'm late for my appointment with Mandrake. And don't say, "You can't go yet." '

'I wasn't going to,' she said indignantly. 'I was going to wish you good luck.'

It was going to take a lot more than luck, Richard thought, looking at Mandrake seated behind a polished expanse of desk. 'I expected you at one,' Mandrake said, looking pointedly at his watch. 'Now, I'm afraid I have another—'

The phone rang. 'Excuse me,' Mandrake said and picked it up. 'Maurice Mandrake here. A book signing? When?'

Richard looked around the office. It was even more sumptuous than he would have guessed. Huge maroon leather chair, huge mahogany desk, nearly life-sized portrait of himself hanging behind it, bookcase full of copies of *The Light at the End of the Tunnel*, Persian carpet. It would fit right in on the *Titanic*, Richard thought.

Mandrake hung up the phone. 'I'm afraid we'd better make it another day. At two, I have—'

'This won't take long,' Richard said and sat down. 'You said in your eulogy you spoke to Jo – Dr Lander the day she was killed.'

Mandrake folded his hands on the desk. 'That day, and many times since,' he said.

I can't do this, Richard thought.

'I see by your expression that you do not believe the dead communicate with the living,' Mandrake said.

If they did, Joanna would have told me what she discovered in Carl Aspinall's room. 'No,' he said.

'That is because you persist in believing only in what you can see on your RIPT scans,' Mr Mandrake said, and his expression was a smirk. 'Dr Lander, fortunately, came to understand that the near-death experience possessed dimensions that science could never explain. Now, if you'll excuse me, I have another appointment –' He started to stand up.

Richard stayed seated. 'I need to know what she said that day.'

'Exactly what I said in my eulogy, that she had realized the NDE – or rather the NAE, for that is what she had come to realize it was – was not merely a physical hallucination, but instead a spiritual revelation of the Other Side.'

You're lying, Richard thought. 'What did she say? Her exact words?'

Mandrake leaned back in his chair, his hands on the padded arms. 'Why? So you can dismiss her as a crank? I realize it must be difficult, having to face the fact that your partner had reached a different conclusion about the NAE from the one you tried so hard to convince her of.' Mandrake leaned forward. 'Luckily, she was not fooled by your *scientific*,' he put an ugly emphasis on the word, 'arguments and found the truth for herself.' He glanced at the door and then looked pointedly at his watch. 'I'm afraid that's all the time I have.' This time he did stand up.

Richard didn't. 'I need to know what she said.'

Mandrake glanced uneasily at the door again. I wonder who this appointment's with, Richard thought. Obviously someone he doesn't want me to see. Someone he's trying to pump about the project? Mrs Troudtheim? Tish?

'Joanna was on her way to the ER to tell me something,' Richard said. 'I'm trying to find out what it was.'

'I should think it was obvious,' Mandrake said, but his eyes had flickered suddenly with something – fear? guilt?

He knows, Richard thought, and, although it made no sense, Joanna did tell him. 'No,' he said slowly. 'It's not obvious.'

Mandrake's eyes flickered again. 'She was trying to tell you what she has since told me *and* Mrs Davenport, speaking from that afterlife you refuse to believe in, that there are more things in heaven and earth, Dr Wright, than are dreamt of in your RIPT scans.' He walked around the desk and over to the door. 'I'm afraid I can't give you any more time, Dr Wright. A gentleman is scheduled—'

A gentleman? Mr Sage? Good luck getting anything out of him about the project. Or anything else. 'I need to know exactly what she said to you,' Richard repeated.

Mandrake opened the door. 'If you'd care to make an appointment for another day, we could—'

'Joanna died trying to tell me what it was,' Richard said. 'I need to know. It's important.'

'Very well.' He closed the door and went back to his desk and sat down. 'If it's so important to you.'

Richard waited.

'She said, "You were right all along, Mr Mandrake. I realize it now. The NAE is a message from the Other Side." '

'You bastard,' Richard said, coming out of his chair.

There was a knock on the door, and Mr Wojakowski leaned in, wearing his baseball cap. 'Hiya, Manny,' he said to Mandrake, and then to Richard, 'Well, hiya, Doc. Sorry to bust in like this, but I—'

'We're all finished here,' Mandrake said.

'That's right,' Richard said. 'Finished.' He strode out of the office, past Mr Wojakowski and down the hall.

'Wait up, Doc,' Mr Wojakowski said, catching up to him. 'You're just the guy I wanted to see.'

'It doesn't look like it,' Richard said, jerking his thumb in the direction of Mandrake's door. 'It looks like he's the guy you wanted to see, Mr Wojakowski.'

'Ed,' he corrected. 'Yeah, he called me the other day, said he wanted to talk to me about your project. I said I hadn't worked on it for a while, but he said that didn't matter, he wanted to talk to me anyway, so I said okay, but I had to talk to you first and see if it was okay, sometimes the docs don't want you blabbing about their research, and I've been trying ever since to get in touch with you.'

He slapped his knee. 'Boy, you sure are a hard guy to get ahold of. I been trying every way I could think of so I could ask you if it was okay. I know you've had other stuff on your mind, what with poor Doc Lander and all, but I was about to give up hope of ever getting ahold of you. Like Norm Pichette. Did I ever tell you about him? Got left behind when we abandoned the *Yorktown*, down in sick bay, and when he comes to, here he is on a ship that's going down, so he hollers at the *Hughes*,' he said, cupping his hands around his mouth, 'but she's too far away to hear him, so he tries to think of some way to signal them. He waves his arms like crazy, he screams and whistles and hollers, but nothing works.'

Richard thought of Maisie, trying to signal him, trying to get Nurse Lucille to page him, to let her call, bribing Eugene to carry a message, finally telling her mother about the project as a last resort.

'So then he tries to use the radio,' Mr Wojakowski was saying, 'but the door to the radio room's locked. Can you imagine that? Locking the doors on a sinking ship? Who do they think's gonna get in?'

Locked. Himself, yanking frantically at the locked door, kicking at it, trying to get back to the lab, and Joanna, trying the door to the aft stairway and finding it locked, going down to the mail room to get the key to the locker with the rockets in it. The key. Amelia saying, 'I had to find the key.'

'Pichette went all over that ship,' Mr Wojakowski said, 'looking for something he can get their attention with.'

All over the ship. Joanna going up to the Boat Deck, down to the Promenade Deck, along Scotland Road. Running all over. Up to the lab to tell him about Coma Carl, and, when he wasn't there, up to Dr Jamison's office, down to the ER.

And he and Kit and Vielle, running all over, too. Up to Timberline and over to four-east, asking nurses and taxi drivers, mapping stairways, trying to find out where Joanna had gone, who she had talked to. Going over the transcripts and through *Mazes and Mirrors*, graphing the scans, searching the hospital and their memories and the *Titanic*, trying everything they could think of.

'Pichette tries everything he can think of,' Mr Wojakowski said. 'He even takes off his shirt and waves it like a flag, but that doesn't work either, and the ship's sinking. He's gotta think of some way to signal 'em before it's too late.'

Some way to signal them. Mr Briarley sending up rockets. The quartermaster working the Morse lamp. The wireless operator tapping out messages to the *Carpathia* and the *Californian* and the *Frankfurt*. Messages. The bearded man sending the steward with a message to Mr Briarley, and the mail clerk dragging sacks of wet letters up to the Boat Deck, and J. H. Rogers writing a note to his sister.

'Messages,' Richard murmured. 'It's about messages.' His NDE had been full of them: the wireless operator taking down the names of the survivors, and the secretary with the telephone to her ear and Joanna's number on his pager.

Mr Sage heard a telephone ringing, he thought suddenly. And Mrs Davenport got a telegram, telling her to come back. 'There's got to be some common thread between all these NDEs,' Kit had said, and this must be it. Messages. The NDEs were all about messages.

But there hadn't been any telegrams in Amelia Tanaka's NDE, or rockets, or telephones. There weren't any messages in it at all, just a test and a locked cupboard full of chemicals. And she had tried one key after another, one chemical after another, trying to find the one that would work.

Like Joanna – he had a sudden vision of the crash team working over her, trying CPR, paddles, epinephrine, trying technique after technique. Looking for something that would work, he thought, and had the feeling Joanna had described, of almost, *almost* knowing.

'I know it has something to do with the *Titanic*,' Joanna had said. The *Titanic*, which had sent up rockets, lowered lifeboats, tapped out Morse code, looking for something that would work.

'So, anyway, I'm standing on the deck of the *Hughes*, looking down in the water,' Mr Wojakowski said, but Richard shut his voice out, trying to hold on to the knowledge he nearly had, that was almost within reach.

Morse code. Code. 'It was like the labels were written in code,' Amelia had said. And Maisie, gleefully telling him why she'd set the time at two-ten, 'I sent it in code.' Code. Chemical formulas and metaphors and 'some strange language.' Dots and dashes and 'Rosabelle, remember.' Code.

'Tell Richard it's … SOS,' Joanna had said, and he had thought she'd tried to tell him something and failed. But she hadn't. That was the message. 'It's an SOS.'

An SOS. A message sent out in all directions in the hope that somebody hears it. A message tapped out by the dying brain to the frontal cortex, the amygdala, the hippocampus, trying to get somebody to come to the rescue.

'Pretty damned ingenious, huh?' Mr Wojakowski was saying.

'What? I'm sorry,' Richard said. 'I didn't hear how he finally got their attention.'

'Sounds like you're the one needs to sign up for that hearing study,' he said, and slapped Richard on the shoulder. 'With a machine gun. See, I'm standing there on the *Hughes* looking down at the water for Jap subs, and all of a sudden I see these little fountains. 'Sub!' I shout, and the lieutenant comes over and looks at it and says, 'A sub doesn't make the water fly up like that. That's a depth charge,' but I'm looking at the splashes and they don't look like a depth charge either, they're in a straight line, and I look to see where they're coming from, and there's a guy up on the catwalk, leaning over the railing and firing a machine gun into the water. I can't hear it, it's too far, and he knows that, he knows he's gotta—'

Too far, and the way's blocked. Half of the synapses have already shut down from lack of oxygen, half the pathways are locked or have 'Closed for Repair' signs on them. So the temporal lobe tries one route after another, one chemical after another, carnosine, NPK, amiglycine, trying to find a short-cut, trying to get the signal through to the motor cortex to start the heart, the lungs. 'It was really late,' Amelia had said. 'All I wanted was to find the right chemical and go home,' and Mrs Brandeis's angel had said, 'You must return to earth. It is not yet your time.'

'The command to return is in over sixty percent of them,' Joanna had said, but it wasn't a command. It was a message that had finally gotten through, a chemical that had finally connected, a synapse that had finally fired, like a key turning over in the ignition. The NDE's a survival mechanism, Richard thought, a last-ditch effort by the brain to jump-start the system. The body's version of a crash team.

He looked blindly at Mr Wojakowski, who was still talking. 'So we take a boat over to get him and throw him up a ladder,' he said, 'but he won't come, he keeps shouting something down at us, only we can't hear over the motor. We think he must be in too bad a shape to climb down the ladder, so the first mate sends me up after him, and he is in bad shape, shot in the gut and lost a lot of blood, but that isn't what he was trying to tell us. Seems there's *another* guy down in sick bay, and he's *really* in bad shape, unconscious from a skull fracture.' He shook his head. 'He'd 'a' been a goner if Pichette hadn't thought of that machine gun.'

Down the hall, a door opened. Richard looked up and saw Mandrake coming. And knew suddenly what Joanna had said to Mandrake. The orderly had said Joanna had laughed, and of course she had. 'You were right,' she'd told him. 'The NDE *is* a message.'

But not from the Other Side. From this side, as the brain, going down, made a last valiant effort to save itself, trying everything in its arsenal: endorphins, to block out the pain and fear and clear the decks for action, adrenaline to strengthen the signals, acetylcholine to open up pathways and connectors. Pretty damned ingenious.

But the acetylcholine had a side effect. It increased the associative abilities of the cerebral cortex, too, and long-term memory, struggling to make sense of the sensations and sights and emotions pouring over it, turned them into tunnels and angels and the *Titanic*. Into metaphors that people mistook for reality. But the reality was a complex system of signals sent to the hippocampus to activate a neurotransmitter that could jump-start the system.

And I know what it is, Richard thought in a kind of wonder. I've been looking right at it all this time. That's why it was in all of Mrs Troudtheim's NDEs and the one where Joanna kicked out. I was looking for an inhibitor, and I was right, theta-asparcine's not an inhibitor. It's an activator. It's the key.

'What are you telling my subject, Dr Wright?' Mandrake demanded. 'That

NDEs aren't real, that they're nothing but a physical phenomenon?' He turned to Mr Wojakowski. 'Dr Wright doesn't believe in miracles.'

I do, Richard thought, I do.

'Dr Wright refuses to believe that the dead communicate with us,' Mandrake said. 'Is that what he was telling you?'

'He wasn't telling me anything,' Mr Wojakowski said. 'I was telling the doc here about this time on the *Yorktown*—'

'I'm sure Dr Wright will let you tell him some other time,' Mandrake said. 'I have a very busy schedule, and if we're going to meet—'

Mr Wojakowski turned to Richard. 'Is it okay if I talk to him, Doc?'

'It's fine. You tell him anything you want,' Richard said and started for the elevator. He needed to set up tests to see if theta-asparcine could bring subjects out of the NDE-state on its own, or whether it was the combination of theta-asparcine and acetylcholine and cortisol. I need to call Amelia, he thought. She said she'd be willing to go under.

He punched the 'up' button on the elevator. I need to look at the scans, and talk to Dr Jamison. And Maisie's mother, he thought, and looked back down the hall. Mr Wojakowski and Mandrake were almost to his office. Richard sprinted after them. 'Mr Wojakowski. Ed,' he said, catching up to them. 'What happened to him?'

'Dr Wright,' Mr Mandrake said, 'you have already taken up more than half of my appointment time with Mr Wojakowski here –'

Richard ignored him. 'What happened to the sailor, the one who fired the machine gun?' he said to Mr Wojakowski.

'Norm Pichette? Didn't make it.' He shook his head.

Didn't make it.

'Dr Wright,' Mandrake said, 'if this is your way of undermining my research—'

'Peritonitis,' Mr Wojakowski said. 'Died the next day.'

'What happened to the other one?'

'Dr *Wright*,' Mandrake bellowed.

'The one out cold in sick bay? George Weise?' Mr Wojakowski said. 'He recovered fine. Got a letter about him from Soda Pop Papachek the other day.'

'You mean a message,' Richard said gaily. 'You were right, Mandrake, it *is* a message.'

Mandrake pursed his lips. 'What are you talking about?'

Richard clapped him on the shoulder. 'You wouldn't understand. There are more things in heaven and earth, Manny, old boy, than are dreamt of in your philosophy. And you're about to find out what they are.'

57

'I am ... I ... a sea of ... alone.'
— ALFRED HITCHCOCK, shortly before his death

After a long time, the darkness seemed to diminish a little, the blackness taking on a tinge of gray, the stars beginning to dim. 'The sun is coming up,' Joanna said to the little French bulldog, though she still couldn't see him, and began to scan the sky to the east for a telltale pallor along the horizon. But she could not make out the horizon, and the light, if that was what it was, leaked evenly from all directions into the sky, if that was what it was.

It grew light so slowly that Joanna thought she had been mistaken, that she had only imagined the diminishing of the blackness, but after an endless time, the stars went out, not one by one, but all together, and the sky turned charcoal and then slate. A little wind came up, and the night took on an early-morning chill.

It's four o'clock, Joanna thought. That was when the *Carpathia* had steamed up, having come fifty-eight miles in three hours at pushing, punishing speed. The people in the lifeboats had seen it in the black-gray of near dawn, first her light and then the tall stack, streaming smoke. But though Joanna stared, squinting, toward the southwest, there was no light, no smoke.

There's nothing out there at all, she thought, but as the darkness continued to diminish, she could make out a jagged horizon, as of distant mountains. The Blessed Realm, she thought, hope fluttering up in her. Or the Isle of Avalon.

'Maybe we're saved after all,' she said, looking down at the dog, and when she did, she saw that it was not the French bulldog she was holding after all, but the little girl from the Hartford circus fire, Little Miss 1565. Her face was smudged with soot, and ash had caught in her sausage curls.

'I never had a dog,' the little girl said. 'What's his name?' and Joanna saw that the little girl was holding the French bulldog in her arms.

Joanna brushed a flake of ash from the little girl's hair. 'I don't know,' she said.

'I will give you a name then,' the little girl said to the dog, holding him up, her smudged hands clutching it around its fat middle. 'I will call you Ulla.'

Ulla. 'Who are you?' Joanna asked, 'What's your name?' and waited, afraid, for the answer. Not Maisie. Please don't let it be Maisie.

'I don't know,' the little girl said, dandling the dog by its paws. 'Can you do tricks, Ulla?' she said, and then to Joanna, 'The dog at the circus could jump through a hoop. He had a purple collar. That color.'

She pointed, and Joanna saw that the sky had turned a pale, lovely lavender, and all around them, lavender-pink in the growing light, were glittering icebergs. 'The ice field,' Joanna murmured, and looked down at the hyacinth water.

They were sitting on the grand piano from the À La Carte Restaurant, the wide walnut top with its curving sides floating steadily on the surface. A piece of sheet music still stood open against the music stand. 'I guess pianos do float, after all,' Joanna said, and saw that the keyboard was underwater, the keys shimmering pale pink and black through the lavender water.

'There was a tuba at the circus,' the little girl said. 'And a big drum. Is the *Carpathia* going to come save us?'

No, Joanna thought. Because this isn't the Atlantic, in spite of the water, in spite of the icebergs, and even if it were, it was too late. The *Carpathia* had steamed up well before dawn.

The sun would be up any minute, staining the sky and the ice and the water rose-pink, and then flooding the east with light. The icebergs would flare into snowy brilliance. Maybe that's what Mr Mandrake's subjects saw, Joanna thought. They believed it was an Angel of Light, but it wasn't. It was the ice field, glittering like diamonds and sapphires and rubies in the blinding light of the sun.

'Jump!' the little girl commanded. She circled her arms into a hoop. 'Jump!'

The bulldog looked curiously at her, his head to one side.

The little girl dropped her arms. 'What will happen when the *Carpathia* gets here?' she asked.

The *Carpathia* isn't coming, Joanna thought. It's too far for her to come, too far for anyone or anything to come and save us.

'They check your name off on a list when you go on board,' the little girl said. She had taken off her hair ribbon and was tying it around the dog's neck. 'What'll I tell them when they say, "What's your name, little girl?"' She tied the hair ribbon into a bow. It was singed at the ends. 'If you don't know your name, they don't let you on.'

It doesn't matter, it isn't coming, Joanna thought, but she said, 'How about if I give you a name, like you named Ulla?'

The little girl looked skeptical. 'What name?'

Not Maisie, Joanna thought. The name of some child who had been on the *Titanic*. Lorraine. But Lorraine Allison had gone down, the only child in First Class who had not been saved. Not Lorraine. Not the name of any child who'd died on the *Titanic*. Not Beatrice Sandstrom or Nina Harper or Sigrid Anderson.

The little girl who had been on the *Lusitania* who had gotten separated from her mother – what was her name? – the little girl the stranger had saved. 'He threw her into the boat,' she could hear Maisie's voice saying, 'and then he jumped in, and they were both saved.'

Helen. Her name had been Helen. 'Helen,' Joanna said. 'I'm going to call you Helen.'

The little girl picked up the dog's front paw. 'How do you do?' she said. 'My name is Helen.' She dropped her voice to a gruff bass. 'How do you do? My name's Ulla.' She let go of his paw. 'Roll over, Ulla!' she commanded, 'Play dead!'

The French bulldog sat, his ear cocked, not understanding. The wind that had sprung up as it grew light died down, and the water, already smooth as glass, became even smoother, but the sky did not change. It remained pink, reflecting its rosy light on the water and the ice and the polished walnut of the piano. 'Stay!' Helen said to the unmoving dog, and they all obeyed, the sky and the water and the sea.

An eon went by. Helen stopped trying to teach the dog tricks and took him onto her lap. The wind that had sprung up as it grew light, died down, and the water stilled even more, till it was imperceptible from the pink sky. But the sun did not come up. And no ship appeared on the horizon.

'Is this still the NDE?' Helen asked. She had set the dog down and was leaning over the side of the piano, staring down into the water.

'I don't know,' Joanna said.

'How come we're just sitting here?'

'I don't know.'

'I bet we're becalmed,' Helen said, trailing her hand lazily back and forth in the still water. 'Like in that poem.'

'What poem?'

'*You* know, the one with the bird.'

'"The Rime of the Ancient Mariner"?' Joanna said and remembered Mr Briarley saying, '"The Rime of the Ancient Mariner" is not, contrary to the way it is popularly taught, a poem about similes and alliteration and ono-matopoeia. Neither is it about albatrosses and oddly spelled words. It is a poem about resurrection.'

And Purgatory, Joanna thought, the ship eternally becalmed, the crew all dead, 'alone on a wide, wide sea,' and wondered if that was what this was, a place of punishment and penance. In 'The Rime of the Ancient Mariner,' a rain had come, and a breeze, washing away sin, setting them free. Joanna scanned the sky, but there were no clouds, no wind. It was still as death.

'How come we're becalmed?' Helen asked.

'I don't know,' Joanna said.

'*I* bet we're waiting for somebody,' Helen said.

No, Joanna thought, not Maisie. Don't let it be Maisie we're waiting for.

'We have to be waiting for something,' Helen said, trailing her hand lazily back and forth in the pink water. 'Otherwise something would happen.'

Something *was* happening. The light was changing, jagged peaks of ice going from pink to peach, the sea turning from rose to coral. The sun's going down, Joanna thought, though there had been no sun, only the pink, even light.

'What's happening?' Helen asked, creeping closer to Joanna.

'It's getting dark,' Joanna said, thinking hopefully of the clear, shining stars.

Helen shook her head, her dark curls bobbing. 'Hunh-unnh,' she said. 'It's getting *red*.'

It was, staining the water the red of sandstone mesas, the red of canyons. 'It got red in the big top,' Helen said. 'All around.'

Joanna put her arm around her, around Ulla, pulling them close, shielding them from the sky. 'Don't let it be Maisie,' she whispered. 'Please.'

The sky continued to redden, till it was the color of fire, the color of blood. The red of disaster.

58

'It's all right, little girl. You go. I will stay.'
– Last words spoken to Mary Marvin by her husband,
DANIEL, as he put her into one of the *Titanic*'s lifeboats

Maisie was really good. She didn't push the button on her pager, even though Dr Wright didn't come see her for a really long time.

After a whole week, she started worrying that maybe something had happened to him, like Joanna, and she asked Nurse Lucille to call him, she had a question about her pager she had to ask him, and Nurse Lucille told her he couldn't come right now, he was busy working on something important, and asked her if she wanted to watch a video.

Maisie said no, but Nurse Lucille put in *The Sound of Music* anyway. She always put in *The Sound of Music*, every time. It was her favorite video, probably because she looked just like the wrinkly old nuns.

Finally, Kit came. She looked really pretty and excited. 'Did Dr Wright talk to Mr Mandrake?' Maisie asked her.

'Yes,' Kit said. 'This is a present from Richard – Dr Wright. He said it's to thank you for telling him about Mr Mandrake.' She handed Maisie a package wrapped in red paper that looked like a video.

'What did Mr Mandrake say?' Maisie said. 'He *did* talk to Joanna that day, didn't he? Did she tell him the thing Dr Wright was trying to find out?'

'Open your present, and then I'll tell you everything.' Kit walked swiftly to the door and pulled the curtains together. 'Dr Wright said to open it and get it put away before your mother comes back.'

'Really? What is it?' She began ripping the paper off. '*The Hindenburg!*' she said, looking happily at the picture of the flaming Zeppelin on the box.

'Dr Wright said to warn you the movie's not exactly like the real *Hindenburg* crash. He says they changed the ending so the dog survives.'

'I don't *care!*' Maisie said, clasping the video to her chest. 'It's perfect!'

'Where do you want me to put it?' Kit asked.

'Get one of my videos on the bottom of the nightstand No, not *The Secret Garden*. Nurse Evelyn loves *The Secret Garden*. She puts it in every time she's on shift.'

'How about *Winnie the Pooh*?'

'Yeah, that's good.'

Kit handed her the plastic video case. Maisie handed her *The Hindenburg*. 'Here, open this,' she said, opened *Winnie the Pooh*, and took the video out.

Kit tore the cellophane off *The Hindenburg* and handed it back to Maisie, and she slid it out of its box, put it in the *Winnie the Pooh* box, and handed Kit the *Winnie the Pooh* video. 'Put it on the bottom,' she said.

Kit slid it under the bottom video of the stack. 'And I suppose you want me to take this home with me?' she asked, holding out the *Hindenburg* box. Maisie nodded. 'You know, Maisie,' Kit said seriously, 'after you get your new heart, you're going to have to stop lying and tricking your mother.'

'What did Mr Mandrake say?' Maisie said. 'Did he tell Dr Wright what Joanna said?'

'No,' Kit said, 'but Richard found out anyway. Joanna was trying to tell us the NDE was a kind of SOS. It's a message the brain sends out to the different chemicals in the brain to find one that will signal the heart to start beating and the patient to start breathing.'

'After they code,' Maisie said.

'Yes, and now that Richard knows what it is, he can design a method to send those same chemicals to—'

'He really does have a coding treatment?' Maisie asked excitedly. 'I just made that up.'

Kit shook her head. 'Not yet, but he's working on it. He's developed a prototype, but it still has to be tested,' her face got real serious, 'and even if it works—'

'He might not do it in time,' Maisie said, and was afraid Kit was going to lie and say, 'Of course he will,' but she didn't.

'He said to tell you that, no matter what happens, you did something important,' Kit said. 'You helped make a discovery that may save lots and lots of lives.'

A few days later Richard came and asked the nurses a whole bunch of questions about what she weighed and stuff. He hardly talked to Maisie at all, except right when he was leaving, he looked up at the TV and he said, 'Seen any good movies lately?'

'Yes!' she said, 'this *really* good movie, except for they made the dog a Dalmatian instead of a German shepherd. And they left out the guy who had the NDE, but the rest is pretty good. I love the part where the guy goes and lets the dog out.'

She watched it over and over. She had the meal guy put it in for her when he came to get her supper tray and had the night shift nurse's aide take it out before she went to sleep.

Sometimes she didn't feel like watching TV or anything. It was hard to breathe, and she got all puffed up in spite of the dopamine. Her heart doctors came in and told her they were going to put her on dobutamine, and after that she felt a little better and felt like talking to Kit when she came to see her.

'Do you still have your pager?' Kit asked.

'Yes,' Maisie said and showed her how she had it clipped to her dog tags chain.

'It's very important that you wear it all the time,' Kit said. 'If you start to feel like you did before you coded, or if you hear your monitor start to beep, you push the button. Don't wait. Push it right away.'

'What if then I don't code?' Maisie asked. 'Will I get in trouble?'

'No,' Kit said, 'not at all. You push it, and then you try to hang on. Dr Wright will come right away.'

'What if he's not in the hospital?'

'He'll be in the hospital.'

'But what if he's a long way away, like the *Carpathia*?' Maisie persisted. 'It's a really big hospital.'

'He knows all the shortcuts,' Kit said.

Dr Wright came again with three of Maisie's heart doctors and her mom's lawyer, and they asked her how she was feeling and looked at her monitors and then went out in the hall. Maisie could see them talking, though they were too far away for her to hear what they were saying. Dr Wright talked for a little while, and then her heart doctor talked a lot, and then the lawyer talked for a really long time and handed them a lot of papers, and everybody left.

A couple of days after that, Vielle came to see her. She was wearing a pager, too. 'They won't let me work in the ER until my hand gets better,' she said, looking mad only not really, 'so they sent me up here to take care of you.' Vielle looked up at the TV. 'What *is* that?' She made a face. '*The Sound of*

Music? I hate *The Sound of Music.* I always thought Maria was way too cheerful. Don't you have any good videos around here? I can see I'm going to have to bring in some of mine.'

She did, but Maisie didn't get to watch them because her mom had started staying in her room all the time, even at night. It didn't matter. Most of the time she was too tired to even watch *The Sound of Music* and she just lay there and thought about Joanna.

They kept having to take her down to have echocardiograms and one of the times when they were getting her into position, the button on her pager got pressed, and Vielle and a crash cart and about a hundred doctors and nurses showed up, and a couple of minutes later Dr Wright came running in, all panting and out of breath, and after that she didn't feel so worried, but she still felt terrible. It was hard to breathe, even with the oxygen mask, and her head hurt.

Her heart doctors came in and told her they were going to put a special pump in that would help her heart do its work. 'An L-VAD or a bivad?' she asked.

'An L-VAD,' they said, but then they didn't.

'They've decided to wait till you're feeling better,' her mom said. 'And, anyway, your new heart's going to be here any day now.'

'When they put a new heart in,' Maisie asked Vielle the next time she came in to check her vitals, 'do they cut your chest open?'

'Yes,' Vielle said, 'but it won't hurt.'

'And your arms have IVs in them and stuff?' Maisie said.

'Yes, but you'll be under the anesthetic. You won't feel a thing.'

'Can I have some adhesive tape?' Maisie asked. 'And some scissors?' and when her mom went down to the cafeteria for dinner, Maisie took her dog tags off and went to work.

The next day her mom said, 'You have to think positive thoughts, sweetie. You have to say to yourself, "My new heart's going to come in just a few days, and then this will all be over, and I'll forget all about feeling uncomfortable. I'll get to go to school again and play soccer!"'

And a little while later, Vielle came in and said, 'You just have to hang on a little longer, honey,' but she couldn't. She was too tired, even, to push the button on her special pager, and then she was in the tunnel.

There was no smoke this time, and no light either. The tunnel was totally black. Maisie put her hand out, trying to feel the wall, and touched a narrow metal strut. Next to it there was nothing for a little ways and then another metal strut, at a different angle, and another.

'I'll bet this is the *Hindenburg*,' she said. 'I'll bet I'm up inside the zeppelin.' She looked up, trying to see the inside of the big silver balloon far overhead, but it was too dark, and the floor she was walking on wasn't a metal catwalk, it was soft, and too wide. Even when she took hold of the metal strut and stretched out both arms as far as they would reach, she couldn't feel anything but space on the other side of the tunnel.

So it must not be the *Hindenburg*, she thought, but she didn't dare let go of the strut for fear it was and she would fall.

She worked her way along, walking carefully along the soft floor and holding on to one strut and then the next one, and after a few minutes the struts on the side she was on disappeared, and there was nothing to hold on to on either side of her. I must be at the end of the tunnel, she thought, peering into the darkness.

A light shone suddenly, mercilessly, in her eyes. She put up her hand to protect her eyes, but it was too bright. 'The explosion!' she thought.

The light swung suddenly away from her. She could see its long beam as it swung, like the beam from a flashlight. There were little specks of dust in it. It swung around in a big arc, lighting the struts behind her as it went, and she could see they were the underneath part of a grandstand, full of people. Up above the tunnel where she had been standing was a big red-and-gold sign that said 'Main Entrance.'

The light swung in front of her and then stopped and shone on a man standing on a round box dressed all in white. Even his boots were white, and his top hat. The light made a circle around him. 'La-deez and gentlemen!' he said, really loud. 'Kindly direct your attention to the center ring!'

'I like this part the best,' someone said. Maisie turned. A little girl was standing next to her. She had on a white dress and a big blue sash. She was holding a fluffy pink puff of cotton candy on a paper cone. 'My name's Pollyanna,' the little girl said. 'What's yours?'

'Maisie.'

'I love the circus, don't you, Mary?' Pollyanna said, eating cotton candy.

'Not Mary,' Maisie said. *'Maisie.'*

'Ladeez and gentlemen!' the ringmaster said, real loud, 'we now present, for your entertainment, an act so sensational, so stupendous, so amazing, it has never been attempted anywhere!' He pointed his whip with a flourish, and the spotlight swung again so that its smoky beam shone straight up at a little platform at the top of a narrow ladder. There were people standing on it, dressed in fancy white leotards.

Maisie stood staring up at them, her mouth open. They looked like Barbie dolls, they were such a long way up. Their leotards sparkled in the smoky bluish light of the spotlight. '... those wizards of the tent top,' the ringmaster was saying, 'those heroes of the high wire!'

A band struck up a fanfare, and Maisie looked across the ring to see where the band was. They were sitting in a big white bandstand, wearing bright red jackets with gold decorations on their shoulders. One of them had a tuba.

'Look!' Pollyanna said, pointing up with her cotton candy. Maisie looked up again. The people on the platform were bowing and smiling, waving one of their arms in big wide swoops and hanging on to the ladder with the other one.

'We proudly present,' the ringmaster was saying, 'the daring, the dazzling, the devil-may-care ...' He paused, and the band played another fanfare. '... death-defying ... Wallendas!'

'Oh, no,' Maisie said.

The band started playing a slow, pretty song, and one of the girl Wallendas picked up a long white pole and stepped onto the end of the high wire. She had short blond hair like Kit's. 'You have to get down!' Maisie shouted up to her.

The girl Wallenda started out across the high wire, holding her pole in both hands. 'There's going to be a disaster!' Maisie shouted. 'Go back! Go back!'

The girl continued to walk, placing her feet in their flat white shoes carefully, carefully. Maisie tilted her head back, trying to see the top of the tent. She could see the Wallendas, waiting for their turns to go out on the high wire, but everything above them was black, like there wasn't a tent above them at all, just sky.

If it was the sky, there'd be stars, she thought, and just then she saw one. It glittered, a tiny white point of light, high above the Wallendas' heads. So maybe it's all right, Maisie thought, looking at the star. It glittered again, and then flared brightly, brighter even than the spotlight, and turned red.

'Fire!' Maisie shouted, but the Wallendas didn't pay any attention. The girl Wallenda reached the middle of the wire, and a man Wallenda started out toward her.

Maisie ran as hard as she could across the center ring, her feet sinking in the sawdust, over to the bandstand. 'The big top's on fire!' she shouted, but the band didn't pay any attention to her either.

She ran over to the conductor. 'You have to play the duck song!' she cried, 'the song that means the circus is in trouble! "The Stars and Stripes Forever!"' but he didn't even turn around. 'See!' Maisie said, yanking on his sleeve and pointing up at the fire. It was burning a line down the roof of the tent now, making a jagged red tear.

'Get down!' she shouted to the Wallendas, pointing, and one of the Wallendas saw the fire and started climbing down the ladder. The girl Wallenda who looked like Kit was still out in the middle of the wire. One of the men Wallendas threw her a rope, and she dropped her white pole and grabbed it. She wrapped her legs around it, and slid down.

'Fire!' somebody shouted in the grandstand, and all the people looked up, their mouths open like Maisie's had been, and began to run down off the grandstand.

The fire burned along the high wire, along the rigging, moving lines of flame. Like messages, Maisie thought. Like SOSs. Somebody grabbed Maisie's arm. She turned around. It was Pollyanna. 'We have to get out of here!' Pollyanna said, tugging Maisie back across the ring toward the main entrance.

'We can't get out that way!' Maisie said, resisting. 'The animal run's in the way.'

'Hurry, Molly!' Pollyanna said.

'Not Molly,' Maisie said. 'Maisie!' but the band had started playing 'The Stars and Stripes Forever' and Pollyanna couldn't hear her.

'Look,' Maisie said, reaching inside the neck of her hospital gown. 'My name is Maisie. It's all written right here, on my dog tags.'

They weren't there. She fumbled wildly at her neck, searching for her dog tags. They must have fallen off, back there while she was standing in the entranceway, looking up at the Wallendas.

'Well, Margie or whatever your name is, we better get out of here,' Pollyanna said. She took Maisie's hand.

'No!' Maisie said, wrenching it away from her. 'I have to find them!' She ran wildly back across the center ring. 'I have to,' she shouted over her shoulder as she ran, 'or they won't know who I am when they find my body.'

'I thought you said we can't get out that way,' Pollyanna called to her. 'I thought you said it wasn't clear.'

'Clear,' her heart doctor said, and the jolt jerked her really hard, but it must not have worked. The heart monitor was still whining.

'All right,' her heart doctor said. 'If you've got anything, now's the time to try it,' and Dr Wright said, 'Start the theta-asparcine. Start the acetylcholine.'

'Hang on, honey,' Vielle said. 'Don't leave us,' but she had to find her dog tags. They weren't in the main entrance. She dropped to her knees and dug in the sawdust, sifting it in her hands.

A lady ran by, kicking sawdust onto Maisie's hands. 'Don't –' she said, and a big girl ran by, and a man carrying a little boy. 'Stop it,' she said. 'You're mashing it! I have to find my dog tags!'

But they didn't listen. They ran past her into the darkness of the tunnel. 'You can't get out that way!' Maisie said, grabbing at the big girl's skirt. 'The animal run is in the way.'

'It's on fire!' the big girl said and yanked the tail of her skirt away so hard it tore.

'You have to go out the performers' entrance!' Maisie said, but the big girl had already disappeared into the darkness, and a whole bunch of people were running after her, kicking the sawdust all over, trampling it, stepping on Maisie's hands.

'You're messing it all up,' Maisie said, cradling her bruised fingers in her other hand. She struggled to her feet. 'This isn't the way out!' she shouted, holding up her hands to make the people stop, but they couldn't hear her. They were screaming and shrieking so loud she couldn't even hear the band playing 'The Stars and Stripes Forever.' They were stumbling against her, shoving her, pushing her into the tunnel.

It was dark in the tunnel and full of smoke. Somebody shoved Maisie, still on one knee, and she fell forward, her hands out, and came up against hard metal bars. The animal run, she thought, and tried to pull herself up to standing, but they were pressing her flat against the bars, mashing her chest.

'Open the cage!' somebody shouted.

'No! The lions and tigers will get out,' she tried to shout, but the smoke was too thick, her ribs were being crushed into the bars of the cage, and if she didn't get out of there they were going to push her chest right through the bars.

She started to climb up the side of the run, pulling up with one hand and then the other, trying to get above the pushing people. If she could get up on top of the animal run, maybe she could crawl over it to the door.

But it was too high. She climbed and climbed, and there were still bars. She pulled herself up hand over hand, away from the screaming people, and now she could hear the band. They were playing a different song. A German song, like the one in *The Sound of Music*, only it wasn't the band, it was a piano with a light, tinny sound, like the one on the *Hindenburg*.

She had been wrong. It was the *Hindenburg*, after all. It wasn't the animals' run, she was in the rigging inside the balloon, and she had to hold on tight or she would fall out of the sky. Like Ulla.

Far below her, in New Jersey, the children piled up against the cage, screaming. 'You can't get out that way,' she shouted down to them. The fire was all around her, the roaring flames like snowy fields, so bright you couldn't look at them, and she knew if she let go, she would fall and fall, and they wouldn't know her name.

'My name is Maisie,' she said, 'Maisie Nellis,' but there was no air left in her lungs, only the smoke, thick as fog, and the bars were hot, she couldn't hold on much longer, they were melting under her hands. The snowy fields under her got brighter, and she saw it wasn't snow, it was apple blossoms. Beautiful, soft white apple blossoms.

If I fell onto them, it wouldn't hurt at all, she thought. But she couldn't let go. They wouldn't know who she was. They would bury her in a grave that only had a number on it, and nobody would ever know what had happened to her. 'Joanna!' she shouted. 'Joanna!'

'Nothing,' Maisie's heart doctor said.

'Increase the acetylcholine,' Dr Wright said.

'It's been four minutes,' the heart doctor said. 'I think it's time.'

'No,' Dr Wright said, sounding mad. 'Come on, Maisie, you're a whiz at stalling. Now's the time to stall.'

'Hang on, honey,' Vielle said, holding tight to her white, lifeless hand. 'Hang on.'

'Let go,' somebody down below her said. Maisie looked down. She couldn't see anything but smoke.

'Just let go,' the voice said, and a hand reached up through the smoke, a hand with a white glove on.

'It's too far,' Maisie said. 'I have to wait till the *Hindenburg* gets closer to the ground.'

'There isn't time,' he said. 'Let go.' He reached his gloved hand up farther, and she could see a raggedy black sleeve.

Maisie scrunched her eyes up, trying to see him through the smoke, trying to see if he had a red nose and a banged-up black hat. 'Are you Emmett Kelly?' she called down to him.

'There's nothing to be afraid of, kiddo,' he said. 'I'll catch you.' He stretched his white-gloved hand up really far, but it was still a long way underneath. 'We have to get you out of here.'

'I can't,' she said, clinging to the burning bars. 'When they find me, they won't know who I am.'

'*I* know who you are, Maisie,' he said, and she let go. And fell and fell and fell.

'No pulse,' Vielle said.

'Her heart was just too damaged,' her heart doctor said. 'It just couldn't stand the strain.'

'Clear,' Dr Wright said. 'Again. Clear.'

'It's been five minutes.'

'Increase the acetylcholine.'

He caught her. She couldn't see him for the smoke, but she could feel his arms under her. And then all of a sudden the smoke cleared, and she could see his face – the red nose, the brown painted-on beard, the white down-turned mouth. 'You *are* Emmett Kelly,' she said, squinting at him, trying to see his real face under the clown makeup. 'Aren't you?'

He put her down so she was standing in the sawdust, and tipped his banged-up hat and made a funny bow. 'There isn't much time,' he said. He took her hand in his white gloved one, and started running across the big top toward the performers' entrance, dragging Maisie with him.

The whole roof was on fire now, and the poles holding up the tent, and the rigging. A big piece of burning canvas came crashing down right in front of the band, and the man playing the tuba made a funny 'bla-a-a-t-t-t' and then went on playing.

Emmett Kelly ran with Maisie past the band, his big clown shoes making a flapping up-and-down noise. A clown in a funny fireman's hat ran past them dragging a big fire hose. An elephant ran past, and a German shepherd.

Emmett Kelly led her between them, pulling Maisie out of the way of a white horse. Its tail was on fire. 'There's the performers' entrance,' he said, pointing at a door with a black curtain across it as he ran. 'We're almost there.'

He suddenly stopped, pulling Maisie up short. 'Why'd you do that?' Maisie asked, and one of the on-fire poles came crashing down, bringing the performers' entrance crashing down with it, and the ladder the Wallendas had stood on. The roof of the tent came down on top of all of it, on fire, covering it up, and smoke boiled up.

The clown in the funny fireman's hat shouted, 'There's no way out!'

'Yes, there is, kiddo,' Emmett Kelly said. 'And you know what it is.'

'There isn't any way out. The main entrance is blocked,' she said. 'The animal run's in the way.'

'You know the way out,' he said, bending down and gripping her by the shoulders. 'You told me, remember? When we were looking at your book?'

'The tent,' Maisie said. 'They could've got out by crawling under the tent.'

Emmett Kelly led Maisie, running, back across the ring to the far side of the tent. 'There's a Victory garden on the far side of the lot,' he said as they ran. 'I want you to go over there and wait till your mother comes.'

Maisie looked at him. 'Aren't you coming with me?'

He shook his head. 'Women and children only.'

They reached the side of the tent. The canvas was tied down with stakes. Emmett Kelly squatted down in his funny, too-big pants and untied the rope. He lifted up the canvas so Maisie could go under. 'I want you to run to the Victory garden.' He raised the canvas up higher.

Maisie looked out under the canvas. It was dark outside, darker even than the tunnel. 'What if I get lost?' she said and started to cry. 'They won't know who I am.'

Emmett Kelly stood up and reached in one of his tattered pockets and pulled out a purple spotted handkerchief. He started to wipe Maisie's eyes with it, but it wouldn't come all the way out of his pocket. He yanked on it, and the end of it came out in a big knot, tied to a red bandanna. He pulled on the bandanna, and a green handkerchief came out and then an orange one, all knotted together.

Maisie laughed.

He pulled and pulled, looking surprised, and a lavender handkerchief came out, and a yellow one, and a white one with apple blossoms on it. And a chain with Maisie's dog tags on the end of it.

He put the chain around her neck. 'Now hurry,' he said. 'The whole place is on fire.'

It was. Up above, the roof of the tent was one big flame, and the grandstands and the center ring and the bandstand were all burning, but the band was still playing, blowing on their trumpets and tubas in their red uniforms. They weren't playing 'The Stars and Stripes Forever,' though. They were playing a really slow, sad song. 'What is that?' Maisie asked.

' "Nearer, My God, to Thee," ' Emmett Kelly said.

'Like on the *Titanic*,' Maisie said.

'Like on the *Titanic*,' he said. 'It means it's time to go.'

'I don't want to,' Maisie said. 'I want to stay here with you. I know a lot about disasters.'

'That's why you have to go,' he said. 'So you can become a disasterologist.'

'Why can't you come, too?'

'I have to stay here,' he said, and she saw that he was holding a water bucket.

'And save people's lives,' Maisie said.

He smiled under his painted-on, sad-looking expression. 'And save people's lives.' He squatted down and lifted up the canvas again. 'Now go, kiddo. I want you to run lickety-split.'

Maisie ducked under the canvas and stood poised in the opening a moment, clutching her dog tags, and then looked back at him.

'I know who you are,' she said. 'You're not really Emmett Kelly, are you? That's just a metaphor.'

The clown put his gloved finger up to his wide white mouth in a sh-shhing motion. 'I want you to run straight for the Victory garden,' he said.

Maisie smiled at him. 'You can't fool me,' she said. 'I know who you really are,' and ran into the darkness, as fast as she could.

59

> 'There! If the boat goes down, you'll remember me.'
> – Words spoken to Minnie Coutts by a crewman on the *Titanic*
> who had given his lifejacket to her little boy

Two days after successfully reviving Maisie, Richard's special pager went off again. This time, trying not to think of what the strain of two codes in three days might do to Maisie's system or what deadly side effect the theta-asparcine might have produced, he made it up to CICU in three minutes flat.

Evelyn met him as he skidded into the unit, all smiles. 'Her heart's here,' she said. 'Maisie's in being prepped. I tried to call you.'

'My special pager went off,' he said, still not convinced there wasn't a disaster, and Evelyn said, unruffled, 'She was quite insistent that you and Vielle Howard be informed, and I guess she took matters into her own hands.'

She had, in more ways than one. After the transplant surgery, which took eight hours and went without a hitch, one of the attending nurses told him Maisie had taped her dog tags to the bottom of her foot and was furious that they'd been removed. 'What if I'd died?' she'd demanded indignantly as soon as her airway was removed, and, in spite of the danger of infection due to the immunosuppressants she was taking, she was allowed to wear her dog tags, swabbed with disinfectant, wrapped around her wrist, 'just in case.'

Maisie's mother, absolutely impossible now that her faith in positive thinking had been confirmed, had, according to the nurse, tried to talk her out of them, to no avail.

'I need them,' Maisie had said. 'In case I get complications. I might get a blood clot or reject my new heart.'

'You won't do any such thing,' her mother had said. 'You're going to get well and come home and go back to school. You're going to take ballet lessons' – something Richard could not in his wildest dreams imagine Maisie doing, unless a ballet-related flood or volcanic eruption was involved – 'and grow up and have children of your own.' To which Maisie, ever the realist, had replied, 'I'll still die sometime. Everybody dies sooner or later.'

After a week of family only, Maisie was allowed visitors, provided they wore paper gowns, booties, and masks, and limited their visits to five minutes, and visited two at a time. That meant her mother was always present, which cramped Maisie's style considerably, although she still told Richard plenty of grisly details about her surgery. 'So then they crack your chest open,' she demonstrated, 'and they cut your heart out and put the new one in. Did you know it comes in a cooler, like beer?'

'Maisie –' her mother protested. 'Let's talk about something cheerful. You need to thank Dr Wright. He revived you after you coded.'

'That's right,' Evelyn said, coming in to check the numerous monitors. 'Dr Wright saved your life.'

'No, he didn't,' Maisie said.

'I know he didn't do your transplant surgery, like Dr Templeton,' Mrs Nellis said, looking embarrassed, 'but he helped by starting your heart again so you could get your new heart.'

'I know,' Maisie said, 'but—'

'A lot of people worked together to get you your new heart, didn't they?' Mrs Nellis said. 'Your Peds nurses and Dr—'

'Maisie,' Richard said, leaning forward, 'who did save your life?'

Maisie opened her mouth to answer, and Evelyn, adjusting her IV, said, 'I know who she means. You mean the person who donated your heart, don't you, Maisie?'

'Yes,' Maisie said after a moment, and Richard thought, That isn't what she was going to say. 'I wish they told you what their name was,' Maisie said. 'They don't tell you anything, not how they died or whether they were a boy or a girl or anything.'

'That's because they don't want you to worry about it,' Mrs Nellis said. 'You're supposed to be thinking positive thoughts to help you get well.'

'It's positive they saved my life,' Maisie said.

'Cheerful topics,' Mrs Nellis admonished. 'Tell Dr Wright what Dr Murrow brought you.'

Dr Murrow had brought her a giant Mylar balloon with a heart on it. 'It's got helium in it, not hydrogen, so you don't have to worry about it blowing up like the *Hindenburg*,' Maisie told him and had to be cautioned again about cheerful topics.

In the week that followed, the red heart balloon was joined by Mylar balloons with smiley-faces and teddy bears on them (no regular balloons allowed in CICU, and no flowers), and Maisie's room filled up with dolls and stuffed animals and visitors. Barbara came up from Peds to see her and stopped by the lab afterward to tell Richard Maisie wanted to see him and to thank him. 'You saved her life,' she said, and it reminded him of what Maisie had said, or, rather, not said, on his first visit.

He wondered if that was what she wanted to see him about. 'Was her mother there when you visited her?' he asked Barbara.

'Yes,' she said, rolling her eyes. 'I wouldn't go down there right now. Mr Mandrake was going in as I was coming out. I'd steer clear of him if I were you. He's in a foul mood these days, thanks to Mabel Davenport.'

'Mabel Davenport? You mean Mrs Davenport?' Richard asked. 'Why? What did she do?'

'You mean you haven't heard?' She leaned confidentially toward him. 'You will not *believe* what's happened. His new book, *Messages from the Other Side*, is coming out next month,' she paused expectantly, 'the twentieth, to be exact.'

'Wonderful,' Richard said, wondering what there was in that news to make her smile so smugly. 'And?'

'And *Communications from Beyond* is coming out on the tenth. With a nationwide book tour and, rumor has it, an even bigger advance than Mr Mandrake's.'

'*Communications from Beyond*?'

'By Mabel R. Davenport. Mr Mandrake says she made the whole thing up. *She* says he tried to make her remember things she never saw and he's got it all wrong, there's no Angel of Light, no Life Review, just a golden aura that confers psychic powers, which Mrs Davenport claims she has. She says she's been in contact with Houdini and Amelia Earhart. I can't believe you haven't heard about this. It's been all over the tabloids. Mr Mandrake's furious. So I'd wait till this afternoon before I went down to see Maisie.'

He did, but when he went down Ms Sutterly was there, and he had the feeling Maisie wanted to speak to him in private, so he merely waved at her from the door and went back that evening, but then, and for the next several days, her room was jammed with people, in spite of the two-visitors rule, and he was busy, too, meeting with the head of research and the grant proposals people about further research on theta-asparcine. He had to settle for keeping tabs on Maisie by calling CICU.

The nurses' reports were almost as optimistic as Maisie's mother's. Maisie was showing no signs of rejection, the fluid in her lungs was steadily diminishing, and she was beginning to eat (this last reported by Eugene, who, being in charge of her menus, took a personal responsibility for her appetite).

When Richard went down Monday, the entire Peds staff was there, and Tuesday and Wednesday, her mother. Finally, on Friday, he ran into Mrs Nellis leaving the CICU, pulling her mask and gown off as she went. 'Oh, good, Dr Wright, you're here,' she said hurriedly. 'I have to meet with Dr Templeton, and I was nervous about leaving Maisie with –' she shot a glance back toward Maisie's room, 'but I know I can trust you to keep the conversation upbeat and positive.'

He went in, curious to see who he was supposed to be protecting Maisie from, and hoping it wasn't Mandrake. It wasn't. It was Mr Wojakowski, in a mask and baseball cap. '– and he did it, he laid that bomb right on the flight deck of the *Shokaku*,' Mr Wojakowski was saying.

'And he was already dead?' Maisie said, her eyes wide with excitement.

'He was already dead. But he did it.' Mr Wojakowski looked up. 'Hiya, Doc. I was just telling Maisie here about Jo-Jo Powers.'

'I didn't know you two knew each other,' Richard said.

'Mr Wojakowski made me my dog tags that Joanna gave me,' Maisie said. 'He was on the *Yorktown*. He tells the *best* stories.'

That he does, Richard thought, and he has found the perfect audience. Someone should have thought of this before. 'I can't stop,' he said. 'I just came to see how you're doing.'

'Really good,' Maisie said. 'Nurse Vielle brought me a *Charlie's Angels* poster, and my mom's lawyer brought me that balloon,' she pointed to a Mylar balloon with a butterfly on it, 'and Eugene brought me this,' Maisie said, pulling a bright pink baseball cap out from under her pillow. 'Back from the Grave and Ready to Party' was written on it in purple letters. Richard laughed.

'I *know*,' Maisie said. 'I think it's really cool, but my mom won't let me wear it. She says I'm supposed to be thinking about positive things, not graves and stuff. Everybody's been to see me except Kit. She couldn't come 'cause she has to take care of her uncle, but she said tomorrow you're all bringing me a surprise.'

We are? Richard thought.

'What is it?' Maisie demanded, and then appraisingly, 'I think I already have enough balloons. And teddy bears.'

'It's a surprise. You'll have to wait till tomorrow,' he said. He'd better call Kit and find out what this was about.

'It looks like you two have a lot of visiting to do, so I'll be moseying along,' Mr Wojakowski said.

'No, wait!' Maisie protested. 'You have to tell me about the time the York-town got all shot up.' She turned back to Richard. 'The Japanese thought they'd sunk her, and they had to fix her really fast.'

'In three days flat,' Mr Wojakowski said, sitting down again. 'And the ship's carpenter says, "Three days!" and threw his hammer so hard it went right through the bulkhead, and the harbormaster says, "That's just one more hole you're gonna have to fix," and –' They didn't even notice Richard leaving. A match made in heaven.

He called Kit as soon as he got back to the lab. 'Maisie told Vielle she'd always wished she could go to Dish Night,' Kit said, 'so we're setting it up for her. The nurses are letting us hold it in the CICU conference room tomor-row at four, after *considerable* negotiations, and I was wondering if you could pick up the videos. Vielle thought maybe *Volcano* or *The Towering Inferno.*'

'What about Maisie's mother?' Richard asked.

'Not a problem. She has a meeting with Daniels, Dutton, and Walsh at four. She's fighting to get Maisie into a clinical trial for a new antirejection drug.'

He rented *Volcano* and, since *The Towering Inferno* was checked out, *Twister*. 'Disasters, huh?' the short kid who waited on him said. 'You should rent *Titanic.*'

'I've seen it,' Richard said.

When he got up to CICU, Kit and Vielle were already in Maisie's room in their masks and gowns, and Maisie was higher than her Mylar balloons. 'He's here!' she said the second he walked in. 'They said I had to wait till you got here to find out what the surprise is. So what is it?'

'We'll tell you when we get there,' Vielle said, bringing in a wheelchair. Evelyn came in to get Maisie's heart monitor and IVs ready to go. Richard and Kit helped her into the wheelchair, and Richard wheeled her three doors down to the conference room.

'Dish Night!' Maisie said when she saw the movie posters.

'Not only Dish Night,' Kit said, 'but a Disaster Double Feature.' Richard held up the videos.

'Actually, Dr Templeton says you can only watch one today,' Evelyn said.

'Then we'll have to watch the other one at our next Dish Night,' Kit said, 'after you get out of the hospital.'

'I get to go to a *real* Dish Night?' Maisie said, transported, and Richard hoped this wasn't too much excitement for her. He handed her the videos, and Kit and Vielle bent over her, one on each side, discussing which one to watch and explaining the rules of Dish Night.

'Rule Number One, no talking about work,' Kit said. 'For you that means no talking about your transplant.'

'Or rib cages. Or beer coolers,' Vielle said. 'Rule Number Two, only movie food can be eaten.'

'Dr Templeton said no popcorn yet,' Kit said. 'We'll have that at our next Dish Night. For now he said you could have a snow cone.' She produced a cone of shaved ice and two bottles of syrup. 'Red or blue?'

'Blue!' Maisie said.

Richard leaned against the door, watching them. The bandage on Vielle's arm had been taken off, though she still had the one on her hand, and the bruised, beaten look was gone from her eyes. Kit was in nearly as high spirits as Maisie. She was still very thin, but there was color in her cheeks. He remembered her standing in the lab, pale and determined, clutching the text-book, saying, 'Joanna saved my life.'

She saved all our lives, Richard thought, and wondered if that was what Maisie had meant when she said he hadn't been the one who saved her life, if she realized it had been Joanna's last words that had saved her life.

'Rule Number Three, no Woody Allen movies,' Kit said.

'And no Kevin Costner,' Vielle said.

'And *no* Disney movies,' Maisie said vehemently.

Richard watched them, thinking about Joanna that first Dish Night, laughing, saying, 'This is a *Titanic*-free zone.'

'There's a reason I'm seeing the *Titanic*,' she'd told him, and she was right. The *Titanic* had been the perfect metaphor for the brain's distress calls sent out frantically in all directions, by every method available, but he wondered, leaning against the door and looking at Maisie and Vielle and Kit, if that was the only connection. Because the *Titanic* wasn't primarily about messages. It was about people who had, in the middle of the ocean, in the middle of the night, put forth a superhuman effort to save wives, sweethearts, friends, babies, children, dogs, and the first-class mail. To save something besides themselves.

Joanna had wanted to die like W. S. Gilbert, and the *Titanic* was full of Gilberts. Assistant Engineer Harvey and Edith Evans and Jay Yates. Daniel Buckley shepherding the girls he had promised to take care of up through the First-Class Dining Saloon, up the Grand Staircase, into the boats, Robert Norman giving his lifejacket to a woman and her child, John Jacob Astor plunking a flowered hat on a ten-year-old boy and saying, 'Now he's a girl and now he can go.' Captain Smith, swimming toward one of the boats with a baby in his arms. And Jack Phillips. And the band. And firemen, stokers, engineers, trimmers, working to keep the boilers going and the dynamos running and the wireless working, the lights on. So it wouldn't get dark.

'Turn off the lights,' Vielle was saying. 'We need to get this show on the road. It's already four-thirty.'

'She has a date,' Maisie said wisely.

'How did *you* find out?' Vielle asked Maisie, her hands on her hips.

'You have a date?' Kit said. 'Who with? Please tell me it's not with Harvey the Embalmer.'

'It's not,' Maisie said. 'It's with a cop.'

'The one who looks like Denzel Washington?' Kit asked. 'You finally met him?'

Vielle nodded. 'I called him to see if he could help me find the taxi Joanna took,' she said, 'and just how did you find out, Little Miss Gossip?'

Maisie turned to Richard. 'So I guess you and Kit will have to eat at the cafeteria, just the two of you,' she said.

'I think it's time to start the movie,' Kit said, whacking Maisie with the *Volcano* box. She handed Vielle the video, and Vielle turned the TV on and slid the video into the slot.

'Wait! Don't start yet! I forgot my "Back from the Grave and Ready to Party" hat Eugene gave me,' Maisie said and added defensively, 'I have to have it. It's a party.'

'I'll go get it,' Richard said.

'No,' Maisie said. 'I have to get it,' and to Richard, 'You don't know where it is.'

'You could tell me,' Richard started to say and then got a look at Maisie's face, innocent and determined. She obviously had a reason for wanting to go back to her room, even if it meant wheeling her monitor and IV pole back, too. 'We'll be right back,' Richard said and maneuvered her and her equipment back down the hall.

As soon as they got inside the room, Maisie said, 'My hat's under the pillow. Push me up to the nightstand.' She opened the drawer and brought out several tablet pages, folded into quarters. 'It's my NDE from when I coded,' she said, handing them to him. 'I couldn't write it down right away.'

'That's all right,' Richard said, touched that she had written the whole thing down. 'It doesn't matter.'

'Joanna said you should always write it down right away,' Maisie said disapprovingly, 'so you won't confabulate.'

'That's true,' Richard said, 'but you can't always. This will be very useful.'

Maisie looked mollified. 'Do you think Mr Wojakowski tells the truth?'

Out of left field. 'The truth?' Richard said, stalling. He wondered if she had begun to catch Mr Wojakowski in inconsistencies, like Joanna had.

'Uh-huh,' Maisie said. 'I asked him if Jo-Jo Powers, that's the guy who said he was going to lay his bomb right on the flight deck, if he knew he did it. Hit the *Shokaku*, I mean. 'Cause he'd already died when it hit. And Mr Wojakowski said, "You bet he knew it! He was standing there at the pearly gates watching the whole thing." Do you think he was?'

'Was standing at the pearly gates?' Richard said.

'No, was telling the *truth*. It's like a dream, right? The NDE? Vielle told me it's like signals your brain is sending out to make your heart start, and you make the signals into a kind of dream. A symbol, Vielle said.'

'That's right,' Richard said.

'So it's not real.'

'No,' he said. 'It feels like it's really happening, but it's not.'

Maisie thought about that. 'I kind of figured that out 'cause of Pollyanna being there. She's not a real person, and none of the animals really got loose. At the Hartford circus fire,' she said at his bewildered look. 'That's where I went. In my NDE.'

My God. The Hartford circus fire.

'And after the NDE, there's nothing,' she said, 'and you don't even know you're dead. 'Cause of brain death.'

He nodded.

'But you don't know that for sure. Joanna said nobody knows for sure what happens after you die, except people who've died, and they can't tell you,' Maisie said, and then, following some private line of reasoning of her own, 'and the thing the dream stands for is real, even if the dream isn't.'

'Maisie, did you see Joanna in your NDE?' he asked.

'Hunh-unh,' she said, and then, 'Mr Mandrake says people who've died can tell us stuff. Do you think they can?'

She wants Joanna to still be here, to be talking to her, he thought. And who can blame her? 'They speak to us in our hearts,' he said carefully.

'I don't mean like *that*,' Maisie said. 'I mean really.'

'No.'

Maisie nodded. 'I told Mr Mandrake they couldn't 'cause if they could, Little Miss 1565 would have told them who she was.'

And Joanna would have told me what her last words meant, Richard thought. But she had. Maisie was the living proof of that. And if he didn't get her back to Dish Night, Kit and Vielle would have a fit. 'We'd better get going so we can watch the movie,' he said and plunked the pink 'Back from the Grave' hat on her head.

Maisie nodded, but as he came around to push her wheelchair out of the room, she said, 'Wait, we can't go yet. When I said it wasn't you who saved my life, I didn't mean the kid who gave me my heart either.'

'Who did you mean?'

'Emmett Kelly.'

So far out in left field there was no way to follow the ball. 'Emmett Kelly?'

'Yeah, you know,' Maisie said, 'the sad-looking clown with the raggedy clothes and it looks like he didn't shave. He saved this little girl at the Hartford circus fire. He told her to go stand in the Victory garden. And he told me to, too, and showed me how to get out of the tent, so that's why I said he saved my life.'

Richard nodded, trying to understand.

'Only it wasn't really him. It looked like him and everything, but it wasn't. It was like how Vielle said the NDE was, and Emmett Kelly was a symbol for who it was really. But just because you want something to be true doesn't mean it is.'

'Who was it really, Maisie?'

'But Joanna said just because you want it to be true doesn't mean it isn't, either,' she said, still following some private line of reasoning, 'and I think it *was* real, even though Pollyanna and the fire and stuff wasn't.'

'Maisie, who saved you?'

She gave him her it-is-so-obvious look. *'Joanna,'* she said.

60

'Guesses, of course, only guesses. If they are not true, something better will be.'

— C. S. LEWIS, writing about resurrection in
Letters to Malcolm, Chiefly on Prayer

'Look,' Helen said. She had been sitting close to Joanna, with the little French bulldog on her lap, untying the hair ribbon around its neck and then retying it, ignoring the steadily reddening sky, but now she looked up. 'I think something's happening.'

The red's getting darker, Joanna thought, looking fearfully up at the bloody sky. The light's going, and this time it won't be a night of clear and sparkling stars, but the color was not deepening, it was changing, the hue shifting from blood-red to carmine.

'Not the *sky*,' Helen said, pointing down over the side of the piano. 'The water!'

Joanna looked down at the water, and it was carmine, too, the burning orange-red of flames. '"But the fearful and unbelieving shall have their part in the lake which burneth with fire,"' Joanna thought, remembering her sister quoting from the Bible, '"which is the second death."'

She reached to pull Helen closer, but Helen wriggled out of her arms and went over to the edge. She flopped down on her stomach, the little dog beside her, and trailed her hand in the water. 'I think we're unbecalmed,' she said, but the flame-red water was still as smooth as glass, so still Helen's hand, trailing through it, left no wake at all.

'We are too unbecalmed,' Helen said as if Joanna had spoken. 'Look!' She bobbed her head toward the ice field, and she was right, because, even though the piano had not drifted, even though the water was still smooth and still, they were no longer surrounded by ice. The bergs lay far behind them, their sharp peaks copper against the burning sky.

We've drifted out of the ice field, Joanna thought. They'll never find us now.

'I told you we were unbecalmed,' Helen said, and stood up, rocking the piano so the water lapped at its sides. 'I bet whatever we were waiting for must have happened.'

No, Joanna thought. Please.

'What do you think will –?' Helen said and stopped, looking back toward the ice field.

Joanna followed her gaze. She could no longer see the icebergs. On all sides, stretching out to an endless horizon, lay the still, burnished water.

'What do you think will happen now?' Helen said again.

'I don't know.'

'I think we will find land soon,' Helen said, and sat down crosslegged in the center of the piano. She put her curled hands up to her eye as if they were a telescope and gazed earnestly at the horizon, searching for land. 'Look!' she shouted and pointed to the east. 'There it is!'

At first Joanna couldn't see anything, but then she spotted a tiny speck on the horizon. She leaned forward, squinting. It's a lifeboat, she thought, and strained to see, hoping it was Mr Briarley and Mrs Woollam, safe in Collapsible D.

'It's a ship!' Helen shouted, and, as Joanna looked, the speck resolved itself into an oblong, like a smokestack. 'It's the *Carpathia*!' Helen said happily.

It can't be, Joanna thought. It's too far for her to come. And the *Carpathia* had steamed up from the southwest.

'I bet it is, though,' Helen said as if Joanna had spoken. 'What else could it be?'

The *Mackay-Bennett*, Joanna thought, watching the ship steam toward them. Coming out from Halifax with a minister and a hold full of ice to pick up the corpses, to bury them at sea. It must be near the end, Joanna thought, looking across the water at the ship. The sky was changing again, darkening, yellowing, like decaying flesh.

The last neurons must be dying, the last cells of the cerebral cortex and the hippocampus and the amygdala going out, shutting down, the synapses flickering faintly, failing to arc. V ... V ... and then what? Irreversible brain death, she thought, and the *Mackay-Bennett*.

'If it's the *Carpathia*, then we're saved,' Helen said happily, and gathered the little bulldog up as if she were collecting her luggage, getting ready to disembark.

The sky had turned a dull, uneasy brass. The *Mackay-Bennett*'s stack stood out blackly against it. They won't know who we are, Joanna thought, and looked for her hospital ID, but it had fallen off in the water. I should have had Mr Wojakowski make me a set of dog tags, too, she thought.

They had known John Jacob Astor by the initials embroidered inside his collar. She fumbled in her pockets, looking for a pen to write Helen's name in the collar of her dress, but there was nothing at all in her pockets, not even a coin for Charon the boatman.

'I think you were right,' Helen said, 'it doesn't look at all like the *Carpathia*.'

Joanna looked up, bracing herself to see the deck stacked with coffins, the embalmer standing ready. The ship was still a long way off, but its shape was clearly defined against the brassy sky. What she had first thought was its smokestack was instead its central island, spiky with masts and antennas, and under it the broad, flat deck and the incurving triangular prow.

'Is it the *Carpathia*?' Helen asked.

'No,' Joanna said wonderingly. 'It's the *Yorktown*.'

'The *Yorktown*?' Helen said. 'I thought the *Yorktown* sank in the Coral Sea.'

'It did,' Joanna said. She could see the wireless shack now, high up on the island, and the antennas, shaped like crosses. And was raised again in three days.

'What's it doing here?'

'I don't know.'

'How do you know it's the *Yorktown*, if you can't read the name?' Helen said, but there was no mistaking it now. She could see the planes. Sailors lined the railing of the flight deck, their white uniforms blindingly bright.

'Do you think they'll see us?' Helen asked. 'Maybe we should signal them or something.'

'We have,' Joanna said. 'SOS. SOS.' She stood up and faced the ship as if it were a firing squad.

'Are we saved?' Helen asked, looking up at Joanna.

'I don't know,' Joanna said. This could be some final synapse firing, some last attempt to make sense of dying and death, some final metaphor. Or something else altogether. She looked up at the sky. It was changing again, deepening, brightening to gold. The *Yorktown* plowed toward them, impossibly huge, impossibly fast, its narrow prow cutting like a knife through the shining water.

'Are you scared?' Helen asked.

The *Yorktown* was nearly upon them. Flags were flying from the tower and the masts and the antennas, and on the flight deck, sailors stood at the railing, waving. In the center, the captain, all in white, held up a pair of binoculars and looked toward them, the lenses glinting gold.

'Are you?' Helen demanded.

'Yes,' Joanna said. 'No. Yes.'

'I'm scared, too,' Helen said.

Joanna put her arm around her. The sailors were shouting from the railing, waving their white hats in the air. Behind them, above the tower, the sun came out, blindingly bright, gilding the crosses and the captain.

'What if it sinks again?' Helen asked fearfully. 'The *Yorktown* went down at Midway.'

Joanna smiled down at her, at the little bulldog, and then looked back at the *Yorktown*. 'All ships sink sooner or later,' she said, and raised her hand to wave in greeting. 'But not today. Not today.'

If you've enjoyed these books and would
like to read more, you'll find literally thousands
of classic Science Fiction & Fantasy titles
through the **SF Gateway**

✳

For the new home of
Science Fiction & Fantasy . . .

✳

For the most comprehensive collection
of classic SF on the internet . . .

✳

Visit the SF Gateway

www.sfgateway.com

Connie Willis (1945–)

Constance Elaine Trimmer Willis was born in Denver, Colorado, in 1945. Having earned a BA in English and elementary education from the University of North Colorado, she spent a brief stint in the late 1960s working as a teacher, until she left to raise her first child. During this period she began writing SF, with her first publication, 'The Secret of Santa Titicaca', appearing in *Worlds of Fantasy* in 1971. Willis is a highly decorated author and has won, among other accolades, ten Hugo Awards and six Nebula Awards for works of all lengths: short stories, novellas, novelettes and novels alike. She was recently named an SFWA Grand Master. Willis currently lives in Greeley, Colorado with her family.